THE

WAVERLEY NOVELS

BY

SIR WALTER SCOTT, BART.

Red Gauntlet
Quentin Durward

NEW YORK
THOMAS Y. CROWELL & COMPANY
PUBLISHERS

REDGAUNTLET.

INTRODUCTION TO REDGAUNTLET

THE Jacobite enthusiasm of the 18th century, particularly during the rebellion of 1745, afforded a theme, perhaps the finest that could be selected for fictitious composition, founded upon real or probable incident. This civil war, and its remarkable events, were remembered by the existing generation without any degree of the bitterness of spirit which seldom fails to attend internal dissension. The Highlanders, who formed the principal strength of Charles Edward's army, were an ancient and high-spirited race, peculiar in their habits of war and of peace, brave to romance, and exhibiting a character turning upon points more adapted to poetry than to the prose of real life. Their prince, young, valiant, patient of fatigue, and despising danger, heading his army on foot in the most toilsome marches, and defeating a regular force in three battles—all these were circumstances fascinating to the imagination, and might well be supposed to seduce young and enthusiastic minds to the cause in which they were found united, although wisdom and reason frowned upon the enterprise.

The adventurous Prince, as is well known, proved to be one of those personages who distinguish themselves during some single and extraordinarily brilliant period of their lives, like the course of a shooting star, at which men wonder, as well on account of the briefness as the brilliancy of its splendor. A long trace of darkness overshadowed the subsequent life of a man who, in his youth, showed himself so capable of great undertakings ; and, without the painful task of tracing his course further, we may say the latter pursuits and habits of this unhappy prince are those painfully evincing a broken heart, which seeks refuge from its own thoughts in sordid enjoyments.

Still, however, it was long ere Charles Edward appeared to be—perhaps it was long ere he altogether became—so much degraded from his original self, as he enjoyed for a time the luster attending the progress and termination of his enterprise. Those who thought they discerned in his

subsequent conduct an insensibility to the distresses of his
followers, coupled with that egotistical attention to his own
interests which has been often attributed to the Stuart
family, and which is the natural effect of the principles of
divine right in which they were brought up, were now generally considered as dissatisfied and splenetic persons, who,
displeased with the issue of their adventure, and finding
themselves involved in the ruins of a falling cause, indulged
themselves in undeserved reproaches against their leader.
Indeed, such censures were by no means frequent among
those of his followers who, if what was alleged had been
just, had the best right to complain. Far the greater number of those unfortunate gentlemen suffered with the most
dignified patience, and were either too proud to take notice
of ill treatment on the part of their prince, or so prudent as
to be aware their complaints would meet with little sympathy from the world. It may be added, that the greater
part of the banished Jacobites, and those of high rank and
consequence, were not much within reach of the influence of
the Prince's character and conduct, whether well regulated
or otherwise.

In the meantime, that great Jacobite conspiracy, of which
the insurrection of 1745–46 was but a small part, precipitated into action on the failure of a far more general
scheme, was resumed and again put into motion by
the Jacobites of England, whose force had never been
broken, as they had prudently avoided bringing it into the
field. The surprising effect which had been produced by
small means in 1745–46 animated their hopes for more important successes, when the whole Nonjuring interest of
Britain, identified as it then was with a great part of the
landed gentlemen, should come forward to finish what had
been gallantly attempted by a few Highland chiefs.

It is probable, indeed, that the Jacobites of the day were
incapable of considering that the very small scale on which
the effort was made was in one great measure the cause of
its unexpected success. The remarkable speed with which
the insurgents marched, the singularly good discipline
which they preserved, the union and unanimity which for
some time animated their councils, were all in a considerable degree produced by the smallness of their numbers.
Notwithstanding the discomfiture of Charles Edward, the
Nonjurors of the period long continued to nurse unlawful
schemes, and to drink treasonable toasts, until age stole
upon them. Another generation arose, who did not share

the sentiments which they cherished; and at length the sparkles of disaffection, which had long smoldered, but had never been heated enough to burst into actual flame, became entirely extinguished. But in proportion as the political enthusiasm died gradually away among men of ordinary temperament, it influenced those of warm imaginations and weak understandings, and hence wild schemes were formed, as desperate as they were adventurous.

Thus a young Scotchman of rank is said to have stooped so low as to plot the surprisal of St. James's Palace, and the assassination of the royal family. While these ill-digested and desperate conspiracies were agitated among the few Jacobites who still adhered with more obstinacy to their purpose, there is no question but that other plots might have been brought to an open explosion, had it not suited the policy of Sir Robert Walpole rather to prevent or disable the conspirators in their projects than to promulgate the tale of danger, which might thus have been believed to be more widely diffused than was really the case.

In one instance alone this very prudential and humane line of conduct was departed from, and the event seemed to confirm the policy of the general course. Doctor Archibald Cameron, brother of the celebrated Donald Cameron of Lochiel, attainted for the rebellion of 1745, was found by a party of soldiers lurking with a comrade in the wilds of Loch Katrine, five or six years after the battle of Culloden, and was there seized. There were circumstances in his case, so far as was made known to the public, which attracted much compassion, and gave to the judicial proceedings against him an appearance of cold-blooded revenge on the part of government; and the following argument of a zealous Jacobite in his favor was received as conclusive by Dr. Johnson and other persons who might pretend to impartiality. Dr. Cameron had never borne arms, although engaged in the Rebellion, but used his medical skill for the service, indifferently, of the wounded of both parties. His return to Scotland was ascribed exclusively to family affairs. His behavior at the bar was decent, firm, and respectful. His wife threw herself, on three different occasions, before George II. and the members of his family, was rudely repulsed from their presence, and at length placed, it was said, in the same prison with her husband, and confined with unmanly severity.

Dr. Cameron was finally executed, with all the severities of the law of treason; and his death remains in popular es-

timation a dark blot upon the memory of George II., being
almost publicly imputed to a mean and personal hatred of
Donald Cameron of Lochiel, the sufferer's heroic brother.
Yet the fact was, that whether the execution of Archibald
Cameron was political or otherwise, it might certainly have
been justified, had the King's ministers so pleased, upon
reasons of a public nature. The unfortunate sufferer had
not come to the Highlands solely upon his private affairs, as
was the general belief; but it was not judged prudent by
the English ministry to let it be generally known that he
came to inquire about a considerable sum of money which
had been remitted from France to the friends of the exiled
family. He had also a commission to hold intercourse with
the well-known McPherson of Cluny, chief of the clan
Vourich, whom the Chevalier had left behind at his departure from Scotland in 1746, and who remained during ten
years of proscription and danger, skulking from place to
place in the Highlands, and maintaining an uninterrupted
correspondence between Charles and his friends. That Dr.
Cameron should have held a commission to assist this chief
in raking together the dispersed embers of disaffection is in
itself sufficiently natural, and, considering his political principles, in no respect dishonorable to his memory. But
neither ought it to be imputed to George II. that he suffered
the laws to be enforced against a person taken in the act of
breaking them. When he lost his hazardous game, Dr.
Cameron only paid the forfeit which he must have calculated
upon. The ministers, however, thought it proper to leave
Dr. Cameron's new schemes in concealment, lest by divulg-
ing them they had indicated the channel of communication
which, it is now well known, they possessed to all the plots
of Charles Edward. But it was equally ill-advised and ungenerous to sacrifice the character of the King to the policy
of the administration. Both points might have been gained
by sparing the life of Dr. Cameron after conviction, and
limiting his punishment to perpetual exile.

These repeated and successive Jacobite plots rose and
burst like bubbles on a fountain; and one of them, at least,
the Chevalier judged of importance enough to induce him
to risk himself within the dangerous precincts of the British
capital. This appears from Dr. King's *Anecdotes of his Own
Times* :—

September 1750.—I received a note from my Lady Primrose, who
desired to see me immediately. As soon as I waited on her, she led
me into her dressing room, and presented me to ——. [The Chev-

alier, doubtless.] If I was surprised to find him there, I was still more astonished when he acquainted me with the motives which had induced him to hazard a journey to England at this juncture. The impatience of his friends who were in exile had formed a scheme which was impracticable ; but although it had been as feasible as they had represented it to him, yet no preparation had been made, nor was anything ready to carry it into execution. He was soon convinced that he had been deceived ; and therefore, after a stay in London of five days only, he returned to the place from whence he came [pp. 196, 197].

Dr. King was in 1750 a keen Jacobite, as may be inferred from the visit made by him to the Prince under such circumstances, and from his being one of that unfortunate person's chosen correspondents. He, as well as other men of sense and observation, began to despair of making their fortune in the party which they had chosen. It was indeed sufficiently dangerous ; for, during the short visits just described, one of Dr. King's servants remarked the stranger's likeness to Prince Charles, whom he recognized from the common busts.

The occasion taken for breaking up the Stuart interest we shall tell in Dr. King's own words :—

When he (Charles Edward) was in Scotland, he had a mistress whose name is Walkenshaw, and whose sister was at that time, and is still, housekeeper at Leicester House. Some years after he was released from his prison, and conducted out of France, he sent for this girl, who soon acquired such a dominion over him that she was acquainted with all his schemes, and trusted with his most secret correspondence. As soon as this was known in England, all those persons of distinction who were attached to him were greatly alarmed ; they imagined that this wench had been placed in his family by the English ministers ; and, considering her sister's situation, they seemed to have some ground for their suspicion ; wherefore, they despatched a gentleman to Paris, where the Prince then was, who had instructions to insist that Mrs. Walkenshaw should be removed to a convent for a certain term ; but her gallant absolutely refused to comply with this demand ; and although Mr. M'Namara, the gentleman who was sent to him, who has a natural eloquence and an excellent understanding, urged the most cogent reasons, and used all the arts of persuasion, to induce him to part with his mistress, and even proceeded so far as to assure him, according to his instructions, that an immediate interruption of all correspondence with his most powerful friends in England, and, in short, that the ruin of his interest, which was now daily increasing, would be the infallible consequence of his refusal, yet he continued inflexible, and all M'Namara's entreaties and remonstrances were ineffectual. M'Namara staid in Paris some days beyond the time prescribed him, endeavoring to reason the Prince into better temper ; but finding him obstinately persevere in his first answer, he took his leave with concern and indignation, saying, as he passed out, " What has your family done, sir, thus to draw down the vengeance of Heaven on every branch of it, through so many ages ? "

It is worthy of remark, that in all the conferences which M'Namara had with the Prince on this occasion, the latter declared that it was not a violent passion, or indeed any particular regard, which attached him to Mrs. Walkenshaw, and that he could see her removed from him without any concern ; but he would not receive directions in respect to his private conduct from any man alive. When M'Namara returned to London and reported the Prince's answer to the gentlemen who had employed him. they were astonished and confounded. However, they soon resolved on the measures which they were to pursue for the future, and determined no longer to serve a man who could not be persuaded to serve himself, and chose rather to endanger the lives of his best and most faithful friends than part with an harlot whom, as he often declared, he neither loved nor esteemed [pp. 204-209].

From this anecdote, the general truth of which is indubitable, the principal fault of Charles Edward's temper is sufficiently obvious. It was a high sense of his own importance, and an obstinate adherence to what he had once determined on—qualities which, if he had succeeded in his bold attempt, gave the nation little room to hope that he would have been found free from the love of prerogative and desire of arbitrary power which characterized his unhappy grandfather. He gave a notable instance how far this was the leading feature of his character when, for no reasonable cause that can be assigned, he placed his own single will in opposition to the necessities of France, which, in order to purchase a peace become necessary to the kingdom, was reduced to gratify Britain by prohibiting the residence of Charles within any part of the French dominions. It was in vain that France endeavored to lessen the disgrace of this step by making the most flattering offers, in hopes to induce the Prince of himself to anticipate this disagreeable alternative, which, if seriously enforced, as it was likely to be, he had no means whatever of resisting, by leaving the kingdom as of his own free-will. Inspired, however, by the spirit of hereditary obstinacy, Charles preferred a useless resistance to a dignified submission, and by a series of idle bravadoes laid the French court under the necessity of arresting their late ally, and sending him to close confinement in the Bastile, from which he was afterwards sent out of the French dominions, much in the manner in which a convict is transported to the place of his destination.

In addition to these repeated instances of a rash and inflexible temper, Dr. King also adds faults alleged to belong to the Prince's character of a kind less consonant with his noble birth and high pretensions. He is said by this author to have been avaricious, or parsimonious at least, to such a degree of meanness as to fail, even when he had ample means, in relieving the sufferers who had lost their fortune and sacrificed all in his ill-fated attempt.* We must receive, however, with some degree of jealousy what is said by Dr. King on this subject, recollecting that he had left at least, if he did not desert, the standard of the unfortunate prince, and was not therefore a person who was likely to form the fairest estimate of his virtues and faults. We must also remember that, if the exiled prince gave little, he had but little to give, especially considering how late he nourished the scheme of another expedition to Scotland, for which he was long endeavoring to hoard money.

The case, also, of Charles Edward must be allowed to have been a difficult one. He had to satisfy numerous persons, who, having lost their all in his cause, had, with that all, seen the extinction of hopes which they accounted nearly as good as certainties ; some of these were perhaps clamorous in their applications, and certainly ill pleased with their want of success. Other parts of the Chevalier's conduct may have afforded grounds for charging him with coldness to the sufferings of his devoted followers. One of these was a sentiment which has nothing in it that is generous, but it was certainly a principle in which the young prince was trained, and which may be too probably denominated peculiar to his family, educated in all the high notions of passive obedience and non-resistance. If the unhappy prince gave implicit faith to the professions of statesmen holding such notions, which is implied by his whole conduct, it must have led to the natural, though ungracious, inference that the services of a subject could not, to whatever degree of ruin they might bring the individual, create a debt against his sovereign. Such a person could only boast that he had done his duty ; nor was he entitled to be a claimant for a greater reward than it was convenient for the prince to bestow, or to hold his sovereign his debtor for losses which he had sustained through his loyalty. To a certain extent the Jacobite principles inevitably led to this cold and egotistical mode of reasoning on the part of the sovereign ; nor, with all our natural pity for the situation of royalty in distress, do we feel entitled to affirm that Charles did not use this opiate to his feelings, on viewing the misery of his followers, while he certainly possessed, though in no great degree, the means of affording them more relief

* See Prince Charles Edward's Love of Money. Note 1.

than he practised. His own history, after leaving France, is brief and melancholy. For a time he seems to have held the firm belief that Providence, which had borne him through so many hazards, still reserved him for some distant occasion, in which he should be empowered to vindicate the honors of his birth. But opportunity after opportunity slipped by unimproved, and the death of his father gave him the fatal proof that none of the principal powers of Europe were, after that event, likely to interest themselves in his quarrel. They refused to acknowledge him under the title of the King of England, and, on his part, he declined to be then recognized as the Prince of Wales.

Family discord came to add its sting to those of disappointed ambition ; and, though a humiliating circumstance, it is generally acknowledged that Charles Edward, the adventurous, the gallant, and the handsome, the leader of a race of pristine valor, whose romantic qualities may be said to have died along with him, had, in his latter days, yielding to those humiliating habits of intoxication in which the meanest mortals seek to drown the recollection of their disappointments and miseries. Under such circumstances, the unhappy Prince lost the friendship even of those faithful followers who had most devoted themselves to his misfortunes, and was surrounded, with some honorable exceptions, by men of a lower description, regardless of the character which he was himself no longer able to protect.

It is a fact consistent with the Author's knowledge, that persons totally unentitled to, and unfitted for, such a distinction were presented to the unfortunate Prince in moments unfit for presentation of any kind. Amid these clouds was at length extinguished the torch which once shook itself over Britain with such terrific glare, and at last sunk in its own ashes, scarce remembered and scarce noted.

Meantime, while the life of Charles Edward was gradually wasting in disappointed solitude, the number of those who had shared his misfortunes and dangers had shrunk into a small handful of veterans, the heroes of a tale which had been told. Most Scottish readers who can count the number of sixty years must recollect many respected acquaintances of their youth who, as the established phrase gently worded it, had been "out in the forty-five." It may be said that their political principles and plans no longer either gained proselytes or attracted terror : those who held them had ceased to be the subjects either of fear or opposition. Jacobites were looked upon in society as men who had proved their sincerity by sacrificing their interest to their principles ; and in well regulated companies it was held a piece of ill-breeding to injure their feelings or ridicule the compromises by which they endeavored to keep themselves abreast of the current of the day. Such, for example, was the evasion of a gentleman of fortune in Perthshire, Mr. Oliphant of Gask, who, in having the newspapers read to him, caused the King and Queen to be designated by the initial letters of "K" and "Q," as if, by naming the full word, he might imply an acquiescence in the usurpation of the family of Hanover. George III., having heard of this gentleman's custom in the above and other particulars, commissioned the member for Perthshire to carry his compliments to the steady Jacobite. "That is," said the excellent old king, "not the compliments of the King of England, but those of the Elector of Hanover, and tell him how much I respect him for the steadiness of his principles."

Those who remember such old men will probably agree that the progress of time, which has withdrawn all of them from the field, has removed, at the same time, a peculiar and striking feature of ancient manners. Their love of past times, their tales of bloody battles fought against romantic odds, were all dear to the imagination, and their little idolatry of locks of hair, pictures, rings, ribbons, and other memorials of the time in which they still seemed to live, was an interesting enthusiasm ; and although their political principles, had they existed in the relation of fathers, might have rendered them dangerous to the existing dynasty, yet, as we now recollect them, there could not be on the earth supposed to exist persons better qualified to sustain the capacity of innocuous and respectable grandsires.

It was while reflecting on these things that the novel of *Redgauntlet* was undertaken. But various circumstances in the composition induced the Author to alter its purport considerably as it passed through his hands, and to carry the action to that point of time when the Chevalier Charles Edward, though fallen into the sere and yellow leaf, was yet meditating a second attempt, which could scarcely have been more hopeless than his first ; although one to which, as we have seen, the unfortunate Prince, at least as late as 1753, still looked with hope and expectation.*

1*st April*, 1832.

* [See Lockhart's *Life of Scott*, vol. vii. pp. 213, 214.]

REDGAUNTLET

LETTER I

DARSIE LATIMER TO ALAN FAIRFORD

DUMFRIES.

Cur me exanimas querelis tuis? In plain English, Why do
you deafen me with your croaking? The disconsolate tone
in which you bade me farewell at Noble House,* and
mounted your miserable hack to return to your law drudgery, still sounds in my ears. It seemed to say, "Happy
dog! you can ramble at pleasure over hill and dale, pursue
every object of curiosity that presents itself, and relinquish
the chase when it loses interest; while I, your senior and
your better, must, in this brilliant season, return to my
narrow chamber and my musty books."

Such was the import of the reflections with which you
saddened our parting bottle of claret, and thus I must needs
interpret the terms of your melancholy adieu.

And why should this be so, Alan? Why the deuce should
you not be sitting precisely opposite to me at this moment,
in the same comfortable George Inn, thy heels on the fender,
and thy juridical brow expanding its plications as a pun
rose in your fancy? Above all, why, when I fill this very
glass of wine, cannot I push the bottle to you, and say,
"Fairford, you are chased!" "Why, I say, should not all
this be, except because Alan Fairford has not the same true
sense of friendship as Darsie Latimer, and will not regard
our purses as common as well as our sentiments?

I am alone in the world: my only guardian writes to me
of a large fortune which will be mine when I reach the age

* The first stage on the road from Edinburgh to Dumfries, *via*
Moffat.

1

of twenty-five complete ; my present income is, thou knowest, more than sufficient for all my wants ; and yet thou,
traitor as thou art to the cause of friendship, dost deprive
me of the pleasure of thy society, and submittest, besides,
to self-denial on thine own part, rather than my wanderings should cost me a few guineas more ! Is this regard for
my purse or for thine own pride ? Is it not equally absurd
and unreasonable, whichever source it springs from ? For
myself, I tell thee, I have, and shall have, more than enough
for both. This same methodical Samuel Griffiths, of Iron-
monger Lane, Guildhall, London, whose letter arrives as
duly as quarter-day, has sent me, as I told thee, double allowance for this my twenty-first birthday, and an assurance,
in his brief fashion, that it will be again doubled for the
succeeding years, until I enter into possession of my own
property. Still I am to refrain from visiting England until
my twenty-fifth year expires ; and it is recommended that I
shall forbear all inquiries concerning my family, and so forth,
for the present.

Were it not that I recollect my poor mother in her deep
widow's weeds, with a countenance that never smiled but
when she looked on me, and then in such wan and woful
sort as the sun when he glances through an April cloud—
were it not, I say, that her mild and matron-like form and
countenance forbid such a suspicion, I might think myself
the son of some Indian director or rich citizen who had more
wealth than grace, and a handful of hypocrisy to boot, and
who was breeding up privately, and obscurely enriching, one
of whose existence he had some reason to be ashamed. But,
as I said before, I think on my mother, and am convinced
as much as of the existence of my own soul that no touch of
shame could arise from aught in which she was implicated.
Meantime, I am wealthy and I am alone, and why does my
friend scruple to share my wealth ?

Are you not my only friend, and have you not acquired a
right to share my wealth ? Answer me that, Alan Fairford.
When I was brought from the solitude of my mother's dwelling into the tumult of the Gait's Class at the High School—
when I was mocked for my English accent—salted with
snow as a Southern pig—rolled in the gutter for a Saxon
pock-pudding, who, with stout arguments and stouter blows,
stood forth my defender ? Why, Alan Fairford. Who beat
me soundly when I brought the arrogance of an only son,
and of course a spoiled urchin, to the forms of the little
republic ? Why, Alan. And who taught me to smoke a

cobbler, pin a losen, head a bicker, and hold the bannets ? *
Alan, once more. If I became the pride of the "yards"
and the dread of the hucksters in the High School Wynd, it
was under thy patronage ; and, but for thee, I had been contented with humbly passing through the Cowgate Port,
without climbing over the top of it, and had never seen the
Kittle Nine Steps † nearer than from Bareford's Parks.
You taught me to keep my fingers off the weak and to clench
my fist against the strong, to carry no tales out of school, to
stand forth like a true man, obey the stern order of a " *Pande
manum*," and endure my pawmies without wincing, like one
that is determined not to be the better for them. In a word,
before I knew thee, I knew nothing.

At college it was the same. When I was incorrigibly idle,
your example and encouragement roused me to mental exertion, and showed me the way to intellectual enjoyment.
You made me an historian, a metaphysician (*invita
Minerva*)—nay, by Heaven ! you had almost made an advocate of me as well as of yourself. Yes, rather than part
with you, Alan, I attended a weary season at the Scotch
Law Class, a wearier at the Civil ; and with what excellent
advantage, my note-book filled with caricatures of the professors and my fellow-students, is it not yet extant to
testify :

Thus far have I held on with thee untired ;

and, to say truth, purely and solely that I might travel the
same road with thee. But it will not do, Alan. By my
faith, man, I could as soon think of being one of those
ingenious traders who cheat little Master Jackies on the
outside of the partition with tops, balls, bats, and battle-
dores as a member of the long-robed fraternity within, who
impose on grown country gentlemen with bouncing brocards
of law.‡ Now, don't you read this to your worthy father,
Alan ; he loves me well enough, I know, of a Saturday
night, but he thinks me but idle company for any other
day of the week. And here, I suspect, lies your real objection to taking a ramble with me through the southern
counties in this delicious weather. I know the good gentleman has hard thoughts of me for being so unsettled as to
leave Edinburgh before the session rises ; perhaps, too, he

---

* Break a window, head a skirmish with stones, and hold the
bonnet or handkerchief which used to divide High School boys
when fighting.
† See Note 2.   ‡ See Parliament House, Edinburgh. Note 3.

quarrels a little—I will not say, with my want of ancestry, but with my want of connections. He reckons me a lone thing in this world, Alan, and so in good truth I am; and it seems a reason to him why you should not attach yourself to me, that I can claim no interest in the general herd. Do not suppose I forget what I owe him for permitting me to shelter for four years under his roof. My obligations to him are not the less, but the greater, if he never heartily loved me. He is angry, too, that I will not, or cannot, be a lawyer, and, with reference to you, considers my disinclination that way as *pessemi exempli*, as he might say.

But he need not be afraid that a lad of your steadiness will be influenced by such a reed shaken by the winds as I am. You will go on doubting with Dirleton, and resolving those doubts with Stewart,* until the cramp-speech has been spoken *moré solito* from the corner of the bench, and with covered head—until you have sworn to defend the liberties and privileges of the College of Justice, until the black gown is hung on your shoulders, and you are free as any of the faculty to sue or defend. Then will I step forth, Alan, and in a character which even your father will allow may be more useful to you than had I shared this splendid termination of your legal studies. In a word, if I cannot be a counsel, I am determined to be a *client*—a sort of person without whom a lawsuit would be as dull as a supposed case. Yes, I am determined to give you your first fee. One can easily, I am assured, get into a lawsuit—it is only the getting out which is sometimes found troublesome; and, with your kind father for an agent, and you for my counsel learned in the law, and the worshipful Master Samuel Griffiths to back me, a few sessions shall not tire my patience. In short, I will make my way into court, even it should cost me the making a *delict*, or at least a *quasi delict*. You see all is not lost of what Erskine wrote and Wallace taught.

Thus far I have fooled it off well enough; and yet, Alan, all is not at ease within me. I am affected with a sense of loneliness, the more depressing that it seems to me to be a solitude peculiarly my own. In a country where all the world have a circle of consanguinity, extending to sixth cousins at least, I am a solitary individual, having only one kind heart to throb in unison with my own. If I were condemned to labor for my bread, methinks I should less regard

<hr>

* See Note 4.　　　　　† S ee Note 5,

this peculiar species of deprivation. The necessary communication of master and servant would be at least a tie
which would attach me to the rest of my kind ; as it is, my
very independence seems to enhance the peculiarity of
my situation. I am in the world as a stranger in the
crowded coffee-house, where he enters, calls for what refreshments he wants, pays his bill, and is forgotten so soon as
the waiter's mouth has pronounced his "Thank ye, sir."
I know your good father would term this "sinning my
mercies," and ask how I should feel if, instead of being able
to throw down my reckoning, I were obliged to deprecate
the resentment of the landlord for consuming that which I
could not pay for. I cannot tell how it is ; but, though this
very reasonable reflection comes across me, and though I do
confess that four hundred a-year in possession, eight hundred in near prospect, and the L—d knows how many
hundreds more in the distance, are very pretty and comfortable things, yet I would freely give one-half of them to
call your father "father," though he should scold me for my
idleness every hour of the day, and to call you "brother,"
though a brother whose merits would throw my own so
completely into the shade.

The faint, yet not improbable, belief often has come
across me that your father knows something more about my
birth and natural condition than he is willing to communicate ; it is so unlikely that I should have been left in
Edinburgh at six years old, without any other recommendation than the regular payment of my board to old M—— *
of the High School. Before that time, as I have often told
you, I have but a recollection of unbounded indulgence on
my mother's part, and the most tyrannical exertion of caprice on my own. I remember still how bitterly she sighed,
how vainly she strove to soothe me, while, in the full energy
of despotism, I roared like ten bull calves for something
which it was impossible to procure for me. She is dead,
that kind, that ill-rewarded mother ! I remember the long
faces, the darkened room, the black hangings, the mysterious impression made upon my mind by the hearse and
mourning-coaches, and the difficulty which I had to reconcile all this to the disappearance of my mother. I do not

* Probably Matheson, the predecessor of Dr. Adam, to whose
memory the Author and his contemporaries owe a deep debt of
gratitude.—Alexander Matheson was rector of the High School
from 1759 to 1768, and was succeeded by Dr. Alexander Adam, who
survived till 1809 (*Laing*).

think I had before this event formed any idea of death, or
that I had even heard of that final consummation of all that
lives. The first acquaintance which I formed with it
deprived me of my only relation.

A clergyman of venerable appearance, our only visitor,
was my guide and companion in a journey of considerable
length ; and in the charge of another elderly man substituted in his place, I know not how or why, I completed my
journey to Scotland—and this is all I recollect.

I repeat the little history now, as I have a hundred times
done before, merely because I would wring some sense out
of it. Turn, then, thy sharp, wire-drawing, lawyer-like
ingenuity to the same task—make up my history as though
thou wert shaping the blundering allegations of some blue-
bonneted, hard-headed client into a condescendence of
facts and circumstance, and thou shalt be, not my Apollo—
qaid tibi cum lyra ?—but my Lord Stair. Meanwhile, I
have written myself out of my melancholy and blue devils,
merely by prosing about them ; so I will now converse half
an hour with Roan Robin in his stall ; the rascal knows me
already, and snickers whenever I cross the threshold of the
stable.

The black which you bestrode yesterday morning promises
to be an admirable roadster, and ambled as easily with Sam
and the portmanteau as with you and your load of law-
learning. Sam promises to be steady, and has hitherto
been so. No long trial, you will say. He lays the
blame of former inaccuracies on evil company—the
people who were at the livery-stable were too seduc-
tive, I suppose ; he denies he ever did the horse injustice—would rather have wanted his own dinner, he says.
In this I believe him, as Roan Robin's ribs and coat show
no marks of contradiction. However, as he will meet with
no saints in the inns we frequent, and as oats are sometimes
as speedily converted into ale as John Barleycorn himself, I
shall keep a lookout after Master Sam. Stupid fellow !
had he not abused my good-nature, I might have chatted to
him to keep my tongue in exercise, whereas now I must
keep him at a distance.

Do you remember what Mr. Fairford said to me on this
subject—it did not become my father's son to speak in that
manner to Sam's father's son ? I asked you what your
father could possibly know of mine, and you answered, " As
much, you supposed, as he knew of Sam's—it was a proverbial expression." This did not quite satisfy me, though

I am sure I cannot tell why it should not. But I am returning to a fruitless and exhausted subject. Do not be afraid that I shall come back on this well-trodden yet pathless field of conjecture. I know nothing so useless, so utterly feeble and contemptible, as the groaning forth one's helpless lamentations into the ears of our friends.

I would fain promise you that my letters shall be as entertaining as I am determined they shall be regular and well filled. We have an advantage over the dear friends of old, every pair of them. Neither David and Jonathan, nor Orestes and Pylades, nor Damon and Pythias—although, in the latter case particularly, a letter by post would have been very acceptable—ever corresponded together ; for they probably could not write, and certainly had neither posts nor franks to speed their effusions to each other ; whereas yours, which you had from the old peer, being handled gently and opened with precaution, may be returned to me again, and serve to make us free of his Majesty's post-office during the whole time of my proposed tour.* Mercy upon us, Alan, what letters I shall have to send you, with an account of all that I can collect, of pleasant or rare, in this wild-goose jaunt of mine ! All I stipulate is, that you do not communicate them to the *Scots Magazine ;* † for though you used, in a left-handed way, to compliment me on my attainments in the lighter branches of literature, at the expense of my deficiency in the weightier matters of the law, I am not yet audacious enough to enter the portal which the learned Ruddiman so kindly opened for the acolytes of the Muses. *Vale, sis memor mei.* D. L.

P. S.—Direct to the post-office here. I shall leave orders to forward your letters wherever I may travel.

* See Franking Letters. Note 6.   † See Note 7.

LETTER II

ALAN FAIRFORD TO DARSIE LATIMER

NEGATUR, my dear Darsie—you have logic and law enough to understand the word of denial—I deny your conclusion. The premises I admit, namely, that when I mounted on that infernal hack I might utter what seemed a sigh, although I deemed it lost amid the puffs and groans of the broken-winded brute, matchless in the complication of her complaints by any save she, the poor man's mare,* renowned in song, that died

A mile aboon Dundee.

But credit me, Darsie, the sigh which escaped me concerned thee more than myself, and regarded neither the superior mettle of your cavalry nor your greater command of the means of traveling. I could certainly have cheerfully ridden on with you for a few days ; and assure yourself I would not have hesitated to tax your better-filled purse for our joint expenses. But you know my father considers every moment taken from the law as a step downhill ; and I owe much to his anxiety on my account, although its effects are sometimes troublesome. For example.

I found, on my arrival at the shop in Brown's Square, that the old gentleman had returned that very evening, impatient, it seems, of remaining a night out of the guardianship of the domestic Lares. Having this information from James, whose brow wore rather an anxious look on the occasion, I despatched a Highland chairman to the livery stable with my Bucephalus, and slunk, with as little noise, as might be, into my own den, where I began to mumble certain half-gnawed and not half-digested doctrines of our municipal code. I was not long seated when my father's visage was thrust, in a peering sort of way, through the half-opened door ; and withdrawn, on seeing my occupation, with a half-articulated " humph !" which seemed to convey

* See " The Auld Man's Mare's Dead." Note 8.

a doubt of the seriousness of my application. If it were so, I cannot condemn him ; for recollection of thee occupied me so entirely during an hour's reading, that although Stair laid before me, and notwithstanding that I turned over three or four pages, the sense of his lordship's clear and perspicuous style so far escaped me that I had the mortification to find my labor was utterly in vain.

Ere I had brought up my leeway, James appeared with his summons to our frugal supper—radishes, cheese, and a bottle of the old ale—only two plates though—and no chair set for Mr. Darsie by the attentive James Wilkinson. Said James, with his long face, lank hair, and a very long pigtail in its leathern strap, was placed, as usual, at the back of my father's chair, upright as a wooden sentinel at the door of a puppet-show. "You may go down, James," said my father ; and exit Wilkinson. "What is to come next ?" thought I ; "for the weather is not clear on the paternal brow."

My boots encountered his first glance of displeasure, and he asked me, with a sneer, which way I had been riding. He expected me to answer, "Nowhere," and would then have been at me with his usual sarcasm, touching the humor of walking in shoes at twenty shillings a pair. But I answered with composure that I had ridden out to dinner as far as Noble House. He started (you know his way), as if I had said that I had dined at Jericho ; and as I did not choose to seem to observe his surprise, but continued munching my radishes in tranquillity, he broke forth in ire.

"To Noble House, sir ! and what had you to do at Noble House, sir ? Do you remember you are studying law, sir ? that your Scots law trials are coming on, sir ? that every moment of your time just now is worth hours at another time ? and have you leisure to go to Noble House, sir ? and to throw your books behind you for so many hours ? Had it been a turn in the Meadows, or even a game at golf—but Noble House, sir !"

"I went so far with Darsie Latimer, sir, to see him begin his journey."

"Darsie Latimer !" he replied in a softened tone. "Humph ! Well, I do not blame you for being kind to Darsie Latimer ; but it would have done as much good if you had walked with him as far as the toll-bar, and then made your farewells ; it would have saved horse-hire—and your reckoning, too, at dinner."

"Latimer paid that, sir," I replied, thinking to soften the matter ; but I had much better left it unspoken.

"The reckoning, sir!" replied my father. "And did you sponge upon any man for a reckoning? Sir, no man should enter the door of a public-house without paying his lawing."

"I admit the general rule, sir," I replied; "but this was a parting-cup between Darsie and me, and I should conceive it fell under the exception of *doch an dorroch.*"

"You think yourself a wit," said my father, with as near an approach to a smile as ever he permits to gild the solemnity of his features; but, I reckon you did not eat your dinner standing, like the Jews at their Passover? and it was decided in a case before the town bailies of Cupar-Angus, when Luckie Simpson's cow had drunk up Luckie Jameson's browst of ale, while it stood in the door to cool, that there was no damage to pay, because the crummie drank without sitting down; such being the very circumstances constituting *doch an dorroch,* which is a standing drink, for which no reckoning is paid. Ha, sir! what says your advocateship—*fieri*—to that? *Exceptio firmat regulam.* But come, fill your glass, Alan; I am not sorry ye have shown this attention to Darsie Latimer, who is a good lad, as times go; and having now lived under my roof since he left the school, why, there is really no great matter in coming under this small obligation to him."

As I saw my father's scruples were much softened by the consciousness of his superiority in the legal argument, I took care to accept my pardon as a matter of grace rather than of justice; and only replied, "We should feel ourselves duller of an evening, now that you were absent." I will give you my father's exact words in reply, Darsie. You know him so well that they will not offend you; and you are also aware that there mingles with the good man's preciseness and formality a fund of shrewd observation and practical good sense.

"It is very true," he said, "Darsie was a pleasant companion; but over waggish—over waggish, Alan, and somewhat scatter-brained. By the way, Wilkinson must get our ale bottled in English pints now, for a quart bottle is too much, night after night, for you and me, without his assistance. But Darsie, as I was saying, is an arch lad, and somewhat light in the upper story. I wish him well through the world; but he has little solidity, Alan—little solidity."

I scorn to desert an absent friend, Darsie, so I said for you a little more than my conscience warranted; but your defection from your legal studies had driven you far to leeward in my father's good opinion.

"Unstable as water, he shall not excel," said my father;

"or, as the Septuagint hath it, *Effusa est sicut aqua, non crescat.* He goeth to dancing-houses, and readeth novels—*sat e*t."

I endeavored to parry these texts by observing that the dancing houses amounted only to one night at La Pique's ball, the novels (so far as matter of notoriety, Darsie) to an odd volume of *Tom Jones.*

"But he danced from night to morning," replied my father, "and he read the idle trash, which the author should have been scourged for, at least twenty times over. It was never out of his hand."

I then hinted that in all probability your fortune was now so easy as to dispense with your prosecuting the law any farther than you had done ; and therefore you might think you had some title to amuse yourself. This was the least palatable argument of all.

"If he cannot amuse himself with the law," said my father, snappishly, "it is the worse for him. If he needs not law to teach him to make a fortune, I am sure he needs it to teach him how to keep one ; and it would better become him to be learning this than to be scouring the country like a landlouper, going he knows not where, to see he knows not what, and giving treats at Noble House to fools like himself (an angry glance at poor me). Noble House, indeed !" he repeated, with elevated voice and sneering tone, as if there were something offensive to him in the very name, though I will venture to say that any place in which you had been extravagant enough to spend five shillings would have stood as deep in his reprobation.

Mindful of your idea that my father knows more of your real situation than he thinks proper to mention, I thought I would hazard a fishing observation. "I did not see," I said, "how the Scottish law would be useful to a young gentleman whose fortune would seem to be vested in England."

I really thought my father would have beat me.

"D'ye mean to come round me, sir, *per ambages,* as Counselor Pest says ? What is it to you where Darsie Latimer's fortune is vested, or whether he hath any fortune, ay or no ? And what ill would the Scottish law do to him, though he had as much of it as either Stair or Bankton, sir ? Is not the foundation of our municipal law the ancient code of the Roman Empire, devised at a time when it was so much renowned for its evil polity, sir, and wisdom ? Go to your bed, sir, after your expedition to Noble House, and see that your lamp be burning, and your book before you, ere the sun peeps. *Ars longa, vita brevis*—were it not a sin to call the divine science of the law by the inferior name of art."

So my lamp did burn, dear Darsie, the next morning, though the owner took the risk of a domiciliary visitation, and lay snug in bed, trusting its glimmer might, without farther inquiry, be received as sufficient evidence of his vigilance. And now, upon this the third morning after your departure, things are but little better; for though the lamp burns in my den, and Voet, *On the Pandects,* hath his wis. dom spread open before me, yet, as I only use him as a reading-desk on which to scribble this sheet of nonsense to Darsie Latimer, it is probable the vicinity will be of little furtherance to my studies.

And now, methinks, I hear thee call me an affected hypocritical varlet, who, living under such a system of distrust and restraint as my father chooses to govern by, nevertheless pretends not to envy you your freedom and independence.

Latimer, I will tell you no lies. I wish my father would allow me a little more exercise of my free will, were it but that I might feel the pleasure of doing what would please him of my own accord. A little more spare time, and a little more money to enjoy it, would, besides, neither misbecome my age nor my condition; and it is, I own, provoking to see so many in the same situation winging the air at freedom, while I sit here, caged up like a cobbler's linnet, to chant the same unvaried lesson from sunrise to sunset, not to mention the listening to so many lectures against idleness, as if I enjoyed or was making use of the means of amusement! But then I cannot at heart blame either the motive or the object of this severity.

For the motive—it is and can only be my father's anxious, devoted, and unremitting affection and zeal for my improvement, with a laudable sense of the honor of the profession to which he has trained me. As we have no near relations, the tie betwixt us is of even unusual closeness, though in itself one of the strongest which nature can form. I am, and have all along been, the exclusive object of my father's anxious hopes, and his still more anxious and engrossing fears: so what title have I to complain, although now and then these fears and hopes lead him to take a troublesome and incessant charge of all my motions? Besides, I ought to recollect, and, Darsie, I do recollect, that my father, upon various important occasions, has shown that he can be indulgent as well as strict. The leaving his old apartments in the Luckenbooths was to him like divorcing the soul from the body ; yet Dr. R——* did but hint that the better air of this new district was more favorable to my health, as I was then suffering under the penalties of too rapid a growth, when he exchanged his old and beloved quarters, adjacent to the very Heart of Midlothian, for one of those new tenements, entire within themselves, which modern taste has so lately introduced.† Instance also the inestimable favor which he conferred on me by receiving you into his honse, when you had only the unpleasant alternative of remaining, though a grown-up lad, in the society of mere boys. This was a thing so contrary to all my father's ideas of seclusion, of economy, and of the safety to my morals and industry which he wished to attain, by preserving me from the society of other young people, that, upon my word, I am always rather astonished how I should have had the impudence to make the request than that he should have complied with it.

Then for the object of his solicitude. Do not laugh, or hold up your hands, my good Darsie ; but, upon my word, I like the profession to which I am in the course of being educated, and am serious in prosecuting the preliminary studies. The law is my vocation—in an especial, and, I may say, in an hereditary way, my vocation ; for although I have not the honor to belong to any of the great families who form in Scotland, as in France, the noblesse of the robe, and, with us at least, carry their heads as high, or rather higher, than the noblesse of the sword—for the former consist more frequently of the " first-born of Egypt "—yet my grandfather, who, I daresay, was a most excellent person, had the honor to sign a bitter protest against the Union, in the respectable character of town-clerk to the ancient borough of Birlthegroat ; and there is some reason—shall I say to hope, or to suspect ?—that he may have been a natural son of a first cousin of the then Fairford of that Ilk, who had been long numbered among the minor barons. Now my father mounted a step higher on the ladder of legal promotion, being, as you know as well as I do, an eminent and respected Writer to his Majesty's Signet ; and I myself am destined to mount a round higher still, and wear the honored robe which is sometimes supposed, like charity, to cover a multitude of sins. I have, therefore, no choice but to climb upwards, since we have mounted thus high, or else to fall down at the imminent risk of my neck. So that I reconcile myself to my destiny ;

* See Note 9.   † See Brown's Square, Edinburgh.   Note 10.

and while you are looking from mountain peaks at distant
lakes and friths, I am, *de apicibus juris,* consoling myself
with visions of crimson and scarlet gowns—with the appen-
dages of handsome cowls, well lined with salary.

You smile, Darsie, *more tuo,* and seem to say it is little
worth while to cozen one's self with such vulgar dreams ;
yours being, on the contrary, of a high and heroic character,
bearing the same resemblance to mine that a bench, covered
with purple cloth and plentifully loaded with session papers,
does to some Gothic throne, rough with barbaric pearl and
gold. But what would you have ? *Sua quemque trahit
voluptas.* And my visions of preferment, though they may
be as unsubstantial at present, are nevertheless more capable
of being realized than your aspirations after the Lord knows
what. What says my father's proverb ? " Look to a gown
of gold, and you will at least get a sleeve of it." Such is my
pursuit ; but what dost thou look to ? The chance that the
mystery, as you call it, which at present overclouds your
birth and connections will clear up into something inexpressibly and inconceivably brilliant ; and this without any effort
or exertion of your own, but purely by the good-will of Fortune. I know the pride and naughtiness of thy heart, and
sincerely do I wish that thou hadst more beatings to thank
me for than those which thou dost acknowledge so grate-
fully. Then had I thumped these Quixotical expectations
out of thee, and thou hadst not, as now, conceived thyself to
be the hero of some romantic history, and converted, in thy
vain imagination, honest Griffiths, citizen and broker, who
never bestows more than the needful upon his quarterly
epistles, into some wise Alcander or sage Alquife, the mys-
tical and magical protector of thy peerless destiny. But I
know not how it was, thy skull got harder, I think, and my
knuckles became softer ; not to mention that at length thou
didst begin to show about thee a spark of something dangerous, which I was bound to respect at least, if I did not
fear it.

And while I speak of this, it is not much amiss to advise
thee to correct a little this cock-a-hoop courage of thine. I
fear much that, like a hot-mettled horse, it will carry the
owner into some scrape, out of which he will find it difficult
to extricate himself, especially if the daring spirit which bore
thee thither should chance to fail thee at a pinch. Remember, Darsie, thou art not naturally courageous ; on the contrary, we have long since agreed that, quiet as I am, I have
the advantage in this important particular. My courage

consists, I think, in strength of nerves and constitutional indifference to danger; which, though it never pushes me on adventure, secures me in full use of my recollection and tolerably complete self-possession, when danger actually arrives. Now, thine seems more what may be called intellectual courage—highness of spirit and desire of distinction; impulses which render thee alive to the love of fame, and deaf to the apprehension of danger, until it forces itself suddenly upon thee. I own that, whether it is from my having caught my father's apprehensions, or that I have reason to entertain doubts of my own, I often think that this wildfire chase of romantic situation and adventure may lead thee into some mischief; and then what would become of Alan Fairford? They might make whom they pleased Lord Advocate or Solicitor-General, I should never have the heart to strive for it. All my exertions are intended to vindicate myself one day in your eyes; and I think I should not care a farthing for the embroidered silk gown, more than for an old woman's apron, unless I had hopes that thou shouldst be walking the boards to admire, or perhaps to envy, me.

That this may be the case, I prithee—beware! See not a Dulcinea in every slipshod girl, who, with blue eyes, fair hair, a tattered plaid, and a willow-wand in her gripe, drives out the village cows to the loaning. Do not think you will meet a gallant Valentine in every English rider, or an Orson in every Highland drover. View things as they are, and not as they may be magnified through thy teeming fancy. I have seen thee look at an old gravel pit, till thou madest out capes, and bays, and inlets, crags, and precipices, and the whole stupendous scenery of the isle of Feroe, in what was to all ordinary eyes a mere horse-pond. Besides, did I not once find thee gazing with respect at a lizard, in the attitude of one who looks upon a crocodile? Now this is, doubtless, so far a harmless exercise of your imagination, for the puddle cannot drown you, nor the Lilliputian alligator eat you up. But it is different in society, where you cannot mistake the character of those you converse with, or suffer your fancy to exaggerate their qualities, good or bad, without exposing yourself not only to ridicule, but to great and serious inconveniences. Keep guard, therefore, on your imagination, my dear Darsie; and let your old friend assure you, it is the point of your character most pregnant with peril to its good and generous owner. Adieu! let not the franks of the worthy peer remain unemployed; above all, *Sis memor mei*

A. F.

LETTER III

SHEPHERD'S BUSH.

I HAVE received thine absurd and most conceited epistle. It is well for thee that, Lovelace and Belford like, we came under a convention to pardon every species of liberty which we may take with each other ; since, upon my word, there are some reflections in your last which would otherwise have obliged me to return forthwith to Edinburgh, merely to show you I was not what you took me for.

Why, what a pair of prigs hast thou made of us ! I plunging into scrapes, without having courage to get out of them ; thy sagacious self, afraid to put one foot before the other, lest it should run away from its companion, and so standing still like a post, out of mere faintness and coldness of heart, while all the world were driving full speed past thee. Thou a portrait-painter ! I tell thee, Alan, I have seen a better seated on the fourth round of a ladder, and painting a bare-breeched Highlander, holding a pint-stoup as big as himself, and a booted Lowlander, in a bob-wig, supporting a glass of like dimensions ; the whole being designed to represent the sign of the Salutation.

How hadst thou the heart to represent thine own individual self with all thy motions, like those of a great Dutch doll, depending on the pressure of certain springs, as duty, reflection, and the like, without the impulse of which thou wouldst doubtless have me believe thou wouldst not budge an inch ? But have I not seen Gravity out of his bed at midnight ? And must I, in plain terms, remind thee of certain mad pranks ? Thou hadst ever, with the gravest sentiments in thy mouth, and the most starched reserve in thy manner, a kind of a lumbering proclivity towards mischief, although with more inclination to set it a-going than address to carry it through ; and I cannot but chuckle internally when I think of having seen my most venerable monitor, the future president of some high Scottish court, puffing, blowing, and floundering like a clumsy cart-horse in a bog where his efforts to extricate himself only plunged him deeper at every awkward struggle, till some one—I myself, for example—took compassion on the moaning monster and dragged him out by mane and tail.

As for me, my portrait is, if possible, even more scandalously caricatured. *I* fail or quail in spirit at the upcome ! Where canst thou show me the least symptom of the recreant temper with which thou hast invested me (as I trust), merely to set off the solid and impassible dignity of thine own stupid indifference? If you ever saw me tremble, be assured that my flesh, like that of the old Spanish general, only quaked at the dangers into which my spirit was about to lead it. Seriously, Alan, this imputed poverty of spirit is a shabby charge to bring against your friend. I have examined myself as closely as I can, being, in very truth, a little hurt at your having such hard thoughts of me, and on my life I can see no reason for them. I allow you have, perhaps, some advantage of me in the steadiness and indifference of your temper ; but I should despise myself if I were conscious of the deficiency in courage which you seem willing enough to impute to me. However, I suppose this ungracious hint proceeds from sincere anxiety for my safety ; and so viewing it, I swallow it as I would do medicine from a friendly doctor, although I believed in my heart he had mistaken my complaint.

This offensive insinuation disposed of, I thank thee, Alan, for the rest of thy epistle. I thought I heard your good father pronouncing the words "Noble House" with a mixture of contempt and displeasure, as if the very name of the poor little hamlet were odious to him, or, as if you had selected, out of all Scotland, the very place at which you had no call to dine. But if he had had any particular aversion to that blameless village and very sorry inn, is it not his own fault that I did not accept the invitation of the laird of Glengallacher to shoot a buck in what he emphatically calls his "country"? Truth is, I had a strong desire to have complied with his lairdship's invitation. To shoot a buck ! Think how magnificent an idea to one who never shot anything but hedge-sparrows, and that with a horse-pistol, purchased at a broker's stand in the Cowgate ! You, who stand upon your courage, may remember that I took the risk of firing the said pistol for the first time, while you stood at twenty yards' distance ; and that when you were persuaded it would go off without bursting, forgetting all law but that of the biggest and strongest, you possessed yourself of it ex-

2

clusively for the rest of the holidays. Such a day's sport
was no complete introduction to the noble art of deer-stalk-
ing, as it is practised in the Highlands ; but I should not
have scrupled to accept honest Glengallacher's invitation at
the risk of firing a rifle for the first time, had it not been
for the outcry which your father made at my proposal, in
the full ardor of his zeal for King George, the Hanover
succession, and the Presbyterian faith. I wish I had stood
out, since I have gained so little upon his good opinion by
submission. All his impressions concerning the Highlanders are taken from the recollections of the Forty-five, when
he retreated from the West Port with his brother volun-
teers, each to the fortalice of his own separate dwelling, so
soon as they heard the Adventurer was arrived with his
clans as near them as Kirkliston. The flight of Falkirk—
parma non bene selecta—in which I think your sire had his
share with the undaunted western regiment, does not seem
to have improved his taste for the company of the Highlanders (*quære*, Alan, dost thou derive the courage thou
makest such boast of from an hereditary source ?) ; and stories of Rob Roy MacGregor and Sergeant Alan Mohr Cameron* have served to paint them in still more sable colors
to his imagination.

Now, from all I can understand, these ideas, as applied to
the present state of the country, are absolutely chimerical.
The Pretender is no more remembered in the Highlands than
if the poor gentleman were gathered to his hundred and
eight fathers, whose portraits adorn the ancient walls of
Holyrood ; the broadswords have passed into other hands ;
the targets are used to cover the butter-churns ; and the
race has sunk, or is fast sinking, from ruffling bullies into
tame cheaters. Indeed, it was partly my conviction that
there is little to be seen in the North which, arriving at your
father's conclusion, though from different premises, inclined my course in this direction, where perhaps I shall see
as little.

One thing, however, I *have* seen ; and it was with pleasure
the more indescribable, that I was debarred from treading
the land which my eyes were permitted to gaze upon, like
those of the dying prophet from the top of Mount Pisgah.
I have seen, in a word, the fruitful shores of merry England
—merry England ! of which I boast myself a native, and on

* Of Rob Roy we have had more than enough. Alan Cameron,
commonly called Sergeant Mohr, a freebooter of the same period,
was equally remarkable for strength, courage and generosity.

which I gaze, even while raging floods and unstable quicksands divide us, with the filial affection of a dutiful son.

Thou canst not have forgotten, Alan—for when didst thou ever forget what was interesting to thy friend ?—that the same letter from my friend Griffiths which doubled my income, and placed my motions at my own free disposal, contained a prohibitary clause, by which, reason none assigned, I was interdicted, as I respected my present safety and future fortunes, from visiting England ; every other part of the British dominions, and a tour, if I pleased, on the Continent, being left to my own choice. Where is the tale, Alan, of a covered dish in the midst of a royal banquet, upon which the eyes of every guest were immediately fixed, neglecting all the dainties with which the table was loaded ? This clause of banishment from England—from my native country—from the land of the brave, and the wise, and the free—affects me more than I am rejoiced by the freedom and independence assigned to me in all other respects. Thus, in seeking this extreme boundary of the country which I am forbidden to tread, I resemble the poor tethered horse, which, you may have observed, is always grazing on the very verge of the circle to which it is limited by its halter.

Do not accuse me of romance for obeying this impulse towards the South ; nor suppose that, to gratify the imaginary longing of an idle curiosity, I am in any danger of risking the solid comforts of my present condition. Whoever has hitherto taken charge of my motions has shown me, by convincing proofs, more weighty than the assurances which they have withheld, that my real advantage is their principal object. I should be, therefore, worse than a fool did I object to their authority, even when it seems somewhat capriciously exercised ; for assuredly, at my age, I might—entrusted as I am with the care and management of myself in every other particular—expect that the cause of excluding me from England should be frankly and fairly stated for my own consideration and guidance. However, I will not grumble about the matter. I shall know the whole story one day, I suppose ; and perhaps, as you sometimes surmise, I shall not find there is any mighty matter in it after all.

Yet one cannot help wondering—but, plague on it, if I wonder any longer, my letter will be as full of wonders as one of Katterfelto's advertisements. I have a month's mind, instead of this damnable iteration of guesses and forebodings, to give thee the history of a little adventure which befell me yesterday ; though I am sure you will, as usual, turn the opposite end of the spy-glass on my poor narrative, and reduce, *more tuo*, to the most petty trivialities the circumstances to which thou accusest me of giving undue consequence. Hang thee, Alan, thou art as unfit a confidant for a youthful gallant with some spice of imagination as the old taciturn secretary of Facardin of Trebizond. Nevertheless, we must each perform our separate destinies. I am doomed to see, act, and tell; thou, like a Dutchman, inclosed in the same diligence with a Gascon, to hear and shrug thy shoulders.

Of Dumfries, the capital town of this county, I have but little to say, and will not abuse your patience by reminding you that it is built on the gallant river Nith, and that its churchyard, the highest place of the whole town, commands an extensive and fine prospect. Neither will I take the traveler's privilege of inflicting upon you the whole history of Bruce poniarding the Red Comyn in the church of the Dominicans at this place, and becoming a king and patriot, because he had been a church-breaker and a murderer. The present Dumfriezers remember and justify the deed, observing, it was only a Papist church; in evidence whereof, its walls have been so completely demolished that no vestiges of them remain. They are a sturdy set of true-blue Presbyterians, these burghers of Dumfries; men after your father's own heart, zealous for the Protestant succession, the rather that many of the great families around are suspected to be of a different way of thinking, and shared, a great many of them, in the insurrection of the Fifteen, and some in the more recent business of the Forty-five. The town itself suffered in the latter era; for Lord Elcho, with a large party of the rebels, levied a severe contribution upon Dumfries, on account of the citizens having annoyed the rear of the Chevalier during his march into England.

Many of these particulars I learned from Provost C——, who, happening to see me in the market-place, remembered that I was an intimate of your father's, and very kindly asked me to dinner. Pray tell your father that the effects of his kindness to me follow me everywhere. I became tired, however, of this pretty town in the course of twenty-four hours, and crept along the coast eastwards, amusing myself with looking out for objects of antiquity, and sometimes making, or attempting to make, use of my new angling-rod. By the way, old Cotton's instructions, by which I hoped to qualify myself for one of the gentle society of anglers, are not worth a farthing for this meridian. I learned this by mere accident, after I had waited four mortal hours. I shall never forget an impudent urchin, a cowherd, about twelve years old, without either brogue or bonnet, barelegged, and with a very indifferent pair of breeches— how the villain grinned in scorn at my landing-net, my plummet, and the gorgeous jury of flies which I had assembled to destroy all the fish in the river. I was induced at last to lend the rod to the sneering scoundrel, and, to see what he would make of it ; and he not only half filled my basket in an hour, but literally taught me to kill two trouts with my own hand. This, and Sam having found the hay and oats, not forgetting the ale, very good at this small inn, first made me take the fancy of resting here for a day or two ; and I have got my grinning blackguard of a *piscator* leave to attend on me, by paying sixpence a-day for a herd-boy in his stead.

A notably clean Englishwoman keeps this small house, and my bedroom is sweetened with lavender, has a clean sash-window, and the walls are, moreover, adorned with ballads of fair Rosamond and Cruel Barbara Allan. The woman's accent, though uncouth enough, sounds yet kindly in my ear ; for I have never yet forgotten the desolate effect produced on my infant organs when I heard on all sides your slow and broad Northern pronunciation, which was to me the tone of a foreign land. I am sensible I myself have since that time acquired Scotch in perfection, and many a Scotticism withal. Still the sound of the English accentuation comes to my ears as the tones of a friend ; and even when heard from the mouth of some wandering beggar, it has seldom failed to charm forth my mite. You Scotch, who are so proud of your own nationality, must make due allowance for that of other folks.

On the next morning, I was about to set forth to the stream where I had commenced angler the night before, but was prevented, by a heavy shower of rain, from stirring abroad the whole forenoon ; during all which time I heard my varlet of a guide as loud with his blackguard jokes in the kitchen as a footman in the shilling gallery ; so little are modesty and innocence the inseparable companions of of rusticity and seclusion.

When after dinner the day cleared, and we at length sallied out to the riverside, I found myself subjected to a new trick on the part of my accomplished preceptor. Apparently he liked fishing himself better than the trouble of instructing an awkward novice such as I ; and in hopes of exhausting my patience, and inducing me to resign the rod, as I had done on the preceding day, my friend contrived to keep me thrashing the water more than an hour with a pointless hook. I detected this trick at last, by observing the rogue grinning with delight when he saw a large trout rise and dash harmless away from the angle. I gave him a sound cuff, Alan ; but the next moment was sorry, and, to make amends, yielded possession of the fishing-rod for the rest of the evening, he undertaking to bring me home a dish of trouts for my supper, in atonement for his offenses.

Having thus got honorably rid of the trouble of amusing myself in a way I cared not for, I turned my steps towards the sea, or rather the Solway Firth, which here separates the two sister kingdoms, and which lay at about a mile's distance, by a pleasant walk over sandy knolls, covered with short herbage, which you call links, and we English downs.

But the rest of my adventure would weary out my fingers, and must be deferred until to-morrow, when you shall hear from me by way of continuation ; and, in the meanwhile, to prevent overhasty conclusions, I must just hint to you, we are but yet on the verge of the adventure which it is my purpose to communicate.

LETTER IV

THE SAME TO THE SAME

I MENTIONED in my last that, having abandoned my fishing-rod as an unprofitable implement, I crossed over the open downs which divided me from the margin of the Solway. When I reached the banks of the great estuary, which are here very bare and exposed, the waters had receded from the large and level space of sand, through which a stream, now feeble and fordable, found its way to the ocean. The whole was illuminated by the beams of the low and setting sun, who showed his ruddy front, like a warrior prepared for defense, over a huge battlemented and turreted wall of crimson and black clouds, which appeared like an immense Gothic fortress, into which the lord of day was descending. His setting rays glimmered bright upon the wet surface of the sands and the numberless pools of water by which it was covered, where the inequality of the ground had occasioned their being left by the tide.

The scene was animated by the exertions of a number of horsemen, who were actually employed in hunting salmon. Ay, Alan, lift up your hands and eyes as you will, I can give their mode of fishing no name so appropriate : for they chased the fish at full gallop, and struck them with their barbed spears, as you see hunters spearing boars in the old tapestry. The salmon, to be sure, take the thing more quietly than the boars ; but they are so swift in their own element, that to pursue and strike them is the task of a good horseman, with a quick eye, a determined hand, and full command both of his horse and weapon. The shouts of the fellows as they galloped up and down in the animating exercise, their loud bursts of laughter when any of their number caught a fall, and still louder acclamations when any of the party made a capital stroke with his lance, gave so much animation to the whole scene, that I caught the enthusiasm of the sport, and ventured forward a considerable space on the sands. The feats of one horseman, in particular, called forth so repeatedly the clamorous applause of his companions, that the very banks rang again with their shouts. He was a tall man, well mounted on a strong black horse, which he caused to turn and wind like a bird in the air, carried a longer spear than the others, and wore a sort of fur cap or bonnet, with a short feather in it, which gave him on the whole rather a superior appearance to the other fishermen. He seemed to hold some sort of authority among them, and occasionally directed their motions both by voice and hand ; at which times I thought his gestures were striking, and his voice uncommonly sonorous and commanding.

The riders began to make for the shore, and the interest of the scene was almost over, while I lingered on the sands, with my looks turned to the shores of England, still gilded by the sun's last rays, and, as it seemed, scarce distant a mile from me. The anxious thoughts which haunt me began to muster in my bosom, and my feet slowly and insensibly approached the river which divided me from the forbidden precincts, though without any formed intention, when my steps were arrested by the sound of a horse galloping ; and as I turned the rider, the same fisherman whom I had formerly distinguished, called out to me, in an abrupt manner, "Soho, brother ! you are too late for Bowness to-night—the tide will make presently."

I turned my head and looked at him without answering ; for, to my thinking, his sudden appearance, or rather, I should say, his unexpected approach, had, amidst the gathering shadows and lingering light, something in it which was wild and ominous.

"Are you deaf ?" he added, "or are you mad ? or have you a mind for the next world ?"

"I am a stranger," I answered, "and had no other purpose than looking on at the fishing ; I am about to return to the side I came from."

"Best make haste then," said he. "He that dreams on the bed of the Solway may wake in the next world. The sky threatens a blast that will bring in the waves three feet abreast."

So saying, he turned his horse and rode off, while I began to walk back towards the Scottish shore, a little alarmed at what I had heard ; for the tide advances with such rapidity upon these fatal sands, that well-mounted horsemen lay aside hopes of safety if they see its white surge advancing while they are yet at a distance from the bank.

These recollections grew more agitating, and, instead of walking deliberately, I began a race as fast as I could, feel-

ing, or thinking I felt, each pool of salt water through which
1 splashed grow deeper and deeper. At length the surface
of the sand did seem considerably more intersected with pools
and channels full of water—either that the tide was really
beginning to influence the bed of the estuary, or, as I must
own is equally probable, that I had, in the hurry and confusion of my retreat, involved myself in difficulties which I
had avoided in my more deliberate advance. Either way, it
was rather an unpromising state of affairs, for the sands at the
same time turned softer, and my footsteps, so soon as I had
passed, were instantly filled with water. I began to have
odd recollections concerning the snugness of your father's
parlor, and the secure footing afforded by the pavement of
Brown's Square and Scot's Close, when my better genius,
the tall fisherman, appeared once more close to my side, he
and his sable horse looming gigantic in the now darkening
twilight.

"Are you mad?" he said, in the same deep tone which
had before thrilled on my ear, "or are you weary of your
life? You will be presently amongst the quicksands." I
professed my ignorance of the way, to which he only replied,
"There is no time for prating; get up behind me."

He probably expected me to spring from the ground with
the activity which these Borderers have, by constant practise, acquired in everything relating to horsemanship; but
as I stood irresolute, he extended his hand, and grasping
mine, bid me place my foot on the toe of his boot, and thus
raised me in a trice to the croupe of his horse. I was scarce
securely seated ere he shook the reins of his horse, who instantly sprung forward; but annoyed, doubtless, by the
unusual burden, treated us to two or three bounds, accompanied by as many flourishes of his hind heels. The rider
sat like a tower, notwithstanding that the unexpected plunging of the animal threw me forward upon him. The horse
was soon compelled to submit to the discipline of the spur
and bridle, and went off at a steady hand gallop; thus short-
ening the devious, for it was by no means a direct, path by
which the rider, avoiding the loose quicksands, made for the
northern bank.

My friend, perhaps I may call him my preserver—for, to
a stranger, my situation was fraught with real danger—continued to press on at the same speedy pace, but in perfect
silence, and I was under too much anxiety of mind to disturb
him with any questions. At length we arrived at a part of
the shore with which I was utterly unacquainted, when I

alighted and began to return, in the best fashion I could, my thanks for the important service which he had just rendered me.

The stranger only replied by an impatient "Pshaw!" and was about to ride off and leave me to my own resources, when I implored him to complete his work of kindness by directing me to Shepherd's Bush, which was, as I informed him, my home for the present.

"To Shepherd's Bush!" he said. "It is but three miles but if you know not the land better than the sand, you may break your neck before you get there; for it is no road for a moping boy in a dark night; and, besides, there are the brook and the fens to cross."

I was a little dismayed at this communication of such difficulties as my habits have not called on me to contend with. Once more the idea of thy father's fireside came across me; and I could have been well contented to have swopped the romance of my situation, together with the glorious independence of control which I possessed at the moment, for the comforts of the chimney-corner, though I were obliged to keep my eyes chained to Erskine's larger *Institutes*.

I asked my new friend whether he could not direct me to any house of public entertainment for the night; and supposing it probable he was himself a poor man, I added, with the conscious dignity of a well-filled pocket-book, that I could make it worth any man's while to oblige me. The fisherman making no answer, I turned away from him with as gallant an appearance of indifference as I could command, and began to take, as I thought, the path which he had pointed out to me.

His deep voice immediately sounded after me to recall me. "Stay, young man—stay, you have mistaken the road already. I wonder your friends send out such an inconsiderate youth, without some one wiser than himself to take care of him."

"Perhaps they might not have done so," said I, "if I had any friends who cared about the matter."

"Well, sir," he said, "it is not my custom to open my house to strangers, but your pinch is like to be a smart one; for, besides the risk from bad roads, fords, and broken ground, and the night, which looks both black and gloomy, there is bad company on the road sometimes—at least it has a bad name, and some have come to harm; so that I think I must for once make my rule give way to your necessity, and give you a night's lodging in my cottage."

Why was it, Alan, that I could not help giving an involuntary shudder at receiving an invitation so seasonable in itself, and so suitable to my naturally inquisitive disposition ? I easily suppressed this untimely sensation ; and, as I returned thanks, and expressed my hope that I should not disarrange his family, I once more dropped a hint of my desire to make compensation for any trouble I might occasion. The man answered very coldly, " Your presence will no doubt give me trouble, sir, but it is of a kind which your purse cannot compensate ; in a word, although I am content to receive you as my guest, I am no publican to call a reckoning."

I begged his pardon, and, at his instance, once more seated myself behind him upon the good horse, which went forth steady as before—the moon, whenever she could penetrate the clouds, throwing the huge shadow of the animal, with its double burden, on the wild and bare ground over which we passed.

Thou mayst laugh till thou lettest the letter fall if thou wilt, but it reminded me of the magician Atlantes on his hippogriff, with a knight trussed up behind him, in the manner Ariosto has depicted that matter. Thou art, I know, matter-of-fact enough to affect contempt of that fascinating and delicious poem ; but think not that, to conform with thy bad taste, I shall forbear any suitable illustration which now or hereafter may occur to me.

On we went, the sky blackening around us, and the wind beginning to pipe such a wild and melancholy tune as best suited the hollow sounds of the advancing tide, which I could hear at a distance, like the roar of some immense monster defrauded of its prey.

At length, our course was crossed by a deep dell or dingle, such as they call in some parts of Scotland a den, and in others a cleuch, or narrow glen. It seemed, by the broken glances which the moon continued to throw upon it, to be steep, precipitous, and full of trees, which are, generally speaking, rather scarce upon these shores. The descent by which we plunged into this dell was both steep and rugged, with two or three abrupt turnings ; but neither danger nor darkness impeded the motion of the black horse, who seemed rather to slide upon his haunches than to gallop down the pass, throwing me again on the shoulders of the athletic rider, who, sustaining no inconvenience by the circumstance, continued to press the horse forward with his heel, steadily supporting him at the same time by raising

his bridle-hand, until we stood in safety at the bottom of
the steep—not a little to my consolation, as, friend Alan,
thou mayst easily conceive.

A very short advance up the glen, the bottom of which
we had attained by this ugly descent, brought us in front of
two or three cottages, one of which another blink of moonshine enabled me to rate as rather better than those of the
Scottish peasantry in this part of the world ; for the sashes
seemed glazed, and there were what are called storm-win-
dows in the roof, giving symptoms of the magnificence of a
second story. The scene around was very interesting ; for
the cottages, and the yards or crofts annexed to them, occupied a " haugh," or holm, of two acres, which a brook
of some consequence (to judge from its roar) had left upon
one side of the little glen while finding its course close to the
further bank, and which appeared to be covered and darkened with trees, while the level space beneath enjoyed such
stormy smiles as the moon had that night to bestow.

I had little time for observation, for my companion's loud
whistle, seconded by an equally loud halloo, speedily brought
to the door of the principal cottage a man and a woman, together with two large Newfoundland dogs, the deep baying
of which I had for some time heard. A yelping terrier or
two, which had joined the concert, were silent at the presence of my conductor, and began to whine, jump up, and
fawn upon him. The female drew back when she beheld a
stranger ; the man, who had a lighted lantern, advanced,
and, without any observation, received the horse from my
host, and led him, doubtless, to stable, while I followed my
conductor into the house. When he had passed the hallan,
we entered a well-sized apartment, with a clean brick floor,
where a fire blazed (much to my contentment) in the ordinary projecting sort of chimney common in Scottish houses.
There were stone seats within the chimney ; and ordinary
utensils, mixed with fishing-spears, nets, and similar implement of sport, were hung around the walls of the place. The
female who had first appeared at the door had now retreated
into a side apartment. She was presently followed by my
guide, after he had silently motioned me to a seat ; and their
place was supplied by an elderly woman, in a gray stuff gown,
with a check apron and " toy," obviously a menial, though
neater in her dress than is usual in her apparent rank—an
advantage which was counterbalanced by a very forbidding
aspect. But the most singular part of her attire, in this
very Protestant country, was a rosary, in which the smaller

beads were black oak, and those indicating the *paternoster* of silver, with a crucifix of the same metal.

This person made preparations for supper, by spreading a clean though coarse cloth over a large oaken table, placing trenchers and salt upon it, and arranging the fire to receive a gridiron. I observed her motions in silence; for she took no sort of notice of me, and as her looks were singularly forbidding, I felt no disposition to commence conversation.

When this duenna had made all preliminary arrangements, she took from the well-filled pouch of my conductor, which he had hung up by the door, one or two salmon, or grilses, as the smaller sort are termed, and selecting that which seemed best, and in highest season, began to cut it into slices and to prepare a grillade, the savory smell of which affected me so powerfully that I began sincerely to hope that no delay would intervene between the platter and the lip.

As this thought came across me the man who had conducted the horse to the stable entered the apartment, and discovered to me a countenance yet more uninviting than that of the old crone who was performing with such dexterity the office of cook to the party. He was perhaps sixty years old; yet his brow was not much furrowed, and his jet-black hair was only grizzled, not whitened, by the advance of age. All his motions spoke strength unabated; and, though rather undersized, he had very broad shoulders, was square-made, thin-flanked, and apparently combined in his frame muscular strength and activity; the last somewhat impaired perhaps by years, but the first remaining in full vigor. A hard and harsh countenance; eyes far sunk under projecting eyebrows, which were grizzled like his hair; a wide mouth, furnished from ear to ear with a range of unimpaired teeth, of uncommon whiteness, and a size and breadth which might have become the jaws of an ogre, completed this delightful portrait. He was clad like a fisherman, in jacket and trousers of the blue cloth commonly used by seamen, and had a Dutch case-knife, like that of a Hamburgh skipper, stuck into a broad buff belt, which seemed as if it might occasionally sustain weapons of a description still less equivocally calculated for violence.

This man gave me an inquisitive, and, as I thought, a sinister, look upon entering the apartment; but, without any farther notice of me, took up the office of arranging the table, which the old lady had abandoned for that of cooking the fish, and, with more address than I expected from a person of his coarse appearance, placed two chairs at the head of the table, and two stools below ; accommodating each seat to a cover, beside which he placed an allowance of barley-bread, and a small jug, which he replenished with ale from a large black-jack. Three of these jugs were of ordinary earthenware, but the fourth, which he placed by the right-hand cover at the upper end of the table, was a flagon of silver, and displayed armorial bearings. Beside this flagon he placed a salt-cellar of silver, handsomely wrought, containing salt of exquisite whiteness, with pepper and other spices. A sliced lemon was also presented on a small silver salver. The two large water-dogs, who seemed perfectly to understand the nature of the preparations, seated themselves one on each side of the table, to be ready to receive their portion of the entertainment. I never saw finer animals, or which seemed to be more influenced by a sense of decorum, excepting that they slobbered a little as the rich scent from the chimney was wafted past their noses. The small dogs ensconced themselves beneath the table.

I am aware that I am dwelling upon trivial and ordinary circumstances, and that perhaps I may weary out your patience in doing so. But conceive me alone in this strange place, which seemed, from the universal silence, to be the very temple of Harpocrates ; remember that this is my first excursion from home ; forget not that the manner in which I had been brought hither had the dignity of danger and something the air of an adventure, and that there was a mysterious incongruity in all I had hitherto witnessed ; and you will not, I think, be surprised that these circumstances, though trifling, should force themselves on my notice at the time, and dwell in my memory afterwards.

That a fisher, who pursued the sport perhaps for his amusement as well as profit, should be well mounted and better lodged than the lower class of peasantry had in it nothing surprising ; but there was something about all that I saw which seemed to intimate that I was rather in the abode of a decayed gentleman, who clung to a few of the forms and observances of former rank, than in that of a common peasant, raised above his fellows by comparative opulence.

Besides the articles of plate which I have already noticed, the old man now lighted and placed on the table a silver lamp, or " cruisie," as the Scottish term it, filled with very pure oil, which in burning diffused an aromatic fragrance, and gave me a more perfect view of the cottage walls, which I had hitherto only seen dimly by the light of the fire. The bink, with its usual arrangement of pewter and earthenware, which was most strictly and critically clean, glanced back the flame of the lamp merrily from one side of the apartment. In a recess, formed by the small bow of a latticed window, was a large writing-desk of walnut-tree wood, curiously carved, above which arose shelves of the same, which supported a few books and papers. The opposite side of the recess contained (as far as I could discern, for it lay in shadow, and I could not at any rate have seen it but imperfectly from the place where I was seated) one or two guns, together with swords, pistols, and other arms—a collection which, in a poor cottage, and in a country so peaceful, appeared singular at least, if not even somewhat suspicious.

All these observations, you may suppose, were made much sooner than I have recorded, or you (if you have not skipped) have been able to read them. They were already finished, and I was considering how I should open some communication with the mute inhabitants of the mansion, when my conductor re-entered from the side door by which he had made his exit.

He had now thrown off his rough riding-cap and his coarse jockey-coat, and stood before me in a gray jerkin trimmed with black, which sat close to, and set off, his large and sinewy frame, and a pair of trousers of a lighter color, cut as close to the body as they are used by Highlandmen. His whole dress was of finer cloth than that of the old man ; and his linen, so minute was my observation, clean and unsullied, His shirt was without ruffles, and tied at the collar with a black ribbon, which showed his strong and muscular neck rising from it, like that of an ancient Hercules. His head was small, with a large forehead and well-formed ears. He wore neither peruke nor hair-powder ; and his chestnut locks, curling close to his head, like those of an antique statue, showed not the least touch of time, though the owner must have been at least fifty. His features were high and prominent in such a degree that one knew not whether to term them harsh or handsome. In either case, the sparkling gray eye, aquiline nose, and well-formed mouth combined to render his physiognomy noble and expressive. An air of sadness, or severity, or of both, seemed to indicate a melancholy, and, at the same time, a haughty, temper. I could not help running mentally over the ancient heroes to whom I might assimilate the noble form and countenance before me. He was too young, and evinced too little resignation to his fate, to resemble Belisarius. Coriolanus standing by the hearth of Tullus Aufidius came nearer the mark ; yet the gloomy and haughty look of the stranger, had, perhaps, still more of Marius seated among the ruins of Carthage.

While I was lost in these imaginations, my host stood by the fire, gazing on me with the same attention which I paid to him, until, embarrassed by his look, I was about to break silence at all hazards. But the supper, now placed upon the table, reminded me, by its appearance, of those wants which I had almost forgotton while I was gazing on the fine form of my conductor. He spoke at length, and I almost started at the deep rich tone of his voice, though what he said was but to invite me to sit down to the table. He himself assumed the seat of honor, beside which the silver flagon was placed, and beckoned to me to sit beside him.

Thou knowest thy father's strict and excellent domestic discipline has trained me to hear the invocation of a blessing before we break the daily bread, for which we are taught to pray ; I paused a moment, and without designing to do so, I suppose my manner made him sensible of what I expected. The two domestics, or inferiors, as I should have before observed, were already seated at the bottom of the table, when my host shot a glance of a very peculiar expression towards the old man, observing, with something approaching to a sneer, " Cristal Nixon, say grace ; the gentleman expects one."

" The foul fiend shall be clerk and say "amen," when I turn chaplain," growled out the party addressed, in tones which might have become the condition of a dying bear. " If the gentleman is a Whig, he may please himself with his mummery. My faith is neither in word nor writ, but in barley bread and brown ale."

" Mabel Moffat," said my guide looking at the old woman, and raising his sonorous voice, probably because she was hard of hearing, " canst thou ask a blessing upon our victuals."

The old woman shook her head, kissed the cross which hung from her rosary, and was silent.

" Mabel will say grace for no heretic," said the master of the house, with the same latent sneer on his brow and in his accent.

At the same moment, the side-door already mentioned opened, and the young woman (so she proved) whom I had first seen at the door of the cottage advanced a little way into the room, then stopped bashfully, as if she had observed that I was looking at her, and asked the master of the house " if he had called."

"Not louder than to make old Mabel hear me," he replied. "And yet," he added, as she turned to retire, "it is a shame a stranger should see a house where not one of the family can or will say grace ; do thou be our chaplain."

The girl, who was really pretty, came forward with timid modesty, and, apparently unconscious that she was doing anything uncommon, pronounced the benediction in a silver-toned voice, and with affecting simplicity, her cheek coloring just so much as to show that, on a less solemn occasion, she would have felt more embarrassed.

Now, if thou expectest a fine description of this young woman, Alan Fairford, in order to entitle thee to taunt me with having found a Dulcinea in the inhabitant of a fisherman's cottage on the Solway Firth, thou shalt be disappointed ; for, having said she seemed very pretty, and that she was a sweet and gentle-speaking creature, I have said all concerning her that I can tell thee. She vanished when the benediction was spoken.

My host, with a muttered remark on the cold of our ride, and the keen air of the Solway sands, to which he did not seem to wish an answer, loaded my plate from Mabel's grillade, which, with a large wooden bowl of potatoes, formed our whole meal. A sprinkling from the lemon gave a much higher zest than the usual condiment of vinegar ; and I promise you that whatever I might hitherto have felt, either of curiosity or suspicion, did not prevent me from making a most excellent supper, during which little passed betwixt me and my entertainer, unless that he did the usual honors of the table with courtesy, indeed, but without even the affectation of hearty hospitality which those in his (apparent) condition generally affect on such occasions, even when they do not actually feel it. On the contrary, his manner seemed that of a polished landlord towards an unexpected and un-welcome guest, whom, for the sake of his own credit, he receives with civility, but without either good-will or cheerfulness.

If you ask how I learned all this, I cannot tell you ; nor, were I to write down at length the insignificant intercourse which took place between us, would it perhaps serve to justify these observations. It is sufficient to say that, in helping his dogs, which he did from time to time with great liberality, he seemed to discharge a duty much more pleasing to himself than when he paid the same attention to his guest. Upon the whole, the result on my mind was as I tell it you.

When supper was over, a small case-bottle of brandy, in a

curious frame of silver filigree, circulated to the guests. I had already taken a small glass of the liquor, and, when it had passed to Mabel and to Cristal, and was again returned to the upper end of the table, I could not help taking the bottle in my hand, to look more at the armorial bearings, which were chased with considerable taste on the silver framework. Encountering the eye of my entertainer, I instantly saw that my curiosity was highly distasteful; he frowned, bit his lip, and showed such uncontrollable signs of impatience that, setting the bottle immediately down, I attempted some apology. To this he did not deign either to reply or even to listen; and Cristal at a signal from his master removed the object of my curiosity, as well as the cup, upon which the same arms were engraved.

There ensued an awkward pause, which I endeavored to break by observing, that "I feared my intrusion upon his hospitality had put his family to some inconvenience."

"I hope you see no appearance of it, sir," he replied, with cold civility. "What inconvenience a family so retired as ours may suffer from receiving an unexpected guest is like to be trifling, in comparison of what the visitor himself sustains from want of his accustomed comforts. So far, therefore, as our connection stands, our accounts stand clear."

Notwithstanding this discouraging reply, I blundered on, as is usual in such cases, wishing to appear civil, and being, perhaps, in reality the very reverse. "I was afraid," I said, "that my presence had banished one of the family (looking at the side-door) from this table."

"If," he coldly replied, "I meant the young woman whom I had seen in the apartment, he bid me observe that there was room enough at the table for her to have seated herself, and meat enough, such as it was, for her supper. I might, therefore, be assured, if she had chosen it, she would have supped with us."

There was no dwelling on this or any other topic longer; for my entertainer, taking up the lamp, observed, that "My wet clothes might reconcile me for the night to their custom of keeping early hours; that he was under the necessity of going abroad by peep of day to-morrow morning, and would call me up at the same time, to point out the way by which I was to return to the Shepherd's Bush."

This left no opening for further explanation; nor was there room for it on the usual terms of civility; for, as he neither asked my name nor expressed the least interest

The supper party at **Redgauntlet Cottage.**

concerning my condition, I—the obliged person—had no pretense to trouble him with such inquiries on my part.

He took up the lamp and led me through the side-door into a very small room, where a bed had been hastily arranged for my accommodation, and, putting down the lamp, directed me to leave my wet clothes on the outside of the door, that they might be exposed to the fire during the night. He then left me having muttered something which was meant to pass for " Good-night. "

I obeyed his directions with respect to my clothes, the rather that, in spite of the spirits which I had drank, I felt my teeth begin to chatter, and received various hints from an aguish feeling that a town-bred youth, like myself, could not at once rush into all the hardihood of country sports with impunity. But my bed, though coarse and hard, was dry and clean ; and I soon was so little occupied with my heats and tremors as to listen with interest to a heavy foot, which seemed to be that of my landlord, traversing the boards (there was no ceiling, as you may believe) which roofed my apartment. Light, glancing through these rude planks, became visible as soon as my lamp was extinguished ; and the noise of the slow, solemn, and regular step continued, and I could distinguish that the person turned and returned as he reached the end of the apartment, it seemed clear to me that the walker was engaged in no domestic occupation, but merely pacing to and fro for his own pleasure. " An odd amusement this," 1 thought, " for one who has been engaged at least a part of the preceding day in violent exercise, and who talked of rising by the peep of dawn on the ensuing morning."

Meantime I heard the storm, which had been brewing during the evening, begin to descend with a vengeance ; sounds as of distant thunder (the noise of the more distant waves, doubtless on the shore) mingled with the roaring of the neighboring torrent, and with the crashing, groaning, and even screaming of the trees in the glen, whose boughs were tormented by the gale. Within the house, windows clattered and doors clapped, and the walls, though sufficiently substantial for a building of the kind, seemed to me to totter in the tempest.

But still the heavy steps perambulating the apartment over my head were distinctly heard, amid the roar and fury of the elements. I thought more than once I even heard a groan ; but I frankly own that, placed in this unusual situation, my fancy may have misled me. I was tempted several times to call aloud, and ask whether the turmoil around us did not threaten danger to the building which we inhabited ; but when I thought of the secluded and unsocial master of the dwelling, who seemed to avoid human society, and to remain unperturbed amid the elemental war, it seemed that to speak to him at that moment would have been to address the spirit of the tempest himself, since no other being, I thought, could have remained calm and tranquil while winds and waters were thus raging around.

In process of time, fatigue prevailed over anxiety and curiosity. The storm abated, or my senses became deadened to its terrors, and I fell asleep ere yet the mysterious paces of my host had ceased to shake the flooring over my head.

It might have been expected that the novelty of my situation, although it did not prevent my slumbers, would have at least diminished their profoundness and shortened their duration. It proved, otherwise, however ; for I never slept more soundly in my life, and only awoke when, at morning dawn, my landlord shook me by the shoulder, and dispelled some dream, of which, fortunately for you, I have no recollection, otherwise you would have been favored with it, in hopes you might have proved a second Daniel upon the occasion.

"You sleep sound," said his full deep voice ; "ere five years have rolled over your head, your slumbers will be lighter—unless ere then you are wrapped in the sleep which is never broken."

"How !" said I, starting up in the bed ; "do you know anything of me—of my prospects—of my views in life ?"

"Nothing," he answered, with a grim smile ; "but it is evident you are entering upon the world young, inexperienced, and full of hopes, and I do but prophesy to you what I would to any one in your condition. But come ; there lie your clothes ; a brown crust and a draught of milk wait you, if you choose to break your fast ; but you must make haste."

"I must first," I said, "take the freedom to spend a few minutes alone, before beginning the ordinary works of the day."

"Oh ! humph ! I cry your devotions pardon," he replied, and left the apartment.

Alan, there is something terrible about this man.

I joined him, as I had promised, in the kitchen where we had supped over night, where I found the articles which he had offered me for breakfast, without butter or any other addition.

He walked up and down, while I partook of the bread and milk ; and the slow, measured, weighty step seemed identified with those which I had heard last night. His pace, from its funereal slowness, seemed to keep time with some current of internal passion, dark, slow, and unchanged. "We run and leap by the side of a lively and bubbling brook," thought I, internally, "as if we would run a race with it ; but beside waters deep, slow, and lonely our pace is sullen and silent as their course. What thoughts may be now corresponding with that furrowed brow and bearing time with that heavy step !"

"If you have finished," said he, looking up to me with a glance of impatience, as he observed that I ate no longer, but remained with my eyes fixed upon him, "I wait to show you the way."

We went out together, no individual of the family having been visible excepting my landlord. I was disappointed of the opportunity which I watched for of giving some gratuity to the domestics, as they seemed to be. As for offering any recompense to the master of the household, it seemed to me impossible to have attempted it.

What would I have given for a share of thy composure, who wouldst have thrust half-a-crown into a man's hand whose necessities seemed to crave it, conscious that you did right in making the proffer, and not caring sixpence whether you hurt the feelings of him whom you meant to serve ! I saw thee once give a penny to a man with a long beard, who, from the dignity of his exterior, might have represented Solon. I had not thy courage, and therefore I made no tender to my mysterious host, although, notwithstanding his display of silver utensils, all around the house bespoke narrow circumstances, if not actual poverty.

We left the place together. But I hear thee murmur thy very new and appropriate ejaculation, *Ohe jam satis !* The rest for another time. Perhaps I may delay farther communication till I learn how my favors are valued.

LETTER V

I HAVE thy two last epistles, my dear Darsie, and, expecting the third, have been in no hurry to answer them. Do not think my silence ought to be ascribed to my failing to take interest in them, for, truly, they excel (though the task was difficult) thy usual excellings. Since the moon-calf who earliest discovered the Pandemonium of Milton in an expiring woodfire, since the first ingenious urchin who blew bubbles out of soap and water, thou, my best of friends, hast the highest knack at making histories out of nothing. Wert thou to plant the bean in the nursery tale, thou wouldst make out, so soon as it began to germinate, that the castle of the giant was about to elevate its battlements on the top of it. All that happens to thee gets the touch of the wonderful and the sublime from thy own rich imagination. Didst ever see what artists call a Claude Lorraine glass, which spreads its own particular hue over the whole landscape which you see through it ? Thou beholdest ordinary events just through such a medium.

I have looked carefully at the facts of thy last long letter, and they are just such as might have befallen any little truant of the High School who had got down to Leith sands, gone beyond the "prawn dub," wet his hose and shoon, and, finally, had been carried home, in compassion, by some high-kilted fishwife, cursing all the while the trouble which the brat occasioned her.

I admire the figure which thou must have made, clinging for dear life behind the old fellow's back, thy jaws chattering with fear, thy muscles cramped with anxiety. Thy execrable supper of broiled salmon, which was enough to ensure the nightmare's regular visits for a twelvemonth, may be termed a real affliction ; but as for the storm of Thursday last (such, I observe, was the date), it roared, whistled, howled, and bellowed as fearfully amongst the old chimney-heads in the Candlemaker Row as it could on the Solway shore, for the very wind of it—*teste me per totam noctem vigilante.* And then in the morning again, when—

Lord help you !—in your sentimental delicacy you bid the poor man adieu without even tendering him half-a-crown for supper and lodging ! You laugh at me for giving a penny (to be accurate, though, thou shouldst have said sixpence) to an old fellow whom thou, in thy high flight, wouldst have sent home supperless because he was like Solon or Belisarius. But you forget that the affront descended like a benediction into the pouch of the old gaberlunzie, who overflowed in blessings upon the generous donor. Long ere he would have thanked thee, Darsie, for thy barren veneration of his beard and his bearing. Then you laugh at my good father's retreat from Falkirk, just as if it were not time for a man to trudge when three or four mountain knaves, with naked claymores, and heels as light as their fingers, were scampering after him crying "furinish." You remember what he said himself when the laird of Bucklivat told him that "furinish" signified, "stay awhile." "What the devil," he said, surprised out of his Presbyterian correctness by the unreasonableness of such a request under the circumstances, "would the scoundrels have had me stop to have my head cut off ? "

Imagine such a train at your own heels, Darsie, and ask yourself whether you would not exert your legs as fast as you did in flying from the Solway tide. And yet you impeach my father's courage ! I tell you he has courage enough to do what is right and to spurn what is wrong—courage enough to defend a righteous cause with hand and purse, and to take the part of the poor man against his oppressor, without fear of the consequences to himself. This is civil courage, Darsie ; and it is of little consequence to most men in this age and country whether they ever possess military courage or no.

Do not think I am angry with you, though I thus attempt to rectify your opinions on my father's account. I am well aware that, upon the whole, he is scarce regarded with more respect by me than by thee. And while I am in a serious humor, which it is difficult to preserve with one who is perpetually tempting me to laugh at him, pray, dearest Darsie, let not thy ardor for adventnre carry thee into more such scrapes as that of the Solway sands. The rest of the story is a mere imagination ; but that stormy evening might have proved, as the clown says to Lear, a "naughty night to swim in."

As for the rest, if you can work mysterious and romantic heroes out of old cross-grained fishermen, why, I for one will reap some amusement by the metamorphosis. Yet hold! even there, there is some need of caution. This same female chaplain—thou sayest so little of her, and so much of every one else, that it excites some doubt in my mind. " Very pretty " she is, it seems, and that is all thy discretion informs me of. There are cases in which silence implies other things than consent. Wert thou ashamed or afraid, Darsie, to trust thyself with the praises of the very pretty grace-sayer? As I live, thou blushest! Why, do I not know thee an inveterate squire of dames? and have I not been in thy confidence? An elegant elbow, displayed when the rest of the figure was muffled in a cardinal, or a neat, well-turned ankle and instep, seen by chance as its owner tripped up the Old Assembly Close,* turned thy brain for eight days. Thou wert once caught, if I remember rightly, with a single glance of a single matchless eye, which, when the fair owner withdrew her veil, proved to be single in the literal sense of the word. And, besides, were you not another time enamored of a voice—a new voice, that mingled in the psalmody at the Old Greyfriars' church— until you discovered the proprietor of that dulcet organ to be Miss Dolly MacIzzard, who is both " back and breast," as our saying goes?

All these things considered, and contrasted with thy artful silence on the subject of this grace-saying Nereid of thine, I must beg thee to be more explicit upon that subject in thy next, unless thou wouldst have me form the con clusion that thou thinkest more of her than thou carest to talk of.

You will not expect much news from this quarter, as you know the monotony of my life, and are aware it must at present be devoted to uninterrupted study. You have said a thousand times that I am only qualified to make my way by dint of plodding, and therefore plod I must.

My father seems to be more impatient of your absence than he was after your first departure. He is sensible, I believe, that our solitary meals want the light which your gay humor was wont to throw over them, and feels melancholy, as men do when the light of the sun is no longer upon the landscape. If it is thus with him, thou mayst imagine it is much more so with me, and canst conceive how heartily I wish that thy frolic were ended, and thou once more our inmate.

* Of old this almost deserted alley formed the most common access betwixt the High Street and the southern suburbs

I resume my pen, after a few hours' interval, to say that
an incident has occurred on which you will yourself be
building a hundred castles in the air, and which even I,
jealous as I am of such baseless fabrics, cannot but own
affords ground for singular conjecture.

My father has of late taken me frequently along with him
when he attends the courts, in his anxiety to see me properly initiated into the practical forms of business. I own I
feel something on his account and my own from this over-
anxiety, which, I daresay renders us both ridiculous. But
what signifies my repugnance? My father drags me up to
his counsel learned in the law. "Are you quite ready to
come on to-day, Mr. Crossbite? This is my son, designed
for the bar; I take the liberty to bring him with me to-day
to the consultation, merely that he may see how these things
are managed."

Mr. Crossbite smiles and bows, as a lawyer smiles on the
solicitor who employs him, and, I daresay, thrusts his
tongue into his cheek and whispers into the first great wig
that passes him, "What the d—l does old Fairford mean by
letting loose his whelp on me?"

As I stood beside them, too much vexed at the childish
part I was made to play to derive much information from
the valuable arguments of Mr. Crossbite, I observed a rather
elderly man, who stood with his eyes firmly bent on my
father, as if he only waited an end of the business in which
he was engaged to address him. There was something, I
thought, in the gentleman's appearance which commanded
attention. Yet his dress was not in the present taste, and
though it had once been magnificent, was now antiquated
and unfashionable. His coat was of branched velvet, with a
satin lining, a waistcoat of violet-colored silk, much embroidered; his breeches the same stuff as the coat. He
wore square-toed shoes, with foretops, as they are called;
and his silk stockings were rolled up over his knee, as you
may have seen in pictures, and here and there on some of
those originals who seem to pique themselves on dressing
after the mode of Methuselah. A *chapeau bras* and sword
necessarily completed his equipment, which, though out of
date, showed that it belonged to a man of distinction.

The instant Mr. Crossbite had ended what he had to say,
this gentleman walked up to my father with, "Your servant, Mr. Fairford; it is long since you and I met."

My father, whose politeness, you know, is exact and formal, bowed and hemmed, and was confused, and at length

professed that the distance since they had met was so great that though he remembered the face perfectly, the name, he was sorry to say, had—really—somehow—escaped his memory.

" Have you forgot Herries of Birrenswork ? " said the gentleman, and my father bowed even more profoundly than before ; though I think his reception of his old friend seemed to lose some of the respectful civility which he bestowed on him while his name was yet unknown. It now seemed to be something like the lip-courtesy which the heart would have denied had ceremony permitted.

My father, however, again bowed low, and hoped he saw him well.

" So well, my good Mr. Fairford, that I come hither determined to renew my acquaintance with one or two old friends, and with you in the first place. I halt at my old resting-place ; you must dine with me to-day at Paterson's, at the head of the Horse Wynd ; it is near your new fashionable dwelling, and I have business with you."

My father excused himself respectfully, and not without embarrassment—" He was particularly engaged at home."

" Then I will dine with you, man," said Mr. Herries of Birrenswork ; " the few minutes you can spare me after dinner will suffice for my business ; and I will not prevent you a moment from minding your own—I am no bottle-man."

You have often remarked that my father, though a scrupulous observer of the rites of hospitality, seems to exercise them rather as a duty than as a pleasure ; indeed, but for a conscientious wish to feed the hungry and receive the stranger, his doors would open to guests much seldomer than is the case. I never saw so strong an example of this peculiarity (which I should otherwise have said is caricatured in your description) as in his mode of homologating the self-given invitation of Mr. Herries. The embarrassed brow, and the attempt at a smile which accompanied his " We will expect the honor of seeing you in Brown Square at three o'clock," could not deceive any one, and did not impose upon the old laird. It was with a look of scorn that he replied, " I will relieve you then till that hour, Mr. Fairford ;' and his whole manner seemed to say, " It is my pleasure to dine with you, and I care not whether I am welcome or no."

When he turned away, I asked my father who he was.

" An unfortunate gentleman," was the reply.

" He looks pretty well on his misfortunes," replied I. " I should not have suspected that so gay an outside was lacking a dinner."

" Who told you that he does ? " replied my father. " He is *omni suspicione major,* so far as worldly circumstances are concerned. It is to be hoped he makes a good use of them, though, if he does, it will be for the first time in his life."

" He has then been an irregular liver ? " insinuated I.

My father replied by that famous brocard with which he silences all unacceptable queries, turning in the slightest degree upon the failings of our neighbors—" If we mend our own faults, Alan, we shall all of us have enough to do, without sitting in judgment upon other folks."

Here I was again at fault ; but rallying once more I observed, he had the air of a man of high rank and family.

" He is well entitled," said my father, " representing Herries of Birrenswork—a branch of that great and once powerful family of Herries, the elder branch whereof merged in the house of Nithsdale at the death of Lord Robin the Philosopher, Anno Domini sixteen hundred and sixty-seven."

" Has he still," said I, " his patrimonial estate of Birrenswork ? "

" No," replied my father ; " so far back as his father's time, it was a mere designation, the property being forfeited by Herbert Herries's following his kinsman the Earl of Derwentwater to the Preston affair in 1715. But they keep up the designation, thinking, doubtless, that their claims may be revived in more favorable times for Jacobites and for Popery ; and folks who in no way partake of their fantastic capriccios do yet allow it to pass unchallenged, *ex comitate,* if not *ex misericordia.* But were he the Pope and the Pretender both, we must get some dinner ready for him, since he has thought fit to offer himself. So hasten home, my lad, and tell Hannah, Cook Epps, and James Wilkinson to do their best ; and do thou look out a pint or two of Maxwell's best. It is in the fifth bin ; there are the keys of the winecellar. Do not leave them in the lock. You know poor James's failing, though he is an honest creature under all other temptations ; and I have but two bottles of the old brandy left, we must keep it for medicine, Alan."

Away went I—made my preparations ; the hour of dinner came, and so did Mr. Herries of Birrenswork.

If I had thy power of imagination and description, Darsie, I could make out a fine, dark, mysterious, Rembrandt-looking portrait of this same stranger, which should be as far superior to thy fisherman as a shirt of chain-mail is to a herring-net. I can assure you there is some matter for description about him ; but knowing my own imperfections, I can only say, I thought him eminently disagreeable and ill-bred. No, "ill-bred" is not the proper word ; on the contrary, he appeared to know the rules of good breeding perfectly, and only to think that the rank of the company did not require that he should attend to them—a view of the matter infinitely more offensive than if his behavior had been that of uneducated and proper rudeness. While my father said grace, the laird did all but whistle aloud ; and when I, at my father's desire, returned thanks, he used his toothpick, as if he had waited that moment for its exercise.

So much for kirk ; with king matters went even worse. My father, thou knowest, is particularly full of deference to his guests ; and in the present case he seemed more than usually desirous to escape every cause of dispute. He so far compromised his loyalty as to announce merely "The King" as his first toast after dinner, instead of the emphatic "King George" which is his usual formula. Our guest made a motion with his glass, so as to pass it over the water-decanter which stood beside him, and added, "Over the water."

My father colored, but would not seem to hear this. Much more there was of careless and disrespectful in the stranger's manner and tone of conversation ; so that, though I know my father's prejudices in favor of rank and birth, and though I am aware his otherwise masculine understanding has never entirely shaken off the slavish awe of the great which in his earlier days they had so many modes of commanding, still I could hardly excuse him for enduring so much insolence—such it seemed to be—as this self-invited guest was disposed to offer to him at his own table.

One can endure a traveler in the same carriage, if he treads upon your toes by accident, or even through negligence ; but it is very different when, knowing that they are rather of a tender description, he continues to pound away at them with his hoofs. In my poor opinion—and I am a man of peace—you can, in that case, hardly avoid a declaration of war.

I believe my father read my thoughts in my eye ; for, pulling out his watch, he said, "Half-past four, Alan—you should be in your own room by this time ; Birrenswork will excuse you."

Our visitor nodded carelessly, and I had no longer any pretense to remain. But as I left the room I heard this magnate of Nithsdale distinctly mention the name of "Latimer." I lingered ; but at length a direct hint from my

father obliged me to withdraw ; and when, an hour afterwards, I was summoned to partake of a cup of tea, our guest
had departed. He had business that evening in the High
Street, and could not spare time even to drink tea. I could
not help saying, I considered his departure as a relief from
incivility. " What business has he to upbraid us," I said,
" with the change of our dwelling from a more inconvenient to a better quarter of the town ? What was it to
him if we chose to imitate some of the conveniences or lux-
uries of an English dwelling-house, instead of living piled
up above each other in flats ? Have his patrician birth and
aristocratic fortunes given him any right to censure those
who dispose of the fruits of their own industry according to
their own pleasure ? "

My father took a long pinch of snuff, and replied, " Very
well, Alan—very well indeed. I wish Mr. Crossbite or Counselor Pest had heard you ; they must have acknowledged
that you have a talent for forensic elocution ; and it may
not be amiss to try a little declamation at home now and
then, to gather audacity and keep yourself in breath. But
touching the subject of this paraffle of words, it's not worth
a pinch of tobacco. D'ye think that I care for Mr. Herries
of Birrenswork more than any other gentleman who comes
here about business, although I do not care to go tilting at
his throat, because he speaks like a gray goose as he is ?
But to say no more about him, I want to have Darsie Latimer's present direction ; for it is possible I may have to
write the lad a line with my own hand—and yet I do not
well know—but give me the direction at all events."

I did so, and if you have heard from my father accordingly, you know more, probably, about the subject of this
letter than I who write it. But if you have not, then shall
I have discharged a friend's duty, in letting you know that
there certainly is something afloat between this disagreeable
laird and my father in which you are considerably interested.

Adieu ! and although I have given thee a subject for
waking dreams, beware of building a castle too heavy for the
foundation, which, in the present instance, is barely the
word " Latimer " occurring in a conversation betwixt a
gentleman of Dumfriesshire and a W. S. of Edinburgh.
Cætera prorsus ignoro.

LETTER VI

DARSIE LATIMER TO ALAN FAIRFORD

(In continuation of Letters III. and IV.)

I TOLD thee I walked out into the open air with my grave and stern landlord. I could now see more perfectly than on the preceding night the secluded glen, in which stood the two or three cottages which appeared to be the abode of him and his family.

It was so narrow, in proportion to its depth, that no ray of the morning sun was likely to reach it till it should rise high in the horizon. Looking up the dell, you saw a brawling brook issuing in foaming haste from a covert of underwood, like a race-horse impatient to arrive at the goal; and, if you gazed yet more earnestly, you might observe part of a high waterfall glimmering through the foliage, and giving occasion, doubtless, to the precipitate speed of the brook. Lower down, the stream became more placid, and opened into a quiet piece of water, which afforded a rude haven to two or three fishermen's boats, then lying high and dry on the sand, the tide being out. Two or three miserable huts could be seen beside this little haven, inhabited probably by the owners of the boats, but inferior in every respect to the establishment of mine host, though that was miserable enough,

I had but a minute or two to make these observations, yet during that space my companion showed symptoms of impatience, and more than once shouted, "Cristal—Cristal Nixon," until the old man of the preceding evening appeared at the door of one of the neighboring cottages or outhouses, leading the strong black horse which I before commemorated, ready bridled and saddled. My conductor made Cristal a sign with his finger, and, turning from the cottage door, led the way up the steep path or ravine which connected the sequestered dell with the open country.

Had I been perfectly aware of the character of the road down which I had been hurried with so much impetuosity on the preceding evening, I greatly question if I should have ventured the descent; for it deserved no better name

than the channel of a torrent, now in a good measure filled
with water, that dashed in foam and fury into the dell, being
swelled with the rains of the preceding night. I ascended
this ugly path with some difficulty, although on foot, and
felt dizzy when I observed, from such traces as the rains had
not obliterated, that the horse seemed almost to have slid
down it upon his haunches the evening before.

My host threw himself on his horse's back without placing
a foot in the stirrup, passed me in the perilous ascent,
against which he pressed his steed as if the animal had had
the footing of a wildcat. The water and mud splashed from
his heels in his reckless course, and a few bounds placed him
on the top of the bank, where I presently joined him, and
found the horse and rider standing still as a statue; the
former panting and expanding his broad nostrils to the
morning wind, the latter motionless, with his eye fixed on
the first beams of the rising sun, which already began to
peer above the eastern horizon, and gild the distant mountains of Cumberland and Liddesdale.

He seemed in a reverie, from which he started at my approach, and putting his horse in motion, led the way at a
leisurely pace, through a broken and sandy road, which traversed a waste, level, and uncultivated tract of downs, intermixed with morass, much like that in the neighborhood
of my quarters at Shepherd's Bush. Indeed, the whole
open ground of this district, where it approaches the sea,
has, except in a few favored spots, the same uniform and
dreary character.

Advancing about a hundred yards from the brink of the
glen, we gained a still more extensive command of this desolate prospect, which seemed even more dreary, as contrasted with the opposite shores of Cumberland, crossed and
intersected by ten thousand lines of trees growing in hedge-
rows, shaded with groves and woods of considerable extent,
and animated by hamlets and villas, from which thin clouds
of smoke already gave sign of human life and human industry.

My conductor had extended his arm, and was pointing the
road to Shepherd's Bush, when the step of a horse was heard
approaching us. He looked sharply around, and having observed who was approaching, proceeded in his instructions
to me, planting himself at the same time in the very middle
of the path, which, at the place where we halted, had a
slough on the one side and a sandbank on the other.

I observed that the rider who approached us slackened his

horse's pace from a slow trot to a walk, as if desirous to suffer us to proceed, or at least to avoid passing us at a spot where the difficulty of doing so must have brought us very close to each other. You know my old failing, Alan, and that I am always willing to attend to anything in preference to the individual who has for the time possession of the conversation.

Agreeably to this amiable propensity, I was internally speculating concerning the cause of the rider keeping aloof from us, when my companion, elevating his deep voice so suddenly and so sternly as at once to recall my wandering thoughts, exclaimed, "In the name of the devil, young man, do you think that others have no better use for their time than you have, that you oblige me to repeat the same thing to you three times over? Do you see, I say, yonder thing at a mile's distance, that looks like a finger-post. or rather like a gallows? I would it had a dreaming fool hanging upon it, as an example to all meditative mooncalves! Yon gibbet-looking pole will guide you to the bridge, whêre you must pass the large brook; then proceed straight forwards, till several roads divide at a cairn. Plague on thee, thou art wandering again!"

It is indeed quite true that at this moment the horseman approached us, and my attention was again called to him as I made way to let him pass. His whole exterior at once showed that he belonged to the Society of Friends, or, as the world and the world's law call them, Quakers. A strong and useful iron-gray galloway showed, by its sleek and good condition, that the merciful man was merciful to his beast. His accouterments were in the usual unostentatious, but clean and serviceable, order which characterizes these sectaries. His long surtout of dark-gray superfine cloth descended down to the middle of his leg, and was buttoned up to his chin to defend him against the morning air. As usual, his ample beaver hung down without button or loop, and shaded a comely and placid countenance, the gravity of which appeared to contain some seasoning of humor, and had nothing in common with the pinched Puritanical air affected by devotees in general. The brow was open and free from wrinkles, whether of age or hypocrisy. The eye was clear, calm, and considerate, yet appeared to be disturbed by apprehension, not to say fear, as pronouncing the usual salutation of " I wish thee a good morrow, friend," he indicated by turning his palfrey close to one side of the path a wish to glide past us with as little trouble as possible, just

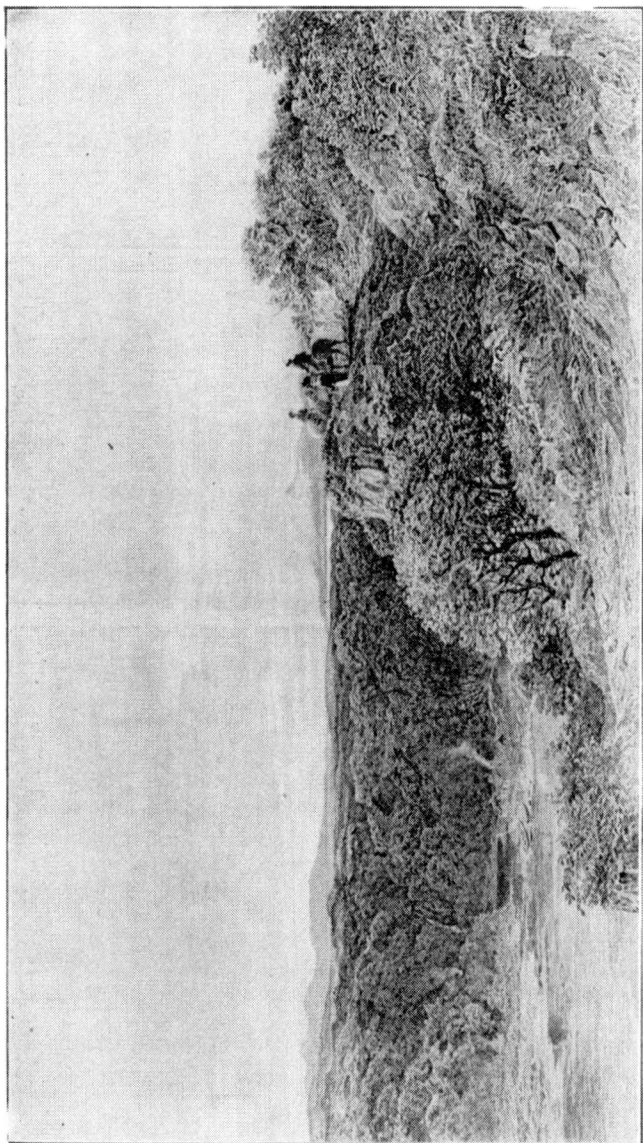

Redgauntlet and Dairsie Latimer on their way to Shepherd's Bush, intercepted by Joshua Geddes.

as a traveler would choose to pass a mastiff of whose peaceable intentions he is by no means confident.

But my friend, not meaning, perhaps, that he should get off so easily, put his horse quite across the path, so that, without plunging into the slough or scrambling up the bank, the Quaker could not have passed him. Neither of these was an experiment without hazard greater than the passenger seemed willing to incur. He halted, therefore, as if waiting till my companion should make way for him ; and, as they sat fronting each other, I could not help thinking that they might have formed no bad emblem of Peace and War ; for although my conductor was unarmed, yet the whole of his manner, his stern look, and his upright seat on horseback were entirely those of a soldier in undress. He accosted the Quaker in these words—" So ho ! friend Joshua, thou art early to the road this morning. Has the Spirit moved thee and thy righteous brethren to act with some honesty and pull down yonder tide-nets that keep the fish from coming up the river ? "

" Surely, friend, not so," answered Joshua, firmly, but good-humoredly at the same time ; " thou canst not expect that our own hands should pull down what our own purses established. Thou killest the fish with spear, line, and coble-net ; and we with snares and with nets, which work by the ebb and the flow of the tide. Each doth what seems best in his eyes to secure a share of the blessing which Providence hath bestowed on the river, and that within his own bounds. I prithee seek no quarrel against us, for thou shalt have no wrong at our hand."

" Be assured I will take none at the hand of any man, whether his hat be cocked or broad-brimmed," answered the fisherman. " I tell you in fair terms, Joshua Geddes, that you and your partners are using unlawful craft to destroy the fish in the Solway by stake-nets and wears ; and that we, who fish fairly, and like men, as our fathers did, have daily and yearly less sport and less profit. Do not think gravity or hypocrisy can carry it off as you have done. The world knows you, and we know you. You will destroy the salmon which make the livelihood of fifty poor families, and then wipe your mouth and go to make a speech at meeting. But do not hope it will last thus. I give you fair warning, we will be upon you one morning soon, when we will not leave a stake standing in the pools of the Solway ; and down the tide they shall every one go, and well if we do not send a lessee along with them."

"Friend," replied Joshua, with a constrained smile, "but that I know thou dost not mean as thou say'st, I would tell thee we are under the protection of this country's laws ; nor do we the less trust to obtain their protection, that our principles permit us not, by any act of violent resistance, to protect ourselves."

"All villainous cant and cowardice," exclaimed the fisherman, "and assumed merely as a cloak to your hypocritical avarice."

"Nay, say not cowardice, my friend," answered the Quaker, "since thou knowest there may be as much courage in enduring as in acting ; and I will be judged by this youth, or by any one else, whether there is not more cowardice— even in the opinion of that world whose thoughts are the breath in thy nostrils—in the armed oppressor who doth injury than in the defenseless and patient sufferer who endureth it with constancy."

"I will change no more words with you on the subject," said the fisherman, who, as if something moved at the last argument which Mr. Geddes had used, now made room for him to pass forward on his journey. "Do not forget, however," he added, "that you have had fair warning, nor suppose that we will accept of fair words in apology for foul play. These nets of yours are unlawful, they spoil our fishings, and we will have them down at all risks and hazards. I am a man of my word, friend Joshua."

"I trust thou art," said the Quaker ; but thou art the rather bound to be cautious in rashly affirming what thou wilt never execute. For I tell thee, friend, that though there is as great a difference between thee and one of our people as there is between a lion and a sheep, yet I know and believe that thou hast so much of the lion in thee that thou wouldst scarce employ thy strength and thy rage upon that which professeth no means of resistance. Report says so much good of thee, at least, if it says little more."

"Time will try," answered the fisherman ; "and hark thee, Joshua, before we part I will put in thee the way of doing one good deed, which, credit me, is better than twenty moral speeches. Here is a stranger youth, whom Heaven has so scantily gifted with brains that he will bewilder himself in the sands, as he did last night, unless thou wilt kindly show him the way to Shepherd's Bush ; for I have been in vain endeavoring to make him comprehend the road thither. Hast thou so much charity under thy simplicity, Quaker, as to do this good turn ?"

"Nay, it is thou, friend," answered Joshua, "that dost lack charity, to suppose any one unwilling to do so simple a kindness."

"Thou art right; I should have remembered it can cost thee nothing. Young gentleman, this pious pattern of primitive simplicity will teach thee the right way to the Shepherd's Bush—ay, and will himself shear thee like a sheep, if you come to buying and selling with him."

He then abruptly asked me how long I intended to remain at Shepherd's Bush.

I replied I was at present uncertain—as long, probably, as I could amuse myself in the neighborhood.

"You are fond of sport?" he added, in the same tone of brief inquiry.

I answered in the affirmative, but added, I was totally inexperienced.

"Perhaps, if you reside here for some days," he said, "we may meet again, and I may have the chance of giving you a lesson."

Ere I could express either thanks or assent, he turned short round with a wave of his hand, by way of adieu, and rode back to the verge of the dell from which we had emerged together; and as he remained standing upon the banks I could long hear his voice while he shouted down to those within its recesses.

Meanwhile the Quaker and I proceeded on our journey for some time in silence; he restraining his sober-minded steed to a pace which might have suited a much less active walker than myself, and looking on me from time to time with an expression of curiosity, mingled with benignity. For my part, I cared not to speak first. It happened I had never before been in company with one of this particular sect, and, afraid that in addressing him I might unwittingly infringe upon some of their prejudices or peculiarities, I patiently remained silent. At length he asked me whether I had been long in the service of the Laird, as men called him.

I repeated the words "in his service" with such an accent of surprise as induced him to say, "Nay, but, friend, I mean no offense; perhaps I should have said in his society —an inmate, I mean, in his house?"

"I am totally unknown to the person from whom we have just parted," said I, "and our connection is only temporary. He had the charity to give me his guidance from the sands, and a night's harborage from the tempest. So our acquaintance began, and there is likely to end : for you may observe that our friend is by no means apt to encourage familiarity."

"So little so," answered my companion, "that thy case is, I think, the first in which I ever heard of his receiving any one into his house; that is, if thou hast really spent the night there."

"Why should you doubt it?" replied I ; "there is no motive I can have to deceive you, nor is the object worth it."

"Be not angry with me," said the Quaker ; "but thou knowest that thine own people do not, as we humbly endeavor to do, confine themselves within the simplicity of truth, but employ the language of falsehood, not only for profit, but for compliment, and sometimes for mere diversion. I have heard various stories of my neighbor, of most of which I only believe a small part, and even then they are difficult to reconcile with each other. But this being the first time I ever heard of his receiving a stranger within his dwelling made me express some doubts. I pray thee let them not offend thee."

"He does not," said I, "appear to possess in much abundance the means of exercising hospitality, and so may be excused from offering it in ordinary cases."

"That is to say, friend," replied Joshua, "thou hast supped ill, and perhaps breakfasted worse. Now my small tenement, called Mount Sharon, is nearer to us by two miles than thine inn ; and although going thither may prolong thy walk, as taking thee off the straighter road to Shepherd's Bush, yet methinks exercise will suit thy youthful limbs, as well as a good plain meal thy youthful appetite. What sayst thou, my young acquaintance ?"

"If it puts you not to inconvenience," I replied ; for the invitation was cordially given, and my bread and milk had been hastily swallowed, and in small quantity.

"Nay," said Joshua, "use not the language of compliment with those who renounce it. Had this poor courtesy been very inconvenient, perhaps I had not offered it."

"I accept the invitation then," said I, "in the same good spirit in which you give it."

The Quaker smiled, reached me his hand ; I shook it, and we traveled on in great cordiality with each other. The fact is, I was much entertained by contrasting in my own mind the open manner of the kind-hearted Joshua Geddes with the abrupt, dark, and lofty demeanor of my entertainer on the preceding evening. Both were blunt and unceremonious ; but the plainness of the Quaker had the

character of devotional simplicity, and was mingled with
the more real kindness, as if honest Joshua was desirous of
atoning by his sincerity for the lack of external courtesy.
On the contrary, the manners of the fisherman were those
of one to whom the rules of good behavior might be
familiar, but who, either from pride or misanthropy, scorned
to observe them.   Still I thought of him with interest and
curiosity, notwithstanding so much about him that was re-
pulsive ; and I promised myself, in the course of my conversation with the Quaker, to learn all he knew on the subject.
He turned the conversation, however, into a different channel, and inquired into my own condition of life, and views
in visiting this remote frontier.

I only thought it necessary to mention my name, and add,
that I had been educated to the law, but finding myself possessed of some independence, I had of late permitted myself
some relaxation, and was residing at Shepherd's Bush to
enjoy the pleasure of angling.

"I do thee no harm, young man," said my new friend,
" in wishing thee a better employment for thy grave hours,
and a more humane amusement, if amusement thou must
have, for those of a lighter character."

"You are severe, sir," I replied.   "I heard you but a
moment since refer yourself to the protection of the laws
of the country ; if there be laws, there must be lawyers to
explain and judges to administer them."

Joshua smiled, and pointed to the sheep which were grazing
on the downs over which we were traveling.   " Were a wolf,"
he said, " to come even now upon yonder flocks, they would
crowd for protection, doubtless, around the shepherd and
his dogs ; yet they are bitten and harassed daily by the one,
shorn and finally killed and eaten, by the other.   But I say
not this to shock you ; for, though laws and lawyers are
evils, yet they are necessary evils in this probationary state
of society, till man shall learn to render unto his fellows
that which is their due, according to the light of his own
conscience, and through no other compulsion.   Meanwhile
I have known many righteous men who have followed thy
intended profession in honesty and uprightness of walk.
The greater their merit who walk erect in a path which so
many find slippery."

"And angling," said I, " you object to that also as an
amusement—you who, if I understand rightly what passed
between you and my late landlord, are yourself a proprietor
of fisheries ? "

"Not a proprietor," he replied, "I am only, in copartnery with others, a tacksman or lessee of some valuable salmon-fisheries a little down the coast. But mistake me not. The evil of angling, with which I class all sports, as they are called, which have the sufferings of animals for their end and object, does not consist in the mere catching and killing those animals with which the bounty of Providence hath stocked the earth for the good of man, but in making their protracted agony a principle of delight and enjoyment. I do indeed cause these fisheries to be conducted for the necessary taking, killing, and selling the fish ; and, in the same way, were I a farmer, I should send my lambs to market. But I should as soon think of contriving myself a sport and amusement out of the trade of the butcher as out of that of the fisher."

We argued this point no further ; for, though I thought his arguments a little too high-strained, yet, as my mind acquitted me of having taken delight in aught but the theory of field-sports, I did not think myself called upon stubbornly to advocate a practise which had afforded me so little pleasure.

We had by this time arrived at the remains of an old finger-post, which my host had formerly pointed out as a landmark. Here a ruinous wooden bridge, supported by long posts resembling crutches, served me to get across the water, while my new friend sought a ford a good way higher up, for the stream was considerably swelled.

As I paused for his rejoining me, I observed an angler at a little distance pouching trout after trout, as fast almost as he could cast his line ; and I own, in spite of Joshua's lecture on humanity, I could not but envy his adroitness and success—so natural is the love of sport to our minds, or so easily are we taught to assimilate success in field-sports with ideas of pleasure, and with the praise due to address and agility. I soon recognized in the successful angler little Benjie, who had been my guide and tutor in that gentle art, as you have learned from my former letters. I called—I whistled. The rascal recognized me, and, starting like a guilty thing, seemed hesitating whether to approach or to run away ; and when he determined on the former, it was to assail me with a loud, clamorous, and exaggerated report of the anxiety of all at the Shepherd's Bush for my personal safety—how my landlady had wept, how Sam and the hostler had not the heart to go to bed, but sat up all night drinking, and how he himself had been up long before daybreak to go in quest of me.

"And you were switching the water, I suppose," said I, "to discover my dead body?"

This observation produced a long " Na—a—a " of acknowledged detection ; but, with his natural impudence, and confidence in my good-nature, he immediately added, "That he thought I would like a fresh trout or twa for breakfast, and the water being in such rare trim for the saumon raun,* he couldna help taking a cast."

While we were engaged in this discussion, the honest Quaker returned to the further end of the wooden bridge to tell me he could not venture to cross the brook in its present state, but would be under the necessity to ride round by the stone bridge, which was a mile and a half higher up than his own house. He was about to give me directions how to proceed without him, and inquire for his sister, when I suggested to him that, if he pleased to trust his horse to little Benjie, the boy might carry him round by the bridge, while we walked the shorter and more pleasant road.

Joshua shook his head, for he was well acquainted with Benjie, who, he said, was the naughtiest varlet in the whole neighborhood. Nevertheless, rather than part company, he agreed to put the pony under his charge for a short season, with many injunctions that he should not attempt to mount, but lead the pony, even Solomon, by the bridle, under the assurances of sixpence in case of proper demeanor, and penalty that, if he transgressed the orders given him, "verily he should be scourged."

Promises cost Benjie nothing, and he showered them out wholesale ; till the Quaker at length yielded up the bridle to him, repeating his charges, and enforcing them by holding up his forefinger. On my part, I called to Benjie to leave the fish he had taken at Mount Sharon, making, at the same time, an apologetic countenance to my new friend, not being quite aware whether the compliment would be agreeable to such a condemner of field-sports.

He understood me at once, and reminded me of the practical distinction betwixt catching the animals as an object of cruel and wanton sport and eating them as lawful and gratifying articles of food after they were killed. On the latter point he had no scruples ; but, on the contrary, assured me that this brook contained the real red trout, so highly esteemed by all connoisseurs, and that, when eaten within an hour of their being caught, they had a peculiar

* The bait made of salmon-row salted and preserved. In a swollen river, and about the month of October, it is a most deadly bait.

firmness of substance and delicacy of flavor which rendered them an agreeable addition to a morning meal, especially when earned, like ours, by early rising and an hour or two's wholesome exercise.

But, to thy alarm be it spoken, Alan, we did not come so far as the frying of our fish without farther adventure. So it is only to spare thy patience, and mine own eyes, that I pull up for the present, and send thee the rest of my story in a subsequent letter.

LETTER VII

THE SAME TO THE SAME

(*In continuation*)

LITTLE BENJIE, with the pony, having been sent off on the left side of the brook, the Quaker and I sauntered on, like the cavalry and infantry of the same army occupying the opposite banks of a river, and observing the same line of march. But, while my worthy companion was assuring me of a pleasant greensward walk to his mansion, little Benjie, who had been charged to keep in sight, chose to deviate from the path assigned him, and turning to the right, led his charge, Solomon, out of our vision.

"The villain means to mount him!" cried Joshua, with more vivacity than was consistent with his profession of passive endurance.

I endeavored to appease his apprehensions, as he pushed on, wiping his brow with vexation, assuring him that, if the boy did mount, he would, for his own sake, ride gently.

"You do not know him," said Joshua, rejecting all consolation; "*he* do anything gently! no, he will gallop Solomon—he will misuse the sober patience of the poor animal who has borne me so long! Yes, I was given over to my own devices when I ever let him touch the bridle, for such a little miscreant there never was before him in this country!"

He then proceeded to expatiate on every sort of rustic enormity of which he accused Benjie. He had been suspected of snaring partridges; was detected by Joshua himself in liming singing-birds; stood fully charged with having worried several cats, by aid of a lurcher which attended him, and which was as lean, and ragged, and mischievous as his master. Finally, Benjie stood accused of having stolen a duck, to hunt it with the said lurcher, which was as dexterous on water as on land. I chimed in with my friend, in order to avoid giving him further irritation, and declared, I should be disposed, from my own experience, to give up Benjie as one of Satan's imps. Joshua Geddes began to censure the phrase as too much exaggerated, and otherwise

unbecoming the mouth of a reflecting person ; and, just as
I was apologizing for it, as being a term of common par-
lance, we heard certain sounds on the opposite side of the
brook, which seemed to indicate that Solomon and Benjie
were at issue together. The sand-hills behind which Benjie
seemed to take his course had concealed from us, as
doubtless he meant they should, his ascent into the forbidden saddle, and, putting Solomon to his mettle, which he
was seldom called upon to exert, they had cantered away
together in great amity, till they came near to the ford
from which the palfrey's legitimate owner had already
turned back.

Here a contest of opinions took place between the horse
and his rider. The latter, according to his instructions,
attempted to direct Solomon towards the distant bridge of
stone ; but Solomon opined that the ford was the shortest
way to his own stable. The point was sharply contested,
and we heard Benjie gee-hupping, tchek-tcheking, and,
above all, flogging in great style ; while Solomon, who,
docile in his general habits, was now stirred beyond his
patience, made a great trampling and recalcitration ; and it
was their joint noise which we heard, without being able to
see, though Joshua might too well guess, the cause of it.

Alarmed at these indications, the Quaker began to shout
out, " Benjie, thou varlet !—Solomon, thou fool !" when
the couple presented themselves in full drive, Solomon having now decidedly obtained the better of the conflict, and
bringing his unwilling rider in high career down to the
ford. Never was there anger changed so fast into humane
fear as that of my good companion. " The varlet will be
drowned !" he exclaimed—"a widow's son !—her only son !
—and drowned ! Let me go——" And he struggled with
me stoutly as I hung upon him, to prevent him from plunging into the ford.

I had no fear whatever for Benjie ; for the blackguard
vermin, though he could not manage the refractory horse,
stuck on his seat like a monkey. Solomon and Benjie
scrambled through the ford with little inconvenience, and
resumed their gallop on the other side.

It was impossible to guess whether on this last occasion
Benjie was running off with Solomon or Solomon with
Benjie ; but, judging from character and motives, I rather
suspected the former. I could not help laughing as the
rascal passed me, grinning betwixt terror and delight,
perched on the very pommel of the saddle, and holding

with extended arms by bridle and mane; while Solomon, the bit secured between his teeth, and his head bored down betwixt his fore-legs, passed his master in this unwonted guise as hard as he could pelt.

"The mischievous bastard!" exclaimed the Quaker, terrified out of his usual moderation of speech—"the doomed gallows-bird! he will break Solomon's wind to a certainty."

I prayed him to be comforted; assured him a brushing gallop would do his favorite no harm; and reminded him of the censure he had bestowed on me a minute before for applying a harsh epithet to the boy.

But Joshua was not without his answer. "Friend youth," he said, "thou didst speak of the lad's soul, which thou didst affirm belonged to the enemy, and of that thou couldst say nothing of thine own knowledge; on the contrary, I did but speak of his outward man, which will assuredly be suspended by a cord, if he mendeth not his manners. Men say that, young as he is, he is one of the Laird's gang."

"Of the Laird's gang!" said I, repeating the words in surprise. "Do you mean the person with whom I slept last night? I heard you call him the Laird. Is he at the head of a gang?"

"Nay, I meant not precisely a gang," said the Quaker, who appeared in his haste to have spoken more than he intended—"a company, or party, I should have said; but thus, it is, friend Latimer, with the wisest men, when they permit themselves to be perturbed with passion, and speak as in a fever, or as with the tongue of the foolish and the forward. And although thou hast been hasty to mark my infirmity, yet I grieve not that thou hast been a witness to it, seeing that the stumbles of the wise may be no less a caution to youth and inexperience than is the fall of the foolish."

This was a sort of acknowledgment of what I had already begun to suspect—that my new friend's real goodness of disposition, joined to the acquired quietism of his religious sect, had been unable entirely to check the effervescence of a temper naturally warm and hasty.

Upon the present occasion, as if sensible he had displayed a greater degree of emotion than became his character, Joshua avoided further allusion to Benjie and Solomon, and proceeded to solicit my attention to the natural objects around us, which increased in beauty and interest as, still

conducted by the meanders of the brook, we left the common behind us, and entered a more cultivated and inclosed
country, where arable and pasture land was agreeably varied
with groves and hedges. Descending now almost close to
the stream, our course lay through a little gate, into a path-
way kept with great neatness, the sides of which were decorated with trees and flowering shrubs of the hardier species ;
until, ascending by a gentle slope, we issued from the grove,
and stood almost at once in front of a low but very neat
building, of an irregular form ; and my guide, shaking me
cordially by the hand, made me welcome to Mount Sharon.

The wood through which we had approached this little
mansion was thrown around it both on the north and northwest, but, breaking off into different directions, was intersected by a few fields, well watered and sheltered. The
house fronted to the south-east, and from thence the pleasure-
ground, or, I should rather say, the gardens, sloped down to
the water. I afterwards understood that the father of the
present proprietor had a considerable taste for horticulture,
which had been inherited by his son, and had formed these
gardens, which, with their shaven turf, pleached alleys,
wildernesses, and exotic trees and shrubs, greatly excelled
anything of the kind which had been attempted in the neighborhood.

If there was a little vanity in the complacent smile with
which Joshua Geddes saw me gaze with delight on a scene
so different from the naked waste we had that day traversed
in company, it might surely be permitted to one who, culti-
vating and improving the beauties of nature, had found
therein, as he said, bodily health and a pleasing relaxation
for the mind. At the bottom of the extended gardens the
brook wheeled round in a wide semicircle, and was itself
their boundary. The opposite side was no part of Joshua's
domain, but the brook was there skirted by a precipitous
rock of limestone, which seemed a barrier of nature's own
erecting around his little Eden of beauty, comfort, and
peace.

"But I must not let thee forget," said the kind Quaker,
"amidst thy admiration of these beauties of our little inheritance, that thy breakfast has been a light one."

So saying, Joshua conducted me to a small sashed door
opening under a porch amply mantled by honeysuckle and
clematis, into a parlor of moderate size ; the furniture of
which, in plainness and excessive cleanliness, bore the characteristic marks of the sect to which the owner belonged.

Thy father's Hannah is generally allowed to be an exception to all Scottish housekeepers, and stands unparalleled for cleanliness among the women of Auld Reekie ; but the cleanliness of Hannah is sluttishness compared to the scrupulous purifications of these people, who seem to carry into the minor decencies of life that conscientious rigor which they affect in their morals.

The parlor would have been gloomy, for the windows were small and the ceiling low ; but the present proprietor had rendered it more cheerful by opening one end into a small conservatory, roofed with glass, and divided from the parlor by a partition of the same. I have never before seen this very pleasing manner of uniting the comforts of an apartment with the beauties of the garden, and I wonder it is not more practised by the great. Something of the kind is hinted at in a paper of the *Spectator*.

As I walked towards the conservatory to view it more closely, the parlor chimney engaged my attention. It was a pile of massive stone, entirely out of proportion to the size of the apartment. On the front had once been an armorial scutcheon ; for the hammer, or chisel, which had been employed to deface the shield and crest had left uninjured the scroll beneath, which bore the pious motto, " Trust in God." Black-letter, you know, was my early passion, and the tombstones in the Greyfriars' churchyard early yielded up to my knowledge as a decipherer what little they could tell of the forgotten dead.

Joshua Geddes paused when he saw my eye fixed on this relic of antiquity. " Thou canst read it ? " he said.

I repeated the motto, and added, there seemed vestiges of a date.

" It should be 1537," said he ; " for so long ago, at the least computation, did my ancestors, in the blinded times of Papistry, possess these lands, and in that year did they build their house."

" It is an ancient descent," said I, looking with respect upon the monument. " I am sorry the arms have been defaced."

It was perhaps impossible for my friend, Quaker as he was, to seem altogether void of respect for the pedigree which he began to recount to me, disclaiming all the while the vanity usually connected with the subject ; in short, with the air of mingled melancholy, regret, and conscious dignity with which Jack Fawkes used to tell us, at college, of his ancestor's unfortunate connection with the Gunpowder Plot.

"Vanity of vanities, saith the preacher," thus harangued Joshua Geddes of Mount Sharon, "if we ourselves are nothing in the sight of Heaven, how much less than nothing must be our derivation from rotten bones and moldering dust, whose immortal spirits have long since gone to their private account! Yes, friend Latimer, my ancestors were renowned among the ravenous and bloodthirsty men who then dwelt in this vexed country ; and so much were they famed for successful freebooting, robbery, and bloodshed, that they are said to have been called Geddes, as likening them to the fish called a jack, pike, or luce, and in our country tongue, a "ged." A goodly distinction truly for Christian men ! Yet did they paint this shark of the fresh water upon their shields, and these profane priests of a wicked idolatry, the empty boasters called heralds, who make engraven images of fishes, fowls, and four-footed beasts, that men may fall down and worship them, assigned the ged for the device and escutcheon of my fathers, and hewed it over their chimneys, and placed it above their tombs ; and the men were elated in mind, and became yet more ged-like, slaying, leading into captivity, and dividing the spoil, until the place where they dwelt obtained the name of Sharing Knowe, from the booty which was there divided amongst them and their accomplices. But a better judgment was given to my father's father, Philip Geddes, who, after trying to light his candle at some of the vain wildfires then held aloft at different meetings and steeple-houses, at length obtained a spark from the lamp of the blessed George Fox, who came into Scotland spreading light among darkness, as he himself hath written, as plentifully as fly the sparkles from the hoof of the horse which gallops swiftly along the stony road." Here the good Quaker interrupted himself with, "And that is very true, I must go speedily to see after the condition of Solomon."

A Quaker servant here entered the room with a tray, and inclining his head towards his master, but not after the manner of one who bows, said composedly, "Thou art welcome home, friend Joshua, we expected thee not so early ; but what hath befallen Solomon thy horse ?"

"What hath befallen him, indeed," said my friend, "hath he not been returned hither by the child whom they call Benjie ?"

"He hath," said his domestic, "but it was after a strange fashion ; for he came hither at a swift and furious pace, and flung the child Benjie from his back, upon the heap of dung which is in the stable-yard."

"I am glad of it," said Joshua, hastily—"glad of it, with all my heart and spirit! But stay, he is the child of the widow—hath the boy any hurt?"

"Not so," answered the servant, "for he rose and fled swiftly."

Joshua muttered something about a scourge, and then inquired after Solomon's present condition.

"He seetheth like a steaming cauldron," answered the servant; "and Bauldie, the lad, walketh him about the yard with a halter, lest he take cold."

Mr. Geddes hastened to the stable-yard to view personally the condition of his favorite, and I followed, to offer my counsel as a jockey—don't laugh, Alan; sure I have jockey-ship enough to assist a Quaker—in this unpleasing predicament.

The lad who was leading the horse seemed to be no Quaker, though his intercourse with the family had given him a touch of their prim sobriety of look and manner. He assured Joshua that his horse had received no injury, and I even hinted that the exercise would be of service to him. Solomon himself neighed towards his master, and rubbed his head against the good Quaker's shoulder, as if to assure him of his being quite well; so that Joshua returned in comfort to his parlor, where breakfast was now about to be displayed.

I have since learned that the affection of Joshua for his pony is considered as inordinate by some of his own sect; and that he has been much blamed for permitting it to be called by the name of Solomon, or any other name whatever; but he has gained so much respect and influence among them that they overlook these foibles.

I learned from him (whilst the old servant, Jehoiachim, entering and re-entering, seemed to make no end of the materials which he brought in for breakfast) that his grandfather Philip, the convert of George Fox, had suffered much from the persecution to which these harmless devotees were subjected on all sides during that intolerant period, and much of their family estate had been dilapidated. But better days dawned on Joshua's father, who, connecting himself by marriage with a wealthy family of Quakers in Lancashire, engaged successfully in various branches of commerce, and redeemed the remnants of the property, changing its name in sense, without much alteration of sound, from the Border appellation of Sharing Knowe to the evangelical appellation of Mount Sharon.

This Philip Geddes, as I before hinted, had imbibed the taste for horticulture and the pursuits of the florist which are not uncommon among the peaceful sect he belonged to. He had destroyed the remnants of the old peel-house, substituting the modern mansion in its place ; and while he reserved the hearth of his ancestors, in memory of their hospitality, as also the pious motto which they had chanced to assume, · he failed not to obliterate the worldly and military emblems displayed upon the shield and helmet, together with all their blazonry.

In a few minutes after Mr. Geddes had concluded the account of himself and his family, his sister Rachel, the only surviving member of it, entered the room. Her appearance is remarkably pleasing, and although her age is certainly thirty at least, she still retains the shape and motion of an earlier period. The absence of everything like fashion or ornament was, as usual, atoned for by the most perfect neatness and cleanliness of her dress ; and her simple close cap was particularly suited to eyes which had the softness and simplicity of the dove's. Her features were also extremely agreeable, but had suffered a little through the ravages of that professed enemy to beauty, the small-pox—a disadvantage which was in part counterbalanced by a well-formed mouth, teeth like pearls, and a pleasing sobriety of smile, that seemed to wish good here and hereafter to every one she spoke to. You cannot make any of your vile inferences here, Alan, for I have given a full-length picture of Rachel Geddes ; so that you cannot say in this case, as in the letter I have just received, that she was passed over as a subject on which I feared to dilate. More of this anon.

Well, we settled to our breakfast after a blessing, or rather an extempore prayer, which Joshua made upon the occasion, and which the Spirit moved him to prolong rather more than I felt altogether agreeable. Then, Alan, there was such a despatching of the good things of the morning as you have not witnessed since you have seen Darsie Latimer at breakfast. Tea and chocolate, eggs, ham, and pastry, not forgetting the broiled fish, disappeared with a celerity which seemed to astonish the good-humored Quakers, who kept loading my plate with supplies, as if desirous of seeing whether they could by any possibility tire me out. One hint, however, I received which put me in mind where I was. Miss Geddes had offered me some sweet-cake, which, at the moment, I declined; but presently afterwards, seeing it within my reach, I naturally enough helped myself to a slice, and had just deposited it beside my plate, when Joshua, mine host, not with the authoritative air of Sancho's doctor, Tirtea Fuera, but in a very calm and quiet manner, lifted it away and replaced it on the dish, observing only, "Thou didst refuse it before, friend Latimer."

These good folks, Alan, make no allowance for what your father calls the Aberdeen man's privilege of "taking his word again," or what the wise call second thoughts.

Bating this slight hint that I was among a precise generation, there was nothing in my reception that was peculiar— unless, indeed, I were to notice the solicitous and uniform kindness with which all the attentions of my new friends were seasoned, as if they were anxious to assure me that the neglect of worldly compliments interdicted by their sect only served to render their hospitality more sincere. At length my hunger was satisfied, and the worthy Quaker, who, with looks of great good-nature, had watched my progress, thus addressed his sister :

" This young man, Rachel, hath last night sojourned in the tents of our neighbor, whom men call the Laird. I am sorry I had not met him the evening before, for our neighbor's hospitality is too unfrequently exercised to be well prepared with the means of welcome."

" Nay, but, Joshua," said Rachel, " if our neighbor hath done a kindness, thou shouldst not grudge him the opportunity ; and if our young friend hath fared ill for a night, he will the better relish what Providence may send him of better provisions."

" And that he may do so at leisure," said Joshua, " we will pray him, Rachel, to tarry a day or twain with us ; he is young, and is but now entering upon the world, and our habitation may, if he will, be like a resting-place, from which he may look abroad upon the pilgrimage which he must make and the path which he has to travel. What sayest thou, friend Latimer ? We constrain not our friends to our ways, and thou art, I think, too wise to quarrel with us for following our own fashions ; and if we should even give thee a word of advice, thou wilt not, I think, be angry, so that it is spoken in season."

You know, Alan, how easily I am determined by anything resembling cordiality ; and so, though a little afraid of the formality of my host and hostess, I accepted their invitation,

5

provided I could get some messenger to send to Shepherd's Bush for my servant and portmanteau.

"Why, truly, friend," said Joshua, "thine outward frame would be improved by cleaner garments; but I will do thine errand myself to the Widow Gregson's house of reception, and send thy lad hither with thy clothes. Meanwhile, Rachel will show thee these little gardens, and then will put thee in some way of spending thy time usefully, till our meal calls us together at the second hour afternoon. I bid thee farewell for the present, having some space to walk, seeing I must leave the animal Solomon to his refreshing rest."

With these words, Mr. Joshua Geddes withdrew. Some ladies we have known would have felt, or at least affected, reserve or embarrassment at being left to do the honors of the grounds to—(it will be out, Alan)—a smart young fellow, an entire stranger. She went out for a few minutes, and returned in her plain cloak and bonnet, with her beaver gloves, prepared to act as my guide, with as much simplicity as if she had been to wait upon thy father. So forth I sallied with my fair Quaker.

If the house at Mount Sharon be merely a plain and convenient dwelling, of moderate size, and small pretensions, the gardens and offices, though not extensive, might rival an earl's in point of care and expense. Rachel carried me first to her own favorite resort, a poultry-yard, stocked with a variety of domestic fowls, of the more rare as well as the more ordinary kinds, furnished with every accommodation which may suit their various habits. A rivulet, which spread into a pond for the convenience of the aquatic birds, trickled over gravel as it passed through the yards dedicated to the land poultry, which were thus amply supplied with the means they use for digestion.

All these creatures seemed to recognize the presence of their mistress, and some especial favorites hastened to her feet, and continued to follow her as far as their limits permitted. She pointed out their peculiarities and qualities, with the discrimination of one who had made natural history her study; and I own I never looked on barn-door fowls with so much interest before—at least until they were boiled or roasted. I could not help asking the trying question, how she could order the execution of any of the creatures of which she seemed so careful.

"It was painful," she said, "but it was according to the law of their being. They must die; but they knew not when death was approaching; and in making them comfortable while they lived, we contributed to their happiness as much as the conditions of their existence permitted to us."

I am not quite of her mind, Alan. I do not believe either pigs or poultry would admit that the chief end of their being was to be killed and eaten. However, I did not press the argument from which my Quaker seemed rather desirous to escape ; for, conducting me to the greenhouse, which was extensive, and filled with the choicest plants, she pointed out an aviary which occupied the farther end, where, she said, she employed herself with attending the inhabitants, without being disturbed with any painful recollections concerning their future destination.

I will not trouble you with any account of the various hot-houses and gardens and their contents. No small sum of money must have been expanded in erecting and maintaining them in the exquisite degree of good order which they exhibited. The family, I understood, were connected with that of the celebrated Millar, and had imbibed his taste for flowers and for horticulture. But instead of murdering botanical names, I will rather conduct you to the policy, or pleasure-garden, which the taste of Joshua or his father had extended on the banks betwixt the house and river. This also, in contradistinction to the prevailing simplicity, was ornamented in an unusual degree. There were various compartments, the connection of which was well managed, and although the whole ground did not exceed five or six acres, it was so much varied as to seem four times larger. The space contained close alleys and open walks, a very pretty artificial waterfall, a fountain also, consisting of a considerable *jet d'eau*, whose streams glittered in the sunbeams and exhibited a continual rainbow. There was a " cabinet of verdure," as the French call it, to cool the summer heat, and there was a terrace sheltered from the northeast by a noble holly hedge, with all its glittering spears, where you might have the full advantage of the sun in the clear frosty days of winter.

I know that you, Alan, will condemn all this as bad and antiquated ; for, ever since Dodsley has described the Leasowes, and talked of Brown's imitations of nature, and Horace Walpole's late *Essay on Gardening*, you are all for simple nature—condemn walking up and down stairs in the open air, and declare for wood and wilderness. But *ne quid nimis*. I would not deface a scene of natural grandeur or beauty by the introduction of crowded artificial decorations ; yet such may, I think, be very interesting where the situation, in its natural state, otherwise has no particular charm. So that when I have a country-house—who can say how soon ?—you may look for grottoes, and cascades, and fountains ; nay, if you vex me by contradiction, perhaps I may go the length of the temple. So provoke me not, for you see of what enormities I am capable.

At any rate, Alan, had you condemned as artificial the rest of friend Geddes's grounds, there is a willow walk by the very verge of the stream so sad, so solemn, and so silent that it must have commanded your admiration. The brook, restrained at the ultimate boundary of the grounds by a natural dam-dike or ledge of rocks, seemed, even in its present swollen state, scarcely to glide along ; and the pale willow trees, dropping their long branches into the stream, gathered around them little coronals of the foam that floated down from the more rapid stream above. The high rock which formed the opposite bank of the brook was seen dimly through the branches, and its pale and splintered front, garlanded with long streamers of briers and other creeping plants, seemed a barrier between the quiet path which we trod and the toiling and bustling world beyond. The path itself, following the sweep of the stream, made a very gentle curve ; enough, however, served by its inflection completely to hide the end of the walk until you arrived at it. A deep and sullen sound, which increased as you proceeded, prepared you for this termination, which was indeed only a plain root-seat, from which you looked on a fall of about six or seven feet, where the brook flung itself over the ledge of natural rock I have already mentioned, which there crossed its course.

The quiet and twilight seclusion of this walk rendered it a fit scene for confidential communing ; and having nothing more interesting to say to my fair Quaker, I took the liberty of questioning her about the Laird ; for you are, or ought to be, aware that, next to discussing the affairs of the heart, the fair sex are most interested in those of their neighbors.

I did not conceal either my curiosity or the check which it had received from Joshua, and I saw that my companion answered with embarrassment. "I must not speak otherwise than truly," she said ; "and therefore I tell thee that my brother dislikes, and that I fear, the man of whom thou hast asked me. Perhaps we are both wrong ; but he is a man of violence, and hath great influence over many, who, following the trade of sailors and fishermen, become as rude as the elements with which they contend. He hath no certain name among them, which is not unusual, their rude fashion being to distinguish each other by nicknames ; and they have called him the Laird of the Lakes—not remembering there should be no one called Lord, save one only— in idle derision, the pools of salt water left by the tide among the sands being called the Lakes of Solway."

"Has he no other revenue than he derives from these sands ?" I asked.

"That I cannot answer," replied Rachel : " men say that he wants not money though he lives like an ordinary fisherman, and that he imparts freely of his means to the poor around him. They intimate that he is a man of consequence, once deeply engaged in the unhappy affair of the rebellion, and even still too much in danger from the government to assume his own name. He is often absent from his cottage at Brokenburn Cliffs for weeks and months."

" I should have thought," said I, " that the government would scarce, at this time of day, be likely to proceed against any one even of the most obnoxious rebels. Many years have passed away——"

" It is true," she replied ; " yet such persons may understand that their being connived at depends on their living in obscurity. But indeed there can nothing certain be known among these rude people. The truth is not in them ; most of them participate in the unlawful trade betwixt these parts and the neighboring shore of England, and they are familiar with every species of falsehood and deceit."

" It is a pity," I remarked, " that your brother should have neighbors of such a description, especially as I understand he is at some variance with them."

" Where, when, and about what matter ?" answered Miss Geddes, with an eager and timorous anxiety, which made me regret having touched on the subject.

I told her, in a way as little alarming as I could devise, the purport of what had passed betwixt this Laird of the Lakes and her brother at their morning's interview.

" You affright me much," answered she ; " it is this very circumstance which has scared me in the watches of the night. When my brother Joshua withdrew from an active share in the commercial concerns of my father, being satisfied with the portion of worldly substance which he already possessed, there were one or two undertakings in which he retained an interest, either because his withdrawing might have been prejudicial to friends or because he wished to retain some mode of occupying his time. Amongst the more important of these is a fishing-station on the coast, where by certain improved modes of erecting snares opening at the advance of the tide and shutting at the reflux, many more fish are taken than can be destroyed by those who, like the men of Brokenburn, use only the boat-net and spear, or fishing-rod. They complain of these tide-nets, as men call them, as an innovation, and pretend to a right to remove and destroy them by the strong hand. I fear me, this man of violence, whom they call the Laird, will execute these his threats, which cannot be without both loss and danger to my brother."

"Mr. Geddes," said I, "ought to apply to the civil magistrate ; there are soldiers at Dumfries who would be detached for his protection."

"Thou speakest, friend Latimer," answered the lady, " as one who is still in the gall of bitterness and bond of iniquity. God forbid that we should endeavor to preserve nets of flax and stakes of wood, or the Mammon of gain which they procure for us, by the hands of men of war, and at the risk of spilling human blood ! "

"I respect your scruples," I replied ; " but since such is your way of thinking, your brother ought to avert the danger by compromise or submission."

"Perhaps it would be best," answered Rachel ; " but what can *I* say ? Even in the best-trained temper there may remain some leaven of the old Adam ; and I know not whether it is this or a better spirit that maketh my brother Joshua determine that, though he will not resist force by force, neither will he yield up his right to mere threats, or encourage wrong to others by yielding to menaces. His partners, he says, confide in his steadiness, and that he must not disappoint them by yielding up their right for the fear of the threats of man, whose breath is in his nostrils."

This observation convinced me that the spirit of the old sharers of the spoil was not utterly departed even from the bosom of the peaceful Quaker ; and I could not help confessing internally that Joshua had the right, when he averred that there was as much courage in sufferance as in exertion.

As we approached the further end of the willow walk, the sullen and continuous sound of the dashing waters became still more and more audible, and at length rendered it difficult for us to communicate with each other. The conversation dropped, but apparently my companion continued to dwell upon the apprehensions which it had excited. At the bottom of the walk we obtained a view of the cascade, where the swollen brook flung itself in foam and tumult over the natural barrier of rock, which seemed in vain to attempt to bar its course. I gazed with delight, and, turning to express my sentiments to my companion, I observed that she had folded her hands in an attitude of sorrowful resignation, which showed her thoughts were far from the scene which lay before her. When she saw that her abstraction was observed, she resumed her former placidity of manner; and having given me sufficient time to admire this termination of our sober and secluded walk, proposed that we should return to the house through her brother's farm. "Even we Quakers, as we are called, have our little pride," she said; "and my brother Joshua would not forgive me were I not to show thee the fields which he taketh delight to cultivate after the newest and best fashion; for which, I promise thee, he had received much praise from good judges, as well as some ridicule from those who think it folly to improve on the customs of our ancestors."

As she spoke, she opened a low door, leading through a moss and ivy-covered wall, the boundary of the pleasure-ground, into the open fields; through which we moved by a convenient path, leading, with good taste and simplicity, by stile and hedge-row, through pasturage, and arable, and woodland; so that, in all ordinary weather, the good man might, without even soiling his shoes, perform his perambulation round the farm. There were seats also, on which to rest; and though not adorned with inscriptions, nor quite so frequent in occurrence as those mentioned in the account of the Leasowes, their situation was always chosen with respect to some distant prospect to be commanded, or some home-view to be enjoyed.

But what struck me most in Joshua's domain was the quantity and the tameness of the game. The hen partridge scarce abandoned the roost at the foot of the hedge where she had assembled her covey, though the path went close beside her; and the hare, remaining on her form, gazed at us as we passed, with her full black eye, or, rising lazily and hopping to a little distance, stood erect to look at us with more curiosity than apprehension. I observed to Miss Geddes the extreme tameness of these timid and shy animals, and she informed me that their confidence arose from protection in the summer and relief during the winter. .

"They are pets," she said, "of my brother, who considers them as the better entitled to this kindness that they are a race persecuted by the world in general. He denieth himself," she said, "even the company of a dog, that these creatures may here at least enjoy undisturbed security. Yet this harmless or humane propensity, or humor, hath given offense," she added, "to our dangerous neighbor."

She explained this, by telling me that my host of the preceding night was remarkable for his attachment to field-sports, which he pursued without much regard to the wishes of the individuals over whose property he followed them. The undefined mixture of respect and fear with which he was generally regarded induced most of the neighboring landholders to connive at what they would perhaps in another have punished as a trespass ; but Joshua Geddes would not permit the intrusion of any one upon his premises, and as he had before offended several country neighbors, who, because he would neither shoot himself nor permit others to do so, compared him to a dog in the manger, so he now aggrevated the displeasure which the Laird of the Lakes had already conceived against him, by positively debarring him from pursuing his sport over his grounds. "So that," said Rachel Geddes, "I sometimes wish our lot had been cast elsewhere than in these pleasant borders, where, if we had less of beauty around us, we might have had a neighborhood of peace and good-will."

We at length returned to the house, where Miss Geddes showed me a small study, containing a little collection of books, in two separate presses.

"These," said she, pointing to a smaller press, "will, if thou bestowest thy leisure upon them, do thee good ; and these," pointing to the other and larger cabinet, "can, I believe, do thee little harm. Some of our people do indeed hold that every writer who is not with us is against us ; but brother Joshua is mitigated in his opinions, and correspondeth with our friend John Scot of Amwell, who hath himself constructed verses well approved of even in the world. I wish thee many good thoughts till our family meet at the hour of dinner."

Left alone, I tried both collections ; the first consisted entirely of religious and controversial tracts, and the latter formed a small collection of history, and of moral writers, both in prose and verse.

Neither collection promising much amusement, thou hast, in these close pages, the fruits of my tediousness ; and truly, I think, writing history (one's self being the subject) is as amusing as reading that of foreign countries at any time.

Sam, still more drunk than sober, arrived in due time with my portmanteau, and enabled me to put my dress into order better befitting this temple of cleanliness and decorum, where (to conclude) I believe I shall be a sojourner for more days than one.*

P. S.—I have noted your adventure, as you home-bred youths may perhaps term it, concerning the visit of your doughty laird. We travelers hold such an incident of no great consequence, though it may serve to embellish the uniform life of Brown's Square. But art thou not ashamed to attempt to interest one who is seeing the world at large, and studying human nature on a large scale, by so bad a narrative ? Why, what does it amount to, after all, but that a Tory laird dined with a Whig lawyer ? no very uncommon matter, especially as you state Mr. Herries to have lost the estate, though retaining the designation. The laird behaves with haughtiness and impertinence—nothing out of character in that ; is *not* kicked downstairs, as he ought to have been, were Alan Fairford half the man that he would wish his friends to think him. Ay, but then, as the young lawyer, instead of showing his friend the door, chose to make use of it himself, he overheard the laird aforesaid ask the old lawyer concerning Darsie Latimer—no doubt earnestly inquiring after the handsome, accomplished inmate of his family, who has so lately made Themis his bow, and declined the honor of following it farther. You laugh at me for my air-drawn castles ; but confess, have they not surer footing, in general, than two words spoken by such a man as Herries ? And yet—and yet, I would rally the matter off, Alan, but in dark nights even the glow-worm becomes an object of lustre, and to one plunged in my uncertainty and ignorance the slightest gleam that promises intelligence is interesting. My life is like the subterranean river in the Peak of Derby, visible only where it crosses the celebrated cavern. I am here, and this much I know ; but where I have sprung from, or whither my course of life is like to tend, who shall tell me ? Your father, too, seemed interested and alarmed, and talked of writing. Would to Heaven he may ! I send daily to the post-town for letters.

* See Author's Residence with Quakers. Note 11.

LETTER VIII

THOU mayst clap thy wings and crow as thou pleasest. You go in search of adventures, but adventures come to me unsought for ; and oh ! in what a pleasing shape came mine, since it arrived in the form of a client, and a fair client to boot ! What think you of that, Darsie, you who are such a sworn squire of dames ? Will this not match my adventures with thine, that hunt salmon on horseback, and will it not, besides, eclipse the history of a whole tribe of broadbrims ? But I must proceed methodically.

When I returned to-day from the college, I was surprised to see a broad grin distending the adust countenance of the faithful James Wilkinson, which, as the circumstance seldom happens above once a-year, was matter of some surprise. Moreover, he had a knowing glance with his eye, which I should have as soon expected from a dumb-waiter—an article of furniture to which James, in his usual state, may be happily assimilated. " What the devil is the matter, James ? "

" The devil may be in the matter, for aught I ken," said James, with another provoking grin ; " for here has been a woman calling for you, Maister Alan."

" A woman calling for me ! " said I in surprise ; for you know well that, excepting old Aunt Peggy, who comes to dinner of a Sunday, and the still older Lady Bedrocket, who calls ten times a-year for the quarterly payment of her jointure of four hundred merks, a female scarce approaches our threshold, as my father visits all his female clients at their own lodgings. James protested, however, that there had been a lady calling, and for me. " As bonny a lass as I have seen," added James, " since I was in the Fusileers, and kept company with Peg Baxter." Thou knowest all James's gay recollections go back to the period of his military service, the years he has spent in ours having probably been dull enough.

" Did the lady leave no name nor place of address ? "

" No," replied James ; " but she asked when ye wad be at

74

hame, and I appointed her for twelve o'clock, when the
house wad be quiet, and your father at the bank."

"For shame, James! how can you think my father's
being at home or abroad could be of consequence? The
lady is of course a decent person?"

"I'se uphaud her that, sir; she is nane of your—whew
(here James supplied a blank with a low whistle); but I
didna ken—my maister makes an unco work if a woman
comes here."

I passed into my own room, not ill-pleased that my father
was absent, notwithstanding that I had thought it proper to
rebuke James for having so contrived it. I disarranged my
books, to give them the appearance of a graceful confusion
on the table, and laying my foils (useless since your departure) across the mantelpiece, that the lady might see I was
tam Marte quam Mercurio, I endeavored to dispose my
dress so as to resemble an elegant morning dishabille, gave
my hair the general shade of powder which marks the
gentleman, laid my watch and seals on the table, to hint
that I understood the value of time; and when I had made
all these arrangements, of which I am a little ashamed when
I think of them, I had nothing better to do than to watch
the dial-plate till the index pointed to noon. Five minutes
elapsed, which I allowed for variation of clocks; five minutes more rendered me anxious and doubtful; and five
minutes more would have made me impatient.

Laugh as thou wilt, but remember, Darsie, I was a lawyer
expecting his first client; a young man, how strictly bred
up I need not remind you, expecting a private interview
with a young and beautiful woman. But ere the third term
of five minutes had elapsed, the door-bell was heard to
tinkle low and modestly, as if touched by some timid
hand.

James Wilkinson, swift in nothing, is, as thou knowest,
peculiarly slow in answering the door-bell; and I reckoned
on five minutes good ere his solemn step should have ascended
the stair. Time enough, thought I, for a peep through the
blinds, and was hastening to the window accordingly. But
I reckoned without my host, for James, who had his own
curiosity as well as I, was lying *perdu* in the lobby, ready to
open the door at the first tinkle; and there was, "This
way ma'am. Yes, ma'am. The lady, Mr. Alan,' before I
could get to the chair in which I proposed to be discovered,
seated in all legal dignity. The consciousness of being half
caught in the act of peeping, joined to that native air of

awkward bashfulness of which I am told the law will soon free me, kept me standing on the floor in some confusion ; while the lady, disconcerted on her part, remained on the threshold of the room. James Wilkinson, who had his senses most about him, and was perhaps willing to prolong his stay in the apartment, busied himself in setting a chair for the lady, and recalled me to my good breeding by the hint. I invited her to take possession of it, and bid James withdraw.

My visitor was undeniably a lady, and probably considerably above the ordinary rank ; very modest, too, judging from the mixture of grace and timidity with which she moved, and at my entreaty sat down. Her dress was, I should suppose, both handsome and fashionable ; but it was much concealed by a walking-cloak of green silk, fancifully embroidered ; in which, though heavy for the season, her person was enveloped, and which, moreover, was furnished with a hood.

The devil take that hood, Darsie ! for I was just able to distinguish that, pulled as it was, over the face, it concealed from me, as I was convinced, one of the prettiest countenances I have seen, and which, from a sense of embarrassment, seemed to be crimsoned with a deep blush. I could see her complexion was beautiful, her chin finely turned, her lips coral, and her teeth rivals to ivory. But further the deponent sayeth not ; for a clasp of gold, ornamented with a sapphire, closed the envious mantle under the incognita's throat, and the cursed hood concealed entirely the upper part of the face.

I ought to have spoken first, that is certain ; but ere I could get my phrases well arranged, the young lady, rendered desperate, I suppose, by my hesitation, opened the conversation herself.

" I fear I am an intruder, sir ; I expected to meet an elderly gentleman."

This brought me to myself. " My father, madam, perhaps ? But you inquired for Alan Fairford ; my father's name is Alexander."

" It is Mr. Alan Fairford, undoubtedly, with whom I wished to speak," she said, with greater confusion ; " but I was told that he was advanced in life."

"Some mistake, madam, I presume, betwixt my father and myself; our Christian names have the same initials, though the terminations are different. I—I—I would esteem it a most fortunate mistake, if I could have the honor of supplying my father's place in anything that would be of service to you."

"You are very obliging, sir." A pause, during which she seemed undetermined whether to rise or sit still.

"I am just about to be called to the bar, madam," said I, in hopes to remove her scruples to open her case to me; "and if my advice or opinion could be of the slightest use, although I cannot presume to say that they are much to be depended upon, yet——"

The lady arose. "I am truly sensible of your kindness, sir; and I have no doubt of your talents. I will be very plain with you—it *is* you whom I came to visit; although, now that we have met, I find it will be much better that I should commit my communication to writing."

"I hope, madam, you will not be so cruel—so tantalizing, I would say. Consider, you are my first client, your business my first consultation; do not do me the displeasure of withdrawing your confidence because I am a few years younger than you seem to have expected. My attention shall make amends for my want of experience."

"I have no doubt of either," said the lady, in a grave tone, calculated to restrain the air of gallantry with which I had endeavored to address her. "But when you have received my letter, you will find good reasons assigned why a written communication will best suit my purpose. I wish, you, sir, a good morning." And she left the apartment, her poor baffled counsel scraping, and bowing, and apologizing for anything that might have been disagreeable to her, although the front of my offense seems to be my having been discovered to be younger than my father.*

The door was opened, out she went, walked along the pavement, turned down the close, and put the sun, I believe, into her pocket when she disappeared, so suddenly did dulness and darkness sink down on the square, when she was no longer visible. I stood for a moment as if I had been senseless, not recollecting what a fund of entertainment I must have supplied to our watchful friends on the other side of the green. Then it darted on my mind that I might dog her, and ascertain at least who or what she was. Off I set, ran down the close, where she was no longer to be seen, and demanded of one of the dyer's lads whether he had seen a lady go down the close, or had observed which way she turned.

"A leddy!" said the dyer, staring at me with a rainbow

* See Green Mantle. Note 12.

countenance. "Mr. Alan, what takes you out, rinning like daft, without your hat?"

"The devil take my hat!" answered I, running back, however, in quest of it, snatched it up and again sallied forth. But as I reached the head of the close once more, I had sense enough to recollect that all pursuit would be now in vain. Besides, I saw my friend, the journeyman dyer, in close confabulation with a pea-green personage of his own profession, and was conscious, like Scrub, that they talked of me, because they laughed consumedly. I had no mind, by a second sudden appearance, to confirm the report that Advocate Fairford was "gaen daft," which had probably spread from Campbell's Close foot to the Mealmarket Stairs, and so slunk back within my own hole again.

My first employment was to remove all traces of that elegant and fanciful disposition of my effects from which I had hoped for so much credit; for I was now ashamed and angry at having thought an instant upon the mode of receiving a visit which had commenced so agreeably, but terminated in a manner so unsatisfactory. I put my folios in their places, threw the foils into the dressing closet, tormenting myself all the while with the fruitless doubt whether I had missed an opportunity or escaped a stratagem, or whether the young person had been really startled, as she seemed to intimate, by the extreme youth of her intended legal adviser. The mirror was not unnaturally called into aid; and that cabinet counselor pronounced me rather short, thick-set, with a cast of features fitter, I trust, for the bar than for a ball; not handsome enough for blushing virgins to pine for my sake, or even to invent sham cases to bring them to my chambers, yet not ugly enough, either, to scare those away who came on real business; dark, to be sure, but *nigri sunt hyacinthi*; there are pretty things to be said in favor of that complexion.

At length—as common sense will get the better in all cases when a man will but give it fair play—I began to stand convicted in my own mind as an ass before the interview, for having expected too much; an ass during the interview, for having failed to extract the lady's real purpose; and an especial ass now that it was over, for thinking so much about it. But I can think of nothing else, and therefore I am determined to think of this to some good purpose.

You remember Murtough O'Hara's defense of the Catholic doctrine of confession; because, "by his soul, his sins were always a great burden to his mind till he had told them to the priest; and once confessed, he never thought more about them." I have tried this receipt, therefore; and having poured my secret mortification into thy trusty ear, I will think no more about this maid of the mist,

Who, with no face, as 'twere, outfaced me.

————————

————Four o'clock.

Plague on her green mantle, she can be nothing better than a fairy; she keeps possession of my head yet! All during dinner-time I was terribly absent; but luckily, my father gave the whole credit of my reverie to the abstract nature of the doctrine, *Vinco vincentem, ergo vinco te;* upon which brocard of law the professor this morning lectured. So I got an early dismissal to my own crib, and here am I studying, in one sense, *vincere vincentem*, to get the better of the silly passion of curiosity—I think—I think it amounts to nothing else—which has taken such possession of my imagination, and is perpetually worrying me with the question—Will she write or no? She will not—she will not! So says Reason, and adds, Why should she take the trouble to enter into correspondence with one who, instead of a bold, alert, prompt gallant, proved a chicken-hearted boy, and left her the whole awkwardness of explanation, which he should have met half-way? But then, says Fancy, she *will* write, for she was not a bit that sort of person whom you, Mr. Reason, in your wisdom, take her to be. She was disconcerted enough, without my adding to her distress by an impudent conduct on my part. And she will write, for——

By Heaven, she HAS written, Darsie, and with a vengeance! Here is her letter, thrown into the kitchen by a cadie, too faithful to be bribed, either by money or whisky, to say more than that he received it, with sixpence, from an ordinary-looking woman, as he was plying on his station near the Cross.

" For ALAN FAIRFORD, ESQUIRE, BARRISTER.

" SIR—Excuse my mistake of to-day. I had accidentally learned that Mr. Darsie Latimer had an intimate friend and associate in a Mr. A. Fairford. When I inquired for such a person, he was pointed out to me at the Cross, as I think the exchange of your city is called, in the character of a respectable elderly man—your father, as I now understand. On inquiry at Brown Square, where I understood he resided,

I used the full name of Alan, which naturally occasioned you the trouble of this day's visit. Upon further inquiry, I am led to believe that you are likely to be the person most active in the matter to which I am now about to direct your attention ; and I regret much that circumstances, arising out of my own particular situation, prevent my communicating to you personally what I now apprise you of in this manner.

"Your friend, Mr. Darsie Latimer, is in a situation of considerable danger. You are doubtless aware that he has been cautioned not to trust himself in England. Now, if he has not absolutely transgressed this friendly injunction, he has at least approached as nearly to the menaced danger as he could do, consistently with the letter of the prohibition. He has chosen his abode in a neighborhood very perilous to him ; and it is only by a speedy return to Edinburgh, or at least by a removal to some more remote part of Scotland, that he can escape the machinations of those whose enmity he has to fear. I must speak in mystery, but my words are not the less certain ; and, I believe, you know enough of your friend's fortunes to be aware that I could not write this much without being even more intimate with them than you are.

"If he cannot, or will not, take the advice here given, it is my opinion that you should join him, if possible, without delay, and urge, by your personal presence, and entreaty, the arguments which may prove ineffectual in writing. One word more, and I implore of your candor to take it as it is meant. No one supposes that Mr. Fairford's zeal in his friend's service needs to be quickened by mercenary motives. But report says that Mr. Alan Fairford, not having yet entered on his professional career, may, in such a case as this, want the means, though he cannot want the inclination, to act with promptitude. The inclosed note Mr. Alan Fairford must be pleased to consider as his first professional emolument ; and she who sends it hopes it will be the omen of unbounded success, though the fee comes from a hand so unknown as that of GREEN MANTLE."

A bank-note of £20 was the enclosure, and the whole incident left me speechless with astonishment. I am not able to read over the beginning of my own letter, which forms the introduction to this extraordinary communication. I only know that, though mixed with a quantity of foolery (God knows, very much different from my present feelings),

it gives an account sufficiently accurate of the mysterious
person from whom this letter comes, and that I have neither
time nor patience to separate the absurd commentary from
the text, which it is so necessary you should know.

Combine this warning, so strangely conveyed, with the
caution impressed on you by your London correspondent,
Griffiths, against your visiting England ; with the character
of your Laird of the Solway Lakes ; with the lawless habits
of the people on that frontier country, where warrants are
not easily executed, owing to the jealousy entertained by
either country of the legal interference of the other ; remember, that even Sir John Fielding said to my father that he
could never trace a rogue beyond the Briggend of Dumfries ;
think that the distinctions of Whig and Tory, Papist and
Protestant, still keep that country in a loose and comparatively lawless state—think of all this, my dearest Darsie,
and remember that, while at this Mount Sharon of yours,
you are residing with a family who are actually menaced
with forcible interference, and who, while their obstinacy
provokes violence, are by principle bound to abstain from
resistance.

Nay, let me tell you, professionally, that the legality of
the mode of fishing practised by your friend Joshua is
greatly doubted by our best lawyers ; and that, if the stake-
nets be considered as actually an unlawful obstruction
raised in the channel of the estuary, an assembly of persons
who shall proceed, *via facti*, to pull down and destroy them
would not, in the eye of the law, be esteemed guilty of a riot.
So, by remaining where you are, you are likely to be engaged in a quarrel with which you have nothing to do, and
thus to enable your enemies, whoever these may be, to
execute, amid the confusion of a general hubbub, whatever
designs they may have against your personal safety. Black-
fishers, poachers, and smugglers are a sort of gentry that
will not be much checked, either by your Quaker's texts or by
your chivalry. If you are Don Quixote enough to lay lance
in rest in defense of those of the stake-net and of the sad-
colored garment, I pronounce you but a lost knight ; for, as
I said before, I doubt if these potent redressors of wrongs,
the justices and constables, will hold themselves warranted
to interfere. In a word, return my dear Amadis ; the
adventure of the Solway nets is not reserved for your worship. Come back and I will be your faithful Sancho Panza
upon a more hopeful quest. We will beat about together in
search of this Urganda, the Unknown She of the Green

6

Mantle, who can read this, the riddle of thy fate, better
than wise Eppie of Buckhaven,* or Cassandra herself.

I would fain trifle, Darsie ; for, in debating with you,
jests will sometimes go farther than arguments ; but I am
sick at heart, and cannot keep the ball up. If you have
a moment's regard for the friendship we have so often
vowed to each other, let my wishes for once prevail over
your own venturous and romantic temper. I am quite
serious in thinking that the information communicated to
my father by this Mr. Herries and the admonitory letter of
the young lady bear upon each other ; and that, were you
here, you might learn something from one or other, or from
both, that might throw light on your birth and parentage.
You will not, surely, prefer an idle whim to the prospect
which is thus held out to you ?

I would, agreeably to the hint I have received in the
young lady's letter (for I am confident that such is her condition), have ere now been with you to urge these things,
instead of pouring them out upon paper. But you know
that the day for my trial is appointed ; I have already gone
through the form of being introduced to the examiners,
and have gotten my titles assigned me. All this should not
keep me at home, but my father would view any irregularity upon this occasion as a mortal blow to the hopes
which he has cherished most fondly during his life, viz., my
being called to the bar with some credit. For my own part,
I know there is no great difficulty in passing these formal
examinations, else how have some of our acquaintance got
through them ? But to my father these formalities compose an august and serious solemnity, to which he has long
looked forward, and my absenting myself at this moment
would wellnigh drive him distracted. Yet I shall go altogether distracted myself if I have not an instant assurance
from you that you are hastening hither. Meanwhile,
I have desired Hannah to get your little crib into the
best order possible. I cannot learn that my father has yet
written to you ; nor has he spoken more of his communication with Birrenswork ; but when I let him have some
inkling of the dangers you are at present incurring, I know
my request that you will return immediately will have his
cordial support.

Another reason yet—I must give a dinner, as usual, upon
my admission, to our friends ; and my father, laying aside

---

* Well known in the chap-book called the *History of Buckhaven.*

all his usual considerations of economy, has desired it may be in the best style possible. Come hither then, dear Darsie ! or I protest to you, I shall send examination, admission-dinner, and guests to the devil, and come in person · to fetch you with a vengeance. Thine, in much anxiety.

A. F.

LETTER IX

ALEXANDER FAIRFORD, W.S., TO MR. DARSIE LATIMER

DEAR MR. DARSIE :

Having been your *factor loco tutoris*, or rather, I ought to say in correctness, since I acted without warrant from the court, your *negotiorum gestor*, that connection occasions my present writing. And although, having rendered an account of my intromissions, which have been regularly approved of, not only by yourself (whom I could not prevail upon to look at more than the docket and sum total), but also by the worthy Mr. Samuel Griffiths of London, being the hand through whom the remittances were made, I may, in some sense, be considered as to you *functus officio*, yet, to speak facetiously, I trust you will not hold me accountable as a vicious intromitter, should I still consider myself as occasionally interested in your welfare. My motives for writing at this time are twofold.

I have met with a Mr. Herries of Birrenswork, a gentleman of very ancient descent, but who hath in time past been in difficulties, nor do I know if his affairs are yet well redd. Birrenswork says that he believes he was very familiar with your father, whom he states to have been called Ralph Latimer of Langcote Hall, in Westmoreland ; and he mentioned family affairs which it may be of the highest importance to you to be acquainted with ; but as he seemed to decline communicating them to me, I could not civilly urge him thereanent. This much I know, that Mr. Herries had his own share in the late desperate and unhappy matter of 1745, and was in trouble about it, although that is probably now over. Moreover, although he did not profess the Popish religion openly, he had an eye that way. And both of these are reasons why I have hesitated to recommend him to a youth who maybe hath not altogether so well founded his opinious concerning kirk and state that they might not be changed by some sudden wind of doctrine. For I have observed ye, Master Darsie, to be rather tinctured with the old leaven of prelacy—this under your leave : and although God forbid that you should be in any manner dis-

84

affected to the Protestant Hanoverian line, yet ye have ever loved to hear the blawing, bleezing stories which the Hieland gentlemen tell of those troublous times, which, if it were their will, they had better pretermit, as tending rather to shame than to honor. It is come to me also by a sidewind, as I may say, that you have been neighboring more than was needful among some of the pestilent sect of Quakers—a people who own neither priest, nor king, nor civil magistrate, nor the fabric of our law, and will not depone either *in civilibus* or *criminalibus*, be the loss to the lieges what it may. Anent which heresies, it were good ye read *The Snake in the Grass*, or *The Foot out of the Snare*, being both well-approved tracts touching these doctrines.

Now, Mr. Darsie, ye are to judge for yourself whether ye can safely to your soul's weal remain longer among these Papists and Quakers—these defections on the right hand and fallings away on the left; and truly if you can confidently resist these evil examples of doctrine, I think ye may as well tarry in the bounds where ye are, until you see Mr. Herries of Birrenswork, who does assuredly know more of your matters than I thought had been communicated to any man in Scotland. I would fain have precognosced him myself on these affairs, but found him unwilling to speak out, as I have partly intimated before.

To call a new cause—I have the pleasure to tell you, that Alan has passed his private Scots Law examinations with good approbation, a great relief to my mind, especially as worthy Mr. Pest told me in my ear there was no fear of the "callant," as he familiarly calls him, which gives me great heart. His public trials, which are nothing in comparison save a mere form, are to take place, by order of the Honorable Dean of Faculty, on Wednesday first; and on Friday he puts on the gown, and gives a bit chack of dinner to his friends and acquaintances, as is, you know, the custom. Your company will be wished for there, Master Darsie, by more than him, which I regret to think is impossible to have, as well by your engagements as that our cousin, Peter Fairford, comes from the west on purpose, and we have no place to offer him but your chamber in the wall. And to be plain with you, after my use and wont, Master Darsie, it may be as well that Alan and you do not meet till he is hefted as it were to his new calling. You are a pleasant gentleman, and full of daffing, which may well become you, as you have enough (as I understand) to uphold your merry

humor. If you regard the matter wisely, you would perchance consider that a man of substance should have a douce
and staid demeanor ; yet you are so far from growing grave
and considerate with the increase of your annual income,
that the richer you become, the merrier I think you grow.
But this must be at your own pleasure, so far as you are
concerned. Alan, however (overpassing my small savings),
has the world to win ; and louping and laughing, as he and
you were wont to do, would soon make the powder flee out
of his wig and the pence out of his pocket. Nevertheless, I
trust you will meet when you return from your rambles ; for
there is a time, as the wise man sayeth, for gathering and a
time for casting away ; it is always the part of a man of
sense to take the gathering time first. I remain, dear sir,
your well-wishing friend, and obedient to command.

ALEXANDER FAIRFORD.

P.S.—Alan's thesis * is upon the title *De periculo et commodo rei venditæ*, and is a very pretty piece of Latinity.
Ross House, in our neighborhood, is nearly finished, and is
thought to excel Duff House in ornature.

* See Note 13.

LETTER X

DARSIE LATIMER TO ALAN FAIRFORD

THE plot thickens, Alan. I have your letter, and also one from your father. The last makes it impossible for me to comply with the kind request which the former urges. No, I cannot be with you, Alan ; and that for the best of all reasons—I cannot and ought not to counteract your father's anxious wishes. I do not take it unkind of him that he desires my absence. It is natural that he should wish for his son, what his son so well deserves, the advantage of a wiser and steadier companion than I seem to him. And yet I am sure I have often labored hard enough to acquire that decency of demeanor which can no more be suspected of breaking bounds than an owl of catching a butterfly.

But it was in vain that I have knitted my brows till I had the headache, in order to acquire the reputation of a grave, solid, and well-judging youth. Your father always has discovered, or thought that he discovered, a hare-brained eccentricity lying folded among the wrinkles of my forehead, which rendered me a perilous associate for the future counselor and ultimate judge. Well, Corporal Nym's philosophy must be my comfort, "Things must be as they may." I cannot come to your father's house, where he wishes not to see me ; and as to your coming hither—by all that is dear to me, I vow that, if you are guilty of such a piece of reckless folly—not to say undutiful cruelty, considering your father's thoughts and wishes—I will never speak to you again as long as I live ! I am perfectly serious. And besides, your father, while he in a manner prohibits me from returning to Edinburgh, gives me the strongest reasons for continuing a little while longer in this country, by holding out the hope that I may receive from your old friend, Mr. Herries of Birrenswork, some particulars concerning my origin, with which that ancient recusant seems to be acquainted.

That gentleman mentioned the name of a family in Westmoreland, with which he supposes me connected. My inquiries here after such a family have been ineffectual, for the Borderers, on either side, know little of each other. But I shall doubtless find some English person of whom to make inquiries, since the confounded fetterlock clapped on my movements by old Griffiths prevents me repairing to England in person. At least, the prospect of obtaining some information is greater here than elsewhere ; it will be an apology for my making a longer stay in this neighborhood, a line of conduct which seems to have your father's sanction, whose opinion must be sounder than that of your wandering damoiselle.

If the road were paved with dangers which leads to such a discovery, I cannot for a moment hesitate to tread it. But in fact there is no peril in the case. If the tritons of the Solway shall proceed to pull down honest Joshua's tide-nets, I am neither Quixote enough in disposition nor Goliath enough in person to attempt their protection. I have no idea of attempting to prop a fallen house, by putting my shoulders against it. And indeed Joshua gave me a hint that the company which he belongs to, injured in the way threatened (some of them being men who thought after the fashion of the world), would pursue the rioters at law, and recover damages, in which probably his own ideas of non-resistance will not prevent his participating. Therefore the whole affair will take its course as law will, as I only mean to interfere when it may be necessary to direct the course of the plaintiffs to thy chambers ; and I request they may find thee intimate with all the Scottish statutes concerning salmon-fisheries, from the *Lex Aquarum* downward.

As for the Lady of the Mantle, I will lay a wager that the sun so bedazzled thine eyes on that memorable morning that everything thou didst look upon seemed green ; and notwithstanding James Wilkinson's experience in the Fusileers, as well as his negative whistle, I will venture to hold a crown that she is but a what-shall-call-'um after all. Let not even the gold persuade you to the contrary. She may make a shift to cause you to disgorge that, and (immense spoil !) a session's fees to boot, if you look not all the sharper about you. Or if it should be otherwise, and if indeed there lurk some mystery under this visitation, credit me, it is one which thou canst not penetrate, nor can I as yet even attempt to explain it ; since, if I prove mistaken, and mistaken I may easily be, I would be fain to creep into Phalaris's bull, were it standing before me ready heated, rather than be roasted with thy raillery. Do not tax me with want of confidence ; for the instant I can throw any

light on the matter thou shalt have it ; but while I am only
blundering about in the dark, I do not choose to call wise
folks to see me, perchance, break my nose against a post.
So if you marvel at this,

E'en marvel on till time makes all things plain.

In the meantime, kind Alan, let me proceed in my
diurnal.

On the third or fourth day after my arrival at Mount
Sharon, Time, that bald sexton to whom I have just referred
you, did certainly limp more heavily along with me than he
had done at first. The quaint morality of Joshua and
Huguenot simplicity of his sister began to lose much of
their raciness with their novelty, and my mode of life, by
dint of being very quiet, began to feel abominably dull. It
was, as thou say'st, as if the Quakers had put the sun in
their pockets : all around was soft and mild, and even pleasant ; but there was, in the whole routine, a uniformity, a
want of interest, a helpless and hopeless languor, which
rendered life insipid. No doubt, my worthy host and hostess
felt none of this void, this want of excitation, which was
becoming oppressive to their guest. They had their little
round of occupations, charities, and pleasures ; Rachel had
her poultry-yard and conservatory, and Joshua his garden.
Besides this, they enjoyed, doubtless, their devotional meditations ; and, on the whole, time glided softly and imperceptibly on with them, though to me, who long for stream
and cataract, it seemed absolutely to stand still. I meditated
returning to Shepherd's Bush, and began to think, with
some hankering, after little Benjie and the rod. The imp
has ventured hither, and hovers about to catch a peep of
me now and then ; I suppose the little sharper is angling for
a few more sixpences. But this would have been, in
Joshua's eyes, a return of the washed sow to wallowing in
the mire, and I resolved, while I remained his guest, to
spare him so violent a shock to his prejudices. The next
point was, to shorten the time of my proposed stay ; but,
alas ! that I felt to be equally impossible. I had named a
week ; and however rashly my promise had been pledged, it
must be held sacred, even according to the letter, from
which the Friends permit no deviation.

All these considerations wrought me up to a kind of impatience yesterday evening ; so that I snatched up my hat,
and prepared for a sally beyond the cultivated farm and

ornamented grounds of Mount Sharon, just as if I were desirous to escape from the realms of art into those of free and unconstrained nature. I was scarcely more delighted when I first entered this peaceful demesne than I now was—such is the instability and inconsistency of human nature!—when I escaped from it to the open downs, which had formerly seemed so waste and dreary. The air I breathed felt purer and more bracing. The clouds, riding high upon a summer breeze, drove, in gay succession, over my head, now obscuring the sun, now letting its rays stream in transient flashes upon various parts of the landscape, and especially upon the broad mirror of the distant Firth of Solway.

I advanced on the scene with the light step of a liberated captive ; and, like John Bunyan's Pilgrim, could have found in my heart to sing as I went on my way. It seemed as if my gaiety had accumulated while suppressed, and that I was, in my present joyous mood, entitled to expend the savings of the previous week. But just as I was about to uplift a merry stave, I heard, to my joyous surprise, the voices of three or more choristers, singing, with considerable success, the lively old catch :

" For all our men were very, very merry,
    And all our men were drinking :
There were two men of mine,
Three men of thine,
And three that belong'd to old Sir Thom o' Lyne ;
As they went to the ferry, they were very, very merry,
    And all our men were drinking." *

As the chorus ended, there followed a loud and hearty laugh by way of cheers. Attracted by sounds which were so congenial to my present feelings, I made towards the spot from which they came, cautiously, however, for the downs, as had been repeatedly hinted to me, had no good name ; and the attraction of the music, without rivaling that of the syrens in melody, might have been followed by similarly inconvenient consequences to an incautious amateur.

I crept on, therefore, trusting that the sinuosities of the ground, broken, as it was, into knolls and sand-pits, would permit me to obtain a sight of the musicians before I should be observed by them. As I advanced, the old ditty was again raised. The voices seemed those of a man and two boys ; they were rough, but kept good time, and were man-

* See " All our men were very, very merry." Note 14.

aged with too much skill to belong to the ordinary country
people.

> " Jack look'd at the sun, and cried, ' Fire, fire, fire ; '
> Jem stabled his keffel in Birkendale mire ;
> Tom startled a calf, and halloo'd for a stag ;
> Will mounted a gate-post, instead of his nag ;
> For all our men were very, very merry,
>   And all our men were drinking ;
> There were two men of mine,
> Three men of thine,
> And three that belong'd to old Sir Thom o' Lyne ;
> As they went to the ferry, they were very, very merry,
>   For all our men were drinking."

The voices, as they mixed in their several parts, and ran
through them, untwisting and again entwining all the links
of the merry old catch, seemed to have a little touch of
the bacchanalian spirit which they celebrated, and showed
plainly that the musicians were engaged in the same joyous
revel as the " menyie " of old Sir Thom o' Lyne. At length
I came within sight of them, three in number, where they
sat cosily niched into what you might call a " bunker "—a
little sand-pit, dry and snug, and surrounded by its banks
and a screen of whins in full bloom.

The only one of the trio whom I recognized as a personal
acquaintance was the notorious little Benjie, who, having
just finished his stave, was cramming a huge luncheon of
pie-crust into his mouth with one hand, while in the other
he held a foaming tankard, his eyes dancing with all the glee
of a forbidden revel ; and his features, which have at all
times a mischievous archness of expression, confessing the
full sweetness of stolen waters and bread eaten in secret.

There was no mistaking the profession of the male and
female, who were partners with Benjie in these merry
doings. The man's long, loose-bodied greatcoat (wrap-
rascal, as the vulgar term it), the fiddle-case, with its straps,
which lay beside him, and a small knapsack which might
contain his few necessaries ; a clear gray eye ; features
which, in contending with many a storm, had not lost a
wild and careless expression of glee, animated at present,
when he was exercising for his own pleasure the arts which
he usually practised for bread—all announced one of those
peripatetic followers of Orpheus whom the vulgar call a
strolling fiddler. Gazing more attentively, I easily discovered that, though the poor musician's eyes were open, their
sense was shut, and that the ecstasy with which he turned
them up to Heaven only derived its apparent expression

from his own internal emotions, but received no assistance from the visible objects around. Beside him sat his female companion, in a man's hat, a blue coat, which seemed also to have been an article of male apparel, and a red petticoat. She was cleaner, in person and in clothes, than such itinerants generally are ; and, having been in her day a strapping *bona roba,* she did not even yet neglect some attention to her appearance : wore a large amber necklace and silver ear-rings, and had her plaid fastened across her breast with a brooch of the same metal.

The man also looked clean, notwithstanding the meanness of his attire, and had a decent silk hankerchief well knotted about his throat, under which peeped a clean owrelay. His beard, also, instead of displaying a grizzly stubble, unmowed for several days, flowed in thick and comely abundance over the breast, to the length of six inches, and mingled with his hair, which was but beginning to exhibit a touch of age. To sum up his appearance, the loose garment which I have described was secured around him by a large old-fashioned belt, with brass studs, in which hung a dirk, with a knife and fork, its usual accompaniments. Altogether, there was something more wild and adventurous-looking about the man than I could have expected to see in an ordinary modern crowder ; and the bow which he now and then drew across the violin, to direct his little choir, was decidedly that of no ordinary performer.

You must understand, that many of these observations were the fruits of after remark ; for I had scarce approached so near as to get a distinct view of the party, when my friend Benjie's lurching attendant, which he calls by the appropriate name of Hemp, began to cock his tail and ears, and, sensible of my presence, flew, barking like a fury, to the place where I had meant to lie concealed till I heard another song. I was obliged, however, to jump on my feet, and intimidate Hemp, who would otherwise have bit me, by two sound kicks on the ribs, which sent him howling back to his master.

Little Benjie seemed somewhat dismayed at my appearance ; but, calculating on my placability, and remembering, perhaps, that the ill-used Solomon was no palfrey of mine, he speedily affected great glee, and almost in one breath assured the itinerants that I was "a grand gentleman, and had plenty of money, and was very kind to poor folk ; " and informed me that this was " Willie Steenson—Wandering Willie —the best fiddler that ever kittled thairm with horsehair."

The woman rose and courtesied ; and Wandering Willie
sanctioned his own praises with a nod, and the ejaculation,
" All is true that the little boy says."

I asked him if he was of this country.

" *This* country !" replied the blind man. " I am of every
country in broad Scotland, and a wee bit of England to the
boot. But yet I am, in some sense, of this country ; for I
was born within hearing of the roar of Solway. Will I give
your honor a touch of the auld bread-winner ? "

He preluded as he spoke, in a manner which really excited
my curiosity ; and then taking the old tune of " Galashiels "
for his theme, he graced it with a number of wild, complicated, and beautiful variations ; during which it was
wonderful to observe how his sightless face was lighted up
under the conscious pride and heartfelt delight in the exercise of his own very considerable powers.

" What think you of that, now, for threescore and
twa ? "

I expressed my surprise and pleasure.

" A rant, man—an auld rant," said Willie ; " naething like
the music ye hae in your ball-houses and your playhouses in
Edinbro' ; but it's weel aneugh anes in a way at a dike-side.
Here's another ; its no a Scots tune, but it passes for ane.
Oswald made it himsell, I reckon ; he has cheated mony ane,
but he canna cheat Wandering Willie."

He then played your favorite air of " Roslin Castle," with
a number of beautiful variations, some of which I am certain
were almost extempore.

" You have another fiddle there, my friend," said I.
" Have you a comrade ? " But Willie's ears were deaf, or
his attention was still busied with the tune.

The female replied in his stead, " O ay, sir, troth we have
a partner—a gangrel body like oursells. No but my hinnie
might have been better if he had liked ; for mony a bein
nook in mony a braw house has been offered to my
hinnie Willie, if he wad but just bide still and play to the
gentles."

" Whisht, woman—whisht !" said the blind man, angrily,
shaking his locks ; " dinna deave the gentleman wi' your
havers. Stay in a house and play to the gentles !—strike up
when my lady pleases, and lay down the bow when my lord
bids ! Na—na, that's nae life for Willie. Look out, Maggie
—peer out, woman, and see if ye can see Robin coming.
Deil be in him ! he has got to the lee-side of some smuggler's
punch-bowl, and he wunna budge the night, I doubt."

"That is your consort's instrument," said I. "Will you give me leave to try my skill?" I slipped at the same time a shilling into the woman's hand.

"I dinna ken whether I dare trust Robin's fiddle to ye," said Willie, bluntly. His wife gave him a twitch. "Hout awa', Maggie," he said, in contempt of the hint, "though the gentleman may hae gien ye siller, he may have nae bowhand for a' that, and I'll no trust Robin's fiddle wi' an ignoramus. But that's no sae muckle amiss," he added, as I began to touch the instrument; "I am thinking ye have some skill o' the craft."

To confirm him in this favorable opinion, I began to execute such a complicated flourish as I thought must have turned Crowdero into a pillar of stone with envy and wonder. I scaled the top of the finger-board, to dive at once to the bottom, skipped with flying fingers, like Timotheus, from shift to shift, struck arpeggios and harmonic tones; but without exciting any of the astonishment which I had expected.

Willie indeed listened to me with considerable attention; but I was no sooner finished than he immediately mimicked on his own instrument the fantastic complication of tones which I had produced, and made so whimsical a parody of my performance that, although somewhat angry, I could not help laughing heartily, in which I was joined by Benjie, whose reverence for me held him under no restraint; while the poor dame, fearful, doubtless, at my taking offense at this familiarity, seemed divided betwixt her conjugal reverence for her Willie and her desire to give him a hint for his guidance.

At length the old man stopped of his own accord, and, as if he had sufficiently rebuked me by his mimicry, he said, "But for a' that, ye will play very weel wi' a little practise and some gude teaching. But ye maun learn to put the heart into it, man—to put the heart into it."

I played an air in simpler taste, and received more decided approbation.

"That's something like it, man. Od, ye are a clever birkie!"

The woman touched his coat again. "The gentleman is a gentleman, Willie; ye maunna speak that gate to him, hinnie."

"The deevil I maunna!" said Willie; "and what for maunna I? If he was ten gentles, he canna draw a bow like me, can he?"

"Indeed I cannot, my honest friend," said I ; "and if you will go with me to a house hard by, I would be glad to have a night with you."

Here I looked round, and observed Benjie smothering a laugh, which I was sure had mischief in it. I seized him suddenly by the ear, and made him confess that he was laughing at the thoughts of the reception which a fiddler was likely to get from the Quakers at Mount Sharon. I chucked him from me, not sorry that his mirth had reminded me in time of what I had for the moment forgotten ; and invited the itinerant to go with me to Shepherd's Bush, from which I proposed to send word to Mr. Geddes that I should not return home that evening. But the minstrel declined this invitation also. He was engaged for the night, he said, to a dance in the neighborhood, and vented a round execration on the laziness or drunkenness of his comrade, who had not appeared at the place of rendezvous.

"I will go with you instead of him," said I, in a sudden whim ; "and I will give you a crown to introduce me as your comrade."

"*You* gang instead of Rob the Rambler ! My certie, freend, ye are no blate !" answered Wandering Willie, in a tone which announced death to my frolic.

But Maggie, whom the offer of the crown had not escaped, began to open on that scent with a maundering sort of lecture. "O Willie ! hinnie Willie, when will ye learn to be wise ? There's a crown to be won for naething but saying ae man's name instead of anither. And, wae's me ! I hae just a shilling of this gentleman's gieing and a boddle of my ain ; and ye wunna bend your will sae muckle as to take up the siller that's flung at your feet ! Ye will die the death of a cadger's powney in a wreath of drift ! and what can I do better than lie doun and die wi' you ! for ye winna let me win siller to keep either you or mysell leevin."

"Haud your nonsense tongue, woman," said Willie, but less absolutely than before. "Is he a real gentleman, or ane of the player-men ?"

"I'se uphaud him a real gentleman," said the woman.

"I'se uphaud ye ken little of the matter," said Willie ; let us see haud of your hand, neebor, gin ye like."

I gave him my hand. He said to himself, "Ay—ay, here are fingers that have seen canny service." Then running his hand over my hair, my face, and my dress, he went on with his soliloquy—"Ay—ay, muisted hair, braid-claith o' the best, and se'enteen hundred linen on his back, at the least o' it. And how do you think, my braw birkie, that ye are to pass for a tramping fiddler ?"

" My dress is plain," said I—indeed, I had chosen my most ordinary suit, out of compliment to my Quaker friends —" and I can easily pass for a young farmer out upon a frolic. Come, I will double the crown I promised you."

" Damn your crowns !" said the disinterested man of music. " I would like to have a round wi' you, that's certain ; but a farmer, and with a hand that never held pleughstilt or pettle, that will never do. Ye may pass for a trades lad from Dumfries, or a student upon the ramble, or the like o' that. But hark ye, lad ; if ye expect to be ranting amang the queans o' lasses where ye are gaun, ye will come by the waur, I can tell ye ; for the fishers are wild chaps, and will bide nae taunts."

I promised to be civil and cautious ; and, to smooth the good woman, I slipped the promised piece into her hand. The acute organs of the blind man detected this little maneuver.

" Are ye at it again wi' the siller, ye jaud ? I'll be sworn ye wad rather hear ae twalpenny clink against another than have a spring from Rory Dall,* if he was coming alive again anes errand. Gang doun the gate to Luckie Gregson's and get the things ye want, and bide there till ele'en hours in the morn ; and if ye see Robin, send him on to me."

" Am I no gaun to the ploy, then ?" said Maggie, in a disappointed tone.

" And what for should ye ?" said her lord and master ; " to dance a' night, I'se warrant, and no to be fit to walk your tae's-length the morn, and we have ten Scots miles afore us ? Na, na. Stable the steed, and pit your wife to bed, when there's night wark to do."

" Aweel—aweel, Willie hinnie, ye ken best ; but O, take an unco care o' yoursell, and mind ye hae nae the blessing o' sight."

" Your tongue gars me whiles tire of the blessing of hearing, woman," replied Willie, in answer to this tender exhortation.

But I now put in for my interest. " Halloo, good folks, remember that I am to send the boy to Mount Sharon, and if you go to the Shepherd's Bush, honest woman, how the deuce am I to guide the blind man where he is going ? I know little or nothing of the country."

---

* Blind Rorie, a famous performer, according to tradition.

"And ye ken mickle less of my hinnie, sir," replied Maggie, "that think he needs ony guiding : he's the best guide himsell that ye'll find between Criffell and Carlisle. Horse-road and footpath, parish-road and kirk-road, high-road and cross-road, he kens ilka foot of ground in Nithsdale."

"Ay, ye might have said in braid Scotland, gudewife," added the fiddler. "But gang your ways, Maggie, that's the first wise word ye hae spoke the day. I wish it was dark night, and rain, and wind, for the gentleman's sake, that I might show him there is whiles when ane had better want een than have them ; for I am as true a guide by darkness as by daylight." *

Internally as well pleased that my companion was not put to give me this last proof of his skill, I wrote a note with a pencil, desiring Samuel to bring my horses at midnight, when I thought my frolic would be well-nigh over, to the place to which the bearer should direct him, and I sent little Benjie with an apology to the worthy Quakers.

As we parted in different directions, the good woman said, "Oh, sir, if ye wad but ask Willie to tell ye ane of his tales to shorten the gate ! He can speak like ony minister frae the pulpit, and he might have been a minister him-sell,——"

"Haud your tongue, ye fule !" said Willie. "But stay, Meg—gie me a kiss ; we maunna part in anger, neither." And thus our society separated.

* See Faculties of the Blind. Note 15.

7

LETTER XI

You are now to conceive us proceeding in our different directions across the bare downs. Yonder flies little Benjie to the northward, with Hemp scampering at his heels, both running as if for dear life so long as the rogue is within sight of his employer, and certain to take the walk very easy so soon as he is out of ken. Stepping westward, you see Maggie's tall form and high-crowned hat, relieved by the fluttering of her plaid upon the left shoulder, darkening as the distance diminishes her size, and as the level sunbeams begin to sink upon the sea. She is taking her quiet journey to the Shepherd's Bush.

Then, stoutly striding over the lea, you have a full view of Darsie Latimer, with his new acquaintance, Wandering Willie, who, bating that he touched the ground now and then with his staff, not in a doubtful groping manner, but with the confident air of an experienced pilot, heaving the lead when he has the soundings by heart, walks as firmly and boldly as if he possessed the eyes of Argus. There they go, each with his violin slung at his back, but one of them at least totally ignorant whither their course is directed.

And wherefore did you enter so keenly into such a mad frolic? says my wise counselor. Why, I think, upon the whole, that as a sense of loneliness, and a longing for that kindness which is interchanged in society, led me to take up my temporary residence at Mount Sharon, the monotony of my life there, the quiet simplicity of the conversation of the Geddeses, and the uniformity of their amusements and employments, wearied out my impatient temper, and prepared me for the first escapade which chance might throw in my way.

What would I have given that I could have procured that solemn grave visage of thine, to dignify this joke, as it has done full many a one of thine own! Thou hast so happy a knack of doing the most foolish things in the wisest manner, that thou mightst pass thy extravagancies for rational actions, even in the eyes of prudence herself.

From the direction which my guide observed, I began to suspect that the dell at Brokenburn was our probable destination ; and it became important to me to consider whether I could, with propriety, or even perfect safety, intrude myself again upon the hospitality of my former host. I therefore asked Willie whether we were bound for the Laird's, as folk called him

" Do ye ken tne Laird ? " said Willie, interrupting a sonata of Corelli, of which he had whistled several bars with great precision.

" I know the Laird a little, said I ; " and therefore I was doubting whether I ought to go to his town in disguise."

" And I should doubt, not a little only, but a great deal, before I took ye there, my chap," said Wandering Willie ; " for I am thinking it wad be worth little less than broken banes baith to you and me. Na—na, chap, we are no ganging to the Laird's, but to a blythe birling at the Brokenburn-foot, where there will be mony a braw lad and lass ; and maybe there may be some of the Laird's folk, for he never comes to sic splores himsell. He is all for fowling-piece and salmon spear, now that pike and musket are out of the question."

" He has been a soldier, then ? " said I.

" I'se warrant him a soger," answered Willie ; " but take my advice, and speer as little about him as he does about you. Best to let sleeping dogs lie. Better sae naething about the Laird, my man, and tell me instead, what sort of a chap ye are, that are sae ready to cleik in with an auld gaberlunzie fiddler ? Maggie says ye're gentle, but a shilling maks a' the difference that Maggie kens between a gentle and a semple, and your crowns wad mak ye a prince of the blood in her een. But I am ane that kens full weel that ye may wear good claithes, and have a saft hand, and yet that may come of idleness as weel as gentrice."

I told him my name, with the same addition I had formerly given to Mr. Joshua Geddes—that I was a law student, tired of my studies, and rambling about for exercise and amusement.

" And are ye in the wont of drawing up wi' a' the gangrel bodies that ye meet on the highroad, or find cowering in a sand-bunker upon the links ? " demanded Willie.

" Oh no ; only with honest folks like yourself, Willie," was my reply.

" Honest folks like me ! How do ye ken whether I am honest, or what I am ? I may be the deevil himsell for what ye ken, for he has power to come disguised like an angel of light ; and. besides, he is a prime fiddler. He played a sonata to Corelli, ye ken."

There was something odd in this speech and the tone in which it was said. It seemed as if my companion was not always in his constant mind, or that he was willing to try if he could frighten me. I laughed at the extravagance of his language, however, and asked him in reply if he was fool enough to believe that the foul fiend would play so silly a masquerade.

" Ye ken little about it—little about it," said the old man, shaking his head and beard, and knitting his brows. " I could tell ye something about that."

What his wife mentioned of his being a tale-teller as well as a musician now occurred to me ; and as you know I like tales of superstition, I begged to have a specimen of his talent as we went along.

" It is very true," said the blind man, " that when I am tired of scraping thairm or singing ballants, I whiles make a tale serve the turn among the country bodies ; and I have some fearsome anes, that make the auld carlines shake on the settle, and the bits o' bairns skirl on their minnies out frae their beds. But this that I am gaun to tell you was a thing that befell in our ain house in my father's time—that is, my father was then a hafflins callant ; and I tell it to you, that it may be a lesson to you, that are but a young, thoughtless chap, wha ye draw up wi' on a lonely road ; for muckle was the dool and care that came o't to my gudesire."

He commenced his tale accordingly, in a distinct narrative tone of voice, which he raised and depressed with considerable skill—at times sinking almost into a whisper, and turning his clear but sightless eyeballs upon my face, as if it had been possible for him to witness the impression which his narrative made upon my features. I will not spare you a syllable of it, although it be of the longest ; so I make a dash—and begin.

Wandering Willie's Tale

Ye maun have heard of Sir Robert Redgauntlet of that Ilk, who lived in these parts before the dear years. The country will lang mind him ; and our fathers used to draw breath thick if ever they heard him named. He was out wi' the Hielandmen in Montrose's time ; and again he was in the

hills wi' Glencairn in the saxteen hundred and fifty-twa;
and sae when King Charles the Second came in, wha was in
sic favor as the Laird of Redgauntlet? He was knighted at
Lonon court, wi' the King's ain sword; and being a red-hot
prelatist, he came down here, rampauging like a lion, with
commissions of lieutenancy (and of lunacy, for what I ken),
to put down a' the Whigs and Covenanters in the country.
Wild wark they made of it; for the Whigs were as dour as
the Cavaliers were fierce, and it was which should first tire
the other. Redgauntlet was aye for the strong hand; and
his name is kenn'd as wide in the country as Claverhouse's or
Tam Dalyell's. Glen, nor dargle, nor mountain, nor cave
could hide the puir Hill-folk when Redgauntlet was out with
bugle and bloodhound after them, as if they had been sae
mony deer. And troth when they fand them, they didna
mak muckle mair ceremony than a Hielandman wi' a roe-
buck. It was just, " Will ye tak the test?" If not, " Make
ready—present—fire! " and there lay the recusant.

Far and wide was Sir Robert hated and feared. Men
thought he had a direct compact with Satan; that he was
proof against steel, and that bullets happed aff his buff-coat
like hailstanes from a hearth; that he had a mear that would
turn a hare on the side of Carrifra Gauns—and muckle to the
same purpose, of whilk mair anon. The best blessing they
wared on him was, " Deil scowp wi' Redgauntlet! " He
wasna a bad maister to his ain folk though, and was weel
aneugh liked by his tenants; and as for the lackies and
troopers that raid out wi' him to the persecutions, as the
Whigs ca'd those killing times, they wad hae drunken them-
sells blind to his health at ony time.

Now you are to ken that my gudesire lived on Redgauntlet's grund; they ca' the place Primrose Knowe. We had
lived on the grund, and under the Redgauntlets, since the
riding days, and lang before. It was a pleasant bit; and I
think the air is callerer and fresher there than onywhere else
in the country. It's a' deserted now; and I sat on the broken
door-cheek three days since, and was glad I couldna see the
plight the place was in; but that's a' wide o' the mark.
There dwelt my gudesire, Steenie Steenson, a rambling,
rattling chiel he had been in his young days, and could play
weel on the pipes; he was famous at " Hoopers and Girders,"
a' Cumberland couldna touch him at " Jockie Lattin," and
he had the finest finger for the back-lilt between Berwick
and Carlisle. The like o' Steenie wasna the sort that they
made Whigs o'. And so he became a Tory, as they ca' it,

which we now ca' Jacobites, just out of a kind of need-
cessity, that he might belang to some side or other. He
had nae ill to the Whig bodies, and liked little to see the
bluid rin, though, being obliged to follow Sir Robert in
hunting and hosting, watching and warding, he saw muckle
mischief, and maybe did some that he couldna avoid.

Now Steenie was a kind of favorite with his master, and
kenn'd a' the folks about the castle, and was often sent for
to play the pipes when they were at their merriment. Auld
Dougal MacCallum, the butler, that had followed Sir Robert
through gude and ill, thick and thin, pool and stream, was
specially fond of the pipes, and aye gae my gudesire his gude
word wi' the laird ; for Dougal could turn his master round
his finger.

Weel, round came the Revolution, and it had like to have
broken the hearts baith of Dougal and his master. But the
change was not a'thegither sae great as they feared, and
other folk thought for. The Whigs made an unco crawing
what they wad do with their auld enemies, and in special
wi' Sir Robert Redgauntlet. But there were ower mony
great folks dipped in the same doings to mak a spick and
span new warld. So Parliament passed it a' ower easy ; and
Sir Robert, bating that he was held to hunting foxes instead
of Covenanters, remained just the man he was. His revel
was as loud, and his hall as weel lighted, as ever it had been,
though maybe he lacked the fines of the Nonconformists,
that used to come to stock his larder and cellar ; for it is
certain he began to be keener about the rents than his tenants used to find him before, and they behooved to be prompt
to the rent-day, or else the laird wasna pleased. And he
was sic an awsome body that naebody cared to anger him ;
for the oaths he swore and the rage that he used to get into,
and the looks that he put on, made men sometimes think
him a devil incarnate.*

Weel, my gudesire was nae manager—no that he was a
very great misguider—but he hadna the saving gift, and he
got twa terms' rent in arrear. He got the first brash at
Whitsunday put ower wi' fair word and piping ; but when
Martinmas came, there was a summons from the grund-
officer to come wi' the rent on a day preceese, or else Steenie
behooved to flit. Sair wark he had to get the siller ; but he
was weel-freended, and at last he got the haill scraped thegither—a thousand merks ; the maist of it was from a neigh-

---

* See William III. and the Covenanters. **Note 16.**

bor they ca'd Laurie Lapraik—a sly tod. Laurie had walth o' gear—could hunt wi' the hound and rin wi' the hare—and be Whig or Tory, saunt or sinner, as the wind stood. He was a professor in this Revolution warld ; but he liked an orra sough of this warld, and a tune on the pipes weel aneugh at a bye-time ; and abune a', he thought he had gude security for the siller he lent my gudesire ower the stocking at Primrose Knowe.

Away trots my gudesire to Redgauntlet Castle, wi' a heavy purse and a light heart, glad to be out of the laird's danger. Weel, the first thing he learned at the castle was that Sir Robert had fretted himsell into a fit of the gout, because he did not appear before twelve o'clock. It wasna a'thegither for sake of the money, Dougal thought ; but because he didna like to part wl' my gudesire aff the grund. Dougal was glad to see Steenie, and brought him into the great oak parlor, and there sat the laird his leesome lane, excepting that he had beside him a great ill-favored jackanape, that was a special pet of his—a cankered beast it was, and mony an ill-natured trick it played ; ill to please it was, and easily angered—ran about the haill castle, chattering and yowling, and pinching and biting folk, especially before ill weather, or disturbances in the state. Sir Robert ca'd it Major Weir, after the warlock that was burnt ;* and few folk liked either the name or the conditions of the creature—they thought there was something in it by ordinar—and my gudesire was not just easy in his mind when the door shut on him, and he saw himself in the room wi naebody but the laird, Dougal MacCallum, and the major, a thing that hadna chanced to him before.

Sir Robert sat, or, I should say, lay, in a great armed chair, wi' his grand velvet gown, and his feet on a cradle ; for he had baith gout and gravel, and his face looked as gash and ghastly as Satan's. Major Weir sat opposite to him, in a red laced coat, and the laird's wig on his head ; and aye as Sir Robert girned wi' pain, the jackanape girned too, like a sheep's-head between a pair of tangs—an ill-faured, fearsome couple they were. The laird's buff-coat was hung on a pin behind him, and his broadsword and his pistols within reach ; for he keepit up the auld fashion of having the weapons ready, and a horse saddled day and night, just as he used to do when he was able to loup on horseback, and away after ony of the Hill-folk he could get

---

* A celebrated wizard, executed [1670] at Edinburgh for sorcery and other crimes.

speerings of. Some said it was for fear of the Whigs taking vengeance, but I judge it was just his auld custom—he wasna gien to fear onything. The rental-book, wi' its black cover and brass clasps, was lying beside him ; and a book of sculduddry sangs was put betwixt the leaves, to keep it open at the place where it bore evidence against the goodman of Primrose Knowe, as behind the hand with his mails and duties. Sir Robert gave my gudesire a look as if he would have withered his heart in his bosom. Ye maun ken he had a way of bending his brows that men saw the visible mark of a horse-shoe in his forehead, deep-dinted, as if it had been stamped there.

"Are ye come light-handed, ye son of a toom whistle ?" said Sir Robert. "Zounds, if you are——"

My gudesire, with as gude a countenance as he could put on, made a leg, and placed the bag of money on the table wi' a dash, like a man that does something clever. The laird drew it to him hastily. "Is it all here, Steenie, man ?"

"Your honor will find it right," said my gudesire.

"Here, Dougal," said the laird, " gie Steenie a tass of brandy downstairs, till I count the siller and write the receipt."

But they werena weel out of the room when Sir Robert gied a yelloch that garr'd the castle rock. Back ran Dougal —in flew the livery-men—yell on yell gied the laird, ilk ane mair awfu' than the ither. My gudesire knew not whether to stand or flee, but he ventured back into the parlor, where a' was gaun hirdie-girdie—naebody to say "come in" or "gae out." Terribly the laird roared for cauld water to his feet, and wine to cool his throat ; and "Hell, hell, hell, and its flames," was aye the word in his mouth. They brought him water, and when they plunged his swoln feet into the tub, he cried out it was burning ; and folk say that it *did* bubble and sparkle like a seething cauldron. He flung the cup at Dougal's head, and said he had given him blood instead of burgundy ; and sure aneugh, the lass washed clotted blood aff the carpet the neist day. The jackanape they ca'd Major Weir, it jibbered and cried as if it was mocking its master. My gudesire's head was like to turn ; he forgot baith siller and receipt, and downstairs he banged ; but as he ran, the shrieks came faint and fainter ; there was a deep-drawn shivering groan, and word gaed through the castle that the laird was dead.

Weel, away came my gudesire wi' his finger in his mouth, and his best hope was that Dougal had seen the money-bag, and heard the laird speak of writing the receipt. The young laird, now Sir John, came from Edinburgh to see things put to rights. Sir John and his father never gree'd weel. Sir John had been bred an advocate, and afterwards sat in the last Scots Parliament and voted for the Union, having gotten, it was thought, a rug of the compensations ; if his father could have come out of his grave he would have brained him for it on his awn hearthstane. Some thought it was easier counting with the auld rough knight than the fair-spoken young ane—but mair of that anon.

Dougal MacCallum, poor body, neither grat nor graned, but gaed about the house looking like a corpse, but directing, as was his duty, a' the order of the grand funeral. Now, Dougal looked aye waur and waur when night was coming, and was aye the last to gang to his bed, whilk was in a little round just opposite the chamber of dais, whilk his master occupied while he was living, and where he now lay in state, as they ca'd it, weel-a-day ! The night before the funeral, Dougal could keep his awn counsel nae langer ; he came doun with his proud spirit, and fairly asked auld Hutcheon to sit in his room with him for an hour. When they were in the round, Dougal took ae tass of brandy to himsell and gave another to Hutcheon, and wished him all health and lang life, and said that, for himsell, he wasna lang for this world ; for that, every night since Sir Robert's death, his silver call had sounded from the state chamber, just as it used to do at nights in his lifetime, to call Dougal to help to turn him in his bed. Dougal said that, being alone with the dead on that floor of the tower (for naebody cared to wake Sir Robert Redgauntlet like anether corpse), he had never daured to answer the call, but that now his conscience checked him for neglecting his duty ; for, " though death breaks service," said MacCallum, " it shall never break my service to Sir Robert ; and I will answer his next whistle, so be you will stand by me Hutcheon."

Hutcheon had nae will to the wark, but he had stood by Dougal in battle and broil, and he wad not fail him at this pinch ; so down the carles sat ower a stoup of brandy, and Hutcheon, who was something of a clerk, would have read a chapter of the Bible ; but Dougal would hear naething but a blaud of Davie Lindsay, whilk was the waur preparation.

When midnight came, and the house was quiet as the grave, sure aneugh the silver whistle sounded as sharp and shrill as if Sir Robert was blowing it, and up gat the twa auld serving-men and tottered into the room where the dead

man lay. Hutcheon saw aneugh at the first glance ; for
there were torches in the room, which showed him the foul
fiend in his ain shape, sitting on the laird's coffin ! Ower
he couped as if he had been dead. He could not tell how
lang he lay in a trance at the door, but when he gathered
himself he cried on his neighbor, and getting nae answer,
roused the house, when Dougal was found lying dead within
twa steps of the bed where his master's coffin was placed.
As for the whistle, it was gaen anes and aye ; but mony a
time was it heard at the top of the house on the bartizan,
and amang the auld chimneys and turrets, where the howlets have their nests. Sir John hushed the matter up, and
the funeral passed ower without mair bogle-wark.

But when a' was ower, and the laird was beginning to
settle his affairs, every tenant was called up for his arrears,
and my gudesire for the full sum that stood against him in
the rental-book. Weel, away he trots to the castle, to tell
his story, and there he is introduced to Sir John, sitting in
his father's chair, in deep mourning, with weepers and
hanging cravat, and a small walking rapier by his side,
instead of the auld broadsword that had a hundredweight of
steel about it, what with blade, chape, and basket-hilt. I
have heard their communing so often tauld ower, that I
almost think I was there mysell, though I couldna be born
at the time. (In fact, Alan, my companion mimicked, with
a good deal of humor, the flattering, conciliating tone of the
tenant's address, and the hypocritical melancholy of the
laird's reply. His grandfather, he said, had, while he
spoke, his eye fixed on the rental-book, as if it were a
mastiff-dog that he was afraid would spring up and bite him).

" I wuss ye joy, sir, of the head seat, and the white loaf,
and the braid lairdship. Your father was a kind man to
friends and followers ; muckle grace to you, **Sir John**, to
fill his shoon—his boots, I suld say, for he seldom wore
shoon, unless it were muils when he had the gout."

" Ay, Steenie," quoth the laird, sighing deeply, and putting his napkin to his een, " his was a sudden call, and he
will be missed in the country ; no time to set his house in
order : weel prepared Godward, no doubt, which is the root
of the matter, but left us behind a tangled hesp to wind,
Steenie. Hem ! hem ! We maun go to business, Steenie ;
much to do, and little time to do it in."

Here he opened the fatal volume. I have heard of a thing
they call Doomsday Book—I am clear it has been a rental of
back-ganging tenants.

Steenie Steenson demanding a receipt for his rent from Sir Robert Redgauntlet.
(Wandering Willie's Tale.)

"Stephen," said Sir John, still in the same soft sleekit tone of voice—"Stephen Stevenson, or Steenson, ye are down here for a year's rent behind the hand, due at last term."

Stephen. "Please your honor, Sir John, I paid it to your father."

Sir John. "Ye took a receipt then, doubtless, Stephen, and can produce it?"

Stephen. "Indeed I hadna time, an it like your honor; for nae sooner had I set doun the siller, and just as his honor Sir Robert, that's gaen, drew it till him to count it, and write out the receipt, he was ta'en wi' the pains that removed him."

"That was unlucky," said Sir John, after a pause. "But ye maybe paid it in the presence of somebody. I want but a *talis qualis* evidence, Stephen. I would go ower strictly to work with no poor man."

Stephen. "Troth, Sir John, there was naebody in the room but Dougal MacCallum, the butler. But, as your honor kens, he has e'en followed his auld master."

"Very unlucky again, Stephen," said Sir John, without altering his voice a single note. "The man to whom ye paid the money is dead; and the man who witnessed the payment is dead too; and the siller, which should have been to the fore, is neither seen nor heard tell of in the repositories. How am I to believe a' this?"

Stephen. "I dinna ken, your honor; but there is a bit memorandum note of the very coins—for, God help me! I had to borrow out of twenty purses—and I am sure that ilka man there set down will take his grit oath for what purpose I borrowed the money."

Sir John. "I have little doubt ye *borrowed* the money, Steenie. It is the *payment* to my father that I want to have some proof of."

Stephen. "The siller maun be about the house, Sir John. And since your honor never got it, and his honor that was canna have taen it wi' him, maybe some of the family may have seen it."

Sir John. "We will examine the servants, Stephen; that is but reasonable."

But lackey and lass, and page and groom, all denied stoutly that they had ever seen such a bag of money as my gudesire described. What was waur, he had unluckily not mentioned to any living soul of them his purpose of paying his rent. Ae quean had noticed something under his arm, but she took it for the pipes.

Sir John Redgauntlet ordered the servants out of the room, and then said to my gudesire, "Now, Steenie, ye see you have fair play ; and, as I have little doubt ye ken better where to find the siller than ony other body, I beg, in fair terms, and for your own sake, that you will end this fasherie ; for, Stephen, ye maun pay or flit."

"The Lord forgie your opinion," said Stephen, driven almost to his wit's end—"I am an honest man."

"So am I, Stephen," said his honor ; "and so are all the folks in the house, I hope. But if there be a knave amongst us, it must be he that tells the story he cannot prove." He paused, and then added, mair sternly, "If I understand your trick, sir, you want to take advantage of some malicious reports concerning things in this family, and particularly respecting my father's sudden death, thereby to cheat me out of the money, and perhaps take away my character, by insinuating that I have received the rent I am demanding. Where do you suppose this money to be? I insist upon knowing."

My gudesire saw everything look sae muckle against him that he grew nearly desperate ; however, he shifted from one foot to another, looked to every corner of the room, and made no answer.

"Speak out, sirrah," said the laird, assuming a look of his father's—a very particular ane, which he had when he was angry : it seemed as if the wrinkles of his frown made that selfsame fearful shape of a horse's shoe in the middle of his brow—"speak out, sir! I *will* know your thoughts. Do you suppose that I have this money?"

"Far be it frae me to say so," said Stephen.

"Do you charge any of my people with having taken it?"

"I wad be laith to charge them that may be innocent," said my gudesire ; "and if there be any one that is guilty, I have nae proof."

"Somewhere the money must be, if there is a word of truth in your story," said Sir John ; "I ask where you think it is, and demand a correct answer?"

"In hell, if you *will* have my thoughts of it," said my gudesire, driven to extremity—"in hell ! with your father, his jackanape, and his silver whistle."

Down the stairs he ran, for the parlor was nae place for him after such a word, and he heard the laird swearing blood and wounds behind him, as fast as ever did Sir Robert, and roaring for the bailie and the baron-officer.

Away rode my gudesire to his chief creditor, him they ca'd

Laurie Lapraik, to try if he could make onything out of
him ; but when he tauld his story he got but the warst word
in his wame—thief, beggar, and dyvour were the safest
terms ; and to the boot of these hard terms, Laurie brought
up the old story of his dipping his hand in the blood of
God's saunts, just as if a tenant could have helped riding
with the laird, and that a laird like Sir Robert Redgauntlet.
My gudesire was by this time far beyond the bounds of
patience, and while he and Laurie were at deil speed the
liars, he was wanchancie aneugh to abuse Lapraik's doctrine
as weel as the man, and said things that garr'd folks' flesh
grue that heard them ; he wasna just himsell, and he had
lived wi' a wild set in his day.

At last they parted, and my gudesire was to ride hame
through the wood of Pitmurkie, that is a' fou of black firs,
as they say. I ken the wood, but the firs may be black or
white for what I can tell. At the entry of the wood there is
a wild common, and on the edge of the common a little
lonely change-house, that was keepit then by a hostler-wife
—they suld hae ca'd her Tibbie Faw—and there puir Steenie
cried for a mutchkin of brandy, for he had had no refreshment the haill day. Tibbie was earnest wi' him to take a
bite o' meat, but he couldna think o't, nor would he take his
foot out of the stirrup, and took off the brandy wholely at
twa draughts, and named a toast at each—the first was, the
memory of Sir Robert Redgauntlet, and might he never lie
quiet in his grave till he had righted his poor bond-tenant ;
and the second was, a health to Man's Enemy, if he would
but get back the pock of siller, or tell him what came o't,
for he saw the haill world was like to regard him as a thief
and a cheat, and he took that waur than even the ruin of his
house and hauld.

On he rode, little caring where. It was a dark night
turned, and the trees made it yet darker, and he let the
beast take its ain road through the wood ; when, all of a
sudden, from tired and wearied that it was before, the nag
began to spring, and flee, and stend, that my gudesire could
hardly keep the saddle ; upon the whilk, a horseman, suddenly riding up beside him, said, "That's a mettle beast of
yours, freend ; will you sell him ? " So saying, he touched
the horse's neck with his riding wand, and it fell into its
auld heigh-ho of a stumbling trot. "But his spunk's soon
out of him, I think," continued the stranger, "and that is
like mony a man's courage, that thinks he wad do great
things till he come to the proof."

My gudesire scarce listened to this, but spurred his horse, with "Gude e'en to you, freend."

But it's like the stranger was ane that doesna lightly yield his point ; for, ride as Steenie liked, he was aye beside him at the selfsame pace. At last my gudesire, Steenie Steenson, grew half angry, and, to say the truth, half feared.

"What is it that ye want with me, freend ?" he said. "If ye be a robber, I have nae money ; if ye be a leal man, wanting company, I have nae heart to mirth or speaking ; and if ye want to ken the road, I scarce ken it mysell."

"If you will tell me your grief," said the stranger, "I am one that, though I have been sair misca'd in the world, am the only hand for helping my freends."

So my gudesire, to ease his ain heart, mair than from any hope of help, told him the story from beginning to end.

"It's a hard pinch," said the stranger ; "but I think I can help you."

"If you could lend me the money, sir, and take a lang day—I ken nae other help on earth," said my gudesire.

"But there may be some under the earth," said the stranger. "Come, I'll be frank wi' you ; I could lend you the money on bond, but you would maybe scruple my terms. Now, I can tell you that your auld laird is disturbed in his grave by your curses, and the wailing of your family, and if ye daur venture to go to see him, he will give you the receipt."

My gudesire's hair stood on end at this proposal, but he thought his companion might be some humorsome chield that was trying to frighten him, and might end with lending him the money. Besides, he was bauld wi' brandy, and desperate wi' distress ; and he said he had courage to go to the gate of hell, and a step farther, for that receipt. The stranger laughed.

Weel, they rode on through the thickest of the wood, when, all of a sudden, the horse stopped at the door of a great house ; and, but that he knew the place was ten miles off, my father would have thought he was at Redgauntlet Castle. They rode into the outer courtyard, through the muckle faulding yetts, and aneath the auld portcullis ; and the whole front of the house was lighted, and there were pipes and fiddles, and as much dancing and deray within as used to be in Sir Robert's house at Pace and Yule, and such high seasons. They lap off, and my gudesire, as seemed to him, fastened his horse to the very ring he had tied him to that morning, when he gaed to wait on the young Sir John. .

"God!" said my gudesire, "if Sir Robert's death be but a dream!"

He knocked at the ha' door just as he was wont, and his auld acquaintance, Dougal MacCallum, just after his wont, too, came to open the door, and said, "Piper Steenie, are ye there, lad? Sir Robert has been crying for you."

My gudesire was like a man in a dream; he looked for the stranger, but he was gane for the time. At last he just tried to say, "Ha! Dougal Driveower, are ye living? I thought ye had been dead."

"Never fash yoursell wi' me," said Dougal, "but look to yoursell; and see ye take naething frae onybody here, neither meat, drink, or siller, except just the receipt that is your ain."

So saying, he led the way through halls and trances that were weel kenn'd to my gudesire, and into the auld oak parlor; and there was as much singing of profane sangs, and birling of red wine, and speaking blasphemy and sculduddry, as had ever been in Redgauntlet Castle when it was at the blythest.

But, Lord take us in keeping! what a set of ghastly revelers they were that sat round that table! My gudesire kenn'd mony that had long before gane to their place, for often had he piped to the most part in the hall of Redgauntlet. There was the fierce Middleton, and the dissolute Rothes, and the crafty Lauderdale; and Dalyell, with his bald head and a beard to his girdle; and Earlshall, with Cameron's blude on his hand; and wild Bonshaw, that tied blessed Mr. Cargill's limbs till the blude sprung; and Dumbarton Douglas, the twice-turned traitor baith to country and king. There was the Bluidy Advocate MacKenyie, who, for his worldly wit and wisdom, had been to the rest as a god. And there was Claverhouse, as beautiful as when he lived, with his long, dark, curled locks, streaming down over his laced buff-coat, and his left-hand always on his right spule-blade, to hide the wound that the silver bullet had made.* He set apart from them all, and looked at them with a melancholy, haughty countenance; while the rest hallooed, and sung, and laughed, that the room rang. But their smiles were fearfully contorted from time to time; and their laughter passed into such wild sounds as made my gudesire's very nails grow blue, and chilled the marrow in his banes.

They that waited at the table were just the wicked serv-

* See Persecutors of the Covenanters. Note 17.

ing-men and troopers that had done their work and cruel bidding on earth. There was the Lang Lad of the Nether-town, that helped to take Argyle ; and the bishop's sum-moner, that they called the Deil's Rattle-bag ; and the wicked guardsmen, in their laced coats ; and the savage Highland Amorites, that shed blood like water ; and mony a proud serving-man, haughty of heart and bloody of hand, cringing to the rich, and making them wickeder than they would be ; grinding the poor to powder, when the rich had broken them to fragments. And mony, mony mair were coming and ganging, a' as busy in their vocation as if they had been alive.

Sir Robert Redgauntlet, in the midst of a' this fearful riot, cried, wi' a voice like thunder, on Steenie Piper to come to the board-head, where he was sitting, his legs stretched out before him, and swathed up with flannel, with his holster pistols aside him, while the great broadsword rested against his chair, just as my gudesire had seen him the last time upon earth—the very cushion for the jackanape was close to him, but the creature itsell was not there ; it wasna its hour, it's likely ; for he heard them say as he came forward, " Is not the major come yet ? " And another answered, " The jackanape will be here betimes the morn." And when my gudesire came forward, Sir Robert, or his ghaist, or the deevil in his likeness, said, " Weel, piper, hae ye settled wi' my son for the year's rent ? "

With much ado my father gat breath to say that Sir John would not settle without his honor's receipt.

" Ye shall hae that for a tune of the pipes, Steenie," said the appearance of Sir Robert. " Play us up, ' Weel hoddled, Luckie.' "

Now this was a tune my gudesire learned frae a warlock, that heard it when they were worshiping Satan at their meetings, and my gudesire had sometimes played it at the ranting suppers in Redgauntlet Castle, but never very will-ingly ; and now he grew cauld at the very name of it, and said, for excuse, he hadna his pipes wi' him.

" MacCallum, ye limb of Beelzebub," said the fearfu' Sir Robert, " bring Steenie the pipes that I am keeping for him."

MacCallum brought a pair of pipes might have served the piper of Donald of the Isles. But he gave my gudesire a nudge as he offered them ; and looking secretly and closely, Steenie saw that the chanter was of steel, and heated to a white heat ; so he had fair warning not to trust his fingers

with it. So he excused himself again, and said he was faint
and frightened, and had not wind aneugh to fill the bag.

" Then ye maun eat and drink, Steenie," said the figure ;
"for we do little else here ; and it's ill speaking between a fou
man and a fasting."

Now these were the very words that the bloody Earl of
Douglas said to keep the king's messenger in hand, while he
cut the head off MacLellan of Bombie, at the Threave
Castle,* and that put Steenie mair and mair on his guard.
So he spoke up like a man, and said he came neither to eat,
or drink, or make minstrelsy, but simply for his ain—to ken
what was come o' the money he had paid, and to get a discharge for it ; and he was so stout hearted by this time, that
he charged Sir Robert for conscience' sake (he had no power
to say the holy name), and as he hoped for peace and rest, to
spread no snares for him, but just to give him his ain.

The appearance gnashed its teeth and laughed, but it took
from a large pocketbook the receipt, and handed it to
Steenie. " There is your receipt, ye pitiful cur ; and for the
money, my dog whelp of a son may go look for it in the Cat's
Cradle."

My gudesire uttered mony thanks, and was about to retire
when Sir Robert roared aloud, " Stop though, thou sack-
doudling son of a whore ! I am not done with thee. HERE
we do nothing for nothing ; and you must return on this
very day twelvemonth to pay your master the homage that
you owe me for my protection."

My father's tongue was loosed of a suddenty, and he said
aloud, " I refer mysell to God's pleasure, and not to yours."

He had no sooner uttered the word than all was dark
around him, and he sunk on the earth with such a sudden
shock, that he lost both breath and sense.

How lang Steenie lay there, he could not tell ; but when
he came to himsell, he was lying in the auld kirkyard of Redgauntlet parochine, just at the door of the family aisle, and
the scutcheon of the auld knight, Sir Robert, hanging over
his head. There was a deep morning fog on grass and
gravestane around him, and his horse was feeding quietly
beside the minister's twa cows. Steenie would have thought
the whole was a dream, but he had the receipt in his hand,
fairly written and signed by the auld laird ; only the last
letters of his name were a little disorderly, written like one
seized with sudden pain.

* The reader is referred for particulars to Pitscottie's *History of
Scotland,*

Sorely troubled in his mind, he left that dreary place, rode through the mist to Redgauntlet Castle, and with much ado he got speech of the laird.

" Well, you dyvour bankrupt," was the first word, "have you brought me my rent ? "

" No," answered my gudesire, "I have not ; but I have brought your honor Sir Robert's receipt for it."

" How, sirrah ? Sir Robert's receipt ! You told me he had not given you one."

" Will your honor please to see if that bit line is right ? "

Sir John looked at every line, and at every letter, with much attention, and at last at the date, which my gudesire had not observed—" ' From my appointed place,' he read, ' this twenty-fifth of November.' What ! That is yesterday ! Villain, thou must have gone to Hell for this ! "

" I got it from your honor's father ; whether he be in Heaven or Hell, I know not," said Steenie.

" I will delate you for a warlock to the privy council ! " said Sir John. " I will send you to your master, the devil, with the help of a tar-barrel and a torch ! "

" I intend to delate mysell to the presbytery," said Steenie, " and tell them all I have seen last night, whilk are things fitter for them to judge of than a borrel man like me."

Sir John paused, composed himsell, and desired to hear the full history ; and my gudesire told it him from point to point, as I have told it you—word for word, neither more nor less."

Sir John was silent again for a long time, and at last he said, very composedly, "Steenie, this story of yours concerns the honor of many a noble family besides mine ; and if it be a leasing-making, to keep yourself out of my danger, the least you can expect is to have a red-hot iron driven through your tongue, and that will be as bad as scauding your fingers with a red-hot chanter. But yet it may be true, Steenie ; and if the money cast up, I shall not know what to think of it. But where shall we find the Cat's Cradle ? There are cats enough about the old house, but I think they kitten without the ceremony of bed or cradle."

" We were best ask Hutcheon," said my gudesire ; "he kens a' the odd corners about as weel as—another serving man that is now gane, and that I wad not like to name."

Aweel, Hutcheon, when he was asked, told them that a ruinous turret, lang disused, next to the clock-house, only accessible by a ladder, for the opening was on the outside, and far above the battlements, was called of old, the Cat's Cradle.

"There will I go immediately," said Sir John ; and he took (with what purpose, Heaven kens) one of his father's pistols from the hall-table, where they had lain since the night he died, and hastened to the battlements. It was a dangerous place to climb, for the ladder was auld and frail, and wanted ane or twa rounds. However, up got Sir John, and entered at the turret door, where his body stopped the only little light that was in the bit turret. Something flees at him wi' a vengeance, maist dang him back ower ; bang gaed the knight's pistol, and Hutcheon, that held the ladder, and my gudesire that stood beside him, hears a loud skelloch. A minute after, Sir John flings the body of the jackanape down to them, and cries that the siller is fund, and that they should come up and help him. And there was the bag of siller sure aneugh, and mony orra things besides that had been missing for mony a day. And Sir John, when he had riped the turret weel, led my gude-sire into the dining-parlor, and took him by the hand, and spoke kindly to him, and said he was sorry he should have doubted his word, and that he would hereafter be a good master to him, to make amends.

"And now, Steenie," said Sir John, " although this vision of yours tends, on the whole to my father's credit, as an honest man, that he should, even after his death, desire to see justice done to a poor man like you, yet you are sensible that ill-dispositioned men might make bad constructions upon it, concerning his soul's health. So, I think, we had better lay the haill dirdum on that ill-deedie creature, Major Weir, and say naething about your dream in the wood of Pitmurkie. You had taken ower muckle brandy to be very certain about ony thing ; and, Steenie, this receipt (his hand shook while he held it out), it's but a queer kind of document, and we will do best, I think, to put it quietly in the fire."

" Od, but for as queer as it is, it's a' the voucher I have for my rent," said my gudesire, who was afraid, it may be, of losing the benefit of Sir Robert's discharge.

"I will bear the contents to your credit in the rental-book, and give you a discharge under my own hand," said Sir John, " and that on the spot. And, Steenie, if you can hold your tongue about this matter, you shall sit, from this term downward, at an easier rent."

" Mony thanks to your honor," said Steenie, who saw

easily in what corner the wind was; "doubtless I will be comfortable to all your honor's commands; only I would willingly speak wi' some powerful minister on the subject, for I do not like the sort of soumons of appointment whilk your honor's father——"

"Do not call the phantom my father!" said Sir John, interrupting him.

"Weel, then, the thing that was so like him," said my gudesire; "he spoke of my coming back to him this time twelvemonth, and it's a weight on my conscience."

"Aweel, then," said Sir John, "if you be so much distressed in mind, you may speak to our minister of the parish; he is a douce man, regards the honor of our family, and the mair that he may look for some patronage from me."

Wi' that my gudesire readily agreed that the receipt should be burned, and the laird threw it into the chimney with his ain hand. Burn it would not for them, though; but away it flew up the lum, wi' a lang train of sparks at its tail, and a hissing noise like a squib.

My gudesire gaed down to the manse, and the minister, when he had heard the story, said it was his real opinion that, though my gudesire had gaen very far in tampering with dangerous matters, yet, as he had refused the devil's arles (for such was the offer of meat and drink), and had refused to do homage by piping at his bidding, he hoped, that if he held a circumspect walk hereafter, Satan could take little advantage by what was come and gane. And, indeed, my gudesire, of his ain accord, lang forswore baith the pipes and the brandy; it was not even till the year was out, and the fatal day passed, that he would so much as take the fiddle, or drink usquebaugh or tippenny.

Sir John made up his story about the jackanape as he liked himsell; and some believe till this day there was no more in the matter than the filching nature of the brute. Indeed, ye'll no hinder some to threap that it was nane o' the Auld Enemy that Dougal and my gudesire [Hutcheon] saw in the laird's room, but only that wanchancie creature, the major, capering on the coffin; and that, as to the blawing on the laird's whistle that was heard after he was dead, the filthy brute could do that as weel as the laird himsell, if no better. But Heaven kens the truth, whilk first came out by the minister's wife, after Sir John and her ain gudeman were baith in the molds. And then, my gudesire, wha was failed in his limbs, but not in his judgment or memory—at least nothing to speak of—was obliged to tell the real narrative to his freends for the credit of his good name. He might else have been charged for a warlock.*

THE shades of evening were growing thicker around us as my conductor finished his long narrative with this moral— "Ye see, birkie, it is nae chancy thing to tak a stranger traveler for a guide when ye are in an uncouth land."

"I should not have made that inference," said I. "Your grandfather's adventure was fortunate for himself, whom it saved from ruin and distress ; and fortunate for his landlord also, whom it prevented from committing a gross act of injustice."

"Ay, but they had baith to sup the sauce o't sooner or later," said Wanderer Willie. "What was fristed wasna forgiven. Sir John died before he was much over three-score ; and it was just like of a moment's illness. And for my gudeshire, though he departed in fulness of years, yet there was my father, a yauld man of forty-five, fell down betwixt the stilts of his pleugh, and raise never again, and left nae bairn but me, a puir, sightless, fatherless, motherless creature, could neither work nor want. Things gaed weel aneugh at first ; for Sir Redwald Redgauntlet, the only son of Sir John, and the oye of auld Sir Robert, and, wae's me ! the last of the honorable house, took the farm off our hands, and brought me into his household to have care of me. He liked music, and I had the best teachers baith England and Scotland could gie me. Mony a merry year was I wi' him ; but wae's me ! he gaed out with other pretty men in the Forty-five—— I'll say nae mair about it. My head never settled weel since I lost him ; and if I say another word about it, deil a bar will I have the heart to play the night. Look out, my gentle chap," he resumed, in a different tone, "ye should see the lights in Brokenburn Glen by this time."

* See Excessive Lamentation. Note 18.

LETTER XII

Tam Luter was their minstrel meet,
  Gude Lord as he could lance,
He played sae shrill and sang sae sweet,
  Till Towsie took a trance.
Auld Lightfoot there he did forleet,
  And counterfeited France ;
He used himself as man discreet,
  And took up Morrice danse
            Sae loud,
At Christ's Kirk on the Green that day.
                          KING JAMES I.

I CONTINUE to scribble at length, though the subject may seem somewhat deficient in interest. Let the grace of the narrative, therefore, and the concern we take in each other's matters, make amends for its tenuity. We fools of fancy, who suffer ourselves, like Malvolio, to be cheated with our own visions, have, nevertheless, this advantage over the wise ones of the earth, that we have our whole stock of enjoyments under our own command, and can dish for ourselves an intellectual banquet with most moderate assistance from external objects. It is, to be sure, something like the feast which the Barmecide served up to Alnaschar ; and we cannot be expected to get fat upon such diet. But then, neither is there repletion nor nausea, which often succeed the grosser and more material revel. On the whole, I still pray, with the *Ode to Castle-Building*—

Give me thy hope which sickens not the heart ;
  Give me thy wealth which has no wings to fly ;
Give me the bliss thy visions can impart ;
  Thy friendship give me, warm in poverty !

And so, despite thy solemn smile and sapient shake of the head, I will go on picking such interest as I can out of my trivial adventures, even though that interest should be the creation of my own fancy ; nor will I cease to inflict on thy devoted eyes the labor of perusing the scrolls in which I shall record my narrative.

My last broke off as we were on the point of descending

118

into the glen at Brokenburn by the dangerous track which I
had first traveled *en croupe* behind a furious horseman, and
was now again to brave under the precarious guidance of a
blind man.

It was now getting dark ; but this was no inconvenience to
my guide, who moved on, as formerly, with instinctive security of step, so that we soon reached the bottom, and I could
see lights twinkling in the cottage which had been my place
of refuge on a former occasion. It was not thither, however,
that our course was directed. We left the habitation of the
Laird to the left, and turning down the brook, soon approached the small hamlet which had been erected at the
mouth of the stream, probably on account of the convenience
which it afforded as a harbor to the fishing-boats. A large
low cottage, full in our front, seemed highly illuminated ;
for the light not only glanced from every window and aperture in its frail walls, but was even visible from rents and
fractures in the roof, composed of tarred shingles, repaired
in part by thatch and divot.

While these appearances engaged my attention, that of my
companion was attracted by a regular succession of sounds,
like a bouncing on the floor, mixed with a very faint noise
of music, which Willie's acute organs at once recognized and
accounted for, while to me it was almost inaudible. The
old man struck the earth with his staff in a violent passion.
" The whoreson fisher rabble ! They have brought another
violer upon my walk ! They are such smuggling blackguards, that they must run in their very music ; but I'll sort
them waur than ony gauger in the country. Stay—hark—
it's no a fiddle neither ; it's the pipe and tabor bastard,
Simon of Sowport, frae the Nicol Forest ; but I'll pipe and
tabor him ! Let me hae ance my left hand on his cravat,
and ye shall see what my right will do. Come away, chap—
come away, gentle chap ; nae time to be picking and waling
your steps." And on he passed with long and determined
strides, dragging me along with him.

I was not quite easy in his company ; for now, that his
minstrel pride was hurt, the man had changed from the quiet,
decorous, I might almost say respectable, person which he
seemed while he told his tale, into the appearance of a
fierce, brawling, dissolute stroller ; so that when he entered
the large hut, where a great number of fishers, with their
wives and daughters, were engaged in eating, drinking, and
dancing, I was somewhat afraid that the impatient violence
of my companion might procure us an indifferent reception,

But the universal shout of welcome with which Wandering Willie was received—the hearty congratulations—the repeated " Here's t'ye, Willie ! "—" Whare hae ye been, ye blind deevil ? " and the call upon him to pledge them—above all, the speed with which the obnoxious pipe and tabor were put to silence, gave the old man such effectual assurance of undiminished popularity and importance as at once put his jealousy to rest, and changed his tone of offended dignity into one better fitted to receive such cordial greetings. Young men and women crowded round to tell how much they were afraid some mischance had detained him, and how two or three young fellows had set out in quest of him.

" It was nae mischance, praised be Heaven," said Willie, " but the absence of the lazy loon Rob the Rambler, my comrade, that didna come to meet me on the links ; but I hae gotten a braw consort in his stead, worth a dozen of him, the unhanged blackguard."

" And wha is't tou's gotten, Wullie, lad ? " said half a score of voices, while all eyes were turned on your humble servant, who kept the best countenance he could, though not quite easy at becoming the center to which all eyes were pointed.

" I ken him by his hemmed cravat," said one fellow ; "it's Gil Hobson, the souple tailor frae Burgh. Ye are welcome to Scotland, ye prick-the-clout loon," he said, thrusting forth a paw much the color of a badger's back, and of most portentous dimensions.

" Gil Hobson ! Gil whoreson ! " exclaimed Wandering Willie ; " it's a gentle chap that I judge to be an apprentice wi' auld Joshua Geddes to the Quaker trade."

" What trade be's that, man ? " said he of the badger-colored fist.

" Canting and lying," said Willie, which produced a thundering laugh ; " but I am teaching the callant a better trade, and that is feasting and fiddling."

Willie's conduct in thus announcing something like my real character was contrary to compact ; and yet I was rather glad he did so, for the consequence of putting a trick upon these rude and ferocious men might, in case of discovery, have been dangerous to us both, and I was at the same time delivered from the painful effort to support a fictitious character. The good company, except perhaps one or two of the young women, whose looks expressed some desire for better acquaintance, gave themselves no farther trouble about me; but, while the seniors resumed their places near an immense bowl, or rather reeking caldron of brandy-punch, the younger arranged themselves on the floor, and called loudly on Willie to strike up.

With a brief caution to me to "mind my credit, for fishers have ears, though fish have none," Willie led off in capital style, and I followed, certainly not so as to disgrace my companion, who every now and then gave me a nod of approbation. The dances were, of course, the Scottish jigs, and reels, and "twasome dances," with a strathspey or hornpipe for interlude; and the want of grace, on the part of the performers, was amply supplied by truth of ear, vigor and decision of step, and the agility proper to the Northern performers. My own spirits rose with the mirth around me, and with old Willie's admirable execution, and frequent "weel dune, gentle chap, yet!" and, to confess the truth, I felt a great deal more pleasure in this rustic revel than I have done at the more formal balls and concerts in your famed city, to which I have sometimes made my way. Perhaps this was because I was a person of more importance to the presiding matron of Brokenburn-foot than I had the means of rendering myself to the far-famed Miss Nickie Murray, the patroness of your Edinburgh assemblies. The person I mean was a buxom dame of about thirty, her fingers loaded with many a silver ring, and three or four of gold; her ankles liberally displayed from under her numerous blue, white, and scarlet short petticoats, and attired in hose of the finest and whitest lamb's-wool, which arose from shoes of Spanish cordwain, fastened with silver buckles. She took the lead in my favor, and declared "that the brave young gentleman should not weary himself to death wi' playing, but take the floor for a dance or twa."

"And what's to come of me, Dame Martin?" said Willie.

"Come o' thee?" said the dame; "mischanter on the auld beard o' ye! ye could play for twenty hours on end, and tire out the haill countryside wi' dancing before ye laid down your bow, saving for a bye-drink or the like o' that."

"In troth, dame," answered Willie, "ye are nae sae far wrang; sae if my comrade is to take his dance, ye maun gie me my drink, and then bob it away like Madge of Middlebie."

The drink was soon brought, but while Willie was partaking of it, a party entered the hut, which arrested my attention at once, and intercepted the intended gallantry with which I had proposed to present my hand to the fresh-

colored, well-made, white-ankled Thetis, who had obtained
me manumission from my musical task.

This was nothing less than the sudden appearance of the
old woman whom the Laird had termed Mabel; Cristal
Nixon, his male attendant; and the young person who had
said grace to us when I supped with him.

This young person—Alan, thou art in thy way a bit of a
conjurer—this young person whom I *did not* describe, and
whom you, for that very reason, suspected was not an indifferent object to me—is, I am sorry to say it, in very fact not
so much so as in prudence she ought. I will not use the
name of "love" on this occasion; for I have applied it too
often to transient whims and fancies to escape your satire,
should I venture to apply it now. For it is a phrase, I must
confess, which I have used—a romancer would say profaned
—a little too often, considering how few years have passed
over my head. But seriously, the fair chaplain of Brokenburn has been often in my head when she had no business
there; and if this can give thee any clue for explaining my
motives in lingering about the country, and assuming the
character of Willie's companion, why, hang me, thou art
welcome to make use of it—a permission for which thou
needest not thank me much, as thou wouldst not have failed
to assume it, whether it were given or no.

Such being my feelings, conceive how they must have
been excited when, like a beam upon a cloud, I saw this
uncommonly beautiful girl enter the apartment in which
they were dancing; not, however, with the air of an equal,
but that of a superior, come to grace with her presence the
festival of her dependants. The old man and woman
attended, with looks as sinister as hers were lovely, like two
of the worst winter months waiting upon the bright-eyed
May.

When she entered—wonder if thou wilt—she wore *a green
mantle*, such as thou hast described as the garb of thy fair
client, and confirmed what I had partly guessed from thy
personal description, that my chaplain and thy visitor were
the same person. There was an alteration on her brow the
instant she recognized me. She gave her cloak to her
female attendant, and, after a momentary hesitation, as if
uncertain whether to advance or retire, she walked into the
room with dignity and composure, all making way, the men
unbonneting and the women courtesying respectfully, as she
assumed a chair which was reverently placed for her
accommodation, apart from others.

There was then a pause, until the bustling mistress of the
ceremonies, with awkward but kindly courtesy, offered the
young lady a glass of wine, which was at first declined, and
at length only thus far accepted, that, bowing round to the
festive company, the fair visitor wished them all health and
mirth, and, just touching the brim with her lip, replaced it
on the salver. There was another pause; and I did not
immediately recollect, confused as I was by this unexpected
apparition, that it belonged to me to break it. At length a
murmur was heard around me, being expected to exhibit—
nay, to lead down the dance—in consequence of the previous
conversation.

"Deil's in the fiddler lad," was muttered from more
quarters than one—"saw folk ever sic a thing as a shame-
faced fiddler before?"

At length a venerable triton, seconding his remonstrances
with a hearty thump on my shoulder, cried out, "To the
floor—to the floor, and let us see how ye can fling; the
lassies are a' waiting."

Up I jumped, sprung from the elevated station which
constituted our orchestra, and, arranging my ideas as
rapidly as I could, advanced to the head of the room, and,
instead of offering my hand to the white-footed Thetis
aforesaid, I venturously made the same proposal to her of
the Green Mantle.

The nymph's lovely eyes seemed to open with astonishment
at the audacity of this offer; and, from the murmurs I
heard around me, I also understood that it surprised, and
perhaps offended, the bystanders. But after the first
moment's emotion, she wreathed her neck, and drawing herself haughtily up, like one who was willing to show that she
was sensible of the full extent of her own condescension,
extended her hand towards me, like a princess gracing a
squire of low degree.

There is affectation in all this, thought I to myself, if the
Green Mantle has borne true evidence, for young ladies do
not make visits, or write letters to counsel learned in the
law, to interfere in the motions of those whom they hold as
cheap as this nymph seems to do me; and if I am cheated
by a resemblance of cloaks, still I am interested to show
myself in some degree worthy of the favor she has granted
with so much state and reserve. The dance to be performed
was the old Scots jig, in which you are aware I used to play
no sorry figure at La Pique's, when thy clumsy movements
used to be rebuked by raps over the knuckles with that great

professor's fiddlestick. The choice of the tune was left to my comrade Willie, who, having finished his drink, feloniously struck up to the well known and popular measure.

> Merrily danced the Quaker's wife,
> And merrily danced the Quaker.

An astounding laugh arose at my expense, and I should have been annihilated, but that the smile which mantled on the lip of my partner had a different expression from that of ridicule, and seemed to say, " Do not take this to heart." And I did not, Alan. My partner danced admirably, and I like one who was determined, if outshone, which I could not help, not to be altogether thrown into the shade.

I assure you our performance, as well as Willie's music, deserved more polished spectators and auditors ; but we could not then have been greeted with such enthusiastic shouts of applause as attended while I handed my partner to her seat, and took my place by her side, as one who had a right to offer the attentions usual on such an occasion. She was visibly embarrassed, but I was determined not to observe her confusion, and to avail myself of the opportunity of learning whether this beautiful creature's mind was worthy of the casket in which nature had lodged it.

Nevertheless, however courageously I formed this resolution, you cannot but too well guess the difficulties I must needs have felt in carrying it into execution ; since want of habitual intercourse with the charmers of the other sex has rendered me a sheepish cur, only one grain less awkward than thyself. Then she was so very beautiful, and assumed an air of so much dignity, that I was like to fall under the fatal error of supposing she should only be addressed with something very clever ; and in the hasty racking which my brains underwent in this persuasion, not a single idea occurred that common sense did not reject as fustian on the one hand, or weary, flat, and stale triticism on the other. I felt as if my understanding were no longer my own, but was alternately under the dominion of Aldiborontiphoscophornio, and that of his facetious friend Rigdumfunnidos.* How did I envy at that moment our friend Jack Oliver, who produces with such happy complacence his fardel of small talk, and who, as he never doubts his own powers of affording amusement, passes them current with every pretty woman

---

* These jocular names, by way of contrast, were given by Scott to the two brothers, James and John Ballantyne (*Laing*).

he approaches, and fills up the intervals of chat by his complete acquaintance with the exercise of the fan, the *flaçon*,
and the other duties of the *cavaliere servente*. Some of
these I attempted, but I suppose it was awkwardly ; at least
the Lady Greenmantle received them as a princess accepts
the homage of a clown.

Meantime the floor remained empty, and as the mirth of
the good meeting was somewhat checked, I ventured, as a
dernier ressort, to propose a minuet. She thanked me, and
told me, haughtily enough, " She was here to encourage the
harmless pleasures of these good folks, but was not disposed
to make an exhibition of her own indifferent dancing for
their amusement."

She paused a moment, as if she expected me to suggest
something ; and as I remained silent and rebuked, she bowed
her head more graciously, and said, "Not to affront you,
however, a country dance, if you please."

What an ass was I, Alan, not to have anticipated her
wishes ! Should I not have observed that the ill-favored
couple, Mabel and Cristal, had placed themselves on each
side of her seat, like the supporters of the royal arms ? The
man, thick, short, shaggy, and hirsute, as the lion ; the
female, skin-dried, tight-laced, long, lean, and hungry-
faced, like the unicorn. I ought to have recollected that
under the close inspection of two such watchful slavages our
communication, while in repose, could not have been easy ;
that the period of dancing a minuet was not the very choicest
time for conversation ; but that the noise, the exercise, and
the mazy confusion of a country dance, where the inexperienced performers were every now and then running against
each other, and compelling the other couples to stand still
for a minute at a time, besides the more regular repose
afforded by the intervals of the dance itself, gave the best
possible openings for a word or two spoken in season, and
without being liable to observation.

We had but just led down when an opportunity of the kind
occurred, and my partner said, with great gentleness and
modesty, " It is not perhaps very proper in me to acknowledge an acquaintance that is not claimed ; but I believe I
speak to Mr. Darsie Latimer ?"

" Darsie Latimer was indeed the person that had now the
honor and happiness——"

I would have gone on in the false gallop of compliment,
but she cut me short. " And why," she said, " is Mr. Latimer here, and in disguise, or at least assuming an office

unworthy of a man of education ? I beg pardon," she continued ; "I would not give you pain, but surely making an associate of a person of that description——"

She looked towards my friend Willie, and was silent. I felt heartily ashamed of myself, and hastened to say it was an idle frolic, which want of occupation has suggested, and which I could not regret, since it had procured me the pleasure I at present enjoyed.

Without seeming to notice my compliment, she took the next opportunity to say, "Will Mr. Latimer permit a stranger who wishes him well to ask whether it is right that, at his active age, he should be in so far void of occupation as to be ready to adopt low society for the sake of idle amusement ?"

"You are severe, madam," I answered ; "but I cannot think myself degraded by mixing with any society where I meet——"

Here I stopped short, conscious that I was giving my answer an unhandsome turn. The *argumentum ad hominem*, the last to which a polite man has recourse, may, however, be justified by circumstances, but seldom or never the *argumentum ad fœminam*.

She filled up the blank herself which I had left. "Where you meet *me*, I suppose you would say ? But the case is different. I am, from my unhappy fate, obliged to move by the will of others, and to be in places which I would by my own will gladly avoid. Besides, I am, except for these few minutes, no participator of the revels—a spectator only, and attended by my servants. Your situation is different ; you are here by choice, the partaker and minister of the pleasures of a class below you in education, birth, and fortunes. If I speak harshly, Mr. Latimer," she added, with much sweetness of manner, "I mean kindly."

I was confounded by her speech, "severe in youthful wisdom" ; all of naive or lively, suitable to such a dialogue, vanished from my recollection, and I answered, with gravity like her own, "I am, indeed, better educated than these poor people ; but you, madam, whose kind admonition I am grateful for, must know more of my condition than I do myself ; I dare not say I am their superior in birth, since I know nothing of my own, or in fortunes, over which hangs an impenetrable cloud."

"And why should your ignorance on these points drive you into low society and idle habits ?" answered my female monitor. "Is it manly to wait till fortune cast her beams

upon you, when by exertion of your own energy you might
distinguish yourself ? Do not the pursuits of learning lie
open to you—of manly ambition—of war ? But no—not of
war, that has already cost you too dear."

" I will be what you wish me to be," I replied with eagerness. " You have but to choose my path, and you shall see
if I do not pursue it with energy, were it only because you
command me."

" Not because I command you," said the maiden, " but
because reason, common sense, manhood, and, in one word,
regard for your own safety, give the same counsel."

" At least permit me to reply, that reason and sense never
assumed a fairer form—of persuasion," I hastily added ; for
she turned from me, nor did she give me another opportunity
of continuing what I had to say till the next pause of the
dance, when, determined to bring our dialogue to a point, I
said, " You mentioned manhood also, madam, and, in the
same breath, personal danger. My ideas of manhood suggest that it is cowardice to retreat before dangers of a doubtful character. You, who appear to know so much of my
fortunes that I might call you my guardian angel, tell me
what these dangers are, that I may judge whether manhood
calls on me to face or to fly them."

She was evidently perplexed by this appeal.

" You make me pay dearly for acting as your humane
adviser," she replied at last. " I acknowledge an interest
in your fate, and yet I dare not tell you whence it arises ;
neither am I at liberty to say why, or from whom, you are
in danger ; but it is not less true that danger is near and
imminent. Ask me no more, but, for your own sake,
begone from this country. Elsewhere you are safe ; here
you do but invite your fate."

" But am I doomed to bid thus farewell to almost the only
human being who has showed an interest in my welfare ?
Do not say so ; say that we shall meet again, and the hope
shall be the leading star to regulate my course ! "

" It is more than probable," she said—" much more than
probable that we may never meet again. The help which I
now render you is all that may be in my power ; it is such
as I should render to a blind man whom I might observe
approaching the verge of a precipice ; it ought to excite no
surprise, and requires no gratitude."

So saying, she again turned from me, nor did she address
me until the dance was on the point of ending, when she
said, " Do not attempt to speak to or approach me again in

the course of the night ; leave the company as soon as you can, but not abruptly, and God be with you."

I handed her to her seat, and did not quit the fair palm I held without expressing my feelings by a gentle pressure. She colored slighty, and withdrew her hand, but not angrily. Seeing the eyes of Cristal and Mabel sternly fixed on me, I bowed deeply, and withdrew from her ; my heart saddening, and my eyes becoming dim in spite of me, as the shifting crowd hid us from each other.

It was my intention to have crept back to my comrade Willie, and resumed my bow with such spirit as I might, although at the moment I would have given half my income for an instant's solitude. But my retreat was cut off by Dame Martin with the frankness—if it is not an inconsistent phrase—of rustic coquetry, that goes straight up to the point.

" Ay, lad, ye seem unco sune weary, to dance sae lightly? Better the nag that ambles a'the day than him that makes a brattle for a mile, and then's dune wi' the road."

This was a fair challenge, and I could not decline accepting it. Besides, I could see Dame Martin was queen of the revels ; and so many were the rude and singular figures about me, that I was by no means certain whether I might not need some protection. I seized on her willing hand, and we took our places in the dance, where, if I did not acquit myself with all the accuracy of step and movement which I had before attempted, I at least came up to the expectations of my partner, who said, and almost swore, " I was prime at it "; while, stimulated to her utmost exertions, she herself frisked like a kid, snapped her fingers like castanets, whooped like a Bacchanal, and bounded from the floor like a tennis-ball—ay, till the color of her garters was no particular mystery. She made the less secret of this, perhaps, that they were sky-blue, and fringed with silver.

The time has been that this would have been special fun ; or rather, last night was the only time I can recollect these four years when it would *not* have been so ; yet, at this moment, I cannot tell you how I longed to be rid of Dame Martin. I almost wished she would sprain one of those " many-twinkling " ankles, which served her so alertly ; and when, in the midst of her exuberant caprioling, I saw my former partner leaving the apartment, and with eyes, as I thought, turning towards me, this unwillingness to carry on the dance increased to such a point, that I was almost about to feign a sprain or a dislocation myself, in order to put an

end to the performance. But there were around me scores
of old women, all of whom looked as if they might have
some sovereign recipe for such an accident ; and, remembering Gil Blas and his pretented disorder in the robbers'
cavern, I thought it as wise to play Dame Martin fair, and
dance till she thought proper to dismiss me. What I did I
resolved to do strenuously, and in the latter part of the
exhibition I cut and sprang from the floor as high and as
perpendicularly as Dame Martin herself ; and received, I
promise you, thunders of applause, for the common people
always prefer exertion and agility to grace. At length Dame
Martin could dance no more, and, rejoicing at my release, I
led her to a seat, and took the privilege of a partner to
attend her.

"Hegh, sirs," exclaimed Dame Martin, "I am sair forfoughten ! Troth, callant, I think ye hae been amaist the
death o' me."

I could only atone for the alleged offense by fetching her
some refreshment, of which she readily partook.

"I have been lucky in my partners," I said, "first that
pretty young lady, and then you, Mrs. Martin."

"Hout wi' your fleeching," said Dame Martin. "Gae
wa—gae wa, lad ; dinna blaw in folks' lugs that gate ; me
and Miss Lilias even'd thegither ! Na—na, lad ; od, she is
maybe four or five years younger than the like o'me—by and
attour her gentle havings."

"She is the Laird's daughter ?" said I, in as careless a
tone of inquiry as I could assume.

"His daughter, man ! Na—na, only his niece ; and sib
aneugh to him, I think."

"Ay, indeed," I replied ; "I thought she had borne his
name ?"

"She bears her ain name, and that's Lilias."

"And has she no other name ?" asked I.

"What needs she another till she gets a gudeman ?"
answered my Thetis, a little miffed perhaps—to use the
women's phrase—that I turned the conversation upon my
former partner, rather than addressed it to herself.

There was a short pause, which was interrupted by Dame
Martin observing, "They are standing up again."

"True," said I, having no mind to renew my late violent
capriole, "and I must go help old Willie."

Ere I could extricate myself, I heard poor Thetis address
herself to a sort of merman in a jacket of seaman's blue and
a pair of trowsers (whose hand, by the way, she had rejected

Q

at an earlier part of the evening), and intimate that she was now disposed to take a trip.

" Trip away then, dearie," said the vindictive man of the waters, without offering his hand ; " there," pointing to the floor, " is a roomy berth for you. "

Certain I had made one enemy, and perhaps two, I hastened to my original seat beside Willie, and began to handle my bow. But I could see that my conduct had made an unfavorable impression : the words, " flory conceited chap," " hafflins gentle," and at length the still more alarming epithet of " spy," began to be buzzed about, and I was heartily glad when the apparition of Sam's visage at the door, who was already possessed of and draining a can of punch, gave me assurance that my means of retreat were at hand. I intimated as much to Willie, who probably had heard more of the murmurs of the company than I had, for he whispered, " Ay, ay,—awa' wi' ye—ower lang here ; slide out canny—dinna let them see ye are on the tramp."

I slipped half-a-guinea into the old man's hand, who answered, " Truts, pruts, nonsense ! but I'se no refuse, trusting ye can afford it. Awa' wi' ye ; and if onybody stops ye, cry on me."

I glided, by his advice, along the room as if looking for a partner, joined Sam, whom I disengaged with some difficulty from his can, and we left the cottage together in a manner to attract the least possible observation. The horses were tied in a neighboring shed, and as the moon was up and I was now familiar with the road, broken and complicated as it is, we soon reached the Shepherd's Bush, where the old landlady was sitting up waiting for us, under some anxiety of mind, to account for which she did not hesitate to tell me that some folks had gone to Brokenburn from her house or neighboring towns that did not come so safe back again. " Wandering Willie," she said, " was doubtless a kind of protection."

Here Willie's wife, who was smoking in the chimney-corner, took up the praises of her " hinnie," as she called him, and endeavored to awaken my generosity afresh, by describing the dangers from which, as she was pleased to allege, her husband's countenance had assuredly been the means of preserving me. I was not, however, to be fooled out of more money at this time, and went to bed in haste, full of various cogitations.

I have since spent a couple of days betwixt Mount Sharon and this place, and betwixt reading, writing to thee this

momentous history, forming plans for seeing the lovely
Lilias, and—partly, I think, for the sake of contradiction—
angling a little in spite of Joshua's scruples, though I am
rather liking the amusement better as I begin to have some
success in it.

And now, my dearest Alan, you are in full possession of
my secret—let me as frankly into the recesses of your bosom.
How do you feel towards this fair *ignis fatuus*, this lily of
the desert ? Tell me honestly ; for however the recollection
of her may haunt my own mind, my love for Alan Fairford
surpasses the love of woman. I know, too, that when you
do love it will be to

Love once and love no more.

A deep consuming passion, once kindled in a breast so
steady as yours, would never be extinguished but with life.
I am of another and more volatile temper, and though I
shall open your next with a trembling hand and uncertain
heart, yet let it bring a frank confession that this fair unknown has made a deeper impression on your gravity than
you reckoned for, and you will see I can tear the arrow from
my own wound, barb and all. In the meantime, though I
have formed schemes once more to see her, I will, you may
rely on it, take no step for putting them into practise. I
have refrained from this hitherto, and I give you my word
of honor I shall continue to do so ; yet why should you
need any further assurance from one who is so entirely yours
as   D. L.

P.S.—I shall be on thorns till I receive your answer. I
read and re-read your letter, and cannot for my soul discover
what your real sentiments are. Sometimes I think you
write of her as one in jest, and sometimes I think that cannot be. Put me at ease as soon as possible.

LETTER XIII

ALAN FAIRFORD TO DARSIE LATIMER

I WRITE on the instant, as you direct; and in a tragi-comic humor, for I have a tear in my eye and a smile on my cheek. Dearest Darsie, sure never a being but yourself could be so generous—sure never a being but yourself could be so absurd! I remember when you were a boy you wished to make your fine new whip a present to old aunt Peggy, merely because she admired it; and now, with like unreflecting and unappropriate liberality, you would resign your beloved to a smoke-dried young sophister, who cares not one of the hairs which it is his occupation to split for all the daughters of Eve. *I* in love with your Lilias—your green-mantle—your unknown enchantress! why I scarce saw her for five minutes, and even then only the tip of her chin was distinctly visible. She was well made, and the tip of her chin was of a most promising cast for the rest of the face; but, Heaven save you! she came upon business! and for a lawyer to fall in love with a pretty client on a single consul-tation would be as wise as if he became enamored of a par-ticularly bright sunbeam which chanced for a moment to gild his bar-wig. I give you my word I am heart-whole; and, moreover, I assure you that, before I suffer a woman to sit near my heart's core, I must see her full face, without mask or mantle, ay, and know a good deal of her mind into the bargain. So never fret yourself on my account, my kind and generous Darsie; but, for your own sake, have a care, and let not an idle attachment, so lightly taken up, lead you into serious danger.

On this subject I feel so apprehensive, that now when I am decorated with the honors of the gown, I should have abandoned my career at the very starting to come to you, but for my father having contrived to clog my heels with fetters of a professional nature. I will tell you the matter at length, for it is comical enough; and why should not you list to my juridical adventures, as well as I to those of your fiddling knight-errantry?

It was after dinner, and I was considering how I might

best introduce to my father the private resolution I had
formed to set off for Dumfriesshire, or whether I had not
better run away at once, and plead my excuse by letter,
when, assuming the peculiar look with which he commu-
nicates any of his intentions respecting me that he suspects
may not be altogether acceptable, "Alan," he said, "ye
now wear a gown—ye have opened shop, as we would say
of a more mechanical profession—and, doubtless, ye think
the floor of the court is strewed with guineas, and that ye
have only to stoop down to gather them ?"

"I hope I am sensible, sir," I replied, "that I have some
knowledge and practise to acquire, and must stoop for that
in the first place."

"It is well said," answered my father ; and, always afraid
to give too much encouragement, added—"very well said,
if it be well acted up to. Stoop to get knowledge and practise is the very word. Ye know very well, Alan, that, in
the other faculty who study the *ars medendi*, before the
young doctor gets to the bedsides of palaces, he must, as
they call it, walk the hospitals, and cure Lazarus of his sores,
before he be admitted to prescribe for Dives, when he has
gout or indigestion——"

"I am aware, sir, that——"

"Whisht—do not interrupt the court. Well, also the
chirurgeons have an useful practise, by which they put their
apprentices and *tyrone*s to work upon senseless dead bodies,
to which, as they can do no good, so they certainly can do
as little harm ; while at the same time the *tyro*, or apprentice, gains experience, and becomes fit to whip off a leg or
arm from a living subject as cleanly as ye would slice an
onion."

"I believe I guess your meaning, sir," answered I ; "and
were it not for a very particular engagement——"

"Do not speak to me of engagements ; but whisht, there
is a good lad, and do not interrupt the court."

My father, you know, is apt—be it said with all filial duty
—to be a little prolix in his harangues. I had nothing for
it but to lean back and listen.

"Maybe you think, Alan, because I have, doubtless, the
management of some actions in dependence, whilk my
worthy clients have entrusted me with, that I may think of
airting them your way instanter ; and so setting you up in
practise, so far as my small business or influence may go ;
and, doubtless, Alan, that is a day whilk I hope may come
round. But then, before I give, as the proverb hath it,

"My own fish-guts to my own sea-maws," I must, for the sake of my own character, be very sure that my sea-maw can pick them to some purpose. What say ye?"

"I am so far," answered I, "from wishing to get early into practise, sir, that I would willingly bestow a few days——"

"In farther study, ye would say, Alan. But that is not the way either; ye must walk the hospitals—ye must cure Lazarus—ye must cut and carve on a departed subject, to show your skill."

"I am sure," I replied, "I will undertake the cause of any poor man with pleasure, and bestow as much pains upon it as if it were a duke's; but for the next two or three days——"

"They must be devoted to close study, Alan—very close study indeed; for ye must stand primed for a hearing, *in presentia dominorum*, upon Tuesday next."

"I sir!" I replied in astonishment. "I have not opened my mouth in the Outer House yet!"

"Never mind the Court of the Gentiles, man," said my father; "we will have you into the sanctuary at once—over shoes, over boots."

"But, sir, I should really spoil any cause thrust on me so hastily."

"Ye cannot spoil it, Alan," said my father, rubbing his hands with much complacency; "that is the very cream of the business, man: it is just, as I said before, a subject upon whilk all the *tyrones* have been trying their whittles for fifteen years, and as there have been about ten or a dozen agents concerned, and each took his own way, the case is come to that pass that Stair or Arniston could not mend it. And I do not think even you, Alan, can do it much harm; ye may get credit by it, but ye can lose none."

"And pray what is the name of my happy client, sir?" said I, ungraciously enough, I believe.

"It is a well-known name in the Parliament House," replied my father. "To say the truth, I expect him every moment; it is Peter Peebles."*

"Peter Peebles!" exclaimed I, in astonishment; "he is an insane beggar, 'as poor as Job and as mad as a March hare!"

"He has been pleaing in the court for fifteen years," said my father, in a tone of commiseration, which seemed to

* See Note 19.

acknowledge that this fact was enough to account for the poor man's condition both in mind and circumstances.

" Besides, sir," I added, "he is on the poor's roll ; and you know there are advocates regularly appointed to manage those cases ; and for me to presume to interfere——"

"Whisht, Alan !—never interrupt the court ; all *that* is managed for ye like a tee'd ball (my father sometimes draws his similes from his once favorite game of golf). You must know, Alan, that Peter's cause was to have been opened by young Dumtoustie—ye may ken the lad, a son of Dumtoustie of that Ilk, member of Parliament for the county of ——, and a nephew of the laird's younger brother, worthy Lord Bladderskate, whilk ye are aware sounds as like being akin to a peatship* and a sheriffdom as a sieve is sib to a riddle. Now, Saunders [Peter] Drudgeit, my lord's clerk, came to me this morning in the House, like ane bereft of his wits ; for it seems that young Dumtoustie is ane of the poor's lawyers, and Peter Peebles's process had been remitted to him of course. But so soon as the hare-brained goose saw the pokes—as, indeed, Alan, they are none of the least—he took fright, called for his nag, lap on, and away to the country is he gone ; " and so," said Saunders, " my lord is at his wit's end wi' vexation and shame, to see his nevoy break off the course at the very starting." " I'll tell you, Saunders," said I, " were I my lord, and a friend or kinsman of mine should leave the town while the court was sitting, that kinsman, or be he what he liked, should never darken my door again." And then, Alan, I thought to turn the ball our own way ; and I said that you were a gey sharp birkie, just off the irons, and if it would oblige my lord, and so forth, you would open Peter's cause on Tuesday, and make some handsome apology for the necessary absence of your learned friend, and the loss which your client and the court had sustained, and so forth. Saunders lap at the proposition like a cock at a grossart ; for, he said, the only chance was to get a new hand, that did not ken the charge he was taking upon him ; for there was not a lad of two sessions' standing that was not dead-sick of Peter Peebles and his cause ; and he advised me to break the matter gently to you at the first ; but I told him you were a good bairn, Alan, and had no will and pleasure in these matters but mine."

* Formerly, a lawyer, supposed to be under the peculiar patronage of any particular judge, was invidiously termed his " peat" or " pet."

What could I say, Darsie, in answer to this arrangement, so very well meant—so very vexatious at the same time ? To imitate the defection and flight of young Dumtoustie was at once to destroy my father's hopes of me for ever ; nay, such is the keenness with which he regards all connected with his profession, it might have been a step to breaking his heart. I was obliged, therefore, to bow in sad acquiescence, when my father called to James Wilkinson to bring the two bits of pokes he would find on his table.

Exit James, and presently re-enters, bending under the load of two huge leathern bags, full of papers to the brim, and labeled on the greasy backs with the magic impress of the clerks of court, and the title, " Peebles against Plainstanes." This huge mass was deposited on the table, and my father, with no ordinary glee in his countenance, began to draw out the various bundles of papers, secured by none of your red tape or whipcord, but stout, substantial casts of tarred rope, such as might have held small crafts at their moorings.

I made a last and desperate effort to get rid of the impending job. " I am really afraid, sir, that this case seems so much complicated, and there is so little time to prepare, that we had better move the court to supersede it till next session."

" How, sir ! how, Alan ! " said my father. " Would you approbate and reprobate, sir ? You have accepted the poor man's cause, and if you have not his fee in your pocket, it is because he has none to give you ; and now would you approbate and reprobate in the same breath of your mouth ? Think of your oath of office, Alan, and your duty to your father. my dear boy."

Once more, what could I say ? I saw, from my father's hurried and alarmed manner, that nothing could vex him so much as failing in the point he had determined to carry, and once more intimated my readiness to do my best, under every disadvantage.

" Well—well, my boy," said my father, " the Lord will make your days long in the land for the honor you have given to your father's gray hairs. You may find wiser advisers, Alan, but none that can wish you better."

My father, you know, does not usually give way to expressions of affection, and they are interesting in proportion to their rarity. My eyes began to fill at seeing his glisten ; and my delight at having given him such sensible gratification would have been unmixed, but for the thoughts of you.

These out of the question, I could have grappled with the bags, had they been as large as corn-sacks. But, to turn what was grave into farce, the door opened, and Wilkinson ushered in Peter Peebles.

You must have seen this original, Darsie, who, like others in the same predicament, continues to haunt the courts of justice, where he has made shipwreck of time, means, and understanding. Such insane paupers have sometimes seemed to me to resemble wrecks lying upon the shoals on the Goodwin Sands, or in Yarmouth Roads, warning other vessels to keep aloof from the banks on which they have been lost ; or rather such ruined clients are like scarecrows and potato-bogles, distributed through the courts to scare away fools from the scene of ligitation.

The identical Peter wears a huge greatcoat, threadbare and patched itself, yet carefully so disposed and secured by what buttons remains, and many supplementary pins, as to conceal the still more infirm state of his under-garments. The shoes and stockings of a plowman were, however, seen to meet at his knees with a pair of brownish, blackish breeches ; a rusty-colored handkerchief, that has been black in its day, surrounded his throat, and was an apology for linen. His hair, half gray, half black, escaped in elf-locks around a huge wig, made of tow, as it seemed to me, and so much shrunk that it stood up on the very top of his head ; above which he plants, when covered, an immense cocked hat, which, like the chieftain's banner in an ancient battle, may be seen any sederunt day betwixt nine and ten, high towering above all the fluctuating and changeful scene in the Outer House, where his eccentricities often make him the centre of a group of petulant and teazing boys, who exercise upon him every art of ingenious torture. His countenance, originally that of a portly, comely burgess, is now emaciated with poverty and anxiety, and rendered wild by an insane lightness about the eyes ; a withered and blighted skin and complexion ; features begrimed with snuff, charged with the self-importance peculiar to insanity ; and a habit of perpetually speaking to himself. Such was my unfortunate client; and I must allow, Darsie, that my profession had need to do a great deal of good, if, as is much to be feared, it brings many individuals to such a pass.

After we had been, with a good deal of form, presented to each other, at which time I easily saw by my father's manner that he was desirous of supporting Peter's character in my eyes as much as circumstances would permit, "Alan," he said, "this is the gentleman who has agreed to accept of you as his counsel, in place of young Dumtoustie."

"Entirely out of favor to my old acquaintance your father," said Peter, with a benign and patronizing countenance—"out of respect to your father, and my old intimacy with Lord Bladderskate. Otherwise, by the *Regiam Majestatem!* I would have presented a petition and complaint against Daniel Dumtoustie, advocate, by name and surname —I would, by all the practiques! I know the forms of process, and I am not to be trifled with."

My father here interrupted my client, and reminded him that there was a good deal of business to do, as he proposed to give the young counsel an outline of the state of the conjoined process, with a view to letting him into the merits of the cause, disencumbered from the points of form. "I have made a short abbreviate, Mr. Peebles," said he; "having sat up late last night and employed much of this morning in wading through these papers, to save Alan some trouble, and I am now about to state the result."

"I will state it myself," said Peter, breaking in without reverence upon his solicitor.

"No, by no means," said my father; "I am your agent for the time."

"Mine eleventh in number," said Peter; "I have a new one every year; I wish I could get a new coat as regularly."

"Your agent for the time," resumed my father; "and you, who are acquainted with the forms know that the client states the cause to the agent, the agent to the counsel——"

"The counsel to the lord ordinary," continued Peter, once set a-going, like the peal of an alarm clock, "the ordinary to the Inner House, the president to the bench. It is just like the rope to the man, the man to the ax, the ax to the ox, the ox to the water, the water to the fire——"

"Hush, for Heaven's sake, Mr. Peebles," said my father, cutting his recitation short; "time wears on, we must get to business; you must not interrupt the court, you know. Hem—hem! From this abbreviate it appears——"

"Before you begin," said Peter Peebles, "I'll thank you to order me a morsel of bread and cheese, or some cauld meat, or broth, or the like alimentary provision, I was so anxious to see your son that I could not eat a mouthful of dinner."

Heartily glad, I believe, to have so good a chance of stopping his client's mouth effectually, my father ordered some cold meat ; to which James Wilkinson, for the honor of the house, was about to add the brandy bottle, which remained on the sideboard, but, at a wink from my father, supplied its place with small beer. Peter charged the provisions with the rapacity of a famished lion ; and so well did the diversion engage him, that though, while my father stated the case, he looked at him repeatedly, as if he meant to interrupt his statement, yet he always found more agreeable employment for his mouth, and returned to the cold beef with an avidity which convinced me he had not had such an opportunity for many a day of satiating his appetite. Omitting much formal phraseology and many legal details, I will endeavor to give you, in exchange for your fiddler's tale, the history of a litigant, or rather, the history of his lawsuit.

"Peter Peebles and Paul Plainstanes," said my father, "entered into partnership in the year ——, as mercers and linen-drapers, in the Luckenbooths, and carried on a great line of business to mutual advantage. But the learned counsel needeth not to be told, *societas est mater discordiarum:* partnership oft makes pleaship. The company being dissolved by mutual consent in the year ——, the affairs had to be wound up, and after certain attempts to settle the matter extra-judicially, it was at last brought into the court, and has branched out into several distinct processes, most of whilk have been conjoined by the ordinary. It is to the state of these processes that counsel's attention is particularly directed. There is the original action of Peebles *v.* Plainstanes, convening him for payment of £3000, less or more, as alleged balance due by Plainstanes. 2dly, There is a counter action, in which Plainstanes is pursuer and Peebles defender, for £2500, less or more, being balanced alleged *per contra* to be due by Peebles. 3dly, Mr. Peebles's seventh agent advised an action of compt and reckoning at his instance, wherein what balance should prove due on either side might be fairly struck and ascertained. 4thly, To meet the hypothetical case, that Peebles might be found liable in a balance to Plainstanes, Mr. Wildgoose, Mr. Peeble's eighth agent, recommended a multiplepoinding, to bring all parties concerned into the field."

My brain was like to turn at this account of lawsuit within lawsuit, like a next of chip-boxes, with all of which I was expected to make myself acquainted.

"I understand," I said, "that Mr. Peebles claims a sum

of money from Plainstanes—how then can he be his debtor ? And if not his debtor, how can he bring a multiplepoinding, the very summons of which sets forth that the pursuer does owe certain monies, which he is desirous to pay by warrant of a judge ? "

" Ye know little of the matter, I doubt, friend," said Mr. Peebles ; " a multiplepoinding is the safest *remedium juris* in the whole form of process. I have known it conjoined with a declarator of marriage. Your beef is excellent," he said to my father, who in vain endeavored to resume his legal disquisition, " but something highly powdered ; and the twopenny is undeniable, but it is small swipes—small swipes—more of hop than malt ; with your leave I'll try your black bottle."

My father started to help him with his own hand, and in due measure ; but, infinitely to my amusement, Peter got possession of the bottle by the neck, and my father's ideas of hospitality were far too scrupulous to permit his attempting, by any direct means, to redeem it ; so that Peter returned to the table triumphant, with his prey in his clutch.

" Better have a wine-glass, Mr. Peebles," said my father, in an admonitory tone ; " you will find it pretty strong."

" If the kirk is ower muckle, we can sing mass in the quire," said Peter, helping himself in the goblet out of which he had been drinking the small beer. " What is it, usquebaugh ?—BRANDY, as I am an honest man ! I had almost forgotten the name and taste of brandy. Mr. Fairford, elder, your good health (a mouthful of brandy). Mr. Alan Fairford, wishing you well through your arduous undertaking (another go-down of the comfortable liquor). And now, though you have given a tolerable breviate of this great lawsuit, of whilk everybody has heard something that has walked the boards in the Outer House—here's to ye again, by way of interim decreet—yet ye have omitted to speak a word of the arrestments."

" I was just coming to that point, Mr. Peebles."

" Or of the action of suspension of the charge on the bill."

" I was just coming to that."

" Or the advocation of the sheriff court process."

" I was just coming to it."

" As Tweed comes to Melrose, I think," said the litigant ; and then filling his goblet about a quarter full of brandy, as if in· absence of mind, " Oh, Mr. Alan Fairford, ye are a lucky man to buckle to such a cause as mine at the very

Peter Peebles capturing Allan Fairford.

outset ! It is like a specimen of all causes, man. By the
Regiam, there is not a *remedium juris* in the practiques but
ye'll find a spice o't. Here's to your getting weel through
with it. Pshut—I am drinking naked spirits, I think.
But if the heathen be ower strong, we'll christen him with
the brewer," here he added a little small beer to his beverage, paused, rolled his eyes, winked, and proceeded. " Mr.
Fairford—the action of assault and battery, Mr. Fairford,
when I compelled the villain Plainstanes to pull my nose
within two steps of King Charles's statue, in the Parliament Close, there I had him in a hose-net. Never man
could tell me how to shape that process ; no counsel that
ever selled wind could condescend and say whether it were
best to proceed by way of petition and complaint, *ad vindictam publicam*, with consent of his Majesty's advocate, or
by action on the statute for battery, *pendente lite*, whilk
would be the winning my plea at once, and so getting a
back-door out of court. By the Regiam, that beef and
brandy is unco het at my heart—I maun try the ale again
(sipped a little beer), and the ale's but cauld, I maun e'en
put in the rest of the brandy."

He was as good as his word, and proceeded in so loud and
animated a style of elocution, thumping the table, drinking
and snuffing alternately, that my father, abandoning all attempts to interrupt him, sat silent and ashamed, suffering
and anxious for the conclusion of the scene.

" And then to come back to my pet process of all—my
battery and assault process, when I had the good luck to provoke him to pull my nose at the very threshold of the court
whilk was the very thing I wanted. Mr. Pest—ye ken him,
Daddie Fairford ?—old Pest was for making it out " hamesucken," for he said the court might be said—said—ugh !—
to be my dwelling-place. I dwell mair there than ony gate
else, and the essence of hamesucken is to strike a man in his
dwelling-place—mind that, young advocate—and so there's
hope Plainstanes may be hanged, as many has for a less
matter ; " for, my lords "—will Pest say to the justiciary
bodies—" my lords, the Parliament House is Peebles's place
of dwelling," says he, " being *commune forum*, and *commune
fornm est commune domicilium*." Lass, fetch another glass
of whisky, and score it—time to gae hame—by the practiques, I cannot find the jug—yet there's twa of them, I
think. By the Regiam, Fairford—Daddie Fairford—lend
us twal pennies to buy sneeshing, mine is done. Macer; call
another cause."

The box fell from his hands, and his body would at the same time have fallen from the chair, had I not supported him.

"This is intolerable," said my father. "Call a chairman, James Wilkinson, to carry this degraded, worthless, drunken beast home."

When Peter Peebles was removed from this memorable consultation, under the care of an able-bodied Celt, my father hastily bundled up the papers, as a showman whose exhibition has miscarried hastes to remove his booth. "Here are my memoranda, Alan," he said in a hurried way ; "look them carefully over, compare them with the processes, and turn it in your head before Tuesday. Many a good speech has been made for a beast of a client ; and harkye, lad— harkye, I never intended to cheat you of your fee when all was done, though I would have liked to have heard the speech first ; but there is nothing like corning the horse before the journey. Here are five goud guineas in a silk purse—of your poor mother's netting, Alan ; she would have been a blythe woman to have seen her young son with a gown on his back. But no more of that ; be a good boy, and to the work like a tiger."

I did set to work, Darsie ; for who could resist such motives ? With my father's assistance, I have mastered the details, confused as they are ; and on Tuesday I shall plead as well for Peter Peebles as I could for a duke. Indeed, I feel my head so clear on the subject as to be able to write this long letter to you ; into which, however, Peter and his lawsuit have insinuated themselves so far as to show you how much they at present occupy my thoughts. Once more, be careful of yourself, and mindful of me, who am ever thine, while

ALAN FAIRFORD."

From circumstances to be hereafter mentioned, it was long ere this letter reached the person to whom it was addressed.

CHAPTER I

NARRATIVE

THE advantage of laying before the reader, in the words of the actors themselves, the adventures which we must otherwise have narrated in our own has given great popularity to the publication of epistolary correspondence, as practised by various great authors, and by ourselves in the preceding chapters. Nevertheless, a genuine correspondence of this kind (and Heaven forbid it should be in any respect sophisticated by interpolations of our own!) can seldom be found to contain all in which it is necessary to instruct the reader for his full comprehension of the story. Also it must often happen that various prolixities and redundancies occur in the course of an interchange of letters which must hang as a dead weight on the progress of the narrative. To avoid this dilemma, some biographers have used the letters of the personages concerned, or liberal extracts from them, to describe particular incidents, or express the sentiments which they entertained; while they connect them occasionally with such portions of narrative as may serve to carry on the thread of the story.

It is thus that the adventurous travelers who explore the summit of Mont Blanc now move on through the crumbling snow-drift so slowly that their progress is almost imperceptible; and anon abridge their journey by springing over the intervening chasms which cross their path with the assistance of their pilgrim-staves. Or, to make a briefer simile, the course of story-telling which we have for the present adopted resembles the original discipline of the dragoons, who were trained to serve either on foot or horseback, as the emergencies of the service required. With this explanation, we shall proceed to narrate some circumstances which Alan Fairford did not, and could not, write to his correspondent.

Our reader, we trust, has formed somewhat approaching to a distinct idea of the principal characters who have appeared before him during our narrative; but in case our good opinion of his sagacity has been exaggerated, and in order to satisfy such as are addicted to the laudable practise of

143

"skipping" (with whom we have at times a strong fellow-feeling) the following particulars may not be superfluous.
Mr. Saunders Fairford, as he was usually called, was a man of business of the old school, moderate in his charges, economical and even niggardly in his expenditure, strictly honest in conducting his own affairs and those of his clients, but taught by long experience to be wary and suspicious in observing the motions of others. Punctual as the clock of St. Giles tolled nine, the neat dapper form of the little hale old gentleman was seen at the threshold of the court hall, or, at farthest, at the head of the back stairs, trimly dressed in a complete suit of snuff-colored brown, with stockings of silk or woolen, as suited the weather ; a bobwig and a small cocked hat ; shoes blacked as Warren would have blacked them ; silver shoe-buckles, and a gold stock-buckle. A nosegay in summer and a sprig of holly in winter completed his well-known dress and appearance. His manners corresponded with his attire, for they were scrupulously civil, and not a little formal. He was an elder of the kirk, and, of course, zealous for King George and the government even to slaying, as he had showed by taking up arms in their cause. But then, as he had clients and connections of business among families of opposite political tenets, he was particularly cautious to use all the conventional phrases which the civility of the time had devised as an admissible mode of language betwixt the two parties. Thus he spoke sometimes of the Chevalier, but never either of the Prince, which would have been sacrificing his own principles, or of the Pretender, which would have been offensive to those of others. Again, he usually designated the rebellion as the 'affair' of 1745, and spoke of any one engaged in it as a person who had been 'out' at a certain period.* So that, on the whole, Mr. Fairford was a man much liked and respected on all sides, though his friends would not have been sorry if he had given a dinner more frequently, as his little cellar contained some choice old wine, of which, on such rare occasions, he was no niggard.

The whole pleasure of this good, old-fashioned man of method, besides that which he really felt in the discharge of his daily business, was the hope to see his son Alan, the only fruit of a union which death early dissolved, attain what in the father's eyes was the proudest of all distinctions—the rank and fame of a well-employed lawyer.

Every profession has its peculiar honors, and Mr. Fair-

* See Old-fashioned Scottish Civility. Note 20.

ford's mind was constructed upon so limited and exclusive a
plan, that he valued nothing save the objects of ambition
which his own represented. He would have shuddered at
Alan's acquiring the renown of a hero, and laughed with
scorn at the equally barren laurels of literature ; it was by
the path of the law alone that he was desirous to see him rise
to eminence, and the probabilities of success or disappointment were the thoughts of his father by day and his dream
by night.

The disposition of Alan Fairford, as well as his talents,
were such as to encourage his father's expectations. He had
acuteness of intellect, joined to habits of long and patient
study, improved no doubt by the discipline of his father's
house ; to which, generally speaking, he conformed with
the utmost docility, expressing no wish for greater or more
frequent relaxation than consisted with his father's anxious
and severe restriction. When he did indulge in any juvenile
frolics, his father had the candor to lay the whole blame
upon his more mercurial companion, Darsie Latimer.

This youth, as the reader must be aware, had been received as an inmate into the family of Mr. Fairford, senior,
at a time when some of the delicacy of constitution which
had abridged the life of his consort began to show itself in
the son, and when the father was, of course, peculiarly disposed to indulge his slightest wish. That the young Englishman was able to pay a considerable board was a matter of no
importance to Mr. Fairford ; it was enough that his presence
seemed to make his son cheerful and happy. He was compelled to allow that " Darsie was a fine lad, though unsettled,"
and he would have had some difficulty in getting rid of him,
and the apprehensions which his levities excited, had it not
been for the voluntary excursion which gave rise to the preceding correspondence, and in which Mr. Fairford secretly
rejoiced, as affording the means of separating Alan from his
gay companion, at least until he should have assumed, and
become accustomed to, the duties of his dry and laborious
profession.

But the absence of Darsie was far from promoting the end
which the elder Mr. Fairford had expected and desired. The
young men were united by the closest bonds of intimacy ; and
the more so, that neither of them sought nor desired to admit
any others into their society. Alan Fairford was averse to
general company, from a disposition naturally reserved, and
Darsie Latimer from a painful sense of his own unknown
origin, peculiarly afflicting in a country where high and low

10

are professed genealogists. The young men were all in all to each other ; it is no wonder, therefore, that their separation was painful, and that its effects upon Alan Fairford, joined to the anxiety occasioned by the tenor of his friend's letters, greatly exceeded what the senior had anticipated. The young man went through his usual duties, his studies, and the examinations to which he was subjected, but with nothing like the zeal and assiduity which he had formerly displayed ; and his anxious and observant father saw but too plainly that his heart was with his absent comrade.

A philosopher would have given way to this tide of feeling, in hopes to have diminished its excess, and permitted the youths to have been some time together, that their intimacy might have been broken off by degrees ; but Mr. Fairford only saw the more direct mode of continued restraint, which, however, he was desirous of veiling under some plausible pretext. In the anxiety which he felt on this occasion, he had held communication with an old acquaintance, Peter Drudgeit, with whom the reader is partly acquainted. "Alan," he said, "was ance wud and aye waur ; and he was expecting every moment when he would start off in a wildgoose chase after the callant Latimer ; Will Sampson, the horse-hirer in Candlemaker Row, had given him a hint that Alan had been looking for a good hack, to go to the country for a few days. And then to oppose him downright—he could not but think on the way his poor mother was removed. Would to Heaven he was yoked to some tight piece of business, no matter whether well or ill paid, but some job that would hamshackle him at least vntil the courts rose, if it were but for decency's sake."

Peter Drudgeit sympathized, for Peter had a son who, reason or none, would needs exchange the torn and inky fustian sleeves for the blue jacket and white lapels ; and he suggested, as the reader knows, the engaging our friend Alan in the matter of Poor Peter Peebles, just opened by the desertion of young Dumtoustie, whose defection would be at the same time concealed ; and this, Drudgeit said, " would be felling two dogs with one stone."

With these explanations, the reader will hold a man of the elder Fairford's sense and experience free from the hazardous and impatient curiosity with which boys fling a puppy into a deep pond, merely to see if the creature can swim. However confident in his son's talents, which were really considerable, he would have been very sorry to have involved him in the duty of pleading a complicated and difficult

case, upon his very first appearance at the bar, had he not
resorted to it as an effectual way to prevent the young man
from taking a step which his habits of thinking represented
as a most fatal one at his outset of life.

Betwixt two evils, Mr. Fairford chose that which was in
his own apprehension the least ; and, like a brave officer
sending forth his son to battle, rather chose he should die
upon the breach than desert the conflict with dishonor.
Neither did he leave him to his own unassisted energies
Like Alpheus preceding Hercules, he himself encountered the
Augean mass of Peter Peebles's law-matters. It was to the
old man a labor of love to place in a clear and undistorted
view the real merits of this case, which the carelessness and
blunders of Peter's former solicitors had converted into a
huge chaotic mass of unintelligible technicality ; and such
was his skill and industry, that he was able, after the severe
toil of two or three days, to present to the consideration of
the young counsel the principal facts of the case, in a light
equally simple and comprehensible. With the assistance of
a solicitor so affectionate and indefatigable, Alan Fairford
was enabled, when the day of trial arrived, to walk towards
the court, attended by his anxious yet encouraging parent,
with some degree of confidence that he would lose no reputation upon this arduous occasion.

They were met at the door of the court by Poor Peter
Peebles, in his usual plenitude of wig and celsitude of hat.
He seized on the young pleader like a lion on his prey.
"How is a' wi' you, Mr. Alan—how is a' wi' you, man ?
The awfu' day is come at last—a day that will be lang mind-
ed in this house. Poor Peter Peebles against Plainstanes—
conjoined processes—hearing in presence—stands for the
Short Roll for this day. I have not been able to sleep for a
week for thinking of it, and, I dare to say, neither has the
Lord President himsell—for such a cause ! But your father
garr'd me tak a wee drap ower muckle of his pint bottle the
other night ; it's no right to mix brandy wi' business, Mr.
Fairford. I would have been the waur o' liquor if I would
have drunk as muckle as you twa would have had me. But
there's a time for a' things, and if ye will dine with me after
the case is heard, or, whilk is the same, or maybe better, *I'll*
gang my ways hame wi' *you*, and I winna object to a cheerfu'
glass, within the bounds of moderation."

Old Fairford shrugged his shoulders and hurried past the
client, saw his son wrapt in the sable bombazine, which, in
his eyes, was more venerable than an archbishop's lawn, and

could not help fondly patting his shoulder, and whispering to him to take courage, and show he was worthy to wear it. The party entered the Outer Hall of the court, once the place of meeting of the ancient Scottish Parliament, and which corresponds to the use of Westminster Hall in England, serving as a vestibule to the Inner House, as it is termed, and a place of dominion to certain sedentary personages called Lords Ordinary.

The earlier part of the morning was spent by old Fairford in reiterating his instructions to Alan, and in running from one person to another, from whom he thought he could still glean some grains of information, either concerning the point at issue or collateral cases. Meantime Poor Peter Peebles, whose shallow brain was altogether unable to bear the importance of the moment, kept as close to his young counsel as shadow to substance, affected now to speak loud, now to whisper in his ear, now to deck his ghastly countenance with wreathed smiles, now to cloud it with a shade of deep and solemn importance, and anon to contort it with the sneer of scorn and derision. These moods of the client's mind were accompanied with singular "mopings and mowings," fantastic gestures, which the man of rags and litigation deemed appropriate to his changes of countenance. Now he brandished his arm aloft, now thrust his fist straight out, as if to knock his opponent down ; now he laid his open palm on his bosom, and now flinging it abroad, he gallantly snapped his fingers in the air.

These demonstrations, and the obvious shame and embarrassment of Alan Fairford, did not escape the observation of the juvenile idlers in the hall. They did not, indeed, approach Peter with their usual familiarity, from some feeling of deference towards Fairford, though many accused him of conceit in presuming to undertake at this early stage of his practise a case of considerable difficulty. But Alan, notwithstanding this forbearance, was not the less sensible that he and his companion were the subjects of many a passing jest and many a shout of laughter, with which that region at all times abounds.

At length the young counsel's patience gave way, and as it threatened to carry his presence of mind and recollection along with it, Alan frankly told his father that, unless he was relieved from the infliction of his client's personal presence and instructions, he must necessarily throw up his brief and decline pleading the case.

"Hush—hush, my dear Alan," said the old gentleman,

almost at his own wit's end upon hearing this dilemma ; "dinna mind the silly ne'er-do-weel ; we cannot keep the man from hearing his own cause, though he be not quite right in the head."

" On my life, sir," answered Alan, " I shall be unable to go on : he drives everything out of my remembrance ; and if I attempt to speak seriously of the injuries he has sustained, and the condition he is reduced to, how can I expect but that the very appearance of such an absurd scarecrow will turn it all into ridicule ? "

" There is something in that," said Saunders Fairford, glancing a look at Poor Peter, and then cautiously inserting his forefinger under his bobwig, in order to rub his temple and aid his invention ; " he is no figure for the fore-bar to see without laughing. But how to get rid of him ? To speak sense, or anything like it, is the last thing he will listen to. Stay, ay—Alan, my darling, hae patience ; I'll get him off on the instant, like a gowff ba'."

So saying, he hastened to his ally, Peter Drudgeit, who, on seeing him with marks of haste in his gait and care upon his countenance, clapped his pen behind his ear, with " What's the stir now, Mr. Saunders ? Is there aught wrang ? "

" Here's a dollar, man," said Mr. Saunders ; " now or never, Peter, do me a good turn. Yonder's your namesake, Peter Peebles, will drive the swine through our bonny hanks of yarn ; * get him over to John's Coffee-house, man—gie him his meridian—keep him there, drunk or sober, till the hearing is ower."

" Eneugh said," quoth Peter Drudgeit, no way displeased with his own share in the service required. " We'se do your bidding."

Accordingly, the scribe was presently seen whispering in the ear of Peter Peebles, whose responses came forth in the following broken form :—

" Leave the court for ae minute on this great day of judgment !—not I, by the Reg—— Eh ! what ? Brandy, did ye say—Franch Brandy ? Couldna ye fetch a stoup to the bar under your coat, man ? Impossible ! Na, if it's clean impossible, and if we have an hour good till they get through the single bills and the summar-roll, I carena if I cross the close wi' you ; I am sure I need something to keep my heart up this awful day ; but I'll no stay above an instant—not above a minute of time—nor drink aboon a single gill."

In a few minutes afterwards, the two Peters were seen

* See Swine in Hanks of Yarn. Note 21.

moving through the Parliament Close (which newfangled affectation has termed a Square), the triumphant Drudgeit leading captive the passive Peebles, whose legs conducted him towards the dram-shop, while his reverted eyes were fixed upon the court. They dived into the Cimmerian abysses of John's Coffee-house,* formerly the favorite rendezvous of the classical and genial Doctor Pitcairn, and were for the present seen no more.

Relieved from his tormentor, Alan Fairford had time to rally his recollections, which, in the irritation of his spirits, had nearly escaped him, and to prepare himself for a task the successful discharge or failure in which must, he was aware, have the deepest influence upon his fortunes. He had pride, was not without a consciousness of talent, and the sense of his father's feelings upon the subject impelled him to the utmost exertion. Above all, he had that sort of self-command which is essential to success in every arduous undertaking, and he was constitutionally free from that feverish irritability by which those whose over-active imaginations exaggerate difficulties render themselves incapable of encountering such when they arrive.

Having collected all the scattered and broken associations which were necessary, Alan's thoughts reverted to Dumfriesshire and the precarious situation in which he feared his beloved friend had placed himself ; and once and again he consulted his watch, eager to have his present task commenced and ended, that he might hasten to Darsie's assistance. The hour and moment at length arrived. The macer shouted, with all his well-remembered brazen strength of lungs, " Poor Peter Peebles *versus* Plainstanes, *per* Dumtoustie *et* Tough.—Maister Da-a-niel Dumtoustie ! " Dumtoustie answered not the summons, which, deep and swelling as it was, could not reach across the Queensferry ; but our Maister Alan Fairford appeared in his place.

The court was very much crowded ; for much amusement had been received on former occasions when Peter had volunteered his own oratory, and had been completely successful in routing the gravity of the whole procedure, and putting to silence, not indeed the counsel of the opposite party, but his own.

Both bench and audience seemed considerably surprised at the juvenile appearance of the young man who appeared in the room of Dumtoustie, for the purpose of opening this complicated and long-depending process, and the common

* See John's Coffee-house.　Note 22.

herd were disappointed at the absence of Peter the client, the Punchinello of the expected entertainment. The judges looked with a very favorable countenance on our friend Alan, most of them being acquainted, more of less, with so old a practitioner as his father, and all, or almost all, affording, from civility, the same fair play to the first pleading of a counsel which the House of Commons yields to the maiden speech of one of its members.

Lord Bladderskate was an exception to this general expression of benevolence. He scowled upon Alan from beneath his large, shaggy, gray eyebrows, just as if the young lawyer had been usurping his nephew's honors, instead of covering his disgrace ; and, from feelings which did his lordship little honor, he privately hoped the young man would not succeed in the cause which his kinsman had abandoned.

Even Lord Bladderskate, however, was, in spite of himself, pleased with the judicious and modest tone in which Alan began his address to the court, apologizing for his own presumption, and excusing it by the sudden illness of his learned brother, for whom the labor of opening a cause of some difficulty and importance had been much more worthily designed. He spoke of himself as he really was, and of young Dumtoustie as what he ought to have been, taking care not to dwell on either topic a moment longer than was necessary. The old judge's looks became benign ; his family pride was propitiated, and, pleased equally with the modesty and civility of the young man whom he had thought forward and officious, he relaxed the scorn of his features into an expression of profound attention, the highest compliment, and the greatest encouragement, which a judge can render to the counsel addressing him.

Having succeeded in securing the favorable attention of the court, the young lawyer, using the lights which his father's experience and knowledge of business had afforded him, proceeded, with an address and clearness unexpected from one of his years, to remove from the case itself those complicated formalities with which it had been loaded, as a surgeon strips from a wound the dressings which have been hastily wrapped round it, in order to proceed to his cure *secundum artem.* Developed of the cumbrous and complicated technicalities of litigation, with which the perverse obstinacy of the client, the inconsiderate haste or ignorance of his agent, and the evasions of a subtle adversary, had invested the process, the cause of Poor Peter Peebles, stand. ing upon its simple merits, was no bad subject for the declamation of a young counsel, nor did our friend Alan fail to avail himself of its strong points.

He exhibited his client as a simple-hearted, honest, well-meaning man, who, during a copartnership of twelve years, had gradually become impoverished, while his partner (his former clerk), having no funds but his share of the same business, into which he had been admitted without any advance of stock, had become gradually more and more wealthy.

"Their association," said Alan, and the little flight was received with some applause, "resembled the ancient story of the fruit which was carved with a knife poisoned on one side of the blade only, so that the individual to whom the envenomed portion was served drew decay and death from what afforded savor and sustenance to the consumer of the other moiety." He then plunged boldly into the *mare magnum* of accompts between the parties ; he pursued each false statement from the waste-book to the day-book, from the day-book to the bill-book, from the bill-book to the ledger ; placed the artful interpolations and insertions of the fallacious Plainstanes in array against each other, and against the fact ; and, availing himself to the utmost of his father's previous labors, and his own knowledge of accompts, in which he had been sedulously trained, he laid before the court a clear and intelligible statement of the affairs of the copartnery, showing with precision that a large balance must, at the dissolution, have been due to his client, sufficient to have enabled him to have carried on business on his own account, and thus to have retained his situation in society as an independent and industrious tradesman. "But, instead of this justice being voluntarily rendered by the former clerk to his former master—by the party obliged to his benefactor—by one honest man to another, his wretched client had been compelled to follow his quondam clerk, his present debtor, from court to court ; had found his just claims met with well-invented but unfounded counter-claims ; had seen his party shift his character of pursuer or defender as often as harlequin effects his transformations, till, in a chase so varied and so long, the unhappy litigant had lost substance, reputation, and almost the use of reason itself, and came before their lordships an object of thoughtless derision to the unreflecting, of compassion to the better-hearted, and of awful meditation to every one who considered that, in a country where excellent laws were administered by upright and incorruptible judges, a man might pursue an almost indisputable claim through all the mazes of litigation, lose fortune, reputation, and reason itself in the chase, and at length come before the Supreme Court of his country in the wretched condition of his unhappy client, a victim to protracted justice and to that hope delayed which sickens the heart."

The force of this appeal to feeling made as much impression on the bench as had been previously effected by the clearness of Alan's argument. The absurd form of Peter himself, with his tow-wig, was fortunately not present to excite any ludicrous emotion, and the pause that took place when the young lawyer had concluded his speech was followed by a murmur of approbation, which the ears of his father drank in as the sweetest sounds that had ever entered them. Many a hand of gratulation was thrust out to his grasp, trembling as it was with anxiety, and finally with delight; his voice faltering as he replied, " Ay—ay, I kenn'd Alan was the lad to make a spoon or spoil a horn." *

The counsel on the other side arose, an old practitioner, who had noted too closely the impression made by Alan's pleadings not to fear the consequences of an immediate decision. He paid the highest compliments to his very young brother—" the Benjamin, as he would presume to call him, of the learned faculty ; said the alleged hardships of Mr. Peebles were compensated by his being placed in a situation where the benevolence of their lordships had assigned him gratuitously such assistance as he might not otherwise have obtained at a high price ; and allowed his young brother had put many things in such a new point of view that, although he was quite certain of his ability to refute them, he was honestly desirous of having a few hours to arrange his answer, in order to be able to follow Mr. Fairford from point to point. He had further to observe, there was one point of the case to which his brother, whose attention had been otherwise so wonderfully comprehensive, had not given the consideration which he expected ; it was founded on the interpretation of certain correspondence which had passed betwixt the parties soon after the dissolution of the copartnery."

The court having heard Mr. Tough, readily allowed him two days for preparing himself, hinting, at the same time, that he might find his task difficult ; and affording the young counsel, with high encomiums upon the mode in which he

---

* Said of an adventurous gipsy, who resolves at all risks to convert a sheep's horn into a spoon.

had acquitted himself, the choice of speaking either now or
at next calling of the cause upon the point which Plainstanes's lawyer had adverted to.

Alan modestly apologized for what in fact had been an
omission very pardonable in so complicated a case, and professed himself instantly ready to go through that correspondence, and prove that it was in form and substance exactly
applicable to the view of the case he had submitted to their
lordships. He applied to his father, who sat behind him, to
hand him from time to time the letters, in the order in
which he meant to read and comment upon them.

Old Counselor Tough had probably formed an ingenious
enough scheme to blunt the effect of the young lawyer's
reasoning, by thus obliging him to follow up a process of
reasoning, clear and complete in itself, by a hasty and extem-
porary appendix. If so, he seemed likely to be disappointed ;
for Alan was well prepared on this, as on other parts of the
cause, and recommenced his pleading with a degree of animation and spirit which added force even to what he had
formerly stated, and might perhaps have occasioned the old
gentleman to regret his having again called him up ; when
his father, as he handed him the letters, put one into his
hand which produced a singular effect on the pleader.

At the first glance, he saw that the paper had no reference to the affairs of Peter Peebles ; but the first glance also
showed him what, even at that time and in that presence,
he could not help reading ; and which, being read, seemed
totally to disconcert his ideas. He stopped short in his
harangue, gazed on the paper with a look of surprise and
horror, uttered an exclamation, and, flinging down the brief
which he had in his hand, hurried out of court without returning a single word of answer to the various questions—
"What was the matter ?" "Was he taken unwell ?"
"Should not a chair be called ?" etc. etc. etc.

The elder Mr. Fairford, who remained seated, and looking
as senseless as if he had been made of stone, was at length
recalled to himself by the anxious inquiries of the judges
and the counsel after his son's health. He then rose with
an air in which was mingled the deep habitual reverence in
which he held the court with some internal cause of agitation, and with difficulty mentioned something of a mistake
—a piece of bad news. Alan, he hoped, would be well
enough to-morrow. But unable to proceed farther, he
clasped his hands together, exclaiming, " My son ! my son !"
and left the court hastily, as if in pursuit of him.

" What's the matter with the auld bitch next ?"* said an acute metaphysical judge, though somewhat coarse in his manners, aside to his brethren. "This is a daft cause, Bladderskate. First, it drives the poor man mad that aught it ; then your nevoy goes daft with fright, and flies the pit ; then this smart young hopeful is aff the hooks with too hard study, I fancy ; and now auld Saunders Fairford is as lunatic as the best of them. What say ye till't, ye bitch ?"

" Nothing, my lord," answered Bladderskate, much too formal to admire the levities in which his philosophical brother sometimes indulged—" I say nothing, but pray to Heaven to keep our own wits."

" Amen—amen," answered his learned brother ; " for some of us have but few to spare."

The court then arose, and the audience departed, greatly wondering at the talent displayed by Alan Fairford at his first appearance, in a case so difficult and so complicated, and assigning an hundred conjectural causes, each different from the others, for the singular interruption which had clouded his day of success. The worst of the whole was, that six agents, who had each come to the separate resolution of thrusting a retaining fee into Alan's hand as he left the court, shook their heads as they returned the money into their leathern pouches, and said, " That the lad was clever, but they would like to see more of him before they engaged him in the way of business ; they did not like his louping away like a flea in a blanket."

* Tradition ascribes this whimsical style of language to the in-genious and philosophical Lord Kaimes.

CHAPTER II

HAD our friend Alexander Fairford known the consequences of his son's abrupt retreat from the court, which are mentioned in the end of the last chapter, it might have accomplished the prediction of the lively old judge and driven him to utter distraction. As it was, he was miserable enough. His son had risen ten degrees higher in his estimation than ever, by his display of juridical talents, which seemed to assure him that the applause of the judges and professors of the law, which, in his estimation, was worth that of all mankind besides, authorized to the fullest extent the advantageous estimate which even his parental partiality had been induced to form of Alan's powers. On the other hand he felt that he was himself a little humbled, from a disguise which he had practised towards this son of his hopes and wishes.

The truth was that, on the morning of this eventful day, Mr. Alexander Fairford had received from his correspondent and friend, Provost Crosbie of Dumfries, a letter of the following tenor:—

"DEAR SIR—Your respected favor of 25th ultimo, per favor of Mr. Darsie Latimer, reached me in safety, and I showed to the young gentleman such attentions as he was pleased to accept of. The object of my present writing is twofold. First, the council are of opinion that you should now begin to stir in the thirlage cause ; and they think they will be able, from evidence *noviter repertum*, to enable you to amend your condescendence upon the use and wont of the burgh, touching the *grana invecta et illata.* So you will please consider yourself as authorized to speak to Mr. Pest, and lay before him the papers which you will receive by the coach. The council think that a fee of two guineas may be sufficient on this occasion, as Mr. Pest had three for drawing the original condescendence.

"I take the opportunity of adding, that there has been great riot among the Solway fishermen, who have destroyed, in a masterful manner, the stake nets set up near the mouth of this river ; and have besides attacked the house of Quaker Geddes, one of the principal partners of the Tide-net Fishing Company, and done a great deal of damage. Am sorry to add, young Master Latimer was in the fray and has not since been heard of. Murder is spoke of, but that may be a word of course. As the young gentleman has behaved rather oddly while in these parts, as in declining to dine with me more than once, and going about the country with strolling fiddlers and such-like, I rather hope that his present absence is only occasioned by a frolic ; but as his servant has been making inquiries of me respecting his master, I thought it best to acquaint you in course of post. I have only to add, that our sheriff has taken a precognition, and committed one or two of the rioters. If I can be useful in this matter, either by advertising for Mr. Latimer as missing, publishing a reward, or otherwise, I will obey your respected instructions, being your most obedient to command,

"WILLIAM CROSBIE."

When Mr. Fairford received this letter, and had read it to an end, his first idea was to communicate it to his son, that an express might be instantly despatched, or a king's messenger sent with proper authority to search after his late guest.

The habits of the fishers were rude, as he well knew, though not absolutely sanguinary or ferocious ; and there had been instances of their transporting persons who had interfered in their smuggling trade to the Isle of Man and elsewhere, and keeping them under restraint for many weeks. On this account Mr. Fairford was naturally led to feel anxiety concerning the fate of his late inmate ; and, at a less interesting moment, would certainly have set out himself, or licensed his son to go, in pursuit of his friend.

But, alas ! he was both a father and an agent. In the one capacity, he looked on his son as dearer to him than all the world besides ; in the other, the lawsuit which he conducted was to him like an infant to its nurse, and the case of Poor Peter Peebles against Plainstanes was, he saw, adjourned, perhaps *sine die*, should this document reach the hands of his son. The mutual and enthusiastical affection betwixt the young men was well known to him ; and he concluded that, if the precarious state of Latimer were made known to Alan Fairford, it would render him not only unwilling, but totally unfit, to discharge the duty of the day, to which the old gentleman attached such ideas of importance.

On mature reflection, therefore, he resolved, though not without some feelings of compunction, to delay communicating to his son the disagreeable intelligence which he had received, until the business of the day should be ended. The delay, he persuaded himself, could be of little consequence to Darsie Latimer, whose folly, he dared to say, had led him into some scrape which would meet an appropriate punishment in some accidental restraint, which would be thus prolonged for only a few hours longer. Besides, he would have time to speak to the sheriff of the county, perhaps to the King's Advocate, and set about the matter in a regular manner, or, as he termed it, as summing up the duties of a solicitor, to "agé as accords."

The scheme, as we have seen, was partially successful, and was only ultimately defeated, as he confessed to himself with shame, by his own very unbusiness-like mistake of shuffling the provost's letter, in the hurry and anxiety of the morning, among some papers belonging to Peter Peebles's affairs, and then handing it to his son, without observing the blunder. He used to protest, even till the day of his death, that he never had been guilty of such an inaccuracy as giving a paper out of his hand without looking at the docketing, except on that unhappy occasion, when, of all others, he had such particular reason to regret his negligence.

Disturbed by these reflections, the old gentleman had, for the first time in his life, some disinclination, arising from shame and vexation, to face his own son ; so that, to protract for a little the meeting which he feared would be a painful one, he went to wait upon the sheriff-depute, who he found had set off for Dumfries, in great haste, to superintend in person the investigation which had been set on foot by his substitute. This gentleman's clerk could say little on the subject of the riot, excepting that it had been serious, much damage done to property, and some personal violence offered to individuals, but, as far as he had yet heard, no lives lost on the spot.

Mr. Fairford was compelled to return home with this intelligence ; and on inquiring at James Wilkinson where his son was, received for answer, that "Maister Alan was in his own room, and very busy."

"We must have our explanation over," said Saunders Fairford to himself. "Better a finger off as aye wagging" ; and going to the door of his son's apartment, he knocked at first gently, then more loudly, but received no answer. Somewhat alarmed at this silence, he opened the door of the chamber ; it was empty—clothes lay mixed in confusion with the law-books and papers, as if the inmate had been engaged in hastily packing for a journey. As Mr. Fairford looked around in alarm, his eye was arrested by a sealed letter lying upon his son's writing-table, and addressed to himself. It contained the following words :—

" My Dearest Father—

" You will not, I trust, be surprised, nor perhaps very much displeased, to learn that I am now on my way to Dumfriesshire, to learn, by my own personal investigation, the present state of my dear friend, and afford him such relief as may be in my power, and which, I trust, will be effectual. I do not presume to reflect upon you, dearest sir, for concealing from me information of so much consequence to my peace of mind and happiness ; but I hope your having done so will be, if not an excuse, at least some mitigation, of my present offense, in taking a step of consequence without consulting your pleasure ; and, I must further own, under circumstances which perhaps might lead to your disapprobation of my purpose. I can only say, in further apology, that if anything unhappy, which Heaven forbid ! shall have occurred to the person who, next to yourself, is dearest to me in this world, I shall have on my heart, as a subject of eternal regret, that, being in a certain degree warned of his danger, and furnished with the means of obviating it, I did not instantly hasten to his assistance, but preferred giving my attention to the business of this unlucky morning. No view of personal distinction, nothing, indeed, short of your earnest and often expressed wishes, could have detained me in town till this day, and having made this sacrifice to filial duty, I trust you will hold me excused, if I now obey the calls of friendship and humanity. Do not be in the least anxious on my account ; I shall know, I trust, how to conduct myself with due caution in any emergence which may occur, otherwise my legal studies for so many years have been to little purpose. I am fully provided with money, and also with arms, in case of need ; but you may rely on my prudence in avoiding all occasions of using the latter, short of the last necessity. God Almighty bless you, my dearest father ! and grant that you may forgive the first, and, I trust, the last, act approaching towards premeditated disobedience of which I either have now or shall hereafter have to accuse myself. I remain, till death, your dutiful and affectionate son,

" Alan Fairford."

" *P. S.*—I shall write with the utmost regularity, acquainting you with my motions, and requesting your advice. I trust my stay will be very short, and I think it possible that I may bring back Darsie along with me.

The paper dropped from the old man's hand when he was thus assured of the misfortune which he apprehended. His first idea was to get a post-chaise and pursue the fugitive ; but he recollected that, upon the very rare occasions when Alan had shown himself indocile to the *patria potestas*, his natural ease and gentleness of disposition seemed hardened into obstinacy, and that now, entitled, as arrived at the years of majority, and a member of the learned faculty, to direct his own motions, there was great doubt whether, in the event of his overtaking his son, he might be able to prevail upon him to return back. In such a risk of failure, he thought it wiser to desist from his purpose, especially as even his success in such a pursuit would give a ridiculous *éclat* to the whole affair, which could not be otherwise than prejudicial to his son's rising character.

Bitter, however, were Saunders Fairford's reflections as, again picking up the fatal scroll, he threw himself into his son's leathern easy-chair, and bestowed upon it a disjointed commentary. "Bring back Darsie! little doubt of that : the bad shilling is sure enough to come back again. I wish Darsie no worse ill than that he were carried where the silly fool Alan should never see him again. It was an ill hour that he darkened my doors in, for, ever since that, Alan has given up his ain old-fashioned mother wit for the t'other's capernoited maggots and nonsense. Provided with money ! You must have more than I know of, then, my friend, for I trow I kept you pretty short for your own good. Can he have gotten more fees ? or does he think five guineas has neither beginning nor end ? Arms ! What would he do with arms, or what would any man do with them that is not a regular soldier under government, or else a thief taker ? I have had enough of arms, I trow, although I carried them for King George and the government. But this is a worse strait than Falkirk field yet ! Gude guide us, we are poor, inconsistent creatures ! To think the lad should have made so able an appearance, and then bolted off this gate, after a glaiket ne'er-do-weel, like a hound upon a false scent ! Las-a-day ! it's a sore thing to see a stunkard cow kick down the pail when it's reaming fou. But, after all, it's an ill bird that defiles its ain nest. I must cover up the scandal as well as I can. What's the matter now, James ?"

"A message, sir," said James Wilkinson, "from my Lord President, and he hopes Mr. Alan is not seriously indisposed."

"From the Lord President ? the Lord preserve us ! I'll send an answer this instant ; bid the lad sit down, and ask him to drink, James. Let me see," continued he, taking a sheet of gilt paper, " how we are to draw our answers."

Ere his pen had touched the paper, James was in the room again.

"What now, James ? "

"Lord Bladderskate's lad is come to ask how Mr. Alan is, as he left the court——"

"Ay—ay—ay," answered Saunders, bitterly ; " he has e'en made a moonlight flitting, like my lord's ain nevoy."

"Shall I say sae, sir ? " said James, who, as an old soldier, was literal in all things touching the service.

"The devil ! no—no ! Bid the lad sit down and taste our ale. I will write his lordship an answer."

Once more the gilt paper was resumed, and once more the door was opened by James.

"Lord —— sends his servitor to ask after Mr. Alan."

"Oh, the deevil take their civility !" said poor Saunders. "Set him down to drink too. I will write to his lordship."

"The lads will bide your pleasure, sir, as lang as I keep the bicker fou ; but this ringing is like to wear out the bell, I think ; there are they at it again."

He answered the fresh summons accordingly, and came back to inform Mr. Fairford that the Dean of Faculty was below, inquiring for Mr. Alan. "Will I set him down to drink too ? " said James.

"Will you be an idiot, sir ?" said Mr. Fairford. "Show Mr. Dean into the parlor."

In going slowly down-stairs, step by step, the perplexed man of business had time enough to reflect that, if it be possible to put a fair gloss upon a true story, the verity always serves the purpose better than any substitute which ingenuity can devise. He therefore told his learned visitor that, although his son had been incommoded by the heat of the court, and the long train of hard study, by day and night, preceding his exertions, yet he had fortunately so far recovered as to be in condition to obey upon the instant a sudden summons which had called him to the country on a matter of life and death.

"It should be a serious matter indeed that takes my young friend away at this moment," said the good-natured Dean. "I wish he had stayed to finish his pleading, and put down

old Tough. Without compliment, Mr. Fairford, it was as
fine a first appearance as I ever heard. I should be sorry
your son did not follow it up in a reply. Nothing like
striking while the iron is hot."

Mr. Saunders Fairford made a bitter grimace as he acquiesced in an opinion which was indeed decidedly his own ;
but he thought it most prudent to reply, "That the affair
which rendered his son Alan's presence in the country absolutely necessary regarded the affairs of a young gentleman
of great fortune, who was a particular friend of Alan's, and
who never took any material step in his affairs without consulting his counsel learned in the law."

"Well—well, Mr. Fairford, you know best," answered the
learned Dean ; "if there be death or marriage in the case, a
will or a wedding is to be preferred to all other business. I
am happy Mr. Allan is so much recovered as to be able for
travel, and wish you a very good morning."

Having thus taken his ground to the Dean of Faculty,
Mr. Fairford hastily wrote cards in answer to the inquiry of
the three judges, accounting for Alan's absence in the same
manner. These, being properly sealed and addressed, he
delivered to James, with directions to dismiss the parti-
colored gentry, who, in the meanwhile, had consumed a
gallon of twopenny ale while discussing points of law, and
addressing each other by their masters' titles.*

The exertions which these matters demanded, and the
interest which so many persons of legal distinction appeared
to have taken in his son, greatly relieved the oppressed spirit
of Saunders Fairford, who continued to talk mysteriously of
the very important business which had interfered with his
son's attendance during the brief remainder of the session.
He endeavored to lay the same unction to his own heart ;
but here the application was less fortunate, for his conscience
told him that no end, however important, which could be
achieved in Darsie Latimer's affairs could be balanced against
the reputation which Alan was like to forfeit by deserting
the cause of Poor Peter Peebles.

In the meanwhile, although the haze which surrounded
the cause, or causes, of that unfortunate litigant had been
for a time dispelled by Alan's eloquence, like a fog by the
thunder of artillery, yet it seemed once more to settle down
upon the mass of litigation, thick as the palpable darkness
of Egypt, at the very sound of Mr. Tough's voice, who,
on the second day of Mr. Alan's departure, was heard in

* See titles of Scottish Judges. Note 23.

answer to the opening counsel. Deep-mouthed, long-breathed, and pertinacious, taking a pinch of snuff betwixt [after] every sentence, which otherwise seemed interminable, the veteran pleader prosed over all the themes which had been treated so luminously by Fairford; he quietly and imperceptibly replaced all the rubbish which the other had cleared away; and succeeded in restoring the veil of obscurity and unintelligibility which had for many years darkened the case of Peebles against Plainstanes; and the matter was once more hung up by a remit to an accountant, with instruction to report before answer. So different a result from that which the public had been led to expect from Alan's speech gave rise to various speculations.

The client himself opined that it was entirely owing, first, to his own absence during the first day's pleading, being, as he said, deboshed with brandy, usquebaugh, and other strong waters, at John's Coffee-house, *per ambayes* of Peter Drudgeit, employed to that effect by and through the device, counsel, and covyne of Saunders Fairford, his agent, or pretended agent; secondly, by the flight and voluntary desertion of the younger Fairford, the advocate; on account of which he served both father and son with a petition and complaint against them, for malversation in office. So that the apparent and most probable issue of this cause seemed to menace the melancholy Mr. Saunders Fairford with additional subject for plague and mortification which was the more galling, as his conscience told him that the case was really given away, and that a very brief resumption of the former argument, with reference to the necessary authorities and points of evidence, would have enabled Alan, by the mere breath, as it were, of his mouth, to blow away the various cobwebs with which Mr. Tough had again invested the proceedings. But it went, he said, just like a decreet in absence, and was lost for want of a contradictor.

In the meantime, nearly a week passed over without Mr. Fairford hearing a word directly from his son. He learned, indeed, by a letter from Mr. Crosbie, that the young counselor had safely reached Dumfries, but had left that town upon some ulterior researches, the purpose of which he had not communicated. The old man, thus left to suspense and to mortifying recollections, deprived also of the domestic society to which he had been habituated, began to suffer in body as well as in mind. He had formed the determination of setting out in person for Dumfriesshire, when, after having been dogged, peevish, and snappish to his clerks and domestics to an unusual and almost intolerable degree, the acrimonious humors settled in a hissing-hot fit of the gout, which is a well-known tamer of the most froward spirits, and under whose discipline we shall, for the present, leave him, as the continuation of this history assumes, with the next division, a form somewhat different from direct narrative and epistolary correspondence, though partaking of the character of both.

CHAPTER III

JOURNAL OF DARSIE LATIMER

The following address is written on the inside of the envelope which
contained the Journal.

INTO what hands soever these leaves may fall, they will instruct him, during a certain time at least, in the history of
the life of an unfortunate young man, who, in the heart of
a free country, and without any crime being laid to his charge,
has been, and is, subjected to a course of unlawful and violent
restraint. He who opens this letter is therefore conjured to
apply to the nearest magistrate, and, following such indications as the papers may afford, to exert himself for the relief
of one who, while he possesses every claim to assistance which
oppressed innocence can give, has, at the same time, both
the inclination and the means of being grateful to his de-
liverers. Or, if the person obtaining these letters shall want
courage or means to effect the writer's release, he is, in that
case, conjured, by every duty of a man to his fellow-mortals,
and of a Christian towards one who professes the same holy
faith, to take the earliest measures for conveying them with
speed and safety to the hands of Alan Fairford, Esq., advocate, residing in the family of his father, Alexander
Fairford, Esq., Writer to the Signet, Brown's Square, Edinburgh. He may be assured of a liberal reward, besides the
consciousness of having discharged a real duty to humanity.

MY DEAREST ALAN—

Feeling as warmly towards you in doubt and in distress as I ever did in the brightest days of our intimacy, it is
to you whom I address a history which may perhaps fall into
very different hands. A portion of my former spirit descends
to my pen when I write your name, and indulging the happy
thought that you may be my deliverer from my present uncomfortable and alarming situation, as you have been my
guide and counselor on every former occasion, I will subdue
the dejection which would otherwise overwhelm me. There-

fore, as, Heaven knows, I have time enough to write, I will
endeavor to pour my thoughts out, as fully and freely as of
old, though probably without the same gay and happy levity.
If the papers should reach other hands than yours, still I
will not regret this exposure of my feelings ; for, allowing
for an ample share of the folly incidental to youth and inexperience, I fear not that I have much to be ashamed of in
my narrative ; nay, I even hope that the open simplicity and
frankness with which I am about to relate every singular and
distressing circumstance may prepossess even a stranger in
my favor ; and that, amid the multitude of seemingly trivial
circumstances which I detail at length, a clue may be found
to effect my liberation.

Another chance certainly remains—the Journal, as I may
call it, may never reach the hands either of the dear friend
to whom it is addressed or those of an indifferent stranger,
but may become the prey of the persons by whom I am at
present treated as a prisoner. Let it be so—they will learn
from it little but what they already know ; that, as a man
and an Englishman, my soul revolts at the usage which I
have received ; that I am determined to essay every possible
means to obtain my freedom ; that captivity has not broken
my spirit ; and that, although they may doubtless complete
their oppression by murder, I am still willing to bequeath
my cause to the justice of my country. Undeterred, therefore, by the probability that my papers may be torn from
me, and subjected to the inspection of one in particular,
who, causelessly my enemy already, may be yet farther incensed at me for recording the history of my wrongs, I
proceed to resume the history of events which have befallen
me since the conclusion of my last letter to my dear Alan
Fairford, dated, if I mistake not, on the 5th day of this still
current month of August.

Upon the night preceding the date of that letter, I had
been present, for the purpose of an idle frolic, at a dancing
party at the village of Brokenburn, about six miles from
Dumfries ; many persons must have seen me there, should
the fact appear of importance sufficient to require investigation. I danced, played on the violin, and took part in the
festivity till about midnight, when my servant, Samuel Owen,
brought me my horses, and I rode back to a small inn called
Shepherd's Bush, kept by Mrs. Gregson, which had been
occasionally my residence for about a fortnight past. I spent
the earlier part of the forenoon in writing a letter which I
have already mentioned, to you, my dear Alan, and which,

I think, you must have received in safety. Why did I not follow your advice, so often given me? Why did I linger in the neighborhood of a danger to which a kind voice had warned me? These are now unavailing questions. I was blinded by a fatality, and remained fluttering like a moth around the candle, until I have been scorched to some purpose.

The greater part of the day * had passed, and time hung heavy on my hands. I ought perhaps to blush at recollecting what has been often objected to me by the dear friend to whom this letter is addressed, viz. the facility with which I have in moments of indolence, suffered my motions to be directed by any person who chanced to be near me, instead of taking the labor of thinking or deciding for myself. I had employed for some time, as a sort of guide and errand-boy, a lad named Benjamin, the son of one Widow Coltherd, who lives near the Shepherd's Bush, and I cannot but remember that, upon several occasions, I had of late suffered him to possess more influence over my motions than at all became difference of our age and condition. At present he exerted himself to persuade me that it was the finest possible sport to see the fish taken out from the nets placed in the Solway at the reflux of the tide, and urged my going thither this evening so much, that, looking back on the whole circumstances, I cannot but think he had some especial motive for his conduct. These particulars I have mentioned, that, if these papers fall into friendly hands, the boy may be sought after and submitted to examination.

His eloquence being unable to persuade me that I should take any pleasure in seeing the fruitless struggles of the fish when left in the nets and deserted by the tide, he artfully suggested that Mr. and Miss Geddes, a respectable Quaker family well known in the neighborhood, and with whom I had contracted habits of intimacy, would possibly be offended if I did not make them an early visit. Both, he said, had been particularly inquiring the reasons of my leaving their house rather suddenly on the previous day. I resolved, therefore, to walk up to Mount Sharon and make my apologies; and I agreed to permit the boy to attend upon me, and wait my return from the house, that I might fish on my way homeward to Shepherd's Bush, for which amusement, he assured me, I would find the evening most favorable. I mention this minute circumstance because I strongly suspect that this boy had a presentiment how the evening was to

* ["A couple of days," on p. 130]

terminate with me, and entertained the selfish though childish wish of securing to himself an angling-rod which he had often admired, as a part of my spoils. I may do the boy wrong, but I had before remarked in him the peculiar art of pursuing the trifling objects of cupidity proper to his age with the systematic address of much riper years. When we had commenced our walk, I upbraided him with the coolness of the evening, considering the season, the easterly wind, and other circumstances, unfavorable for angling. He presisted in his own story, and made a few casts, as if to convince me of my error, but caught no fish ; and, indeed, as I am now convinced, was much more intent on watching my motions than on taking any. When I ridiculed him once more on his fruitless endeavors, he answered, with a sneering smile, that " the trouts would not rise because there was thunder in the air "—an intimation which, in one sense, I have found too true.

I arrived at Mount Sharon ; was received by my friends there with their wonted kindness ; and after being a little rallied on my having suddenly left them on the preceding evening, I agreed to make atonement by staying all night, and dismissed the lad who attended with my fishing-rod to carry that information to Shepherd's Bush. It may be doubted whether he went thither or in a different direction.

Betwixt eight and nine o'clock, when it began to become dark, we walked on the terrace to enjoy the appearance of the firmament, glittering with ten million of stars, to which slight touch of early frost gave tenfold luster. As we gazed on this splendid scene, Miss Geddes, I think, was the first to point out to our admiration a shooting or falling star, which, she said, drew a long train after it. Looking to the part of the heavens which she pointed out, I distinctly observed two successive sky-rockets arise and burst in the sky.

" These meteors," said Mr. Geddes, in answer to his sister's observation, " are not formed in heaven, nor do they bode any good to the dwellers upon earth."

As he spoke, I looked to another quarter of the sky, and a rocket, as if a signal in answer to those which had already appeared, rose high from the earth, and burst apparently among the stars.

Mr. Geddes seemed very thoughtful for some minutes, and then said to his sister, " Rachel, though it waxes late, I must go down to the fishing-station and pass the night in the overseer's room there."

" Nay, then," replied the lady, " I am but too well assured

that the sons of Belial are menacing these nets and devices.
Joshua, art thou a man of peace, and wilt thou willingly and
wittingly thrust thyself where thou mayst be tempted by the
old man Adam within thee to enter into debate and strife ?"

"I am a man of peace, Rachel," answered Mr. Geddes,
" even to the utmost extent which our friends can demand of
humanity ; and neither have I ever used, nor, with the help
of God, will I at any future time employ, the arm of flesh to
repel or to revenge injuries. But if I can, by mild reasons
and firm conduct, save those rude men from committing a
crime, and the property belonging to myself and others from
sustaining damage, surely I do but the duty of a man and a
Christian."

With these words, he ordered his horse instantly ; and his
sister, ceasing to argue with him, folded her arms upon her
bosom, and looked up to heaven with a resigned and yet
sorrowful countenance.

These particulars may appear trivial, but it is better in my
present condition to exert my faculties in recollecting the
past, and in recording it, than waste them in vain and anxious anticipations of the future.

It would have been scarcely proper in me to remain in the
house from which the master was thus suddenly summoned
away, and I therefore begged permission to attend him to the
fishing-station, assuring his sister that I would be a guarantee for his safety.

The proposal seemed to give much pleasure to Miss Geddes.

" Let it be so, brother," she said, " and let the young man
have the desire of his heart, that there may be a faithful witness to stand by thee in the hour of need, and to report how
it shall fare with thee."

" No, Rachel," said the worthy man, " thou art to blame
in this, that, to quiet thy apprehensions on my account, thou
shouldst thrust into danger—if danger it shall prove to be—
this youth, our guest, for whom, doubtless, in case of mishap, as many hearts will ache as may be afflicted on our account."

"Nay my good friend," said I, taking Mr. Geddes's hand
"I am not so happy as you suppose me. Were my span to
be concluded this evening, few would so much as know that
such a being had existed for twenty years on the face of the
earth ; and of these few, only one would sincerely regret me.
Do not, therefore, refuse me the privilege of attending you,
and of showing, by so trifling an act of kindness, that, if I
have few friends, I am at least desirous to serve them."

"Thou hast a kind heart, I warrant thee," said Joshua Geddes, returning the pressure of my hand. " Rachel, the young man shall go with me. Why should he not face danger, in order to do justice and preserve peace ? There is that within me," he added, looking upwards, and with a passing enthusiasm which I had not before observed, and the absence of which perhaps rather belonged to the sect than to his own personal character—" I say, I have that within which assures me that, though the ungodly may rage even like the storm of the ocean, they shall not have freedom to prevail against us."

Having spoken thus, Mr. Geddes appointed a pony to be saddled for my use ; and having taken a basket with some provisions, and a servant to carry back the horses, for which there was no accommodation at the fishing-station, we set off about nine o'clock at night, and after three-quarters of an hour's riding arrived at our place of destination.

The station consists, or then consisted, of huts for four or five fishermen, a cooperage and sheds, and a better sort of cottage, at which the superintendent resided. We gave our horses to the servant, to be carried back to Mount Sharon, my companion expressing himself humanely anxious for their safety, and knocked at the door of the house. At first we only heard a barking of dogs ; but these animals became quiet on snuffing beneath the door, and acknowledging the presence of friends. A hoarse voice than demanded, in rather unfriendly accents, who we were and what we wanted ; and it was not until Joshua named himself, and called upon his superintendent to open, that the latter appeared at the door of the hut, attended by three large dogs of the Newfoundland breed. He had a flambeau in his hand, and two large, heavy ship-pistols stuck into his belt. He was a stout, elderly man, who had been a sailor, as I learned, during the earlier part of his life, and was now much confided in by the Fishing Company, whose concerns he directed under the orders of Mr. Geddes.

"Thou didst not expect me to-night, friend Davies ?" said my friend to the old man, who was arranging seats for us by the fire.

"No, Master Geddes," answered he, " I did not expect you, nor, to speak the truth, did I wish for you either."

"These are plain terms, John Davies," answered Mr. Geddes.

"Ay—ay, sir, I know your worship loves no holyday speeches."

" Thou dost guess, I suppose, what brings us here so late, John Davies ? " said Mr. Geddes.

" I do suppose, sir," answered the superintendent, " that it was because these d—d smuggling wreckers on the coast are showing their lights to gather their forces, as they did the night before they broke down the dam-dike and wears up the country ; but if that same be the case, I wish once more you had staid away, for your worship carries no fighting tackle aboard, I think, and there will be wórk for such ere morning, your worship."

" Worship is due to Heaven only, John Davies," said Geddes. " I have often desired these to desist from using that phrase to me."

" I won't then," said John ; " no offense meant. But how the devil can a man stand picking his words, when he is just going to come to blows ? "

" I hope not, John Davies," said Joshua Geddes. " Call in the rest of the men, that I may give them their instructions."

" I may cry till doomsday, Master Geddes, ere a soul answers : the cowardly lubbers have all made sail—the cooper, and all the rest of them—so soon as they heard the enemy were at sea. They have all taken to the long-boat, and left the ship among the breakers, except little Phil and myself— they have by—— ! "

" Swear not at all, John Davies ; thou art an honest man, and I believe, without an oath, that thy comrades love their own bones better than my goods and chattels. And so thou hast no assistance but little Phil against a hundred men or two ? "

" Why, there are the dogs, your honor knows, Neptune and Thetis, and the puppy may do something ; and then though your worship—I beg pardon—though your honor be no great fighter, this young gentleman may bear a hand."

" Ay, and I see you are provided with arms," said Mr. Geddes ; " let me see them."

" Ay—ay, sir ; here be a pair of buffers will bite as well as bark—these will make sure of two rogues at least. It would be a shame to strike without firing a shot. Take care, your honor, they are double-shotted."

" Ay, John Davies, I will take care of them," throwing the pistols into a tub of water beside him ; " and I wish I could render the whole generation of them useless at the same moment."

A deep shade of displeasure passed over John Davis's

weatherbeaten countenance. "Belike your honor is going to
take the command yourself, then ?" he said, after a pause.
"Why, I can be of little use now ; and since your worship,
or your honor, or whatever you are, means to strike quietly,
I believe you will do it better without me than with me, for
I am like enough to make mischief, I admit ; but I'll never
leave my post without orders."

"Then you have mine, John Davies, to go to Mount
Sharon directly, and take the boy Phil with you. Where is
he ?"

"He is on the outlook for these scums of the earth," answered Davies ; but it is to no purpose to know when they
come, if we are not to stand to our weapons."

"We will use none but those of sense and reason, John."

"And you may just as well cast chaff against the wind as
speak sense and reason to the like of them."

"Well—well, be it so," said Joshua. "And now, John
Davies, I know thou art what the world calls a brave fellow,
and I have ever found thee an honest one. And now I command you to go to Mount Sharon, and let Phil lie on the bank-
side—see the poor boy hath a sea-cloak, though—and watch
what happens here, and let him bring you the news ; and if
any violence shall be suffered to the property there, I trust
to your fidelity to carry my sister to Dumfries, to the house of
our friends the Corsacks, and inform the civil authorities of
what mischief hath befallen."

The old seaman paused a moment. "It is hard lines for
me," he said, " to leave your honor in tribulation ; and yet,
staying here, I am only like to make bad worse ; and your
honor's sister, Miss Rachel, must be looked to, that's certain ;
for if the rogues once get their hand to mischief, they will
come to Mount Sharon after they have wasted and destroyed
this here snug little roadstead, where I thought to ride at
anchor for life."

"Right—right, John Davies," said Joshua Geddes ; "and
best call the dogs with you."

"Ay—ay, sir," said the veteran, "for they are something
of my mind, and would not keep quiet if they saw mischief
doing ; so maybe they might come to mischief, poor dumb
creatures. So God bless your honor—I mean your worship—
I cannot bring my mouth to say 'fare you well.' Here, Neptune, Thetis ! come, dogs—come."

So saying, and with a very crestfallen countenance, John
Davies left the hut.

"Now, there goes one of the best and most faithful crea-

tures that ever was born," said Mr. Geddes, as the superin-
tendant shut the door of the cottage. "Nature made him
with a heart that would not have suffered him to harm a fly ;
but thou seest, friend Latimer, that, as men arm their bull-
dogs with spiked collars, and their game-cocks with steel
spurs, to aid them in fight, so they corrupt, by education,
the best and mildest natures, until fortitude and spirit become stubbornness and ferocity. Believe me, friend Latimer, I would as soon expose my faithful household dog to a
vain combat with a herd of wolves as yon trusty creature to
the violence of the enraged multitude. But I need say little
on this subject to thee, friend Latimer, who, I doubt not,
art trained to believe that courage is displayed and honor
attained, not by doing and suffering, as becomes a man, that
which fate calls us to suffer, and justice commands us to do,
but because thou art ready to retort violence for violence,
and considerest the lightest insult as a sufficient cause for the
spilling of blood, nay, the taking of life. But, leaving these
points of controversy to a more fit season, let us see what
our basket of provision contains ; for in truth, friend Latimer, I am one of those whom neither fear nor anxiety deprive of their ordinary appetite."

We found the means of good cheer accordingly, which Mr.
Geddes seemed to enjoy as much as if it had been eaten in a
situation of perfect safety ; nay, his conversation appeared
to be rather more gay than on ordinary occasions. After
eating our supper, we left the hut together, and walked for
a few minutes on the banks of the sea. It was high water,
and the ebb had not yet commenced. The moon shone
broad and bright upon the placid face of the Solway Firth,
and showed a slight ripple upon the stakes, the tops of which
were just visible above the waves, and on the dark-colored
buoys which marked the upper edge of the enclosure of nets.
At a much greater distance—for the estuary is here very wide
—the line of the English coast was seen on the verge of the
water, resembling one of those fog-banks on which mariners
are said to gaze, uncertain whether it be land or atmospher-
ical delusion."

"We shall be undisturbed for some hours," said Mr.
Geddes : "they will not come down upon us till the state of
the tide permits them to destroy the tide-nets. Is it not
strange to think that human passions will so soon transform
such a tranquil scene as this into one of devastation and
confusion ?"

It was indeed a scene of exquisite stillness ; so much so,

that the restless waves of the Solway seemed, if not absolutely
to sleep, at least to slumber. On that shore no night-bird
was heard ; the cock had not sung his first matins ; and we
ourselves walked more lightly than by day, as if to suit the
sound of our own paces to the serene tranquillity around us.
At length the plaintive cry of a dog broke the silence, and
on our return to the cottage we found that the younger of
the three animals which had gone along with John Davies,
unaccustomed, perhaps, to distant journeys, and the duty of
following to heel, had strayed from the party, and, unable to
rejoin them, had wandered back to the place of its birth.

"Another feeble addition to our feeble garrison," said Mr.
Geddes, as he caressed the dog and admitted it into the cottage. " Poor thing ! as thou art incapable of doing any mischief, I hope thou wilt sustain none. At least, thou mayst
do us the good service of a sentinel, and permit us to enjoy a
quiet repose, under the certainty that thou wilt alarm us
when the enemy is at hand."

There were two beds in the superintendent's room, upon
which we threw ourselves. Mr. Geddes, with his happy equanimity of temper, was asleep in the first five minutes. I lay
for some time in doubtful and anxious thoughts, watching
the fire and the motions of the restless dog, which, disturbed
probably at the absence of John Davies, wandered from the
hearth to the door and back again, then came to the bedside
and licked my hands and face, and at length, experiencing no
repulse to its advances, established itself at my feet, and
went to sleep, an example which I soon afterwards followed.

The rage of narration, my dear Alan—for I will never relinquish the hope that what I am writing may one day reach
your hands—has not forsaken me even in my confinement,
and the extensive though unimportant details into which I
have been hurried render it necessary that I commence
another sheet. Fortunately, my pigmy characters comprehends a great many words within a small space of paper.

CHAPTER IV

THE morning was dawning, and Mr. Geddes and I myselt were still sleeping soundly, when the alarm was given by my canine bedfellow, who first growled deeply at intervals, and at length bore more decided testimony to the approach of some enemy. I opened the door of the cottage, and perceived, at the distance of about two hundred yards, a small but close column of men, which I would have taken for a dark hedge, but that I could perceive it was advancing rapidly and in silence.

The dog flew towards them, but instantly ran howling back to me, having probably been chastised by a stick or a stone. Uncertain as to the plan of tactics or of treaty which Mr. Geddes might think proper to adopt, I was about to retire into the cottage, when he suddenly joined me at the door, and, slipping his arm through mine, said, " Let us go to meet them manfully ; we have done nothing to be ashamed of. " Friends," he said, raising his voice as we approached them, " who and what are you, and with what purpose are you here on my property ? "

A loud cheer was the answer returned, and a brace of fiddlers who occupied the front of the march immediately struck up the insulting air the words of which begin

> " Merily danced the Quaker's wife,
> And merrily danced the Quaker."

Even at that moment of alarm, I think I recognized the tones of the blind fiddler, known by the name of Wandering Willie, from his itinerant habits. They continued to advance swiftly and in great order, in their front

> The fiery fiddlers playing martial airs ;

when, coming close up, they surrounded us by a single movement, and there was a universal cry, " Whoop, Quaker— whoop, Quaker ! Here have we them both, the wet Quaker and the dry one."

"Hang up the wet Quaker to dry, and wet the dry one with a ducking," answered another voice. "Where is the sea-otter, John Davies, that destroyed more fish than any sealgh upon Ailsay Craig?" exclaimed a third voice. "I have an old crow to pluck with him, and a pock to put the feathers in."

We stood perfectly passive ; for, to have attempted resistance against more than a hundred men, armed with guns, fish-spears, iron crows, spades, and bludgeons would have been an act of utter insanity. Mr. Geddes, with his strong sonorous voice, answered the question about the superintendent in a manner the manly indifference of which compelled them to attend to him.

"John Davies," he said, "will, I trust, soon be at Dumfries——"

"To fetch down redcoats and dragoons against us, you canting old villain !"

A blow was, at the same time, leveled at my friend, which I parried by interposing the stick I had in my hand. I was instantly struck down, and have a faint recollection of hearing some crying, "Kill the young spy !" and others, as I thought, interposing on my behalf. But a second blow on the head, received in the scuffle, soon deprived me of sense and consciousness, and threw me into a state of insensibility, from which I did not recover immediately. When I did come to myself, I was lying on the bed from which I had just risen before the fray, and my poor companion, the Newfoundland puppy, its courage entirely cowed by the tumult of the riot, had crept as close to me as it could, and lay trembling and whining, as if under the most dreadful terror. I doubted at first whether I had not dreamed of the tumult, until, as I attempted to rise, a feeling of pain and dizziness assured me that the injury I had sustained was but too real. I gathered together my senses—listened—and heard at a distance the shouts of the rioters, busy, doubtless, in their work of devastation.* I made a second effort to rise, or at least to turn myself, for I lay with my face to the wall of the cottage, but I found that my limbs were secured, and my motions effectually prevented—not indeed by cords, but by linen or cloth bandages swathed around my ankles, and securing my arms to my sides. Aware of my utterly captive condition, I groaned betwixt bodily pain and mental distress.

A voice by my bedside whispered, in a winning tone, "Whisht a-ye, hinnie—whisht a-ye ; haud your tongue, like

* See Attack upon the Dam-dike. Note 24.

a gude bairn. Ye have cost us dear aneugh already. My hinnie's clean gane now.'

Knowing, as I thought, the phraseology of the wife of the itinerant musician, I asked her where her husband was, and whether he had been hurt.

" Broken," answered the dame—"all broken to pieces : fit for nought but to be made spunks of—the best blood that was in Scotland."

" Broken !—blood ! Is your husband wounded—has there been bloodshed—broken limbs?"

" Broken limbs ! I wish," answered the beldam, " that my hinnie had broken the best bane in his body, before he had broken his fiddle, that was the best blood in Scotland ; it was a cremony, for aught that I ken."

" Pshaw—only his fiddle !" said I.

" I dinna ken what waur your honor could have wished him to do, unless he had broken his neck ; and this is muckle the same to my hinnie Willie and me. Chaw, indeed ! It is easy to say ' chaw,' but wha is to gie us onything to chaw ? The bread-winner's gane, and we may e'en sit down and starve."

" No—no," I said, " I will pay you for twenty such fiddles."

" Twenty such ! is that a' ye ken about it ? the country hadna the like o't. But if your honor were to pay us, as nae doubt wad be to your credit here and hereafter, where are ye to get the siller ?"

" I have enough of money," said I, attempting to reach my hand towards my side-pocket ; " unloose these bandages, and I will pay you on the spot."

This hint appeared to move her, and she was approaching the bedside, as I hoped, to liberate me from my bonds, when a nearer and more desperate shout was heard, as if the rioters were close by the hut.

" I daurna—I daurna," said the poor woman ; "they would murder me and my hinnie Willie baith, and they have misguided us aneugh already ; but if there is anything worldly I could do for your honor, leave out loosing ye ?"

What she said recalled me to my bodily suffering. Agitation, and the effects of the usage I had received, had produced a burning thirst. I asked for a drink of water.

" Heaven Almighty forbid that Epps [Maggie] Ainslie should gie ony sick gentleman cauld well-water, and him in a fever. Na—na, hinnie, let me alane, I'll do better for ye than the like of that."

"Give me what you will," I replied ; "let it but be liquid and cool."

The woman gave me a large horn accordingly, filled with spirits and water, which, without minute inquiry concerning the nature of its contents, I drained at a draught. Either the spirits taken in such a manner acted more suddenly than usual on my brain, or else there was some drug mixed with the beverage. I remember little after drinking it off, only that the appearance of things around me became indistinct ; that the woman's form seemed to multiply itself, and to flit in various figures around me, bearing the same lineaments as she herself did. I remember also that the discordant noises and cries of those without the cottage seemed to die away in a hum like that with which a nurse hushes her babe. At length I fell into a deep sound sleep, or rather, a state of absolute insensibility.

I have reason to think this species of trance lasted for many hours ; indeed, for the whole subsequent day and part of the night. It was not uniformly so profound, for my recollection of it is checkered with many dreams, all of a painful nature, but too faint and too indistinct to be remembered. At length the moment of waking came, and my sensations were horrible.

A deep sound, which, in the confusion of my senses, I identified with the cries of the rioters, was the first thing of which I was sensible ; next, I became conscious that I was carried violently forward in some conveyance, with an unequal motion, which gave me much pain. My position was horizontal, and when I attempted to stretch my hands in order to find some mode of securing myself against this species of suffering, I found I was bound as before, and the horrible reality rushed on my mind that I was in the hands of those who had lately committed a great outrage on property, and were now about to kidnap, if not to murder, me. I opened my eyes, it was to no purpose : all around me was dark, for a day had passed over during my captivity. A dispiriting sickness oppressed my head, my heart seemed on fire, while my feet and hands were chilled and benumbed with want of circulation. It was with the utmost difficulty that I at length, and gradually, recovered in a sufficient degree the power of observing external sounds and circumstances ; and when I did so, they presented nothing consolatory.

Groping with my hands, as far as the bandages would permit, and receiving the assistance of some occasional glances of the moonlight, I became aware that the carriage in which I was transported was one of the light carts of the country, called "tumblers," and that a little attention had been paid to my accomodation, as I was laid upon some sacks, covered with matting and filled with straw. Without these, my condition would have been still more intolerable, for the vehicle, sinking now on one side and now on the other, sometimes sticking absolutely fast, and requiring the utmost exertions of the animal which drew it to put it once more in motion, was subjected to jolts in all directions, which were very severe. At other times it rolled silently and smoothly over what seemed to be wet sand ; and, as I heard the distant roar of the tide, I had little doubt that we were engaged in passing the formidable estuary which divides the two kingdoms.

There seemed to be at least five or six people about the cart, some on foot, others on horseback ; the former lent assistance whenever it was in danger of upsetting, or sticking fast in the quicksand ; the others rode before and acted as guides, often changing the direction of the vehicle as the precarious state of the passage required.

I addressed myself to the men around the cart, and endeavored to move their compassion. I had harmed, I said, no one, and for no action in my life had deserved such cruel treatment. I had no concern whatever in the fishing-station which had incurred their displeasure, and my acquaintance with Mr. Geddes was of a very late date. Lastly, and as my strongest argument, I endeavored to excite their fears, by informing them that my rank in life would not permit me to be either murdered or secreted with impunity : and to interest their avarice, by the promises I made them of reward, if they would effect my deliverance. I only received a scornful laugh in reply to my threats ; my promises might have done more, for the fellows were whispering together as if in hesitation, and I began to reiterate and increase my offers, when the voice of one of the horsemen, who had suddenly come up, enjoined silence to the men on foot, and approaching the side of the cart, said to me, with a strong and determined voice, " Young man, there is no personal harm designed to you. If you remain silent and quiet, you may reckon on good treatment ; but if you endeavor to tamper with these men in the execution of their duty, I will take such measures for silencing you as you shall remember the longest day you have to live."

I thought I knew the voice which uttered these threats ; but, in such a situation, my perceptions could not be supposed to be perfectly accurate. I was contented to reply, "Whoever you are that speak to me, I entreat the benefit of the meanest prisoner, who is not to be subjected legally to greater hardship than is necessary for the restraint of his person. I entreat that these bonds, which hurt me so cruelly, may be slackened at least, if not removed altogether."

"I will slacken the belts," said the former speaker; "nay, I will altogether remove them, and allow you to pursue your journey in a more convenient manner, provided you will give me your word of honor that you will not attempt an escape."

"Never!" I answered, with an energy of which despair alone could have rendered me capable—"I will never submit to loss of freedom a moment longer than I am subjected to it by force."

"Enough," he replied; "the sentiment is natural, but do not on your side complain that I, who am carrying on an important undertaking, use the only means in my power for ensuring its success."

I entreated to know what it was designed to do with me; but my conductor, in a voice of menacing authority, desired me to be silent on my peril; and my strength and spirits were too much exhausted to permit my continuing a dialogue so singular, even if I could have promised myself any good result by doing so.

It is proper here to add that, from my recollections at the time, and from what has since taken place, I have the strongest possible belief that the man with whom I held this expostulation was the singular person residing at Brokenburn in Dumfriesshire, and called by the fishers of that hamlet the Laird of the Solway Lochs. The cause for his inveterate persecution I cannot pretend even to guess at.

In the meantime, the cart was dragged heavily and wearily on, until the nearer roar of the advancing tide excited the apprehension of another danger. I could not mistake the sound, which I had heard upon another occasion, when it was only the speed of a fleet horse which saved me from perishing in the quicksands. Thou, my dear Alan, canst not but remember the former circumstances; and now, wonderful contrast! the very man, to the best of my belief, who then saved me from peril was the leader of the lawless band who had deprived me of my liberty. I conjectured that the danger grew imminent; for I heard some words and circumstances which made me aware that a rider hastily

fastened his own horse to the shafts of the cart, in order to
assist the exhausted animal which drew it, and the vehicle
was now pulled forward at a faster pace, which the horses
were urged to maintain by blows and curses. The men,
however, were inhabitants of the neighborhood ; and I had
strong personal reason to believe that one of them, at least,
was intimately acquainted with all the depths and shallows
of the perilous paths in which we were engaged. But they
were in eminent danger themselves ; and if so, as, from the
whispering and exertions to push on with the cart, was much
to be apprehended, there was little doubt that I should be
left behind as a useless encumbrance, and that while I was
in a condition which rendered every chance of escape impracticable. These were awful apprehensions ; but it pleased
Providence to increase them to a point which my brain was
scarcely able to endure.

As we approached very near to a black line, which, dimly
visible as it was, I could make out to be the shore, we heard
two or three sounds which appeared to be the report of
fire-arms. Immediately all was bustle among our party to
get forward. Presently a fellow galloped up to us, crying
out, "Ware hawk !—ware hawk ! the land-sharks are out
from Burgh, and Allonby Tom will lose his cargo if you do
not bear a hand."

Most of my company seemed to make hastily for the shore
on receiving this intelligence. A driver was left with the
cart ; but at length, when, after repeated and hairbreadth
escapes, it actually stuck fast in a slough or quicksand, the
fellow with an oath cut the harness, and, as I presume,
departed with the horses, whose feet I heard splashing over
the wet sand and through the shallows, as he galloped off.

The dropping sound of firearms was still continued, but
lost almost entirely in the thunder of the advancing surge.
By a desperate effort I raised myself in the cart, and attained
a sitting posture, which served only to show me the extent
of my danger. There lay my native land—my own England
—the land where I was born, and to which my wishes, since
my earliest age, had turned with all the prejudices of national
feeling—there it lay, within a furlong of the place where I
yet was ; that furlong, which an infant would have raced
over in a minute, was yet a barrier effectual to divide me forever from England and from life. I soon not only heard
the roar of this dreadful torrent, but saw, by the fitful moonlight, the foamy crests of the devouring waves, as they advanced with the speed and fury of a pack of hungry wolves.

The consciousness that the slightest ray of hope, or power of struggling, was not left me, quite overcame the constancy which I had hitherto maintained. My eyes began to swim ; my head grew giddy and mad with fear ; I chattered and howled to the howling and roaring sea. One or two great waves already reached the cart, when the conductor of the party, whom I have mentioned so often, was, as if by magic, at my side. He sprang from his horse into the vehicle, cut the ligatures which restrained me, and bade me get up and mount in the fiend's name.

Seeing I was incapable of obeying, he seized me, as if I had been a child of six months old, threw me across the horse, sprung on behind, supporting me with one hand, while he directed the animal with the other. In my helpless and painful posture, I was unconscious of the degree of danger which we incurred ; but I believe at one time the horse was swimming, or 'nearly so, and that it was with difficulty that my stern and powerful assistant kept my head above water. I remember particularly the shock which I felt when the animal, endeavoring to gain the bank, reared, and very nearly fell back on his burden. The time during which I continued in this dreadful condition did not probably exceed two or three minutes, yet so strongly were they marked with horror and agony, that they seem to my recollection a much more considerable space of time.

When I had been thus snatched from destruction, I had only power to say to my protector or oppressor, for he merited neither name at my hands—" You do not, then, design to murder me ? "

He laughed as he replied, but it was a sort of laughter which I scarce desire to hear again—" Else you think I had let the waves do their work ? But remember, the shepherd saves his sheep from the torrent—is it to preserve its life ? Be silent, however, with questions or entreaties. What I mean to do, thou canst no more discover or prevent than a man with his bare palm can scoop dry the Solway."

I was too much exhausted to continue the argument ; and, still numbed and torpid in all my limbs, permitted myself without reluctance to be placed on a horse brought for the purpose. My formidable conductor rode on the one side, and another person on the other, keeping me upright in the saddle. In this manner we traveled forward at a considerable rate, and by bye-roads, with which my attendant seemed as familiar as with the perilous passages of the Solway.

At length, after stumbling through a labyrinth of dark

and deep lanes, and crossing more than one rough and barren heath, we found ourselves on the edge of a highroad, where a chaise and four awaited, as it appeared, our arrival. To my great relief, we now changed our mode of conveyance ; for my dizziness and headache had returned in so strong a degree, that I should otherwise have been totally unable to keep my seat on horseback, even with the support which I received.

My doubted and dangerous companion signed to me to enter the carriage ; the man who had ridden on the left side of my horse stepped in after me, and, drawing up the blinds of the vehicle, gave the signal for instant departure.

I had obtained a glimpse of the countenance of my new companion, as by the aid of a dark lantern the drivers opened the carriage-door, and I was well-nigh persuaded that I recognized in him the domestic of the leader of this party, whom I had seen at his house in Brokenburn on a former occasion. To ascertain the truth of my suspicion, I asked him whether his name was not Cristal Nixon.

" What is other folks' names to you," he replied, gruffly, " who cannot tell your own father and mother ? "

" You know them, perhaps ? " I exclaimed, eagerly. " You know them ! and with that secret is connected the treatment which I am now receiving ? It must be so, for in my life have I never injured any one. Tell me the cause of my misfortunes, or rather, help me to my liberty, and I will reward you richly."

" Ay—ay," replied my keeper ; " but what use to give you liberty, who know nothing how to use it like a gentleman, but spend your time with Quakers and fiddlers, and such-like raff ? If I was your—hem, hem, hem ! "

Here Cristal stopped short, just on the point, as it appeared, when some information was likely to escape him. I urged him once more to be my friend, and promised him all the stock of money which I had about me, and it was not inconsiderable, if he would assist in my escape.

He listened, as if to a proposition which had some interest, and replied, but in a voice rather softer than before, " Ay, but men do not catch old birds with chaff, my master. Where have you got the rhino you are so flush of ? "

" I will give you earnest directly, and that in banknotes," said I ; but thrusting my hand into my side-pocket, I found my pocketbook was gone. I would have persuaded myself that it was only the numbness of my hands which prevented my finding it ; but Cristal Nixon, who bears in

his countenance that cynicism which is especially entertained with human misery, no longer suppressed his
laughter.

"Oh, ho ! my young master," he said ; "we have taken
good enough care you have not kept the means of bribing
poor folks' fidelity. What, man, they have souls as well as
other people, and to make them break trust is a deadly sin.
And as for me, young gentleman, if you would fill St. Mary's
kirk with gold, Cristal Nixon would mind it no more than
so many chucky-stones."

I would have persisted, were it but in hopes of his letting
drop that which it concerned me to know, but he cut off
further communication by desiring me to lean back in the
corner and go to sleep.

"Thou art cockbrained enough already," he added, "and
we shall have thy young pate addled entirely, if you do not
take some natural rest."

I did indeed require repose, if not slumber ; the draught
which I had taken continued to operate, and satisfied in my
own mind that no attempt on my life was designed, the fear
of instant death no longer combated the torpor which crept
over me ; I slept, and slept soundly, but still without refreshment.

When I awoke, I found myself extremely indisposed ; images of the past, and anticipations of the future, floated
confusedly through my brain. I perceived, however, that
my situation was changed, greatly for the better. I was in
a good bed, with the curtains drawn round it ; I heard the
lowered voice and cautious step of attendants, who seemed
to respect my repose ; it appeared as if I was in the hands
either of friends or of such as meant me no personal
harm.

I can give but an indistinct account of two or three
broken and feverish days which succeeded, but if they were
checkered with dreams and visions of terror, other and more
agreeable objects were also sometimes presented. Alan
Fairford will understand me when I say, I am convinced I
saw G. M. during this interval of oblivion. I had medical attendance, and was bled more than once. I also remember
a painful operation performed on my head, where I had
received a severe blow on the night of the riot. My hair
was cut short, and a bone of the skull examined, to discover if the cranium had received any injury.

On seeing the physician, it would have been natural to
have appealed to him on the subject of my confinement, and

I remember more than once attempting to do so. But the fever lay like a spell upon my tongue, and when I would have implored the doctor's assistance, I rambled from the subject, and spoke I know not what—nonsense. Some power, which I was unable to resist, seemed to impel me into a different course of conversation from what I intended, and though conscious, in some degree, of the failure, I could not mend it ; and resolved, therefore, to be patient, until my capacity of steady thought and expressions was restored to me with my ordinary health, which had sustained a severe shock from the vicissitudes to which I had been exposed.

CHAPTER V

Two or three days, perhaps more, perhaps less, had been spent in bed, where I was carefully attended, and treated, I believe, with as much judgment as the case required, and I was at length allowed to quit my bed, though not the chamber. I was now more able to make some observation on the place of my confinement.

The room, in appearance and furniture, resembled the best apartment in a farmer's house ; and the window, two stories high, looked into a back-yard, or court, filled with poultry. There were the usual domestic offices about this yard. I could distinguish the brewhouse and the barn, and I heard, from a more remote building, the lowing of the cattle and other rural sounds, announcing a large and well-stocked farm. These were sights and sounds qualified to dispel any apprehension of immediate violence. Yet the building seemed ancient and strong : a part of the roof was battlemented, and the walls were of great thickness ; lastly, 1 observed with some unpleasant sensations, that the windows of my chamber had been lately secured with iron stanchions, and that the servants who brought me victuals, or visited my apartment to render other menial offices, always locked the door when they retired.

The comfort and cleanness of my chamber were of true English growth, and such as I had rarely seen on the other side of the Tweed ; the very old wainscot which composed the floor and the paneling of the room was scrubbed with a degree of labor which the Scottish housewife rarely bestows on her most costly furniture.

The whole apartments appropriated to my use consisted of the bedroom, a small parlor adjacent, within which was a still smaller closet, having a narrow window, which seemed anciently to have been used as a shot-hole, admitting, indeed, a very moderate portion of light and air, but without its being possible to see anything from it except the blue sky, and that only by mounting on a chair. There were appearances of a separate entrance into this cabinet besides

that which communicated with the parlor, but it had been
recently built up, as I discovered by removing a piece of
tapestry which covered the fresh mason-work. I found
some of my clothes here, with linen and other articles, as well
as my writing-case, containing pen, ink, and paper, which
enables me, at my leisure (which, God knows, is undisturbed
enough), to make this record of my confinement. It may
be well believed, however, that I do not trust to the security
of the bureau, but carry the written sheets about my person,
so that I can only be deprived of them by actual violence.
I also am cautious to write in the little cabinet only, so that
I can hear any person approach me through the other apartments, and have time enough to put aside my journal before
they come upon me.

The servants, a stout country fellow and a very pretty
milkmaid-looking lass, by whom I am attended, seem of the
true Joan and Hodge school, thinking of little, and desire
ing nothing, beyond the very limited sphere of their own
duties or enjoyments, and having no curiosity whatever
about the affairs of others. Their behavior to me, in particular, is at the same time very kind and very provoking.
My table is abundantly supplied, and they seem anxious to
comply with my taste in that department. But whenever I
make inquiries beyond " What's for dinner ? " the brute of
a lad baffles me by his " anan " and his " dunne knaw," and,
if hard pressed, turns his back on me composedly and
leaves the room. The girl, too, pretends to be as simple as
he ; but an arch grin, which she cannot always suppress,
seems to acknowledge that she understands perfectly well
the game which she is playing, and is determined to keep
me in ignorance. Both of them, and the wench in particular, treat me as they would do a spoiled child, and never
directly refuse me anything which I ask, taking care, at the
same time, not to make their words good by effectually
granting my request. Thus, if I desire to go out, I am
promised by Dorcas that I shall walk in the park at night
and see the cows milked, just as she would propose such an
amusement to a child. But she takes care never to keep
her word, if it is in her power to do so.

In the meantime, there has stolen on me insensibly an
indifference to freedom, a carelessness about my situation,
for which I am unable to account, unless it be the consequence of weakness and loss of blood. I have read of men
who, immured as I am, have surprised the world by the
address with which they have successfully overcome the

most formidable obstacles to their escape ; and when I have
heard such anecdotes, I have said to myself that no one who
is possessed only of a fragment of freestone, or a rusty nail,
to grind down rivets and to pick locks, having his full leisure
to employ in the task, need continue the inhabitant of a
prison. Here, however, I sit day after day without a single
effort to effect my liberation.

Yet my inactivity is not the result of despondency, but
arises, in part at least, from feelings of a very different
cast. My story, long a mysterious one, seems now upon
the verge of some strange development ; and I feel a solemn
impression that I ought to wait the course of events, to
struggle against which is opposing my feeble efforts to the
high will of fate. Thou, my Alan, wilt treat as timidity
this passive acquiescence, which has sunk down on me like a
benumbing torpor ; but if thou hast remembered by what
visions my couch was haunted, and dost but think of the
probability that I am in the vicinity, perhaps under the
same roof with G. M., thou wilt acknowledge that other
feelings than pusillanimity have tended in some degree to
reconcile me to my fate.

Still I own it is unmanly to submit with patience to this
oppressive confinement. My heart rises against it, especially when I sit down to record my sufferings in this Journal ;
and I am determined, as the first step to my deliverance, to
have my letters sent to the post-house.

I am disappointed. When the girl Dorcas, upon whom
I had fixed for a messenger, heard me talk of sending a
letter, she willingly offered her services, and received the
crown which I gave her (for my purse had not taken flight
with the more valuable contents of my pocketbook) with a
smile which showed her whole set of white teeth.

But when, with the purpose of gaining some intelligence
respecting my present place of abode, I asked to which
post town she was to send or carry the letter, a stolid " anan "
showed me she was either ignorant of the nature of a post-
office, or that, for the present, she chose to seem so.
·" Simpleton ! " I said, with some sharpness.

" O Lord, sir ! " answered the girl, turning pale, which
they always do when I show any sparks of anger. " Don't
put yourself in a passion ! I'll put the letter in the post."

" What ! and not know the name of the post-town ? "
said I, out of patience. " How on earth do you propose to
manage that ? "

"La you there, good master. What need you frighten a poor girl that is no schollard, bating what she learned at the charity school of St. Bees?"

"Is St. Bees far from this place, Dorcas? Do you send your letters there?" said I, in a manner as insinuating, and yet careless as I could assume.

"St. Bees! La, who but a madman—begging your honor's pardon—it's a matter of twenty years since fader lived at St. Bees, which is twenty, or forty, or I dunna know not how many miles from this part to the west, on the coast-side; and I would not have left St. Bees, but that fader——"

"Oh, the devil take your father!" replied I.

To which she answered, "Nay, but thof your honor be a little how-come-so, you shouldn't damn folks' faders; and I won't stand to it, for one."

"Oh, I beg you a thousand pardons. I wish your father no ill in the world—he was a very honest man in his way."

"*Was* an honest man!" she exclaimed; for the Cumbrians are, it would seem, like their neighbors the Scotch, ticklish on the point of ancestry. "He *is* a very honest man, as ever led nag with halter on head to Staneshaw Bank Fair. Honest! He is a horse-couper."

"Right—right," I replied; "I know it—I have heard of your father—as honest as any horse-couper of them all. Why, Dorcas, I mean to buy a horse of him."

"Ah, your honor," sighed Dorcas, "he is the man to serve your honor well, if ever you should get round again —or, thof you were a bit off the hooks, he would no more cheat you than——"

"Well—well, we will deal, my girl, you may depend on't. But tell me now, were I to give you a letter, what would you do to get it forward?"

"Why, put it into Squire's own bag that hangs in hall," answered poor Dorcas. "What else could I do? He sends it to Brampton, or to Carloisle, or where it pleases him, once a week, and that gate."

"Ah!" said I; "and I suppose your sweetheart John carries it?"

"Noa—disn't now; and Jan is no sweetheart of mine, ever since he danced at his mother's feast with Kitty Rutledge, and let me sit still—that a did."

"It was most abominable in Jan, and what I could never have thought of him," I replied.

"O, but a did though—a let me sit still on my seat a did."

"Well—well, my pretty May, you will get a handsomer fellow than Jan. Jan's not the fellow for you, I see that."

"Noa—noa," answered the damsel ; "but he is weel aneugh for a' that, mon. But I carena a button for him ; for there is the miller's son, that suitored me last Appleby Fair, when I went wi' my oncle, is a gway canny lad as you will see in the sunshine."

"Ay, a fine stout fellow. Do you think he would carry my letter to Carlisle ?"

"To Carloisle ! 'Twould be all his life is worth ; he maun wait on clap and hopper as they say. Od, his father would brain him if he went to Carloisle, bating to wrestling for the belt or sic-loike. But I ha' more bachelors than him ; there is the schoolmaster can write almaist as weel as tou canst, mon."

"Then he is the very man to take charge of a letter ; he knows the trouble of writing one."

"Ay, marry does he, an tou comest to that, mon ; only it takes him four hours to write as mony lines. Tan, it is a great round hand loike, that one can read easily, and not loike your honor's that are like midge's taes. But for ganging to Carloisle, he's dead foundered, mon, as cripple as Eckie's mear."

"In the name of God," said I, "how is it that you propose to get my letter to the post ?"

"Why, just to put it into Squire's bag loike," reiterated Dorcas ; "he sends it by Cristal Nixon to post, as you call it, when such is his pleasure."

Here I was then, not much edified by having obtained a list of Dorcas's bachelors ; and by finding myself with respect to any information which I desired just exactly at the point where I set out. It was of consequence to me, however, to accustom the girl to converse with me familiarly. If she did so, she could not always be on her guard, and something, I thought, might drop from her which I could turn to advantage.

"Does not the Squire usually look into his letter-bag, Dorcas ?" said I, with as much indifference as I could assume.

"That a does," said Dorcas ; "and a threw out a letter of mine to Raff Miller, because a said——"

"Well—well, I won't trouble him with mine," said I, "Dorcas ; but, instead, I will write to himself, Dorcas. But how shall I address him ?"

"Anan ?" was again Dorcas's resource.

" I mean, how is he called ? What is his name ? "

" Sure your honor should know best," said Dorcas.

" I know ? The devil ! You drive me beyond patience."

" Noa—Noa ! donna your honor go beyond patience— donna ye now," implored the wench. " And for his neame, they say he has mair nor ane in Westmoreland and on the Scottish side. But he is but seldom wi' us, excepting in the cocking-season ; and then we just call him Squoire loike ; and so do my measter and dame."

" And is he here at present ? " said I.

" Not he—not he ; he is a buck-hoonting, as they tell me, somewhere up the Patterdale way ; but he comes and gangs like a flap of a whirlwind, or sic-loike."

I broke off the conversation, after forcing on Dorcas a little silver to buy ribbons, with which she was so much delighted, that she exclaimed, " God ! Cristal Nixon may say his worst on thee, but thou art a civil gentleman for all him, and a quoit man wi' woman-folk loike."

There is no sense in being too quiet with women folk, so I added a kiss with my crown-piece ; and I cannot help thinking that I have secured a partisan in Dorcas. At least she blushed, and pocketed her little compliment with one hand, while, with the other, she adjusted her cherry-colored ribbons, a little disordered by the struggle it cost me to attain the honor of a salute."

As she unlocked the door to leave the apartment, she turned back, and looking on me with a strong expression of compassion, added the remarkable words, " La—be'st mad or no, thou'se a mettled lad, after all."

There was something very ominous in the sound of these farewell words, which seemed to afford me a clue to the pretext under which I was detained in confinement. My demeanor was probably insane enough, while I was agitated at once by the frenzy incident to the fever and the anxiety arising from my extraordinary situation. But is it possible they can now establish any cause for confining me, arising out of the state of my mind ? "

If this be really the pretext under which I am restrained from my liberty, nothing but the sedate correctness of my conduct can remove the prejudices which these circumstances may have excited in the minds of all who have approached me during my illness. I have heard—dreadful thought !—of men who, for various reasons, have been trepanned into the custody of the keepers of private madhouses, and whose brain, after years of misery, became at length unsettled, through irresistible sympathy with the wretched beings among whom they were classed. This shall not be my case, if, by strong internal resolution, it is in human nature to avoid the action of exterior and contagious sympathies.

Meantime, I sat down to compose and arrange my thoughts for my purposed appeal to my jailer—so I must call him—whom I addressed in the following manner; having at length, and after making several copies, found language to qualify the sense of resentment which burned in the first draughts of my letter, and endeavored to assume a tone more conciliating. I mentioned the two occasions on which he had certainly saved my life, when at the utmost peril; and I added that, whatever was the purpose of the restraint now practised on me, as I was given to understand, by his authority, it could not certainly be with any view to ultimately injuring me. He might, I said, have mistaken me for some other person; and I gave him what account I could of my situation and education, to correct such an error. I supposed it next possible that he might think me too weak for traveling, and not capable of taking care of myself; and I begged to assure him that I was restored to perfect health, and quite able to endure the fatigue of a journey. Lastly, I reminded him in firm though measured terms that the restraint which I sustained was an illegal one, and highly punishable by the laws which protect the liberties of the subject. I ended by demanding that he would take me before a magistrate; or, at least, that he would favor me with a personal interview, and explain his meaning with regard to me.

Perhaps this letter was expressed in a tone too humble for the situation of an injured man, and I am inclined to think so when I again recapitulate its tenor. But what could I do? I was in the power of one whose passions seem as violent as his means of gratifying them appear unbounded. I had reason, too, to believe—this to thee, Alan—that all his family did not approve of the violence of his conduct towards me; my object, in fine, was freedom, and who would not sacrifice much to attain it?

I had no means of addressing my letter excepting, "For the Squire's own hand." He could be at no great distance, for in the course of twenty-four hours I received an answer. It was addressed to Darsie Latimer, and contained these words: "You have demanded an interview with me. You have required to be carried before a magistrate. Your first wish shall be granted, perhaps the second also. Meanwhile, be assured that you are a prisoner for the time by competent authority, and that such authority is supported by adequate power. Beware, therefore, of struggling with a force sufficient to crush you, but abandon yourself to that train of events by which we are both swept along, and which it is impossible that either of us can resist."

These mysterious words were without signature of any kind, and left me nothing more important to do than to prepare myself for the meeting which they promised. For that purpose I must now break off, and make sure of the manuscript—so far as I can, in my present condition, be sure of anything—by concealing it within the lining of my coat, so as not to be found without strict search.

13

CHAPTER VI

THE important intervie v expected at the conclusion of my
last took place sooner than I had calculated ; for the very
day I received the letter, and just when my dinner was
finished, the Squire, or whatever he is called, entered the
room so suddenly that I almost thought I beheld an apparition. The figure of this man is peculiarly noble and
stately, and his voice has that deep fulness of accent which
implies unresisted authority. I had risen involuntarily as he
entered ; we gazed on each other for a moment in silence,
which was at length broken by my visitor.

" You have desired to see me," he said. "I am here ;
if you have aught to say, let me hear it ; my time is too
brief to be consumed in childish dumb-show."

"I would ask of you," said I, " by what authority I am
detained in this place of confinement, and for what
purpose ?"

"I have told you already," said he, "that my authority
is sufficient, and my power equal to it; this is all which it
is necessary for you at present to know.

" Every British subject has a right to know why he suffers
restraint," I replied ; "nor can he be deprived of liberty
without a legal warrant. Show me that by which you confine me thus."

" You shall see more," he said ; "you shall see the magistrate by whom it is granted, and that without a moment's
delay."

This sudden proposal fluttered and alarmed me ; I felt,
nevertheless, that I had the right cause, and resolved to plead
it boldly, although I could well have desired a little further
time for preparation. He turned, however, threw open the
door of the apartment, and commanded me to follow him.
I felt some inclination, when I crossed the threshold of my
prison chamber, to have turned and run for it ; but I knew
not where to find the stairs ; had reason to think the outer
doors would be secured ; and, to conclude, so soon as I had
quitted the room to follow the proud step of my conductor,

I observed that I was dogged by Cristal Nixon, who suddenly
appeared within two paces of me, and with whose great personal strength, independent of the assistance he might have
received from his master, I saw no chance of contending. I
therefore followed, unresistingly and in silence, along one or
two passages of much greater length than consisted with the
ideas I had previously entertained of the size of the house.
At length a door was flung open, and we entered a large,
old-fashioned parlor, having colored glass in the windows,
oaken paneling on the wall, a huge grate, in which a large
fagot or two smoked under an arched chimney-piece of
stone, which bore some armorial device, whilst the walls
were adorned with the usual number of heroes in armor, with
large wigs instead of helmets, and ladies in sacques, smelling
to nosegays.

Behind a long table, on which were several books, sat a
smart, underbred-looking man, wearing his own hair tied in
a club, and who, from the quire of paper laid before him,
and the pen which he handled at my entrance, seemed prepared to officiate as clerk. As I wish to describe these
persons as accurately as possible, I may add, he wore a dark-
colored coat, corduroy breeches, and spatterdashes. At the
upper end of the same table, in an ample easy-chair, covered
with black leather, reposed a fat personage, about fifty years
old, who either was actually a country justice or was well
selected to represent such a character. His leathern breeches
were faultless in make, his jockey boots spotless in the var-
nish, and a handsome and flourishing pair of boot-garters, as
they are called, united the one part of his garments to the
other ; in fine, a richly-laced scarlet waistcoat, and a purple
coat, set off the neat though corpulent figure of the little
man, and threw an additional bloom upon his plethoric aspect.
I suppose he had dined, for it was two hours past noon,
and he was amusing himself, and aiding digestion, with a
pipe of tobacco. There was an air of importance in his
manner which corresponded to the rural dignity of his exterior, and a habit which he had of throwing out a number of
interjectional sounds, uttered with a strange variety of into-
nation, running from bass up to treble in a very extraordinary manner, or breaking off his sentences with a whiff
of his pipe, seemed adopted to give an air of thought and
mature deliberation to his opinions and decisions. Notwithstanding all this, Alan, it might be "dooted," as our old
professor used to say, whether the Justice was anything more
than an ass. Certainly, besides a great deference for the

legal opinion of his clerk, which might be quite according to the order of things, he seemed to be wonderfully under the command of his brother squire, if squire either of them were, and indeed much more than was consistent with so much assumed consequence of his own.

"Ho—ha—ay—so—so. Hum—humph—this is the young man, I suppose. Hum—ay—seems sickly. Young gentleman, you may sit down."

I used the permission given, for I had been much more reduced by my illness than I was aware of, and felt myself really fatigued, even by the few paces I had walked, joined to the agitation I suffered.

"And your name, young man, is—humph—ay—ah—what is it?"

"Darsie Latimer."

"Right—ay—humph—very right. Darsie Latimer is the very thing—ha—ay—where do you come from?"

"From Scotland, sir," I replied.

"A native of Scotland—a—humph—eh—how is it?"

"I am an Englishman by birth, sir."

"Right—ay—yes, you are so. But pray, Mr. Darsie Latimer, have you always been called by that name, or have you any other? Nick, write down his answers, Nick."

"As far as I remember, I never bore any other," was my answer.

"How, no? Well, I should not have thought so. Hey, neighbor, would you?"

Here he looked towards the other squire, who had thrown himself into a chair; and with his legs stretched out before him, and his arms folded on his bosom, seemed carelessly attending to what was going forward. He answered the appeal of the Justice by saying, that perhaps the young man's memory did not go back to a very early period.

"Ah—eh—ha—you hear the gentleman. Pray, how far may your memory be pleased to run back to—umph?"

"Perhaps, sir, to the age of three years, or a little farther."

"And will you presume to say, sir," said the Squire, drawing himself suddenly erect in his seat, and exerting the strength of his powerful voice, "that you *then* bore your present name?"

I was startled at the confidence with which this question was put, and in vain rummaged my memory for the means of replying. "At least," I said, "I always remember being called Darsie ; children, at that early age seldom get more than their Christian name."

"O, I thought so," he replied, and again stretched himself on his seat, in the same lounging posture as before.

"So you were called Darsie in your infancy," said the Justice ; "and hum—ay—when did you first take the name of Latimer ?"

"I did not take it, sir ; it was given to me."

"I ask you," said the lord of the mansion, but with less severity in his voice than formerly, "whether you can remember that you were ever called Latimer until you had that name given you in Scotland ?"

"I will be candid. I cannot recollect an instance that I was so called when in England, but neither can I recollect when the name was first given me ; and if anything is to be founded on these queries and my answers, I desire my early childhood may be taken into consideration."

"Hum—ay—yes," said the Justice ; "all that requires consideration shall be duly considered. Young man—eh—I beg to know the name of your father and mother ?"

This was galling a wound that has festered for years, and I did not endure the question so patiently as those which preceded it ; but replied, "I demand, in my turn, to know if I am before an English justice of the peace ?"

"His worship, Squire Foxley of Foxley Hall, has been of the quorum these twenty years," said Master Nicholas.

"Then he ought to know, or you, sir, as his clerk, should inform him," said I, "that I am the complainer in this case, and that my complaint ought to be heard before I am subjected to cross-examination."

"Humph—boy—what, ay—there is something in that, neighbor," said the poor justice, who, blown about by every wind of doctrine, seemed desirous to attain the sanction of his brother squire.

"I wonder at you, Foxley," said his firm-minded acquaintance ; "how can you render the young man justice unless you know who he is ?"

"Ha—yes—egad that's true," said Mr. Justice Foxley ; "and now—looking into the matter more closely—there is, eh, upon the whole, nothing at all in what he says ; so, sir, you must tell your father's name and surname."

"It is out of my power, sir ; they are not known to me, since you must needs know so much of my private affairs."

The Justice collected a great afflatus in his cheeks, which

puffed them up like those of a Dutch cherub, while his eyes
seemed flying out of his head, from the effort with which he
retained his breath. He then blew it forth with—' Whew !
hoom—poof—ha ! not know your parents, youngster ? Then
I must commit you for a vagrant, I warrant you. *Omne
ignotum pro terribili,* as we used to say at Appleby school ;
that is, every one that is not known to the justice is a rogue
and a vagabond. Ha ! ay, you may sneer, sir ; but I question
if you would have known the meaning of that Latin unless I
had told you."

I acknowledged myself obliged for a new edition of the
adage, and an interpretation which I could never have
reached alone and unassisted. I then proceeded to state my
case with greater confidence. The Justice was an ass, that
was clear ; but it was scarcely possible he could be so utterly
ignorant as not known what was necessary in so plain a case
as mine. I therefore informed him of the riot which had
been committed on the Scottish side of the Solway Firth ;
explained how I came to be placed in my present situation ;
and requested of his worship to set me at liberty. I pleaded
my cause with as much earnestness as I could, casting an eye
from time to time upon the opposite party, who seemed entirely indifferent to all the animation with which I accused
him.

As for the Justice, when at length I had ceased, as really
not knowing what more to say in a case so very plain, he
replied, " Ho—ay—ay—yes—wonderful ! And so this is all
the gratitude you show to this good gentleman for the great
charge and trouble he hath had with respect to and concerning of you ?'

" He saved my life, sir, I acknowledge, on one occasion certainly, and most probably on two ; but his having done so
gives him no right over my person. I am not, however, asking for any punishment or revenge ; on the contrary, I am
content to part friends with the gentleman, whose motives I
am unwilling to suppose are bad, though his actions have
been, towards me, unauthorized and violent."

This moderation, Alan, thou wilt comprehend, was not entirely dictated by my feelings towards the individual of whom
I complained ; there were other reasons, in which regard for
him had little share. It seemed, however, as if the mildness
with which I pleaded my cause had more effect upon him
than anything I had yet said. He was moved to the point
of being almost out of countenance ; and took snuff repeatedly, as if to gain time to stifle some degree of emotion.

But on Justice Foxley, on whom my eloquence was particularly designed to make impression, the result was much less favorable. He consulted in a whisper with Mr. Nicholas, his clerk, pshawed, hemmed, and elevated his eyebrows, as if in scorn of my supplication. At length, having apparently made up his mind, he leaned back in his chair and smoked his pipe with great energy, with a look of defiance, designed to make me aware that all my reasoning was lost on him.

At length when I stopped, more from lack of breath than want of argument, he opened his oracular jaws and made the following reply, interrupted by his usual interjectional ejaculations, and by long volumes of smoke :—" Hem—ay—eh—poof. And, youngster, do you think Matthew Foxley, who has been one of the quorum for these twenty years, is to be come over with such trash as would hardly cheat an apple-woman? Poof--poof—eh ! Why, man—eh—dost thou know the charge is not a bailable matter, and that—hum—ay—the greatest man—poof—the Baron of Graystock himself, must stand committed ? And yet you pretend to have been kidnapped by this gentleman, and robbed of property, and what not ; and—eh—poof—you would persuade me all you want is to get away from him ? I do believe—eh—that it *is* all you want. Therefore, as you are a sort of a slipstring gentleman, and—ay—hum—a kind of idle apprentice, and something cockbrained withal, as the honest folks of the house tell me, why, you must e'en remain under custody of your guardian till your coming of age, or my Lord Chancellor's warrant, shall give you the management of your own affairs, which, if you can gather your brains again, you will even then not be—ay—hem—poof—in particular haste to assume."

The time occupied by his worship's hums, and haws, and puffs of tobacco smoke, together with the slow and pompous manner in which he spoke, gave me a minute's space to collect my ideas, dispersed as they were by the extraordinary purport of this annunciation.

" I cannot conceive, sir," I replied, " by what singular tenure this person claims my obedience as a guardian ; it is a barefaced imposture : I never in my life saw him until I came unhappily to this country, about four weeks since."

" Ay, sir,—we—eh—know, and are aware—that—poof—you do not like to hear some folks' names ; and that—eh—you understand me—there are things, and sounds, and matters, conversation about names, and such-like, which put you off the hooks—which I have no humor to witness. Nevertheless, Mr. Darsie—or—poof—Mr. Darsie Latimer—or—

poof, poof—eh—ay—Mr. Darsie without the Latimer—you have acknowledged as much to-day as assures me you will best be disposed of under the honorable care of my friend here ; all your confessions—besides that—poof—eh—I know him to be a most responsible person—a—hay—ay—most responsible and honorable person. Can you deny this ?"

"I know nothing of him," I repeated, "not even his name ; and I have not, as I told you, seen him in the course of my whole life till a few weeks since."

"Will you swear to that ?" said the singular man, who seemed to await the result of this debate, secure as a rattlesnake is of the prey which has once felt its fascination. And while he said these words in a deep undertone, he withdrew his chair a little behind that of the Justice, so as to be unseen by him or his clerk, who sat upon the same side ; while he bent on me a frown so portentous that no one who has witnessed the look can forget it during the whole of his life. The furrows of the brows above the eyes became livid and almost black, and were bent into a semicircular, or rather elliptical, form above the junction of the eyebrows. I had heard such a look described in an old tale of *diablerie* which it was my chance to be entertained with not long since, when this deep and gloomy contortion of the frontal muscles was not unaptly described as forming the representation of a small horseshoe.

The tale, when told, awakened a dreadful vision of infancy, which the withering and blighting look now fixed on me again forced on my recollection, but with much more vivacity. Indeed, I was so much surprised, and, I must add, terrified, at the vague ideas which were awakened in my mind by this fearful sign, that I kept my eyes fixed on the face in which it was exhibited, as on a frightful vision ; until, passing his handkerchief a moment across his countenance, this mysterious man relaxed at once the look which had for me something so appalling. "The young man will no longer deny that he has seen me before," said he to the Justice, in a tone of complacency ; "and I trust he will now be reconciled to my temporary guardianship, which may end better for him than he expects."

"Whatever I expect," I replied, summoning my scattered recollections together, "I see I am neither to expect justice nor protection from this gentleman, whose office it is to render both to the lieges. For you, sir, how strangely you have wrought yourself into the fate of an unhappy young man, or what interest you can pretend in me, you yourself

only can explain. That I have seen you before is certain ;
for none can forget the look with which you seem to have the
power of blighting those upon whom you cast it."

The Justice seemed not very easy under this hint. "Ho !—
ay," he said ; "it is time to be going, neighbor. I have a
many miles to ride, and I care not to ride darkling in these
parts. You and I, Mr. Nicholas, must be jogging."

The·Justice fumbled with his gloves, in endeavoring to
draw them on hastily, and Mr. Nicholas bustled to get his
greatcoat and whip. Their landlord endeavored to detain
them, and spoke of supper and beds. Both, pouring forth
many thanks for his invitation, seemed as if they would
much rather not ; and Mr. Justice Foxley was making a score
of apologies, with at least a hundred cautionary hems and
eh-ehs, when the girl Dorcas burst into the room, and announced a gentleman on justice business.

"What gentleman ? and whom does he want ? "

"He is cuome post on his ten toes," said the wench, "and
on justice business to his worship loike. I'se uphald him a
gentleman, for he speaks as good Latin as the schulemeaster ;
but, lack-a-day ! he has gotten a queer mop of a wig."

The gentleman thus announced and described, bounced
into the room. But I have already written as much as fills
a sheet of my paper, and my singular embarrassments press
so hard on me that I have matter to fill another from what
followed the intrusion of, my dear Alan, your crazy client—
Poor Peter Peebles !

CHAPTER VII

Sheet 2

I HAVE rarely in my life, till the last alarming days, known what it was to sustain a moment's real sorrow. What I called such was, I am now well convinced, only the weariness of mind which, having nothing actually present to complain of, turns upon itself, and becomes anxious about the past and the future; those periods with which human life has so little connection, that Scripture itself hath said, " Sufficient for the day is the evil thereof."

If, therefore, I have sometimes abused prosperity, by murmuring at my unknown birth and uncertain rank in society, I will make amends by bearing my present real adversity with patience and courage, and, if I can, even with gaiety. What can they—dare they, do to me? Foxley, I am persuaded, is a real justice of peace and country gentleman of estate, though (wonderful to tell!) he is an ass notwithstanding; and his functionary in the drab coat must have a shrewd guess at the consequences of being accessary to an act of murder or kidnapping. Men invite not such witnesses to deeds of darkness. I have also—Alan, I *have* hopes, arising out of the family of the oppressor himself. I am encouraged to believe that G. M. is likely again to enter on the field. More I dare not here say; nor must I drop a hint which another eye than thine might be able to construe. Enough, my feelings are lighter than they have been; and though fear and wonder are still around me, they are unable entirely to overcloud the horizon.

Even when I saw the spectral form of the old scarecrow of the Parliament house rush into the apartment where I had undergone so singular an examination, I thought of thy connection with him, and could almost have parodied Lear—

Death! . . . nothing could have thus subdued nature
To such a lowness but his "learned lawyers."

He was e'en as we have seen him of yore, Alan, when, rather to keep thee company than to follow my own bent, I formerly frequented the halls of justice. The only addition to his dress, in the capacity of a traveler, was a pair of boots, that seemed as if they might have seen the field of Sheriff Moor ; so large and heavy that, tied as they were to the creature's wearied hams with large bunches of worsted tape of various colors, they looked as if he had been dragging them along, either for a wager or by way of penance.

Regardless of the surprised looks of the party on whom he thus intruded himself, Peter blundered into the middle of the apartment, with his head charged like a ram's in the act of butting, and saluted them thus :—

"Gude day to ye—gude day to your honors. Is't here they sell the fugie warrants ? "

I observed that, on his entrance, my friend—or enemy— drew himself back, and placed himself as if he would rather avoid attracting the observation of the newcomer. I did the same myself, as far as I was able ; for I thought it likely that Mr. Peebles might recognize me, and indeed I was too frequently among the group of young juridical aspirants who used to amuse themselves by putting cases for Peter's solution, and playing him worse tricks ; yet I was uncertain whether I had better avail myself of our acquaintance to have the advantage, such as it might be, of his evidence before the magistrate, or whether to make him, if possible, bearer of a letter which might procure me more effectual assistance. I resolved, therefore, to be guided by circumstances, and to watch carefully that nothing might escape me. I drew back as far as I could and even reconnoitred the door and passage, to consider whether absolute escape might not be practicable. But there paraded Cristal Nixon, whose little black eyes, sharp as those of a basilisk, seemed, the instant when they encountered mine, to penetrate my purpose.

I sat down, as much out of sight of all parties as I could, and listened to the dialogue which followed—a dialogue how much more interesting to me than any I could have conceived in which Peter Peebles was to be one of the *dramatis personæ!*

"Is it here where ye sell warrants—the fugies, ye ken ? " said Peter.

"Hey—eh—what ? " said Justice Foxley ; "what the devil does the fellow mean ? What would you have a warrant for ? "

"It is to apprehend a young lawyer that is *in meditatione fugæ;* for he has ta'en my memorial and pleaded my cause, and a good fee I gave him, and as muckle brandy as he could drink that day at his father's house—he loes the brandy ower weel for sae youthful a creature."

"And what has this drunken young dog of a lawyer done to you, that you are come to me—eh—ha? Has he robbed you? Not unlikely, if he be a lawyer—eh—Nick—ha?" said Justice Foxley.

"He has robbed me of himself, sir," answered Peter—"of his help, comfort, aid, maintenance, and assistance, whilk, as a counsel to a client, he is bound to yield me *ratione officii*—that is it, ye see. He has pouched my fee, and drucken a mutchkin of brandy, and now he's ower the march, and left my cause, half won, half lost—as dead a heat as e'er was run ower the back-sands. Now, I was advised by some cunning laddies that are used to crack a bit law wi' me in the House, that the best thing I could do was to take heart o' grace and set out after him; so I have taken post on my ain shanks, forbye a cast in a cart, or the like. I got wind of him in Dumfries, and now I have run him ower to the English side, and I want a fugie warrant against him."

How did my heart throb at this information, dearest Alan! Thou art near me, then, and I well know with what kind purpose; thou hast abandoned all to fly to my assistance; and no wonder that, knowing thy friendship and faith, thy sound sagacity and persevering disposition, 'my bosom's lord should now sit lightly on his throne'; that gaiety should almost involuntarily hover on my pen; and that my heart should beat like that of a general, responsive to the drums of his advancing ally, without whose help the battle must have been lost.

I did not suffer myself to be startled by this joyous surprise, but continued to bend my strictest attention to what followed among this singular party. That Poor Peter Peebles had been put upon this wildgoose chase by some of his juvenile advisers in the Parliament House he himself had intimated; but he spoke with much confidence, and the Justice, who seemed to have some secret apprehension of being put to trouble in the matter, and, as sometimes occurs on the English frontier, a jealousy lest the superior acuteness of their Northern neighbors might overreach their own simplicity, turned to his clerk with a perplexed countenance.

"Eh—oh—Nick—d—n thee. Hast thou got nothing to say? This is more Scots law, I take it, and more Scotsmen. (Here he cast a side-glance at the owner of the mansion, and winked to his clerk.) I would Solway were as deep as it is wide, and we had then some chance of keeping of them out."

Nicholas conversed an instant aside with the supplicant, and then reported—

"The man wants a Border warrant, I think ; but they are only granted for debt—now he wants one to catch a lawyer."

"And what for no ?" answered Peter Peebles, doggedly— "what for no, I'll be glad to ken ? If a day laborer refuses to work, ye'll grant a warrant to gar him do out his daurg ; if a wench quean rin away from her hairst, ye'll send her back to her heuck again ; if sae mickle as a collier or a salter* make a moonlight flitting, ye will cleek him by the back-spaul in a minute of time, and yet the damage canna amount to mair than a creelfu' of coals, and a forpit or twa of saut ; and here is a chield taks leg from his engagement, and damages me to the tune of sax thousand punds sterling ; that is, three thousand that I should win and three thousand mair that I am like to lose ; and you that ca' yoursell a justice canna help a poor man to catch the rinaway ? A bonny like justice I am like to get amang ye !"

"The fellow must be drunk," said the clerk.

"Black-fasting from all but sin," replied the supplicant. "I havena had mair than a mouthful of cauld water since I passed the Border, and deil a ane of ye is like to say to me, ' Dog, will ye drink ?'"

The Justice seemed moved by this appeal. "Hem—tush, man," replied he ; "thou speak'st to us as if thou wert in presence of one of thine own beggarly justices ; get downstairs—get something to eat, man—with permission of my friend to make so free in his house—and a mouthful to drink, and I will warrant we get ye such justice as will please ye."

"I winna refuse your neighborly offer," said Poor Peter Peebles, making his bow ; "muckle grace be wi' your honor, and wisdom to guide ye in this extraordinary cause."

When I saw Peter Peebles about to retire from the room, I could not forbear an effort to obtain from him such evidence as might give me some credit with the Justice. I stepped forward, therefore, and saluting him, asked him if he remembered me.

* See Note 25.

After a stare or two, and a long pinch of snuff, recollection seemed suddenly to dawn on Peter Peebles. "Recollect ye!" he said: "by my troth do I. Haud him a grip, gentleman!—constables, keep him fast! Where that ill-deedy hempy is, ye are sure that Alan Fairford is not far off. Haud him fast, Master Constable; I charge ye wi' him, for I am mista'en if he is not at the bottom of this rinaway business. He was aye getting the silly callant Alan awa' wi gigs, and horse, and the like of that, to Roslin, and Prestonpans, and a' the idle gates he could think of. He's a rinaway apprentice, that ane."

"Mr. Peebles," I said, "do not do me wrong. I am sure you can say no harm of me justly, but can satisfy these gentlemen, if you will, that I am a student of law in Edinburgh—Darsie Latimer by name."

"Me satisfy! how can I satisfy the gentlemen," answered Peter, "that am sae far from being satisfied mysell? I ken naething about your name, and can only testify, *nihil novit in causa.*"

"A pretty witness you have brought forward in your favor," said Mr. Foxley. "But—ha—ay—I'll ask him a question or two. Pray, friend, will you take your oath to this youth being a runaway apprentice?"

"Sir," said Peter, "I will make oath to onything in reason; when a case comes to my oath it's a won cause. But I am in some haste to prie your worship's good cheer;" for Peter had become much more respectful in his demeanor towards the Justice since he had heard some intimation of dinner.

"You shall have—eh—hum—ay—a bellyful, if it be possible to fill it. First let me know if this young man be really what he pretends. Nick, make his affidavit."

"Ou, he is just a wud harum-scarum creature, that wad never take to his studies; daft, sir—clean daft."

"Deft!" said the Justice; "what d'ye mean by deft—eh?"

"Just fifish," replied Peter—"wowf—a wee bit by the East Nook or sae; it's a common case: the tae half of the warld thinks the tither daft. I have met with folk in my day that thought I was daft mysell; and, for my part, I think our Court of Session clean daft, that have had the great cause of Peebles against Plainstanes before them for this score of years, and have never been able to ding the bottom out of it yet."

"I cannot make out a word of his cursed brogue," said the

Cumbrian justice; "can you, neighbor—eh? What can he mean by 'deft'?"

"He means 'mad,' said the party appealed to, thrown off his guard by impatience of this protracted discussion.

"Ye have it—ye have it," said Peter; "that is, not clean skivie, but——"

Here he stopped, and fixed his eye on the person he addressed with an air of joyful recognition. "Ay—ay, Mr. Herries of Birrenswork, is this your ainsell in blood and bane? I thought ye had been hanged at Kennington Common, or Hairiebie, or some of these places, after the bonny ploy ye made in the Forty-five."

"I believe you are mistaken, friend," said Herries, sternly, with whose name and designation I was thus made unexpectedly acquainted.

"The deil a bit," answered the undaunted Peter Peebles. "I mind ye weel, for ye lodged in my house the great year of forty-five, for a great year it was; the Grand Rebellion broke out, and my cause—the great cause—Peebles against Plainstanes, *et per contra*—was called in the beginning of the winter session, and would have been heard, but that there was a surcease of justice, with your plaids, and your piping, and your nonsense."

"I tell you, fellow," said Herries, yet more fiercely, "you have confused me with some of the other furniture of your crazy pate."

"Speak like a gentleman, sir," answered Peebles: "these are not legal phrases, Mr. Herries of Birrenswork. Speak in form of law, or I sall bid ye gude-day, sir. I have nae pleasure in speaking to proud folk, though I am willing to answer onything in a legal way; so if you are for a crack about auld langsyne, and the splores that you and Captain Redgimlet used to breed in my house, and the girded cask of brandy that ye drank and ne'er thought of paying for it—not that I minded it muckle in thae days, though I have felt a lack of it sinsyne—why, I will waste an hour on ye at ony time. And where is Captain Redgimlet now? He was a wild chap, like yoursell, though they are nae sae keen after you poor bodies for these some years bye-gane: the heading and hanging is weel ower now—awful job—awful job—will ye try my sneeshing?"

He concluded his desultory speech by thrusting out his large bony paw, filled with a Scottish mull of huge dimensions, which Herries, who had been standing like one petrified by the assurance of this unexpected address, rejected with a contemptuous motion of his hand, which spilled some of the contents of the box.

"Aweel—aweel," said Peter Peebles, totally unabashed by the repulse, "e'en as ye like, a wilful man maun hae his way; but," he added, stooping down and endeavoring to gather the spilt snuff from the polished floor, "I canna afford to lose my sneeshing for a' that ye are gumple-foisted wi' me."

My attention had been keenly awakened during this extraordinary and unexpected scene. I watched, with as much attention as my own agitation permitted me to command, the effect produced on the parties concerned. It was evident that our friend, Peter Peebles, had unwarily let out something which altered the sentiments of Justice Foxley and his clerk towards Mr. Herries, with whom, until he was known and acknowledged under that name, they had appeared to be so intimate. They talked with each other aside, looked at a paper or two which the clerk selected from the contents of a huge black pocketbook, and seemed, under the influence of fear and uncertainty, totally at a loss what line of conduct to adopt.

Herries made a different and a far more interesting figure. However little Peter Peebles might resemble the angel Ithuriel, the appearance of Herries, his high and scornful demeanor, vexed at what seemed detection, yet fearless of the consequence, and regarding the whispering magistrate and his clerk with looks in which contempt predominated over anger or anxiety, bore, in my opinion, no slight resemblance to

> The regal port
> And faded splendor wan

with which the poet has invested the detected King of the Powers of the Air.

As he glanced round, with a look which he had endeavored to compose to haughty indifference, his eye encountered mine, and, I thought, at the first glance sunk beneath it. But he instantly rallied his natural spirit, and returned me one of those extraordinary looks by which he could contort so strangely the wrinkles on his forehead. I started; but, angry at myself for my pusillanimity, I answered him by a look of the same kind, and, catching the reflection of my countenance in a large antique mirror which stood before me, I started again at the real or imaginary resemblance which my countenance, at that moment, bore to that of Herries. Surely my fate is somehow strangely interwoven with that

of this mysterious individual. I had no time at present to
speculate upon the subject, for the subsequent conversation
demanded all my attention.

The Justice addressed Herries, after a pause of about five
minutes, in which all parties seemed at some loss how to proceed. He spoke with embarrassment, and his faltering voice,
and the long intervals which divided his sentences, seemed
to indicate fear of him whom he addressed.

"Neighbor," he said, "I could not have thought this ; or,
if *I*—eh—*did* think—in a corner of my own mind as it were
—that you, I say—that you might have unluckily engaged
in—eh—the matter of the Forty-five—there was still time to
have forgot all that."

"And is it so singular that a man should have been out in
the Forty-five ?" said Herries, with contemptuous composure. "Your father, I think, Mr. Foxley, was out with
Derwentwater in the Fifteen."

"And lost half of his estate," answered Foxley, with more
rapidity than usual ; "and was very near—hem—being
hanged into the boot. But this is—another-guess job—for
—eh—fifteen is not forty-five ; and my father had a remission, and you, I take it, have none."

"Perhaps I have," said Herries, indifferently ; "or, if I
have not, I am but in the case of half a dozen others whom
government do not think worth looking after at this time of
day, so they give no offense or disturbance."

"But you have given both, sir," said Nicholas Faggot, the
clerk, who, having some petty provincial situation, as I have
since understood, deemed himself bound to be zealous for
government. "Mr. Justice Foxley cannot be answerable
for letting you pass free, now your name and surname have
been spoken plainly out. There are warrants out against
you from the Secretary of State's office."

"A proper allegation, Mr. Attorney, that, at the distance
of so many years, the Secretary of State should trouble
himself about the unfortunate relics of a ruined cause ! "
answered Mr. Herries.

"But if it be so," said the clerk, who seemed to assume
more confidence upon the composure of Herries's demeanor,
"and if cause has been given by the conduct of a gentleman
himself, who hath been, it is alleged, raking up old matters,
and mixing them with new subjects of disaffection—I say,
if it be so, I should advise the party, in his wisdom, to surrender himself quietly into the lawful custody of the next
justice of peace—Mr. Foxley, suppose—where, and by whom,

14

the matter should be regularly inquired into. I am only putting a case," he added, watching with apprehension the effect which his words were likely to produce upon the party to whom they were addressed.

"And were I to receive such advice," said Herries, with the same composure as before—"putting the case, as you say, Mr. Faggot—I should request to see the warrant which countenanced such a scandalous proceeding."

Mr. Nicholas, by way of answer, placed in his hand a paper, and seemed anxiously to expect the consequences which were to ensue. Mr. Herries looked it over with the same equanimity as before, and then continued, "And were such a scrawl as this presented to me in my own house, I would throw it into the chimney, and Mr. Faggot upon the top of it."

Accordingly, seconding the word with the action, he flung the warrant into the fire with one hand, and fixed the other, with a stern and irresistible gripe, on the breast of the attorney, who, totally unable to contend with him, in either personal strength or mental energy, trembled like a chicken in the raven's clutch. He got off, however, for the fright ; for Herries, having probably made him fully sensible of the strength of his grasp, released him, with a scornful laugh.

"Deforcement—spulzie—stouthrief—masterful rescue !" exclaimed Peter Peebles, scandalized at the resistance offered to the law in the person of Nicholas Faggot. But his shrill exclamations were drowned in the thundering voice of Herries, who, calling upon Cristal Nixon, ordered him to take the bawling fool downstairs, fill his belly, and then give him a guinea, and thrust him out of doors. Under such injunctions, Peter easily suffered himself to be withdrawn from the scene.

Herries then turned to the Justice, whose visage, wholly abandoned by the rubicund hue which so lately beamed upon it, hung out the same pale livery as that of his dismayed clerk. "Old friend and acquaintance," he said, "you came here at my request, on a friendly errand, to convince this silly young man of the right which I have over his person for the present. I trust you do not intend to make your visit the pretext of disquieting me about other matters ? All the world knows that I have been living at large, in these northern counties, for some months, not to say years, and might have been apprehended at any time, had the necessities of the state required, or my own behavior deserved, it. But no English magistrate has been ungenerous enough to trouble a gentleman under misfortune, on account of political opinions and disputes which have been long ended by the success of the reigning powers. I trust, my good friend, you will not endanger yourself by taking any other view of the subject than you have done ever since we were acquainted ? "

The Justice answered with more readiness, as well as more spirit, than usual, " Neighbor Ingoldsby—what you say—is —eh—in some sort true ; and when you were coming and going at markets, horse-races, and cock-fights, fairs, hunts, and such-like—it was—eh—neither my business nor my wish to dispel—I say—to inquire into and dispel the mysteries which hung about you ; for while you were a good companion in the field, and over a bottle now and then—I did not—eh—think it necessary to ask—into your private affairs. And if I thought you were—ahem—somewhat unfortunate in former undertakings, and enterprises, and connections, which might cause you to live unsettledly and more private, I could have—eh—very little pleasure—to aggravate your case by interfering, or requiring explanations, which are often more easily asked than given. But when there are warrants and witnesses to names—and those names, Christian and surname, belong to—eh—an attainted person—charged —I trust falsely—with—ahem—taking advantage of modern broils and heart-burnings to renew our civil disturbances, the case is altered ; and I must—ahem—do my duty."

The Justice got on his feet as he concluded this speech, and looked as bold as he could. I drew close beside him and his clerk, Mr. Faggot, thinking the moment favorable for my own liberation, and intimated to Mr. Foxley my determination to stand by him. But Mr. Herries only laughed at the menacing posture which we assumed. " My good neighbor," said he, " you talk of a witness. Is yon crazy beggar a fit witness in an affair of this nature ? "

" But you do not deny that you are Mr. Herries of Birrenswork, mentioned in the Secretary of State's warrant ? " said Mr. Foxley.

" How can I deny or own anything about it ? " said Herries, with a sneer. " There is no such warrant in existence now ; its ashes, like the poor traitor whose doom it threatened, have been dispersed to the four winds of Heaven. There is now no warrant in the world."

" But you will not deny," said the Justice, " that you were the person named in it, and that—eh—your own act destroyed it ? "

"I will neither deny my name nor my actions, Justice," replied Mr. Herries, "when called upon by competent authority to avow or defend them. But I will resist all impertinent attempts either to intrude into my private motives or to control my person. I am quite well prepared to do so; and I trust that you, my good neighbor and brother sportsman, in your expostulation, and my friend Mr. Nicholas Faggot here, in his humble advice and petition that I should surrender myself, will consider yourselves as having amply discharged your duty to King George and government."

The cold and ironical tone in which he made this declaration, the look and attitude, so nobly expressive of absolute confidence in his own superior strength and energy, seemed to complete the indecision which had already shown itself on the side of those whom he addressed.

The justice looked to the clerk, the clerk to the justice; the former "ha'd," "eh'd," without bringing forth an articulate syllable; the latter only said, "As the warrant is destroyed, Mr. Justice, I presume you do not mean to proceed with the arrest?"

"Hum—ay—why no—Nicholas—it would not be quite advisable—and as the Forty-five was an old affair—and—hem—as my friend here will, I hope, see his error—that is, if he has not seen it already—and renounce the Pope, the Devil, and the Pretender—I mean no harm, neighbor—I think we—as we have no *posse*, or constables, or the like —should order our horses—and, in one word, look the matter over."

"Judiciously resolved," said the person whom this decision affected; "but before you go, I trust you will drink and be friends?"

"Why," said the Justice, rubbing his brow, "our business has been—hem—rather a thirsty one."

"Cristal Nixon," said Mr. Herries, "let us have a cool tankard instantly, large enough to quench the thirst of the whole commission."

While Cristal was absent on this genial errand, there was a pause, of which I endeavored to avail myself, by bringing back the discourse to my own concerns. "Sir," I said to Justice Foxley, "I have no direct business with your late discussion with Mr. Herries, only just thus far: you leave me, a loyal subject of King George, an unwilling prisoner in the hands of a person whom you have reason to believe unfriendly to the king's cause. I humbly submit that this is

contrary to your duty as a magistrate, and that you ought
to make Mr. Herries aware of the illegality of his proceedings, and take steps for my rescue, either upon the spot,
or, at least, as soon as possible after you have left this
case——"

"Young man," said Mr. Justice Foxley, "I would have
you remember you are under the power—the lawful power
—ahem—of your guardian."

"He calls himself so, indeed," I replied; "but he has
shown no evidence to establish so absurd a claim; and if
he had, his circumstances, as an attainted traitor excepted
from pardon, would void such a right, if it existed. I do
therefore desire you, Mr. Justice, and you, his clerk, to consider my situation, and afford me relief at your peril."

"Here is a young fellow now," said the Justice, with
much embarrassed looks, "thinks that I carry the whole
statute law of England in my head, and a *posse comitatus* to
execute them in my pocket! Why, what good would my
interference do? But—hum—eh—I will speak to your
guardian in your favor."

He took Mr. Herries aside, and seemed indeed to urge
something upon him with much earnestness; and perhaps
such a species of intercession was all which, in the circumstances, I was entitled to expect from him.

They often looked at me as they spoke together; and as
Cristal Nixon entered with a huge four-pottle tankard, filled
with the beverage his master had demanded, Herries turned
away from Mr. Foxley somewhat impatiently, saying with
emphasis, "I give you my word of honor that you have not
the slightest reason to apprehend anything on his account."
He then took up the tankard, and saying aloud in Gaelic,
"*Slaint an rey*," just tasted the liquor, and handed the tankard to Justice Foxley, who, to avoid the dilemma of pledging him to what might be the Pretender's health, drank to
Mr. Herries's own, with much pointed solemnity, but in a
draught far less moderate.

The clerk imitated the example of his principal, and I was
fain to follow their example, for anxiety and fear are at least
as thirsty as sorrow is said to be. In a word, we exhausted
the composition of ale, sherry, lemon-juice, nutmeg, and
other good things, stranded upon the silver bottom
of the tankard, the huge toast, as well as the roasted
orange, which had whilome floated jollily upon the brim,
and rendered legible Dr. Byrom's celebrated lines engraved
thereon—

" God bless the King ! God bless the faith's defender !
God bless—no harm in blessing—the Pretender.
Who that pretender is, and who that king,
God bless us all ! is quite another thing."

I had time enough to study this effusion of the Jacobite
muse, while the Justice was engaged in the somewhat tedious
ceremony of taking leave. That of Mr. Faggot was less ceremonious ; but I suspect something besides empty compliment passed betwixt him and Mr. Herries ; for I remarked
that the latter slipped a piece of paper into the hand of the
former, which might perhaps be a little atonement for the
rashness with which he had burned the warrant, and imposed
no gentle hand on the respectable minion of the law by whom
it was exhibited ; and I observed that he made this propitia-
tion in such a manner as to be secret from the worthy clerk's
principal.

When this was arranged, the party took leave of each
other, with much formality on the part of Squire Foxley,
amongst whose adieus the following phrase was chiefly
remarkable : " I presume you do not intend to stay long in
these parts ? "

" Not for the present, Justice, you may be sure ; there
are good reasons to the contrary. But I have no doubt of
arranging my affairs so that we shall speedily have sport
together again."

He went to wait upon the Justice to the courtyard ; and,
as he did so, commanded Cristal Nixon to see that I returned
into my apartment. Knowing it would be to no purpose to
resist or tamper with that stubborn functionary, I obeyed
in silence, and was once more a prisoner in my former
quarters.

CHAPTER VIII

I SPENT more than an hour, after returning to the apartment which I may call my prison, in reducing to writing the singular circumstances which I had just witnessed. Methought I could now form some guess at the character of Mr. Herries, upon whose name and situation the late scene had thrown considerable light ; one of those fanatical Jacobites, doubtless, whose arms, not twenty years since, had shaken the British throne, and some of whom, though their party daily diminished in numbers, energy, and power, retained still an inclination to renew the attempt they had found so desperate. He was indeed perfectly different from the sort of zealous Jacobites whom it had been my luck hitherto to meet with. Old ladies of family over their hyson, and gray-haired lairds over their punch, I had often heard utter a little harmless treason ; while the former remembered having led down a dance with the Chevalier, and the latter recounted the feats they had performed at Preston, Clifton, and Falkirk.

The disaffection of such persons was too unimportant to excite the attention of government. I had heard, however, that there still existed partizans of the Stuart family, of a more daring and dangerous description—men who, furnished with gold from Rome, moved, secretly and in disguise, through the various classes of society, and endeavored to keep alive the expiring zeal of their party.

I had no difficulty in assigning an important post among this class of persons, whose agency and exertion are only doubted by those who look on the surface of things, to this Mr. Herries, whose mental energies, as well as his personal strength and activity, seemed to qualify him well to act so dangerous a part ; and I knew that, all along the Western Border, both in England and Scotland, there are so many Nonjurors, that such a person may reside there with absolute safety, unless it becomes, in a very especial degree, the object of the government to secure his person ; and which purpose, even then, might be disappointed by early intelligence, or, as in the case of Mr. Foxley, by the unwillingness of provincial magistrates to interfere in what is now considered an invidious pursuit of the unfortunate.

There have, however, been rumors lately, as if the present state of the nation, or at least of some discontented provinces, agitated by a variety of causes, but particularly by the unpopularity of the present administration, may seem to this species of agitators a favorable period for recommencing their intrigues ; while, on the other hand, government may not, at such a crisis, be inclined to look upon them with the contempt which a few years ago would have been their most appropriate punishment.

That men should be found rash enough to throw away their services and lives in a desperate cause is nothing new in history, which abounds with instances of similar devotion ; that Mr. Herries is such an enthusiast is no less evident ; but all this explains not his conduct towards *me.* Had he sought to make me a proselyte to his ruined cause, violence and compulsion were arguments very unlikely to prevail with any generous spirit. But even if such were his object, of what use to him could be the acquisition of a single reluctant partizan, who could bring only his own person to support any quarrel which he might adopt ! He had claimed over me the rights of a guardian ; he had more than hinted that I was in a state of mind which could not dispense with the authority of such a person. Was this man, so sternly desperate in his purpose—he who seemed willing to take on his own shoulders the entire support of a cause which had been ruinous to thousands—was he the person that had the power of deciding on my fate ? Was it from him those dangers flowed, to secure me against which I had been educated under such circumstances of secrecy and precaution ?

And if this was so, of what nature was the claim which he asserted ? Was it that of propinquity ? And did I share the blood, perhaps the features, of this singular being ? Strange as it may seem, a thrill of awe, which shot across my mind at that instant, was not unmingled with a wild and mysterious feeling of wonder, almost amounting to pleasure. I remembered the reflection of my own face in the mirror at one striking moment during the singular interview of the day, and I hastened to the outward apartment to consult a glass which hung there, whether it were possible for my countenance to be again contorted into the peculiar frown which so much resembled the terrific look of Herries. But

I folded my brows in vain into a thousand complicated
wrinkles, and I was obliged to conclude, either that the supposed mark on my brow was altogether imaginary, or that
it could not be called forth by voluntary effort ; or, in fine,
what seemed most likely, that it was such a resemblance as
the imagination traces in the embers of a wood fire, or among
the varied veins of marble, distinct at one time, and obscure
or invisible at another, according as the combination of lines
strikes the eye or impresses the fancy.

While I was molding my visage like a mad player, the door
suddenly opened, and the girl of the house entered.   Angry
and ashamed at being detected in my singular occupation, I
turned round sharply, and, I suppose, chance produced the
change on my features which I had been in vain laboring to
call forth.

The girl started back with her " Don't ye look so now—
don't ye, for love's sake ; you be as like the ould squoire
as—— But here a comes," said she, huddling away out of
the room ; "and if you want a third, there is none but ould
Harry, as I know of, that can match ye for a brent broo ! "

As the girl muttered this exclamation and hastened out
of the room, Herries entered.   He stopped on observing that
I had looked again to the mirror, anxious to trace the look
by which the wench had undoubtedly been terrified.   He
seemed to guess what was passing in my mind, for, as I
turned towards him, he observed, "Doubt not that it is
stamped on your forehead—the fatal mark of our race ;
though it is not now so apparent as it will become when
age and sorrow, and the traces of stormy passions, and of
bitter penitence, shall have drawn their furrows on your
brow."

" Mysterious man," I replied, " I know not of what you
speak : your language is as dark as your purposes."

" Sit down, then," he said, " and listen ; thus far, at
least, must the veil of which you complain be raised.   When
withdrawn, it will only display guilt and sorrow—guilt, followed by strange penalty ; and sorrow, which Providence
has entailed upon the posterity of the mourners."

He paused a moment, and commenced his narrative which,
he told with the air of one who, remote as the events were
which he recited, took still the deepest interest in them.
The tone of his voice, which I have already described as
rich and powerful, aided by its inflections the effect of his
story, which I will endeavor to write down, as nearly as possible, in the very words which he used.

"It was not of late years that the English nation learned that their best chance of conquering their independent neighbors must be by introducing amongst them division and civil war. You need not be reminded of the state of thraldom to which Scotland was reduced by the unhappy war betwixt the domestic factions of Bruce and Baliol ; nor how, after Scotland had been emancipated from a foreign yoke, by the conduct and valor of the immortal Bruce, the whole fruits of the triumphs of Bannockburn were lost in the dreadful defeats of Dupplin and Halidon ; and Edward Baliol, the minion and feudatory of his namesake of England, seemed, for a brief season, in safe and uncontested possession of the throne, so lately occupied by the greatest general and wisest prince in Europe. But the experience of Bruce had not died with him. There were many who had shared his martial labors, and all remembered the successful efforts by which, under circumstances as disadvantageous as those of his son, he had achieved the liberation of Scotland.

"The usurper, Edward Baliol, was feasting with a few of his favorite retainers in the Castle of Annan, when he was suddenly surprised by a chosen band of insurgent patriots. Their chiefs were Douglas, Randolph, the young Earl of Moray, and Sir Simon Fraser ; and their success was so complete, that Baliol was obliged to fly for his life, scarcely clothed, and on a horse which there was no leisure to saddle. It was of importance to seize his person, if possible, and his flight was closely pursued by a valiant knight of Norman descent, whose family had been long settled in the marches of Dumfriesshire. Their Norman appellation was Fitz-Aldin, but this knight, from the great slaughter which he had made of the Southron, and the reluctance which he had shown to admit them to quarter during the former wars of that bloody period, had acquired the name of Redgauntlet, which he transmitted to his posterity——"

"Redgauntlet !" I involuntarily repeated.

"Yes, Redgauntlet," said my alleged guardian looking at me keenly ; "does that name recall any associations to your mind ?"

"No," I replied, "except that I lately heard it given to the hero of a supernatural legend."

"There are many such current concerning the family," he answered ; and then proceeded in his narrative.

"Alberick Redgauntlet, the first of his house so termed, was, as may be supposed from his name, of a stern and implacable disposition, which had been rendered more so by family discord. An only son, now a youth of eighteen, shared so much the haughty spirit of his father, that he became impatient of domestic control, resisted paternal authority, and finally fled from his father's house, renounced his political opinions, and awakened his mortal displeasure by joining the adherents of Baliol. It was said that his father cursed in his wrath his degenerate offspring, and swore that, if they met, he should perish by his hand. Meantime, circumstances seemed to promise atonement for this great deprivation. The lady of Alberick Redgauntlet was again, after many years, in a situation which afforded her husband the hope of a more dutiful heir.

" But the delicacy and deep interest of his wife's condition did not prevent Alberick from engaging in the undertaking of Douglas and Moray. He had been the most forward in the attack of the castle, and was now foremost in the pursuit of Baliol, eagerly engaged in dispersing or cutting down the few daring followers who endeavored to protect the usurper in his flight.

" As these were successively routed or slain, the formidable Redgauntlet, the mortal enemy of the house of Baliol, was within two lances' length of the fugitive Edward Baliol, in a narrow pass, when a youth, one of the last who attended the usurper in his flight, threw himself between them, received the shock of the pursuer, and was unhorsed and overthrown. The helmet rolled from his head, and the beams of the sun, then rising over the Solway, showed Redgauntlet the features of his disobedient son, in the livery, and wearing the cognizance, of the usurper.

" Redgauntlet beheld his son lying before his horse's feet ; but he also saw Baliol, the usurper of the Scottish crown, still, as it seemed, within his grasp, and separated from him only by the prostrate body of his overthrown adherent. Without pausing to inquire whether young Edward was wounded, he dashed his spurs into his horse, meaning to leap over him, but was unhappily frustrated in his purpose. The steed made indeed a bound forward, but was unable to clear the body of the youth, and with its hind foot struck him in the forehead, as he was in the act of rising. The blow was mortal. It is needless to add that the pursuit was checked, and Baliol escaped.

" Redgauntlet, ferocious as he is described, was yet overwhelmed with the thoughts of the crime he had committed. When he returned to his castle, it was to encounter new domestic sorrows. His wife had been prematurely seized with

the pangs of labor upon hearing the dreadful catastrophe
which had taken place. The birth of an infant boy had cost
her her life. Redgauntlet sat by her corpse for more than
twenty-four hours without changing either feature or posture, so far as his terrified domestics could observe. The
abbot of Dundrennan preached consolation to him in vain.
Douglas, who came to visit in his affliction a patriot of such
distinguished zeal, was more successful in arousing his attention. He caused the trumpets to sound an English point
of war in the courtyard, and Redgauntlet at once sprung to
his arms, and seemed restored to the recollection which had
been lost in the extent of his misery.

"From that moment, whatever he might feel inwardly,
he gave way to no outward emotion. Douglas caused his
infant to be brought ; but even the iron-hearted soldiers
were struck with horror to observe that, by the mysterious
law of nature, the cause of his mother's death, and the evidence of his father's guilt, was stamped on the innocent
face of the babe, whose brow was distinctly marked by the
miniature resemblance of a horseshoe. Redgauntlet himself pointed it out to Douglas, saying, with a ghastly smile,
"It should have been bloody."

"Moved as he was to compassion for his brother-in-arms,
and steeled against all softer feelings by the habits of civil
war, Douglas shuddered at this sight, and displayed a desire
to leave the house which was doomed to be the scene of such
horrors. As his parting advice, he exhorted Alberick Redgauntlet to make a pilgrimage to St. Ninian's of Whiteherne,
then esteemed a shrine of great sanctity ; and departed with
a precipitation which might have aggravated, had that been
possible, the forlorn state of his unhappy friend. But that
seems to have been incapable of admitting any addition.
Sir Alberick caused the bodies of his slaughtered son and
the mother to be laid side by side in the ancient chapel of
his house, after he had used the skill of a celebrated surgeon of that time to embalm them ; and it was said that for
many weeks he spent some hours nightly in the vault where
they reposed.

"At length he undertook the proposed pilgrimage to
Whiteherne, where he confessed himself for the first time
since his misfortune, and was shrived by an aged monk,
who afterwards died in the odor of sanctity. It is said that
it was then foretold to the Redgauntlet that, on account of
his unshaken patriotism, his family should continue to be
powerful amid the changes of future times ; but that, in de-

testation of his unrelenting cruelty to his own issue, Heaven had decreed that the valor of his race should always be fruitless, and that the cause which they espoused should never prosper.

"Submitting to such penance as was there imposed, Sir Alberick went, it is thought, on a pilgrimage either to Rome or to the Holy Sepulchre itself. He was universally considered as dead ; and it was not till thirteen years afterwards that, in the great battle of Durham, fought between David Bruce and Queen Philippa of England, a knight, bearing a horseshoe for his crest, appeared in the van of the Scottish army, distinguishing himself by his reckless and desperate valor, who, being at length overpowered and slain, was finally discovered to be the brave and unhappy Sir Alberick Redgauntlet."

"And has the fatal sign," said I, when Herries had ended his narrative, "descended on all the posterity of this unhappy house ? "

"It has been so handed down from antiquity, and is still believed," said Herries. "But perhaps there is, in the popular evidence, something of that fancy which creates what it sees. Certainly, as other families have peculiarities by which they are distinguished, this of Redgauntlet is marked in most individuals by a singular indenture of the forehead, supposed to be derived from the son of Alberick, their ancestor, and brother to the unfortunate Edward, who had perished in so piteous a manner. It is certain there seems to have been a fate upon the house of Redgauntlet, which has been on the losing side in almost all the civil broils which have divided the kingdom of Scotland from David Bruce's days till the late valiant and unsuccessful attempt of the Chevalier Charles Edward."

He concluded with a deep sigh, as one whom the subject had involved in a train of painful reflections.

"And am I then," I exclaimed, "descended from this unhappy race ? Do you too belong to it ? And if so, why do I sustain restraint and hard usage at the hands of a relation ? "

"Inquire no farther for the present," he said. "The line of conduct which I am pursuing towards you is dictated not by choice, but by necessity. You were withdrawn from the bosom of your family, and the care of your legal guardian, by the timidity and ignorance of a doting mother, who was incapable of estimating the arguments or feelings of those who prefer honor and principle to fortune, and even to life. The young hawk, accustomed only to the fostering care of its dam, must be tamed by darkness and sleeplessness ere it is trusted on the wing for the purpose of the falconer."

I was appalled at this declaration, which seemed to threaten a long continuance, and a dangerous termination, of my captivity. I deemed it best, however, to show some spirit, and at the same time to mingle a tone of conciliation. "Mr. Herries," I said, "if I call you rightly by that name, let us speak upon this matter without the tone of mystery and fear in which you seem inclined to envelope it. I have been long, alas! deprived of the care of that affectionate mother to whom you allude, long under the charge of strangers, and compelled to form my own resolutions upon the reasoning of my own mind. Misfortune —early deprivation—has given me the privilege of acting for myself; and constraint shall not deprive me of an Englishman's best privilege."

"The true cant of the day," said Herries, in a tone of scorn. "The privilege of free action belongs to no mortal : we are tied down by the fetters of duty, our moral path is limited by the regulations of honor, our most indifferent actions are but meshes of the web of destiny by which we are all surrounded."

He paced the room rapidly, and proceeded in a tone of enthusiasm which, joined to some other parts of his conduct, seems to intimate an over-excited imagination, were it not contradicted by the general tenor of his speech and conduct.

"Nothing," he said, in an earnest yet melancholy voice— "nothing is the work of chance, nothing is the consequence of free-will : the liberty of which the Englishman boasts gives as little real freedom to its owner as the despotism of an Eastern sultan permits to his slave. The usurper, William of Nassau, went forth to hunt, and thought, doubtless, that it was by an act of his own royal pleasure that the horse of his murdered victim was prepared for his kingly sport. But Heaven had other views ; and before the sun was high, a stumble of that very animal over an obstacle so inconsiderable as a mole-hillock cost the haughty rider his life and his usurped crown. Do you think an inclination of the rein could have avoided that trifling impediment ? I tell you, it crossed his way as inevitably as all the long chain of Caucasus could have done. Yes, young man, in doing and suffering we play but the part allotted by Destiny, the man-

ager of this strange drama, stand bound to act no more than
is prescribed, to say no more than is set down for us ; and
yet we mouth about free-will, and freedom of thought and
action, as if Richard must not die, or Richmond conquer,
exactly where the author has decreed it shall be so ! ''

He continued to pace the room after this speech, with
folded arms and downcast looks ; and the sound of his steps
and tone of his voice brought to my remembrance that I
had heard this singular person, when I met him on a former
occasion, uttering such soliloquies in his solitary chamber.
I observed that, like other Jacobites, in his inveteracy
against the memory of King William, he had adopted the
party opinion that the monarch, on the day he had his fatal
accident, rode upon a horse once the property of the unfortunate Sir John Friend, executed for high treason in
1696.

It was not my business to aggravate, but, if possible,
rather to soothe him in whose power I was so singularly
placed. When I conceived that the keenness of his feelings
had in some degree subsided, I answered him as follows :—
"I will not—indeed I feel myself incompetent to argue a
question of such metaphysical subtlety as that which in-
volves the limits betwixt free-will and predestination. Let
us hope we may live honestly and die hopefully, without being obliged to form a decided opinion upon a point so far
beyond our comprehension."

"Wisely resolved," he interrupted, with a sneer ; "there
came a note from some Geneva sermon."

"But," I proceeded, "I call your attention to the fact
that I, as well as you, am acted upon by impulses, the result either of my own free-will or the consequences of the
part which is assigned to me by destiny. These may be—
nay, at present they are—in direct contradiction to those
by which you are actuated ; and how shall we decide which
shall have precedence ? *You* perhaps feel yourself destined
to act as my jailer. I feel myself, on the contrary, destined
to attempt and effect my escape. One of us must be wrong,
but who can say which errs till the event has decided betwixt
us ? ''

" I shall feel myself destined to have recourse to severe
modes of restraint," said he, in the same tone of half jest,
half earnest which I had used.

"In that case," I answered, "it will be my destiny to
attempt everything for my freedom."

"And it may be mine, young man," he replied, in a deep

and stern tone, "to take care that you should rather die than attain your purpose."

This was speaking out indeed, and I did not allow him to go unanswered. "You threaten me in vain," said I: "the laws of my country will protect me; or whom they cannot protect, they will avenge."

I spoke this firmly, and he seemed for a moment silenced; and the scorn with which he at last answered me had something of affectation in it.

"The laws!" he said; "and what, stripling, do you know of the laws of your country? Could you learn jurisprudence under a base-born blotter of parchment such as Saunders Fairford; or from the empty pedantic coxcomb, his son, who now, forsooth, writes himself advocate? When Scotland was herself, and had her own king and legislature, such plebeian cubs, instead of being called to the bar of her Supreme Courts, would scarce have been admitted to the honor of bearing a sheepskin process-bag."

Alan, I could not bear this, but answered indignantly, that he knew not the worth and honor from which he was detracting.

"I know as much of these Fairfords as I do of you," he replied.

"As much," said I, "and as little; for you can neither estimate their real worth nor mine. I know you saw them when last in Edinburgh."

"Ha!" he exclaimed, and turned on me an inquisitive look.

"It is true," said I, "you cannot deny it; and having thus shown you that I know something of your motions, let me warn you I have modes of communication with which you are not acquainted. Oblige me not to use them to your prejudice."

"Prejudice me!" he replied. "Young man, I smile at and forgive your folly. Nay, I will tell you that of which you are not aware, namely, that it was from letters received from these Fairfords that I first suspected, what the result of my visit to them confirmed, that you were the person whom I had sought for years."

"If you learned this," said I, "from the papers which were about my person on the night when I was under the necessity of becoming your guest at Brokenburn, I do not envy your indifference to the means of acquiring information. It was dishonorable to——"

"Peace, young man," said Herries, more calmly than I

might have expected ; " the word dishonor must not be mentioned as in conjunction with my name. Your pocketbook was in the pocket of your coat, and did not escape the curiosity of another, though it would have been sacred from mine. My servant, Cristal Nixon, brought me the intelligence after you were gone. I was displeased with the manner in which he had acquired his information ; but it was not the less my duty to ascertain its truth, and for that purpose I went to Edinburgh. I was in hopes to persuade Mr. Fairford to have entered into my views ; but I found him too much prejudiced to permit me to trust him. He is a wretched yet a timid slave of the present government, under which our unhappy country is dishonorably enthralled ; and it would have been altogether unfit and unsafe to have entrusted him with the secret either of the right which I possess to direct your actions or of the manner in which I purpose to exercise it."

I was determined to take advantage of his communicative humor, and obtain, if possible, more light upon his purpose. He seemed most accessible to being piqued on the point of honor, and I resolved to avail myself, but with caution, of his sensibility upon that topic. " You say," I replied, that you are not friendly to indirect practises, and disapprove of the means by which your domestic obtained information of my name and quality. Is it honorable to avail yourself of that knowledge which is dishonorably obtained ?"

" It is boldly asked," he replied ; " but, within certain necessary limits, I dislike not boldness of expostulation. You have, in this short conference, displayed more character and energy than I was prepared to expect. You will, I trust, resemble a forest plant, which has indeed by some accident been brought up in the greenhouse, and thus rendered delicate and effeminate, but which regains its native firmness and tenacity when exposed for a season to the winter air. I will answer your question plainly. In business, as in war, spies and informers are necessary evils, which all good men detest, but which yet all prudent men must use, unless they mean to fight and act blindfold. But nothing can justify the use of falsehood and treachery in our own person."

" You said to the elder Mr. Fairford," continued I, with the same boldness, which I began to find was my best game, "that I was the son of Ralph Latimer of Langcote Hall ? How do you reconcile this with your late assertion that my name is not Latimer ?"

He colored as he replied, " the doting old fool lied, or per-

15

haps mistook my meaning. I said that the gentleman *might* be your father. To say the truth, I wished you to visit England, your native country ; because, when you might do so, my rights over you would revive."

This speech fully led me to understand a caution which had been often impressed upon me, that if I regarded my safety I should not cross the southern Border ; and I cursed my own folly, which kept me fluttering like a moth around the candle, until I was betrayed into the calamity with which I had dallied. " What are these rights," I said, " which you claim over me ? To what end do you propose to turn them ? "

" To a weighty one, you may be certain," answered Mr. Herries ; " but I do not, at present, mean to communicate to you either its nature or extent. You may judge of its importance, when, in order to entirely possess myself of your person, I condescended to mix myself with the fellows who destroyed the fishing-station of yon wretched Quaker. That I held him in contempt, and was displeased at the greedy devices with which he ruined a manly sport, is true enough ; but, unless as it favored my designs on you, he might have, for me, maintained his stake-nets until Solway should cease to ebb and flow."

" Alas ! " I said, " it doubles my regret to have been the unwilling cause of misfortune to an honest and friendly man."

" Do not grieve for that," said Herris : " honest Joshua is one of those who, by dint of long prayers, can possess themselves of widows' houses ; he will quickly repair his losses. When he sustains any mishap, he and the other canters set it down as a debt against Heaven, and, by the way of set-off, practise rogueries without computation, till they make the balance even, or incline it to the winning side. Enough of this for the present. I must immediately shift my quarters ; for, although I do not fear the over-zeal of Mr. Justice Foxley or his clerk will lead them to any extreme measure, yet that mad scoundrel's unhappy recognition of me may make it more serious for them to connive at me, and I must not put their patience to an over-severe trial. You must prepare to attend me, either as a captive or a companion ; if as the latter, you must give your parol of honor to attempt no escape. Should you be so ill-advised as to break your word once pledged, be assured that I will blow your brains out without a moment's scruple."

" I am ignorant of your plans and purposes," I replied,

" and cannot but hold them dangerous. I do not mean to aggravate my present situation by any unavailing resistance to the superior force which detains me ; but I will not renounce the right of asserting my natural freedom should a favorable opportunity occur. I will, therefore, rather be your prisoner than your confederate."

" That is spoken fairly," he said ; and yet not without the canny caution of one brought up in the Gude Town of Edinburgh. On my part, I will impose no unnecessary hardship upon you ; but, on the contrary, your journey shall be made as easy as is consistent with your being kept safely. Do you feel strong enough to ride on horseback as yet, or would you prefer a carriage ? The former mode of traveling is best adapted to the country through which we are to travel, but you are at liberty to choose between them."

I said, " I felt my strength gradually returning, and that I should much prefer traveling on horseback. A carriage," I added, " is so close——"

" And so easily guarded," replied Herries with a look as if he would have penetrated my very thoughts, " that, doubtless, you think horseback better calculated for an escape."

" My thoughts are my own," I answered ; " and though you keep my person prisoner, these are beyond your control."

" O, I can read the book," he said, " without opening the leaves. But I would recommend to you to make no rash attempt, and it will be my care to see that you have no power to make any that is likely to be effectual. Linen, and all other necessaries for one in your circumstances, are amply provided. Cristal Nixon will act as your valet—I should rather, perhaps, say *femme de chambre*. Your traveling-dress you may perhaps consider as singular, but it is such as the circumstances require ; and if you object to use the articles prepared for your use, your mode of journeying will be as personally unpleasant as that which conducted you hither. Adieu. We now know each other better than we did ; it will not be my fault if the consequences of farther intimacy be not a more favorable mutual opinion."

He then left me with a civil " good-night," to my own reflections, and only turned back to say, that we should proceed on our journey at daybreak next morning, at farthest ; perhaps earlier, he said ; but complimented me by supposing that, as I was a sportsman, I must always be ready for a sudden start.

We are then at issue, this singular man and myself. His personal views are to a certain point explained. He has chosen an antiquated and desperate line of politics, and he claims, from some pretended tie of guardianship or relationship which he does not design to explain, but which he seems to have been able to pass current on a silly country justice and his knavish clerk, a right to direct and to control my motions. The danger which awaited me in England, and which I might have escaped had I remained in Scotland, was doubtless occasioned by the authority of this man. But what my poor mother might fear for me as a child, what my English friend, Samuel Griffiths, endeavored to guard against during my youth and nonage, is now, it seems, come upon me ; and, under a legal pretext, I am detained in what must be a most illegal manner, by a person, too, whose own political immunities have been forfeited by his conduct. It matters not ; my mind is made up, neither persuasion nor threats shall force me into the desperate designs which this man meditates. Whether I am of the trifling consequence which my life hitherto seems to intimate, or whether I have, as would appear from my adversary's conduct, such importance, by birth or fortune, as may make me a desirable acquisition to a political faction, my resolution is taken in either case. Those who read this Journal, if it shall be perused by impartial eyes, shall judge of me truly ; and if they consider me as a fool in encountering danger unnecessarily, they shall have no reason to believe me a coward or a turncoat when I find myself engaged in it. I have been bred in sentiments of attachment to the family on the throne, and in these sentiments I will live and die. I have, indeed, some idea that Mr. Herries has already discovered that I am made of different and more unmalleable metal than he had at first believed. There were letters from my dear Alan Fairford, giving a ludicrous account of my instability of temper, in the same pocketbook which, according to the admission of my pretended guardian, fell under the investigation of his domestic during the night I passed at Brokenburn, where, as I now recollect, my wet clothes, with the contents of my pockets, were, with the thoughtlessness of a young traveler, committed too rashly to the care of a strange servant. And my kind friend and hospitable landlord, Mr. Alexander Fairford, may also, and with justice, have spoken of my levities to this man. But he shall find he has made a false estimate upon these plausible grounds, since——

But I must break off for the present.

CHAPTER IX

THERE is at length a halt—at length I have gained so much privacy as to enable me to continue my Journal. It has become a sort of task of duty to me, without the discharge of which I do not feel that the business of the day is performed. True, no friendly eye may ever look upon these labors, which have amused the solitary hours of an unhappy prisoner. Yet, in the meanwhile, the exercise of the pen seems to act as a sedative upon my own agitated thoughts and tumultuous passions. I never lay it down but I rise stronger in resolution, more ardent in hope. A thousand vague fears, wild expectations, and indigested schemes, hurry through one's thoughts in seasons of doubt and of danger. But by arresting them as they flit across the mind, by throwing them on paper, and even by that mechanical act compelling ourselves to consider them with scrupulous and minute attention, we may perhaps escape becoming the dupes of our own excited imagination ; just as a young horse is cured of the vice of starting, by being made to stand still and look for some time without any interruption at the cause of its terror.

There remains but one risk, which is that of discovery. But, besides the small characters in which my residence in Mr. Fairford's house enabled me to excel, for the purpose of transferring as many scroll sheets as possible to a huge sheet of stamped paper, I have, as I have elsewhere intimated, had hitherto the comfortable reflection that, if the record of my misfortunes should fall into the hands of him by whom they are caused, they would, without harming any one, show him the real character and disposition of the person who has become his prisoner, perhaps his victim. Now, however, that other names and other characters are to be mingled with the register of my own sentiments, I must take additional care of these papers, and keep them in such a manner that, in case of the least hazard of detection, I may be able to destroy them at a moment's notice. I shall not soon or easily forget the lesson I have been taught by the prying disposition which Cristal Nixon, this man's agent and confederate. manifested

229

at Brokenburn, and which proved the original cause of my sufferings.

My laying aside the last sheet of my Journal hastily was occasioned by the unwonted sound of a violin in the farmyard beneath my windows. It will not appear surprising to those who have made music their study that, after listening to a few notes, I became at once assured that the musician was no other than the itinerant formerly mentioned as present at the destruction of Joshua Geddes's stake-nets, the superior delicacy and force of whose execution would enable me to swear to his bow amongst a whole orchestra. I had the less reason to doubt his identity, because he played twice over the beautiful Scottish air called "Wandering Willie"; and I could not help concluding that he did so for the purpose of intimating his own presence, since what the French call the *nom de guerre* of the performer was described by the tune.

Hope will catch at the most feeble twig for support in extremity. I knew this man, though deprived of sight, to be bold, ingenious, and perfectly capable of acting as a guide. I believed I had won his good-will by having, in a frolic, assumed the character of his partner ; and I remembered that, in a wild, wandering, and disorderly course of life, men, as they become loosened from the ordinary bonds of civil society, hold those of comradeship more closely sacred ; so that honor is sometimes found among thieves, and faith and attachment in such as the law has termed vagrants. The history of Richard Cœur-de-Lion and his minstrel, Blondel, rushed at the same time, on my mind, though I could not even then suppress a smile at the dignity of the example, when applied to a blind fiddler and myself. Still, there was something in all this to awaken a hope that, if I could open a correspondence with this poor violer, he might be useful in extricating me from my present situation.

His profession furnished me with some hope that this desired communication might be attained ; since it is well known that, in Scotland, where there is so much national music, the words and airs of which are generally known, there is a kind of freemasonry amongst performers, by which they can, by the mere choice of a tune, express a great deal to the hearers. Personal allusions are often made in this manner, with much point and pleasantry ; and nothing is more usual at public festivals than that the air played to accompany a particular health or toast is made the vehicle of compliment, of wit, and sometimes of satire.*

* See Tunes and Toasts. Note 26.

While these things passed through my mind rapidly, I heard my friend beneath recommence, for the third time, the air from which his own name had been probably adopted, when he was interrupted by his rustic auditors.

"If thou canst play no other spring but that, mon, ho hadst best put up ho's pipes and be jogging. Squoire will be back anon, or Master Nixon, and we'll see who will pay poiper then."

"Oho," thought I, "if I have no sharper ears than those of my friends Jan and Dorcas to encounter, I may venture an experiment upon them ;" and, as most expressive of my state of captivity, I sung two or three lines of the 137th Psalm—

> "By Babel's streams we sat and wept."

The country people listened with attention, and when I ceased, I heard them whisper together in tones of commiseration, "Lack-a-day, poor soul! so pretty a man to be beside his wits !"

"An he be that gate," said Wandering Willie, in a tone calculated to reach my ears, "I ken naething will raise his spirits like a spring." And he struck up with great vigor and spirit the lively Scottish air, the words of which instantly occurred to me—

> "Oh whistle and I'll come t'ye, my lad,
> Oh whistle and I'll come t'ye, my lad ;
> Though father and mother and a' should gae mad,
> Oh whistle and I'll come t'ye, my lad."

I soon heard a clattering noise of feet in the courtyard, which I concluded to be Jan and Doras dancing a jig in their Cumberland wooden clogs. Under cover of this din I endeavored to answer Willie's signal by whistling, as loud as I could—

> "Come back again and loe me
> When a' the lave are gane."

He instantly threw the dancers out, by changing his air to

> "There's my thumb, I'll ne'er beguile thee."

I no longer doubted that a communication betwixt us was happily established, and that, if I had an opportunity of speaking to the poor musician, I should find him willing to take my letter to the post, to invoke the assistance of some active magistrate, or of the commanding officer of Carlisle

Castle, or, in short, to do whatever else I could point out, in the compass of his power, to contribute to my liberation. But to obtain speech of him I must have run the risk of alarming the suspicions of Dorcas, if not yet of her more stupid Corydon. My ally's blindness prevented his receiving any communication by signs from the window, even if I could have ventured to make them, consistently with prudence ; so that, notwithstanding the mode of intercourse we had adopted was both circuitous and peculiarly liable to misapprehension, I saw nothing I could do better than to continue it, trusting my own and my correspondent's acuteness in applying to the airs the meaning they were intended to convey. I thought of singing the words themselves of some significant song, but feared I might, by doing so, attract suspicion. I endeavored, therefore, to intimate my speedy departure from my present place of residence by whistling the well-known air with which festive parties in Scotland usually conclude the dance—

> " Good-night and joy be wi' ye a',
> For here nae langer maun I stay ;
> There's neither friend nor foe of mine
> But wishes that I were away."

It appeared that Willie's powers of intelligence were much more active than mine, and that, like a deaf person, accustomed to be spoken to by signs, he comprehended, from the very first notes, the whole meaning I intended to convey ; and he accompanied me in the air with his violin, in such a manner as at once to show he understood my meaning, and to prevent my whistling from being attended to.

His reply was almost immediate, and was conveyed in the old martial air of " Hey, Johnnie lad, cock up your beaver." I ran over the words, and fixed on the following stanza as most applicable to my circumstances :—

> " Cock up your beaver, and cock it fu' sprush,
> We'll over the Border and give them a brush
> There's somebody there we'll teach better behavior—
> Hey, Johnnie lad, cock up your beaver."

If these sounds alluded, as I hope they do, to any chance of assistance from my Scottish friends, I may indeed consider that a door is open to hope and freedom. I immediately replied with,

" My heart's in the Highlands, my heart is not here;
My heart's in the Highlands, a-chasing the deer—
A-chasing the wild deer, and following the roe;
My heart's in the Highlands wherever I go.

Farewell to the Highlands! farewell to the North!
The birthplace of valor, the cradle of worth;
Wherever I wander, wherever I rove,
The hills of the Highlands for ever I love."

Willie instantly played with a degree of spirit which might
have awakened hope in Despair herself, if Despair could be
supposed to understand Scottish music, the fine old Jacobite
air,

" For a' that, and a' that,
And twice as much as a' that."

I next endeavored to intimate my wish to send notice of
my condition to my friends ; and, despairing to find an air
sufficiently expressive of my purpose, I ventured to sing a
verse, which, in various forms, occurs so frequently in old
ballads—

" Wharo will I get a bonny boy
That will win hose and shoon ;
That will gae down to Durisdeer,
And bid my merry-men come ? "

He drowned the latter part of the verse by playing, with
much emphasis,

" Kind Robin lose me."

Of this, though I ran over the verses of the song in my
mind, I could make nothing ; and before I could contrive
any mode of intimating my uncertainty, a cry arose in the
courtyard that Cristal Nixon was coming. My faithful
Willie was obliged to retreat ; but not before he had half-
played, half-hummed, by way of farewell,

" Leave thee—leave thee, lad ?
I'll never leave thee.
The stars shall gae withershins
Ere I will leave thee."

I am thus, I think, secure of my one trusty adherent in
my misfortunes ; and, however whimsical it may be to rely
much on the man of his idle profession, and deprived of
sight withal, it is deeply impressed on my mind that his
services may be both useful and necessary. There is another

quarter from which I look for succor, and which I have indicated to thee, Alan, in more than one passage of my
Journal.   Twice, at the early hours of daybreak, I have seen
the individual alluded to in the court of the farm, and twice
she made signs of recognition in answer to the gestures by
which I endeavored to make her comprehend my situation ;
but on both occasions she pressed her fingers on her lips, as
expressive of silence and secrecy.

The manner in which G. M. entered upon the scene for
the first time seems to assure me of her good-will, so far as
her power may reach ; and I have many reasons to believe it
is considerable.   Yet she seemed hurried and frightened
during the very transitory moments of our interview, and I
think was, upon the last occasion, startled by the entrance
of some one into the farmyard, just as she was on the point
of addressing me.   You must not ask whether I am an early
riser, since such objects are to be seen at daybreak ; and
although I have never again seen her, yet I have reason to
think she is not distant.   It was but three nights ago that,
worn out by the uniformity of my confinement, I had manifested more symptoms of despondence than I had before
exhibited, which I conceive may have attracted the attention
of the domestics, through whom the circumstance might
transpire.   On the next morning the following lines lay on
my table ; but how conveyed there I cannot tell.   The hand
in which they are written is a beautiful Italian manuscript :—

> " As lords their laborers' hire delay,
>   Fate quits our toil with hopes to come,
> Which, if far short of present pay,
>   Still owns a debt and names a sum
>
> Quit not the pledge, frail sufferer then,
>   Although a distant date be given ;
> Despair is treason towards man,
>   And blasphemy to Heaven."

That these lines are written with the friendly purpose of
inducing me to keep up my spirits I cannot doubt ; and I
trust the manner in which I shall conduct myself may show
that the pledge is accepted.

The dress is arrived in which it seems to be my self-elected
guardian's pleasure that I shall travel ; and what does it
prove to be ?   A skirt, or upper petticoat, or camlet, like
those worn by country ladies of moderate rank when on
horseback, with such a riding-mask as they frequently use
on journeys to preserve their eyes and complexion from the

sun and dust, and sometimes, it is suspected, to enable them to play off a little coquetry. From the gayer mode of employing the mask, however, I suspect I shall be precluded ; for instead of being only pasteboard, covered with black velvet, I observe with anxiety that mine is thickened with a plate of steel, which, like Quixote's visor, serves to render it more strong and durable.

This apparatus, together with a steel clasp for securing the mask behind me with a padlock, gave me fearful recollections of the unfortunate being who, never being permitted to lay aside such a visor, acquired the well-known historical epithet of the Man in the Iron Mask. I hesitated a moment whether I should so far submit to the acts of oppression designed against me as to assume this disguise, which was, of course, contrived to aid their purposes. But then I remembered Mr. Herries's threat, that I should be kept close prisoner in a carriage unless I assumed the dress which should be appointed for me ; and I considered the comparative degree of freedom which I might purchase by wearing the mask and female dress as easily and advantageously purchased. Here, therefore, I must pause for the present, and await what the morning may bring forth.

To carry on the story from the documents before us, we think it proper here to drop the Journal of the captive Darsie Latimer, and adopt, instead, a narrative of the proceedings of Alan Fairford in pursuit of his friend, which forms another series in this history.

CHAPTER X

NARRATIVE OF ALAN FAIRFORD

THE reader ought, by this time, to have formed some idea of the character of Alan Fairford. He had a warmth of heart which the study of the law and of the world could not chill, and talents which they had rendered unusually acute. Deprived of the personal patronage enjoyed by most of his contemporaries, who assumed the gown under the protection of their aristocratic alliances and descents, he early saw that he should have that to achieve for himself which fell to them as a right of birth. He labored hard in silence and solitude, and his labors were crowned with success. But Alan doted on his friend Darsie, even more than he loved his profession, and, as we have seen, threw everything aside when he thought Latimer in danger ; forgetting fame and fortune, and hazarding even the serious displeasure of his father, to rescue him whom he loved with an elder brother's affection. Darsie, though his parts were more quick and brilliant than those of his friend, seemed always to the latter a being under his peculiar charge, whom he was called upon to cherish and protect, in cases where the youth's own experience was unequal to the exigency ; and now, when the fate of Latimer seemed worse than doubtful, and Alan's whole prudence and energy were to be exerted in his behalf, an adventure which might have seemed perilous to most youths of his age had no terrors for him. He was well acquainted with the laws of his country, and knew how to appeal to them ; and, besides his professional confidence, his natural disposition was steady, sedate, persevering, and, undaunted. With these requisites he undertook a quest which, at that time, was not unattended with actual danger, and had much in it to appal a more timid disposition.

Fairford's first inquiry concerning his friend was of the chief magistrate of Dumfries, Provost Crosbie, who had sent the information of Darsie's disappearance. On his first application, he thought he discerned in the honest dignitary a desire to get rid of the subject. The provost spoke of the riot at the fishing-station as an "outbreak among those

lawless loons the fishermen, which concerned the sheriff,"
he said, " more than us poor town-council bodies, that have
enough to do to keep peace within burgh, amongst such a
set of commoners as the town are plagued with."

" But this is not all, Provost Crosbie," said Mr. Alan
Fairford : " a young gentleman of rank and fortune has
disappeared amongst their hands. You know him—my
father gave him a letter to you—Mr. Darsie Latimer."

" Lack-a-day, yes !—lack-a-day, yes !" said the provost.
" Mr. Darsie Latimer. He dined at my house. I hope he
is well ?"

" I hope so too," said Alan, rather indignantly ; " but I
desire more certainty on that point. You yourself wrote
my father that he had disappeared."

" Troth, yes, and that is true," said the provost. " But
did he not go back to his friends in Scotland ? It was not
natural to think he would stay here."

" Not unless he is under restraint," said Fairford, surprised at the coolness with which the provost seemed to
take up the matter.

" Rely on it, sir," said Mr. Crosbie, " that if he has not
returned to his friends in Scotland, he must have gone to his
friends in England."

" I will rely on no such thing," said Alan ; " if there is
law or justice in Scotland, I will have the thing cleared to
the very bottom."

" Reasonable—reasonable," said the provost, " so far as is
possible ; but you know I have no power beyond the ports
of the burgh."

" But you are in the commission besides, Mr. Crosbie—a
justice of peace for the county."

" True—very true ; that is," said the cautious magistrate,
" I will not say but my name may stand on the list, but I
cannot remember that I have ever qualified."*

" Why, in that case," said young Fairford, " there are ill-
natured people might doubt your attachment to the Protestant line, Mr. Crosbie."

" God forbid, Mr. Fairfold ! I who have done and suffered in the Forty-five ! I reckon the Highlandmen did me
damage to the amount of £100 Scots, forbye all they ate and
drank. No—no, sir, I stand beyond challenge ; but as for
plaguing myself with county business, let them that aught
the mare shoe the mare. The Commissioners of Supply
would see my back broken before they would help me in the

* By taking the oath to government.

burgh's work, and all the world kens the difference of the weight between public business in burgh and landward. What are their riots to me ? Have we not riots enough of our own ? But I must be getting ready, for the council meets this forenoon. I am blythe to see your father's son on the causeway of our ancient burgh, Mr. Alan Fairford. Were you a twelvemonth aulder, we would make a burgess of you, man. I hope you will come and dine with me before you go away. What think you of to-day at two o'clock —just a roasted chucky and a drappit egg ? "

Alan Fairford resolved that his friend's hospitality should not, as it seemed the inviter intended, put a stop to his queries. " I must delay you for a moment," he said, " Mr. Crosbie. This is a serious affair : a young gentleman of high hopes, my own dearest friend, is missing ; you cannot think it will be passed over slightly, if a man of your high character and known zeal for the government do not make some active inquiry. Mr. Crosbie, you are my father's friend, and I respect you as such ; but to others it will have a bad appearance."

The withers of the provost were not unwrung : he paced the room in much tribulation, repeating, " But what can I do, Mr. Fairford ? I warrant your friend casts up again ; he will come back again, like the ill shilling—he is not the the sort of gear that tynes—a hellicat boy, running through the country with a blind fiddler, and playing the fiddle to a parcel of blackguards, who can tell where the like of him may have scampered to ? "

" There are persons apprehended and in the jail of the town, as I understand from the sheriff-substitute," said Mr. Fairford ; " you must call them before you and inquire what they know of this young gentleman."

" Ay—ay, the sheriff-depute did commit some poor creatures, I believe—wretched, ignorant fishermen bodies, that had been quarreling with Quaker Geddes and his stake-nets, whilk, under favor of your gown be it spoken, Mr. Fairford, are not over and above lawful, and the town-clerk thinks they may be lawfully removed *via facti*—but that is by the by. But, sir, the creatures were a' dismissed for want of evidence : the Quaker would not swear to them, and what could the sheriff and me do but just let them loose ? Come awe', cheer up, Master Alan, and take a walk till dinnertime. I must really go to the council."

" Stop a moment, provost," said Alan ; " I lodge a complaint before you, as a magistrate, and you will find it serious to slight it over. You must have these men apprehended again."

"Ay, ay—easy said ; but catch them that can," answered the provost ; " they are ower the march by this time, or by the Point of Cairn. Lord help ye ! they are a kind of amphibious deevils, neither land nor water beasts—neither English nor Scots—neither county nor stewartry, as we say —they are dispersed like so much quicksilver. You may as well try to whistle a sealgh out of the Solway as to get hold of one of them till all the fray is over."

"Mr. Crosbie, this will not do," answered the young counselor ; " there is a person of more importance than such wretches as you describe concerned in this unhappy business : I must name to you a certain Mr. Herries."

He kept his eye on the provost as he uttered the name, which he did rather at a venture, and from the connection which that gentleman, and his real or supposed niece, seemed to have with the fate of Darsie Latimer, than from any distinct cause of suspicion which he entertained. He thought the provost seemed embarrassed, though he showed much desire to assume an appearance of indifference, in which he partly succeeded.

"Herries !" he said. " What Herries ? There are many of that name ; not so many as formerly, for the old stocks are wearing out, but there is Herries of Heathgill, and Herries of Auchintulloch, and Herries——"

"To save you farther trouble, this person's designation is Herries of Birrenswork."

"Of Birrenswork !" said Mr. Crosbie. " I have you now, Mr. Alan. Could you not as well have said, the laird of Redgauntlet ? "

Fairford was too wary to testify any surprise at this identification of names, however unexpected. "I thought," said he, " he was more generally known by the name of Herries. I have seen and been in company with him under that name, I am sure."

"O ay ; in Edinburgh, belike. You know Redgauntlet was unfortunate a great while ago, and though he was maybe not deeper in the mire than other folk, yet, for some reason or other, he did not get so easily out."

"He was attainted, I understand, and has no remission," said Fairford.

The cautious provost only nodded, and said, " You may guess, therefore, why it is so convenient he should hold his mother's name, which is also partly his own, when he is

about Edinburgh. To bear his proper name might be accounted a kind of flying in the face of government, ye understand. But he has been long connived at—the story is
an old story ; and the gentleman has many excellent qualities, and is of a very ancient and honorable house—has
cousins among the great folk—counts kin with the advocate
and with the sheriff : hawks, you know, Mr. Alan, will not
pike out hawks' een. He is widely connected—*my* wife is
a fourth cousin of Redgauntlet's."

"*Hinc illæ lachrymæ !*" thought Alan Fairford to himself ; but the hint presently determined him to proceed by
soft means, and with caution. "I beg you to understand,"
said Fairford, "that, in the investigation which I am about
to make, I design no harm to Mr. Herries, or Redgauntlet,
call him what you will. All I wish is to ascertain the safety
of my friend. I know that he was rather foolish in once
going upon a mere frolic, in disguise, to the neighborhood
of this same gentleman's house. In his circumstances, Mr.
Redgauntlet may have misinterpreted the motives, and considered Darsie Latimer as a spy. His influence, I believe,
is great among the disorderly people you spoke of but now ? "

The provost answered with another sagacious shake of his
head, that would have done honor to Lord Burleigh in *The
Critic.*

"Well, then," continued Fairford, "is it not possible
that, in the mistaken belief that Mr. Latimer was a spy,
he may, upon such suspicion, have caused him to be carried
off and confined somewhere ? Such things are done at elec-
tions, and on occasions less pressing than when men think
their lives are in danger from an informer."

"Mr. Fairford," said the provost, very earnestly, "I
scarce think such a mistake possible ; or if, by any extraordinary chance it should have taken place, Redgauntlet,
whom I cannot but know well, being, as I have said, my
wife's first cousin—fourth cousin, I should say—is altogether
incapable of doing anything harsh to the young gentleman :
he might send him ower to Ailsay for a night or two, or
maybe land him on the north coast of Ireland, or in Islay,
or some of the Hebrides ; but depend upon it, he is incapable of harming a hair of his head."

"I am determined not to trust to that, provost," answered
Fairford, firmly ; "and I am a good deal surprised at your
way of talking so lightly of such an aggression on the
liberty of the subject. You are to consider, and Mr. Herries
or Mr. Redgauntlet's friends would do very well also to con-

sider, how it will sound in the ears of an English **Secretary**
of State, that an attainted traitor, for such is this gentleman, has not only ventured to take up his abode in this
realm against the king of which he has been in arms, but is
suspected of having proceeded, by open force and violence,
against the person of one of the lieges, a young man who is
neither without friends nor property to secure his being
righted."

The provost looked at the young counselor with a face
in which distrust, alarm, and vexation seemed mingled.
" A fashious job," he said at last—" a fashious job ; and it
will be dangerous meddling with it. I should like ill to see
your father's son turn informer against an unfortunate
gentleman."

" Neither do I mean it," answered Alan, " provided that
unfortunate gentleman and his friends give me a quiet opportunity of securing *my* friend's safety. If I could speak
with Mr. Redgauntlet, and hear his own explanation, I
should probably be satisfied. If I am forced to denounce
him to government, it will be in his new capacity of a kid-
napper. I may not be able, nor is it my business, to prevent his being recognized in his former character of an
attainted person, excepted from the general pardon."

" Master Fairford," said the provost, " would ye ruin
the poor innocent gentleman on an idle suspicion ? "

" Say no more of it, Mr. Crosbie ; my line of conduct is
determined unless that suspicion is removed."

" Weel, sir," said the provost, " since so it be, and since
you say that you do not seek to harm Redgauntlet personally, I'll ask a man to dine with us to-day that kens as much
about his matters as most folk. You must think, Mr.
Alan Fairford, though Redgauntlet be my wife's dear relative, and though, doubtless, I wish him weel, yet I am not
the person who is like to be entrusted with his incomings
and outgoings. I am not a man for that. I keep the kirk,
and I abhor Popery. I have stood up for the house of Hanover, and for liberty and property. I carried arms, sir,
against the Pretender, when three of the Highlandmen's
baggage-carts were stopped at Ecclefechan ; and I had an
especial loss of a hundred pounds——"

" Scots," interrupted Fairford. " You forget you told me
all this before."

" Scots or English, it was too much for me to lose," said
the provost ; " so you see I am not a person to pack or peel
with Jacobites, and such unfreemen as poor Redgauntlet."

16

"Granted—granted, Mr. Crosbie; and what then? said Alan Fairford.

"Why, then, it follows that, if I am to help you at this pinch, it cannot be by and through my ain personal knowledge, but through some fitting agent or third person."

"Granted again," said Fairford. "And pray who may this third person be?"

"Wha but Pate Maxwell of Summertrees—him they call Pate-in-Peril?"

"An old Forty-five man, of course?" said Fairford.

"Ye may swear that," replied the provost—"as black a Jacobite as the auld leaven can make him; but a sonsy, merry companion, that none of us think it worth while to break wi' for all his brags and his clavers. You would have thought, if he had had but his own way at Derby, he would have marched Charlie Stuart through between Wade and the Duke, as a thread goes through the needle's ee, and seated him in St. James's before you could have said 'haud your hand.' But though he is a windy body when he gets on his auld-warld stories, he has mair gumption in him than most people—knows business, Mr. Alan, being bred to the law; but never took the gown, because of the oaths, which kept more folk out then than they do now—the more's the pity."

"What! are you sorry, provost, that Jacobitism in upon the decline?" said Fairford.

"No—no," answered the provost; "I am only sorry for folks losing the tenderness of conscience which they used to have. I have a son breeding to the bar, Mr. Fairford; and, no doubt, considering my services and sufferings, I might have looked for some bit postie to him; but if the muckle tikes come in—I mean a' these Maxwells, and Johnstones, and great lairds, that the oaths used to keep out lang syne— the bits o' messan doggies, like my son, and maybe like your father's son, Mr. Alan, will be sair put to the wall."

"But to return to the subject, Mr. Crosbie," said Fairford, "do you really think it likely that this Mr. Maxwell will be of service in this matter?"

"It's very like he may be, for he is the tongue of the trump to the whole squad of them," said the provost; "and Redgauntlet, though he will not stick at times to call him a fool, takes more of his counsel than any man's else that I am aware of. If Pate can bring him to a communing, the business is done. He's a sharp chield, Pate-in-Peril."

"Pate-in-Peril!" repeated Alan—"a very singular name."

"Ay, and it was in as queer a way he got it ; but I'll say naething about that," said the provost, " for fear of forestalling his market ; for ye are sure to hear it once at least, however oftener, before the punch-bowl gives place to the tea-pot. And now, fare ye weel ; for there is the council-bell clinking in earnest ; and if I am not there before it jows in, Bailie Laurie will be trying some of his maneuvers."

The provost, repeating his expectation of seeing Mr. Fairford at two o'clock, at length effected his escape from the young counselor, and left him at a considerable loss how to proceed. The sheriff, it seems, had returned to Edinburgh, and he feared to find the visible repugnance of the provost to interfere with this laird of Birrenswork, or Redgauntlet, much stronger amongst the country gentlemen, many of whom were Catholics as well as Jacobites, and most others unwilling to quarrel with kinsmen and friends, by prosecuting with severity political offenses which had almost run a prescription.

To collect all the information in his power, and not to have recourse to the higher authorities until he could give all the light of which the case was capable, seemed the wiser proceeding in a choice of difficulties. He had some conversation with the procurator-fiscal, who, as well as the provost, was an old correspondent of his father. Alan expressed to that officer a purpose of visiting Brokenburn, but was assured by him that it would be a step attended with much danger to his own person, and altogether fruitless ; that the individuals who had been ringleaders in the riot were long since safely sheltered in their various lurking-holes in the Isle of Man, Cumberland, and elsewhere ; and that those who might remain would undoubtedly commit violence on any who visited their settlement with the purpose of inquiring into the late disturbances.

There were not the same objections to his hastening to Mount Sharon, where he expected to find the latest news of his friend ; and there was time enough to do so before the hour appointed for the provost's dinner. Upon the road, he congratulated himself on having obtained one point of almost certain information. The person who had in a manner forced himself upon his father's hospitality, and had appeared desirous to induce Darsie Latimer to visit England, against whom, too, a sort of warning had been received from an individual connected with and residing in his own family, proved to be a promoter of the disturbance in which Darsie had disappeared.

What could be the cause of such an attempt on the liberty of an inoffensive and amiable man? It was impossible it could be merely owing to Redgauntlet's mistaking Darsie for a spy; * for though that was the solution which Fairford had offered to the provost, he well knew that, in point of fact, he himself had been warned by his singular visitor of some danger to which his friend was exposed, before such suspicion could have been entertained; and the injunctions received by Latimer from his guardian, or him who acted as such, Mr. Griffiths of London, pointed to the same thing. He was rather glad, however, that he had not let Provost Crosbie into his secret farther than was absolutely necessary; since it was plain that the connection of his wife with the suspected party was likely to affect his impartiality as a magistrate.

When Alan Fairford arrived at Mount Sharon, Rachel Geddes hastened to meet him, almost before the servant could open the door. She drew back in disappointment when she beheld a stranger, and said, to excuse her precipitation, that "She had thought it was her brother Joshua returned from Cumberland."

"Mr. Geddes is then absent from home?" said Fairford, much disappointed in his turn.

"He hath been gone since yesterday, friend," answered Rachel, once more composed to the quietude which characterizes her sect, but her pale cheek and red eye giving contradiction to her assumed equanimity.

"I am," said Fairford, hastily, "the particular friend of a young man not unknown to you, Miss Geddes—the friend of Darsie Latimer—and am come hither in the utmost anxiety, having understood from Provost Crosbie that he had disappeared in the night when a destructive attack was made upon the fishing-station of Mr. Geddes."

"Thou dost afflict me, friend, by thy inquiries," said Rachel, more affected than before; "for although the youth was like those of the worldly generation, wise in his own conceit, and lightly to be moved by the breath of vanity, yet Joshua loved him, and his heart clave to him as if he had been his own son. And when he himself escaped from the sons of Belial, which was not until they had tired themselves with reviling, and with idle reproach, and the jests of the scoffer, Joshua, my brother, returned to them once and again, to give ransom for the youth called Darsie Latimer, with offers of money and with promise of remission, but

* See Trepanning and Concealment. Note 27.

they would not hearken to him. Also, he went before the
head judge, whom men call the sheriff, and would have told
him of the youth's peril ; but he would in no way hearken
to him unless he would swear unto the truth of his words,
which thing he might not do without sin, seeing it is written,
"Swear not at all ;" also, the our "conversation shall be
yea or nay." Therefore, Joshua returned to me disconsolate,
and said, "Sister Rachel, this youth hath run into peril for
my sake ; assuredly I shall not be guiltless if a hair of his
head be harmed, seeing I have sinned in permitting him to
go with me to the fishing-station when such evil was to be
feared. Therefore, I will take my horse, even Solomon, and
ride swiftly into Cumberland, and I will make myself friends
with mammon of unrighteousness among the magistrates of
the Gentiles, and among their mighty men ; and it shall
come to pass that Darsie Latimer shall be delivered, even if
it were at the expense of half my substance." And I said,
"Nay, my brother, go not, for they will but scoff at and
revile thee ; but hire with thy silver one of the scribes, who
are eager as hunters in pursuing their prey, and he shall
free Darsie Latimer from the men of violence by his cunning, and thy soul shall be guiltless of evil towards the lad."
But he answered and said, "I will not be controlled in this
matter." And he is gone forth, and hath not returned, and
I fear me that he may never return ; for though he be
peaceful, as becometh one who holds all violence as offense
against his own soul, yet neither the floods of water, nor the
fear of the snare, nor the drawn sword of the adversary
brandished in the path will overcome his purpose ; wherefore the Solway may swallow him up, or the sword of the
enemy may devour him. Nevertheless, my hope is better
in Him who directeth all things, and ruleth over the waves
of the sea, and overruleth the devices of the wicked, and
who can redeem us even as a bird from the fowler's net."

This was all that Fairford could learn from Miss Geddes ;
but he heard with pleasure that the good Quaker, her brother,
had many friends among those of his own profession in Cumberland, and without exposing himself to so much danger,
as his sister seemed to apprehend, he trusted he might be
able to discover some traces of Darsie Latimer. He himself
rode back to Dumfries, having left with Miss Geddes his
direction in that place, and an earnest request that she
would forward thither whatever information she might
obtain from her brother.

On Fairford's return to Dumfries, he employed the brief

interval which remained before dinner-time in writing an account of what had befallen Latimer, and of the present uncertainty of his condition, to Mr. Samuel Griffiths, through whose hands the remittances for his friend's service had been regularly made, desiring he would instantly acquaint him with such parts of his history as might direct him in the search which he was about to institute through the Border counties, and which he pledged himself not to give up until he had obtained news of his friend, alive or dead. The young lawyer's mind felt easier when he had despatched this letter. He could not conceive any reason why his friend's life should be aimed at ; he knew Darsie had done nothing by which his liberty could be legally affected ; and although, even of late years, there had been singular histories of men, and women also, who had been trepanned, and concealed in solitudes and distant islands, in order to serve some temporary purpose, such violences had been chiefly practised by the rich on the poor, and by the strong on the feeble ; whereas, in the present case, this Mr. Herries, or Redgauntlet, being amenable, for more reasons than one, to the censure of the law, must be the weakest in any struggle in which it could be appealed to. It is true that his friendly anxiety whispered that the very cause which rendered this oppressor less formidable might make him more desperate. Still, recalling his language, so strikingly that of the gentleman, and even of the man of honor, Alan Fairford concluded that, though, in his feudal pride, Redgauntlet might venture on the deeds of violence exercised by the aristocracy in other times, he could not be capable of any action of deliberate atrocity. And in these convictions he went to dine with Provost Crosbie with a heart more at ease than might have been expected.

CHAPTER XI

FIVE minutes had elapsed after the town-clock struck two before Alan Fairford, who had made a small detour to put his letter into the post-house, reached the mansion of Mr. Provost Crosbie, and was at once greeted by the voice of that civic dignitary, and the rural dignitary his visitor, as by the voices of men impatient for their dinner.

"Come away, Mr. Fairford—the Edinburgh time is later than ours," said the provost.

And, "Come away, young gentleman," said the laird. "I remember your father weel, at the Cross, thirty years ago. I reckon you are as late in Edinburgh as at London—four o'clock hours, eh?"

"Not quite so degenerate," replied Fairford; "but certainly many Edinburgh people are so ill-advised as to postpone their dinner till three, that they may have full time to answer their London correspondents."

"London correspondents!" said Mr. Maxwell; "and pray, what the devil have the people of Auld Reekie to do with London correspondents?"*

"The tradesmen must have their goods," said Fairford.

"Can they not buy our own Scottish manufactures, and pick their customers' pockets in a more patriotic manner?"

"Then the ladies must have fashions," said Fairford.

"Can they not busk the plaid over their heads, as their mothers did? A tartan screen, and once a-year a new cockernony from Paris, should serve a countess. But ye have not many of them left, I think; Mareschal, Airley, Winton, Wemyss, Balmerino, all passed and gone! Ay, ay, the countesses and ladies of quality will scarce take up too much of your ball-room floor with their quality hoops nowadays."

"There is no want of crowding, however, sir," said Fairford; "they begin to talk of a new Assembly Room."

"A new Assembly Room!" said the old Jacobite laird. "Umph—I mind quartering three hundred men in the old

Assembly Room.* But come—come, I'll ask no more questions ; the answers all smell of new lords, new lands, and do but spoil my appetite, which were a pity, since here comes Mrs. Crosbie to say our mutton's ready."

It was even so. Mrs. Crosbie had been absent, like Eve, "on hospitable cares intent"—a duty which she did not conceive herself exempted from, either by the dignity of her husband's rank in the municipality, or the splendor of her Brussels silk gown, or even by the more highly prized luster of her birth ; for she was born a Maxwell, and allied, as her husband often informed his friends, to several of the first families in the county. She had been handsome, and was still a portly, good-looking woman of her years ; and though her peep into the kitchen had somewhat heightened her complexion, it was no more than a modest touch of rouge might have done.

The provost was certainly proud of his lady, nay, some said he was afraid of her ; for, of the females of the Redgauntlet family there went a rumor that, ally where they would, there was a gray mare as surely in the stables of their husbands as there is a white horse in Wouverman's pictures. The good dame, too, was supposed to have brought a spice of politics into Mr. Crosbie's household along with her ; and the provost's enemies at the council-table of the burgh used to observe, that he uttered there many a bold harangue against the Pretender, and in favor of King George and government, of which he dared not have pronounced a syllable in his own bedchamber ; and that, in fact his wife's predominating influence had now and then occasioned his acting, or forbearing to act, in a manner very different from his general professions of zeal for Revolution principles. If this was in any respect true, it was certain, on the other hand, that Mrs. Crosbie, in all external points, seemed to acknowledge the "lawful sway and right supremacy" of the head of the house, and if she did not in truth reverence her husband, she at least seemed to do so.

This stately dame received Mr. Maxwell—a cousin of course—with cordiality, and Fairford with civility ; answering, at the same time, with respect, to the magisterial complaints of the provost, that dinner was just coming up. "But since you changed poor Peter MacAlpin, that used to

---

* I remember hearing this identical answer given by an old Highland gentleman of the Forty-five, when he heard of the opening of the New Assembly Rooms in George Street,

take care of the town-clock, my dear, it has never gone well a single day."

"Peter MacAlpin, my dear," said the provost, "made himself too busy for a person in office, and drunk healths and so forth, which it became no man to drink or to pledge, far less one that is in point of office a servant of the public. I understand that he lost the music-bells in Edingurgh for playing "Ower the water to Charlie" upon the 10th of June. He is a black sheep, and deserves no encouragement."

"Not a bad tune, though, after all," said Summertrees; and, turning to the window, he half hummed, half whistled the air in question, then sang the last verse aloud :

> "Oh I loe weel my Charlie's name,
>   Though some there be that abhor him ;
> But oh to see the deil gang hame
>   Wi' a' the Whigs before him !
> Over the water, and over the sea,
>   And over the water to Charlie ;
> Come weal, come woe, we'll gather and go,
>   And live or die with Charlie."

Mrs. Crosbie smiled furtively on the laird, wearing an aspect at the same time of deep submission ; while the provost, not choosing to hear his visitor's ditty, took a turn through the room, in unquestioned dignity and independence of authority.

"Aweel—aweel, my dear," said the lady, with a quiet smile of submission, "ye ken these matters best, and you will do your pleasure—they are far above my hand—only, I doubt if ever the town-clock will go right, or your meals be got up so regular as I should wish, till Peter MacAlpin gets his office back again. The body's auld, and can neither work nor want, but he is the only hand to set a clock."

It may be noticed in passing that, notwithstanding this prediction, which, probably, the fair Cassandra had the full means of accomplishing, it was not till the second council-day thereafter that the misdemeanours of the Jacobite clock-keeper were passed over, and he was once more restored to his occupation of fixing the town's time, and the provost's dinner-hour.

Upon the present occasion the dinner passed pleasantly away. Summertrees talked and jested with the easy indifference of a man who holds himself superior to his company. He was indeed an important person, as was testified by his portly appearance ; his hat laced with *point d' Espagne* ; his coat and waistcoat once richly embroidered, though now almost threadbare ; the splendor of his solitaire and lace ruffles though the first were sorely creased and the other sullied ; not to forget the length of his silver-headed rapier. His wit, or rather humor, bordered on the sarcastic, and intimated a discontented man ; and although he showed no displeasure when the provost attempted a repartee; yet it seemed that he permitted it upon mere sufferance, as a fencing-master, engaged with a pupil, will sometimes permit the tyro to hit him, solely by way of encouagement. The laird's own jests, in the meanwhile, were eminently successful, not only with the provost and his lady, but with the red-cheeked and red-ribboned servant-maid who waited at table, and who could scarce perform her duty with propriety, so effectual were the explosions of Summertrees. Alan Fairford alone was unmoved among all this mirth, which was the less wonderful that, besides the important subject which occupied his thoughts, most of the laird's good things consisted in sly allusions to little parochial or family incidents with which the Edinburgh visitor was totally unacquainted ; so that the laughter of the party sounded in his ear like the idle crackling of thorns under the pot, with this difference, that they did not accompany or second any such useful operation as the boiling thereof.

Fairford was glad when the cloth was withdrawn ; and when Provost Crosbie (not without some points of advice from his lady touching the precise mixture of the ingredients) had accomplished the compounding of a noble bowl of punch, at which the old Jacobite's eyes seemed to glisten, the glasses were pushed round, filled, and withdrawn each by its owner, when the provost emphatically named the toast, "The king," with an important look at Fairford, which seemed to say, "You can have no doubt whom I mean, and therefore there is no occasion to particularize the individual."

Summertrees repeated the toast with a sly wink to the lady, while Fairford drank his glass in silence.

"Well, young advocate," said the landed proprietor, "I am glad to see there is some shame, if there is little honesty, left in the faculty. Some of your black-gowns, nowadays, have as little of the one as of the other."

"At least, sir," replied Mr. Fairford, "I am so much of a lawyer as not willingly to enter into disputes which I am not retained to support ; it would be but throwing away both time and argument."

"Come—come," said the lady, "we will have no argu-

ment in this house about Whig and Tory; the provost kens
what he maun *say*, and I ken what he should *think*; and for
a' that has come and gane yet, there may be a time coming
when honest men may say what they think, whether they be
provosts or not."

"D'ye hear that, provost?" said Summertrees; "your
wife's a witch, man: you should nail a horseshoe on your
chamber door. Ha, ha, ha!"

This sally did not take quite so well as former efforts of
the laird's wit. The lady drew up, and the provost said,
half aside, "The sooth bourd is nae bourd. You will find
the horseshoe hissing hot, Summertrees."

"You can speak from experience, doubtless, provost," answered the laird; "but I crave pardon—I need not tell Mrs.
Crosbie that I have all respect for the auld and honorable
house of Redgauntlet."

"And good reason ye have, that are sae sib to them,"
quoth the lady, "and kenn'd weel baith them that are here,
and them that are gane."

"In troth, and ye may say sae, madam," answered the
laird; "for poor Harry Redgauntlet that suffered at Carlisle
was hand and glove with me; and yet we parted on short
leave-taking."

"Ay, Summertrees," said the provost; "that was when you
played cheat-the-woodie, and gat the bye-name of Pate-in-
Peril. I wish you would tell the story to my young friend
here. He likes weel to hear of a sharp trick, as most lawyers
do."

"I wonder at your want of circumspection, provost," said
the laird, much after the manner of a singer, when declining
to sing the song that is quivering upon his tongue's very end.
"Ye should mind there are some auld stories that cannot be
ripped up again with entire safety to all concerned. *Tace*
is Latin for a candle."

"I hope," said the lady, "you are not afraid of anything
being said out of the house to your prejudice, Summertrees?
I have heard the story before, but the oftener I hear it, the
more wonderful I think it."

"Yes, madam; but it has been now a wonder of more than
nine days, and it is time it should be ended," answered
Maxwell.

"Fairford now thought it civil to say, "That he had often
heard of Mr. Maxwell's wonderful escape, and that nothing
could be more agreeable to him than to hear the right version
of it."

But Summertrees was obdurate, and refused to take up the time of the company with such "auld-warld nonsonse."

"Weel—weel," said the provost, "a wilful man maun hae his way. What do you folk in the country think about the disturbances that are beginning to spunk out in the colonies?"

"Excellent, sir—excellent. When things come to the worst they will mend; and to the worst they are coming. But as to that nonsense ploy of mine, if ye insist on hearing the particulars——" said the laird, who began to be sensible that the period of telling his story gracefully was gliding fast away.

"Nay," said the provost, "it is not for myself, but this young gentleman."

"Aweel, what for should I not pleasure the young gentleman? I'll just drink to honest folk at hame and abroad, and deil ane else. And then—but you have heard it before, Mrs. Crosbie?"

"Not so often as to think it tiresome, I assure ye," said the lady; and without further preliminaries, the laird addressed Alan Fairford.

"Ye have heard of a year they call the Forty-five, young gentleman; when the Southrons' heads made their last acquaintance with Scottish claymores? There was a set of rampanging chields in the country then that they called rebels —I never could find out what for. Some men should have been wi' them that never came, provost—Skye and the Bush aboon Traquair for that, ye ken. Weel, the job was settled at last. Cloured crowns were plenty, and raxed necks came into fashion. I dinna mind very weel what I was doing, swaggering about the country with dirk and pistol at my belt for five or six months, or thereaway; but I had a weary waking out of a wild dream. Then did I find myself on foot in a misty morning, with my hand, just for fear of going astray, linked into a handcuff, as they call it, with poor Harry Redgauntlet's fastened into the other; and there we were, trudging along, with about a score more that had thrust their horns ower deep in the bog, just like ourselves, and a sergeant's guard of redcoats, with twa file of dragoons, to keep all quiet, and give us heart to the road. Now, if this mode of traveling was not very pleasant, the object did not particularly recommend it; for you understand, young man, that they did not trust these poor rebel bodies to be tried by juries of their ain kindly countrymen, though ane would have thought they would have found Whigs enough in Scotland to hang us all ; but they behoved to trounce us away to be tried at Carlisle, where the folk had been so frightened that, had you brought a whole Highland clan at once into the court, they would have put their hands upon their een, and cried, ' hang them a', just to be quit of them."

" Ay—ay," said the provost, " that was a snell law, I grant ye."

" Snell ! " said his wife—" snell ! I wish they that passed it had the jury I would recommend them to ! "

" I suppose the young lawyer thinks it all very right," said Summertrees, looking at Fairford; " an *old* lawyer might have thought otherwise. However, the cudgel was to be found to beat the dog, and they choose a heavy one. Well, I kept my spirits better than my companion, poor fellow ; for I had the luck to have neither wife nor child to think about, and Harry Redgauntlet had both one and t'other. You have seen Harry, Mrs. Crosbie ? "

" In troth have I," said she, with the sigh which we give to early recollections, of which the object is no more. " He was not so tall as his. brother, and a gentler lad every way. After he married the great English fortune, folk called him less of a Scotchman than Edward."

" Folk lee'd, then," said Summertrees ; " poor Harry was none of your bold-speaking, ranting reivers, that talk about what they did yesterday, or what they will do to-morrow : it was when something was to do at the moment that you should have looked at Harry Redgauntlet. I saw him at Culloden, when all was lost, doing more than twenty of these bleezing braggarts, till the very soldiers that took him, cried not to hurt him—for all somebody's orders, provost—for he was the bravest fellow of them all. Weel, as I went by the side of Harry, and felt him raise my hand up in the mist of the morning, as if he wished to wipe his eye—for he had not that freedom without my leave—my very heart was like to break for him, poor fellow. In the meanwhile, I had been trying and trying to make my hand as fine as a lady's, to see if I could slip it out of my iron wrist-band. You may think," he said, laying his broad bony hand on the table, " I had work enough with such a shoulder-of-mutton fist ; but if you observe, the shackle-bones are of the largest, and so they were obliged to keep the handcuff wide ; at length I got my hand slipped out, and slipped in again ; and poor Harry was sae deep in his ain thoughts I could not make him sensible what I was doing."

"Why not?" said Alan Fairford, for whom the tale began to have some interest.

"Because there was an unchancy beast of a dragoon riding close beside us on the other side ; and if I had let him into my confidence as well as Harry, it would not have been long before a pistol-ball slapped through my bonnet. Well, I had little for it but to do the best I could for myself ; and by my conscience, it was time, when the gallows was staring me in the face. We were to halt for breakfast at Moffat. Well did I know the moors we were marching over, having hunted and hawked on every acre of ground in very different times. So I waited, you see, till I was on the edge of Errickstane Brae. Ye ken the place they call the Marquis's Beef-Stand, because the Annandale loons used to put their stolen cattle in them ?"

Fairford intimated his ignorance.

"Ye must have seen it as you cam this way ; it looks as if four hills were lying their heads together to shut out day-light from the dark hollow space between them. A d—d deep, black, blackguard-looking abyss of a hole it is, and goes straight down from the roadside, as perpendicular as it can do, to be a heathery brae. At the bottom there is a small bit of a brook, that you would think could hardly find its way out from the hills that are so closely jammed round it."

"A bad pass indeed," said Alan.

"You may say that," continued the laird. "Bad as it was, sir, it was my only chance ; and though my very flesh creeped when I thought what a rumble I was going to get, yet I kept my heart up all the same. And so just when we came on the edge of this Beef-Stand of the Johnstones, I slipped out my hand from the handcuff, cried to Harry Gauntlet " Follow me !" whisked under the belly of the dragoon horse, flung my plaid round me with the speed of lightening, threw myself on my side, for there was no keep-ing my feet, and down the brae hurled I, over heather and fern, and blackberries, like a barrel down Chalmers's Close in Auld Reekie. G—, sir, I never could help laughing when I think how the scoundrel redcoats must have been bum-bazed ; for the mist being, as I said, thick, they had little notion, I take it, that they were on the verge of such a dilemma. I was half-way down—for rowing is faster wark than rinning—ere they could get at their arms ; and then it was flash, flash, flash,—rap, rap, rap—from the edge of the road ; but my head was too jumbled to think anything either of that or the hard knocks I got among the stones. I kept my senses thegither, whilk has been thought wonderful by all that ever saw the place ; and I helped myself with my hands as gallantly as I could, and to the bottom I came. There I lay for half a moment ; but the thoughts of a gallows is worth all the salts and scent-bottles in the world for bringing a man to himself. Up I sprung like a four-year auld colt. All the hills were spinning round with me like so many great big humming-tops. But there was nae time to think of that neither, more especially as the mist had risen a little with the firing. I could see the villains, like sae mony craws on the edge of the brae : and I reckon that they saw me, for some of the loons were beginning to crawl down the hill, but liker auld wives in their red cloaks coming frae a field-preaching than such a souple lad as I was. Accordingly they soon began to stop and load their pieces. Goode'en to you, gentlemen, thought I, if that is to be the gate of it. If you have any further word with me, you maun come as far as Carrifra Gauns. And so off I set, and never buck went faster ower the braes than I did ; and I never stopped till I had put three waters, reasonably deep, as the season was rainy, half a dozen mountains, and a few thousand acres of the worst moss and ling in Scotland betwixt me and my friends the redcoats."

" It was that job which got you the name of ' Pate-in-Peril.' " said the provost, filling the glasses, and exclaiming with great emphasis, while his guest, much animated with the recollections which the exploit excited, looked round with an air of triumph for sympathy and applause, " Here is to your good health ; and may you never put your neck in such a venture again." *

" Humph ! I do not know," answered Summertrees. " I am not like to be tempted with another opportunity.† Yet, who knows ? " And then he made a deep pause.

" May I ask what became of your friend, sir ? " said Alan Fairford.

" Ah, poor Harry ! " said Summertrees. " I'll tell you what, sir, it takes time to make up one's mind to such a venture, as my friend the provost calls it ; and I was told by Neil Maclean, who was next file to us, but had the luck to escape the gallows by some slight-of-hand trick or other, that, upon my breaking off, poor Harry stood like one motionless, although all our brethren in captivity made as

* See escape of Pate-in-Peril. Note 29.
† See Note 30.

much tumult as they could, to distract the attention of the soldiers. And run he did at last ; but he did not know the ground, and either from confusion, or because he judged the descent altogether perpendicular, he fled up the hill to the left, instead of going down at once, and so was easily pursued and taken. If he had followed my example, he would have found enough among the shepherds to hide him, and feed him, as they did me, on bearmeal scones and braxy mutton,* till better days came round again."

" He suffered, then, for his share in the insurrection ? " said Alan.

" You may swear that," said Summertrees. " His blood was too red to be spared when that sort of paint was in request. He suffered, sir, as you call it—that is, he was murdered in cold blood, with many a pretty fellow besides. Well, we may have our day next ; what is fristed is not forgiven ; they think us all dead and buried, but——" Here he filled his glass, and muttering some indistinct denunciations, drank it off, and assumed his usual manner, which had been a little disturbed towards the end of the narrative.

" What became of Mr. Redgauntlet's child ? " said Fairford.

"*Mister* Redgauntlet !   He was Sir Henry Redgauntlet, as his son, if the child now lives, will be Sir Arthur.   I called him Harry from intimacy, and Redgauntlet as the chief of his name.   His proper style was Sir Henry Redgauntlet."

" His son, therefore, is dead ? " said Alan Fairford.   " It is a pity so brave a line should draw to a close."

" He has left a brother," said Summertrees, " Edward Hugh Redgauntlet, who has now the representation of the family.   And well it is ; for though he be unfortunate in many respects, he will keep up the honor of the house better than a boy bred up amongst these bitter Whigs, the relations of his elder brother Sir Henry's lady.   Then they are on no good terms with the Redgauntlet line : bitter Whigs they are, in every sense.   It was a runaway match betwixt Sir Henry and his lady.   Poor thing, they would not allow her to see him when in confinement ; they had even the meanness to leave him without pecuniary assistance ; and as all his own property was seized upon and plundered, he would have wanted common necessaries, but for the attachment of a fellow who was a famous fiddler—a blind man.   I have

* See Note 31.

seen him with Sir Henry myself, both before the affair broke
out and while it was going on.   I have heard that he fiddled
in the streets of Carlisle, and carried what money he got to
his master, while he was confined in the castle."

" I do not believe a word of it," said Mrs. Crosbie, kindling with indignation.   " A Redgauntlet would have died
twenty times before he had touched a fiddler's wages."

" Hout fie—hout fie, all nonsense and pride," said the
laird of Summertrees.   " Scornful dogs will eat dirty pud-
dings, cousin Crosbie ; ye little ken what some of your
friends were obliged to do yon time for a soup of brose or a
bit of bannock.   G—d, I carried a cutler's wheel for several
weeks, partly for need and partly for disguise ; there I went
bizz—bizz, whizz—zizz at every auld wife's door ; and if ever
you want your shears sharpened, Mrs. Crosbie, I am the lad
to do it for you, if my wheel was but in order."

" You must ask my leave first," said the provost ; " for I
have been told you had some queer fashions of taking a kiss
instead of a penny, if you liked your customer."

" Come—come, provost," said the lady, rising, " if the
maut gets abune the meal with you, it is time for me to take
myself away.   And you will come to my room, gentlemen,
when you want a cup of tea."

Alan Fairford was not sorry for the lady's departure.   She
seemed too much alive to the honor of the house of Redgauntlet, though only a fourth cousin, not to be alarmed by
the inquiries which he proposed to make after the where-
about of its present head.   Strange, confused suspicions
arose in his mind, from his imperfect recollection of the tale
of Wandering Willie, and the idea forced itself upon him
that his friend Darsie Latimer might be the son of the unfortunate Sir Henry.   But before indulging in such speculations, the point was, to discover what had actually become
of him.   If he were in the hands of his uncle, might there
not exist some rivalry in fortune or rank which might induce
so stern a man as Redgauntlet to use unfair measures towards
a youth whom he would find himself unable to mold to his
purpose ?   He considered these points in silence during
several revolutions of the glasses as they wheeled in galaxy
round the bowl, waiting until the provost, agreeably to his
own proposal, should mention the subject for which he had
.expressly introduced him to Mr. Maxwell of Summertrees.

Apparently the provost had forgot his promise, or at least
was in no great haste to fulfil it.   He debated with great
earnestness upon the Stamp Act, which was then impending

17

over the American colonies, and upon other political subjects of the day, but said not a word of Redgauntlet. Alan soon saw that the investigation he meditated must advance, if at all, on his own special motion, and determined to proceed accordingly.

Acting upon this resolution, he took the first opportunity afforded by a pause in the discussion of colonial politics to say, " I must remind you, Provost Crosbie, of your kind promise to procure some intelligence upon the subject I am so anxious about."

" Gadso ! " said the provost, after a moment's hesitation, " it is very true. Mr. Maxwell, we wish to consult you on a piece of important business. You must know—indeed, I think you must have heard—that the fishermen at Brokenburn and higher up the Solway have made a raid upon Quaker Geddes's stake-nets and leveled all with the sands."

" In troth I heard it, provost, and I was glad to hear the scoundrels had so much pluck left as to right themselves against a fashion which would make the upper heritors a sort of clocking-hens to hatch the fish that folk below them were to catch and eat."

" Well, sir," said Alan, " that is not the present point. But a young friend of mine was with Mr. Geddes at the time this violent procedure took place, and he has not since been heard of. Now, our friend, the provost, thinks that you may be able to advise——"

Here he was interrupted by the provost and Summertrees speaking out both at once, the first endeavoring to disclaim all interest in the question, and the last to evade giving an answer.

" Me think ! " said the provost. " I never thought twice about it, Mr. Fairford ; it was neither fish, nor flesh, nor salt herring of mine."

" And I able to advise ! " said Mr. Maxwell of Summertrees. " What the devil can I advise you to do, excepting to send the bellman through the town to cry your lost sheep, as they do spaniel dogs or stray ponies ? "

" With your pardon," said Alan, calmly but resolutely, " I must ask a more serious answer."

" Why Mr. Advocate," answered Summertrees, " I thought it was your business to give advice to the lieges, and not to take it from poor stupid country gentlemen."

" If not exactly advice, it is sometimes our duty to ask questions, Mr. Maxwell."

" Ay, sir, when you have your bag-wig and your gown on,

we must allow you the usual privilege of both gown and petticoat, to ask what questions you please. But when you are out of your canonicals the case is altered. How come you, sir, to suppose that I have any business with this riotous proceeding, or should know more than you do what happened there! The question proceeds on an uncivil supposition."

" I will explain," said Alan, determined to give Mr. Maxwell no opportunity of breaking off the conversation. " You are an intimate of Mr. Redgauntlet—he is accused of having been engaged in this affray, and of having placed under forcible restraint the person of my friend, Darsie Latimer, a young man of property and consequence, whose fate I am here for the express purpose of investigating. This is the plain state of the case : and all parties concerned—your friend, in particular—will have reason to be thankful for the temperate manner in which it is my purpose to conduct the matter, if I am treated with proportionate frankness."

" You have misunderstood me," said Maxwell, with a tone changed to more composure : " I told you I was the friend of the late Sir Henry Redgauntlet, who was executed in 1745, at Hairibie, near Carlisle, but I know no one who at present bears the name of Redgauntlet."

" You know Mr. Herries of Birrenswork," said Alan, smiling, " to whom the name of Redgauntlet belongs ? "

Maxwell darted a keen, reproachful look towards the provost, but instantly smoothed his brow and changed his tone to that of confidence and candor.

" You must not be angry, Mr. Fairford, that the poor persecuted Nonjurors are a little upon the *qui vive* when such clever young men as you are making inquires after us. I myself now, though I am quite out of the scrape, and may cock my hat at the Cross as I best like, sunshine or moonshine, have been yet so much accustomed to walk with the lap of my cloak cast over my face, that, faith, if a redcoat walk suddenly up to me, I wish for my wheel and whetstone again for a moment. Now Redgauntlet, poor fellow, is far worse off : he is, you may have heard, still under the lash of the law—the mark of the beast is still on his forehead, poor gentleman ; and that makes us cautious—very cautious—which I am sure there is no occasion to be towards you, as no one of your appearance and manners would wish to trepan a gentleman under misfortune."

" On the contrary, sir," said Fairford, " I wish to afford Mr. Redgauntlet's friends an opportunity to get him out of the scrape, by procuring the instant liberation of my friend Darsie Latimer. I will engage that, if he has sustained no greater bodily harm than a short confinement, the matter may be passed over quietly, without inquiry ; but to attain this end, so desirable for the man who has committed a great and recent infraction of the laws, which he had before grievously offended, very speedy reparation of the wrong must be rendered."

Maxwell seemed lost in reflection, and exchanged a glance or two, not of the most comfortable or congratulatory kind, with his host the provost. Fairford rose and walked about the room, to allow them an opportunity of conversing together : for he was in hopes that the impression he had visibly made upon Summertrees was likely to ripen into something favorable to his purpose. They took the opportunity, and engaged in whispers to each other, eagerly and reproachfully on the part of the laird, while the provost answered in an embarrassed and apologetical tone. Some broken words of the conversation reached Fairford, whose presence they seemed to forget, as he stood at the bottom of the room, apparently intent upon examining the figures upon a fine Indian screen, a present to the provost from his brother, captain of a vessel in the Company's service. What he overheard made it evident that his errand, and the obstinacy with which he pursued it, occasioned altercation between the whisperers.

Maxwell at length let out the words, " A good fright "— " and so send him home with his tail scalded, like a dog that has come a-privateering on strange premises."

The provost's negative was strongly interposed—" Not to be thought of "—" making bad worse "—" my situation "— " my utility "—" you cannot conceive how obstinate—just like his father."

They then whispered more closely, and at length the provost raised his drooping crest and spoke in a cheerful tone. " Come, sit down to your glass, Mr. Fairford ; we have laid our heads thegither, and you shall see it will not be our fault if you are not quite pleased, and Mr. Darsie Latimer let loose to take his fiddle under his neck again. But Summertrees thinks it will require you to put yourself into some bodily risk, which may be you may not be so keen of."

" Gentlemen," said Fairford, " I will not certainly shun any risk by which my object may be accomplished ; but I bind it on your consciences—on yours, Mr. Maxwell, as a man of honor and a gentleman, and on yours, provost, as a magistrate and a loyal subject—that you do not mislead me in this matter."

"Nay, as for me," said Summertrees, "I will tell you the truth at once, and fairly own that I can certainly find you the means of seeing Redgauntlet, poor man ; and that I will do, if you require it, and conjure him also to treat you as your errand requires ; but poor Redgauntlet is much changed —indeed, to say truth, his temper never was the best in the world ; however, I will warrant you from any very great danger."

"I will warrant myself from such," said Fairford, "by carrying a proper force with me."

"Indeed," said Summertrees, "you will do no such thing ; for, in the first place, do you think that we will deliver up the poor fellow into the hands of the Philistines, when, on the contrary, my only reason for furnishing you with the clue I am to put into your hands is to settle the matter amicably on all sides ? And secondly, his intelligence is so good, that were you coming near him with soldiers, or constables, or the like, I shall answer for it, you will never lay salt on his tail."

Fairford mused for a moment. He considered that to gain sight of this man, and knowledge of his friend's condition, were advantages to be purchased at every personal risk ; and he saw plainly that were he to take the course most safe for himself, and call in the assistance of the law, it was clear he would either be deprived of the intelligence necessary to guide him, or that Redgauntlet would be apprised of his danger, and might probably leave the country, carrying his captive along with him. He therefore repeated, "I put myself on your honor, Mr. Maxwell ; and I will go alone to visit your friend. I have little doubt I shall find him amenable to reason, and that I shall receive from him a satisfactory account of Mr. Latimer."

"I have little doubt that you will," said Mr. Maxwell of Summertrees ; "but still I think it will be only in the long-run, and after having sustained some delay and inconvenience. My warrandice goes no farther."

"I will take it as it is given," said Alan Fairford. "But let me ask, would it not be better, since you value your friend's safety so highly, and surely would not willingly compromise mine, that the provost or you should go with me to this man, if he is within any reasonable distance, and try to make him hear reason ?"

"Me! I will not go my foot's length," said the provost; "and that, Mr. Alan, you may be well assured of. Mr. Redgauntlet is my wife's fourth cousin, that is undeniable; but were he the last of her kin and mine both, it would ill befit my office to be communing with rebels."

"Ay, or drinking with Nonjurors," said Maxwell, filling his glass. "I would as soon expect to have met Claverhouse at a field-preaching. And as for myself, Mr. Fairford, I cannot go for just the opposite reason. It would be *infra dig.* in the provost of this most flourishing and loyal town to associate with Redgauntlet; and for me, it would be *noscitur a socio.* There would be post to London with the tidings that two such Jacobites as Redgauntlet and I had met on a braeside; the Habeas Corpus would be suspended; fame would sound a charge from Carlisle to the Land's-End; and who knows but the very wind of the rumor might blow my estate from between my fingers, and my body over Errickstane Brae again? No—no; bide a gliff, I will go into the provost's closet and write a letter to Redgauntlet, and direct you how to deliver it."

"There is pen and ink in the office," said the provost, pointing to the door of an inner apartment, in which he had his walnut-tree desk and east-country cabinet.

"A pen that can write, I hope?" said the old laird.

"It can write and spell baith—in right hands," answered the provost, as the laird retired and shut the door behind him.

CHAPTER XII

NARRATIVE OF ALAN FAIRFORD, CONTINUED

THE room was no sooner deprived of Mr. Maxwell of Summertree's presence than the provost looked very warily above, beneath, and around the apartment, hitched his chair towards that of his remaining guest, and began to speak in a whisper which could not have startled "the smallest mouse that creeps on floor."

"Mr. Fairford," said he, "you are a good lad; and, what is more, you are my auld friend your father's son. Your father has been agent for this burgh for years, and has a good deal to say with the council; so there have been a sort of obligations between him and me; it may have been now on this side and now on that, but obligations there have been. I am but a plain man, Mr. Fairford; but I hope you understand me?"

"I believe you mean me well, provost; and I am sure," replied Fairford, "you can never better show your kindness than on this occasion."

"That's it—that's the very point I would be at, Mr. Alan," replied the provost; "besides, I am, as becomes well my situation, a stanch friend to kirk and king, meaning this present establishment in church and state; and so, as I was saying, you may command my best—advice."

"I hope for your assistance and co-operation also," said the youth.

"Certainly—certainly," said the wary magistrate. "Well, now, you see one may love the kirk, and yet not ride on the rigging of it; and one may love the king, and yet not be cramming him eternally down the throat of the unhappy folk that may chance to like another king better. I have friends and connections among them, Mr. Fairford, as your father may have clients; they are flesh and blood like ourselves, these poor Jacobite bodies—sons of Adam and Eve, after all; and therefore—I hope you understand me? I am a plain-spoken man."

"I am afraid I do *not* quite understand you," said Fairford; "and if you have anything to say to me in private, my dear provost, you had better come quickly out with it, for the laird of Summertrees must finish his letter in a minute or two."

"Not a bit, man : Pate is a long-headed fellow, but his pen does not clear the paper as his greyhound does the Tinwald furs. I gave him a wipe about that, if you noticed : I can say anything to Pate-in-Peril. Indeed, he is my wife's near kinsman."

"But your advice, provost," said Alan, who perceived that, like a shy horse, the worthy magistrate always started off from his own purpose just when he seemed approaching to it.

"Weel, you shall have it in plain terms, for I am a plain man. Ye see, we will suppose that any friend like yourself were in the deepest hole of the Nith, and making a sprattle for your life. Now, you see, such being the case, I have little chance of helping you, being a fat, short-arm man, and no swimmer, what would be the use of my jumping in after you ?"

"I understand you, I think," said Alan Fairford. "You think that Darsie Latimer is in danger of his life."

"Me ! I think nothing about it, Mr. Alan ; but if he were, as I trust he is not, he is nae drap's blood akin to you, Mr. Alan."

"But here your friend, Summertree," said the young lawyer, "offers me a letter to this Redgauntlet of yours. What say you to that ?"

"Me !" ejaculated the provost—"me, Mr. Alan ? I say neither bluff nor style to it. But we dinna ken what it is to look a Redgauntlet in the face ; better try my wife, who is but a fourth cousin, before ye venture on the Laird himself —just say something about the Revolution, and see what a look she can gie you."

"I shall leave you to stand all the shots from that battery, provost," replied Fairford. "But speak out like a man. Do you think Summertrees means fairly by me ?"

"Fairly—he is just coming—fairly ! I am a plain man, Mr. Fairford—but ye said 'fairly' !"

"I do so," replied Alan, "and it is of importance to me to know, and to you to tell me if such is the case ; for if you do not, you may be an accomplice to murder before the fact, and that under circumstances which may bring it near to murder under trust."

"Murder ! Who spoke of murder ?" said the provost. "No danger of that, Mr. Alan ; only, if I were you—to

speak my plain mind——" Here he approached his mouth
to the ear of the young lawyer, and, after another acute pang of
travail, was safely delivered of his advice in the following
abrupt words :—"Take a keek into Pate's letter before ye
deliver it."

Fairford startled, looked the provost hard in the face, and
was silent; while Mr. Crosbie, with the self-approbation of
one who was at length brought himself to the discharge of a
great duty, at the expense of a considerable sacrifice, nodded
and winked to Alan, as if enforcing his advice; and then
swallowing a large glass of punch, concluded, with the sigh
of a man released from a heavy burden, "I am a plain man,
Mr. Fairford."

"A plain man!" said Maxwell, who entered the room at
that moment, with the letter in his hand. "Provost, I
never heard you make use of the word but when you had
some sly turn of your own to work out."

The provost looked silly enough, and the laird of Summertrees directed a keen and suspicious glance upon Alan Fairford, who sustained it with professional intrepidity. There
was a moment's pause.

"I was trying," said the provost, "to dissuade our young
friend from his wildgoose expedition."

"And I, said Fairford, "am determined to go through
with it. Trusting myself to you, Mr. Maxwell, I conceive
that I rely, as I before said, on the words of a gentleman."

"I will warrant you," said Maxwell, "from all serious
consequences; some inconveniences you must look to
suffer."

"To these I shall be resigned," said Fairford, "and stand
prepared to run my risk."

"Well, then," said Summertrees, "you must go——"

"I will leave you to yourselves, gentlemen," said the
provost, rising; "when you have done with your crack, you
will find me at my wife's tea-table."

"And a more accomplished old woman never drank cat-
lap," said Maxwall, as he shut the door. "The last word
has him, speak it who will; and yet, because he is a whilly-
wha body, and has a plausible tongue of his own, and is well
enough connected, and especially because nobody could ever
find out whether he is Whig or Tory, this is the third time they
have made him provost! But to the matter in hand. This
letter, Mr. Fairford," putting a sealed one into his hand,
"is addressed, you observe, to Mr. H—— of B——, and
contains your credentials for that gentleman, who is also

known by his family name of Redgauntlet, but less frequently addressed by it, because it is mentioned something invidiously in a certain Act of Parliament. I have little doubt he will assure you of your friend's safety, and in a short time place him at freedom—that is, supposing him under present restraint. But the point is, to discover where he is; and, before you are made acquainted with this necessary part of the business, you must give me your assurance of honor that you will acquaint no one, either by word or by letter, with the expedition which you now propose to yourself."

"How, sir?" answered Alan; "can you expect that I will not take the precaution of informing some person of the route I am about to take, that, in case of accident, it may be known where I am, and with what purpose I have gone thither?"

"And can you expect," answered Maxwell, in the same tone, "that I am to place my friend's safety, not merely in your hands, but in those of any person you may choose to confide in, and who may use the knowledge to his destruction? Na —na, I have pledged my word for your safety, and you must give me yours to be private in the matter. ' Giff-gaff,' you know."

Alan Fairford could not help thinking that this obligation to secrecy gave a new and suspicious coloring to the whole transaction; but, considering that his friend's release might depend upon his accepting the condition, he gave it in the terms proposed, and with the resolution of abiding by it.

"And now, sir," he said, "whither am I to proceed with this letter? Is Mr. Herries at Brokenburn?"

"He is not. I do not think he will come thither again until the business of the stake-nets be hushed up, nor would I advise him to do so: the Quakers, with all their demureness, can bear malice as long as other folk; and though I have not the prudence of Mr. Provost, who refuses to ken where his friends are concealed during adversity, lest, perchance, he should be asked to contribute to their relief, yet I do not think it necessary or prudent to inquire into Redgauntlet's wanderings, poor man, but wish to remain at perfect freedom to answer, if asked at, that I ken nothing of the matter. You must, then, go to old Tom Trumbull's, at Annan—Tam Turnpenny. as they call him; and he is sure either to know where Redgauntlet is himself or to find some one who can give a shrewd guess. But you must attend that old Turnpenny will answer no question on such a subject without you give him the password, which at present you must do by asking him the age of the moon; if he answers, "Not light enough to land a cargo," you are to answer, "Then plague on Aberdeen almanacks," and upon that he will hold free intercourse with you. And now, I would advise you to lose no time, for the parole is often changed ; and take care of yourself among these moonlight lads, for laws and lawyers do not stand very high in their favor."

"I will set out this instant," said the young barrister : "I will but bid the provost and Mrs. Crosbie farewell, and then get on horseback so soon as the hostler of the George Inn can saddle him ; as for the smugglers, I am neither gauger nor supervisor, and, like the man who met the devil, if they have nothing to say to me, I have nothing to say to them."

"You are a mettled young man," said Summertrees, evidently with increasing good-will, on observing an alertness and contempt of danger which perhaps he did not expect from Alan's appearance and profession—"a very mettled young fellow, indeed ! and it is almost a pity——" Here he stopped short.

"What is a pity ?" said Fairford.

"It is almost a pity that I cannot go with you myself, or at least send a trusty guide."

They walked together to the bedchamber of Mrs. Crosbie, for it was in that asylum that the ladies of the period dispensed their tea, when the parlor was occupied by the punch-bowl.

"You have been good bairns to-night, gentlemen," said Mrs. Crosbie. "I am afraid, Summertrees, that the provost have given you a bad browst : you are not used to quit the lee-side of the punch-bowl in such a hurry. I say nothing to you, Mr. Fairford, for you are too young a man yet for stoup and bicker ; but I hope you will not tell the Edinburgh fine folk that the provost has scrimped you of your cogie, as the sang says ?"

"I am much obliged for the provost's kindness and yours, madam," replied Alan ; "but the truth is, I have still a long ride before me this evening, and the sooner I am on horseback the better."

"This evening ?" said the provost, anxiously. "Had you not better take daylight with you to-morrow morning ?"

"Mr. Fairford will ride as well in the cool of the evening," said Summertrees, taking the word out of Alan's mouth.

The provost said no more, nor did his wife ask any questions, nor testify any surprise at the suddenness of their guest's departure.

Having drank tea, Alan Fairford took leave with the usual ceremony. The laird of Summertrees seemed studious to prevent any further communication between him and the provost, and remained lounging on the landing-place of the stair while they made their adieus ; heard the provost ask if Alan proposed a speedy return, and the latter reply, that his stay was uncertain ; and witnessed the parting shake of the hand, which, with a pressure more warm than usual, and a tremulous "God bless and prosper you !" Mr. Crosbie bestowed on his young friend. Maxwell even strolled with Fairford as far as the George, although resisting all his attempts at further inquiry into the affairs of Redgauntlet, and referring him to Tom Trumbull, *alias* Turnpenny, for the particulars which he might find it necessary to inquire into.

At length Alan's hack was produced—an animal long in neck and high in bone, accoutered with a pair of saddle-bags containing the rider's traveling-wardrobe. Proudly surmounting his small stock of necessaries, and no way ashamed of a mode of traveling which a modern Mr. Silvertongue would consider as the last of degradations, Alan Fairford took leave of the old Jacobite, Pate-in-Peril, and set forward on the road to the royal burgh of Annan. His reflections during his ride were none of the most pleasant. He could not disguise from himself that he was venturing rather too rashly into the power of outlawed and desperate persons ; for with such only a man in the situation of Redgauntlet could be supposed to associate. There were other grounds for apprehension. Several marks of intelligence betwixt Mrs. Crosbie and the laird of Summertrees had not escaped Alan's acute observation ; and it was plain that the provost's inclinations towards him, which he believed to be sincere and good, were not firm enough to withstand the influence of this league between his wife and friend. The provost's adieus, like Macbeth's "amen," had stuck in his throat, and seemed to intimate that he apprehended more than he dared give utterance to.

Laying all these matters together, Alan thought, with no little anxiety, on the celebrated lines of Shakspeare,

> A drop,
> That in the ocean seeks another drop, etc.

But pertinacity was a strong feature in the young lawyer's character. He was, and always had been, totally unlike the "horse hot at hand," who tires before noon through his own over-eager exertions in the beginning of the day. On the contrary, his first efforts seemed frequently inadequate to accomplishing his purpose, whatever that for the time might be ; and it was only as the difficulties of the task increased that his mind seemed to acquire the energy necessary to combat and subdue them. If, therefore, he went anxiously forward upon his uncertain and perilous expedition, the reader must acquit him of all idea, even in a passing thought, of the possibility of abandoning his search and resigning Darsie Latimer to his destiny.

A couple of hours' riding brought him to the little town of Annan, situated on the shores of the Solway, between eight and nine o'clock. The sun had set, but the day was not yet ended ; and when he had alighted and seen his horse properly cared for at the principal inn of the place, he was readily directed to Mr. Maxwell's friend, old Tom Trumbull, with whom everybody seemed well acquainted. He endeavored to fish out from the lad that acted as a guide something of this man's situation and profession ; but the general expressions of " a very decent man," " a very honest body," " weel to pass in the world," and such-like, were all that could be extracted from him ; and while Fairford was following up the investigation with closer interrogatories, the lad put an end to them by knocking at the door of Mr. Trumbull, whose decent dwelling was a little distance from the town, and considerably nearer to the sea. It was one of a little row of houses running down to the waterside, and having gardens and other accommodations behind. There was heard within the uplifting of a Scottish psalm ; and the boy, saying, " They are at exercise, sir," gave intimation they might not be admitted till prayers were over.

When, however, Fairford repeated the summons with the end of his whip, the singing ceased, and Mr. Trumbull himself, with his psalm-book in his hand, kept open by the insertion of his forefinger between the leaves, came to demand the meaning of this unseasonable interruption.

Nothing could be more different than his whole appearance seemed to be from the confidant of a desperate man and the associate of outlaws in their unlawful enterprises. He was a tall, thin, bony figure, with white hair combed straight down on each side of his face, and an iron-gray hue of complexion ; where the lines, or rather, as Quin said of Macklin, the cordage, of his countenance were so sternly adapted to a devotional and even ascetic expression, that they left no room for any indication of reckless daring or sly dissimulation. In short, Trumbull appeared a perfect specimen of the rigid old Covenanter, who said only what he thought right, acted on no other principle but that of duty, and, if he committed errors, did so under the full impression that he was serving God rather than man.

"Do you want me, sir?" he said to Fairford, whose guide had slunk to the rear, as if to escape the rebuke of the severe old man. "We were engaged, and it is the Saturday night."

Alan's Fairford's preconceptions were so much deranged by this man's appearance and manner that he stood for a moment bewildered, and would as soon have thought of giving a cant password to a clergyman descending from the pulpit as to the respectable father of a family just interrupted in his prayers for and with the objects of his care. Hastily concluding Mr. Maxwell had passed some idle jest on him, or rather that he had mistaken the person to whom he was directed, he asked if he spoke to Mr. Trumbull.

"To Thomas Trumbull," answered the old man. "What may be your business, sir?" And he glanced his eye to the book he held in his hand, with a sigh like that of a saint desirous of dissolution.

"Do you know Mr. Maxwell of Summertrees?" said Fairford.

"I have heard of such a gentleman in the countryside, but have no acquaintance with him," answered Mr. Trumbull. "He is, as I have heard, a Papist; for the whore that sitteth on the seven hills ceaseth not yet to pour forth the cup of her abomination on these parts."

"Yet he directed me hither, my good friend," said Alan. "Is there another of your name in this town of Annan?"

"None," replied Mr. Trumbull, "since my worthy father was removed; he was indeed a shining light. I wish you good-even, sir."

"Stay one single instant," said Fairford; "this is a matter of life and death."

"Not more than the casting the burden of our sins where they should be laid," said Thomas Trumbull, about to shut the door in the inquirer's face.

"Do you know," said Alan Fairford, "the Laird of Redgauntlet?"

"Now Heaven defend me from treason and rebellion!" exclaimed Trumbull. "Young gentleman, you are importunate. I live here among my own people, and do not consort with Jacobites and mass-mongers."

He seemed about to shut the door, but did *not* shut it—a circumstance which did not escape Alan's notice.

"Mr. Redgauntlet is sometimes," he said, "called Herries of Birrenswork ; perhaps you may know him under that name."

"Friend, you are uncivil," answered Mr. Trumbull. "Honest men have enough to do to keep one name undefiled ; I ken nothing about those who have two. Good-even to you, friend."

He was now about to slam the door in his visitor's face without further ceremony, when Alan, who had observed symptoms that the name of Redgauntlet did not seem altogether so indifferent to him as he pretended, arrested his purpose by saying in a low voice, "At least you can tell me what age the moon is ? "

The old man started, as if from a trance, and, before answering, surveyed the querist with a keen penetrating glance, which seemed to say, " Are you really in possession of this key to my confidence, or do you speak from mere accident ? "

To this keen look of scrutiny, Fairford replied by a smile of intelligence.

The iron muscles of the old man's face did not, however, relax, as he dropped, in a careless manner, the countersign, "Not light enough to land a cargo."

"Then plague of all Aberdeen almanacks ! "

"And plague of all fools that waste time," said Thomas Trumbull. " Could you not have said as much at first ? And standing wasting time, and encouraging lookers-on, in the open street too ? Come in bye—in bye."

He drew his visitor into the dark entrance of the house, and shot the door carefully ; then putting his head into an apartment which the murmurs within announced to be filled with the family, he said aloud, "A work of necessity and mercy. Malachi, take the book ; you will sing six double verses of the hundred and nineteen ; and you may lecture out of the Lamentations. And, Malachi "—this he said in an undertone—" see you give them a screed of doctrine that will last them till I come back ; or else these inconsiderate lads will be out of the house, and away to the publics, wasting their precious time, and, it may be, putting themselves in the way of missing the morning tide."

An articulate answer from within intimated Malachi's acquiescence in the commands imposed ; and Mr. Trumbull, shutting the door, muttered something about " fast bind, fast find," turned the key, and put it into his pocket ; and then bidding his visitor have a care of his steps, and make no noise, he led him through the house, and out of a back-door, into a little garden. Here a plaited alley conducted them, without the possibility of their being seen by any neighbor, to a door in the garden-wall, which, being opened, proved to be a private entrance into a three-stalled stable ; in one of which was a horse, that whinnied on their entrance. "Hush —hush!" cried the old man, and presently seconded his exhortations to silence by throwing a handful of corn into the manger, and the horse soon converted his acknowledgment of their presence into the usual sound of munching and grinding his provender.

As the light was now failing fast, the old man, with much more alertness than might have been expected from the rigidity of his figure, closed the window-shutters in an instant, produced phosphorus and matches, and lighted a stable-lantern, which he placed on the corn-bin, and then addressed Fairford. "We are private here, young man ; and as some time has been wasted already, you will be so kind as to tell me what is your errand. Is it about the way of business, or the other job ?"

"My business with you, Mr. Trumbull, is to request you will find me the means of delivering this letter from Mr. Maxwell of Summertrees to the Laird of Redgauntlet."

"Humph—fashious job ! Pate Maxwell will still be the auld man—always Pate-in-Peril—Craig-in-Peril, for what I know. Let me see the letter from him."

He examined it with much care, turning it up and down, and looking at the seal very attentively. "All's right, I see ; it has the private mark for haste and speed. I bless my Maker that I am no great man, or great man's fellow ; and so I think no more of those passages than just to help them forward in the way of business. You are an utter stranger in these parts, I warrant ?"

Fairford answered in the affirmative.

"Ay—I never saw them make a wiser choice. I must call some one to direct you what to do. Stay, we must go to him, I believe. You are well recommended to me, friend, and doubtless trusty ; otherwise you may see more than I would like to show, or am in the use of showing in the common line of business."

Saying this, he placed his lantern on the ground, beside the post of one of the empty stalls, drew up a small spring-bolt which secured it to the floor, and then forcing the post to one side, discovered a small trap-door. "Follow me," he said, and dived into the subterranean descent to which this secret aperture gave access.

Fairford plunged after him, not without apprehensions of more kinds than one, but still resolved to prosecute the adventure. The descent, which was not above six feet, led to a very narrow passage, which seemed to have been constructed for the precise purpose of excluding every one who chanced to be an inch more in girth than was his conductor. A small vaulted room, of about eight feet square, received them at the end of this lane. Here Mr. Trumbull left Fairford alone, and returned for an instant, as he said, to shut his concealed trap-door.

Fairford liked not his departure, as it left him in utter darkness ; besides that his breathing was much affected by a strong and stifling smell of spirits, and other articles of a savor more powerful than agreeable to the lungs. He was very glad, therefore, when he heard the returning steps of Mr. Trumbull, who, when once more by his side, opened a strong though narrow door in the wall, and conveyed Fairford into an immense magazine of spirit-casks and other articles of contraband trade.

There was a small light at the end of this range of well-stocked subterranean vaults, which, upon a low whistle, began to flicker and move towards them. An undefined figure, holding a dark lantern, with the light averted, approached them, whom Mr. Trumbull thus addressed : " Why were you not at worship, Job, and this Saturday at e'en ? "

" Swanston was loading the ' Jenny,' sir, and I stayed to serve out the article."

" True—a work of necessity, and in the way of business. Does the ' Jumping Jenny ' sail this tide ? "

" Ay—ay, sir ; she sails for—— "

" I did not ask you *where* she sails for, Job," said the old gentleman, interrupting him. " I thank my Maker, I know nothing of their incomings or outgoings. I sell my article fairly and in the ordinary way of business ; and I wash my hands of everything else. But what I wished to know is, whether the gentleman called the Laird of the Solway Lakes is on the other side of the Border even now ? "

" Ay—ay," said Job, " the Laird is something in my own line, you know—a little contraband or so. There is a statute for him. But no matter ; he took the sands after the splore at the Quaker's fish-traps yonder ; for he has a

18

leal heart, the Laird, and is always true to the countryside. But avast—is all snug here?"

So saying, he suddenly turned on Alan Fairford the light side of the lantern he carried, who, by the transient gleam which it threw in passing on the man who bore it, saw a huge figure, upwards of six feet high, with a rough hairy cap on his head, and a set of features corresponding to his bulky frame. He thought also he observed pistols at his belt.

"I will answer for this gentleman," said Mr. Trumbull; "he must be brought to speech of the Laird."

"That will be kittle steering," said the subordinate personage; "for I understood that the Laird and his folk were no sooner on the other side than the land-sharks were on them, and some mounted lobsters from Carlisle; and so they were obliged to split and squander. There are new brooms out to sweep the country of them, they say; for the brush was a hard one, and they say there was a lad drowned; he was not one of the Laird's gang, so there was the less matter."

"Peace! prithee—peace, Job Rutledge," said honest, pacific Mr. Trumbull. "I wish thou couldst remember, man, that I desire to know nothing of your roars and splores, your brooms and brushes. I dwell here among my own people; and I sell my commodity to him who comes in the way of business; and so wash my hands of all consequences, as becomes a quiet subject and an honest man. I never take payment, save in ready money."

"Ay—ay," muttered he with the lantern, "your worship, Mr. Trumbull, understands that in the way of business."

"Well, I hope you will one day know, Job," anwered Mr. Trumbull, "the comfort of a conscience void of offense, and that fears neither gauger nor collector, neither excise nor customs. The business is to pass this gentleman to Cumberland upon earnest business. and to procure him speech with the Laird of the Solway Lakes—I suppose that can be done? Now I think Nanty Ewart, if he sails with the brig this morning tide, is the man to set him forward."

"Ay—ay,—truly is he," said Job; "never man knew the Border, dale and fell, pasture and plowland, better than Nanty; and he can always bring him to the Laird, too, if you are sure the gentleman's right. But indeed that's his own lookout; for were he the best man in Scotland, and the chairman of the d—d Board to boot, and had fifty men

at his back, he were as well not visit the Laird for anything but good. As for Nanty, he is word and blow a d—d
deal fiercer than Cristie Nixon that they keep such a din
about. I have seen them both tried by——"

Fairford now found himself called upon to say something; yet his feelings, upon finding himself thus completely in the power of a canting hypocrite and of his retainer, who had so much the air of a determined ruffian,
joined to the strong and abominable fume which they
snuffed up with indifference, while it almost deprived him
of respiration, combined to render utterance difficult. He
stated, however, that he had no evil intentions towards the
Laird, as they called him, but was only the bearer of a
letter to him on particular bnsiness from Mr. Maxwell of
Summertrees.

"Ay—ay," said Job, "that may be well enough; and if
Mr. Trumbull is satisfied that the scrive is right, why, we
will give you a cast in the 'Jumping Jenny' this tide and
Nanty Ewart will put you on a way of finding the Laird, I
warrant you."

"I may for the present return, I presume, to the inn
where I have left my horse?" said Fairford.

"With pardon," replied Mr. Trumbull, "you have been
ower far ben with us for that; but Job will take you to a
place where you may sleep rough till he calls you. I will
bring you what little baggage you can need; for those who
go on such errands must not be dainty. I will myself see
after your horse; for a merciful man is merciful to his
beast—a matter too often forgotten in our way of business."

"Why, Master Trumbull," replied Job, "you know that
when we are chased it's no time to shorten sail, and so the
boys do ride whip and spur——" He stopped in his speech,
observing the old man had vanished through the door by
which he had entered. "That's always the way with old
Turnpenny," he said to Fairford; "he cares for nothing
of the trade but the profit; now, d—me, if I don't think
the fun of it is better worth while. But come along, my
fine chap; I must stow you away in safety until it is time
to go aboard."

CHAPTER XIII

FAIRFORD followed his gruff guide among a labyrinth of barrels and puncheons, on which he had more than once like to have broken his nose, and from thence into what, by the glimpse of the passing lantern upon a desk and writing-materials, seemed to be a small office for the despatch of business. Here there appeared no exit ; but the smuggler, or smuggler's ally, availing himself of a ladder, removed an old picture, which showed a door about seven feet from the ground, and Fairford, still following Job, was involved in another tortuous and dark passage, which involuntarily reminded him of Peter Peebles's lawsuit. At the end of this labyrinth, when he had little guess where he had been conducted, and was, according to the French phrase, totally *desorienté*, Job suddenly set down the lantern, and availing himself of the flame to light two candles which stood on the table, asked if Alan would choose anything to eat, recommending, at all events, a slug of brandy to keep out the night air. Fairford declined both, but inquired after his baggage.

"The old master will take care of that himself," said Job Rutledge ; and drawing back in the direction in which he had entered, he vanished from the further end of the apartment, by a mode which the candles, still shedding an imperfect light, gave Alan no means of ascertaining. Thus the adventurous young lawyer was left alone in the apartment to which he had been conducted by so singular a passage.

In this condition, it was Alan's first employment to survey, with some accuracy, the place where he was ; and accordingly, having trimmed the lights, he walked slowly round the apartment, examining its appearance and dimensions. If seemed to be such a small dining-parlor as is usually found in the house of the better class of artisans, shopkeepers, and such persons, having a recess at the upper end, and the usual furniture of an ordinary description. He found a door, which he endeavored to open, but it was locked on the outside. A corresponding door on the same side of the apartment admitted him into a closet, upon the front shelves of which were punch-bowls, glasses, tea-cups, and the like, while on one side was hung a horseman's greatcoat of the coarsest materials, with two great horse-pistols peeping out of the pocket, and on the floor stood a pair of well-spattered jack-boots, the usual equipment of the time, at least for long journeys.*

Not greatly liking the contents of the closet, Alan Fairford shut the door, and resumed his scrutiny round the walls of the apartment, in order to discover the mode of Job Rutledge's retreat. The secret passage was, however, too artificially concealed, and the young lawyer had nothing better to do than to meditate on the singularity of his present situation. He had long known that the excise laws had occasioned an active contraband trade betwixt Scotland and England, which then, as now, existed, and will continue to exist until the utter abolition of the wretched system which establishes an inequality of duties † betwixt the different parts of the same kingdom—a system, be it said in passing, mightily resembling the conduct of a pugilist who should tie up one arm that he might fight the better with the other. But Fairford was unprepared for the expensive and regular establishments by which the illicit traffic was carried on, and could not have conceived that the capital employed in it should have been adequate to the erection of these extensive buildings, with all their contrivances for secrecy of communication. He was musing on these circumstances, not without some anxiety for the progress of his own journey, when suddenly, as he lifted his eyes, he discovered old Mr. Trumbull at the upper end of the apartment, bearing in one hand a small bundle, in the other his dark lantern, the light of which, as he advanced, he directed full upon Fairford's countenance.

Though such an apparition was exactly what he expected, yet he did not see the grim, stern old man present himself thus suddenly without emotion, especially when he recollected, what to a youth of his pious education was peculiarly shocking, that the grizzled hypocrite was probably that instant arisen from his knees to Heaven, for the purpose of engaging in the mysterious transactions of a desperate and illegal trade.

The old man, accustomed to judge with ready sharpness of the physiognomy of those with whom he had business,

* See Concealments for Theft and Smuggling. Note 32.
† These duties were equalized in 1855 (*Laing*).

did not fail to remark something like agitation in Fairford's demeanor. "Have ye taken the rue?" said he. "Will ye take the sheaf from the mare, and give up the venture?" "Never!" said Fairford, firmly, stimulated at once by his natural spirit and the recollection of his friend—"never, while I have life and strength to follow it out!"

"I have brought you," said Trumbull, "a clean shirt and some stockings, which is all the baggage you can conveniently carry, and I will cause one of the lads lend you a horseman's coat, for it is ill sailing or riding without one; and, touching your valise, it will be as safe in my poor house, were it full of the gold of Ophir, as if it were in the depth of the mine."

"I have no doubt of it," said Fairford.

"And now," said Trumbull again, "I pray you to tell me by what name I am to name you to Nanty (which is Antony) Ewart?"

"By the name of Alan Fairford," answered the young lawyer.

"But that," said Mr. Trumbull, in reply, "is your own proper name and surname."

"And what other should I give?" said the young man. "Do you think I have any occasion for an *alias*? And, besides, Mr. Trumbull," added Alan, thinking a little raillery might intimate confidence of spirit, "you blessed yourself, but a little while since, that you had no acquaintance with those who defiled their names so far as to be obliged to change them."

"True—very true," said Mr. Trumbull; "nevertheless, young man, my gray hairs stand unreproved in this matter; for, in my line of business, when I sit under my vine and my fig-tree, exchanging the strong waters of the North for the gold which is the price thereof, I have, I thank Heaven, no disguises to keep with any man, and wear my own name of Thomas Trumbull, without any chance that the same may be polluted; whereas thou, who art to journey in miry ways, and amongst a strange people, mayst do well to have two names, as thou hast two shirts, the one to keep the other clean."

Here he emitted a chuckling grunt, which lasted for two vibrations of the pendulum exactly, and was the only approach towards laughter in which old Turnpenny, as he was nicknamed, was ever known to indulge.

"You are witty, Mr. Trumbull," said Fairford; "but jests are no arguments. I shall keep my own name."

"At your own pleasure," said the merchant; "there is but one name which," etc. etc. etc.

We will not follow the hypocrite through the impious cant which he added, in order to close the subject.

Alan followed him, in silent abhorrence, to the recess in which the beaufet was placed, and which was so artificially made as to conceal another of those traps with which the whole building abounded. This concealment admitted them to the same winding passage by which the young lawyer had been brought thither. The path which they now took amid these mazes differed from the direction in which he had been guided by Rutledge. It led upwards, and terminated beneath a garret window. Trumbull opened it, and, with more agility than his age promised, clambered out upon the leads. If Fairford's journey had been hitherto in a stifled and subterranean atmosphere, it was now open, lofty, and airy enough; for he had to follow his guide over leads and slates, which the old smuggler traversed with the dexterity of a cat. It is true, his course was facilitated by knowing exactly where certain stepping-places and holdfasts were placed, of which Fairford could not so readily avail himself; but after a difficult and somewhat perilous progress along the roofs of two or three houses, they at length descended by a skylight into a garret room, and from thence by the stairs into a public house; for such it appeared by the ringing of bells, whistling for waiters and attendance, bawling of "House—house, here!" chorus of sea-songs, and the like noises.

Having descended to the second story, and entered a room there, in which there was a light, old Mr. Trumbull rung the bell of the apartment thrice, with an interval betwixt each, during which he told deliberately the number twenty. Immediately after the third ringing, the landlord appeared, with stealthy step, and an appearance of mystery on his buxom visage. He greeted Mr. Trumbull, who was his landlord as it proved, with great respect, and expressed some surprise at seeing him so late, as he termed it, "on Saturday at e'en."

"And I, Robin Hastie," said the landlord to the tenant, "am more surprised than pleased to hear sae muckle din in your house, Robie, so near the honorable Sabbath; and I must mind you that it is contravening the terms of your tack, whilk stipulate that you should shut your public on Saturday at nine o'clock, at latest."

"Yes, sir," said Robin Hastie, no way alarmed at the

gravity of the rebuke, "but you must take tent that I have
admitted naebody but you, Mr. Trumbull—who, by the way,
admitted yoursell—since nine o'clock; for the most of the
folk have been here for several hours about the lading, and
so on, of the brig. It is not full tide yet, and I cannot put
the men out into the street. If I did, they would go to
some other public, and their souls would be nane the better,
and my purse muckle the waur; for how am I to pay the
rent if I do not sell the liquor?"

"Nay, then," said Thomas Trumbull, "if it is a work of
necessity, and in the honest independent way of business,
no doubt there is balm in Gilead. But prithee, Robin, wilt
thou see if Nanty Ewart be, as is most likely, amongst these
unhappy topers; and if so, let him step this way cannily,
and speak to me and this young gentleman. And it's dry
talking, Robin, you must minister to us a bowl of punch;
ye ken my gage."

"From a mutchin to a gallon, I ken your honor's taste,
Mr. Thomas Trumbull," said mine host; "and ye shall
hang me over the sign-post if there be a drap mair lemon or
a curn less sugar than just suits you. There are three of
you; you will be for the auld Scots peremptory pint-stoup *
for the success of the voyage?"

"Better pray for it than drink for it, Robin," said Mr.
Trumbull. "Yours is a dangerous trade, Robin: it hurts
mony a ane, baith host and guest. But ye will get the blue
bowl, Robin—the blue bowl, that will sloken all their drouth,
and prevent the sinful repetition of whipping for an eke of a
Saturday at e'en. Ay, Robin, it is a pity of Nanty Ewart.
Nanty likes the turning up of his little finger unco weel, and
we maunna stint him, Robin, so as we leave him sense to
steer by."

"Nanty Ewart could steer through the Pentland Firth
though he were as drunk as the Baltic Ocean," said Robin
Hastie; and instantly tripping downstairs, he speedily returned with the materials for what he called his "browst,"
which consisted of two English quarts of spirits in a huge
blue bowl, with all the ingredients for punch, in the same
formidable proportion. At the same time he introduced
Mr. Antony or Nanty Ewart, whose person, although he was
a good deal flustered with liquor, was different from what
Fairford expected. His dress was what is emphatically
termed the shabby genteel—a frock with tarnished lace, a
small cocked hat, ornamented in a similar way, a scarlet

* See Pint Measure. Note 33.

waistcoat, with faded embroidery, breeches of the same, with silver knee-bands, and he wore a smart hanger and a pair of pistols in a sullied sword-belt.

"Here I come, patron," he said, shaking hands with Mr. Trumbull. "Well, I see you have got some grog aboard."

"It is not my custom, Mr. Ewart." said the old gentleman, "as you well know, to become a chamberer or carouser thus late on Saturday at e'en ; but I wanted to recommend to your attention a young friend of ours that is going upon a something particular journey, with a letter to our friend the Laird, from Pate-in-Peril, as they call him."

"Ay—indeed ? he must be in high trust for so young a gentleman. I wish you joy, sir," bowing to Fairford. "By'r lady, as Shakspeare says, you are bringing up a neck to a fair end. Come, patron, we will drink to Mr. What-shall-call-um. What is his name ? Did you tell me ? And have I forgot it already ?"

"Mr. Alan Fairford," said Trumbull.

"Ay, Mr. Alan Fairford—a good name for a fair trader—Mr. Alan Fairford ; and may he long be withheld from the topmost round of ambition, which I take to be the highest round of a certain ladder."

While he spoke, he seized the punch ladle and began to fill the glasses. But Mr. Trumbull arrested his hand, until he had, as he expressed himself, sanctified the liquor by a long grace ; during the pronunciation of which he shut indeed his eyes, but his nostrils became dilated, as if he were snuffing up the fragrant beverage with peculiar complacency.

When the grace was at length over, the three friends sat down to their beverage, and invited Alan Fairford to partake. Anxious about his situation, and disgusted as he was with his company, he craved, and with difficulty obtained permission, under the allegation of being fatigued, heated, and the like, to stretch himself on a couch which was in the apartment, and attempted at least to procure some rest before high water, when the vessel was to sail.

He was at length permitted to use his freedom, and stretched himself on the couch, having his eyes for some time fixed on the jovial party he had left, and straining his ears to catch if possible a little of their conversation. This he soon found was to no purpose ; for what did actually reach his ears was disguised so completely by the use of cant words, and the theives' Latin called slang, that, even when he caught the words, he found himself as far as ever from the sense of their conversation. At length he fell asleep.

It was after Alan had slumbered for three or four hours that he was wakened by voices bidding him rise up and prepare to be jogging. He started up accordingly, and found himself in presence of the same party of boon companions, who had just despatched their huge bowl of punch. To Alan's surprise, the liquor had made but little innovation on the brains of men who were accustomed to drink at all hours, and in the most inordinate quantities. The landlord indeed spoke a little thick, and the texts of Mr. Thomas Trumbull stumbled on his tongue; but Nanty was one of those topers who, becoming early what *bon-vivants* term flustered, remain whole nights and days at the same point of intoxication; and in fact, as they are seldom entirely sober, can be as rarely seen absolutely drunk. Indeed, Fairford, had he not known how Ewart had been engaged whilst he himself was asleep, would almost have sworn when he awoke that the man was more sober than when he first entered the room.

He was confirmed in this opinion when they descended below, where two or three sailors and ruffian-looking fellows awaited their commands. Ewart took the whole direction upon himself, gave his orders with briefness and precision, and looked to their being executed with the silence and celerity which that peculiar crisis required. All were now dismissed for the brig, which lay, as Fairford was given to understand, a little farther down the river, which is navigable for vessels of light burden, till almost within a mile of the town.

When they issued from the inn, the landlord bid them good-bye. Old Trumbull walked a little way with them, but the air had probably considerable effect on the state of his brain; for, after reminding Alan Fairford that the next day was the honorable Sabbath, he became extremely excursive in an attempt to exhort him to keep it holy. At length, being perhaps sensible that he was becoming unintelligible, he thrust a volume into Fairford's hand, hiccupping at the same time—"Good book—good book—fine hymn-book—fit for the honorable Sabbath, whilk awaits us to-morrow morning." Here the iron tongue of time told five from the town-steeple of Annan, to the further confusion of Mr. Trumbull's already disordered ideas. "Ay! is Sunday come and gone already? Heaven be praised! Only it is a marvel the afternoon is sae dark for the time of the year. Sabbath has slipped ower quietly, but we have reason to bless oursells it has not been altogether misemployed. I heard a little of the preaching— a cauld moralis, I doubt, served that out; but, eh—the

prayer I mind it as if I had said the words mysell." Here
he repeated one or two petitions, which were probably a part
of his family devotions, before he was summoned forth to
what he called the way of business. " I never remember a
Sabbath pass so cannily off in my life." Then he recollected
himself a little, and said to Alan, " You may read that book,
Mr. Fairford, to-morrow, all the same, though it be Monday;
for, you see, it was Saturday when we were thegither, and
now it's Sunday, and it's dark night; so the Sabbath has
slipped clean away through our fingers, like water through
a sieve, which abideth not ; and we have to begin again to-
morrow morning in the weariful, base, mean, earthly employments whilk are unworthy of an immortal spirit—always
excepting the way of business."

Three of the fellows were now returning to the town, and,
at Ewart's command, they cut short the patriarch's exhortation by leading him back to his own residence. The rest of
the party then proceeded to the brig, which only waited their
arrival to get under weigh and drop down the river. Nanty
Ewart betook himself to steering the brig, and the very touch
of the helm seemed to dispel the remaining influence of the
liquor which he had drunk, since, through a troublesome and
intricate channel, he was able to direct the course of his little
vessel with the most perfect accuracy and safety.

Alan Fairford for some time availed himself of the clearness of the summer morning to gaze on the dimly seen shores
betwixt which they glided, becoming less and less distinct as
they receded from each other, until at length, having adjusted
his little bundle by way of pillow, and wrapped around him
the greatcoat with which old Trumbull had equipped him, he
stretched himself on the deck, to try to recover the slumber
out of which he had been awakened. Sleep had scarce begun
to settle on his eyes ere he found something stirring about his
person. With ready presence of mind he recollected his situation, and resolved to show no alarm until the purpose of this
became obvious ; but he was soon relieved from his anxiety
by finding it was only the result of Nanty's attention to his
comfort, who was wrapping around him, as softly as he could,
a great boat-cloak, in order to defend him from the morning
air.

" Thou art but a cockerel," he muttered, " but 'twere pity
thou were knocked off the perch before seeing a little more
of the sweet and sour of this world ; though, faith, if thou
hast the usual luck of it, the best way were to leave thee to
the chance of a seasoning fever."

These words, and the awkward courtesy with which the skipper of the little brig tucked the sea-coat round Fairford, gave him a confidence of safety which he had not yet thoroughly possessed. He stretched himself in more security on the hard planks, and was speedily asleep, though his slumbers were feverish and unrefreshing.

It has been elsewhere intimated that Alan Fairford inherited from his mother a delicate constitution, with a tendency to consumption ; and, being an only child, with such a cause for apprehension, care, to the verge of effeminacy, was taken to preserve him from damp beds, wet feet, and those various emergencies to which the Caledonian boys of much higher birth, but more active habits, are generally accustomed. In man, the spirit sustains the constitutional weakness, as in the winged tribes, the feathers bear aloft the body. But there is a bound to these supporting qualities ; and as the pinions of the bird must at length grow weary, so the *vis animi* of the human struggler becomes broken down by continued fatigue.

When the voyager was awakened by the light of the sun now riding high in Heaven, he found himself under the influence of an almost intolerable headache, with heat, thirst, shootings across the back and loins, and other symptoms intimating violent cold, accompanied with fever. The manner in which he had passed the preceding day and night, though perhaps it might have been of little consequence to most young men, was to him, delicate in constitution and nurture, attended with bad, and even perilous, consequences. He felt this was the case, yet would fain have combated the symptoms of indisposition, which, indeed, he imputed chiefly to sea-sickness. He sat up on deck, and looked on the scene around, as the little vessel, having borne down the Solway Firth, was beginning, with a favorable northerly breeze, to bear away to the southward, crossing the entrance of the Wampool river, and preparing to double the most northerly point of Cumberland.

But Fairford felt annoyed with deadly sickness, as well as by pain of a distressing and oppressive character ; and neither Criffell, rising in majesty on the one hand, nor the distant yet more picturesque outline of Skiddaw and Glaramara upon the other, could attract his attention in the manner which it was usually fixed by beautiful scenery, and especially that which had in it something new as well as striking. Yet it was not in Alan Fairford's nature to give way to despondence, even when seconded by pain. He had recourse, in the first place, to his pocket; but instead of the little Sallust he had brought with him, that the perusal of a favorite classical author might help to pass away a heavy hour, he pulled out the supposed hymn-book with which he had been presented a few hours before by that temperate and scrupulous person, Mr. Thomas Trumbull, *alias* Turnpenny. The volume was bound in sable, and its exterior might have become a psalter. But what was Alan's astonishment to read on the title-page the following words :— *Merry Thoughts for Merry Men ; or Mother Midnight's Miscellany for the Small Hours ;* and, turning over the leaves, he was disgusted with profligate tales, and more profligate songs, ornamented with figures corresponding in infamy with the letterpress.

" Good God ! " he thought, " and did this hoary reprobate summon his family together, and, with such a disgraceful pledge of infamy in his bosom, venture to approach the throne of his Creator ? It must be so ; the book is bound after the manner of those dedicated to devotional subjects, and doubtless, the wretch, in his intoxication, confounded the books he carried with him, as he did the days of the week." Seized with the disgust with which the young and generous usually regard the vices of advanced life, Alan, having turned the leaves of the book over in hasty disdain, flung it from him, as far as he could, into the sea. He then had recourse to the Sallust, which he had at first sought for in vain. As he opened the book, Nanty Ewart, who had been looking over his shoulder, made his own opinion heard.

" I think now, brother, if you are so much scandalized at a little piece of sculduddery, which, after all, does nobody any harm, you had better have given it to me than have flung it into the Solway,"

" I hope, sir," answered Fairford, civilly, " you are in the habit of reading better books."

" Faith," answered Nanty, " with help of a little Geneva text, I could read my Sallust as well as you can ; " and snatching the book from Alan's hand, he began to read, in the Scottish accent : ' " *Igitur ex divitiis juventutum luxuria atque avaritia cum superbiâ invasere ; rapere, consumere ; sua parvi pendere, aliena cupere ; pudorem, amicitiam, pudicitiam, divina atque humana promiscna, nihil pensi neque moderati habere.* " * There is a slap in the face now for an honest fellow that has been buccaneering ! Never could keep a groat of what he got, or hold his

* See Translations from Sallust. Note. 34.

fingers from what belonged to another, said you ? Fie—fie, friend Crispus, thy morals are as crabbed and austere as thy style—the one has as little mercy as the other has grace. By my soul, it is unhandsome to make personal reflections on an old acquaintance, who seeks a little civil intercourse with you after nigh twenty years' separation. On my soul, Master Sallust deserves to float on the Solway better than Mother Midnight herself."

"Perhaps, in some respects, he may merit better usage at our hands," said Alan ; "for if he has described vice plainly, it seems to have been for the purpose of rendering it generally abhorred."

"Well," said the seaman, "I have heard of the *sortes Virgilianæ*, and I daresay the *sortes Sallustianæ* are as true every tittle. I have consulted honest Crispus on my own account, and have had a cuff for my pains. But now see, I open the book on your behalf, and behold what occurs first to my eye ! Lo you there—' *Catilina . . . omnium flagitiosorum atque facinorosorum circum se . . . habebat.*' And then again—'*Etiam si quis a culpa vacuus in amicitiam ejus inciderat, quotidiano usu par . . . similisque cæteris efficiebatur.*' That is what I call plain speaking on the part of the old Roman, Mr. Fairford. By the way, that is a capital name for a lawyer."

"Lawyer as I am," said Fairford, "I do not understand your innuendo."

"Nay, then," said Ewart, "I can try it another way, as well as the hypocritical old rascal Turnpenny himself could do. I would have you to know that I am well acquainted with my Bible-book, as well as with my friend Sallust." He then, in a snuffling and canting tone, began to repeat the Scripture text—"'David therefore departed thence, and went to the cave of Adullam. And every one that was in distress, and every one that was in debt, and every one that was discontented, gathered themselves together unto him, and he became a captain over them.' What think you of that ?" he said, suddenly changing his manner. "Have I touched you now, sir ?"

"You are as far off as ever," replied Fairford.

"What the devil ! and you a repeating frigate between Summertrees and the Laird ! Tell that to the marines, the sailors won't believe it. But you are right to be cautious, since you can't say who are right, who not. But you look ill ; it's but the cold morning air. Will you have a can of flip, or a jorum of hot rumbo, or will you splice the main-

brace (showing a spirit-flask) ? Will you have a quid, or a
pipe, or a cigar ?—a pinch of snuff, at least, to clear your
brains and sharpen your apprehension ?"

Fairford rejected all these friendly propositions.

"Why, then," continued Ewart, "if you will do nothing
for the free trade, I must patronize it myself."

So saying, he took a large glass of brandy.

"A hair of the dog that bit me," he continued—"of the
dog that will worry me one day soon ; and yet, and be d—d
to me for an idiot, I must always have him at my throat.
But," says the old catch—here he sung, and sung well—

> "Let's drink—let's drink, while life we have ;
> We'll find but cold drinking—cold drinking in the grave.

All this," he continued, "is no charm against the headache.
I wish I had anything that could do you good. Faith, and
we have tea and coffee aboard ! I'll open a chest or a bag,
and let you have some in an instant. You are at the age to
like such cat-lap better than better stuff."

Fairford thanked him, and accepted his offer of tea.

Nanty Ewart was soon heard calling about, "Break open
yon chest ; take out your capful, you bastard of a powder-
monkey, we may want it again. No sugar ! all used up for
grog, say you ! Knock another loaf to pieces, can't ye ?
And get the kettle boiling, ye hell's baby, in no time at all !"

By dint of these energetic proceedings, he was in a short
time able to return to the place where his passenger lay sick
and exhausted with a cup, or rather a canful, of tea ; for
everything was on a large scale on board of the "Jumping
Jenny." Alan drank it eagerly, and with so much appearance of being refreshed, that Nanty Ewart swore he would
have some too, and only laced it, as his phrase went, with a
single glass of brandy.

CHAPTER XIV

NARRATIVE OF ALAN FAIRFORD, CONTINUED

WE left Alan Fairford on the deck of the little smuggling brig, in that disconsolate situation when sickness and nausea attack a heated and fevered frame and an anxious mind. His share of sea-sickness, however, was not so great as to engross his sensations entirely, or altogether to divert his attention from what was passing around. If he could not delight in the swiftness and agility with which the "little frigate" walked the waves, or amuse himself by noticing the beauty of the sea-views around him, where the distant Skiddaw raised his brow, as if in defiance of the clouded eminence of Criffel, which lorded it over the Scottish side of the estuary, he had spirits and composure enough to pay particular attention to the master of the vessel, on whose character his own safety in all probability was dependent.

Nanty Ewart had now given the helm to one of his people, a bald-pated, grizzled old fellow, whose whole life had been spent in evading the revenue laws, with now and then the relaxation of a few months' imprisonment, for deforcing officers, resisting seizure, and the like offenses.

Nanty himself sat down by Fairford, helped him to his tea, with such other refreshments as he could think of, and seemed in his way sincerely desirous to make his situation as comfortable as things admitted. Fairford had thus an opportunity to study his countenance and manners more closely.

It was plain, Ewart, though a good seaman, had not been bred upon that element. He was a reasonably good scholar, and seemed fond of showing it, by recurring to the subject of Sallust and Juvenal ; while, on the other hand, sea-phrases seldom checkered his conversation. He had been in person what is called a smart little man ; but the tropical sun had burned his originally fair complexion to a dusty red, and the bile which was diffused through his system had stained it with a yellowish-black : what ought to have been the white part of his eyes, in particular, had a hue as deep as the

topaz. He was very thin, or rather emaciated, and his countenance, though still indicating alertness and activity, showed
a constitution exhausted with excessive use of his favorite
stimulus.

"I see you look at me hard," said he to Fairford. "Had
you been an officer of the d—d customs, my terriers' backs
would have been up," He opened his breast, and showed
Alan a pair of pistols disposed between his waistcoat and
jacket, placing his finger at the same time upon the cock of
one of them. "But come, you are an honest fellow, though
you're a close one I daresay you think me a queer customer ;
but I can tell you, they that see the ship leave harbor know
little of the seas she is to sail through. My father, honest
old gentleman, never would have thought to see me master
of the 'Jumping Jenny.'"

Fairford said, "It seemed very clear indeed that Mr.
Ewart's education was far superior to the line he at present
occupied."

"O, Criffel to Solway Moss !" said the other. "Why,
man, I should have been an expounder of the Word, with a
wig like a snow-wreath, and a stipend like—like—like a
hundred pounds a-year, I suppose. I can spend thrice as
much as that, though, being such as I am." Here he sung
a scrap of an old Northumbrian ditty, mimicking the burr
of the natives of that county :—

> " Willy Foster's gone to sea,
> Siller buckles at his knee,
> He'll come back and marry me—
> Canny Willy Foster."

"I have no doubt," said Fairford, "your present occupation is more lucrative ; but I should have thought the church
might have been more——"

He stopped, recollecting that it was not his business to
say anything disagreeable.

"More respectable, you mean, I suppose ? " said Ewart,
with a sneer, and squirting the tobacco-juice through his
front teeth ; then was silent for a moment, and proceeded in
a tone of candor which some internal touch of conscience
dictated, "And so it would, Mr. Fairford, and happier, too,
by a thousand degrees, though I have had my pleasures too.
But there was my father. God bless him—a true chip of
the old Presbyterian block, walked his parish like a captain
on the quarter-deck, and was always ready to do good to rich
and poor. Off went the laird's hat to the minister as fast as

19

the poor man's bonnet. When the eye saw him—— Pshaw!
what have I to do with that now? Yes, he was, as Virgil
hath it, "*Vir sapientia et pietate gravis.*" But he might
have been the wiser man had he kept me at home, when hᴜ
sent me at nineteen to study divinity at the head of the highest stair in the Covenant Close. It was a cursed mistake in
the old gentleman. What though Mrs. Cantrips of Kittlebasket, for she wrote herself no less, was our cousin five
times removed, and took me on that account to board and
lodging at six shillings instead of seven shillings a week? it
was a d—d bad saving, as the case proved. Yet her very
dignity might have kept me in order; for she never read a
chapter except out of a Cambridge Bible, printed by Daniel,
and bound in embroidered velvet. I think I see it at this
moment! And on Sundays, when we had a quart of twopenny ale, instead of buttermilk, to our porridge, it was always
served up in a silver posset-dish. Also she used silver-
mounted spectacles, whereas even my father's were cased in
mere horn. These things had their impression at first, but
we got used to grandeur to degrees. Well sir! Gad, I can
scarce get on with my story—it sticks in my throat—must
take a trifle to wash it down. Well, this dame had a daughter, Jess Cantrips—a black-eyed, bouncing wench—and as
the devil would have it, there was the d—d five-story stair—
her foot was never from it, whether I went or came home
from the divinity hall. I would have eschewed her, sir—I
would, on my soul, for I was as innocent a lad as ever came
from Lammermuir; but there was no possibility of escape,
retreat, or flight, unless I could have got a pair of wings,
or made use of a ladder seven stories high, to scale the window of my attic. It signifies little talking—you may suppose
how all this was to end. I would have married the girl, and
taken my chance—I would, by Heaven! for she was a pretty
girl, and a good girl, until she and I met; but you know the
old song, 'Kirk would not let us be.' A gentleman, in my
case, would have settled the matter with the kirk-treasurer
for a small sum of money; but the poor stibbler, the penni-
less dominie, having married his cousin of Kittlebasket, must
next have proclaimed her frailty to the whole parish, by
mounting the throne of Presbyterian penance, and proving,
as Othello says, 'his love a whore,' in face of the whole
congregation.

"In this extremity I dared not stay where I was, and so
thought to go home to my father. But first I got Jack
Hadaway, a lad from the same parish, and who lived in the

same infernal stair, to make some inquiries how the old gentleman had taken the matter. I soon, by way of answer, learned, to the great increase of my comfortable reflections, that the good old man made as much clamor as if such a thing as a man's eating his wedding dinner without saying grace had never happened since Adam's time. He did nothing for six days but cry out " Ichabod—Ichabod, the glory is departed from my house!" and on the seventh he preached a sermon, in which he enlarged on this incident as illustrative of one of the great occasions for humiliation and causes of national defection. I hope the course he took comforted himself ; I am sure it made me ashamed to show my nose at home. So I went down to Leith, and, exchanging my hodden-gray coat of my mother's spinning for such a jacket as this, I entered my name at the rendezvous as an able-bodied landsman, and sailed with the tender round to Portsmouth, where they were fitting out a squadron for the West Indies. There I was put aboard the " Fearnought," Captain Daredevil, among whose crew I soon learned to fear Satan, the terror of my early youth, as little as the toughest Jack on board. I had some qualms at first, but I took the remedy (tapping the case-bottle) which I recommended to you, being as good for sickness of the soul as for sickness of the stomach. What, you won't? Very well, I must, then. Here is to ye."

" You would, I am afraid, find your education of little use in your new condition?" said Fairford.

" Pardon me, sir," resumed the captain of the " Jumping Jenny " ; " my handful of Latin and small pinch of Greek were as useless as old junk, to be sure ; but my reading, writing, and accompting stood me in good stead, and brought me forward. I might have been schoolmaster—ay, and master, in time ; but that valiant liquor, rum, made a conquest of me rather too often, and so, make what sail I could, I always went to leeward. We were four years boiling in that blasted climate, and I came back at last with a little prize-money. I always had thoughts of putting things to rights in the Covenant Close, and reconciling myself to my father. I found out Jack Hadaway, who was " tuptowing " away with a dozen of wretched boys, and a fine string of stories he had ready to regale my ears withal. My father had lectured on what he called " my falling away" for seven Sabbaths, when, just as his parishoners began to hope that that the course was at an end, he was found dead in his bed on the eighth Sunday morning. Jack Hadaway assured me that, if I wished to atone for my errors by undergoing the

fate of the first martyr, I had only to go to my native village
where the very stones of the street would rise up against me
as my father's murderer. Here was a pretty item. Well,
my tongue clove to my mouth for an hour, and was only able
at last to utter the name of Mrs. Cantrips. O, this was a
new theme for my Job's comforter. My sudden departure,
my father's no less sudden death, had prevented the payment of the arrears of my board and lodging. The landlord
was a haberdasher, with a heart as rotten as the muslin
wares he dealt in. Without respect to her age and gentle
kin, my Lady Kittlebasket was ejected from her airy habitation ; her porridge-pot, silver posset-dish, silver-mounted
spectacles, and Daniel's Cambridge Bible sold, at the Cross
of Edinburgh, to the cadie who would bid highest for them,
and she herself driven to the workhouse, where she got in
difficulty, but was easily enough lifted out, at the end of the
month, as dead as her friends could desire. Merry tidings
this to me, who had been the d—d (he paused a moment)
origo mali. Gad, I think my confession would sound better
in Latin than in English."

"But the best jest was behind. I had just power to stammer out something about Jess—by my faith he *had* an answer *!*
I had taught Jess one trade, and, like a prudent girl, she had
found out another for herself ; unluckily, they were both
contraband, and Jess Cantrips, daughter of the Lady Kittlebasket, had the honor to be transported to the plantations for
street-walking and pocket-picking about six months before
I touched shore."

He changed the bitter tone of affected pleasantry into an
attempt to laugh ; then drew his swarthy hand across his
swarthy eyes, and said in a more natural accent, "Poor
Jess !"

There was a pause, until Fairford, pitying the poor man's
state of mind, and believing he saw something in him that,
but for early error and subsequent profligacy, might have
been excellent and noble, helped on the conversation by asking, in a tone of commiseration, how he had been able to
endure such a load of calamity.

"Why, very well," answered the seaman—"exceedingly
well—like a tight ship in a brisk gale. Let me recollect. I
remember thanking Jack, very composedly, for the interesting and agreeable communication. I then pulled out my
canvas pouch with my hoard of moidores, and taking out
two pieces, I bid Jack keep the rest till I came back, as I
was for a cruise about Auld Reekie. The poor devil looked

anxiously, but I shook him by the hand and ran downstairs in such confusion of mind that, notwithstanding what I had heard, I expected to meet Jess at every turning.

"It was market-day, and the usual number of rogues and fools were assembled at the Cross. I observed everybody looked strange on me, and I thought some laughed. I fancy I had been making queer faces enough, and perhaps talking to myself. When I saw myself used in this manner, I held out my clenched fists straight before me, stooped my head, and, like a ram when he makes his race, darted off right down the street, scattering groups of weatherbeaten lairds and periwigged burgesses, and bearing down all before me. I heard the cry of "Seize the madman!" echoed, in Celtic sounds, from the City Guard, with "Ceaze ta matman!" but pursuit and opposition were in vain. I pursued my career ; the smell of the sea, I suppose, led me to Leith, where, soon after, I found myself walking very quietly on the shore, admiring the tough round and sound cordage of the vessels, and thinking how a loop, with a man at the end of one of them, would look, by way of tassel.

"I was opposite to the rendezvous, formerly my place of refuge ; in I bolted—found one or two old acquaintances, made half a dozen new ones—drank for two days—was put aboard the tender—off to Portsmouth—then landed at the Haslaar hospital in a fine hissing-hot fever. Never mind, I got better : nothing can kill me. The West Indies were my lot again, for, since I did not go where I deserved in the next world, I had something as like such quarters as can be had in this—black devils for inhabitants, flames and earthquakes, and so forth, for your element. Well, brother, something or other I did or said—I can't tell what. How the devil should I, when I was as drunk as David's sow, you know ? But I was punished, my lad—made to kiss the wench that never speaks but when she scolds, and that's the gunner's daughter, comrade. Yes, the minister's son of— no matter where—has the cat's scratch on his back ! This roused me, and when were ashore with the boat I gave three inches of the dirk, after a stout tussle, to the fellow I blamed most, and so took the bush for it. There were plenty of wild lads then along-shore ; and—I don't care who knows— I went on the account, look you—sailed under the black flag and marrow-bones—was a good friend to the sea and an enemy to all that sailed on it."

Fairford, though uneasy in his mind at finding himself, a lawyer, so close to a character so lawless, thought it best,

nevertheless, to put a good face on the matter, and asked
Mr. Ewart, with as much unconcern as he could assume,
" Whether he was fortunate as a rover ? "

" No—no, d—n it, no," replied Nanty ; " the devil a crumb
of butter was ever churned that would stick upon my bread.
There was no order among us : he that was captain to-day
was swabber to-morrow ; and as for plunder—they say old
Avery* and one or two close hunks made money, but in my
time all went as it came ; and reason good, for if a fellow
had saved five dollars his throat would have been cut in his
hammock. And then it was a cruel, bloody work. Pah—
we'll say no more about it. I broke with them at last, for
what they did on board of a bit of a snow—no matter what it
was—bad enough, since it frightened me. I took French
leave, and came in upon the proclamation, so I am free of
all that business. And here I sit, the skipper of the " Jumping Jenny "—a nutshell of a thing, but goes through the
water like a dolphin. If it were not for you hypocritical
scoundrel at Annan, who has the best end of the profit and
takes none of the risk, I should be well enough—as well as
I want to be. Here is no lack of my best friend," touching
his case-bottle ; " but, to tell you a secret, he and I have
got so used to each other, I begin to think he is like a professed joker, that makes your sides sore with laughing if
you see him but now and then, but if you take up house
with him he can only make your head stupid. But I warrant the old fellow is doing the best he can for me, after
all."

" And what may that be ? " said Fairford.

" He is KILLING me," replied Nanty Ewart ; " and I am
only sorry he is so long about it."

So saying he jumped on his feet, and tripping up and
down the deck, gave his orders with his usual clearness and
decision, notwithstanding the considerable quantity of spirits
which he had contrived to swallow while recounting his
history.

Although far from feeling well, Fairford endeavored to
rouse himself and walk to the head of the brig, to enjoy the
beautiful prospect, as well as to take some note of the course
which the vessel held. To his great surprise, instead of
standing across to the opposite shore from which she had
departed, the brig was going down the firth, and apparently
steering into the Irish Sea. He called to Nanty Ewart, and
expressed his surprise at the course they were pursuing, and

* See Note 35.

asked why they did not stand straight across the firth for some port in Cumberland.

"Why, this is what I call a reasonable question, now," answered Nanty ; " as if a ship could go as straight to its port as a horse to the stable, or a free-trader could sail the Solway as securely as a king's cutter ! Why, I'll tell ye, brother, if I do not see a smoke on Bowness, that is the village upon the headland yonder, I must stand out to sea for twenty-four hours at least, for we must keep the weather-gage if there are hawks abroad."

"And if you do see the signal of safety, Master Ewart, what is to be done then ? "

" Why then, and in that case, I must keep off till night, and then run you, with the kegs and the rest of the lumber, ashore at Skinburness."

" And then I am to meet with this same laird whom I have the letter for ? " continued Fairford.

" That," said Ewart, " is thereafter as it may be : the ship has its course, the fair-trader has his port, but it is not so easy to say where the Laird may be found. But he will be within twenty miles of us, off or on ; and it will be my business to guide you to him."

Fairford could not withstand the passing impulse of terror which crossed him when thus reminded that he was so absolutely in the power of a man who, by his own account, had been a pirate, and who was at present, in all probability, an outlaw as well as a contraband trader. Nanty Ewart guessed the cause of his involuntary shuddering.

" What the devil should I gain," he said, " by passing so poor a card as you are ? Have I not had ace of trumps in my hand, and did I not play it fairly ? Ay, I say the " Jumping Jenny " can run in other ware as well as kegs. Put *sigma* and *tau* to " Ewart," and see how that will spell. D'ye take me now ? "

" No, indeed," said Fairford : " I am utterly ignorant of what you allude to."

" Now, by Jove ! " said Nanty Ewart, " thou art either the deepest or the shallowest fellow I ever met with—or you are not right after all. I wonder where Summertrees could pick up such a tender along-shore. Will you let me see his letter ? "

Fairford did not hesitate to gratify his wish, which, he was aware he could not easily resist. The master of the " Jumping Jenny " looked at the direction very attentively, then turned the letter to and fro, and examined each flourish of the pen, as if he were judging of a piece of ornamented manuscript ; then handed it back to Fairford, without a single word or remark.

" Am I right now ? " said the young lawyer.

" Why, for that matter," answered Nanty, " the letter is right, sure enough ; but whether *you* are right or not is your own business, rather than mine." And, striking upon a flint with the back of a knife, he kindled a cigar as thick as his finger, and began to smoke away with great perseverance.

Alan Fairford continued to regard him with a melancholy feeling divided betwixt the interest he took in the unhappy man and a not unnatural apprehension for the issue of his own adventure.

Ewart, notwithstanding the stupefying nature of his pastime, seemed to guess what was working in his passenger's mind ; for, after they had remained some time engaged in silently observing each other, he suddenly dashed his cigar on the deck, and said to him, " Well, then, if you are sorry for me, I am sorry for you. D—n me, if I have cared a button for man or mother's son since two years since, when I had another peep of Jack Hadaway. The fellow was got as fat as a Norway whale ; married to a great Dutch-built quean that had brought him six children. I believe he did not know me, and thought I was come to rob his house ; however, I made up a poor face, and told him who I was. Poor Jack would have given me shelter and clothes, and began to tell me of the moidores that were in bank, when I wanted them. Egad, he changed his note when I told him what my life had been, and only wanted to pay me my cash and get rid of me. I never saw so terrified a visage. I burst out a-laughing in his face, told him it was all a humbug, and that the moidores were all his own, henceforth and forever, and so ran off. I caused one of our people send him a bag of tea and a keg of brandy before I left. Poor Jack ! I think you are the second person these ten years that has cared a tobacco-stopper for Nanty Ewart."

" Perhaps, Mr. Ewart," said Fairford, " you live chiefly with men too deeply interested for their own immediate safety to think much upon the distress of others ? "

" And with whom do you yourself consort, I pray ? " replied Nanty, smartly. " Why, with plotters that can make no plot to better purpose than their own hanging ; and incendiaries, that are snapping the flint upon wet tinder. You'll as soon raise the dead as raise the Highlands ; you'll as soon get a grunt from a dead sow as any comfort from

Wales or Cheshire. You think, because the pot is boiling, that no scum but yours can come uppermost ; I know better, by ——. All these rackets and riots that you think are trending your way have no relation at all to your interest ; and the best way to make the whole kingdom friends again at once would be the alarm of such an undertaking as these mad old fellows are trying to launch into."

"I really am not in such secrets as you seem to allude to," said Fairford ; and, determined at the same time to avail himself as far as possible of Nanty's communicative disposition, he added, with a smile, "And if I were, I should not hold it prudent to make them much the subject of conversation. But I am sure so sensible men as Summertrees and the Laird may correspond together without offense to the state."

"I take you, friend—I take you," said Nanty Ewart, upon whom, at length, the liquor and tobacco-smoke began to make considerable innovation. "As to what gentlemen may or may not correspond about, why, we may pretermit the question, as the old professor used to say at the hall ; and as to Summertrees, I will say nothing, knowing him to be an old fox. But I say that this fellow the Laird is a firebrand in the country ; that he is stirring up all the honest fellows who should be drinking their brandy quietly, by telling them stories about their ancestors and the Forty-five ; and that he is trying to turn all waters into his own mill-dam, and to set his sails to all winds. And because the London people are roaring about for some pinches of their own, he thinks to win them to his turn with a wet finger. And he gets encouragement from some because they want a spell of money from him ; and from others because they fought for the cause once, and are ashamed to go back ; and others because they have nothing to lose ; and others because they are discontented fools. But if he has brought you, or any one, I say not whom, into this scrape, with the hope of doing any good, he's a d—d decoy-duck, and that's all I can say for him ; and you are geese, which is worse than being decoy-ducks, or lame ducks either. And so here is to the prosperity of King George the Third, and the true Presbyterian religion, and confusion to the Pope, the Devil, and the Pretender ! I'll tell you what, Mr. Fairbairn, I am but tenth owner of this bit of a craft, the "Jumping Jenny."—but tenth owner, and must sail by her own owners' directions. But if I were whole owner, I would not have the brig be made a ferryboat for your Jacobitical, old-fashioned Popish riff-raff, Mr. Fairport—I would not, by my soul : they should walk the plank, by the gods, as I have seen better men do when I sailed under the what-d'ye-callum colors. But being contraband good, and on board my vessel, and I with my sailing orders in my hand, why, I am to forward them as directed. I say, John Robers, keep her up a bit with the helm. And so, Mr. Fairweather, what I do is, as the d—d villain Turnpenny says, " all in the way of business."

He had been speaking with difficulty for the last five minutes, and now at length dropped on the deck fairly silenced by the quantity of spirits which he had swallowed, but without having shown any glimpse of the gaiety, or even of the extravagance, of intoxication.

The old sailor stepped forward and flung a sea-cloak over the slumberer's shoulders, and added, looking at Fairford, " Pity of him he should have this fault ; for without it, he would have been as clever a fellow as ever trode a plank with ox leather."

" And what are we to do now ? " said Fairford.

" Stand off and on, to be sure, till we see the signal, and then obey orders."

So saying, the old man turned to his duty, and left the passenger to amuse himself with his own meditations. Presently afterward a light column of smoke was seen rising from the little headland..

" I can tell you what we are to do now, master," said the sailor. " We'll stand out to sea, and then run in again with the evening tide, and make Skinburness ; or, if there's not light, we can run into the Wampool river, and put you ashore about Kirkbride or Leaths with the long-boat."

Fairford, unwell before, felt this destination condemned him to an agony of many hours, which his disordered stomach and aching head were ill able to endure. There was no remedy, however, but patience, and the recollection that he was suffering in the cause of friendship. As the sun rose high, he became worse ; his sense of smell appeared to acquire a morbid degree of acuteness, for the mere purpose of inhaling and distinguishing all the various odors with which he was surrounded, from that of pitch to all the complicated smells of the hold. His heart, too, throbbed under the heat, and he felt as if in full progress towards a high fever.

The seamen, who were civil and attentive, considering their calling, observed his distress, and one contrived to make an awning out of an old sail, while another compounded some lemonade, the only liquor which their passenger could be prevailed upon to touch. After drinking it off, he obtained, but could not be said to enjoy, a few hours of troubled slumber.

CHAPTER XV

ALAN FAIRFORD's spirit was more ready to encounter labor than his frame was adequate to support it. In spite of his exertions, when he awoke, after five or six hours' slumber, he found that he was so much disabled by dizziness in his head and pains in his limbs that he could not raise himself without assistance. He heard with some pleasure that they were now running right for the Wampool river, and that he would be put on shore in a very short time. The vessel accordingly lay to, and presently showed a weft in her ensign, which was hastily answered by signals from on shore. Men and horses were seen to come down the broken path which leads to the shore, the latter all properly tackled for carrying their loading. Twenty fishing-barks were pushed afloat at once, and crowded round the brig with much clamor, laughter, cursing, and jesting. Amidst all this apparent confusion there was the essential regularity. Nanty Ewart again walked his quarter-deck as if he had never tasted spirits in his life, issued the necessary orders with precision, and saw them executed with punctuality. In half an hour the loading of the brig was in a great measure disposed in the boats ; in a quarter of an hour more, it was landed on the beach · and another interval of about the same duration was sufficient to distribute it on the various strings of pack-horses which waited for that purpose, and which instantly dispersed, each on its own proper adventure. More mystery was observed in loading the ship's boat with a quantity of small barrels, which seemed to contain ammunition. This was not done until the commercial customers had been dismissed ; and it was not until this was performed that Ewart proposed to Alan, as he lay stunned with pain and noise, to accompany him ashore.

It was with difficulty that Fairford could get over the side of the vessel, and he could not seat himself on the stern of the boat without assistance from the captain and his people. Nanty Ewart, who saw nothing in this worse than an ordinary fit of sea-sickness, applied the usual topics of con-

solation. He assured his passenger that he would be quite
well by and by, when he had been half an hour on terra
firma, and that he hoped to drink a can and smoke a pipe
with him at Father Crackenthorp's, for all that he felt a
little out of the way for riding the wooden horse.

"Who is Father Crackenthorp?" said Fairford, though
scarcely able to articulate the question.

"As honest a fellow as is of a thousand," answered Nanty.
"Ah, how much good brandy he and I have made little of
in our day! By my soul, Mr. Fairbird, he is the prince of
skinkers, and the father of the free trade ; not a stingy,
hypocritical devil like old Turnpenny Skinflint, that drinks
drunk on other folks' cost, and thinks it sin when he has to
pay for it, but a real hearty old cock. The sharks have been
at and about him this many a day, but Father Crackenthorp
knows how to trim his sails—never a warrant but he hears
of it before the ink's dry. He is *bonus socius* with head-
borough and constable. The King's Exchequer could not
bribe a man to inform against him. If any such rascal were
to cast up, why, he would miss his ears next morning, or be
sent to seek them in the Solway. He is a statesman, though
he keeps a public ; but, indeed, that is only for convenience,
and to excuse his having cellarage and folk about him ; his
wife's a canny woman, and his daughter Doll too. Gad,
you'll be in port there till you get round again ; and I'll
keep my word with you, and bring you to speech of the
Laird. Gad, the only trouble I shall have is to get you out
of the house ; for Doll is a rare wench, and my dame a funny
old one, and Father Crackenthorp the rarest companion !
He'll drink you a bottle of rum or brandy without starting,
but never wet his lips with that nasty Scottish stuff that the
canting old scoundrel Turnpenny has brought into fashion.
He is a gentleman, every inch of him, old Crackenthorp—
in his own way, that is ; and besides, he has a share in the
'Jumping Jenny,' and many a moonlight outfit besides.
He can give Doll a pretty penny, if he likes the tight fellow
that would turn in with her for life."

In the midst of this prolonged panegyric on Father Crackenthorp, the boat touched the beach, the rowers backed
their oars to keep her afloat, whilst the other fellows jumped
into the surf, and, with the most rapid dexterity, began to
hand the barrels ashore.

"Up with them higher on the beach, my hearties," exclaimed Nanty Ewart. "High and dry—high and dry ; this
gear will not stand wetting. Now, out with our spare hand

here—high and dry with him too. What's that ? the galloping of horse ! Oh, I hear the jingle of the pack-saddles :
they are our own folk."

By this time all the boat's load was ashore, consisting of
the little barrels ; and the boat's crew, standing to their
arms, ranged themselves in front, waiting the advance of the
horses which came clattering along the beach. A man, overgrown with corpulence, who might be distinguished in the
moonlight, panting with his own exertions, appeared at the
head of the cavalcade, which consisted of horses linked together, and accommodated with pack-saddles, and chains for
securing the kegs, which made a dreadful clattering.

"How now, Father Crackenthorp ?" said Ewart. "Why
this hurry with your horses ? We mean to stay a night with
you, and taste your old brandy and my dame's home-brewed.
The signal is up, man, and all is right."

"All is wrong Captain Nanty," cried the man to whom
he spoke ; "and you are the lad that is like to find it so, unless you bundle off. There are new brooms bought at
Carlisle yesterday to sweep the country of you and the like
of you ; so you were better be jogging inland."

"How many rogues are the officers ? If not more than
ten, I will make fight."

"The devil you will !" answered Crackenthorp. "You
were better not, for they have the bloody-backed dragoons
from Carlisle with them."

"Nay, then," said Nanty, "we must make sail. Come,
Master Fairlord, you must mount and ride. He does not
hear me : he has fainted, I believe. What the devil shall I
do ? Father Crackenthorp, I must leave this young fellow
with you till the gale blows out. Hark ye—goes between
the Laird and the t'other old one. He can neither ride nor
walk—I must send him up to you."

"Send him up to the gallows !" said Crackenthorp.
"There is Quartermaster Thwacker, with twenty men, up
yonder ; an he had not some kindness for Doll, I had never
got hither for a start ; but you must get off, or they will be
here to seek us, for his orders are woundy particular ; and
these kegs contain worse than whisky—a hanging matter,
I take it."

"I wish they were at the bottom of Wampool river, with
them they belong to," said Nanty Ewart. "But they are
part of cargo ; and what to do with the poor young
fellow——"

"Wny, many a better fellow has roughed it on the grass,

with a cloak o'er him,' said Crackenthorp. "If he hath a fever, nothing is so cooling as the night air."

" Yes, he would be cold enough in the morning, no doubt ; but it's a kind heart, and shall not cool so soon, if I can help it," answered the captain of the "Jumping Jenny."

"Well, captain, and ye will risk your own neck for another man's, why not take him to the old girls at Fairladies ? "

"What, the Miss Arthurets! The Papist jades! But never mind, it will do ; I have known them take in a whole sloop's crew that were stranded on the sands."

" You may run some risk, though, by turning up to Fairladies ; for I tell you they are all up through the country."

" Never mind, I may chance to put some of them down again," said Nanty, cheerfully. " Come, lads, bustle to your tackle. Are you all loaded ? "

" Ay—ay, captain ; we will be ready in a jiffy," answered the gang.

" D—n your ' captains ! ' Have you a mind to have me hanged if I am taken ? All's hail-fellow here."

" A sup at parting," said Father Crackenthorp, extending a flask to Nanty Ewart.

" Not the twentieth part of a drop," said Nanty. " No Dutch courage for me : my heart is always high enough when there's a chance of fighting ; besides, if I live drunk, I should like to die sober. Here, old Jephson—you are the best-natured brute amongst them—get the lad between us on a quiet horse, and we will keep him upright, I warrant."

As they raised Fairford from the ground, he groaned heavily, and asked faintly, where they were taking him to.

" To a place where you will be as snug and quiet as a mouse in his hole," said Nanty, " if so be that we can get you there safely. Good-by, Father Crackenthorp ; poison the quartermaster, if you can."

The loaded horses then sprang forward at a hard trot, following each other in a line, and every second horse being mounted by a stout fellow in a smock-frock, which served to conceal the arms with which most of these desperate men were provided. Ewart followed in the rear of the line, and, with the occasional assistance of old Jephson, kept his young charge erect in the saddle. He groaned heavily from time to time ; and Ewart, more moved with compassion for his situation than might have been expected from his own habits, endeavored to amuse him and comfort him, by some

account of the place to which they were conveying him, his
words of consolation being, however, frequently interrupted
by the necessity of calling to his people, and many of them
being lost amongst the rattling of the barrels, and clinking
of the tackle and small chains by which they are secured on
such occasions.

" And you see, brother, you will be in safe quarters at Fairladies—good old scrambling house—good old maids enough,
if they were not Papists. Halloo, you, Jack Lowther ; keep
the line, can't ye, and shut your rattle-trap, you broth of
a——! And so, being of a good family, and having enough,
the old lasses have turned a kind of saints, and nuns, and so
forth. The place they live in was some sort of nun-shop
long ago, as they have them still in Flanders ; so folk call
them the Vestals of Fairladies ; that may be or may not be,
and I care not whether it be or no. Blinkinsop, hold your
tongue, and be d—d ! And so, betwixt great alms and good
dinners, they are well thought of by rich and poor, and their
trucking with Papists is looked over. There are plenty of
priests, and stout young scholars, and such-like about the
house : it's a hive of them. More shame that government
send dragoons out after a few honest fellows that bring the
old women of England a drop of brandy, and let these raga-
muffins smuggle in as much Papistry and—— Hark ! was
that a whistle ? No, it's only a plover. You, Jem Collier,
keep a look-out a-head ; we'll meet them at the High Whins
or Brotthole Bottom, or nowhere. Go a furlong a-head, I
say, and look sharp. These Miss Arthurets feed the
hungry, and clothe the naked, and such-like acts ; which
my poor father used to say were filthy rags, but he dressed
himself out with as many of them as most folk. D—n that
stumbling horse ! Father Crackenthorp should be d—d
himself for putting an honest fellow's neck in such jeopardy."

Thus, and with much more to the same purpose, Nanty
ran on, increasing, by his well-intended annoyance, the
agony of Alan Fairford, who, tormented by racking pain
along the back and loins, which made the rough trot of the
horse torture to him, had his aching head still further
rended and split by the hoarse voice of the sailor, close to his
ear. Perfectly passive, however, he did not even essay to
give any answer ; and indeed his own bodily distress was
now so great and engrossing that to think of his situation
was impossible, even if he could have mended it by doing so.

Their course was inland, but in what direction Alan had
no means of ascertaining. They passed at first over heaths

and sandy downs ; they crossed more than one brook, or
" beck," as they are called in that country—some of them of
considerable depth—and at length reached a cultivated
country, divided, according to the English fashion of agri-
culture, into very small fields or closes, by high banks, overgrown with underwood and surmounted by hedgerow trees,
amongst which winded a number of impracticable and complicated lanes, where the boughs, projecting from the
embankments on each side, intercepted the light of the
moon and endangered the safety of the horsemen. But
through this labyrinth the experience of the guides conducted them without a blunder, and without even the slackening of their pace. In many places, however, it was
impossible for three men to ride abreast, and therefore the
burden of supporting Alan Fairford fell alternately to old
Jephson and to Nanty ; and it was with much difficulty that
they could keep him upright in his saddle.

At length, when his powers of sufferance were quite worn
out, and he was about to implore them to leave him to his
fate in the first cottage or shed, or under a haystack or a
hedge, or anywhere, so he was left at ease, Collier, who rode
a-head, passed back the word that they were at the avenue
to Fairladies. "Was he to turn up ?"

Committing the charge of Fairford to Jephson, Nanty
dashed up to the head of the troop and gave his orders.
" Who knows the house best ?"

"Sam Skelton's a Catholic," said Lowther.

"A d—d bad religion," said Nanty, of whose Presbyterian
education a hatred of Popery seemed to be the only remnant.
" But I'm glad there is one amongst us, anyhow. You, Sam,
being a Papist, know Fairladies and the old maidens, I daresay ; so do you fall out of the line and wait here with me ;
and do you, Collier, carry on to Walinford Bottom, then
turn down the beck till you come to the old mill, and Goodman Grist, the miller, or old Peel-the-Causeway will tell you
where to stow ; but I will be up with you before that."

The string of loaded horses then struck forward at their
former pace, while Nanty, with Sam Skelton, waited by the
roadside till the rear came up, when Jephson and Fairford
joined them ; and, to the great relief of the latter, they
began to proceed at an easier pace than formerly, suffering
the gang to precede them, till the clatter and clang attending their progress began to die away in the distance. They
had not proceeded a pistol-shot from the place where they
parted, when a short turning brought them in front of an

20

old moldering gateway, whose heavy pinnacles were decorated in the style of the 17th century, with clumsy architectural ornaments, several of which had fallen down from decay, and lay scattered about, no further care having been taken than just to remove them out of the direct approach to the avenue. The great stone pillars, glimmering white in the moonlight, had some fanciful resemblance to supernatural apparitions ; and the air of neglect all around gave an uncomfortable idea of the habitation to those who passed its avenue.

"There used to be no gate here," said Skelton, finding their way unexpectedly stopped.

"But there is a gate now, and a porter too," said a rough voice from within. "Who be you, and what do you want at this time of night ?"

"We want to come to speech of the ladies—of the Miss Arthurets," said Nanty ; "and to ask lodging for a sick man."

"There is no speech to be had of the Miss Arthurets at this time of night, and you may carry your sick man to the doctor," answered the fellow from within, gruffly ; "for, as sure as there is savor in salt and scent in rosemary, you will get no entrance. Put your pipes up and be jogging on."

"Why, Dick Gardener," said Skelton, "be thou then turned porter ?"

"What, do you know who I am ?" said the domestic, sharply.

"I know you by your bye-word," answered the other. "What, have you forgot little Sam Skelton and the brock in the barrel ?"

"No, I have not forgotten you," answered the acquaintance of Sam Skelton ; "but my orders are peremptory to let no one up the avenue this night, and therefore——"

"But we are armed, and will not be kept back," said Nanty. "Harkye, fellow, were it not better for you to take a guinea and let us in than to have us break the door first and thy pate afterwards ? for I won't see my comrade die at your door, be assured of that."

"Why, I dunna know," said the fellow ; "but what cattle were those that rode by in such hurry ?"

"Why, some of our folks from Browness, Stoniecultrum, and thereby," answered Skelton : "Jack Lowther, and old Jephson, and broad Will Lamplugh, and such-like."

"Well," said Dick Gardener, "as sure as there is savor in

salt and scent in rosemary, I thought it had been the troopers from Carlisle and Wigton, and the sound brought my heart to my mouth."

" Had thought thou wouldst have known the clatter of a cask from the clash of a broadsword as well as e'er a quaffer in Cumberland," answered Skelton.

" Come, brother, less of your jaw and more of your legs, if you please," said Nanty : " every moment we stay is a moment lost. Go to the ladies, and tell them that Nanty Ewart, of the ' Jumping Jenny,' has brought a young gentleman, charged with letters from Scotland to a certain gentleman of consequence in Cumberland ; that the soldiers are out, and the gentleman is very ill, and if he is not received at Fairladies, he must be left either to die at the gate or to be taken, with all his papers about him, by the redcoats."

Away ran Dick Gardener with this message ; and in a few minutes lights were seen to flit about, which convinced Fairford, who was now, in consequence of the halt, a little restored to self-possession, that they were traversing the front of a tolerably large mansion house.

" What if thy friend, Dick Gardener, comes not back again ? " said Jephson to Skelton.

" Why, then," said the person addressed, " I shall owe him just such a licking as thou, old Jephson, hadst from Dan Cooke, and will pay as duly and truly as he did."

The old man was about to make an angry reply, when his doubts were silenced by the return of Dick Gardener, who announced that Miss Arthuret was coming herself as far as the gateway to speak with them.

Nanty Ewart cursed in a low tone, the suspicion of old maids and the churlish scruples of Catholics, that made so many obstacles to helping a fellow-creature, and wished Miss Arthuret a hearty rheumatism or toothache as the reward of her excursion ; but the lady presently appeared, to cut short farther grumbling. She was attended to by a waiting-maid with a lantern, by means of which she examined the party on the outside, as closely as the imperfect light and the spars of the newly-erected gate would permit.

" I am sorry we have disturbed you so late, Madam Arthuret," said Nanty ; " but the case is this——"

" Holy Virgin," said she, " why do you speak so loud ? Pray, are you not the captain of the ' Sainte Genevieve ' ? "

" Why, ay, ma'am," answered Ewart, " they call the brig so at Dunkirk, sure enough ; but alongshore here they call her the ' Jumping Jenny.' "

"You brought over the holy Father Buonaventure, did you not ?"

"Ay—ay, madam, I have brought over enough of them black cattle," answered Nanty.

"Fie ! fie ! friend," said Miss Arthuret ; "it is a pity that the saints should commit these good men to a heretic's care."

"Why, no more they would, ma'am," answered Nanty, "could they find a Papish lubber that knew the coast as I do. Then I am trusty as steel to owners, and always look after cargo—live lumber, or dead flesh, or spirits, all is one to me ; and your Catholics have such d—d large hoods, with pardon, ma'am, that they can sometimes hide two faces under them. But here is a gentleman dying, with letters about him from the Laird of Summertrees to the Laird of the Lochs, as they call him, along Solway, and every minute he lies here is a nail in his coffin."

"St Mary ! what shall we do ?" said Miss Arthuret.

"We must admit him, I think, at all risks. You, Richard Gardener, help one of these men to carry the gentleman up to the Place ; and you, Selby, see him lodged at the end of the long gallery. You are a heretic, captain, but I think you are trusty, and I know you have been trusted ; but if you are imposing on me——"

"Not I, madam—never attempt to impose on ladies of your experience : my practise that way has been all among the young ones. Come, cheerly, Mr. Fairford—you will be taken good care of ; try to walk."

Alan did so ; and, refreshed by his halt, declared himself able to walk to the house with the sole assistance of the gardener.

"Why, that's hearty. Thank thee, Dick, for lending him thine arm," and Nanty slipped into his hand the guinea he had promised. "Farewell, then, Mr. Fairford, and farewell, Madam Arthuret, for I have been too long here."

So saying, he and his two companions threw themselves on horseback, and went off at a gallop. Yet, even above the clatter of their hoofs did the incorrigible Nanty halloo out the old ballad—

> "A lovely lass to a friar came,
>   To confession a-morning early ;—
> 'In what, my dear, are you to blame,
>   Come tell me most sincerely ?'
> 'Alas ! my fault I dare not name—
>   But my lad he loved me dearly.'"

"Holy Virgin !" exclaimed Miss Seraphina, as the unhallowed sounds reached her ears ; "what profane heathens be these men, and what frights and pinches we be put to among them ! The saints be good to us, what a night has this been ! the like never seen at Fairladies. Help me to make fast the gate, Richard, and thou shalt come down again to wait on it, lest there come more unwelcome visitors. Not that you are unwelcome, young gentleman, for it is sufficient that you need such assistance as we can give you to make you welcome to Fairladies—only, another time would have done as well ; but, hem ! I daresay it is all for the best. The avenue is none of the smoothest, sir, look to your feet. Richard Gardener should have had it mown and leveled, but he was obliged to go on a pilgrimage to St. Winifred's Well, in Wales." Here Dick gave a short dry cough, which, as if he had found it betrayed some internal feeling a little at variance with what the lady said, he converted into a muttered "*Sancta Winifreda ora pro nobis.*" Miss Arthuret, meantime, proceeded—" We never interfere with our servants' vows or penances, Master Fairford—I know a very worthy father of your name, perhaps a relation —I say, we never interfere with our servants' vows. Our Lady forbid they should not know some difference between our service and a heretic's. Take care, sir, you will fall if you have not a care. Alas, by night and day there are many stumbling-blocks in our paths !"

With more talk to the same purpose, all of which tended to show a charitable and somewhat silly woman, with a strong inclination to her superstitious devotion, Miss Arthuret entertained her new guest, as, stumbling at every obstacle which the devotion of his guide, Richard, had left in the path, he at last, by ascending some stone steps decorated on the side with griffins, or some such heraldic anomalies, attained a terrace extending in front of the Place of Fairladies—an old-fashioned gentleman's house of some consequence, with its range of notched gable-ends and narrow windows, relieved by here and there an old turret about the size of a pepper-box. The door was locked during the brief absence of the mistress ; a dim light glimmered through the sashed door of the hall, which opened beneath a huge stone porch, loaded with jessamine and other creepers. All the windows were dark as pitch.

Miss Arthuret tapped at the door. "Sister—sister Angelica !"

"Who is there ?" was answered from within ; "is it you, sister Seraphina ?"

"Yes—yes, undo the door. Do you not know my voice ?"

"No doubt, sister," said Angelica, undoing bolt and bar; "but you know our charge, and the enemy is watchful to surprise us : *incedit sicut leo vorans*, saith the breviary. Whom have you brought here ? Oh, sister, what have you done ?"

"It is a young man," said Seraphina, hastening to interrupt her sister's remonstrance, "a relation, I believe, of our worthy Father Fairford, left at the gate by the captain of that blessed vessel the 'Sainte Genevieve'—almost dead, and charged with despatches to——"

She lowered her voice as she mumbled over the last words.

"Nay, then, there is no help," said Angelica ; "but it is unlucky."

During this dialogue between the vestals of Fairladies, Dick Gardener deposited his burden in a chair, where the young [er] lady, after a moment of hesitation, expressing a becoming reluctance to touch the hand of a stranger, put her finger and thumb upon Fairford's wrist and counted his pulse.

"There is fever here, sister," she said ; "Richard must call Ambrose, and we must send some of the febrifuge."

Ambrose arrived presently, a plausible and respectable-looking old servant, bred in the family, and who had risen from rank to rank in the Arthuret service, till he was become half-physician, half-almoner, half-butler, and entire governor ; that is, when the father confessor, who frequently eased him of the toils of government, chanced to be abroad. Under the direction, and with the assistance. of this venerable personage, the unlucky Alan Fairford was conveyed to a decent apartment at the end of a long gallery, and, to his inexpressible relief, consigned to a comfortable bed. He did not attempt to resist the prescription of Mr. Ambrose, who not only presented him with the proposed draught, but proceeded so far as to take a considerable quantity of blood from him, by which last operation he probably did his patient much service.

CHAPTER XVI

NARRATIVE OF ALAN FAIRFORD, CONTINUED

ON the next morning, when Fairford awoke, after no very refreshing slumbers, in which were mingled many wild dreams of his father, and of Darsie Latimer, of the damsel in the green mantle, and the vestals of Fairladies, of drinking small beer with Nanty Ewart, and being immersed in the Solway with the "Jumping Jenny," he found himself in no condition to dispute the order of Mr. Ambrose, that he should keep his bed, from which, indeed, he could not have raised himself without assistance. He became sensible that his anxiety, and his constant efforts for some days past, had been too much for his health, and that, whatever might be his impatience, he could not proceed in his undertaking until his strength was re-established.

In the meanwhile, no better quarters could have been found for an invalid. The attendants spoke under their breath, and moved only on tiptoe ; nothing was done unless *par ordonnance du médecin :* Esculapius reigned paramount in the premises at Fairladies. Once a-day the ladies came in great state to wait upon him and inquire after his health, and it was then that Alan's natural civility, and the thankfulness which he expressed for their timely and charitable assistance, raised him considerably in their esteem. He was on the third day removed to a better apartment than that in which he had been at first accommodated. When he was permitted to drink a glass of wine, it was of the first quality—one of those curious old-fashioned cobwebbed bottles being produced on the occasion which are only to be found in the crypts of old country seats, where they may have lurked undisturbed for more than half a century.

But, however delightful a residence for an invalid, Fairladies, at its present inmate became soon aware, was not so agreeable to a convalesent. When he dragged himself to the window so soon as he could crawl from bed, behold it was closely grated, and commanded no view except of a little paved court. This was nothing remarkable, most old Border houses having their windows so secured ; but then Fairford observed that whoever entered or left the room always locked the door with great care and circumspection ; and some proposals which he made to take a walk in the gallery, or even in the garden, were so coldly received, both by the ladies and their prime minister, Mr. Ambrose, that he saw plainly such an extension of his privileges as a guest would not be permitted.

Anxious to ascertain whether this excessive hospitality would permit him his proper privilege of free agency, he announced to this important functionary, with grateful thanks for the care with which he had been attended, his purpose to leave Fairladies next morning, requesting only, as a continuance of the favors with which he had been loaded, the loan of a horse to the next town ; and, assuring Mr. Ambrose that his gratitude would not be limited by such a trifle, he slipped three guineas into his hand, by way of seconding his proposal. The fingers of that worthy domestic closed as naturally upon the *honorarium* as if a degree in the learned faculty had given him a right to clutch it, but his answer concerning Alan's proposed departure was at first evasive, and when he was pushed it amounted to a peremptory assurance that he could not be permitted to depart to-morrow ; it was as much as his life was worth, and his ladies would not authorize it.

"I know best what my own life is worth," said Alan ; "and I do not value it in comparison to the business which requires my instant attention."

Receiving still no satisfactory answer from Mr. Ambrose, Fairford thought it best to state his resolution to the ladies themselves, in the most measured, respectful, and grateful terms, but still such as expressed a firm determination to depart on the morrow, or next day at farthest. After some attempts to induce him to stay, on the alleged score of health, which were so expressed that he was convinced they were only used to delay his departure, Fairford plainly told them that he was entrusted with despatches of consequence to the gentleman known by the name of Herries, Redgauntlet, and the Laird of the Lochs ; and that it was matter of life and death to deliver them early.

"I daresay, sister Angelica," said the elder Miss Arthuret, " that the gentleman is honest ; and if he is really a relation of Father Fairford, we can run no risk."

" Jesu Maria !" exclaimed the younger. " Oh, fie, sister Seraphina ! Fie—fie ! *Vade retro*—get thee behind me !"

" Well—well ; but sister—sister Angelica—let me speak with you in the gallery."

So out the ladies rustled in their silks and tissues, and it was a good half-hour ere they rustled in again, with importance and awe on their countenances.

"To tell you the truth, Mr. Fairford, the cause of our desire to delay you is, there is a religious gentleman in this house at present——"

"A most excellent person indeed," said the sister Angelica.

"An anointed of his Master!" echoed Seraphina; "and we should be glad that, for conscience' sake, you would hold some discourse with him before your departure."

"Oho!" thought Fairford, "the murder is out : here is a design of conversion! I must not affront the good old ladies, but I shall soon send off the priest, I think." He then answered aloud, "That he should be happy to converse with any friend of theirs ; that in religious matters he had the greatest respect for every modification of Christianity, though, he must say, his belief was made up to that in which he had been educated ; nevertheless, if his seeing the religious person they recommended could in the least show his respect——"

"It is not quite that," said sister Seraphina, "although I am sure the day is too short to hear him—Father Buonaventure, I mean—speak upon the concerns of our souls ; but——"

"Come—come, sister Seraphina," said the younger, "it is needless to talk so much about it. His—his Eminence— I mean, Father Buonaventure—will himself explain what he wants this gentleman to know."

"His Eminence," said Fairford, surprised. "Is this gentleman so high in the Catholic Church ? The title is given only to cardinals, I think."

"He is not a cardinal as yet," answered Seraphina ; "but I assure you, Mr. Fairford, he is as high in rank as he is eminently endowed with good gifts, and——"

"Come away," said sister Angelica. "Holy Virgin, how you do talk! What has Mr. Fairford to do with Father Buonaventure's rank ? Only, sir, you will remember that the father has been always accustomed to be treated with the most profound deference ; indeed——"

"Come away, sister," said sister Seraphina, in her turn. "Who talks now, I pray you ? Mr. Fairford will know how to comport himself."

"And we had best both leave the room," said the younger lady, "for here his Eminence comes."

She lowered her voice to a whisper as she pronounced the last words ; and as Fairford was about to reply by assuring her that any friend of hers should be treated by him with all the ceremony he could expect, she imposed silence on him by holding up her finger.

A solemn and stately step was now heard in the gallery ; it might have proclaimed the approach not merely of a bishop or cardinal, but of the Sovereign Pontiff himself. Nor could the sound have been more respectfully listened to by the two ladies had it announced that the Head of the Church was approaching in person. They drew themselves, like sentinels on duty, one on each side of the door by which the long gallery communicated with Fairford's apartment, and stood there immovable, and with countenances expressive of the deepest reverence.

The approach of Father Buonaventure was so slow, that Fairford had time to notice all this, and to marvel in his mind what wily and ambitious priest could have contrived to subject his worthy bnt simple-minded hostesses to such superstitious trammels. Father Buonaventure's entrance and appearance in some degree accounted for the whole.

He was a man of middle life, about forty or upwards ; but either care, or fatigue, or indulgence had brought on the appearance of premature old age, and given to his fine features a cast of seriousness or even sadness. A noble countenance, however, still remained ; and though his complexion was altered, and wrinkles stamped upon his brow in many a melancholy fold, still the lofty forehead, the full and well-opened eye, and the well-formed nose showed how handsome in better days he must have been. He was tall, but lost the advantage of his height by stooping ; and the cane which he wore always in his hand, and occasionally used, as well as his slow though majestic gait, seemed to intimate that his form and limbs felt already some touch of infirmity. The color of his hair could not be discovered, as, according to the fashion, he wore a periwig. He was handsomely, though gravely, dressed in a secular habit, and had a cockade in his hat—circumstances which did not surprise Fairford, who knew that a military disguise was very often assumed by the seminary priests, whose visits to England, or residence there, subjected them to legal penalties.

As this stately person entered the apartment, the two ladies facing inward, like soldiers on their post when about to salute a superior officer, dropped on either hand of the father a courtesy so profound, that the hoop petticoats which performed the feat seemed to sink down to the very floor, nay, through it, as if a trap-door had opened for the decent of the dames who performed this act of reverence.

The father seemed accustomed to such homage, profound as it was ; he turned his person a little way first towards one sister, and then towards the other, while, with a gracious inclination of his person, which certainly did not amount to a bow, he acknowledged their courtesy. But he passed forward without addressing them, and seemed by doing so to intimate that their presence in the apartment was unnecessary.

They accordingly glided out of the room, retreating backwards, with hands clasped and eyes cast upwards, as if imploring blessings on the religious man whom they venerated so highly. The door of the apartment was shut after them, but not before Fairford had perceived that there were one or two men in the gallery, and that, contrary to what he had before observed, the door, though shut, was not locked on the outside.

" Can the good souls apprehend danger from me to this god of their idolatry ? " thought Fairford. But he had no time to make farther observations, for the stranger had already reached the middle of the apartment.

Fairford rose to receive him respectfully, but as he fixed his eyes on the visitor, he thought that the father avoided his looks. His reasons for remaining incognito were cogent enough to account for this, and Fairford hastened to relieve him, by looking downwards in his turn ; but when again he raised his face, he found the broad light eye of the stranger so fixed on him, that he was almost put out of countenance be the steadiness of his gaze. During this time they remained standing.

" Take yonr seat, sir," said the father : " you have been an invalid."

He spoke with the tone of one who desires an inferior to be seated in his presence, and his voice was full and melodious.

Fairford, somewhat surprised to find himself overawed by the airs of superiority, which could be only properly exercised towards one over whom religion gave the speaker influence, sat down at his bidding, as if moved by springs, and was at a loss how to assert the footing of equality on which he felt that they ought to stand. The stranger kept the advantage which he had obtained.

" Your name, sir, I am informed, is Fairford ? " said the father.

Alan answered by a bow.

"Called to the Scottish bar," continued his visitor. "There is, I believe, in the West, a family of birth and rank called Fairford of Fairford."

Alan thought this a strange observation from a foreign ecclesiastic, as his name intimated Father Buonaventure to be ; but only answered, he believed there was such a family.

"Do you count kindred with them, Mr. Fairford ?" continued the inquirer.

"I have not the honor to lay such a claim," said Fairford. "My father's industry has raised his family from a low and obscure situation : I have no hereditary claim to distinction of any kind. May I ask the cause of these inquiries ?"

"You will learn it presently," said Father Buonaventure, who had given a dry and dissatisfied "hem" at the young man's acknowledging a plebeian descent. He then motioned to him to be silent, and proceeded with his queries.

"Although not of condition, you are, doubtless, by sentiments and education, a man of honor and a gentleman ?"

"I hope so, sir," said Alan, coloring with displeasure. "I have not been accustomed to have it questioned."

"Patience, young man," said the unperturbed querist : "we are on serious business, and no idle etiquette must prevent its being discussed seriously. You are probably aware that you speak to a person proscribed by the severe and unjust laws of the present government ?"

"I am aware of the statute 1700, chapter 3," said Alan, "banishing from the realm priests and trafficking Papists, and punishing by death, on summary conviction, any such person who being so banished may return. The English law, I believe, is equally severe. But I have no means of knowing you, sir, to be one of those persons ; and I think your prudence may recommend to you to keep your own counsel."

"It is sufficient, sir ; and I have no apprehensions of disagreable consequences from your having seen me in this house," said the priest.

"Assuredly no," said Alan. "I consider myself as indebted for my life to the mistresses of Fairladies ; and it would be a vile requital on my part to pry into or make known what I may have seen or heard under this hospitable roof. If I were to meet the Pretender himself in such a situation, he should, even at the risk of a little stretch to my loyalty, be free from any danger from my indiscretion."

"The Pretender !" said the priest, with some angry emphasis ; but immediately softened his tone and added, " No doubt, however, that person *is* a pretender ; and sôme people think his pretensions are not ill founded. But before running into politics, give me leave to say, that I am surprised to find a gentleman of your opinions in habits of intimacy with Mr. Maxwell of Summertrees and Mr. Redgauntlet, and the medium of conducting the intercourse betwixt them."

"Pardon me, sir," replied Alan Fairford ; "I do not aspire to the honor of being reputed their confidant or go-between. My concern with those gentlemen is limited to one matter of business, dearly interesting to me, because it concerns the safety—perhaps the life--of my dearest friend."

" Would you have any objections to entrust me with the cause of your journey ?" said Father Buonaventure. " My advice may be of service to you, and my influence with one or both these gentlemen is considerable."

Fairford hesitated a moment, and hastily revolving all circumstances, concluded that he might perhaps receive some advantage from propitiating this personage ; while, on the other hand, he endangered nothing by communicating to him the occasion of his journey. He, therefore, after stating shortly that he hoped Mr. Buonaventure would render him the same confidence which he required on his part, gave a short account of Darsie Latimer—of the mystery which hung over his family, and of the disaster which had befallen him, finally, of his own resolution to seek for his friend, and to deliver him, at the peril of his own life.

The Catholic priest, whose manner it seemed to be to avoid all conversation which did not arise from his own express motion, made no remarks upon what he had heard, but only asked one or two abrupt questions, where Alan's narrative appeared less clear to him ; then rising from his seat, he took two turns through the apartment, muttering between his teeth, with emphasis, the word " Madman !" But apparently he was in the habit of keeping all violent emotions under restraint ; for he presently addressed Fairford with the most perfect indifference.

"If," said he, " you thought you could do so without breach of confidence, I wish you would have the goodness to show me the letter of Mr. Maxwell of Summertrees. I desire to look particularly at the address."

Seeing no cause to decline this extension of his confidence, Alan, without hesitation, put the letter into his hand. Having turned it round as old Trumbull and Nanty Ewart had formerly done, and, like them, having examined the address

with much minuteness, he asked whether he had observed
these words, pointing to a pencil-writing upon the under
side of the letter.   Fairford answered in the negative, and
looking at the letter, read with surprise, " *Cave ne literas
Bellerophontis adferres* "—a caution which coincided so exactly with the provost's admonition, that he would do well
to inspect the letter of which he was bearer, that he was
about to spring up and attempt an escape, he knew not
wherefore or from whom.

" Sit still, young man," said the father, with the same
tone of authority which reigned in his whole manner, although mingled with stately courtesy.   " You are in no
danger : my character shall be a pledge for your safety.   By
whom do you suppose these words have been written ? "

Fairford could have answered, " By Nanty Ewart," for
he remembered seeing that person scribble something with a
pencil, although he was not well enough to observe with
accuracy where or upon what.   But not knowing what suspicions, or what worse consequences, the seaman's interest
in his affairs might draw upon him, he judged it best to
answer that he knew not the hand.

Father Buonaventure was again silent for a moment or
two, which he employed in surveying the letter with the
strictest attention ; then stepped to the window, as if to
examine the address and writing of the envelope with the
assistance of a stronger light, and Alan Fairford beheld him,
with no less amazement than high displeasure, coolly and
deliberately break the seal, open the letter, and peruse the
contents.

" Stop, sir—hold ! " he exclaimed, so soon as his astonishment permitted him to express his resentment in words ;
" by what right do you dare——"

" Peace, young gentleman," said the father, repelling him
with a wave of his hand ; " be assured I do not act without
warrant : nothing can pass betwixt Mr. Maxwell and Mr.
Redgauntlet that I am not fully entitled to know."

" It may be so," said Alan, extremely angry ; " but though
you may be these gentlemen's father confessor, you are not
mine ; and in breaking the seal of a letter entrusted to my
care, you have done me——"

" No injury, I assure you," answered the unperturbed
priest ; " on the contrary, it may be a service."

" I desire no advantage at such a rate, or to be obtained
in such a manner," answered Fairford ; " restore me the
letter instantly, or——"

" As you regard your own safety," said the priest, "forbear all injurious expressions and all menacing gestures. I am not one who can be threatened or insulted with impunity ; and there are enough within hearing to chastise any injury or affront offered to me, in case, I may think it unbecoming to protect or avenge myself with my own hand."

In saying this, the father assumed an air of such fearlessness and calm authority, that the young lawyer, surprised and overawed, forbore, as he had intended, to snatch the letter from his hand, and confined himself to bitter complaints of the impropriety of his conduct, and of the light in which he himself must be placed to Redgauntlet, should he present him a letter with a broken seal.

" That," said Father Buonaventure, " shall be fully cared for. I will myself write to Redgauntlet, and inclose Maxwell's letter, provided always you continue to desire to deliver it, after perusing the contents."

He then restored the letter to Fairford, and, observing that he hesitated to peruse it, said emphatically, " Read it, for it concerns you."

This recommendation, joined to what Provost Crosbie had formerly recommended, and to the warning which he doubted not that Nanty intended to convey by his classical allusion, decided Fairford's resolution. "If these correspondents," he thought, "are conspiring against my person, I have a right to counterplot them ; self-preservation, as well as my friend's safety, require that I should not be too scrupulous."

So thinking, he read the letter, which was in the following words :—

"Dear Rugged and Dangerous—

" Will you never cease meriting your old nickname ? You have springed your dottrel, I find, and what is the consequence ? Why, that there will be hue and cry after you presently. The bearer is a pert young lawyer, who has brought a formal complaint against you, which, luckily, he has preferred in a friendly court. Yet, favorable as the judge was disposed to be, it was with the utmost difficulty that cousin Jenny and I could keep him to his tackle. He begins to be timid, suspicious, and intractable, and I fear Jenny will soon bend her brows on him in vain. I know not what to advise. The lad who carries this is a good lad, active for his friend ; and I have pledged my honor he shall have no personal ill-usage. Pledged my honor, remark these words, and remember I can be rugged and dangerous as well as my neighbors. But I have not ensured him against a short captivity, and as he is a stirring, active fellow, I see no remedy but keeping him out of the way till this business of the good Father B—— is safely blown over, which God send it were! Always thine, even should I be once more

"CRAIG-IN-PERIL."

"What think you, young man, of the danger you have been about to encounter so willingly?"

"As strangely," replied Alan Fairford, "as of the extraordinary means which you have been at present pleased to use for the discovery of Mr. Maxwell's purpose."

"Trouble not yourself to account for my conduct," said the father; "I have a warrant for what I do, and fear no responsibility. But tell me what is your present purpose."

"I should not perhaps name it to you, whose own safety may be implicated."

"I understand you," answered the father: "you would appeal to the existing government? That can at no rate be permitted; we will rather detain you at Fairladies by compulsion."

"You will probably," said Fairford, "first weigh the risk of such a proceeding in a free country."

"I have incurred more formidable hazard," said the priest, smiling; "yet I am willing to find a milder expedient. Come—let us bring the matter to a compromise." And he assumed a conciliating graciousness of manner which struck Fairford as being rather too condescending for the occasion. "I presume you will be satisfied to remain here in seclusion for a day or two longer, provided I pass my solemn word to you that you shall meet with the person whom you seek after—meet with him in perfect safety, and, I trust, in good health, and be afterwards both at liberty to return to Scotland, or dispose of yourselves as each of you may be minded?"

"I respect the *verbum sacerdotis* as much as can reasonably be expected from a Protestant," answered Fairford; "but, methinks, you can scarce expect me to repose so much confidence in the word of an unknown person as is implied in the guarantee which you offer me."

"I am not accustomed, sir," said the father, in a very haughty tone, "to have my word disputed. But," he added, while the angry hue passed from his cheek, after a moment's reflection, "you know me not, and ought to be excused. I will repose more confidence in your honor than you seem willing to rest upon mine ; and since we are so situated that one must rely upon the other's faith, I will cause you to be set presently at liberty, and furnished with the means of delivering your letter as addressed, provided that now, knowing the contents, you think it safe for yourself to execute the commission."

Alan Fairford paused. "I cannot see," he at length replied, "how I can proceed with respect to the accomplishment of my sole purpose, which is the liberation of my friend, without appealing to the law, and obtaining the assistance of a magistrate. If I present this singular letter of Mr. Maxwell, with the contents of which I have become so unexpectedly acquainted, I shall only share his captivity."

"And if you apply to a magistrate, young man, you will bring ruin on these hospitable ladies, to whom, in all human probability, you owe your life. You cannot obtain a warrant for your purpose without giving a clear detail of all the late scenes through which you have passed. A magistrate would oblige you to give a complete account of yourself, before arming you with his authority against a third party,; and in giving such an account the safety of these ladies will necessarily be compromised. A hundred spies have had, and still have, their eyes upon this mansion ; but God will protect His own." He crossed himself devoutly, and then proceeded. "You can take an hour to think of your best plan, and I will pledge myself to forward it thus far, provided it be not asking you to rely more on my word than your prudence can warrant. You shall go to Redgauntlet —I name him plainly, to show my confidence in you—and you shall deliver him this letter of Mr. Maxwell's with one from me, in which I will enjoin him to set your friend at liberty, or at least to make no attempts upon your own person, either by detention or otherwise. If you can trust me thus far," he said, with a proud emphasis on the words, "I will on my side see you depart from this place with the most perfect confidence that you will not return armed with powers to drag its inmates to destruction. You are young and inexperienced, bred to a profession also which sharpens suspicion, and gives false views of human nature. I have seen much of the world, and have known better than most men how far mutual confidence is requisite in managing affairs of consequence."

He spoke with an air of superiority, even of authority, by which Fairford, notwithstanding his own internal struggles,

21

was silenced and overawed so much that it was not till the father had turned to leave the apartment that he found words to ask him, what the consequences would be should he decline to depart on the terms proposed.

" You must then, for the safety of all parties, remain for some days an inhabitant of Fairladies, where we have the means of detaining you, which self-preservation will in that case compel us to make use of. Your captivity will be short ; for matters cannot long remain as they are. The cloud must soon rise, or it must sink upon us forever. *Benedicite !* "

With these words he left the apartment.

Fairford, upon his departure, felt himself much at a loss what course to pursue. His line of education, as well as his father's tenets in matters of church and state, had taught him a holy horror of Papists, and a devout belief in whatever had been said of the punic faith of Jesuits, and of the expedients of mental reservation by which the Catholic priests in general were supposed to evade keeping faith with heretics. Yet there was something of majesty, depressed indeed, and overclouded, but still grand and imposing, in the manner and words of Father Buonaventure, which it was difficult to reconcile with those preconceived opinions which imputed subtlety and fraud to his sect and order. Above all, Alan was aware that, if he accepted not his freedom upon the terms offered him, he was likely to be detained by force ; so that, in every point of view, he was a gainer by adopting them.

A qualm, indeed, came across him, when he considered, as a lawyer, that his father was probably, in the eye of law, a traitor, and that there was an ugly crime on the statute book, called misprision of treason. On the other hand, whatever he might think or suspect, he could not take upon him to say that the man was a priest, whom he had never seen in the dress of his order, or in the act of celebrating mass ; so that he felt himself at liberty to doubt of that respecting which he possessed no legal proof. He therefore arrived at the conclusion that he would do well to accept his liberty, and proceed to Redgauntlet under the guaranty of Father Buonaventure, which he scarce doubted would be sufficient to save him from personal inconvenience. Should he once obtain speech of that gentleman, he felt the same confidence as formerly that he might be able to convince him of the rashness of his conduct, should he not consent to liberate Darsie Latimer. At all events, he should learn where his friend was, and how circumstanced,

Having thus made up his mind, Alan waited anxiously for the expiration of the hour which had been allowed him for deliberation, He was not kept on the tenter-hooks of impatience an instant longer than the appointed moment arrived, for, even as the clock struck, Ambrose appeared at the door of the gallery, and made a sign that Alan should follow him. He did so, and after passing through some of the intricate avenues common in old houses, was ushered into a small apartment, commodiously fitted up, in which he found Father Buonaventure reclining on a couch, in the attitude of a man exhausted by fatigue or indisposition. On a small table beside him, a silver embossed salver sustained a Catholic book of prayer, a small flask of medicine, a cordial, and little tea-cup of old china. Ambrose did not enter the room ; he only bowed profoundly, and closed the door with the least possible noise so soon as Fairford had entered.

" Sit down, young man," said the father, with the same air of condescension which had before surprised, and rather offended, Fairford. " You have been ill, and I know too well by my own case that indisposition requires indulgence. Have you," he continued, so soon as he saw him seated, " resolved to remain or to depart ? "

" To depart," said Alan, " under the agreement that you will guarantee my safety with the extraordinary person who has conducted himself in such a lawless manner towards my friend, Darsie Latimer."

" Do not judge hastily, young man," replied the father. " Redgauntlet has the claims of a guardian over his ward in respect to the young gentleman, and a right to dictate his place of residence, although ·he may have been injudicious in selecting the means by which he thinks to enforce his authority."

" His situation as an attainted person abrogates such rights," said Fairford, hastily.

" Surely," replied the priest, smiling at the young lawyer's readiness, " in the eye of those who acknowledge the justice of the attainder ; but that do not I. However, sir, here is the guaranty ; look at its contents, and do not again carry the letters of Uriah."

Fairford read these words :—

" Good Friend—We send you hither a young man desirous to know the situation of your ward since he came under your paternal authority, and hopeful of dealing with you for having your relative put at large. This we recommend to your prudence, highly disapproving, at the same time, of any force or coercion, when such can be avoided, and wishing, therefore, that the bearer's negotiation may be successful. At all rates, however, the bearer hath our pledged word for his safety and freedom, which, therefore, you are to see strictly observed, as you value our honor and your own. We farther wish to converse with you, with as small loss of time as may be, having matters of the utmost confidence to impart. For this purpose we desire you to repair hither with all haste, and thereupon we bid you heartily farewell.

"P. B."

"You will understand sir," said the father, when he saw that Alan had perused his letter, "that, by accepting charge of this missive, you bind yourself to try the effect of it before having recourse to any legal means, as you term them, for your friend's release."

"There are a few ciphers added to this letter," said Fairford, when he had perused the paper attentively; "may I inquire what their import is?"

"They respect my own affairs," answered the father, briefly; "and have no concern whatever with yours."

"It seems to me, however," replied Alan, "natural to suppose——"

"Nothing must be supposed incompatible with my honor," replied the priest, interrupting him; "when such as I am confer favors, we expect that they shall be accepted with gratitude or declined with thankful respect, not questioned or discussed."

"I will accept your letter then," said Fairford, after a minute's consideration, "and the thanks you expect shall be most liberally paid if the result answer what you teach me to expect."

"God only commands the issue," said Father Buonventure. "Man uses means. You understand that, by accepting this commission, you engage yourself in honor to try the effect of my letter upon Mr. Redgauntlet before you have recourse to informations or legal warrants?"

"I hold myself bound, as a man of good faith and honor, to do so," said Fairford.

"Well, I trust you," said the father. "I will now tell you that an express, despatched by me last night, has, I hope, brought Redgauntlet to a spot many miles nearer this place, where he will not find it safe to attempt any violence on your friend, should he be rash enough to follow the advice of Mr. Maxwell of Summertrees rather than my commands. We now understand each other."

He extended his hand towards Alan, who was about to pledge his faith in the usual form by grasping it with his own, when the father drew back hastily. Ere Alan had time to comment upon this repulse, a small side-door, covered with tapestry, was opened ; the hangings were drawn aside, and a lady as if by sudden apparition, glided into the apartment. It was neither of the Miss Arthurets, but a woman in the prime of life, and in the full-blown expansion of female beauty, tall, fair, and commanding in her aspect. Her locks, of paly gold, were taught to fall over a brow which, with the stately glance of the large, open, blue eyes, might have become Juno herself ; her neck and bosom were admirably formed, and of a dazzling whiteness. She was rather inclined to *embonpoint*, but not more than became her age, of apparently thirty years. Her step was that of a queen, but it was of Queen Vashti, not Queen Esther—the bold and commanding, not the retiring, beauty.

Father Buonaventure raised himself on the couch, angrily, as if displeased by this intrusion. " How now, madam," he said with some sternness—" why have we the honor of your company ? "

" Because it is my pleasure," answered the lady, composedly.

" Your pleasure, madam ! " he repeated, in the same angry tone.

" My pleasure, sir," she continued, " which always keeps exact pace with my duty. I had heard you were unwell ; let me hope it is only business which produces this seclusion."

" I am well," he replied—" perfectly well, and I thank you for your care ; but we are not alone, and this young man——"

" That young man ! " she said, bending her large and serious eye on Alan Fairford, as if she had been for the first time aware of his presence—" may I ask who he is ? "

" Another time, madam. You shall learn his history after he is gone. His presence renders it impossible for me to explain farther."

" After he is gone may be too late," said the lady ; " and what is his presence to me when your safety is at stake ? He is the heretic lawyer whom those silly fools, the Arthurets, admitted into this house at a time when they should have let their own father knock at the door in vain, though the night had been a wild one. You will not surely dismiss him ? "

" Your own impatience can alone make that step perilous," said the father. " I have resolved to take it ; do not let your indiscreet zeal, however excellent its motive, add any unnecessary risk to the transaction."

" Even so ? " said the lady, in a tone of reproach, yet mingled with respect and apprehension. " And thus you will still go forward, like a stag upon the hunter's snares, with undoubting confidence, after all that has happened ? "

" Peace, madam," said Father Buonaventure, rising up : " be silent, or quit the apartment ; my designs do not admit of female criticism."

To this peremptory command the lady seemed about to make a sharp reply ; but she checked herself, and pressing her lips strongly together, as if to secure the words from bursting from them which were already formed upon her tongue, she made a deep reverence, partly as it seemed in reproach, partly in respect, and left the room as suddenly as she had entered it.

The father looked disturbed at this incident, which he seemed sensible could not but fill Fairford's imagination with an additional throng of bewildering suspicions : he bit his lip, and muttered something to himself as he walked through the apartment ; then suddenly turned to his visitor with a smile of much sweetness, and a countenance in which every rougher expression was exchanged for those of courtesy and kindness.

" The visit we have just been honored with, my young friend, has given you," he said, " more secrets to keep than I would have wished you burdened with. The lady is a person of condition—of rank and fortune ; but, nevertheless, is so circumstanced that the mere fact of her being known to be in this country would occasion many evils. I should wish you to observe secrecy on this subject, even to Redgauntlet or Maxwell, however much I trust them in all that concerns my own affairs."

" I can have no occasion," replied Fairford, " for holding any discussion with these gentlemen, or with any others, on the circumstance which I have just witnessed ; it could only have become the subject of my conversation by mere accident, and I will now take care to avoid the subject entirely."

" You will do well, sir, and I thank you," said the father, throwing much dignity into the expression of obligation which he meant to convey. "The time may perhaps come when you will learn what it is to have obliged one of my condition. As to the lady, she has the highest merit, and nothing can be said of her justly which would not redound to her praise. Nevertheless—in short, sir, we wander at present as in a morning mist ; the sun will, I trust, soon rise and dispel it, when all that now seems mysterious will be fully revealed ; or it will sink into rain," he added, in a solemn tone, "and then explanation will be of little consequence. Adieu, sir ; I wish you well."

He made a graceful obeisance, and vanished through the same side-door by which the lady had entered ; and Alan thought he heard their voices high in dispute in the adjoining apartment.

Presently afterwards, Ambrose entered, and told him that a horse and guide waited him beneath the terrace.

"The good Father Buonaventure," added the butler, "has been graciously pleased to consider your situation, and desired me to inquire whether you have any occasion for a supply of money ? "

"Make my respects to his reverence," answered Fairford, "and assure him I am provided in that particular. I beg you also to make my acknowledgments to the Miss Arthurets, and assure that their kind hospitality, to which I probably owe my life, shall be remembered with gratitude as long as that life lasts. You yourself, Mr. Ambrose, must accept of my kindest thanks for your skill and attention."

Mid these acknowledgments they left the house, descended the terrace, and reached the spot where the gardener, Fairford's old acquaintance, waited for him, mounted upon one horse and leading another.

Bidding adieu to Ambrose, our young lawyer mounted, and rode down the avenue, often looking back to the melancholy and neglected dwelling in which he had witnessed such strange scenes, and musing upon the character of its mysterious inmates, especially the noble and almost regal seeming priest, and the beautiful but capricious dame, who, if she was really Father Buonaventure's penitent, seemed less docile to the authority of the church than, as Alan conceived, the Catholic discipline permitted. He could not indeed help being sensible that the whole deportment of these persons differed much from his preconceived notions of a priest and devotee. Father Buonaventure, in particular, had more natural dignity and less art and affectation in his manner than accorded with the idea which Calvinists were taught to entertain of that wily and formidable person, a Jesuitical missionary.

While reflecting on these things, he looked back so frequently at the house that Dick Gardener, a forward, talkative fellow, who began to tire of silence, at length said to him, "I think you will know Fairladies when you see it again, sir."

"I daresay I shall, Richard," answered Fairford, goodhumoredly. "I wish I knew as well where I am to go next. But you can tell me perhaps?"

"Your worship should know better than I," said Dick Gardener; "nevertheless, I have a notion you are going where all you Scotsmen should be sent, whether you will or no."

"Not to the devil, I hope, good Dick?" said Fairford.

"Why, no. That is a road which you may travel as heretics; but, as Scotsmen, I would only send you three-fourths of the way, and that is back to Scotland again—always craving your honor's pardon?"

"Does our journey lie that way?" said Fairford.

"As far as the water-side," said Richard. "I am to carry you to old Father Crackenthrop's, and then you are within a spit and a stride of Scotland, as the saying is. But mayhap you may think twice of going thither, for all that; for Old England is fat feeding-ground for north-country cattle."

CHAPTER XVII

NARRATIVE OF DARSIE LATIMER

OUR history must now, as the old romancers wont to say, "leave to tell" of the quest of Alan Fairford, and instruct our readers of the adventures which befell Darsie Latimer, left as he was in the precarious custody of his self-named tutor, the Laird of the Lochs of Solway, to whose arbitrary pleasure he found it necessary for the present to conform himself.

In consequence of this prudent resolution, and although he did not assume such a disguise without some sensations of shame and degradation, Darsie permitted Cristal Nixon to place over his face, and secure by a string, one of those silk masks which ladies frequently wore to preserve their complexions, when exposed to the air during long journeys on horseback. He remonstrated somewhat more vehemently against the long riding-skirt, which converted his person from the waist into the female guise, but was obliged to concede this point also.

The metamorphosis was then complete ; for the fair reader must be informed that in those rude times the ladies, when they honored the masculine dress by assuming any part of it, wore just such hats, coats, and waistcoats as the male animals themselves made use of, and had no notion of the elegant compromise betwixt male and female attire which has now acquired, *par excellence*, the name of a "habit." Trolloping things our mothers must have looked, with long, square-cut coats, lacking collars, and with waistcoats plentifully supplied with a length of pocket, which hung far downwards from the middle. But then they had some advantage from the splendid colors, lace, and gay embroidery which masculine attire then exhibited ; and, as happens in many similar instances, the finery of the materials made amends for the want of symmetry and grace of form in the garments themselves. But this is a digression.

In the court of the old mansion, half manor-place, half farm-house, or rather a decayed manor-house, converted into an abode for a Cumberland tenant, stood several saddled horses. Four or five of them were mounted by servants of inferior retainers, all of whom were well armed with sword, pistol, and carabine. But two had riding-furniture for the use of females—the one being accoutred with a side-saddle, the other with a pillion attached to the saddle.

Darsie's heart beat quicker within him ; he easily comprehended that one of these was intended for his own use, and his hopes suggested that the other was designed for that of the fair Green Mantle, whom, according to his established practise, he had adopted for the queen of his affections, although his opportunities of holding communication with her had not exceeded the length of a silent supper * on one occasion, and the going down a country dance on another. This, however, was no unwonted mood of passion with Darsie Latimer, upon whom Cupid was used to triumph only in the degree of a Mahratta conqueror, who overruns a province with the rapidity of lightning, but finds it impossible to retain it beyond a very brief space. Yet this new love was rather more serious than the scarce skinned-up wounds which his friend Fairford used to ridicule. The damsel had shown a sincere interest in his behalf ; and the air of mystery with which that interest was veiled gave her, to his lively imagination, the character of a benevolent and protecting spirit, as much as that of a beautiful female.

At former times, the romance attending his short-lived attachments had been of his own creating, and had disappeared [as] soon as ever he approached more closely to the object with which he had invested it. On the present occasion, it really flowed from external circumstances, which might have interested less susceptible feelings, and an imagination less lively, than that of Darsie Latimer, young, inexperienced, and enthusiastic as he was.

He watched, therefore, anxiously to whose service the palfrey bearing the lady's saddle was destined. But ere any female appeared to occupy it, he was himself summoned to take his seat on the pillion behind Cristal Nixon, amid the grins of his old acquaintance Jan, who helped him to horse, and the unrestrained laughter of Cicely (Dorcas), who displayed on the occasion a case of teeth which might have rivalled ivory.

Latimer was at an age when being an object of general ridicule, even to clowns and milkmaids, was not a matter of indifference, and he longed heartily to have laid his horsewhip across Jan's shoulders. That, however, was a solace-

* [Read 'short grace." *Compare* p. 33.]

ment of his feelings which was not at the moment to be thought of; and Cristal Nixon presently put an end to his unpleasant situation by ordering the riders to go on. He himself kept the center of the troop, two men riding before and two behind him, always, as it seemed to Darsie, having their eye upon him, to prevent any attempt to escape. He could see from time to time, when the straight line of the road or the advantage of an ascent permitted him, that another troop of three or four riders followed them at about a quarter of a mile's distance, amongst whom he could discover the tall form of Redgauntlet, and the powerful action of his gallant black horse. He had little doubt that Green Mantle made one of the party, though he was unable to distinguish her from the others.

In this manner they traveled from six in the morning until nearly ten of the clock, without Darsie's exchanging a word with any one; for he loathed the very idea of entering into conversation with Cristal Nixon, against whom he seemed to feel an instinctive aversion; nor was that domestic's saturnine and sullen disposition such as to have encouraged advances, had he thought of making them.

At length the party halted for the purpose of refreshment; but as they had hitherto avoided all villages and inhabited places upon their route, so they now stopped at one of those large, ruinous Dutch barns which are sometimes found in the fields, at a distance from the farm-houses to which they belong. Yet in this desolate place some preparations had been made for their reception. There were in the end of the barn racks filled with provender for the horses, and plenty of provisions for the party were drawn from the trusses of straw, under which the baskets that contained them had been deposited. The choicest of these were selected and arranged apart by Cristal Nixon, while the men of the party threw themselves upon the rest, which he abandoned to their discretion. In a few minutes afterwards the rearward party arrived and dismounted, and Redgauntlet himself entered the barn with the green-mantled maiden by his side. He presented her to Darsie with these words:

"It is time you two should know each other better. I promised you my confidence, Darsie, and the time is come for reposing it. But first we will have our breakfast; and then, when once more in the saddle, I will tell you that which it is necessary that you should know. Salute Lilias, Darsie."

The command was sudden, and surprised Latimer, whose confusion was increased by the perfect ease and frankness

with which Lilias offered at once her cheek and her hand,
and pressing his, as she rather took it than gave her own,
said very frankly, " Dearest Darsie, how rejoiced I am that
our uncle has at last permitted us to become acquainted!"
Darsie's head turned round ; and it was perhaps well that
Redgauntlet called on him to sit down, as even that movement served to hide his confusion. There is an old song
which says—

> When ladies are willing.
> A man can but look like a fool.

And on the same principle Darsie Latimer's looks at this
unexpected frankness of reception would have formed an
admirable vignette for illustrating the passage. " Dearest
Darsie," and such a ready, nay, eager salute of lip and hand !
It was all very gracious, no doubt, and ought to have been
received with much gratitude ; but, constituted as our
friend's temper was, nothing could be more inconsistent with
his tone of feeling. If a hermit had proposed to him to club
for a pot of beer, the illusion of his reverend sanctity could
not have been dispelled more effectually than the divine
qualities of Green Mantle faded upon the ill-imagined frank-
heartedness of poor Lilias. Vexed with her forwardness,
and affronted at having once more cheated himself, Darsie
could hardly help muttering two lines of the song we have
already quoted :—

> "The fruit that must fall without shaking
> Is rather too mellow for me."

And yet it was pity of her too : she was a very pretty young
woman, his fancy had scarce overrated her in that respect ;
and the slight derangement of the beautiful brown locks
which escaped in natural ringlets from under her riding hat,
with the bloom which exercise had brought into her cheek,
made her even more than usually fascinating. Redgauntlet
modified the sternness of his look when it was turned towards
her, and, in addressing her, used a softer tone than his usual
deep bass. Even the grim features of Cristal Nixon relaxed
when he attended on her, and it was then, if ever, that his
misanthropical visage expressed some sympathy with the rest
of humanity.

" How can she," thought Latimer, " look so like an angel,
yet be so mere a mortal after all ? How could so much
seeming modesty have so much forwardness of manner, when
she ought to have been most reserved ? How can her con-

duct be reconciled to the grace and ease of her general deportment ? "

The confusion of thoughts which occupied Darsie's imagination gave to his looks a disordered appearance, and his inattention to the food which was placed before him, together with his silence and absence of mind, induced Lilias solicitously to inquire whether he did not feel some return of the disorder under which he had suffered so lately. This led Mr. Redgauntlet, who seemed also lost in his own contemplations, to raise his eyes and join in the same inquiry with some appearance of interest. Latimer explained to both that he was perfectly well.

"It is well it is so," answered Redgauntlet ; "for we have that before us which will brook, no delay from indisposition : we have not, as Hotspur says, leisure to be sick."

Lilias, on her part, endeavored to prevail upon Darsie to partake of the food which she offered him, with a kindly and affectionate courtesy corresponding to the warmth of the interest she had displayed at their meeting, but so very natural, innocent, and pure in its character, that it would have been impossible for the vainest coxcomb to have mistaken it for coquetry, or a desire of captivating a prize so valuable as his affections. Darsie, with no more than the reasonable share of self-opinion common to most youths when they approach twenty-one, knew not how to explain her conduct. Sometimes he was tempted to think that his own merits had, even during the short intervals when they had seen each other, secured such a hold of the affections of a young person who had probably been bred up in ignorance of the world and its forms that she was unable to conceal her partiality. Sometimes he suspected that she acted by her guardian's order, who, aware that he, Darsie, was entitled to a considerable fortune, might have taken this bold stroke to bring about a marriage betwixt him and so near a relative

But neither of these suppositions was applicable to the character of the parties. Miss Lilias's manners, however soft and natural, displayed in their ease and versatility considerable acquaintance with the habits of the world, and in the few words she said during the morning repast there were mingled a shrewdness and good sense which could scarce belong to a miss capable of playing the silly part of a love-smitten maiden so broadly. As for Redgauntlet, with his stately bearing, his fatal frown, his eye of threat and of command, it was impossible, Darsie thought, to suspect him

of a scheme having private advantage for its object : he could
as soon have imagined Cassius picking Cæsar's pocket, instead of drawing his poniard on the dictator.

While he thus mused, unable either to eat, drink, or answer to the courtesy of Lilias, she soon ceased to speak to
him, and sat silent as himself.

They had remained nearly an hour in their halting-place,
when Redgauntlet said aloud, " Look out, Cristal Nixon.
If we hear nothing from Fairladies, we must continue our
journey."

Cristal went to the door, and presently returned and said
to his master, in a voice as harsh as his features, " Gilbert
Gregson is coming, his horse as white with foam as if a fiend
had ridden him."

Redgauntlet threw from him the plate on which he had
been eating, and hastened towards the door of the barn,
which the courier at that moment entered—a smart jockey
with a black velvet hunting-cap, and a broad belt drawn
tight round his waist, to which was secured his express-bag.
The variety of mud with which he was splashed from cap to
spur showed he had had a rough and rapid ride.   He delivered a letter to Mr. Redgauntlet, with an obeisance, and
then retired to the end of the barn, where the other attendants were sitting or lying upon the straw, in order to get
some refreshment.

Redgauntlet broke the letter open with haste, and read it
with anxious and discomposed looks.   On a second perusal,
his displeasure seemed to increase, his brow darkened, and
was distinctly marked with the fatal sign peculiar to his
family and house.   Darsie had never before observed his
frown bear such a close resemblance to the shape which
tradition assigned it.

Redgauntlet held out the open letter with one hand, and
struck it with the forefinger of the other, as, in a suppressed
and displeased tone, he said to Cristal Nixon, " Counter-
manded—ordered northward once more! Northward, when all
our hopes lie to the south—a second Derby direction, when we
turned our back on glory, and marched in quest of ruin ! "

Cristal Nixon took the letter and ran it over, then returned it to his master with the cold observation, "A female
influence predominates."

" But it shall predominate no longer," said Redgauntlet :
" it shall wane as ours rises in the horizon.   Meanwhile, I
will on before ; and you, Cristal, will bring the party to the
place assigned in the letter.   You may now permit the

young persons to have unreserved communication together ; only mark that you watch the young man closely enough to prevent his escape, if he should be idiot enough to attempt it, but not approaching so close as to watch their free conversation."

" I care nought about their conversation," said Nixon, surlily.

" You hear my commands, Lilias," said the Laird, turning to the young lady. " You may use my permission and authority to explain so much of our family matters as you yourself know. At our next meeting I will complete the task of disclosure, and I trust I shall restore one Redgauntlet more to the bosom of our ancient family. Let Latimer, as he calls himself, have a horse to himself ; he must for some time retain his disguise. My horse—my horse ! "

In two minutes they heard him ride off from the door of the barn, followed at speed by two of the armed men of his party.

The commands of Cristal Nixon, in the meanwhile, put all the remainder of the party in motion, but the Laird himself was long out of sight ere they were in readiness to resume their journey. When at length they set out, Darsie was accommodated with a horse and side-saddle, instead of being obliged to resume his place on the pillion behind the detestable Nixon. He was obliged, however, to retain his riding-skirt, and to reassume his mask. Yet, notwithstanding this disagreeable circumstance, and although he observed that they gave him the heaviest and slowest horse of the party, and that, as a farther precaution against escape, he was closely watched on every side, yet riding in company with the pretty Lilias was an advantage which overbalanced these inconveniences.

It is true, that this society, to which that very morning he would have looked forward as a glimpse of heaven, had, now that it was thus unexpectedly indulged, something much less rapturous than he had expected.

It was in vain that, in order to avail himself of a situation so favorable for indulging his romantic disposition, he endeavored to coax back, if I may so express myself, that delightful dream of ardent and tender passion ; he felt only such a confusion of ideas at the difference between the being whom he had imagined and her with whom he was now in contact, that it seemed to him like the effect of witchcraft. What most surprised him was, that this sudden flame should have died away so rapidly, notwithstanding that the maiden's personal beauty was even greater than he had expected, her demeanor, unless it should be deemed over kind towards himself, as graceful and becoming as he could have fancied it, even in his gayest dreams. It were judging hardly of him to suppose, that the mere belief of his having attracted her affections more easily than he expected was the cause of his ungratefully undervaluing a prize too lightly won, or that his transient passion played around his heart with the flitting radiance of a wintry sunbeam flashing against an icicle, which may brighten it for a moment, but cannot melt it. Neither of these was precisely the case, though such fickleness of disposition might also have some influence in the change.

The truth is, perhaps, that the lover's pleasure, like that of the hunter, is in the chase ; and that the brightest beauty loses half its merit, as the fairest flower its perfume, when the willing hand can reach it too easily. There must be doubt, there must be danger, there must be difficulty ; and if, as the poet says, the course of ardent affection never does run smooth, it is perhaps because, without some intervening obstacle, that which is called the romantic passion of love, in its high poetical character and coloring, can hardly have an existence, any more than there can be a current in a river without the stream being narrowed by steep banks or checked by opposing rocks.

Let not those, however, who enter into a union for life without those embarrassments which delight a Darsie Latimer or a Lydia Languish, and which are perhaps necessary to excite an enthusiastic passion in breasts more firm than theirs, augur worse of their future happiness because their own alliance is formed under calmer auspices. Mutual esteem, an intimate knowledge of each other's character, seen, as in their case, undisguised by the mists of too partial passion, a suitable proportion of parties in rank and fortune, in taste and pursuits, are more frequently found in a marriage of reason than in a union of romantic attachment, where the imagination, which probably created the virtues and accomplishments with which it invested the beloved object, is frequently afterwards employed in magnifying the mortifying consequences of it own delusion, and exasperating all the stings of disappointment. Those who follow the banners of reason are like the well-disciplined battalion which, wearing a more sober uniform, and making a less dazzling show, than the light troops commanded by imagination, enjoy more safety, and even more honor, in the con-

flicts of human life. All this, however, is foreign to our
present purpose.

Uncertain in what manner to address her whom he had
been lately so anxious to meet with, and embarrassed by a
tête-à tête to which his own timid inexperience gave some
awkwardness, the party had proceeded more than a hundred
yards before Darsie assumed courage to accost, or even to
look at, his companion. Sensible, however, of the impropriety of his silence, he turned to speak to her ; and observing that, although she wore her mask, there was something
like disappointment and dejection in her manner, he was
moved by self-reproach for his own coldness, and hastened
to address her in the kindest tone he could assume.

" You must think me cruelly deficient in gratitude, Miss
Lilias, that I have been thus long in your company without
thanking you for the interest which you have deigned to
take in my unfortunate affairs ? "

" I am glad you have at length spoken," she said, " though
I own it is more coldly than I expected. *Miss* Lilias !
Deign to take interest ! In whom, dear Darsie, *can* I take
interest but in you ? and why do you put this barrier of
ceremony betwixt us, whom adverse circumstances have
already separated for such a length of time ? "

Darsie was again confounded at the extra candor, if we
may use the term, of this frank avowal. " One must love
partridge very well," thought he, " to accept it when thrown
in one's face : if this is not plain speaking, there is no such
place as downright Dunstable in being ! "

Embarrassed with these reflections, and himself of a
nature fancifully, almost fastidiously, delicate, he could only
in reply stammer forth an acknowledgment of his companion's goodness, and his own gratitude. She answered in a
tone partly sorrowful and partly, impatient, repeating, with
displeased emphasis, the only distinct words he had been
able to bring forth—" Goodness—gratitude ! O Darsie,
should these be the phrases between you and me ? Alas ! I
am too sure you are displeased with me, though I cannot
even guess on what account. Perhaps you think I have
been too free in venturing upon my visit to your friend.
But then remember it was in your behalf, and that I knew no
better way to put you on your guard against the misfortunes
and restraint which you have been subjected to, and are still
enduring."

" Dear lady——" said Darsie, rallying his recollection,
and suspicious of some error in apprehension—a suspicion

32

which his mode of address seemed at once to communicate to Lilias, for she interrupted him—

"*Lady!* dear *lady!* For whom or for what, in Heaven's name, do you take me, that you address me so formally ?"

Had the question been asked in that enchanted hall in Fairyland where all interrogations must be answered with absolute sincerity, Darsie had certainly replied that he took her for the most frank-hearted and ultra-liberal lass that had ever lived since Mother Eve eat the pippin without paring. But as he was still on middle-earth, and free to avail himself of a little polite deceit, he barely answered, that he believed he had the honor of speaking to the niece of Mr. Redgauntlet.

"Surely," she replied ; "but were it not as easy for you to have said, to your own only sister ?"

. Darsie started in his saddle as if he had received a pistol-shot.

"My sister !" he exclaimed.

"And you did *not* know it, then ?"said she. "I thought your reception of me was cold and indifferent !"

A kind and cordial embrace took place betwixt the relatives ; and so light was Darsie's spirit, that he really felt himself more relieved by getting quit of the embarrassments of the last half hour, during which he conceived himself in danger of being persecuted by the attachment of a forward girl, than disappointed by the vanishing of so many day-dreams as he had been in the habit of encouraging during the time when the green-mantled maiden was goddess of his idolatry. He had been already flung from his romantic Pegasus, and was too happy at length to find himself with bones unbroken, though with his back on the ground. He was, besides, with all his whims and follies, a generous, kind-hearted youth, and was delighted to acknowledge so beautiful and amiable a relative, and to assure her in the warmest terms of his immediate affection and future protection, so soon as they should be extricated from their present situation. Smiles and tears mingled on Lilias's cheeks, like showers and sunshine in April weather.

"Out on me," she said, "that I should be so childish as to cry at what makes me so sincerely happy ! since, God knows, family love is what my heart has most longed after, and to which it has been most a stranger. My uncle says that you and I, Darsie, are but half Redgauntlets, and that the metal of which our father's family was made has been softened to effeminacy in our mother's offspring."

" Alas !" said Darsie, " I know so little of our family story that I almost doubted that I belonged to the house of Redgauntlet, although the chief of the family himself intimated so much to me."

"The chief of the family ? " said Lilias. " You must know little of your own descent indeed, if you mean my uncle by that expression. You yourself, my dear Darsie, are the heir and representative of our ancient house, for our father was the elder brother—that brave and unhappy Sir Henry Darsie Redgauntlet who suffered at Carlisle in the year 1746. He took the name of Darsie, in conjunction with his own, from our mother, heiress to a Cumberland family of great wealth and antiquity, of whose large estates you are the undeniable heir, although those of your father have been involved in the general doom of forfeiture. But all this must be necessarily unknown to you."

" Indeed, I hear it for the first time in my life," answered Darsie.

" And you knew not that I was your sister ? " said Lilias. " No wonder you received me so coldly. What a strange, wild, forward young person you must have thought me— mixing myself in the fortunes of a stranger whom I had only once spoken to—corresponding with him by signs. Good Heaven ! what can you have supposed me ? "

" And how should I have come to the knowledge of our connection ? " said Darsie. " You are aware I was not acquainted with it when we danced together at Brokenburn."

" I saw that with concern, and fain I would have warned you," answered Lilias ; " but I was closely watched, and before I could find or make an opportunity of coming to a full explanation with you on a subject so agitating, I was forced to leave the room. What I did say was, you may remember, a caution to leave the southern border, for I foresaw what has since happened. But since my uncle has had you in his power, I never doubted he had communicated to you our whole family history."

" He has left me to learn it from you, Lilias ; and assure yourself that I will hear it with more pleasure from your lips than from his. I have no reason to be pleased with his conduct towards me."

" Of that," said Lilias, " you will judge better when you have heard what I have to tell you ; and she began her communication in the following manner.

CHAPTER XVIII

"THE house of Redgauntlet," said the young lady, "has for centuries been supposed to lie under a doom, which has rendered vain their courage, their talents, their ambition, and their wisdom. Often making a figure in history, they have been ever in the situation of men striving against both wind and tide, who distinguish themselves by their desperate exertions of strength, and their persevering endurance of toil, but without being able to advance themselves upon their course, by either vigor or resolution. They pretend to trace this fatality to a legendary history, which I may tell you at a less busy moment."

Darsie intimated that he had already heard the tragic story of Sir Alberick Redgauntlet.

"I need only say, then," proceeded Lilias, "that our father and uncle felt the family doom in its full extent. They were both possessed of considerable property, which was largely increased by our father's marriage, and were both devoted to the service of the unhappy house of Stuart; but, as our mother at least supposed, family considerations might have withheld her husband from joining openly in the affair of 1745, had not the high influence which the younger brother possessed over the elder, from his more decided energy of character, hurried him along with himself into that undertaking.

"When, therefore, the enterprise came to the fatal conclusion which bereaved our father of his life and consigned his brother to exile, Lady Redgauntlet fled from the north of England, determined to break off all communication with her late husband's family, particularly his brother, whom she regarded as having, by their insane political enthusiasm, been the means of his untimely death, and determined that you, my brother, an infant, and that I, to whom she had just given birth, should be brought up as adherents of the present dynasty. Perhaps she was too hasty in this determination—too timidly anxious to exclude, if possible, from the knowledge of the very spot where we existed a relation

340

so nearly connected with us as our father's only brother.
But you must make allowance for what she had suffered.
See, brother," she said, pulling her glove off, " these five
blood-specks on my arm are a mark by which mysterious
nature has impressed on an unborn infant a record of its
father's violent death and its mother's miseries." *

"You were not, then, born when my father suffered ?"
said Darsie.

" Alas, no ! " she replied ; " nor were you a twelvemonth
old. It was no wonder that my mother, after going through
such scenes of agony, became irresistibly anxious for the
sake of her children—of her son in particular ; the more
especially as the late Sir Henry, her husband, had, by a
settlement of his affairs, confided the custody of the persons
of her children, as well as the estates which descended to
them, independently of those which fell under his forfeiture,
to his brother Hugh, in whom he placed unlimited confidence."

" But my mother had no reason to fear the operation of
such a deed, conceived in favor of an attainted man," said
Darsie.

" True," replied Lilias ; " but our uncle's attainder might
have been reversed, like that of so many other persons, and
our mother, who both feared and hated him, lived in continual terror that this would be the case, and that she should
see the author, as she thought him, of her husband's death
come armed with legal powers, and in a capacity to use
them, for the purpose of tearing her children from her protection. Besides, she feared, even in his incapacitated
condition, the adventurous and pertinacious spirit of her
brother-in-law, Hugh Redgauntlet, and felt assured that he
would make some attempt to possess himself of the persons
of the children. On the other hand, our uncle, whose proud
disposition might, perhaps, have been soothed by the offer
of her confidence, revolted against the distrustful and sus·
picious manner in which Lady Darsie Redgauntlet acted
towards him. She basely abused, he said, the unhappy
circumstances in which he was placed, in order to deprive
him of his natural privilege of protecting and educating the
infants whom nature and law, and the will of their father,
had committed to his charge, and he swore solemnly he
would not submit to such an injury. Report of his threats
was made to Lady Redgauntlet, and tended to increase those
fears, which proved but too well founded. While you and

* See Prenatal Marks. Note 36.

I, children at that time of two or three years old, were playing together in a walled orchard adjacent to our mother's
residence, which she had fixed somewhere in Devonshire,
my uncle suddenly scaled the wall with several men, and I
was snatched up and carried off to a boat which waited for
them. My mother, however, flew to your rescue, and as
she seized on and held you fast, my uncle could not, as he
has since told me, possess himself of your person without
using unmanly violence to his brother's widow. Of this he
was incapable; and, as people began to assemble upon my
mother's screaming, he withdrew, after darting upon you
and her one of those fearful looks which, it is said, remain
with our family as a fatal bequest of Sir Alberick, our
ancestor."

"I have some recollection of the scuffle which you mention," said Darsie; "and I think it was my uncle himself,
since my uncle he is, who recalled the circumstance to my
mind on a late occasion. I can now account for the guarded
seclusion under which my poor mother lived, for her frequent
tears, her starts of hysterical alarm, and her constant and
deep melancholy. Poor lady! what a lot was hers, and what
must have been her feelings when it approached to a close!"

"It was then that she adopted," said Lilias, "every precaution her ingenuity could suggest to keep your very existence concealed from the person whom she feared—nay,
from yourself; for she dreaded, as she is said often to have
expressed herself, that the wildfire blood of Redgauntlet
would urge you to unite your fortunes to those of your uncle,
who was well known still to carry on political intrigues,
which most other persons had considered as desperate. It
was also possible that he, as well as others, might get his
pardon, as government showed every year more lenity towards the remnant of the Jacobites, and then he might
claim the custody of your person as your legal guardian.
Either of these events she considered as the direct road to
your destruction."

"I wonder she had not claimed the protection of Chan-
cery for me," said Darsie: "or confided me to the care of
some powerful friend."

"She was on indifferent terms with her relations on account of her marriage with our father," said Lilias, "and
trusted more to secreting you from your uncle's attempts
than to any protection which law might afford against them.
Perhaps she judged unwisely, but surely not unnaturally,
for one rendered irritable by so many misfortunes and so

many alarms. Samuel Griffiths, an eminent banker, and a worthy clergyman now dead were, I believe, the only persons whom she entrusted with the execution of her last will ; and my uncle believes that she made them both swear to observe profound secrecy concerning your birth and pretensions until you should come to the age of majority, and, in the mean time, to breed you up in the most private way possible, and that which was most likely to withdraw you from my uncle's observation."

"And I have no doubt," said Darsie, " that, betwixt change of name and habitation, they might have succeeded perfectly, but for the accident—lucky or unlucky, I know not which to term it—which brought me to Brokenburn, and into contact with Mr. Redgauntlet. I see also why I was warned against England, for in England——"

" In England alone, if I understand rightly," said Miss Redgauntlet, " the claims of your uncle to the custody of your person could have been enforced, in case of his being replaced in the ordinary rights of citizenship, either by the lenity of the government or by some change in it. In Scotland, where you possess no property, I understand his authority might have been resisted, and measures taken to put you under the protection of the law. But, pray, think it not unlucky that you have taken the step of visiting Brokenburn ; I feel confident that the consequences must be ultimately fortunate, for, have they not already brought us into contact with each other ? "

So saying, she held out her hand to her brother, who grasped it with a fondness of pressure very different from the manner in which they first clasped hands that morning. There was a moment's pause, while the hearts of both were overflowing with a feeling of natural affection, to which circumstances had hitherto rendered them strangers.

At length Darsie broke silence. " I am ashamed," he said, " my dearest Lilias, that I have suffered you to talk so long about matters concerning myself only, while I remain ignorant of your story and your present situation."

" The former is none of the most interesting, nor the latter the most safe or agreeable," answered Lilias ; " but now, my dearest brother, I shall have the inestimable support of your countenance and affection ; and were I but sure that we could weather the formidable crisis which I find so close at hand, I should have little apprehensions for the future."

" Let me know," said Darsie, " what our present situation

is ; and rely upon my utmost exertions both in your defense and my own. For what reason can my uncle desire to detain me a prisoner ? If in mere opposition to the will of my mother, she has long been no more ; and I see not why he should wish, at so much trouble and risk, to interfere with the free-will of one to whom a few months will give a privilege of acting for himself with which he will have no longer any pretense to interfere."

" My dearest Arthur," answered Lilias—" for that name, as well as Darsie, properly belongs to you—it is the leading feature in my uncle's character that he has applied every energy of his powerful mind to the service of the exiled family of Stuart. The death of his brother, the dilapidation of his own fortunes, have only added to his hereditary zeal for the house of Stuart a deep and almost personal hatred against the present reigning family. He is, in short, a political enthusiast of the most dangerous character, and proceeds in his agency with as much confidence as if he felt himself the very Atlas who is alone capable of supporting a sinking cause."

"And where or how did you, my Lilias, educated doubtless, under his auspices, learn to have a different view of such subjects ?"

" By a singular chance," replied Lilias, " in the nunnery where my uncle placed me. Although the abbess was a person exactly after his own heart, my education as a pensioner devolved much on an excellent old mother who had adopted the tenets of the Jansenists, with perhaps a still further tendency towards the Reformed doctrines than those of Porte Royale. The mysterious secrecy with which she inculcated these tenets gave them charms to my young mind, and I embraced them the rather that they were in direct opposition to the doctrines of the abbess, whom I hated so much for her severity that I felt a childish delight in setting her control at defiance, and contradicting in my secret soul all that I was openly obliged to listen to with reverence. Freedom of religious opinion brings on, I suppose, freedom of political creed ; for I had no sooner renounced the Pope's infallibility than I began to question the doctrine of hereditary and indefeasible right. In short, strange as it may seem, I came out of a Parisian convent not indeed an instructed Whig and Protestant, but with as much inclination to be so as if I had been bred up, like you, within the Presbyterian sounds of St. Giles's chimes."

" More so, perhaps," replied Darsie, " for the nearer the

church——— The proverb is somewhat musty. But how did these liberal opinions of yours agree with the very opposite prejudices of my uncle ? "

" They would have agreed like fire and water," answered Lilias, " had I suffered mine to become visible ; but as that would have subjected me to constant reproach and upbraiding, or worse, I took great care to keep my own secret ; so that occasional censures for coldness and lack of zeal for the good cause were the worst I had to undergo, and these were bad enough."

" I applaud your caution," said Darsie.

" You have reason," replied his sister ; " but I got so terrible a specimen of my uncle's determination of character, before I had been acquainted with him for much more than a week, that it taught me at what risk I should contradict his humor. I will tell you the circumstances ; for it will better teach you to appreciate the romantic and resolved nature of his character than anything which I could state of his rashness and enthusiasm.

" After I had been many a long year at the convent, I was removed from thence, and placed with a meager old Scottish lady of high rank, the daughter of an unfortunate person whose head had in the year 1715 been placed on Temple Bar. She subsisted on a small pension from the French court, aided by an occasional gratuity from the Stuarts ; to which the annuity paid for my board formed a desirable addition. She was not ill-tempered, nor very covetous—neither beat me nor starved me ; but she was so completely trammeled by rank and prejudices, so awfully profound in genealogy, and so bitterly keen, poor lady, in British politics, that I sometimes thought it pity that the Hanoverians, who murdered, as she used to tell me, her poor dear father, had left his dear daughter in the land of the living. Delighted, therefore, was I when my uncle made his appearance, and abruptly announced his purpose of conveying me to England. My extravagant joy at the idea of leaving Lady Rachel Rougedragon was somewhat qualified by observing the melancholy look, lofty demeanor, and commanding tone of my near relative. He held more communication with me on the journey, however, than consisted with his taciturn demeanor in general, and seemed anxious to ascertain my tone of character, and particularly in point of courage. Now, though I am a tamed Redgauntlet, yet I have still so much of our family spirit as enables me to be as composed in danger as most of my sex ; and upon two occasions in the course of our journey—a threatened attack by banditti and the overturn of our carriage—I had the fortune so to conduct myself as to convey to my uncle a very favorable idea of my intrepidity. Probably this encouraged him to put into execution the singular scheme which he had in agitation.

"Ere we reached London we changed our means of conveyance, and altered the route by which we approached the city more than once ; then, like a hare which doubles repeatedly at some distance from the seat she means to occupy, and at last leaps into her form from a distance as great as she can clear by a spring, we made a forced march, and landed in private and obscure lodgings in a little old street in Westminster, not far distant from the cloisters.

"On the morning of the day on which we arrived my uncle went abroad, and did not return for some hours. Meantime I had no other amusement than to listen to the tumult of noises which succeeded each other, or reigned in confusion together, during the whole morning. Paris I had thought the most noisy capital in the world, but Paris seemed midnight silence compared to London. Cannon thundered near· and at a distance ; drums, trumpets, and military music of every kind rolled, flourished, and pierced the clouds, almost without intermission. To fill up the concert, bells pealed incessantly from a hundred steeples. The acclamations of an immense multitude were heard from time to time, like the roaring of a mighty ocean, and all this without my being able to glean the least idea of what was going on, for the windows of our apartment looked upon a waste back-yard, which seemed totally deserted. My curiosity became extreme, for I was satisfied, at length, that it must be some festival of the highest order which called forth these incessant sounds.

"My uncle at length returned, and with him a man of an exterior singularly unprepossessing, I need not describe him to you, for—do not look round—he rides behind us at this moment."

"That respectable person, Mr. Cristal Nixon, I suppose ?" said Darsie.

"The same," answered Lilias ; "make no gesture that may intimate we are speaking of him."

Darsie signified that he understood her, and she pursued her relation.

"They were both in full dress, and my uncle, taking a bundle from Nixon, said to me, ' Lilias, I am come to carry you to see a grand ceremony ; put on as hastily as you can

the dress you will find in that parcel, and prepare to attend
me.' I found a female dress, splendid and elegant, but
somewhat bordering upon the antique fashion. It might be
that of England, I thought, and I went to my apartment full
of curiosity, and dressed myself with all speed.

" My uncle surveyed me with attention. " ' She may pass
for one of the flower girls,' " he said to Nixon, who only answered with a nod.

" We left the house together, and such was their knowledge of the lanes, courts, and bye-paths that, though there
was the roar of the multitude in the broad streets, those
which we traversed were silent and deserted ; and the stroll-
ers whom we met, tired of gazing upon gayer figures, scarcely
honored us with a passing look, although at any other time
we should, among these vulgar suburbs, have attracted a
troublesome share of observation. We crossed at length
a broad street, where many soldiers were on guard, while
others, exhausted with previous duty, were eating, drinking,
smoking, and sleeping beside their piled arms.

" ' One day, Nixon,' whispered my uncle, ' we will make
these redcoated gentry stand to their muskets more watch-
fully.'

" ' Or it will be the worse for them,' answered his attendant, in a voice as unpleasant as his physiognomy.

" Unquestioned and unchallenged by any one, we crossed
among the guards, and Nixon tapped thrice at a small postern door in a huge ancient building which was straight
before us. It opened, and we entered without my perceiving
by whom we were admitted. A few dark and narrow passages at length conveyed us into an immense Gothic hall, the
magnificence of which baffles my powers of description.

" It was illuminated by ten thousand wax lights, whose
splendor at first dazzled my eyes, coming as we did from
these dark and secret avenues. But when my sight began
to become steady, how shall I describe what I beheld !
Beneath were huge ranges of tables, occupied by princes and
nobles in their robes of state ; high officers of the crown,
wearing their dresses and badges of authority ; reverend
prelates and judges, the sages of the church and law, in their
more somber, yet not less awful robes, with others whose
antique and striking costume announced their importance,
though I could not even guess who they might be. But at
length the truth burst on me at once ; it was, and the murmurs around confirmed it, the coronation feast. At a table
above the rest, and extending across the upper end of the

hall, sat enthroned the youthful sovereign himself, surrounded by the princes of the blood and other dignitaries, and receiving the suit and homage of his subjects. Heralds and pursuivants, blazing in their fantastic yet splendid armorial habits, and pages of honor, gorgeously arrayed in the garb of other days, waited upon the princely banqueters. In the galleries with which this spacious hall was surrounded shone all, and more than all, that my poor imagination could conceive of what was brilliant in riches or captivating in beauty. Countless rows of ladies, whose diamonds, jewels, and splendid attire were their least powerful charms, looked down from their lofty seats on the rich scene beneath, themselves forming a show as dazzling and as beautiful as that of which they were spectators. Under these galleries and behind the banqueting tables, were a multitude of gentlemen, dressed as if to attend a court, but whose garb, although rich enough to have adorned a royal drawing-room, could not distinguish them in such a high scene as this. Amongst these we wandered for a few minutes, undistinguished and unregarded. I saw several young persons dressed as I was, so was under no embarrassment from the singularity of my habit, and only rejoiced, as I hung on my uncle's arm, at the magical splendor of such a scene, and at his goodness for procuring me the pleasure of beholding it.'

" By and by, I perceived that my uncle had acquaintances among those who were under the galleries, and seemed, like ourselves, to be mere spectators of the solemnity. They recognized each other with a single word, sometimes only with a grip of the hand—exchanged some private signs, doubtless —and gradually formed a little group, in the center of which we were placed.

" ' Is it not a grand sight, Lilias ? ' said my uncle. ' All the noble, and all the wise, and all the wealthy of Britain are there assembled.

" ' It is indeed,' said I, ' all that my mind could have fancied of regal power and splendor.'

" ' Girl,' he whispered—and my uncle can make his whispers as terribly emphatic as his thundering voice or his blighting look—' all that is noble and worthy in this fair land are there assembled, but it is to bend like slaves and sycophants before the throne of a new usurper.'

" I looked at him, and the dark hereditary frown of our unhappy ancestor was black upon his brow. ·

" ' For God's sake,' I whispered, ' consider where we are.'

" 'Fear nothing,' he said : ' we are surrounded by friends.' As he proceeded, his strong and muscular frame shook with suppressed agitation. 'See,' he said, ' yonder bends Norfolk, renegade to his Catholic faith ; there stoops the Bishop of ——, traitor to the Church of England ; and— shame of shames ! yonder the gigantic form of Errol bows his head before the grandson of his father's murderer ! But a sign shall be seen this night amongst them : *"Mene, Mene, Tekel, Upharsin"* shall be read on these walls as distinctly as the spectral handwriting made them visible on those of Belshazzar !'

" ' For God's sake,' said I, dreadfully alarmed, ' it is impossible you can meditate violence in such a presence !'

" ' None is intended, fool,' he answered, ' nor can the slightest mischance happen, provided you will rally your boasted courage and obey my directions. But do it coolly and quickly, for there are an hundred lives at stake.'

" ' Alas ! what can I do ?' I asked in the utmost terror.

" ' Only be prompt to execute my bidding,' said he ; ' it is but to lift a glove. Here, hold this in your hand—throw the train of your dress over it—be firm, composed, and ready—or, at all events, I step forward myself.'

" ' If there is no violence designed,' I said, taking, mechanically, the iron glove he put into my hand.

" I could not conceive his meaning ; but, in the excited state of mind in which I beheld him, I was convinced that disobedience on my part would lead to some wild explosion. I felt, from the emergency of the occasion, a sudden presence of mind, and resolved to do anything that might avert violence and bloodshed. I was not long held in suspense. A loud flourish of trumpets, and the voice of heralds, were mixed with the clatter of horse's hoofs, while a champion armed at all points, like those I had read of in romances, attended by squires, pages, and the whole retinue of chivalry, pranced forward, mounted upon a barbed steed. His challenge, in defiance of all who dared impeach the title of the new sovereign, was recited aloud—once and again.

" ' Rush in at the third sounding,' said my uncle to me ; ' bring me the parader's gage, and leave mine in lieu of it.'

" I could not see how this was to be done, as we were surrounded by people on all sides. But, at the third sounding of the trumpets, a lane opened, as if by word of command, betwixt me and the champion, and my uncle's voice said, ' Now, Lilias, now !'

" With a swift and yet steady step, and with a presence of

mind for which I have never since been able to account, I discharged the perilous commission. I was hardly seen, I believe, as I exchanged the pledges of battle, and in an instant retired. 'Nobly done, my girl!' said my uncle, at whose side I found myself, shrouded as I was before, by the interposition of the bystanders. 'Cover our retreat, gentlemen,' he whispered to those around him.

"Room was made for us to approach the wall, which seemed to open, and we were again involved in the dark passages through which we had formerly passed. In a small ante-room, my uncle stopped, and hastily muffling me in a mantle which was lying there, we passed the guards, threaded the labyrinth of empty streets and courts, and reached our retired lodgings without attracting the least attention."

"I have often heard," said Darsie, "that a female, supposed to be a man in disguise—and yet, Lilias, you do not look very masculine—had taken up the champion's gauntlet at the present king's coronation, and left in its place a gage of battle, with a paper, offering to accept the combat, provided a fair field should be allowed for it. I have hitherto considered it as an idle tale. I little thought how nearly I was interested in the actors of a scene so daring. How could you have courage to go through with it?" *

"Had I had leisure for reflection," answered his sister, "I should have refused, from a mixture of principle and of fear. But, like many people who do daring actions, I went on because I had not time to think of retreating. The matter was little known, and it is said the king had commanded that it should not be farther inquired into—from prudence, as I suppose, and lenity, though my uncle chooses to ascribe the forbearance of the Elector of Hanover, as he calls him, sometimes to pusillanimity and somutimes to a presumptuous scorn of the faction who opposes his title."

"And have your subsequent agencies under this frantic enthusiast," said Darsie, "equalled this in danger?"

"No, nor in importance," replied Lilias; "though I have witnessed much of the strange and desperate machinations by which, in spite of every obstacle and in contempt of every danger, he endeavors to awaken the courage of a broken party. I have traversed in his company all England and Scotland, and have visited the most extraordinary and contrasted scenes; now lodging at the castles of the proud gentry of Cheshire and Wales, where the retired aristocrats,

* See Coronation of George III. Note 37.

with opinions as antiquated as their dwellings and their manners, still continue to nourish Jacobitical principles; and the next week, perhaps, spent among outlawed smugglers or Highland banditti. I have known my uncle often act the part of a hero, and sometimes that of a mere vulgar conspirator, and turn himself, with the most surprising flexibility, into all sorts of shapes to attract proselytes to his cause."

"Which, in the present day," said Darsie, "he finds, I presume, no easy task."

"So difficult," said Lilias, "that I believe he has, at different times, disgusted with the total falling away of some friend and the coldness of others, been almost on the point of resigning his undertaking. How often have I known him affect an open brow and a jovial manner, joining in the games of the gentry, and even in the sports of the common people, in order to invest himself with a temporary degree of popularity, while, in fact, his heart was bursting to witness what he called the degeneracy of the times, the decay of activity among the aged, and the want of zeal in the rising generation. After the day has been passed in the hardest exercise, he has spent the night in pacing his solitary chamber, bewailing the downfall of the cause, and wishing for the bullet of Dundee or the ax of Balmerino."

"A strange delusion," said Darsie; "and it is wonderful that it does not yield to the force of reality."

"Ah, but," replied Lilias, "realities of late have seemed to flatter his hopes. The general dissatisfaction with the peace, the unpopularity of the minister, which has extended itself even to the person of his master, the various uproars which have disturbed the quiet of the metropolis, and a general state of disgust and dissatisfaction, which seems to affect the body of the nation, have given unwonted encouragement to the expiring hopes of the Jacobites, and induced many, both at the court of Rome and, if it can be called so, of the Pretender, to lend a more favorable ear than they had hitherto done to the insinuations of those who, like my uncle, hope when hope is lost to all but themselves. Nay, I really believe that at this moment they meditate some desperate effort. My uncle has been doing all in his power of late to conciliate the affections of those wild communities that dwell on the Solway, over whom our family possessed a seigniorial interest before the forfeiture, and amongst whom, on the occasion of 1745, our unhappy father's interest, with his own, raised a considerable body of men. But they are no longer willing to obey his summons ; and, as one apology among others, they allege your absence as their natural head and leader. This has increased his desire to obtain possession of your person, and, if he possibly can, to influence your mind, so as to obtain your authority to his proceedings."

"That he shall never obtain," answered Darsie : "my principles and my prudence alike forbid such a step. Besides, it would be totally unavailing to his purpose. Whatever these people may pretend to evade your uncle's importunities, they cannot, at this time of day, think of subjecting their necks again to the feudal yoke, which was effectually broken by the Act of 1748, abolishing vassalage and hereditary jurisdictions."

" Ay, but that my uncle considers as the act of a usurping government," said Lilias.

" Like enough *he* may think so," answered her brother, " for he is a superior, and loses his authority by the enactment. But the question is, what the vassal will think of it, who have gained their freedom from feudal slavery, and have now enjoyed that freedom for many years ? However, to cut the matter short, if five hundred men would rise at the wagging of my finger, that finger should not be raised in a cause which I disapprove of, and upon that my uncle may reckon."

" But you may temporize," said Lilias, upon whom the idea of her uncle's displeasure made evidently a strong impression—" you may temporize, as most of the gentry in this country do, and let the bubble burst of itself ; for it is singular how few of them venture to oppose my uncle directly. I entreat you to avoid direct collision with him. To hear you, the head of the house of Redgauntlet, declare against the family of Stuart would either break his heart or drive him to some act of desperation."

" Yes, but, Lilias, you forget that the consequences of such an act of complaisance might be, that the house of Redgauntlet and I might lose both our heads at one blow."

" Alas ! " said she,' ' I had forgotten that danger. I have grown familiar with perilous intrigues, as the nurses in a pest-house are said to become accustomed to the air around them, till they forget even that it is noisome."

" And yet," said Darsie, " if I could free myself from him without coming ·to an open rupture—— Tell me Lilias, do you think it possible that he can have any immediate attempt in view ? "

" To confess the truth," answered Lilias, " I cannot doubt

that he has. There has been an unusual bustle among the
Jacobites of late. They have hopes, as I told you, from
circumstances unconnected with their own strength. Just
before you came to the country, my uncle's desire to find
you out became, if possible, more eager than ever—he talked
of men to be presently brought together, and of your name
and influence for raising them. At this very time, your first
visit to Brokenburn took place. A suspicion arose in my
uncle's mind that you might be the youth he sought, and it
was strengthened by papers and letters which the rascal
Nixon did not hesitate to take from your pocket. Yet a
mistake might have occasioned a fatal explosion ; and my
uncle therefore posted to Edinburgh to follow out the clue
he had obtained, and fished enough of information from old
Mr. Fairford to make him certain that you were the person
he sought. Meanwhile, and at the expense of some personal,
and perhaps too bold, exertion, I endeavored, through your
friend young Fairford, to put you on your guard."

" Without success," said Darsie, blushing under his mask,
when he recollected how he had mistaken his sister's meaning.

" I do not wonder that my warning was fruitless," said
she : " the thing was doomed to be. Besides, your escape
would have been difficult. You were dogged the whole time
you were at the Shepherd's Bush and at Mount Sharon by a
spy who scarcely ever left you."

"That wretch little Benjie !" exclaimed Darsie. " I will
wring the monkey's neck round the first time we meet."

" It was he indeed who gave constant information of your
motions to Cristal Nixon," said Lilias.

" And Cristal Nixon—I owe him, too, a day's work in
harvest," said Darsie ; " for I am mistaken if he is not the
person that struck me down when I was made prisoner
among the rioters."

" Like enough ; for he has a head and hand for any villany.
My uncle was very angry about it ; for though the riot was
made to have an opportunity of carrying you off in the confusion, as well as to put the fishermen at variance with the
public law, it would have been his last thought to have injured a hair of your head. But Nixon has insinuated himself into all my uncle's secrets, and some of these are so dark
and dangerous that, though there are few things he would
not dare, I doubt if he dare quarrel with him. And yet I
know that of Cristal would move my uncle to pass his sword
through his body."

23

"What is it, for Heaven's sake?" said Darsie; "1 have a particular desire for wishing to know."

"The old brutal desperado, whose face and mind are a libel upon human nature, has had the insolence to speak to his master's niece as one whom he was at liberty to admire; and when I turned on him with the anger and contempt he merited, the wretch grumbled out something, as if he held the destiny of our family in his hand."

"I thank you, Lilias," said Darsie, eagerly—"I thank you with all my heart for this communication. I have blamed myself as a Christian man for the indescribable longing I felt, from the first moment I saw that rascal, to send a bullet through his head; and now you have perfectly accounted for and justified this very laudable wish. I wonder my uncle, with the powerful sense you describe him to be possessed of, does not see through such a villain."

"I believe he knows him to be capable of much evil," answered Lilias—"selfish, obdurate, brutal, and a man hater. But then he conceives him to possess the qualities most requisite for a conspirator—undaunted courage, imperturbable coolness and address, and inviolable fidelity. In the last particular he may be mistaken. I have heard Nixon blamed for the manner in which our poor father was taken after Culloden."

"Another reason for my innate aversion," said Darsie; "but I will be on my guard with him."

"See, he observes us closely," said Lilias. "What a thing is conscience! He knows we are now speaking of him, though he cannot have heard a word that we have said."

It seemed as if she had guessed truly; for Cristal Nixon at that moment rode up to them, and said, with an affectation of jocularity which sat very ill upon his sullen features, "Come, young ladies, you have had time enough for your chat this morning, and your tongues, I think, must be tired. We are going to pass a village, and I must beg you to separate—you, Miss Lilias, to ride a little behind, and you, Mrs., or Miss, or Master, whichever you choose to be called, to be jogging a little bit before."

Lilias checked her horse without speaking, but not until she had given her brother an expressive look, recommending caution; to which he replied by a signal, indicating that he understood and would comply with her request.

CHAPTER XIX

LEFT to his solitary meditations, Darsie (for we will still term Sir Arthur Darsie Redgauntlet of that Ilk by the name to which the reader is habituated) was surprised not only at the alteration of his own state and condition, but at the equanimity with which he felt himself disposed to view all these vicissitudes.

His fever-fit of love had departed like a morning's dream, and left nothing behind but a painful sense of shame, and a resolution to be more cautious ere he again indulged in such romantic visions. His station in society was changed from that of a wandering, unowned youth, in whom none appeared to take an interest, excepting the strangers by whom he had been educated, to the heir of a noble house, possessed of such influence and such property that it seemed as if the progress or arrest of important political events was likely to depend upon his resolution. Even this sudden elevation, the more than fulfilment of those wishes which had haunted him ever since he was able to form a wish on the subject, was contemplated by Darsie, volatile as his disposition was, without more than a few thrills of gratified vanity.

It is true, there were circumstances in his present situation to counterbalance such high advantages. To be a prisoner in the hands of a man so determined as his uncle was no agreeable consideration, when he was calculating how he might best dispute his pleasure, and refuse to join him in the perilous enterprise which he seemed to meditate. Outlawed and desperate himself, Darsie could not doubt that his uncle was surrounded by men capable of anything, that he was restrained by no personal considerations ; and therefore what degree of compulsion he might apply to his brother's son, or in what manner he might feel at liberty to punish his contumacy, should he disavow the Jacobite cause, must depend entirely upon the limits of his own conscience ; and who was to answer for the conscience of a heated enthusiast, who considers opposition to the party he has espoused as treason to the welfare of his country ? After a short terval, Cristal Nixon was pleased to throw some light upon the subject which agitated him.

When that grim satellite rode up without ceremony close to Darsie's side, the latter felt his very flesh creep with abhorrence, so little was he able to endure his presence, since the story of Lilias had added to his instinctive hatred of the man. His voice, too, sounded like that of a screech-owl, as he said, " So, my young cock of the North, you now know it all, and no doubt are blessing your uncle for stirring you up to such an honorable action."

" I will acquaint my uncle with my sentiments on the subject, before I make them known to any one else," said Darsie, scarcely prevailing on his tongue to utter even these few words in a civil manner.

" Umph," murmured Cristal between his teeth. " Close as wax, I see ; and perhaps not quite so pliable. But take care, my pretty youth," he added, scornfully ; " Hugh Redgauntlet will prove a rough colt-breaker : he will neither spare whipcord nor spur-rowel, I promise you."

" I have already said, Mr. Nixon," answered Darsie, " that I will canvass those matters of which my sister has informed me with my uncle himself, and with no other person."

" Nay, but a word of friendly advice would do you no harm, young master," replied Nixon. " Old Redgauntlet is apter at a blow than a word—likely to bite before he barks— the true man for giving Scarborough warning—first knock you down, then bid you stand. So, methinks, a little kind warning as to consequences were not amiss, lest they come upon you unawares."

" If the warning is really kind, Mr. Nixon," said the young man, " I will hear it thankfully ; and, indeed, if otherwise, I must listen to it whether I will or no, since I have at present no choice of company or of conversation."

" Nay, I have but little to say," said Nixon, affecting to give to his sullen and dogged manner the appearance of an honest bluntness : " I am as little apt to throw away words as any one. But here is the question—Will you join heart and hand with your uncle or no ?"

" What if I should say ' Ay ' ? " said Darsie, determined, if possible, to conceal his resolution from this man.

" Why, then," said Nixon, somewhat surprised at the readiness of his answer, " all will go smooth, of course : you will take share in this noble undertaking, and, when it succeeds, you will exchange your open helmet for an earl's coronet perhaps."

"And how if it fails?" said Darsie.

"Thereafter as it may be," said Nixon : "they who play at bowls must meet with rubbers."

"Well, but suppose, then, I have some foolish tenderness for my windpipe, and that, when my uncle proposes the adventure to me, I should say 'No'—how then, Mr. Nixon?"

"Why, then, I would have you look to yourself, young master. There are sharp laws in France against refractory pupils—*lettres de cachet* are easily come by, when such men as we are concerned with interest themselves in the matter."

"But we are not in France," said poor Darsie, through whose blood ran a cold shivering at the idea of a French prison.

"A fast-sailing lugger will soon bring you there though, snug stowed under hatches, like a cask of moonlight."

"But the French are at peace with us," said Darsie, "and would not dare——"

"Why, who would ever hear of you?" interrupted Nixon. "Do you imagine that a foreign court would call you up for judgment, and put the sentence of imprisonment in the *Courier de l'Europe*, as they do at the Old Bailey? No—no, young gentleman—the gates of the Bastile, and of Mont St. Michel, and the Castle of Vincennes move on d—-d easy hinges when they let folk in : not the least jar is heard. There are cool cells there for hot heads—as calm, and quiet, and dark as you could wish in Bedlam ; and the dismissal comes when the carpenter brings the prisoner's coffin, and not sooner."

"Well, Mr. Nixon," said Darsie, affecting a cheerfulness which he was far from feeling, " mine is a hard case—a sort of hanging choice, you will allow—since I must either offend our own government here, and run the risk of my life for doing so, or be doomed to the dungeons of another country, whose laws I have never offended, since I have never trod its soil. Tell me what you would do if you were in my place."

"I'll tell you what when I *am* there," said Nixon, and, checking his horse, fell back to the rear of the little party.

"It is evident," thought the young man, " that the villain believes me completely noosed, and perhaps has the ineffable impudence to suppose that my sister must eventually succeed to the possessions which have occasioned my loss of freedom, and that his own influence over the destinies of our unhappy family may secure him possession of the heiress ; but he shall perish by my hand first ! I must now be on the alert to make my escape, if possible, before I am forced on shipboard.

Blind Willie will not, I think, desert me without an effort on my behalf, especially if he has learned that I am the son of his late unhappy patron. What a change is mine! Whilst I possessed neither rank nor fortune, I lived safely and unknown, under the protection of the kind and respectable friends whose hearts Heaven had moved towards me. Now that I am the head of an honorable house, and that enterprises of the most daring character wait my decision, and retainers and vassals seem ready to rise at my beck, my safety consists chiefly in the attachment of a blind stroller!"

While he was revolving these things in his mind, and preparing himself for the interview with his uncle, which could not but be a stormy one, he saw Hugh Redgauntlet come riding slowly back to meet them, without any attendants. Cristal Nixon rode up as he approached, and, as they met, fixed on him a look of inquiry.

"The fool, Crackenthorp," said Redgauntlet, "has let strangers into his house. Some of his smuggling comrades, I believe ; we must ride slowly to give him time to send them packing."

"Did you see any of your friends," said Cristal.

"Three, and have letters from many more. They are unanimous on the subject you wot of ; and the point must be conceded to them, or, far as the matter has gone, it will go no farther."

"You will hardly bring the Father to stoop to his flock," said Cristal, with a sneer.

"He must and shall!" answered Redgauntlet, briefly. "Go to the front, Cristal—I will speak with my nephew. I trust, Sir Arthur Redgauntlet, you are satisfied with the manner in which I have discharged my duty to your sister ?"

"There can be no fault found to her manners or sentiments," answered Darsie ; "I am happy in knowing a relative so amiable."

"I am glad of it," answered Mr. Redgauntlet. "I am no nice judge of women's qualifications, and my life has been dedicated to one great object ; so that since she left France she has had but little opportunity of improvement. I have subjected her, however, as little as possible to the inconveniences and privations of my wandering and dangerous life. From time to time she has resided for weeks and months with families of honor and respectability, and I am glad that she has, in your opinion, the manners and behavior which become her birth."

Darsie expressed himself perfectly satisfied, and there was

a little pause, which Redgauntlet broke by solemnly addressing his nephew.

"For you, my nephew, I also hoped to have done much.
The weakness and timidity of your mother sequestered you
from my care, or it would have been my pride and happiness
to have trained up the son of my unhappy brother in those
paths of honor in which our ancestors have always trod."

"Now comes the storm," thought Darsie to himself, and
began to collect his thoughts, as the cautious master of a
vessel furls his sails and makes his ship snug when he dis-
cerns the approaching squall.

"My mother's conduct in respect to me might be mis-
judged," he said, "but it was founded on the most anxious
affection."

"Assuredly," said his uncle, "and I have no wish to
reflect on her memory, though her mistrust has done so
much injury, I will not say to me, but to the cause of my
unhappy country. Her scheme was, I think, to have made
you that wretched pettifogging being which they still continue to call in derision by the once respectable name of
a Scottish advocate—one of those mongrel things that must
creep to learn the ultimate decision of his causes to the bar
of a foreign court, instead of pleading before the independent and august Parliament of his own native kingdom."

"I did prosecute the study of law for a year or two," said
Darsie, "but I found I had neither taste nor talents for the
science."

"And left it with scorn, doubtless," said Mr. Redgauntlet. "Well, I now hold up to you, my dearest nephew, a
more worthy object of ambition. Look eastward—do you
see a monument standing on yonder plain, near a hamlet?"

Darsie replied that he did.

"The hamlet is called Burgh-upon-Sands, and yonder
monument is erected to the memory of the tyrant Edward I.
The just hand of Providence overtook him on that spot, as he
was leading his bands to complete the subjugation of Scotland, whose civil dissensions began under his accursed policy.
The glorious career of Bruce might have been stopped in its
outset, the field of Bannockburn might have remained a
bloodless turf, if God had not removed, in the very crisis,
the crafty and bold tyrant who had so long been Scotland's
scourge. Edward's grave is the cradle of our national freedom. It is within sight of that great landmark of our
liberty that I have to propose to you an undertaking second
in honor and importance to none since the immortal Bruce

stabbed the Red Comyn, and grasped, with his yet bloody hand, the independent crown of Scotland."

He paused for an answer ; but Darsie, overawed by the energy of his manner, and unwilling to commit himself by a hasty explanation, remained silent.

"I will not suppose," said Hugh Redgauntlet, after a pause, "that you are either so dull as not to comprehend the import of my words, or so dastardly as to be dismayed by my proposal, or so utterly degenerate from the blood and sentiments of your ancestors as not to feel my summons as the horse hears the war-trumpet."

"I will not pretend to misunderstand you, sir," said Darsie ; "but an enterprise directed against a dynasty now established for three reigns requires strong arguments, both in point of justice and of expediency, to recommend it to men of conscience and prudence."

"I will not," said Redgauntlet, while his eyes sparkled with anger—"I will not hear you speak a word against the justice of that enterprise for which your oppressed country calls with the voice of a parent, entreating her children for aid ; or against that noble revenge which your father's blood demands from his dishonored grave. His skull is yet standing over the Rikargate,* and even its bleak and moldered jaws command you to be a man. I ask you, in the name of God and of your country, will you draw your sword and go with me to Carlisle, were it but to lay your father's head, now the perch of the obscene owl and carrion crow, and the scoff of every ribald clown, in consecrated earth, as befits his long ancestry ?"

Darsie, unprepared to answer an appeal urged with so much passion, and not doubting a direct refusal would cost him his liberty or life, was again silent.

"I see," said his uncle, in a more composed tone, "that it is not deficiency of spirit, but the groveling habits of a confined education among the poor-spirited class you were condemned to herd with, that keeps you silent. You scarce yet believe yourself a Redgauntlet : your pulse has not yet learned the genuine throb that answers to the summons of honor and of patriotism."

"I trust," replied Darsie at last, "that I shall never be found indifferent to the call of either ; but to answer them with effect—even were I convinced that they now sounded in my ear—I must see some reasonable hope of success in the

* The northern gate of Carlisle was long garnished with the heads of the Scottish rebels executed in 1746.

desperate enterprise in which you would involve me. I look around me, and I see a settled government—an established authority—a born Briton on the throne—the very Highland mountaineers, upon whom alone the trust of the exiled family reposed, assembled into regiments, which act under the orders of the existing dynasty.* France has been utterly dismayed by the tremendous lessons of the last war, and will hardly provoke another. All without and within the kingdom is adverse to encountering a hopeless struggle, and you alone, sir, seem willing to undertake a desperate enterprise."

"And would undertake it were it ten times more desperate ; and have agitated it when ten times the obstacles were interposed. Have I forgot my brother's blood ? Can I—dare I even now repeat the paternoster, since my enemies and the murderers remain unforgiven ? Is there an art I have not practised, a privation to which I have not submitted, to bring on the crisis which I now behold arrived ? Have I not been a vowed and a devoted man, foregoing every comfort of social life, renouncing even the exercise of devotion, unless when I might name in prayer my prince and country, submitting to everything to make converts to this noble cause ? Have I done all this, and shall I now stop short ?" Darsie was about to interrupt him, but he pressed his hand affectionately upon his shoulder, and enjoining, or rather imploring, silence —" Peace," he said, "heir of my ancestors ' fame—heir of all my hopes and wishes ! Peace, son of my slaughtered brother ! I have sought for thee, and mourned for thee, as a mother for an only child. Do not let me again lose you in the moment when you are restored to my hopes. Believe me, I distrust so much my own impatient temper, that I entreat you, as the dearest boon, do nought to awaken it at this crisis."

Darsie was not sorry to reply, that his respect for the person of his relation would induce him to listen to all which he had to apprise him of before he formed any definite resolution upon the weighty subjects of deliberations which he proposed to him.

"Deliberation !" repeated Redgauntlet, impatiently ; "and yet it is not ill said. I wish there had been more warmth in thy reply, Arthur ; but I must recollect were an eagle bred in a falcon's mew, and hooded like a reclaimed hawk, he could not at first gaze steadily on the sun. Listen to me, my dearest Arthur. The state of this nation no more implies prosperity than the florid color of a feverish patient

* See Highland Regiments. Note 38.

is a symptom of health. All is false and hollow : the apparent success of Chatham's administration has plunged the country deeper in debt than all the barren acres of Canada are worth, were they as fertile as Yorkshire ; the dazzling luster of the victories of Minden and Quebec have been dimmed by the disgrace of the hasty peace ; by the war, England, at immense expense, gained nothing but honor, and that she has gratuitously resigned. Many eyes, formerly cold and indifferent, are now looking towards the line of our ancient and rightful monarchs, as the only refuge in the approaching storm ; the rich are alarmed, the nobles are disgusted, the populace are inflamed, and a band of patriots, whose measures are more safe that their numbers are few, have resolved to set up King Charles's standard."

"But the military," said Darsie—"how can you, with a body of unarmed and disorderly insurgents, propose to encounter a regular army ? The Highlanders are now totally disarmed."

"In a great measure, perhaps," answered Redgauntlet ; "but the policy which raised the Highland regiments has provided for that. We have already friends in these corps ; nor can we doubt for a moment what their conduct will be when the white cockade is once more mounted. The rest of the standing army has been greatly reduced since the peace ; and we reckon confidently on our standard being joined by thousands of the disbanded troops."

"Alas !" said Darsie, " and is it upon such vague hopes as these, the inconstant humor of a crowd or of a disbanded soldiery, that men of honor are invited to risk their families, their property, their life ? "

"Men of honor, boy," said Redgauntlet, his eyes glancing with impatience, " set life, property, family, and all at stake when that honor commands it. We are not now weaker than when seven men, landing in the wilds of Moidart, shook the throne of the usurper till it tottered, won two pitched fields, besides overrunning one kingdom and the half of another, and, but for treachery, would have achieved what their venturous successors are now to attempt in their turn."

" And will such an attempt be made in serious earnest ? " said Darsie. " Excuse me, my uncle, if I can scarce believe a fact so extraordinary. Will there really be found men of rank and consequence sufficient to renew the adventure of 1745 ? "

" I will not give you my confidence by halves, Sir Arthur,"

replied his uncle. " Look at that scroll—what say you to
these names ? Are they not the flower of the Western shires,
of Wales, of Scotland ? "

" The paper contains indeed the names of many that are
great and noble," replied Darsie, after perusing it;
" but——"

" But what ? " asked his uncle impatiently. " Do you
doubt the ability of those nobles and gentlemen to furnish
the aid in men and money at which they are rated ? "

" Not their ability certainly," said Darsie, " for of that I
am no competent judge ; but I see in this scroll the name of
Sir Arthur Darsie Redgauntlet of that Ilk rated at an hundred men and upwards—I certainly am ignorant how he is
to redeem that pledge."

" I will be responsible for the men," replied Hugh
Redgauntlet.

" But, my dear uncle," added Darsie, " I hope, for your
sake, that the other individuals whose names are here written have had more acquaintance with your plan that I have
been indulged with."

" For thee and thine I can be myself responsible," said
Redgauntlet ; " for if thou hast not the courage to head the
force of thy house, the leading shall pass to other hands, and
thy inheritance shall depart from thee, like vigor and verdure from a rotten branch. For these honorable persons, a
slight condition there is which they annex to their friendship—something so trifling that it is scarce worthy of men·
tion. This boon granted to them by him who is most interested, there is no question they will take the field in the
manner there stated."

Again Darsie perused the paper, and felt himself still less
inclined to believe that so many men of family and fortune
were likely to embark in an enterprise so fatal. It seemed
as if some rash plotter had put down at a venture the names
of all whom common report tainted with Jacobitism ; or, if
it was really the act of the individuals named, he suspected
they must be aware of some mode of excusing themselves
from compliance with its purport. It was impossible, he
thought, that Englishmen of large fortune, who had failed
to join Charles when he broke into England at the head of
a victorious army, should have the least thoughts of en·
couraging a descent when circumstances were so much less
propitious. He therefore concluded the enterprise would
fall to pieces of itself and that his best way was, in the
meantime, to remain silent, unless the actual approach of a

crisis (which might, however, never arrive) should compel him to give a downright refusal to his uncle's proposition ; and if, in the interim, some door for escape should be opened, he resolved within himself not to omit availing himself of it.

Hugh Redgauntlet watched his nephew's looks for some time, and then, as if arriving from some other process of reasoning at the same conclusion, he said, " I have told you, Sir Arthur, that I do not urge your immediate accession to my proposal ; indeed, the consequences of a refusal would be so dreadful to yourself, so destructive to all the hopes which I have nursed, that I would not risk, by a moment's impatience, the object of my whole life. Yes, Arthur, I have been a self-denying hermit at one time, at another the apparent associate of outlaws and desperadoes, at another the subordinate agent of men whom I felt every way my inferiors —not for any selfish purpose of my own—no, not even to win for myself the renown of being the principal instrument in restoring my king and freeing my country. My first wish on earth is for that restoration and that freedom ; my next, that my nephew, the representative of my house and of the brother of my love, may have the advantage and the credit of all my efforts in the good cause. But," he added, darting on Darsie one of his withering frowns, " if Scotlond and my father's house cannot stand and flourish together, then perish the very name of Redgauntlet ! perish the son of my brother, with every recollection of the glories of my family, of the affections of my youth, rather than my country's cause should be injured in the tithing of a barleycorn ! The spirit of Sir Alberick is alive within me at this moment," he continued, drawing up his stately form and sitting erect in his saddle, while he pressed his finger against his forehead ; " and if you yourself crossed my path in opposition, I swear, by the mark that darkens my brow, that a new deed should be done—a new doom should be deserved ! "

He was silent, and his threats were uttered in a tone of voice so deeply resolute, that Darsie's heart sunk within him, when he reflected on the storm of passion which he must encounter if he declined to join his uncle in a project to which prudence and principle made him equally adverse. He had scarce any hope left but in temporizing until he could make his escape, and resolved to avail himself for that purpose of the delay which his uncle seemed not unwilling to grant. The stern, gloomy look of his companion became relaxed by degrees, and presently afterwards he made a sign

to Miss Redgauntlet to join the party, and began a forced
conversation on ordinary topics; in the course of which
Darsie observed that his sister seemed to speak under the
most cautious restraint, weighing every word before she uttered it, and always permitting her uncle to give the tone to
the conversation, though of the most trifling kind.   This
seemed to him, such an opinion had he already entertained
of his sister's good sense and firmness, the strongest proof he
had yet received of his uncle's peremptory character, since
he saw it observed with so much deference by a young person whose sex might have given her privileges, and who
seemed by no means deficient either in spirit or firmness.

The little cavalcade was now approaching the house of
Father Crackenthorp, situated, as the reader knows, by the
side of the Solway, and not far distant from a rude pier, near
which lay several fishing-boats, which frequently acted in a
different capacity.   The house of the worthy publican was
also adapted to the various occupations which he carried on,
being a large scrambling assemblage of cottages attached to
a house of two stories, roofed with flags of sandstone—the
original mansion, to which the extension of Master Crackenthorp's trade had occasioned his making many additions.
Instead of the single long watering-trough which usually
distinguishes the front of the English public-house of the
second class, there were three conveniences of that kind, for
the use, as the landlord used to say, of the troop-horses,
when the soldiers came to search his house; while a knowing leer and a nod let you understand what species of troops
he was thinking of.   A huge ash-tree before the door, which
had reared itself to a great size and height, in spite of the
blasts from the neighboring Solway, overshadowed, as usual,
the ale-bench, as our ancestors called it, where, though it
was still early in the day, several fellows, who seemed to be
gentlemen's servants, were drinking beer and smoking.   One
or two of them wore liveries which seemed known to Mr.
Redgauntlet, for he muttered between his teeth, " Fools—
fools! were they on a march to hell, they must have their
rascals in livery with them, that the whole world might know
who were going to be damned."

As he thus muttered, he drew bridle before the door of the
place, from which several other lounging guests began to
issue, to look with indolent curiosity, as usual, upon an
" arrival."

Redgauntlet sprung from his horse, and assisted his niece
to dismount; but, forgetting, perhaps, his nephew's disguise,

he did not pay him the attention which his female dress demanded.

The situation of Darsie was indeed something awkward ; for Cristal Nixon, out of caution perhaps to prevent escape, had muffled the extreme folds of the riding-skirt with which he was accoutered around his ankles and under his feet, and there secured it with large corking-pins. We presume that gentlemen-cavaliers may sometimes cast their eyes to that part of the person of the fair equestrian whom they chance occasionally to escort ; and if they will conceive their own feet, like Darsie's, muffled in such a labyrinth of folds and amplitude of robe as modesty doubtless induces the fair creatures to assume upon such occasions, they will allow that, on a first attempt, they might find some awkwardness in dismounting. Darsie, at least, was in such a predicament, for, not receiving adroit assistance from the attendant of Mr. Redgauntlet, he stumbled as he dismounted from the horse, and might have had a bad fall, had it not been broken by the gallant interposition of a gentleman, who probably was, on his part, a little surprised at the solid weight of the distressed fair one whom he had the honor to receive in his embrace. But what was his surprise to that of Darsie's, when the hurry of the moment and of the accident permitted him to see that it was his friend Alan Fairford in whose arms he found himself ! A thousand apprehensions rushed on him, mingled with the full career of hope and joy, inspired by the unexpected appearance of his beloved friend at the very crisis, it seemed, of his fate.

He was about to whisper in his ear, cautioning him at the same time to be silent ; yet he hesitated for a second or two to effect his purpose, since, should Redgauntlet take the alarm from any sudden exclamation on the part of Alan, there was no saying what consequences might ensue.

Ere he could decide what was to be done, Redgauntlet, who had entered the house, returned hastily, followed by Cristal Nixon. " I'll release you of the charge of this young lady, sir," he said, haughtily, to Alan Fairford, whom he probably did not recognize.

" I had no desire to intrude, sir," replied Alan ; " the lady's situation seemed to require assistance, and—but have I not the honor to speak to Mr. Herries of Birrenswork ? "

" You are mistaken, sir," said Redgauntlet, turning short off and making a sign with his hand to Cristal, who hurried Darsie, however unwillingly, into the house, whispering in his ear, " Come, miss, let us have no making of acquaintance from the windows. Ladies of fashion must be private. Show us a room, Father Crackenthorp."

So saying, he conducted Darsie into the house, interposing at the same time his person betwixt the supposed young lady and the stranger of whom he was suspicious, so as to make communication by signs impossible. As they entered, they heard the sound of a fiddle in the stone-floored and well-sanded kitchen, through which they were about to follow their corpulent host, and where several people seemed engaged in dancing to its strains.

"D—n thee," said Nixon to Crackenthorp, "would you have the lady go through all the mob of the parish? Hast thou no more private way to our sitting-room?"

"None that is fit for my traveling," answered the landlord, laying his hand on his portly stomach. "I am not Tom Turnpenny, to creep like a lizard through keyholes."

So saying, he kept moving on through the revelers in the kitchen; and Nixon holding Darsie by his arm, as if to offer the lady support, but in all probability to frustrate any effort at escape, moved through the crowd, which presented a very motley appearance, consisting of domestic servants, country fellows, seamen, and other idlers, whom Wandering Willie was regaling with his music.

To pass another friend without intimation of his presence would have been actual pusillanimity; and just when they were passing the blind man's elevated seat, Darsie asked him, with some emphasis, whether he could not play a Scottish air? The man's face had been the instant before devoid of all sort of expression, going through his performance like a clown through a beautiful country, too much accustomed to consider it as a task to take any interest in the performance, and, in fact, scarce seeming to hear the noise that he was creating. In a word, he might at the time have made a companion to my friend Wilkie's inimitable blind crowder. But with Wandering Willie this was only an occasional and a rare fit of dulness, such as will at times creep over all the professors of the fine arts, arising either from fatigue, or contempt of the present audience, or that caprice which so often tempts painters and musicians and great actors in the phrase of the latter, to " walk through " their part, instead of exerting themselves with the energy which acquired their fame. But when the performer heard the voice of Darsie, his countenance became at once illuminated, and showed the complete mistake of those who suppose that the principal point of expression depends upon the eyes. With his face turned to the point from which the sound came, his upper lip a little curved and quivering with agitation, and with a color which surprise and pleasure had brought at once into his faded cheek, he exchanged the humdrum hornpipe which he had been sawing out with reluctant and lazy bow for the fine Scottish air,

" You're welcome, Charlie Stuart,"

which flew from his strings as if by inspiration, and, after a breathless pause of admiration among the audience, was received with a clamor of applause which seemed to show that the name and tendency, as well as the execution of the tune, was in the highest degree acceptable to all the party assembled.

In the meantime, Cristal Nixon, still keeping hold of Darsie, and following the landlord, forced his way with some difficulty through the crowded kitchen, and entered a small apartment on the other side of it, where they found Lilias Redgauntlet already seated, Here Nixon gave way to his suppressed resentment, and turning sternly on Crackenthorp, threatened him with his master's severest displeasure because things were in such bad order to receive his family, when he had given such special advice that he desired to be private. But Father Crackenthorp was not a man to be browbeaten.

" Why, brother Nixon, thou art angry this morning," he replied : " hast risen from thy wrong side, I think. You know as well as I that most of this mob is of the Squire's own making—gentlemen that come with their servants, and so forth, to meet him in the way of business, as old Tom Turnpenny says : the very last that came was sent down with Dick Gardener from Fairladies."

" But the blind scraping scoundrel yonder," said Nixon, " how dared you take such a rascal as that across your threshold at such a time as this ? If the Squire should dream you have a thought of peaching—I am only speaking for your good, Father Crackenthorp."

" Why, look ye, brother Nixon," said Crackenthorp, turning his quid with great composure, " the Squire is a very worthy gentleman, and I'll never deny it ; but I am neither his servant nor his tenant, and so he need send me none of his orders till he hears I have put on his livery. As for turning away folk from my door, I might as well plug up the ale-tap and pull down the sign ; and as for peaching and

such-like, the Squire will find the folk here are as honest
to the full as those he brings with him."

"How, you impudent lump of tallow," said Nixon,
"what do you mean by that?"

"Nothing," said Crackenthorp, "but that I can tour out
as well as another—you understand me—keep good lights
in my upper story—know a thing or two more than most
folk in this country. If folk will come to my house on
dangerous errands, egad they shall not find Joe Crackenthorp a cat's paw. I'll keep myself clear, you may depend
on it, and let every man answer for his own actions—that's
my way. Anything wanted, Master Nixon?"

"No. Yes—begone!" said Nixon, who seemed embarrassed with the landlord's contumacy, yet desirous to conceal the effect it produced on him.

The door was no sooner closed on Crackenthorp than Miss
Redgauntlet, addressing Nixon, commanded him to leave
the room and go to his proper place.

"How, madam?" said the fellow sullenly, yet with an
air of respect. "Would you have your uncle pistol me for
disobeying his orders?"

"He may perhaps pistol you for some other reason, if
you do not obey mine," said Lilias, composedly.

"You abuse your advantage over me, madam. I really
dare not go; I am on guard over this other miss here; and
if I should desert my post, my life were not worth five minutes' purchase."

"Then know your post, sir," said Lilias, "and watch on
the outside of the door. You have no commission to listen
to our private conversation, I suppose? Begone, sir, without further speech or remonstrance, or I will tell my uncle
that which you would have reason to repent he should
know."

The fellow looked at her with a singular expression of
spite, mixed with deference. "You abuse your advantages, madam," he said, "and act as foolishly in doing so
as I did in affording you such a hank over me. But you
are a tyrant, and tyrants have commonly short reigns."

So saying, he left the apartment.

"The wretch's unparalleled insolence," said Lilias to her
brother, "has given me one great advantage over him. For,
knowing that my uncle would shoot him with as little remorse
as a woodcock if he but guessed at his brazen-faced assurance
towards me, he dares not since that time assume, so far as
I am concerned, the air of insolent domination which the

24

possession of my uncle's secrets, and the knowledge of his most secret plans, have led him to exert over others of his family."

"In the meantime," said Darsie, "I am happy to see that the landlord of the house does not seem so devoted to him as I apprehended ; and this aids the hope of escape which I am nourishing for you and for myself. O, Lilias, the truest of friends, Alan Fairford, is in pursuit of me, and is here at this moment. Another humble, but I think faithful, friend is also within these dangerous walls."

Lilias laid her finger on her lips, and pointed to the door. Darsie took the hint, lowered his voice, and informed her in whispers of the arrival of Fairford, and that he believed he had opened a communication with Wandering Willie. She listened with the utmost interest, and had just begun to reply, when a loud noise was heard in the kitchen, caused by several contending voices, amongst which Darsie thought he could distinguish that of Alan Fairford.

Forgetting how little his own condition permitted him to become the assistant of another, Darsie flew to the door of the room, and finding it locked and bolted on the outside, rushed against it with all his force, and made the most desperate efforts to burst it open, notwithstanding the entreaties of his sister that he would compose himself, and recollect the condition in which he was placed. But the door, framed to withstand attacks from excisemen, constables, and other personages, considered as worthy to use what are called the king's keys, "and therewith to make lockfast places open and patent," set his efforts at defiance. Meantime, the noise continued without, and we are to give an account of its origin in our next chapter.

CHAPTER XX

NARRATIVE OF DARSIE LATIMER, CONTINUED

JOE CRACKENTHORP'S public-house had never, since it first reared its chimneys on the banks of the Solway, been frequented by such a miscellaneous group of visitors as had that morning become its guests. Several of them were persons whose quality seemed much superior to their dresses and modes of traveling. The servants who attended them contradicted the inferences to be drawn from the garb of their masters, and, according to the customs of the knights of the rainbow, gave many hints that they were not people to serve any but men of first-rate consequence. These gentlemen, who had come thither chiefly for the purpose of meeting with Mr. Redgauntlet, seemed moody and anxious, conversed and walked together, apparently in deep conversation, and avoided any communication with the chance travelers whom accident brought that morning to the same place of resort.

As if Fate had set herself to confound the plans of the Jacobite conspirators, the number of travelers was unusually great, their appearance respectable, and they filled the public tap-room of the inn, where the political guests had already occupied most of the private apartments.

Amongst others, honest Joshua Geddes had arrived, traveling, as he said, in the sorrow of the soul, and mourning for the fate of Darsie Latimer as he would for his first-born child. He had skirted the whole coast of the Solway, besides making various trips into the interior, not shunning, on such occasions, to expose himself to the laugh of the scorner, nay, even to serious personal risk, by frequenting the haunts of smugglers, horse-jockeys, and other irregular persons, who looked on his intrusion with jealous eyes, and were apt to consider him as an exciseman in the disguise of a Quaker. All this labor and peril, however, had been undergone in vain. No search he could make obtained the least intelligence of Latimer, so that he began to fear the poor lad had been spirited abroad—for the practise of kidnapping was then not infrequent, especially on the western coast of Britain—if indeed he had escaped a briefer and more bloody fate.

With a heavy heart he delivered his horse, even Solomon, into the hands of the hostler, and walking into the inn, demanded from the landlord breakfast and a private room. Quakers and such hosts as old Father Crackenthorp are no congenial spirits ; the latter looked askew over his shoulder, and replied, " If you would have breakfast here, friend, you are like to eat it where other folk eat theirs."

"And wherefore can I not," said the Quaker, "have an apartment to myself for my money ?"

"Because, Master Jonathan, you must wait till your betters be served, or else eat with your equals."

Joshua Geddes argued the point no farther, but sitting quietly down on the seat which Crackenthorp indicated to him, and calling for a pint of ale, with some bread, butter, and Dutch cheese, began to satisfy the appetite which the morning air had rendered unusually alert.

While the honest Quaker was thus employed, another stranger entered the apartment, and sat down near to the table on which his victuals were placed. He looked repeatedly at Joshua, licked his parched and chopped lips as he saw the good Quaker masticate his bread and cheese, and sucked up his thin chops when Mr. Geddes applied the tankard to his mouth, as if the discharge of these bodily functions by another had awakened his sympathies in an uncontrollable degree. At last, being apparently unable to withstand his longings, he asked, in a faltering tone, the huge landlord, who was tramping through the room in all corpulent impatience, " Whether he could have a plack-pie ?"

" Never heard of such a thing, master," said the landlord, and was about to trudge onward, when the guest, detaining him, said in a strong Scottish tone. " Ye will maybe have nae whey then, nor buttermilk, nor ye couldna exhibit a souter's clod ?"

" Can't tell what ye are talking about, master," said Crackenthorp.

"Then ye will have nae breakfast that will come within the compass of a shilling Scots ?"

" Which is a penny sterling," answered Crackenthorp, with a sneer. " Why, no, Sawney, I can't say as we have— we can't afford it ; but you shall have a bellyful for love, as we say in the bull-ring."

" I shall never refuse a fair offer," said the poverty-stricken guest ; " and I will say that for the English, if they were deils, that they are a ceeveleesed people to gentlemen that are under a cloud."

"Gentlemen!—humph!" said Crackenthorp—"not a blue-cap among them but halts upon that foot." Then seizing on a dish which still contained a huge cantle of what had been once a princely mutton pasty, he placed it on the table before the stranger, saying, "There, master gentleman—there is what is worth all the black pies, as you call them, that were ever made of sheep's head."

"Sheep's head is a gude thing for a' that," replied the guest ; but, not being spoken so loud as to offend his hospitable entertainer, the interjection might pass for a private protest against the scandal thrown out against the standing dish of Caledonia.

This premised, he immediately began to transfer the mutton and pie-crust from his plate to his lips, in such huge gobbets as if he was refreshing after a three days' fast and laying in provisions against a whole Lent to come.

Joshua Geddes in his turn gazed on him with surprise, having never, he thought, beheld such a gaunt expression of hunger in the act of eating. "Friend," he said, after watching him for some minutes, "if thou gorgest thyself in this fashion thou wilt assuredly choke. Wilt thou not take a draught out of my cup to help down all that dry meat ?"

"Troth," said the stranger, stopping and looking at the friendly propounder, "that's nae bad overture, as they say in the General Assembly. I have heard waur motions than that frae wiser counsel."

Mr. Geddes ordered a quart of home-brewed to be placed before our friend Peter Peebles ; for the reader must have already conceived that this unfortunate litigant was the wanderer in question.

The victim of Themis had no sooner seen the flagon than he seized it with the same energy which he had displayed in operating upon the pie, puffed off the froth with such emphasis that some of it lighted on Mr. Geddes's head, and then said, as if with a sudden recollection of what was due to civility, "Here's to ye, friend. What! are ye ower grand to give me an answer, or are ye dull o' hearing ?"

"I prithee drink thy liquor, friend," said the good Quaker ; "thou meanest it in civility, but we care not for these idle fashions."

"What! ye are a Quaker, are ye ?" said Peter ; and without further ceremony reared the flagon to his head, from which he withdrew it not while a single drop of "barley-broo" remained. "That's done you and me muckle gude," he said, sighing as he set down his pot ; "but twa mutchkins o' yill between twa folk is a drappie ower little measure. What say ye to anither pot ? or shall we cry in a blythe Scots pint at ance ? The yill is no amiss."

"Thou mayst call for what thou wilt on thine own charges, friend,' said Geddes ; "for myself, I willingly contribute to the quenching of thy natural thirst ; but I fear it were no such easy matter to relieve thy acquired and artificial drouth."

"That is to say, in plain terms, ye are for withdrawing your caution with the folk of the house ? You Quaker folk are but fause comforters ; but since ye have garred me drink sae muckle cauld yill—me that am no used to the like of it in the forenoon—I think ye might as weel have offered me a glass of brandy or usquabae. I'm nae nice body : I can drink onything that's wet and toothsome."

"Not a drop at my cost, friend," quoth Geddes. "Thou art an old man, and hast, perchance, a heavy and long journey before thee. Thou art, moreover, my countryman, as I judge from thy tongue, and I will not give thee the means of dishonoring thy gray hairs in a strange land."

"Gray hairs, neighbor !" said Peter, with a wink to the bystanders, whom this dialogue began to interest, and who were in hopes of seeing the Quaker played off by the crazed beggar, for such Peter Peebles appeared to be—"gray hairs ! The Lord mend your eyesight, neighbor, that disna ken gray hairs frae a tow wig !"

This jest procured a shout of laughter, and, what was still more acceptable than dry applause, a man who stood beside called out, 'Father Crackenthorp, bring a nipperkin of brandy. I'll bestow a dram on this fellow, were it but for that very word."

The brandy was immediately brought by a wench who acted as barmaid ; and Peter, with a grin of delight, filled a glass, quaffed it off, and then saying, 'God bless me ! I was so unmannerly as not to drink to ye : I think the Quaker has smitten me wi' his ill-bred havings," he was about to fill another, when his hand was arrested by his new friend, who said at the same time, ' No—no, friend, fair play's a jewel —time about if you please,' and filling a glass for himself, emptied it as gallantly as Peter could have done. "What say you to that, friend ?" he continued, addressing the Quaker.

"Nay, friend," answered Joshua, "it went down thy throat, not mine, and I have nothing to say about what concerns me not ; but if thou art a man of humanity, thou wilt not give this poor creature the means of debauchery. Bethink thee that they will spurn him from the door as they would do a houseless and masterless dog, and that he may die on the sands or on the common. And if he has through thy means been rendered incapable of helping himself, thou shalt not be innocent of his blood."

"Faith, broadbrim, I believe thou art right, and the old gentleman in the flaxen jazy shall have no more of the comforter. Besides, we have business in hand to-day, and this fellow, for as mad as he looks, may have a nose on his face after all. Harkye, father, what is your name, and what brings you into such an out-of-the-way corner?"

"I am not just free to condescend on my name," said Peter; "and as for my business—there is a wee dribble of brandy in the stoup, it would be wrang to leave it to the lass: it is learning her bad usages."

"Well, thou shalt have the brandy, and be d—d to thee, if thou wilt tell me what you are making here."

"Seeking a young advocate chap that they ca' Alan Fairford, that has played me a slippery trick, and ye maun ken a' about the cause,' said Peter.

"An advocate, man!" answered the captain of the 'Jumping Jenny,' for it was he, and no other, who had taken compassion on Peter's drought. "Why, Lord help thee, thou art on the wrong side of the firth to seek advocates, whom I take to be Scottish lawyers, not English."

"English lawyers, man!" exclaimed Peter; "the deil a lawyer's in a' England."

"I wish from my soul it were true," said Ewart; "but what the devil put that in your head?"

"Lord, man, I got a grip of ane of their attorneys in Carlisle, and he tauld me that there wasna a lawyer in England, ony mair than himsell, that kenn'd the nature of a multiplepoinding! And when I tauld him how this loopy lad, Alan Fairford, had served me, he said I might bring an action on the case—just as if the case hadna as mony actions already as one case can weel carry. By my word, it is a gude case, and muckle has it borne, in its day, of various procedure; but it's the barley-pickle breaks the naig's back, and wi' my consent it shall not hae ony mair burden laid upon it."

"But this Alan Fairford," said Nanty—"come, sip up the drop of brandy, man, and tell me some more about him, and whether you are seeking him for good or for harm."

"For my ain gude, and for his harm, to be sure," said

Peter. "Think of his having left my cause in the dead-
thraw between the tyneing and the winning, and capering
off into Cumberland here after a wild loup-the-tether lad
they ca' Darsie Latimer."

"Darsie Latimer!" said Mr. Geddes, hastily. "Do you
know anything of Darsie Latimer?"

"Maybe I do and maybe I do not," answered Peter; "I
am no free to answer everybody's interrogatory, unless it is
put judicially and by form of law, specially where folk think
so much of a caup of sour yill or a thimblefu' of brandy.
But as for this gentleman, that has shown himself a gentleman at breakfast, and will show himself a gentleman at the
meridian, I am free to condescend upon any points in the
cause that may appear to bear upon the question at issue."

"Why, all I want to know from you, my friend, is whether
you are seeking to do this Mr. Alan Fairford good or harm;
because, if you come to do him good, I think you could maybe get speech of him; and if to do him harm, I will take
the liberty to give you a cast across the firth, with fair
warning not to come back on such an errand, lest worse come
of it."

The manner and language of Ewart were such that Joshua
Geddes resolved to keep cautious silence till he could more
plainly discover whether he was likely to aid or impede him
in his researches after Darsie Latimer. He therefore determined to listen attentively to what should pass between Peter
and the seaman, and to watch for an opportunity of questioning the former, so soon as he should be separated from his
new acquaintance.

"I wad by no means," said Peter Peebles, "do any substantial harm to the poor lad Fairford, who has had mony a
gowd guinea of mine, as weel as his father before him; but
I wad hae him brought back to the minding of my business
and his ain; and maybe I wadna insist farther in my action
of damages against him than for refunding the fees, and for
some annual rent on the principal sum, due frae the day on
which he should have recovered it for me, plack and bawbee, at the great advising; for, ye are aware, that is the
least that I can ask *nomine damni*; and I have nae thought
to break down the lad bodily a'thegither: we maun live and
let live, forgie and forget."

"The deuce take me, friend broadbrim," said Nanty
Ewart, looking to the Quaker, "if I can make out what this
old scarecrow means. If I thought it was fitting that
Master Fairford should see him, why, perhaps it is a matter

that could be managed. Do you know anything about the old fellow? You seemed to take some charge of him just now."

"No more than I should have done by any one in distress," said Geddes, not sorry to be appealed to; "but I will try what I can do to find out who he is, and what he is about in this country. But are we not a little too public in this open room?"

"It's well thought of," said Nanty; and at his command the barmaid ushered the party into a side-booth, Peter attending them, in the instinctive hope that there would be more liquor drank among them before parting. They had scarce sat down in their new apartment when the sound of a violin was heard in the room which they had just left.

"I'll awa' back yonder," said Peter, rising up again; "yon's the sound of a fiddle, and where there is music there's aye something ganging to eat or drink."

"I am just going to order something here," said the Quaker; "but, in the meantime have you any objection, my good friend, to tell us your name?"

"None in the world, if you are wanting to drink to me by name and surname," answered Peebles; "but, otherwise, I would rather evite your interrogatories."

"Friend," said the Quaker, "it is not for thine own health, seeing thou hast drunk enough already; however—— Here, handmaiden, bring me a gill of sherry."

"Sherry's but shilpit drink, and a gill's a sma' measure for twa gentlemen to crack ower at their first acquaintance. But let us see your sneaking gill of sherry," said Poor Peter, thrusting forth his huge hand to seize on the diminutive pewter measure, which, according to the fashion of the time, contained the generous liquor freshly drawn from the butt.

"Nay, hold, friend," said Joshua, "thou hast not yet told me what name and surname I am to call thee by."

"D—d sly in the Quaker," said Nanty, apart, "to make him pay for his liquor before he gives it him. Now, I am such a fool, that I should have let him get too drunk, to open his mouth, before I thought of asking him a question."

"My name is Peter Peebles, then," said the litigant, rather sulkily, as one who thought his liquor too sparingly meted out to him; "and what have you to say to that?"

"Peter Peebles!" repeated Nanty Ewart, and seemed to muse upon something which the words brought to his remembrance, while the Quaker pursued his examination.

"But I prithee, Peter Peebles, what is thy further designation ? Thou knowest, in our country, that some men are
distinguished by their craft and calling, as cordwainers,
fishers, weavers, or the like, and some by their titles as proprietors of land—which savors of vanity—now, how may you
be distinguished from others of the same name ?"

"As Peter Peebles of the great plea of Poor Peter Peebles
against Plainstanes, *et per contra* ; if I am laird of naething
else, I am aye a *dominus litis.*"

"It's but a poor lairdship, I doubt," said Joshua.

"Pray, Mr. Peebles," said Nanty, interrupting the conversation abruptly, "were you not once a burgess of Edinburgh ?"

"*Was* I a burgess !" said, Peter indignantly, "and *am* I
not a burgess even now ? I have done nothing to forfeit my
right, I trow—once provost and aye ' my lord.'"

"Well, Mr. Burgess, tell me farther ; have you not some
property in the Gude Town ?" continued Ewart.

"Troth have I—that is, before my misfortunes, I had twa
or three bonny bits of mailings amang the closes and wynds,
forbye the shop and the story abune it. But Plainstanes has
put me to the causeway now. Never mind though, I will be
upsides with him yet."

"Had not you once a tenement in the Covenant Close ?"
again demanded Nanty.

"You have hit it, lad, though you look not like a Covenanter," said Peter ; "we'll drink to its memory—Hout !
the heart's at the mouth o' that ill-faur'd bit stoup already !
—it brought a rent, reckoning from the crawstep to the
groundsill, that ye might ca' fourteen punds a year, forbye
the laigh cellar that was let to Luckie Littleworth."

"And do you not remember that you had a poor old lady
for your tenant, Mrs. Cantrips of Kittlebasket ?" said
Nanty, suppressing his emotion with difficulty.

"Remember ! G—d, I have gude cause to remember her,"
said Peter, "for she turned a dyvour on my hands, the auld
besom ! and, after a' that the law could do to make me satisfied and paid, in the way of poinding and distrenyieing, and
sae forth, as the law will, she ran away to the charity workhouse, a matter of twenty punds Scots in my debt ; it's a
great shame and oppression that charity workhouse, taking
in bankrupt dyvours that canna pay their honest creditors."

"Methinks, friend," said the Quaker, "thine own rags
might teach thee compassion for other people's nakedness."

"Rags !' said Peter, taking Joshua's words literally.

"Does ony wise body put on their best coat when they are traveling, and keeping company with Quakers and such other cattle as the road affords."

"The old lady *died*, I have heard," said Nanty, affecting a moderation which was belied by accents that faltered with passion.

"She might live or die, for what I care," answered Peter the Cruel ; "what business have folk to do to live, that canna live as the law will, and satisfy their just and lawful creditors."

"And you—you that are now yourself trodden down in the very kennel, are you not sorry for what you have done ? Do you not repent having occasioned the poor widow woman's death ?"

"What for should I repent ?" said Peter. "The law was on my side—a decreet of the bailies, followed by poinding and an act of warding, a suspension intended, and the letters found orderly proceeded. I followed the auld rudas through twa courts ; she cost me mair money than her lugs were worth."

"Now, by Heaven !" said Nanty, "I would give a thousand guineas, if I had them, to have you worth my beating ! Had you said you repented, it had been between God and your conscience ; but to hear you boast of your villainy ! Do you think it little to have reduced the aged to famine, and the young to infamy—to have caused the death of one woman, the ruin of another, and to have driven a man to exile and despair ? By Him that made me, I can scarce keep hands off you !"

"Off me ! I defy ye," said Peter. "I take this honest man to witness that, if ye stir the neck of my collar, I will have my action for stouthreif, spulzie, oppression, assault and battery. Here's a bra' din, indeed about an auld wife gaun to the grave, a young limmer to the close-heads and causeway, and a sticket stibbler to the sea instead of the gallows !"

"Now, by my soul," said Nanty, "this is too much ! and since you can feel no otherwise, I will try if I cannot beat some humanity into your head and shoulders."

He drew his hanger as he spoke, and although Joshua, who had in vain endeavored to interrupt the dialogue, to which he foresaw a violent termination, now threw himself between Nanty and the old litigant, he could not prevent the latter from receiving two or three sound slaps over the shoulder with the flat side of the weapon.

Poor Peter Peebles, as inglorious in his extremity as he had been presumptuous in bringing it on, now ran and roared, and bolted out of the apartment and house itself, pursued by Nanty, whose passion became high in proportion to his giving way to its dictates, and by Joshua, who still interfered at every risk, calling upon Nanty to reflect on the age and miserable circumstances of the offender, and upon Poor Peter to stand and place himself under his protection. In front of the house, however, Peter Peebles found a more efficient protector than the worthy Quaker.

CHAPTER XXI

NARRATIVE OF ALAN FAIRFORD

OUR readers may recollect that Fairford had been conducted by Dick Gardener from the house of Fairladies to the inn of old Father Crackenthorp, in order, as he had been informed by the mysterious Father Buonaventure, that he might have the meeting which he desired with Mr. Redgauntlet, to treat with him for the liberty of his friend Darsie. His guide, by the special direction of Mr. Ambrose, had introduced him into the public-house by a back-door, and recommended to the landlord to accommodate him with a private apartment, and to treat him with all civility, but in other respects to keep his eye on him, and even to secure his person, if he saw any reason to suspect him to be a spy. He was not, however, subjected to any direct restraint, but was ushered into an apartment, where he was requested to await the arrival of the gentleman with whom he wished to have an interview, and who, as Crackenthorp assured him with a significant nod, would be certainly there in the course of an hour. In the meanwhile, he recommended to him, with another significant sign, to keep his apartment, "as there were people in the house who were apt to busy themselves about other folks' matters."

Alan Fairford complied with the recommendation, so long as he thought it reasonable ; but when, among a large party riding up to the house, he discerned Redgauntlet, whom he had seen under the name of Mr. Herries of Birrenswork, and whom, by his height and strength, he easily distinguished from the rest, he thought it proper to go down to the front of the house, in hopes that, by more closely reconnoitering the party, he might discover if his friend Darsie was among them.

The reader is aware that, by doing so, he had an opportunity of breaking Darsie's fall from his side-saddle, although his disguise and mask prevented his recognizing his friend. It may be also recollected that, while Nixon hurried Miss Redgauntlet and her brother into the house, their uncle, somewhat chafed at an unexpected and inconvenient interruption, remained himself in parley with Fairford, who had already successively addressed him by the names of Herries and Redgauntlet ; neither of which, any more than the acquaintance of the young lawyer, he seemed at the moment willing to acknowledge, though an air of haughty indifference which he assumed could not conceal his vexation and embarrassment.

"If we must needs be acquainted, sir," he said at last— "for which I am unable to see any necessity, especially as I am now particularly disposed to be private—I must entreat you will tell me at once what you have to say, and permit me to attend to matters of more importance."

"My introduction," said Fairford, "is contained in this letter (delivering that of Maxwell). I am convinced that, under whatever name it may be your pleasure for the present to be known, it is into your hands, and yours only, that it should be delivered."

Redgauntlet turned the letter in his hand, then read the contents, then again looked upon the letter, and sternly observed, "The seal of the letter has been broken. Was this the case, sir, when it was delivered into your hand ?"

Fairford despised a falsehood as much as any man, unless, perhaps, as Tom Turnpenny might have said, "in the way of business." He answered readily and firmly, "The seal was whole when the letter was delivered to me by Mr. Maxwell of Summertrees."

"And did you dare, sir, to break the seal of a letter addressed to me ?" said Redgauntlet, not sorry, perhaps, to pick a quarrel upon a point foreign to the tenor of the epistle.

"I have never broken the seal of any letter committed to my charge," said Alan ; "not from fear of those to whom such letter might be addressed, but from respect to myself."

"That is well worded," said Redgauntlet ; "and yet, young Mr. Counselor, I doubt whether your delicacy prevented your reading my letter, or listening to the contents as read by some other person after it was opened."

"I certainly did hear the contents read over," said Fairford ; "and they were such as to surprise me a good deal."

"Now that," said Redgauntlet, "I hold to be pretty much the same, *in foro conscientiæ*, as if you had broken the seal yourself. I shall hold myself excused from entering upon farther discourse with a messenger so faithless ; and you may thank yourself if your journey has been fruitless."

"Stay, sir," said Fairford ; "and know that I became acquainted with the contents of the paper without my consent —I may even say against my will ; Mr. Buonaventure——"

"Who?" demanded Redgauntlet, in a wild and alarmed manner—"*whom* was it you named?"

"Father Buonaventure," said Alan—"a Catholic priest, as I apprehend, whom I saw at the Miss Arthurets' house, called Fairladies."

"Miss Arthurets! Fairladies! A Catholic priest! Father Buonaventure!" said Redgauntlet, repeating the words of Alan with astonishment. "Is it possible that human rashness can reach such a point of infatuation? Tell me the truth, I conjure you, sir. I have the deepest interest to know whether this is more than an idle legend, picked up from hearsay about the country. You are a lawyer, and know the risk incurred by the Catholic clergy whom the discharge of their duty sends to these bloody shores."

"I am a lawyer, certainly," said Fairford; "but my holding such a respectable condition in life warrants that I am neither an informer nor a spy. Here is sufficient evidence that I have seen Father Buonaventure."

He put Buonaventure's letter into Redgauntlet's hand, and watched his looks closely while he read it. "Double-dyed infatuation!" he muttered, with looks in which sorrow, displeasure, and anxiety were mingled. "'Save me from the indiscretion of my friends,' says the Spaniard; 'I can save myself from the hostility of my enemies.'"

He then read the letter attentively, and for two or three minutes was lost in thought, while some purpose of importance seemed to have gathered and sit brooding upon his countenance. He held up his finger towards his satellite, Cristal Nixon, who replied to his signal with a prompt nod; and with one or two of the attendants approached Fairford in such a manner as to make him apprehensive they were about to lay hold of him.

At this moment a noise was heard from withinside of the house and presently rushed forth Peter Peebles, pursued by Nanty Ewart with his drawn hanger, and the worthy Quaker, who was endeavoring to prevent mischief to others, at some risk of bringing it on himself.

A wilder and yet a more absurd figure can hardly be imagined than that of Poor Peter clattering along as fast as his huge boots would permit him, and resembling nothing so much as a flying scarecrow; while the thin emaciated form of Nanty Ewart, with the hue of death on his cheek, and the fire of vengeance glancing from his eye, formed a ghastly contrast with the ridiculous object of his pursuit.

Redgauntlet threw himself between them. "What ex-

travagant folly is this?" he said. "Put up your weapon,
captain. Is this a time to indulge in drunken brawls, or is
such a miserable object as that a fitting antagonist for a man
of courage?"

"I beg your pardon," said the captain, sheathing his weapon. "I was a little bit out of the way to be sure ; but to
know the provocation, a man must read my heart, and that
I hardly dare to do myself. But the wretch is safe from me.
Heaven has done its own vengeance on us both."

While he spoke in this manner, Peter Peebles, who had at
first crept behind Redgauntlet in bodily fear, began now to
reassume his spirits. Pulling his protector by the sleeve,
"Mr. Herries—Mr. Herries," he whispered, eagerly, "ye
have done me mair than ae gude turn, and if ye will but do
me anither at this dead pinch, I'll forgie the girded keg of
brandy that you and Captain Sir Harry Redgimlet drank out
yon time. Ye shall hae an ample discharge and renuncia-
tion, and though I should see you walking at the Cross of
Edinburgh, or standing at the bar of the Court of Justiciary,
no the very thumbikins themselves should bring to my
memory that ever I saw you in arms yon day."

He accompanied this promise by pulling so hard at Redgauntlet's cloak that he at last turned round. "Idiot!
speak in a word what you want."

"Aweel—aweel! in a word then," said Peter Peebles, "I
have a warrant on me to apprehend that man that stands
there, Alan Fairford by name, and advocate by calling. I
bought it from Justice Maister Foxley's clerk, Maister
Nicholas Faggot, wi' the guinea that you gie me."

"Ha!" said Redgauntlet, "hast thou really such a warrant? Let me see it. Look sharp that no one escape,
Cristal Nixon."

Peter produced a huge, greasy, leathern pocketbook, too
dirty to permit its original color to be visible, filled with
scrolls of notes, memorials to counsel, and Heaven knows
what besides. From amongst this precious mass he culled
forth a paper, and placed it in the hands of Redgauntlet or
Herries, as he continued to call him, saying, at the same
time, "It's a formal and binding warrant, proceeding on my
affidavy made, that the said Alan Fairford, being lawfully
engaged in my service, had slipped the tether and fled over
the Border, and was now lurking there and thereabouts, to
elude and evite the discharge of his bounden duty to me ;
and therefore granting warrant to constables and others to
seek for, take, and apprehend him, that he may be brought

before the honorable Justice Foxley for examination, and, if necessary, for commitment. Now, though a' this be fairly set down as I tell ye, yet where am I to get an officer to execute this warrant in sic a country as this, where sword's and pistols flee out at a word's speaking, and folk care as little for the peace of King George as the peace of Auld King Coul? There's that drunken skipper and that wet Quaker enticed me into the public this morning, and because I wouldna gie them as much brandy as wad have made them blind-drunk, they baith fell on me, and were in way of guiding me very ill."

While Peter went on in this manner, Redgauntlet glanced his eye over the warrant, and immediately saw that it must be a trick passed by Nicholas Faggot to cheat the poor insane wretch out of his solitary guinea. But the Justice had actually subscribed it, as he did whatever his clerk presented to him, and Redgauntlet resolved to use it for his own purposes.

Without making any direct answer, therefore, to Peter Peebles, he walked up gravely to Fairford, who had waited quietly for the termination of a scene in which he was not a little surprised to find his client, Mr. Peebles, a conspicuous actor.

"Mr. Fairford," said Redgauntlet, "there are many reasons which might induce me to comply with the request, or rather the injunctions, of the excellent Father Buonaventure, that I should communicate with you upon the present condition of my ward; whom you know under the name of Darsie Latimer; but no man is better aware than you that the law must be obeyed, even in contradiction to our own feelings; now, this poor man has obtained a warrant for carrying you before a magistrate and I am afraid there is a necessity of your yielding to it, although to the postponement of the business which you may have with me."

"A warrant against me!" said Alan, indignantly, "and at that poor miserable wretch's instance? Why, this is a trick—a mere and most palpable trick!"

"It may be so," replied Redgauntlet, with great equanimity, "doubtless you know best; only the writ appears regular, and with that respect for the law which has been," he said, with hypocritical formality, "a leading feature of my character through life, I cannot dispense with giving my poor aid to the support of a legal warrant. Look at it yourself, and be satisfied it is no trick of mine."

Fairford ran over the affidavit and the warrant, and then

25

exclaimed once more that it was an impudent imposition, and that he would hold those who acted upon such a warrant liable in the highest damages. I guess at your motive, Mr. Redgauntlet," he said, " for acquiescing in so ridiculous a proceeding. But be assured you will find that in this country one act of illegal violence will not be covered or atoned for by practising another. You cannot, as a man of sense and honor, pretend to say you regard this as a legal warrant."

"I am no lawyer, sir," said Redgauntlet ; " and pretend not to know what is or is not law : the warrant is quite formal, and that is enough for me."

" Did ever any one hear," said Fairford, " of an advocate being compelled to return to his task, like a collier or a salter * who has deserted his master ? "

" I see no reason why he should not," said Redgauntlet, drily, " unless on the ground that the services of the lawyer are the most expensive and least useful of the two."

" You cannot mean this in earnest," said Fairford—" you cannot really mean to avail yourself of so poor a contrivance to evade the word pledged by your friend, your ghostly father, in my behalf ? I may have been a fool for trusting it too easily, but think what you must be if you can abuse my confidence in this manner. I entreat you to reflect that this usage releases me from all promises of secrecy or connivance at what I am apt to think are very dangerous practises, and that——"

" Harkye, Mr. Fairford," said Redgauntlet, " I must here interrupt you for your own sake. One word of betraying what you may have seen, or what you may have suspected, and your seclusion is like to have either a very distant or a very brief termination—in either case a most undesirable one. At present, you are sure of being at liberty in a very few days, perhaps much sooner."

" And my friend," said Alan Fairford, " for whose sake I have run myself into this danger, what is to become of him ? Dark and dangerous man ! " he exclaimed, raising his voice, " I will not be again cajoled by deceitful promises——"

" I give you my honor that your friend is well," interrupted Redgauntlet ; " perhaps I may permit you to see him, if you will but submit with patience to a fate which is inevitable."

But Alan Fairford, considering his confidence as having been abused, first by Maxwell and next by the priest, raised his voice, and appealed to all the king's lieges within hear-

* [See Note 25.]

ing, against the violence with which he was threatened. He was instantly seized on by Nixon and two assistants, who, holding down his arms and endeavoring to stop his mouth, were about to hurry him away.

The honest Quaker, who had kept out of Redgauntlet's presence, now came boldly forward.

"Friend," said he, "thou dost more than thou canst answer. Thou knowest me well, and thou art aware that in me thou hast a deeply-injured neighbor, who was dwelling beside thee in the honesty and simplicity of his heart."

"Tush, Jonathan," said Redgauntlet—"talk not to me, man : it is neither the craft of a young lawyer nor the *simplicity* of an old hypocrite can drive me from my purpose."

"By my faith," said the captain, coming forward in his turn, "this is hardly fair, General ; and I doubt," he added, "whether the will of my owners can make me a party to such proceedings. Nay, never fumble with your sword-hilt, but out with it like a man, if you are for a tilting." He unsheathed his hanger, and continued—"I will neither see my comrade Fairford nor the old Quaker abused. D—n all warrants, false or true—curse the justice—confound the constable ! and here stands little Nanty Ewart to make good what he says against gentle and simple, in spite of horseshoe or horseradish either."

The cry of "Down with all warrants !" was popular in the ears of the militia of the inn, and Nanty Ewart was no less so. Fishers, hostlers, seamen, smugglers began to crowd to the spot. Crackenthorp endeavored in vain to mediate. The attendants of Redgauntlet began to handle their firearms ; but their master shouted to them to forbear, and, unsheathing his sword as quick as lightning, he rushed on Ewart in the midst of his bravade, and struck his weapon from his hand with such address and force that it flew three yards from him. Closing with him at the same moment, he gave him a severe fall, and waved his sword over his head, to show he was absolutely at his mercy.

"There you drunken vagabond," he said, "I gave you your life ; you are no bad fellow, if you could keep from brawling among your friends. But we all know Nanty Ewart," he said to the crowd around, with a forgiving laugh, which, joined to the awe his prowess had inspired, entirely confirmed their wavering allegiance.

They shouted, "The Laird forever !" while poor Nanty, rising from the earth, on whose lap he had been stretched so

rudely, went in quest of his hanger, lifted it, wiped it, and
as he returned the weapon to the scabbard, muttered between
his teeth, "It is true they say of him, and the devil will
stand his friend till his hour come; I will cross him no
more."

So saying, he slunk from the crowd, cowed, and disheartened by his defeat.

"For you, Joshua Geddes," said Redgauntlet, approaching the Quaker, who, with lifted hands and eyes, had beheld the scene of violence, "I shall take the liberty to arrest
thee for a breach of the peace altogether unbecoming thy
pretended principles; and I believe it will go hard with thee
both in a Court of Justice and among thine own Society of
Friends, as they call themselves, who will be but indifferently pleased to see the quiet tenor of their hypocrisy insulted by such violent proceedings."

"*I* violent!" said Joshua—"*I* do aught unbecoming the
principles of the Friends! I defy thee, man, and I charge
thee, as a Christian, to forbear vexing my soul with such
charges: it is grievous enough to me to have seen violences
which I was unable to prevent."

"Oh, Joshua—Joshua!" said Redgauntlet, with a sardonic
smile, "thou light of the faithful in the town of Dumfries
and the places adjacent, wilt thou thus fall away from the
truth? Hast thou not, before us all, attempted to rescue a
man from the warrant of law? Didst thou not encourage
that drunken fellow to draw his weapon; and didst thou
not thyself flourish thy cudgel in the cause? Think'st thou
that the oaths of the injured Peter Peebles and the conscientious Cristal Nixon, besides those of such gentlemen as look
on this strange scene, who not only put on swearing as a
garment, but to whom, in custom-house matters, oaths are
literally meat and drink—dost thou not think, I say, that
these men's oaths will go farther than thy "Yea" and
"Nay" in this matter?"

"I will swear to anything," said Peter: "all is fair when
it comes to an oath *ad litem.*"

"You do me foul wrong," said the Quaker, undismayed
by the general laugh. "I encouraged no drawing of weapons, though I attempted to move an unjust man by some
use of argument; I brandished no cudgel, although it may
be that the ancient Adam struggled within me, and caused
my hand to grasp mine oaken staff firmer than usual, when
I saw innocence borne down with violence. But why talk I
what is true and just to thee, who hast been a man of vio-

lence from thy youth upwards ? Let me rather speak to thee
such language as thou canst comprehend. Deliver these
young men up to me," he said, when he had led Redgauntlet
a little apart from the crowd, "and I will not only free thee
from the heavy charge of damages which thou hast incurred
by thine outrage upon my property, but I will add ransom
for them and for myself. What would it profit thee to do
the youths wrong, by detaining them in captiviiy ?"

"Mr. Geddes," said Redgauntlet, in a tone more respectful than he had hitherto used to the Quaker, "your language is disinterested, and I respect the fidelity of your
friendship. Perhaps we have mistaken each other's principles and motives ; but if so, we have not at present time for
explanation. Make yourself easy. I hope to raise your
friend Darsie Latimer to a pitch of eminence which you will
witness with pleasure—nay, do not attempt to answer me.
The other young man shall suffer restraint a few days, probably only a few hours ; it is not more than due for his prag-
matical interference in what concerned him not. Do you,
Mr. Geddes, be so prudent as to take your horse and leave
this place, which is growing every moment more unfit for
the abode of a man of peace. You may wait the event in
safety at Mount Sharon."

"Friend," replied Joshua, "I cannot comply with thy
advice : I will remain here, even as thy prisoner, as thou
didst but now threaten, rather than leave the youth, who
hath suffered by and through me and my misfortunes, in his
present state of doubtful safety. Wherefore, I will not
mount my steed Solomon, neither will I turn his head towards Mount Sharon, until I see an end of this matter."

"A prisoner, then, you must be," said Redgauntlet. "I
have no time to dispute the matter farther with you. But
tell me for what you fix your eyes so attentively on yonder
people of mine ?"

"To speak the truth," said the Quaker, "I admire to
behold among them a little wretch of a boy called Benjie, to
whom I think Satan has given the power of transporting
himself wheresoever mischief is going forward, so that it
may be truly said, there is no evil in this land wherein he
hath not a finger, if not a whole hand."

The boy, who saw their eyes fixed on him as they spoke,
seemed embarrassed, and rather desirous of making his
escape ; but at a signal from Redgauntlet he advanced,
assuming the sheepish look and rustic manner with which
the jackanapes covered much acuteness and roguery.

"How long have you been with the party, sirrah," said Redgauntlet.

"Since the raid on the stake-nets," said Benjie, with his finger in his mouth.

"And what made you follow us?"

"I dauredna stay at hame for the constables," replied the boy.

"And what have you been doing all this time?"

"Doing, sir! I dinna ken what ye ca' doing—I have been doing naething," said Benjie; then seeing something in Redgauntlet's eye which was not to be trifled with, he added, "Naething but waiting on Maister Cristal Nixon."

"Hum!—ay—indeed?" muttered Redgauntlet. "Must Master Nixon bring his own retinue into the field? This must be seen to."

He was about to pursue his inquiry, when Nixon himself came to him with looks of anxious haste. "The Father is come," he whispered, "and the gentlemen are getting together in the largest room of the house, and they desire to see you. Yonder is your nephew, too, making a noise like a man in Bedlam."

"I will look to it all instantly," said Redgauntlet. "Is the Father lodged as I directed?"

Cristal nodded.

"Now, then, for the final trial," said Redgauntlet. He folded his hands, looked upwards, crossed himself, and after this act of devotion (almost the first which any one had observed him make use of), he commanded Nixon to keep good watch, have his horses and men ready for every emergence, look after the safe custody of the prisoners, but treat them at the same time well and civilly. And these orders given, he darted hastily into the house.

CHAPTER XXII

NARRATIVE CONTINUED

REDGAUNTLET'S first course was to the chamber of his nephew. He unlocked the door, entered the apartment, and asked what he wanted, that he made so much noise.

"I want my liberty," said Darsie, who had wrought himself up to a pitch of passion in which his uncle's wrath had lost its terrors—"I desire my liberty, and to be assured of the safety of my beloved friend, Alan Fairford, whose voice I heard but now."

"Your liberty shall be your own within half an hour from this period ; your friend shall be also set at freedom in due time, and you yourself be permitted to have access to his place of confinement."

"This does not satisfy me," said Darsie : "I must see my friend instantly ; he is here, and he is here endangered on my account only. I have heard violent exclamations—the clash of swords. You will gain no point with me unless I have ocular demonstration of his safety."

"Arthur—dearest nephew," answered Redgauntlet, "drive me not mad ! Thine own fate—that of thy house— that of thousands—that of Britain herself, are at this moment in the scales ; and you are only occupied about the safety of a poor insignificant pettifogger ! "

"He has sustained injury at your hands, then ?" said Darsie, fiercely. "I know he has ; but if so, not even relationship shall protect you."

"Peace, ungrateful and obstinate fool ! " said Redgauntlet. "Yet stay. Will you be satisfied if you see this Alan Fairford, the bundle of bombazine—this precious friend of yours —well and sound ? Will you, I say, be satisfied with seeing him in perfect safety, without attempting to speak to or converse with him ?" Darsie signfied his assent. "Take hold of my arm, then," said Redgauntlet ; " and do you, niece Lilias, take the other ; and beware, Sir Arthur, how you bear yourself."

Darsie was compelled to acquiesce, sufficiently aware that his uncle would permit him no interview with a friend whose influence would certainly be used against his present earnest wishes, and in some measure contented with the assurance of Fairford's personal safety.

Redgauntlet led them through one or two passages (for the house, as we have before said, was very irregular, and built at different times), until they entered an apartment where a man with shouldered carabine kept watch at the door, but readily turned the key for their reception. In this room they found Alan Fairford and the Quaker, apparently in deep conversation with each other. They looked up as Redgauntlet and his party entered; and Alan pulled off his hat and made a profound reverence, which the young lady, who recognized him—though, masked as she was, he could not know her—returned with some embarrassment, arising probably from the recollection of the bold step she had taken in visiting him.

Darsie longed to speak, but dared not. His uncle only said, "Gentlemen, I know you are as anxious on Mr. Darsie Latimer's account as he is upon yours. I am commissioned by him to inform you that he is as well as you are. I trust you will all meet soon. Meantime, although I cannot suffer you to be at large, you shall be as well treated as is possible under your temporary confinement."

He passed on, without pausing to hear the answers which the lawyer and the Quaker were hastening to prefer; and only waving his hand by way of adieu, made his exit with the real and the seeming lady whom he had under his charge through a door at the upper end of the apartment, which was fastened and guarded like that by which they entered.

Redgauntlet next led the way into a very small room, adjoining which, but divided by a partition, was one of apparently larger dimensions; for they heard the trampling of the heavy boots of the period, as if several persons were walking to and fro, and conversing in low and anxious whispers.

"Here," said Redgauntlet to his nephew, as he disencumbered him from the riding-skirt and the mask, "I restore you to yourself, and trust you will lay aside all effeminate thoughts with this feminine dress. Do not blush at having worn a disguise to which kings and heroes have been reduced. It is when female craft or female cowardice find their way into a manly bosom that he who entertains these sentiments should take eternal shame to himself for thus having resembled womankind. Follow me while Lilias remains here. I will introduce you to those whom I hope to see associated with you in the most glorious cause that hand ever drew sword in."

Darsie paused. " Uncle," he said, " my person is in your hands ; but remember, my will is my own. I will not be hurried into any resolutiou of importance. Remember what I have already said—what I now repeat—that I will take no step of importance but upon conviction."

" But canst thou be convinced, thou foolish boy, without hearing and understanding the grounds on which we act ? "

So saying, he took Darsie by the arm and walked with him to the next room—a large apartment, partly filled with miscellaneous articles of commerce, chiefly connected with contraband trade ; where, among bales and barrels, sat or walked to and fro several gentlemen, whose manners and looks seemed superior to the plain riding-dresses which they wore.

There was a grave and stern anxiety upon their counte-nances, when, on Redgauntlet's entrance, they drew from their separate coteries into one group around him, and saluted him with a formality which had something in it of omi-nous melancholy. As Darsie looked around the circle, he thought he could discern in it few traces of that adventurous hope which urges men upon desperate enterprises ; and began to believe that the conspiracy would dissolve of itself, without the necessity of his placing himself in direct opposition to so violent a character as his uncle, and incurring the hazard with which such opposition must needs be attended.

Mr. Redgauntlet, however, did not, or would not, see any such marks of depression of spirit amongst his coadjutors, but met them with cheerful countenance and a warm greet-ing of welcome. " Happy to meet you here, my lord," he said, bowing low to a slender young man. " I trust you come with the pledges of your noble father of B—— and all that royal house. Sir Richard, what news in the west ? I am told you had two hundred men on foot to have joined when the fatal retreat from Derby was commenced. When the White Standard is again displayed, it shall not be turned back so easily, either by the force of its enemies or the false-hood of his friends. Doctor Grumball, I bow to the repre-sentative of Oxford, the mother of learning and loyalty. Pengwinion, you Cornish chough, has this good wind blown you north ? Ah, my brave Cambro-Britons, when was Wales last in the race of honor ? "

Such and such-like compliments he dealt around, which were in general answered by silent bows ; but when he sal-uted one of his own countrymen by the name of MacKeller, and greeted Maxwell of Summertrees by that of Pate-in-

Peril, the latter replied, "that if Pate were not a fool, he would be Pate-in-Safety'; and the former, a thin old gentleman, in tarnished embroidery, said bluntly, "Ay, troth, Redgauntlet, I am here just like yourself : I have little to lose ; they that took my land the last time may take my life this, and that is all I care about it."

The English gentlemen, who were still in possession of their paternal estates, looked doubtfully on each other, and there was something whispered among them of the fox which had lost his tail.

Redgauntlet hastened to address them. "I think, my lords and gentlemen," he said, "that I can account for something like sadness which has crept upon an assembly gathered together for so noble a purpose. Our numbers seem, when thus assembled, too small and inconsiderable to shake the firm-seated usurpation of a half-century. But do not count us by what we are in thew and muscle, but by what our summons can do among our countrymen. In this small party are those who have power to raise battalions, and those who have wealth to pay them. And do not believe our friends who are absent are cold or indifferent to the cause. Let us once light the signal, and it will be hailed by all who retain love for the Stuart, and by all—a more numerous body—who hate the Elector. Here I have letters from——"

Sir Richard Glendale interrupted the speaker. "We all confide, Redgauntlet, in your valor and skill, we admire your perseverance, and probably nothing short of your strenuous exertions, and the emulation awakened by your noble and disinterested conduct, could have brought so many of us, the scattered remnant of a disheartened party, to meet together once again in solemn consultation—for I take it, gentlemen," he said, looking round, "this is only a consultation."

"Nothing more," said the young lord.

"Nothing more," said Doctor Grumball, shaking his large academical peruke.

And "Only a consultation," was echoed by the others.

Redgauntlet bit his lip. "I had hopes," he said, "that the discourses I have held with most of you, from time to time, had ripened into more maturity than your words imply, and that we were here to execute as well as to deliberate. And for this we stand prepared : I can raise five hundred men with my whistle."

"Five hundred men !" said one of the Welsh squires.

"Cot bless us! and, pray you, what cood could five hundred men do?"

"All that the priming does for the cannon, Mr. Meredith," answered Redgauntlet: "it will enable us to seize Carlisle, and you know what our friends have engaged for in that case."

"Yes, but," said the young nobleman, "you must not hurry us on too fast, Mr. Redgauntlet; we are all, I believe, as sincere and true-hearted in this business as you are, but we will not be driven forward blindfold. We owe caution to ourselves and our families, as well as to those whom we are empowered to represent on this occasion."

"Who hurries you, my lord? Who is it that would drive this meeting forward blindfold? I do not understand your lordship," said Redgauntlet.

"Nay," said Sir Richard Glendale, "at least do not let us fall under our old reproach of disagreeing among ourselves. What my lord means, Redgauntlet, is, that we have this morning heard it is uncertain whether you could even bring that body of men whom you count upon; your countryman, Mr. MacKellar, seemed, just before you came in, to doubt whether your people would rise in any force, unless you could produce the authority of your nephew."

"I might ask," said Redgauntlet, "what right MacKellar, or any one, has to doubt my being able to accomwhat I stand pledged for? But our hopes consist in our unity. Here stands my nephew. Gentlemen, I present to you my kinsman, Sir Arthur Darsie Redgauntlet of that Ilk."

"Gentlemen," said Darsie, with a throbbing bosom, for he felt the crisis a very painful one, "allow me to say that I suspend expressing my sentiments on the important subject under discussion until I have heard those of the present meeting."

"Proceed in your deliberations, gentlemen," said Redgauntlet; "I will show my nephew such reasons for acquiescing in the result as will entirely remove any scruples which may hang around his mind."

Dr. Grumball now coughed, "shook his ambrosial curls," and addressed the assembly.

"The principles of Oxford," he said, "are well understood, since she was the last to resign herself to the Arch-Usurper; since she was condemned, by her sovereign authority, the blasphemous, atheistical, and anarchical tenets of Locke and other deluders of the public mind. Oxford will

give men, money and countenance to the cause of the rightful monarch. But we have been often deluded by foreign
powers, who have availed themselves of our zeal to stir up
civil dissensions in Britain, not for the advantage of our
blessed though banished monarch, but to engender disturbances by which they might profit, while we, their tools,
are sure to be ruined. Oxford, therefore, will not rise unless our sovereign comes in person to claim our allegiance,
in which case, God forbid we should refuse him our best
obedience."

"It is a very good advice," said Mr. Meredith.

"In troth," said Sir Richard Glendale, "it is the very
keystone of our enterprise, and the only condition upon
which I myself and others could ever have dreamt of taking
up arms. No insurrection which has not Charles Edward
himself at its head will ever last longer than till a single
foot-company of redcoats march to disperse it."

"This is my own opinion, and that of all my family," said
the young nobleman already mentioned ; "and I own I am
somewhat surprised at being summoned to attend a dangerous rendezvous such as this, before something certain could
have been stated to us on this most important preliminary
point."

"Pardon me, my lord," said Redgauntlet ; "I have not
been so unjust either to myself or my friends—I had no
means of communicating to our distant confederates, without the greatest risk of discovery, what is known to some of
my honorable friends. As courageous and as resolved as
when, twenty years since, he threw himself into the wilds of
Moidart, Charles Edward has instantly complied with the
wishes of his faithful subjects. Charles Edward is in this
country—Charles Edward is in this house ! Charles Edward
waits but your present decision, to receive the homage of
those who have ever called themselves his loyal liegemen.
He that would now turn his coat and change his note must
do so under the eye of his sovereign."

There was a deep pause. Those among the conspirators
whom mere habit or a desire of preserving consistency had
engaged in the affair now saw with terror their retreat cut
off ; and others, who at a distance had regarded the proposed
enterprise as hopeful, trembled when the moment of actually
embarking in it was thus unexpectedly and almost inevitably
precipitated.

"How now, my lords and gentlemen !" said Redgauntlet.
"Is it delight and rapture that keep you thus silent ?

Where are the eager welcomes that should be paid your rightful king, who a second time confides his person to the care
of his subjects, undeterred by the hairbreadth escapes and
severe privations of his former expeditions? I hope there
is no gentleman here that is not ready to redeem, in his
prince's presence, the pledge of fidelity which he offered in
his absence?"

"I, at least," said the young nobleman, resolutely, and
laying his hand on his sword, "will not be that coward. If
Charles is come to these shores, I will be the first to give
him welcome, and to devote my life and fortune to his
service."

"Before Cot," said Mr. Meredith, "I do not see that Mr.
Redcantlet has left us anything else to do."

"Stay," said Summertrees, "there is yet one other question. Has he brought any of those Irish rapparees with him,
who broke the neck of our last glorious affair?"

"Not a man of them," said Redgauntlet.

"I trust," said Dr. Grumball, "that there are no Catholic
priests in his company? I would not intrude on the private
conscience of my sovereign, but, as an unworthy son of
the Church of England, it is my duty to consider her security."

"Not a Popish dog or cat is there, to bark or mew about
his Majesty," said Redgauntlet. "Old Shaftesbury himself
could not wish a prince's person more secure from Popery—
which may not be the worst religion in the world, notwithstanding. Any more doubts, gentlemen? can no more plausible reasons be discovered for postponing the payment of our
duty, and discharge of our oaths and engagements? Meantime your king waits your declaration—by my faith, he hath
but a frozen reception!"

"Redgauntlet," said Sir Richard Glendale, calmly, "your
reproaches shall not goad me into anything of which my reason disapproves. That I respect my engagement as much
as you do is evident, since I am here, ready to support it
with the best blood in my veins. But has the King really
come hither entirely unattended?"

"He has no man with him but young ——, as aide-de-
camp, and a single valet-de-chambre."

"No *man*—but, Redgauntlet, as you are a gentleman,
has he no *woman* with him?"

Redgauntlet cast his eyes on the ground and replied, "I
am sorry to say—he has."

The company looked at each other, and remained silent

for a moment. At length Sir Richard proceeded. "I need
not repeat to you, Mr. Redgauntlet, what is the well-
grounded opinion of his Majesty's friends concerning that
most unhappy connection : there is but one sense and feeling amongst us upon the subject. I must conclude that our
humble remonstrances were communicated by you, sir, to
the King ? "

"In the same strong terms in which they were couched,"
replied Redgauntlet. "I love his Majesty's cause more than
I fear his displeasure."

"But, apparently, our humble expostulation has produced
no effect. This lady, who has crept into his bosom, has a
sister in the Elector of Hanover's court, and yet we are well
assured that every point of our most private communication
is placed in her keeping."

"*Varium et mutabile semper femina,*" said Dr. Grumball.

"She puts his secrets into her work-bag," said Maxwell,
"and out they fly whenever she opens it. If I must hang,
I would wish it to be in somewhat a better rope than the
string of a lady's hussy."

"Are you, too, turning dastard, Maxwell ? " said Redgauntlet, in a whisper.

"Not I," said Maxwell ; "let us fight for it, and let them
win and wear us ; but to be betrayed by a brimstone like
that——"

"Be temperate, gentlemen," said Redgauntlet ; "the
foible of which you complain so heavily has always been that
of king and heroes, which I feel strongly confident the King
will surmount, upon the humble entreaty of his best servants, and when he sees them ready to peril their all in his
cause, upon the slight condition of his resigning the society
of a female favorite, of whom I have seen reason to think
he hath been himself for some time wearied. But let us not
press upon him rashly with our well-meant zeal. He has a
princely will, as becomes his princely birth, and we, gentlemen, who are loyalists, should be the last to take advantage
of circumstances to limit its exercise. I am as much surprised and hurt as you can be to find that he has made her
the companion of this journey, increasing every chance of
treachery and detection. But do not let us insist upon a
sacrifice so humiliating, while he has scarce placed a foot
upon the beach of his kingdom. Let us act generously by
our sovereign ; and when we have shown what we will do for
him, we shall be able, with better face, to state what it is
we expect him to concede."

"Indeed, I think it is but a pity," said MacKellar, "when so many pretty gentlemen are got together, that they should part without the flash of a sword among them."

"I should be of that gentleman's opinion," said Lord——, "had I nothing to lose but my life ; but I frankly own that the conditions on which our family agreed to join having been, in this instance, left unfulfilled, I will not peril the whole fortunes of our house on the doubtful fidelity of an artful woman."

"I am sorry to see your lordship," said Redgauntlet, "take a course which is more likely to secure your house's wealth than to augment its honors."

"How am I to understand your language, sir ?" said the young nobleman, haughtily.

"Nay, gentlemen," said Dr. Grumball, interposing, "do not let friends quarrel ; we are all zealous for the cause, but truly, although I know the license claimed by the great in such matters, and can, I hope, make due allowance, there is I may say, an indecorum in a prince who comes to claim the allegiance of the Church of England arriving on such an errand with such a companion—*si non caste, caute tamen.*"

"I wonder how the Church of England came to be so heartily attached to his merry old namesake," said Redgauntlet.

Sir Richard Glendale then took up the question, as one whose authority and experience gave him right to speak with much weight.

"We have no leisure for hesitation," he said : "it is full time that we decide what course we are to hold. I feel as much as you, Mr. Redgauntlet, the delicacy of capitulating with our sovereign in his present condition. But I must also think of the total ruin of the cause, the confiscation and bloodshed which will take place among his adherents, and all through the infatuation with which he adheres to a woman who is the pensionary of the present minister, as she was for years Sir Robert Walpole's. Let his Majesty send her back to the continent, and the sword on which I now lay my hand shall instantly be unsheathed, and, I trust, many hundred others at the same moment."

The other persons present testified their unanimous acquiescence in what Sir Richard Glendale had said.

"I see you have taken your resolutions, gentlemen," said Redgauntlet—"unwisely, I think, because I believe that, by softer and more generous proceedings, you would have been more likely to carry a point which I think as desirable as you do. But what is to be done if Charles should refuse, with the inflexibility of his grandfather, to comply with this request of yours? Do you mean to abandon him to his fate?"

"God forbid!" said Sir Richard, hastily; and God forgive you, Mr. Redgauntlet, for breathing such a thought. No; I for one will, with all duty and humility, see him safe back to his vessel, and defend him with my life against whoever shall assail him. But when I have seen his sails spread, my next act will be to secure, if I can, my own safety by retiring to my house; or, if I find our engagement, as is too probable, has taken wind, by surrendering myself to the next justice of peace, and giving security that hereafter I shall live quiet and submit to the ruling powers.'

Again the rest of the persons present intimated their agreement in opinion with the speaker.

"Well, gentlemen," said Redgauntlet, "it is not for me to oppose the opinion of every one; and I must do you the justice to say, that the King has, in the present instance, neglected a condition of your agreement which was laid before him in very distinct terms. The question now is, who is to acquaint him with the result of this conference? for I presume you would not wait on him in a body to make the proposal that he should dismiss a person from his family as the price of your allegiance."

"I think, Mr. Redgauntlet should make the explanation," said Lord ——. "As he has, doubtless, done justice to our remonstrances by communicating them to the King, no one can, with such propriety and force, state the natural and inevitable consequence of their being neglected."

"Now, I think," said Redgauntlet, "that those who make the objection should state it; for I am confident the King will hardly believe, on less authority than that of the heir of the loyal house of B——, that he is the first to seek an evasion of his pledge to join him."

"An evasion, sir!" repeated Lord ——, fiercely. "I have borne too much from you already, and this I will not endure. Favor me with your company to the downs yonder."

Redgauntlet laughed scornfully, and was about to follow the fiery young man, when Sir Richard again interposed. "Are we to exhibit," he said, "the last symptoms of the dissolution of our party, by turning our swords against each other? Be patient, Lord ——; in such conferences as this, much must pass unquestioned which might brook challenge elsewhere, There is a privilege of party as of parliament;

men cannot, in emergency, stand upon picking phrases. Gentlemen, if you will extend your confidence in me so far, I will wait upon his Majesty, and I hope my Lord —— and Mr. Redgauntlet will accompany me. I trust the explanation of this unpleasant matter will prove entirely satisfactory, and that we shall find ourselves at liberty to render our homage to our sovereign without reserve, when I for one will be the first to peril all in his just quarrel."

Redgauntlet at once stepped forward. "My Lord," he said, "if my zeal made me say anything in the slightest degree offensive, I wish it unsaid, and ask your pardon. A gentleman can do no more."

"I could not have asked Mr. Redgauntlet to do so much," said the young nobleman, willingly accepting the hand which Redgauntlet offered. "I know no man living from whom I could take so much reproof without a sense of degradation as from himself."

"Let me then hope, my lord, that you will go with Sir Richard and me to the presence. Your warm blood will heat our zeal ; our colder resolves will temper yours."

The young lord smiled and shook his head. "Alas ! Mr. Redgauntlet," he said, "I am ashamed to say that in zeal you surpass us all. But I will not refuse this mission, provided you will permit Sir Arthur, your nephew, also to accompany us."

"My nephew !" said Redgauntlet, and seemed to hesitate ; then added, "Most certainly. I trust," he said, looking at Darsie, "he will bring to his prince's presence such sentiments as fit the occasion."

It seemed, however, to Darsie that his uncle would rather have left him behind, had he not feared that he might in that case have been influenced by, or might perhaps himself influence, the unresolved confederates with whom he must have associated during his absence.

"I will go," said Redgauntlet, "and request admission." In a moment after he returned, and, without speaking, motioned for the young nobleman to advance. He did so, followed by Sir Richard Glendale and Darsie, Redgauntlet himself bringing up in the rear. A short passage and a few steps brought them to the door of the temporary presence-chamber, in which the Royal Wanderer was to receive their homage. It was the upper loft of one of those cottages which made additions to the old inn, poorly furnished, dusty, and in disorder ; for, rash as the enterprise might be considered, they had been still careful not to draw the

26

attention of strangers by any particular attentions to the personal accommodation of the Prince. He was seated when the deputies, as they might be termed, of his remaining adherents entered ; and as he rose and came forward and bowed in acceptance of their salutation, it was with a dignified courtesy which at once supplied whatever was deficient in external pomp, and converted the wretched garret into a saloon worthy of the occasion.

It is needless to add, that he was the same personage already introduced in the character of Father Buonaventure, by which name he was distinguished at Fairladies. His dress was not different from what he then wore, excepting that he had a loose riding-coat of camlet, under which he carried an efficient cut-and-thrust sword, instead of his walking rapier, and also a pair of pistols.

Redgauntlet presented to him successively the young Lord —— and his kinsman, Sir Arthur Darsie Redgauntlet, who trembled as, bowing and kissing his hand, he found himself surprised into what might be construed an act of high treason, which yet he saw no safe means to avoid.

Sir Richard Glendale seemed personally known to Charles Edward, who received him with a mixture of dignity and affection, and seemed to sympathize with the tears which rushed into that gentleman's eyes as he bid his Majesty welcome to his native kingdom.

" Yes, my good Sir Richard," said the unfortunate prince, in a tone melancholy yet resolved, " Charles Edward is with his faithful friends once more—not, perhaps, with his former gay hopes which undervalued danger, but with the same determined contempt of the worst which can befall him in claiming his own rights and those of his country."

" I rejoice, sire—and yet, alas ! I must also grieve—to see you once more on the British shores," said Sir Richard Glendale, and stopped short, a tumult of contradictory feelings preventing his farther utterance.

" It is the call of my faithful and suffering people which alone could have induced me to take once more the sword in my hand. For my own part, Sir Richard, when I have reflected how many of my loyal and devoted friends perished by the sword and by proscription, or died indigent and neglected in a foreign land, I have often sworn that no view to my personal aggrandizement should again induce me to agitate a title which has cost my followers so dear. But since so many men of worth and honor conceive the cause of England and Scotland to be linked with that of Charles

Stuart, I must follow their brave example, and, laying aside all other considerations, once more stand forward as their deliverer. I am, however, come hither upon your invitation ; and as you are so completely acquainted with circumstances to which my absence must necessarily have rendered me a stranger, I must be a mere tool in the hands of my friends. I know well I never can refer myself implicitly to more loyal hearts or wiser heads than Herries Redgauntlet and Sir Richard Glendale. Give me your advice, then, how we are to proceed, and decide upon the fate of Charles Edward."

Redgauntlet looked at Sir Richard, as if to say, " Can you press an additional or unpleasant condition at a moment like this ?" And the other shook his head and looked down, as if his resolution was unaltered, and yet as feeling all the delicacy of the situation.

There was a silence, which was broken by the unfortunate representative of an unhappy dynasty with some appearance of irritation. " This is strange, gentlemen," he said : " you have sent for me from the bosom of my family to head an adventure of doubt and danger, and when I come, your own minds seem to be still irresolute. I had not expected this on the part of two such men."

" For me, sire," said Redgauntlet, " the steel of my sword is not truer than the temper of my mind."

" My Lord ——'s and mine are equally so," said Sir Richard ; " but you had in charge, Mr. Redgauntlet, to convey our request to his Majesty, coupled with certain conditions."

" And I discharged my duty to his Majesty and to you," said Redgauntlet.

" I looked at no condition, gentlemen," said their king, with dignity, " save that which called me here to assert my rights in person. *That* I have fulfilled at no common risk. Here I stand to keep my word, and I expect of you to be true to yours."

" There was, or should have been, something more than that in our proposal, please your Majesty," said Sir Richard. " There was a condition annexed to it."

" I saw it not," said Charles, interrupting him. " Out of tenderness towards the noble hearts of whom I think so highly, I would neither see nor read anything which could lessen them in my love and my esteem. Conditions can have no part betwixt prince and subject."

" Sire," said Redgauntlet, kneeling on one knee, " I see from Sir Richard's countenance he deems it my fault that your Majesty seems ignorant of what your subjects desired that I should communicate to your Majesty. For Heaven's sake ! for the sake of all my past services and sufferings, leave not such a stain upon my honor ! The Note Number D., of which this is a copy, referred to the painful subject to which Sir Richard again directs your attention."

" You press upon me, gentlemen," said the Prince, coloring highly, " recollections which, as I hold them most alien to your character, I would willingly have banished from my memory. I did not suppose that my loyal subjects would think so poorly of me as to use my depressed circumstances as a reason for forcing themselves into my domestic privacies, and stipulating arrangements with their king regarding matters in which the meanest hinds claim the privilege of thinking for themselves. In affairs of state and public policy, I will ever be guided, as becomes a prince, by the advice of my wisest counselors ; in those which regard my private affections and my domestic arrangements I claim the same freedom of will which I allow to all my subjects, and without which a crown were less worth wearing than a beggar's bonnet."

" May it please your Majesty," said Sir Richard Glendale, "I see it must be my lot to speak unwilling truths, but, believe me, I do so with as much profound respect as deep regret. It is true we have called you to head a mighty undertaking, and that your Majesty, preferring honor to safety, and the love of your country to your own ease, has condescended to become our leader. But we also pointed out as a necessary and indispensable preparatory step to the achievement of our purpose—and, I must say, as a positive condition of our engaging in it—that an individual, supposed—I presume not to guess how truly—to have your Majesty's more intimate confidence, and believed—I will not say on absolute proof, but upon the most pregnant suspicion— to be capable of betraying that confidence to the Elector of Hanover, should be removed from your royal household and society."

" This is too insolent, Sir Richard !" said Charles Edward. " Have you inveigled me into your power to bait me in this unseemly manner ? And you, Redgauntlet, why did you suffer matters to come to such a point as this without making me more distinctly aware what insults were to be practised on me ?"

" My gracious prince," said Redgauntlet, " I am so far to blame in this, that I did not think so slight an impediment as that of a woman's society could have really interrupted an undertaking of this magnitude. I am a plain man, sire, and speak but bluntly—I could not have dreamed but what, within the first five minutes of this interview, either Sir Richard and his friends would have ceased to insist upon a condition so ungrateful to your Majesty, or that your Majesty would have sacrificed this unhappy attachment to the sound advice, or even to the over-anxious suspicions, of so many faithful subjects. I saw no entanglement in such a difficulty which on either side might not have been broken through like a cobweb."

"You were mistaken, sir," said Charles Edward—"entirely mistaken, as much so as you are at this moment, when you think in your heart my refusal to comply with this insolent proposition is dictated by a childish and romantic passion for an individual. I tell you, sir, I could part with that person to-morrow without an instant's regret—that I have had thoughts of dismissing her from my court, for reasons known to myself ; but that I will never betray my rights as a sovereign and a man by taking this step to secure the favor of any one, or to purchase that allegiance which, if you owe it to me at all, is due to me as my birthright."

"I am sorry for this," said Redgauntlet ; "I hope both your Majesty and Sir Richard will reconsider your resolutions, or forbear this discussion in a conjuncture so pressing. I trust your Majesty will recollect that you are on hostile grounds ; that our preparations cannot have so far escaped notice as to permit us now with safety to retreat from our purpose ; insomuch, that it is with the deepest anxiety of heart I foresee even danger to your own royal person, unless you can generously give your subjects the satisfaction which Sir Richard seems to think they are obstinate in demanding."

"And deep indeed your anxiety ought to be," said the Prince. "Is it in these circumstances of personal danger in which you expect to overcome a resolution which is founded on a sense of what is due to me as a man or a prince ? If the ax and scaffold were ready before the windows of Whitehall, I would rather tread the same path with my great-grandfather than concede the slightest point in which my honor is concerned."

He spoke these words with a determined accent, and looked around him on the company, all of whom (excepting Darsie, who saw, he thought, a fair period to a most perilous enterprise) seemed in deep anxiety and confusion. At length Sir Richard spoke in a solemn and melancholy tone.

"If the safety," he said, "of poor Richard Glendale were

alone concerned in this matter, I have never valued my life enough to weigh it against the slightest point of your Majesty's service. Bnt I am only a messenger—a commissioner, who must execute my trust, and upon whom a thousand voices will cry ' Curse and woe ' if I do it not with fidelity. All of your adherents, even Redgauntlet himself, see certain ruin to this enterprise, the greatest danger to your Majesty's person, the utter destruction of all your party and friends, if they insist not on the point which, unfortunately, your Majesty is so unwilling to concede. I speak it with a heart full of anguish, with a tongue unable to utter my emotions ; but it must be spoken—the fatal truth that, if your royal goodness cannot yield to us a boon which we hold necessary to our security and your own, your Majesty with one word disarms ten thousand men, ready to draw their swords in your behalf ; or, to speak yet more plainly, you annihilate even the semblance of a royal party in Great Britain."

"And why do you not add," said the Prince, scornfully, " that the men who have been ready to assume arms in my behalf will atone for their treason to the Elector by delivering me up to the fate for which so many proclamations have destined me ? Carry my head to St. James's, gentlemen ; you will do a more acceptable and more honorable action than, having inaveigled me into a situation which places me so completely in your power, to dishonor yourselves by propositions which dishonor me."

"My God, sire !" exclaimed Sir Richard, clasping his hands together in impatience, " of what great and inexpiable crime can your Majesty's ancestors have been guilty, that they have been punished by the infliction of judicial blindness on their whole generation ! Come, my Lord ——, we must to our friends."

" By your leave, Sir Richard," said the young nobleman, " not till we have learned what measures can be taken for his Majesty's personal safety."

" Care not for me, young man," said Charles Edward ; " when I was in the society of Highland robbers and cattle-drovers, I was safer than I now hold myself among the representatives of the best blood in England. Farewell, gentlemen—I will shift for myself."

"This must never be," said Redgauntlet. " Let me, that brought yon to the point of danger, at least provide for your safe retreat."

So saying, he hastily left the apartment, followed by his

nephew. The Wanderer, averting his eyes from Lord ——
and Sir Richard Glendale, threw himself into a seat at the
upper end of the apartment, while they, in much anxiety,
stood together at a distance from him and conversed in
whispers.

CHAPTER XXIII

WHEN Redgauntlet left the room, in haste and discomposure, the first person he met on the stair, and indeed so close by the door of the apartment that Darsie thought he must have been listening there, was his attendant Nixon.

"What the devil do you here?" he said, abruptly and sternly.

"I wait your orders," said Nixon. "I hope all's right?— excuse my zeal."

"All is wrong, sir. Where is the seafaring fellow—Ewart —what do you call him?"

"Nanty Ewart, sir. I will carry your commands," said Nixon.

"I will deliver them myself to him," said Redgauntlet. "Call him hither."

"But should your honor leave the presence?" said Nixon, still lingering.

"'Sdeath, sir, do you prate to me?" said Redgauntlet, bending his brows. "I, sir, transact my own business; you, I am told, act by a ragged deputy."

Without farther answer, Nixon departed, rather disconcerted, as it seemed to Darsie.

"That dog turns insolent and lazy," said Redgauntlet; "but I must bear with him for a while."

A moment after, Nixon returned with Ewart.

"Is this the smuggling fellow?" demanded Redgauntlet. Nixon nodded.

"Is he sober now? he was brawling anon."

"Sober enough for business," said Nixon.

"Well then, hark ye, Ewart—man your boat with your best hands, and have her by the pier; get your other fellows on board the brig; if you have any cargo left, throw it overboard—it shall be all paid, five times over; and be ready for a start to Wales or the Hebrides, or perhaps for Sweden or Norway."

Ewart answered sullenly enough, "Ay—ay, sir."

"Go with him, Nixon," said Redgauntlet, forcing himself

to speak with some appearance of cordiality to the servant with whom he was offended ; " see he does his duty."

Ewart left the house sullenly, followed by Nixon. The sailor was just in that species of drunken humor which made him jealous, passionate, and troublesome, without showing any other disorder than that of irritability. As he walked towards the beach he kept muttering to himself, but in such a tone that his companion lost not a word, " 'Smuggling fellow'—ay, smuggler—and, 'start your cargo into the sea— and be ready to start for the Hebrides, or Sweden '—or the devil, I suppose. Well, and what if I said in answer— ' Rebel—Jacobite—traitor—I'll make you and your d—d confederates walk the plank.' I have seen better men do it —half a score of a morning—when I was across the Line."

" D—d unhandsome terms those Redgauntlet used to you, brother," said Nixon.

" Which do you mean ? " said Ewart, starting, and recollecting himself. " I have been at my old trade of thinking aloud, have I ? "

" No matter," answered Nixon, " none but a friend heard you. You cannot have forgotten how Redgauntlet disarmed you this morning ? "

" Why, I would bear no malice about that, only he is so cursedly high and saucy," said Ewart.

" And then," said Nixon, " I know you for a true-hearted Protestant."

" That I am, by G—," said Ewart. " No, the Spaniards could never get my religion from me."

" And a friend to King George and the Hanover line of succession," said Nixon, still walking and speaking very slow.

" You may swear I am, excepting in the way of business, as Turnpenny says. I like King George, but I can't afford to pay duties."

" You are outlawed, I believe ? " said Nixon.

" Am I ?—faith, I believe I am," said Ewart. " I wish I were 'inlawed ' again with all my heart. But come along, we must get all ready for our peremptory gentleman, I suppose."

" I will teach you a better trick," said Nixon. " There is a bloody pack of rebels yonder."

" Ay, we all know that," said the smuggler ; " but the snowball's melting, I think."

" There is some one yonder, whose head is worth—thirty —thousand—pounds—of sterling money," said Nixon,

pausing between each word, as if to enforce the magnificence of the sum.

" And what of that ? " said Ewart, quickly.

" Only that if, instead of lying by the pier with your men
on their oars, if you will just carry your boat on board just
now, and take no notice of any signal from the shore, by
G—d, Nanty Ewart, I will make a man of you for life ! "

" Oh, ho ! then the Jacobite gentry are not so safe as they
think themselves ? " said Nanty.

" In an hour or two," replied Nixon, " they will be made
safer in Carlisle Castle."

" The devil they will ! " said Ewart ; " and you have been
the informer, I suppose ? "

" Yes ; I have been ill paid for my service among the Redgauntlets—have scarce got dog's wages, and been treated
worse than ever dog was used. I have the old fox and his
cubs in the same trap now, Nanty ; and we'll see how a
certain young lady will look then. You see I am frank with
you, Nanty."

" And I will be as frank with you," said the smuggler.
" You are a d—d old scoundrel—traitor to the man whose
bread you eat ! Me help to betray poor devils, that have
been so often betrayed myself ! Not if they were a hundred
Popes, Devils, and Pretenders. I will back and tell them
their danger ; they are part of cargo, regularly invoiced,
put under my charge by the owners—I'll back——"

" You are not stark mad ? " said Nixon, who now saw he
had miscalculated in supposing Nanty's wild ideas of honor
and fidelity could be shaken even by resentment, or by his
Protestant partialities. " You shall not go back ; it is all a
joke."

" I'll back to Redgauntlet, and see whether it is a joke he
will laugh at."

" My life is lost if you do," said Nixon ; " hear reason."

They were in a clump or cluster of tall furze at the moment
they were speaking, about half-way between the pier and the
house, but not in a direct line, from which Nixon, whose
object it was to gain time, had induced Ewart to diverge insensibly. He now saw the necessity of taking a desperate
resolution. " Hear reason," he said ; and added, as Nanty
still endeavored to pass him, " Or else hear this ! " discharging a pocket-pistol into the unfortunate man's body.

Nanty staggered, but kept his feet. " It has cut my back-
bone asunder," he said : " you have done me the last good
office, and I will not die ungrateful."

As he uttered the last words, he collected his remaining strength, stood firm for an instant, drew his hanger, and fetching a stroke with both hands, cut Cristal Nixon down. The blow, struck with all the energy of a desperate and dying man, exhibited a force to which Ewart's exhausted frame might have seemed inadequate : it cleft the hat which the wretch wore, though secured by a plate of iron within the lining, bit deep into his skull, and there left a fragment of the weapon, which was broke by the fury of the blow.

One of the seamen of the lugger, who strolled up, attracted by the firing of the pistol, though, being a small one, the report was very trifling, found both the unfortunate men stark dead. Alarmed at what he saw, which he conceived to have been the consequence of some unsuccessful engagement betwixt his late commander and a revenue officer (for Nixon chanced not to be personally known to him), the sailor hastened back to the boat, in order to apprise his comrades of Nanty's fate, and to advise them to take off themselves and the vessel.

Meantime, Redgauntlet, having, as we have seen, despatched Nixon for the purpose of securing a retreat for the unfortunate Charles in case of extremity, returned to the apartment where he had left the Wanderer. He now found him alone.

"Sir Richard Glendale," said the unfortunate prince, " with his young friend, has gone to consult their adherents now in the house. Redgauntlet, my friend, I will not blame you for the circumstances in which I find myself, though I am at once placed in danger and rendered contemptible. But you ought to have stated to me more strongly the weight which these gentlemen attached to their insolent proposition. You should have told me that no compromise would have any effect—that they desired, not a prince to govern them, but one, on the contrary, over whom they were to exercise restraint on all occasions, from the highest affairs of the state down to the most intimate and closest concerns of his own privacy, which the most ordinary men desire to keep secret and sacred from interference."

" God knows," said Redgauntlet, in much agitation, " I acted for the best when I pressed your Majesty to come hither : I never thought that your Majesty, at such a crisis, would have scrupled, when a kingdom was in view, to sacrifice an attachment which——"

"Peace, sir !" said Charles ; " it is not for you to estimate my feelings upon such a subject."

Redgauntlet colored high, and bowed profoundly. "At least," he resumed, "I hoped that some middle way might be found, and it shall—and must. Come with me, nephew. We will to these gentlemen, and I am confident I shall bring back heart-stirring tidings."

"I will do much to comply with them, Redgauntlet. I am loth, having again set my foot on British land, to quit it without a blow for my right. But this which they demand of me is a degradation, and compliance is impossible."

Redgauntlet, followed by his nephew, the unwilling spectator of this extraordinary scene, left once more the apartment of the adventurous Wanderer, and was met on the top of the stairs by Joe Crackenthorp. "Where are the other gentlemen?" he said.

"Yonder, in the west barrack," answered Joe; "but, Master Ingoldsby"—that was the name by which Redgauntlet was most generally known in Cumberland—"I wished to say to you that I must put yonder folk together in one room."

"What folk?" said Redgauntlet, impatiently.

"Why, them prisoner stranger folk, as you bid Cristal Nixon look after. Lord love you! this is a large house enow, but we cannot have separate lock-ups for folks, as they have in Newgate or in Bedlam. Yonder's a mad beggar that is to be a great man when he wins a lawsuit, Lord help him! yonder's a Quaker and a lawyer charged with a riot; and, ecod, I must make one key and one lock keep them, for we are chokeful and you have sent off old Nixon, that could have given one some help in this confusion. Besides, they take up every one a room, and call for noughts on earth—excepting the old man, who calls lustily enough, but he has not a penny to pay shot."

"Do as thou wilt with them," said Redgauntlet, who had listened impatiently to his statement; "so thou dost but keep them from getting out and making some alarm in the country, I care not."

"A Quaker and a lawyer!" said Darsie. "This must be Fairford and Geddes. Uncle, I must request of you——"

"Nay, nephew," interrupted Redgauntlet, "this is no time for asking questions. You shall yourself decide upon their fate in the course of an hour; no harm whatever is designed them."

So saying, he hurried towards the place where the Jacobite gentlemen were holding their council, and Darsie followed him, in the hope that the obstacle which had arisen

to the prosecution of their desperate adventure would prove
unsurmountable, and spare him the necessity of a dangerous and violent rupture with his uncle. The discussions
among them were very eager; the more daring part of the
conspirators, who had little but life to lose, being desirous
to proceed at all hazards, while the others, whom a sense of
honor and a hesitation to disavow long-cherished principles
had brought forward, were perhaps not ill satisfied to have
a fair apology for declining an adventure into which they
had entered with more of reluctance than zeal.

Meanwhile, Joe Crackenthorp, availing himself of the
hasty permission obtained from Redgauntlet, proceeded to
assemble in one apartment those whose safe custody had
been thought necessary; and without much considering the
propriety of the matter, he selected for the common place of
confinement the room which Lilias had since her brother's
departure occupied alone. It had a strong lock, and was
double-hinged, which probably led the preference assigned
to it as a place of security.

Into this, Joe, with little ceremony and a good deal of
noise, introduced the Quaker and Fairford; the first des-
canting on the immorality, the other on the illegality, of
his proceedings, and he turning a deaf ear both to the one
and the other. Next he pushed in, almost in headlong
fashion, the unfortunate litigant, who, having made some
resistance at the threshold, had received a violent thrust in
consequence, and came rushing forward, like a ram in the
act of charging, with such impetus as must have carried him
to top of the room, and struck the cocked hat which sat
perched on the top of his tow wig against Miss Redgauntlet's
person, had not the honest Quaker interrupted his career
by seizing him by the collar and bringing him to a stand.
"Friend," said he, with the real good-breeding which so
often subsists independently of ceremonial, "thou art no
company for that young person; she is, thou seest, frightened at our being so suddenly thrust in hither; and although
that be no fault of ours, yet it will become us to behave
civilly towards her. Wherefore, come then with me to this
window, and I will tell thee what it concerns thee to
know."

"And what for should I no speak to the leddy, friend?"
said Peter, who was now about half seas over. "I have
spoke to leddies before now, man. What for should she be
frightened at me? I am nae bogle, I ween. What are ye
pooin' me that gate for? Ye will rive my coat, and I will

have a good action for having myself made *sartum atque tectum* at your expenses."

Notwithstanding this threat, Mr. Geddes, whose muscles were as strong as his judgment was sound and his temper sedate, led Poor Peter, under the sense of a control against which he could not struggle, to the farther corner of the apartment, where, placing him, whether he would or no, in a chair, he sat down beside him, and effectually prevented his annoying the young lady, upon whom he had seemed bent on conferring the delights of his society.

If Peter had immediately recognized his counsel learned in the law, it is probable that not even the benevolent efforts of the Quaker could have kept him in a state of restraint ; but Fairford's back was turned towards his client, whose op-tics, besides being somewhat dazzled with ale and brandy, were speedily engaged in contemplating a half-crown which Joshua held between his finger and his thumb, saying, at the same time, " Friend, thou art indigent and improvident. This will, well employed, procure thee sustentation of na-ture for more than a single day ; and I will bestow it on thee if thou wilt sit here and keep me company ; for neither thou nor I, friend, are fit company for ladies."

" Speak for yourself, friend," said Peter, scornfully ; " I was aye kenn'd to be agreeable to the fair sex ; and when I was in business I served the leddies wi' anither sort of de-corum than Plainstanes, the d—d awkward scoundrel ! It was one of the articles of dittay between us."

" Well, but, friend," said the Quaker, who observed that the young lady still seemed to fear Peter's intrusion, " I wish to hear thee speak about this great lawsuit of thine, which has been matter of such celebrity."

" Celebrity ! Ye may swear that," said Peter, for the string was touched to which his crazy imagination always vibrated. " And I dinna wonder that folk that judge things by their outward grandeur should think me something worth their envying. It's very true that it is grandeur upon earth to hear ane's name thundered out along the long-arched roof of the Outer House—" *Poor* Peter Peebles against Plain-stanes, *et per contra* " ; a' the best lawyers in the house flee-ing like eagles to the prey—some because they are in the cause, and some because they want to be thought engaged, for there are tricks in other trades bye selling muslins ; to see the reporters mending their pens to take down the de-bate ; the Lords themselves pooin' in their chairs, like folk sitting down to a gude dinner, and crying on the clerks for parts and pendicles of the process, who, puir bodies, can do little mair than cry on their closet-keepers to help them. To see a' this," continued Peter, in a tone of sustained rapture, "and to ken that naething will be said or dune amang a' thae grand folk, for maybe the feck of three hours, saving what concerns you and your business. O, man, nae wonder that ye judge this to be earthly glory ! And yet, neighbor, as I was saying, there be unco drawbacks : I whiles think of my bit house, where dinner, and supper, and breakfast used to come without the crying for, just as if fairies had brought it, and the gude bed at e'en, and the needfu' penny in the pouch. And then to see a' ane's warldly substance capering in the air in a pair of weigh-bauks, now up, now down, as the breath of judge or counsel inclines it for pursuer of defender—troth, man, there are times I rue having ever begun the plea wark, though, maybe, when ye consider the renown and credit I have by it, ye will hardly believe what I am saying."

"Indeed, friend," said Joshua, with a sigh, "I am glad thou hast found anything in the legal contention which compensates thee for poverty and hunger ; but I believe, were other human objects of ambition looked upon as closely their advantages would be found as chimerical as those attending protracted litigation."

"But never mind, friend," said Peter, "I'll tell you the exact state of the conjunct processes, and make you sensible that I can bring mysell round with a wet finger, now I have my finger and my thumb on this loup-the-dyke loon, the lad Fairford."

Alan Fairford was in the act of speaking to the masked lady, for Miss Redgauntlet had retained her riding-vizard, endeavoring to assure her, as he perceived her anxiety, of such protection as he could afford, when his own name, pronounced in a loud tone, attracted his attention. He looked round, and, seeing Peter Peebles, as hastily turned to avoid his notice, in which he succeeded, so earnest was Peter upon his colloquy with one of the most respectable auditors whose attention he had ever been able to engage. And by this little motion, momentary as it was, Alan gained an unexpected advantage ; for while he looked round, Miss Lilias, I could never ascertain why, took the moment to adjust her mask, and did it so awkwardly that, when her companion again turned his head, he recognized as much of her features as authorized him to address her as his fair client, and to press his offers of protection and assistance with the boldness of a former acquaintance.

Lilias Redgauntlet withdrew the mask from her crimsoned cheek. " Mr. Fairford," she said, in a voice almost inaudible, " you have the character of a young gentleman of sense and generosity ; but we have already met in one situation which you must think singular, and I must be exposed to misconstruction, at least, for my forwardness, were it not in a cause in which my dearest affections were concerned."

" Any interest in my beloved friend Darsie Latimer," said Fairford, stepping a little back and putting a marked restraint upon his former advances, " gives me a double right to be useful to——" He stopped short.

" To his sister, your goodness would say," answered Lilias.

" His sister, madam ! " replied Alan, in the extremity of astonishment, " Sister, I presume, in affection only ? "

" No, sir ; my dear brother Darsie and I are connected by the bonds of actual relationship, and I am not sorry to be the first to tell this to the friend he most values."

Fairford's first thought was on the violent passion which Darsie had expressed towards the fair unknown. " Good God ! " he exclaimed, " how did he bear the discovery ? "

" With resignation, I hope," said Lilias, smiling. " A more accomplished sister he might easily have come by, but scarcely could have found one who could love him more than I do."

" I meant—I only meant to say," said the young counselor, his presence of mind failing him for an instant—" that is, I meant to ask where Darsie Latimer is at this moment."

" In this very house, and under the guardianship of his uncle, whom I believe you knew as a visitor of your father, under the name of Mr. Herries of Birrenswork."

" Let me hasten to him," said Fairford. " I have sought him through difficulties and dangers ; I must see him instantly."

" You forget you are a prisoner," said the young lady.

" True—true ; but I cannot be long detained : the cause alleged is too ridiculous."

" Alas ! " said Lilias, " our fate—my brother's and mine, at least—must turn on the deliberations perhaps of less than an hour. For you, sir, I believe and apprehend nothing but some restraint : my uncle is neither cruel nor unjust, though few will go farther in the cause which he has adopted."

" Which is that of the Pretend——"

" For God's sake, speak lower ! " said Lilias, approaching her hand as if to stop him. " The word may cost you your life.

You do not know—indeed you do not—the terrors of the situation in which we at present stand, and in which I fear you also are involved by your friendship for my brother."

"I do not indeed know the particulars of our situation," said Fairford ; "but, be the danger what it may, I shall not grudge my share of it for the sake of my friend, or," he added, with more timidity, "of my friend's sister. Let me hope," he said, "my dear Miss Latimer, that my presence may be of some use to you ; and that it may be so, let me entreat a share of your confidence, which I am conscious I have otherwise no right to ask."

He led her, as he spoke, towards the recess of the farther window of the room, and observing to her that, unhappily, he was particularly exposed to interruption from the mad old man whose entrance had alarmed her, he disposed of Darsie Latimer's riding-skirt, which had been left in the apartment, over the back of two chairs, forming thus a sort of screen, behind which he ensconced himself with the maiden of the green mantle ; feeling at the moment that the danger in which he was placed was almost compensated by the intelligence which permitted those feelings towards her to revive which justice to his friend had induced him to stifle in the birth.

The relative situation of adviser and advised, of protector and protected, is so peculiarly suited to the respective condition of man and woman, that great progress towards intimacy is often made in very short space ; for the circumstances call for confidence on the part of the gentleman, and forbid coyness on that of the lady, so that the usual barriers against easy intercourse are at once thrown down.

Under these circumstances, securing themselves as far as possible from observation, conversing in whispers, and seated in a corner, where they were brought into so close contact that their faces nearly touched each other, Fairford heard from Lilias Redgauntlet the history of her family, particularly of her uncle, his views upon her brother, and the agony which she felt, lest at that very moment he might succeed in engaging Darsie in some desperate scheme, fatal to his fortune, and perhaps to his life.

Alan Fairford's acute understanding instantly connected what he had heard with the circumstances he had witnessed at Fairladies. His first thought was to attempt, at all risks, his instant escape, and procure assistance powerful enough to crush, in the very cradle, a conspiracy of such a determined character. This he did not consider as difficult ; for,

24

though the door was guarded on the outside, the window, which was not above ten feet from the ground, was open for escape, the common on which it looked was uninclosed, and profusely covered with furze. There would, he thought, be little difficulty in effecting his liberty, and in concealing his course after he had gained it.

But Lilias exclaimed against this scheme. Her uncle, she said, was a man who, in his moments of enthusiasm, knew neither remorse nor fear. He was capable of visiting upon Darsie any injury which he might conceive Fairford had rendered him ; he was her near kinsman also, and not an unkind one, and she deprecated any effort, even in her brother's favor, by which his life must be exposed to danger. Fairford himself remembered Father Buonaventure, and made little question but that he was one of the sons of the old Chevalier de St. George ; and with feelings which, although contradictory of his public duty, can hardly be much censured, his heart recoiled from being the agent by whom the last scion of such a long line of Scottish princes should be rooted up. He then thought of obtaining an audience, if possible, of this devoted person, and explaining to him the utter hopelessness of his undertaking, which he judged it likely that the ardor of his partisans might have concealed from him. But he relinquished this design as soon as formed. He had no doubt that any light which he could throw on the state of the country would come too late to be serviceable to one who was always reported to have his own full share of the hereditary obstinacy which had cost his ancestors so dear, and who, in drawing the sword, must have thrown from him the scabbard.

Lilias suggested the advice which, of all others, seemed most suited to the occasion, that yielding, namely, to the circumstances of their situation, they should watch carefully when Darsie should obtain any degree of freedom, and endeavor to open a communication with him, in which case their joint flight might be effected, and without endangering the safety of any one.

Their youthful deliberation had nearly fixed in this point, when Fairford, who was listening to the low sweet whispering tones of Lilias Redgauntlet, rendered yet more interesting by some slight touch of foreign accent, was startled by a heavy hand which descended with full weight on his shoulder, while the discordant voice of Peter Peebles, who had at length broken loose from the well-meaning Quaker, exclaimed in the ear of his truant counsel—"Aha, lad ! I think ye are catched. An' so ye are turned chamber-counsel, are ye ? And ye have drawn up wi' clients in scarfs and hoods ? But bide a wee, billie, and see if I dinna sort ye when my petition and complaint comes to be discussed, with or without answers, under certification."

Alan Fairford had never more difficulty in his life to subdue a first emotion than he had to refrain from knocking down the crazy blockhead who had broken in upon him at such a moment. But the length of Peter's address gave him time, fortunately perhaps for both parties, to reflect on the extreme irregularity of such a proceeding. He stood silent, however, with vexation, while Peter went on.

"Weel, my bonnie man, I see ye are thinking shame o' yoursell, and nae great wonder. Ye maun leave this quean ; the like of her is ower light company for you. I have heard honest Mr. Pest say, that the gown grees ill wi' the petticoat. But come awa' hame to your puir father, and I'll take care of you the haill gate, and keep you company, and deil a word we will speak about, but just the state of the conjoined processes of the great cause of Poor Peebles against Plainstanes."

"If thou canst endure to hear as much of that suit, friend," said the Quaker, "as I have heard out of mere compassion for thee, I think verily thou wilt soon be at the bottom of the matter, unless it be altogether bottomless."

Fairford shook off, rather indignantly, the large bony hand which Peter had imposed upon his shoulder, and was about to say something peevish upon so unpleasant and insolent a mode of interruption, when the door opened, a treble voice saying to the sentinel, "I tell you I maun be in, to see if Mr. Nixon's here ;" and little Benjie thrust in his mop-head and keen black eyes. Ere he could withdraw it Peter Peebles sprang to the door, seized the boy by the collar, and dragged him forward into the room.

"Let me see it," he said, "ye ne'er-do-weel limb of Satan. I'll gar you satisfy the production, I trow : I'll hae first and second diligence against you, ye devil's buckie !"

"What dost thou want ?" said the Quaker, interfering. "Why dost thou frighten the boy, friend Peebles ?"

"I gave the bastard a penny to buy me snuff," said the pauper, "and he has rendered no account of his intromissions ; but I'll gar him as gude."

So saying, he proceeded forcibly to rifle the pockets of Benjie's ragged jacket of one or two snares for game, marbles, a half-bitten apple, two stolen eggs (one of which Peter

broke in the eagerness of his research), and various other
unconsidered trifles, which had not the air of being very
honestly come by. The little rascal, under this discipline,
bit and struggled like a fox-cub, but, like that vermin,
uttered neither cry nor complaint, till a note, which Peter
tore from his bosom, flew as far as Lilias Redgauntlet and
fell at her feet. It was addressed to ' C. N.'

" It is for the villain Nixon," she said to Alan Fairford ;
" open it without scruple : that boy is his emissary. We
shall now see what the miscreant is driving at."

Little Benjie now gave up all farther struggle, and suffered
Peebles to take from him, without resistance, a shilling, out
of which Peter declared he would pay himself principal and
interest, and account for the balance. The boy, whose attention seemed fixed on something very different, only said,
' Maister Nixon will murder me !' "

Alan Fairford did not hesitate to read the little scrap of
paper, on which was written, " All is prepared ; keep them
in play until I come up. You may depend on your reward.
—C. C."

" Alas ! my uncle—my poor uncle !" said Lilias, " this is
the result of his confidence ! Methinks, to give him instant
notice of his confidant's treachery is now the best service we
can render all concerned. If they break up their undertaking, as they must now do, Darsie will be at liberty."

In the same breath, they were both at the half-opened
door of the room, Fairford entreating to speak with the
Father Buonaventure, and Lilias, equally vehemently, requesting a moment's interview with her uncle. While the
sentinel hesitated what to do, his attention was called to a
loud noise at the door, where a crowd had been assembled
in consequence of the appalling cry that the enemy were upon them, occasioned, as it afterward proved, by some stragglers having at length discovered the dead bodies of Nanty
Ewart and of Nixon.

Amid the confusion occasioned by this alarming incident,
the sentinel ceased to attend to his duty ; and, accepting
Alan Fairford's arm, Lilias found no opposition in penetrating even to the inner apartment, where the principal persons
in the enterprise, whose conclave had been disturbed by this
alarming incident, were now assembled in great confusion,
and had been joined by the Chevalier himself.

" Only a mutiny among these smuggling scoundrels," said
Redgauntlet.

" *Only* a mutiny, do you say ?" said Richard Glendale ;

"and the lugger, the last hope of escape for"—he looked towards Charles—" stands out to sea under a press of sail ! "

" Do not concern yourself about me," said the unfortunate prince ; " this is not the worst emergency in which it has been my lot to stand ; and if it were, I fear it not. Shift for yourselves, my lords and gentlemen."

"No, never !" said the young Lord ——. "Our only hope now is in an honorable resistance."

" Most true," said Redgauntlet ; " let despair renew the union amongst us which accident disturbed. I give my voice for displaying the royal banner instantly, and—— How now ?" he concluded, sternly, as Lilias, first soliciting his attention by pulling his cloak, put into his hand the scroll; and added, it was designed for that of Nixon.

Redgauntlet read, and, dropping it on the ground, continued to stare upon the spot where it fell with raised hands and fixed eyes. Sir Richard Glendale lifted the fatal paper, read it, and saying, " Now all is indeed over," handed it to Maxwell, who said aloud, " Black Colin Campbell, by G—d ! I heard he had come post from London last night."

As if in echo to his thoughts, the violin of the blind man was heard playing with spirit, " The Campbells are coming," a celebrated clan-march.

" The Campbells are coming in earnest," said MacKellar : " they are upon us with the whole battalion from Carlisle."

There was a silence of dismay, and two or three of the company began to drop out of the room.

Lord —— spoke with the generous spirit of a young English nobleman. " If we have been fools, do not let us be cowards. We have one here more precious than us all, and come hither on our warranty ; let us save him at least."

" True—most true," answered Sir Richard Glendale. " Let the King be first cared for."

" That shall be my business," said Redgauntlet. " If we have but time to bring back the brig, all will be well ; I will instantly despatch a party in a fishing-skiff to bring her to." He gave his commands to two or three of the most active among his followers. " Let him be once on board," he said, " and there are enough of us to stand to arms and cover his retreat."

" Right—right," said Sir Richard, "and I will look to points which can be made defensible ; and the old powder-plot boys could not have made a more desperate resistance than we shall. Redgauntlet," continued he, " I see some of our friends are looking pale ; but methinks your nephew has

more mettle in his eye now than when we were in cold deliberation, with danger at a distance."

"It is the way of our house," said Redgauntlet : "our
courage ever kindles highest on the losing side. I, too, feel
that the catastrophe I have brought on must not be survived
by its author. Let me first," he said, addressing Charles,
"see your Majesty's sacred person in such safety as can now
be provided for it, and then——"

"You may spare all considerations concerning me, gentlemen," again repeated Charles ; "yon mountain of Criffell
shall fly as soon as I will."

Most threw themselves at his feet with weeping and entreaty ; some one or two slunk in confusion from the apartment, and were heard riding off. Unnoticed in such a scene,
Darsie, his sister, and Fairford drew together, and held each
other by the hands as those who, when a vessel is about to
founder in the storm, determine to take their chance of life
and death together.

Amid this scene of confusion, a gentleman, plainly dressed
in a riding-habit, with a black cockade in his hat, but without any arms except a *couteau-de-chasse*, walked into the
apartment without ceremony. He was a tall, thin, gentle-
manly man, with a look and bearing decidedly military. He
had passed through their guards, if in the confusion they
now maintained any, without stop or question, and now
stood almost unarmed among armed men, who, nevertheless,
gazed on him as on the angel of destruction.

"You look coldly on me, gentlemen," he said. "Sir
Richard Glendale—my Lord ——, we were not always such
strangers. Ha, Pate-in-Peril, how is it with you ? And
you, too, Ingoldsby—I must not call you by any other name
—why do you receive an old friend so coldly ? But you
guess my errand."

"And are prepared for it, General," said Redgauntlet :
"we are not men to be penned up like sheep for the slaughter."

"Pshaw ! you take it too seriously ; let me speak but one
word with you."

"No words can shake our purpose," said Redgauntlet,
"were your whole command, as I suppose is the case, drawn
round the house."

"I am certainly not unsupported," said the General ;
"but if you would hear me——"

"Hear *me*, sir," said the Wanderer, stepping forward.
"I suppose I am the mark you aim at. I surrender myself

willingly, to save these gentlemen's danger; let this at least avail in their favor,"

An exclamation of " Never—never !" broke from the little body of partisans, who threw themselves round the unfortunate prince, and would have seized or struck down Campbell, had it not been that he remained with his arms folded, and a look rather indicating impatience because they would not hear him than the least apprehension of violence at their hand.

At length he obtained a moment's silence. " I do not," he said, " know this gentleman (making a profound bow to the unfortunate prince)—I do not wish to know him ; it is a knowledge which would suit neither of us."

" Our ancestors, nevertheless, have been well acquainted," said Charles, unable to suppress, even in that hour of dread and danger, the painful recollections of fallen royalty.

" In one word, General Campbell," said Redgauntlet, " is it to be peace or war ? You are a man of honor, and we can trust you."

" I thank you, sir," said the General ; " and I reply that the answer to your question rests with yourself. Come, do not be fools, gentlemen ; there was perhaps no great harm meant or intended by your gathering together in this obscure corner, for a bear-bait or a cock-fight, or whatever other amusement you may have intended ; but it was a little imprudent, considering how you stand with government, and it has occasioned some anxiety. Exaggerated accounts of your purpose have been laid before government by the information of a traitor in your own counsels ; and I was sent down post to take the command of a sufficient number of troops, in case these calumnies should be found to have any real foundation. I have come here, of course, sufficiently supported both with cavalry and infantry to do whatever might be necessary ; but my commands are—and I am sure they agree with my inclination—to make no arrests, nay, to make no farther inquiries of any kind, if this good assembly will consider their own interests so far as to give up their immediate purpose and return quietly home to their own houses."

" What !—all ? " exclaimed Sir Richard Glendale—" all, without exception ? "

" ALL, without one single exception," said the General ; " such are my orders. If you accept my terms, say so, and make haste ; for things may happen to interfere with his Majesty's kind purposes towards you all."

"His Majesty's kind purposes!" said the Wanderer. "Do I hear you aright, sir?"

"I speak the King's very words, from his very lips," replied the General. "'I will,' said his Majesty, 'deserve the confidence of my subjects by reposing my security in the fidelity of the millions who acknowledge my title—in the good sense and prudence of the few who continue, from the errors of education, to disown it.' His Majesty will not even believe that the most zealous Jacobites who yet remain can nourish a thought of exciting a civil war, which must be fatal to their families and themselves, besides spreading bloodshed and ruin through a peaceful land. He cannot even believe of his kinsman that he would engage brave and generous, though mistaken, men in an attempt which must ruin all who have escaped former calamities; and he is convinced that, did curiosity or any other motive lead that person to visit this country, he would soon see it was his wisest course to return to the continent; and his Majesty compassionates his situation too much to offer any obstacle to his doing so."

"Is this real?" said Redgauntlet. "Can you mean this? Am I—are all—are any of these gentlemen at liberty, without interruption, to embark in yonder brig, which, I see, is now again approaching the shore?"

"You, sir—all—any of the gentlemen present," said the General—"all whom the vessel can contain, are at liberty to embark uninterrupted by me; but I advise none to go off who have not powerful reasons, unconnected with the present meeting, for this will be remembered against no one."

"Then, gentlemen," said Redgauntlet, clasping his hands together as the words burst from him, "the cause is lost forever!"

General Campbell turned away to the window, as if to avoid hearing what they said. Their consultation was but momentary; for the door of escape which thus opened was as unexpected as the exigence was threatening.

"We have your word of honor for our protection," said Sir Richard Glendale, "if we dissolve our meeting in obedience to your summons?"

"You have, Sir Richard," answered the General.

"And I also have your promise," said Redgauntlet, "that I may go on board yonder vessel with any friend whom I may choose to accompany me?"

"Not only that, Mr. Ingoldsby—or I will call you Redgauntlet once more—you may stay in the offing for a tide, until you are joined by any person who may remain at Fair-ladies. After that, there will be a sloop of war on the station, and I need not say your condition will then become perilous."

" Perilous it should not be, General Campbell," said Red-gauntlet, " or more perilous to others than to us, if others thought as I do even in this extremity."

" You forget yourself, my friend," said the unhappy Adventurer : " you forget that the arrival of this gentleman only puts the copestone on our already adopted resolution to abandon our bull-fight, or by whatever other wild name this headlong enterprise may be termed. I bid you farewell, unfriendly friends ; I bid *you* farewell (bowing to the General), my friendly foe : I leave this strand as I landed upon it, alone, and to return no more !"

" Not alone," said Redgauntlet, " while there is blood in the veins of my father's son."

" Not alone," said the other gentlemen present, stung with feelings which almost overpowered the better reasons under which they had acted. " We will not disown our principles, or see your person endangered."

" If it be only your purpose to see the gentleman to the beach," said General Campbell, " I will myself go with you. My presence among you, unarmed and in your power, will be a pledge of my friendly intentions, and will overawe, should such be offered, any interruption on the part of officious persons."

" Be it so," said the Adventurer, with the air of a prince to a subject, not of one who complied with the request of an enemy too powerful to be resisted.

They left the apartment—they left the house ; an unauthenticated and dubious, but appalling, sensation of terror had already spread itself among the inferior retainers, who had so short time before strutted, and bustled, and thronged the doorway and the passages. A report had arisen, of which the origin could not be traced, of troops advancing towards the spot in considerable numbers ; and men who, for one reason or other, were most of them amenable to the arm of power, had either shrunk into stables or corners or fled the place entirely. There was solitude on the landscape, excepting the small party which now moved towards the rude pier, where a boat lay manned, agreeably to Redgauntlet's orders previously given.

The last heir of the Stuarts leant on Redgauntlet's arm as they walked toward the beach ; for the ground was rough, and he no longer possessed the elasticity of limb and of spirit which had, twenty years before, carried him over many a Highland hill, as light as one of their native deer. His adherents followed, looking on the ground, their feelings struggling against the dictates of their reason.

General Campbell accompanied them with an air of apparant ease and indifference, but watching at the same time, and no doubt with some anxiety, the changing features of those who acted in this extraordinary scene.

Darsie and his sister naturally followed their uncle, whose violence they no longer feared, while his character attracted their respect; and Alan Fairford accompanied them from interest in their fate, unnoticed in a party where all were too much occupied with their own thoughts and feelings, as well as with the impending crisis, to attend to his presence.

Half-way betwixt the house and the beach, they saw the bodies of Nanty Ewart and Cristal Nixon blackening in the sun.

"That was your informer?" said Redgauntlet, looking back to General Campbell, who only nodded his assent. "Caitiff wretch!" exclaimed Redgauntlet; "and yet the name were better bestowed on the fool who could be misled by thee."

"That sound broadsword cut," said the General, "has saved us the shame of rewarding a traitor."

They arrived at the place of embarkation. The Prince stood a moment with folded arms, and looked around him in deep silence. A paper was then slipped into his hands; he looked at it, and said, "I find the two friends I have left at Fairladies are apprised of my destination, and propose to embark from Bowness. I presume this will not be an infringement of the conditions under which we have acted?"

"Certainly not," answered General Campbell, "they shall have all facility to join you."

"I wish, then," said Charles, "only another companion. Redgauntlet, the air of this country is as hostile to you as it is to me. These gentlemen have made their peace, or rather they have done nothing to break it. But you—come you, and share my home where chance shall cast it. We shall never see these shores again; but we will talk of them, and of our disconcerted bull-fight."

"I follow you, sire, through life," said Redgauntlet, "as I would have followed you to death. Permit me one moment."

The Prince then looked round, and seeing the abashed

countenances of his other adherents bent upon the ground, he hastened to say, " Do not think that you, gentlemen, have obliged me less because your zeal was mingled with prudence, entertained, I am sure, more on my own account and on that of your country than from selfish apprehensions."

He stepped from one to another, and, amid sobs and bursting tears, received the adieus of the last remnant which had hitherto supported his lofty pretensions, and addressed them individually, with accents of tenderness and affection.

The General drew a little aloof, and signed to Redgauntlet to speak with him while this scene proceeded. " It is now all over," he said, " and Jacobite will be henceforth no longer a party name. When you tire of foreign parts, and wish to make your peace, let me know. Your restless zeal alone has impeded your pardon hitherto."

" And now I shall not need it," said Redgauntlet. " I leave England forever ; but I am not displeased that you should hear my family adieus. Nephew, come hither. In presence of General Campbell, I tell you that, though to breed you up in my own political opinions has been for many years my anxious wish, I am now glad that it could not be accomplished. You pass under the service of the reigning monarch without the necessity of changing your allegiance— a change, however," he added, looking around him, " which sits more easy on honorable men than I could have anticipated ; but some wear the badge of their loyalty on the sleeve, and others in the heart. You will from henceforth be uncontrolled master of all the property of which forfeiture could not deprive your father—of all that belonged to him— excepting this, his good sword (laying his hand on the weapon he wore), which shall never fight for the house of Hanover ; and as my hand will never draw weapon more, I shall sink it forty fathoms deep in the wide ocean. Bless you, young man ! If I have dealt harshly with you, forgive me. I had set my whole desires on one point—God knows, with no selfish purpose—and I am justly punished by this final termination of my views for having been so little scrupulous in the means by which I pursued them. Niece, farewell, God bless you also ! "

" No, sir," said Lilias, seizing his hand eagerly. " You have been hitherto my protector ; you are now in sorrow, let me be your attendant and your comforter in exile ! "

" I thank you, my girl, for your unmerited affection ; but it cannot and must not be. The curtain here falls between us. I go to the house of another. If I leave it before

I quit the earth, it shall be only for the house of God.
Once more, farewell both ! The fatal doom," he said, with
a melancholy smile, " will, I trust, now depart from the
house of Redgauntlet, since its present representative has
adhered to the winning side. I am convinced he will not
change it, should it in turn become the losing one."

The unfortunate Charles Edward had now given his last
adieus to his downcast adherents. He made a sign with his
hand to Redgauntlet, who came to assist him into the skiff.
General Campbell also offered his assistance, the rest appearing too much affected by the scene which had taken place to
prevent him.

" You are not sorry, General, to do me this last act of
courtesy," said the Chevalier ; " and, on my part, I thank
you for it. You have taught me the principle on which men
on the scaffold feel forgiveness and kindness even for their
executioner. Farewell ! "

They were seated in the boat, which presently pulled off
from the land. The Oxford divine broke out into a loud
benediction, in terms which General Campbell was too
generous to criticise at the time or to remember afterwards ;
nay, it is said that, Whig and Campbell as he was, he could
not help joining in the universal "Amen ! " which resounded
from the shore.

CONCLUSION

BY

DOCTOR DRYASDUST

IN A LETTER TO THE AUTHOR OF *WAVERLEY*

I AM truly sorry, my worthy and much-respected sir, that
my anxious researches have neither in the form of letters,
nor of diaries, or other memoranda been able to discover
more than I have hitherto transmitted of the history of the
Redgauntlet family. But I observe in an old newspaper
called the *Whitehall Gazette*, of which I fortunately possess a file for several years, that Sir Arthur Darsie Redgauntlet was presented to his late Majesty at the drawing-
room by Lieut.-General Campbell; upon which the editor
observes, in the way of comment, that we were going *remis
atque velis* into the interests of the Pretender, since a Scot
had presented a Jacobite at court. I am sorry I have not
room (the frank being only uncial) for his farther observations, tending to show the apprehensions entertained by
many well-instructed persons of the period, that the young
king might himself be induced to become one of the Stuarts'
faction—a catastrophe from which it has pleased Heaven to
preserve these kingdoms.

I perceive also, by a marriage contract in the family repositories, that Miss Lilias Redgauntlet of Redgauntlet,
about eighteen months after the transactions you have commemorated, intermarried with Alan Fairford, Esq., advocate,
of Clinkdollar, who, I think, we may not unreasonably conclude to be the same person whose name occurs so frequently
in the pages of your narration. In my last excursion to
Edinburgh, I was fortunate enough to discover an old cadie,
from whom, at the expense of a bottle of whisky and half a
pound of tobacco, I extracted the important information
that he knew Peter Peebles very well, and had drunk many
a mutchkin with him in Cadie Fraser's time. He said that
he lived ten years after King George's accession, in the
momentary expectation of winning his cause every day in

the session time, and every hour in the day, and at last fell down dead, in what my informer called a " perplexity fit," upon a proposal for a composition being made to him in the Outer House. I have chosen to retain my informer's phrase, not being able justly to determine whether it is a corruption of the word apoplexy, as my friend Mr. Oldbuck supposes, or the name of some peculiar disorder incidental to those who have concerns in the courts of law, as many callings and conditions of men have diseases appropriate to themselves. The same cadie also remembered Blind Willie Stevenson, who was called Wandering Willie, and who ended his days " unco beinly, in Sir Arthur Redgauntlet's ha' neuk." " He had done the family some good turn," he said, "specially when ane of the Argyle gentlemen was coming down on a wheen of them that had the "auld leaven" about them, and wad hae ta'en every man of them, and nae less nor headed and hanged them. But Willie, and a friend they had, called Robin the Rambler, gae them warning, by playing tunes such as " The Campbells are coming," and the like, whereby they got timeous warning to take the wing." I needed not point out to your acuteness, my worthy sir, that this seems to refer to some inaccurate account of the transactions in which you seem so much interested.

Respecting Redgauntlet, about whose subsequent history you are more particularly inquisitive, I have learned from an excellant person, who was a priest in the Scottish monastery of Ratisbon before its suppression, that he remained for two or three years in the family of the Chevalier, and only left it at last in consequence of some discords in that melancholy household. As he had hinted to General Campbell, he exchanged his residence for the cloister, and displayed in the latter part of his life a strong sense of the duties of religion, which in his earlier days he had too much neglected, being altogether engaged in political speculations and intrigues. He rose to the situation of prior in the house which he belonged to, and which was of a very strict order of religion. He sometimes received his countrymen whom accident brought to Ratisbon, and curiosity induced to visit the monastery of ——. But it was remarked, that though he listened with interest and attention when Britain, or particularly Scotland, became the subject of conversation, yet he never either introduced or prolonged the subject, never used the English language, never inquired about English affairs, and, above all, never mentioned his own family. His strict observances of the rules of his order gave

him, at the time of his death, some pretensions to be chosen
a saint, and the brethren of the monastery of —— made
great efforts for that effect, and brought forward some
plausible proofs of miracles. But there was a circumstance
which threw a doubt over the subject, and prevented the
consistory from acceding to the wishes of the worthy brethren. Under his habit, and secured in a small silver box, he
had worn perpetually around his neck a lock of hair, which
the fathers avouched to be a relic. But the *avocato del
diablo,* in combating, as was his official duty, the pretensions
of the candidate for sanctity, made it at least equally probable that the supposed relic was taken from the head of a
brother of a deceased prior, who had been executed for adherence to the Stuart family in 1745-46 ; and the motto,
Haud obliviscendum, seemed to intimate a tone of mundane
feeling and recollection of injuries which made it at least
doubtful whether, even in the quiet and gloom of the cloister,
Father Hugo had forgotten the sufferings and injuries of the
house of Redgauntlet.

NOTES TO REDGAUNTLET.

NOTE 1.—PRINCE CHARLES EDWARD'S LOVE OF MONEY, p. XI

THE repproach is thus expressed by Dr. King, who brings the charge :—" But the most odious part of his character is his love of money—a vice which I do not remember to have been imputed by our historians to any of his ancestors, and is the certain index of a base and little mind. I know it may be urged in his vindication that a prince in exile ought to be an economist. And so he ought; but, nevertheless, his purse should be always open as long as there is anything in it, to relieve the necessities of his friends and adherents. King Charles II., during his banishment, would have shared the last pistole in his pocket with his little family. But I have known this gentleman, with two thousand louis-d'ors in his strong-box, pretend he was in great distress, and borrow money from a lady in Paris who was not in affluent circumstances. His most faithful servants, who had closely attended him in all his difficulties, were ill rewarded." [*Anecdotes of his own Times*, 1818, pp. 201–203.]

NOTE 2.—KITTLE NINE STEPS, p. 3

A pass on the very brink of the Castle rock to the north, by which it is just possible for a goat, or a High School boy, to turn the corner of the building where it rises from the edge of the precipice. This was so favorite a feat with the " hell and neck boys " of the higher classes, that at one time sentinels were posted to prevent its repetition. One of the nine steps was rendered more secure because the climber could take hold of the root of a nettle, so precarious were the means of passing this celebrated spot. The manning the Cowgate Port, especially in snowball time, was also a choice amusement, as it offered an inaccessible station for the boys who used these missiles to the annoyance of the passengers. The gateway is now demolished ; and probably most of its garrison lie as low as the fortress. To recollect that the Author himself, however naturally disqualified, was one of those juvenile dreadnoughts is a sad reflection to one who cannot now step over a brook without assistance.

NOTE 3.—PARLIAMENT HOUSE, EDINBURGH, p. 3

The Hall of the Parliament House of Edinburgh was, in former days, divided into two unequal portions by a partition, the inner side of which was consecrated to the use of the Courts of Justice and the gentlemen of the law ; while the outer division was occupied by the stalls of stationers, toymen, and the like, as in a modern bazaar. From the old play of the *Plain Dealer*, it seems such was formerly the case with Westminster Hall. Minos has now purified his courts in both cities from all traffic but his own.

NOTE 4.—DIRLETON'S *DOUBTS*, p. 4

Sir John Nisbet of Dirleton's *Doubts and Questions upon the Law, especially of Scotland* [1698], and Sir James Stewart's *Dirleton's Doubts and Questions on the Law of Scotland Resolved and Answered*, are works of authority in Scottish jurisprudence. As is generally the case, the *Doubts* are held more in respect than the solution.

NOTE 5.—CRAMP-SPEECH, p. 4

Till of late years, every advocate who entered at the Scottish bar made a Latin address to the court, faculty, and audience, in set terms, and said a few words upon a text of the civil law, to show his Latinity and jurisprudence. He also wore his hat for a minute, in order to vindicate his right of being covered before the court, which is said to have originated from the celebrated lawyer, Sir Thomas Hope, having two sons on the bench while he himself remained at the bar. Of late this ceremony has been dispensed with, as occupying the time of the court unnecessarily. The entrant lawyer merely takes the oaths to government, and swears to maintain the rules and privileges of his order.

NOTE 6.—FRANKING LETTERS, p. 7

It is well known and remembered that, when Members of Parliament enjoyed the unlimited privilege of franking by the mere writing the name on the cover, it was extended to the most extraordinary occasions. One noble lord, to express his regard for a particular regiment, franked a letter for every rank and file. It was customary also to save the covers and return them, in order that the correspondence might be carried on as long as the envelopes could hold together.

NOTE 7.—*SCOTS MAGAZINE*, p. 7

The *Scots Magazine*, commenced in 1739, was really not connected with the Ruddimans. Walter Ruddiman, junior, nephew of Thomas the Grammarian, who died in 1757, started an opposition periodical in 1768, called *The Weekly Magazine or Edinburgh Amusement*. It was carried on till 1784 (*Laing*).

NOTE 8.—" THE AULD MAN'S MARE'S DEAD," p. 8

Alluding, as all Scotsmen know, to the humorous old song :

> The auld man's mare's dead,
> The puir man's mare's dead,
> The auld man's mare's dead,
> A mile aboon Dundee.

—Both the words and air of this popular song are attributed to Patie Birnie, the famous fiddler of Kinghorn, celebrated by Allan Ramsay. See Johnson's *Scots Musical Museum* (*Laing*).

NOTE 9.—DR. RUTHERFORD, p. 13

Probably Dr. John Rutherford, the Author's uncle. He was a professor in the University of Edinburgh, and one of the founders of the Medical School. Scott's father removed from near the top of the College Wynd to George Square soon after Sir Walter's birth (*Laing*).

NOTE 10.—BROWN'S SQUARE EDINBURGH, p. 13

The diminutive and obscure place called Brown's Square was hailed about the time of its erection as an extremely elegant improvement upon the style of designing and erecting Edinburgh residences. Each house was, in the phrase used by appraisers, " finished within itself," or, in the still newer phraseology, " self-contained." It was built about the year 1763–64 ; and the old part of the city being near and accessible, this square soon received many inhabitants, who ventured to remove to so moderate a distance from the High Street.—
The north side of the square now forms part of Chambers Street (*Laing*).

NOTE 11.—AUTHOR'S RESIDENCE WITH QUAKERS, p. 73

In explanation of this circumstance, I cannot help adding a note not very necessary for the reader, which yet I record with pleasure, from recollection of the kindness which it evinces. In early youth I resided for a considerable time in the vicinity of the beautiful village of Kelso, where my life passed in a very solitary manner. I had few acquaintances, scarce any companions, and books, which were at the time almost essential to my happiness, were difficult to come by. It was then that I was particularly indebted to the liberality and friendship of an old lady of the Society of Friends, eminent for her benevolence and charity. Her deceased husband had been a medical man of eminence, and left her, with other valuable property, a small and well-selected library. This the kind old lady permitted me to rummage at pleasure, and carry home what volumes I chose, on condition that I should take, at the same time, some of the tracts printed for encouraging and extending the doctrines of her own sect. She did not even exact any assurance that I would read these performances, being too justly afraid of involving me in a breach of promise, but was merely desirous that I should have the chance of instruction within my reach, in case whim, curiosity, or accident might induce me to have recourse to it.

NOTE 12.—GREEN MANTLE, p. 77

This scene would almost appear to have been founded on an incident in the

Author's own experience, and which is referred to in the following passage from a letter addressed to him about 1790 by an intimate friend :—" Your Quixotism, dear Walter, was highly characteristic. From the description of the blooming fair, as she appeared when she lowered her *manteau vert,* I am hopeful you have not dropt the acquaintance. At least I am certain some of our more rakish friends would have been glad enough of such an introduction." In referring to this letter, Mr. Lockhart says, " Scott's friends discovered that he had, from almost the dawn of the passions, cherished a secret attachment, which continued, through all the most perilous stage of life, to act as a romantic charm in safeguard of virtue. This was the early and innocent affection, however he may have disguised the story, to which we owe the tenderest pages of *Redgauntlet,* and where the heroine has certain distinctive features, drawn from one and the same haunting dream of his manly adolescence."

NOTE 13.—ALAN'S THESIS, p. 86

Mr. Lockhart, referring to the above, say it is easy for us to imagine who the original of the Alan in this letter was. He also informs us, that, when the Author " passed " advocate, the real Darsie (William Clerk) was present at the real Alan's " bit chack of dinner," and the real Alexander Fairford, W. S. (Scott's father), was very joyous on the occasion. Scott's thesis, on the same occasion, was, in fact, on the Ti :le of the Pandects, " Concerning the disposal of the dead bodies of criminals." See the reference to Voet, p. 12 (*Laing*).

NOTE 14.—" ALL OUR MEN WERE VERY, VERY MERRY," p. 90

The original of this catch is to be found in Cowley's witty comedy of *The Guardian,* the first edition [Act ii. sc. 9]. It does not exist in the second and revised edition, called the *Cutter of Coleman Street.*

CAPTAIN BLADE. Ha, ha, boys, another catch.
And all our men were very, very **merry,**
And all our men were drinking.
CUTTER. One man of mine.
DOGREL. Two men of mine.
BLADE. Three men of mine.
CUTTER. And one man of mine.
OMNES. As we went by the way
We were drunk, drunk, damnably **drunk.**
And all our men were very, very merry, etc.

Such are the words, which are somewhat altered and amplified in the text. The play was acted in presence of Charles II., then Prince of Wales, in 1641. The catch in the text has been happily set to music.

NOTE 15.—FACULTIES OF THE BLIND, p. 97

It is certain that in many cases the blind have, by constant exercise of their other organs, learned to overcome a defect which one would think incapable of being supplied. Every reader must remember the celebrated Blind Jack of Knaresborough, who lived by laying out roads.—
This remarkable character, John Metcalf, called the Road-Maker, was born at Knaresborough in 1717. He lost his sight when six years old. An account of his life and undertakings forms an interesting chapter in the *Lives of the Engineers,* by S. Smiles, vol. i. 1861 (*Laing*).

NOTE 16.—WILLIAM III. AND THE COVENANTERS, p. 102

The caution and moderation of King William III., and his principles of unlimited toleration, deprived the Cameronians of the opportunity they ardently desired to retaliate the injuries which they had received during the reign of prelacy, and purify the land, as they called it, from the pollution of blood. They esteemed the Revolution, therefore, only a half measure, which neither comprehended the rebuilding the kirk in its full splendor nor the revenge of the death of the saints on their persecutors.

NOTE 17.—PERSECUTORS OF THE COVENANTERS, p. 111

The personages here mentioned are most of them characters of historical fame ; but those less known and remembered may be found in the tract entitled, *The Judgment and Justice of God Exemplified ; or, a Brief Historical Account of some of the Wicked Lives and Miserable Deaths of some of the most Remark-*

able Apostates and Bloody Persecutors, from the Reformation till after the Revolution. This constitutes a sort of postscript or appendix to John Howie of Lochgoin's *Account of the Lives of the most eminent Scots Worthies.* The author has, with considerable ingenuity, reversed his reasoning upon the inference to be drawn from the prosperity or misfortunes which befall individuals in this world, either in the course of their lives or in the hour of death. In the account of the martyrs' sufferings such inflictions are mentioned only as trials permitted by Providence, for the better and brighter display of their faith and constancy of principle. But when similar afflictions befell the opposite party, they are imputed to the direct vengeance of Heaven upon their impiety. If, indeed, the life of any person obnoxious to the historian's censures happened to have passed in unusual prosperity, the mere fact of its being finally concluded by death is assumed as an undeniable token of the judgment of Heaven, and, to render the conclusion inevitable, his last scene is generally garnished with some singular circumstances. Thus the Duke of Lauderdale is said, through old age but immense corpulence, to have become so sunk in spirits "that his heart was not the bigness of a walnut."

NOTE 18.—EXCESSIVE LAMENTATION, p. 117

I have heard in my youth some such wild tale as that placed in the mouth of the blind fiddler, of which, I think, the hero was Sir Robert Grierson of Lagg, the famous persecutor. But the belief was general throughout Scotland that the excessive lamentation over the loss of friends disturbed the repose of the dead, and broke even the rest of the grave. There are several instances of this in tradition, but one struck me particularly, as I heard it from the lips of one who professed receiving it from those of a ghost-seer. This was a Highland lady named Mrs. C—— of B——, who probably believed firmly in the truth of an apparition which seems to have originated in the weakness of her nerves and strength of her imagination. She had been lately left a widow by her husband, with the office of guardian to their only child. The young man added to the difficulties of his charge by an extreme propensity for a military life, which his mother was unwilling to give way to, while she found it impossible to repress it. About this time the Independent Companies, formed for the preservation of the peace of the Highlands, were in the course of being levied ; and as a gentleman named Cameron, nearly connected with Mrs C——, commanded one o those companies, she was at length persuaded to compromise the matter with her son, by permitting him to enter this company in the capacity of a cadet ; thus gratifying his love of a military life without the dangers of foreign service, to which no one then thought these troops were at all liable to be exposed, while even their active service at home was not likely to be attended with much danger. She readily obtained a promise from her relative that he would be particular in his attention to her son, and therefore concluded she had accommodated matters between her son's wishes and his safety in a way sufficiently attentive to both. She set off to Edinburgh to get what was awanting for his outfit, and shortly afterwards received melancholy news from the Highlands. The Independent Company into which her son was to enter had a skirmish with a party of caterans engaged in some act of spoil, and her friend the captain being wounded, and out of the reach of medical assistance, died in consequence. This news was a thunderbolt to the poor mother, who was at once deprived of her kinsman's advice and assistance, and instructed by his fate of the unexpected danger to which her son's new calling exposed him. She remained also in great sorrow for her relative, whom she loved with sisterly affection. These conflicting causes of anxiety together with her uncertainty whether to continue or change her son's destination, were terminated in the following manner :—

The house in which Mrs. C—— resided in the old town of Edinburgh was a flat or story of a land, accessible, as was then universal, by a common stair. The family who occupied the story beneath were her acquaintances, and she was in the habit of drinking tea with them every evening. It was accordingly about six o'clock, when recovering herself from a deep fit of anxious reflection, she was about to leave the parlor in which she sat in order to attend this engagement. The door through which she was to pass opened, as was very common in Edinburgh, into a dark passage. In this passage, and within a yard of her when she opened the door, stood the apparition of her kinsman, the deceased officer, in his full tartans, and wearing his bonnet. Terrified at what she saw, or thought she saw, she closed the door hastily, and, sinking on her knees by a chair, prayed to be delivered from the horrors of the vision. She remained in that posture till her friends below tapped on the floor to intimate that tea was ready. Recalled to herself by the signal, she arose, and, on opening the apartment door, again was confronted by the visionary Highlander, whose bloody brow bore token, on this second appearance, to the death he had died. Unable to endure this repetition of her terrors, Mrs. C—— sunk on the floor in a swoon. Her friends below, startled with the noise, came upstairs, and, alarmed at the situation in which they found her, insisted on her going to bed and taking some medicine, in order to compose what they took for a nervous attack. They had no sooner left her in quiet than the apparition of the soldier was once more visible in the apartment. This time she took courage and said, " In the name of God, Donald, why do you haunt one who respected and loved you when living ? " To which he answered readily, in Gaelic, " Cousin, why did you not speak sooner ? My rest is disturbed by your unnecessary lamentation—your tears scald me in my shroud. I come to tell you that my untimely death ought to make no difference in your views for your son ; God will raise patrons to supply my place, and he will live to the fulness of years, and die honored and at peace." The lady of course followed her kinsman's advice ; and as she was accounted a person of strict veracity, we may conclude the first apparition an illusion of the fancy, the final one a lively dream suggested by the other two.

NOTE 19.—PETER PEEBLES, p. 134

This unfortunate litigant (for a person named Peter Peebles actually flourished) frequented the courts of justice in Scotland about the year 1792, and the sketch of his appearance is given from recollection. The Author is of opinion that he himself had at one time the honor to be counsel for Peter Peebles, whose voluminous course of litigation served as a sort of assay-pieces to most young men who were called to the bar. The scene of the consultation is entirely imaginary.—
Another character of the same kind, by name Andrew Nicol, who flourished about this time, was probably well known to the Author. He was a weaver of Kinross, who, after years of litigation, neglecting his business, died a pauper in the jail of Cupar-Fife in 1817. See Kay's *Portraits*, vol. i. Nos. 118 and 119. The first represents him with a plan of his middenstead, dated 1804 ; the other, in 1802, consulting a lawyer [listening to John Skene and Mary Walker] (*Laing*).

NOTE 20.—OLD-FASHIONED SCOTTISH CIVILITY, p. 144

Such were literally the points of politeness observed in general society during the Author's youth, where it was by no means unusual in a company assembled by chance to find individuals who had borne arms on one side or the other in the civil broils of 1745. Nothing, according to my recollection, could be more gentle and decorous than the respect these old enemies paid to each other's prejudices. But in this I speak generally. I have witnessed one or two explosions.

NOTE 21.—SWINE IN HANKS OF YARN, p. 149

The simile is obvious, from the old manufacture of Scotland, when the " guidwife's " thrift, as the yarn wrought in the winter was called, when laid down to bleach by the burn-side, was peculiarly exposed to the inroads of the pigs, seldom well regulated about a Scottish farm-house.

NOTE 22.—JOHN'S COFFEE-HOUSE, p. 150

This small dark coffee-house, now burnt down, was the resort of such writers and clerks belonging to the Parliament House above thirty years ago as retained the ancient Scottish custom of a meridian, as it was called, or noontide dram of spirits. If their proceedings were watched, they might be seen to turn fidgety about the hour of noon, and exchange looks with each other from their separate desks, till at length some one of formal and dignified presence assumed the honor of leading the band, when away they went, threading the crowd like a string of wild-fowl, crossed the square or close, and following each other into the coffee-house, received in turn from the hand of the waiter the meridian, which were placed ready at the bar. This they did day by day ; and though they did not speak to each other, they seemed to attach a certain degree of sociability to per-forming the ceremony in company.

NOTE 23.—TITLES OF SCOTTISH JUDGES, p, 162

The Scottish judges are distinguished by the title of " lord " prefixed to their own territorial designation. As the ladies of these official dignitaries do not bear any share in their husbands' honors, they are distinguished only by their lords' family name. They were not always contented with this species of Salique law, which certainly is somewhat inconsistent. But their pretensions to title are said to have been long since repelled by James V., the sovereign who founded the College of Justice. " I," said he, " made the carles lords, but who the devil made the carlines ladies ? "

Note 24.—Attack upon the Dam-dike, p. 176

It may be here mentioned that a violent and popular attack upon what the country people of this district considered as an invasion of their fishing right is by no means an improbable fiction. Shortly after the close of the American war, Sir James Graham of Netherby constructed a dam-dike, or cauld, across the Esk, at a place where it flowed through his estate, though it has its origin and the principal part of its course, in Scotland. The new barrier at Netherby was considered as an encroachment calculated to prevent the salmon from ascending into Scotland ; and the right of erecting it being an international question of law betwixt the sister kingdoms, there was no court in either competent to its decision. In this dilemma, the Scots people assembled in numbers by signal of rocket-lights, and, rudely armed with fowling-pieces, fish-spears, and such rustic weapons, marched to the banks of the river for the purpose of pulling down the dam-dike objected to. Sir James Graham armed many of his own people to protect his property, and had some military from Carlisle for the same purpose. A renewal of the Border wars had nearly taken place in the 18th century, when prudence and moderation on both sides saved much tumult, and perhaps some bloodshed. The English proprietor consented that a breach should be made in his dam-dike sufficient for the passage of the fish, and thus removed the Scottish grievance. I believe the river has since that time taken the matter into its own disposal, and entirely swept away the dam-dike in question.

Note 25.—Collier and Salter, p. 205

The persons engaged in these occupations were at this time bondsmen ; and in case they left the ground of the farm to which they belonged, and as pertaining to which their services were bought or sold, they were liable to be brought back by a summary process. The existence of this species of slavery being thought irreconcilable with the spirit of liberty, colliers and salters were declared free, and put upon the same footing with other servants, by the Act 15 Geo. III, chap, 28th. They were so far from desiring or prizing the blessing conferred on them, that they esteemed the interest taken in their freedom to be a mere decree on the part of the proprietors to get rid of what they called head and herezeld money, payable to them when a female of their number, by bearing a child, made an addition to the live stock of their master's property.

Note 26.—Tunes and Toasts, p. 231

Every one must remember instances of this festive custom, in which the adaptation of the tune to the toast was remarkably felicitous. Old Neil Gow and his son Nathaniel were peculiarly happy on such occasions. [See *St. Ronan's Well*, Glossary, under " Gow."]

Note 27.—Trepanning and Concealment, p. 244

Scotland, in its half-civilized state, exhibited too many examples of the exertion of arbitrary force and violence, rendered easy by the dominion which lairds exerted over their tenants, and chiefs over their clans. The captivity of Lady Grange,* in the desolate cliffs of St. Kilda, is in the recollection of every one. At the supposed date of the novel also, a man of the name of Merrilees, a tanner in Leith, absconded from his country to escape his creditors ; and after having slain his own mastiff dog, and put a bit of red cloth in its mouth, as if it had died in a contest with soldiers, and involved his own existence in as much mystery as possible, made his escape into Yorkshire. Here he was detected by persons sent in search of him, to whom he gave a portentous account of his having been carried off and concealed in various places. Mr. Merrilees was, in short, a kind of male Elizabeth Canning,† but did not trespass on the public credulity quite so long.

---

* [Lady Grange was the wife of a Scottish judge, Lord Grange. When she was on the eve of separating from him after twenty years of married life, she was, on 22d January 1732, carried off from her home by violence by a party of Highlanders, instigated by her husband. She was kept in close confinement for ten years, the last eight of the period in the lonely island of St. Kilda, far out in the Atlantic.]

† [Elizabeth Canning was a London domestic servant, who disappeared suddenly, and without known cause, from her mistress's house in that city, in January 1753. But after a week's absence she returned in a wretched plight, and told a remarkable story of having been kidnapped, forcibly detained, and robbed by persons unknown to her. Two women, whom she pointed out, were arrested and tried for the alleged offence. One of them was sentenced to death ; the other to be branded on the hand and imprisoned for six months. Canning was subse-

NOTE 28.—MAILS TO EDINBURGH, p. 247

Not much in those days, for within my recollection the London post was brought north in a small mail-cart ; and men are yet alive who recollect when it came down with only one single letter for Edinburgh, addressed to the manager of the British Linen Company.

NOTE 29.—ESCAPE OF PATE-IN-PERIL, p. 255

The escape of a Jacobite gentleman, while on the road to Carlisle to take his trial for his share in the affair of 1745, took place at Errickstane Brae, in the singular manner ascribed to the laird of Summertrees in the text. The Author has seen in his youth the gentleman to whom the adventure actually happened. The distance of time makes some indistinctness of recollection, but it is believed the real name was MacEwen or MacMillan.

NOTE 30.—ANOTHER OPPORTUNITY, p. 255

An old gentleman of the Author's name was engaged in the affair of 1715, and with some difficulty was saved from the gallows by the intercession of the Duchess of Buccleugh and Monmouth. Her Grace, who maintained a good deal of authority over her clan, sent for the object of her intercession, and warning him of the risk which he had run, and the trouble she had taken on his account, wound up her lecture by intimating that, in case of such disloyalty again, he was not to expect her interest in his favor. "An it please your Grace," said the stout old Tory, "I fear I am too old to see another opportunity."

NOTE 31.—BRAXY MUTTON, p. 256

The flesh of sheep that has died of disease, not by the hand of the butcher. In pastoral countries it is used as food with little scruple.

NOTE 32.—CONCEALMENTS FOR THEFT AND SMUGGLING, p. 277

I am sorry to say, that the modes of concealment described in the imaginary premises of Mr. Trumbull are of a kind which have been common on the frontiers of late years. The neighborhood of two nations having different laws, though united in government, still leads to a multitude of transgressions on the Border, and extreme difficulty in apprehending delinquents. About twenty years since, as far as my recollection serves, there was along the frontier an organized gang of coiners, forgers, smugglers, and other malefactors, whose operations were conducted on a scale not inferior to what is here described. The chief of the party was one Richard Mendham, a carpenter, who rose to opulence, although ignorant even of the arts of reading and writing. But he had found a short road to wealth, and had taken singular measures for conducting his operations. Amongst these, he found means to build, in a suburb of Berwick called Spittal, a street of small houses, as if for the investment of property. He himself inhabited one of these ; another, a species of public-house, was open to his confederates, who held secret and unsuspected communication with him by crossing the roofs of the intervening houses, and descending by a trap-stair, which admitted them into the alcove of the dining-room of Dick Mendham's private mansion. A vault, too, beneath Mendham's stable, was accessible in the manner mentioned in the novel. The post of one of the stalls turned round on a bolt being withdrawn, and gave admittance to a subterranean place of concealment for contraband and stolen goods, to a great extent. Richard Mendham, the head of this very formidable conspiracy, which involved malefactors of every kind, was tried and executed at Jedburgh, where the Author was present as Sheriff of Selkirkshire. Mendham had previously been tried, but escaped by want of proof and the ingenuity of his counsel.

NOTE 33.—PINT MEASURE, p. 280

The Scottish pint of liquid measure comprehends four English measures of the same denomination. The jest is well known of my poor countryman, who, driven to extremity by the raillery of the Southern on the small denomination of the Scottish coin, at length answered, "Ay—ay ! but the deil tak them that has the *least pint-stoup.*"

NOTE 34.—TRANSLATIONS FROM SALLUST, p, 285

The translation of these passages is thus given by Sir Henry Steuart of Allanton.

___

quently charged with being an impostor. as indeed many suspected all along, convicted, and sentenced to seven years' transportation. The affair created great commotion in London for a time.]

" The youth, taught to look up to riches as the sovereign good, became apt pupils in the school of luxury. Avarice and pride supplied their precepts. Rapacity and profusion went hand in hand. Careless of their own fortunes, and eager to possess those of others, shame and remorse, modesty and moderation, every principle gave way."—*Works of Sallust, with Original Essays*, vol. ii. p. 17.

After enumerating the evil qualities of Catiline's associates, the author adds, " If it happened that any as yet uncontaminated by vice were fatally drawn into his friendship, the effects of intercourse and snares artfully spread subdued every scruple, and early assimilated them to their corruptors.'—*Ibidem*, p. 19

Note 35.—Old Avery, p. 294

Captain Avery, a noted and successful pirate, who married a daughter of the Great Mogul, according to his biographer Charles Johnson ; see his *History of Highwaymen, Pyrates*, etc., 1734, and his earlier *History of the Pyrates (Laing)*.

Note 36.—Prenatal Marks, p. 341

Several persons have brought down to these days the impressions which nature had thus recorded when they were yet babes unborn. One lady of quality, whose father was long under sentence of death posterior to the rebellion, was marked on the back of the neck by the sign of a broad axe. Another, whose kinsmen had been slain in battle and died on the scaffold to the number of seven, bore a child spattered on the right shoulder and down the arm with scarlet drops, as if of blood. Many other instances might be quoted.

Note 37.—Coronation of George III., p. 350

The particulars here given are of course entirely imaginary ; that is, they have no other foundation than what might be supposed probable had such a circumstance actually taken place. Yet a report to such an effect was long and generally current, though now having wholly lost its lingering credit, those who gave it currency, if they did not originate it, being, with the tradition itself, now mouldered in the dust. The attachment to the unfortunate house of Stuart among its adherents continued to exist and to be fondly cherished longer perhaps than in any similar case in another country ; and when reason was baffled, and all hope destroyed, by repeated frustration, the mere dreams of imagination were summoned in to fill up the dreary blank left in so many hearts. Of the many reports set on foot and circulated from this cause, the tradition in question, though amongst the least authenticated, is not the least striking ; and, in excuse of what may be considered as a violent infraction of probability in chapter xviii., the Author is under the necessity of quoting it. It was always said, though with very little appearance of truth, that, upon the coronation of George III., when the Champion of England, Dymock, or his representative, appeared in West-minster Hall, and, in the language of chivalry, solemnly wagered his body to de-fend in single combat the right of the young king to the crown of these realms, at the moment when he flung down his gauntlet as the gage of battle, an unknown female stepped from the crowd and lifted the pledge, leaving another gage in room of it, with a paper expressing that, if a fair field of combat should be al-lowed, a champion of rank and birth would appear with equal arms to dispute the claim of King George to the British kingdoms. The story, as we have said, is probably one of the numerous fictions which were circulated to keep up the spirits of a sinking faction. The incident was, however, possible, if it could be supposed to be attended by any motive adequate to the risk, and might be im-agined to occur to a person of Redgauntlet's enthusiastic character. George III., it is said, had a police of his own, whose agency was so efficient, that the sovereign was able to tell his prime minister upon one occasion, to his great sur-prise, that the Pretender was in London. The prime minister began immediately to talk of measures to be taken, warrants to be procured, messengers and guards to be got in readiness. " Pooh—pooh," said the good-natured sovereign, " since I have found him out, leave me alone to deal with him." " And what," said the minister, " is your Majesty's purpose in so important a case ? " " To leave the young man to himself," said George III. ; " and when he tires he will go back again." The truth of this story does not depend on that of the lifting of the gauntlet ; and while the latter could be but an idle bravado, the former ex-presses George III.'s goodness of heart and soundness of policy.

Note 38.—Highland Regiments, p. 361

The Highland regiments were first employed by the celebrated Earl of Chat-ham, who assumed to himself no small degree of praise for having called forth to the support of the country and the government the valor which had been too often directed against both.

GLOSSARY

OF

WORDS, PHRASES, AND ALLUSIONS

Abunu, aboon, above

Account, went on the, took part in piratical expeditions

Ad litem, in a lawsuit

Adust, parched, sunburnt in the public defence

Ad vindictam publicam,

Age as accords, to do what is fitting—a Scots law phrase

Ailsay, or *Ailsa, Craig,* a rocky island in the Firth of Clyde

Ain, own

Airt, to direct

Alcander, an ancient Greek soothsayer, the son of Munichus, king of the Molossi

Aldiborontiphosc o p h o r-nio, the humorous name given by Scott to James Ballantyne, is borrowed from H. Carey's *Chrononhotonthologus* (1734)

Alquife, a famous enchanter in the mediæval romances of the *Amadis of Gaul* cycle

Amadis, a celebrated hero in the mediæval romances of chivalry

Amaist, almost

Ance, anes, once ; *ance, wud and aye waur,* once he was mad, he would get worse instead of better

Ane, one

Anes errand, for that very purpose

Another-guess, another sort of

Approbate and reprobate, to approve and reject, exercise choice

Argumentum ad hominem, personal recrimination to a man, *ad fœminam,* to a lady

Arles, earnest-money

Arniston, probably Robert Dundas of Arniston, **the Younger (1713-87),**

Lord President of the Scottish courts

Ars longa, vita brevis, art or work is long and life is short

Ars medendi, art of healing, medicine

Atlantes, a magician in Ariosto's *Orlando Furioso*

Attour. See Bye and attour, under Bye

Aught, to own, possess, be chiefly concerned in

Auld Reekie, "Old Smoky," a popular name for Edinburgh

Auld-warld, olden times, days that are gone

Avocato, or *avvocato, del diablo,* Devil's advocate, the official pleader appointed by the Roman Catholic Church to dispute a proposal of canonization

Back-ganging, b e h i n d-hand in paying, getting into debt

Back-sands (p. 205). Horse-races were held on Leith sands for many years previous to their transference to Musselburgh in 1816

Back-spauld, the back part of the shoulder

Ballant, ballad

Balmerino, Lord, beheaded for participating in the Jacobite rebellion of 1745

Bankton, Andrew Macdouall, Lord, Scottish lawyer and judge, author of *Institute of the Laws of Scotland* (1751-53)

Bareford's Parks, now George Street, Edinburgh

Barley-pickle, barley-corn, the last straw

Barmecide's feast to Al-

naschar. See *Arabian Nights,* tale of "Barber's Sixth Brother"

Baron-officer, the police officer of the estate

Bauld, bold

Bearmeal, barley meal

Bein, snug, comfortable

Belford, friend of Lovelace, in Richardson's *Clarissa Harlowe* (1749)

Belisarius, general of the Roman emperor Justinian, lost favor in his old age (548) through the malice of his enemies

Ben, within ; *ower far ben,* too far in, too intimate

Benedicite, my blessing be with you

Bicker, a drinking-bowl

Billie, brother, comrade —a term of familiarity

Bink, dresser for plates

Birkie, a smart fellow

Birling, merry-making, drinking

Bishop's summoner, perhaps William Carmichael, an agent of Archbishop Sharpe's

Black-fasting, being long without food

Black-fisher, a salmon-poacher who fished by night

Black-jack, a jug of waxed leather for holding ale

Blate, bashful

Blaud, a large piece, several verses

Blaw in (the) lugs, to blow in the ears, flatter, cajole

Bleezing, blazing, making an ostentatious show

Blue-cap, a Scotsman

Blue jacket and white lapelle, the uniform of officers in the royal navy

Bluidy Advocate MacKenyie, or *Mackenzie,* Lord Advocate of Scotland under Charles II.

441

and an active persecutor of the Cameronians

Boddle, a Scotch coin = 1-6th penny English

Bogle, bogie, ghost ; scarecrow

Bombazine, a stuff of wool and silk, of which a barrister's gown was made

Bona roba, courtezan, mistress

Bonshaw, James Irvine of, captured Cargill (*q. v.*), at Covington Mill in 1681

Bonus socius, good comrade, good fellow

Borrel, common, simple

Bourd. See Sooth, bourd, etc.

Brash, brush, attack

Brattle, clattering noise, of a horse going at great speed

Brent broo, high, smooth brow

Brocard, maxim

Brock, a badger

Brogue, a light rough leather shoe, worn by Highlanders

Brose, oatmeal over which boiling water has been poured

Brown's imitations of nature. L a n c e l o t Brown, known as "Capability Brown," (1715-83), a celebrated landscape-gardener, fond of formal arrangements and artificial ornaments, caused a small stream, "a rival to the Thames," to flow through the grounds of Blenheim House

Browst, a brewing

Bucephalus, the favorite horse of Alexander the Great

Buckie, imp

Buff nor aye, neither one thing nor another

Bumbazed, stupefied, astonished

Burgh, or **Burgh by Sands,** a village on the Solway, five miles from Carlisle.

Bush aboon Traquair, the title of an old Scottish song. The "bush" itself was pointed out in the grounds of Traquair House, the seat of the Earl of Traquair in Peeblesshire

Bye, besides ; *bye and attour,* over and above ; *by ordinar,* uncommon, unusual ; *bye-time,* now and then, occasionally

Cadie, a messenger, errand-boy

Cairn, Point of. See Point of Cairn

Callant, lad

Caller, fresh, crisp

Cambridge Bible, printed by Buck and Daniel, folio, 1638

Canning Elizabeth. See Elizabeth Canning

Canny, cannily, quiet, quietly

Cantle, fragment

Capernoited, cantankerous, crabbed, irritable

Cargill, Donald, or **Daniel,** founder, with Richard Cameron, of the Cameronians, a Covenanting sect, executed in 1681

Carle, fellow

Carline, witch, old woman

Carrifra Gauns, or **Carrifran Gans,** the precipitous side of a mountain in Moffatdale Dumfries

Cassandra, daughter of Priam, king of Troy, and possessed of the power of prophecy

Cast, lift, short ride

Cateran, freebooter, robber

Cauld, cold

Caup, or **cap,** a cup or wooden bowl

Cavaliere servente, an attentive beau

Cave ne literas, etc. (p. 319), beware of carrying Bellerophon's letters (letters unfavorable to the bearer)

Celsitude, loftiness, height

Cetera prorsus ignora, as for the rest, in short, I know nothing

Chack, a slight repast

Chamber of dais, the best bedroom, state bedroom

Change-house, inn, wayside inn

Chape, the metal mounting of a scabbard ; the scabbard itself

Chapeau bras, a lowcrowned, three-cornered hat

Cheat-the-woodie, cheat the-gallows

Chiel, fellow

Clavers, idle talk, gossip

Cleek, or **cleik,** to lay hold upon ; *cleik in with,* to hook on to, join company with

Cleugh, a steep descent

Close-head, the top of a narrow side-street or

passage, a favorite place for gossips to gather at

Clour, to strike heavily

Cockade, white. *S e e* White cockade

Cockernony, top-knot of hair

Cocking-season, the time for shooting woodcock

Cogie, or **coggie,** small wooden bowl

Commune forum, etc. (p. 142), the common court is a common domicile

Cordwain, or **cordovan,** Spanish leather used for shoes

Corelli, Archangelo, celebrated Italian violinist and musical composer (1653-1713). The *Devil's Sonata* was composed, not by Corelli, but by Tartini (1692-1770), even more famous as a violinist and composer

Coriolanus C. Marcius, a famous old Roman patrician and soldier (5th century), was banished from Rome, and sought shelter at the hearth-stone of his enemy, Tullus Aufidius, the Volscian chief

Corking - pin, the largest kind of pin in use

Corporal Nym's philosophy, in Shakespeare's *Henry V.*, Act ii. sc. 1

Corydon, a rustic swain in Virgil's *Eclogues*

Cotton, Charles, a friend of Izaak Walton, and writer of the second part of *The Complete Angler* (1676)

Councillor Pest, ought probably to be Councillor Peat, according to J. G. Lockhart, in *Life of Scot,* vol. i. p. 251

Coup, or **cowp,** to tumble over, upset

Couteau de chasse, hanger, hunting-knife

Covyne, or **covine,** artifice

Crack, gossip, chat, talk

C r a w s t e p, the step-like edges of a house gable

Creelfu' basketful

C r e m o n y, Cremona, in Italy, where the celebrated violin - makers, the Amati family, lived in the 16th and 17th centuries

C r i f f e l l, a conspicuous mountain in Kirkcudbright, overlooking the estuary of the Nith

Crispus, that is, Sallust, the Roman historian

Crowder, fiddler

Crowdero, a lame fiddler in Butler's *Hudibras*

Cruisie, a lamp

Crummie, a cow

Cur me exanimas, etc. (p. 1), Why do you kill me with your complaints ?

Curn, a grain, particle

Daffing, frolicking, jesting

Daft, crazy ; *gaen daft*, gone crazy

Dais, chamber of. See Chamber of dais

Dalyell. See Tam Dalyell

Dang, knocked over

Daniel. See Cambridge Bible

Dargle. Compare The Dargle, a wooded glen in Wicklow, Ireland. Perhaps, however, the word is a slip of the pen for "dingle," a small valley or dell

Daured, dared

Daurg, or *darg*, a day's work, task

David's sow, the wife of a Welshman, David Lloyd, who was found lying dead drunk beside the sow, when David brought a visitor to see the animal, which had six legs. See Glossary to *The Pirate*, "Drunk as Davy's sow"

Davie Lindsay, or *Sir David Lyndsay of the Mount*, the most popular poet (c. 1490 to c. 1555) of Scotland antecedent to Burn's

Day's work in harvest, owe one a, to owe a good deed in a time of special need—of course used ironically on p. 355

Dead-thraw, death-agony

De apicibus juris, from ticklish points or delicate distinctions of the law

"*Death ... nothing could have,*" etc. (p. 204), from *King Lear*, Act iii. sc. 4

Deave, to deafen

Delate, to accuse

Delict, misdemeanor

Den, a dell or hollow

De periculo et commodo rei venditœ, concerning the risk and profit of things that are sold

Deray, mirthful noise, disorder

Dernier ressort, last remedy, resource

Désorienté, having lost all bearings

Diligence, a writ of execution—a Scots law term

Ding, to knock

Dirdum, uproar, disturbance

Dittay, indictment

Divot, thin flat turf used for thatching

Doch an dorroch, a drink taken standing, for which nothing is paid ; a stirrup-cup. See *Waverley*, Note 10, p. 473

Doctor Pitcairn, or *Pitcairne*, a celebrated Edinburgh doctor (1652-1713), who had a turn for writing Latin verse

Dominus litis, one of the principals in a lawsuit

Donald of the Isles, a powerful chief of the western isles (Hebrides, etc.) of Scotland in the 15th century

Dool, sad consequences

Door-cheek, door-post

Douce, quiet, sensible

Dour, stubborn, obstinate

Downright Dunstable, a proverbial expression for, plain straightforward speech or action. Dunstable is a town in Bedfordshire

Drappie, drop

Drappit egg, an egg dropped in gravy

Dub, a pool, puddle

Dumbarton Douglas, Thomas Douglas, a Covenanting minister, an associate of Cameron and Cargill (*q.v.*)

Dundee, John Graham of Claverhouse, Viscount, was shot whilst urging on the Highlanders for James II. at Killiecrankie in 1689

Dyvour, bankrupt

Earl of Douglas (p. 114). See MacLellan of Bombie

Earlshall, Bruce of, Claverhouse's lieutenant in his campaigns against the Cameronians in the south - west of Scotland

East Nook, a cape or promontory of Fifeshire

Ee, eye ; *een*, eyes

Effusa est, etc. (p. 11), He is poured out like water, he shall not increase

Eke, addition

Elizabeth Canning. See footnote to Note 27, p. 442

Errickstane Brae, a steep hillside, or gully, at the head of the River Annan, in Dumfriesshire

Errol James, fourteenth Earl of, who officiated as constable at the coronation of George III., was the grandson of Lord Kilmarnock. who was beheaded in 1746

Erskine, John, professor of law in Edinburgh University, and author of *Principles of the Law of Scotland* (1754), and *Institutes of the Law of Scotland* (1773), both very important works

Even'd, compared

Exceptio firmat Regulam, the exception confirms the rule

Ex comitate, out of courtesy

Ex Misericordia, out of compassion

Facardin of Trebizond, an allusion to Count Anthony Hamilton's story o *Les Quatre Facardins* (1749)

Factor loco tutoris, an agent acting in the place of a guardian

Falkirk, flight of. See Flight of Falkirk

Fardel, bundle, pack, burden

Fash, fasherie, trouble ; *fashious*, troublesome

Faulding, folding

Faur'd, favored

Fause, false

Feck, space, greater part

Feroe, isle of, or *the Färoe Islands*, North of Scotland, present steep, rugged cliffs to the sea

Fielding, Sir John, halfbrother of Henry Fielding, the novelist, was, as justice of Westminster, a terror to evil-doers, in spite of his being blind from his youth

Fieri, (yet) to be made

Fifish, a little deranged, cracked ; on p. 207 there is a sly allusion to the county of Fife

Flaçon, a smelling-bottle

Fleeching, flattery, cajolery

Flight of Falkirk, General Hawley's defeat by the Highlanders of the Pretender's army on 17th January 1746

Flip, ale or cider, sweetened and spiced, and heated by plunging a hot iron into the liquor

Flory, frothy, empty
Footman in the shilling gallery. In the 18th century, footmen, after keeping their master's or mistress's place in the boxes, were allowed to go up to the second or shilling gallery. The withdrawal of this privilege at Drury Lane, in 1737, in consequence of their bad behavior, occasioned a riot
Foot out of the Snare, a tract against the Quakers, by John Toldervy, Thomas Brooks, and seven others (1656)
Forfoughten, or *forfouchten,* out of breath, distressed
Forleet, leave off, forsake
F o r p i t, or *f o r p e t,* the fourth part of a peck
Fou, full
Four-pottle, a gallon
Fox, George. See George Fox
Friend, Sir John. See Sir John Friend
Fristed, postponed
Fugie warrant, to apprehend a debtor who is presumed to be about to flee
Functus officio, in the position of one whose duty is completed and cannot be performed again
Furnish, stop a bit, stay a while
Furs, furrows
F u s t i a n, bombastic and empty language

Gaberlunzie, a beggar
Gaen daft, gone out of his mind
Gaits', or *Gytes',* Class, the elementary class, boobies' class
Galloway, a horse bred in the old Scotch county of Galloway
Gangrel, wandering, vagrant
Gar, to force, make
Gash, ghastly, deathlike
Gate, way, road
Gaun, going
G e a r, property, thing, goods
Gentrice, honorable birth, gentle blood
George Fox, the founder (1624-90) of the Quakers
Gey, pretty (as an adverb), moderately
Gie, give ; *gied,* gave
Giff-gaff, give and take, mutual obligation

Gil Blas in the robbers' cave. See Lesage, *Gil Blas,* Bk. I. chap. x.
G i r d e d, hooped with twigs, like a barrel
Girn, to grin, cry
Glaiket, giddy, rash
Glaramara, a mountain in the west of Cumberland, 2560 feet high
Glencairn, William Cuningham, Lord, tried to raise the Highlands for Charles (II.) in 1653
Gliff, an instant
Gobbet, a lump, piece
" *God bless the king,*" etc, (p. 215), slightly altered from an extempore piece by Dr. John Byrom (1691-1763)
Gowff ba', golf ball
Grana invecta et illata, grain brought in and imported
Grange, Lady. See Lady Grange
Grat nor graned, wept nor groaned
Greyfriars' Churchyard, in Edinburgh, contains the graves of George Heriot, George Buchanan, Allan Ramsay, Sir George Mackenzie, and many other distinguished Scotsmen
Grillade, a broiled dish
Grossart, gooseberry
G r u e, to creep (of the flesh), shiver
Gudeman, husband, head of the family
Gudesire, grandfather
Guiding, treating, behaving to
Gumple-foisted, sulky, sullen
Gunner's daughter, kiss the, be flogged whilst laid along the breech of a gun
Gyte, or *gait,* contemptuous name for a child, a brat

Hafflins, half-grown
Haill, the whole ; *haill gate,* the whole way
H a i r i b e e, or *Harraby, Hill,* close to Carlisle, where criminals were executed, especially several of the Jacobites of 1745
Hairst, harvest
Hallan, partition in a cottage
Hamesucken, the crime of assaulting a man in his own house

Ha' neuk, a cosy corner beside the hall fireplace
Hank over, an advantage over, ground for compelling obedience
Happed, hopped
Harpocrates, an Egyptian god, (erroneously) conceived by the ancient Greeks to be the God of Silence
Harvest, owe a day's work in. See Day's work, etc.
Haud o b l i v i s c e n d u m, never to be forgotten
H a u g h, a holm, low ground beside a river
Hauld, habitation
Havers, nonsense
Havings, behavior, manners.
Head-borough, petty constable, the head of a borough
Heart of Midlothian, the ancient jail of Edinburgh, stood close beside St. Giles' Cathedral
Hellicat, wild, giddy
Hempy, a rogue
Herezeld, or *Herreyeld,* a fine payable to a feudal superior on the death of a tenant. See *Guy Mannering,* Note 15, p. 431
Heritor, landowner of a Scottish parish
Hesp, hank of yarn
Het, hot
Heuck, sickle, reaping-hook
Hill Folk, Covenanters, so called from their seeking refuge in the hills
Hinc illæ lachrymæ, hence these tears. that's where the shoe pinches
Hinnie, honey, a term of endearment
Hirdie-girdie, topsy-turvy
Hodden-grey, cloth manufactured from undyed wool
Hoddled, waddled
Homologating, ratifying, approving
Hose-net, a small net like a stocking, affixed to a stick and used in rivulets
Hosting, mustering of armed men
Hunks, a miser, niggard
Hussy, lady's needlecase

Ilk, ilka, every, each
Ill deedie, or *ill-deedy* mischievous
Ill-faured, ugly, ill-favored
Incedit sicut leo vorans,

walketh about like a devouring lion

In civilibus vel criminalibus, in civil or criminal matters

In foro conscientiæ, before one's conscience

In meditatione fugæ, meditating flight

In presentia dominorum, before the (law) lords

Invita, unwilling ; *invita Minerva*, against my own natural inclination

Iron Mask. See Man in the Iron Mask

Ithuriel. See Milton's *Paradise Lost*, Bk. iv.

Jansenists, a 17th century party in the Roman Catholic Church, who opposed certain of the Jesuits' doctrines in religion and morality

Jaud, jade

Jazy, or *Jasey*, a wig, originally made of worsted

Jet d'eau, jet or upward stream of water

John Scot of Amwell, a Quaker(1739-83) of Southwark, wrote *Elegies* and the poem *Amwell*, descriptive of his estate in Hertfordshire

Jorum, a drinking-vessel ; the liquor it contains

Jows in, ceases tolling

June 10th of, the birthday, in 1688, of James, the Old Pretender

Junk, old cable and cordage, often cut to pieces to make mats, etc., of

Katterfelto, Gustavus, a well-known conjurer and quack doctor in London (1782-1784), advertised in the newspapers under the heading " Wonders ! Wonders ! Wonders !"

Keek, look, glance

Keffel, or *keffle*, an inferior horse

Kennel, gutter

Kennington Common, on the south side of London, where many who had taken part in the Young Pretender's rebellion of 1745 were executed in the following year

King's keys, crowbar and hatchet

Kittle, ticklish, difficult ; *kittled*, tickled

Knights of the rainbow, lackeys, liveried servants

Lady Grange. See footnote to Note 27, p. 442

Laigh, low

Laith, loth, unwilling

Lance, to make delicate and lively strokes on the violin

Land, a house or building containing several tenements or flats

Landlouper, adventurer, gad-about

Landward, country, rural, as opposed to town or urban

Lap, leaped

Lares, the guardian deities of the family

Lauderdale John Maitland, Duke of, Secretary of State for Charles II. in Scotland (1660-80)

Lave, the remainder

Lawing, inn reckoning

Leasing-making, slander ; literally, seditious words

Leasowes, the house and estate (converted into a landscape-garden) of the poet, William Shenstone, in Worcestershire, which the bookseller, R. Dodsley, described in an essay prefixed to his edition of Shenstone's *Works* (1764-69)

Leesome lane, alone with his own dear self

Lettres de cachet, sealed letters, conferring the most extensive power over the personal liberty of others

Lex aquarum, the law of the waters, water rights

Limmer, a loose woman, jade

Lindsay Davie. See Davie Lindsay

Loaning, an uncultivated tract, near the homestead, where the cows were pastured and frequently milked

Lobsters, redcoats, soldiers

Loe, to love

Loon, fellow, rogue (humorously)

Loopy, crafty, deceitful

Lord Burleigh in The Critic, Sheridan's play ; *see* Act iii. sc. 1

Lord Stair, James Dalrymple, Viscount of Stair, a celebrated Scottish lawyer, and author of *The Institutes of the Law of Scotland* (1681)

Louis d'or, a French gold

coin worth from 16s. 6d. to 18s. 9d.

Loup, to leap ; *loup-the-dyke*, runaway ; *loup-the-tether*, breaking loose from restraint

Lovelace, friend of Belford, in Richardson's *Clarissa Harlowe* (1749)

Luckenbooths, a block of shops and houses formerly in the middle of High Street, Edinburgh, beside St. Giles' Cathedral

Luckie, a title of honor given to an elderly dame

Lum, chimney

Lydia Languish, one of the characters in Sheridan's *Rivals*

MacKenyie Advocate. See Bluidy Advocate Mackenyie

Macklin, Charles, an Irish actor (1697 ?-1797), who excelled as Shylock

MacLellan of Bombie, or *Bunby*, was put to death by Earl Douglas, whilst the messenger, who brought the order for his release, was detained to take refreshment after his journey. *See* Scott's *Tales of a Grandfather*, chap. xxi.

Mailing, a small farm, rented property ; *mails*, rents

Maist, almost ; most

Man in the Iron Mask, a mysterious state prisoner of France, confined in the Bastille and other prisons for thirty years in the reign of Louis XIV. He was a person of not the highest rank, but who is not yet clearly ascertained, in spite of several identifications—a new one even in 1893

March, border, boundary

Mare magnum, vast ocean

Marius, Caius, a famous old Roman soldier (157-86 b. c.), who, being once a fugitive, took refuge amongst the ruins of Carthage

Maun, must ; *maunna*, must not

Maundering, talking incoherently, mumbling

Maut abune the meal, hilarious, when the ale or wine has taken effect

Meadows, a sort of park on

the south side of Edinburgh

Mear, mare

Menyie, retinue

Meridian, a mid-day dram

Merk, a Scotch silver coin =1s. 1½d.

Messan doggies, dogs of inferior breed

Middenstead, the place where the dunghill stands

Middleton, Earl of, an unscrupulous soldier, and commissioner of Charles II. in Scotland

Miffed, piqued

Millar, or *Miller Philip*, gardener (1691-1771) to the Apothecaries Company at Chelsea, and author of several books for gardeners

Minden, 40 miles west of Hanover ; there, in 1759, during the Seven Years War, the Anglo-Hanoverian army defeated the French

Minnie, mamma, mother

Minos, in ancient Creek mythology, judge of the lower world

Mischanter, mischief

Miss Nickie Murray, sister of the Earl of Mansfield, was the presiding genius of the Edinburgh assemblies (public balls) during the middle of the the 18th century

Moidart, or *Kinlochmoidart*, a district in the southwest corner of Inverness-shire, between Skye and Mull, where the Young Pretender landed in 1745 with only seven followers

Moidore, a gold coin of Portugal=27s.

Month's mind, constant prayer for a deceased person during the month immediately following his death—a service in the Roman Catholic Church

Mont St. Michel, an island fortress, close to the north coast of France, east of St. Malo was used as a state-prison from the Revolution until 1863

Moonlight (cask of), more usually *moonshine*, smuggled spirits

More solito, in the usual way ; *more tuo*, in your own way

Muckle, much, large, great

Muckle tikes, big wigs, great folks

Muils, or *mullis*, a kind of slippers made of cloth or velvet and embroidered

Muisted, scented

Mull, a snuff-box

Multiplepoinding, a Scottish legal process for enforcing settlement of competing claims to the same fund, the English interpleader

Murray, Miss Nickie. See Miss Nickie Murray

Negatur, I deny it

Negotiorum gestor, manager of affairs

Neist, next

Ne quid nimis, not too much

Nevoy, nephew

Nicol, or *Nichol, Forest*, a border township of Cumberland

Nigri sunt hyacinthi, there are black hyacinths

Nihil novit in causa, he knows nothing of the case

Nipperkin, a small measure for ale or spirits

Nom de guerre, professional nickname

Nomine damni, in name of damages

Noscitur a socio, known by his associate

Noviter repertum, more newly discovered

Ohe, jamsatis, ho ! enough

Omne ignotum pro terribili, the unknown is always taken to be something terrible

Omni suspicione major, above all suspicion

Origo mali, the cause of the evil

Orra, odd, occasional ; *orra sough*, an occasional whiff, breath

Oswald James, author of *The Caledonian Pocket Companion* (1750, etc.), a collection of Scottish musical airs. The tune of " Roslin Castle " is attributed to him

Owe a day's work in harvest. See Day's work etc.

Owerlay, a neckcloth, cravat

Oye, or *oe*, grandson

Pace, Easter

Pack or peel (peile), said

of a burgh freeman who lends his name for trading purposes to one who has not the freedom of the burgh

Pande manum, hold out your hand

Paraffle, ostentatious display

Parma non bene selecta, a defence not well chosen

Parochine, parish

Par ordonnance du medecin, by the doctor's orders

Patria potestas, paternal authority

Pawmie, a stroke on the palm of the hand

Peel-house, a small square tower, used as a place of refuge and defence on the Scottish borders

Pendente lite, whilst the case is proceeding

Per ambages, by circumlocution, in an ambiguous or indirect way

Per contra, on the other part

Perdu, concealed, lying in wait

Pessimi exempli, a very bad example

Pest, Councillor. See Councillor Pest

Pettle, a stick with which the ploughman removes the soil from his plough

Phalaris's bull, a furnace shaped like a bull, into which the tyrant Phalaris, ruler of Agrigentum in ancient Sicily, used to cast his victims

Pike out, pick out

Pint-stoup, a pint measure, containing 4 pints English. See Notes 33, p. 444

Piscator, fisherman

Pistole, a gold coin worth about 16s.

Plack and bawbee, to the last farthing ; *plack-pie*, a pie sold for a plack = ½d. English

Plain-dealer, a comedy (1677) by Wycherley

Pleached, plashed and woven together

Pleugh - stilt, plow - handle

Ploy, a harmless frolic, sport, fête

Pock, or *poke*, bag, process-bag

Pock-pudding, a contemptuous term applied to an Englishman

Poinding and distrenyie-

ing, distraining, seizing upon and taking possession of a debtor's goods

Point d'Espagne, Spanish lace

Point of Cairn, or *Cairn Head*, a promontory in the south-east of Wigtownshire

Point of war, a signal by trumpet or drum

Pooin', pulling

Porte Royale, a Cistercian abbey, 8 miles southwest of Versailles, gave its name to a body of men and women whose aims were closely identified with those of the Jansenists (*q.v.*)

Posse, or *posse comitatus*, the sheriff's levy of citizens to enable him to execute the law

Pottle, a measure containing 2 quarts

Pound Scots = 1s. 8d. English

Powdered (beef), pickled, sprinkled with salt, spices, etc.

Powder-plot boys. Catesby and his fellow-conspirators of the Gunpowder Plot fought most desperately against the government force sent to take them

Prawn dub, the puddle or pool in which prawns could be caught

Prie, or *pree*, to taste

Procurator-fiscal, public prosecutor for a Scotch county

Pund Scots = 1s. 8d. English

Quean, woman, lass, wench

Quebec, the battle by which General James Wolfe won (1759) Canada for the English

Queensferry, the passage of the Firth of Forth where the Great Forth Bridge now stands

Quid tibi cum lyra? What would you do with poetry?

Quin, James, an English actor (1693–1766), at the head of his profession until supplanted by Garrick

Raff, worthless character, rabble, scum

Rainbow, knights of the. See Knights of the rainbow

Rampauging, raging, violent

Rant, a noisy dance-tune; *ranting*, larking and toying, with dancing and drinking

Rapparee, an Irish plunderer, armed with a rappary or half-pike, a worthless fellow

Ratione officii, by virtue of his position

Raxed, stretched

Reaming, frothing, foaming

Redd, arranged, managed

Regiam Majestatem, an ancient collection of Scottish laws

Reiver, robber, forayer

Remedium juris, remedy at law

Remis atque velis, with might and main

Rhino, money, cash

Richard and Richmond, an allusion to Shakespeare's *Richard III.*

Rigdumfunnidos, the humorous name given by Scott to John Ballantyne, is borrowed from H. Carey's *Chrononhotonthologus* (1734)

Rigging, ridge (of a building)

Riped, searched

Rothes, John, Earl of, a supporter of Lauderdale (*q.v.*)

Row, to roll

Rudas, a jade, scold

Rue, take the, to repent of

Rug, a good share, good thing (out of)

Rumble, a shaking roll, tumble, fall

Rumbo, rum, spirits

Sack-doudling, hugging and squeezing the bagpipes, in order to play the instrument

Sacque, or *sack*, a lady's gown, which had a long loose back depending from the collar-band

Sae, so

St. Giles's, the principal Presbyterian church in Edinburgh, situated on the High Street

St. Ninian's of Whiteherne, in Wigtownshire, now called Whithorn, anciently *Candida Casa* (White House), was sacred to the memory of St. Ninian from the 4th century

St. Winifred's Well in

Wales, at Holywell in Flintshire

Sair, very, much

Salvages, savages, rude, uncouth creatures

Sancho's doctor. See Don Quixote, Part II. chap. xlvii., where the doctor is styled Pedro Rezio de Aguero, a native of Tirteafuera

Sancta Winifreda, ora pro nobis, St. Winifred, pray for us

Sartum atque tectum, repaired and covered

Saut, salt

Scarborough warning, first a blow, then a warning, a phrase traced to a practice that prevailed in that town of lynching robbers; another origin is found in the sudden seizure of the castle at Scarborough by Thomas Stafford in the reign of Queen Mary

Scauding, scalding

Scot of Amwell. See John Scot of Amwell

Scots Mile = nearly 9 furlongs; *Scots pint* = three, sometimes four, pints English; *Scots pund, see* Pund Scots; *Scots shilling, see* Shilling Scots

Scowp, or *scoup*, to leap or run from one place to another; to drink off

Scrive, writing

Scrub, a footman in George Farquhar's *Beaux' Stratagem* (1707)

Sculduddery, loose, immoral

Sealch, or *sealgh*, seal

Secundum artem, according to the recognized rules of the art

Sederunt day, day on which the law courts sit

Se'enteen hundred linen, had the web 1700 threads broad. *Compare* Burns' *Tam o' Shanter*

Semple, a common, ordinary man

Shaftesbury, Anthony Ashley Cooper, Earl of, took dexterous advantage of the Popish Plot of Titus Oates

Sheep's-head between a pair of tangs, held over the fire in order to have the wool singed off

Shilling Scots = 1d. English

Shilpit, weak, insipid

Shoon, shoes
Sib, related
Sic, such
Sigma, the Greek letter of the alphabet answering to " s "
Sin, since
Sinning my mercies, a peculiar Scottish phrase expressive of ingratitude for the favors of Providence
Sinon caste, caute tamen, if not modest, yet (be) prudent
Sir John Friend, a wealthy London brewer, executed for treason in 1696. In the text (p. 224) read " Fenwick " instead of " Friend "
Skelloch, screech
Skinker, one who serves out drink, tapster
Skirl, to scream
Skivie, harebrained
Skye. Sir Alexander MacDonald of Sleat and MacLeod of MacLeod, the principal chiefs in Skye, held aloof from the Young Pretender when he landed in Scotland in 1745
Slaint an rey, or *righ*, the king's health !
Sleekit, smooth
Sloken, quench
Slug, a swallow, mouthful, dram
Small swipes, thin drink, weak stuff
Snake in the Grass (1696), an attack upon the Quakers by Charles Leslie, an Anglo-Irish nonjuror (1650–1722)
Sneeshing, snuff
Snell, sharp, terrible
Snow, a vessel rigged very much like a brig
Societas est mater discordiarum, partnership breeds disagreements
Solon, the statesman and law-giver of the ancient Athenians
Somebody's orders (p. 254), the orders of the Duke of Cumberland to show no mercy after the battle of Culloden
Sonsy, good-humored
Sooth bourd is nae bourd, a true joke is no joke
Sortes Virgilianæ, telling fortunes by opening the *Æneid* of Virgil at random and reading the passage that first catches the eye
Soumons, summons

Souple, supple, agile ; cunning
Souter's clod, a kind of course black bread
Sowp, a spoonful
Speer, inquire, ask ; *speerings*, tidings, intelligence
Splore, a spree, frolic
Sprattle, struggle, scramble
Sprush, spruce
Spule-blade, shoulder-blade
Spulzie, illegal removal of another man's goods
Spunk, a sort of match
Spunk out, get wind, leak out
Staneshaw Bank Fair, was held on the bank of the river Eden, not far from Carlisle
Statesman, a small landed proprietor of Cumberland
Stend, to leap, spring, take long steps
Stewartry, the territory over which the peculiar jurisdiction of the officer called a " steward " extended in Scotland
Stibbler, a ludicrous name for a probationer, or Scotch divinity student ; *sticket stibbler*, a student of divinity who has not been able to complete (stuck in) his studies
Stocking, cattle and implements on a farm
Stoup, a liquid measure
Stouthrief, robbery with violence
Stunkard, sullen, obstinate
Sua quemque trahit voluptas, every one has his own way of pleasure
Summar-roll, the list of summary cases

Tace, be silent. " Tace is Latin for a candle " is a proverbial expression enjoining silence and caution
Taciturn secretary. See Facardin of Trebizond
Tack, lease ; *tacksman*, tenant, lessee
Take the rue, repent of a proposal or undertaking
Talis qualis, of some kind
Tam Dalyell. See Old Mortality, Note 29, p. 424, and Note 33, p. 425
Tam Marte quam Mercurio, a soldier as well as a pleader

Tangs. See Sheep's head, etc.
Tass, a glass
Tau, the Greek letter of the alphabet answering to " t "
Tent, notice, care
Teste me, etc. (p. 40), I can testify by being kept awake the whole night
Thairm, catgut
Themis, the ancient Greek goddess of justice
Thirlage, feudal servitude to a particular mill
Threap, to aver, maintain
Threave Castle. See MacLellan of Bombie
Thumbikins, thumbscrew, an instrument of torture
Timotheus, an ancient Greek musician, made many innovations in playing. See also Pope's Essay on Criticism
Tinwald, a seat in Dumfriesshire
Tippenny, twopenny ale
Tirlea Fuera, See Sancho's doctor
Tod, fox
Tongue of the trump, the speaking part of the instrument (Jews'-harp)
Toom, empty
Tour out, to look about one, keep one's weather-eye open
Town, the house and its outbuildings
Toy, a linen or woollen head-dress hanging down over the shoulders
Trance, passage
Triticism, a trite, hackneyed expression, phrase
Tuptowing, declining the Greek verb *tupto*, which means " I strike, I beat "
Twa, two ; *twasom*, by a couple or pair
Twalpenny, twelve-pence Scotch — one penny English
Tynes, gets lost
Tyrones (sing. *tyro*), beginners, apprentices, novices

Unchancy, unlucky
Unco, uncommon, strange ; particularly
Upcome, literally, promise for the future ; here (at the) pinch
Uphaud, to uphold, maintain
Upsides, quits, evens
Urganda, an enchantress in the mediæval romance, *Amadis of Gaul*

Usquebaugh, or *usquebae,* whisky

Vade retro, get thee behind me
Vale, sis memor mei, farewell, remember me
Varium et mutabile semper femina, woman was always capricious and changeable
Verbum sacerdotis, a priest's word
Via facti, by personal act, by force
Vincennes, Castle of about 4 miles east of Paris, sometimes used as a state-prison
Vinco vincentem, etc. (p. (80) If I beat your opponent in competition at law, I beat you ; *vincere vincentem,* to beat the winning (counsel)
Vir sapientia et pietate gravis, a man full of wisdom and piety
Vis animi, force of the spirit
Voet, Jan, Dutch law professor, wrote a *Compendium* (1693) on the Pandects. *See* Note 13, p. 437

Wad, would
Wade and the Duke, Marshal Wade and the Duke of Cumberland, the royal commanders against the Young Pretender in 1745
Wae's me, woe's me ! alack the pity !

Waling, choosing
Wallace, George, an Edinburgh advocate, author of *Principles of the Law of Scotland* (1760)
Wame, belly, womb
Wanchancie, unlucky
Warding, act of, warrant for imprisonment
Ware, to expend
Warlock, wizard
Warren, a well-known manufacturer of blacking
Waur, worse
Weel-freended, had good friends
Ween, to guess
Weepers, strips of muslin or cambric, stitched to the ends of the sleeves as a sign of mourning
Weft, a signal by waving
Weigh-bauk, scales
West Port, the western city gate of Edinburgh
Wet finger, with a, very easily
Wheen, a few, small number
Whilly-whaw, wheedling, cajoling
White cockade, the badge of the Jacobites
Wilkie's blind crowder, an allusion to the picture " The Blind Fiddler," by Sir David Wilkie
William of Nassau, or *King William III.,* is said to have been riding a horse that had belonged to Sir John Fenwick (not

Sir John Friend, as on p. 224), executed for 1697, when the animal stumbled over a mole hill, and threw its rider, and the fall occasioned the king's death
Windy, boastful, bragging
Withershins, backwards in their courses, in the contrary direction
Withers were not unwrung, (p. 239), from Shakespeare's *Hamlet,* Act. iii. sc. 2. The meaning is, he showed no signs of giving way or yielding
Woundy, very, exceedingly
Wouf, a little deranged, half-cracked
Writer to his Majesty's Signet, a member of a privileged body of Scottish lawyers
W.S., Writer to the signet. *See* above
Wud, mad
Wunna, will not
Wuss, to wish

Yards, the playgrounds of the High School, Edinburgh
Yauld, active, sprightly
Yelloch, yell, scream
Yett, gate
Yill, ale
Yowling, howling
Yule, Christmas

INDEX

QUENTIN DURWARD.

INTRODUCTION TO QUENTIN DURWARD.

THE scene of this romance is laid in the 15th century, when the feudal system, which had been the sinews and nerves of national defense, and the spirit of chivalry, by which, as by a vivifying soul, that system was animated, began to be innovated upon and abandoned by those grosser characters who centered their sum of happiness in procuring the personal objects on which they had fixed their own exclusive attachment. The same egotism had indeed displayed itself even in more primitive ages; but it was now for the first time openly avowed as a professed principle of action. The spirit of chivalry had in it this point of excellence, that however overstrained and fantastic many of its doctrines may appear to us, they were all founded on generosity and self-denial, of which if the earth were deprived, it would be difficult to conceive the existence of virtue among the human race.

Among those who were the first to ridicule and abandon the self-denying principles in which the young knight was instructed, and to which he was so carefully trained up, Louis the Eleventh of France was the chief. That sovereign was of a character so purely selfish—so guiltless of entertaining any purpose unconnected with his ambition, covetousness, and desire of selfish enjoyment, that he almost seems an incarnation of the devil himself, permitted to do his utmost to corrupt our ideas of honor in its very source. Nor is it to be forgotten that Louis possessed to a great extent that caustic wit which can turn into ridicule all that a man does for any other person's advantage but his own, and was, therefore, peculiarly qualified to play the part of a cold-hearted and sneering fiend.

In this point of view, Goethe's conception of the character and reasoning of Mephistopheles, the tempting spirit in the singular play of *Faust*, appears to me more happy than that which has been formed by Byron, and even than the Satan of Milton. These last great authors have given to the Evil Principle something which elevates and dignifies his wickedness—a sustained and unconquerable resistance against Omnipotence itself, a lofty scorn of suffering compared with submission, and all those points of attraction in the Author of Evil which have induced Burns and others to consider him as the hero of the _Paradise Lost._ The great German poet has, on the contrary, rendered his seducing spirit a being who, otherwise totally unimpassioned, seems only to have existed for the purpose of increasing, by his persuasions and temptations, the mass of moral evil, and who calls forth by his seductions those slumbering passions which otherwise might have allowed the human being who was the object of the evil spirit's operations to pass the tenor of his life in tranquility. For this purpose Mephistopheles is, like Louis XI., endowed with an acute and depreciating spirit of caustic wit, which is employed incessantly in undervaluing and vilifying all actions the consequences of which do not lead certainly and directly to self-gratification.

Even an author of works of mere amusement may be permitted to be serious for a moment, in order to reprobate all policy, whether of a public or private character, which rests its basis upon the principles of Machiavel or the practise of Louis XI.

The cruelties, the perjuries, the suspicions, of this prince were rendered more detestable, rather than amended, by the gross and debasing superstition which he constantly practised. The devotion to the Heavenly saints, of which he made such a parade, was upon the miserable principle of some petty deputy in office, who endeavors to hide or atone for the malversations of which he is conscious, by liberal gifts to those whose duty it is to observe his conduct, and endeavors to support a system of fraud by an attempt to corrupt the incorruptible. In no other light can we regard his creating the Virgin Mary a countess and colonel of his guards, or the cunning that admitted to one or two peculiar forms of oath the force of a binding obligation which he denied to all others, strictly preserving the secret, which mode of swearing he really accounted obligatory, as one of the most valuable of state mysteries.

To a total want of scruple, or, it would appear, of any sense whatever of moral obligation, Louis XI. added great natural firmness and sagacity of character, with a system of policy so highly refined, considering the times he lived in, that he sometimes overreached himself by giving way to its dictates.

Probably there is no portrait so dark as to be without its

softer shades. He understood the interests of France, and faithfully pursued them so long as he could identify them with his own. He carried the country safe through the dangerous crisis of war termed for " the public good "; in thus disuniting and dispersing this grand and dangerous alliance of the great crown vassals of France against the sovereign, a king of a less cautious and temporizing character, and of a more bold and less crafty disposition, than Louis XI. would in all probability, have failed. Louis had also some personal accomplishments not inconsistent with his public character. He was cheerful and witty in society ; caressed his victim like the cat, which can fawn when about to deal the most bitter wound ; and none was better able to sustain and extol the superiority of the coarse and selfish reasons by which he endeavored to supply those nobler motives for exertion which his predecessors had derived from the high spirit of chivalry.

In fact that system was now becoming ancient, and had, even while in its perfection, something so overstrained and fantastic in its principles, as rendered it peculiarly the object of ridicule, whenever, like other old fashions, it began to fall out of repute, and the weapons of raillery could be employed against it, without exciting the disgust and horror with which they would have been rejected at an early period as a species of blasphemy. In the 14th century a tribe of scoffers had arisen who pretended to supply what was naturally useful in chivalry by other resources, and threw ridicule upon the extravagant and exclusive principles of honor and virtue which were openly treated as absurd, because, in fact, they were cast in a mould of perfection too lofty for the practice of fallible beings. If an ingenous and high-spirited youth proposed to frame himself on his father's principles of honor, he was vulgarly derided as if he had brought to the field the good old knight's Durindarte or two-handed sword, ridiculous from its antique make and fashion, although its blade might be the Ebro's temper, and its ornaments of pure gold.

In like manner, the principles of chivalry were cast aside, and their aid supplied by baser stimulants. Instead of the high spirit which pressed every man forward in the defence of his country, Louis XI. substituted the exertions of the ever ready mercenary soldier, and persuaded his subjects, among whom the mercantile class began to make a figure, that it was better to leave to mercenaries the risks and labors of war, and to supply the crown with the means of paying

them, than to peril themselves in defense of their own substance. The merchants were easily persuaded by this reasoning. The hour did not arrive, in the days of Louis XI.,
when the landed gentry and nobles could be in like manner
excluded from the ranks of war ; but the wily monarch
commenced that system, which, acted upon by his successors,
at length threw the whole military defence of the state into
the hands of the crown.

He was equally forward in altering the principles which
were wont to regulate the intercourse of the sexes. The
doctrines of chivalry had established in theory, at least, a
system in which Beauty was the governing and remunerating
divinity, Valor her slave, who caught his courage from her
eye, and gave his life for her slightest service. It is true,
the system here, as in other branches, was stretched to
fantastic extravagance, and cases of scandal not unfrequently
arose. Still they were generally such as those mentioned by
Burke, where frailty was deprived of half its guilt by being
purified from all its grossness. In Louis XI.'s practice, it
was far otherwise. He was a low voluptuary, seeking
pleasure without sentiment, and despising the sex from
whom he desired to obtain it ; his mistresses were of inferior
rank, as little to be compared with the elevated though
faulty character of Agnes Sorel, as Louis was to his heroic
father, who freed France from the threatened yoke of England. In like manner, by selecting his favorites and
ministers from among the dregs of the people, Louis showed
the slight regard which he paid to eminent station and high
birth ; and although this might be not only excusable but
meritorious, where the monarch's fiat promoted obscure talent, or called forth modest worth, it was very different when
the King made his favorite associates of such men as Tristan
l'Hermite, the chief of his marshalsea or police ; and it was
evident that such a prince could no longer be, as his descendant Francis elegantly designed himself, " the first gentleman
in his dominions."

Nor were Louis's sayings and actions, in private or public,
of a kind which could redeem such gross offences against the
character of a man of honor. His word, generally accounted the most sacred test of a man's character, and the least
impeachment of which is a capital offence by the code of
honor, was forfeited without scruple on the slightest occasion,
and often accompanied by the perpetration of the most enormous crimes. If he broke his own personal and plighted faith,
he did not treat that of the public with more ceremony. His

sending an inferior person disguised as a herald to Edward IV. was in those days, when heralds were esteemed the sacred depositaries of public and national faith, a daring imposition, of which few save this unscrupulous prince would have been guilty. *

In short, the manners, sentiments, and actions of Louis XI. were such as were inconsistent with the principles of chivalry, and his caustic wit was sufficiently disposed to ridicule a system adopted on what he considered as the most absurd of all bases, since it was founded on the principle of devoting toil, talents, and time to the accomplishment of objects from which no personal advantage could, in the nature of things, be obtained.

It is more than probable that, in thus renouncing almost openly the ties of religion, honor, and morality, by which mankind at large feel themselves influenced, Louis sought to obtain great advantages in his negotiations with parties who might esteem themselves bound, while he himself enjoyed liberty. He started from the goal, he might suppose, like the racer who has got rid of the weights with which his competitors are still encumbered, and expects to succeed of course. But Providence seems always to unite the existence of peculiar danger with some circumstance which may put those exposed to the peril upon their guard. The constant suspicion attached to any public person who becomes badly eminent for breach of faith is to him what the rattle is to the poisonous serpent ; and men come at last to calculate, not so much on what their antagonist says, as upon that which he is likely to do ; a degree of mistrust which tends to counteract the intrigues of such a faithless character more than his freedom from the scruples of conscientious men can afford him advantage. The example of Louis XI. raised disgust and suspicion rather than a desire of imitation among other nations in Europe, and the circumstance of his outwitting more than one of his contemporaries operated to put others on their guard. Even the system of chivalry, though much less generally extended than heretofore, survived this profligate monarch's reign, who did so much to sully its luster, and long after the death of Louis XI. it inspired the Knight without Fear and Reproach and the gallant Francis I.

Indeed, although the reign of Louis had been as successful in a political point of view as he himself could have desired, the spectacle of his death-bed might of itself be a

* See Note 46, p. 448.

warning-piece against the seduction of his example. Jealous
of every one, but chiefly of his own son, he immured himself
in his Castle of Plessis, entrusting his person exclusively to
the doubtful faith of his Scottish mercenaries. He never
stirred from his chamber, he admitted no one into it; and
wearied Heaven and every saint with prayers, not for the
forgiveness of his sins, but for the prolongation of his life.
With a poverty of spirit totally inconsistent with his shrewd
worldly sagacity, he importuned his physicians until they insulted as well as plundered him. In his extreme desire of
life, he sent to Italy for supposed relics, and the yet more
extraordinary importation of an ignorant crack-brained peasant, who, from laziness probably, had shut himself up in a
cave, and renounced flesh, fish, eggs, or the produce of the
dairy. This man, who did not possess the slightest tincture
of letters, Louis reverenced as if he had been the Pope himself, and to gain his good-will founded two cloisters.

It was not the least singular circumstance of this course
of superstition that bodily health and terrestrial felicity
seemed to be his only objects. Making any mention of his
sins when talking on the state of his health was strictly prohibited ; and when at his command a priest recited a prayer
to St. Eutropius, in which he recommended the King's welfare both in body and soul, Louis caused the two last words
to be omitted, saying it was not prudent to importune the
blessed saint by too many requests at once. Perhaps he
thought by being silent on his crimes he might suffer them
to pass out of the recollection of the celestial patrons, whose
aid he invoked for his body.

So great were the well-merited tortures of this tyrant's
death-bed, that Philip des Comines enters into a regular comparison between them and the numerous cruelties inflicted
on others by his order ; and, considering both, comes to express an opinion, that the worldly pangs and agony suffered
by Louis were such as might compensate the crimes he had
committed and that, after a reasonable quarantine in purgatory, he might in mercy be found duly qualified for the superior regions.

Fénelon also has left his testimony against this prince,
whose mode of living and governing he has described in the
following remarkable passage :—

Pygmalion, tourmenté par une soif insatiable des richesses, se
rend de plus en plus misérable et odieux à ses sujets. C'est un
crime à Tyr que d'avoir de grands biens ; l'avarice le rend défiant,
soupçonneux, cruel ; il persécute les riches, et il craint les pauvres.

C'est un crime encore plus grand à Tyr d'avoir de la vertu ; car Pygmalion suppose que le bons ne peuvent souffrir ses injustices et ses infamies ; la vertu le condamne ; il s'aigrit el s'irrite contre elle. Tout l'agite inquète, le ronge ; il a peur de son ombre ; il ne dort ni nuit ni jour ; les Dieux, pour le confondre, l'accablent de trésors dont il n'ose jouir. De qu'il cherche pour être heureux est précisément ce qui l'empêche de l'être. Il regrette tout ce qu'il donne ; il craint toujours de perdre ; il se tourmente pour gagner. On ne le voit presque jamais ; il est seul, triste, abattu, au fond de son palais ; ses amis mêmes n'osent l'aborder, de peur, de lui devenir suspects. Une garde terrible tient toujours des épées nues et des piques levées autour de sa maison. Trent chambres qui communiquent les unes aux autres, et dont chacune a une porte de fer avec six gros verroux, sont le lieu où il se renferme ; on ne sait jamais dans laquelle de ces chambres il couche ; et on assure qu'il ne couche jamais deux nuits de suite dans la même, de peur d'y être égorgé. Il ne connoît ni les doux plaisirs, ni l'amitié encore plus douce. Si on lui parle de chercher la joie, il sent qu'elle fuit loin de lui, et qu'elle refuse d'entrer dans son cœur. Ses yeux creux sont pleins d'un feu âpre et farouche ; ils sont sans cesse errans de tous cotés ; il prête l'oreille au moindre bruit, et se sent tout ému ; il est pâle, défait, et les noirs soucis sont peints sur son visage toujours ridé. Il se tait, il soupire, il tire de son cœur de profonds gémissemens, il ne peut cacher les remords qui déchirent ses entrailles. Les mets les plus exquis le dégoûtent. Ses enfans, loin d'être son espérance, sont le sujet de sa terreur : il en a fait ses plus dangereux ennemis. Il n'a eu toute sa vie aucun moment d'assuré : il ne se conserve qu'à force de répandre le sang de tous ceux qu'il craint. Insensé, qui ne voit pas que sa cruauté, à laquelle il se confie, le fera périr ! Quelqu'un de ses domestiques, aussi défiant que lui, se hâtera de délivrer le monde de ce monstre.

The instructive but appalling scene of this tyrant's sufferings was at length closed by death, 30th August, 1483.

The selection of this remarkable person as the principle character in the romance—for it will be easily comprehended that the little love intrigue of Quentin is only employed as the means of bringing out the story—afforded considerable facilities to the Author. The whole of Europe was, during the 15th century, convulsed with dissensions from such various causes, that it would have required almost a dissertation to have brought the English reader with a mind perfectly alive and prepared to admit the possibility of the strange scenes to which he was introduced.

In Louis XI.'s time, extraordinary commotions existed throughout all Europe. England's civil wars were ended rather in appearance than reality by the short-lived ascendency of the house of York. Switzerland was asserting that freedom which was afterwards so bravely defended. In the Empire and in France the great vassals of the crown were endeavoring to emancipate themselves from its control, while

Charles of Burgundy by main force, and Louis more artfully by indirect means, labored to subject them to subser-
vience to their respective sovereignties. Louis, while with
one hand he circumvented and subdued his own rebellious
vassals, labored secretly with the other to aid and encourage
the large trading towns of Flanders to rebel against the Duke
of Burgundy, to which their wealth and irritability naturally
disposed them. In the more woodland districts of Flanders,
the Duke of Gueldres, and William de la Marck, called from
his ferocity the Wild Boar of Ardennes, were throwing off
the habits of knights and gentlemen, to practise the violences
and brutalities of common bandits.

A hundred secret combinations existed in the different
provinces of France and Flanders ; numerous private emissaries of the restless Louis—Bohemians, pilgrims, beggars,
or agents disguised as such—were everywhere spreading the
discontent which it was his policy to maintain in the dominions of Burgundy.

Amidst so great an abundance of materials, it was
difficult to select such as should be most intelligible and
interesting to the reader ; and the Author had to regret
that, though he made liberal use of the power of departing
from the reality of history, he felt by no means confident of
having brought his story into a pleasing, compact, and
sufficiently intelligible form. The mainspring of the plot
is that which all who know the least of the feudal system can
easily understand, though the facts are absolutely fictitious.

The right of a feudal superior was in nothing more universally acknowledged than in his power to interfere in the
marriage of a female vassal. This may appear to exist as a
contradiction both of the civil and canon law, which declare
that marriage shall be free, while the feudal or muncipal jurisprudence, in case of a fief passing to a female, acknowledges
an interest in the superior of the fief to dictate the choice of
her companion in marriage. This is accounted for on the
principle that the superior was, by his bounty, the original
grantor of the fief, and is still interested that the marriage of
the vassal shall place no one there who may be inimical to
his liege lord. On the other hand, it might be reasonably
pleaded that this right of dictating to the vassal, to a certain
extent, in the choice of a husband, is only competent to the
superior from whom the fief is originally derived. There is
therefore no violent improbability in the vassal of Burgundy
flying to the protection of the King of France, to whom the
Duke of Burgundy himself was vassal ; nor is it a great

stretch of probability to affirm, that Louis, unscrupulous as he was, should have formed the design of betraying the fugitive into some alliance which might prove inconvenient, if not dangerous, to his formidable kinsman and vassal of Burgundy.

I may add, that the romance of *Quentin Durward,* which acquired a popularity at home more extensive than some of its predecessors, found also unusual success on the continent,* where the historical allusions awakened more familar ideas.

ABBOTSFORD 1*st December* 1831.

INTRODUCTION TO FIRST EDITION †

And one who hath had losses—go to !
Much Ado About Nothing.

WHEN honest Dogberry sums up and recites all the claims which he had to respectability, and which, as he opined, ought to have exempted him from the injurious appellation conferred on him by Master Gentleman Conrade, it is remarkable that he lays not more emphasis even upon his double gown (a matter of some importance in a certain *ci-devant* capital which I wot of), or upon his being " a pretty piece of flesh as any in Messina," or even upon the conclusive argument of his being " a *rich* fellow enough," than upon his being one " *that hath had losses.*"

Indeed, I have always observed your children of prosperity, whether by way of hiding their full glow of splendor from those whom fortune has treated more harshly, or whether that to have risen in spite of calamity is as honorable to their fortune as it is to a fortress to have undergone a siege, —however this be, I have observed that such persons never fail to entertain you with an account of the damage they sustain by the hardness of the times. You seldom dine at a well-supplied table, but the intervals between the champagne, the burgundy, and the hock are filled, if your entertainer be a moneyed man, with the fall of interest and the difficulty of finding investments for cash, which is therefore lying idle on his hands ; or, if he be a landed

* [See Lockhart's *Life of Scott,* vol. vii. pp. 161-167.]
† It is scarcely necessary to say, that all that follows is imaginary.

proprietor, with a woeful detail of arrears and diminished
rents. This hath its effects. The guests sigh and shake
their heads in cadence with their landlord, look on the
sideboard loaded with plate, sip once more the rich wines
which flow around them in quick circulation, and think of
the genuine benevolence, which, thus stinted of its means,
still lavishes all that it yet possesses on hospitality, and
what is yet more flattering, on the wealth, which, undiminished by these losses, still continues, like the inexhaustible
hoard of the generous Aboulcasem, to sustain, without im-
poverishment, such copious drains.

This querulous humor, however, hath its limits, like to
the conning of grievances, which all valetudinarians know
is a most fascinating pastime, so long as there is nothing to
complain of but chronic complaints. But I never heard a
man whose credit was actually verging to decay talk of the
diminution of his funds ; and my kind and intelligent
physician assures me, that it is a rare thing with those
afflicted with a good rousing fever, or any such active disorder, which

> With mortal crisis doth pretend
> His life to appropinque an end,

to make their agonies the subject of amusing conversation.

Having deeply considered all these things, I am no longer
able to disguise from my readers that I am neither so un-
popular nor so low in fortune as not to have my share in the
distresses which at present afflict the moneyed and landed interest of these realms. Your authors who live upon a
mutton chop may rejoice that it has fallen to threepence
per pound, and, if they have children, gratulate themselves
that the peck-loaf may be had for sixpence ; but we who
belong to the tribe which is ruined by peace and plenty—
we who have lands and beeves, and sell what these poor
gleaners must buy—we are driven to despair by the very
events which would make all Grub Street illuminate its
attics, if Grub Street could spare candle-ends for the
purpose. I therefore put in my proud claim to share in the
distresses which only affect the wealthy ; and write myself
down, with Dogberry, " a rich fellow enough," but still one
" who hath had losses."

With the same generous spirit of emulation, I have had
lately recourse to the universal remedy for the brief im-
pecuniosity of which I complain—a brief residence in a

southern climate, by which I have not only saved many cart-loads of coals, but have also had the pleasure to excite general sympathy for my decayed circumstances among those who, if my revenue had continued to be spent among them, would have cared little if I had been hanged. Thus, while I drink my *vin ordinaire*, my brewer finds the sale of his small-beer diminished—while I discuss my flask of *cinq francs*, my modicum of port hangs on my wine-merchant's hands—while my *côtelette à la Maintenon* is smoking on my plate, the mighty sirloin hangs on its peg in the shop of my blue-aproned friend in the village. Whatever, in short, I spend here is missed at home; and the few sous gained by the *garçon perruquier*, nay, the very crust I give to his little bare-bottomed, red-eyed poodle, are *autant de perdu* to my old friend the barber, and honest Trusty, the mastiff-dog in the yard. So that I have the happiness of knowing at every turn that my absence is both missed and moaned by those who would care little were I in my coffin, were they sure of the custom of my executors. From this charge of self-seeking and indifference, however, I solemnly except Trusty, the yard-dog, whose courtesies towards me, I have reason to think, were of a more disinterested character than those of any other person who assisted me to consume the bounty of the public.

Alas! the advantage of exciting such general sympathies at home cannot be secured without incurring considerable personal inconvenience. "If thou wishest me to weep, thou must first shed tears thyself," says Horace; and, truly, I could sometimes cry myself at the exchange I have made of the domestic comforts which custom had rendered neces-saries for the foreign substitutes which caprice and love of change had rendered fashionable. I cannot but confess with shame, that my home-bred stomach longs for the genuine steak, after the fashion of Dolly's, hot from the gridiron, brown without, and scarlet when the knife is applied; and that all the delicacies of Very's *carte*, with his thousand va-rious orthographies of *bifticks de mouton*, do not supply the vacancy. Then my mother's son cannot learn to delight in thin potations; and, in these days when malt is had for nothing, I am convinced that a double "straick" of John Barleycorn must have converted "the poor domestic creature, small-beer," into a liquor twenty times more generous than the acid unsubstantial tipple which here bears the honored name of wine, though, in substance and qualities, much similiar to your Seine water. Their higher wines, indeed, are well enough—there is nothing to except against in their Château Margout, or Sillery; yet I cannot but remember the generous qualities of my sound old Oporto. Nay, down to the *garçon* and his poodle, though they are both amusing animals, and play ten thousand monkey tricks which are diverting enough, yet there was more sound humor in the wink with which our village Packwood used to communicate the news of the morning than all Antoine's gambols could have expressed in a week, and more of human and dog-like sympathy in the wag of old Trusty's tail than if his rival, Touton, had stood on his hind-legs for a twelvemonth.

These signs of repentance come perhaps a little late, and I own, for I must be entirely candid with my dear friend the public, that they have been somewhat matured by the perversion of my niece Christy to the ancient Popish faith by a certain whacking priest in our neighborhood, and the marriage of my aunt Dorothy to a *demi-solde* captain of horse, a *ci-devant* member of the Legion of Honor, and who would, he assures us have been a field-marshal by this time had our old friend Bonaparte continued to live and to triumph. For the matter of Christy, I must own her head had been so fairly turned at Edinburgh with five routs a night, that, though I somewhat distrusted the means and medium of her conversation, I was at the same time glad to see that she took a serious thought of any kind; besides, there was little loss in the matter, for the convent took her off my hands for a very reasonable pension. But aunt Dorothy's marriage on earth was a very different matter from Christian's celestial espousals. In the first place, there were two thousand three per cents as much lost to my family as if the sponge had been drawn over the national slate, for who the deuce could have thought aunt Dorothy would have married? Above all, who would have thought a woman of fifty years' experience would have married a French anatomy, his lower branch of limbs corresponding with the upper branch, as if one pair of half-extended compasses had been placed perpendicularly upon the top of another, while the space on which the hinges revolved quite sufficed to represent the body? All the rest was mustache, pelisse, and calico trouser. She might have commanded a polk of real Cossacks in 1815, for half the wealth which she surrendered to this military scarecrow. However, there is no more to be said upon the matter, especially as she had come to the length of quoting Rousseau for sentiment; and so let that pass.

Having thus expectorated my bile against a land which is, notwithstanding, a very merry land, and which I cannot blame, because I sought it and it did not seek me, I come to the more immediate purpose of this Introduction, and which, my dearest public, if I do not reckon too much on the continuance of your favors (though, to say truth, consistency and uniformity of taste are scarce to be reckoned upon by those who court your good graces) may perhaps go far to make my amends for the loss and damage I have sustained by bringing aunt Dorothy to the country of thick calves, slender ankles, black mustachios, bodiless limbs (I assure you the fellow is, as my friend Lord L——said, a complete giblet-pie, all legs and wings), and fine sentiments. If she had taken from the half-pay list a ranting Highlandman, ay, or a dashing son of Erin, I would never have mentioned the subject; but as the affair has happened, it is scarce possible not to resent such a gratuitous plundering of her own lawful heirs and executors. But "be hushed, my dark spirit!" and let us invite our dear public to a more pleasing theme to us, a more interesting one to others.

By dint of drinking acid tiff, as above mentioned, and smoking cigars, in which I am no novice, my public are to be informed that I gradually sipped and smoked myself into a certain degree of acquaintance with *un homme comme il faut*, one of the few fine old specimens of nobility who are still to be found in France, who, like mutilated statues of an antiquated and obsolete worship, still command a certain portion of awe and estimation in the eyes even of those by whom neither one nor other are voluntarily rendered.

On visiting the coffee-house of the village, I was at first struck with the singular dignity and gravity of this gentleman's manners, his sedulous attachment to shoes and stockings in contempt of half-boots and pantaloons, the *croix de St Louis* at his button-hole, and a small white cockade in the loop of his old-fashioned *schakos*. There was something interesting in his whole appearance; and besides, his gravity among the lively group around him seemed like the shade of a tree in the glare of a sunny landscape, more interesting from its rarity. I made such advances towards acquaintance as the circumstances of the place and the manners of the country authorized—that is to say, I drew near him, smoked my cigar by calm and intermitted puffs, which were scarcely visible, and asked him those few questions which good-breeding everywhere, but more especially in France, permits strangers to put without hazarding the imputation of impertinence. The Marquis de Hautlieu, for such was his rank, was as short and sententious as French politeness permitted. He answered every question, but proposed nothing, and encouraged no farther inquiry.

The truth was, that, not very accessible to foreigners of any nation, or even to strangers among his own countrymen, the marquis was peculiarly shy towards the English. A remnant of ancient national prejudice might dictate this feeling; or it might arise from his idea that they are a haughty, purse-proud people, to whom rank united with straitened circumstances, affords as much subject for scorn as for pity; or finally, when he reflected on certain recent events, he might perhaps feel mortified as a Frenchman even for those successes which had restored his master to the throne and himself to a diminished property and dilapidated *château*. His dislike, however, never assumed a more active form than that of alienation from English society. When the affairs of strangers required the interposition of his influence in their behalf, it was uniformly granted with the courtesy of a French gentleman who knew what is due to himself and to national hospitality.

At length, by some chance, the marquis made the discovery that the new frequenter of his ordinary was a native of Scotland—a circumstance which told mightily in my favor. Some of his own ancestors, he informed me, had been of Scottish origin, and he believed his house had still some relations, in what he was pleased to call the province of Hanguisse in that country. The connection had been acknowledged early in the last century on both sides, and he had once almost determined during his exile (for it may be supposed that the marquis had joined the ranks of Condé, and shared all the misfortune and distresses of emigration) to claim the acquaintance and protection of his Scottish friends. But after all, he said, he cared not to present himself before them in circumstances which could do them but small credit, and which they might think entailed some little burden, perhaps even some little disgrace ; so that he thought it best to trust in Providence and do the best he could for his own support. What that was I never could learn ; but I am sure it inferred nothing which could be discreditable of the excellent old man, who held fast his opinions and his loyalty, through good and bad repute, till time restored him, aged, indigent, and broken spirited, to the country which he had left in the prime of youth and health, and sobered by age into patience, instead of that tone of

high resentment which promised speedy vengeance upon
those who expelled him. I might have laughed at some
points of the marquis's character, at his prejudices particularly, both at birth and politics, if I had known him under
more prosperous circumstances ; but, situated as he was,
even if they had not been fair and honest prejudices, turning
on no base or interested motive, one must have respected him
as we respect the confessor of the martyr of a religion which
is not entirely our own.

By degrees we became good friends, drank our coffee,
smoked our cigar, and took our *bavoroise* together, for more
than six weeks, with little interruption from avocations on
either side. Having with some difficulty got the key-note of
his inquiries concerning Scotland, by a fortunate conjecture
that the *province d'Hanguisse* could only be our shire of
Angues, I was enabled to answer the most of his queries concerning his allies there in a manner more or less satisfactory,
and was much surprised to find the marquis much better
acquainted with the genealogy of some of the distinguished
families in that county than I could possibly have expected.

On his part his satisfaction at our intercourse was so great
that he at length wound himself to such a pitch of resolution
as to invite me to dine at the Château de Hautlieu, well deserving the name, as occupying a commanding eminence on the
banks of the Loire. This building lay about three miles from
the town at which I had settled my temporary establishment ;
and when I first beheld it I could easily forgive the mortified
feelings which the owner testified at receiving a guest in the
asylum which he had formed out of the ruins of the palace of
his fathers. He gradually, with much gaiety, which yet
evidently covered a deeper feeling, prepared me for the sort
of place I was about to visit ; and for this he had full opportunity whilst he drove me in his little cabriolet, drawn by a
large heavy Norman horse, towards the ancient building.

Its remains run along a beautiful terrace overhanging the
river Loire, which had been formerly laid out with a succession
of flights of steps, highly ornamented with statues, rockwork,
and other artificial embellishments, descending from one
terrace to another until the very verge of the river was attained. All this architectural decoration, with its accompanying parterres of rich flowers and exotic shrubs, had,
many years since, given place to the more profitable scene of
the vine-dresser's labors ; yet the remains, too massive to be
destroyed, are still visible, and, with the various artificial
slopes and levels of the high bank, bear perfect evidence

how actively art had been here employed to decorate nature.

Few of these scenes are now left in perfection ; for the fickleness of fashion has accomplished in England the total change which devastation and popular fury have produced in the French pleasure-grounds. For my part, I am contented to subscribe to the opinion of the best qualified judge of our time, * who thinks we have carried to an extreme our taste for simplicity, and that the neighborhood of a stately mansion requires some more ornate embellishments than can be derived from the meager accompaniments of grass and gravel. A highly romantic situation may be degraded, perhaps, by an attempt at such artificial ornaments ; but then, in by far the greater number of sites, the intervention of more architectural decoration than is now in use seems necessary to redeem the naked tameness of a large house, placed by itself in the midst of a lawn, where it looks as much unconnected with all around as if it had walked out of town upon an airing.

How the taste came to change so suddenly and absolutely is rather a singular circumstance, unless we explain it on the same principle on which the three friends of the father in Molière's comedy recommend a cure for the melancholy of his daughter—that he should furnish her apartments, viz., with paintings, with tapestry, or with china, according to the different commodities in which each of them was a dealer. Tried by this scale, we may perhaps discover that, of old, the architect laid out the garden and the pleasure-grounds in the neighborhood of the mansion, and, naturally enough, displayed his own art there in statues and vases, and paved terraces and flights of steps with ornamented balustrades ; while the gardener, subordinate in rank, endeavored to make the vegetable kingdom correspond to the prevailing taste, and cut his evergreens into verdant walls, with towers and battlements, and his detached trees into a resemblance of statuary. But the wheel has since revolved, so as to place the landscape-gardener, as he is called, almost upon a level with the architect ; and hence a liberal and somewhat violent use is made of spade and pick-ax, and a conversion of the ostentatious labors of the architect into a *ferme ornee,* as little different from the simplicity of nature, as displayed in the surrounding country, as the comforts of convenient and cleanly walks imperiously demanded in the vicinage of a gentleman's residence can possibly admit.

* See Price on the Picturesque. Note 1.

To return from this digression, which has given the marquis's cabriolet (its activity greatly retarded by the downward
propensities of Jean Roast-Beef, which I suppose the Norman horse cursed as heartily as his countrymen of old time
execrated the stolid obesity of a Saxon slave) time to ascend
the hill by a winding causeway, now much broken, we came in
sight of a long range of roofless buildings connected with the
western extremity of the castle, which was totally ruinous.
" I should apologize," he said, " to you, as an Englishman,
for the taste of my ancestors, in connecting that row of
stables with the architecture of the château. I know in your
country it is usual to remove them to some distance ; but my
family had an hereditary pride in horses, and were fond of
visiting them more frequently than would have been convenient if they had been kept at a greater distance. Before
the Revolution I had thirty fine horses in that ruinous
line of buildings."

This recollection of past magnificence escaped from him
accidentally, for he was generally sparing in alluding to his
former opulence. It was quietly said, without any affectation either of the importance attached to early wealth, or as
demanding sympathy for its having passed away. It
awakened unpleasing reflections, however, and we were both
silent, till, from a partially repaired corner of what had been
a porter's lodge, a lively French *paysanne*, with eyes as black
as jet and as brilliant as diamonds, came out with a smile,
which showed a set of teeth that duchesses might have envied,
and took the reins of the little carriage.

" Madelon must be groom to-day," said the marquis, after
graciously nodding in return for her deep reverence to Monsieur, " for her husband is gone to market ; and for La
Jeunesse, he is almost distracted with his various occupations. Madelon," he continued, as he walked forward under
the entrance-arch, crowned with the mutilated armorial
bearings of former lords, now half-obscured by moss and
rye-grass, not to mention the vagrant branches of some
unpruned shrubs—" Madelon was my wife's god-daughter,
and was educated to be *fille-de-chambre* to my daughter."

This passing intimation, that he was a widowed husband
and childless father, increased my respect for the unfortunate nobleman, to whom every particular attached to his
present situation brought doubtless its own share of food for
melancholy reflection. He proceeded, after the pause of an
instant, with something of a gayer tone—" You will be entertained with my poor La Jeunesse," he said, " who, by the

way, is ten years older than I am (the marquis is above sixty) ; he reminds me of the player in the *Roman Comique*, who acted a whole play in his own proper person ; he insists on being *maître d'hôtel, maître de cuisine, valet-de-chambre,* a whole suite of attendants in his own poor individuality. He sometimes reminds me of a character in the *Bridle of Lammermore*, which you must have read, as it is the work of one of your *gens de lettres, qu'on appelle, je crois, le Chevalier Scott.*" *

"I presume you mean Sir Walter ? "

"Yes—the same—the same," answered the marquis.

We were now led away from more painful recollections ; for I had to put my French friend right in two particulars. In the first I prevailed with difficulty ; for the marquis, though he disliked the English, yet, having been three months in London, piqued himself on understanding the most intricate difficulties of our language, and appealed to every dictionary, from Florio downwards, that *la bride* must mean "the bridle." Nay, so skeptical was he on this point of philology, that when I ventured to hint that there was nothing about a bridle in the whole story, he with great composure, and little knowing to whom he spoke, laid the whole blame of that inconsistency on the unfortunate author. I had next the common candor to inform my friend, upon grounds which no one could know so well as myself, that my distinguished literary countryman, of whom I shall always speak with the respect his talents deserve, was not responsible for the slight works which the humor of the public had too generously, as well as too rashly, ascribed to him. Surprised by the impulse of the moment, I might even have gone farther, and clinched the negative by positive evidence, owning to my entertainer that no one else could possibly have written these works, since I myself was the author, when I was saved from so rash a commitment of myself by the calm reply of the marquis, that he was glad to hear these sort of trifles were not written by a person of condition. "We read them," he said, "as we listen to the pleasantries of a comedian, or as our ancestors did to those of a professed family-jester, with a good deal of amusement, which, however, we should be sorry to derive from the mouth of one who has better claims to our society."

I was completely recalled to my constitutional caution by

---

* It is scarce necessary to remind the reader that this passage was published during the Author's incognito ; and, as Lucio expresses it, spoken "according to the trick."

this declaration, and became so much afraid of committing myself, that I did not even venture to explain to my aristocratic friend that the gentleman whom he had named owed his advancement, for aught I had ever heard, to certain works of his, which may, without injury, be compared to romances in rhyme.

The truth is, that amongst some other unjust prejudices, at which I have already hinted, the marquis had contracted a horror, mingled with contempt, for almost every species of author-craft slighter than that which compounds a folio volume of law or of divinity, and looked upon the author of a romance, novel, fugitive poem, or periodical piece of criticism as men do on a venomous reptile, with fear at once and with loathing. The abuse of the press, he contended, especially in its lighter departments, had poisoned the whole morality of Europe, and was once more gradually regaining an influence which had been silenced amidst the voice of war. All writers except those of the largest and heaviest calibre, he conceived to be devoted to this evil cause, from Rousseau and Voltaire down to Pigault le Brun and the author of the Scotch novels ; and although he admitted he read them *pour passer le temps,* yet like Pistol eating his leek, it was not without execrating the tendency, as he devoured the story, of the work with which he was engaged.

Observing this peculiarity, I backed out of the candid confession which my vanity had meditated, and engaged the marquis in farther remarks on the mansion of his ancestors. "There," he said, "was the theater where my father used to procure an order for the special attendance of some of the principal actors of the Comédie Françoise when the King and Madame Pompadour more than once visited him at this place ; yonder, more to the center, was the baron's hall where his feudal jurisdiction was exercised when criminals were to be tried by the seigneur or his bailiff; for we had, like your old Scottish nobles, the right of pit and gallows, or *fossa cum furca,* as the civilians term it. Beneath that lies the question-chamber, or apartment for torture ; and, truly, I am sorry a right so liable to abuse should have been lodged in the hands of any living creature. But," he added, with a feeling of dignity derived even from the atrocities which his ancestors had committed beneath the grated windows to which he pointed, "such is the effect of superstition that, to this day, the peasants dare not approach the dungeons, in which, it is said, the wrath of my ancestors had perpetrated, in former times, much cruelty."

As we approached the window, while I expressed some curiosity to see this abode of terror, there arose from its subterranean abyss a shrill shout of laughter, which we easily detected as produced by a group of playful children, who had made the neglected vaults a theatre for a joyous romp at Colin Maillard.

The marquis was somewhat disconcerted, and had recourse to his *tabatière;* but, recovering in a moment, observed these were Madelon's children, and familiar with the supposed terrors of the subterranean recesses. " Besides," he added, " to speak the truth, these poor children have been born after the period of supposed illumination, which dispelled our superstition and our religion at once ; and this bids me to remind you, that this is a *jour maigre.* The *curé* of the parish is my only guest, besides yourself, and I would not voluntarily offend his opinions. Besides," he continued more manfully, and throwing off his restraint, " adversity has taught me other thoughts on these subjects than those which prosperity dictated ; and I thank God I am not ashamed to avow that I follow the observances of my church."

I hastened to answer, that, though they might differ from those of my own, I had every possible respect for the religious rules of every Christian community, sensible that we addressed the same Deity, on the same grand principle of salvation, though with different forms ; which variety of worship, had it pleased the Almighty not to permit, our observances would have been as distinctly prescribed to us as they are laid down under the Mosaic law.

The marquis was no shaker of hands, but upon the present occasion he grasped mine and shook it kindly—the only mode of acquiescence in my sentiments which perhaps a zealous Catholic could or ought consistently to have given upon such an occasion.

This circumstance of explanation and remark, with others which arose out of the view of the extensive ruins, occupied us during two or three turns upon the long terrace, and a seat of about a quarter of an hour's duration in a vaulted pavilion of freestone, decorated with the marquis's armorial bearings, the roof of which, though disjointed in some of its groined arches, was still solid and entire. " Here " said he, resuming the tone of a former part of his conversation, " I love to sit, either at noon, when the alcove affords me shelter from the heat, or in the evening, when the sun's beams are dying on the broad face of the Loire—here in the words of your great poet, whom, Frenchman as I am, I am more inti-

mately acquainted with than most Englishmen, I love to rest
myself,

'Showing the code of sweet and bitter fancy.'"

Against this various reading of a well-known passage in
Shakspeare, I took care to offer no protest ; for I suspect
Shakspeare would have suffered in the opinion of so delicate
a judge as the marquis, had I proved his having written
"chewing the cud," according to all other authorities.
Besides, I had had enough of our former dispute, having
been long convinced (though not until ten years after I had
left Edinburgh College) that the pith of conversation does
not consist in exhibiting your own superior knowledge on
matters of small consequence, but in enlarging, improving,
and correcting the information you possess by the authority
of others. I therefore let the marquis *show his code* at his
pleasure, and was rewarded by his entering into a learned
and well-informed disquisition on the florid style of architecture introduced into France during the 17th century. He
pointed out its merits and its defects with considerable taste ;
and having touched on topics similar to those upon which I
have formerly digressed, he made an appeal of a different
kind in their favor, founded on the associations with which
they were combined. "Who," he said, "would willingly
destroy the terraces of the château of Sully, since we cannot
tread them without recalling the image of that statesman,
alike distinguished for severe integrity and for strong and
unerring sagacity of mind ? Were they an inch less broad,
a ton's weight less massive, or were they deprived of their
formality by the slightest inflections, could we suppose them
to remain the scene of his patriotic musings ? Would an
ordinary root-house be a fit scene for the duke occupying an
arm-chair and his duchess a *tabouret,* teaching from thence
lessons of courage and fidelity to his sons, of modesty and
submission to his daughters, of rigid morality to both ; while
the circle of young *noblesse* listened with ears attentive, and
eyes modestly fixed on the ground, in a standing posture,
neither replying nor sitting down without the express command of their Prince and parent ? No, monsieur," he said
with enthusiasm ; " destroy the princely pavilion in which
this edifying family-scene was represented, and you remove
from the mind the vraisemblance, the veracity, of the whole
representation. Or can your mind suppose this distinguished
peer and patriot walking in a *jardin Anglois ?* Why, you
might as well fancy him dressed with a blue frock and white

waistcoat, instead of his Henri Quatre coat and *chapeau-à-plumes.* Consider how he could have moved in the tortuous maze of what you have called a *ferme ornée,* with his usual attendants of two files of Swiss guards preceding and the same number following him. To recall his figure, with his beard, *haut-de-chausses à cannon,* united to his doublet by ten thousand *aiguilettes* and knots of ribbon, you could not, supposing him in a modern *jardin Anglois,* distinguish the picture in your imagination from the sketch of some mad old man, who has adopted the humor of dressing like his great-great-grandfather, and whom a party of *gens-d'armes* were conducting to the *hôpital des fous.* But look on the long and magnificent terrace, if it yet exists, which the loyal and exalted Sully was wont to make the scene of his solitary walk twice a-day, while he pondered over the patriotic schemes which he nourished for advancing the glory of France, or, at a later and more sorrowful period of life, brooded over the memory of his murdered master and the fate of his distracted country : throw in that noble background of arcades, vases, images, urns, and whatever could express the vicinity of a ducal palace, and the landscape becomes consistent at once. The *factionnaires,* with their harquebusses ported, placed at the extremity of the long and level walk, intimate the presence of the feudal prince ; while the same is more clearly shown by the guard of honor which, precede and follow him, their halberds carried upright, their mien martial and stately, as if in the presence of an enemy, yet moved, as it were, with the same soul as their princely superior ; teaching their steps to attend upon his, marching as he marches, halting as he halts, accommodating their pace even to the slight irregularities of pause and advance dictated by the fluctuations of his reverie, and wheeling with military precision before and behind him, who seems the center and animating principle of their armed files, as the heart gives life and energy to the human body. Or, if you smile," added the marquis, looking doubtfully on my countenance, " at a promenade so inconsistent with the light freedom of modern manners, could you bring your mind to demolish that other terrace trod by the fascinating Marchioness de Sévigné, with which are united so many recollections connected with passages in her enchanting letters ? "

A little tired of this disquisition, which the marquis certainly dwelt upon to exalt the natural beauties of his own terrace, which, dilapitated as it was, required no such formal recommendation, I informed my companion that I had just received from England a journal of a tour made in the south of France by a young Oxonian friend of mine, a poet, a draughtsman, and a scholar, in which he gives such an animated and interesting description of the Château Grignan, the dwelling of Madame de Sévigné's beloved daughter, and frequently the place of her own residence, that no one who ever read the book would be within forty miles of the same without going a pilgrimage to the spot. The marquis smiled, seemed very much pleased, and asked the title at length of the work in question ; and writing down to my dictation, *An Itinerary of Provence and the Rhone, made during the year* 1819,* by John Hughes, A.M., of Oriel College, Oxford, observed, he could now purchase no books for the château, but would recommend that the *Itinèraire* should be commissioned for the library to which he was *abonné* in the neighboring town. " And here," he said, " comes the curé to save us farther disquisition ; and I see La Jeunesse gliding round the old portico on the terrace, with the purpose of ringing the dinner-bell—a most unnecessary ceremony for assembling three persons, but which it would break the old man's heart to forego. Take no notice of him at present, as he wishes to perform the duties of the inferior departments incognito ; when the bell has ceased to sound, he will blaze forth on us in the character of major-domo."

As the marquis spoke, we had advanced towards the eastern extremity of the château, which was the only part of the edifice that remained still habitable.

" The *Bande Noire*," said the marquis, " when they pulled the rest of the house to pieces, for the sake of the lead, timber, and other materials, have, in their ravages, done me the undesigned favor to reduce it to dimensions better fitting the circumstances of the owner. There is enough of the leaf left for the catapillar to coil up his chrysalis in, and what needs he care though reptiles have devoured the rest of the bush ?"

As he spoke thus, we reached the door, at which La Jeunesse appeared, with an air at once of prompt service and deep respect, and a countenance which, though puckered by a thousand wrinkles, was ready to answer the first good-natured word of his master with a smile, which showed his white set of teeth firm and fair, in despite of age and suffering. His clean silk stockings, washed till their tint had become yellowish, his cue tied with a rosette, the thin gray curl on either side of his lank cheek, the pearl-colored coat, without a

* See Hughes's *Itinerary.* Note 2.

collar, the solitaire, the *jabot*, the ruffles at the wrist, and
the *chapeau-bras*—all announced that La Jeunesse considered
the arrival of a guest at the château as an unusual event,
which was to be met with a corresponding display of magnificence and parade on his part.

As I looked at the faithful though fantastic follower of his
master, who doubtless inherited his prejudices as well as his
cast-clothes, I could not but own, in my own mind, the resemblance pointed out by the marquis betwixt him and my
own Caleb, the trusty squire of the Master of Ravenswood.
But a Frenchman, a Jack-of-all-trades by nature, can, with
much more ease and suppleness, address himself to a variety
of services, and suffice in his own person to discharge them
all, than is possible for the formality and slowness of a Scottishman.   Superior to Caleb in dexterity, though not in zeal,
La Jeunesse seemed to multiply himself with the necessities
of the occasion, and discharged his several tasks with such
promptitude and assiduity, that farther attendance than his
was neither missed nor wished for.

The dinner, in particular, was exquisite.   The soup,
although bearing the term of *maigre*, which Englishmen use
in scorn, was most delicately flavored, and the matelot of
pike and eels reconciled me, though a Scottishman, to the
latter.   There was even a *petit plat* of *bouilli* for the heretic,
so exquisitely dressed as to retain all the juices, and, at the
same time, rendered so thoroughly tender that nothing could
be more delicate.   The *potage*, with another small dish or
two, was equally well arranged.   But what the old *maître
d'hôtel* valued himself upon as something superb, smiling
with self-satisfaction, and in enjoyment of my surprise, as
he placed it on the table, was an immense *assiettée* of spinage,
not smoothed into a uniform surface, as by our uninaugurated
cooks upon your side of the water, but swelling into hills
and declining into vales, over which swept a gallant stag,
pursued by a pack of hounds in full cry, and a noble field of
horsemen with bugle-horns, and whips held upright, and
brandished after the manner of broadswords—hounds, huntsman, and stag being all very artificially cut out of toasted
bread.   Enjoying the praises which I failed not to bestow on
this *chef d'œuvre*, the old man acknowledged it had cost the
best part of two days to bring it to perfection ; and added,
given honor where honor was due, that an idea so brilliant
was not entirely his own, but that Monsieur himself had
taken the trouble to give him several valuable hints, and
even condescended to assist in the execution of some of the

most capital figures. The marquis blushed a little at this *éclaircissement,* which he might probably have wished to suppress, but acknowledged he had wished to surprise me with a scene from the popular poem of my country, *Miladi Lac.* I answered, that "So splendid a cortege much more resembled a *grand chasse* of Louis Quatorze than of a poor King of Scotland, and that the *paysage* was rather like Fontainebleau than the wilds of Callander." He bowed graciously in answer to this compliment, and acknowledged that recollections of the costume of the old French court, when in its splendor, might have misled his imagination—and so the conversation passed on to other matters.

Our dessert was exquisite : the cheese, the fruits, the salad, the olives, the *cerneaux,* and the delicious white wine, each in their way were *impayables ;* and the good marquis, with an air of great satisfaction, observed, that his guests did sincere homage to their merits. "After all," he said, "and yet it is but confessing a foolish weakness—but, after all, I cannot but rejoice in feeling myself equal to offering a stranger a sort of hospitality which seems pleasing to him. Believe me, it is not entirely out of pride that we *pauvre revenants* live so very retired, and avoid the duties of hospitality. It is true, that too many of us wander about the halls of our fathers, rather like ghosts of their deceased proprietors than like living men restored to their own possessions ; yet it is rather on your account, than to spare our own feelings, that we do not cultivate the society of our foreign visitors. We have an idea that your opulent nation is particularly attached to *faste* and to *grande chère*—to your ease and enjoyment of every kind ; and the means of entertainment left to us are, in most cases, so limited, that we feel ourselves totally precluded from such expense and ostentation. No one wishes to offer his best where he has reason to think it will not give pleasure ; and as many of you publish your journals, *monsier la marquis* would not probably be much gratified by seeing the poor dinner which he was able to present to *milord Anglais* put upon permanent record."

I interrupted the marquis, that were I to wish an account of my entertainment published, it would be only in order to preserve the memory of the very best dinner I ever had eaten in my life. He bowed in return, and presumed that "I either differed much from the national taste, or the accounts of it were greatly exaggerated. He was particularly obliged to me for showing the value of the possessions which remained to him. The useful," he said, "had no doubt survived the sumptuous at Hautlieu as elsewhere. Grottoes, statues, curious conservatories of exotics, temple and tower, had gone to the ground ; but the vineyard, the *potager*, the orchard, the *étange*, still existed " ; and once more he expressed himself " happy to find that their combined productions could make what even a Briton accepted as a tolerable meal. " I only hope," he continued, " that you will convince me your compliments are sincere by accepting the hospitality of the Château de Hautlieu as often as better engagements will permit during your stay in this neighborhood."

I readily promised to accept an invitation offered with such grace as to make the guest appear the person conferring the obligation.

The conversation then changed to the history of the chateau and its vicinity—a subject which was strong ground to the marquis, though he was no great antiquary, and even no very profound historian, when other topics were discussed. The curé, however, chanced to be both, and withal a very conversable, pleasing man, with an air of *prévenance* and ready civility of communication, which I have found a leading characteristic of the Catholic clergy, whether they are well-informed or otherwise. It was from him that I learned there still existed the remnant of a fine library in the Château de Hautlieu. The marquis shrugged his shoulders as the curé gave me this intimation, looked to the one side and the other, and displayed the same sort of petty embarrassment which he had been unable to suppress when La Jeunesse blabbed something of his interference with the arrangements of the *cuisine*. "I should be happy to show the books," he said, "but they are in such a wild condition, so dismantled, that I am ashamed to exhibit them to any one."

"Forgive me, my dear sir," said the curé, "you know you permitted the great English bibliomaniac, Dr. Dibdin, to consult your curious relics, and you know how highly he spoke of them."

"What could I do, my dear friend ?" said the marquis ; " the good doctor had heard some exaggerated account of these remnants of what was once a library ; he had stationed himself in the *auberge* below, determined to carry his point or die under the walls. I even heard of his taking the altitude of the turret in order to provide scaling-ladders. You would not have had me reduce a respectable divine, though of another church, to such an act of desperation ? I could not have answered it in conscience."

"But you know, besides, *monsieur le marquis,*" continued the curé, "that Dr. **Dibdin** was so much grieved at the dilapidation your library had sustained, that he avowedly envied the powers of our church, so much did he long to launch an anathema at the heads of the perpetrators."

"His resentment was in proportion to his disappointment, I suppose," said our entertainer.

"Not so," said the curé; "for he was so enthusiastic on the value of what remains, that I am convinced nothing but your positive request to the contrary prevented the Château of Hautlieu occupying at least twenty pages in that splendid work of which he sent us a copy, and which will remain a lasting monument of his zeal and erudition."

"Dr. Dibdin is extremely polite," said the marquis; "and when we have had our coffee—here it comes—we will go to the turret; and I hope, as monsieur has not despised my poor fare, so he will pardon the state of my confused library, while I shall be equally happy if it can afford anything which can give him amusement. Indeed," he added, "were it otherwise, you, my good father, have every right over books which, without your intervention, would never have returned to the owner."

Although this additional act of courtesy was evidently wrested by the importunity of the curé from his reluctant friend, whose desire to conceal the nakedness of the land, and the extent of his losses, seemed always to struggle with his disposition to be obliging, I could not help accepting an offer which, in strict politeness, I ought perhaps to have refused. But then the remains of a collection of such curiosity as had given to our bibliomaniacal friend the desire of leading the forlorn hope in an escalade—it would have been a desperate act of self-denial to have declined an opportunity of seeing it. La Jeunesse brought coffee, such as we only taste on the continent, upon a salver, covered with a napkin, that it might be *censé* for silver, and *chasse-café* from Martinique on a small waiter, which was certainly so. Our repast thus finished, the marquis led me up an *escalier derobé* into a very large and well-proportioned saloon of nearly one hundred feet in length, but so waste and dilapidated, that I kept my eyes on the ground, lest my kind entertainer should feel himself called upon to apologize for tattered pictures and torn tapestry, and, worse than both, for casements that had yielded, in one or two instances, to the boisterous blast.

"We have contrived to make the turret something more habitable," said the marquis, as he moved hastily through this chamber of desolation. "This," he said, "was the picture gallery in former times, and in the boudoir, beyond, which we now occupy as a book-closet, were preserved some curious cabinet paintings, whose small size required that they should be viewed closely."

As he spoke, he held aside a portion of the tapestry I have mentioned, and we entered the room of which he spoke.

It was octangular, corresponding to the external shape of the turret whose interior it occupied. Four of the sides had latticed windows, commanding each, from a different point, the most beautiful prospect over the majestic Loire and the adjacent country through which it winded ; and the casements were filled with stained glass, through two of which streamed the luster of the setting sun, showing a brilliant assemblage of religious emblems and armorial bearings, which it was scarcely possible to look at with an undazzled eye ; but the other two windows, from which the sunbeams had passed away, could be closely examined, and plainly showed that the lattices were glazed with stained glass, which did not belong to them originally, but, as I afterwards learned, to the profaned and desecrated chapel of the castle. It had been the amusement of the marquis for several months to accomplish this *rifacimento*, with the assistance of the curate and the all-capable La Jeunesse ; and though they had only patched together fragments, which were in many places very minute, yet the stained glass, till examined very closely, and with the eye of an antiquary, produced, on the whole, a very pleasing effect.

The sides of the apartment not occupied by the lattices were, except the space for the small door, fitted up with presses and shelves, some of walnut-tree, curiously carved, and brought to a dark color by time, nearly resembling that of a ripe chestnut, and partly of common deal, employed to repair and supply the deficiencies occasioned by violence and devastation. On these shelves were deposited the wrecks, or rather the precious relics of a most splendid library.

The marquis's father had been a man of information, and his grandfather was famous, even in the court of Louis XIV., where literature was in some degree considered as the fashion, for the extent of his acquirements. Those two proprietors, opulent in their fortunes, and liberal in the indulgence of their taste, had made such additions to a curious old Gothic library, which had descended from their ancestors, that there were few collections in France which could be compared to that of Hautlieu. It had been completely dispersed, in consequence of an ill-judged attempt of the present marquis, in 1790, to defend his château against a revolutionary mob. Luckily, the curé, who, by his charitable and moderate conduct and his evangelical virtues, possessed much interest among the neighboring peasantry, prevailed on many of them to buy, for the petty sum of a few sous, and sometimes at the vulgar rate of a glass of brandy, volumes which had cost large sums, but which were carried off in mere spite by the ruffians who pillaged the castle. He himself also had purchased as many of the books as his funds could possibly reach, and to his care it was owing that they were restored to the turret in which I found them. It was no wonder, therefore, that the good curé had some pride and pleasure in showing the collection to strangers.

In spite of odd volumes, imperfections, and all the other mortifications which an amateur encounters in looking through an ill-kept library, there were many articles in that of Hautlieu calculated, as Bayes says, " to elevate and surprise" the bibliomaniac. There were,

The small rare volume, dark with tarnish'd gold,

as Dr. Ferriar feelingly sings—curious and richly painted missals, manuscripts of 1380, 1320, and even earlier, and works in Gothic type, printed in the 15th and 16th centuries. But of these I intend to give a more detailed account should the marquis grant his permission.

In the meantime, it is sufficient to say that, delighted with the day I had spent at Hautlieu, I frequently repeated my visit, and that the key of the octangular tower was always at my command. In those hours I became deeply enamored of a part of French history, which, although most important to that of Europe at large, and illustrated by an inimitable old historian, I had never sufficiently studied. At the same time, to gratify the feelings of my excellent host, I occupied myself occasionally with some family memorials which had fortunately been preserved, and which contained some curious particulars respecting the connection with Scotland, which first found my favor in the eyes of the Marquis de Hautlieu.

I pondered on these things, *more meo*, until my return to Britain, to beef and sea-coal fires—a change of residence which took place since I drew up these Gallic reminiscences.

At length the result of my meditations took the form of which my readers, if not startled by this preface, will presently be enabled to judge. Should the public receive it with favor, I shall not regret having been for a short time an absentee.

QUENTIN DURWARD

CHAPTER I

THE CONTRAST

Look here upon this picture, and on this,
The counterfeit presentment of two brothers.
Hamlet.

THE latter part of the 15th century prepared a train of
future events, that ended by raising France to that state of
formidable power which has ever since been, from time to
time, the principal object of jealousy to the other European
nations. Before that period she had to struggle for her very
existence with the English, already possessed of her fairest
provinces; while the utmost exertions of her king, and the
gallantry of her people, could scarcely protect the remainder
from a foreign yoke. Nor was this her sole danger. The
princes who possessed the grand fiefs of the crown, and, in
particular, the Dukes of Burgundy and Bretagne, had come to
wear their feudal bonds so lightly, that they had no scruple
in lifting the standard against their liege and sovereign
lord, the King of France, on the slightest pretence. When
at peace, they reigned as absolute princes in their own provinces; and the house of Burgundy, possessed of the district
so called, together with the fairest and richest part of Flanders, was itself so wealthy and so powerful as to yield nothing to the crown, either in splendor or in strength.

In imitation of the grand feudatories, each inferior vassal
of the crown assumed as much independence as his distance
from the sovereign power, the extent of his fief, or the
strength of his château, enabled him to maintain; and these
petty tyrants, no longer amenable to the exercise of the law,
perpetrated with impunity the wildest excesses of fantastic
oppression and cruelty. In Auvergne alone, a report was
made of more than three hundred of these independent nobles,
to whom incest, murder, and rapine were the most ordinary
and familiar actions.

Besides these evils, another, springing out of the long-continued wars betwixt the French and English, added no small misery to this distracted kingdom. Numerous bodies of soldiers, collected into bands, under officers chosen by themselves from among the bravest and most successful adventurers, had been formed in various parts of France out of the refuse of all other countries. These hireling combatants sold their swords for a time to the best bidder ; and, when such service was not to be had, they made war on their own account, seizing castles and towers, which they used as the places of their retreat, making prisoners and ransoming them, exacting tribute from the open villages and the country around them, and acquiring, by every species of rapine, the appropriate epithets of *tondeurs* and *écorcheurs,* that is, " clippers " and " flayers."

In the midst of the horrors and miseries arising from so distracted a state of public affairs, reckless and profuse expense distinguished the courts of the lesser nobles, as well as of the superior princes ; and their dependants, in imitation, expended in rude but magnificent display the wealth which they extorted from the people. A tone of romantic and chivalrous gallantry, which, however, was often disgraced by unbounded license, characterized the intercourse between the sexes ; and the language of knight-errantry was yet used, and its observances followed, though the pure spirit of honorable love and benevolent enterprise which it inculcates had ceased to qualify and atone for its extravagances. The jousts and tournaments, the entertainments and revels, which each petty court displayed invited to France every wandering adventurer ; and it was seldom that, when arrived there, he failed to employ his rash courage and headlong spirit of enterprise in actions for which his happier native country afforded no free stage.

At this period, and as if to save this fair realm from the various woes with which it was menaced, the tottering throne was ascended by Louis XI., whose character, evil as it was in itself, met, combated, and in a great degree neutralized, the mischiefs of the time—as poisons of opposing qualities are said, in ancient books of medicine, to have the power of counteracting each other.

Brave enough for every useful and political purpose, Louis had not a spark of that romantic valor, or of the pride generally associated with it, which fought on for the point of honor, when the point of utility had been long gained. Calm, crafty, and profoundly attentive to his own interest, he made

every sacrifice, both of pride and passion, which could interfere with it. He was careful in disguising his real sentiments
and purposes from all who approached him, and frequently
used the expressions, " That the king knew not how to reign
who knew not how to dissemble ; and that, for himself, if
he thought his very cap knew his secrets, he would throw it
into the fire." No man of his own or of any other time
better understood how to avail himself of the frailties of
others, and when to avoid giving any advantage by the untimely indulgence of his own.

He was by nature vindictive and cruel, even to the extent
of finding pleasure in the frequent executions which he commanded. But, as no touch of mercy ever induced him to
spare when he could with safety condemn, so no sentiment
of vengeance ever stimulated him to a premature violence.
He seldom sprung on his prey till it was fairly within his
grasp, and till all hope of rescue was vain ; and his movements were so studiously disguised, that his success was
generally what first announced to the world the object he
had been manœuvering to attain.

In like manner, the avarice of Louis gave way to apparent
profusion, when it was necessary to bribe the favorite or
minister of a rival prince for averting any impending attack,
or to break up any alliance confederated against him. He
was fond of license and pleasure ; but neither beauty nor
the chase, though both were ruling passions, ever withdrew
him from the most regular attendance to public business and
the affairs of his kingdom. His knowledge of mankind was
profound, and he had sought it in the private walks of life,
in which he often personally mingled ; and, though naturally proud and haughty, he hesitated not, with an inattention to the arbitrary divisions of society which was then
thought something portentously unnatural, to raise from the
lowest rank men whom he employed on the most important
duties, and knew so well how to choose them, that he was
rarely disappointed in their qualities.

Yet there were contradictions in the character of this artful and able monarch ; for human nature is rarely uniform.
Himself the most false and insincere of mankind, some of
the greatest errors of his life arose from too rash a confidence
in the honor and integrity of others. When these errors
took place, they seem to have arisen from an over-refined
system of policy, which induced Louis to assume the appearance of undoubting confidence in those whom it was
his object to overreach ; for, in his general conduct,

he was as jealous and suspicious as any tyrant who ever breathed.

Two other points may be noticed to complete the sketch of this formidable character, by which he rose among the rude chivalrous sovereigns of the period to the rank of a keeper among wild beasts, who, by superior wisdom and policy, by distribution of food, and some discipline by blows, comes finally to predominate over those who, if unsubjected by his arts, would by main strength have torn him to pieces.

The first of these attributes was Louis's excessive superstition—a plague with which Heaven often afflicts those who refuse to listen to the dictates of religion. The remorse arising from his evil actions, Louis never endeavored to appease by any relaxation in his Machiavellian stratagems, but labored, in vain, to soothe and silence that painful feeling by superstitions observances, severe penance, and profuse gifts to the ecclesiastics. The second property, with which the first is sometimes found strangely united, was a disposition to low pleasures and obscure debauchery. The wisest, or at least the most crafty, sovereign of his time, he was fond of low life, and, being himself a man of wit, enjoyed the jests and repartees of social conversation more than could have been expected from other points of his character. He even mingled in the comic adventures of obscure intrigue, with a freedom little consistent with the habitual and guarded jealousy of his character ; and he was so fond of this species of humble gallantry, that he caused a number of its gay and licentious anecdotes to be enrolled in a collection well known to book-collectors, in whose eyes (and the work is unfit for any other) the *right* edition is very precious.*

By means of this monarch's powerful and prudent, though most unamiable, character, it pleased Heaven, who works by the tempest as well as by the soft small rain, to restore to the great French nation the benefits of civil government, which, at the time of his accession, they had nearly lost.

Ere he succeeded to the crown, Louis had given evidence of his vices rather than of his talents. His first wife, Margaret of Scotland, was "done to death by slanderous tongues" in her husband's court, where, but for the encouragement of Louis himself, not a word would have been breathed against that amiable and injured princess. He had been an ungrateful and a rebellious son, at one time conspiring to seize his father's person, and at another levying open war against him. For the first offence, he was banished to his

* See Edition of *Cent Nouvelles.* Note 3.

Louis XI., King of France.

appanage of Dauphiné, which he governed with much sagacity ; for the second, he was driven into absolute exile, and forced to throw himself on the mercy, and almost on the charity, of the Duke of Burgundy and his son, where he enjoyed hospitality, afterwards indifferently requited, until the death of his father in 1461.

In the very outset of his reign, Louis was almost overpowered by a league formed against him by the great vassals of France, with the Duke of Burgundy, or rather his son, the Count de Charalois, at its head. They levied a powerful army, blockaded Paris, fought a battle of doubtful issue under its very walls, and placed the French monarchy on the brink of actual destruction. It usually happens in such cases that the more sagacious general of the two gains the real fruit, though perhaps not the martial fame,of the disputed field. Louis, who had shown great personal bravery during the battle of Montl'hèry, was able, by his prudence, to avail himself of its undecided character, as if it had been a victory on his side. He temporized until the enemy had broken up their leaguer, and showed so much dexterity in sowing jealousies among those great powers, that their alliance "for the public weal," as they termed it, but in reality for the overthrow of all but the external appearance of the French monarchy, dissolved itself, and was never again renewed in a manner so formidable. From this period, Louis, relieved of all danger from England by the civil wars of York and Lancaster, was engaged for several years, like an unfeeling but able physician, in curing the wounds of the body politic, or rather in stopping, now by gentle remedies, now by the use of fire and steel, the progress of those mortal gangrenes with which it was then infected. The *brigandage* of the Free Companies, and the unpunished oppressions of the nobility, he labored to lessen, since he could not actually stop them ; and, by dint of unrelaxed attention, he gradually gained some addition to his own regal authority, or effected some diminution of those by whom it was counterbalanced.

Still the King of France was surrounded by doubt and danger. The members of the league " for the public weal," though not in unison, were in existence, and, like a scotched snake, might re-unite and become dangerous again. But a worse danger was the increasing power of the Duke of Burgundy, then one of the greatest princes of Europe, and little diminished in rank by the very slight dependence of his duchy upon the crown of France.

Charles, surnamed the Bold, or rather the Audacious, for his courage was allied to rashness and frenzy, then wore the ducal coronet of Burgundy, which he burned to convert into a royal and independent regal crown. The character of this duke was in every respect the direct contrast to that of Louis XI.

The latter was calm, deliberate, and crafty, never prosecuting a desperate enterprise, and never abandoning one likely to be successful, however distant the prospect. The genius of the Duke was entirely different. He rushed on danger because he loved it, and on difficulties because he despised them. As Louis never sacrificed his interest to his passion, so Charles, on the other hand, never sacrificed his passion, or even his humor, to any other consideration. Notwithstanding the near relationship that existed between them, and the support which the Duke and his father had afforded to Louis in his exile when Dauphin, there was mutual contempt and hatred betwixt them. The Duke of Burgundy despised the cautious policy of the King, and imputed to the faintness of his courage, that he sought by leagues, purchases, and other indirect means those advantages which, in his place the Duke would have snatched with an armed hand. He likewise hated the King, not only for the ingratitude he had manifested for former kindnesses, and for personal injuries and imputations which the ambassadors of Louis had cast upon him when his father was yet alive, but also, and especially, because of the support which he afforded in secret to the discontented citizens of Ghent, Liege, and other great towns in Flanders. These turbulent cities, jealous of their privileges and proud of their wealth, were frequently in a state of insurrection against their liege lords the Dukes of Burgundy, and never failed to find underhand countenance at the court of Louis, who embraced every opportunity of fomenting disturbance within the dominions of his overgrown vassal.

The contempt and hatred of the Duke were retaliated by Louis with equal energy, though he used a thicker veil to conceal his sentiments. It was impossible for a man of his profound sagacity not to despise the stubborn obstinacy which never resigned its purpose, however fatal perseverance might prove, and the headlong impetuosity which commenced its career without allowing a moment's consideration for the obstacles to be encountered. Yet the King hated Charles even more than he contemned him, and his scorn and hatred were the more intense that they were mingled with

fear ; for he knew that the onset of the mad bull, to whom
he likened the Duke of Burgundy, must ever be formidable
though the animal makes it with shut eyes. It was not
alone the wealth of the Burgundian provinces, the discipline
of the warlike inhabitants, and the mass of their crowded
population, which the King dreaded, for the personal
qualities of their leader had also much in them that was
dangerous. The very soul of bravery, which he pushed to
the verge of rashness, and beyond it, profuse in expenditure,
splendid in his court, his person, and his retinue, in all
which he displayed the hereditary magnificence of the
house of Burgundy, Charles the Bold drew into his service
almost all the fiery spirits of the age whose tempers were congenial ; and Louis saw too clearly what might be attempted
and executed by such a train of resolute adventurers, following a leader of a character as ungovernable as their own.

There was yet another circumstance which increased the
animosity of Louis towards his overgrown vassal : he owed
him favors which he never meant to repay, and was under
the frequent necessity of temporizing with him, and even of
enduring bursts of petulant insolence, injurious to the regal
dignity, without being able to treat him otherwise than as his
" fair cousin of Burgundy."

It was about the year 1468, when their feuds were at the
highest, though a dubious and hollow truce, as frequently
happened, existed for the time betwixt them, that the present
narrative. opens. The person first introduced on the stage
will be found indeed to be of a rank and condition the illustration of whose character scarcely called for a dissertation
on the relative position of two great princes ; but the passions of the great, their quarrels, and their reconciliations,
involve the fortunes of all who approach them ; and it will
be found, on proceeding farther in our story, that this
preliminary chapter is necessary for comprehending the
history of the individual whose adventures we are about to
relate.

CHAPTER II

THE WANDERER

Why then the world is my oyster, which I with sword will open.
Ancient Pistol.

IT was upon a delicious summer morning, before the sun had assumed its scorching power, and while the dews yet cooled and perfumed the air, that a youth, coming from the north-eastward, approached the ford of a small river, or rather a large brook, tributary to the Cher, near to the royal Castle of Plessis-lès-Tours, whose dark and multiplied battlements rose in the background over the extensive forest with which they were surrounded. These woodlands comprised a noble chase, or royal park, fenced by an inclosure, termed, in the Latin of the middle ages, *plexitium*, which gives the name of Plessis to so many villages in France. The castle and village of which we particularly speak was called Plessis-lès-Tours, to distinguish it from others, and was built about two miles to the southward of the fair town of that name, the capital of ancient Touraine, whose rich plain has been termed the Garden of France.

On the bank of the above-mentioned brook, opposite to that which the traveler was approaching, two men, who appeared in deep conversation, seemed, from time to time, to watch his motions ; for, as their station was much more elevated, they could remark him at considerable distance.

The age of the young traveler might be about nineteen, or betwixt that and twenty, and his face and person, which were very prepossessing, did not, however, belong to the country in which he was now a sojourner. His short gray cloak and hose were rather of Flemish than of French fashion, while the smart blue bonnet, with a single sprig of holly and an eagle's feather, was already recognized as the Scottish head-gear. His dress was very neat, and arranged with the precision of a youth conscious of possessing a fine person. He had at his back a satchel, which seemed to contain a few necessaries, a hawking gauntlet on his left hand, though he carried no bird, and in his right a stout

8

hunter's pole. Over his left shoulder hung an embroidered scarf which sustained a small pouch of scarlet velvet, such as was then used by fowlers of distinction to carry their hawks' food, and other matters belonging to that much admired sport. This was crossed by another shoulder-belt, to which was hung a hunting-knife, or *couteau de chasse*. Instead of the boots of the period, he wore buskins of half-dressed deer's-skin.

Although his form had not yet attained its full strength, he was tall and active, and the lightness of the step with which he advanced showed that his pedestrian mode of traveling was pleasure rather than pain to him. His complexion was fair, in spite of a general shade of darker hue, with which the foreign sun, or perhaps constant exposure to the atmosphere in his own country, had in some degree embrowned it.

His features, without being quite regular, were frank, open, and pleasing. A half smile, which seemed to arise from a happy exuberance of animal spirits, showed, now and then, that his teeth were well set, and as pure as ivory; whilst his bright blue eye, with a corresponding gaiety, had an appropriate glance for every object which it encountered, expressing good-humor, lightness of heart, and determined resolution.

He received and returned the salutation of the few travelers who frequented the road in those dangerous times with the action which suited each. The strolling spearman, half soldier, half brigand, measured the youth with his eye, as if balancing the prospect of booty with the chance of desperate resistance ; and read such indications of the latter in the fearless glance of the passenger, that he charged his ruffian purpose for a surly " Good morrow, comrade," which the young Scot answered with as martial, though a less sullen, tone. The wandering pilgrim or the begging friar answered his reverend greeting with a paternal benedicite ; and the dark-eyed peasant girl looked after him for many a step after they had passed each other, and interchanged a laughing "good morrow." In short, there was an attraction about his whole appearance not easily escaping attention, and which was derived from the combination of fearless frankness and good-humor with sprightly looks and a handsome face and person. It seemed, too, as if his whole demeanor bespoke one who was entering on life with no apprehension of the evils with which it is beset, and small means for struggling with its hardships, except a lively spirit and a courageous disposition ; and it is with such tempers that youth most readily sympathizes, and for whom chiefly age and experience feel affectionate and pitying interest.

The youth whom we have described had been long visible to the two persons who loitered on the opposite side of the small river which divided him from the park and the castle ; but as he descended the rugged bank to the water's edge, with the light step of a roe which visits the fountain, the younger of the two said to the other, " It is our man— it is the Bohemian ! If he attempts to cross the ford, he is a lost man : the water is up, and the ford impassable."

" Let him make that discovery himself, gossip," said the elder personage ; " it may, perchance, save a rope, and break a proverb."

" I judge him by the blue cap," said the other, "for I cannot see his face. Hark, sir ; he hallooes to know whether the water be deep."

"Nothing like experience in this world," answered the other : " let him try."

The young man, in the mean while, receiving no hint to the contrary, and taking the silence of those to whom he applied as an encouragement to proceed, entered the stream without farther hesitation than the delay necessary to take off his buskins. The elder person, at the same moment, hallooed to him to beware, adding, in a lower tone, to his companion, " *Mortdieu,* gossip, you have made another mistake : this is not the Bohemian chatterer."

But the intimation to the youth came too late. He either did not hear or could not profit by it, being already in the deep stream. To one less alert and practised in the exercise of swimming, death had been certain, for the brook was both deep and strong.

" By St. Anne ! but he is a proper youth," said the elder man. " Run, gossip, and help your blunder by giving him aid, if thou canst. He belongs to thine own troop ; if old saws speak truth, water will not drown him."

Indeed, the young traveler swam so strongly, and buffeted the waves so well, that, notwithstanding the strength of the current, he was carried but a little way down from the ordinary landing-place.

By this time the younger of the two strangers was hurrying down to the shore to render assistance, while the other followed him at a graver pace, saying to himself as he approached, " I knew water would never drown that young fellow. By my halidome, he is ashore, and grasps his pole! If I make not the more haste, he will beat my gossip for the only charitable action which I ever saw him perform, or attempt to perform, in the whole course of his life."

There was some reason to augur such a conclusion of the adventure, for the bonny Scot had already accosted the younger Samaritan, who was hastening to his assistance, with these ireful words—"Discourteous dog! why did you not answer when I called to know if the passage was fit to be attempted? May the foul fiend catch me, but I will teach you the respect due to strangers on the next occasion!"

This was accompanied with that significant flourish with his pole which is called *le moulinet,* because the artist, holding it in the middle, brandishes the two ends in every direction, like the sails of a windmill in motion. His opponent, seeing himself thus menaced, laid hand upon his sword, for he was one of those who on all occasions are more ready for action than for speech; but his more considerate comrade, who came up, commanded him to forbear, and, turning to the young man, accused him in turn of precipitation in plunging into the swollen ford, and of intemperate violence in quarreling with a man who was hastening to his assistance.

The young man, on hearing himself thus reproved by a man of advanced age and respectable appearance, immediately lowered his weapon, and said, "He would be sorry if he had done them injustice; but, in reality, it appeared to him as if they had suffered him to put his life in peril for want of a word of timely warning, which could be the part neither of honest men nor of good Christians, far less of respectable burgesses, such as they seemed to be."

"Fair son," said the elder person, "you seem, from your accent and complexion, a stranger; and you should recollect your dialect is not so easily comprehended by us as perhaps it may be uttered by you."

"Well, father," answered the youth, "I do not care much about the ducking I have had, and I will readily forgive your being partly the cause, provided you will direct me to some place where I can have my clothes dried; for it is my only suit, and I must keep it somewhat decent."

"For whom do you take us, fair son?" said the elder stranger, in answer to this question.

"For substantial burgesses, unquestionably," said the youth; "or, hold—you, master, may be a money-broker or a corn-merchant, and this man a butcher or grazier."

"You have hit our capacities rarely," said the elder, smiling. "My business is indeed to trade in as much money as I can ; and my gossip's dealings are somewhat of kin to the butcher's. As to your accommodation, we will try to serve you ; but I must first know who you are, and whither you are going ; for, in these times, the roads are filled with travelers on foot and horseback who have anything in their heads but honesty and the fear of God."

The young man cast another keen and penetrating glance on him who spoke, and on his silent companion, as if doubtful whether they, on their part, merited the confidence they demanded ; and the result of his observation was as follows:

The eldest and most remarkable of these men, in dress and appearance, resembled the merchant or shopkeeper of the period. His jerkin, hose, and cloak were of a dark uniform-color, but worn so threadbare that the acute young Scot conceived that the wearer must be either very rich or very poor, probably the former. The fashion of the dress was close and short—a kind of garments which were not then held decorous among gentry, or even the superior class of citizens, who generally wore loose gowns which descended below the middle of the leg.

The expression on this man's countenance was partly attractive and partly forbidding. His strong features, sunken cheeks, and hollow eyes had, nevertheless, an expression of shrewdness and humor congenial to the character of the young adventurer. But then, those same sunken eyes, from under the shroud of thick black eyebrows, had something in them that was at once commanding and sinister. Perhaps this effect was increased by the low fur cap, much depressed on the forehead, and adding to the shade from under which those eyes peered out ; but it is certain that the young stranger had some difficulty to reconcile his looks with the meanness of his appearance in other respects. His cap, in particular, in which all men of any quality displayed either a brooch of gold or of silver, was ornamented with a paltry image of the Virgin, in lead, such as the poorer sort of pilgrims bring from Loretto.

His comrade was a stout-formed, middle-sized man, more than ten years younger than his companion, with a down-looking visage and a very ominous smile, when by chance he gave way to that impulse, which was never, except in reply to certain secret signs that seemed to pass between him and the elder stranger. This man was armed with a sword and dagger ; and, underneath his plain habit, the Scotsman observed that he concealed a *jazeran*, or flexible shirt of linked mail, which, as being often worn by those, even of peaceful professions, who were called upon at that perilous period to be frequently abroad, confirmed the young man in his conjecture that the wearer was by profession a butcher, grazier, or something of that description, called upon to be much abroad.

The young stranger, comprehending in one glance the result of the observation which has taken us some time to express, answered, after a moment's pause, " I am ignorant whom I may have the honor to address," making a slight reverence at the same time ; " but I am indifferent who knows that I am a cadet of Scotland, and that I come to seek my fortune in France, or elsewhere, after the custom of my countrymen."

" *Pasques-dieu!* and a gallant custom it is," said the elder stranger. " You seem a fine young springald, and at the right age to prosper, whether among men or women. What say you ? I am a merchant, and want a lad to assist in my traffic. I suppose you are too much a gentleman to assist in such mechanical drudgery ? "

" Fair sir," said the youth, " if your offer be seriously made, of which I have my doubts, I am bound to thank you for it, and I thank you accordingly ; but I fear I should be altogether unfit for your service."

" What ! " said the senior, " I warrant thou knowest better how to draw the bow than how to draw a bill of charges— canst handle a broadsword better than a pen— ha ! "

" I am, master," answered the young Scot, " a braeman, and therefore, as we say, a bowman. But besides that, I have been in a convent, where the good fathers taught me to read and write, and even to cipher."

" *Pasques-dieu!* that is too magnificent," said the merchant. " By our Lady of Embrun, thou art a prodigy, man ! "

" Rest you merry, fair master," said the youth, who was not much pleased with his new acquaintance's jocularity, " I must go dry myself, instead of standing dripping here, answering questions."

The merchant only laughed louder as he spoke, and answered, " *Pasques-dieu!* the proverb never fails—*fier comme un Ecossois ;* but come, youngster, you are of a country I have a regard for, having traded in Scotland in my time— an honest poor set of folks they are ; and, if you will come

with us to the village, I will bestow on you a cup of burnt
sack and a warm breakfast, to atone for your drenching.
But, *tête-bleau !* what do you with a hunting-glove on your
hand ? Know you not there is no hawking permitted in a
royal chase ? "

" I was taught that lesson," answered the youth, " by a
rascally forester of the Duke of Burgundy. I did but fly
the falcon I had brought with me from Scotland, and that I
reckoned on for bringing me into some note, at a heron near
Péronne, and the rascally *schelm* shot my bird with an
arrow."

" What did you do ? " said the merchant.

" Beat him," said the youngster, brandishing his staff,
" as near to death as one Christian man should belabor another. I wanted not to have his blood to answer for."

" Know you," said the burgess, " that, had you fallen
into the Duke of Burgundy's hands, he would have hung
you up like a chestnut ? "

" Ay, I am told he is as prompt as the King of France for
that sort of work. But, as this happened near Péronne, I
made a leap over the frontiers, and laughed at him. If he
had not been so hasty, I might perhaps have taken service
with him."

" He will have a heavy miss of such a paladin as you are,
if the truce should break off," said the merchant, and threw
a look at his own companion, who answered him with one of
the downcast lowering smiles, which gleamed along his countenance, enlivening it as a passing meteor enlivens a winter
sky.

The young Scot suddenly stopped, pulled his bonnet over
his right eyebrow, as one that would not be ridiculed, and
said firmly, " My masters, and especially you, sir, the elder,
and who should be the wiser, you will find, I presume, no
sound or safe jesting at my expense. I do not altogether
like the tone of your conversation. I can take a jest with
any man, and a rebuke, too, from my elder, and say
' Thank you, sir,' if I know it to be deserved ; but I do
not like being borne in hand as if I were a child, when, God
wot, I find myself man enough to belabor you both, if you
provoke me too far."

The eldest man seemed like to choke with laughter at the
lad's demeanor ; his companion's hand stole to his sword
hilt, which the youth observing dealt him a blow across
the wrist, which made him incapable of grasping it ; while
his companion's mirth was only increased by the incident.

"Hold—hold," he cried, "most doughty Scot, even for thine own dear country's sake ; and you, gossip, forbear your menacing look. *Pasques-dieu!* let us be just traders, and set off the wetting against the knock on the wrist, which was given with so much grace and alacrity. And hark ye, my young friend," he said to the young man with a grave sternness which, in spite of all the youth could do, damped and overawed him, "no more violence. I am no fit object for it, and my gossip, as you may see, has had enough of it. Let me know your name."

"I can answer a civil question civilly," said the youth ; "and will pay fitting respect to your age, if you do not urge my patience with mockery. Since I have been here in France and Flanders, men have called me, in their fantasy, the Varlet with the Velvet Pouch, because of this hawk purse which I carry by my side ; but my true name, when at home, is Quentin Durward."

"Durward!" said the querist ; "is it a gentleman's name?"

"By fifteen descents in our family," said the young man ; "and that makes me reluctant to follow any other trade than arms."

"A true Scot! Plenty of blood, plenty of pride, and right great scarcity of ducats, I warrant thee. Well, gossip," he said to his companion, "go before us, and tell them to have some breakfast ready yonder at the Mulberry Grove ; for this youth will do as much honor to it as a starved mouse to a house-wife's cheese. And for the Bohemian—hark in thy ear——"

His comrade answered by a gloomy but intelligent smile, and set forward at a round pace, while the elder man continued, addressing young Durward—" You and I will walk leisurely forward together, and we may take a mass at St. Hubert's chapel in our way through the forest ; for it is not good to think of our fleshly before our spiritual wants."

Durward, as a good Catholic, had nothing to object against this proposal, although he might probably have been desirous, in the first place, to have dried his clothes and refreshed himself. Meanwhile, they soon lost sight of their downward-looking companion, but continued to follow the same path which he had taken, until it led them into a wood of tall trees, mixed with thickets and brushwood, traversed by long avenues, through which were seen, as through a vista, the deer trotting in little herds with a degree of security which argued their consciousness of being completely protected.

"You asked me if I were a good bowman," said the young Scot. "Give me a bow and a brace of shafts, and you shall have a piece of venison in a moment."

"*Pasques-dieu!* my young friend," said his companion, "take care of that; my gossip yonder hath a special eye to the deer; they are under his charge, and he is a strict keeper."

"He hath more the air of a butcher than of a gay forester," answered Durward. "I cannot think yon hang-dog look of his belongs to any one who knows the gentle rules of woodcraft."

"Ah, my young friend," answered his companion, "my gossip hath somewhat an ugly favor to look upon at the first; but those who become acquainted with him never are known to complain of him."

Quentin Durward found something singularly and disagreeably significant in the tone with which this was spoken; and, looking suddenly at the speaker, thought he saw in his countenance, in the slight smile that curled his upper lip, and the accompanying twinkle of his keen dark eye, something to justify his unpleasing surprise. "I have heard of robbers," he thought to himself, "and of wily cheats and cut-throats; what if yonder fellow be a murderer, and this old rascal his decoy-duck? I will be on my guard; they will get little by me but good Scottish knocks."

While he was thus reflecting, they came to a glade, where the large forest trees were more widely separated from each other, and where the ground beneath, cleared of underwood and bushes, was clothed with a carpet of the softest and most lovely verdure, which, screened from the scorching heat of the sun, was here more beautifully tender than it is usually to be seen in France. The trees in this secluded spot were chiefly beeches and elms of huge magnitude, which rose like great hills of leaves into the air. Amidst these magnificent sons of the earth, there peeped out, in the most open spot of the glade, a lowly chapel, near which trickled a small rivulet. Its architecture was of the rudest and most simple kind; and there was a very small lodge beside it, for the accommodation of a hermit or solitary priest, who remained there for regularly discharging the duty of the altar. In a small niche, over the arched doorway, stood a stone image of St. Hubert,* with the bugle horn around his neck and a leash of

* See Note 4.

greyhounds at his feet. The situation of the chapel in the midst of a park or chase so richly stocked with game made the dedication to the sainted huntsman peculiarly appropriate. Towards this little devotional structure the old man directed his steps, followed by young Durward; and, as they approached, the priest, dressed in his sacerdotal garments, made his appearance, in the act of proceeding from his cell to the chapel, for the discharge, doubtless, of his holy office. Durward bowed his body reverently to the priest, as the respect due to his sacred office demanded; whilst his companion, with an appearance of still more deep devotion, kneeled on one knee to receive the holy man's blessing, and then followed him into church, with a step and manner expressive of the most heartfelt contrition and humility.

The inside of the chapel was adorned in a manner adapted to the occupation of the patron saint while on earth. The richest furs of such animals as are made the objects of the chase in different countries supplied the place of tapestry and hangings around the altar and elsewhere, and the characteristic emblazonments of bugles, bows, quivers, and other-emblems of hunting, surrounded the walls, and were mingled with the heads of deer, wolves, and other animals considered beasts of sport. The whole adornments took an appropriate and silvan character ; and the mass itself, being considerably shortened, proved to be of that sort which is called a " hunting-mass," because in use before the noble and powerful, who, while assisting at the solemnity, are usually impatient to commence their favorite sport.

Yet, during this brief ceremony, Durward's companion seemed to pay the most rigid and scrupulous attention ; while Durward, not quite so much occupied with religious thoughts could not forbear blaming himself in his own mind for having entertained suspicions derogatory to the character of so good and so humble a man. Far from now holding him as a companion and accomplice of robbers, he had much to do to forbear regarding him as a saint-like personage.

When mass was ended, they retired together from the chapel, and the elder said to his young comrade, "It is but a short walk from hence to the village ; you may now break your fast with an unprejudiced conscience ; follow me."

Turning to the right, and proceeding along a path which seemed gradually to ascend, he recommended to his companion by no means to quit the track, but, on the contrary, to keep the middle of it as nearly as he could. Durward could not help asking the cause of this precaution.

"You are now near the court, young man," answered his guide; "and *Pasques dieu!* there is some difference betwixt walking in this region and on your own healthy hills. Every yard of this ground, excepting the path which we now occupy, is rendered dangerous, and well-nigh impracticable, by snares and traps, armed with scythe-blades, which shred off the unwary passenger's limbs as sheerly as a hedge-bill lops a hawthorn-sprig, and calthrops that would pierce your foot through and pitfalls deep enough to bury you in them forever; for you are now within the precincts of the royal demesne, and we shall presently see the front of the château."

"Were I the King of France," said the young man, "I would not take so much trouble with traps and gins, but would try instead to govern so well that no man should dare to come near my dwelling with a bad intent ; and for those who came there in peace and good-will, why, the more of them the merrier we should be."

His companion looked round affecting an alarmed gaze, and said, "Hush—hush, Sir Varlet with the Velvet Pouch ! for I forgot to tell you that one great danger of these precincts is that the very leaves of the trees are like so many ears, which carry all which is spoken to the King's own cabinet."

"I care little for that," answered Quentin Durward ; "I bear a Scottish tongue in my head bold enough to speak my mind to King Louis's face, God bless him ! and for the ears you talk of, if I could see them growing on a human head, I would crop them out of it with my wood-knife."

Quentin Durward.

CHAPTER III

Full in the midst a mighty pile arose,
Where iron-grated gates their strength oppose
To each invading step, and, strong and steep,
The battled walls arose, the fosse sunk deep.
Slow round the fortress rolled the sluggish stream.
And high in middle air the warder's turrets gleam.

Anonymous.

WHILE Durward and his new acquaintance thus spoke, they came in sight of the whole front of the Castle of Plessis-les-Tours, which, even in those dangerous times, when the great found themselves obliged to reside within places of fortified strength, was distinguished for the extreme and jealous care with which it was watched and defended.

From the verge of the wood where young Durward halted with his companion, in order to take a view of this royal residence, extended, or rather arose, though by a very gentle elevation, an open esplanade, devoid of trees and bushes of every description, excepting one gigantic and half-withered old oak. This space was left open, according to the rules of fortification in all ages, in order that an enemy might not approach the walls under cover, or unobserved from the battlements; and beyond it arose the castle itself.

There were three external walls, battlemented and turreted from space to space, and at each angle, the second inclosure rising higher than the first, and being built so as to command the exterior defence in case it was won by the enemy; and being again, in the same manner, itself commanded by the third and innermost barrier. Around the external wall, as the Frenchman informed his young companion (for, as they stood lower than the foundation of the wall, he could not see it), was sunk a ditch of about twenty feet in depth, supplied with water by a damhead on the river Cher, or rather on one of its tributary branches. In front of the second inclosure, he said, there ran another fosse; and a third, both of the same unusual dimensions, was led between the second and the innermost inclosure. The verge, both of the outer and inner circuit of this triple moat, was strongly fenced with palisades of iron, serving the purpose of what are called *chevaux-de-frise* in modern fortification, the top of each pale being divided into a cluster of sharp spikes, which seemed to render any attempt to climb over an act of self-destruction.

From within the innermost enclosure arose the castle itself, containing buildings of different periods, crowded around and united with the ancient and grim-looking donjon-keep, which was older than any of them, and which rose, like a black Ethiopian giant high into the air, while the absence of any windows larger than shot-holes, irregularly disposed for defence, gave the spectator the same unpleasant feeling which we experience on looking at a blind man. The other buildings seemed scarcely better adapted for the purposes of comfort, for the windows opened to an inner and inclosed courtyard ; so that the whole external front looked much more like that of a prison than a palace. The reigning king had even increased this effect ; for, desirous that the additions which he himself had made to the fortifications should be of a character not easily distinguished from the original building (for, like many jealous persons, he loved not that his suspicions should be observed), the darkest-colored brick and freestone were employed, and soot mingled with the lime, so as to give the whole castle the same uniform tinge of extreme and rude antiquity.

This formidable place had but one entrance, at least Durward saw none along the spacious front except where, in the center of the first and outward boundary, arose two strong towers, the usual defences of a gateway ; and he could observe their ordinary accompaniments, portcullis and drawbridge, of which the first was lowered and the last raised. Similar entrance-towers were visible on the second and third bounding wall, but not in the same line with those on the outward circuit ; because the passage did not cut right through the whole three inclosures at the same point, but, on the contrary, those who entered had to proceed nearly thirty yards betwixt the first and second wall, exposed, if their purpose were hostile, to missiles from both ; and again, when the second boundary was passed, they must make a similar digression from the straight line, in order to attain the portal of the third and innermost inclosure ; so that before gaining the outer court, which ran along the front of the building, two narrow and dangerous defiles were to be traversed under a flanking discharge of artillery, and three gates, defended in the strongest manner known to the age, were to be successively forced.

Coming from a country alike desolated by foreign war and internal feuds—a country, too, whose unequal and mountainous surface, abounding in precipices and torrents, affords so many situations of strength—young Durward was sufficiently acquainted with all the various contrivances by which men, in that stern age, endeavored to secure their dwellings ; but he frankly owned to his companion that he did not think it had been in the power of art to do so much for defense, where nature had done so little ; for the situation, as we have hinted was merely the summit of a gentle elevation ascending upwards from the place where they were standing.

To enhance his surprise, his companion told him that the environs of the castle, except the single winding path by which the portal might be safely approached, were, like the thickets through which they had passed, surrounded with every species of hidden pitfall, snare, and gin, to entrap the wretch who should venture thither without a guide ; that upon the walls were constructed certain cradles of iron, called " swallows, nests," from which the sentinels who were regularly posted there could, without being exposed to any risk, take deliberate aim at any who should attempt to enter without the proper signal or password of the day ; and that the archers of the Royal Guard performed that duty day and night, for which they received high pay, rich clothing, and much honor and profit at the hands of King Louis. " And now tell me, young man," he continued, " did you ever see so strong a fortress, and do you think there are men bold enough to storm it ? "

The young man looked long and fixedly on the place, the sight of which interested him so much that he had forgotten, in the eagerness of youthful curiosity, the wetness of his dress. His eye glanced, and his color mounted to his cheek like that of a daring man who meditates an honorable action, as he replied, " It is a strong castle, and strongly guarded ; but there is no impossibility to brave men."

" Are there any in your country who could do such a feat ? " said the elder, rather scornfully.

" I will not affirm that," answered the youth ; " but there are thousands that, in a good cause, would attempt as bold a deed."

" Umph ! " said the senior, " perhaps you are yourself such a gallant ? "

"I should sin if I were to boast where there is no danger," answered young Durward ; " but my father has done as bold an act, and I trust I am no bastard."

"Well," said his companion, smiling, "you might meet your match, and your kindred withal, in the attempt ; for the Scottish Archers of King Louis's Life Guards stand sentinels on yonder walls—three hundred gentlemen of the best blood in your country."

"And were I King Louis," said the youth, in reply, "I would trust my safety to the faith of the three hundred Scottish gentlemen, throw down my bounding walls to fill up the moat, call in my noble peers and paladins, and live as became me, amid breaking of lances in gallant tournaments, and feasting of days with nobles and dancing of nights with ladies, and have no more fear of a foe than I have of a fly."

His companion again smiled, and turning his back on the castle, which, he observed, they had approached a little too nearly, he led the way again into the wood, by a more broad and beaten path than they had yet trodden. "This," he said, "leads us to the village of Plessis, as it is called, where you, as a stranger, will find reasonable and honest accommodation. About two miles onward lies the fine city of Tours, which gives name to this rich and beautiful earldom. But the village of Plessis, or Plessis of the Park, as it is sometimes called, from its vicinity to the royal residence, and the chase with which it is encircled, will yield you nearer, and as convenient, hospitality."

"I thank you, kind master, for your information," said the Scot ; "but my stay will be so short here that, if I fail not in a morsel of meat and a drink of something better than water, my necessities in Plessis, be it of the park or the pool, will be amply satisfied."

"Nay," answered his companion, "I thought you had some friend to see in this quarter."

"And so I have—my mother's own brother," answered Durward ; "and as pretty a man, before he left the braes of Angus, as ever planted brogue on heather."

"What is his name ?" said the senior. "We will inquire him out for you ; for it is not safe for you to go up to the castle, where you might be taken for a spy."

"Now, by my father's hand !" said the youth, "I taken for a spy ! By Heaven, he shall brook cold iron that brands me with such a charge ! But for my uncle's name, I care not who knows it—it is Lesly—Lesly, an honest and noble name !"

"And so it is, I doubt not," said the old man ; "but there are three of the name in the Scottish Guard."

"My uncle's name is Ludovic Lesly," said the young man. "Of the three Leslies," answered the merchant, " two are called Ludovic."

"They call my kinsman Ludovic with the Scar," said Quentin. "Our family names are so common in a Scottish house, that, where there is no land in the case, we always give a 'to-name.'"

"A *nom de guerre*, I suppose you to mean," answered his companion ; "and the man you speak of, we, I think, call *Le Balafré*, from that scar on his face—a proper man and a good soldier. I wish I may be able to help you to an interview with him, for he belongs to a set of gentlemen whose duty is strict, and who do not often come out of garrison, unless in the immediate attendance on the King's person. And now, young man, answer me one question. I will wager you are desirous to take service with your uncle in the Scottish Guard. It is a great thing, if you propose so ; especially as you are very young, and some years' experience is necessary for the high office which you aim at."

"Perhaps I may have thought on some such thing," said Durward, carelessly ; "but if I did, the fancy is off."

"How so, young man ?" said the Frenchman, something sternly. "Do you speak thus of a charge which the most noble of your countrymen feel themselves emulous to be admitted to ?"

"I wish them joy of it," said Quentin, composedly. "To speak plain, I should have liked the service of the French king full well, only, dress me as fine and feed me as high as you will, I love the open air better than being shut up in a cage or a swallow's nest yonder, as you call these same grated pepper-boxes. Besides," he added, in a lower voice, "to speak truth, I love not the castle when the covin-tree* bears such acorns as I see yonder."

"I guess what you mean," said the Frenchman ; "but speak yet more plainly."

"To speak more plainly, then," said the youth, "there grows a fair oak some flight-shot or so from yonder castle ; and on that oak hangs a man in a gray jerkin, such as this which I wear."

"Ay and indeed ! " said the man of France. "*Pasques-dieu !* see what it is to have youthful eyes ! Why, I did see something, but only took it for a raven among the branches.

* See Note 5.

But the sight is no way strange, young man ; when the summer fades into autumn, and moonlight nights are long, and roads become unsafe, you will see a cluster of ten, ay, of twenty such acorns, hanging on that old doddered oak. But what then ? they are so many banners displayed to scare knaves ; and for each rogue that hangs there, an honest man may reckon that there is a thief, a traitor, a robber on the highway, a *pilleur* and oppressor of the people, the fewer in France. These, young man, are signs of our sovereign's justice."

" I would have hung them farther from my palace, though, were I King Louis," said the youth. " In my country, we hang up dead corbies where living corbies haunt, but not in our gardens or pigeon-houses. The very scent of the carrion —faugh—reached my nostrils at the distance where we stood."

"If you live to be an honest and loyal servant of your prince, my good youth," answered the Frenchman, "you will know there is no perfume to match the scent of a dead traitor."

" I shall never wish to live till I lose the scent of my nostrils or the sight of my eyes," said the Scot. " Show me a living traitor, and here are my hand and my weapon ; but when life is out, hatred should not live longer. But here, I fancy, we come upon the village ; where I hope to show you that neither ducking nor disgust have spoiled mine appetite for my breakfast. So, my good friend, to the hostelry, with all the speed you may. Yet, ere I accept of your hospitality, let me know by what name to call you."

" Men call me Maître Pierre," answered his companion. "I deal in no titles. A plain man, that can live on mine own good—that is my designation."

"So be it, Maître Pierre," said Quentin, "and I am happy my good chance has thrown us together ; for I want a word of seasonable advice, and can be thankful for it."

While they spoke thus, the tower of the church and a tall wooden crucifix, rising above the trees, showed that they were at the entrance of the village.

But Maître Pierre, deflecting a little from the road, which had now joined an open and public causeway, said to his companion, that the inn to which he intended to introduce him stood somewhat secluded, and received only the better sort of travelers.

"If you mean those who travel with the better-filled purses," answered the Scot, " I am none of the number, and will rather stand my chance of your flayers on the highway than of your flayers in the hostelry!"

"*Pasques-dieu!*" said his guide, "how cautious your countrymen of Scotland are! An Englishman, now, throws himself headlong into a tavern, eats and drinks of the best, and never thinks of the reckoning till his belly is full. But you forget, Master Quentin, since Quentin is your name— you forget I owe you a breakfast for the wetting which my mistake procured you. It is the penance of my offense towards you."

"In truth," said the light-hearted young man, "I had forgot wetting, offense, and penance, and all. I have walked my clothes dry, or nearly so; but I will not refuse your offer in kindness, for my dinner yesterday was a light one, and supper I had none. You seem an old and respectable burgess, and I see no reason why I should not accept your courtesy."

The Frenchman smiled aside, for he saw plainly that the youth, while he was probably half famished, had yet some difficulty to reconcile himself to the thoughts of feeding at a stranger's cost, and was endeavoring to subdue his inward pride by the reflection that, in such slight obligations, the acceptor performed as complacent a part as he by whom the courtesy was offered.

In the meanwhile, they descended a narrow lane, over-shadowed by tall elms, at the bottom of which a gateway admitted them into the courtyard of an inn of unusual magnitude, calculated for the accommodation of the nobles and suitors who had business at the neighboring castle, where very seldom, and only when such hospitality was altogether unavoidable, did Louis XI. permit any of his court to have apartments. A scutcheon, bearing the *fleur-de-lys*, hung over the principal door of the large irregular building; but there was about the yard and the offices little or none of the bustle which in those days, when attendants were maintained both in public and in private houses, marked that business was alive and custom plenty. It seemed as if the stern and unsocial character of the royal mansion in the neighborhood had communicated a portion of its solemn and terrific gloom even to a place designed, according to universal custom else-where, for the temple of social indulgence, merry society, and good cheer.

Maître Pierre, without calling any one, and even without approaching the principal entrance, lifted the latch of a side door, and led the way into a large room, where a fagot was

blazing on the hearth, and arrangements made for a substantial breakfast.

"My gossip has been careful," said the Frenchman to the
Scot. "You must be cold, and I have commanded a fire;
you must be hungry, and you shall have breakfast presently."
He whistled, and the landlord entered; answered Maître
Pierre's "*bon jour*" with a reverence; but in no respect
showed any part of the prating humor properly belonging
to a French publican of all ages.

"I expected a gentleman," said Maître Pierre, " to order
breakfast. Hath he done so ?"

In answer, the landlord only bowed; and while he continued to bring, and arrange upon the table, the various
articles of a comfortable meal, omitted to extol their merits
by a single word. And yet the breakfast merited such eulo-
giums as French hosts are wont to confer upon their regales,
as the reader will be informed in the next chapter.

CHAPTER IV

THE DEJEUNER

Sacred heaven! what masticators! what bread!
Yorick's Travels.

WE left our young stranger in France situated more comfortably than he had found himself since entering the territories of the ancient Gauls. The breakfast, as we hinted in the conclusion of the last chapter, was admirable. There was a *pâté de Périgord*, over which a gastronome would have wished to live and die, like Homer's lotus-eaters, forgetful of kin, native country, and all social obligations whatever. Its vast walls of magnificent crust seemed raised like the bulwarks of some rich metropolitan city, an emblem of the wealth which they are designed to protect. There was a delicate ragout, with just that *petite pointe de l'ail* which Gascons love and Scottishmen do not hate. There was, besides, a delicate ham, which had once supported a noble wild boar in the neighboring wood of Mountrichart. There was the most exquisite white bread made into little round loaves called *boulez* (whence the bakers took their French name of *boulangers*), of which the crust was so inviting that, even with water alone, it would have been a delicacy. But the water was not alone, for there was a flask of leather called *bottrine*, which contained about a quart of exquisite *vin de Beaulne*. So many good things might have created appetite under the ribs of death. What effect, then, must they have produced upon a youngster of scarce twenty, who (for the truth must be told) had eaten little for the two last days, save the scarcely ripe fruit which chance afforded him an opportunity of plucking, and a very moderate portion of barley-bread? He threw himself upon the ragout, and the plate was presently vacant; he attacked the mighty pasty, marched deep into the bowels of the land, and, seasoning his enormous meal with an occasional cup of wine, returned to the charge again and again, to the astonishment of mine host and the amusement of Maître Pierre.

The latter, indeed, probably because he found himself the

27

author of a kinder action than he had thought of, seemed
delighted with the appetite of the young Scot; and when,
at length, he observed that his exertions began to languish,
endeavored to stimulate him to new efforts, by ordering confections, *darioles,* and any other light dainties he could
think of, to entice the youth to continue his meal. While
thus engaged, Maître Pierre's countenance expressed a kind
of good-humor almost amounting to benevolence, which
appeared remote from its ordinary sharp, caustic, and severe
character. The aged almost always sympathize with the enjoyments of youth, and with its exertions of every kind,
when the mind of the spectator rests on its natural poise,
and is not disturbed by inward envy or idle emulation.

Quentin Durward also, while thus agreeably employed,
could do no otherwise than discover that the countenance of
his entertainer, which he had at first found so unprepossessing, mended when it was seen under the influence of the *vin
de Beaulne,* and there was kindness in the tone with which
he reproached Maître Pierre, that he amused himself with
laughing at his appetite, without eating anything himself.

"I am doing penance," said Maître Pierre, "and may not
eat anything before noon, save some comfiture and a cup of
water. Bid yonder lady," he added, turning to the innkeeper, "bring them hither to me."

The innkeeper left the room, and Maître Pierre proceeded—"Well have I kept faith with you concerning the
breakfast I promised you?"

"The best meal I have eaten," said the youth, "since I
left Glen Houlakin."

"Glen—what?" demanded Maître Pierre; "are you
going to raise the devil, that you use such long-tailed
words?"

"Glen Houlakin," answered Quentin, good-humoredly,
"which is to say the Glen of the Midges, is the name of our
ancient patrimony, my good sir. You have bought the
right to laugh at the sound, if you please."

"I have not the least intention to offend," said the old
man; "but I was about to say, since you like your present
meal so well, that the Scottish Archers of the Guard eat as
good a one, or a better, every day."

"No wonder," said Durward, "for if they be shut up in
the swallows' nests all night, they must needs have a curious
appetite in the morning."

"And plenty to gratify it upon," said Maître Pierre.
"They need not, like the Burgundians, choose a bare back,

that they may have a full belly : they dress like counts, and feast like abbots."

"It is well for them," said Durward.

"And wherefore will you not take service here, young man ? Your uncle might, I daresay, have you placed on the file when there should a vacancy occur. And, hark in your ear, I myself have some little interest, and might be of some use to you. You can ride, I presume, as well as draw the bow ? "

"Our race are as good horsemen as ever put a plated shoe into a steel stirrup ; and I know not but I might accept of your kind offer. Yet, look you, food and raiment are needful things, but, in my case, men think of honor, and advancement, and brave deeds of arms. Your King Louis—God bless him! for he is a friend and ally of Scotland—but he lies here in this castle, or only rides about from one fortified town to another ; and gains cities and provinces by politic embassies, and not in fair fighting. Now, for me, I am of the Douglasses' mind, who always kept the fields, because they loved better to hear the lark sing than the mouse squeak."

"Young man," said Maître Pierre, "do not judge too rashly of the actions of sovereigns. Louis seeks to spare the blood of his subjects, and cares not for his own. He showed himself a man of courage at Montl'héry."

"Ay, but that was some dozen years ago or more," answered the youth. "I should like to follow a master that would keep his honor as bright as his shield, and always venture foremost in the very throng of the battle."

"Why did you not tarry at Brussels, then," said Maître Pierre, "with the Duke of Burgundy ? He would put you in the way to have your bones broken every day ; and rather than fail, would do the job for you himself, especially if he heard that you had beaten his forester."

"Very true," said Quentin ; "my unhappy chance has shut that door against me."

"Nay, there are plenty of dare-devils abroad, with whom mad youngsters may find service," said his adviser. "What think you, for example, of William de la Marck ? "

"What !" exclaimed Durward, "serve Him with the Beard—serve the Wild Boar of Ardennes—a captain of pillagers and murderers, who would take a man's life for the value of his gaberdine, and who slays priests and pilgrims as if they were so many lance-knights and men-at-arms ? It would be a blot on my father's scutcheon forever."

"Well, my young hot-blood," replied Maître Pierre, "if you hold the *Sanglier* too unscrupulous, wherefore not follow the young Duke of Gueldres ? " *

"Follow the foul fiend as soon," said Quentin. "Hark in your ear—he is a burden too heavy for earth to carry : hell gapes for him. Men say that he keeps his own father imprisoned, and that he has even struck him. Can you believe it ? "

Maître Pierre seemed somewhat disconcerted with the naive horror with which the young Scotsman spoke of filial ingratitude, and he answered, " You know not, young man, how short a while the relations of blood subsist amongst those of elevated rank " ; then changed the tone of feeling in which he had begun to speak, and added, gaily, " Besides, if the duke has beaten his father, I warrant you his father hath beaten him of old, so it is but a clearing of scores."

" I marvel to hear you speak thus," said the Scot, coloring with indignation ; " gray hairs such as yours ought to have fitter subjects for jesting. If the old duke did beat his son in childhood, he beat him not enough ; for better he had died under the rod than have lived to make the Christian world ashamed that such a monster had ever been baptized."

" At this rate," said Maitre Pierre, " as you weigh the characters of each prince and leader, I think you had better become a captain yourself ; for where will one so wise find a chieftain fit to command him ? "

" You laugh at me, Maitre Pierre," said the youth, good-humoredly, " and perhaps you are right ; but you have not named a man who is a gallant leader, and keeps a brave party up here, under whom a man might seek service well enough."

" I cannot guess whom you mean."

" Why, he that hangs like Mahomet's coffin—a curse be upon Mahomet !—between the two loadstones ; he that no man can call either French or Burgundian, but who knows to hold the balance between them both, and makes both of them fear and serve him, for as great princes as they be."

" I cannot guess whom you mean," said Maître Pierre, thoughtfully.

" Why, whom should I mean but the noble Louis de Luxembourg, Count of St. Paul, the High Constable of France ? † Yonder he makes his place good, with his gallant little army, holding his head as high as either King

Louis or Duke Charles, and balancing between them, like the boy who stands on the midst of a plank, while two others are swinging on the opposite ends."

"He is in danger of the worst fall of the three," said Maître Pierre. "And hark ye, my young friend, you who hold pillaging such a crime, do you know that your politic Count of St. Paul was the first who set the example of burning the country during the time of war, and that, before the shameful devastation which he committed, open towns and villages, which made no resistance, were spared on all sides?"

"Nay, faith," said Durward, "if that be the case, I shall begin to think no one of these great men is much better than another, and that a choice among them is but like choosing a tree to be hung upon. But this Count de St. Paul, this Constable, hath possessed himself by clean conveyance of the town which takes its name from my honored saint and patron, St. Quentin,* (here he crossed himself), and methinks, were I dwelling there, my holy patron would keep some lookout for me; he has not so many named after him as your more popular saints; and yet he must have forgotten me, poor Quentin Durward, his spiritual god-son, since he lets me go one day without food, and leaves me the next morning to the harborage of St. Julian, and the chance courtesy of a stranger, purchased by a ducking in the renowned river Cher, or one of its tributaries."

"Blaspheme not the saints, my young friend," said Maître Pierre. "St. Julian is the faithful patron of travelers; and, peradventure, the blessed St. Quentin hath done more and better for thee than thou art aware of."

As he spoke, the door opened, and a girl, rather above than under fifteen years old, entered with a platter, covered with damask, on which was placed a small saucer of the dried plums which have always added to the reputation of Tours, and a cup of the curiously chased plate which the goldsmiths of that city were anciently famous for executing with a delicacy of workmanship that distinguished them from the other cities of France, and even excelled the skill of the metropolis. The form of the goblet was so elegant, that Durward thought not of observing closely whether the material was of silver, or, like what had been placed before him-

---

* It was by his possession of the town of St. Quentin that the Constable was able to carry on those political intrigues which finally cost him so dear.

self, of a baser metal, but so well burnished as to resemble the richer ore.

But the sight of the young person by whom this service was executed attracted Durward's attention far more than the petty minutiæ of the duty which she performed. He speedily made the discovery that a quantity of long, black tresses, which, in the maiden fashion of his own country, were unadorned by any ornament, except a single chaplet lightly woven out of ivy leaves, formed a veil around a countenance which, in its regular features, dark eyes, and pensive expression, resembled that of Melpomene, though there was a faint glow on the cheek, and an intelligence on the lips and in the eye, which made it seem that gaiety was not foreign to a countenance so expressive, although it might not be its most habitual expression. Quentin even thought he could discern that depressing circumstances were the cause why a countenance so young and so lovely was graver than belongs to early beauty ; and as the romantic imagination of youth is rapid in drawing conclusions from slight premises, he was pleased to infer, from what follows, that the fate of this beautiful vision was wrapped in silence and mystery.

"How now, Jacqueline !" said Maître Pierre when she entered the apartment. "Wherefore this ? Did I not desire Dame Perette should bring what I wanted ? *Pasquesdieu !* Is she, or does she think herself, too good to serve me ?"

"My kinswoman is ill at ease," answered Jacqueline, in a hurried yet a humble tone—"ill at ease, and keeps her chamber."

"She keeps it *alone*, I hope ?" replied Maître Pierre, with some emphasis. "I am *vieux routier*, and none of those upon whom feigned disorders pass for apologies."

Jacqueline turned pale, and even tottered, at the answer of Maître Pierre ; for it must be owned that his voice and looks, at all times harsh, caustic, and unpleasing, had, when he expressed anger or suspicion, an effect both sinister and alarming.

The mountain chivalry of Quentin Durward was instantly awakened, and he hastened to approach Jacqueline and relieve her of the burden she bore, and which she passively resigned to him, while with a timid and anxious look she watched the countenance of the angry burgess. It was not in nature to resist the piercing and pity-craving expression of her looks, and Maître Pierre proceeded, not merely with an air of diminished displeasure, but with as much gentleness as he could assume in countenance and manner—" I blame not thee, Jacqueline, and thou art too young to be—what it is a pity to think thou must be one day—a false and treacherous thing, like the rest of thy giddy sex.* No man ever lived to man's estate but he had the opportunity to know you all. Here is a Scottish cavalier will tell you the same."

Jacqueline looked for an instant on the young stranger, as if to obey Maître Pierre, but the glance, momentary as it was, appeared to Durward a pathetic appeal to him for support and sympathy ; and with the promptitude dictated by the feelings of youth, and the romantic veneration for the female sex inspired by his education, he answered hastily, " That he would throw down his gage to any antagonist, of equal rank and equal age, who should presume to say that such a countenance as that which he now looked upon could be animated by other than the purest and truest mind."

The young woman grew deadly pale, and cast an apprehensive glance upon Maître Pierre, in whom the bravado of the young gallant seemed to only excite laughter, more scornful than applausive. Quentin, whose second thoughts generally corrected the first, though sometimes after they had found utterance, blushed deeply at having uttered what might be construed into an empty boast, in presence of an old man of a peaceful profession ; and, as a sort of just and appropriate penance, resolved patiently to submit to the ridicule which he had incurred. He offered the cup and trencher to Maître Pierre with a blush in his cheek, and a humiliation of countenance which endeavored to disguise itself under an embarrassed smile.

" You are a foolish young man," said Maître Pierre, " and know as little of women as of princes, whose hearts," he said, crossing himself devoutly, " God keeps in his right hand."

" And who keeps those of the women, then ? " said Quentin, resolved, if he could help it, not to be borne down by the assumed superiority of this extraordinary old man, whose lofty and careless manner possessed an influence over him of which he felt ashamed.

" I am afraid you must ask of them in another quarter," said Maître Pierre composedly.

Quentin was again rebuffed, but not utterly disconcerted. " Surely," he said to himself, " I do not pay this same bur-

---

* It was a part of Louis's very unamiable character, and not the best part of it, that he entertained a great contempt for the understanding, and not less for the character, of the fair sex.

3

gess of Tours all the deference which I yield him on account
of the miserable obligation of a breakfast, though it was a
right good and substantial meal. Dogs and hawks are
attached by feeding only ; man must have kindness, if
you would bind him with the cords of affection and obligation. But he is an extraordinary person ; and that beautiful
emanation that is even now vanishing—surely a thing so fair
belongs not to this mean place, belongs not even to the
money-gathering merchant himself, though he seems to exert
authority over her, as doubtless he does over all whom chance
brings within his little circle. It is wonderful what ideas of
consequence these Flemings and Frenchmen attach to wealth,
so much more than wealth deserves, that I suppose this old
merchant thinks the civility I pay to his age is given to his
money—I, a Scottish gentleman of blood and coat-armor,
and he a mechanic of Tours ! "

Such were the thoughts which hastily traversed the mind
of young Durward ; while Maître Pierre said with a smile,
and at the same time patting Jacqueline's head, from which
hung down her long tresses, " This young man will serve me,
Jacqueline ; thou mayst withdraw. I will tell thy negligent
kinswoman she does ill to expose thee to be gazed on unnecessarily."

" It was only to wait on you," said the maiden, " I trust
you will not be displeased with my kinswoman, since——"

" *Pasques-dieu !* " said the merchant, interrupting her,
but not harshly, " do you bandy words with me, you brat,
or stay you to gaze upon the youngster here ? Begone ; he
is noble, and his services will suffice me."

Jacqueline vanished ; and so much was Quentin Durward
interested in her sudden disappearance, that it broke his previous thread of reflection, and he complied mechanically,
when Maître Pierre said, in a tone of one accustomed to be
obeyed, as he threw himself carelessly upon a large easy
chair, " Place that tray beside me."

The merchant then let his dark eyebrows sink over his
keen eyes, so that the last became scarce visible, or but shot
forth occasionally a quick and vivid ray, like those of the
sun setting behind a dark cloud, through which its beams
are occasionally darted, but singly, and for an instant.

" That is a beautiful creature," said the old man at last,
raising his head, and looking steadily and firmly at Quentin,
when he put the question, " a lovely girl to be the servant of
an *auberge ?* She might grace the board of an honest burgess ; but 'tis a vile education, a base origin."

It sometimes happens that a chance shot will demolish a noble castle in the air, and the architect on such occasions entertains little good-will towards him who fires it, although the damage on the offender's part may be wholly unintentional. Quentin was disconcerted, and was disposed to be angry, he himself knew not why, with this old man for acquainting him that this beautiful creature was neither more nor less than what her occupation announced—the servant of the *auberge*—an upper servant, indeed, and probably a niece of the landlord, or such-like ; but still a domestic, and obliged to comply with the humor of the customers, and particularly of Maître Pierre, who probably had sufficiency of whims, and was rich enough to ensure their being attended to.

The thought, the lingering thought, again returned on him, that he ought to make the old gentleman understand the difference betwixt their conditions, and call on him to mark that, how rich soever he might be, his wealth put him on no level with a Durward o᷃ Glen Houlakin. Yet, whenever he looked on Maître Pierre's countenance with such a purpose, there was, notwithstanding the downcast look, pinched features, and mean and miserly dress, something which prevented the young man from asserting the superiority over the merchant which he conceived himself to possess. On the contrary, the oftener and more fixedly Quentin looked at him, the stronger became his curiosity to know who or what this man actually was ; and he set him down internally for at least a syndic or high magistrate of Tours, or one who was, in some way or other, in the full habit of exacting and receiving deference.

Meantime, the merchant seemed again sunk into a reverie, from which he raised himself only to make the sign of the cross devoutly, and to eat some of the dried fruit, with a morsel of biscuit. He then signed to Quentin to give him the cup, adding, however, by way of question, as he presented it—" You are noble, you say ? "

" I surely am," replied the Scot, " if fifteen descents can make me so. So I told you before. But do not constrain yourself on that account, Maître Pierre : I have always been taught it is the duty of the young to assist the more aged."

" An excellent maxim," said the merchant, availing himself of the youth's assistance in handing the cup, and filling it from a ewer which seemed of the same materials with the goblet, without any of those scruples in point of propriety which, perhaps, Quentin had expected to excite,

"The devil take the ease and familiarity of this old mechanical burgher," said Durward once more to himself ; "he uses the attendance of a noble Scottish gentleman with as little ceremony as I would that of a gillie from Glen Isla."

The merchant, in the meanwhile, having finished his cup of water, said to his companion, " From the zeal with which you seemed to relish the *vin de Beaulne*, I fancy you would not care much to pledge me in this elemental liquor. But I have an elixir about me which can convert even the rock water into the richest wines of France."

As he spoke, he took a large purse from his bosom, made of the fur of the sea otter, and streamed a shower of small silver pieces into the goblet, until the cup, which was but a small one, was more than half full.

" You have reason to be more thankful, young man," said Maître Pierre, " both to your patron St. Quentin and to St. Julian than you seemed to be but now. I would advise you to bestow alms in their name. Remain in this hostelry until you see your kinsman, Le Balafré, who will be relieved from guard in the afternoon. I will cause him to be acquainted that he may find you here, for I have business in the castle."

Quentin Durward would have said something to have excused himself from accepting the profuse liberality of his new friend ; but Maître Pierre, bending his dark brows and erecting his stooping figure into an attitude of more dignity than he had yet seen him assume, said, in a tone of authority, " No reply, young man, but do what you are commanded."

With these words, he left the apartment, making a sign, as he departed, that Quentin must not follow him.

The young Scotsman stood astounded, and knew not what to think of the matter. His first most natural, though perhaps not most dignified, impulse drove him to peep into the silver goblet, which assuredly was more than half full of silver pieces, to the number of several scores, of which perhaps Quentin had never called twenty his own at one time during the course of his whole life. But could he reconcile it to his dignity as a gentleman to accept the money of this wealthy plebeian ? This was a trying question ; for though he had secured a good breakfast, it was no great reserve upon which to travel either back to Dijon, in case he chose to hazard the wrath, and enter the service, of the Duke of Burgundy, or to St. Quentin, if he fixed on that of the Constable St. Paul ; for to one of those powers, if not to the King of France, he was determined to offer his services. He perhaps took the wisest resolution in the circumstances, in resolving to be guided by the advice of his uncle ; and, in the meantime, he put the money into his velvet hawking-pouch, and called for the landlord of the house, in order to restore the silver-cup —resolving, at the same time, to ask him some questions about this liberal and authoritative merchant.

The man of the house appeared presently ; and, if not more communicative, was at least more loquacious than he had been formerly. He positively declined to take back the silver cup. " It was none of his," he said, " but Maître Pierre's, who had bestowed it on his guest. He had, indeed, four silver *hanaps* of his own, which had been left him by his grandmother, of happy memory, but no more like the beautiful carving of that in his guest's hand than a peach was like a turnip : that was one of the famous cups of Tours, wrought by Martin Dominique, an artist who might brag all Paris."

" And, pray, who is this Maître Pierre," said Durward, interrupting him, " who confers such valuable gifts on strangers ? "

" Who is Maître Pierre ? " said the host, dropping the words as slowly from his mouth as if he had been distilling them.

" Ay," said Durward, hastily and peremptorily, " who is this Maître Pierre, and why does he throw about his bounties in this fashion ? And who is the butcherly-looking fellow whom he sent forward to order breakfast ? "

" Why, fair sir, as to who Maître Pierre is, you should have asked the question of himself ; and for the gentleman who ordered breakfast to be made ready, may God keep us from his closer acquaintance ! "

" There is something mysterious in all this," said the young Scot. " This Maître Pierre tells me he is a merchant."

" And if he told you so," said the innkeeper, " surely he is a merchant."

" What commodities does he deal in ! "

" O, many a fair matter of traffic," said the host ; " and especially he has set up silk manufactories here, which match those rich bales that the Venetians bring from India and Cathay. You might see the rows of mulberry-trees as you came hither, all planted by Maître Pierre's commands, to feed the silk-worms."

" And that young person who brought in the confections, who is she, my good friend ! " said the guest.

" My lodger, sir, with her guardian, some sort of aunt or kinswoman, as I think," replied the innkeeper.

"And do you usually employ your guests in waiting on each other?" said Durward; "for I observed that Maître Pierre would take nothing from your hand or that of your attendant."

"Rich men may have their fancies, for they can pay for them," said the landlord; "this is not the first time that Maître Pierre has found the true way to make gentlefolks serve at his beck."

The young Scotsman felt somewhat offended at the insinuation; but disguising his resentment, he asked whether he could be accommodated with an apartment at this place for a day, and perhaps longer.

"Certainly," the innkeeper replied; "for whatever time he was pleased to command it."

"Could he be permitted," he asked, "to pay his respects to the ladies, whose fellow-lodger he was about to become?"

The innkeeper was uncertain. "They went not abroad," he said, "and received no one at home."

"With the exception, I presume, of Maître Pierre?" said Durward.

"I am not at liberty to name any exceptions," answered the man, firmly but respectfully.

Quentin, who carried the notions of his own importance pretty high, considering how destitute he was of means to support them, being somewhat mortified by the innkeeper's reply, did not hesitate to avail himself of a practice common enough in that age. "Carry to the ladies," he said, "a flask of *Auvernat*, with my humble duty; and say, that Quentin Durward, of the house of Glen Houlakin, a Scottish cavalier of honor, and now their fellow-lodger, desires the permission to dedicate his homage to them in a personal interview."

The messenger departed, and returned, almost instantly, with the thanks of the ladies, who declined the proffered refreshment, and with their acknowledgments, to the Scottish cavalier, regretted that, residing there in privacy, they could not receive his visit.

Quentin bit his lip, took a cup of the rejected *Auvernat*, which the host had placed on the table. "By the mass but this is a strange country," said he to himself, "where merchants and mechanics exercise the manners and munificence of nobles, and little traveling damsels, who hold their court in a *cabaret*, keep their state like disguised princesses! I will see that black-browed maiden again, or it will go hard, however"; and having formed this prudent resolution, he demanded to be conducted to the apartment which he was to call his own.

The landlord presently ushered him up a turret staircase, and from thence along a gallery, with many doors opening from it, like those of cells in a convent—a resemblance which our young hero, who recollected, with much *ennui*, an early specimen of a monastic life, was far from admiring. The host paused at the very end of the gallery, selected a key from the large bunch which he carried at his girdle, opened the door, and showed his guest the interior of a turret-chamber, small, indeed, but which, being clean and solitary, and having the pallet bed and the few articles of furniture in unusually good order, seemed, on the whole, a little palace.

"I hope you will find your dwelling agreeable here, fair sir," said the landlord. "I am bound to pleasure every friend of Maître Pierre."

"O happy ducking!" exclaimed Quentin Durward, cutting a caper on the floor so soon as his host had retired. "Never came good luck in a better or a wetter form. I have been fairly deluged by my good fortune."

As he spoke thus, he stepped towards the little window, which, as the turret projected considerably from the principal line of the building, not only commanded a very pretty garden of some extent, belonging to the inn, but overlooked beyond its boundary a pleasant grove of those very mulberry-trees which Maître Pierre was said to have planted for the support of the silk-worm. Besides, turning the eye from these more remote objects, and looking straight along the wall, the turret of Quentin was opposite to another turret, and the little window at which he stood commanded a similar little window in a corresponding projection of the building. Now, it would be difficult for a man twenty years older than Quentin to say why this locality interested him more than either the pleasant garden or the grove of mulberry-trees ; for, alas ! eyes which have been used for forty years and upwards look with indifference on little turret-windows, though the lattice be half open to admit the air, while the shutter is half closed to exclude the sun, or perhaps a too curious eye—nay, even though there hang on the one side of the casement a lute, partly mantled by a light veil of sea-green silk. But, at Durward's happy age, such "accidents," as a painter would call them, form sufficient foundation for a hundred airy visions and mysterious conjectures, at recollection of which the full-grown man smiles while he sighs, and sighs while he smiles.

As it may be supposed that our friend Quentin wished to learn a little more of his fair neighbor, the owner of the lute and veil—as it may be supposed he was at least interested to know whether she might not prove the same whom he had seen in humble attendance on Maître Pierre, it must of course be understood that he did not produce a broad staring visage and person in full front of his own casement. Durward knew better the art of bird-catching ; and it was to his keeping his person skilfully withdrawn on one side of his window, while he peeped through the lattice, that he owed the pleasure of seeing a white, round, beautiful arm take down the instrument, and that his ears had presently after their share in the reward of his dexterous management.

The maid of the little turret, of the veil, and of the lute sung exactly such an air as we are accustomed to suppose flowed from the lips of the high-born dames of chivalry, when knights and troubadours listened and languished. The words had neither so much sense, wit, or fancy as to withdraw the attention from the music, nor the music so much of art as to drown all feeling of the words.   The one seemed fitted to the other ; and if the song had been recited without the notes, or the air played without the words, neither would have been worth noting. It is, therefore, scarcely fair to put upon record lines intended not to be said or read, but only to be sung.   But such scraps of old poetry have always had a sort of fascination for us ; and as the tune is lost forever, unless Bishop happens to find the notes, or some lark teaches Stephens * to warble the air, we will risk our credit, and the taste of the Lady of the Lute, by preserving the verses, simple and even rude as they are.

> "Ah! County Guy, the hour is nigh,
>   The sun has left the lea,
> The orange flower perfumes the bower,
>   The breeze is on the sea.
> The lark, his lay who thrill'd all day,
>   Sits hush'd his partner nigh ;
> Breeze, bird, and flower, confess the hour,
>   But where is County Guy ? "

> " The village maid steals through the shade,
>   Her shepherd's suit to hear ;
> To beauty shy, by lattice high,
>   Sings high born cavalier.

* See Note 8.

The star of Love, all stars above,
Now reigns o'er earth and sky ;
And high and low the influence know—
But where is County Guy ? "

Whatever the reader may think of this simple ditty, it had
a powerful effect on Quentin, when married to heavenly airs,
and sung by a sweet and melting voice, the notes mingling
with the gentle breezes which wafted perfumes from the
garden, and the figure of the songstress being so partially
and obscurely visible as threw a veil of mysterious fascination over the whole.

At the close of the air, the listener could not help showing
himself more boldly than he had yet done, in a rash attempt
to see more than he had yet been able to discover. The
music instantly ceased, the casement was closed, and a dark
curtain, dropped on the inside, put a stop to all farther
observation on the part of the neighbor in the next turret.

Durward was mortified and surprised at the consequence
of his precipitance, but comforted himself with the hope that
the Lady of the Lute could neither easily forego the practise
of an instrument which seemed so familiar to her, nor cruelly
resolve to renounce the pleasures of fresh air and an open
window for the churlish purpose of preserving for her own
exclusive ear the sweet sounds which she created. There
came, perhaps, a little feeling of personal vanity to mingle
with these consolatory reflections. If, as he shrewdly suspected, there was a beautiful, dark-tressed damsel inhabitant
of the one turret, he could not but be conscious that a handsome, young, roving, bright-locked gallant, a cavalier of
fortune, was the tenant of the other ; and romances, those
prudent instructors, had taught his youth that if damsels
were shy, they were yet neither void of interest nor of curiosity in their neighbors' affairs.

Whilst Quentin was engaged in these sage reflections, a
sort of attendant or chamberlain of the inn informed him
that a cavalier desired to speak with him below.

CHAPTER V

Full of strange oaths, and bearded like the pard,
Seeking the bubble reputation even in the cannon's mouth.
As You Like It.

THE cavalier who awaited Quentin Durward's descent into the apartment where he had breakfasted was one of those of whom Louis XI had long since said, that they held in their hands the fortune of France, as to them were entrusted the direct custody and protection of the royal person.

Charles the Sixth had instituted this celebrated body, the Archers, as they were called, of the Scottish Body-Guard, with better reason than can generally be alleged for establishing round the throne a guard of foreign and mercenary troops. The divisions which tore from his side more than half of France, together with the wavering and uncertain faith of the nobility who yet acknowledged his cause, rendered it impolitic and unsafe to commit his personal safety to their keeping. The Scottish nation was the hereditary enemy of the English and the ancient, and, as it seemed, the natural allies of France. They were poor, courageous, faithful ; their ranks were sure to be supplied from the superabundant population of their own country, than which none in Europe sent forth more or bolder adventurers. Their high claims of descent, too, gave them a good title to approach the person of a monarch more closely than other troops, while the comparative smallness of their numbers prevented the possibility of their mutinying, and becoming masters where they ought to be servants.

On the other hand, the French monarchs made it their policy to conciliate the affections of this select band of foreigners, by allowing them honorary privileges and ample pay, which last most of them disposed of with military profusion in supporting their supposed rank. Each of them ranked as a gentleman in place and honor ; and their near approach to the king's person gave them dignity in their own eyes, as well as importance in those of the nation of

France. They were sumptuously armed, equipped, and mounted ; and each was entitled to allowance for a squire, a valet, a page, and two yeomen, one of whom was termed *coutelier*, from the large knife which he wore to despatch those whom in the *mêlée* his master had thrown to the ground. With these followers, and a corresponding equipage, an archer of the Scottish Guard was a person of quality and importance ; and vacancies being generally filled up by those who had been trained in the service as pages or valets, the cadets of the best Scottish families were often sent to serve under some friend and relation in those capacities, until a chance of preferment should occur.

The coutelier and his companion, not being noble or capable of this promotion, were recruited from persons of inferior quality ; but as their pay and appointments were excellent, their masters were easily able to select from among their wandering countrymen the strongest and most courageous to wait upon them in these capacities.

Ludovic Lesly, or, as we shall more frequently call him, Le Balafré, by which name he was generally known in France, was upward of six feet high, robust, strongly compacted in person, and hard-favored in countenance, which latter attribute was much increased by a large and ghastly scar, which, beginning on his forehead, and narrowly missing his right eye, had laid bare the cheek-bone, and descended from thence almost to the tip of his ear, exhibiting a deep seam, which was sometimes scarlet, sometimes purple, sometimes blue, and sometimes approaching to black ; but always hideous, because at variance with the complexion of the face in whatever state it chanced to be, whether agitated or still, flushed with unusual passion, or in its ordinary state of weatherbeaten and sunburnt swarthiness.

His dress and arms were splendid. He wore his national bonnet, crested with a tuft of feathers, and with a Virgin Mary of massive silver for a brooch. These brooches had been presented to the Scottish Guard, in consequence of the King, in one of his fits of superstitious piety, having devoted the swords of his guard to the service of the Holy Virgin, and, as some say, carried the matter so far as to draw out a commission to Our Lady as their captain-general. The archer's gorget, arm-pieces, and gauntlets were of the finest steel, curiously inlaid with silver, and his hauberk, or shirt of mail, was as clear and bright as the frostwork of a winter morning upon fern or brier. He wore a loose surcoat, or cassock, of rich blue velvet, open at the sides like that of a herald, with a large white St. Andrew's cross of embroidered silver bisecting it both before and behind ; his knees and legs were protected by hose of mail and shoes of steel ; a broad strong poniard, called the "mercy of God," hung by his right side; the baldric for his two-handed sword, richly embroidered, hung upon his left shoulder ; but, for convenience, he at present carried in his hand that unwieldy weapon, which the rules of the service forbade him to lay aside.

Quentin Durward, though, like the Scottish youth of the period, he had been early taught to look upon arms and war, thought he had never seen a more martial-looking, or more completely equipped and accomplished, man-at-arms than now saluted him in the person of his mother's brother, called Ludovic with the Scar, or Le Balafré ; yet he could not but shrink a little from the grim expression of his countenance, while, with its rough mustachios, he brushed first the one and then the other cheek of his kinsman, welcomed his nephew to France, and, in the same breath, asked what news from Scotland.

"Little good tidings, dear uncle," replied young Durward; "but I am glad that you know me so readily."

"I would have known thee, boy, in the *landes* of Bourdeaux, had I met thee marching there like a crane on a pair of stilts.* But sit thee down—sit thee down ; if there is sorrow to hear of, we will have wine to make us bear it. Ho! old Pinch-Measure, our good host, bring us of thy best, and that in an instant."

The well-known sound of the Scottish French was as familiar in the taverns near Plessis as that of the Swiss French in the modern *guinguettes* of Paris ; and promptly—ay, with the promptitude of fear and precipitation—was it heard and obeyed. A flagon of champagne stood before them, of which the elder took a draught, while the nephew helped himself only to a moderate sip, to acknowledge his uncle's courtesy, saying, in excuse, that he had already drunk wine that morning,

"That had been a rare good apology in the mouth of thy sister, fair nephew," said Le Balafré ; "you must fear the wine-pot less, if you would wear beard on your face, and write yourself soldier. But come—come, unbuckle your Scottish mail-bag—give us the news of Glen Houlakin. How doth my sister ?"

"Dead, fair uncle," answered Quentin, sorrowfully.

"Dead !" echoed his uncle with a tone rather marked by

* See Use of Stilts. Note 9.

wonder than sympathy; "why, she was five years younger than I, and I was never better in my life. Dead! the thing is impossible. I have never had so much as a headache, unless after reveling out my two or three days' furlough with the brethren of the joyous science; and my poor sister is dead! And your father, fair nephew, hath he married again?"

And ere the youth could reply, he read the answer in his surprise at the question, and said, "What! no? I would have sworn that Allan Durward was no man to live without a wife. He loved to have his house in order, loved to look on a pretty woman too, and was somewhat strict in life withal; matrimony did all this for him. Now, I care little about these comforts; and I can look on a pretty woman without thinking on the sacrament of wedlock; I am scarce holy enough for that."

"Alas! dear uncle, my mother was left a widow a year since, when Glen Houlakin was harried by the Ogilvies. My father, and my two uncles, and my two elder brothers, and seven of my kinsmen, and the harper, and the tasker, and some six more of our people, were killed in defending the castle; and there is not a burning hearth or a standing stone in all Glen Houlakin."

"Cross of St. Andrew!" said de Balafré; "that is what I call an onslaught! Ay, these Ogilvies were ever but sorry neighbors to Glen Houlakin; an evil chance it was, but fate of war—fate of war. When did this mishap befall, fair nephew?" With that he took a deep draught of wine, and shook his head with much solemnity when his kinsman replied that his family had been destroyed upon the festival of St. June last by-past.

"Look ye there," said the soldier, "I said it was all chance. On that very day I and twenty of my comrades carried the Castle of Roche-Noir by storm, from Amaury Bras-de-Fer, a captain of free lances, whom you must have heard of. I killed him on his own threshold, and gained as much gold as made this fair chain, which was once twice as long as it now is; and that minds me to send part of it on an holy errand. Here Andrew—Andrew!"

Andrew, his yeoman, entered, dressed like the archer himself in the general equipment, but without the armor for the limbs; that of the body more coarsely manufactured; his cap without a plume, and his cassock made of serge, or ordinary cloth, instead of rich velvet. Untwining his gold chain from his neck, Balafré twisted off, with his firm and strong-set teeth, about four inches from the one end of it, and said to his attendant, " Here, Andrew, carry this to my gossip, jolly Father Boniface, the monk of St. Martin's ; greet him well from me, by the same token that he could not say ' God save ye ' when we last parted at midnight. Tell my gossip that my brother and sister, and some others of my house, are all dead and gone, and I pray him to say masses for their souls as far as the value of these links will carry him, and to do on trust what else may be necessary to free them from purgatory. And hark ye, as they were just-living people, and free from all heresy, it may be that they are wellnigh out of limbo already, so that a little matter may have them free of the fetlocks : and in that case, look ye, ye will say I desire to take out the balance of the gold in curses upon a generation called the Ogilvies of Angusshire, in what way soever the church may best come at them. You understand all this, Andrew ? "

The coutelier nodded.

" Then look that none of the links find their way to the wine-house ere the monk touches them ; for if it so chance, thou shalt taste of saddle-girth and stirrup-leather, till thou art as raw as St. Bartholomew. Yet hold, I see thy eye has fixed on the wine measure, and thou shalt not go without tasting."

So saying, he filled him a brimful cup, which the coutelier drank off, and retired to do his patron's commission.

" And now, fair nephew, let us hear what was your own fortune in this unhappy matter."

" I fought it out among those who were older and stouter than I was, till we were all brought down," said Durward, " and I received a cruel wound."

" Not a worse slash than I received ten years since myself," said Le Balafré. " Look at this now, my fair nephew," tracing the dark crimson gash which was imprinted on his face. " An Ogilvie's sword never plowed so deep a furrow."

" They ploughed deep enough," answered Quentin, sadly ; " but they were tired at last, and my mother's entreaties procured mercy for me, when I was found to retain some spark of life ; but although a learned monk of Aberbrothock, who chanced to be our guest at the fatal time, and narrowly escaped being killed in the fray, was permitted to bind my wounds, and finally to remove me to a place of safety, it was only on promise, given both by my mother and him, that I should become a monk."

"A monk!" exclaimed the uncle—"Holy St. Andrew! that is what never befell me. No one, from my childhood upwards, ever so much as dreamed of making me a monk. And yet I wonder when I think of it; for you will allow that, bating the reading and writing, which I could never learn; and the psalmody, which I could never endure; and the dress, which, is that of a mad beggar—Our Lady forgive me! (here he crossed himself); and their fasts, which do not suit my appetite, I would have made every whit as good a monk as my little gossip at St. Martin's yonder. But I know not why, none ever proposed the station to me. O so, fair nephew, you were to be a monk, then; and wherefore, I pray you?"

"That my father's house might be ended, either in the cloister or in the tomb," answered Quentin, with deep feeling.

"I see," answered his uncle— "I comprehend. Cunning rogues—very cunning! They might have been cheated, though; for, look ye, fair nephew, I myself remember the canon Robesart who had taken the vows, and afterwards broke out of cloister, and became a captain of Free Companions. He had a mistress, the prettiest wench I ever saw, and three as beautiful children. There is no trusting monks, fair nephew,—no trusting them: they may become soldiers and fathers when you least expect it; but on with your tale."

"I have little more to tell," said Durward, "except that, considering my poor mother to be in some degree a pledge for me, I was induced to take upon me the dress of a novice, and conformed to the cloister rules, and even learned to read and write."

"To read and write!" exclaimed Le Balafré, who was one of that sort of people who think all knowledge is miraculous which chances to exceed their own. "To write, say'st thou, and to read! I cannot believe it: never Durward could write his name that ever I heard of, nor Lesly either. I can answer for one of them: I can no more write than I can fly. Now, in St. Louis's name, how did they teach it you?"

"It was troublesome at first," said Durward, "but become more easy by use; and I was weak with my wounds and loss of blood, and desirous to gratify my preserver, Father Peter, and so I was the more easily kept to my task. But after several months' languishing, my good kind mother died, and as my health was now fully restored, I communicated to my benefactor, who was also sub-prior of the convent, my

reluctance to take the vows ; and it was agreed between us,
since my vocation lay not to the cloister, that I should be
sent out into the world to seek my fortune, and that, to
save the sub-prior from the anger of the Ogilvies, my departure should have the appearance of flight ; and to color
it, I brought off the abbot's hawk with me. But I was regularly dismissed, as will appear from the hand and seal of
the abbot himself."

"That is right—that is well," said his uncle. "Our king
cares little what other theft thou mayest have made, but
hath a horror at anything like a breach of the cloister. And,
I warrant thee, thou hadst no great treasure to bear thy
charges ?"

"Only a few pieces of silver," said the youth ; "for to
you, fair uncle, I must make a free confession."

"Alas !" repeated Le Balafré, "that is hard. Now,
though I am never a hoarder of my pay, because it doth ill
to bear a charge about one in these perilous times, yet I
always have—and I would advise you to follow my example
—some odd gold chain, or bracelet, or carcanet, that serves
for the ornament of my person, and can at need spare a superfluous link or two, or it may be a superfluous stone, for
sale, that can answer any immediate purpose. But you may
ask, fair kinsman, how you are to come by such toys as this ?
(he shook his chain with complacent triumph). They hang
not on every bush ; they grow not in the fields like the
daffodils, with whose stalks children make knights' collars.
What then ? you may get such where I got this, in the service of the good King of France, where there is always
wealth to be found, if a man has but the heart to seek it, at
the risk of a little life or so."

"I understand," said Quentin, evading a decision to which
he felt himself as yet scarcely competent, "that the Duke
of Burgundy keeps a more noble state than the King of
France, and that there is more honor to be won under his
banners, that good blows are struck there, and deeds of
arms done ; while the Most Christian King, they say, gains
his victories by his ambassadors' tongues."

"You speak like a foolish boy, fair nephew," answered
he with the scar ; "and yet, I bethink me, when I came
hither I was nearly as simple : I could never think of a king
but what I supposed him either sitting under the high deas
and feasting amid his high vassals and paladins, eating *blanc-
manger*, with a great gold crown upon his head, or else
charging at the head of his troops like Charlemagne in the

romaunts, or like Robert Bruce or William Wallace in our own true histories, such as Barbour and the Minstrel. Hark in thine ear, man—it is all moonshine in the water. Policy —policy does it all. But what is policy, you will say ? It is an art this French king of ours has found out, to fight with other men's swords, and to wage his soldiers out of other men's purses. Ah! it is the wisest prince that ever put purple on his back ; and yet he weareth not much of that neither : I see him often go plainer than I would think befitted me to do."

" But you meet not my exception, fair uncle," answered young Durward ; " I would serve, since serve I must in a foreign land, somewhere where a brave deed, were it my hap to do one, might work me a name."

" I understand you, my fair nephew," said the royal man-at-arms—" I understand you passing well ; but you are unripe in these matters. The Duke of Burgundy is a hot-brained, impetuous, pudding-headed, iron-ribbed dare-all. He charges at the head of his nobles and native knights, his liegemen of Artois and Hainault ; think you, if you were there, or if I were there myself, that we could be much farther forward than the Duke and all his brave nobles of his own land ? If we were not up with them, we had a chance to be turned on the provost-marshal's hands for being slow in making to ; if we were abreast of them, all would be called well, and we might be thought to have deserved our pay ; and grant that I was a spear's-length or so in the front, which is both difficult and dangerous in such a *mêlée* where all do their best, why, my lord duke says, in his Flemish tongue, when he sees a good blow struck, " Ha! *gut getroffen!* a good lance—a brave Scot ; give him a florin to drink our health ; but neither rank, nor lands, nor treasures come to the stranger in such a service : all goes to the children of the soil."

" And where should it go, in Heaven's name, fair uncle ? " demanded young Durward.

" To him that protects the children of the soil," said Balafré, drawing up his gigantic height. " Thus says King Louis : " My good French peasant—mine honest Jacques Bonhomme—get you to your tools, your plow and your harrow, your pruning-knife and your hoe ; here is my gallant Scot that will fight for you, and you shall only have the trouble to pay him. And you, my most serene duke, my illustrious count, my most mighty marquis, e'en rein up your fiery courage till it is wanted, for it is apt to start out

4

of the course, and to hurt its master ; here are my companies of ordonnance—here are my French Guards—here are, above all, my Scottish Archers, and mine honest Ludovic with the Scar, who will fight, as well or better than you, with all that undisciplined valor which, in your fathers' time, lost Cressy and Azincour." Now, see you not in which of these states a cavalier of fortune holds the highest rank, and must come to the highest honor ? "

"I think I understand you, fair uncle," answered the nephew ; " but, in my mind, honor cannot be won where there is no risk. Sure, this is—I pray you pardon me—an easy and almost slothful life, to mount guard round an elderly man whom no one thinks of harming, to spend summer day and winter night up in yonder battlements, and shut up all the while in iron cages, for fear you should desert your posts ; uncle—uncle, it is but the hawk upon the perch, who is never carried out to the fields ! "

"Now, by St. Martin of Tours, the boy has some spirit— a right touch of the Lesly in him—much like myself, though always with a little more folly in it ! Hark ye, youth—long live the King of France !—scarce a day but there is some commission in hand, by which some of his followers may win both coin and credit. Think not that the bravest and most dangerous deeds are done by daylight. I could tell you of some, as scaling castles, making prisoners, and the like, where one who shall be nameless hath run higher risk, and gained greater favor, than any desperado in the train of desperate Charles of Burgundy. And if it please his Majesty to remain behind and in the background while such things are doing, he hath the more leisure of spirit to admire, and the more liberality of hand to reward, the adventurers, whose dangers, perhaps, and whose feats of arms, he can better judge of than if he had personally shared them. O, 'tis a sagacious and most politic monarch ! "

His nephew paused, and then said, in a low but impressive tone of voice, " The good Father Peter used often to teach me there might be much danger in deeds by which little glory was acquired. I need not say to you, fair uncle, that I do in course suppose that these secret commissions must needs be honorable."

" For whom or for what take you me, fair nephew ? " said Balefré, somewhat sternly ; " I have not been trained, indeed, in the cloister, neither can I write nor read. But I am your mother's brother : I am a loyal Lesly. Think you that I am like to recommend to you anything unworthy ?

The best knight in France, Du Guesclin himself, if he were
alive again, might be proud to number my deeds among his
achievements."

"I cannot doubt your warranty, fair uncle," said the
youth; "you are the only adviser my mishap has left me.
But is it true, as fame says, that this king keeps a meager
court here at his Castle of Plessis? No repair of nobles or
courtiers, none of his grand feudatories in attendance, none
of the high officers of the crown; half solitary sports, shared
only with the menials of his household; secret councils, to
which only low and obscure men are invited; rank and nobility depressed, and men raised from the lowest origin to
the kingly favor—all this seems unregulated, resembles not
the manners of his father, the noble Charles, who tore from
the fangs of the English lion this more than half-conquered
kingdom of France."

"You speak like a giddy child," said Le Balafré; "and
even as a child, you harp over the same notes on a new
string. Look you: if the King employs Oliver Dain, his
barber, to do what Oliver can do better than any peer of
them all, is not the kingdom the gainer? If he bids his
stout provost-marshal, Tristan, arrest such or such seditious
burgher, take off such or such a turbulent noble, the deed
is done and no more of it; when, were the commission given
to a duke or peer of France, he might perchance send the
King back a defiance in exchange. If, again, the King
pleases to give to plain Ludovic le Balafré a commission
which he will execute, instead of employing the high constable, who would perhaps betray it, doth it not show wisdom? Above all, doth not a monarch of such conditions
best suit cavaliers of fortune, who must go where their services are most highly prized and most frequently in demand? No—no, child, I tell thee Louis knows how to
choose his confidants, and what to charge them with, suit-
ing, as they say, the burden to each man's back. He is not
like the King of Castile, who choked of thirst because the
great butler was not beside to hand his cup. But hark to
the bell of St. Martin's! I must hasten back to the castle.
Farewell; make much of yourself, and at eight to-morrow
morning present yourself before the drawbridge, and ask the
sentinel for me. Take heed you step not off the straight
and beaten path in approaching the portal! There are such
traps and snap-haunches as may cost you a limb, which you
will sorely miss. You shall see the King, and learn to judge
him for yourself. Farewell."

So saying, Balafré hastily departed, forgetting, in his hurry, to pay for the wine he had called for—a shortness of memory incidental to persons of his description, and which his host, overawed, perhaps, by the nodding bonnet and ponderous two-handed sword, did not presume to use any efforts for correcting.

It might have been expected that, when left alone, Durward would have again betaken himself to his turret, in order to watch for the repetition of those delicious sounds which had soothed his morning reverie. But that was a chapter of romance, and his uncle's conversation had opened to him a page of the real history of life. It was no pleasing one, and for the present the recollections and reflections which it excited were qualified to overpower other thoughts, and especially all of a light and soothing nature.

Quentin resorted to a solitary walk along the banks of the rapid Cher, having previously inquired of his landlord for one which he might traverse without fear of disagreeable interruption from snares and pitfalls, and there endeavored to compose his turmoiled and scattered thoughts, and consider his future motions, upon which his meeting with his uncle had thrown some dubicty.

CHAPTER VI

THE BOHEMIANS

Sae rantingly, sae wantonly,
Sae dauntingly gaed he,
He play'd a spring and danced a round
Beneath the gallows-tree !

Old Song.

THE manner in which Quentin Durward had been educated was not of a kind to soften the heart, or perhaps to improve the moral feeling. He, with the rest of his family, had been trained to the chase as an amusement, and taught to consider war as their only serious occupation, and that it was the great duty of their lives stubbornly to endure, and fiercely to retaliate, the attacks of their feudal enemies, by whom their race had been at last almost annihilated. And yet there mixed with these feuds a spirit of rude chivalry, and even courtesy, which softened their rigor ; so that revenge, their only justice, was still prosecuted with some regard to humanity and generosity. The lessons of the worthy old monk, better attended to, perhaps, during a long illness and adversity than they might have been in health and success, had given young Durward still farther insight into the duties of humanity towards others ; and, considering the ignorance of the period, the general prejudices entertained in favor of a military life, and the manner in which he himself had been bred, the youth was disposed to feel more accurately the moral duties incumbent on his station than was usual at the time.

He reflected on his interview with his uncle with a sense of embarrassment and disappointment. His hopes had been high ; for although intercourse by letters was out of the question, yet a pilgrim, or an adventurous trafficker, or a crippled soldier, sometimes brought Lesly's name to Glen Houlakin, and all united in praising his undaunted courage, and his success in many petty enterprises which his master had entrusted to him. Quentin's imagination had filled up the sketch in his own way, and assimilated his successful and adventurous uncle (whose exploits probably lost nothing in the telling) to some of the champions and knights-errant of whom minstrels sang, and who won crowns and kings' daughters by dint of sword and lance. He was now compelled to rank his kinsman greatly lower in the scale of chivalry ; but, blinded by the high respect paid to parents and those who approach that character, moved by every early prejudice in his favor, inexperienced besides, and passionately attached to his mother's memory, he saw not, in the only brother of that dear relation, the character he truly held, which was that of an ordinary mercenary soldier, neither much worse nor greatly better than many of the same profession whose presence added to the distracted state of France.

Without being wantonly cruel, Le Balafré was, from habit, indifferent to human life and human suffering ; he was profoundly ignorant, greedy of booty, unscrupulous how he acquired it, and profuse in expending it on the gratification of his passions. The habit of attending exclusively to his own wants and interests had converted him into one of the most selfish animals in the world ; so that he was seldom able, as the reader may have remarked, to proceed far in any subject without considering how it applied to himself, or, as it is called, making the case his own, though not upon feelings connected with the golden rule, but such as were very different. To this must be added, that the narrow round of his duties and his pleasures had gradually circumscribed his thoughts, hopes, and wishes, and quenched in a great measure the wild spirit of honor, and desire of distinction in arms, by which his youth had been once animated. Balafré was, in short, a keen soldier, hardened, selfish, and narrow-minded ; active and bold in the discharge of his duty, but acknowledging few objects beyond it, except the formal observance of a careless devotion, relieved by an occasional debauch with Brother Boniface, his comrade and confessor. Had his genius been of a more extended character, he would probably have been promoted to some important command, for the King, who knew every soldier of his body-guard personally, reposed much confidence in Balafré's courage and fidelity ; and, besides, the Scot had either wisdom or cunning enough perfectly to understand, and ably to humor, the peculiarities of that sovereign. Still, however, his capacity was too much limited to admit of his rising to higher rank, and though smiled on and favored by Louis on many occasions, Balafré continued a mere Life-Guardsman, or Scottish Archer.

Without seeing the full scope of his uncle's character, Quentin felt shocked at his indifference to the disastrous extirpation of his brother-in-law's whole family, and could not help being surprised, moreover, that so near a relative had not offered him the assistance of his purse, which, but for the generosity of Maître Pierre, he would have been under the necessity of directly craving from him. He wronged his uncle, however, in supposing that this want of attention to his probable necessities was owing to avarice. Not precisely needing money himself at that moment, it had not occurred to Balafré that his nephew might be in exigencies ; otherwise, he held a near kinsman so much a part of himself, that he would have provided for the weal of the living nephew, as he endeavored to do for that of his deceased sister and her husband. But, whatever was the motive, the neglect was very unsatisfactory to young Durward, and he wished more than once he had taken service with the Duke of Burgundy before he quarreled with his forester. "Whatever had then become of me," he thought to himself, " I should always have been able to keep up my spirits with the reflection that I had, in case of the worst, a stout back-friend in this uncle of mine. But now I have seen him, and, woe worth him ! there has been more help in a mere mechanical stranger than I have found in my own mother's brother, my countryman and a cavalier. One would think the slash, that has carved all comeliness out of his face, had let at the same time every drop of gentle blood out of his body."

Durward now regretted he had not had an opportunity to mention Maître Pierre to Le Balafré, in the hope of obtaining some farther account of that personage ; but his uncle's questions had followed fast on each other, and the summons of the great bell of St. Martin of Tours had broken off their conference rather suddenly. "That old man," he thought to himself, " was crabbed and dogged in appearance, sharp and scornful in language, but generous and liberal in his actions ; and such a stranger is worth a cold kinsman. What says our old Scottish proverb ? ' Better kind fremit than fremit kindred." * "I will find out that man, which, methinks, should be no difficult task, since he is so wealthy as mine host bespeaks him. He will give me good advice for my governance at least ; and if he goes to strange countries, as many such do, I know not but his may be as adventurous a service as that of those guards of Louis."

As Quentin framed this thought, a whisper from those re-

* See Note 10.

cesses of the heart in which lies much that the owner does
not know of, or will not acknowledge willingly, suggested
that, perchance, the lady of the turret, she of the veil and
lute, might share that adventurous journey.

As the Scottish youth made these reflections, he met two
grave-looking men, apparently citizens of Tours, whom,
doffing his cap with the deference due from youth to age, he
respectfully asked to direct him to the house of Maître
Pierre.

"The house of whom, my fair son ?" said one of the passengers.

"Of Maître Pierre, the great silk merchant, who planted
all the mulberry-trees in the park yonder," said Durward.

"Young man," said one of them who was nearest to him,
"you have taken up an idle trade a little too early."

"And have chosen wrong subjects to practise your fool-
eries upon," said the farther one, still more gruffly. "The
syndic of Tours is not accustomed to be thus talked to by
strolling jesters from foreign parts."

Quentin was so much surprised at the causeless offense
which these two decent-looking persons had taken at a very
simple and civil question, that he forgot to be angry at the
rudeness of their reply, and stood staring after them as they
walked on with amended pace, often looking back at him,
as if they were desirous to get as soon as possible out of his
reach.

He next met a party of vine-dressers and addressed to them
the same question ; and, in reply, they demanded to know
whether he wanted Maître Pierre the schoolmaster, or Maître
Pierre the carpenter, or Maître Pierre the beadle, or half a
dozen of Maître Pierres besides. When none of these corresponded with the description of the person after whom he inquired, the peasants accused him of jesting with them imper-
tinently, and threatened to fall upon him and beat him, in
guerdon of his raillery. The oldest amongst them, who had
some influence over the rest, prevailed on them to desist from
violence.

"You see by his speech and his fool's cap," said he, "that
he is one of the foreign mountebanks who are come into the
country, and whom some call magicians and soothsayers,
and some jugglers, and the like, and there is no knowing
what tricks they have amongst them. I have heard of such
a one paying a liard to eat his bellyful of grapes in a poor
man's vineyard ; and he ate as many as would have loaded a
wain, and never undid a button of his jerkin ; and so let him

pass quietly, and keep his way, as we will keep ours. And you, friend, if you would shun worse, walk quietly on, in the name of God, our Lady of Marmontier, and St. Martin of Tours, and trouble us no more about your Maître Pierre, which may be another name for the devil, for aught we know."

The Scot, finding himself much the weaker party, judged it his wisest course to walk on without reply ; but the peasants, who at first shrunk from him in horror at his supposed talents for sorcery and grape-devouring, took heart of grace as he got to a distance, and having uttered a few cries and curses, finally gave them emphasis with a shower of stones, although at such a distance as to do little or no harm to the object of their displeasure. Quentin, as he pursued his walk, began to think, in his turn, either that he himself lay under a spell or that the people of Touraine were the most stupid, brutal, and inhospitable of the French peasants. The next incident which came under his observation did not tend to diminish this opinion.

On a slight eminence rising above the rapid and beautiful Cher, in the direct line of his path, two or three large chestnut trees were so happily placed as to form a distinguished and remarkable group ; and beside them stood three or four peasants, motionless, with their eyes turned upwards, and fixed, apparently, upon some object amongst the branches of the tree next to them. The meditations of youth are seldom so profound as not to yield to the slightest impulse of curiosity, as easily as the lightest pebble, dropped casually from the hand, breaks the surface of a limpid pool. Quentin hastened his pace, and ran lightly up the rising ground, time enough to witness the ghastly spectacle which attracted the notice of these gazers—which was nothing less than the body of a man, convulsed by the last agony, suspended on one of the branches.

"Why do you not cut him down ?" said the young Scot, whose hand was as ready to assist affliction as to maintain his own honor when he deemed it assailed.

One of the peasants, turning on him an eye from which fear had banished all expression but its own, and a face as pale as clay, pointed to a mark cut upon the bark of the tree, having the same rude resemblance to a *fleur-de-lys* which certain talismanic scratches, well known to our revenue officers, bear to a broad arrow. Neither understanding nor heeding the import of this symbol, young Durward sprung lightly as the ounce up into the tree, drew from his pouch that most necessary implement of a Highlander or woods-man, the trusty *skene dhu,** and calling to those below to receive the body on their hands, cut the rope asunder in less than a minute after he had perceived the exigency.

But his humanity was ill seconded by the bystanders. So far from rendering Durward any assistance, they seemed terrified at the audacity of his action, and took to flight with one consent, as if they feared their merely looking on might have been construed into accession to his daring deed. The body, unsupported from beneath, fell heavily to earth, in such a manner that Quentin, who presently afterwards jumped down, had the mortification to see that the last sparks of life were extinguished. He gave not up his chari-table purpose, however, without farther efforts. He freed the wretched man's neck from the fatal noose, undid the doublet, threw water on the face, and practised the other ordinary remedies resorted to for recalling suspended animation.

While he was thus humanely engaged, a mild clamor of tongues, speaking a language which he knew not, arose around him ; and he had scarcely time to observe that he was surrounded by several men and women of a singular and foreign appearance, when he found himself roughly seized by both arms, while a naked knife at the same moment was offered to his throat.

" Pale slave of Eblis ! " said a man, in imperfect French, " are you robbing him you have murdered ? But we have you, and shall abye it."

There were knives drawn on every side of him as these words were spoken, and the grim and distorted countenances which glared on him were like those of wolves rushing on their prey.

Still the young Scot's courage and presence of mind bore him out. " What mean ye, my masters ? " he said. " If that be your friend's body, I have just now cut him down in pure charity, and you will do better to try to recover his life than to misuse an innocent stranger to whom he owes his chance of escape."

The women had by this time taken possession of the dead body, and continued the attempts to recover animation which Durward had been making use of, though with the like bad success ; so that, desisting from their fruitless efforts, they seemed to abandon themselves to all the Oriental expressions of grief ; the women making a piteous wailing, and tearing

*See Note 11.

their long black hair, while the men seemed to rend their garments and to sprinkle dust upon their heads. They gradually became so much engaged in their mourning rites, that they bestowed no longer any attention on Durward, of whose innocence they were probably satisfied from circumstances. It would certainly have been his wisest plan to have left these wild people to their own courses, but he had been bred in almost reckless contempt of danger, and felt all the eagerness of youthful curiosity.

The singular assemblage,* both male and female, wore turbans and caps, more similar, in general appearance, to his own bonnet than to the hats commonly worn in France. Several of the men had curled black beards, and the complexion of all was nearly as dark as that of Africans. One or two, who seemed their chiefs, had some tawdry ornaments of silver about their necks and in their ears, and wore showy scarfs of yellow, or scarlet, or light green ; but their legs and arms were bare, and the whole troop seemed wretched and squalid in appearance. There were no weapons among them that Durward saw, except the long knives with which they had lately menaced him, and one short crooked saber, or Moorish sword, which was worn by an active-looking young man, who often laid his hand upon the hilt, while he surpassed the rest of the party in his extravagant expressions of grief, and seemed to mingle with them threats of vengeance.

The disordered and yelling group were so different in appearance from any beings whom Quentin had yet seen, that he was on the point of concluding them to be a party of Saracens, of those "heathen hounds" who were the opponents of gentle knights and Christian monarchs in all the romances which he had heard or read, and was about to withdraw himself from a neighborhood so perilous, when a galloping of horse was heard, and the supposed Saracens, who had raised by this time the body of their comrade upon their shoulders, were at once charged by a party of French soldiers.

This sudden apparition changed the measured wailing of the mourners into irregular shrieks of terror. The body was thrown to the ground in an instant, and those who were around it showed the utmost and most dexterous activity in escaping, under the bellies as it were of the horses, from the point of the lances which were leveled at them with exclamations of " Down with the accursed heathen thieves—

* See Gipsies or Bohemians. Note 12.

take and kill—bind them like beasts—spear them like wolves !"

These cries were accompanied with corresponding acts of violence ; but such was the alertness of the fugitives, the ground being rendered unfavorable to the horsemen by thickets and bushes, that only two were struck down and made prisoners, one of whom was the young fellow with the sword, who had previously offered some resistance. Quentin, whom fortune seemed at this period to have chosen for the butt of her shafts, was at the same time seized by the soldiers, and his arms, in spite of his remonstrances, bound down with a cord ; those who apprehended him showing a readiness and despatch in the operation which proved them to be no novices in matters of police.

Looking anxiously to the leader of the horsemen, from whom he hoped to obtain liberty, Quentin knew not exactly whether to be pleased or alarmed upon recognizing in him the down-looking and silent companion of Maître Pierre. True, whatever crime these strangers might be accused of, this officer might know, from the history of the morning, that he, Durward, had no connection with them whatever ; but it was a more difficult question whether this sullen man would be either a favorable judge or a willing witness in his behalf, and he felt doubtful whether he would mend his condition by making any direct application to him.

But there was little leisure for hesitation. "Trois-Eschelles and Petit-André," said the down-looking officer to two of his band, " these same trees stand here quite convenient. I will teach these misbelieving, thieving sorcerers to interfere with the King's justice, when it has visited any of their accursed race. Dismount, my children, and do your office briskly."

Trois-Eschelles and Petit-André were in an instant on foot, and Quentin observed that they had each, at the crupper and pommel of his saddle, a coil or two of ropes, which they hastily undid, and showed that, in fact, each coil formed a halter, with the fatal noose adjusted, ready for execution. The blood ran cold in Quentin's veins when he saw three cords selected, and perceived that it was proposed to put one around his own neck. He called on the officer loudly, reminded him of their meeting that morning, claimed the right of a free-born Scotsman, in a friendly and allied country, and denied any knowledge of the persons along with whom he was seized, or of their misdeeds.

The officer whom Durward thus addressed scarce deigned

to look at him while he was speaking, and took no notice whatever of the claim he preferred to prior acquaintance. He barely turned to one or two of the peasants who were now come forward, either to volunteer their evidence against the prisoners or out of curiosity, and said gruffly, "Was yonder young fellow with the vagabonds ?"

"That he was, sir, and it please your noble provostship," answered one of the clowns ; "he was the very first blasphemously to cut down the rascal whom his Majesty's justice most deservedly hung up, as we told your worship."

"I'll swear by God and St. Martin of Tours to have seen him with their gang," said another, "when they pillaged our *métairie*."

"Nay, but, father," said a boy, "yonder heathen was black, and this youth is fair ; yonder one had short curled hair, and this hath long fair locks."

"Ay, child," said the peasant, "and perhaps you will say yonder one had a green coat and this a gray jerkin. But his worship, the provost, knows that they can change their complexions as easily as their jerkins, so that I am still minded he was the same."

"It is enough that you have seen him intermeddle with the course of the King's justice, by attempting to recover an executed traitor," said the officer. "Trois-Eschelles and Petit-André, despatch."

"Stay, seignior officer !" exclaimed the youth, in mortal agony—"hear me speak—let me not die guiltlessly ; my blood will be required of you by my countrymen in this world, and by Heaven's justice in that which is to follow."

"I will answer for my actions in both," said the provost, coldly, and made a sign with his left hand to the executioners ; then, with a smile of triumphant malice, touched with his forefinger his right arm, which hung suspended in a scarf, disabled probably by the blow which Durward had dealt him that morning.

"Miserable, vindictive wretch !" answered Quentin, persuaded by that action that private revenge was the sole motive of this man's rigor, and that no mercy whatever was to be expected from him.

"The poor youth raves," said the functionary ; "speak a word of comfort to him ere he make his transit, Trois-Eschelles ; thou art a comfortable man in such cases, when a confessor is not to be had. Give him one minute of ghostly advice, and despatch matters in the next. I must proceed on the rounds. Soldiers, follow me !"

The provost rode on, followed by his guard, excepting two or three who were left to assist in the execution. The unhappy youth cast after him an eye almost darkened by despair, and thought he heard, in every tramp of his horse's retreating hoofs, the last slight chance of his safety vanish. He looked around him in agony, and was surprised, even in that moment, to see the stoical indifference of his fellow-prisoners. They had previously testified every sign of fear, and made every effort to escape ; but now, when secured, and destined apparently to inevitable death, they awaited its arrival with the utmost composure. The scene of fate before them gave, perhaps, a more yellow tinge to their swarthy cheeks ; but it neither agitated their features nor quenched the stubborn haughtiness of their eye. They seemed like foxes, which, after all their wiles and artful attempts at escape are exhausted, die with a silent and sullen fortitude, which wolves and bears, the fiercer objects of the chase, do not exhibit.

They were undaunted by the conduct of the fatal executioners, who went about their work with more deliberation than their master had recommended, and which probably arose from their having acquired by habit a kind of pleasure in the discharge of their horrid office. We pause an instant to describe them, because under a tyranny, whether despotic or popular, the character of the hangman becomes a subject of grave importance.

These functionaries were essentially different in their appearance and manners. Louis used to call them Democritus and Heraclitus, and their master, the provost, termed them *Jean qui pleure* and *Jean qui rit.*

Trois-Éschelles was a tall, thin, ghastly man, with a peculiar gravity of visage, and a large rosary round his neck, the use of which he was accustomed piously to offer to those sufferers on whom he did his duty. He had one or two Latin texts continually in his mouth on the nothingness and vanity of human life ; and, had it been regular to have enjoyed such a plurality. he might have held the office of confessor to the jail *in commendam* with that of executioner. Petit-André, on the contrary, was a joyous-looking, round, active little fellow, who rolled about in execution of his duty as if it were the most diverting occupation in the world. He seemed to have a sort of fond affection for his victims, and always spoke of them in kindly and affectionate terms. They were his poor honest fellows, his pretty dears, his gossips, his good old fathers, as their age or sex might be ; and as Trois-Eschelles endeavored to inspire them with a philosophical or religious regard to futurity, Petit-André seldom failed to refresh them with a jest or two, as if to induce them to pass from life as something that was ludicrous, contemptible, and not worthy of serious consideration.

I cannot tell why or wherefore it was, but these two excellent persons, notwithstanding the variety of their talents and the rare occurrence of such among persons of their profession, were both more utterly destested than, perhaps, any creatures of their kind, whether before or since ; and the only doubt of those who knew aught of them was, whether the grave and pathetic Trois-Eschelles or the frisky, comic, alert Petit-André * was the object of the greatest fear or of the deepest execration. It is certain they bore the palm in both particulars over every hangman in France, unless it were perhaps their master, Tristan l'Hermite, the renowned provost-marshal, or *his* master, Louis XI.

It must not be supposed that these reflections were of Quentin Durward's making. Life, death, time, and eternity were swimming before his eyes—a stunning and overwhelming prospect, from which human nature recoiled in its weakness, though human pride would fain have borne up. He addressed himself to the God of his fathers ; and when he did so, the little rude and unroofed chapel, which now held almost all his race but himself, rushed on his recollection. " Our feudal enemies gave my kindred graves in our own land," he thought, " but I must feed the ravens and kites of a foreign land, like an excommunicated felon ! " The tears gushed involuntarily from his eyes. Trois-Eschelles, touching one shoulder, gravely congratulated him on his Heavenly disposition for death, and pathetically exclaiming, *"Beati qui in Domino moriuntur,"* remarked the soul was happy that left the body while the tear was in the eye. Petit-André, slapping the other shoulder, called out, " Courage, my fair son ! since you must begin the dance, let the ball open gaily, for all the rebecs are in tune," twitching the halter at the same time, to give point to his joke. As the youth turned his dismayed looks first on one and then on the other, they made their meaning plainer by gently urging him forward to the fatal tree, and bidding him be of good courage, for it would be over in a moment.

In this fatal predicament, the youth cast a distracted look around him. " Is there any good Christian who hears me," he said, "that will tell Ludovic Lesly of the Scottish Guard,

* See Note 13.

called in this country Le Balafré, that his nephew is here basely murdered ? "

The words were spoken in good time, for an archer of the Scottish Guard, attracted by the preparations for the execution, was standing by, with one or two other chance passengers, to witness what was passing.

" Take heed what you do," he said to the executioners ; " if this young man be of Scottish birth, I will not permit him to have foul play."

" Heaven forbid, sir cavalier," said Trois-Eschelles ; " but we must obey our orders," drawing Durward forward by one arm.

" The shortest play is ever the fairest," said Petit-André, pulling him onward by the other.

But Quentin had heard words of comfort, and, exerting his strength, he suddenly shook off both the finishers of the law, and, with his arms still bound, ran to the Scottish archer. " Stand by me, countryman," he said in his own language, " for the love of Scotland and St. Andrew ! I am innocent—I am your own native landsman. Stand by me, as you shall answer at the last day ! "

" By St. Andrew ! they shall make at you through me," said the archer, and unsheathed his sword.

" Cut my bonds, countryman," said Quentin, " and I will do something for myself."

This was done with a touch of the archer's weapon ; and the liberated captive, springing suddenly on one of the provost's guard, wrested from him a halberd with which he was armed. " And now," he said, " come on, if you dare ! "

The two officers whispered together.

" Ride thou after the provost-marshal," said Trois-Eschelles, " and I will detain them here, if I can. Soldiers of the provost's guard, stand to your arms."

Petit-André mounted his horse and left the field, and the other marshals-men in attendance drew together so hastily at the command of Trois-Eschelles, that they suffered the other two prisoners to make their escape during the confusion. Perhaps they were not very anxious to detain them ; for they had of late been sated with the blood of such wretches, and, like other ferocious animals, were, through long slaughter, become tired of carnage. But the pretext was, that they thought themselves immediately called upon to attend to the safety of Trois-Eschelles ; for there was a jealousy which occasionally led to open quarrels betwixt the Scot-

tish Archers and the marshal's guards, who executed the
orders of their provost.

"We are strong enough to beat the proud Scots twice
over, if it be your pleasure," said one of the soldiers to Trois-
Eschelles.

But that cautious official made a sign to him to remain
quiet, and addressed the Scottish archer with great civility.
"Surely, sir, this is a great insult to the provost-marshal,
that you should presume to interfere with the course of the
King's justice, duly and lawfully committed to his charge ;
and it is no act of justice to me, who am in lawful possession
of my criminal. Neither is it a well-meant kindness to the
youth himself, seeing that fifty opportunities of hanging him
may occur, without his being found in so happy a state of
preparation as he was before your ill-advised interference."

"If my young countryman," said the Scot, smiling, "be
of opinion I have done him an injury, I will return him to
your charge without a word more dispute."

"No, no!—for the love of Heaven, no!" exclaimed
Quentin. "I would rather you swept my head off with your
long sword ; it would better become my birth than to die by
the hands of such a foul churl."

"Hear how he revileth !" said the finisher of the law.
"Alas ! how soon our best resolutions pass away ! He was
in a blessed frame for departure, but now, and in two minutes he has become a contemner of authorities."

"Tell me at once," said the archer, "what has this young ·
man done ?"

"Interfered," answered Trois-Eschelles, with some earnestness, "to take down the dead body of a criminal, when
the *fleur-de-lys* was marked on the tree where he was hung
with my own proper hand."

"How is this, young man ?" said the archer ; "how came
you to have committed such an offense ?"

"As I desire your protection," answered Durward, "I will
tell you the truth as if I were at confession. I saw a man
struggling on the tree, and I went to cut him down out of
mere humanity. I thought neither of *fleur-de-lys* nor of
clove-gilliflower, and had no more idea of offending the King
of France than our father the Pope."

"What a murrain had you to do with the dead body,
then ?" said the archer. "You'll see them hanging, in the
rear of this gentleman, like grapes on every tree, and you will
have enough to do in this country if you go a-gleaning after
the hangman. However, I will not quit a countryman's

5

cause if I can help it. Hark ye, master marshals-man, you see this is entirely a mistake. You should have some compassion on so young a traveler. In our country at home he has not accustomed to see such active proceedings as yours and your master's."

"Not for want of need of them, seignior archer," said Petit-André, who returned at this moment. "Stand fast, Trois-Eschelles, for here comes the provost-marshal; we shall presently see how he will relish having his work taken out of his hand before it is finished."

"And in good time," said the archer, "here come some of my comrades."

Accordingly, as the Provost Tristan rode up with his patrol on one side of the little hill which was the scene of the altercation, four or five Scottish Archers came as hastily up on the other, and at their head the Balafré himself.

Upon this urgency, Leslie showed none of that indifference towards his nephew of which Quentin had in his heart accused him; for he no sooner saw his comrade and Durward standing upon their defense than he exclaimed, "Cunningham, I thank thee. Gentleman—comrades, lend me your aid. It is a young Scottish gentleman—my nephew. Lindesay—Guthrie—Tyrie, draw and strike in !"

There was now every prospect of a desperate scuffle between the parties, who were not so disproportioned in numbers but that the better arms of the Scottish cavaliers gave them an equal chance of victory. But the provost-marshal, either doubting the issue of the conflict or aware that it would be disagreeable to the King, made a sign to his followers to forbear from violence, while he demanded of Balafré, who now put himself forward as the head of the other party, "What he, a cavalier of the King's Body-Guard, purposed by opposing the execution of a criminal ?"

"I deny that I do so," answered the Balafré. "St. Martin ! there is, I think, some difference between the execution of a criminal and the slaughter of my own nephew ?"

"Your nephew may be a criminal as well as another, seignior," said the provost-marshal; "and every stranger in France is amenable to the laws of France."

"Yes, but we have privileges, we Scottish Archers," said Balafré; "have we not, comrades ?"

"Yes—yes," they all exclaimed together. "Privileges—privileges ! Long live King Louis—long live the bold Balafré—long live the Scottish Guard—and death to all who would infringe our privileges !"

"'And now,' he said, 'come on, if you dare.'"

" Take reason with you, gentlemen cavaliers," said the provost-marshal ; " consider my commission."

" We will have no reason at your hand," said Cunningham ; " our own officer shall do us reason. We will be judged by the King's grace, or by our own captain, now that the Lord High Constable is not in presence."

" And we will be hanged by none," said Lindesay, " but Sandie Wilson, the auld marshals-man of our ain body."

" It would be a positive cheating of Sandie, who is as honest a man as ever tied noose upon hemp, did we give way to any other proceeding, " said the Balafré. " Were I to be hanged myself, no other should tie tippet about my craig."

" But here ye," said the provost-marshal, " this young fellow belongs not to you, and cannot share what you call your privileges."

" What we *call* our privileges all shall admit to be such," said Cunningham.

" We will not hear them questioned !" was the universal cry of the archers.

" Ye are mad, my masters," said Tristan l'Hermite. " No one disputes your priveliges ; but this youth is not one of you."

" He is *my* nephew," said the Balafré, with a triumphant air.

" But no Archer of the Guard, I think," retorted Tristan l'Hermite.

The archers looked on each other in some uncertainty.

" Stand to it yet, comrade," whispered Cunningham to Balafré. " Say he is engaged with us."

" St. Martin ! you say well, fair countryman," answered Lesly ; and, raising his voice, swore that he had that day enrolled his kinsman as one of his own retinue.

This declaration was a decisive argument.

" It is well, gentlemen," said the Provost Tristan, who was aware of the King's nervous apprehension of disaffection creeping in among his Guards. " You know, as you say, your privileges, and it is not my duty to have brawls with the King's Guards, if it is to be avoided. But I will report this matter for the King's own decision ; and I would have you to be aware that, in doing so, I act more mildly than perhaps my duty warrants me."

So saying he put his troop into motion, while the archers, remaining on the spot, held a hasty consultation what was next to be done.

" We must report the matter to Lord Crawford, our

captain, in the first place, and have the young fellow's name put on the roll."

" But, gentlemen, and my worthy friends and preservers," said Quentin, with some hesitation, " I have not yet determined whether to take service with you or no."

" Then settle in your own mind," said his uncle, " whether you choose to do so or be hanged ; for I promise you that, nephew of mine as you are, I see no other chance of your 'scaping the gallows."

This was an unanswerable argument, and reduced Quentin at once to acquiesce in what he might have otherwise considered as no very agreeable proposal ; but the recent escape from the halter, which had been actually around his neck, would probably have reconciled him to a worse alternative than was proposed.

" He must go home with us to our *caserne*," said Cunningham ; " there is no safety for him out of our bounds, whilst these man hunters are prowling about."

"May I not then abide for this night at the hostelry where I breakfasted, fair uncle ? " said the youth, thinking, perhaps, like many a new recruit, that even a single night of freedom was something gain d.

" Yes, fair nephew," answered his uncle, ironically, " that we may have the pleasure of fishing you out of some canal or moat, or perhaps out of a loop of the Loire, knit up in a sack, for the greater convenience of swimming, for that is like to be the end on't. The provost-marshal smiled on us when we parted," continued he, addressing Cunningham, " and that is a sign his thoughts were dangerous."

" I care not for his danger," said Cunningham ; " such game as we are beyond his bird-bolts. But I would have thee tell the whole to the Devil's Oliver, who is always a good friend to the Scottish Guard, and will see Father Louis before the provost can, for he is to shave him to-morrow."

" But hark you," said Balafré, " it is ill going to Oliver empty handed, and I am as bare as the birch in December."

" So are we all," said Cunningham ; " Oliver must not scruple to take our Scottish words for once. We will make up something handsome among us against the next pay-day ; and if *he* expects to share, let me tell you, the pay-day will come about all the sooner."

" And now for the château," said Balafré ; " and my nephew shall tell us by the way how he brought the provost-marshal on his shoulders, that we may know how to frame our report both to Crawford and Oliver."

CHAPTER VII

THE ENROLMENT

Justice of Peace. Here, hand me down the statute—
     read the articles—
Swear, kiss the book—subscribe, and be a hero ;
Drawing a portion from the public stock
For deeds of valor to be done hereafter—
Sixpence per day, subsistence and arrears.
                 The Recruiting Officer.

An attendant upon the archers having been dismounted, Quentin Durward was accommodated with his horse, and, in company of his martial countrymen, rode at a round pace towards the Castle of Plessis, about to become, although on his own part involuntarily, an inhabitant of that gloomy fortress, the outside of which had, that morning, struck him with so much surprise.

In the meanwhile, in answer to his uncle's repeated interrogations, he gave him an exact account of the accident which had, that morning, brought him into so much danger. Although he himself saw nothing in his narrative save what was affecting, he found it was received with much laughter by his escort.

"And yet it is no good jest either," said his uncle, "for what, in the devil's name, could lead the senseless boy to meddle with the body of a cursed misbelieving Jewish Moorish pagan !"

"Had he quarreled with the marshals-men about a pretty wench, as Michael of Moffat did, there had been more sense in it," said Cunningham.

"But I think it touches our honor, that Tristan and his people pretend to confound our Scottish bonnets with these pilfering vagabonds' *tocques* and *turbands*, as they call them," said Lindesay. "If they have not eyes to see the difference, they must be taught by rule of hand. But it's my belief, Tristan but pretends to mistake, that he may snap up the kindly Scots that come over to see their kinsfolks."

"May I ask, kinsman," said Quentin, "what sort of people these are of whom you speak ?"

"In troth you may ask," said his uncle, "but I know not,

fair nephew, who is able to answer you. Not I, I am sure, although I know it may be, as much as other people ; but they have appeared in this land within a year or two, just as a flight of locusts might do."

" Ay," said Lindesay, " and Jacques Bonhomme—that is our name for the peasant, young man—you will learn our way of talk in time—honest Jacques, I say, cares little what wind either brings them or the locusts, so he but knows any gale that would carry them away again."

" Do they do so much evil ?" asked the young man.

" Evil ! why, boy, they are heathens, or Jews, or Mahommedans at the least, and neither worship Our Lady nor the saints (crossing himself), and steal what they can lay hands on, and sing, and tell fortunes," added Cunningham.

" And they say there are some goodly wenches amongst these women," said Guthrie ; " but Cunningham knows that best."

" How, brother !" said Cunningham ; " I trust ye mean me no reproach ? "

" I am sure I said ye none," answered Guthrie.

" I will be judged by the company," said Cunningham. " Ye said as much as that I, a Scottish gentleman, and living within pale of holy church, had a fair friend among these off-scourings of heathenesse."

" Nay—nay," said Balafré, " he did but jest. We will have no quarrels among comrades."

" We must have no such jesting then," said Cunningham, murmuring as if he had been speaking to his own beard.

" Be there such vagabonds in other lands than France ?" said Lindesay.

" Ay, in good sooth, are there : tribes of them have appeared in Germany, and in Spain, and in England," answered Balafré. " By the blessing of good St. Andrew, Scotland is free of them yet."

" Scotland," said Cunningham, " is too cold a country for locusts, and too poor a country for thieves."

" Or perhaps John Highlander will suffer no thieves to thrive there but his own," said Guthrie.

" I let you all know," said Balafré, " that I come from the braes of Angus, and have gentle Highland kin in Glen Isla, and I will not have the Highlanders slandered."

" You will not deny that they are cattle lifters ?" said Guthrie.

" To drive a spreagh or so is no thievery," said Balafré, " and that I will maintain when and how you dare."

"For shame, comrade," said Cunningham, "who quarrels now? The young man should not see such mad misconstruction. Come, here we are at the chateau. I will bestow a runlet of wine to have a rouse in friendship, and drink to Scotland, Highland and Lowland both, if you will meet me at dinner at my quarters."

"Agreed—agreed," said Balafré ; "and I will bestow another, to wash away unkindness, and to drink a health to my nephew on his first entrance to our corps."

At their approach, the wicket was opened and the drawbridge fell. One by one they entered ; but when Quentin appeared, the sentinels crossed their pikes, and commanded him to stand, while bows were bent, and harquebusses aimed at him from the walls—a rigor of vigilance used notwithstanding that the young stranger came in company of a party of the garrison, nay of the very body which furnished the sentinels who were then upon duty.

Le Balafré, who had remained by his nephew's side on purpose, gave the necessary explanations, and, after some considerable hesitation and delay, the youth was conveyed under a strong guard to the Lord Crawford's apartment.

This Scottish nobleman was one of the last relics of the gallant band of Scottish lords and knights who had so long and so truly served Charles VI. in those bloody wars which decided the independence of the French crown and the expulsion of the English. He had fought, when a boy, abreast with Douglas and with Buchan, had ridden beneath the banner of the Maid of Arc, and was perhaps one of the last of those associates of Scottish chivalry who had so willingly drawn their swords for the *fleur-de-lys* against their "auld enemies of England." Changes which had taken place in the Scottish kingdom, and perhaps his having become habituated to French climate and manners, had induced the old baron to resign all thoughts of returning to his native country, the rather that the high office which he held in the household of Louis, and his own frank and loyal character, had gained a considerable ascendency over the King, who, though in general no ready believer in human virtue or honor, trusted and confided in those of the Lord Crawford, and allowed him the greater influence, because he was never known to interfere excepting in matters which concerned his charge.

Balafré and Cunningham followed Durward and the guard to the apartment of their officer, by whose dignified appearance, as well as with the respect paid to him by these proud soldiers, who seemed to respect no one else, the young man was much and strongly impressed.

Lord Crawford was tall, and through advanced age had become gaunt and thin ; yet retaining in his sinews the strength, at least, if not the elasticity, of youth, he was able to endure the weight of his armor during a march as well as the youngest man who rode in his band. He was hard-favored, with a scarred and weather-beaten countenance, and an eye that had looked upon death as his playfellow in thirty pitched battles, but which nevertheless expressed a calm contempt of danger, rather than the ferocious courage of a mercenary soldier. His tall, erect figure was at present wrapped in a loose chamber-gown, secured around him by his buff belt, in which was suspended his richly-hilted poniard. He had round his neck the collar and badge of the order of St. Michael. He sat upon a couch covered with deer's hide, and with spectacles on his nose (then a recent invention) was laboring to read a huge manuscript, called the *Rosier de la Guerre*—a code of military and civil policy which Louis had compiled for the benefit of his son the Dauphin, and upon which he was desirous to have the opinion of the experienced Scottish warrior.

Lord Crawford laid the book somewhat peevishly aside upon the entrance of these unexpected visitors, and demanded, in his broad national dialect, " What, in the foul fiend's name, they lacked now ? "

Le Balafré, with more respect than perhaps he would have showñ to Louis himself, stated at full length the circumstances in which his nephew was placed, and humbly requested his lordship's protection. Lord Crawford listened very attentively. He could not but smile at the simplicity with which the youth had interfered in behalf of the hanged criminal, but he shook his head at the account which he received of the ruffle betwixt the Scottish Archers and the provost-marshal's guard.*

" How often," he said, " will you bring me such ill-winded pirns to ravel out ? How often must I tell you, and especially both you, Ludovic Lesly, and you, Archie Cunning-ham, that the foreign soldier should bear himself modestly and decorously towards the people of the country, if you would not have the whole dogs of the town at your heels ? However, if you must have a bargain,† I would rather it were with that loon of a provost than any one else ; and I

* See Quarrels of Scottish Archers.   Note 14.
† A quarrel, videlicet.

blame you less for this onslaught than for other frays that you have made, Ludovic, for it was but natural and kind-like to help your young kinsman. This simple bairn must come to no skaith neither; so give me the roll of the company yonder down from the shelf, and we will even add his name to the troop, that he may enjoy the privileges."

"May it please your lordship," said Durward——

"Is the lad crazed!" exclaimed his uncle. "Would you speak to his lordship without a question asked?"

"Patience, Ludovic," said Lord Crawford, "and let us hear what the bairn has to say."

"Only this, if it may please your lordship," replied Quentin, "that I told my uncle formerly I had some doubts about entering this service. I have now to say that they are entirely removed, since I have seen the noble and experienced commander under whom I am to serve; for there is authority in your look."

"Weel said, my bairn," said the old lord, not insensible to the compliment; "we have had some experience, had God sent us grace to improve by it, both in service and in command. There you stand, Quentin, in our honorable corps of Scottish Body-Guards, as esquire to your uncle, and serving under his lance. I trust you will do well, for you should be a right man-at-arms, if all be good that is upcome,* and you are come of a gentle kindred. Ludovic, you will see that your kinsman follow his exercise diligently, for we will have spears-breaking one of these days."

"By my hilts, and I am glad of it, my lord; this peace makes cowards of us all. I myself feel a sort of decay of spirit, closed up in this cursed dungeon of a castle."

"Well, a bird whistled in my ear," continued Lord Crawford, "that the old banner will be soon dancing in the field again."

"I will drink a cup the deeper this evening to that very tune," said Balafré.

"Thou wilt drink to any tune," said Lord Crawford; "and I fear me, Ludovic, you will drink a bitter browst of your own brewing one day."

Lesly, a little abashed, replied, "That it had not been his wont for many a day; but his lordship knew the use of the company to have a carouse to the health of a new comrade."

"True," said the old leader, "I had forgot the occasion. I will send a few stoups of wine to assist your carouse; but

* That is, if your courage corresponds with your personal appearance.

let it be over by sunset. And, hark ye—let the soldiers for duty be carefully pricked off ; and see that none of them be more or less partakers of your debauch."

"Your lordship shall be lawfully obeyed," said Ludovic ; "and your health duly remembered."

"Perhaps," said Lord Crawford, "I may look in myself upon your mirth, just to see that all is carried decently."

"Your lordship shall be most dearly welcome," said Ludovic ; and the whole party retreated in high spirits to prepare for their military banquet, to which Lesly invited about a score of his comrades, who were pretty much in the habit of making their mess together.

A soldier's festival is generally a very extempore affair, providing there is enough of meat and drink to be had ; but on the present occasion Ludovic bustled about to procure some better wine than ordinary, observing, that the "old lord was the surest gear in their aught, and that, while he preached sobriety to them, he himself, after drinking at the royal table as much wine as he could honestly come by, never omitted any creditable opportunity to fill up the evening over the wine-pot. So you must prepare, comrades," he said, "to hear the old histories of the battles of Vernoil and Beaugé." *

The Gothic apartment in which they generally met was, therefore, hastily put into the best order : their grooms were despatched to collect green rushes to spread upon the floor ; and banners, under which the Scottish Guard had marched to battle, or which they had taken from the enemies' ranks, were displayed, by way of tapestry, over the table, and around the walls of the chamber.

The next point was to invest the young recruit as hastily as possible with the dress and appropriate arms of the Guard, that he might appear in every respect the sharer of its important privileges, in virtue of which, and by the support of his countrymen, he might freely brave the power and the displeasure of the provost-marshal, although the one was known to be as formidable as the other was unrelenting.

The banquet was joyous in the highest degree ; and the guests gave vent to the whole current of their national partiality on receiving into their ranks a recruit from their beloved fatherland. Old Scottish songs were sung, old tales of Scottish heroes told ; the achievements of their fathers, and the scenes in which they were wrought, were recalled to mind ; and for a time the rich plains of Touraine seemed

* See Scottish Auxiliaries. Note 15.

converted into the mountainous and sterile regions of Caledonia. When their enthusiasm was at high flood, and each was endeavoring to say something to enhance the dear remembrance of Scotland, it received a new impulse from the arrival of Lord Crawford, who, as Le Balafré had well prophesied, sat as it were on thorns at the royal board until an opportunity occurred of making his escape to the revelry of his own countrymen. A chair of state had been reserved for him at the upper end of the table ; for, according to the manners of the age, and the constitution of that body, although their leader and commander under the King and High Constable, the members of the corps, as we should now say, the privates, being all ranked as noble by birth, their captain sat with them at the same table without impropriety, and might mingle when he chose in their festivity, without derogation from his dignity as commander.

At present, however, Lord Crawford declined occupying the seat prepared for him, and bidding them " hold themselves merry," stood looking on the revel with a countenance which seemed greatly to enjoy it.

" Let him alone," whispered Cunningham to Lindesay, as the latter offered the wine to their noble captain—"let him alone—hurry no man's cattle—let him take it of his own accord."

In fact, the old lord, who at first smiled, shook his head, and placed the untasted wine-cup before him, began presently, as if it were in absence of mind, to sip a little of the contents, and, in doing so, fortunately recollected that it would be ill-luck did he not drink a draught to the health of the gallant lad who had joined them this day. The pledge was filled and answered, as may be well supposed, with many a joyous shout, when the old leader proceeded to acquaint them that he had possessed Master Oliver with an account, of what had passed that day. " And as," he said, " the scraper of chins hath no great love for the stretcher of throats, he has joined me in obtaining from the King an order commanding the provost to suspend all proceedings, under whatever pretense, against Quentin Durward, and to respect, on all occasions, the privileges of the Scottish Guard."

Another shout broke forth, the cups were again filled till the wine sparkled on the brim, and there was an acclaim to the health of the noble Lord Crawford, the brave conservator of the privileges and rights of his countrymen. The

good old lord could not but in courtesy do reason to this
pledge also, and gliding into the ready chair, as it were
without reflecting what he was doing, he caused Quentin to
come up beside him, and assailed him with many more
questions concerning the state of Scotland, and the great
families there, than he was well able to answer ; while ever
and anon, in the course of his queries, the good lord kissed
the wine-cup by way of parenthesis, remarking that sociality
became Scottish gentlemen, but that young men like Quentin ought to practise it cautiously, lest it might degenerate
into excess ; upon which occasion he uttered many excellent things, until his own tongue, although employed in the
praises of temperance, began to articulate something thicker
than usual. It was now that, while the military ardor of
the company augmented with each flagon which they emptied, Cunningham called on them to drink the speedy
hoisting of the *Oriflamme,* the royal banner of France.

"And a breeze of Burgundy to fan it !" echoed Lindesay.

" With all the soul that is left in this worn body do I accept the pledge, bairns," echoed Lord Crawford ; "and as
old as I am, I trust I may see it flutter yet. Hark ye, my
mates (for wine had made him something communicative),
ye are all true servants to the French crown, and wherefore should ye not know there is an envoy come from
Duke Charles of Burgundy, with a message of an angry
favor."

" I saw the Count of Crévecœur's equipage, horses and
retinue," said another of the guests, "down at the inn
yonder, at the Mulberry Grove. They say the King will not
admit him into the castle."

"Now, Heaven send him an ungracious answer !" said
Guthrie ; " but what is it he complains of ?"

"A world of grievances upon the frontier," said Lord Crawford ; "and latterly, that the King hath received under his
protection a lady of his land, a young countess, who hath fled
from Dijon because, being a ward of the Duke, he would
have her marry his favorite, Campo-basso."

"And hath she actually come hither alone, my lord?" said
Lindesay.

" Nay, not altogether alone, but with the old countess,.
her kinswoman, who hath yielded to her cousin's wishes in
this matter."

"And will the King," said Cunningham, " he being the
Duke's feudal sovereign, interfere between the Duke and his
ward, over whom Charles hath the same right which, were

he himself dead, the King would have over the heiress of Burgundy?"

"The King will be ruled, as he is wont, by rules of policy; and you know," continued Crawford, "that he hath not publicly received these ladies, nor placed them under the protection of his daughters, the Lady of Beaujeau or the Princess Joan, so, doubtless, he will be guided by circumstances. He is our master; but it is no treason to say, he will chase with the hounds and run with the hare with any prince in Christendom."

"But the Duke of Burgundy understands no such doubling," said Cunningham.

"No," answered the old lord; "and, therefore, it is likely to make work between them."

"Well—St. Andrew further the fray!" said Le Balafré. "I had it foretold me ten, ay, twenty years since, that I was to make the fortune of my house by marriage. Who knows what may happen, if once we come to fight for honor and ladies' love, as they do in the old romaunts?"

"*Thou* name ladies' love, with such a trench in thy visage!" said Guthrie.

"As well not love at all, as love a Bohemian woman of heathenesse," retorted La Balafré.

"Hold there, comrades," said Lord Crawford: "no tilting with sharp weapons, no jesting with keen scoffs—friends all. And for the lady, she is too wealthy to fall to a poor Scottish lord, or I would put in my own claim, fourscore years and all, or not very far from it. But here is her health, nevertheless, for they say she is a lamp of beauty."

"I think I saw her," said another soldier, "when I was upon guard this morning at the inner barrier; but she was more like a dark lantern than a lamp, for she and another were brought into the château in close litters."

"Shame!—shame! Arnot!" said Lord Crawford; "a soldier on duty should say naught of what he sees. Besides," he added after a pause, his own curiosity prevailing over the show of discipline which he had thought it necessary to exert, "why should these litters contain this very same Countess Isabelle de Croye?"

"Nay, my lord," replied Arnot, "I know nothing of it save this, that my coutelier was airing my horses in the road to the village, and fell in with Doguin the muleteer who brought back the litters to the inn, for they belong to the fellow of the Mulberry Grove yonder—he of the Fleur-de-Lys, I mean—and so Doguin asked Saunders Steed to take a

cup of wine, as they were acquainted, which he was no doubt
willing enough to do——"

"No doubt—no doubt," said the old lord, "it is a thing
I wish were corrected among you, gentlemen ; but all your
grooms and couteliers, and jackmen, as we should call them
in Scotland, are but too ready to take a cup of wine with
any one. It is a thing perilous in war, and must be amended.
But Andrew Arnot, this is a long tale of yours, and we will
cut it with a drink, as the Highlander says *Skeoch doch nan
skial* *—and that's good Gaelic. Here is to the Countess
Isabelle of Croye, and a better husband to her than Campo-
basso, who is a base Italian cullion ! And now, Andrew
Arnot, what said the muleteer to this yeoman of thine ? "

"Why he told him in secrecy, if it please your lordship,"
continued Arnot, "that these two ladies whom he had presently before convoyed up to the castle in the close litters
were great ladies, who had been living in secret at his master's house for some days, and that the King had visited them
more than once very privately, and had done them great
honor ; and that they had fled up to the castle, as he believed
for fear of the Count de Crèvecœur, the Duke of Burgundy's
ambassador, whose approach was just announced by an advance courier."

"Ay, Andrew, come you there to me ? " said Guthrie ;
"then I will be sworn it was the Countess whose voice I
heard singing to the lute, as I came even now through the
inner court. The sound came from the bay-windows of the
Dauphin's Tower ; and such melody was there as no one ever
heard before in the Castle of Plessis of the Park. By my
faith, I thought it was the music of the fairy Melusina's
making. There I stood, though I knew your board was covered and that you were all impatient—there I stood like——"

"Like an ass, Johnny Guthrie," said his commander ;
"thy long nose smelling the dinner, thy long ears hearing
the music, and thy short discretion not enabling thee to
decide which of them thou didst prefer. Hark ! is not that
the cathedral bell tolling to vespers ? Sure it cannot be
that time yet ? The mad old sexton has toll'd evensong an
hour too soon."

"In faith, the bell rings but too justly the hour," said
Cunningham ; "yonder the sun is sinking on the west side
of the fair plain."

"Ay," said the Lord Crawford, "is it even so ? Well,

---

* "Cut a tale with a drink," an expression used when a man
preaches over his liquor, as *bons vivants* say in England.

lads, we must live within compass. Fair and soft goes far
—slow fire makes sweet malt—to be merry and wise is a
sound proverb. One other rouse to the weal of old Scotland,
and then each man to his duty."

The parting-cup was emptied, and the guests dismissed ;
the stately old baron taking the Balafré's arm, under pretense of giving him some instructions concerning his nephew,
but perhaps, in reality, lest his own lofty pace should seem
in the public eye less steady than became his rank and high
command. A serious countenance did he bear as he passed
through the two courts which separated his lodgings from
the festal chamber, and solemn as the gravity of a hogshead
was the farewell caution with which he prayed Ludovic to
attend his nephew's motions, especially in the matter of
wenches and wine-cups.

Meanwhile, not a word that was spoken concerning the
beautiful Countess Isabelle had escaped the young Durward,
who, conducted into a small cabin, which he was to share
with his uncle's page, made his new and lowly abode the
scene of much high musing. The reader will easily imagine
that the young soldier should build a fine romance on such a
foundation as the supposed, or rather assumed, identification
of the maiden of the turret, to whose lay he had listened
with so·much interest, and the fair cup-bearer of Maître
Pierre, with a fugitive countess of rank and wealth, flying
from the pursuit of a hated lover, the favorite of an oppressive
guardian, who abused his feudal power. There was an interlude in Quentin's vision concerning Maître Pierre, who
seemed to exercise such authority even over the formidable
officer from whose hands he had that day, with much difficulty, made his escape. At length the youth's reveries,
which had been respected by little Will Harper, the companion of his cell, were broken in upon by the return of his
uncle, who commanded Quentin to bed, that he might arise
betimes in the morning, and attend him to his Majesty's
ante-chamber, to which he was called by his hour of duty,
along with five of his comrades.

CHAPTER VIII

THE ENVOY

Be thou as lightning in thee yes of France;
For ere thou canst report I will be there,
The thunder of my cannon shall be heard.
So, hence! Be thou the trumpet of our wrath.
King John.

HAD sloth been a temptation by which Durward was easily
beset, the noise with which the *caserne* of the guards resounded after the first toll of primes had certainly banished
the siren from his couch ; but the discipline of his father's
tower and of the convent of Aberbrothock had taught him
to start with the dawn ; and he did on his clothes gaily, amid
the sounding of bugles and the clash of armor, which announced the change of the viligant guards—some of whom
were returning to barracks after their nightly duty, whilst
some were marching out to that of the morning ; and others,
again, amongst whom was his uncle, were arming for immediate attendance upon the person of Louis. Quentin
Durward soon put on, with the feelings of so young a man
on such an occasion, the splendid dress and arms appertaining to his new situation ; and his uncle, who looked with
great accuracy and interest to see that he was completely
fitted out in every respect, did not conceal his satisfaction
at the improvement which had been thus made in his nephew's appearance. " If thou dost prove as faithful and bold
as thou art well-favored, I shall have in thee one of the
handsomest and best esquires in the guard, which cannot
but be an honor to thy mother's family. Follow me to the
presence-chamber ; and see thou keep close at my shoulder."

So saying, he took up a partizan, large, weighty, and
beautifully inlaid and ornamented, and directing his nephew
to assume a lighter weapon of a similar description, they
proceeded to the inner court of the palace, where their comrades, who were to form the guard of the interior apartments, were already drawn up and under arms—the squires
each standing behind their masters, to whom they thus
formed a second rank. Here were also in attendance many

yeomen-prickers, with gallant horses and noble dogs, on
which Quentin looked with such inquisitive delight that his
uncle was obliged more than once to remind him that the
animals were not there for his private amusement, but for
the King's, who had a strong passion for the chase, one of
the few inclinations which he indulged, even when coming
in competition with his course of policy ; being so strict a
proctector of the game in the royal forests, that it was currently said you might kill a man with greater impunity
than a stag.

On a signal given, the guards were put into motion by the
command of Le Balafré, who acted as officer upon the occasion ; and, after some minutiæ of word and signal, which
all served to show the extreme and punctilious jealousy
with which their duty was performed, they marched into the
hall of audience, where the King was immediately expected.

New as Quentin was to scenes of splendor, the effect of
that which was now before him rather disappointed the expectations which he had formed of the brilliancy of a court.
There were household officers, indeed, richly attired, there
were guards gallantly armed, and there were domestics of
various degrees ; but he saw none of the ancient counselors
of the kingdom, none of the high officers of the crown ;
heard none of the names which in those days sounded an
alarm to chivalry ; saw none either of those generals or leaders who, possessed of the full prime of manhood, were the
strength of France, or of the more youthful and fiery nobles,
those early aspirants after honor, who were her pride. The
jealous habits, the reserved manners, the deep and artful
policy of the King, had estranged this splendid circle from
the throne, and they were only called around it upon certain stated and formal occasions, when they went reluctantly, and returned joyfully, as the animals in the fable
are supposed to have approached and left the den of the
lion.

The very few persons who seemed to be there in the character of counselors were mean looking men, whose countenances sometimes expressed sagacity, but whose manners
showed they were called into a sphere for which their previous education and habits had qualified them but indifferently. One or two persons, however, did appear to Durward to possess a more noble mien, and the strictness of the
present duty was not such as to prevent his uncle communicating the names of those whom he thus distinguished.

With the Lord Crawford, who was in attendance, dressed
6

in the rich habit of his office, and holding a leading staff of silver in his hand, Quentin, as well as the reader, was already acquainted. Among others who seemed of quality, the most remarkable was the Count de Dunois, the son of that celebrated Dunois, known by the name of the Bastard of Orleans, who, fighting under the banner of Jeanne d'Arc, acted such a distinguished part in liberating France from the English yoke. His son well supported the high renown which had descended to him from such an honored source; and, notwithstanding his connection with the royal family, and his hereditary popularity both with the nobles and the people, Dunois had, upon all occasions, manifested such an open, frank loyalty of character that he seemed to have escaped all suspicion, even on the part of the jealous Louis, who loved to see him near his person, and sometimes even called him to his councils. Although accounted complete in all the exercises of chivalry, and possessed of much of the character of what was then termed a perfect knight, the person of the count was far from being a model of romantic beauty. He was under the common size, though very strongly built, and his legs rather curved outwards into that make which is more convenient for horseback than elegant in a pedestrian. His shoulders were broad, his hair black, his complexion swarthy, his arms remarkably long and nervous. The features of his countenance were irregular, even to ugliness; yet, after all, there was an air of conscious worth and nobility about the Count de Dunois which stamped, at the first glance, the character of the high-born nobleman and the undaunted soldier. His mien was bold and upright, his step free and manly, and the harshness of his countenance was dignified by a glance like an eagle and a frown like a lion. His dress was a hunting-suit, rather sumptuous than gay, and he acted on most occasions as Grand Huntsman, though we are not inclined to believe that he actually held the office.

Upon the arm of his relation Dunois, walking with a step so slow and melancholy that he seemed to rest on his kinsman and supporter, came Louis Duke of Orleans, the first prince of the blood royal (afterwards King, by the name of Louis XII.), and to whom the guards and attendants rendered their homage as such. The jealously-watched object of Louis's suspicions, this prince, who, failing the King's offspring, was heir to the kingdom, was not suffered to absent himself from court, and, while residing there, was alike denied employment and countenance. The dejection which

his degraded and almost captive state naturally impressed on
the deportment of this unfortunate prince was at this moment greatly increased by his consciousness that the King
meditated, with respect to him, one of the most cruel and
unjust actions which a tyrant could commit, by compelling
him to give his hand to the Princess Joan of France, the
younger daughter of Louis, to whom he had been contracted
in infancy, but whose deformed person rendered the insist-
ing upon such an agreement an act of abominable rigor.*

The exterior of this unhappy prince was in no respect distinguished by personal advantages ; and in mind he was of a
gentle, mild, and beneficent disposition, qualities which were
visible even through the veil of extreme dejection with which
his natural character was at present obscured. Quentin observed that the Duke studiously avoided even looking at the
Royal Guards, and when he returned their salute, that he
kept his eyes bent on the ground, as if he feared the King's
jealousy might have construed that gesture of ordinary
courtesy as arising from the purpose of establishing a
separate and personal interest among them.

Very different was the conduct of the proud cardinal and
prelate, John of Balue, the favorite minister of Louis for the
time, whose rise and character bore as close a resemblance to
that of Wolsey as the difference betwixt the crafty and politic
Louis and the headlong and rash Henry VIII. of England
would permit. The former had raised his minister from the
lowest rank to the dignity, or at least to the emoluments, of
Grand Almoner of France, loaded him with benefices, and
obtained for him the hat of a cardinal ; and although he was
too cautious to repose in the ambitious Balue the unbounded
power and trust which Henry placed in Wolsey, yet he was
more influenced by him than by any other of his avowed
counselors. The cardinal, accordingly, had not escaped the
error incidental to those who are suddenly raised to power
from an obscure situation, for he entertained a strong persuasion, dazzled doubtless by the suddenness of his elevation,
that his capacity was equal to intermeddling with affairs of
every kind, even those most foreign to his profession and
studies. Tall and ungainly in his person, he affected gallantry and admiration of the fair sex, although his manners
rendered his pretensions absurd, and his profession marked
them as indecorous. Some male or female flatterer had, in
evil hour, possessed him with the idea that there was much
beauty of contour in a pair of huge, substantial legs, which

* See Note 19, p. 440.

he had derived from his father, a carman of Limoges, or according to other authorities, a miller of Verdun ; and with this idea he had become so infatuated, that he always had his cardinal's robe a little looped up on one side, that the sturdy proportion of his limbs might not escape observation. As he swept through the stately apartment in his crimson dress and rich cope, he stopped repeatedly to look at the arms and appointments of the cavaliers on guard, asked them several questions in an authoritative tone, and took upon him to censure some of them for what he termed irregularities of discipline, in language to which these experienced soldiers dared no reply, although it was plain they listened to it with impatience and with contempt.

" Is the King aware," said Dunois to the cardinal, " that the Burgundian envoy is peremptory in demanding an audience ?"

" He is," answered the cardinal ; " and here, as I think, comes the all-sufficient Oliver Dain * to let us know the royal pleasure."

As he spoke, a remarkable person, who then divided the favor of Louis with the proud cardinal himself, entered from the inner apartment, but without any of that important and consequential demeanor which marked the fullblown dignity of the churchman. On the contrary, this was a little, pale, meager man, whose black silk jerkin and hose, without either coat, cloak, or cassock, formed a dress ill qualified to set off to advantage a very ordinary person. He carried a silver basin in his hand, and a napkin flung over his arm indicated his menial capacity. His visage was penetrating and quick, although he endeavored to banish such expression from his features, by keeping his eyes fixed on the ground, while, with the stealthy and quiet pace of a cat, he seemed modestly rather to glide than to walk through the apartment. But, though modesty may easily obscure worth, it cannot hide court favor : and all attempts to steal unperceived through the presence-chamber were vain on the part of one known to have such possession of the King's ear as had been attained by his celebrated barber and groom of the chamber, Oliver le Dain, called sometimes Oliver le Mauvais, and sometimes Oliver le Diable—epithets derived from the unscrupulous cunning with which he assisted in the execution of the schemes of his master's tortuous policy. At present he spoke earnestly for a few moments with the Count de Dunois, who instantly left the chamber, while the

* See Note 16.

tonsor glided quietly back towards the royal apartment whence he had issued, every one giving place to him ; which civility he only acknowledged by the most humble inclination of the body, excepting in a very few instances, where he made one or two persons the subject of envy to all the other courtiers by whispering a single word in their ear ; and at the same time muttering something of the duties of his place, he escaped from their replies, as well as from the eager solicitations of those who wished to attract his notice. Ludovic Lesly had the good fortune to be one of the individuals who, on the present occasion, was favored by Oliver with a single word, to assure him that his matter was fortunately terminated.

Presently afterwards, he had another proof of the same agreeable tidings ; for Quentin's old acquaintance, Tristan l'Hermite, the provost-marshal of the royal household, entered the apartment, and came straight to the place where Le Balafré was posted. This formidable officer's uniform, which was very rich, had only the effect of making his sinister countenance and bad mien more strikingly remarkable, and the tone which he meant for conciliatory was like nothing so much as the growling of a bear. The import of his words, however, was more amicable than the voice in which they were pronounced. He regretted the mistake which had fallen between them on the preceding day, and observed it was owing to the Sieur Le Balafré's nephew not wearing the uniform of his corps, or announcing himself as belonging to it, which had led him into the error for which he now asked forgiveness.

Ludovic Lesly made the necessary reply, and as soon as Tristan had turned away, observed to his nephew that they had now the distinction of having a mortal enemy from henceforward in the person of this dreaded officer. " But we are above his *votée :* a soldier," said he, " who does his duty may laugh at the provost-marshal."

Quentin could not help being of his uncle's opinion, for as Tristan parted from them, it was with the look of angry defiance which the bear casts upon the hunter whose spear has wounded him. Indeed, even when less strongly moved, the sullen eye of this official expressed a malevolence of purpose which made men shudder to meet his glance ; and the thrill of the young Scot was the deeper and more abhorrent, that he seemed to himself still to feel on his shoulders the grasp of the two deathdoing functionaries of this fatal officer.

Meanwhile, Oliver, after he had prowled around the room in the stealthy manner which we have endeavored to describe —all, even the highest officers, making way for him, and loading him with their ceremonious attentions, which his modesty seemed desirous to avoid—again entered the inner apartment, the doors of which were presently thrown open, and King Louis entered the presence-chamber.

Quentin, like all others, turned his eyes upon him; and started so suddenly that he almost dropt his weapon, when he recognized in the King of France that silk-merchant, Maître Pierre, who had been the companion of his morning walk. Singular suspicions respecting the real rank of this person had at different times crossed his thoughts; but this, the proved reality, was wilder than his wildest conjecture.

The stern look of his uncle, offended at this breach of the decorum of his office, recalled him to himself; but not a little was he astonished when the King, whose quick eye had at once discovered him, walked straight to the place where he was posted, without taking notice of any one else. "So," he said, "young man, I am told you have been brawling on your first arrival in Touraine; but I pardon you, as it was chiefly the fault of a foolish old merchant, who thought your Caledonian blood required to be heated in the morning with *vin de Beaulne*. If I can find him, I will make him an example to those who debauch my Guards. Balafré," he added, speaking to Lesly, "your kinsman is a fair youth, though a fiery. We love to cherish such spirits, and mean to make more than ever we did of the brave men who are around us. Let the year, day, hour, and minute of your nephew's birth be written down and given to Oliver Dain."

Le Balafré bowed to the ground and reassumed his erect military position, as one who would show by his demeanor his promptitude to act in the King's quarrel or defence. Quentin, in the meantime, recovered from his first surprise, studied the King's appearance more attentively, and was surprised to find how differently he now construed his deportment and features than he had done at their first interview.

These were not much changed in exterior, for Louis, always a scorner of outward show, wore on the present occasion, an old dark-blue hunting-dress, not much better than the plain burgher-suit of the preceding day, and garnished with a huge rosary of ebony, which had been sent to him by no less a personage than the Grand Seignior, with an attestation that it had been used by a Coptic hermit on Mount Lebanon, a personage of profound sanctity. And instead of

his cap with a single image, he now wore a hat the band of
which was garnished with at least a dozen of little paltry
figures of saints stamped in lead. But those eyes which, according to Quentin's former impression, only twinkled with
the love of gain, had, now that they were known to be the
property of an able and powerful monarch, a piercing and
majestic glance ; and those wrinkles on the brow,which he had
supposed were formed during a long series of petty schemes
of commerce, seemed now the furrows which sagacity had
worn.while toiling in meditation upon the fate of nations.

Presently after the King's appearance, the Princesses of
France, with the ladies of their suite, entered the apartment.
With the eldest, afterwards married to Peter of Bourbon, and
known in French history by the name of the Lady of Beaujeau, our story has but little to do. She was tall, and rather
handsome, possessed eloquence, talent, and much of her
father's sagacity, who reposed great confidence in her, and
loved her as well perhaps as he loved any one.

The younger sister, the unfortunate Joan, the destined
bride of the Duke of Orleans, advanced timidly by the side of
her sister, conscious of a total want of those external qualities
which women are most desirous of possessing, or being thought
to possess. She was pale, thin, and sickly in her complexion ; her shape visibly bent to one side, and her gait so unequal that she might be called lame. A fine set of teeth, and
eyes which were expressive of melancholy, softness, and resignation, with a quantity of light brown locks, were the only
redeeming points which flattery itself could have dared to
number to counteract the general homeliness of her face and
figure. To complete the picture, it was easy to remark, from
the Princess's negligence in dress and the timidity of her
manner, that she had an unusual and distressing consciousness of her own plainness of appearance, and did not dare to
make any of those attempts to mend by manners or by art
what nature had left amiss, or in any other way to exert a
power of pleasing. The King, who loved her not, stepped
hastily to her as she entered. " How now ! " he said, " our
world-contemning daughter. Are you robed for a hunting-
party or for the convent this morning ? Speak—answer."

" For which your Highness pleases, sire," said the Princess,
scarce raising her voice above her breath.

" Ay, doubtless you would persuade me it is your desire
to quit the court, Joan, and renounce the world and its
vanities. Ha ! maiden, wouldst thóu have it thought that
we, the first-born of holy church, would refuse our daughter

to Heaven ? Our Lady and St. Martin forbid we should
refuse the offering, were it worthy of the altar, or were thy
vocation in truth thitherward ! "

So saying, the King crossed himself devoutly, looking, in
the meantime, as appeared to Quentin, very like a cunning
vassal, who was depreciating the merit of something which
he was desirous to keep to himself, in order that he might
stand excused for not offering it to his chief or superior.
" Dares he thus play the hypocrite with Heaven," thought
Durward, " and sport with God and the saints, as he may
safely do with men, who dare not search his nature too
closely ? "

Louis meantime resumed, after a moment's mental devotion—" No, fair daughter, I and another know your real
mind better. Ha ! fair cousin of Orleans, do we not ?
Approach, fair sir, and lead this devoted vestal of ours to her
horse."

Orleans started when the King spoke, and hastened to
obey him ; but with such precipitation of step and confusion
that Louis called out, " Nay, cousin, rein your gallantry,
and look before you. Why, what a headlong matter a gallant's haste is on some occasions ! You had wellnigh taken
Anne's hand instead of her sister's. Sir, must I give Joan's
to you myself ? "

The unhappy prince looked up, and shuddered like a child,
when forced to touch something at which it has instinctive
horror ; then making an effort, took the hand, which the
Princess neither gave nor yet withheld. As they stood, her
cold damp fingers inclosed in his trembling hand, with their
eyes looking on the ground, it would have been difficult to
say which of these two youthful beings was rendered more
utterly miserable—the duke, who felt himself fettered to the
object of his aversion by bonds which he durst not tear
asunder, or the unfortunate young woman, who too plainly
saw that she was an object of abhorrence to him to gain
whose kindness she would willingly have died.

" And now to horse, gentlemen and ladies. We will ourselves lead forth our daughter of Beaujeau," said the King ;
" and God's blessing and St. Hubert's be on our morning
sport ! "

" I am, I fear, doomed to interrupt it, sire," said the
Compte de Dunois—" the Burgundian envoy is before the
gates of the castle, and demands an audience."

" *Demands* an audience, Dunois ! " replied the King.
" Did you not answer him, as we sent you word by Oliver,

that we were not at leisure to see him to-day ; and that to-morrow was the festival of St. Martin, which, please Heaven, we would disturb by no earthly thoughts ; and that on the succeeding day we were designed for Amboise ; but that we would not fail to appoint him as early an audience, when we returned, as our pressing affairs would permit ? "

" All this I said," answered Dunois ; " but yet, sire——"

" *Pasques-dieu!* man, what is it that thus sticks in thy throat ? " said the King. " This Burgundian's terms must have been hard of digestion."

" Had not my duty, your Grace's commands, and his character as an envoy restrained me," said Dunois, " he should have tried to digest them himself ; for, by our Lady of Orleans, I had more mind to have made him eat his own words than to have brought them to your Majesty."

" Body of me, Dunois," said the King, " it is strange that thou, one of the most impatient fellows alive, shouldst have so little sympathy with the like infirmity in our blunt and fiery cousin, Charles of Burgundy. Why, man, I mind his blustering messages no more than the towers of this castle regard the whistling of the northeast wind, which comes from Flanders, as well as this brawling envoy."

" Know then, sire," replied Dunois, " that the Count of Crèvecœur tarries below, with his retinue of pursuivants and trumpets, and says that, since your Majesty refuses him the audience which his master has instructed him to demand, upon matters of most pressing concern, he will remain there till midnight, and accost your Majesty at whatever hour you are pleased to issue from your castle, whether for business, exercise, or devotion ; and that no consideration, except the use of absolute force, shall compel him to desist from this resolution."

" He is a fool," said the King, with much composure. " Does the hot-headed Hainaulter think it any penance for a man of sense to remain for twenty-four hours quiet within the walls of his castle, when he hath the affairs of a kingdom to occupy him ? These impatient coxcombs think that all men, like themselves, are miserable, save when in saddle and stirrup. Let the dogs be put up and well looked to, gentle Dunois. We will hold council to day, instead of hunting."

" My liege," answered Dunois, " you will not thus rid yourself of Crèvecœur ; for his master's instructions are, that, if he hath not this audience which he demands, he shall nail his gauntlet to the palisades before the castle, in token of mortal defiance on the part of his master, shall renounce the Duke's fealty to France, and declare instant war."

" Ay," said Louis, without any perceptible alteration of voice, but frowning until his piercing dark eyes became almost invisible under his shaggy eyebrows, " is it even so ?— will oûr ancient vassal prove so masterful—our dear cousin treat us thus unkindly ? Nay then, Dunois, we must unfold the *Oriflamme*, and cry ' *Denis Montejoye!* '"

" Marry and amen, and in a most happy hour ! " said the martial Dunois ; and the guards in the hall, unable to resist the same impulse, stirred each upon his post, so as to produce a low but distinct sound of clashing arms. The King cast his eye proudly round, and for a moment thought and looked like his heroic father.

But the excitement of the moment presently gave way to the host of political considerations which, at that conjuncture, rendered an open breach with Burgundy so peculiarly perilous. Edward IV., a brave and victorious king, who had in his own person fought thirty battles, was now established on the throne of England, was brother to the Duchess of Burgundy, and, it might well be supposed, waited but a rupture between his near connection and Louis to carry into France, through the ever-open gate of Calais, those arms which had been triumphant in the English civil wars, and to obliterate the recollection of internal dissensions by that most popular of all occupations amongst the English, an invasion of France. To this consideration was added the uncertain faith of the Duke of Bretagne and other weighty subjects of reflection. So that, after a deep pause, when Louis again spoke, although in the same tone, it was with an altered spirit. " But God forbid," he said, " that aught less than necessity should make us, the Most Christian King, give cause to the effusion of Christian blood, if anything short of dishonor may avert such a calamity. We tender our subjects' safety dearer than the ruffle which our own dignity may receive from the rude breath of a malapert ambassador, who hath perhaps exceeded the errand with which he was charged. Admit the envoy of Burgundy to our presence."

" *Beati pacifici,*" said the Cardinal Balue.

" True ; and your eminence knoweth that they who humble themselves shall be exalted," added the King.

The cardinal spoke an " Amen," to which few assented ; for even the pale cheek of Orleans kindled with shame, and

Balafré suppressed his feelings so little as to let the butt-end of his partizan fall heavily on the floor—a movement of impatience for which he underwent a bitter reproof from the cardinal, with a lecture on the mode of handling his arms when in presence of the sovereign. The King himself seemed unusually embarrassed at the silence around him. "You are pensive, Dunois," he said. "You disapprove of our giving way to this hot-headed envoy."

"By no means," said Dunois : "I meddle not with matters beyond my sphere. I was but thinking of asking a boon of your Majesty."

"A boon, Dunois—what is it ? You are an unfrequent suitor, and may count on our favor."

"I would, then, your Majesty would send me to Évreux to regulate the clergy," said Dunois, with military frankness.

"That were indeed beyond thy sphere," replied the King, smiling.

"I might order priests as well," replied the count, "as my Lord Bishop of Évreux, or my lord cardinal, if he likes the title better, can exercise the soldiers of your Majesty's Guard."

The King smiled again, and more mysteriously, while he whispered Dunois, "The time may come when you and I will regulate the priests together. But this is for the present a good conceited animal of a bishop. Ah, Dunois ! Rome—Rome puts him and other burdens upon us. But patience, cousin, and shuffle the cards, till our hand is a stronger one." *

The flourish of trumpets in the courtyard now announced the arrival of the Burgundian nobleman. All in the presence-chamber made haste to arrange themselves according to their proper places of precedence, the King and his daughters remaining in the center of the assembly.

The Count of Crèvecœur, a renowned and undaunted warrior, entered the apartment ; and, contrary to the usage among the envoys of friendly powers, he appeared all armed, excepting his head, in a gorgeous suit of the most superb Milan armor, made of steel, inlaid and embossed with gold, which was wrought into the fantastic taste called the arabesque. Around his neck, and over his polished cuirass, hung his master's order of the Golden Fleece,† one of the most honored associations of chivalry then known in Chris-

* See Card-Playing. Note 17.
† See Note 18.

tendom. A handsome page bore his helmet behind him, a
herald preceded him, bearing his letters of credence, which
he offered on his knee to the King; while the ambassador
himself paused in the midst of the hall, as if to give all present time to admire his lofty look, commanding stature, and
undaunted composure of countenance and manner. The
rest of his attendants waited in the ante-chamber, or courtyard.

"Approach, Seignior Count de Crèvecœur," said Louis,
after a moment's glance at his commission ; " we need not
our cousin's letters of credence either to introduce to us a
warrior so well known or to assure us of your highly deserved credit with your master. We trust that your fair
partner, who shares some of our ancestral blood, is in good
health. Had you brought her in your hand, seignior count,
we might have thought you wore your armor, on this unwonted occasion, to maintain the superiority of her charms
against the amorous chivalry of France. As it is, we cannot guess the reason of this complete panoply."

"Sire," replied the ambassador, "the Count of Crèvecœur must lament his misfortune, and entreat your forgiveness, that he cannot, on this occasion, reply with such
humble deference as is due to the royal courtesy with which
your Majesty has honored him. But, although it is only
the voice of Philip Crèvecœur de Cordès which speaks, the
words which he utters must be those of his gracious lord
and sovereign the Duke of Burgundy."

"And what has Crèvecœur to say in the words of Burgundy ?" said Louis, with an assumption of sufficient dignity. "Yet hold—remember, that in this presence Philip
Crèvecœur de Cordès speaks to him who is his sovereign's
sovereign."

Crèvecœur bowed, and then spoke aloud : "King of
France, the mighty Duke of Burgundy once more sends
you a written schedule of the wrongs and oppressions committed on his frontiers by your Majesty's garrisons and officers ; and the first point of inquiry is, whether it is your
Majesty's purpose to make him amends for these injuries ?"

The King, looking slightly at the memorial which the
herald delivered to him upon his knee, said, "These matters have been already long before our council. Of the injuries complained of, some are in requital of those sustained
by my subjects, some are affirmed without any proof, some
have been retaliated by the Duke's garrisons and soldiers ;
and if there remain any which fall under none of those pre-

dicaments, we are not, as a Christian prince, averse to make satisfaction for wrongs actually sustained by our neighbor, though committed not only without our countenance but against our express order."

"I will convey your Majesty's answer," said the ambassador, "to my most gracious master; yet, let me say that, as it is in no degree different from the evasive replies which have already been returned to his just complaints, I cannot hope that it will afford the means of re-establishing peace and friendship betwixt France and Burgundy."

"Be that at God's pleasure," said the King. "It is not for dread of thy master's arms, but for the sake of peace only, that I return so temperate an answer to his injurious reproaches. Proceed with thine errand."

"My master's next demand," said the ambassador, "is, that your Majesty will cease your secret and underhand dealings with his towns of Ghent, Liege, and Malines. He requests that your Majesty will recall the secret agents by whose means the discontents of his good citizens of Flanders are inflamed; and dismiss from your Majesty's dominions, or rather deliver up to the condign punishment of their liege lord, those traitorous fugitives who, having fled from the scene of their machinations, have found too ready a refuge in Paris, Orleans, Tours, and other French cities."

"Say to the Duke of Burgundy," replied the King, "that I know of no such indirect practises as those with which he injuriously charges me; that my subjects of France have frequent intercourse with the good cities of Flanders, for the purpose of mutual benefit by free traffic, which it would be as much contrary to the Duke's interest as mine to interrupt; and that many Flemings have residence in my kingdom, and enjoy the protection of my laws, for the same purpose; but none, to our knowledge, for those of treason or mutiny against the Duke. Proceed with your message; you have heard my answer."

"As formerly, sire, with pain," replied the Count of Crèvecœur; "it not being of that direct or explicit nature which the Duke, my master, will accept, in atonement for a long train of secret machinations, not the less certain though now disavowed by your Majesty. But I proceed with my message. The Duke of Burgundy further requires the King of France to send back to his dominions without delay, and under a secure safeguard, the persons of Isabelle Countess of Croye, and of her relation and guardian the Countess Hameline, of the same family, in respect the said Countess Isabelle, being, by the law of the country and the feudal tenure of her estates, the ward of the said Duke of Burgundy, hath fled from his dominions, and from the charge which he, as a careful guardian, was willing to extend over her, and is here maintained in secret by the King of France, and by him fortified in her contumacy to the Duke, her natural lord and guardian, contrary to the laws of God and man, as they ever have been acknowledged in civilized Europe. Once more I pause for your Majesty's reply."

"You did well, Count de Crèvecœur," said Louis, scornfully, "to begin your embassy at an early hour ; for if it be your purpose to call on me to account for the flight of every vassal whom your master's heady passion may have driven from his dominions, the bead-roll may last till sunset. Who can affirm that these ladies are in my dominions ? Who can presume to say, if it be so, that I have either countenanced their flight hither or have received them with offers of protection ? Nay, who is it will assert that, if they are in France, their place of retirement is within my knowledge ?"

"Sire," said Crèvecœur, "may it please your Majesty, I *was* provided with a witness on this subject—one who beheld these fugitive ladies in the inn called the Fleur-de-Lys, not far from this castle ; one who saw your Majesty in their company, though under the unworthy disguise of a burgess of Tours ; one who received from them, in your royal presence, messages and letters to their friends in Flanders—all which he conveyed to the hand and ear of the Duke of Burgundy."

"Bring him forward," said the King ; "place the man before my face who dares maintain these palpable falsehoods."

"You speak in triumph, sire ; for you are well aware that this witness no longer exists. When he lived, he was called Zamet Maugrabin, by birth one of those Bohemian wanderers. He was yesterday, as I have learned, executed by a party of your Majesty's provost-marshal, to prevent, doubtless, his standing here to verify what he said of this matter to the Duke of Burgundy, in presence of his council, and of me, Philip Crèvecœur de Cordès."

"Now, by our Lady of Embrun !" said the King, "so gross are these accusations, and so free of consciousness am I of aught that approaches them, that, by the honor of a king, I laugh rather than am wroth at them. My provost-guard daily put to death, as is their duty, thieves and vagabonds; and is my crown to be slandered with whatever these thieves and vagabonds may have said to our hot cousin of Burgundy and his wise counselors? I pray you, tell my kind cousin, if he loves such companions, he had best keep them in his own estates; for here they are like to meet short shrift and a tight cord."

"My master needs no such subjects, sir king," answered the count, in a tone more disrespectful than he had yet permitted himself to make use of; "for the noble Duke uses not to inquire of witches, wandering Egyptians, or others upon the destiny and fate of his neighbors and allies."

"We have had patience enough and to spare," said the King, interrupting him; "and since thy sole errand here seems to be for the purpose of insult, we will send some one in our name to the Duke of Burgundy—convinced, in thus demeaning thyself towards us, thou hast exceeded thy commission, whatever that may have been."

"On the contrary," said Crèvecœur, "I have not yet acquitted myself of it. Hearken, Louis of Valois, King of France. Hearken, nobles and gentlemen who may be present. Hearken, all good and true men. And thou, Toison d'Or," addressing the herald, "make proclamation after me. I, Philip Crèvecœur of Cordès, Count of the Empire, and Knight of the honorable and princely Order of the Golden Fleece, in the name of the most puissant Lord and Prince, Charles, by the grace of God, Duke of Burgundy and Lotharingia, of Brabant and Limbourg, of Luxembourg and of Gueldres, Earl of Flanders and of Artois, Count Palatine of Hainault, of Holland, Zealand, Namur, and Zutphen, Marquis of the Holy Empire, Lord of Friezeland, Salines, and Malines, do give you, Louis, King of France, openly to know, that, you having refused to remedy the various griefs, wrongs, and offenses done and wrought by you, or by and through your aid, suggestion, and instigation, against the said Duke and his loving subjects, he, by my mouth, renounces all allegiance and fealty towards your crown and dignity, pronounces you false and faithless, and defies you as a prince and as a man. There lies my gage, in evidence of what I have said."

So saying, he plucked the gauntlet off his right hand and flung it down on the floor of the hall.

Until this last climax of audacity, there had been a deep silence in the royal apartment during the extraordinary scene; but no sooner had the clash of the gauntlet, when cast down, been echoed by the deep voice of Toison d'Or, the Burgundian herald, with the ejaculation, "Vive Bourgogne" than there was a general tumult. While Dunois, Orleans, old Lord Crawford, and one or two others, whose rank authorized their interference, contended which should lift up the gauntlet, the others in the hall exclaimed, "Strike him down! Cut him to pieces! Comes he here to insult the King of France in his own palace?"

But the King appeased the tumult by exclaiming, in a voice like thunder, which overawed and silenced every other sound, "Silence, my lieges! lay not a hand on the man, not a finger on the gage. And you, sir count, of what is your life composed or how is it warranted, that you thus place it on the cast of a die so perilous? Or is your duke made of a different metal from other princes, since he thus asserts his pretended quarrel in a manner so unusual?"

"He is indeed framed of a different and more noble metal than the other princes of Europe," said the undaunted Count of Crèvecœur; "for, when not one of them dared to give shelter to you—to *you*, I say, King Louis—when you were yet only Dauphin, an exile from France, and pursued by the whole bitterness of your father's revenge and all the power of his kingdom, you were received and protected like a brother by my noble master, whose generosity of disposition you have so grossly misused. Farewell, sire, my mission is discharged."

So saying, the Count de Crèvecœur left the apartment abruptly, and without farther leave-taking.

"After him—after him—take up the gauntlet and after him!" said the King. "I mean not you, Dunois, nor you, my Lord of Crawford, who, methinks, may be too old for such hot frays; nor you, cousin of Orleans, who are too young for them. My lord cardinal—my Lord Bishop of Auxerre—it is your holy office to make peace among princes; do you lift the gauntlet, and remonstrate with Count Crèvecœur on the sin he has committed, in thus insulting a great monarch in his own court, and forcing us to bring the miseries of war upon his kingdom and that of his neighbor."

Upon this direct personal appeal, the Cardinal Balue proceeded to lift the gauntlet, with such precaution as one would touch an adder—so great was apparently his aversion to this symbol of war—and presently left the royal apartment to hasten after the challenger.

Louis paused and looked round the circle of his courtiers, most of whom, except such as we have already distinguished, being men of low birth, and raised to their rank in the

King's household for other gifts than courage or feats of
arms, looked pale on each other, and had obviously received
an unpleasant impression from the scene which had been
just acted. Louis gazed on them with contempt, and then
said aloud, "Although the Count of Crèvecœur be presumptuous and overweening, it must be confessed that in
him the Duke of Burgundy hath as bold a servant as ever
bore message for a prince. I would I knew where to find as
faithful an envoy to carry back my answer."

"You do your French nobles injustice, sire," said Dunois ;
"not one of them but would carry a defiance to Burgundy
on the point of his sword."

"And, sire," said old Crawford, "you wrong also the
Scottish gentlemen who serve you. I, or any of my followers, being of meet rank, would not hesitate a moment to
call yonder proud count to a reckoning ; my own arm is yet
strong enough for the purpose, if I had but your Majesty's
permission."

"But your Majesty," continued Dunois, "will employ us
in no service through which we may win honor to ourselves,
to your Majesty, or to France."

"Say, rather," said the King, "that I will not give way,
Dunois, to the headlong impetuosity which, on some punc-
tilio of chivalry, would wreck yourselves, the throne,
France, and all. There is not one of you who knows not
how precious every hour of peace is at this moment, when so
necessary to heal the wounds of a distracted country ; yet
there is not one of you who would not rush into war on account
of the tale of a wandering gipsy, or of some errant damosel,
whose reputation, perhaps, is scarce higher. Here comes
the cardinal, and we trust with more pacific tidings. How
now, my lord—have you brought the count to reason and to
temper ?"

"Sire," said Balue, "my task hath been difficult. I put
it to yonder proud count, how he dared to use towards your
Majesty the presumptuous reproach with which his audience
had broken up, and which must be understood as proceeding, not from his master, but from his own insolence, and
as placing him therefore in your Majesty's discretion, for
what penalty you might think proper."

"You said right," replied the King ; "and what was his
answer ?"

"The count," continued the cardinal, "had at that moment his foot in the stirrup, ready to mount ; and, on hearing my expostulation, he turned his head without altering

7

his position. "Had I," said he, " been fifty leagues distant, and had heard by report that a question vituperative of my prince had been asked by the King of France, I had, even at that distance, instantly mounted, and returned to disburden my mind of the answer which I gave him but now."

" I said, sirs," said the King, turning around, without any show of angry emotion, "that in the Count Philip of Crèvecœur, our cousin the Duke possesses as worthy a servant as ever rode at a prince's right hand. But you prevailed with him to stay ?"

" To stay for twenty-four hours ; and in the meanwhile to receive again his gage of defiance," said the cardinal : " he has dismounted at the Fleur-de-Lys."

" See that he be nobly atttended and cared for at our charges," said the King ; "such a servant is a jewel in a a prince's crown. "Twenty-four hours !" he added, muttering to himself, and looking as if he were stretching his eyes to see into futurity—" twenty-four hours ! 'tis of the shortest. Yet twenty-four hours, ably and skilfully employed, may be worth a year in the hand of indolent or incapable agents. Well. To the forest—to the forest, my gallant lords ! Orleans, my fair kinsman, lay aside that modesty, though it becomes you ; mind not my Joan's coyness. The Loire may as soon avoid mingling with the Cher as she from favoring your suit, or you from preferring it," he added, as the unhappy prince moved slowly on after his betrothed bride. " And now for your boar-spears, gentlemen ; for Allegre, my pricker, hath harbored one that that will try both dog and man. Dunois, lend me your spear ; take mine, it is too weighty for me ; but when did *you* complain of such a fault in your lance ? To horse—to horse, gentlemen."

And all the chase rode on.

CHAPTER IX

THE BOAR-HUNT

I will converse with unrespective boys
And iron-witted fools. None are for me
That look into me with suspicious eyes.
                                    King Richard.

ALL the experience which the cardinal had been able to collect of his master's disposition did not, upon the present occasion, prevent his falling into a great error of policy. His vanity induced him to think that he had been more successful in prevailing upon the Count of Crèvecœur to remain at Tours than any other moderator whom the King might have employed would, in all probability, have been. And as he was well aware of the importance which Louis attached to the postponement of a war with the Duke of Burgundy, he could not help showing that he conceived himself to have rendered the King great and acceptable service. He pressed nearer to the King's person than he was wont to do, and endeavored to engage him in conversation on the events of the morning.

This was injudicious in more respects than one ; for princes love not to see their subjects approach them with an air conscious of deserving, and thereby seeming desirous to extort acknowledgment and recompense for their services ; and Louis, the most jealous monarch that ever lived, was peculiarly averse and inaccessible to any one who seemed either to presume upon service rendered or to pry into his secrets.

Yet, hurried away, as the most cautious sometimes are, by the self-satisfied humor of the moment, the cardinal continued to ride on the King's right hand, turning the discourse, whenever it was possible, upon Crèvecœur and his embassy ; which, although it might be the matter at that moment most in the King's thoughts, was nevertheless precisely that which he was least willing to converse on. At length Louis, who had listened to him with attention, yet without having returned any answer which could tend to prolong the conversation, signed to Dunois, who rode at no great distance, to come up on the other side of his horse.

" We came hither for sport and exercise," said he, " but the reverend father here would have us hold a council of state."

" I hope your Highness will excuse my assistance," said Dunois ; " I am born to fight the battles of France, and have heart and hand for that, but I have no head for her councils."

" My lord cardinal hath a head turned for nothing else, Dunois," answered Louis ; " he hath confessed Crèvecœur at the castle gate, and he hath communicated to us his whole shrift. Said you not the *whole ?* " he continued, with an emphasis on the word, and a glance at the cardinal, which shot from betwixt his long dark eyelashes, as a dagger gleams when it leaves the scabbard.

The cardinal trembled, as, endeavoring to reply to the King's jest, he said, " That though his order were obliged to conceal the secrets of their penitents in general, there was no *sigillum confessionis* which could not be melted at his Majesty's breath."

" And as his Eminence," said the King, " is ready to communicate the secrets of others to us, he naturally expects that we should be equally communicative to him ; and, in order to get upon this reciprocal footing, he is very reasonably desirous to know if these two Ladies of Croye be actually in our territories. We are sorry we cannot indulge his curiosity, not ourselves knowing in what precise place errant damsels, disguised princesses, distressed countesses, may lie leaguer within our dominions, which are, we thank God and our Lady of Embrun, rather too extensive for us to answer easily his Eminence's most reasonable inquiries. But supposing they were with us, what say you, Dunois, to our cousin's peremptory demand ? "

" I will answer you, my liege, if you will tell me in sincerity whether you want war or peace," replied Dunois, with a frankness which, while it arose out of his own native openness and intrepidity of character, made him from time to time a considerable favorite with Louis, who, like all astucious persons, was as desirous of looking into the hearts of others as of concealing his own.

" By my halidome," said he, " I should be as well contented as thyself, Dunois, to tell thee my purpose, did I myself but know it exactly. But say I declared for war, what should I do with this beautiful and wealthy young heiress, supposing her to be in my dominions ? "

" Bestow her in marriage on one of your own gallant fol-

lowers, who has a heart to love and an arm to protect her,"
said Dunois.

"Upon thyself, ha?" said the King. "*Pasques-dieu!*
thou art more politic than I took thee for, with all thy
bluntness."

"Nay, sire," answered Dunois, "I am aught except politic. By our Lady of Orleans, I come to the point at once,
as I ride my horse at the ring. Your Majesty owes the
house of Orleans at least one happy marriage."

"And I will pay it, count—*Pasques-dieu*, I will pay it!
See you not yonder fair couple?"

The King pointed to the unhappy Duke of Orleans and
the Princess, who, neither daring to remain at a greater distance from the King nor in his sight appear separate from
each other, were riding side by side, yet with an interval of
two or three yards betwixt them—a space which timidity on
the one side and aversion on the other prevented them from
diminishing, while neither dared to increase it.

Dunois looked in the direction of the King's signal, and
as the situation of his unfortunate relative and the destined
bride reminded him of nothing so much as of two dogs,
which, forcibly linked together, remain nevertheless as
widely separated as the length of their collars will permit,
he could not help shaking his head, though he ventured not
on any other reply to the hypocritical tyrant. Louis seemed
to guess his thoughts.

"It will be a peaceful and quiet household they will keep
—not much disturbed with children, I should augur.* But
these are not always a blessing."

It was, perhaps, the recollection of his own filial ingratitude that made the King pause as he uttered the last reflection, and which converted the sneer that trembled on his
lip into something resembling an expression of contrition.
But he instantly proceeded in another tone.

"Frankly, my Dunois, much as I revere the holy sacrament of matrimony (here he crossed himself), I would rather
the house of Orleans raised for me such gallant soldiers as
thy father and thyself, who share the blood-royal of France
without claiming its rights, than that the country should be
torn to pieces, like to England, by wars arising from the
rivalry of legitimate candidates for the crown. The lion
should never have more than cub."

Dunois sighed and was silent, conscious that contradicting
his arbitrary sovereign might well hurt his kinsman's inter-

* See Louis and his daughter. Note 19.

ests, but could do him no service; yet he could not forbear adding, in the next moment—

"Since your Majesty has alluded to the birth of my father, I must needs own that, setting the frailty of his parents on one side, he might be termed happier, and more fortunate, as the son of lawless love than of conjugal hatred."

"Thou art a scandalous fellow, Dunois, to speak thus of holy wedlock," answered Louis, jestingly. "But to the devil with the discourse, for the boar is unharbored. Lay on the dogs, in the name of the holy St. Hubert! Ha! ha! tra-la-la-lira-la!" And the King's horn rung merrily through the woods as he pushed forward on the chase, followed by two or three of his guards, amongst whom was our friend Quentin Durward. And here it was remarkable that, even in the keen prosecution of his favorite sport, the King, in indulgence of his caustic disposition, found leisure to amuse himself by tormenting Cardinal Balue.

It was one of that able statesman's weaknesses, as we have elsewhere hinted, to suppose himself, though of low rank and limited education, qualified to play the courtier and the man of gallantry. He did not, indeed, actually enter the lists of chivalrous combat, like Becket, or levy soldiers like Wolsey. But gallantry, in which they also were proficients, was his professed pursuit; and he likewise affected great fondness for the martial amusement of the chase. Yet, however well he might succeed with certain ladies, to whom his power, his wealth, and his influence as a statesman might atone for deficiencies in appearance and manners, the gallant horses, which he purchased at almost any price, were totally insensible to the dignity of carrying a cardinal, and paid no more respect to him that they would have done to his father, the carter, miller, or tailor, whom he rivaled in horsemanship. The King knew this, and, by alternately exciting and checking his own horse, he brought that of the cardinal, whom he kept close by his side, into such a state of mutiny against his rider that it became apparent they must soon part company; and then, in the midst of its starting, bolting, rearing, and lashing out alternately, the royal tormentor rendered the rider miserable, by questioning him upon many affairs of importance, and hinting his purpose to take that opportunity of communicating to him some of those secrets of state which the cardinal had but a little while before seemed so anxious to learn.*

A more awkward situation could hardly be imagined than

* See Balue's Horsemanship. Note 20.

that of a privy-councilor forced to listen to and reply to his sovereign while each fresh gambade of his unmanageable horse placed him in a new and more precarious attitude—his violet robe flying loose in every direction, and nothing securing him from an instant and perilous fall save the depth of the saddle, and its height before and behind. Dunois laughed without restraint ; while the King, who had a private mode of enjoying his jest inwardly, without laughing aloud, mildly rebuked his minister on his eager passion for the chase, which would not permit him to dedicate a few moments to business. " I will no longer be your hinderance to a course," continued he, addressing the terrified cardinal, and giving his own horse the rein at the same time.

Before Balue could utter a word by way of answer or apology, his horse, seizing the bit with his teeth, went forth at an uncontrollable gallop, soon leaving behind the King and Dunois, who followed at a more regulated pace, enjoying the statesman's distressed predicament. If any of our readers has chanced to be run away with in his time, as we ourselves have in ours, he will have a full sense at once of the pain, peril, and absurdity of the situation. Those four limbs of the quadruped, which, no way under the rider's control, nor sometimes under that of the creature they more properly belong to, fly at such a rate as if the hindermost meant to overtake the foremost ; those clinging legs of the biped which we so often wish safely planted on the greensward, but which now only augment our distress by pressing the animal's sides; the hands which have forsaken the bridle for the mane ; the body which, instead of sitting upright on the center of gravity, as old Angelo used to recommend, or stooping forward like a jockey's at Newmarket, lies, rather than hangs, crouched upon the back of the animal, with no better chance of saving itself than a sack of corn—combine to make a picture more than sufficiently ludicrous to spectators, however uncomfortable to the exhibiter. But add to this some singularity of dress or appearance on the part of the unhappy cavalier—a robe of office, a splendid uniform, or any other peculiarity of costume—and let the scene of action be a racecourse, a review, a procession, or any other place of concourse and public display, and if the poor wight would escape being the object of a shout of inextinguishable laughter, he must contrive to break a limb or two, or, which will be more effectual, to be killed on the spot ; for on no slighter condition will his fall excite anything like serious sympathy. On the present occasion, the short violet-colored gown of the

cardinal, which he used as a riding-dress (having changed
his long robes before he left the castle), his scarlet stockings
and scarlet hat, with the long strings hanging down, together
with his utter helplessness, gave infinite zest to his exhibition of horsemanship.

The horse, having taken matters entirely into his own hand,
flew rather than galloped up a long green avenue, overtook
the pack in hard pursuit of the boar, and then, having over-
turned one or two yeomen-prickers, who little expected to
be charged in the rear, having ridden down several dogs, and
greatly confused the chase, animated by the clamorous expostulations and threats of the huntsman, carried the terrified
cardinal past the formidable animal itself, which was rushing
on at a speedy trot, furious and embossed with the foam which
he churned around his tusks.   Balue, on beholding himself
so near the boar, set up a dreadful cry for help, which, or
perhaps the sight of the boar, produced such an effect on his
horse, that the animal interrupted its headlong career by
suddenly springing to one side ; so that the cardinal, who had
long kept his seat only because the motion was straight forward, now fell heavily to the ground.   The conclusion of
Balue's chase took place so near the boar that, had not the
animal been at that moment too much engaged about his
own affairs, the vicinity might have proved as fatal to the
cardinal as it is said to have done to Favila, king of the
Visigoths, of Spain.   The powerful churchman got off, however, for the fright, and, crawling as hastily as he could out
of the way of hounds and huntsmen, saw the whole chase
sweep by him without affording him assistance ; for hunters
in those days were as little moved by sympathy for such
misfortunes as they are in our own.

The King, as he passed, said to Dunois, " Yonder lies his
Eminence low enough ; he is no great huntsman, though for
a fisher, when a secret is to be caught, he may match St.
Peter himself.   He has, however, for once, I think, met with
his match."

The cardinal did not hear the words, but the scornful look
with which they were spoken led him to suspect their general
import.   The devil is said to seize such opportunities of
temptation as was now afforded by the passions of Balue,
bitterly moved as they had been by the scorn of the King.
The momentary fright was over as soon as he had assured
himself that his fall was harmless ; but mortified vanity, and
resentment against his sovereign, had a much longer influence
on his feelings.

After all the chase had passed him, a single cavalier, who seemed rather to be a spectator than a partaker of the sport, rode up with one or two attendants, and expressed no small surprise to find the cardinal upon the ground, without a horse or attendants, and in such a plight as plainly showed the nature of the accident which had placed him there. To dismount and offer his assistance in this predicament, to cause one of his attendants resign a staid and quiet palfrey for the cardinal's use, to express his surprise at the customs of the French court, which thus permitted them to abandon to the danger of the chase, and forsake in his need, their wisest statesman, were the natural modes of assistance and consolation which so strange a rencontre supplied to Crèvecœur; for it was the Burgundian ambassador who came to the assistance of the fallen cardinal.

He found the minister in a lucky time and humor for essaying some of those practises on his fidelity to which it is well known that Balue had the criminal weakness to listen. Already in the morning, as the jealous temper of Louis had suggested, more had passed betwixt them than the cardinal durst have reported to his master. But although he had listened with gratified ears to the high value which, he was assured by Crèvecœur, the Duke of Burgundy placed upon his person and talents, and not without a feeling of temptation, when the count hinted at the munificence of his master's disposition, and the rich benefices of Flanders, it was not until the accident, as we have related, had highly irritated him, that, stung with wounded vanity, he resolved in a fatal hour, to show Louis XI. that no enemy can be so dangerous as an offended friend and confidant.

On the present occasion, he hastily requested Crèvecœur to separate from him, lest they should be observed, but appointed him a meeting for the evening in the abbey of St. Martin's at Tours, after vesper service, and that in a tone which assured the Burgundian that his master had obtained an advantage hardly to have been hoped for, except in such a moment of exasperation.

In the meanwhile, Louis, who, though the most politic prince of his time, upon this, as upon other occasions, had suffered his passions to interfere with his prudence, followed contentedly the chase of the wild boar, which was now come to an interesting point. It had so happened that a sounder (*i e.*, in the language of the period, a boar of only two years old) had crossed the track of the proper object of the chase, and withdrawn in pursuit of him all the dogs, except two or three couple of old stanch hounds, and the greater part of the huntsmen. The King saw, with internal glee, Dunois, as well as others, follow upon this false scent, and enjoyed in secret the thought of triumphing over that accomplished knight in the art of venerie, which was then thought almost as glorious as war. Louis was well mounted and followed close on the hounds ; so that when the original boar turned to bay in a marshy piece of ground, there was no one near him but the king himself.

Louis showed all the bravery and expertness of an experienced huntsman ; for, unheeding the danger, he rode up to the tremendous animal, which was defending itself with fury against the dogs, and struck him with his boar-spear ; yet, as the horse shied from the boar, the blow was not so effectual as either to kill or disable him. No effort could prevail on the horse to charge the second time ; so that the King, dismounting, advanced on foot against the furious animal, holding naked in his hand one of those short, sharp, straight, and pointed swords which huntsmen used for such encounters. The boar instantly quitted the dogs to rush on his human enemy, while the King, taking his station, and posting himself firmly, presented the sword, with the purpose of aiming it at the boar's throat, or rather chest, within the collar-bone ; in which case, the weight of the beast, and the impetuosity of its career, would have served to accelerate its own destruction. But, owing to the wetness of the ground, the King's foot slipped, just as this delicate and perilous maneuver ought to have been accomplished, so that the point of the sword encountering the cuirass of bristles on the outside of the creature's shoulder, glanced off without making any impression, and Louis fell flat on the ground. This was so far fortunate for the monarch, because the animal, owing to the King's fall, missed his blow in his turn, and in passing only rent with his tusk the King's short hunting-cloak, instead of ripping up his thigh. But when, after running a little ahead in the fury of his course, the boar turned to repeat his attack on the King at the moment when he was rising, the life of Louis was in imminent danger. At this critical moment, Quentin Durward, who had been thrown out in the chase by the slowness of his horse, but who, nevertheless, had luckily distinguished and followed the blast of the King's horn, rode up and transfixed the animal with his spear.

The King, who had by this time recovered his feet, came in turn to Durward's assistance, and cut the animal's throat with his sword. Before speaking a word to Quentin, he measured the huge creature not only by paces, but even by feet ; then wiped the sweat from his brow and the blood from his hands ; then took off his hunting-cap, hung it on a bush, and devoutly made his orisons to the little leaden images which it contained ; and at length, looking upon Durward, said to him, " Is it thou, my young Scot ? Thou hast begun thy woodcraft well, and Maître Pierre owes thee as good entertainment as he gave thee at the Fleur-de Lys, yonder. Why dost thou not speak ? Thou hast lost thy forwardness and fire, methinks, at the court where others find both."

Quentin, as shrewd a youth as ever Scottish breeze breathed caution into, had imbibed more awe than confidence towards his dangerous master, and was far too wise to embrace the perilous permission of familiarity which he seemed thus invited to use. He answered in very few and well-chosen words, that if he ventured to address his Majesty at all, it could be but to crave pardon for the rustic boldness with which he had conducted himself when ignorant of his high rank.

"Tush ! man," said the King ; "I forgive thy sauciness for thy spirit and shrewdness. I admired how near thou didst hit upon my gossip Tristan's occupation. You have nearly tasted of his handiwork since, as I am given to understand. I bid thee beware of him ; he is a merchant who deals in rough bracelets and tight necklaces. Help me to my horse. I like thee, and will do thee good. Build on no man's favor but mine—not even on thine uncle's or Lord Crawford's ; and say nothing of thy timely aid in this matter of the boar, for if a man makes boast that he has served a king in such a pinch, he must take the braggart humor for its own recompense."

The king then winded his horn, which brought up Dunois and several attendants, whose compliments he received on the slaughter of such a noble animal, without scrupling to appropriate a much greater share of merit than actually belonged to him ; for he mentioned Durward's assistance as slightly as a sportsman of rank, who, in boasting of the number of birds which he has bagged, does not always dilate upon the presence and assistance of the gamekeeper. He then ordered Dunois to see that the boar's carcass was sent to the brotherhood of St. Martin, at Tours, to mend their fare on holydays, and that they might remember the King in their private devotions.

"And," said Louis, "who hath seen his Eminence, my lord cardinal ? Methinks it were but poor courtesy, and cold regard to holy church, to leave him afoot here in the forest."

" May it please you, sire," said Quentin, when he saw that all were silent, " I saw his lordship the cardinal accommodated with a horse, on which he left the forest."

" Heaven cares for its own," replied the King. "Set forward to the castle, my lords ; we'll hunt no more this morning. You, sir squire," addressing Quentin, "reach me my wood-knife; it has dropped from the sheath besides the quarry there. Ride on, Dunois ; I follow instantly."

Louis, whose lightest motions were often conducted like stratagems, thus gained an opportunity to ask Quentin privately, " My bonny Scot, thou hast an eye, I see. Canst thou tell me who helped the cardinal to a palfrey ? Some stranger, I should suppose ; for, as *I* passed without stopping, the courtiers would likely be in no hurry to do him such a timely good turn."

"I saw those who aided his Eminence but an instant, sire," said Quentin ; " it was only a hasty glance, for I had been unluckily thrown out, and was riding fast, to be in my place ; but I think it was the ambassador of Burgundy and his people."

"Ha !" said Louis. " Well, be it so ; France will match them yet."

There was nothing more remarkable happened, and the King, with his retinue, returned to the castle.

CHAPTER X

THE SENTINEL

Where should this music be ? i' the air or the earth ?
The Tempest.
I was all ear,
And took in strains that might create a soul
Under the ribs of death.
Comus.

QUENTIN had hardly reached his little cabin, in order to make some necessary changes in his dress, when his worthy relative required to know the full particulars of all that had befallen him at the hunt.

The youth, who could not help thinking that his uncle's hand was probably more powerful than his understanding, took care, in his reply, to leave the King in full possession of the victory which he had seemed desirous to appropriate. Le Balafré's reply was a boast of how much better he himself would have behaved in the like circumstances, and it was mixed with a gentle censure of his nephew's slackness, in not making in to the King's assistance, when he might be in imminent peril. The youth had prudence, in answer, to abstain from all farther vindication of his own conduct, except that, according to the rules of woodcraft, he held it ungentle to interfere with the game attacked by another hunter, unless he was specially called upon for his assistance. This discussion was scarcely ended, when occasion was afforded Quentin to congratulate himself for observing some reserve towards his kinsman. A low tap at the door announced a visitor ; it was presently opened, and Oliver Dain, or Mauvais, or Diable, for by all these names he was known, entered the apartment.

This able but most unprincipled man has been already described, in so far as his exterior is concerned. The aptest resemblance of his motions and manners might perhaps be to those of the domestic cat, which, while couching in seeming slumber, or gliding through the apartment with slow, stealthy, and timid steps, is now engaged in watching the hole of some unfortunate mouse, now in rubbing herself with

apparent confidence and fondness against those by whom she
desires to be caressed, and, presently after, is flying upon her
prey, or scratching perhaps, the very object of her former
cajolements.

He entered with stooping shoulders, a humble and modest
look, and threw such a degree of civility into his address to
the Seignior Balafré that no one, who saw the interview,
could have avoided concluding that he came to ask a boon
of the Scottish Archer. He congratulated Lesly on the excellent conduct of his young kinsman in the chase that day,
which he observed, had attracted the King's particular
attention. He here paused for a reply ; and with his eyes
fixed on the ground, save just when once or twice they stole
upwards to take a side glance at Quentin, he heard Balafré
observe, " That his Majesty had been unlucky in not having
himself by his side instead of his nephew, as he would ques-
tionless have made in and speared the brute, a matter which
he understood Quentin had left upon his Majesty's royal
hands, so far as he could learn the story. But it will be a
lesson to his Majesty," he said, " while he lives, to mount
a man of my inches on a better horse ; for how could my
great hill of a Flemish dray-horse keep up with his Majesty's
Norman runner ? I am sure I spurred till his sides were
furrowed. It is ill considered, Master Oliver, and you must
represent it to his Majesty."

Master Oliver only replied to this observation by turning
towards the bold bluff speaker one of those slow, dubious
glances which, accompanied by a slight motion of the hand
and a gentle depression of the head to one side, may be
either interpreted as a mute assent to what is said or as a
cautious deprecation of farther prosecution of the subject.
It was a keener, more scrutinizing glance which he bent on
the youth, as he said, with an ambiguous smile, " So, young
man, is it the wont of Scotland to suffer your princes to be
endangered for the lack of aid, in such emergencies as this
of to-day ?"

" It is our custom," answered Quentin, determined to
throw no farther light on the subject, " not to encumber
them with assistance in honorable pastimes, when they
can aid themselves without it. We hold that a prince in a
hunting-field must take his chance with others, and that he
comes there for the very purpose. What were woodcraft .
without fatigue and without danger ?"

" You hear the silly boy," said his uncle ; " that is always
the way with him : he hath an answer or a reason ready to

be rendered to every one. I wonder whence he hath caught the gift ; I never could give a reason for anything I have ever done in my life, except for eating when I was a-hungry, calling the muster-roll, and such points of duty as the like."

"And pray, worthy seignior," said the royal tonsor, looking at him from under his eyelids, "what might your reason be for calling the muster-roll, on such occasions ?"

"Because the captain commanded me," said Le Balafré. "By St. Giles, I know no other reason ! If he had commanded Tyrie or Cunningham, they must have done the same."

"A most military final cause !" said Oliver. "But Seignior Le Balafré, you will be glad, doubtless, to learn that his Majesty is so far from being displeased with your nephew's conduct, that he hath selected him to execute a piece of duty this afternoon."

"Selected *him ?*" said Balafré in great surprise. "Selected *me*, I suppose you mean ?"

"I mean precisely as I speak," replied the barber in a mild but decided tone : "the King hath a commission with which to entrust your nephew."

"Why, wherefore, and for what reason ?" said Balafré. "Why doth he choose the boy, and not me ?"

"I can go no farther back than your own ultimate cause, Seignior Le Balafré : such are his Majesty's commands. But," said he, "if I might use the presumption to form a conjecture, it may be his Majesty hath work to do fitter for a youth like your nephew than for an experienced warrior like yourself, Seignior Balafré. Wherefore, young gentleman, get your weapons and follow me. Bring with you a harquebuss, for you are to mount sentinel."

"Sentinel !" said the uncle ; "are you sure you are right, Master Oliver ? The inner guards of the castle have ever been mounted by those only who have, like me, served twelve years in our honorable body."

"I am quite certain of his Majesty's pleasure," said Oliver, "and must no longer delay executing it."

"But," said Le Balafré, "my nephew is not even a free archer, being only an esquire, serving under my lance."

"Pardon me," answered Oliver, "the King sent for the register not half an hour since, and enrolled him among the Guard. Have the goodness to assist to put your nephew in order for the service."

Balafré, who had no ill-nature, or even much jealousy, in his disposition. hastily set about adjusting his nephew's dress, and giving him directions for his conduct under arms, but was unable to refrain from larding them with interjections of surprise at such luck chancing to fall upon the young man so early.

" It had never-taken place before in the Scottish Guard," he said, " not even in his own instance. But doubtless his service must be to mount guard over the popinjays and Indian peacocks which the Venetian ambassador had lately presented to the King—it could be nothing else ; and such duty being only fit for a beardless boy (here he twirled his own grim mustachios), he was glad the lot had fallen on his fair nephew."

Quick and sharp of wit, as well as ardent in fancy, Quentin saw visions of higher importance in this early summons to the royal presence, and his heart beat high at the anticipation of rising into speedy distinction. He determined carefully to watch the manners and language of his conductor, which he suspected must, in some cases at least, be interpreted by contraries, as soothsayers are said to discover the interpretation of dreams. He could not but hug himself on having observed strict secrecy on the events of the chase, and then formed a resolution which, for so young a person, had much prudence in it, that, while he breathed the air of this secluded and mysterious court, he would keep his thoughts locked in his bosom, and his tongue under the most careful regulation.

His equipment was soon complete, and with his harquebuss on his shoulder (for though they retained the name of archers, the Scottish Guard very early substituted firearms for the long bow, in the use of which their nation never excelled), he followed Master Oliver out of the barrack.

His uncle looked long after him with a countenance in which wonder was blended with curiosity ; and though neither envy nor the malignant feelings which it engenders entered into his honest meditation, there was yet a sense of wounded or diminished self-importance which mingled with the pleasure excited by his nephew's favorable commencement of service.

He shook his head gravely, opened a privy cupboard, took out a large *bottrine* of stout old wine, shook it to examine how low the contents had ebbed, filled and drank a hearty cup ; then took his seat, half-reclining, on the great oaken settle, and having once again slowly shaken his head, received so much apparent benefit from the oscillation, that, like the toy called a mandarin, he continued the motion until he dropped into a slumber, from which he was first roused by the signal to dinner.

When Quentin Durward left his uncle to these sublime meditations, he followed his conductor, Master Oliver, who, without crossing any of the principal courts, led him partly through private passages exposed to the open air, but chiefly through a maze of stairs, vaults, and galleries, communicating with each other by secret doors and at unexpected points, into a large and spacious latticed gallery, which, from its breadth, might have been almost termed a hall, hung with tapestry more ancient than beautiful, and with a very few of the hard, cold, ghastly-looking pictures belonging to the first dawn of the arts, which preceded their splendid sunrise. These were designed to represent the paladins of Charlemagne, who made such a distinguished figure in the romantic history of France ; and as the gigantic form of the celebrated Orlando constituted the most prominent figure, the apartment acquired from him the title of Roland's Hall, or Roland's Gallery.*

" You will keep watch here," said Oliver, in a low whisper, as if the hard delineations of monarchs and warriors around could have been offended at the elevation of his voice, or as if he had feared to awaken the echoes that lurked among the groined vaults and Gothic drop-work on the ceiling of this huge and dreary apartment.

" What are the orders and signs of my watch ? " answered Quentin, in the same suppressed tone.

" Is your harquebuss loaded ? " replied Oliver, without answering his query.

" That," answered Quentin, " is soon done "; and proceeded to charge his weapon, and to light the slow-match, by which when necessary it was discharged, at the embers of a wood fire, which was expiring in the huge hall chimney— a chimney itself so large that it might have been called a Gothic closet or chapel appertaining to the hall.

When this was performed, Oliver told him that he was ignorant of one of the high privileges of his own corps, which only received orders from · the King in person, or the High Constable of France, in lieu of their own officers. " You are placed here by his Majesty's command, young man," added Oliver, " and you will not be long here without knowing wherefore you are summoned. Meantime, your walk extends along this gallery. You are permitted to stand still while you list, but on no account to sit down or

*See Louis XI. and Charlemagne. Note 21.

17

quit your weapon. You are not to sing aloud or whistle upon any account; but you may, if you list, mutter some of the church's prayers, or what else you list that has no offense in it, in a low voice. Farewell, and keep good watch."

"Good watch!" thought the youthful soldier, as his guide stole away from him with that noiseless, gliding step which was peculiar to him, and vanished through a side door behind the arras—"good watch! but upon whom, and against whom? for what, save bats or rats, are there here to contend with, unless these grim old representatives of humanity should start into life for the disturbance of my guard? Well, it is my duty, I suppose, and I must perform it."

With the vigorous purpose of discharging his duty, even to the very rigor, he tried to while away the time with some of the pious hymns which he had learned in the convent in which he had found shelter after the death of his father—allowing in his own mind that, but for the change of a novice's frock for the rich military dress which he now wore, his soldierly walk in the royal gallery of France resembled greatly those of which he had tired excessively in the cloistered seclusion of Aberbrothock.

Presently, as if to convince himself he now belonged not to the cell but to the world, he chanted to himself, but in such tone as not to exceed the license given to him, some of the ancient rude ballads which the old family harper had taught him, of the defeat of the Danes at Aberlemno and Forres, the murder of King Duffus at Forfar, and other pithy sonnets, and lays, which appertained to the history of his distant native country, and particularly of the district to which he belonged. This wore away a considerable space of time, and it was now more than two hours past noon, when Quentin was reminded by his appetite that the good fathers of Aberbrothock, however strict in demanding his attendance upon the hours of devotion, were no less punctual in summoning him to those of refection; whereas here, in the interior of a royal palace, after a morning spent in exercise and a noon exhausted in duty, no man seemed to consider it as a natural consequence that he must be impatient for his dinner.

There are, however, charms in sweet sounds which can lull to rest even the natural feelings of impatience by which Quentin was now visited. At the opposite extremities of the long hall or gallery were two large doors, ornamented with heavy architraves, probably opening into different suites of apartments, to which the gallery served as a medium of mutual communication. As the sentinel directed his solitary walk betwixt these two entrances, which formed the boundary of his duty, he was startled by a strain of music, which was suddenly waked near one of those doors, and which, at least in his imagination, was a combination of the same lute and voice by which he had been enchanted on the preceding day. All the dreams of yesterday morning, so much weakened by the agitating circumstances which he had since undergone, again rose more vivid from their slumber, and, planted on the spot where his ear could most conveniently drink in the sounds, Quentin remained, with his harquebuss shouldered, his mouth half open, ear, eye, and soul directed to the spot, rather the picture of a sentinel than a living form—without any other idea than that of catching, if possible, each passing sound of the dulcet melody.

These delightful sounds were but partially heard : they languished, lingered, ceased entirely, and were from time to time renewed after uncertain intervals. But, besides that music, like beauty, is often most delightful, or at least most interesting to the imagination, when its charms are but partially displayed, and the imagination is left to fill up what is from distance but imperfectly detailed, Quentin had matter enough to fill up his reverie during the intervals of fascination. He could not doubt, from the report of his uncle's comrades and the scene which had passed in the presence-chamber that morning, that the siren who thus delighted his ears was not, as he had profanely supposed, the daughter or kinswoman of a base *cabaretier*, but the same disguised and distressed countess for whose cause kings and princes were now about to buckle on armor and put lance in rest. A hundred wild dreams, such as romantic and adventurous youth readily nourished in a romantic and adventurous age, chased from his eyes the bodily presentment of the actual scene, and substituted their own bewildering delusions, when at once, and rudely, they were banished by a rough grasp laid upon his weapon, and a harsh voice which exclaimed, close to his ear, " Ha ! *Pasques-dieu*, sir squire, methinks you keep sleepy ward here ! "

The voice was tuneless, yet impressive and ironical, tone of Maître Pierre, and Quentin, suddenly recalled to himself, saw, with shame and fear, that he had, in his reverie, permitted Louis himself—entering probably by some secret door, and gliding along by the wall or behind the tapes-

try—to approach him so nearly as almost to master his
weapon.

The first impulse of his surprise was to free his harquebuss
by a violent exertion, which made the King stagger backward into the hall. His next apprehension was, that in obeying the animal instinct, as it may be termed, which prompts
a brave man to resist an attempt to disarm him, he had
aggravated, by a personal struggle with the King, the displeasure produced by the negligence with which he had
performed his duty upon guard ; and, under this impression,
he recovered his harquebuss without almost knowing what
he did, and, having again shouldered it, stood motionless
before the monarch, whom he had reason to conclude he had
mortally offended.

Louis, whose tyrannical disposition was less founded on
natural ferocity or cruelty of temper than on cold-blooded
policy and jealous suspicion, had, neverthless, a share of that
caustic severity which would have made him a despot in
private conversation, and always seemed to enjoy the pain
which he inflicted on occasions like the present. But he did
not push his triumph far, and contented himself with saying
—"Thy service of the morning hath already overpaid some
negligence in so young a soldier. Hast thou dined ? "

Quentin, who rather looked to be sent to the provost-marshal than greeted with such a compliment, answered humbly
in the negative.

"Poor lad," said Louis, in a softer tone than he usually
spoke in, "hunger hath made him drowsy. I know thine
appetite is a wolf," he continued, "and I will save thee from
one wild beast as thou didst me from another. Thou hast
been prudent, too, in that matter, and I thank thee for it.
Canst thou yet hold out an hour without food ? "

"Four-and-twenty, sire," replied Durward, "or I were no
true Scot."

"I would not for another kingdom be the pasty which
should encounter thee after such a vigil," said the King ;
"but the question now is, not of thy dinner, but of my own.
I admit to my table this day, and in strict privacy, the Cardinal Balue and this Burgundian—this Count de Crèvecœur,
and something may chance : the devil is most busy when foes
meet on terms of truce."

He stopped, and remained silent, with a deep and gloomy
look. As the King was in no haste to proceed, Quentin at
length ventured to ask what his duty was to be in these circumstances.

"To keep watch at the beauffet, with thy loaded weapon," said Louis; "and if there is treason, to shoot the traitor dead."

"Treason, sire! and in this guarded castle!" exclaimed Durward.

"You think it impossible," said the King, not offended, it would seem, by his frankness; "but our history has shown that treason can creep into an auger-hole. Treason excluded by guards! O thou silly boy! *Quis custodiat ipsos custodes* —who shall exclude the treason of those very warders?"

"Their Scottish honor," answered Durward boldly.

"True—most true," thou pleasest me," said the King cheerfully; "the Scottish honor was ever true, and I trust it accordingly. But treason!" here he relapsed into his former gloomy mood, and traversed the apartment with unequal steps—" she sits at our feasts, she sparkles in our bowls, she wears the beard of our councilors, the smiles of our courtiers, the crazy laugh of our jesters—above all she lies hid under the friendly air of a reconciled enemy. Louis of Orleans trusted John of Burgundy: he was murdered in the Rue Barbette. John of Burgundy trusted the faction of Orleans: he was murdered on the bridge of Montereau. I will trust no one—no one. Hark ye; I will keep my eye on that insolent count; ay, and on the churchman too, whom I hold not too faithful. When I say, "*Écosse, en avant,*" shoot Crèvecœur dead on the spot."

"It is my duty," said Quentin, "your Majesty's life being endangered."

"Certainly—I mean it no otherwise," said the King. "What should I get by slaying this insolent soldier? Were it to the Constable St. Paul indeed——" Here he paused, as if he thought he had said a word too much, but resumed, laughing—"There's our brother-in-law, James of Scotland —your own James Quentin—poniarded the Douglas* when on a hospitable visit, within his own royal castle of Skirling."

"Of Stirling," said Quentin, "and so please your Highness. It was a deed of which came little good."

"Stirling call you the castle?" said the King, overlooking the latter part of Quentin's speech. "Well, let it be Stirling; the name is nothing to the purpose. But I meditate no injury to these men—none. It would serve me nothing. They may not purpose equally fair for me. I rely on thy harquebuss."

* See Murder of Douglas. Note 22.

"I shall be prompt at the signal," said Quentin; "but yet——"

"You hesitate," said the King. "Speak out; I give thee full leave. From such as thou art, hints may be caught that are right valuable."

"I would only presume to say," replied Quentin, "that your Majesty having occasion to distrust this Burgundian, I marvel that you suffer him to approach so near your person, and that in privacy."

"O content you, sir squire," said the King. "There are some dangers which, when they are braved, disappear, and which yet, when there is an obvious and apparent dread of them displayed, become certain and inevitable. When I walk boldly up to a surly mastiff and caress him, it is ten to one I soothe him to good temper; if I show fear of him, he flies on me and rends me. I will be thus far frank with thee. It concerns me nearly that this man returns not to his headlong master in a resentful humor. I run my risk, therefore. I have never shunned to expose my life for the weal of my kingdom. Follow me."

Louis led his young Life Guardsman, for whom he seemed to have taken a special favor, through the side door by which he had himself entered, saying, as he showed it him, "He who would thrive at court must know the private wickets and concealed staircases—ay, and the traps and pitfalls of the palace, as well as the principal entrances, folding-doors, and portals."

After several turns and passages, the King entered a small vaulted room, where a table was prepared for dinner with three covers. The whole furniture and arrangements of the room were plain almost to meanness. A beauffet, or folding and movable cupboard, held a few pieces of gold and silver plate, and was the only article in the chamber which had, in the slightest degree, the appearance of royalty. Behind this cupboard, and completely hidden by it, was the post which Louis assigned to Quentin Durward; and after having ascertained, by going to different parts of the room, that he was invisible from all quarters, he gave him his last charge—"Remember the word, "*Écosse, en avant*"; and so soon as ever I utter these sounds, throw down the screen—spare not for cup or goblet, and be sure thou take good aim at Crève-cœur. If thy piece fail, cling to him, and use thy knife. Oliver and I can deal with the cardinal."

Having thus spoken, he whistled aloud, and summoned into the apartment Oliver, who was premier valet of the

chamber as well as barber, and who, in fact, performed all
offices immediately connected with the King's person, and who
now appeared, attended by two old men, who were the only
assistants or waiters at the royal table. So soon as the King
had taken his place, the visitors were admitted ; and Quentin,
though himself unseen, was so situated as to remark all the
particulars of the interview.

The King welcomed his visitors with a degree of cordiality
which Quentin had the utmost difficulty to reconcile with
the directions which he had previously received, and the purpose for which he stood behind the beauffet with his deadly
weapon in readiness. Not only did Louis appear totally free
from apprehension of any kind, but one would have supposed that those visitors whom he had done the high honor
to admit to his table were the very persons in whom he
could most unreservedly confide, and whom he was most
willing to honor. Nothing could be more dignified, and at
the same time more courteous, than his demeanor. While
all around him, including even his own dress, was far beneath the splendor which the petty princes of the kingdom
displayed in their festivities, his own language and manners
were those of a mighty sovereign in his most condescending
mood. Quentin was tempted to suppose either the whole of
his previous conversation with Louis had been a dream, or
that the dutiful demeanor of the cardinal, and the frank,
open, and gallant bearing of the Burgundian noble, had entirely erased the King's suspicion.

But whilst the guests, in obedience to the King, were in
the act of placing themselves at the table, his Majesty darted
one keen glance on them, and then instantly directed his
look to Quentin's post. This was done in an instant ; but
the glance conveyed so much doubt and hatred toward his
guests, such a peremptory injunction on Quentin to be watchful in attendance and prompt in execution, that no room
was left for doubting that the sentiments of Louis continued
unaltered, and his apprehensions unabated. He was, therefore more than ever astonished at the deep veil under which
that monarch was able to conceal the movements of his
jealous disposition.

Appearing to have entirely forgotten the language which
Crèvecœur had held towards him in the face of his court,
the King conversed with him of old times, of events which
had occurred during his own exile in the territories of Burgundy, and inquired respecting all the nobles with whom he
had been then familiar, as if that period had indeed been

the happiest of his life, and as if he retained towards all who had contributed to soften the term of his exile the kindest and most grateful sentiments.

" To an ambassador of another nation," he said, " I would have thrown something of state into our reception ; but to an old friend, who often shared my board at the Castle of Genappes,* I wished to show myself, as I love best to live, old Louis of Valois, as simple and plain as any of his Parisian *badauds.* But I directed them to make some better cheer than ordinary for you, sir count, for I know your Burgundian proverb, " *Mieux vault bon repas que bel habit* " ; and therefore I bid them have some care of our table. For our wine, you know well it is the subject of an old emulation betwixt France and Burgundy, which we will presently reconcile ; for I will drink to you in Burgundy, and you, sir count, shall pledge me in champagne. Here, Oliver, let me have a cup of *vin d'Auxerre* ; " and he hummed gaily a song then well known—

" Auxerre est la boisson des rois.

Here, sir count, I drink to the health of the noble Duke of Burgundy, our kind and loving cousin. Oliver, replenish yon golden cup with *vin de Rhetms,* and give it to the count on your knee ; he represents our loving brother. My lord cardinal, we will ourself fill your cup."

" You have already, sire, even to overflowing," said the cardinal, with the lowly mien of a favorite towards an indulgent master.

" Because we know that your Eminence can carry it with a steady hand," said Louis. " But which side do you espouse in the great controversy—Sillery or Auxerre—France or Burgundy ? "

" I will stand neutral, sire," said the cardinal, " and replenish my cup with Auvernat."

" A neutral has·a perilous part to sustain," said the King ; but as he observed the cardinal color somewhat, he glided from the subject, and added, " But you prefer the Auvernat, because it is so noble a wine it endures not water. You, sir count, hesitate to empty your cup. I trust you have found no national bitterness at the bottom."

" I would, sir," said the Count de Crèvecœur, " that all

---

* During his residence in Burgundy, in his father's lifetime, Genappes was the usual abode of Louis. This period of exile is often alluded to in the novel.

national quarrels could be as pleasantly ended as the rivalry betwixt our vineyards."

"With time, sir count," answered the King—"with time —such time as you have taken to your draught of champagne. And now that it is finished, favor me by putting the goblet in your bosom, and keeping it as a pledge of our regard. It is not to every one that we would part with it. It belonged of yore to that terror of France, Henry V. of England, and was taken when Rouen was reduced, and those islanders expelled from Normandy by the joint arms of France and Burgundy. It cannot be better bestowed than on a noble and valiant Burgundian, who well knows that on the union of these two nations depends the continuance of the freedom of the Continent from the English yoke."

The count made a suitable answer, and Louis gave unrestrained way to the satirical gaiety of disposition which sometimes enlivened the darker shades of his character. Leading, of course, the conversation, his remarks, always shrewd and caustic, and often actually witty, were seldom good-natured, and the anecdotes with which he illustrated them were often more humorous than delicate; but in no one word, syllable, or letter did he betray the state of mind of one who, apprehensive of assassination, hath in his apartment an armed soldier, with his piece loaded, in order to prevent or anticipate an attack on his person.

The Count of Crèvecœur gave frankly into the King's humor; while the smooth churchman laughed at every jest, and enhanced every ludicrous idea, without exhibiting any shame at expressions which made the rustic young Scot blush even in his place of concealment.* In about an hour and a half the tables were drawn; and the King, taking courteous leave of his guests, gave the signal that it was his desire to be alone.

So soon as all, even Oliver, had retired, he called Quentin from his place of concealment; but with a voice so faint, that the youth could scarce believe it to be the same which had so lately given animation to the jest and zest to the tale. As he approached, he saw an equal change in his countenance. The light of assumed vivacity had left the King's eyes, the smile had deserted his face, and he exhibited all the fatigue of a celebrated actor, when he has finished the exhausting representation of some favorite character, in which, while upon the stage, he had displayed the utmost vivacity.

"Thy watch is not yet over," said he to Quentin. "Re-

* See Louis's Humor. Note 23.

fresh thyself for an instant—yonder table affords the means —I will then instruct thee in thy farther duty.   Meanwhile, it is ill talking between a full man and a fasting."

He threw himself back on the seat, covered his brow with his hand, and was silent.

CHAPTER XI

THE HALL OF ROLAND

Painters show Cupid blind. Hath Hymen eyes?
Or is his sight warp'd by those spectacles
Which parents, guardians, and advisers lend him,
That he may look through them on lands and mansions,
On jewels, gold, and all such rich dotations,
And see their value ten times magnified?
Methinks 'twill brook a question.
The Miseries of Enforced Marriage.

LOUIS the XI. of France, though the sovereign in Europe who was fondest and most jealous of power, desired only its substantial enjoyment; and though he knew well enough, and at times exacted strictly, the observances due to his rank, was in general singularly careless of show.

In a prince of sounder moral qualities, the familiarity with which he invited subjects to his board—nay, occasionally sat at theirs—must have been highly popular; and even such as he was, the King's homeliness of manners atoned for many of his vices with that class of his subjects who were not particularly exposed to the consequences of his suspicion and jealousy. The *tiers état*, or commons, of France, who rose to more opulence and consequence under the reign of this sagacious prince, respected his person, though they loved him not; and it was resting on their support that he was enabled to make his party good against the hatred of the nobles, who conceived that he diminished the honor of the French crown, and obscured their own splendid privileges, by that very neglect of form which gratified the citizens and commons.

With patience, which most other princes would have considered as degrading, and not without a sense of amusement, the monarch of France waited till his Life Guardsman had satisfied the keenness of a youthful appetite. It may be supposed, however, that Quentin had too much sense and prudence to put the royal patience to a long or tedious proof; and indeed he was repeatedly desirous to break off his repast ere Louis would permit him. " I see it in thine eye," he said, good-naturedly, "that thy courage is not half abated. Go on—God and St. Denis !—charge again. I tell thee that meat and mass (crossing himself) never hindered the work of a good Christian man. Take a cup of wine ; but mind thou be cautious of the wine-pot ; it is the vice of thy countrymen as well as of the English, who, lacking that folly, are the choicest soldiers ever wore armor. And now wash speedily ; forget not thy benedicite, and follow me."

Quentin obeyed, and, conducted by a different, but as mazelike an approach as he had formerly passed, he followed Louis into the Hall of Roland.

"Take notice," said the King, imperatively, "thou hast never left this post—let that be thine answer to thy kinsman and comrades ; and, hark thee, to bind the recollection on thy memory, I give thee this gold chain (flinging on his arm one of considerable value). If I go not brave myself, those whom I trust have ever the means to ruffle it with the best. But, when such chains as these bind not the tongue from wagging too freely, my gossip, L'Hermite, hath an amulet for the throat, which never fails to work a certain cure. And now attend. No man, save Oliver or I myself, enters here this evening ; but ladies will come hither, perhaps from the one extremity of the hall, perhaps from the other, perhaps one from each. You may answer if they address you, but, being on duty, your answer must be brief ; and you must neither address them in your turn nor engage in any prolonged discourse. But hearken to what they say. Thine ears, as well as thy hands, are mine : I have bought thee, body and soul. Therefore, if thou hearest aught of their conversation, thou must retain it in memory until it is communicated to me, and then forget it. And, now I think better on it, it will be best that thou pass for a Scottish recruit, who hath come straight down from his mountains, and hath not yet acquired our most Christian language. Right. So, if they speak to thee, thou wilt *not* answer ; this will free you from embarrassment, and lead them to converse without regard to your presence. You understand me. Farewell. Be wary, and thou hast a friend."

The King had scarce spoken these words ere he disappeared behind the arras, leaving Quentin to meditate on what he had seen and heard. The youth was in one of those situations from which it is pleasanter to look forward than to look back ; for the reflection that he had been planted like a marksman in a thicket who watches for a stag, to take the life of the noble Count of Crèvecœur, had in it nothing en-

nobling. It was very true, that the King's measures seemed
on this occasion merely cautionary and defensive ; but how
did the youth know but he might be soon commanded on
some offensive operation of the same kind ? This would be
an unpleasant crisis, since it was plain, from the character of
his master, that there would be destruction in refusing, while
his honor told him there would be disgrace in complying.
He turned his thoughts from this subject of reflection, with
the sage consolation so often adopted by youth when pros-
pective dangers intrude themselves on their mind, that it
was time enough to think what was to be done when the
emergence actually arrived, and that sufficient for the day
was the evil thereof.

Quentin made use of this sedative reflection the more easily,
that the last commands of the King had given him something more agreeable to think of than his own condition.
The lady of the lute was certainly one of those to whom his
attention was to be dedicated ; and well in his mind did he
promise to obey one part of the King's mandate, and listen
with diligence to every word that might drop from her lips,
that he might know if the magic of her conversation equalled
that of her music. But with as much sincerity did he swear
to himself, that no part of her discourse should be reported
by him to the King which might affect the fair speaker
otherwise than favorably.

Meantime there was no fear of his again slumbering on
his post. Each passing breath of wind which, finding its
way through the open lattice, waved the old arras, sounded
like the approach of the fair object of his expectation. He
felt, in short, all that mysterious anxiety and eagerness of
expectation which is always the companion of love, and
sometimes hath a considerable share in creating it.

At length, a door actually creaked and jingled, for the
doors even of palaces did not in the 15th century turn on
their hinges so noiseless as ours ; but, alas ! it was not at
that end of the hall from which the lute had been heard.
It opened, however, and a female figure entered, followed
by two others, whom she directed by a sign to remain without, while she herself came forward into the hall. By her
imperfect and unequal gait, which showed to peculiar disadvantage as she traversed this long gallery, Quentin at once
recognized the Princess Joan, and, with the respect which
became his situation, drew himself up in a fitting attitude
of silent vigilance, and lowered his weapon to her as she
passed. She acknowledged the courtesy by a gracious in-

clination of her head, and he had an opportunity of seeing her countenance more distinctly than he had in the morning. There was little in the features of this ill-fated princess to atone for the misfortune of her shape and gait. Her face was, indeed, by no means disagreeable in itself, though destitute of beauty ; and there was a meek expression of suffering patience in her large blue eyes, which were commonly fixed upon the ground. But, besides that she was extremely pallid in complexion, her skin had the yellowish, discolored tinge which accompanies habitual bad health ; and though her teeth were white and regular, her lips were thin and pale. The Princess had a profusion of flaxen hair, but it was so light-colored as to be almost of a bluish tinge ; and her tire-woman, who doubtless considered the luxuriance of her mistress's tresses as a beauty, had not greatly improved matters by arranging them in curls around her pale countenance, to which they added an expression almost corpse-like and unearthly. To make matters still worse, she had chosen a vest or cymar of a pale green silk, which gave her, on the whole, a ghastly and even spectral appearance.

While Quentin followed this singular apparition with eyes in which curiosity was blended with compassion, for every look and motion of the Princess seemed to call for the latter feeling, two ladies entered from the upper end of the apartment.

One of these was the young person who, upon Louis's summons, had served him with fruit, while Quentin made his memorable breakfast at the Fleur-de-Lys. Invested now with all the mysterious dignity belonging to the nymph of the veil and lute, and proved, beside, at least in Quentin's estimation, to be the high-born heiress of a rich earldom, her beauty made ten times the impression upon him which it had done when he beheld in her one whom he deemed the daughter of a paltry innkeeper, in attendance upon a rich and humorous old burgher. He now wondered what fascination could ever have concealed from him her real character. Yet her dress was nearly as simple as before, being a suit of deep mourning, without any ornaments. Her head-dress was but a veil of crape, which was entirely thrown back, so as to leave her face uncovered ; and it was only Quentin's knowledge of her actual rank which gave in his estimation new elegance to her beautiful shape, a dignity to her step which had before remained unnoticed, and to her regular features, brilliant complexion, and dazzling eyes an air of conscious nobleness that enhanced their beauty.

Had death been the penalty, Durward must needs have rendered to this beauty and her companion the same homage which he had just paid to the royalty of the Princess. They received it as those who were accustomed to the deference of inferiors, and returned it with courtesy ; but he thought—perhaps it was but a youthful vision—that the young lady colored slightly, kept her eyes on the ground, and seemed embarrassed, though in a trifling degree, as she returned his military salutation. This must have been owing to her recollection of the audacious stranger in the neighboring turret at the Fleur-de-Lys ; but did that discomposure express displeasure ? This question he had no means to determine.

The companion of the youthful countess, dressed like herself simply, and in deep mourning, was at the age when women are apt to cling most closely to that reputation for beauty which has for years been diminishing. She had still remains enough to show what the power of her charms must once have been, and, remembering past triumphs, it was evident from her manner that she had not relinquished the pretensions to future conquests. She was tall and graceful, though somewhat haughty in her deportment, and returned the salute of Quentin with a smile of gracious condescension, whispering, the next instant, something into her companion's ear, who turned towards the soldier, as if to comply with some hint from the elder lady, but answered, nevertheless, without raising her eyes. Quentin could not help suspecting that the observation called on the young lady to notice his own good mien ; and he was (I do not know why) pleased with the idea that the party referred to did not choose to look at him in order to verify with her own eyes the truth of the observation. Probably he thought there was already a sort of mysterious connection beginning to exist between them, which gave importance to the slightest trifle.

This reflection was momentary, for he was instantly wrapped up in attention to the meeting of the Princess Joan with these stranger ladies. She had stood still upon their entrance, in order to receive them, conscious, perhaps, that motion did not become her well ; and as she was somewhat embarrassed in receiving and repaying their compliments, the elder stranger, ignorant of the rank of the party whom she addressed, was led to pay her salutation in a manner rather as if she conferred than received an honor through the interview.

" I rejoice, madam," she said, with a smile, which was

meant to express condescension at once and encouragement, " that we are at length permitted the society of such a respectable person of our own sex as you appear to be. I must say that my niece and I have had but little for which to thank the hospitality of King Louis. Nay, niece, never pluck my sleeve. I am sure I read in the looks of this young lady, sympathy for our situation. Since we came hither, fair madam, we have been used little better than mere prisoners ; and after a thousand invitations to throw our cause and our persons under the protection of France, the Most Christian King has afforded us at first but a base inn for our residence, and now a corner of this moth-eaten palace, out of which we are only permitted to creep towards sunset, as if we were bats or owls, whose appearance in the sunshine is to be held matter of ill omen."

" I am sorry," said the Princess, faltering with the awkward embarrassment of the interview, " that we have been unable, hitherto, to receive you according to your deserts. Your niece, I trust, is better satisfied ? "

" Much—much better than I can express," answered the youthful countess. " I sought but safety, and I have found solitude and secrecy besides. The seclusion of our former residence, and the still greater solitude of that now assigned to us, augment, in my eye, the favor which the King vouchsafed to us unfortunate fugitives."

" Silence, my silly cousin," said the elder lady, " and let us speak according to our conscience, since at last we are alone with one of our own sex—I say alone, for that handsome young soldier is a mere statue, since he seems not to have the use of his limbs, and I am given to understand he wants that of his tongue, at least in civilized language—I say, since no one but this lady can understand us, I must own there is nothing I have regretted equal to taking this French journey. I looked for a splendid reception, tournaments, carousals, pageants, and festivals ; and instead of which, all has been seclusion and obscurity ! and the best society whom the King introduced to us was a Bohemian vagabond, by whose agency he directed us to correspond with our friends in Flanders. Perhaps," said the lady, " it is his politic intention to mew us up here until our lives' end, that he may seize on our estates, after the extinction of the ancient house of Croye. The Duke of Burgundy was not so cruel : he offered my niece a husband, though he was a bad one."

" I should have thought the veil preferable to an evil husband," said the Princess, with difficulty finding opportunity to interpose a word.

"One would at least wish to have the choice, madam," replied the voluble dame. "It is, Heaven knows, on account of my niece that I speak; for myself, I have long laid aside thoughts of changing my condition. I see you smile but, by my halidome, it is true; yet that is no excuse for the King, whose conduct, like his person, hath more resemblance to that of old Michaud, the money-changer of Ghent, than to the successor of Charlemagne."

"Hold!" said the Princess, with some asperity in her tone; "remember you speak of my father."

"Of your father!" replied the Burgundian lady in surprise.

"Of my father!" repeated the Princess, with dignity. "I am Joan of France. But fear not, madam," she continued, in the gentle accent which was natural to her, "you designed no offense, and I have taken none. Command my influence to render your exile and that of this interesting young person more supportable. Alas! it is but little I have in my power; but it is willingly offered."

Deep and submissive was the reverence with which the Countess Hameline de Croye, so was the elder lady called, received the obliging offer of the Princess's protection. She had been long the inhabitant of courts, was mistress of the manners which are there acquired, and held firmly the established rule of courtiers of all ages, who, although their usual private conversation turns upon the vices and follies of their patrons, and on the injuries and neglect which they themselves have sustained, never suffer such hints to drop from them in the presence of the sovereign or those of his family. The lady was, therefore, scandalized to the last degree at the mistake which had induced her to speak so indecorously in presence of the daughter of Louis. She would have exhausted herself in expressing regret and making apologies, had she not been put to silence and restored to equanimity by the Princess, who requested, in the most gentle manner, yet which, from a daughter of France, had the weight of a command, that no more might be said in the way either of excuse or of explanation.

The Princess Joan then took her own chair with a dignity which became her, and compelled the two strangers to sit, one on either hand, to which the younger consented with unfeigned and respectful diffidence, and the elder with an affectation of deep humility and deference, which was intended

9

for such. They spoke together, but in such a low tone that the sentinel could not overhear the discourse, and only remarked, that the Princess seemed to bestow much of her regard on the younger and more interesting lady ; and that the Countess Hameline, though speaking a great deal more, attracted less of the Princess's attention by her full flow of conversation and compliment than did her kinswoman by her brief and modest replies to what was addressed to her.

The conversation of the ladies had not lasted a quarter of an hour, when the door at the lower end of the hall opened, and a man entered shrouded in a riding-cloak. Mindful of the King's injunction, and determined not to be a second time caught slumbering, Quentin instantly moved towards the intruder, and, interposing between him and the ladies, requested him to retire instantly.

" By whose command ? " said the stranger, in a tone of contemptuous surprise.

" By that of the King," said Quentin, firmly, " which I am placed here to enforce."

" Not against Louis of Orleans," said the duke, dropping his cloak.

The young man hesitated a moment ; but how enforce his orders against the first prince of the blood, about to be allied, as the report now generally went, with the King's own family ?

" Your Highness," he said, " is too great that your pleasure should be withstood by me. I trust your Highness will bear me witness that I have done the duty of my post, so far as your will permitted."

" Go to—you shall have no blame, young soldier," said Orleans ; and passing forward, paid his compliments to the Princess with that air of constraint which always marked his courtesy when addressing her.

" He had been dining," he said, " with Dunois, and understanding there was society in Roland's Gallery, he had ventured on the freedom of adding one to the number."

The color which mounted into the pale cheek of the unfortunate Joan, and which for the moment spread something of beauty over her features, evinced that this addition to the company was anything but indifferent to her. She hastened to present the Prince to the two Ladies of Croye, who received him with the respect due to his eminent rank ; and the Princess, pointing to a chair, requested him to join their conversation party.

The duke declined the freedom of assuming a seat in such

society ; but taking a cushion from one of the settles, he laid it at the feet of the beautiful young Countess of Croye, and so seated himself that, without appearing to neglect the Princess, he was enabled to bestow the greater share of his attention on her lovely neighbor.

At first, it seemed as if this arrangement rather pleased than offended his destined bride. She encouraged the duke in his gallantries towards the fair stranger, and seemed to regard them as complimentary to herself. But the Duke of Orleans, though accustomed to subject his mind to the stern yoke of his uncle when in the King's presence, had enough of princely nature to induce him to follow his own inclinations whenever that restraint was withdrawn ; and his high rank giving him a right to overstep the ordinary ceremonies and advance at once to familiarity, his praises of the Countess Isabelle's beauty became so energetic, and flowed with such unrestrained freedom, owing perhaps to his having drunk a little more wine than usual, for Dunois was no enemy to the worship of Bacchus, that at length he seemed almost impassioned, and the presence of the Princess appeared wellnigh forgotten.

The tone of compliment which he indulged was grateful only to one individual in the circle ; for the Countess Hameline already anticipated the dignity of an alliance with the first prince of the blood, by means of her whose birth, beauty, and large possessions rendered such an ambitious consummation by no means impossible, even in the eyes of a less sanguine projector, could the views of Louis XI. have been left out of the calculation of chances. The younger countess listened to the duke's gallantries with anxiety and embarrassment, and ever and anon turned an entreating look towards the Princess, as if requesting her to come to her relief. But the wounded feelings and the timidity of Joan of France rendered her incapable of an effort to make the conversation more general ; and at length, excepting a few interjectional civilities of the Lady Hameline, it was maintained almost exclusively by the duke himself, though at the expense of the younger Countess of Croye, whose beauty formed the theme of his high-flown eloquence.

Nor must I forget that there was a third person, the unregarded sentinel, who saw his fair visions melt away like wax before the sun, as the duke persevered in the warm tenor of his passionate discourse. At length the Countess Isabelle de Croye made a determined effort to cut short what was becoming intolerably disagreeable to her, especially from the pain to which the conduct of the duke was apparently subjecting the Princess.

Addressing the latter, she said, modestly, but with some firmness, that the first boon she had to claim from her promised protection was, "That her Highness would undertake to convince the Duke of Orleans that the ladies of Burgundy, though inferior in wit and manners to those of France, were not such absolute fools as to be pleased with no other conversation than that of extravagant compliment."

"I grieve, lady," said the Duke, preventing the Princess's answer, "that you will satirize, in the same sentence, the beauty of the dames of Burgundy and the sincerity of the knights of France. If we are hasty and extravagant in the expression of our admiration, it is because we love as we fight, without letting cold deliberation come into our bosoms, and surrender to the fair with the same rapidity with which we defeat the valiant."

"The beauty of our countrywomen," said the young countess, with more of reproof than she had yet ventured to use towards the high-born suitor, "is as unfit to claim such triumphs as the valor of the men of Burgundy is incapable of yielding them."

"I respect your patriotism, countess," said the duke ; "and the last branch of your theme shall not be impugned by me till a Burgundian knight shall offer to sustain it with lance in rest. But for the injustice which you have done to the charms which your land produces, I appeal from yourself to yourself. Look there," he said, pointing to a large mirror, the gift of the Venetian republic, and then of the highest rarity and value, "and tell me as you look, what is the heart that can resist the charms there represented ?"

The Princess, unable to sustain any longer the neglect of her lover, here sank backwards on her chair with a sigh, which at once recalled the duke from the land of romance, and induced the Lady Hameline to ask whether her Highness found herself ill.

"A sudden pain shot through my forehead," said the Princess, attempting to smile ; "but I shall be presently better."

Her increasing paleness contradicted her words, and induced the Lady Hameline to call for assistance, as the Princess was about to faint.

The duke, biting his lip and cursing the folly which could not keep guard over his tongue, ran to summon the Princess's attendants, who were in the next chamber ; and when they came hastily with the usual remedies, he could not but, as a cavalier and gentleman, give his assistance to support and to recover her. His voice, rendered almost tender by pity and self-reproach, was the most powerful means of recalling her to herself, and just as the swoon was passing away the King himself entered the apartment.

CHAPTER XII

THE POLITICIAN

This is a lecturer so skill'd in policy,
That (no disparagement to Satan's cunning)
He well might read a lesson to the devil,
And teach the old seducer new temptations.
Old Play.

As Louis entered the gallery, he bent his brows in the manner we have formerly described as peculiar to him, and sent,
from under his gathered and gloomy eyebrows, a keen look
on all around ; in darting which, as Quentin afterwards declared, his eyes seemed to turn so small, so fierce, and so
piercing, as to resemble those of an aroused adder looking
through the bush of heath in which he lies coiled.

When, by this momentary and sharpened glance, the King
had reconnoitred the cause of the bustle which was in the
apartment, his first address was to the Duke of Orleans.

"You here, my fair cousin ?" he said ; and turning to
Quentin, added sternly, "Had you not charge ?"

"Forgive the young man, sire," said the Duke ; "he did
not neglect his duty ; but I was informed that the Princess
was in this gallery."

"And I warrant you would not be withstood when you
came hither to pay your court," said the King, whose detestable hypocrisy persisted in representing the duke as participating in a passion which was felt only on the side of his
unhappy daughter ; "and it is thus you debauch the sentinels of my Guard, young man ? But what cannot be
pardoned to a gallant who only lives *par amours !* "

The Duke of Orleans raised his head, as if about to reply
in some manner which might correct the opinion conveyed
in the King's observation ; but the instinctive reverence, not
to say fear, of Louis, in which he had been bred from childhood, chained up his voice.

"And Joan hath been ill ?" said the King. "But do not
be grieved, Louis, it will soon pass away ; lend her your arm
to her apartment, while I will conduct these strange ladies
to theirs."

The order was given in a tone which amounted to a command, and Orleans accordingly made his exit with the Princess at one extremity of the gallery, while the King, ungloving his right hand, courteously handed the Countess Isabelle and her kinswoman to their apartment, which opened from the other. He bowed profoundly as they entered, and remained standing on the threshold for a minute after they had disappeared ; then, with great composure, shut the door by which they had retired, and turning the huge key, took it from the lock and put it into his girdle—an appendage which gave him still more perfectly the air of some old miser, who cannot journey in comfort unless he bear with him the key of his treasure closet.

With slow and pensive step, and eyes fixed on the ground, Louis now paced towards Quentin Durward, who, expecting his share of the royal displeasure, viewed his approach with no little anxiety.

" Thou hast done wrong," said the King, raising his eyes, and fixing them firmly on him when he had come within a yard of him—" thou hast done foul wrong, and deservest to die. Speak not a word in defense ! What hadst thou to do with dukes or princesses ? what with *any* thing but my order ? "

" So please your Majesty," said the young soldier, " what could I do ? "

" What couldst thou do when thy post was forcibly passed ? " answered the King, scornfully. " What is the use of that weapon on thy shoulder ? Thou shouldst have leveled thy piece, and if the presumptuous rebel did not retire on the instant, he should have died within this very hall ! Go—pass into these farther apartments. In the first thou wilt find a large staircase, which leads to the inner bailey ; there thou wilt find Oliver Dain. Send him to me ; do thou begone to thy quarters. As thou dost value thy life, be not so loose of thy tongue as thou hast been this day slack of thy hand."

Well pleased to escape so easily, yet with a soul which revolted at the cold-blooded cruelty which the King seemed to require from him in the execution of his duty, Durward took the road indicated, hastened downstairs, and communicated the royal pleasure to Oliver, who was waiting in the court beneath. The wily tonsor bowed, sighed, and smiled, as, with a voice even softer than ordinary, he wished the youth a good evening ; and they parted, Quentin to his quarters, and Oliver to attend the King.

In this place, the Memoirs which we have chiefly followed
in compiling this true history were unhappily defective ; for,
founded chiefly on information supplied by Quentin, they do
not convey the purport of the dialogue which in his absence,
took place between the King and his secret counselor. Fortunately, the library of Hautlieu contains a manuscript
copy of the *Chronique Scandaleuse* of Jean de Troyes, much
more full than that which has been printed ; to which are
added several curious memoranda, which we incline to think
must have been written down by Oliver himself after the death
of his master, and before he had the happiness to be rewarded
with the halter which he had so long merited. From this
we have been able to extract a very full account of the
obscure favorite's conversations with Louis upon the present
occasion, which throws a light upon the policy of that
prince which we might otherwise have sought for in vain.

When the favorite attendant entered the Gallery of Roland,
he found the King pensively seated upon the chair which
his daughter had left some minutes before. Well acquainted
with his temper, he glided on with his noiseless step until
he had just crossed the line of the King's sight, so as to
make him aware of his presence, then shrank modestly backward and out of sight, until he should be summoned to speak
or to listen. The monarch's first address was an unpleasant
one : " So, Oliver, your fine schemes are melting like snow
before the south wind ! I pray to our Lady of Embrun
that they resemble not the ice-heaps of which the Switzer
churls tell such stories, and come rushing down upon our
heads."

" I have heard with concern that all is not well, sire,"
answered Oliver.

" Not well ! " exclaimed the King, rising and hastily marching up and down the gallery. " All is ill, man, as ill nearly
as possible ; so much for thy fond romantic advice that I,
of all men, should become a protector of distressed damsels !
I tell thee Burgundy is arming, and on the eve of closing an
alliance with England. And Edward, who hath his hands
idle at home, will pour his thousands upon us through that
unhappy gate of Calais. Singly, I might cajole or defy them ;
but united—united, and with the discontent and treachery
of that villain St. Paul ! All thy faults, Oliver, who counseled me to receive the women, and to use the services of
that damned Bohemian to carry messages to their vassals."

" My liege," said Oliver, " you know my reasons. The
countess's domains lie between the frontiers of Burgundy

and Flanders, her castle is almost impregnable, her rights over neighboring estates are such as, if well supported, cannot but give much annoyance to Burgundy, were the lady but wedded to one who should be friendly to France."

"It is—it is a tempting bait," said the King ; "and could we have concealed her being here, we might have arranged such a marriage for this rich heiress as would have highly profited France. But that cursed Bohemian, how couldst thou recommend such a heathen hound for a commission which required trust ?"

"Please you," said Oliver, "to remember it was your Majesty's self who trusted him too far—much farther than I recommended. He would have borne a letter trustily enough to the countess's kinsman, telling him to hold out her castle, and promising speedy relief ; but your Highness must needs put his prophetic powers to the test ; and thus he became possessed of secrets which were worth betraying to Duke Charles."

"I am ashamed—I am ashamed," said Louis. "And yet, Oliver, they say that these heathen people are descended from the sage Chaldeans, who did read the mysteries of the stars in the plains of Shinar."

Well aware that his master, with all his acuteness and sagacity, was but the more prone to be deceived by soothsayers, astrologers, diviners, and all that race of pretenders to occult science, and that he even conceived himself to have some skill in these arts, Oliver dared to press this point no farther ; and only observed that the Bohemian had been a bad prophet on his own account, else he would have avoided returning to Tours, and saved himself from the gallows he had merited.

"It often happens that those who are gifted with prophetic knowledge," answered Louis, with much gravity, "have not the power of foreseeing those events in which they themselves are personally interested."

"Under your Majesty's favor," replied the confidant, "that seems as if a man could not see his own hand by means of the candle which he holds, and which shows him every other object in the apartment."

"He cannot see his own features by the light which shows the faces of others," replied Louis ; "and that is the more faithful illustraion of the case. But this is foreign to my purpose at present. The Bohemian hath had his reward, and peace be with him. But these ladies—not only does Burgundy theaten us with war for harboring them, but their presence is like to interfere with my projects in my own family. My simple cousin of Orleans hath barely seen this damsel, and I venture to prophesy that the sight of her is like to make him less pliable in the matter of his alliance with Joan."

"Your Majesty," answered the counselor, "may send the Ladies of Croye back to Burgundy, and so make your peace with the Duke. Many might murmur at this as dishonorable ; but if necessity demands the sacrifice——"

"If profit demanded the sacrifice, Oliver, the sacrifice should be made without hesitation," answered the King. "I am an old experienced salmon, and use not to gulp the angler's hook because it is busked up with a feather called honor. But what is worse than a lack of honor, there were, in returning those ladies to Burgundy, a forfeiture of those views of advantage which moved us to give them an asylum. It were heart-breaking to renounce the opportunity of planting a friend to ourselves and an enemy to Burgundy in the very center of his dominions, and so near to the discontented cities of Flanders. Oliver, I cannot relinquish the advantages which our scheme of marrying the maiden to a friend of our own house seems to hold out to us."

"Your Majesty," said Oliver, after a moment's thought, "might confer her hand on some right trusty friend, who would take all blame on himself, and serve your Majesty secretly, while in public you might disown him."

"And where am I to find such a friend ?" said Louis. "Were I to bestow her upon any one of our mutinous and ill-ruled nobles, would it not be rendering him independent ? and hath it not been my policy for years to prevent them from becoming so ? Dunois indeed—him, and him only, I might perchance trust. He would fight for the crown of France, whatever were his condition. But honors and wealth change men's natures. Even Dunois I will not trust."

"Your Majesty may find others," said Oliver, in his smoothest manner, and in a tone more insinuating than that which he usually employed in conversing with the King, who permitted him considerable freedom : "men dependent entirely on your own grace and favor, and who could no more exist without your countenance than without sun or air, men rather of head than of action, men who——"

"Men who resemble thyself, ha !" said King Louis. "No, Oliver, by my faith that arrow was too rashly shot ! What ! because I indulge thee with my confidence, and let thee in reward, poll my lieges a little now and then, dost thou think it makes thee fit to be the husband of that beautiful vision, and a count of the highest class to the boot ?— thee, thee, I say, low-born and lower-bred, whose wisdom is at best a sort of cunning, and whose courage is more than doubtful ?"

"Your Majesty imputes to me a presumption of which I am not guilty, in supposing me to aspire so highly," said Oliver.

"I am glad to hear it, man," replied the King ; "and truly, I hold your judgment the healthier that you disown such a reverie. But methinks thy speech sounded strangely in that key. Well, to return. I dare not wed this beauty to one of my subjects ; I dare not return her to Burgundy ; I dare not transmit her to England or to Germany, where she is likely to become the prize of some one more apt to unite with Burgundy than with France, and who would be more ready to discourage the honest malcontents in Ghent and Liege than to yield them that wholesome countenance which might always find Charles the Hardy enough to exercise his valor on, without stirring from his own domains— and they were in so ripe a humor for insurrection, the men of Liege in especial, that they alone, well heated and supported, would find my fair cousin work for more than a twelvemonth ; and backed by a warlike Count of Croye— O, Oliver ! the plan is too hopeful to be resigned without a struggle. Cannot thy fertile brain devise some scheme ?"

" Oliver paused for a long time ; then at last replied, " What if a bridal could be accomplished betwixt Isabelle of Croye and young Adolphus, the Duke of Gueldres ?"

" What !" said the King, in astonishment ; "sacrifice her, and she, too, so lovely a creature, to the furious wretch who deposed, imprisoned, and has often threatened to murder, his own father ! No, Oliver—no, that were too unutterably cruel even for you and me, who look so steadfastly to our excellent end, the peace and the welfare of France, and respect so little the means by which it is attained. Besides, he lies distant from us, and is detested by the people of Ghent and Liege. No—no, I will none of Adolphus of Gueldres ; think on some one else."

"My invention is exhausted, sire," said the counselor ; " I can remember no one who, as husband to the Countess of Croye, would be likely to answer your Majesty's views. He must unite such various qualities—a friend to your Majesty, an enemy to Burgundy, of policy enough to conciliate the

Gauntois and Liegeois, and of valor sufficient to defend his
little dominions against the power of Duke Charles ; of noble
birth besides—that your Highness insists upon ; and of excellent and most virtuous character, to the boot of all."

" Nay, Oliver," said the King, " I learned not so much—
that in, so *very* much, on character ; but methinks Isabelle's
bridegroom should be something less publicly and generally
abhorred than Adolphus of Gueldres. For example, since
I myself must suggest some one, why not William de la
Marck ?"

" On my halidome, sire," said Oliver, " I cannot complain of your demanding too high a standard of moral excellence in the happy man, if the Wild Boar of Ardennes can
serve your turn. De la Marck ! why, he is the most notorious robber and murderer on all the frontiers, excommunicated
by the Pope for a thousand crimes."

" We will have him released from the sentence, friend
Oliver ; holy church is merciful."

" Almost an outlaw," continued Oliver, " and under the
ban of the Empire, by an ordinance of the Chamber at
Ratisbon."

" We will have the ban taken off, friend Oliver," continued
the King in the same tone ; " the Imperial Chamber will
hear reason."

" And admitting him to be of noble birth," said Oliver,
" he hath the manners, the face, and the outward form, as
well as the heart, of a Flemish butcher. She will never
accept of him."

" His mode of wooing, if I mistake him not," said Louis,
" will render it difficult for her to make a choice."

" I was far wrong, indeed, when I taxed your Majesty with
being over scrupulous," said the counselor. " On my life,
the crimes of Adolphus are but virtues to those of De la
Marck ! And then how is he to meet with his bride ? Your
Majesty knows he dare not stir far from his own Forest of
Ardennes."

" That must be cared for," said the King ; " and, in the
first place, the two ladies must be acquainted privately that
they can be no longer maintained at this court, except at the
expense of a war between France and Burgundy, and that,
unwilling to deliver them up to my fair cousin of Burgundy,
I am desirous they should secretely depart from my dominions."

" They will demand to be conveyed to England," said
Oliver ; " and we shall have her return to Flanders with an

island lord, having a round fair face, long brown hair, and three thousand archers at his back."

"No—no," replied the King : "we dare not—you understand me—so far offend our fair cousin of Burgundy as to let her pass to England. It would bring his displeasure as certainly as our maintaining her here. No—no, to the safety of the church alone we will venture to commit her ; and the utmost we can do is to connive at the Ladies Hameline and Isabelle de Croye departing in disguise, and with a small retinue, to take refuge with the Bishop of Liege, who will place the fair Isabelle for the time under the safeguard of a convent."

"And if that convent protect her from William de la Marck, when he knows of your Majesty's favorable intentions, I have mistaken the man."

"Why, yes," answered the King, "thanks to our secret supplies of money, De la Marck hath together a handsome handful of as unscrupulous soldiery as ever were outlawed, with which he contrives to maintain himself among the woods, in such a condition as makes him formidable both to the Duke of Burgundy and the Bishop of Liege. He lacks nothing but some territory which he may call his own ; and this being so fair an opportunity to establish himself by marriage, I think that, *Pasques-dieu !* he will find means to win and wed, without more than a hint on our part. The Duke of Burgundy will then have such a thorn in his side as no lancet of our time will easily cut out from his flesh. The Boar of Ardennes, whom he has already outlawed, strengthened by the possession of that fair lady's lands, castles, and seigniory, with the discontented Liegeois to boot, who, by my faith, will not be in that case unwilling to choose him for their captain and leader—let Charles then think of wars with France when he will, or rather let him bless his stars if she war not with him. How dost thou like the scheme, Oliver, ha ?"

"Rarely," said Oliver, "save and except the doom which confers that lady on the Wild Boar of Ardennes. By my halidome, saving in a little outward show of gallantry, Tristan, the provost-marshal, were the more proper bridegroom of the two."

"Anon thou didst propose Master Oliver, the barber," said Louis ; "but friend Oliver and gossip Tristan, though excellent men in the way of counsel and execution, are not the stuff that men make counts of. Know you not that the burghers of Flanders value birth in other men, precisely because

they have it not themseves ? A plebeian mob ever desire
an aristocratic leader. Yonder Ked, or Cade—how called
they him ?—in England, was fain to lure his rascal rout after
him by pretending to the blood of the Mortimers. William
de la Marck comes of the blood of the princes of Sedan, as
noble as mine own. And now to business. I must determine the Ladies of Croye to a speedy and secret flight, under
sure guidance. This will be easily done : we have but to
hint the alternative of surrendering them to Burgundy.
Thou must find means to let William de la Marck know of
their motions, and let him choose his own time and place to
push his suit. I know a fit person to travel with them."

" May I ask to whom your Majesty commits such an important charge ? " asked the tonsor.

" To a foreigner, be sure," replied the King, " one who
has neither kin nor interest in France, to interfere with the
execution of my pleasure ; and who knows too little of the
country and its factions to suspect more of my purpose than
I choose to tell him—in a word, I design to employ the
young Scot who sent you hither but now."

Oliver paused in a manner which seemed to imply a doubt
of the prudence of the choice, and then added, " Your
Majesty has reposed confidence in that stranger boy earlier
than is your wont."

" I have my reasons," answered the King. " Thou knowest
(and he crossed himself) my devotion for the blessed St.
Julian. I had been saying my orisons to that holy saint late
in the night before last, wherein, as he is known to be the
guardian of travelers, I made it my humble petition that he
would augment my household with such wandering foreigners as might best establish throughout our kingdom unlimited devotion to our will ; and I vowed to the good saint
in guerdon that I would, in his name, receive, and relieve,
and maintain them."

" And did St. Julian," said Oliver, " send your Majesty
this long-legged importation from Scotland in answer to
your prayers ? "

Although the barber, who well knew that his master had
superstition in a large proportion to his want of religion,
and that on such topics nothing was more easy than to offend
him—although, I say, he knew the royal weakness, and
therefore carefully put the preceding question in the softest
and most simple tone of voice, Louis felt the innuendo
which it contained, and regarded the speaker with high
displeasure.

"Sirrah," he said, "thou art well called Oliver the Devil, who darest thus to sport at once with thy master and with the blessed saints. I tell thee, wert thou one grain less necessary to me, I would have thee hung up on yonder oak before the castle, as an example to all who scoff at things holy! Know, thou infidel slave, that mine eyes were no sooner closed than the blessed St. Julian was visible to me, leading a young man, whom he presented to me, saying, that his fortune should be to escape the sword, the cord, the river, and to bring good fortune to the side which he should espouse, and to the adventures in which he should be engaged. I walked out on the succeeding morning, and I met with this youth, whose image I had seen in my dream. In his own country he hath escaped the sword, amid the massacre of his whole family, and here, within the brief compass of two days, he hath been strangely rescued from drowning and from the gallows, and hath already, on a particular occasion, as I but lately hinted to thee, been of the most material service to me. I receive him as sent hither by St. Julian, to serve me in the most difficult, the most dangerous, and even the most desperate services."

The King, as he thus expressed himself, doffed his hat, and selecting from the numerous little leaden figures with which the hat-band was garnished that which represented St. Julian, he placed it on the table, as was often his wont when some peculiar feeling of hope, or perhaps of remorse, happened to thrill across his mind, and, kneeling down before it, muttered, with an appearance of profound devotion, "*Sancte Juliane, adsis precibus nostris! Ora—ora pro nobis!*"

This was one of those ague fits of superstitious devotion which often seized on Louis in such extraordinary times and places that they gave one of the most sagacious monarchs who ever reigned the appearance of a madman, or at least of one whose mind was shaken by some deep consciousness of guilt.

While he was thus employed, his favorite looked at him with an expression of sarcastic contempt, which he scarce attempted to disguise. Indeed, it was one of this man's peculiarities that, in his whole intercourse with his master, he laid aside that fondling, purring affectation of officiousness and humility which distinguished his conduct to others; and if he still bore some resemblance to a cat, it was when the animal is on its guard—watchful, animated, and alert for sudden exertion. The cause of this change was probably

Oliver's consciousness that his master was himself too profound a hypocrite not to see through the hypocrisy of others.

" The features of this youth, then, if I may presume to speak," said Oliver, " resemble those of him whom your dream exhibited ? "

" Closely and intimately," said the King, whose imagination, like that of superstitious people in general, readily imposed upon itself. " I have had his horoscope cast, besides, by Galeotti Martivalle, and I have plainly learned, through his art and mine own observation, that in many respects, this unfriended youth has his destiny under the same constellation with mine."

Whatever Oliver might think of the causes thus boldly assigned for the preference of an inexperienced stripling, he dared make no farther objections, well knowing that Louis, who, while residing in exile, had bestowed much of his attention on the supposed science of judicial astrology, would listen to no raillery of any kind which impeached his skill. He therefore only replied, that " He trusted the youth would prove faithful in the discharge of a task so delicate."

" We will take care he hath no opportunity to be otherwise," said Louis ; " for he shall be privy to nothing save that he is sent to escort the Ladies of Croye to the residence of the Bishop of Liege. Of the probable interference of William de la Marck he shall know as little as they themselves. None shall know that secret but the guide ; and Tristan or thou must find one fit for our purpose."

" But in that case," said Oliver, " judging of him from his country and his appearance, the young man is like to stand to his arms so soon as the Wild Boar comes on them, and may not come off so easily from the tusks as he did this morning."

" If they rend his heart-strings," said Louis, composedly, " St. Julian, blessed be his name ! can send me another in his stead. It skills as little that the messenger is slain after his duty is executed as that the flask is broken when the wine is drunk out. Meanwhile, we must expedite the ladies' departure, and then persuade the Count de Crèvecœur that it has taken place without our connivance, we having been desirous to restore them to the custody of our fair cousin, which their sudden departure has unhappily prevented."

" The count is perhaps too wise, and his master too prejudiced, to believe it."

" Holy Mother ! " said Louis, " what unbelief would that

be in Christian men! But, Oliver, they *shall* believe us. We will throw into our whole conduct towards our fair cousin, Duke Charles, such thorough and unlimited confidence that, not to believe we have been sincere with him in every respect, he must be worse than an infidel. I tell thee, so convinced am I that I could make Charles of Burgundy think of me in every respect as I would have him, that, were it necessary for silencing his doubts, I would ride unarmed, and on a palfrey, to visit him in his tent, with no better guard about me than thine own simple person, friend Oliver."

" And I," said Oliver, " though I pique not myself upon managing steel in any other shape than that of a razor, would rather charge a Swiss battalion of pikes than I would accompany your Highness upon such a visit of friendship to Charles of Burgundy, when he hath so many grounds to be well assured that there is enmity in your Majesty's bosom against him."

" Thou art a fool, Oliver," said the King, " with all thy pretensions to wisdom, and art not aware that deep policy must often assume the appearance of the most extreme simplicity, as courage occasionally shrouds itself under the show of modest timidity. Were it needful, full surely would I do what I have said—the saints always blessing our purpose, and the heavenly constellations bringing round, in their course, a proper conjuncture for such an exploit."

In these words did King Louis XI. give the first hint of the extraordinary resolution which he afterwards adopted in order to dupe his great rival, the subsequent execution of which had very nearly proved his own ruin.

He parted with his counselor, and presently afterwards went to the apartment of the Ladies of Croye. Few persuasions beyond his mere license would have been necessary to determine their retreat from the court of France, upon the first hint that they might not be eventually protected against the Duke of Burgundy ; but it was not so easy to induce them to choose Liege for the place of their retreat. They entreated and requested to be transferred to Bretagne or Calais, where, under protection of the Duke of Bretagne, or King of England, they might remain in a state of safety until the sovereign of Burgundy should relent in his rigorous purpose towards them. But neither of these places of safety at all suited the plans of Louis, and he was at last successful in inducing them to adopt that which did coincide with them.

The power of the Bishop of Liege for their defense was not

10

to be questioned, since his ecclesiastical dignity gave him the means of protecting the fugitives against all Christian princes; while on the other hand, his secular forces, if not numerous, seemed at least sufficient to defend his person and all under his protection from any sudden violence. The difficulty was to reach the little court of the bishop in safety ; but for this Louis promised to provide, by spreading a report that the Ladies of Croye had escaped from Tours by night, under fear of being delivered up to the Burgundian envoy, and had taken their flight towards Bretagne. He also promised them the attendance of a small but faithful retinue and letters to the commanders of such towns and fortresses as they might pass, with instructions to use every means for protecting and assisting them in their journey.

The Ladies of Croye, although internally resenting the ungenerous and discourteous manner in which Louis thus deprived them of the promised asylum in his court, were so far from objecting to the hasty departure which he proposed, that they even anticipated his project by entreating to be permitted to set forward that same night. The Lady Hameline was already tired of a place where there were neither admiring courtiers nor festivities to be witnessed ; and the Lady Isabelle thought she had seen enough to conclude that, were the temptation to become a little stronger, Louis XI., not satisfied with expelling them from his court, would not hesitate to deliver her up to her irritated suzerain, the Duke of Burgundy. Lastly, Louis himself readily acquiesced in their hasty departure, anxious to preserve peace with Duke Charles, and alarmed lest the beauty of Isabelle should interfere with and impede the favorite plan which he had formed for bestowing the hand of his daughter Joan upon his cousin of Orleans.

CHAPTER XIII

THE JOURNEY

Talk not of kings—I scorn the poor comparison ;
I am a SAGE, and can command the elements,
At least men think I can ; and on that thought
I found unbounded empire.

Albumazar.

OCCUPATION and adventure might be said to crowd upon
the young Scottishman with the force of a spring-tide ; for
he was speedily summoned to the apartment of his captain,
the Lord Crawford, where, to his astonishment, he again beheld the King. After a few words respecting the honor and
trust which were about to be reposed in him, which made
Quentin internally afraid that they were again about to propose to him such a watch as he had kept upon the Count of
Crevecœur, or perhaps some duty still more repugnant to
his feelings, he was not relieved merely, but delighted, with
hearing that he was selected, with the assistance of four
others under his command, one of whom was a guide, to
escort the Ladies of Croye to the little court of their relative,
the Bishop of Liege, in the safest and most commodious,
and at the same time the most secret, manner possible. A
scroll was given him, in which were set down directions for
his guidance, for the places of halt (generally chosen in obscure villages, solitary monasteries, and situations remote
from towns), and for the general precautions which he was
to attend to, especially on approaching the frontier of Burgundy. He was sufficiently supplied with instructions what
he ought to say and do to sustain the personage of the *maître
d'hotel* of two English ladies of rank, who had been on a
pilgrimage to St. Martin of Tours, and were about to visit
the holy city of Cologne, and worship the relics of the sage
Eastern monarchs who came to adore the nativity of Bethlehem ; for under that character the Ladies of Croye were
to journey.

Without having any defined notions of the cause of his
delight, Quentin Durward's heart leaped for joy at the idea of
approaching thus nearly to the person of the beauty of the

147

turret, and in a situation which entitled him to her confidence, since her protection was in so great a degree entrusted to his conduct and courage. He felt no doubt in
his own mind that he should be her successful guide through
the hazards of her pilgrimage. Youth seldom thinks of
dangers ; and bred up free, and fearless, and self-confiding,
Quentin, in particular, only thought of them to defy them.
He longed to be exempted from the restraint of the royal
presence, that he might indulge the secret glee with which
such unexpected tidings filled him, and which prompted
him to bursts of delight which would have been totally un-
fitting for that society.

But Louis had not yet done with him. That cautious
monarch had to consult a counselor of a different stamp
from Oliver le Diable, and who was supposed to derive his
skill from the superior and astral intelligences, as men,
judging from their fruits, were apt to think the counsels of
Oliver sprung from the devil himself.

Louis therefore led the way, followed by the impatient
Quentin, to a separate tower of the Castle of Plessis, in
which was installed, in no small ease and splendor, the celebrated astrologer, poet, and philosopher, Galeotti Marti, or
Martius, or Martivalle,* a native of Narni, in Italy, the author of the famous treatise, *De Vulgo Incognitis,*† and the
subject of his age's admiration, and of the panegyrics of
Paulus Jovius. He had long flourished at the court of the
celebrated Matthias Corvinus, king of Hungary, from whom
he was in some measure decoyed by Louis, who grudged the
Hungarian monarch the society and the counsels of a sage
accounted so skilful in reading the decrees of Heaven.

Martivalle was none of those ascetic, withered, pale professors of mystic learning of those days, who bleared their
eyes over the midnight furnace, and macerated their bodies
by out-watching the polar bear. He indulged in all courtly
pleasures, and, until he grew corpulent, had excelled in all
martial sports and gymnastic exercises, as well as in the use
of arms ; insomuch, that Janus Pannonius has left a Latin
epigram, upon a wrestling-match betwixt Galeotti and a renowned champion of that art, in the presence of the Hungarian king and court, in which the astrologer was completely victorious.

The apartments of this courtly and martial sage were far
more splendidly furnished than any which Quentin had yet

* See Note 24.
† Concerning Things Unknown to the Generality of Mankind.

seen in the royal place ; and the carving and ornamented woodwork of his library, as well as the magnificence displayed in the tapestries, showed the elegant taste of the learned Italian. Out of his study one door opened to his sleeping-apartment, another led to the turret which served as his observatory. A large oaken table, in the midst of the chamber, was covered with a rich Turkey carpet, the spoils of the tent of a pacha after the great battle of Jaiza, where the astrologer had fought abreast with the valiant champion of Christendom, Matthias Corvinus. On the table lay a variety of mathematical and astrological instruments, all of the most rich materials and curious workmanship. His astrolabe of silver was the gift of the Emperor of Germany, and his Jacob's staff of ebony, jointed with gold and curiously inlaid, was a mark of esteem from the reigning Pope.

There were various other miscellaneous articles disposed on the table, or hanging around the walls ; amongst others, two complete suits of armor, one of mail, the other of plate, both of which, from their great size, seemed to call the gigantic astrologer their owner, a Spanish toledo, a Scottish broadsword, a Turkish scimitar, with bows, quivers, and other warlike weapons, musical instruments of several different kinds, a silver crucifix, a sepulchral antique vase, and several of the little brazen Penates of the ancient heathens, with other curious nondescript articles, some of which, in the superstitious opinions of that period, seemed to be designed for magical purposes. The library of this singular character was of the same miscellaneous description with his other effects. Curious manuscripts of classic antiquity lay mingled with the voluminous labors of Christian divines, and of those painstaking sages who professed the chemical science, and proffered to guide their students into the most secret recesses of nature by means of the Hermetical philosophy. Some were written in the Eastern character, and others concealed their sense or nonsense under the veil of hieroglyphics and cabalistic characters. The whole apartment, and its furniture of every kind, formed a scene very impressive on the fancy, considering the general belief then indisputably entertained concerning the truth of the occult sciences ; and that effect was increased by the manners and appearance of the individual himself, who, seated in a huge chair, was employed in curiously examining a specimen, just issued from the Frankfort press, of the newly invented art of printing.*

* See Invention of Printing. Note 25.

Galeotti Martivalle was a tall, bulky, yet stately man, considerably past his prime, and whose youthful habits of exercise, though still occasionally resumed, had not been able to contend with his natural tendency to corpulence, increased by sedentary study and indulgence in the pleasures of the table. His features, though rather overgrown, were dignified and noble, and a santon might have envied the dark and downward sweep of his long-descending beard. His dress was a chamber-robe of the richest Genoa velvet, with ample sleeves, clasped with frogs of gold, and lined with sables. It was fastened round his middle by a broad belt of virgin parchment, round which were represented in crimson characters the signs of the zodiac. He rose and bowed to the King, yet with the air of one to whom such exalted society was familiar, and who was not at all likely, even in the royal presence, to compromise the dignity then especially affected by the pursuers of science.

"You are engaged, father," said the King, " and, as I think, with the new-fashioned art of multiplying manuscripts by the intervention of machinery. Can things of such mechanical and terrestrial import interest the thoughts of one before whom Heaven has unrolled her own celestial volumes ? "

" My brother," replied Martivalle—" for so the tenant of this cell must term even the King of France when he deigns to visit him as a disciple—believe me that, in considering the consequences of this invention, I read with as certain augury as by any combination of the heavenly bodies the most awful and portentous changes. When I reflect with what slow and limited supplies the stream of science hath hitherto descended to us, how difficult to be obtained by those most ardent in its search, how certain to be neglected by all who regard their ease, how liable to be diverted, or altogether dried up, by the invasions of barbarism—can I look forward without wonder and astonishment to the lot of a succeeding generation, on whom knowledge will descend like the first and second rain, uninterrupted, unabated, unbounded, fertilizing some grounds and overflowing others, changing the whole form of social life, establishing and overthrowing religions, erecting and destroying kingdoms——"

" Hold, Galeotti," said Louis—" shall these changes come in our time ? "

" No, my royal brother," replied Martivalle ; " this invention may be likened to a young tree which is now newly planted, but shall, in succeeding generations, bear fruit as fatal, yet as precious, as that of the Garden of Eden—the knowledge, namely, of good and evil."

Louis answered, after a moment's pause, " Let futurity look to what concerns them ; we are men of this age, and to this age we will confine our care. Sufficient for the day is the evil thereof. Tell me, hast thou proceeded farther in the horoscope which I sent to thee, and of which you made me some report ? I have brought the party hither, that you may use palmistry, or chiromancy, if such is your pleasure. The matter is pressing."

The bulky sage arose from his seat, and, approaching the young soldier, fixed on him his keen large dark eyes, as if he were in the act of internally spelling and dissecting every lineament and feature. Blushing and borne down by this close examination on the part of one whose expression was so reverent at once and commanding, Quentin bent his eyes on the ground, and did not again raise them till in the act of obeying the sonorous command of the astrologer—" Look up and be not afraid, but hold forth thy hand."

When Martivalle had inspected his palm, according to the form of the mystic arts which he practiced, he led the King some steps aside. " My royal brother," he said, " the physiognomy of this youth, together with the lines impressed on his hand, confirm, in a wonderful degree, the report which I founded on his horoscope, as well as that judgment which your own proficiency in our sublime arts induced you at once to form of him. All promises that this youth will be brave and fortunate."

" And faithful ? " said the King ; " for valor and fortune square not always with fidelity."

" And faithful also," said the astrologer ; " for there is manly firmness in look and eye, and his *linea vitæ* is deeply marked and clear, which indicates a true and upright adherence to those who do benefit or lodge trust in him. But yet——"

" But what ? " said the King. " Father Galeotti, wherefore do you now pause ? "

" The ears of kings," said the sage, " are like the palates of those dainty patients which are unable to endure the bitterness of the drugs necessary for their recovery."

" My ears and my palate have no such niceness," said Louis ; " let me hear what is useful counsel, and swallow what is wholesome medicine. I quarrel not with the rudeness of the one or the harsh taste of the other. I have not been cockered in wantonness or indulgence. My youth was one of exile and suffering. My ears are used to harsh counsel, and take no offense at it."

"Then plainly, sire," replied Galeotti, "if you have aught in your purposed commission which—which, in short, may startle a scrupulous conscience—entrust it not to this youth —at least, not till a few years' exercise in your service has made him as unscrupulous as others."

"And is this what you hesitated to speak, my good Galeotti? and didst thou think thy speaking it would offend me?" said the King. "Alack, I know that thou art well sensible that the path of royal policy cannot be always squared, as that of private life ought invariably to be, by the abstract maxims of religion and of morality. Wherefore do we, the princes of the earth, found churches and monasteries, make pilgrimages, undergo penances, and perform devotions, with which others may dispense, unless it be because the benefit of the public, and the welfare of our kingdoms, force us upon measures which grieve our consciences as Christians? But Heaven has mercy, the church an unbounded stock of merits, and the intercession of Our Lady of Embrun and the blessed saints is urgent, everlasting, and omnipotent." He laid his hat on the table, and devoutly kneeling before the images stuck into the hatband, repeated, in an earnest tone, "*Sancte Huberte, Sancte Juliane, Sancte Martine, Sancta Rosalia, Sancti quotquot adesti, orate pro me peccatore !*" He then smote his breast, arose, reassumed his hat, and continued—"Be assured, good father, that, whatever there may be in our commission of the nature at which you have hinted, the execution shall not be entrusted to this youth, nor shall he be privy to such part of our purpose."

"In this," said the astrologer, "you, my royal brother, will walk wisely. Something may be apprehended likewise from the rashness of this your young commissioner—a failing inherent in those of sanguine complexion. But I hold that, by the rules of art, this chance is not to be weighed against the other properties discovered from his horoscope and otherwise."

"Will this next midnight be a propitious hour in which to commence a perilous journey?" said the King. "See, here is your ephemerides ; you see the position of the moon in regard to Saturn and the ascendence of Jupiter. That should argue, methinks, in submission to your better art, success to him who sends forth the expedition at such an hour."

"To him who *sends forth* the expedition," said the astrologer, after a pause, "this conjunction doth indeed promise success ; but methinks that Saturn, being combust, threatens danger and infortune to the party *sent ;* whence I infer that the errand may be perilous, or even fatal, to those who are to journey. Violence and captivity, methinks, are intimated in that adverse conjunction."

"Violence and captivity to those who are sent," answered the King, "but success to the wishes of the sender. Runs it not thus, my learned father !"

"Even so," replied the astrologer.

The King paused, without giving any further indication how far this presaging speech (probably hazarded by the astrologer from his conjecture that the commission related to some dangerous purpose) squared with his real object, which, as the reader is aware, was to betray the Countess Isabelle of Croye into the hands of William de la Marck, a nobleman indeed of high birth, but degraded by his crimes into a leader of banditti, distinguished for his turbulent disposition and ferocious bravery.

The King then pulled forth a paper from his pocket, and, ere he gave it to Martivalle, said, in a tone which resembled that of an apology—"Learned Galeotti, be not suprised that, possessing in you an oracular treasure superior to that lodged in the breast of any now alive, not excepting the great Nostradamus himself, I am desirous frequently to avail myself of your skill in those doubts and difficulties which beset every prince who hath to contend with rebellion within his land and with external enemies, both powerful and inveterate."

"When I was honored with your request, sire," said the philosopher, "and abandoned the court of Buda for that of Plessis, it was with the resolution to place at the command of my royal patron whatever my art had that might be of service to him."

"Enough, good Martivalle—I pray thee attend to the import of this question." He proceeded to read from the paper in his hand : "A person having on hand a weighty controversy, which is like to draw to debate either by law or by force of arms, is desirous, for the present, to seek accommodation by a personal interview with his antagonist. He desires to know what day will be propitious for the execution of such a purpose ; also what is likely to be the success of such a negotiation, and whether his adversary will be moved to answer the confidence thus reposed in him with gratitude and kindness, or may rather be likely to abuse the opportunity and advantage which such meeting may afford him ?"

"It is an important question," said Martivalle, when the King had done reading, "and requires that I should set a planetary figure, and give it instant and deep consideration."

"Let it be so, my good father in the sciences, and thou shalt know what it is to oblige a King of France. We are determined, if the constellations forbid not—and our own humble art leads us to think that they approve our purpose—to hazard something, even in our own person, to stop these anti-Christian wars."

"May the saints forward your Majesty's pious intent," said the astrologer, "and guard your sacred person !"

"Thanks, learned father. Here is something, the while, to enlarge your curious library."

He placed under one of the volumes a small purse of gold ; for, economical even in his superstitions, Louis conceived the astrologer sufficiently bound to his service by the pensions he had assigned him, and thought himself entitled to the use of his skill at a moderate rate, even upon great exigencies.

Louis, having thus, in legal phrase, added a refreshing fee to his general retainer, turned from him to address Durward. "Follow me," he said, "my bonny Scot, as one chosen by destiny and a monarch to accomplish a bold adventure. All must be got ready that thou mayst put foot in stirrup the very instant the bell of St. Martin's tolls twelve. One minute sooner, one minute later, were to forfeit the favorable aspect of the constellations which smile on your adventure."

Thus saying, the King left the apartment, followed by his young Guardsman ; and no sooner were they gone than the astrologer gave way to very different feelings from those which seemed to animate him during the royal presence.

"The niggardly slave !" he said, weighing the purse in his hand, for, being a man of unbounded expense, he had almost constant occasion for money—"the base, sordid scullion! A coxswain's wife would give more to know that her husband had crossed the narrow seas in safety. *He* acquire any tincture of humane letters ! yes, when prowling foxes and yelling wolves become musicians. *He* read the glorious blazoning of the firmament ! ay, when sordid moles shall become lynxes. *Post tot promissa*—after so many promises made, to entice me from the court of the magnificent Matthias, where Hun and Turk, Christian and infidel, the Czar of Muscovia and the Cham of Tartary themselves,

contended to load me with gifts, doth he think I am to abide
in this old castle, like a bullfinch in a cage, fain to sing as
oft as he chooses to whistle, and all for seed and water?
Not so—*aut inveniam viam, aut faciam:* I will discover or contrive a remedy. The Cardinal Balue is politic and liberal;
this query shall to him, and it shall be his Eminence's own
fault if the stars speak not as he would have them."

He again took the despised guerdon and weighed it in his
hand. " It may be," he said, " there is some jewel or pearl of
price concealed in this paltry case. I have heard he can be liberal even to lavishness when it suits his caprice or interest."

He emptied the purse, which contained neither more nor
less than ten gold pieces. The indignation of the astrologer
was extreme. "Thinks he that for such paltry rate of hire
I will practise that celestial science which I have studied
with the Armenian abbot of Istrahoff, who had not seen the
sun for forty years; with the Greek Dubravius, who is said
to have raised the dead, and have even visited the Scheik
Ebn Hali in his cave in the deserts of Thebais? No, by
Heaven! he that contemns art shall perish through his own
ignorance. Ten pieces! a pittance which I am half ashamed
to offer to Toinette, to buy her new breast-laces."

So saying, the indignant sage nevertheless plunged the
contemned pieces of gold into a large pouch which he wore
at his girdle, which Toinette and other abettors of lavish
expense generally contrived to empty fully faster than the
philosopher, with all his art, could find the means of filling.

CHAPTER XIV

THE JOURNEY

I see thee yet, fair France : thou favor'd land
Of art and nature, thou art still before me ;
Thy sons, to whom their labor is a sport,
So well thy grateful soil returns its tribute ;
Thy sun-burned daughters, with their laughing eyes
And glossy raven-locks. But, favor'd France,
Thou hast had many a tale of woe to tell,
In ancient times as now.

Anonymous.

AVOIDING all conversation with any one, for such was his
charge, Quentin Durward proceeded hastily to array himself
in a strong but plain cuirass, with thigh and arm pieces,
and placed on his head a good steel cap without any visor.
To these was added a handsome cassock of chamois leather,
finely dressed, and laced down the seams with some embroidery, such as might become a superior officer in a noble
household.

These were brought to his apartment by Oliver, who,
with his quiet, insinuating smile and manner, acquainted
him that his uncle had been summoned to mount guard
purposely that he might make no inquiries concerning these
mysterious movements.

"Your excuse will be made to your kinsman," said Oliver,
smiling again ; "and, my dearest son, when you return
safe from the execution of this pleasing trust, I doubt not
you will be found worthy of such promotion as will dispense with your accounting for your motions to any one,
while it will place you at the head of those who must render
an account of theirs to you."

So spoke Oliver le Diable, calculating, probably, in his
own mind the great chance there was that the poor youth
whose hand he squeezed affectionately as he spoke must
necessarily encounter death or captivity in the commission
intrusted to his charge. He added to his fair words a small
purse of gold, to defray necessary expenses on the road, as
a gratuity on the King's part.

At a few minutes before twelve at midnight, Quentin, according to his directions, proceeded to the second courtyard, and paused under the Dauphin's Tower, which, as the reader knows, was assigned for the temporary residence of the Countesses of Croye. He found, at this place of rendezvous, the men and horses appointed to compose the retinue, leading two sumpter mules already loaded with baggage, and holding three palfreys for the two countesses and a faithful waiting-woman, with a stately war-horse for himself, whose steel-plated saddle glanced in the pale moonlight. Not a word of recognition was spoken on either side. The men sat still in their saddles, as if they were motionless: and by the same imperfect light Quentin saw with pleasure that they were all armed, and held long lances in their hands. They were only three in number; but one of them whispered to Quentin, in a strong Gascon accent, that their guide was to join them beyond Tours.

Meantime, lights glanced to and fro at the lattices of the tower, as if there was bustle and preparation among its inhabitants. At length, a small door, which led from the bottom of the tower to the court, was unclosed, and three females came forth, attended by a man wrapped in a cloak. They mounted in silence the palfreys which stood prepared for them, while their attendant on foot led the way, and gave the passwords and signals to the watchful guards, whose posts they passed in succession. Thus they at length reached the exterior of those formidable barriers. Here the man on foot, who had hitherto acted as their guide, paused, and spoke low and earnestly to the two foremost females.

" May Heaven bless you, sire," said a voice which thrilled upon Quentin Durward's ear, " and forgive you, even if your purposes be more interested than your words express ! To be placed in safety under the protection of the good Bishop of Liege is the utmost extent of my desire."

The person whom she thus addressed muttered an inaudible answer, and retreated back through the barrier-gate, while Quentin thought that, by the moon-glimpse, he recognized in him the King himself, whose anxiety for the departure of his guests had probably induced him to give his presence, in case scruples should arise on their part or difficulties on that of the guards of the castle.

When the riders were beyond the castle, it was necessary for some time to ride with great precaution, in order to avoid the pitfalls, snares, and similar contrivances which were placed for the annoyance of strangers. The Gascon

was, however, completely possessed of the clue to this
labyrinth, and in a quarter of an hour's riding they found
themselves beyond the limits of Plessis le Parc, and not far
distant from the city of Tours.

The moon, which had now extricated herself from the
clouds through which she was formerly wading, shed a full
sea of glorious light upon a landscape equally glorious.
They saw the princely Loire rolling his majestic tide through
the richest plain in France, and sweeping along between
banks ornamented with towers, and terraces, and with olives
and vineyards. They saw the walls of the city of Tours,
the ancient capital of Touraine, raising their portal towers
and embattlements white in the moonlight, while from within their circle rose the immense Gothic mass which the devotion of the sainted Bishop Perpetuus erected as early as
the 5th century, and which the zeal of Charlemagne and his
successors had enlarged with such architectural splendors as
rendered it the most magnificent church in France. The
towers of the church of St. Gatien were also visible, and the
gloomy strength of the castle, which was said to have been,
in ancient times, the residence of the Emperor Valentinian.

Even the circumstances in which he was placed, though of
a nature so engrossing, did not prevent the wonder and
delight with which the young Scottishman, accustomed to
the waste though impressive landscape of his own mountains,
and the poverty even of his country's most stately scenery,
looked on a scene which art and nature seemed to have vied
in adorning with their richest splendor. But he was recalled
to the business of the moment by the voice of the elder lady,
pitched at least an octave higher than those soft tones which
bid adieu to King Louis, demanding to speak with the
leader of the band. Spurring his horse forward, Quentin
respectfully presented himself to the ladies in that capacity,
and thus underwent the interrogatories of the Lady Hameline.

" What was his name, and what his degree ? "

He told both.

" Was he perfectly acquainted with the road ? "

" He could not," he replied, " pretend to much knowledge
of the route, but he was furnished with full instructions,
and he was, at their first resting-place to be provided with a
guide in all respects competent to the task of directing their
farther journey ; meanwhile, a horseman who had just joined
them, and made the number of their guard four, was to be
their guide for the first stage."

"And wherefore were you selected for such a duty, young gentleman ? " said the lady. " I am told you are the same youth who was lately upon guard in the gallery in which we met the Princess of France. You seem young and inexperienced for such a charge; a stranger, too, in France, and speaking the language as a foreigner."

" I am bound to obey the commands of the King, madam, but am not qualified to reason on them," answered the young soldier.

" Are you of noble birth ? " demanded the same querist.

" I may safely affirm so, madam," replied Quentin.

" And are you not," said the younger lady, addressing him in her turn, but with a timorous accent, " the same whom I saw when I was called to wait upon the King at yonder inn ? "

Lowering his voice, perhaps from similar feelings of timidity, Quentin answered in the affirmative.

" Then, methinks, my cousin," said the Lady Isabelle, addressing the Lady Hameline, " we must be safe under this young gentleman's safeguard ; he looks not, at least, like one to whom the execution of a plan of treacherous cruelty upon two helpless women could be with safety intrusted."

" On my honor, madam," said Durward, " by the fame of my house, by the bones of my ancestry, I could not, for France and Scotland laid into one, be guilty of treachery or cruelty towards you ! "

" You speak well, young man," said the Lady Hameline ; " but we are accustomed to hear fair speeches from the King of France and his agents. It was by these that we were induced, when the protection of the Bishop of Liege might have been attained with less risk than now, or when we might have thrown ourselves on that of Wenceslaus of Germany or of Edward of England, to seek refuge in France. And in what did the promises of the King result ? In an obscure and shameful concealing of us, under plebeian names, as a sort of prohibited wares, in yonder paltry hostelry, when we, who, as thou knowest, Marthon (addressing her domestic), never put on our head-tire save under a canopy, and upon a dais of three degrees, were compelled to attire ourselves standing on the simple floor, as if we had been two milkmaids."

Marthon admitted that her lady spoke a most melancholy truth.

" I would that had been the sorest evil, dear kinswoman,"

said the Lady Isabelle ; " I could gladly have dispensed with state."

" But not with society," said the elder countess ; " that, my sweet cousin, was impossible."

" I would have dispensed with all, my dearest kinswoman," answered Isabelle, in a voice which penetrated to the very heart of her young conductor and guard—" with all, for a safe and honorable retirement. I wish not—God knows, I never wished—to occasion war betwixt France and my native Burgundy, or that lives should be lost for such as I am. I only implored permission to retire to the convent of Marmoutier or to any other holy sanctuary."

" You spoke then like a fool, my cousin," answered the elder lady, " and not like a daughter of my noble brother. It is well there is still one alive who hath some of the spirit of the noble house of Croye. How should a high-born lady be known from a sunburnt milkmaid save that spears are broken for the one and only hazel-poles shattered for the other ? I tell you, maiden, that while I was in the very earliest bloom, scarcely older than yourself, the famous passage of arms at Haflinghem was held in my honor ; the challengers were four, the assailants so many as twelve. It lasted three days, and cost the lives of two adventurous knights, the fracture of one back-bone, one collar-bone, three legs and two arms, besides flesh-wounds and bruises beyond the heralds' counting ; and thus have the ladies of our house ever been honored. Ah ! had you but half the heart of your noble ancestry, you would find means at some court, where ladies' love and fame in arms are still prized, to maintain a tournament, at which your hand should be the prize, as was that of your great-grandmother of blessed memory at the spear-running of Strasbourg ; and thus should you gain the best lance in Europe to maintain the rights of the house of Croye, both against the oppression of Burgundy and the policy of France."

" But, fair kinswoman," answered the younger countess, " I have been told by my old nurse that, although the Rhinegrave was the best lance at the great tournament at Strasbourg, and so won the hand of my hand of my respected ancestor, yet the match was no happy one, as he used often to scold, and sometimes even to beat, my great-grandmother of blessed memory."

" And wherefore not ? " said the elder countess, in her romantic enthusiasm for the profession of chivalry—" why should those victorious arms, accustomed to deal blows when abroad, be bound to restrain their energies at home ? A thousand times rather would I be beaten twice a-day by a husband whose arm was as much feared by others as by me than be the wife of a coward, who dared neither to lift hand to his wife nor to any one else."

"I should wish you joy of such an active mate, fair aunt," replied Isabelle, "without envying you ; for if broken bones be lovely in tourneys, there is nothing less amiable in ladies' bower."

"Nay, but the beating is no necessary consequence of wedding with a knight of fame in arms," said the Lady Hameline ; "though it is true that our ancestor of blessed memory, the Rhinegrave Gottfried, was something rough-tempered, and addicted to the use of *Rheinwein.* The very perfect knight is a lamb among ladies and a lion among lances. There was Thibault of Montigni—God be with him ! —he was the kindest soul alive, and not only was he never so discourteous as to lift hand against his lady, but, by our good dame, he who beat all enemies without doors found a fair foe who could belabor him within. Well, 'twas his own fault. He was one of the challengers at the passage of Haflinghem, and so well bestirred himself that, if it had pleased Heaven, and your grandfather, there might have been a lady of Montigni who had used his gentle nature more gently."

The Countess Isabelle, who had some reason to dread this passage of Haflinghem, it being a topic upon which her aunt was at all times very diffuse, suffered the conversation to drop ; and Quentin, with the natural politeness of one who had been gently nurtured, dreading lest his presence might be a restraint on their conversation, rode forward to join the guide, as if to ask him some questions concerning their route.

Meanwhile, the ladies continued their journey in silence, or in such conversation as is not worth narrating, until day began to break ; and as they had then been on horseback for several hours, Quentin, anxious lest they should be fatigued, became impatient to know their distance from the nearest resting-place.

"I will show it you," answered the guide, "in half an hour."

"And then you leave us to other guidance ?" continued Quentin.

"Even so, seignior archer," replied the man ; "my journeys are always short and straight. When you and

II

others, seignior archer, go by the bow, I always go by the cord."

The moon had by this time long been down, and the lights of dawn were beginning to spread bright and strong in the east, and to gleam on the bosom of a small lake, on the verge of which they had been riding for a short space of time. This lake lay in the midst of a wide plain, scattered over with single trees, groves, and thickets ; but which might be yet termed open, so that objects began to be discerned with sufficient accuracy. Quentin cast his eye on the person whom he rode beside, and, under the shadow of a slouched overspreading hat, which resembled the sombrero of a Spanish peasant, he recognized the facetious features of the same Petit-André whose fingers, not long since, had, in concert with those of his lugubrious brother, Trois-Eschelles, been so unpleasantly active about his throat. Impelled by aversion not altogether unmixed with fear (for in his own country the executioner is regarded with almost superstitious horror), which his late narrow escape had not diminished, Durward instinctively moved his horse's head to the right, and pressing him at the same time with the spur, made a demi-volte, which separated him eight feet from his hateful companion.

"Ho, ho, ho, ho !" exclaimed Petit-André ; "by our Lady of the Grève, our young soldier remembers us of old. What ! comrade, you bear no malice, I trust ? Every one wins his bread in this country. No man need be ashamed of having come through my hands, for I will do my work with any that ever tied a living weight to a dead tree. And God hath given me grace to be such a merry fellow withal. Ha ! ha ! ha ! I could tell you such jests I have cracked between the foot of the ladder and the top of the gallows, that, by my halidome, I have been obliged to do my job rather hastily, for fear the fellows should die with laughing, and so shame my mystery !"

As he thus spoke, he edged his horse sideways, to regain the interval which the Scot had left between them, saying at the same time, " Come, seignior archer, let there be no unkindness betwixt us ! For my part, I always do my duty without malice, and with a light heart, and I never love a man better than when I have put my scant-of-wind collar about his neck, to dub him knight of the order of St. Patibularius, as the provost's chaplain, the worthy Father Vaconeldiablo, is wont to call the patron saint of the provostry."

" Keep back, thou wretched object ! " exclaimed Quentin, as the finisher of the law again sought to approach him closer, " or I shall be tempted to teach you the distance that should be betwixt men of honor and such an outcast."

" La you there, how hot you are ! " said the fellow. " Had you said men of *honesty*, there had been some savor of truth in it ; but for men of *honor*, good lack, I have to deal with them every day, as nearly and closely as I was about to do business with you. But peace be with you, and keep your company to yourself. I would have bestowed a flagon of Auvernat upon you to wash away every unkindness ; but 'tis like you scorn my courtesy. Well. Be as churlish as you list ; I never quarrel with my customers—my jerry-come-tumbles, my merry dancers, my little playfellows, as Jacques Butcher says to his lambs—those, in fine, who, like your seigniorship, have H. E. M. P. written on their foreheads. No—no, let them use me as they list, they shall have my good service at last ; and yourself shall see, when you next come under Petit-André's hands, that he knows how to forgive an injury."

So saying, and summing up the whole with a provoking wink and such an interjectional *tchick* as men quicken a dull horse with, Petit-André drew off to the other side of the path, and left the youth to digest the taunts he had treated him with, as his proud Scottish stomach best might. A strong desire had Quentin to have belabored him while the staff of his lance could hold together ; but he put a restraint on his passion, recollecting that a brawl with such a character could be creditable at no time or place, and that a quarrel of any kind, on the present occasion, would be a breach of duty, and might involve the most perilous consequences. He therefore swallowed his wrath at the ill-timed and professional jokes of Mons. Petit-André, and contented himself with devoutly hoping that they had not reached the ears of his fair charge, on which they could not be supposed to make an impression in favor of himself, as one obnoxious to such sarcasms. But he was speedily aroused from such thoughts by the cry of both the ladies at once, " Look back —look back ! For the love of Heaven look to yourself and us ; we are pursued ! "

Quentin hastily looked back, and saw that two armed men were in fact following them, and riding at such a pace as must soon bring them up with their party. " It can," he said, " be only some of the provostry making their rounds in the forest. Do thou look," he said to Petit-André, "and see what they may be."

Petit-André obeyed ; and rolling himself jocosely in the saddle after he had made his observations, replied, " These, fair sir, are neither your comrades nor mine—neither archers nor marshal's-men ; for I think they wear helmets, with visors lowered, and gorgets of the same. A plague upon these gorgets, of all other pieces of armor ! I have fumbled with them an hour before I could undo the rivets."

" Do you, gracious ladies," said Durward, without attend-ing to Petit-André, " ride forward, not so fast as to raise an opinion of your being in flight, and yet fast enough to avail yourselves of the impediment which I shall presently place between you and these men who follow us."

The Countess Isabelle looked to their guide, and then whispered to her aunt, who spoke to Quentin thus—" We have confidence in your care, fair archer, and will rather abide the risk of whatever may chance in your company than we will go onward with that man, whose mein is, we think, of no good augury."

" Be it as you will, ladies," said the youth. " There are but two who come after us ; and though they be knights, as their arms seem to show, they shall, if they have any evil purpose, learn how a Scottish gentleman can do his devoir in the presence and for the defense of such as you. Which of you there," he continued, addressing the guards whom he commanded, " is willing to be my comrade, and to break a lance with these gallants ? "

Two of the men, obviously faltered in resolution ; but the third, Bertrand Guyot, swore " that *cap de Diou*, were they knights of King Arthur's Round Table, he would try their mettle for the honor of Gascony."

While he spoke, the two knights—for they seemed of no less rank—came up with the rear of the party, in which Quentin, with his sturdy adherent, had by this time sta-tioned himself. They were fully accoutered in excellent armor of polished steel, without any device by which they could be distinguished.

One of them, as they approached, called out to Quentin, " Sir squire, give place ; we come to relieve you of a charge which is above your rank and condition. You will do well to leave these ladies in our care, who are fitter to wait upon them, especially as we know that in yours they are little better than captives.

" In return to your demands, sirs," replied Durward,

"know, in the first place, that I am discharging the duty imposed upon me by the present sovereign ; and next, that however unworthy I may be, the ladies desire to abide under my protection."

"Out, sirrah !" exclaimed one of the champions ; "will you, a wandering beggar, put yourself on terms of resistance against belted knights ?"

"They are indeed terms of resistance," said Quentin, "since they oppose your insolent and unlawful aggression ; and if there be difference of rank between us, which as yet I know not, your discourtesy has done it away. Draw your sword, or, if you will use the lance, take ground for your career."

While the knights turned their horses and rode back to the distance of about a hundred and fifty yards, Quentin, looking to the ladies, bent low on his saddle-bow, as if desiring their favorable regard, and as they streamed towards him their kerchiefs in token of encouragement, the two assailants had gained the distance necessary for their charge.

Calling to the Gascon to bear himself like a man, Durward put his steed into motion ; and the four horsemen met in full career in the midst of the ground which at first separated them. The shock was fatal to the poor Gascon ; for his adversary, aiming at his face, which was undefended by a visor, ran him through the eye into his brain, so that he fell dead from his horse.

On the other hand, Quentin, though laboring under the same disadvantage, swayed himself in the saddle so dexterously that the hostile lance, slightly scratching his cheek, passed over his right shoulder ; while his own spear, striking his antagonist fair upon the breast, hurled him to the ground. Quentin jumped off, to unhelm his fallen opponent ; but the other knight, who had never yet spoken, seeing the misfortune of his companion, dismounted still more speedily than Durward, and bestriding his friend, who lay senseless, exclaimed, "In the name of God and St. Martin, mount, good fellow, and get thee gone with thy woman's ware ! *Ventre St. Gris,* they have caused mischief enough this morning."

"By your leave, sir knight," said Quentin, who could not brook the menacing tone in which this advice was given, "I will first see who I have had to do with, and learn who is to answer for the death of my comrade."

"That shalt thou never live to know or tell," answered the knight. "Get thee back in peace, good fellow. If we were fools for interrupting your passage, we have had the worst, for thou hast done more evil than the lives of thou and thy whole band could repay. Nay, if thou *wilt* have it (for Quentin now drew his sword and advanced on him), take it with vengeance !"

So saying, he dealt the Scot such a blow on the helmet as till that moment, though bred where good blows were plenty, he had only read of in romance. It descended like a thunder-bolt, beating down the guard which the young soldier had raised to protect his head, and reaching his helmet of proof, cut it through so far as to touch his hair, but without far-ther injury ; while Durward, dizzy, stunned, and beaten down upon one knee, was for an instant at the mercy of the knight, had it pleased him to second his blow. But compassion for Quentin's youth, or admiration of his courage, or a generous love of fair play, made him withhold from taking such ad-vantage ; while Durward, collecting himself, sprung up and attacked his antagonist with the energy of one determined to conquer or die, and at the same time with the presence of mind necessary for fighting the quarrel out to the best ad-vantage. Resolved not again to expose himself to such dreadful blows as he had just sustained, he employed the advantage of superior agility, increased by the comparative lightness of his armor, to harass his antagonist, by traversing on all sides, with a suddenness of motion and rapidity of attack against which the knight, in his heavy panoply, found it difficult to defend himself without much fatigue.

It was in vain that this generous antagonist called aloud to Quentin, "That there now remained no cause of fight be-twixt them, and that he was loth to be constrained to do him injury." Listening only to the suggestions of a passionate wish to redeem the shame of his temporary defeat, Durward continued to assail him with the rapidity of lightning—now menacing him with the edge, now with the point of his sword ; and ever keeping such an eye on the motions of his opponent, of whose superior strength he had had terrible proof, that he was ready to spring backward, or aside, from under the blows of his tremendous weapon.

"Now the devil be with thee for an obstinate and pre-sumptuous fool," muttered the knight, "that cannot be quiet till thou art knocked on the head !" So saying, he changed his mode of fighting, collected himself as if to stand on the defensive, and seemed contented with parrying, in-stead of returning, the blows which Quentin unceasingly aimed at him, with the internal resolution that, the instant when either loss of breath or any false or careless pass of the

young soldier should give an opening, he would put an end
to the fight by a single blow. It is likely he might have
succeeded in this artful policy, but Fate had ordered it
otherwise.

The duel was still at the hottest, when a large party of
horse rode up, crying, "Hold, in the King's name!" Both
champions stepped back; and Quentin saw with surprise
that his captain, Lord Crawford, was at the head of the
party who had thus interrupted their combat. There was
also Tristan l'Hermite, with two or three of his followers;
making, in all, perhaps, twenty horse.

CHAPTER XV

THE GUIDE

He was a son of Egypt, as he told me,
And one descended from those dread magicians,
Who waged rash war, when Israel dwelt in Goshen
With Israel and her Prophet—matching rod
With his the sons of Levi's—and encountering
Jehovah's miracles with incantations,
Till upon Egypt came the avenging angel,
And those 1 oud sages wept for their first-born,
As wept the unletter'd peasant.

Anonymous.

THE arrival of Lord Crawford and his guard put an immediate end to the engagement which we endeavored to describe in the last chapter ; and the knight, throwing off his helmet, hastily gave the old lord his sword, saying, " Crawford, I render myself. But hither, and lend me your ear—a word, for God's sake—save the Duke of Orleans ! "

" How ! What ? the Duke of Orleans ! " exclaimed the Scottish commander. " How came this, in the name of the foul fiend ? It will ruin the callant with the King forever and a day."

" Ask no question," said Dunois, " for it was no other than he ; it was all my fault. See, he stirs. I came forth but to have a snatch at yonder damsel, and make myself a landed and a married man, and see what is come on't. Keep back your canaille ; let no man look upon him." So saying, he opened the visor of Orleans, and threw water on his face, which was afforded by the neighboring lake.

Quentin Durward, meanwhile, stood like one planet-struck, so fast did new adventures pour in upon him. He had now, as the pale features of his first antagonist assured him, borne to the earth the first prince of the blood in France, and had measured swords with her best champion, the celebrated Dunois—both of them achievements honorable in themselves, but whether they might be called good service to the King, or so esteemed by him, was a very different question.

The Duke had now recovered his breath, and was able to

168

sit up and give attention to what passed betwixt Dunois and Crawford, while the former pleaded eagerly that there was no occasion to mention in the matter the name of the most · noble Orleans, while he was ready to take the whole blame on his own shoulders, and to avouch that the duke had only come thither in friendship to him.

Lord Crawford continued listening, with his eyes fixed on the ground, and from time to time he sighed and shook his head. At length he said, looking up, "Thou knowest, Dunois, that for thy father's sake, as well as thine own, I would full fain do thee a service."

"It is not for myself I demand anything," answered Dunois. "Thou hast my sword, and I am your prisoner ; what needs more ? But it is for this noble prince, the only .hope of France, if God should call the Dauphin. He only came hither to do me a favor—in an effort to make my fortune—in a matter which the King had partly encouraged."

"Dunois," replied Crawford, "if another had told me thou hadst brought the noble prince into this jeopardy to serve any purpose of thine own, I had told him it was false. And now that thou dost pretend so thyself, I can hardly believe it is for the sake of speaking the truth."

"Noble Crawford," said Orleans, who had now entirely recovered from his swoon, "you are too like in character to your friend Dunois not to do him justice. It was indeed I that dragged him hither, most unwillingly, upon an enterprise of hare-brained passion, suddenly and rashly undertaken. Look on me all who will," he added, rising up and turning to the soldiery ; "I am Louis of Orleans, willing to pay the penalty of my own folly. I trust the King will limit his displeasure to me, as is but just. Meanwhile, as a child of France must not give up his sword to any one—not even to you, brave Crawford—fare thee well, good steel."

So saying, he drew his sword from its scabbard and flung it into the lake. It went through the air like a stream of lightning, and sunk in the flashing waters, which speedily closed over it. All remained standing in irresolution and astonishment, so high was the rank, and so much esteemed was the character, of the culprit ; while, at the same time, all were conscious that the consequences of his rash enterprise, considering the views which the King had upon him, were likely to end in his utter ruin.

Dunois was the first who spoke, and it was in the chiding tone of an offended and distrusted friend ; "So ! your Highness hath judged it fit to cast away your best sword, in the same morning when it was your pleasure to fling away the King's favor and to slight the friendship of Dunois ? "

" My dearest kinsman," said the duke, " when or how was it in my purpose to slight your friendship, by telling the truth, when it was due to your safety and my honor ? "

" What had you to do with my safety my most princely cousin, I would pray to know ? " answered Dunois, gruffly. " What, in God's name, was it to you if I had a mind to be hanged, or strangled, or flung into the Loire, or poniarded, or broken on the wheel, or hung up alive in an iron cage, or buried alive in a castle fosse, or disposed of in any other way in which it might please King Louis to get rid of his faithful subject ? You need not wink and frown, and point to Tristan l'Hermite ; I see the scoundrel as well as you do. But it would not have stood so hard with me. And so much for my safety. And then for your own honor—by the blush of St. Magdalene, I think the honor would have been to have missed this morning's work, or kept it out of sight. Here has your Highness got yourself unhorsed by a wild Scottish boy."

" Tut—tut ! " said Lord Crawford ; " never shame his Highness for that. It is not the first time a Scottish boy hath broke a good lance. I am glad the youth hath borne him well."

" I will say nothing on the contrary," said Dunois ; " yet, had your lordship come something later than you did, there might have been a vacancy in your band of archers."

"Ay—ay," answered Lord Crawford ; " I can read your handwriting in that cleft morion. Some one take it from the lad, and give him a bonnet, which, with its steel lining, will keep his head better than that broken loom. And let me tell your lordship, that your own armor of proof is not without some marks of good Scottish handwriting. But, Dunois, I must now request the Duke of Orleans and you to take horse and accompany me, as I have power and commission to convey you to a place different from that which my good-will might assign you."

" May I not speak one word, my Lord of Crawford, to yonder fair ladies ? " said the Duke of Orleans.

" Not one syllable," answered Lord Crawford ; " I am too much a friend of your Highness to permit such an act of folly." Then addressing Quentin, he added, " You, young man, have done your duty. Go on to obey the charge with which you are entrusted."

" Under favor, my lord," said Tristan, with his usual

brutality of manner, "the youth must find another guide. I cannot do without Petit-André when there is so like to be business on hand for him."

"The young man," said Petit-André, now coming forward, "has only to keep the path which lies straight before him, and it will conduct him to a place where he will find the man who is to act as his guide. I would not for a thousand ducats be absent from my chief this day! I have hanged knights and squires many a one, and wealthy echevins, and burgomasters to boot—even counts and marquisses have tasted of my handiwork but, a-humph——" He looked at the duke, as if to intimate that he would have filled up the blank with "a prince of blood!" "Ho, ho, ho! Petit-André, thou wilt be read of in chronicle!"

"Do you permit your ruffians to hold such language in such a presence?" said Crawford, looking sternly to Tristan.

"Why do you not correct him yourself, my lord?" said Tristan, sullenly.

"Because thy hand is the only one in this company that can beat him without being degraded by such an action."

"Then rule your own men, my lord, and I will be answerable for mine," said the provost-marshal.

Lord Crawford seemed about to give a passionate reply; but, as if he had thought better of it, turned his back short upon Tristan, and requesting the Duke of Orleans and Dunois to ride one on either hand of him, he made a signal of adieu to the ladies, and said to Quentin, "God bless thee, my child; thou hast begun thy service valiantly, though in an unhappy cause." He was about to go off, when Quentin could hear Dunois whisper to Crawford, "Do you carry us to Plessis?"

"No, my unhappy and rash friend," answered Crawford, with a sigh, "to Loches."

"To Loches!" The name of a castle, or rather a prison, yet more dreaded than Plessis itself, fell like a death-toll upon the ear of the young Scotchman. He had heard it described as a place destined to the workings of those secret acts of cruelty with which even Louis shamed to pollute the interior of his own residence. There were in this place of terror dungeons under dungeons, some of them unknown even to the keepers themselves—living graves, to which men were consigned with little hope of farther employment during the rest of their life than to breathe impure air and feed on bread and water. At this formidable castle were also those dreadful places of confinement called "cages," in which the wretched prisoners could neither stand upright nor stretch himself at length—an invention, it is said, of the Cardinal Balue.* It is no wonder that the name of this place of horrors, and the consciousness that he had been partly the means of despatching thither two such illustrious victims, struck so much sadness into the heart of the young Scot that he rode for some time with his head dejected, his eyes fixed on the ground, and his heart filled with the most painful reflections.

As he was now again at the head of the little troop, and pursuing the road which had been pointed out to him, the Lady Hameline had an opportunity to say to him—

"Methinks, fair sir, you regret the victory which your gallantry has attained in our behalf ?"

There was something in the question which sounded like irony, but Quentin had tact enough to answer simply and with sincerity—

"I can regret nothing that is done in the service of such ladies as you are ; but, methinks, had it consisted with your safety, I had rather fallen by the sword of so good a soldier as Dunois than have been the means of consigning that renowned knight and his unhappy chief, the Duke of Orleans, to yonder fearful dungeons."

"It *was*, then, the Duke of Orleans," said the elder lady, turning to her niece. " I thought so, even at the distance from which we beheld the fray. You see, kinswoman, what we might have been, had this sly and avaricious monarch permitted us to be seen at his court. The first prince of the blood of France, and the valiant Dunois, whose name is known as wide as that of his heroic father ! This young gentleman did his devoir bravely and well ; but methinks 'tis pity that he did not succumb with honor, since his ill-advised gallantry has stood betwixt us and these princely rescuers."

The Countess Isabelle replied in a firm and almost a displeased tone, with an energy, in short, which Quentin had not yet observed her use.

"Madam," she said, "but that I know you jest, I would say your speech is ungrateful to our brave defender, to whom we owe more, perhaps, than you are aware of. Had these gentlemen succeeded so far in their rash enterprise as to have defeated our escort, is it not still evident that, on the arrival of the Royal Guard, we must have shared their captivity ? For my own part, I give tears, and will soon bestow

* Who himself tenanted one of these dens for more than eleven years.

masses, on the brave man who has fallen, and, I trust," she continued, more timidly, " that he who lives will accept my grateful thanks."

As Quentin turned his face towards her, to return the fitting acknowledgments, she saw the blood which streamed down on one side of his face, and exclaimed, in a tone of deep feeling, " Holy Virgin, he is wounded ! he bleeds ! Dismount, sir, and let your wound be bound up."

In spite of all that Durward could say of the slightness of his hurt, he was compelled to dismount, and to seat himself on a bank and unhelmet himself, while the Ladies of Croye, who, according to a fashion not as yet antiquated, pretended to some knowledge of leechcraft, washed the wound, stanched the blood, and bound it with the kerchief of the younger countess, in order to exclude the air, for so their practice prescribed.

In modern times, gallants seldom or never take wounds for ladies' sake, and damsels on their side never meddle with the cure of wounds. Each has a danger the less. That which the men escape will be generally acknowledged ; but the peril of dressing such a slight wound as that of Quentin's, which involved nothing formidable or dangerous, was perhaps as real in its way as the risk of encountering it.

We have already said the patient was eminently handsome ; and the removal of his helmet, or, more properly, of his morion, had suffered his fair locks to escape in profusion around a countenance in which the hilarity of youth was qualified by a blush of modesty at once and pleasure. And then the feelings of the younger countess, when compelled to hold the kerchief to the wound, while her aunt sought in their baggage for some vulnerary remedy, were mingled at once with a sense of delicacy and embarrassment—a thrill of pity for the patient and of gratitude for his services, which exaggerated, in her eyes, his good mien and handsome features. In short, this incident seemed intended by Fate to complete the mysterious communication which she had, by many petty and apparently accidental circumstances, established betwixt two persons who, though far different in rank and fortune, strongly resembled each other in youth, beauty, and the romantic tenderness of an affectionate disposition. It was no wonder, therefore, that from this moment the thoughts of the Countess Isabelle, already so familiar to his imagination, should become paramount in Quentin's bosom, nor that, if the maiden's feelings were of a less decided character, at least so far as known to herself, she should think of her young defender, to whom she had just rended a service so interesting, with more emotion than of any of the whole band of high-born nobles who had for two years past besieged her with their adoration. Above all, when the thought of Campobasso, the unworthy favorite of Duke Charles, with his hypocritical mien, his base, treacherous spirit, his wry neck, and his squint, occurred to her, his portrait was more disgustingly hideous than ever, and deeply did she resolve no tyranny should make her enter into so hateful a union.

In the meantime, whether the good Lady Hameline of Croye understood and admired masculine beauty as much as when she was fifteen years younger (for the good countess was at least thirty-five, if the records of that noble house speak the truth), or whether she thought she had done their young protector less justice than she ought, in the first view which she had taken of his services, it is certain that he began to find favor in her eyes.

"My niece," she said, "has bestowed on you a kerchief for the binding of your wound ; I will give you one to grace your gallantry, and to encourage you in your farther progress in chivalry."

So saying, she gave him a richly embroidered kerchief of blue and silver, and pointing to the housing of her palfrey and the plumes in her riding-cap, desired him to observe that the colors were the same.

The fashion of the time prescribed one absolute mode of receiving such a favor, which Quentin followed accordingly, by tying the napkin round his arm ; yet his manner of acknowledgment had more of awkwardness and less of gallantry in it than perhaps it might have had at another time and in another presence ; for though the wearing of a lady's favor, given in such a manner, was merely matter of general compliment, he would much rather have preferred the right of displaying on his arm that which bound the wound inflicted by the sword of Dunois.

Meantime, they continued their pilgrimage, Quentin now riding abreast of the ladies, into whose society he seemed to be tacitly adopted. He did not speak much, however, being filled by the silent consciousness of happiness, which is afraid of giving too strong vent to its feelings. The Countess Isabelle spoke still less, so that the conversation was chiefly carried on by the Lady Hameline, who showed no inclination to let it drop ; for, to initiate the young archer, as she said, into the principles and practice of chivalry, she detailed to him, at full length, the passage of arms at Haflinghem, where she had distributed the prizes among the victors.

Not much interested, I am sorry to say, in the description of this splendid scene, or in the heraldic bearings of the different Flemish and German knights, which the lady blazoned with pitiless accuracy, Quentin began to entertain some alarm lest he should have passed the place where his guide was to join him—a most serious disaster, and from which, should it really have taken place, the very worst consequences were to be apprehended.

While he hesitated whether it would be better to send back one of his followers to see whether this might not be the case, he heard the blast of a horn, and looking in the direction from which the sound came, beheld a horseman riding very fast towards them. The low size and wild, shaggy, untrained state of the animal reminded Quentin of the mountain breed of horses in his own country ; but this was much more finely limbed, and, with the same appearance of hardiness, was more rapid in its movements. The head particularly, which in the Scottish pony is often lumpish and heavy, was small and well placed in the neck of this animal, with thin jaws, full sparkling eyes, and expanded nostrils.

The rider was even more singular in his appearance than the horse which he rode, though that was extremely unlike the horses of France. Although he managed his palfrey with great dexterity, he sat with his feet in broad stirrups, something resembling shovels, so short in the leathers that his knees were wellnigh as high as the pommel of his saddle. His dress was a red turban of small size, in which he wore a sullied plume, secured by a clasp of silver ; his tunic, which was shaped like those of the Estradiots—a sort of troops whom the Venetians at that time levied in the provinces on the eastern side of their gulf—was green in color and tawdrily laced with gold ; he wore very wide drawers or trowsers of white, though none of the cleanest, which gathered beneath the knee, and his swarthy legs were quite bare, unless for the complicated laces which bound a pair of sandals on his feet ; he had no spurs, the edge of his large stirrups being so sharp as to serve to goad the horse in a very severe manner. In a crimson sash this singular horseman wore a dagger on the right side, and on the left a short crooked Moorish sword ; and by a tarnished baldric over the shoulder hung the horn which announced his approach. He had a swarthy and sunburnt visage, with a thin beard, and piercing dark eyes, a well-formed mouth and nose, and other features which might have been pronounced handsome, but for the black elf-locks which hung around his face, and the air of wildness and emaciation, which rather seemed to indicate a savage than a civilized man.

" He also is a Bohemian ! " said the ladies to each other. " Holy Mary, will the King again place confidence in these outcasts ? "

" I will question the man, if it be your pleasure," said Quentin, " and assure myself of his fidelity as I best may."

Durward, as well as the Ladies of Croye, had recognized in this man's dress and appearance the habit and the manners of those vagrants with whom he had nearly been confounded by the hasty proceedings of Trois-Eschelles and Petit-André, and he, too, entertained very natural apprehensions concerning the risk of reposing trust in one of that vagrant race.

" Art thou come hither to seek us ? " was his first question.

The stranger nodded.

" And for what purpose ? "

" To guide you to the palace of him of Liege."

" Of the bishop ? "

The Bohemian again nodded.

" What token canst thou give me that we should yield credence to thee ? "

" Even the old rhyme, and no other," answered the Bohemian—

" The page slew the boar,
The peer had the gloire."

" A true token," said Quentin. " Lead on, good fellow ; I will speak further with thee presently." Then falling back to the ladies, he said, " I am convinced this man is the guide we are to expect, for he hath brought me a password known, I think, but to the King and me. But I will discourse with him further, and endeavor to ascertain how far he is to be trusted."

CHAPTER XVI

THE VAGRANT

I am as free as Nature first made man,
Ere the base laws of servitude began,
When wild in woods the noble savage ran.
The Conquest of Granada.

WHILE Quentin held the brief communication with the ladies necessary to assure them that this extraordinary addition to their party was the guide whom they were to expect on the King's part, he noticed, for he was as alert in observing the motions of the stranger as the Bohemian could be on his part, that the man not only turned his head as far back as he could to peer at them, but that, with a singular sort of agility more resembling that of a monkey than of a man, he had screwed his whole person around on the saddle, so as to sit almost side-long upon the horse, for the convenience, as it seemed, of watching them more attentively.

Not greatly pleased with this maneuver, Quentin rode up to the Bohemian, and said to him, as he suddenly assumed his proper position on the horse, "Methinks, friend, you will prove but a blind guide if you look at the tail of your horse rather than his ears."

"And if I were actually blind," answered the Bohemian, "I could not the less guide you through any county in this realm of France or in those adjoining to it."

"Yet you are no Frenchman born," said the Scot.

"I am not," answered the guide.

"What countryman, then, are you?" demanded Quentin.

"I am of no country," answered the guide.

"How! of no country?" repeated the Scot.

"No," answered the Bohemian, "of none. I am a Zingaro, a Bohemian, an Eygptian, or whatever the Europeans, in their different languages, may choose to call our people; but I have no country."

"Are you a Christian?" asked the Scotchman.

The Bohemian shook his head.

"Dog!" said Quentin, for there was little toleration in

the spirit of Catholicism in those days, "dost thou worship Mahound ?"

"No," was the indifferent and concise answer of the guide, who neither seemed offended or surprised at the young man's violence of manner.

"Are you a pagan, then, or what are you ?"

"I have no religion," * answered the Bohemian.

Durward started back ; for, though he had heard of Saracens and idolaters, it had never entered into his ideas or belief that any body of men could exist who practised no mode of worship whatever. He recovered from his astonishment, to ask his guide where he usually dwelt.

"Wherever I chance to be for the time," replied the Bohemian. I have no home."

"How do you guard your property ?"

"Excepting the clothes which I wear and the horse I ride on, I have no property."

"Yet you dress gaily and ride gallantly," said Durward. "What are your means of subsistence ?"

"I eat when I am hungry, drink when I am thirsty, and have no other means of subsistence than chance throws in my way," replied the vagabond.

"Under whose laws do you live ?"

"I acknowledge obedience to none, but as it suits my pleasure or my necessities," said the Bohemian.

"Who is your leader, and commands you ?

"The father of our tribe, if I choose to obey him," said the guide ; "otherwise I have no commander."

"You are then," said the wondering querist, "destitute of all that other men are combined by : you have no law, no leader, no settled means of subsistence, no house or home. You have, may Heaven compassionate you, no country ; and may Heaven enlighten and forgive you, you have no God ! What is it that remains to you, deprived of government, domestic happiness, and religion ?" "I have liberty," said the Bohemian. "I crouch to no one—obey no one—respect no one. I go where I will—live as I can—and die when my day comes."

"But you are subject to instant execution, at the pleasure of the judge ?"

"Be it so," returned the Bohemian ; "I can but die so much the sooner."

"And to imprisonment also," said the Scot ; "and where then is your boasted freedom ?"

* See Religion of the Bohemians. Note 26.

"In my thoughts," said the Bohemian, "which no chains can bind; while yours, even when your limbs are free, remain fettered by your laws and your superstitions, your dreams of local attachment and your fantastic visions of civil policy. Such as I are free in spirit when our limbs are chained. You are imprisoned in mind, even when your limbs are most at freedom."

"Yet the freedom of your thoughts," said the Scot, "relieves not the pressure of the gyves on your limbs."

"For a brief time that may be endured," answered the vagrant; "and if within that period I cannot extricate myself and fail of relief from my comrades, I can always die, and death is the most perfect freedom of all."

There was a deep pause of some duration, which Quentin at length broke by resuming his queries.

"Yours is a wandering race, unknown to the nations of Europe. Whence do they derive their origin?"

"I may not tell you," answered the Bohemian.

"When will they relieve this kingdom from their presence, and return to the land from whence they came?" said the Scot.

"When the day of their pilgrimage shall be accomplished," replied the vagrant guide.

"Are you not sprung from those tribes of Israel which were carried into captivity beyond the river Euphrates?" said Quentin, who had not forgotten the lore which had been taught him at Aberbrothock.

"Had we been so," answered the Bohemian, "we had followed their faith and practised their rites."

"What is thine own name?" said Durward.

"My proper name is only known to my brethren. The men beyond our tents call me Hayraddin Maugrabin, that is Hayraddin the African Moor."

"Thou speakest too well for one who hath lived always in thy filthy horde," said the Scot.

"I have learned some of the knowledge of this land," said Hayraddin. "When I was a little boy, our tribe was chased by the hunters after human flesh. An arrow went through my mother's head, and she died. I was entangled in the blanket on her shoulders, and was taken by the pursuers. A priest begged me from the provost's archers, and trained me up in Frankish learning for two or three years."

"How came you to part with him?" demanded Durward.

"I stole money from him—even the god which he worshiped," answered Hayraddin, with perfect composure;

 he detected me, and beat me; I stabbed him with my knife, fled to the woods, and was again united to my people."

"Wretch!" said Durward, "did you murder your benefactor?"

"What had he to do to burden me with his benefits? The Zingaro boy was no house-bred cur, to dog the heels of his master, and crouch beneath his blows, for scraps of food. He was the imprisoned wolf-whelp, which at the first opportunity broke his chain, rended his master, and returned to his wilderness."

There was another pause, when the young Scot, with a view of still farther investigating the character and purpose of this suspicious guide, asked Hayraddin, "whether it was not true that his people, amid their ignorance, pretended to a knowledge of futurity which was not given to the sages, philosophers, and divines of more polished society?"

"We pretend to it," said Hayraddin. "And it is with justice."

"How can it be that so high a gift is bestowed on so abject a race?" said Quentin.

"Can I tell you?" answered Hayraddin. "Yes, I may indeed; but it is when you shall explain to me why the dog can trace the footsteps of a man, while man, the nobler animal, hath not power to trace those of the dog. These powers, which seem to you so wonderful, are instinctive in our race. From the lines on the face and on the hand we can tell the future fate of those who consult us, even as surely as you know from the blossom of the tree in spring what fruit it will bear in the harvest."

"I doubt of your knowledge, and defy you to the proof."

"Defy me not, sir squire," said Hayraddin Maugrabin. "I can tell you that, say what you will of your religion, the goddess whom you worship rides in this company."

"Peace!" said Quentin, in astonishment: "on thy life, not a word farther, but in answer to what I ask thee. Canst thou be faithful?"

"I can; all men can," said the Bohemian.

"But *wilt* thou be faithful?"

"Wouldst thou believe me the more should I swear it?" answered Maugrabin, with a sneer.

"Thy life is in my hand," said the young Scot.

"Strike, and see whether I fear to die," answered the Bohemian.

"Will money render thee a trusty guide?" demanded Durward.

"If I be not such without it, no," replied the heathen.

"Then what will bind thee?" asked the Scot.

"Kindness," replied the Bohemian.

"Shall I swear to show thee such, if thou art true guide to us on this pilgrimage?"

"No," replied Hayraddin, "it were extragavant waste of a commodity so rare. To thee I am bound already."

"How!" exclaimed Durward, more surprised than ever.

"Remember the chestnut-trees on the banks of the Cher. The victim whose body thou didst cut down was my brother, Zamet, the Maugrabin."

"And yet," said Quentin, "I find you in correspondence with those very officers by whom your brother was done to death; for it was one of them who directed me where to meet with you—the same, doubtless, who procured yonder ladies your services as a guide."

"What can we do?" answered Hayraddin, gloomily. "These men deal with us as the sheep-dogs do with the flock: they protect us for a while, drive us hither and thither at their pleasure, and always end by guiding us to the shambles."

Quentin had afterwards occasion to learn that the Bohemian spoke truth in this particular, and that the provost-guard, employed to suppress the vagabond bands by which the kingdom was invested, entertained correspondence among them, and forbore, for a certain time, the exercise of their duty, which always at last ended in conducting these allies to the gallows. This is a sort of political relation between thief and officer, for the profitable exercise of their mutual professions, which has subsisted in all countries, and is by no means unknown to our own.

Durward, parting from the guide, fell back to the rest of the retinue, very little satisfied with the character of Hayraddin, and entertaining little confidence in the professions of gratitude which he had personally made to him. He proceeded to sound the other two men who had been assigned him for attendants, and he was concerned to find them stupid, and as unfit to assist him with counsel as in the rencounter they had shown themselves reluctant to use their weapons.

"It is all the better," said Quentin to himself, his spirit rising with the apprehended difficulties of his situation; "that lovely young lady shall owe all to me. What one hand—ay, and one head—can do, methinks I can boldly count upon. I have seen my father's house on fire, and him and my brothers lying dead amongst the flames. I gave not an inch back, but fought it out to the last. Now I am two years older, and have the best and fairest cause to bear me well that ever kindled mettle within a brave man's bosom."

Acting upon this resolution the attention and activity which Quentin bestowed during the journey had in it something that gave him the appearance of ubiquity. His principal and most favorite post was of course by the side of the ladies, who, sensible of his extreme attention to their safety, began to converse with him in almost the tone of familiar friendship, and appeared to take great pleasure in the naïveté, yet shrewdness, of his conversation. But Quentin did not suffer the fascination of this intercourse to interfere with the vigilant discharge of his duty.

If he was often by the side of the countesses, laboring to describe to the natives of a level country the Grampian Mountains, and, above all, the beauties of Glen Houlakin, he was as often riding with Hayraddin in the front of the cavalcade, questioning him about the road and the resting-places and recording his answers in his mind, to ascertain whether upon cross-examination he could discover anything like meditated treachery. As often again he was in the rear, endeavoring to secure the attachment of the two horsemen, by kind words, gifts, and promises of additional recompense when their task should be accomplished.

In this way they traveled for more than a week, through by-paths and unfrequented districts, and by circuitous routes, in order to avoid large towns. Nothing remarkable occurred, though they now and then met strolling gangs of Rohemians, who respected them as under the conduct of one of their tribe; straggling soldiers, or perhaps banditti, who deemed their party too strong to be attacked ; or parties of the Maréchaussée, as they would now be termed, whom Louis, who searched the wounds of the land with steel and cautery, employed to suppress the disorderly bands which infested the interior. These last suffered them to pursue their way unmolested, by virtue of a password with which Quentin had been furnished for that purpose by the King himself.

Their resting-places were chiefly the monasteries, most of which were obliged by the rules of their foundation to receive pilgrims, under which character the ladies traveled, with hospitality, and without any troublesome inquiries into their ranks and character, which most persons of distinction were desirous of concealing while in the discharge of their vows. The pretence of weariness was usually em-

ployed by the Countesses of Croye as an excuse for instantly
retiring to rest, and Quentin, as their major-domo, arranged
all that was necessary betwixt them and their entertainers
with a strewdness which saved them all trouble, and an
alacrity that failed not to excite a corresponding degree of
good-will on the part of those who were thus sedulously
attended to.

One circumstance gave Quentin peculiar trouble, which
was the character and nation of his guide, who, as a heathen
and an infidel vagabond, addicted, besides, to occult arts (the
badge of all his tribe), was often looked upon as a very improper guest for the holy resting-places at which the company usually halted, and was not in consequence admitted
within even the outer circuit of their walls save with extreme
reluctance. This was very embarrassing; for, on the one
hand, it was necessary to keep in good humor a man who
was possessed of the secret of their expedition ; and on the
other, Quentin deemed it indispensable to maintain a vigilant
though secret watch on Hayraddin's conduct, in order that,
as far as might be, he should hold no communication with
any one without being observed. This, of course, was impossible if the Bohemian was lodged without the precincts
of the convent at which they stopped, and Durward could
not help thinking that Hayraddin was desirous of bringing
about this latter arrangement, for, instead of keeping himself still and quiet in the quarters allotted to him, his conversation, tricks and songs were at the same time so entertaining to the novices and younger brethren and so unedifying in
the opinion of the seniors of the fraternity, that, in more
cases than one, it required all the authority, supported by
threats, which Quentin could exert over him to restrain his
irreverent and untimeous jocularity, and all the interest he
could make with the superiors to prevent the heathen hound
from being thrust out of doors. He succeeded, however, by
the adroit manner in which he apologized for the acts of indecorum committed by their attendant, and the skill with
which he hinted the hope of his being brought to a better
sense of principles and behavior by the neighborhood of holy
relics, consecrated buildings, and above all, of men dedicated
to religion.

But upon the tenth or twelfth day of their journey, after
they had entered Flanders and were approaching the town
of Namur, all the efforts of Quentin became inadequate to
suppress the consequences of the scandal given by his heathen
guide. The scene was a Franciscan convent, and of a strict

and reformed order, and the prior a man who afterwards died in the odor of sanctity. After rather more than the usual scruples, which were indeed in such a case to be expected, had been surmounted, the obnoxious Bohemian at length obtained quarters in an outhouse inhabited by a lay brother who acted as gardener. The ladies retired to their apartment, as usual, and the prior, who chanced to have some distant alliances and friends in Scotland, and who was fond of hearing foreigners tell of their native countries, invited Quentin, with whose mien and conduct he seemed much pleased, to a slight monastic refection in his own cell. Finding the father a man of intelligence, Quentin did not neglect the opportunity of making himself acquainted with the state of affairs in the country of Liege, of which, during the last two days of their journey, he had heard such reports as made him very apprehensive for the security of his charge during the remainder of their route, nay, even of the bishop's power to protect them when they should be safely conducted to his residence. The replies of the prior were not very consolatory.

He said that "The people of Liege were wealthy burghers who, like Jeshurun of old, had waxed fat and kicked ; that they were uplifted in heart because of their wealth and their privileges ; that they had divers disputes with the Duke of Burgundy, their liege lord, upon the subject of imposts and immunities ; and that they had repeatedly broken out into open mutiny, whereat the Duke was so much incensed, as being a man of hot and fiery nature, that he had sworn by St. George, on the next provocation, he would make the city of Liege like to the desolation of Babylon and the downfall of Tyre, a hissing and a reproach to the whole territory of Flanders."

"And he is a prince, by all report, likely to keep such a vow," said Quentin, "so the men of Liege will probably beware how they give him occasion."

"It were to be so hoped," said the prior ; "and such are the prayers of the godly in the land, who would not that the blood of the citizens were poured forth like water, and that they should perish, even as utter castaways, ere they make their peace with Heaven. Also the good bishop labors night and day to preserve peace, as well becometh a servant of the altar ; for it is written in Holy Scripture, *Beati pacifici.* But——" here the good prior stopped with a deep sigh.

Quentin modestly urged the great importance of which it was to the ladies whom he attended to have some assured information respecting the internal state of the country, and what an act of Christian charity it would be if the worthy and reverend father would enlighten them upon that subject.

" It is one," said the prior, " on which no man speaks with willingness ; for those who speak evil of the powerful, *etiam in cubiculo,* may find that a winged thing shall carry the matter to his ears. Nevertheless, to render you, who seem an ingenuous youth, and your ladies, who are devout votaresses accomplishing a holy pilgrimage, the little service that is in my power, I will be plain with you."

He then looked cautiously round, and lowered his voice, as if afraid of being overheard.

" The people of Liege," he said, " are privily instigated to their frequent mutinies by men of Belial, who pretend, but, as I hope, falsely, to have commission to that effect from our Most Christian King, whom, however, I hold to deserve that term better than were consistent with his thus disturbing the peace of a neighboring state. Yet so it is, that his name is freely used by those who uphold and inflame the discontents at Liege. There is, moreover, in the land a nobleman of good descent and fame in warlike affairs, but otherwise, so to speak, *lapis offensionis et petra scandali*—a stumbling-block of offense to the countries of Burgundy and Flanders. His name is William de la Marck."

" Called William with the Beard ? " said the young Scot, " or the Wild Boar of Ardennes ? "

" And rightly so called, my son," said the prior ; " because he is as the wild boar of the forest, which treadeth down with his hoofs and rendeth with his tusks. And he hath formed to himself a band of more than a thousand men, all, like himself, contemners of civil and ecclesiastical authority, and holds himself independent of the Duke of Burgundy, and maintains himself and his followers by rapine and wrong, wrought without distinction upon churchmen and laymen. *Imposuit manus in Christos Domini :* he hath stretched forth his hand upon the Anointed of the Lord, regardless of what is written—' Touch not mine Anointed, and do my prophets no wrong.' Even to our poor house did he send for sums of gold and sums of silver as a ransom for our lives and those of our brethren ; to which we returned a Latin supplication, stating our inability to answer his demand, and exhorting him in the words of the preacher, *Ne moliaris amico tuo malum, cum habet in te fiduciam.* Nevertheless, this Gulielmus Barbatus, this William de la

Marck, as completely ignorant of humane letters as of humanity itself, replied, in his ridiculous jargon, ' *Si non payatis, brulabo monasterium vestrum.*'"*

" Of which rude Latin, however, you, my good father," said the youth, " were at no loss to conceive the meaning."

" Alas! my son," said the prior, " fear and necessity are shrewd interpreters ; and we were obliged to melt down the silver vessels of our altar to satisfy the rapacity of this cruel chief. May Heaven requite it to him sevenfold ! *Pereat improbus. Amen—amen, anathema esto !* "

" I marvel," said Quentin, " that the Duke of Burgundy, who is so strong and powerful, doth not bait this boar to purpose, of whose ravages I have already heard so much."

" Alas ! my son," said the prior, " the Duke Charles is now at Péronne, assembling his captains of hundreds and his captains of thousands, to make war against France ; and thus, while Heaven hath set discord between the hearts of those great princes, the country is misused by such subordinate oppressors. But it is in evil time that the Duke neglects the cure of these internal gangrenes ; for this William de la Marck hath of late entertained open communication with Rouslaer and Pavillon, the chiefs of the discontented at Liege, and it is to be feared he will soon stir them up to some desperate enterprise."

" But the Bishop of Liege," said Quentin, " he hath still power enough to subdue this disquieted and turbulent spirit, hath he not, good father ? Your answer to this question concerns me much."

" The bishop, my child," replied the prior, " hath the sword of St. Peter as well as the keys. He hath power as a secular prince, and he hath the protection of the mighty house of Burgundy ; he hath also spiritual authority as a prelate, and he supports both with a reasonable force of good soldiers and men-at-arms. This William de la Marck was bred in his household, and bound to him by many benefits. But he gave vent, even in the court of the bishop, to his fierce and bloodthirsty temper, and was expelled thence for a homicide, committed on one of the bishop's chief domestics. From thenceforward, being banished from the good prelate's presence, he hath been his constant and unrelenting foe ; and now, I grieve to say, he hath girded his loins and strengthened his horn against him."

* A similar story is told of the Duke of Vendôme, who answered in this sort of macaronic Latin the classical expostulations of a German convent against the imposition of a contribution.

"You consider, then, the situation of the worthy prelate as being dangerous?" said Quentin, very anxiously.

"Alas! my son," said the good Franciscan, "what or who is there in this weary wilderness whom we may not hold as in danger? But Heaven forefend I should speak of the reverend prelate as one whose peril is imminent. He has much treasure, true counselors, and brave soldiers; and, moreover, a messenger who passed hither to the eastward yesterday saith that the Duke of Burgundy hath despatched, upon the bishop's request, an hundred men-at-arms to his assistance. This reinforcement, with the retinue belonging to each lance, are enough to deal with William de la Marck, on whose name be sorrow! Amen."

At this crisis their conversation was interrupted by the sacristan, who, in a voice almost inarticulate with anger, accused the Bohemian of having practised the most abominable arts of delusion among the younger brethren. He had added to their nightly meal cups of a heady and intoxicating cordial of ten times the strength of the most powerful wine, under which several of the fraternity had succumbed; and, indeed, although the sacristan had been strong to resist its influence, they might yet see, from his inflamed countenance and thick speech, that even he, the accuser himself, was in some degree affected by this unhallowed potation. Moreover, the Bohemian had sung songs of worldly vanity and impure pleasures; he had derided the cord of St. Francis, made jest of his miracles, and termed his votaries fools and lazy knaves. Lastly, he had practised palmistry, and foretold to the young Father Cherubin that he was beloved by a beautiful lady, who should make him father to a thriving boy.

The father prior listened to these complaints for some time in silence, as struck with mute horror by their enormous atrocity. When the sacristan had concluded, he rose up, descended to the court of the convent, and ordered the lay brethren, on pain of the worst consequences of spiritual disobedience, to beat Hayraddin out of the sacred precincts with their broom-staves and cart-whips.

This sentence was executed accordingly, in the presence of Quentin Durward, who, however vexed at the occurrence, easily saw that his interference would be of no avail.

The discipline inflicted upon the delinquent, notwithstanding the exhortations of the superior, was more ludicrous than formidable. The Bohemian ran hither and thither through the court, amongst the clamor of voices and noise of blows, some of which reached him not, because purposely misaimed ; others, sincerely designed for his person, were eluded by his activity ; and the few that fell upon his back and shoulders he took without either complaint or reply. The noise and riot was the greater, that the inexperienced cudgel-players, among whom Hayraddin ran the gauntlet, hit each other more frequently than they did him ; till at length, desirous of ending a scene which was more scandalous than edifying, the prior commanded the wicket to be flung open, and the Bohemian, darting through it with the speed of lightning, fled forth into the moonlight.

During this scene, a suspicion which Durward had formerly entertained recurred with additional strength. Hayraddin had, that very morning, promised him more modest and discreet behavior than he was wont to exhibit when they rested in a convent on their journey ; yet he had broken his engagement, and had been even more offensively obstreperous than usual. Something probably lurked under this ; for whatever were the Bohemian's deficiencies, he lacked neither sense nor, when he pleased, self-command ; and might it not be probable that he wished to hold some communication, either with his own horde or some one else, from which he was debarred in the course of the day by the vigilance with which he was watched by Quentin, and had recourse to this stratagem in order to get himself turned out of the convent ?

No sooner did this suspicion dart once more through Durward's mind than, alert as he always was in his motions, he resolved to follow his cudgeled guide, and observe, secretly if possible, how he disposed of himself. Accordingly, when the Bohemian fled, as already mentioned, out at the gate of the convent, Quentin, hastily explaining to the prior the necessity of keeping sight of his guide, followed in pursuit of him.

CHAPTER XVII

THE ESPIED SPY

What, the rue ranger? and spied spy? Hands off—
You are for no such rustics.
    BEN JONSON'S *Tale of Robin Hood.*

WHEN Quentin sallied from the convent, he could mark the precipitate retreat of the Bohemian, whose dark figure was seen in the fair moonlight, flying with the speed of a flogged hound quite through the street of the little village, and across the level meadow that lay beyond.

"My friend runs fast," said Quentin to himself; "but he must run faster yet to escape the fleetest foot that ever pressed the heather of Glen Houlakin."

Being fortunately without his cloak and armor, the Scottish mountaineer was at liberty to put forth a speed which was unrivaled in his own glens, and which, notwithstanding the rate at which the Bohemian ran, was likely soon to bring his pursuer up with him. This was not, however, Quentin's object; for he considered it more essential to watch Hayraddin's motions than to interrupt them. He was the rather led to this by the steadiness with which the Bohemian directed his course; and which continuing, even after the impulse of the violent expulsion had subsided, seemed to indicate that his career had some more certain goal for its object than could have suggested itself to a person unexpectedly turned out of good quarters when midnight was approaching, to seek a new place of repose. He never even looked behind him; and consequently Durward was enabled to follow him unobserved. At length the Bohemian having traversed the meadow, and attained the side of a little stream, the banks of which were clothed with alders and willows, Quentin observed that he stood still, and blew a low note on his horn, which was answered by a whistle at some little distance.

"This is a rendezvous," thought Quentin; "but how shall I come near enough to overhear the import of what passes? The sound of my steps, and the rustling of the boughs through which I must force my passage, will betray me, unless I am cautious. I will stalk them, by St. Andrew, as if they were Glen Isla deer ; they shall learn that I have not conned woodcraft for naught. Yonder they meet, the two shadows—and two of them there are—odds against me if I am discovered, and if their purpose be unfriendly, as is much to be doubted. And then the Countess Isabelle loses her poor friend ! Well, and he were not worthy to be called such, if he were not ready to meet a dozen in her behalf. Have I not crossed swords with Dunois, the best knight in France, and shall I fear a tribe of yonder vagabonds ? Pshaw ! God and St. Andrew to friend, they will find me both stout and wary."

Thus resolving, and with a degree of caution taught him by his silvan habits, our friend descended into the channel of the little stream, which varied in depth, sometimes scarce covering his shoes, sometimes coming up to his knees, and so crept along, his form concealed by the boughs overhanging the bank, and his steps unheard amid the ripple of the water. (We have ourselves, in the days of yore, thus approached the nest of the wakeful raven.) In this manner, the Scot drew near unperceived, until he distinctly heard the voices of those who were the subject of his observation, though he could not distinguish the words. Being at this time under the drooping branches of a magnificent weeping willow, which almost swept the surface of the water, he caught hold of one of its boughs, by the assistance of which, exerting at once much agility, dexterity, and strength, he raised himself up into the body of the tree, and sat, secure from discovery, among the central branches.

From this situation he could discover that the person with whom Hayraddin was now conversing was one of his own tribe, and, at the same time, he perceived, to his great disappointment, that no approximation could enable him to comprehend their language, which was totally unknown to him. They laughed much ; and as Hayraddin made a sign of skipping about, and ended by rubbing his shoulder with his hand, Durward had no doubt that he was relating the story of the bastinading which he had sustained previous to his escape from the convent.

On a sudden, a whistle was again heard in the distance, which was once more answered by a low tone or two of Hayraddin's horn. Presently afterwards, a tall, stout, soldierly-looking man, a strong contrast in point of thews and sinews to the small and slender-limbed Bohemians, made his appearance. He had a broad baldric over his shoulder, which sustained a sword that hung almost across his person ; his hose were much slashed, through which slashes was drawn silk or tiffany of various colors ; they were tied by at least five hundred points or strings, made of ribbon, to the tight buff jacket which he wore, and the right sleeve of which displayed a silver boar's head, the crest of his captain. A very small hat sat jauntily on one side of his head, from which descended a quantity of curled hair, which fell on each side of a broad face, and mingled with as broad a beard, about four inches long. He held a long lance in his hand ; and his whole equipment was that of one of the German adventurers, who were known by the name of *lanzknechts,* in English " spearmen," who constituted a formidable part of the infantry of the period. These mercenaries were, of course, a fierce and rapacious soldiery, and having an idle tale current among themselves that a *lanzknecht* was refused admittance into Heaven on account of his vices, and into Hell on the score of his tumultuous, mutinous, and insubordinate disposition, they manfully acted as if they neither sought the one nor eschewed the other.

" *Donner and Blitz!* " was his first salutation, in a sort of German-French, which we can only imperfectly imitate, " why have you kept me dancing in attendance dis dree nights ? "

" I could not see you sooner, Meinherr," said Hayraddin, very submissively : " there is a young Scot, with as quick an eye as the wild-cat, who watches my least motions. He suspects me already, and, should he find his suspicion confirmed, I were a dead man on the spot, and he would carry back the women into France again."

" *Was henker!* " said the lanzknecht ; " we are three— we will attack them to-morrow, and carry the women off without going farther. You said the two valets were cowards ; you and your comrade may manage them, and the *Teufel* shall hold me, but I match your Scots wild-cat."

" You will find that foolhardy," said Hayraddin ; " for, besides that we ourselves count not much in fighting, this spark hath matched himself with the best knight in France, and come off with honor : I have seen those who saw him press Dunois hard enough."

" *Hagel and sturmwetter!* It is but your cowardice that speaks," said the German soldier.

" I am no more a coward than yourself," said Hayraddin ; " but my trade is not fighting. If you keep the appointment

where it was laid, it is well ; if not, I guide them safely to
the bishop's palace, and William de la Marck may easily possess himself of them there, provided he is half as strong as
he pretended a week since."

"*Potz tausend !* " said the soldier, " we are as strong and
stronger ; but we hear of a hundred of the lances of Burgundy—*das ist,* see you, five men to a lance do make five
hundreds, and then hold me the devil, they will be fainer to
seek for us than we to seek for them ; for *der bischoff* hath a
goot force on footing—ay, indeed ! "

" You must then hold to the ambuscade at the Cross of the
Three Kings, or give up the adventure," said the Bohemian.

" *Geb* up—*geb* up the adventure of the rich bride for our
noble *hauptmann.   Teufel !* I will charge through hell first.
Mein soul, we will be all princes and *hertzogs,* whom they
call dukes, and we will hab a snab at the *weinkeller,* and at
the mouldy French crowns, and it may be at the pretty
graces, too, when He with de Beard is weary on them."

" The ambuscade at the Cross of the Three Kings then
still holds ? " said the Bohemian.

" *Mein Gott,* ay,—you will swear to bring them there ; and
when they are on their knees before the cross and down from
off their horses, which all men do, except such black heathens
as thou, we will make in on them, and they are ours."

" Ay, but I promised this piece of necessary villainy only
on one condition," said Hayraddin. "I will not have a
hair of the young man's head touched. If you swear this to
me, by your Three Dead Men of Cologne, I will swear to
you by the Seven Night Walkers, that I will serve you truly
as to the rest. And if you break your oath, the Night
Walkers shall wake you seven nights from your sleep, between night and morning, and, on the eighth, they shall
strangle and devour you."

" But, *donner and hagel,* what need you be so curious about
the life of this boy, who is neither your bloot nor kin ? " said
the German.

" No matter for that, honest Heinrich ; some men have
pleasure in cutting throats, some in keeping them whole.
So swear to me that you will spare him life and limb, or, by
the bright star Aldebaran, this matter shall go no further.
Swear, and by the Three Kings, as you call them, of Cologne;
I know you care for no other oath."

"*Du bist ein comischer mann,*" said the lanzknecht, "I
swear——"

" Not yet," said the Bohemian. " Faces about, brave

lanzknecht, and look to the east, else the kings may not hear you."

The soldier took the oath in the manner prescribed, and then declared that he would be in readiness, observing the place was quite convenient, being scarce five miles from their present leaguer.

" But, were it not making sure work to have a *fahnlein* of riders on the other road, by the left side of the inn, which might trap them if they go that way ? "

The Bohemian considered a moment, and then answered, " No ; the appearance of their troops in that direction might alarm the garrison of Namur, and then they would have a doubtful fight, instead of assured success. Besides, they shall travel on the right bank of the Maes, for I can guide them which way I will ; for, sharp as this same Scottish mountaineer is, he hath never asked any one's advice save mine upon the direction of their route. Undoubtedly, I was assigned to him by an assured friend, whose words no man mistrusts till they come to know him a little."

" Hark ye, friend Hayraddin," said the soldier, " I would ask you somewhat. You and your *bruder* were, as you say yourself, *gross sternendeuter*, that is, star-lookers and *geister-seers*. Now, what *henker* was it made you not foresee him, your *bruder* Zamet, to be hanged ? "

" I will tell you, Heinrich," said Hayraddin ; " if I could have known my brother was such a fool as to tell the counsel of King Louis to Duke Charles of Burgundy, I could have foretold his death as sure as I can foretell fair weather in July. Louis hath both ears and hands at the court of Burgundy, and Charles's counselors love the chink of French gold as well as thou dost the clatter of a wine-pot. But fare thee well, and keep appointment ; I must await my early Scot a bow-shot without the gate of the den of the lazy swine yonder, else will he think me about some excursion which bodes no good to the success of his journey."

" Take a draught of comfort first," said the lanzknecht, tendering him a flask ; " but I forget, thou art beast enough to drink nothing but water, like a vile vassal of Mahound and Termagund."

" Thou art thyself a vassal of the wine-measure and the flagon," said the Bohemian. " I marvel not that thou art only trusted with the bloodthirsty and violent part of execu-ting what better heads have devised. He must drink no wine who would know the thoughts of others or hide his own. But why preach to thee, who hast a thirst as eternal as **a**

13

sandbank in Arabia ? Fare thee well. Take my comrade Tuisco with thee ; his appearance about the monastery may breed suspicion."

The two worthies parted, after each had again pledged himself to keep the rendezvous at the Cross of the Three Kings.

Quentin Durward watched until they were out of sight, and then descended from his place of concealment, his heart throbbing at the narrow escape which he and his fair charge had made—if, indeed, it could yet be achieved—from a deep-laid plan of villainy. Afraid, on his return to the monastery, of stumbling upon Hayraddin, he made a long detour, at the expense of traversing some very rough ground, and was thus enabled to return to his asylum on a different point from that by which he left it.

On the route, he communed earnestly with himself concerning the safest plan to be pursued. He had formed the resolution, when he first heard Hayraddin avow his treachery, to put him to death so soon as the conference broke up, and his companions were at a sufficient distance ; but when he heard the Bohemian express so much interest in saving his own life, he felt it would be ungrateful to execute upon him, in its rigor, the punishment his treachery had deserved. He therefore resolved to spare his life, and even, if possible, still to use his services as a guide, under such precautions as should ensure the security of the precious charge, to the preservation of which his own life was internally devoted.

But whither were they to turn ? The Countesses of Croye could neither obtain shelter in Burgundy, from which they had fled, nor in France, from which they had been in a manner expelled. The violence of Duke Charles in the one country was scarcely more to be feared than the cold and tyrannical policy of King Louis in the other. After deep thought, Durward could form no better or safer plan for their security than that, evading the ambuscade, they should take the road to Liege by the left hand of the Maes, and throw themselves, as the ladies originally designed, upon the protection of the excellent bishop. That prelate's will to protect them could not be doubted, and, if reinforced by this Burgundian party of men-at-arms, he might be considered as having the power. At any rate, if the dangers to which he was exposed from the hostility of William de la Marck, and from the troubles in the city of Liege, appeared imminent, he would still be able to protect the unfortunate ladies until they could be despatched to Germany with a suitable escort.

To sum up this reasoning—for when is a mental argument conducted without some reference to selfish considerations ? —Quentin imagined that the death or captivity to which King Louis had, in cold blood, consigned him set him at liberty from his engagements to the crown of France ; which, therefore, it was his determined purpose to renounce. The Bishop of Liege was likely, he concluded, to need soldiers, and he thought that, by the interposition of his fair friends who now, especially the elder countess, treated him with much familiarity, he might get some command, and perhaps might have the charge of conducting the Ladies of Croye to some place more safe than the neighborhood of Liege. And, so conclude, the ladies had talked, although almost in a sort of jest, of raising the countess's own vassals, and, as others did in those stormy times, fortifying her strong castle against all assailants whatever ; they had jestingly asked Quentin, whether he would accept the perilous office of their seneschal ; and, on his embracing the office with ready glee and devotion, they had, in the same spirit, permitted him to kiss both their hands on that confidential and honorable appointment. Nay, he thought that the hand of the Countess Isabelle, one of the best formed and most beautiful to which true vassal ever did such homage, trembled when his lips rested on it a moment longer than ceremony required, and that some confusion appeared on her cheek and in her eye as she withdrew it. Something might come of all this ; and what brave man, at Quentin Durward's age, but would gladly have taken the thoughts which it awakened into the considerations which were to determine his conduct ?

This point settled, he had next to consider in what degree he was to use the further guidance of the faithless Bohemian. He had renounced his first thought of killing him in the wood, and if he took another guide and dismissed him alive, it would be sending the traitor to the camp of William de la Marck with intelligence of their motions. He thought of taking the prior into his counsels, and requesting him to detain the Bohemian by force until they should have time to reach the bishop's castle ; but, on reflection, he dared not hazard such a proposition to one who was timid both as an old man and a friar, who held the safety of his convent the most important object of his duty, and who trembled at the mention of the Wild Boar of Ardennes.

At length Durward settled a plan of operation, on which

he could the better reckon, as the execution rested entirely upon himself ; and, in the cause in which he was engaged, he felt himself capable of everything. With a firm and bold heart, though conscious of the dangers of his situation, Quentin might be compared to one walking under a load, of the weight of which he is conscious, but which yet is not beyond his strength and power of endurance. Just as his plan was determined, he reached the convent.

Upon knocking gently at the gate, a brother, considerately stationed for that purpose by the prior, opened it, and acquainted him that the brethren were to be engaged in the choir till daybreak, praying Heaven to forgive to the community the various scandals which had that evening taken place among them.

The worthy friar offered Quentin permission to attend their devotions ; but his clothes were in such a wet condition that the young Scot was obliged to decline the opportunity, and request permission instead to sit by the kitchen fire, in order to his attire being dried before morning, as he was particularly desirous that the Bohemian, when they should next meet, should observe no traces of his having been abroad during the night. The friar not only granted his request, but afforded him his own company, which fell in very happily with the desire which Durward had to obtain information concerning the two routes which he had heard mentioned by the Bohemian in his conversation with the lanzknecht. The friar, entrusted upon many occasions with the business of the convent abroad, was the person in the fraternity best qualified to afford him the information he requested ; but observed that, as true pilgrims, it became the duty of the ladies whom Quentin escorted to take the road on the right side of the Maes, by the Cross of the Kings where the blessed relics of Caspar, Melchior, and Balthasar, as the Catholic Church has named the eastern Magi who came to Bethlehem with their offerings, had rested as they were transported to Cologne, and on which spot they had wrought many miracles.

Quentin replied that the ladies were determined to observe all the holy stations with the utmost punctuality, and would certainly visit that of the Cross either in going to or returning from Cologne, but they had heard reports that the road by the right side of the river was at present rendered unsafe by the soldiers of the ferocious William de la Marck.

"Now may Heaven forbid," said Father Francis, " that the Wild Boar of Ardennes should again make his lair so near us ! Nevertheless, the broad Maes will be a good barrier betwixt us, even should it so chance."

" But it will be no barrier between my ladies and the marauder, should we cross the river and travel on the right bank," answered the Scot.

" Heaven will protect its own, young man," said the friar ; " for it were hard to think that the kings of yonder blessed city of Cologne, who will not endure that a Jew or infidel should even enter within the walls of their town, could be oblivious enough to permit their worshipers, coming to their shrine as true pilgrims, to be plundered and misused by such a miscreant dog as this Boar of Ardennes, who is worse than a whole desert of Saracen heathens and all the ten tribes of Israel to boot."

Whatever reliance Quentin, as a sincere Catholic, was bound to rest upon the special protection of Melchior, Caspar, and Balthasar, he could not but recollect that, the pilgrim habits of the ladies being assumed out of mere earthly policy, he and his charge could scarcely expect their countenance on the present occasion ; and therefore resolved, as far as possible, to avoid placing the ladies in any predicament where miraculous interposition might be necessary ; whilst, in the simplicity of his good faith, he himself vowed a pilgrimage to the Three Kings of Cologne in his own proper person, provided the simulate design of those over whose safety he was now watching should be permitted by those reasonable and royal, as well as sainted, personages to attain the desired effect.

That he might enter into this obligation with all solemnity, he requested the friar to show him into one of the various chapels which opened from the main body of the church of the convent, where, upon his knees, and with sincere devotion, he ratified the vow which he had made internally. The distant sound of the choir, the solemnity of the deep and dead hour which he had chosen for this act of devotion, the effect of the glimmering lamp with which the little Gothic building was illuminated, all contributed to throw Quentin's mind into the state when it most readily acknowledges its human frailty, and seeks that supernatural aid and protection which, in every worship, must be connected with repentance for past sins and resolutions of future amendment. That the object of his devotion was misplaced was not the fault of Quentin ; and, its purpose being sincere, we can scarce suppose it unacceptable to the only true Deity, who regards the motives and not the forms of prayer, and in whose eyes the sincere devotion of a heathen is more estimable than the specious hypocrisy of a Pharisee.

Having commended himself and his helpless companions to the saints and to the keeping of Providence, Quentin at length retired to rest, leaving the friar much edified by the depth and sincerity of his devotion.

CHAPTER XVIII

PALMISTRY

When many a merry tale and many a song
Cheer'd the rough road, we wish'd the rough road long.
The rough road, then, returning in a round,
Mock'd our enchanted steps, for all was fairy ground.
                                        SAMUEL JOHNSON.

BY peep of day Quentin Durward had forsaken his little
cell, had roused the sleepy grooms, and, with more than his
wonted care, seen that everything was prepared for the day's
journey. Girths and bridles, the horse furniture, and the
shoes of the horses themselves, were carefully inspected with
his own eyes, that there might be as little chance as possible
of the occurrence of any of those casualties which, petty as
they seem, often interrupt or disconcert traveling. The
horses were also, under his own inspection, carefully fed, so
as to render them fit for a long day's journey, or, if that
should be necessary, for a hasty flight.

Quentin then betook himself to his own chamber, armed
himself with unusual care, and belted on his sword with the
feeling at once of approaching danger and of stern determination to dare it to the uttermost.

These generous feelings gave him a loftiness of step and a
dignity of manner which the Ladies of Croye had not yet
observed in him, though they had been highly pleased and
interested by the grace, yet naïveté, of his general behavior
and conversation, and the mixture of shrewd intelligence
which naturally belonged to him, with the simplicity arising
from his secluded education and distant country. He let
them understand that it would be necessary that they should
prepare for their journey this morning rather earlier than
usual ; and, accordingly, they left the convent immediately
after a morning repast, for which, as well as the other hospital-
ities of the house, the ladies made acknowledgment by a don-
ation to the altar befitting rather their rank than their appearance. But this excited no suspicion, as they were supposed
to be Englishwomen ; and the attribute of superior wealth
attached at that time to the insular character as strongly as
in our own day.

The prior blessed them as they mounted to depart, and congratulated Quentin on the absence of his heathen guide, "for," said the venerable man, "better stumble in the path than be upheld by the arm of a thief or robber."

Quentin was not quite of his opinion ; for, dangerous as he knew the Bohemian to be, he thought he could use his services, and at the same time baffle his treasonable purpose, now that he saw clearly to what it tended. But his anxiety upon this subject was soon at an end, for the little cavalcade was not an hundred yards from the monastery and the village before Maugrabin joined it, riding as usual on his little active and wild-looking jennet. Their road led them along the side of the same brook where Quentin had overheard the mysterious conference of the preceding evening, and Hayraddin had not long rejoined them ere they passed under the very willow-tree which had afforded Durward the means of concealment when he became an unsuspected hearer of what then passed betwixt that false guide and the lanzknecht.

The recollections which the spot brought back stirred Quentin to enter abruptly into conversation with his guide, whom hitherto he had scarce spoken to.

"Where hast thou found night-quarter, thou profane knave ?" said the Scot.

"Your wisdom may may guess by looking on my gaberdine," answered the Bohemian, pointing to his dress, which was covered with the seeds of hay.

"A good hay-stack," said Quentin, "is a convenient bed for an astrologer, and a much better than a heathen scoffer at our blessed religion and its ministers ever deserves."

"It suited my Klepper better than me, though," said Hayraddin, patting his horse on the neck, "for he had food and shelter at the same time. The old bald fools turned him loose, as if a wise man's horse could have infected with wit or sagacity a whole convent of asses. Lucky that Klepper knows my whistle, and follows me as truly as a hound, or we had never met again, and you in your turn might have whistled for a guide."

"I have told thee more than once," said Durward, sternly, "to restrain thy ribaldry when thou chancest to be in worthy men's company, a thing which, I believe, hath rarely happened to thee in thy life before now ; and I promise thee that, did I hold thee as faithless a guide as I esteem thee a blasphemous and worthless caitiff, my Scottish dirk and thy heathenish heart had ere now been acquainted, although the doing such a deed were as ignoble as the sticking of swine."

"A wild boar is near akin to a sow," said the Bohemian, without flinching from the sharp look with which Quentin regarded him or altering, in the slightest degree, the caustic indifference which he affected in his language; "and many men," he subjoined, "find both pride, pleasure, and profit in sticking them."

Astonished at the man's ready confidence, and uncertain whether he did not know more of his own history and feelings than was pleasant for him to converse upon, Quentin broke off a conversation in which he had gained no advantage over Maugrabin, and fell back to his accustomed post beside the ladies.

We have already observed that a considerable degree of familiarity had begun to establish itself between them. The elder countess treated him, being once well assured of the nobility of his birth, like a favored equal ; and though her niece showed her regard to their protector less freely, yet, under every disadvantage of bashfulness and timidity, Quentin thought he could plainly perceive that his company and conversation were not by any means indifferent to her.

Nothing gives such life and soul to youthful gaiety as the consciousness that it is successfully received ; and Quentin had accordingly, during the former period of their journey, amused his fair charge with the liveliness of his conversation, and the songs and tales of his country, the former of which he sung in his native language, while his efforts to render the latter into his foreign and imperfect French gave rise to a hundred little mistakes and errors of speech, as diverting as the narratives themselves. But on this anxious morning he rode beside the Ladies of Croye without any of his usual attempts to amuse them, and they could not help observing his silence as something remarkable.

"Our young companion has seen a wolf," said the Lady Hamelin, alluding to an ancient superstition,* "and he has lost his tongue in consequence."

"To say I had tracked a fox were nearer the mark," thought Quentin, but gave the reply no utterance.

"Are you well, Seignior Quentin ?" said the Countess Isabelle, in a tone of interest at which she herself blushed, while she felt that it was something more than the distance between them warranted.

"He hath sat up carousing with the jolly friars, and the

* See Wolf Superstition. Note 27.

Lady Hameline. The Scots are like the Germans, **who spend all their mirth** over the *Rheinwein,* and bring only their staggering steps to the dance in the evening, and their aching heads to the ladies' bower in the morning."

" Nay, gentle ladies," said Quentin, " I deserve not your reproach. The good friars were at their devotions almost all night ; and for myself, my drink was barely a cup of their thinnest and most ordinary wine."

" It is the badness of his fare that has put him out of humor," said the Countess Isabelle. " Cheer up, Seignior Quentin ; and should we ever visit my ancient Castle of Bracquemont together, if I myself should stand your cupbearer and hand it to you, you shall have a generous cup of wine that the like never grew upon the vines of Hochheim or Johannisberg."

" A glass of water, noble lady, from *your* hand——" Thus far did Quentin begin, but his voice trembled ; and Isabelle continued, as if she had been insensible of the tenderness of the accentuation, upon the personal pronoun.

" The wine was stocked in the deep vaults of Bracquemont by my great-grandfather, the Rhinegrave Godfrey," said the Countess Isabelle.

" Who won the hand of her great-grandmother," interjected the Lady Hameline, interrupting her niece, " by proving himself the best son of chivalry, at the great tournament of Strasbourg. Ten knights were slain in the lists. But those days are over, and no one now thinks of encountering peril for the sake of honor, or to relieve distressed beauty."

To this speech, which was made in the tone in which a modern beauty, whose charms are rather on the wane, may be heard to condemn the rudeness of the present age, Quentin took upon him to reply, " That there was no lack of that chivalry which the Lady Hameline seemed to consider as extinct, and that, were it eclipsed everywhere else, it would still glow in the bosoms of the Scottish gentlemen."

" Hear him !" said the Lady Hameline ; " he would have us believe that in his cold and bleak country still lives the noble fire which has decayed in France and Germany ! The poor youth is like a Swiss mountaineer, mad with partiality to his native land ; he will next tell us of the vines and olives of Scotland."

" No, madam," said Durward ; " of the wine and the oil of our mountains I can say little, more than that our swords can compel these rich productions as tribute from our wealthier neighbors. But for the unblemished faith and unfaded honor of Scotland, I must now put to the proof how far you can repose trust in them, however mean the individual who can offer nothing more as a pledge of your safety."

"You speak mysteriously—you know of some pressing and present danger," said the Lady Hameline.

"I have read it in his eye for this hour past!" exclaimed the Lady Isabelle, clasping her hands. "Sacred Virgin, what will become of us?"

"Nothing, I hope, but what you would desire," answered Durward. "And now I am compelled to ask—gentle ladies, can you trust me?"

"Trust you!" answered the Countess Hameline, "certainly. But why the question? Or how far do you ask our confidence?"

"I, on my part," said the Countess Isabelle, "trust you implicitly and without condition. If you can deceive us, Quentin, I will no more look for truth, save in Heaven."

"Gentle lady," replied Durward, highly gratified, "you do me but justice. My object is to alter our route, by proceeding directly by the left bank of the Maes to Liege, instead of crossing at Namur. This differs from the order assigned by King Louis and the instructions given to the guide. But I heard news in the monastery of marauders on the right bank of the Maes, and of the march of Burgundian soldiers to suppress them. Both circumstances alarm me for your safety. Have I your permission so far to deviate from the route of your journey?"

"My ample and full permission," answered the younger lady.

"Cousin," said the Lady Hameline, "I believe with you that the youth means us well; but bethink you—we transgress the instructions of King Louis, so positively iterated."

"And why should we regard his instructions?" said the Lady Isabelle. "I am, I thank Heaven for it, no subject of his; and, as a suppliant, he has abused the confidence he induced me to repose in him. I would not dishonor this young gentleman by weighing his word for an instant against the injunctions of yonder crafty and selfish despot."

"Now, may God bless you for that very word, lady," said Quentin, joyously; "and if I deserve not the trust it expresses, tearing with wild horses in this life, and eternal tortures in the next, were e'en too good for my deserts."

So saying, he spurred his horse and rejoined the Bohemian. This worthy seemed of a remarkably passive if not a forgiving, temper. Injury or threat never dwelt, or at least seemed not to dwell, on his recollection ; and he entered into the conversation which Durward presently commenced just as if there had been no unkindly word betwixt them in the course of the morning.

" The dog," thought the Scot, "snarls not now, because he intends to clear scores with me at once and forever, when he can snatch me by the very throat ; but we will try for once whether we cannot foil a traitor at his own weapons. Honest Hayraddin," he said, "thou hast traveled with us for ten days, yet hast never shown us a specimen of your skill in fortune-telling ; which you are, nevertheless, so fond of practising, that you must needs display your gifts in every convent at which we stop, at the risk of being repaid by a night's lodging under a hay-stack."

"You have never asked me for a specimen of my skill," said the gipsy. "You are like the rest of the world, contented to ridicule those mysteries which they do not understand."

" Give me then a present proof of your skill," said Quentin ; and, ungloving his hand, he held it out to the Zingaro.

Hayraddin carefully regarded all the lines which crossed each other on the Scotchman's palm, and noted, with equally scrupulous attention, the little risings or swellings at the roots of the fingers, which were then believed as intimately connected with the disposition, habits, and fortunes of the individual as the organs of the brain are pretended to be in our own time.

" Here is a hand," said Hayraddin, " which speaks of toils endured and dangers encountered. I read in it an early acquaintance with the hilt of the sword ; and yet some acquaintance also with the clasps of the mass-book."

" This of my past life you may have learned elsewhere," said Quentin ; " tell me something of the future."

" This line from the hill of Venus," said the Bohemian, "not broken off abruptly, but attending and accompanying the line of life, argues a certain and large fortune by marriage, whereby the party shall be raised among the wealthy and the noble by the influence of successful love."

" Such promises you make to all who ask your advice," said Quentin ; " they are part of your art."

" What I tell you is as certain," said Hayraddin, " as that you shall in a brief space be menaced with mighty danger ; which I infer from this bright blood-red line cutting the table-line transversely, and intimating stroke of sword or other violence, from which you shall only be saved by the attachment of a faithful friend."

"Thyself, ha?" said Quentin, somewhat indignant that the chiromantist should thus practise on his credulity, and endeavor to found a reputation by predicting the consequences of his own treachery.

"My art," replied the Zingaro, "tells me naught that concerns myself."

"In this then the seers of my land," said Quentin, "excel your boasted knowledge; for their skill teaches them the dangers by which they are themselves beset. I left not my hills without having felt a portion of the double vision with which their inhabitants are gifted; and I will give thee a proof of it, in exchange for thy specimen of palmistry. Hayraddin, the danger which threatens me lies on the right bank of the river; I will avoid it by traveling to Liege on the left bank."

The guide listened with an apathy which, knowing that circumstances in which Maugrabin stood, Quentin could not by any means comprehend. "If you accomplish your purpose," was the Bohemian's reply, "the dangerous crisis will be transferred from your lot to mine."

"I thought," said Quentin, "that you said but now that you could not presage your own fortune?"

"Not in the manner in which I have but now told you yours," answered Hayraddin; "but it requires little knowledge of Louis of Valois to presage that he will hang your guide because your pleasure was to deviate from the road which he recommended."

"The attaining with safety the purpose of the journey, and ensuring its happy termination," said Quentin, "must atone for a deviation from the exact line of the prescribed route."

"Ay," replied the Bohemian, "if you are sure that the King had in his own eye the same termination of the pilgrimage which he insinuated to you."

"And of what other termination is it possible that he could have been meditating? or why should you suppose he had any purpose in his thought other than was avowed in his direction?" inquired Quentin.

"Simply," replied the Zingaro, "that those who know aught of the most Christian King are aware that the purpose about which he is most anxious is always that which he is least willing to declare. Let our gracious Louis send twelve embassies, and I will forfeit my neck to the gallows a year before it is due, if in eleven of them there is not something at the bottom of the ink-horn more than the pen has written in the letters of credence."

"I regard not your foul suspicion," answered Quentin; "my duty is plain and peremptory—to convey these ladies in safety to Liege; and I take it on me to think that I best discharge that duty in changing our prescribed route, and keeping the left side of the river Maes. It is likewise the direct road to Liege. By crossing the river, we should lose time and incur fatigue to no purpose. Wherefore should we do so?"

"Only because pilgrims, as they call themselves, destined for Cologne," said Hayraddin, "do not usually descend the Maes so low as Liege; and that the route of the ladies will be accounted contradictory of their professed destination."

"If we are challenged on that account," said Quentin, "we will say that alarms of the wicked Duke of Gueldres, or of William de la Marck, or of the *écorcheurs* and lanz-knechts, on the right side of the river, justify our holding by the left, instead of our intended route."

"As you will, my good seignior," replied the Bohemian. "I am, for my part, equally ready to guide you down the left as down the right side of the Maes. Your excuse to your master you must make out for yourself."

Quentin, although rather surprised, was at the same time pleased with the ready, or at least the unrepugnant, acquiescence of Hayraddin in their change of route, for he needed his assistance as a guide, and yet had feared that the disconcerting of his intended act of treachery would have driven him to extremity. Besides, to expel the Bohemian from their society would have been the ready mode to bring down William de la Marck, with whom he was in correspondence, upon their intended route; whereas, if Hayraddin remained with them, Quentin thought he could manage to prevent the Moor from having any communication with strangers, unless he was himself aware of it.

Abandoning, therefore, all thoughts of their original route, the little party followed that by the left bank of the broad Maes so speedily and successfully that the next day early brought them to the purposed end of their journey. They found that the Bishop of Liege, for the sake of his health, as he himself alleged, but rather, perhaps, to avoid being surprised by the numerous and mutinous population of the city, had established his residence in his beautiful Castle of Schonwaldt, about a mile without Liege.

"They saw the prelates returning in long procession from the neighboring city."

Just as they approached the castle, they saw the prelate returning in long procession from the neighboring city, in which he had been officiating at the performance of high mass. He was at the head of a splendid train of religious, civil, and military men, mingled together, or, as the old ballad-maker expresses it—

> With many a cross-bearer before,
> And many a spear behind.

The procession made a noble appearance, as, winding along the verdant banks of the broad Maes, it wheeled into, and was as it were devoured by, the hugh Gothic portal of the episcopal residence.

But when the party came more near, they found that circumstances around the castle argued a doubt and sense of insecurity, which contradicted that display of pomp and power which they had just witnessed. Strong guards of the bishop's soldiers were heedfully maintained all around the mansion and its immediate vicinity ; and the prevailing appearance, in an ecclesiastical residence, seemed to argue a sense of danger in the reverend prelate, who found it necessary thus to surround himself with all the defensive precautions of war. The Ladies of Croye, when announced by Quentin, were reverently ushered into the great hall, where they met with the most cordial reception from the bishop, who met them there at the head of his little court. He would not permit them to kiss his hand, but welcomed them with a salute, which had something in it of gallantry on the part of a prince to fine women, and something also of the holy affection of a pastor to the sisters of his flock.

Louis of Bourbon, the reigning Bishop of Liege, was in truth a generous and kind-hearted prince, whose life had not indeed been always confined, with precise strictness, within the bounds of his clerical profession ; but who, notwithstanding, had uniformly maintained the frank and honorable character of the house of Bourbon, from which he was descended.

In later times, as age advanced, the prelate had adopted habits more beseeming a member of the hierarchy than his early reign had exhibited, and was loved among the neighboring princes as a noble ecclesiastic, generous and magnificent in his ordinary mode of life, though preserving no very ascetic severity of character, and governing with an easy indifference which, amid his wealthy and mutinous subjects, rather encouraged than subdued rebellious purposes.

The bishop was so fast an ally of the Duke of Burgundy, that the latter claimed almost a joint sovereignty in his bishopric, and repaid the good-natured ease with which the prelate admitted claims which he might easily have disputed, by taking his part on all occasions, with the determined and furious zeal which was a part of his character. He used to say, " He considered Liege as his own, the bishop as his brother (indeed they might be accounted such, in consequence of the Duke having married for his first wife the bishop's sister), and that he who annoyed Louis of Bourbon had to do with Charles of Burgundy "—a threat which, considering the character and the power of the prince who used it, would have been powerful with any but the rich and discontented city of Liege, where much wealth had, according to the ancient proverb, made wit waver.

The prelate, as we have said, assured the Ladies of Croye of such intercession as his interest at the court of Burgundy, used to the uttermost, might gain for them, and which, he hoped, might be the more effectual, as Campo-basso, from some late discoveries, stood rather lower than formerly in the Duke's personal favor. He promised them also such protection as it was in his power to afford ; but the sigh with which he gave the warrant seemed to allow that his power was more precarious than in words he was willing to admit.

" At every event, my dearest daughters," said the bishop, with an air in which, as in his previous salute, a mixture of spiritual unction qualified the hereditary gallantry of the house of Bourbon, " Heaven forbid I should abandon the lamb to the wicked wolf, or noble ladies to the oppression of faitours. I am a man of peace, though my abode now rings with arms ; but be assured I will care for your safety as for my own ; and should matters become yet more distracted here, which, with Our Lady's grace, we trust will be rather pacified than inflamed, we will provide for your safe-conduct to Germany ; for not even the will of our brother and protector, Charles of Burgundy, shall prevail with us to dispose of you in any respect contrary to your own inclinations. We cannot comply with your request of sending you to a convent; for, alas ! such is the influence of the sons of Belial among the inhabitants of Liege, that we know no retreat to which our authority extends, beyond the bounds of our own castle and the protection of our soldiery. But here you are most welcome, and your train shall have all honorable entertainment ; especially this youth, whom you recommend so particularly to our countenance, and on whom in especial we bestow our blessing."

Quentin kneeled, as in duty bound, to receive the episcopal benediction.

" For yourselves," proceeded the good prelate, " you shall reside here with my sister Isabelle, a canoness of Triers, and with whom you may dwell in all honor, even under the roof of so gay a bachelor as the Bishop of Liege."

He gallantly conducted the ladies to his sister's apartment, as he concluded the harangue of welcome ; and his master of the household, an officer who, having taken deacon's orders, held something between a secular and ecclesiatical character, entertained Quentin with the hospitality which his master enjoined, while the other personages of the retinue of the Ladies of Croye were committed to the inferior departments.

In this arrangement Quentin could not help remarking, that the presence of the Bohemian, so much objected to in country convents, seemed, in the household of this wealthy, and perhaps we might say worldly, prelate, to attract neither objection nor remark.

14

CHAPTER XIX

THE CITY

Good friends, sweet friends, let me not stir you up
To any sudden act of mutiny !
                                          Julius Cæsar.

SEPARATED from the Lady Isabelle, whose looks had been
for so many days his loadstar, Quentin felt a strange vacancy
and chillness of the heart, which he had not yet experienced
in any of the vicissitudes to which his life had subjected
him. No doubt the cessation of the close and unavoidable
intercourse and intimacy betwixt them was the necessary
consequence of the countess having obtained a place of
settled residence ; for, under what pretext could she, had
she meditated such an impropriety, have had a gallant
young squire such as Quentin in constant attendance upon
her ?

But the shock of the separation was not the more welcome
that it seemed unavoidable, and the proud heart of Quentin
swelled at finding he was parted with like an ordinary pos-
tilion, or an escort whose duty is discharged ; while his eyes
sympathized so far as to drop a secret tear or two over the
ruins of all those airy castles, so many of which he had employed himself in constructing during their too interesting
journey. He made a manly, but at first a vain, effort to
throw off this mental dejection ; and so, yielding to the
feelings he could not suppress, he sat him down in one of
the deep recesses formed by a window which lighted the
great Gothic hall of Schonwaldt, and there mused upon his
hard fortune, which had not assigned him rank or wealth
sufficient to prosecute his daring suit.

Quentin tried to dispel the sadness which overhung him
by despatching Chatlet, one of the valets, with letters to the
court of Louis, announcing the arrival of the Ladies of
Croye at Liege. At length his natural buoyancy of temper
returned, much excited by the title of an old romaunt which
had been just printed at Strasbourg, and which lay beside
him in the window, the title of which set forth—

How the squire of lowe degree,
Loved the king's daughter of Hongarie.*

While he was tracing the "letters blake" of the ditty so congenial to his own situation, Quentin was interrupted by a touch on the shoulder, and, looking up, beheld the Bohemian standing by him.

Hayraddin, never a welcome sight, was odious from his late treachery, and Quentin sternly asked him, "Why he dared take the freedom to touch a Christian and a gentleman."

"Simply," answered the Bohemian, "because I wished to know if the Christian gentleman had lost his feeling as well as his eyes and ears. I have stood speaking to you these five minutes, and you have stared on that scrap of yellow paper as if it were a spell to turn you into a statue, and had already wrought half its purpose."

"Well, what dost thou want? Speak, and begone!"

"I want what all men want, though few are satisfied with it," said Hayraddin: "I want my due—my ten crowns of gold for guiding the ladies hither."

"With what face darest thou ask any guerdon beyond my sparing thy worthless life?" said Durward, fiercely; "thou knowest that it was thy purpose to have betrayed them on the road."

"But I did *not* betray them," said Hayraddin; "if I had, I would have asked no guerdon from you or from them, but from him whom their keeping upon the right-hand side of the river might have benefited. The party that I have served is the party who must pay me."

"Thy guerdon perish with thee, then, traitor!" said Quentin, telling out the money. "Get thee to the Boar of Ardennes, or to the devil! but keep hereafter out of my sight, lest I send thee thither before thy time."

"The Boar of Ardennes!" repeated the Bohemian, with a stronger emotion of surprise than his features usually expressed; "it was then no vague guess—no general suspicion —which made you insist on changing the road? Can it be—are there really in other lands arts of prophecy more sure than those of our wandering tribes? The willow-tree under which we spoke could tell no tales. But no—no— no—— Dolt that I was! I have it—I have it! The willow by the brook near yonder convent—I saw you look towards it as you passed it, about half a mile from yon hive of drones

*See Note 28.

—that could not indeed speak, but it might hide one who could hear! I will hold my councils in an open plain henceforth ; not a bunch of thistles shall be near me for a Scot to shroud amongst. Ha! ha! the Scot hath beat the Zingaro at his own subtle weapons. But know, Quentin Durward, that you have foiled me to the marring of thine own fortune. Yes! the fortune I told thee of, from the lines on thy hand, had been richly accomplished but for thine own obstinacy."

"By St. Andrew," said Quentin, "thy impudence makes me laugh in spite of myself. How or in what should thy successful villainy have been of service to me? I heard, indeed, that you did stipulate to save my life, which condition your worthy allies would speedily have forgotten had we once come to blows ; but in what thy betrayal of these ladies could have served me, but by exposing me to death or captivity, is a matter beyond human brains to conjecture."

"No matter thinking of it, then," said Hayraddin, "for I mean still to surprise you with my gratitude. Had you kept back my hire, I should have held that we were quit, and had left you to your own foolish guidance. As it is, I remain your debtor for yonder matter on the banks of the Cher."

"Methinks I have already taken out the payment in cursing and abusing thee," said Quentin.

"Hard words or kind ones," said the Zingaro, "are but wind, which make no weight in the balance. Had you struck me, indeed, instead of threatening——"

"I am likely enough to take out payment in that way, if you provoke me longer."

"I would not advise it," said the Zingaro ; "such payment, made by a rash hand, might exceed the debt, and unhappily leave a balance on your side, which I am not one to forget or forgive. And now farewell, but not for a long space ; I go to bid adieu to the Ladies of Croye."

"Thou," said Quentin in astonishment—"*thou* be admitted to the presence of the ladies, and here, where they are in a manner recluses under the protection of the bishop's sister, a noble canoness! It is impossible."

"Marthon, however, waits to conduct me to their presence," said the Zingaro, with a sneer ; "and I must pray your forgiveness if I leave you something abruptly."

He turned as if to depart, but instantly coming back, said, with a tone of deep and serious emphasis, "I know your hopes ; they are daring, yet not vain if I aid them. I know your fears ; they should teach prudence, not timidity.

Every woman may be won. A count is but a nickname, which will befit Quentin as well as the other nickname of duke befits Charles, or that of king befits Louis."

Ere Durward could reply, the Bohemian had left the hall. Quentin instantly followed ; but, better acquainted than the Scot with the passages of the house, Hayraddin kept the advantage which he had gotten ; and the pursuer lost sight of him as he descended a small back staircase. Still Durward followed, though without exact consciousness of his own purpose in doing so. The staircase terminated by a door opening into the alley of a garden, in which he again beheld the Zingaro hastening down a pleached walk.

On two sides, the garden was surrounded by the buildings of the castle—a huge old pile, partly castellated and partly resembling an ecclesiastical building ; on the other two sides, the inclosure was a high embattled wall. Crossing the alleys of the garden to another part of the building, where a postern-door opened behind a large massive buttress, overgrown with ivy, Hayraddin looked back, and waved his hand in signal of an exulting farewell to his follower, who saw that in effect the postern-door was open by Marthon, and that the vile Bohemian was admitted into the precincts, as he naturally concluded, of the apartment of the Countesses of Croye. Quentin bit his lips with indignation, and blamed himself severely that he had not made the ladies sensible of the full infamy of Hayraddin's character, and acquainted with his machinations against their safety. The arrogating manner in which the Bohemian had promised to back his suit added to his anger and his disgust ; and he felt as if even the hand of the Countess Isabelle would be profaned, were it possible to attain it by such patronage. "But it is all a deception," he said—"a turn of his base juggling artifice. He has procured access to these ladies upon some false pretence, and with some mischievous intention. It is well I have learned where they lodge. I will watch Marthon, and solicit an interview with them, were it but to place them on their guard. It is hard that I must use artifice and brook delay when such as he have admittance openly and without scruple. They shall find, however, that, though I am excluded from their presence, Isabelle's safety is still the chief subject of my vigilance."

While the young lover was thus meditating, an aged gentleman of the bishop's household approached him from the same door by which he had himself entered the garden, and made him aware, though with the greatest civility of manner, that the garden was private, and reserved only for the use of the bishop and guests of the very highest distinction.

Quentin heard him repeat this information twice ere he put the proper construction upon it ; and then starting as from a reverie, he bowed and hurried out of the garden, the official person following him all the way, and overwhelming him with formal apologies for the necessary discharge of his duty. Nay, so pertinacious was he in his attempts to remove the offense which he conceived Durward to have taken, that he offered to bestow his own company upon him, to contribute to his entertainment ; until Quentin, internally cursing his formal foppery, found no better way of escape than pretending a desire of visiting the neighboring city, and setting off thither at such a round pace as speedily subdued all desire in the gentleman-usher to accompany him farther than the drawbridge. In a few minutes Quentin was within the walls of the city of Liege, then one of the richest in Flanders, and of course in the world.

Melancholy, even love-melancholy, is not so deeply seated, at least in minds of a manly and elastic character, as the soft enthusiasts who suffer under it are fond of believing. It yields to unexpected and striking impressions upon the senses, to change of place, to such scenes as create new trains of association, and to the influence of the busy hum of mankind. In a few minutes, Quentin's attention was as much engrossed by the variety of objects presented in rapid succession by the busy streets of Liege as if there had neither been a Countess Isabelle nor a Bohemian in the world.

The lofty houses ; the stately, though narrow and gloomy, streets ; the splendid display of the richest goods and most gorgeous armor in the warehouses and shops around ; the walks crowded by busy citizens of every description, passing and repassing with faces of careful importance or eager bustle ; the huge wains, which transported to and fro the subjects of export and import, the former consisting of broadcloths and serge, arms of all kinds, nails and iron-work, while the latter comprehended every article of use or luxury intended either for the consumption of an opulent city or received in barter and destined to be transported elsewhere —all these objects combined to form an engrossing picture of wealth, bustle, and splendor, to which Quentin had been hitherto a stranger. He admired also the various streams and canals drawn from and communicating with the Maes, which, traversing the city in various directions, offered to every quarter the commercial facilities of water-carriage; and he failed not to hear a mass in the venerable old church of St. Lambert, said to have been founded in the 8th century.

It was upon leaving this place of worship that Quentin began to observe that he, who had been hitherto gazing on all around him with the eagerness of unrestrained curiosity, was himself the object of attention to several groups of substantial looking burghers, who seemed assembled to look upon him as he left the church, and amongst whom arose a buzz and whisper, which spread from one party to another; while the number of gazers continued to augment rapidly, and the eyes of each who added to it were eagerly directed to Quentin, with a stare which expressed much interest and curiosity, mingled with a certain degree of respect.

At length he now formed the center of a considerable crowd, which yet yielded before him while he continued to move forward; while those who followed or kept pace with him studiously avoided pressing on him or impeding his motions. Yet his situation was too embarrassing to be long endured, without making some attempt to extricate himself, and to obtain some explanation.

Quentin looked around him, and fixing upon a jolly, stout-made, respectable man, whom, by his velvet cloak and gold chain, he concluded to be a burgher of eminence, and perhaps a magistrate, he asked him, " Whether he saw anything particular in his appearance, to attract public attention in a degree so unusual? or whether it was the ordinary custom of the people of Liege thus to throng around strangers who chanced to visit their city? "

" Surely not, good seignior," answered the burgher; "the Liegeois are neither so idly curious as to practise such a custom, nor is there anything in your dress or appearance, saving that which is most welcome to this city, and which our townsmen are both delighted to see and desirous to honor."

" This sounds very polite, worthy sir," said Quentin; "but, by the cross of St. Andrew, I cannot even guess at your meaning."

" Your oath, sir," answered the merchant of Liege, "as well as your accent, convinces me that we are right in our conjecture."

" By my patron St. Quentin!" said Durward, " I am farther off from your meaning than ever."

" There again now," rejoined the Liegeois, looking, as he

spoke, most provokingly, yet most civilly, politic and intelligent. "It is surely not for us to see that which you, worthy seignior, deem it proper to conceal. But why swear by St. Quentin, if you would not have me construe your moaning? We know the good Count of St. Paul, who lies there at present, wishes well to our cause."

"On my life," said Quentin, "you are under some delusion : I know nothing of St. Paul."

"Nay, we question you not, said the burgher; although, hark ye—I say, hark in your ear—my name is Pavillon."

"And what is my business with that, Seignior Pavillon ?" said Quentin.

"Nay, nothing ; only methinks it might satisfy you that I am trustworthy. Here is my colleague Rouslaer, too."

Rouslaer advanced, a corpulent dignitary, whose fair round belly, like a battering-ram, "did shake the press before him," and who, whispering caution to his neighbor, said in a tone of rebuke, "You forget, good colleague, the place is too open ; the seignior will retire to your house or mine, and drink a glass of Rhenish and sugar, and then we shall hear more of our good friend and ally, whom we love with all our honest Flemish hearts."

"I have no news for any of you," said Quentin, impatiently ; "I will drink no Rhenish ; and I only desire of you, as men of account and respectability, to disperse this idle crowd, and allow a stranger to leave your town as quietly as he came into it."

"Nay, then, sir," said Rouslaer, "since you stand so much on your incognito, and with us, too, who are men of confidence, let me ask you roundly, wherefore wear you the badge of your company if you would remain unknown in Liege ?"

"What badge and what order ?" said Quentin. "You look like reverend men and grave citizens, yet, on my soul, you are either mad yourselves or desire to drive me so."

"Sapperment !" said the other burgher, "this youth would make St. Lambert swear ! Why, who wear bonnets with the St. Andrew's cross and *fleur-de-lys* save the Scottish Archers of King Louis's Guards ?"

"And supposing I am an archer of the Scottish Guard, why should you make a wonder of my wearing the badge of my company ?" said Quentin, impatiently.

"He has avowed it—he has avowed it !" said Rouslaer and Pavillon, turning to the assembled burghers in attitudes of congratulation, with waving arms, extended palms, and large

round faces radiating with glee. " He hath avowed himself
an archer of Louis's Guard—of Louis, the guardian of the
liberties of Liege ! "

A general shout and cry now arose from the multitude, in
which were mingled the various sounds of " Long live Louis
of France ! Long live the Scottish Guard ! Long live the
valiant ar¢her ! Our liberties, our privileges, or death ! No
imposts ! Long live the valiant Boar of Ardennes ! Down
with Charles of Burgundy ! and confusion to Bourbon and
his bishopric ! "

Half-stunned by the noise, which began anew in one quarter
as soon as it ceased in another, rising and falling like the
billows of the sea, and augmented by thousands of voices
which roared in chorus from distant streets and market-
places, Quentin had yet time to form a conjecture concerning the meaning of the tumult, and a plan for regulating his
own conduct.

He had forgotten that, after his skirmish with Orleans and
Dunois, one of his comrades had, at Lord Crawford's command, replaced the morion, cloven by the sword of the latter
with one of the steel-lined bonnets which formed a part of
the proper and well-known equipment of the Scotch Guards.
That an individual of this body, which was always kept very
close to Louis's person, should have appeared in the streets
of a city whose civil discontents had been aggravated by the
agents of that king, was naturally enough interpreted by the
burghers of Liege into a determination on the part of Louis
openly to assist their cause ; and the apparition of an individual archer was magnified into a pledge of immediate and
active support from Louis—nay, into an assurance that his
auxiliary forces were actually entering the town at one or
other, though no one could distinctly tell which, of the city
gates.

To remove a conviction so generally adopted, Quentin
easily saw was impossible—nay, that any attempt to un-
deceive men so obstinately prepossessed in their belief would
be attended with personal risk, which, in this case, he saw
little use of incurring. He therefore hastily resolved to
temporize, and to get free the best way he could ; and this
resolution he formed while they were in the act of conducting him to the *stadt-house*, where the notables of the town
were fast assembling, in order to hear the tidings which he
was presumed to have brought, and to regale him with a
splendid banquet.

In spite of all his opposition, which was set down to modesty, he was on every side surrounded by the donors of popularity, the unsavory tide of which now floated around him. His two burgomaster friends, who were *schoppen* [*schöffen*], or syndics, of the city, had made fast both his arms. Before him, Nikkel Blok, the chief of the butcher's incorporation, hastily summoned from his office in the shambles, brandished his death-doing ax, yet smeared with blood and brains, with a courage and grace which *brantwein* alone could inspire. Behind him came the tall, lean, raw-boned, very drunk, and very patriotic, figure of Claus Hammerlein, president of the mystery of the workers in iron, and followed by at least a thousand unwashed artificers of his class. Weavers, nailers, ropemakers, artisans of every degree and calling, thronged forward to join the procession from every gloomy and narrow street. Escape seemed a desperate and impossible adventure.

In this dilemma, Quentin appealed to Rouslaer, who held one arm, and to Pavillon, who had secured the other, and who were conducting him forward at the head of the ovation of which he had so unexpectedly become the principal object. He hastily acquainted them " with his having thoughtlessly adopted the bonnet of the Scottish Guard, on an accident having occurred to the head-piece in which he had proposed to travel ; he regretted that, owing to this circumstance and the sharp wit with which the Liegeois drew the natural inference of his quality and the purpose of his visit, these things had been publicly discovered : and he intimated that, if just now conducted to the *stadt-house*, he might unhappily feel himself under the necessity of communicating to the assembled notables certain matters which he was directed by the King to reserve for the private ears of his excellent gossips, Meinherrs Rouslaer and Pavillon of Leige."

This last hint operated like magic on the two citizens, who were the most distinguished leaders of the insurgent burghers, and were, like all demagogues of their kind, desirous to keep everything within their own management, so far as possible. They therefore hastily agreed that Quentin should leave the town for the time, and return by night to Liege, and converse with them privately in the house of Rouslaer, near the gate opposite to Schonwaldt. Quentin hesitated not to tell them that he was at present residing in the bishop's palace, under pretense of bearing despatches from the French court, although his real errand was, as they had well conjectured, designed to the citizens of Liege ;

and this tortuous mode of conducting a communication, as well as the character and rank of the person to whom it was supposed to be entrusted, was so consonant to the character of Louis as neither to excite doubt nor surprise.

Almost immediately after this *éclaircissement* was completed, the progress of the multitude brought them opposite to the door of Pavillon's house, in one of the principal streets, but which communicated from behind with the Maes by means of a garden, as well as an extensive manufactory of tan-pits and other conveniences for dressing hides ; for the patriotic burgher was a felt-dresser, or currier.

It was natural that Pavillon should desire to do the honors of his dwelling to the supposed envoy of Louis, and a halt before his house excited no surprise on the part of the multitude, who, on the contrary, greeted Meinherr Pavillon with a loud *vivat* as he ushered in his distinguished guest. Quentin speedily laid aside his remarkable bonnet for the cap of a feltmaker, and flung a cloak over his other apparel. Pavillon then furnished him with a passport to pass the gates of the city, and to return by night or day as should suit his convenience ; and, lastly, committed him to the charge of his daughter, a fair and smiling Flemish lass, with instructions how he was to be disposed of, while he himself hastened back to his colleague to amuse their friends at the *stadthouse* with the best excuses which they could invent for the disappearance of King Louis's envoy. We cannot, as the footman says in the play, recollect the exact nature of the lie which the bellwethers told the flock ; but no task is so easy as that of imposing upon a multitude whose eager prejudices have more than half done the business, ere the impostor has spoken a word.

The worthy burgess was no sooner gone than his plump daughter, Trudchen, with many a blush and many a wreathed smile, which suited very prettily with lips like cherries, laughing blue eyes, and a skin transparently pure, escorted the handsome stranger through the pleached alleys of the Sieur Pavillon's garden, down to the water-side, and there saw him fairly embarked in a boat, which two stout Flemings, in their trunkhose, fur caps, and many-buttoned jerkins, had got in readiness with as much haste as their Low-Country nature would permit.

As the pretty Trudchen spoke nothing but German, Quentin—no disparagement to his loyal affection to the Countess Croye—could only express his thanks by a kiss on those same cherry lips, which was very gallantly bestowed, and accepted with all modest gratitude ; for gallants with a form and face like our Scottish Archer were not of every-day occurrence among the *bourgeoisie* of Liege.

While the boat was rowed up the sluggish waters of the Maes, and passed the defenses of the town, Quentin had time enough to reflect what account he ought to give of his adventure in Liege, when he returned to the bishop's palace of Schonwaldt ; and disdaining alike to betray any person who had reposed confidence in him, although by misapprehension, or to conceal from the hospitable prelate the mutinous state of his capital, he resolved to confine himself to so general an account as might put the bishop upon his guard, while it should point out no individual to his vengeance.

He was landed from the boat within half a mile of the castle, and rewarded his rowers with a guilder, to their great satisfaction.   Yet, short as was the space which divided him from Schonwaldt, the castle bell had tolled for dinner, and Quentin found, moreover, that he had approached the castle on a different side from that of the principal entrance, and that to go round would throw his arrival considerably later. He therefore made straight towards the side that was nearest him, as he discerned that it presented an embattled wall, probably that of the little garden already noticed, with a postern opening upon the moat, and a skiff moored by the postern, which might serve, he thought, upon summons, to pass him over.   As he approached, in hopes to make his entrance this way, the postern opened, a man came out, and, jumping into the boat, made his way to the farther side of the moat, and then with a long pole pushed the skiff back towards the place where he had embarked.   As he came near, Quentin discerned that this person was the Bohemian, who, avoiding him, as was not difficult, held a different path towards Liege, and was presently out of his ken.

Here was new subject for meditation.   Had this vagabond heathen been all this while with the Ladies of Croye, and for what purpose should they so far have graced him with their presence ?   Tormented with this thought, Durward became doubly determined to seek an explanation with them, for the purpose at once of laying bare the treachery of Hayraddin and announcing to them the perilous state in which their protector, the bishop, was placed by the mutinous state of his town of Liege.*

As Quentin thus resolved, he entered the castle by the

* See Quentin's Adventure at Liege.   Note 29.

principal gate, and found that part of the family who assembled for dinner in the great hall, including the bishop's attendant clergy, officers of the household, and strangers below the rank of the very first nobility, were already placed at their meal. A seat at the upper end of the board had, however, been reserved beside the bishop's domestic chaplain, who wolcomed the stranger with the old college jest of "*Sero venientibus ossa*," while he took care so to load his plate with dainties as to take away all appearance of that tendency to reality which, in Quentin's country, is said to render a joke either no joke or at best an unpalatable one.*

In vindicating himself from the suspicion of ill-breeding, Quentin briefly described the tumult which had been occasioned in the city by his being discovered to belong to the Scottish Archer Guard of Louis, and endeavored to give a ludicrous turn to the narrative, by saying that he had been with difficulty extricated by a fat burgher of Liege and his pretty daughter.

But the company were too much interested in the story to taste the jest. All operations of the table were suspended while Quentin told his tale; and when he had ceased, there was a solemn pause, which was only broken by the major-domo saying, in a low and melancholy tone, "I would to God that we saw those hundred lances of Burgundy!"

"Why should you think so deeply on it?" said Quentin. "You have many soldiers here, whose trade is arms; and your antagonists are only the rabble of a disorderly city, who will fly before the first flutter of a banner with men-at-arms arrayed beneath it."

"You do not know the men of Liege," said the chaplain, "of whom it may be said that, not even excepting those of Ghent, they are at once the fiercest and the most untameable in Europe. Twice has the Duke of Burgundy chastised them for their repeated revolts against their bishop, and twice hath he suppressed them with much severity, abridged their privileges, taken away their banners, and established rights and claims to himself which were not before competent over a free city of the Empire. Nay, the last time he defeated them with much slaughter near St. Tron, where Liege lost nearly six thousand men, what with the sword, what with those drowned in the flight; and, thereafter, to disable them from farther mutiny, Duke Charles refused to enter at any of the gates which they had surrendered, but, beating to the ground forty cubits breadth of their city wall, marched into

* "A sooth boord (true joke) is no boord," says the Scot.

Liege as a conqueror, with visor closed and lance in rest, at the head of his chivalry, by the breach which he had made. Nay, well were the Liegeois then assured that, but for the intercession of his father, Duke Philip the Good, this Charles, then called Count of Charalois, would have given their town up to spoil. And yet, with all these fresh recollections, with their breaches unrepaired, and their arsenals scarcely supplied, the sight of an archer's bonnet is sufficient again to stir them to uproar. May God amend all ! but I fear there will be bloody work between so fierce a population and so fiery a sovereign ; and I would my excellent and kind master had a see of lesser dignity and more safety, for his miter is lined with thorns instead of ermine. This much I say to you, seignior stranger, to make you aware that, if your affairs detain you not at Schonwaldt, it is a place from which each man of sense should depart as speedily as possible. I apprehend that your ladies are of the same opinion ; for one of the grooms who attended them on the route has been sent back by them to the court of France with letters, which, doubtless, are intended to announce their going in search of a safer asylum."

CHAPTER XX

THE BILLET

Go to—thou art made, if thou desirest to be so. If not, let me see
thee still the fellow of servants, and not fit to touch Fortune's
fingers.

Twelfth Night.

WHEN the tables were drawn, the chaplain, who seemed to
have taken a sort of attachment to Quentin Durward's
society, or who perhaps desired to extract from him farther
information concerning the meeting of the morning, led him
into a withdrawing-apartment, the windows of which, on
one side, projected into the garden ; and as he saw his companion's eye gaze rather eagerly upon the spot, he proposed
to Quentin to go down and take a view of the curious foreign
shrubs with which the bishop had enriched its parterres.

Quentin excused himself, as unwilling to intrude, and
therewithal communicated the check which he had received
in the morning. The chaplain smiled, and said, " That
there was indeed some ancient prohibition respecting the
bishop's private garden ; but this," he added, with a smile,
" was when our reverend father was a princely young prelate of not more than thirty years of age, and when many
fair ladies frequented the castle for ghostly consolation.
Need there was," he said, with a downcast look, and a smile,
half simple and half intelligent, " that these ladies, pained
in conscience, who were ever lodged in the apartments now
occupied by the noble canoness, should have some space for
taking the air, secure from the intrusion of the profane.
But of late years," he added, " this prohibition, although
not formally removed, has fallen entirely out of observance,
and remains but as the superstition which lingers in the
brain of a superannuated gentleman-usher. If you please,"
he added, " we will presently descend, and try whether the
place be haunted or no."

Nothing could have been more agreeable to Quentin than
the prospect of a free entrance into the garden, through
means of which, according to a chance which had hitherto
attended his passion, he hoped to communicate with, or at

223

least obtain sight of, the object of his affections, from some such turret or balcony-window, or similar " coign of vantage," as at the hostelry of the Fleur-de-Lys, near Plessis, or the Dauphin's Towers, within that castle itself. Isabelle seemed still destined, wherever she made her abode, to be the " lady of the turret."

When Durward descended with his new friend into the garden, the latter seemed a terrestrial philosopher, entirely busied with the things of the earth ; while the eyes of Quentin, if they did not seek the heavens, like those of the astrologer, ranged at least all around the windows, balconies, and especially the turrets, which projected on every part from the inner front of the old building, in order to discover that which was to be his cynosure.

While thus employed, the young lover heard with total neglect, if indeed he heard at all, the enumeration of plants, herbs, and shrubs, which his reverend conductor pointed out to him ; of which this was choice, because of prime use in medicine ; and that more choice, for yielding a rare flavor to pottage ; and a third choicest of all, because possessed of no merit but its extreme scarcity. Still it was necessary to preserve some semblance at least of attention ; which the youth found so difficult, that he fairly wished at the devil the officious naturalist and the whole vegetable kingdom. He was relieved at length by the striking of a clock, which summoned the chaplain to some official duty.

The reverend man made many unnecessary apologies for leaving his new friend, and concluded by giving him the agreeable assurance that he might walk in the garden till supper, without much risk of being disturbed.

" It is," said he, " the place where I always study my own homilies, as being more sequestered from the resort of strangers. I am now about to deliver one of them in the chapel, if you please to favor me with your audience. I have been thought to have some gift—but the glory be where it is due ! "

Quentin excused himself for this evening, under pretense of a severe headache, which the open air was likely to prove the best cure for ; and at length the well-meaning priest left him to himself.

It may be well imagined, that in the curious inspection which he now made, at more leisure, of every window or aperture which looked into the garden, those did not escape which were in the immediate neighborhood of the small door by which he had seen Marthon admit Hayraddin, as he pretended, to the apartment of the countess. But nothing stirred or showed itself, which could either confute or confirm the tale which the Bohemian had told, until it was becoming dusky ; and Quentin began to be sensible, he scarce knew why, that his sauntering so long in the garden might be subject of displeasure or suspicion.

Just as he had resolved to depart, and was taking what he had destined for his last turn under the windows which had such attraction for him, he heard above him a slight and cautious sound, like that of a cough as intended to call his attention, and to avoid the observation of others. As he looked up in joyful surprise, a casement opened—a female hand was seen to drop a billet, which fell into a rosemary bush that grew at the foot of the wall. The precaution used in dropping this letter prescribed equal prudence and secrecy in reading it. The garden, surrounded, as we have said, upon two sides by the buildings of the palace, was commanded, of course, by the windows of many apartments ; but there was a sort of grotto of rock-work, which the chaplain had shown Durward with much complacency. To snatch up the billet, thrust it into his bosom, and hie to this place of secrecy, was the work of a single minute. He there opened the precious scroll, and blessed, at the same time, the memory of the monks of Aberbrothock, whose nurture had rendered him capable of deciphering its contents.

The first line cotained the injunction, " Read this in secret,"—and the contents were as follows : " What your eyes have too boldly said mine have perhaps too rashly understood! But unjust persecution makes its victims bold, and it were better to throw myself on the gratitude of one than to remain the object of pursuit to many. Fortune has her throne upon a rock ; but brave men fear not to climb. If you dare do aught for one that hazards much, you need but pass into this garden at prime to-morrow, wearing in your cap a blue and white feather ; but expect no farther communication. Your stars have, they say, destined you for greatness, and disposed you to gratitude. Farewell—be faithful, prompt, and resolute, and doubt not thy fortune." Within this letter was enclosed a ring with a table-diamond, on which were cut, in form of a lozenge, the ancient arms of the house of Croye.

The first feeling of Quentin upon this occasion was unmingled ecstasy—a pride and joy which seemed to raise him to the stars,—a determination to do or die, influenced by which he treated with scorn the thousand obstacles that placed themselves betwixt him and the goal of his wishes.

15

In this mood of rapture, and unable to endure any interruption which might withdraw his mind, were it but for a
moment, from so ecstatic a subject of contemplation, Durward, retiring to the interior of the castle, hastily assigned
his former pretext of a headache for not joining the household of the bishop at the supper-meal, and, lighting his lamp,
betook himself to the chamber which had been assigned him,
to read and to read again and again, the precious billet, and
to kiss a thousand times the no less precious ring.

But such high-wrought feelings could not remain long in
the same ecstatic tone. A thought pressed upon him, though
he repelled it as ungrateful—as even blasphemous, that the
frankness of the confession implied less delicacy, on the part
of her who made it, than was consistent with the high
romantic feeling of adoration with which he had hitherto
worshiped the Lady Isabelle. No sooner did this ungracious
thought intrude itself than he hastened to stifle it, as he
would have stifled a hissing and hateful adder that had intruded itself into his couch. Was it for him—him the
favored, on whose account she had stooped from her sphere,
to ascribe blame to her for the very act of condescension,
without which he dared not have raised his eyes towards her ?
Did not her very dignity of birth and of condition reverse,
in her case, the usual rules which impose silence on the lady
until her lover shall have first spoken ? To these arguments,
which he boldly formed into syllogisms, and avowed to himself, his vanity might possibly suggest one which he cared
not to embody even mentally with the same frankness—that
the merit of the party beloved might perhaps warrant, on
the part of the lady, some little departure from common
rules ; and, after all, as in the case of Malvolio, there was
example for it in chronicle. The squire of low degree, of
whom he had just been reading, was, like himself, a gentleman void of land and living, and yet the generous Princess of
Hungary bestowed on him, without scruple, more substantial
marks of her affection than the billet he had just received :—

> " Welcome," she said, " my swete squyre,
> My heartis roote, my soule's desire ;
> I will give thee kisses three,
> And als five hundrid poundis in fee."

And again the same faithful history made the King of
Hongrie himself avouch,

> " I have known many a page
> Come to be prince by marriage."

So that, upon the whole, Quentin generously and magnanimously reconciled himself to a line of conduct on the countess's part by which he was likely to be so highly benefited.

But this scruple was succeeded by another doubt, harder of digestion. The traitor Hayraddin had been in the apartments of the ladies, for aught Quentin knew, for the space of four hours, and, considering the hints which he had thrown out, of possessing an influence of the most interesting kind over the fortunes of Quentin Durward, what should assure him that this train was not of his laying? and if so, was it not probable that such a dissembling villain had set it on foot to conceal some new plan of treachery—perhaps to seduce Isabelle out of the protection of the worthy bishop? This was a matter to be closely looked into, for Quentin felt a repugnance to this individual proportioned to the unabashed impudence with which he had avowed his profligacy, and could not bring himself to hope, that anything in which he was concerned could ever come to an honorable or happy conclusion.

These various thoughts rolled over Quentin's mind like misty clouds, to dash and obscure the fair landscape which his fancy had at first drawn, and his couch was that night a sleepless one. At the hour of prime, ay, and an hour before it, was he in the castle-garden, where no one now opposed either his entrance or his abode, with a feather of the assigned color, as distinguished as he could by any means procure in such haste. No notice was taken of his appearance for nearly two hours; at length he heard a few notes of the lute, and presently the lattice opened right above the little posterndoor at which Marthon had admitted Hayraddin, and Isabelle, in maidenly beauty, appearing at the opening, greeted him half-kindly half-shyly, colored extremely at the deep and significant reverence with which he returned her courtesy, shut the casement and disappeared.

Daylight and champaign could discover no more! The authenticity of the billet was ascertained; it only remained what was to follow, and of this the fair writer had given him no hint. But no immediate danger impended. The countess was in a strong castle, under the protection of a prince, at once respectable for his secular and venerable for his ecclesiastical authority. There was neither immediate room nor occasion for the exulting squire interfering in the adventure; and it was sufficient if he kept himself prompt to execute her commands whenever they should be communicated to him.

But Fate proposed to call him into action sooner than he was aware of.

It was the fourth night after his arrival at Schonwaldt, when Quentin had taken measures for sending back on the morrow, to the court of Louis, the remaining groom who had accompanied him on his journey, with letters from himself to his uncle and Lord Crawford, renouncing the service of France, for which the treachery to which he had been exposed by the private instructions of Hayraddin gave him an excuse, both in honor and prudence ; and he betook himself to his bed with all the rosy-colored ideas around him which flutter about the couch of a youth when he loves dearly, and thinks his love as sincerely repaid.

But Quentin's dreams, which at first partook of the nature of those happy influences under which he had fallen asleep, began by degrees to assume a more terrific character.

He walked with the Countess Isabelle beside a smooth and inland lake, such as formed the principal characteristic of his native glen ; and he spoke to her of his love, without any consciousness of the impediments which lay between them. She blushed and smiled when she listened, even as he might have expected from the tenor of the letter, which, sleeping or waking, lay nearest to his heart. But the scene suddenly changed from summer to winter, from calm to tempest ; the winds and the waves rose with such a contest of surge and whirlwind, as if the demons of the water and of the air had been contending for their roaring empires in rival strife. The rising waters seemed to cut off their advance and their retreat ; the increasing tempest which dashed them against each other, seemed to render their remaining on the spot impossible ; and the tumultuous sensations produced by the apparent danger awoke the dreamer.

He awoke ; but although the circumstances of the vision had disappeared, and given place to reality, the noise, which had probably suggested them, still continued to sound in his ears.

Quentin's first impulse was to sit erect in bed, and listen with astonishment to sounds, which, if they had announced a tempest, might have shamed the wildest that ever burst down from the Grampians ; and again in a minute he became sensible, that the tumult was not excited by the fury of the elements, but by the wrath of men.

He sprung from bed, and looked from the window of his apartment ; but it opened into the garden, and on that side all was quiet, though the opening of the casement made him still more sensible, from the shouts which reached his ears, that the outside of the castle was beleaguered and assaulted, and that by a numerous and determined enemy. Hastily collecting his dress and arms, and putting them on with such celerity as darkness and surprise permitted, his attention was solicited by a knocking at the door of his chamber. As Quentin did not immediately answer, the door, which was a slight one, was forced open from without, and the intruder, announced by his peculiar dialect to be the Bohemian, Hay-raddin Maugrabin, entered the apartment. A phial, which he held in his hand, touched by a match, produced a dark flash of ruddy fire, by means of which he kindled a lamp, which he took from his bosom.

"The horoscope of your destinies," he said energetically to Durward, without any farther greeting, "now turns upon the determination of a minute."

"Caitiff!" said Quentin, in reply, "there is treachery around us ; and where there is treachery, thou *must* have a share in it."

"You are mad," answered Maugrabin ; "I never betrayed any one but to gain by it, and wherefore should I betray you, by whose safety I can take more advantage than by your destruction ? Hearken for a moment, if it be possible for you, to one note of reason ere it is sounded into your ear by the death shot of ruin. The Liegeois are up ; William de la Marck with his band leads them. Were there means of resistance, their numbers and his fury would overcome them ; but there are next to none. If you would save the countess and your own hopes, follow me in the name of her who sent you a table-diamond, with three leopards engraved on it !"

"Lead the way," said Quentin, hastily. "In that name I dare every danger !"

"As I shall manage it," said the Bohemian, "there is no danger, if you can but withhold your hand from strife which does not concern you ; for, after all, what is it to you whether the bishop, as they call him, slaughters his flock, or the flock slaughters the shepherd ? Ha ! ha ! ha ! Follow me but with caution and patience ; subdue your own courage, and confide in my prudence ; and my debt of thankfulness is paid, and you have a countess for your spouse. Follow me."

"I follow," said Quentin, drawing his sword ; "but the moment in which I detect the least sign of treachery, thy head and body are three yards separate !"

Without more conversation, the Bohemian, seeing that

Quentin was now fully armed and ready, ran down the stairs before him, and winded hastily through various side-passages, until they gained the little garden.   Scarce a light was to be seen on that side, scarce any bustle was to be heard ; but no sooner had Quentin entered the open space than the noise on the opposite side of the castle became ten times more stunningly audible, and he could hear the various war-cries of " Liege ! Liege ! Sanglier ! Sanglier !" shouted by the assailants, while the feebler cry of " Our Lady for the Prince Bishop !" was raised in a faint and faltering tone, by those of the prelete's soldiers who had hastened, though surprised and at disadvantage, to the defense of the walls.

But the interest of the fight, notwithstanding the martial character of Quentin Durward, was indifferent to him in comparison of the fate of Isabelle of Croye, which, he had reason to fear, would be a dreadful one, unless rescued from the power of the dissolute and cruel freebooter who was now, as it seemed, bursting the gates of the castle.   He reconciled himself to the aid of the Bohemian as men in a desperate illness refuse not the remedy prescribed by quacks and mountebanks, and followed across the garden, with the intention of being guided by him until he should discover symptoms of treachery, and then piercing him through the heart, or striking his head from his body.   Hayraddin seemed himself conscious that his safety turned on a featherweight, for he forbore, from the moment they entered the open air, all his wonted gibes and quirks, and seemed to have made a vow to act at once with modesty, courage, and activity.

At the opposite door, which led to the ladies' apartments, upon a low signal made by Hayraddin, appeared two women, muffled in the black silk veils which were then, as now, worn by the women in the Netherlands.   Quentin offered his arm to one of them, who clung to it with trembling eagerness, and indeed hung upon him so much that had her weight been greater, she must have much impeded their retreat.   The Bohemian, who conducted the other female, took the road straight for the postern which opened upon the moat, through the garden-wall, close to which the little skiff was drawn up, by means of which Quentin had formerly observed Hayraddin himself retreating from the castle.

As they crossed, the shouts of storm and successful violence seemed to announce that the castle was in the act of being taken ; and so dismal was the sound in Quentin's ears,

that he could not help swearing aloud, " But that my blood
is irretrievably devoted to the fulfilment of my present duty
I would back to the wall, take faithful part with the hospitable bishop, and silence some of those knaves whose throats
are full of mutiny and robbery ! "

The lady, whose arm was still folded in his, pressed it
lightly as he spoke, as if to make him understand that there
was a nearer claim on his chivalry than the defense of
Schonwaldt ; while the Bohemian exclaimed, loud enough
to be heard, " Now, that I call right Christian frenzy, which
would turn back to fight, when love and fortune both demand that we should fly. On—on, with all the haste you
can make. Horses wait us in yonder thicket of willows."

" There are but two horses," said Quentin, who saw them
in the moonlight.

" All that I could procure without exciting suspicion, and
enough, besides," replied the Bohemian. " You two must
ride for Tongres ere the way becomes unsafe ; Marthon will
abide with the women of our horde, with whom she is an old
acquaintance. Know, she is a daughter of our tribe, and
only dwelt among you to serve our purpose as occasion
should fall.

" Marthon ! " exclaimed the countess, looking at the veiled
female with a shriek of surprise ; " is not this my kinswoman ? "

" Only Marthon," said Hayraddin. " Excuse me that
little piece of deceit. I dared not carry off *both* the Ladies
of Croye from the Wild Boar of Ardennes."

" Wretch ! " said Quentin, emphatically ; " but it is not
—shall not—be too late : I will back to rescue the Lady
Hameline."

" Hameline," whispered the Lady, in a disturbed voice,
" hangs on thy arm to thank thee for her rescue."

" Ha ! what ! How is this ? " said Quentin, extricating
himself from her hold, and with less gentleness than he
would at any other time have used towards a female of any
rank. " Is the Lady Isabelle then left behind ? Farewell
—farewell."

As he turned to hasten back to the castle, Hayraddin laid
hold of him. " Nay, hear you—hear you—you run upon
your death ! What the foul fiend did you wear the colors
of the old one for ? I will never trust blue and white silk
again. But she has almost as large a dower—has jewel and
gold—hath pretensions, too, upon the earldom."

While he spoke thus, panting on in broken sentences, the

Bohemian struggled to detain Quentin, who at length laid his hand on his dagger, in order to extricate himself.

"Nay, if that be the case," said Hayraddin, unloosing his hold, "go, and the devil, if there be one, go along with you!" And, soon as freed from his hold, the Scot shot back to the castle with the speed of the wind.

Hayraddin then turned round to the Countess Hameline, who had sunk down on the ground, between shame, fear, and disappointment.

"Here has been a mistake," he said. "Up, lady, and come with me; I will provide you, ere morning comes a gallanter husband than this smock-faced boy; and if one will not serve, you shall have twenty."

The Lady Hameline was as violent in her passions as she was vain and weak in her understanding. Like many other persons, she went tolerably well through the ordinary duties of life; but in a crisis like the present, she was entirely incapable of doing aught, save pouring forth unavailing lamentations, and accusing Hayraddin of being a thief, a base slave, an impostor, a murderer.

"Call me Zingaro," returned he, composedly, "and you have said all at once."

"Monster! you said the stars had decreed our union, and caused me to write—O wretch that I was!" exclaimed the unhappy lady.

"And so they *had* decreed your union," said Hayraddin, "had both parties been willing; but think you the blessed constellations can make any one wed against his will? I was led into error with your accursed Christian gallantries, and fopperies of ribbons and favors, and the youth prefers veal to beef, I think, that's all. Up and follow me; and take notice, I endure neither weeping nor swooning."

"I will not stir a foot," said the countess, obstinately.

"By the bright welkin, but you shall, though!" exclaimed Hayraddin. "I swear to you, by all that ever fools believed in, that you have to do with one who would care little to strip you naked, bind you to a tree, and leave you to your fortune!"

"Nay," said Marthon, interfering, "by your favor she shall not be misused. I wear a knife as well as you, and can use it. She is a kind woman, though a fool. And you, madam, rise up and follow us. Here has been a mistake; but it is something to have saved life and limb. There are many in yonder castle would give all the wealth in the world to stand where we do now."

As Marthon spoke, a clamor, in which the shouts of victory were mingled with screams of terror and despair, was wafted to them from the castle of Schonwaldt.

" Hear that, lady ! " said Hayraddin, "and be thankful you are not adding your treble pipe to yonder concert. Believe me, I will care for you honestly, and the stars shall keep their words, and find you a good husband."

Like some wild animal, exhausted and subdued by terror and fatigue, the Countess Hameline yielded herself up to the conduct of her guides, and suffered herself to be passively led whichever way they would. Nay, such was the confusion of her spirits and the exhaustion of her strength, that the worthy couple, who half bore, half led her, carried on their discourse in her presence without her even understanding it.

"I ever thought your plan was folly," said Marthon. " Could you have brought the *young* people together, indeed, we might have had a hold on their gratitude, and a footing in their castle. But what chance of so handsome a youth wedding this old fool ? "

" Rizpah," said Hayraddin, " you have borne the name of a Christian, and dwelt in the tents of those besotted people, till thou hast become a partaker in their follies. How could I dream that he would have made scruples about a few years, youth or age, when the advantages of the match were so evident ? And thou knowest, there would have been no moving yonder coy wench to be so frank as this coming countess here, who hangs on our arms as dead a weight as a woolpack. I loved the lad, too, and would have done him a kindness : to wed him to this old woman was to make his fortune; to unite him to Isabelle de Croye was to have brought on him De la Marck, Burgundy, France—every one that challenges an interest in disposing of her hand. And this silly woman's wealth being chiefly in gold and jewels, we should have had our share. But the bow-string has burst and the arrow failed. Away with her ; we will bring her to William with the Beard, by the time he has gorged himself with wassail, as is his wont, he will not know an old countess from a young one. Away, Rizpah ; bear a gallant heart. The bright Aldebaran still influence the destinies of the Children of the Desert ! "

CHAPTER XXI

THE SACK

The gates of mercy shall be all shut up,
And the flesh'd soldier, rough and hard of heart,
In liberty of bloody hand shall range,
With conscience wide as hell.

Henry V.

THE surprised and affrighted garrison of the castle of Schonwaldt had, nevertheless, for some time, made good the defense against the assailants; but the immense crowds which, issuing from the city of Liege, thronged to the assault like bees, distracted their attention and abated their courage.

There was also disaffection at least, if not treachery, among the defenders; for some called out to surrender, and others, deserting their posts, tried to escape from the castle. Many threw themselves from the walls into the moat, and such as escaped drowning flung aside their distinguishing badges, and saved themselves by mingling among the motley crowd of assailants. Some few, indeed, from attachment to the bishop's person, drew around him, and continued to defend the great keep, to which he had fled; and others, doubtful of receiving quarter, or from an impulse of desperate courage, held out other detached bulwarks and towers of the extensive building. But the assailants had got possession of the courts and lower parts of the edifice, and were busy pursuing the vanquished and searching for spoil, while one individual, as if he sought for that death from which all others were flying, endeavored to force his way into the scene of tumult and horror, under apprehensions still more horrible to his imagination than the realities around were to his sight and senses. Whoever had seen Quentin Durward that fatal night, not knowing the meaning of his conduct, had accounted him a raging madman; whoever had appreciated his motives had ranked him nothing beneath a hero of romance.

Approaching Schonwaldt on the same side from which he had left it, the youth met several fugitives making for the wood, who naturally avoided him as an enemy, because he

234

came in an opposite direction from that which they had adopted. When he came nearer, he could hear, and partly see, men dropping from the garden-wall into the castle fosse, and others who seemed precipitated from the battlements by the assailants. His courage was not staggered, even for an instant. There was not time to look for the boat, even had it been practicable to use it, and it was in vain to approach the postern of the garden, which was crowded with fugitives, who ever and anon, as they were thrust through it by the pressure behind, fell into the moat which they had no means of crossing.

Avoiding that point, Quentin threw himself into the moat, near what was called the little gate of the castle, and where there was a drawbridge, which was still elevated. He avoided with difficulty the fatal grasp of more than one sinking wretch, and, swimming to the drawbridge, caught hold of one of the chains which was hanging down, and, by a great exertion of strength and activity, swayed himself out of the water, and attained the platform from which the bridge was suspended. As with hands and knees he struggled to make good his footing, a lanzknecht, with his bloody sword in his hand, made towards him, and raised his weapon for a blow, which must have been fatal.

" How now, fellow ! " said Quentin, in a tone of authority. " Is that the way in which you assist a comrade ? Give me your hand."

The soldier in silence, and not without hesitation, reached him his arm, and helped him upon the platform, when without allowing him time for reflection, the Scot continued in the same tone of command—" To the western tower, if you would be rich : the priest's treasury is in the western tower."

These words were echoed on every hand : " To the western tower, the treasure is in the western tower ! " And the stragglers who were within hearing of the cry, took, like a herd of raging wolves, the direction opposite to that which Quentin, come life, come death, was determined to pursue.

Bearing himself as if he were one, not of the conquered, but of the victors, he made a way into the garden, and pushed across it, with less interruption than he could have expected ; for the cry of " To the western tower ! " had carried off one body of the assailants, and another was summoned together, by a war-cry and trumpet-sound, to assist in repelling a desperate sally, attempted by the defenders of the keep, who had hoped to cut their way out of the castle, bearing the bishop along with them. Quentin, therefore, crossed the garden with an eager step and throbbing heart, commending himself to those Heavenly powers which had protected him through the numberless perils of his life, and bold in his determination to succeed, or leave his life in this desperate undertaking. Ere he reached the garden, three men rushed on him with leveled lances, crying, " Liege— Liege !"

Putting himself in defense, but without striking, he replied, " France—France, friend to Liege !"

" *Vivat France!* " cried the burghers of Liege, and passed on. The same signal proved a talisman to avert the weapons of four or five of La Marck's followers, whom he found straggling in the garden, and who set upon him, crying, " Sanglier !"

In a word, Quentin began to hope that his character as an emissary of King Louis, the private instigator of the insurgents of Liege, and the secret supporter of William de la Marck, might possibly bear him through the horrors of the night.

On reaching the turret, he shuddered when he found the little side-door, through which Marthon and the Countess Hameline had shortly before joined him, was now blockaded with more than one dead body.

Two of them he dragged hastily aside, and was stepping over the third body, in order to enter the portal, when the supposed dead man laid hand on his cloak, and entreated him to stay and assist him to rise. Quentin was about to use rougher methods than struggling to rid himself of this untimely obstruction, when the fallen man continued to exclaim, " I am stifled here, in mine own armor ! I am the Syndic Pavillon of Liege ! If you are for us, I will enrich you—if you are for the other side, I will protect you ; but do not—do not leave me to die the death of a smothered pig ! "

In the midst of this scene of blood and confusion, the presence of mind of Quentin suggested to him, that this dignitary might have the means of protecting their retreat. He raised him on his feet, and asked him if he was wounded.

" Not wounded—at least I think not," answered the burgher ; " but much out of wind."

" Sit down then on this stone, and recover your breath," said Quentin ; " I will return instantly."

" For whom are you ? " said the burgher, still detaining him.

" For France—for France," answered Quentin, studying to get away.

" What ! my lively young archer ? " said the worthy syndic.
" Nay, if it has been my fate to find a friend in this fearful
night, I will not quit him, I promise you. Go where you
will, I follow ; and, could I get some of the tight lads of our
guildry together, I might be able to help you in turn ; but
they are all squandered abroad like so many pease. Oh, it
is a fearful night ! "

During this time, he was dragging himself on after
Quentin, who, aware of the importance of securing the
countenance of a person of such influence, slackened his
pace to assist him, although cursing in his heart the encumbrance that retarded him.

At the top of the stair was an ante-room, with boxes and
trunks, which bore marks of having been rifled, as some of
the contents lay on the floor. A lamp, dying in the chimney,
shed a feeble beam on a dead or senseless man, who lay
across the hearth.

Bounding from Pavillon, like a greyhound from his
keeper's leash, and with an effort which almost overthrew
him, Quentin sprung through a second and a third room,
the last of which seemed to be the bedroom of the Ladies of
Croye. No living mortal was to be seen in either of them.
He called upon the Lady Isabelle's name, at first gently,
then more loudly, and then with an accent of despairing
emphasis ; but no answer was returned. He wrung his
hands, tore his hair, and stamped on the earth with desperation. At length, a feeble glimmer of light, which shone
through a crevice in the wainscoting of a dark nook in the
bedroom, announced some recess or concealment behind the
arras. Quentin hastened to examine it. He found there
was indeed a concealed door, but it resisted his hurried
efforts to open it. Heedless of the personal injury he might
sustain, he rushed at the door with his whole force and
weight of his body ; and such was the impetus of an effort
made betwixt hope and despair, that it would have burst
much stronger fastenings.

He thus forced his way, almost headlong, into a small
oratory, where a female figure, which had been kneeling in
agonizing supplication before the holy image, now sunk at
length on the floor, under the new terrors implied in this
approaching tumult. He hastily raised her from the
ground, and, joy of joys ! it was she whom he sought to
save—the Countess Isabelle. He pressed her to his bosom
—he conjured her to awake—entreated her to be of good
cheer—for that she was now under the protection of one

who had heart and hand enough to defend her against armies.

"Durward!" she said, as she at length collected herself, "is it indeed you? Then there is some hope left. I thought all living and mortal friends had left me to my fate. Do not again abandon me."

"Never—never!" said Durward. "Whatever shall happen—whatever danger shall approach, may I forfeit the benefits purchased by yonder blessed sign, if I be not the sharer of your fate until it is again a happy one!"

"Very pathetic and touching, truly," said a rough, broken, asthmatic voice behind. "A love affair, I see; and, from my soul, I pity the tender creature as if she were my own Trudchen."

"You must do more than pity us," said Quentin, turning towards the speaker; "you must assist in protecting us, Meinher Pavillon. Be assured this lady was put under my especial charge by your ally the King of France; and, if you aid me not to shelter her from every species of offense and violence, your city will lose the favor of Louis of Valois. Above all, she must be guarded from the hands of William de la Marck."

"That will be difficult," said Pavillon, "for these *schelms* of lanzknechts are very devils at rummaging out the wenches; but I'll do my best. We will to the other apartment, and there I will consider. It is but a narrow stair, and you can keep the door with a pike, while I look from the window, and get together some of my brisk boys of the curriers' guildry or Liege, that are as true as the knives they wear in their girdles. But first undo me these clasps; for I have not worn this corslet since the battle of St. Tron,* and I am three stone heavier since that time, if there be truth in Dutch beam and scale."

The undoing of the iron inclosure gave great relief to the honest man, who, in putting it on, had more considered his zeal to the cause of Liege than his capacity of bearing arms. It afterwards turned out that, being, as it were, borne forward involuntarily, and hoisted over the walls by his company as they thronged to the assault, the magistrate had been carried here and there, as the tide of attack and defense flowed or ebbed, without the power, latterly, of even uttering a word; until, as the sea casts a log of driftwood ashore in the first creek, he had been ultimately thrown down in the entrance to the Ladies of Croye's apartments, where the encumbrance of his own armor, with the superincum-

* See Note 30.

bent weight of two men slain in the entrance, and who fell above him, might have fixed him down long enough, had he not been relieved by Durward.

The same warmth of temper, which rendered Hermann Pavillon a hot-headed and intemperate zealot in politics, had the more desirable consequence of making him, in private, a good-tempered, kind-hearted man, who, if sometimes a little misled by vanity, was always well-meaning and benevolent. He told Quentin to have an especial care of the poor pretty *yungfrau ;* and, after this unnecessary exhortation, began to halloo from the window, " Liege, Liege, for the gallant skinners' guild of curriers ! "

One or two of his immediate followers collected at the summons, and at the peculiar whistle with which it was accompanied (each of the crafts having such a signal among themselves), and, more joining them, established a guard under the window from which their leader was bawling, and before the postern-door.

Matters seemed now settling into some sort of tranquility. All opposition had ceased, and the leaders of the different classes of assailants were taking measures to prevent indiscriminate plunder. The great bell was tolled, as summons to a military council, and its iron tongue, communicating to Liege the triumphant possession of Schonwaldt by the insurgents, was answered by all the bells in that city, whose distant and clamorous voices seemed to cry, " Hail to the victors ! " It would have been natural, that Meinherr Pavillon should now have sallied from his fastness ; but, either in reverent care of those whom he had taken under his protection, or perhaps for the better assurance of his own safety, he contented himself with despatching messenger on messenger, to command his lieutenant, Peterkin Geislaer, to attend him directly.

Peterkin came at length, to his great relief, as being the person upon whom, on all pressing occasions, whether of war, politics, or commerce, Pavillon was most accustomed to repose confidence. He was a stout, squat figure, with a square face and broad black eyebrows, that announced him to be opinionative and disputatious,—an advice-giving countenance, so to speak. He was endued with a buff jerkin, wore a broad belt and cutlass by his side, and carried a halberd in his hand.

" Peterkin, my dear lieutenant," said his commander, " this has been a glorious day—night, I should say ; I trust . thou art pleased for once ? "

"I am well enough pleased that you are so," said the doughty lieutenant; "though I should not have thought of your celebrating the victory, if you call it one, up in this garret by yourself, when you are wanted in council."

"But *am* I wanted there?" said the syndic.

"Ay, marry are you, to stand up for the rights of Liege, that are in more danger than ever," answered the lieutenant.

"Pshaw, Peterkin," answered his principal, "thou art ever such a frampold grumbler——"

"Grumbler! not I," said Peterkin; "what pleases other people will always please me. Only I wish we have not got King Stork, instead of King Log, like the *fabliau* that the clerk of St. Lambert's used to read us out of Meister Æsop's book."

"I cannot guess your meaning, Peterkin," said the syndic.

"Why then, I tell you, Master Pavillon, that this Boar, or Bear, is like to make his own den of Schonwaldt, and 'tis probable to turn out as bad a neighbor to our town as ever was the old bishop and worse. Here has he taken the whole conquest in his own hand, and is only doubting whether he should be called prince or bishop; and it is a shame to see how they have mishandled the old man among them."

"I will not permit it, Peterkin," said Pavillon, bustling up; "I disliked the miter, but not the head that wore it. We are ten to one in the field, Peterkin, and will not permit these courses."

"Ay, ten to one in the field, but only man to man in the castle; besides that Nikkel Blok the butcher, and all the rabble of the suburbs, take part with William de la Marck, partly for *saus* and *braus*, for he had broached all the ale-tubs and wine-casks, and partly for old envy towards us, who are the craftsmen, and have privileges."

"Peter," said Pavillon, "we will go presently to the city. I will stay no longer in Schonwaldt."

"But the bridges of this castle are up, master," said Geislaer; "the gates locked, and guarded by these lanz-knechts; and, if it were to try to force our way, these fellows, whose everyday business is war, might make wild work of us, that only fight of a holyday."

"But why has he secured the gates?" said the alarmed burgher; "or what business hath he to make honest men prisoners?"

"I cannot tell—not I," said Peter. "Some noise there

is about the Ladies of Croye, who have escaped during the storm of the castle. That first put the Man with the Beard beside himself with anger, and now he's beside himself with drink also."

The burgomaster cast a disconsolate look towards Quentin, and seemed at a loss what to resolve upon. Durward, who had not lost a word of the conversation, which alarmed him very much, saw nevertheless that their only safety depended on his preserving his own presence of mind, and sustaining the courage of Pavillon. He struck boldly into the conversation, as one who had a right to have a voice in the deliberation. "I am ashamed," he said, "Meinherr Pavillon, to observe you hesitate what to do on this occasion. Go boldly to William de la Marck, and demand free leave to quit the castle, you, your lieutenant, your squire, and your daughter. He can have no pretense for keeping you prisoner."

"For me and my lieutenant—that is myself and Peter—good ; but who is my squire ? "

"I am, for the present," replied the undaunted Scot.

"You ! " said the embarrassed burgess ; "but are you not the envoy of King Louis of France ? "

"True, but my message is to the magistrates of Liege, and only in Liege will I deliver it. Were I to acknowledge my quality before William de la Marck, must I not enter into negotiation with him—ay, and, it is like, be detained by him ? You must get me secretly out of the castle in the capacity of your squire."

"Good—my squire. But you spoke of my daughter ; my daughter is, I trust, safe in my house in Liege—where I wish her father was, with all my heart and soul."

"This lady," said Durward, "will call you father while we are in this place."

"And for my whole life afterwards," said the countess, throwing herself at the citizen's feet and clasping his knees. "Never shall the day pass in which I will not honor you, love you, and pray for you as a daughter for a father, if you will but aid me in this fearful strait. Oh, be not hard-hearted ! think your own daughter may kneel to a stranger, to ask him for life and honor—think of this, and give *me* the protection you would wish *her* to receive ! "

"In troth," said the good citizen, much moved with her pathetic appeal, "I think, Peter, that this pretty maiden hath a touch of our Trudchen's sweet look,—I thought so from the first ; and that this brisk youth here, who is so ready with his advice, is somewhat like Trudchen's bachelor.

16

I wager a groat, Peter, that this is a true-love matter, and it is a sin not to further it."

"It were shame and sin both," said Peter, a good-natured Fleming, notwithstanding all his self-conceit; and as he spoke he wiped his eyes with the sleeve of his jerkin.

"She *shall* be my daughter, then," said Pavillon, "well wrapped up in her black silk veil ; and if there are not enough of true-hearted skinners to protect her, being the daughter of their syndic, it were pity they should ever tug leather more. But hark ye, questions must be answered. How if I am asked what should my daughter make here at such an onslaught ? "

"What should half the women in Liege make here when they followed us to the castle ? " said Peter ; "they had no other reason, sure, but that it was just the place in the world that they should *not* have come to. Our *yungfràu* Trudchen has come a little farther than the rest, that is all."

"Admirably spoken," said Quentin : "only be bold, and take this gentleman's good counsel, noble Meinherr Pavillon, and, at no trouble to yourself, you will do the most worthy action since the days of Charlemagne. Here, sweet lady, wrap yourself close in this veil," for many articles of female apparel lay scattered about the apartment ; be but confident, and a few minutes will place you in freedom and safety. Noble sir," he added, addressing Pavillon, "set forward."

"Hold—hold—hold a minute," said Pavillon, "my mind misgives me ! This De la Marck is a fury—a perfect boar in his nature as in his name ; what if the young lady be one of those of Croye ? and what if he discovers her, and be addicted to wrath ? "

"And if I were one of those unfortunate women," said Isabelle, again attempting to throw herself at his feet, "could you for that reject me in this moment of despair ? Oh, that I had been indeed your daughter, or the daughter of the poorest burgher ! "

"Not so poor—not so poor neither, young lady ; we pay as we go," said the citizen.

"Forgive me, noble sir," again began the unfortunate maiden.

"Not noble, nor sir neither," said the syndic ; "a plain burgher of Liege, that pays bills of exchange in ready guilders. But that is nothing to the purpose. Well, say you *be* a countess, I will protect you nevertheless."

"You are bound to protect her, were she a duchess," said Peter, "having once passed your word."

"Right, Peter, very right," said the syndic ; "it is our old Low Dutch fashion, *ein wort, eiu mann ;* and now let us to this gear. We must take leave of this William de la Marck ; and yet I know not, my mind misgives me when I think of him ; and were it a ceremony which could be waived, I have no stomach to go through it."

"Were you not better, since you have a force together, make for the gate and force the guard ?" said Quentin.

But with united voice, Pavillon and his advisers exclaimed against the propriety of such an attack upon their ally's soldiers, with some hints concerning its rashness, which satisfied Quentin that it was not a risk to be hazarded with such associates. They resolved, therefore, to repair boldly to the great hall of the castle, where, as they understood, the Wild Boar of Ardennes held his feast, and demand free egress for the syndic of Liege and his company, a request too reasonable, as it seemed, to be denied. Still the good burgomaster groaned when he looked on his companions, and exclaimed to his faithful Peter, "See what it is to have too bold and too tender a heart ! Alas ! Perkin, how much have courage and humanity cost me ! and how much may I yet have to pay for my virtues before Heaven makes us free of this damned castle of Schonwoldt !"

As they crossed the court, still strewed with the dying and dead, Quentin, while he supported Isabelle through the scene of horrors, whispered to her courage and comfort, and reminded her that her safety depended entirely on her firmness and presence of mind.

"Not on mine—not on mine," she said, "but on yours— on yours only. O, if I but escape this fearful night, never shall I forget him who saved me ! One favor more only let me implore at your hand, and I conjure you to grant it, by your mother's fame and your father's honor !"

"What is it you can ask that I could refuse ?" said Quentin in a whisper.

"Plunge your dagger in my heart," said she, "rather than leave me captive in the hands of these monsters."

Quentin's only answer was a pressure of the young countess's hand, which seemed as if, but for terror, it would have returned the caress. And, leaning on her youthful protector, she entered the fearful hall, preceded by Pavillon and his lieutenant, and followed by a dozen of the *kurschenschaft* [*kürschnerschaft*] or skinner's trade, who attended as a guard of honor on the syndic.

As they approached the hall, the yells of acclamation and

bursts of wild laughter, which proceeded from it, seemed rather to announce the revel of festive demons rejoicing after some accomplished triumph over the human race than of mortal beings who had succeeded in a bold design. An emphatic tone of mind, which despair alone could have inspired, supported the assumed courage of the Countess Isabelle; undaunted spirits, which rose with the extremity, maintained that of Durward ; while Pavillon and his lieutenant made a virtue of necessity, and faced their fate like bears bound to a stake, which must necessarily stand the dangers of the course.

CHAPTER XXII

THE REVELERS

Cade. Where's Dick, the butcher of Ashford?
Dick. Here, sir.
Cade. They fell before thee like sheep and oxen; and thou behavedst thyself as if thou hadst been in thine own slaughter-house.
                                   King Henry VI., Part II.

THERE could hardly exist a more strange and horrible change than had taken place in the castle-hall of Schonwalt since Quentin had partaken of the noontide meal there; and it was indeed one which painted, in the extremity of their dreadful features, the miseries of war—more especially when waged by those most relentless of all agents, the mercernary soldiers of a barbarous age—men who, by habit and profession, had become familiarized with all that was cruel and bloody in the art of war, while they were devoid alike of patriotism and of the romantic spirit of chivalry.

Instead of the orderly, decent, and somewhat formal meal, at which civil and ecclesiastical officers had, a few hours before, sat mingled in the same apartment, where a light jest could only be uttered in a whisper, and where, even amid superfluity of feasting and of wine, there reigned a decorum which almost amounted to hypocrisy, there was now such a scene of wild and roaring debauchery as Satan himself, had he taken the chair as founder of the feast, could scarcely have improved.

At the head of the table sat, in the bishop's throne and state, which had been hastily brought thither from his great council-chamber, the redoubted Boar of Ardennes himself, well deserving that dreaded name, in which he affected to delight and which he did as much as he could think of to deserve. His head was unhelmeted, but he wore the rest of his ponderous and bright armor, which indeed he rarely laid aside. Over his shoulders hung a strong surcoat, made of the dressed skin of a huge wild boar, the hoofs being of solid silver and the tusks of the same. The skin of the head was so arranged that, drawn over the casque when the baron was armed, or over his bare head, in the fashion of a hood,

245

as he often affected when the helmet was laid aside, and as he now wore it, the effect was that of a grinning, ghastly monster ; and yet the countenance which it overshadowed scarce required such horrors to improve those which were natural to its ordinary expression.

The upper part of De la Marck's face, as nature had formed it, almost gave the lie to his character ; for though his hair when uncovered, resembled the rude and wild bristles of the hood he had drawn over it, yet an open, high, and manly forehead, broad ruddy cheeks, large, sparkling, light-colored eyes, and a nose hooked like the beak of the eagle, promised something valiant and generous. But the effect of these more favorable traits was entirely overpowered by his habits of violence and insolence, which, joined to debauchery and intemperance, had stamped upon the features a character inconsistent with the rough gallantry which they would otherwise have exhibited. The former had, from habitual indulgence, swollen the muscles of the cheeks and those around the eyes, in particular the latter ; evil practises and habits had dimmed the eyes themselves, reddened the part of them that should have been white, and given the whole face a hideous likeness of the monster which it was the terrible baron's pleasure to resemble. But from an odd sort of contradiction, De la Marck, while he assumed in other respects the appearance of the wild boar, and even seemed pleased with the name, yet endeavored, by the length and growth of his beard, to conceal the circumstance that had originally procured him that denomination. This was an unusual thickness and projection of the mouth and upper jaw, which, with the huge projecting side teeth, gave that resemblance to the bestial creation which, joined to the delight which De la Marck had in haunting the forest so called, originally procured for him the name of the Boar of Ardennes. The beard, broad, grisly, and uncombed, neither concealed the natural horrors of the countenance nor dignified its brutal expression.

The soldiers and officers sat around the table, intermixed with the men of Liege, some of them of the very lowest description ; among whom Nikkel Blok, the butcher, placed near De la Marck himself, was distinguished by his tucked-up sleeves, which displayed arms smeared to the elbows with blood, as was the cleaver which lay on the table before him. The soldiers wore, most of them, their beards long and grisly, in imitation of their leader ; had their hair plaited and turned upwards in the manner that might best improve the natural ferocity of their appearance ; and intoxicated, as many of them seemed to be, partly with the sense of triumph, and partly with the long libations of wine which they had been quaffing, presented a spectacle at once hideous and disgusting. The language which they held, and the songs which they sung, without even pretending to pay each other the compliment of listening, were so full of license and blasphemy, that Quentin blessed God that the extremity of the noise prevented them from being intelligible to his companion.

It only remains to say, of the better class of burghers who were associated with William de la Marck's soldiers in this fearful revel, that the wan faces and anxious mien of the greater part showed that they either disliked their entertainment or feared their companions ; while some of lower education, or a nature more brutal, saw only in the excesses of the soldier a gallant bearing, which they would willingly imitate, and the tone of which they endeavored to catch so far as was possible, and stimulated themselves to the task by swallowing immense draughts of wine and *schwarzbier*— indulging a vice which at all times was too common in the Low Countries.

The preparations for the feast had been as disorderly as the quality of the company. The whole of the bishop's plate—nay, even that belonging to the service of the church, for the Boar of Ardennes regarded not the imputation of sacrilege—was mingled with blackjacks, or huge tankards made of leather, and drinking-horns of the most ordinary description.

One circumstance of horror remains to be added and accounted for ; and we willingly leave the rest of the scene to the imagination of the reader. Amidst the wild license assumed by the soldiers of De la Marck, one who was excluded from the table—a lanzknecht, remarkable for his courage and for his daring behavior during the storm of the evening—had impudently snatched up a large silver goblet and carried it off, declaring it should atone for his loss of the share of the feast. The leader laughed till his sides shook at a jest so congenial to the character of the company ; but when another, less renowned, it would seem, for audacity in battle, ventured on using the same freedom, De la Marck instantly put a check to a jocular practise which would soon have cleared his table of all the more valuable decorations. " Ho ! by the spirit of the thunder !" he exclaimed, " those who dare not be men when they face the enemy must not

pretend to be thieves among their friends. What! thou
frontless dastard, thou—thou who didst wait for opened
gate and lowered bridge, when Conrade Horst forced his
way over moat and wall, must *thou* be malapert? Knit him
up to the stanchions of the hall-window! He shall beat
time with his feet while we drink a cup to his safe passage
to the devil."

The doom was scarce sooner pronounced than accomplished ; and in a moment the wretch wrestled out his last
agonies, suspended from the iron bars. His body still hung
there when Quentin and the others entered the hall, and in-
tercepting the pale moonbeam, threw on the castle-floor an
uncertain shadow, which dubiously, yet fearfully intimated
the nature of the substance that produced it.

When the syndic Pavillon was announced from mouth to
mouth in this tumultuous meeting, he endeavored to assume,
in right of his authority and influence, an air of importance
and equality, which a glance at the fearful object at the
window, and at the wild scene around him, rendered it very
difficult for him to sustain, notwithstanding the exhortations
of Peter, who whispered in his ear, with some perturbation,
" Up heart, master, or we are but gone men!"

The syndic maintained his dignity, however, as well as he
could, in a short address, in which he complimented the
company upon the great victory gained by the soldiers of De
la Marck and the good citizens of Liege.

"Ay," answered De la Marck, sarcastically, " we have
brought down the game at last, quoth my lady's brach to
the wolf-hound. But ho! sir burgomaster, you come like
Mars, with beauty by your side. Who is this fair one?
Unveil—unveil ; no woman calls her beauty her own to-
night."

" It is my daughter, noble leader," answered Pavillion ;
" and I am to pray your forgiveness for her wearing a veil.
She has a vow for that effect to the Three Blessed Kings."

" I will absolve her of it presently," said De la Marck ;
" for here, with one stroke of a cleaver, will I consecrate myself Bishop of Liege ; and I trust one living bishop is worth
three dead kings."

There was a shuddering and murmur among the guests ;
for the community of Liege, and even some of the rude
soldiers, reverenced the Kings of Cologne, as they were commonly called, though they respected nothing else.

" Nay, I mean no treason against their defunct majesties,"
said De la Marck ; " only bishop I am determined to be. A

prince both secular and ecclesiastical, having power to bind
and loose, will best suit a band of reprobates such as you, to
whom no one else would give absolution. But come hither,
noble burgomaster, sit beside me, when you shall see me make
a vacancy for my own preferment. Bring in our predecessor in the holy seat."

A bustle took place in the hall, while Pavillon, excusing
himself from the proffered seat of honor, placed himself near
the bottom of the table, his followers keeping close behind
him, not unlike a flock of sheep which, when a stranger dog
is in presence, may be sometimes seen to assemble in the
rear of an old bellwether, who is, from office and authority,
judged by them to have rather more courage than themselves.
Near the spot sat a very handsome lad, a natural son, as was
said, of the ferocious De la Marck, and towards whom he
sometimes showed affection, and even tenderness. The
mother of the boy, a beautiful concubine, had perished by a
blow dealt her by the ferocious leader in a fit of drunkenness
or jealousy ; and her fate had caused her tyrant as much
remorse as he was capable of feeling. His attachment to
the surviving orphan might be partly owing to these circumstances. Quentin, who had learned this point of the leader's
character from the old priest, planted himself as close as he
could to the youth in question ; determined to make him, in
some way or other, either a hostage or a protector, should
other means of safety fail them.

While all stood in a kind of suspense, waiting the event of
the orders which the tyrant had issued, one of Pavillon's followers whispered Peter, " Did not our master call that wench
his daughter ? Why, it cannot be our Trudchen. This
strapping lass is taller by two inches ; and there is a black
lock of her hair peeps forth yonder from under her veil.
By St. Michael of the market-place, you might as well call a
black bullock's hide a white heifer's ! "

" Hush ! hush ! " said Peter, with some presence of mind.
" What if our master hath a mind to steal a piece of doe-
venison out of the bishop's park here without our good
dame's knowledge ? And is it for thee or me to be a spy on
him ? "

" That will not I, brother," answered the other, " though
I would not have thought of his turning deer-stealer at his
years. *Sapperment*—what a shy fairy it is ! See how she
crouches down on yonder seat, behind folk's backs, to escape the gaze of the Marckers. But hold—hold ; what are
they about to do with the poor old bishop ? "

As he spoke, the Bishop of Liege, Louis of Bourbon, was dragged into the hall of his own palace by the brutal soldiery. The disheveled state of his hair, beard, and attire bore witness to the ill treatment he had already received ; and some of his sacerdotal robes, hastily flung over him, appeared to have been put on in scorn and ridicule of his quality and character. By good fortune, as Quentin was compelled to think it, the Countess Isabelle, whose feelings at seeing her protector in such an extremity might have betrayed her own secret and compromised her safety, was so situated as neither to hear nor see what was about to take place ; and Durward sedulously interposed his own person before her, so as to keep her from observing alike, and from observation.

The scene which followed was short and fearful. When the unhappy prelate was brought before the footstool of the savage leader, although in former life only remarkable for his easy and good-natured temper, he showed in this extremity a sense of his dignity and noble blood, well becoming the high race from which he was descended. His look was composed and undismayed ; his gesture, when the rude hands which dragged him forward were unloosed, was noble, and at the same time resigned, somewhat between the bearing of a feudal noble and of a Christian martyr ; and so much was even De la Marck himself staggered by the firm demeanor of his prisoner, and recollection of the early benefits he had received from him, that he seemed irresolute, cast down his eyes, and it was not until he had emptied a large goblet of wine, that, resuming his haughty insolence of look and manner, he thus addressed his unfortunate captive :—"Louis of Bourbon," said the truculent soldier, drawing hard his breath, clenching his hands, setting his teeth, and using the other mechanical actions to rouse up and sustain his native ferocity of temper, "I sought your friendship, and you rejected mine. What would you now give that it had been otherwise ? Nikkel, be ready."

The butcher rose, seized his weapon, and stealing round behind De la Marck's chair, stood with it uplifted in his bare and sinewy arms.

"Look at that man, Louis of Bourbon," said De la Marck again ; "what terms wilt thou now offer to escape this dangerous hour ?"

The bishop cast a melancholy but unshaken look upon the grisly satellite, who seemed prepared to execute the will of the tyrant, and then he said with firmness, "Hear me, William De la Marck ; and good men all, if there be any here who deserve that name, hear the only terms I can offer to this ruffian. William de la Marck, thou hast stirred up to sedition an imperial city, hast assaulted and taken the palace of a prince of the Holy German Empire, slain his people, plundered his goods, maltreated his person ; for this thou art liable to the ban of the Empire—hast deserved to be declared outlawed and fugitive, landless and rightless. Thou hast done more than all this. More than mere human laws hast thou broken, more than mere human vengeance hast thou deserved. Thou hast broken into the sanctuary of the Lord, laid violent hands upon a father of the church, defiled the house of God with blood and rapine, like a sacrilegious robber——"

"Hast thou yet done ?" said De la Marck ; fiercely interrupting him, and stamping with his foot.

"No," answered the prelate, "for I have not yet told thee the terms which you demanded to hear from me."

"Go on," said De la Marck ; "and let the terms please me better than the preface, or woe to thy gray head !" And flinging himself back to his seat, he grinded his teeth till the foam flew from his lips, as from the tusks of the savage animal whose name and spoils he wore.

"Such are thy crimes," resumed the bishop, with calm determination ; "now hear the terms which, as a merciful prince and a Christian prelate, setting aside all personal offense, forgiving each peculiar injury, I condescend to offer. Fling down thy leading-staff, renounce thy command, unbind thy prisoners, restore thy spoil, distribute what else thou hast of goods to relieve those whom thou hast made orphans and widows, array thyself in sackcloth and ashes, take a palmer's staff in thy hand, and go barefooted on pilgrimage to Rome, and we will ourselves be intercessors for thee with the Imperial chamber at Ratisbon for thy life, with our Holy Father the Pope for thy miserable soul."

While Louis of Bourbon proposed these terms in a tone as decided as if he still occupied his episcopal throne, and as if the usurper kneeled a suppliant at his feet, the tyrant slowly raised himself in his chair, the amazement with which he was at first filled giving way gradually to rage, until, as the bishop ceased, he looked to Nikkel Blok, and raised his finger, without speaking a word. The ruffian struck, as if he had been doing his office in the common shambles, and the murdered bishop sunk, without a groan, at the foot of his own episcopal throne.* The Liegeois, who were not prepared

* See Murder of the Bishop of Liege. Note 31.

for so a horrible a catastrophe, and who had expected to hear
the conference end in some terms of accommodation, started
up unanimously, with cries of execration, mingled with
shouts of vengeance.

But William de la Marck, raising his tremendous voice
above the tumult, and shaking his clenched hand and extended arm, shouted aloud, " How now, ye porkers of Liege !
ye wallowers in the mud of the Maes ! do ye dare to mate
yourselves with the Wild Boar of Ardennes ? Up, ye Boar's
brood ! (an expression by which he himself and others often
designated his soldiers) let these Flemish hogs see your
tusks ! "

Every one of his followers started up at the command, and
mingled as they were among their late allies, prepared too
for such a surprisal, each had, in an instant, his next neighbor by the collar, while his right hand brandished a broad
dagger that glimmered against lamplight and moonshine.
Every arm was uplifted, but no one struck ; for the victims
were too much surprised for resistance, and it was probably
the object of De la Marck only to impose terror on his civic
confederates.

But the courage of Quentin Durward, prompt and alert
in resolution beyond his years, and stimulated at the moment
by all that could add energy to his natural shrewdness and
resolution, gave a new turn to the scene. Imitating the
action of the followers of De la Marck, he sprung on Carl
Eberson, the son of their leader, and mastering him with
ease, held his dirk at the boy's throat, while he exclaimed,
" Is that your game ? then here I play my part."

" Hold ! hold ! " exclaimed De la Marck, " It is a jest—a
jest. Think you I would injure my good friends and allies
of the city of Liege ? Soldiers, unloose your holds ; sit
down : take away the carrion (giving the bishop's corpse a
thrust with his foot), which hath caused this strife among
friends, and let us drown unkindness in a fresh carouse."

All unloosened their holds, and the citizens and soldiers
stood gazing on each other, as if they scarce knew whether
they were friends or foes.

Quentin Durward took advantage of the moment. " Hear
me," he said, " William de la Marck, and you, burghers and
citizens of Liege ; and do you, young sir, stand still," for
the boy Carl was attempting to escape from his gripe, " no
harm shall befall you, unless another of these sharp jests
shall pass round."

" Who art thou, in the fiend's name," said the astonished

De la Marck, " who art come to hold terms and take hostages from us in our own lair—from us, who exact pledges from others, but yield them to no one ? "

" I am a servant of King Louis of France," said Quentin boldly ; " an archer of the Scottish Guard, as my language and dress may partly tell you. I am here to behold and to report your proceedings ; and I see with wonder that they are those of heathens rather than Christians—of madmen rather than men possessed of reason. The hosts of Charles of Burgundy will be instantly in motion against you all ; and if you wish assistance from France, you must conduct yourselves in a different manner. For you, men of Liege, I advise your instant return to your own city ; and if there is any obstruction offered to your departure, I denounce those by whom it is so offered foes to my master, his most gracious Majesty of France."

" France and Liege ! France and Liege ! " cried the followers of Pavillon, and several other citizens, whose courage began to rise at the bold language held by Quentin.

" France and Liege, and long live the gallant archer ! We will live and die with him ! "

William de la Marck's eyes sparkled, and he grasped his dagger as if about to launch it at the heart of the audacious speaker ; but glancing his eye around, he read something in the looks of his soldiers, which even *he* was obliged to respect. Many of them were Frenchmen, and all of them knew the private support which William had received, both in men and in money, from that kingdom ; nay, some of them were rather startled at the violent and sacrilegious action which had been just committed. The name of Charles of Burgundy, a person likely to resent to the utmost the deeds of that night, had an alarming sound, and the extreme impolicy of at once quarreling with the Liegeois and provoking the monarch of France, made an appalling impression on their minds, confused as their intellects were. De la Marck, in short, saw he would not be supported, even by his own band, in any farther act of immediate violence, and relaxing the terrors of his brow and eye, declared that " he had not the least design against his good friends of Liege, all of whom were at liberty to depart from Schonwaldt at their pleasure, although he had hoped they would revel one night with him, at least, in honor of their victory." He added, with more calmness than he commonly used, that " he would be ready to enter into negotiation concerning the partition of spoil, and the arrangement of measures for their mutual defense, either the next day, or as soon after as they would. Meantime, he trusted that the Scottish gentleman would honor his feast by remaining all night at Schonwaldt."

The young Scot returned his thanks, but said his motions must be determined by those of Pavillon, to whom he was directed particularly to attach himself ; but that, unquestionably, he would attend him on his next return to the quarters of the valiant William de la Marck.

"If you depend on my motions," said Pavillon, hastily and aloud, "you are likely to quit Schonwaldt without an instant's delay ; and, if you do not come back to Schonwaldt, save in my company, you are not likely to see it again in a hurry."

This last part of the sentence the honest citizen muttered to himself, afraid of the consequences of giving audible vent to feelings which, nevertheless, he was unable altogether to suppress.

"Keep close about me, my brisk *kürschner* lads," he said to his body-guard, "and we will get as fast as we can out of this den of thieves."

Most of the better classes of the Liegeois seemed to entertain similar opinions with the syndic, and there had been scarce so much joy amongst them at the obtaining possession of Schonwaldt, as now seemed to arise from the prospect of getting safe out of it. They were suffered to leave the castle without opposition of any kind ; and glad was Quentin when he turned his back on those formidable walls.

For the first time since they had entered that dreadful hall, Quentin ventured to ask the young countess how she did.

"Well—well," she answered, in feverish haste, "excellently well ; do not stop to ask a question ; let us not lose an instant in words. Let us fly—let us fly ! "

She endeavored to mend her pace as she spoke ; but with so little success that she must have fallen from exhaustion had not Durward supported her. With the tenderness of a mother, when she conveys her infant out of danger, the young Scot raised his precious charge in his arms ; and, while she encircled his neck with one arm, lost to every other thought save the desire of escaping, he would not have wished one of the risks of the night unencountered, since such had been the conclusion.

The honest burgomaster was, in his turn, supported and dragged forward by his faithful counselor Peter and another of his clerks ; and thus, in breathless haste, they reached banks of the river, encountering many strolling bands of citizens, who were eager to know the event of the siege, and the truth of certain rumors already afloat, that the conquerors had quarreled among themselves.

Evading their curiosity as they best could, the exertions of Peter and some of his companions at length procured a boat for the use of the company, and with it an opportunity of enjoying some repose, equally welcome to Isabelle, who continued to lie almost motionless in the arms of her preserver, and to the worthy burgomaster, who, after delivering a broken string of thanks to Durward, whose mind was at the time too much occupied to answer him, began a long harangue, which he addressed to Peter, upon his own courage and benevolence, and the dangers to which these virtues had exposed him on this and other occasions.

" Peter—Peter," he said, resuming the complaint of the preceding evening, " if I had not had a bold heart, I would never have stood out against paying the burghers' twentieths, when every other living soul was willing to pay the same. Ay, and then a less stout heart had not seduced me into that other battle of St. Tron, where a Hainault man-at-arms thrust me into a muddy ditch with his lance, which neither heart nor hand that I had could help me out of till the battle was over. Ay, and then, Peter, this very night my courage seduced me, moreover, into too strait a corslet, which would have been the death of me but for the aid of this gallant young gentleman, whose trade is fighting, whereof I wish him heartily joy. And then for my tenderness of heart, Peter, it has made a poor man of me—that is, it would have made a poor man of me, if I had not been tolerably well to pass in this wicked world ; and Heaven knows what trouble it is like to bring on me yet, with ladies, countesses, and keeping of secrets, which, for aught I know, may cost me half my fortune, and my neck into the bargain !"

Quentin could remain no longer silent, but assured him that, whatever danger or damage he should incur on the part of the young lady now under his protection should be thankfully acknowledged, and, as far as was possible, repaid.

" I thank you, young master squire archer—I thank you," answered the citizen of Liege ; " but who was it told you that I desired any repayment at your hand for doing the duty of an honest man ? I only regretted that it might cost me so and so ; and I hope I may have leave to say so

much to my lieutenant, without either grudging my loss or
my peril."

Quentin accordingly concluded that his present friend was
one of the numerous class of benefactors to others, who take
out their reward in grumbling, without meaning more than,
by showing their grievances, to exalt a little the idea of the
valuable service by which they have incurred them, and therefore prudently remained silent, and suffered the syndic to
maunder on to his lieutenant concerning the risk and the
loss he had encountered by his zeal for the public good, and
his disinterested services to individuals, until they reached
his own habitation.

The truth was, that the honest citizen felt that he had lost
a little consequence, by suffering the young stranger to take
the lead at the crisis which had occurred at the castle-hall of
Schonwaldt ; and, however delighted with the effect of Durward's interference at the moment, it seemed to him, on
reflection, that he had sustained a diminution of importance,
for which he endeavored to obtain compensation, by exagge-
rating the claims which he had upon the gratitude of his
country in general, his friends in particular, and more
especially still, on the Countess of Croye and her youthful
protector.

But when the boat stopped at the bottom of his garden,
and he had got himself assisted on shore by Peter, it seemed
as if the touch of his own threshold had at once dissipated
those feelings of wounded self-opinion and jealousy, and converted the discontented and obscured demagogue into the
honest, kind, hospitable, and friendly host. He called loudly
for Trudchen, who presently appeared ; for fear and anxiety
would permit few within the walls of Liege to sleep during
that eventful night. She was charged to pay the utmost attention to the care of the beautiful and half-fainting stranger ;
and, admiring her personal charms, while she pitied her distress, Gertrude discharged the hospitable duty with the zeal
and affection of a sister.

Late as it now was, and fatigued as the syndic appeared,
Quentin, on his side, had difficulty to escape a flask of choice
and costly wine, as old as the battle of Azincour ; and must
have submitted to take his share, however unwilling, but for
the appearance of the mother of the family, whom Pavillon's
loud summons for the keys of the cellar brought forth from
her bedroom. She was a jolly little roundabout woman,
who had been pretty in her time, but whose principal
characteristics for several years had been a red and sharp

nose, a shrill voice, and a determination that the syndic, in consideration of the authority which he exercised when abroad, should remain under the rule of due discipline at home.

So soon as she understood the nature of the debate between her husband and his guest, she declared roundly, that the former, instead of having occasion for more wine, had got too much already ; and far from using, in furtherance of his request, any of the huge bunch of keys which hung by a silver chain at her waist, she turned her back on him without cere- mony, and ushered Quentin to the neat and pleasant apartment in which he was to spend the night, amid such appliances to rest and comfort as probably he had till that moment been entirely a stranger to ; so much did the wealthy Flemings excel, not merely the poor and rude Scots, but the French themselves, in all the conveniences of domestic life.

17

CHAPTER XXIII

THE FLIGHT

> Now bid me run,
> And I will strive with things impossible—
> Yea, get the better of them.
>
> .   .   .   .
>
> Set on your foot ;
> And, with a heart new fired, I follow you
> To do I know not what.
>
> *Julius Cæsar.*

IN spite of a mixture of joy and fear, doubt, anxiety, and other agitating passions, the exhausting fatigues of the preceding day were powerful enough to throw the young Scot into a deep and profound repose, which lasted until late on the day following ; when his worthy host entered the apartment, with looks of care on his brow.

He seated himself by his guest's bedside, and began a long and complicated discourse upon the domestic duties of a married life, and especially upon the awful power and right supremacy which it became married men to sustain in all differences of opinion with their wives. Quentin listened with some anxiety. He knew that husbands, like other belligerent powers, were sometimes disposed to sing *Te Deum*, rather to conceal a defeat than to celebrate a victory ; and he hastened to probe the matter more closely, " by hoping their arrival had been attended with no inconvenience to the good lady of the household."

" Inconvenience ! no," answered the burgomaster. " No woman can be less taken unawares than Mother Mabel— always happy to see her friends—always a clean lodging and a handsome meal ready for them, with God's blessing on bed and board. No woman on earth so hospitable ; only 'tis pity her temper is something particular."

" Our residence here is disagreeable to her, in short ? " said the Scot, starting out of bed, and beginning to dress himself hastily. " Were I but sure the Lady Isabelle were fit for travel after the horrors of last night, we would not increase the offense by remaining here an instant longer."

258

"Nay," said Pavillon, "that is just what the young lady herself said to Mother Mabel ; and truly I wish you saw the color that came to her face as she said it—a milkmaid that has skated five miles to market against the frost-wind is a lily compared to it—I do not wonder Mother Mabel may be a little jealous, poor dear soul."

"Has the Lady Isabelle then left her apartment ?" said the youth, continuing his toilette operations with more despatch than before.

"Yes," replied Pavillon ; "and she expects your approach with much impatience, to determine which way you shall go, since you are both determined on going. But I trust you will tarry breakfast ?"

"Why did you not tell me this sooner ?" said Durward impatiently.

"Softly—softly," said the syndic ; "I have told it you too soon, I think, if it puts you into such a hasty fluster. Now I have some more matter for your ear, if I saw you had some patience to listen to me."

"Speak it, worthy sir, as soon and as fast as you can ; I listen devoutly."

"Well, then," resumed the burgomaster, "I have but one word to say, and that is, that Trudchen, who is as sorry to part with yonder pretty lady as if she had been some sister of hers, wants you to take some other disguise ; for there is word in the town that the Ladies of Croye travel the country in pilgrim's dresses, attended by a French life-guardsman of the Scottish Archers ; and it is said one of them was brought into Schonwaldt last night by a Bohemian after we had left it ; and it was said still farther, that this same Bohemian had assured William de la Marck that you were charged with no message either to him or to the good people of Liege, and that you had stolen away the young countess, and traveled with her as her paramour. And all this news hath come from Schonwaldt this morning ; and it has been told to us and the other counselors, who know not well what to advise ; for though our own opinion is that William de la Marck has been a thought too rough both with the bishop and with ourselves, yet there is a great belief that he is a good-natured soul at bottom—that is, when he is sober— and that he is the only leader in the world to command us against the Duke of Burgundy—and, in truth, as matters stand, it is partly my own mind that we must keep fair with him, for we have gone too far to draw back."

"Your daughter advises well," said Quentin Durward,

abstaining from reproaches or exhortations, which he saw
would be alike unavailing to sway a resolution, which had
been adopted by the worthy magistrate in compliance at
once with the prejudices of his party and the inclination of
his wife ; "your daughter counsels well. We must part in
disguise and that instantly. We may, I trust, rely upon
you for the necessary secrecy, and for the means of escape ?"
" With all my heart—with all my heart," said the honest
citizen, who, not much satisfied with the dignity of his own
conduct, was eager to find some mode of atonement. " I
cannot but remember that I owed you my life last night,
both for unclasping that accursed steel doublet, and helping
me through the other scrape, which was worse ; for yonder
Boar and his brood look more like devils than men. So I will
be true to you as blade to haft, as our cutlers say, who are the
best in the whole world. Nay, now you are ready, come
this way, you shall see how far I can trust you."
The syndic led him from the chamber in which he had
slept to his own counting-room, in which he transacted his
affairs of business ; and after bolting the door, and casting a
piercing and careful eye around him, he opened a concealed
and vaulted closet behind the tapestry, in which stood more
than one iron chest. He proceeded to open one which was
full of guilders, and placed it at Quentin's discretion to take
whatever sum he might think necessary for his companion's
expenses and his own.

As the money with which Quentin was furnished on leaving Plessis was now nearly expended, he hesitated not to accept the sum of two hundred guilders ; and by doing so took
a great weight from the mind of Pavillon, who considered
the desperate transaction in which he thus voluntarily became the creditor, as an atonement for the breach of hospitality which various considerations in a great measure compelled him to commit.

Having carefully locked his treasure-chamber, the wealthy
Fleming next conveyed his guest to the parlor, where, in
full possession of her activity of mind and body, though pale
from the scenes of the preceding night, he found the countess attired in the fashion of a Flemish maiden of the mid-
dling class. No other was present excepting Trudchen, who
was sedulously employed in completing the countess's dress,
and instructing her how to bear herself. She extended her
hand to him, which, when he had reverently kissed, she said
to him, " Seignior Quentin, we must leave our friends here,
unless I would bring on them a part of the misery which

has pursued me ever since my father's death. You must change your dress and go with me, unless you also are tired of befriending a being so unfortunate."

"I!—I tired of being your attendant! To the end of the earth will I guard you! But you—you yourself—are you equal to the task you undertake? Can you, after the terrors of last night——"

"Do not recall them to my memory," answered the countess; "I remember but the confusion of a horrid dream. Has the excellent bishop escaped?"

"I trust he is in freedom," said Quentin, making a sign to Pavillon, who seemed about to enter on the dreadful narrative, to be silent.

"Is it possible for us to rejoin him? Hath he gathered any power?" said the lady.

"His only hopes are in Heaven," said the Scot; "but wherever you wish to go, I stand by your side, a determined guide and guard."

"We will consider," said Isabelle; and after a moment's pause, she added, "A convent would be my choice, but that I fear it would prove a weak defense against those who pursue me."

"Hem! hem!" said the syndic, "I could not well recommend a convent within the district of Liege; because the Boar of Ardennes, though in the main a brave leader, a trusty confederate, and a well-wisher to our city, has, nevertheless, rough humors, and payeth, on the whole, little regard to cloisters, convents, nunneries, and the like. Men say that there are a score of nuns—that is, such as were nuns—who march always with his company."

"Get yourself in readiness hastily, Seignior Durward," said Isabelle, interrupting this detail, "since to your faith I must needs commit myself."

No sooner had the syndic and Quentin left the room than Isabelle began to ask of Gertrude various questions concerning the roads, and so forth, with such clearness of spirit and pertinence that the latter could not help exclaiming, "Lady, I wonder at you! I have heard of masculine firmness, but yours appears to me more than belongs to humanity."

"Necessity," answered the countess—"necessity, my friend, is the mother of courage, as of invention. No long time since, I might have fainted when I saw a drop of blood shed from a trifling cut; I have since seen life-blood flow around me, I may say, in waves, yet I have retained my senses and my self-possession. Do not think it was an easy task," she added, laying on Gertrude's arm a trembling hand, although she still spoke with a firm voice ; "the little world within me is like a garrison besieged by a thousand foes, whom nothing but the most determined resolution can keep from storming it on every hand, and at every moment. Were my situation one whit less perilous than it is—were I not sensible that my only chance to escape a fate more horrible than death is to retain my recollection and self-possession— Gertrude, I would at this moment throw myself into your arms, and relieve my bursting bosom by such a transport of tears and agony of terror as never rushed from a breaking heart !"

"Do not do so, lady !" said the sympathizing Fleming ; "take courage, tell your beads, throw yourself on the care of Heaven ; and surely, if ever Heaven sent a deliverer to one ready to perish, that bold and adventurous young gentleman must be designed for yours. There is one, too," she added, blushing deeply, "in whom I have some interest. Say nothing to my father ; but I have ordered my bachelor, Hans Glover, to wait for you at the eastern gate, and never to see my face more, unless he brings word that he has guided you safe from the territory."

To kiss her tenderly was the only way in which the young countess could express her thanks to the frank and kind-hearted city-maiden, who returned the embrace affectionately, and added, with a smile, "Nay, if two maidens and their devoted bachelors cannot succeed in a disguise and an escape, the world is changed from what I am told it wont to be."

A part of this speech again called the color into the countess's pale cheeks, which was not lessened by Quentin's sudden appearance. He entered completely attired as a Flemish boor of the better class, in the holiday suit of Peter, who expressed his interest in the young Scot by the readiness with which he parted with it for his use ; and swore, at the same time, that, were he to be curried and tugged worse than ever was bullock's hide, they should make nothing out of him, to the betraying of the young folks. Two stout horses had been provided by the activity of Mother Mabel, who really desired the countess and her attendant no harm, so that she could make her own house and family clear of the dangers which might attend upon harboring them. She beheld them mount and go off with great satisfaction, after telling them that they would find their way to the east gate by keeping their eye on Peter, who was to walk in that direction as their guide, but without holding any visible communication with them.

The instant her guests had departed, Mother Mabel took the opportunity to read a long practical lecture to Trudchen upon the folly of reading romances, whereby the flaunting ladies of the court were grown so bold and venturous, that, instead of applying to learn some honest housewifery, they must ride, forsooth, a damsel-erranting through the country, with no better attendant than some idle squire, debauched page, or rakehelly archer from foreign parts, to the great danger of their health, the impoverishing of their substance, and the irreparable prejudice of their reputation.

All this Gertrude heard in silence, and without reply ; but, considering her character, it might be doubted whether she derived from it the practical inference which it was her mother's purpose to enforce.

Meantime, the travelers had gained the eastern gate of the city, traversing crowds of people, who were fortunately too much busied in the political events and rumors of the hour to give any attention to a couple who had so little to render their appearance remarkable. They passed the guards in virtue of a permission obtained for them by Pavillon, but in the name of his colleague Rouslaer, and they took leave of Peter Geislaer with a friendly though brief exchange of good wishes on either side. Immediately afterwards they were joined by a stout young man, riding a good gray horse, who presently made himself known as Hans Glover, the bachelor of Trudchen Pavilion. He was a young fellow with a good Flemish countenance—not, indeed, of the most intellectual cast, but arguing more hilarity and good-humor than wit, and, as the countess could not help thinking, scarce worthy to be bachelor to the generous Trudchen. He seemed, however, fully desirous to second the views which she had formed in their favor ; for, saluting them respectfully, he asked of the countess in Flemish, on which road she desired to be conducted.

" Guide me," said she, " towards the nearest town on the frontiers of Brabant."

" You have then settled the end and object of your journey ? " said Quentin, approaching his horse to that of Isabelle, and speaking French, which their guide did not understand.

" Surely," replied the young lady ; " for situated as I now am, it must be of no small detriment to me if I were to prolong a journey in my present circumstances, even though the termination should be a rigorous prison."

" A prison ! " said Quentin.

" Yes, my friend, a prison ; but I will take care that you shall not share it."

" Do not talk—do not think of me," said Quentin. " Saw I you but safe, my own concerns are little worth minding."

" Do not speak so loud," said the Lady Isabelle ; " you will surprise our guide—you see he has already rode on before us " ; for, in truth, the good-natured Fleming, doing as he desired to be done by, had removed from them the constraint of a third, person upon Quentin's first motion towards the lady. " Yes," she continued, when she noticed they were free from observation, " to you, my friend, my protector—why should I be ashamed to call you what Heaven has made you to me ?—to you it is my duty to say, that my resolution is taken to return to my native country, and to throw myself on the mercy of the Duke of Burgundy. It was mistaken, though well-meant, advice which induced me ever to withdraw from his protection, and place myself under that of the crafty and false Louis of France."

" And you resolve to become the bride, then, of the Count of Campo-basso, the unworthy favorite of Charles ? "

Thus spoke Quentin, with a voice in which internal agony struggled with his desire to assume an indifferent tone, like that of the poor condemned criminal, when, affecting a firmness which he is far from feeling, he asks if the death-warrant be arrived.

" No, Durward, no," said the Lady Isabelle, sitting up erect in her saddle, " to that condition all Burgundy's power shall not sink a daughter of the house of Croye. Burgundy may seize on my lands and fiefs, he may imprison my person in a convent ; but that is the worst I have to expect ; and worse than that I will endure ere I give my hand to Campo-basso."

" The worst ! " said Quentin ; " and what worse can there be than plunder and imprisonment ? Oh, think, while you have God's free air around you, and one by your side who will hazard life to conduct you to England, to Germany, even to Scotland, in all of which you shall find generous protectors. O, while this is the case, do not resolve so rashly to abandon the means of liberty, the best gift that Heaven gives ! O, well sung a poet of my own land—

> Ah, freedom is a noble thing ;
> Freedom makes man to have liking ;
> Freedom the zest to pleasure gives ;
> He lives at ease who freely lives.

Grief, sickness, poortith, want, are all
Summ'd up within the name of thrall.*

She listened with a melancholy smile to her guide's tirade
in praise of liberty ; and then answered after a moment's
pause, " Freedom is for man alone ; woman must ever seek
a protector, since nature made her incapable to defend herself. And where am I to find one ? In that voluptuary
Edward of England—in the inebriated Wenceslaus of
Germany—in Scotland ? Ah, Durward, were I your sister,
and could you promise me shelter in some of those mountain-
glens which you love to describe, where, for charity, or for
the few jewels I have preserved, I might lead an unharassed
life, and forget the lot I was born to—could you promise me
the protection of some honored matron of the land—of some
baron whose heart was as true as his sword—that were indeed a prospect, for which it were worth the risk of farther
censure to wander farther and wider ! "

There was a faltering tenderness of voice with which the
Countess Isabelle made this admission, that at once filled
Quentin with a sensation of joy, and cut him to the very
heart. He hesitated a moment ere he made an answer,
hastily reviewing in his mind the possibility there might be
that he could procure her shelter in Scotland ; but the
melancholy truth rushed on him, that it would be alike base
and cruel to point out to her a course which he had not the
most distant power or means to render safe. " Lady," he
said at last, " I should act foully against my honor and
oath of chivalry did I suffer you to ground any plan upon
the thoughts that I have the power in Scotland to afford you
other protection than that of the poor arm which is now by
your side. I scarce know that my blood flows in the veins
of an individual who now lives in my native land. The
Knight of Innerquharity stormed our castle at midnight,
and cut off all that belonged to my name. Were I again in
Scotland, our feudal enemies are numerous and powerful, I
single and weak ; and even had the king a desire to do me
justice, he dared not, for the sake of redressing the wrongs
of a poor individual, provoke a chief who rides with five
hundred horse."

" Alas ! " said the countess, " there is then no corner of
the world safe from oppression, since it rages as unrestrained

---

* These noble lines form the commencement of the metrical life
of Robert the Bruce, by Barbour, Archdeacon of Aberdeen in the
year 1375 (*Laing*).

amongst those wild hills which afford so few objects to covet, as in our rich and abundant lowlands!"

"It is a sad truth, and I dare not deny it," said the Scot, "that, for little more than the pleasure of revenge and the lust of bloodshed, our hostile clans do the work of executioners on each other; and Ogilvies and the like act the same scenes in Scotland as De la Marck and his robbers do in this country."

"No more of Scotland, then," said Isabelle, with a tone of indifference, either real or affected—"no more of Scotland, which indeed I mentioned but in jest, to see if you really dared recommend to me, as a place of rest, the most distracted kingdom in Europe. It was but a trial of your sincerity, which I rejoice to say may be relied on, even when your partialities are most strongly excited. So, once more, I will think of no other protection than can be afforded by the first honorable baron holding of Duke Charles, to whom I am determined to render myself."

"And why not rather betake yourself to your own estates, and to your own strong castle, as you designed when at Tours?" said Quentin. "Why not call around you the vassals of your father, and make treaty with Burgundy, rather than surrender yourself to him? Surely there must be many a bold heart that would fight in your cause; and I know at least one who would willingly lay down his life to give example."

"Alas!" said the countess, "that scheme, the suggestion of the crafty Louis, and, like all which he ever suggested, designed more for his advantage than for mine, has become impracticable, since it was betrayed to Burgundy by the double traitor Zamet Maugrabin. My kinsman was then imprisoned, and my houses garrisoned. Any attempt of mine would but expose my dependents to the vengeance of Duke Charles; and why should I occasion more bloodshed than has already taken place on so worthless an account? No, I will submit myself to my sovereign as a dutiful vassal, in all which shall leave my personal freedom of choice uninfringed; the rather that I trust my kinswoman, the Countess Hameline, who first counseled, and indeed urged my flight, has already taken this wise and honorable step."

"Your kinswoman!" repeated Quentin, awakened to recollections to which the young countess was a stranger, and which the rapid succession of perilous and stirring events had, as matters of nearer concern, in fact banished from his memory.

" Ay, my aunt, the Countess Hameline of Croye—know
you aught of her ? " said the Countess Isabelle ; " I trust
she is now under the protection of the Burgundian banner.
You are silent ! Know you aught of her ? "

The last question, urged in a tone of the most anxious
inquiry, obliged Quentin to give some account of what he
knew of the countess's fate. He mentioned that he had
been summoned to attend her in a flight from Liege, which
he had no doubt the Lady Isabelle would be partaker in ; he
mentioned the discovery that had been made after they had
gained the forest ; and finally, he told his own return to the
castle, and the circumstances in which he found it. But he
said nothing of the views with which it was plain the Lady
Hameline had left the castle of Schonwaldt, and as little
about the floating report of her having fallen into the hands
of William de la Marck. Delicacy prevented his even hinting at the one, and regard for the feelings of his companion,
at a moment when strength and exertion were most demanded of her, prevented him from alluding to the latter,
which had, besides, only reached him as a mere rumor.

This tale, though abridged of those important particulars,
made a strong impression on the Countess Isabelle, who,
after riding some time in silence, said at last, with a tone of
cold displeasure, " And so you abandoned my unfortunate
relative in a wild forest, at the mercy of a vile Bohemian and
a traitorous waiting-woman ? Poor kinswoman, thou wert
wont to praise this youth's good faith ! "

" Had I not done so, madam," said Quentin, not unreasonably offended at the turn thus given to his gallantry,
" what had been the fate of one to whose service I was far
more devoutly bound ? Had I *not* left the Countess Hameline of Croye to the charge of those whom she had herself
selected as counselors and advisers, the Countess Isabelle had
been ere now the bride of William de la Marck, the Wild
Boar of Ardennes."

" You are right," said the Countess Isabelle, in her usual
manner ; " and I, who have the advantage of your unhesi-
tating devotion, have done you foul and ungrateful wrong.
But oh, my unhappy kinswoman ! and the wretch Marthon,
who enjoyed so much of her confidence, and deserved it so
little—it was she that introduced to my kinswoman the
wretched Zamet and Hayraddin Maugrabin, who, by their
pretended knowledge in soothsaying and astrology, obtained
a great ascendency over her mind ; it was she who, strength-
ening their predictions, encouraged her in—I know not what

to call them—delusions concerning matches and lovers,
which my kinswoman's age rendered ungraceful and improbable. I doubt not that, from the beginning, we had
been surrounded by these snares by Louis of France, in
order to determine us to take refuge at his court, or rather
to put ourselves into his power; after which rash act on our
part, how unkingly, unknightly, ignobly, ungentlemanlike,
he hath conducted himself towards us, you, Quentin
Durward, can bear witness. But alas! my kinswoman—
what think you will be her fate?"

Endeavoring to inspire hopes which he scarce felt, Durward answered, that " The avarice of these people was stronger than any other passion ; that Marthon, even when he
left them, seemed to act rather as the Lady Hameline's pro-
tectress ; and, in fine, that it was difficult to conceive any
object these wretches could accomplish by the ill usage or
murder of the countess, whereas they might be gainers by
treating her well, and putting her to ransom."

To lead the Countess Isabelle's thoughts from this melancholy subject, Quentin frankly told her the treachery of
the Maugrabin, which he had discovered in the night-
quarter near Namur, and which appeared the result of an
agreement betwixt the King and William de la Marck.
Isabelle shuddered with horror, and then recovering herself,
said, " I am ashamed, and I have sinned in permitting myself so far to doubt of the saints' protection, as for an instant
to have deemed possible the accomplishment of a scheme to
utterly cruel, base, and dishonorable, while there are pitying
eyes in Heaven to look down on human miseries. It is not
a thing to be thought of with fear or abhorrence, but to be
rejected as such a piece of incredible treachery and villainy
as it were atheism to believe could ever be successful. But
I now see plainly why that hypocritical Marthon often
seemed to foster every seed of petty jealousy or discontent
betwixt my poor kinswoman and myself, whilst she always
mixed with flattery, addressed to the individual who was
present, whatever could prejudice her against her absent
kinswoman. Yet never did I dream she could have proceeded as far as to have caused my once affectionate kinswoman to have left me behind in the perils of Schonwaldt,
while she made her own escape."

" Did the Lady Hameline not mention to you, then," said
Quentin, " her intended flight ?"

" No," replied the countess, " but she alluded to some
communication which Marthon was to make to me. To say

truth, my poor kinswoman's head was so turned by the mysterious jargon of the miserable Hayraddin, whom that day she had admitted to a long and secret conference, and she threw out so many strange hints, that—that—in short, I cared not to press on her, when in that humor, for any explanation. Yet it was cruel to leave me behind her."

"I will excuse the Lady Hameline from intending such unkindness," said Quentin ; "for such was the agitation of the moment," and the darkness of the hour, that I believe the Lady Hameline as certainly conceived herself accompanied by her niece, as I at the same time, deceived by Marthon's dress and demeanor, supposed I was in the company of both the Ladies of Croye—and of *her* especially," he added, with a low but determined voice, "without whom the wealth of worlds would not have tempted me to leave Schonwaldt."

Isabelle stooped her head forward, and seemed scarce to hear the emphasis with which Quentin had spoken. But she turned her face to him again when he began to speak of the policy of Louis ; and it was not difficult for them, by mutual communication, to ascertain that the Bohemian brothers, with their accomplice Marthon, had been the agents of that crafty monarch, although Zamet, the elder of them, with a perfidy peculiar to his race, had attempted to play a double game, and had been punished accordingly. In the same humor of mutual confidence, and forgetting the singularity of their own situation, as well as the perils of the road, the travelers pursued their journey for several hours, only stopping to refresh their horses at a retired *dorff*, or hamlet, to which they were conducted by Hans Glover, who, in all other respects, as well as in leaving them much to their own freedom in conversation, conducted himself like a person of reflection and discretion.

Meantime, the artificial distinction which divided the two lovers, for such we may now term them, seemed dissolved, or removed, by the circumstances in which they were placed ; for if the countess boasted the higher rank, and was by birth entitled to a fortune incalculably larger than that of the youth, whose revenue lay in his sword, it was to be considered that, for the present, she was as poor as he, and for her safety, honor, and life exclusively indebted to his presence of mind, valor, and devotion. They *spoke* not indeed of love, for though the young lady, her heart full of gratitude and confidence, might have pardoned such a declaration, yet Quentin, on whose tongue there was laid a check, both by natural timidity and by the sentiments of chivalry,

would have held it an unworthy abuse of her situation had
he said anything which could have the appearance of taking
undue advantage of the opportunities which it afforded them.
They *spoke* not then of love, but the thoughts of it were on
both sides unavoidable ; and thus they were placed in that
relation to each other in which sentiments of mutual regard
are rather understood than announced, and which, with the
freedoms which it permits, and the uncertainties that attend it, often forms the most delightful hours of human
existence, and as frequently leads to those which are darkened by disappointment, fickleness, and all the pains of
blighted hope and unrequited attachment.

It was two hours after noon, when the travelers were
alarmed by the report of the guide, who, with paleness and
horror in his countenance, said that they were pursued by
a party of De la Marck's *Schwarzreiters*.* These soldiers,
or rather banditti, were bands levied in the Lower Circles
of Germany, and resembled the lanzknechts in every particular, except that the former acted as light cavalry. To
maintain the name of Black Troopers, and to strike additional terror into their enemies, they usually rode on black
chargers, and smeared with black ointment their arms and
accoutrements, in which operation their hands and faces
often had their share. In morals and in ferocity these
schwarzreiters emulated their pedestrian brethren the
lanzknechts.

On looking back, and discovering along the level road
which they had traversed a cloud of dust advancing, with
one or two of the headmost troopers riding furiously in
front of it, Quentin addressed his companion, "Dearest
Isabelle, I have no weapon left save my sword ; but since
I cannot fight for you, I will fly with you. Could we gain
yonder wood that is before us ere they come up, we may
easily find means to escape."

"So be it, my only friend," said Isabelle, pressing her
horse to the gallop ; "and thou, good fellow," she added,
addressing Hans Glover, "get thee off to another road, and
do not stay to partake our misfortune and danger."

The honest Fleming shook his head, and answered her
generous exhortation with '*Nein, nein! das geht nicht*," † and
continued to attend them, all three riding towards the
shelter of the wood as fast as their jaded horses could go,
pursued, at the same time, by the schwarzreiters, who in-

* See Note 32.

† "No, no ! that must not be."

creased their pace when they saw them fly. But notwithstanding the fatigue of the horses, still the fugitives being unarmed, and riding lighter in consequence, had considerably the advantage of their pursuers, and were within about a quarter of a mile of the wood, when a body of men-at-arms, under a knight's pennon, was discovered advancing from the cover, so as to intercept their flight.

"They have bright armor," said Isabelle ; "they must be Burgundians. Be they who will, we must yield to them rather than to the lawless miscreants who pursue us."

A moment after she exclaimed, looking on the pennon, "I know the cloven heart which it displays ! It is the banner of the Count of Crèvecœur, a noble Burgundian ; to him I will surrender myself."

Quentin Durward sighed ; but what other alternative remained ? and how happy would he have been but an instant before, to have been certain of the escape of Isabelle, even under worse terms ? They soon joined the band of Crèvecœur, and the countess demanded to speak to the leader, who had halted his party till he should reconnoiter the black troopers ; and as he gazed on her with doubt and uncertainty, she said, "Noble count, Isabelle of Croye, the daughter of your old companion in arms, Count Reinold of Croye, renders herself, and asks protection from your valor for her and hers."

"Thou shalt have it, fair kinswoman, were it against a host, always excepting my liege Lord of Burgundy. But there is a little time to talk of it. These filthy-looking fiends have made a halt, as if they intended to dispute the matter. By St. George of Burgundy, they have the insolence to advance against the banner of Crèvecœur ! What ! will not the knaves be ruled ? Damian, my lance. Advance banner. Lay your spears in the rest. Crèvecœur to the rescue !"

Crying his war-cry, and followed by his men-at-arms, he galloped rapidly forward to charge the schwarzreiters.

CHAPTER XXIV

THE SURRENDER

Rescue or none, sir knight, I am your captive;
Deal with me what your nobleness suggests,
Thinking the chance of war may one day place you
Where I must now be reckoned—i' the roll
Of melancholy prisoners.

Anonymous.

THE skirmish betwixt the schwarzreiters and the Burgundian men-at-arms lasted scarcely five minutes, so soon were the former put to the rout by the superiority of the latter in armor, weight of horse, and military spirit. In less than the space we have mentioned, the Count of Crèvecœur, wiping his bloody sword upon his horse's mane ere he sheathed it, came back to the verge of the forest, where Isabelle had remained a spectator of the combat. One part of his people followed him, while the other continued to pursue the flying enemy for a little space along the causeway.

"It is shame," said the count, "that the weapons of knights and gentlemen should be soiled by the blood of those brutal swine."

So saying, he returned his weapon to the sheath and added, "This is a rough welcome to your home, my pretty cousin; but wandering princesses must expect such adventures. And well I came up in time, for, let me assure you, the black troopers respect a countess's coronet as little as a country wench's coif, and I think your retinue is not qualified for much resistance."

"My lord count," said the Lady Isabelle, "without farther preface, let me know if I am a prisoner, and where you are to conduct me?"

"You know, you silly child," answered the count, "how I would answer that question, did it rest on my own will. But you and your foolish match-making, marriage-hunting aunt have made such wild use of your wings of late, that I fear you must be contented to fold them up in a cage for a

272

little while. For my part, my duty, and it is a sad one, will be ended when I have conducted you to the court of the Duke at Péronne ; for which purpose I hold it necessary to deliver the command of this reconnoitering party to my nephew, Count Stephen, while I return with you thither, as I think you may need an intercessor. And I hope the young giddy-pate will discharge his duty wisely."

" So please you, fair uncle," said Count Stephen, " if you doubt my capacity to conduct the men-at-arms, even remain with them yourself, and I will be the servant and guard of the Countess Isabelle of Croye."

" No doubt, fair nephew," answered his uncle, " this were a goodly improvement on my scheme ; but methinks I like it as well in the way I planned it. Please you, therefore, to take notice, that your business here is not to hunt after and stick these black hogs, for which you seemed but now to have felt an especial vocation, but to collect and bring to me true tidings what is going forward in the country of Liege, concerning which we hear such wild rumors. Let some half score of lances follow me, and the rest remain with my banner under your guidance."

" Yet one moment, cousin of Crèvecœur," said the Countess Isabelle, " and let me, in yielding myself prisoner, stipulate at least for the safety of those who have befriended me in my misfortunes. Permit this good fellow, my trusty guide, to go back unharmed to his native town of Liege."

" My nephew," said Crèvecœur, after looking sharply at Glover's honest breadth of countenance, " shall guard this good fellow, who seems, indeed, to have little harm in him, as far into the territory as he himself advances, and then leave him at liberty."

" Fail not to remember me to the kind Gertrude," said the countess to her guide ; and added, taking a string of pearls from under her veil, " Pray her to wear this in remembrance of her unhappy friend."

Honest Glover took the string of pearls, and kissed, with clownish gesture but with sincere kindness, the fair hand which had found such a delicate mode of remunerating his own labors and peril.

" Umph ! signs and tokens !" said the count ; " any farther bequests to make, my fair cousin ? It is time we were on our way."

" Only," said the countess, making an effort to speak, " that you will be pleased to be favorable to this—this young gentleman."

18

"Umph!" said Crèvecœur, casting the same penetrating glance on Quentin which he had bestowed on Glover, but apparently with a much less satisfactory result, and mimicking, though not offensively, the embarrassment of the countess—"umph! Ay, this is a blade of another temper. And pray, my cousin, what has this—this *very* young gentleman done to deserve such intercession at your hands?"

"He has saved my life and honor," said the countess, reddening with shame and resentment.

Quentin also blushed with indignation, but wisely concluded that to give vent to it might only make matters worse.

"Life and honor! Umph!" said again the Count Crèvecœur; "methinks it would have been as well, my cousin, if you had not put yourself in the way of lying under such obligations to this very young gentleman. But let it pass. The young gentleman may wait on us, if his quality permit, and I will see he has no injury ; only I will myself take in future the office of protecting your life and honor, and may perhaps find for him some fitter duty than that of being a squire of the body to damosels errant."

"My lord count," said Durward, unable to keep silence any longer, "lest you should talk of a stranger in slighter terms than you might afterwards think becoming, I take leave to tell you that I am Quentin Durward, an archer of the Scottish Body-Guard, in which, as you well know, none but gentlemen and men of honor, are enrolled."

"I thank you for your information, and I kiss your hands, seignoir archer," said Crèvecœur, in the same tone of raillery. "Have the goodness to ride with me to the front of the party."

As Quentin moved onward at the command of the count, who had now the power, if not the right, to dictate his motions, he observed that the Lady Isabelle followed his motions with a look of anxious and timid interest, which amounted almost to tenderness, and the sight of which brought water into his eyes. But he remembered that he had a man's part to sustain before Crèvecœur, who, perhaps, of all the chivalry, in France or Burgundy, was the least likely to be moved to anything but laughter by a tale of true-love sorrow. He determined, therefore, not to wait his addressing him, but to open the conversation in a tone which should assert his claim to fair treatment, and to more respect than the count, offended perhaps at finding a person of such inferior note placed so near the confidence of his high-born and wealthy cousin, seemed disposed to entertain for him.

"My Lord Count of Crèvecœur," he said in a temperate but firm tone of voice, "may I request of you, before our interview goes farther, to tell me if I am at liberty, or am I to account myself your prisoner?"

"A shrewd question," replied the count, "which at present I can only answer by another. Are France and Burgundy, think you, at peace or war with each other?"

"That," replied the Scot, "you, my lord, should certainly know better than I. I have been absent from the court of France and have heard no news for some time."

"Look you there," said the count, "you see how easy it is to ask questions, but how difficult to answer them. Why, I myself, who have been at Peronne with the Duke for this week and better, cannot resolve this riddle any more than you; and yet, sir squire, upon the solution of that question depends the said point whether you are prisoner or free man; and, for the present, I must hold you as the former. Only, if you have really and honestly been of service to my kinswoman, and if you are candid in your answers to the questions I shall ask, affairs shall stand the better with you."

"The Countess of Croye," said Quentin, "is best judge if I have rendered any service, and to her I refer you on that matter. My answers you will yourself judge of when you ask me your questions."

"Umph! haughty enough," muttered the Count of Crèvecœur, "and very like one that wears a lady's favor in his hat, and thinks he must carry things with a high tone, to honor the precious remnant of silk and tinsel. Well, sir, I trust it will be no abatement of your dignity if you answer me how long you have been about the person of Lady Isabelle of Croye?"

"Count of Crèvecœur," said Quentin Durward, "if I answer questions which are asked in a tone approaching towards insult, it is only lest injurious inferences should be drawn from my silence respecting one to whom we are both obliged to render justice. I have acted as escort to the Lady Isabelle since she left France to retire into Flanders."

"Ho! ho!" said the count; "and that is to say, since she fled from Plessis-lè-Tours? You, an archer of the Scottish Guard, accompanied her, of course, by the express orders of King Louis?"

However little Quentin thought himself indebted to the King of France, who, in contriving the surprisal of the Countess Isabelle by William de la Marck, had probably calculated on the young Scotchman being slain in her defense, he did not yet conceive himself at liberty to betray any trust which Louis had reposed, or had seemed to repose, in him, and therefore replied to Count Crèvecœur's inference, " That it was sufficient for him to have the authority of his superior officer for what he had done, and he inquired no farther."

" It is quite sufficient," said the count. " We know the King does not permit his officers to send the archers of his Guard to prance like paladins by the bridle-rein of wandering ladies, unless he hath some politic purpose to serve. It will be difficult for King Louis to continue to aver so boldly that he knew not of the Ladies of Croye's having escaped from France, since they were escorted by one of his own life-guard. And whither, sir archer, was your retreat directed ? "

" To Liege, my lord," answered the Scot ; " where the ladies desired to be placed under the protection of the late bishop."

" The *late* bishop ! " exclaimed the Count of Crèvecœur ; " is Louis of Bourbon dead ? Not a word of his illness had reached the Duke. Of what did he die ? "

" He sleeps in a bloody grave, my lord—that is, if his murderers have conferred one on his remains."

" Murdered ! " exclaimed Crèvecœur again. " Holy Mother of Heaven ! Young man, it is impossible ! "

" I saw the deed done with my own eyes, and many an act of horror besides."

" Saw it, and made not in to help the good prelate ! " exclaimed the count, " or to raise the castle against his murderers ? Know'st thou not, that even to look on such a deed, without resisting it, is profane sacrilege ? "

" To be brief, my lord," said Durward, " ere this act was done, the castle was stormed by the bloodthirsty William de la Marck, with help of the insurgent Liegois."

" I am struck with thunder ! " said Crèvecœur. " Liege in insurrection ! Schonwaldt taken ! The bishop murdered ! Messenger of sorrow, never did one man unfold such a packet of woes ! Speak—knew you of this assault— of this insurrection—of this murder ? Speak—thou art one of Louis's trusted archers, and it is he that has aimed this painful arrow. Speak, or I will have thee torn with wild horses ! "

" And if I *am* so torn, my lord, there can be nothing rent out of me that may not become a true Scottish gentleman. I know no more of these villainies than you—was so far from

being partaker in them, that I would have withstood them
to the uttermost, had my means, in a twentieth degree,
equaled my inclination. But what could I do ? they were
hundreds and I but one. My only care was to rescue the
Countess Isabelle, and in that I was happily successful. Yet,
had I been near enough when the ruffian deed was so cruelly
done on the old man, I had saved his gray hairs, or I had
avenged them ; and as it was, my abhorrence was spoken
loud enough to prevent other horrors."

"I believe thee, youth," said the count ; " thou art neither
of an age nor nature to be trusted with such bloody work,
however well fitted to be the squire of dames. But alas ! for
the kind and generous prelate, to be murdered on the hearth
where he so often entertained the stranger with Christian
charity and princely bounty ; and that by a wretch—a monster—a portentous growth of blood and cruelty—bred up in
the very hall where he has imbrued his hands in his benefactor's blood ! But I know not Charles of Burgundy—nay,
I should doubt of the justice of Heaven—if vengeance be not
as sharp, and sudden, and severe as this villainy has been
unexampled in atrocity. And, if no other shall pursue the
murderer"—here he paused, grasped his sword, then quitting
his bridle, struck both gauntleted hands upon his breast,
until his corslet clattered, and finally held them up to
Heaven, as he solemnly continued—" I—I, Philip Crèvecœur
of Cordès, make a vow to God, St. Lambert, and the Three
Kings of Cologne, that small shall be my thought of other
earthly concerns till I take full revenge on the murderers of
the good Louis of Bourbon, whether I find them in forest or
field, in city or in country, in hill or plain, in king's court
or in God's church ; and thereto I pledge lands and living,
friends and followers, life and honor. So help me God and
St. Lambert of Liege, and the Three Kings of Cologne !"

When the Count of Crèvecœur had made his vow, his
mind seemed in some sort relieved from the overwhelming
grief and astonishment with which he had heard the fatal
tragedy that had been acted at Schonwaldt, and he proceeded
to question Durward more minutely concerning the particulars of that disastrous affair, which the Scot, nowise desirous
to abate the spirit of revenge which the count entertained
against William de la Marck, gave him at full length.

"But those blind, unsteady, faithless, fickle beasts, the
Liegeois," said the count, " that they should have combined
themselves with this inexorable robber and murderer to put
to death their lawful prince !"

Durward here informed the enraged Burgundian that the
Liegeois, or at least the better class of them, however rashly
they had run into the rebellion against their bishop, had no
design, so far as appeared to him, to aid in the execrable
deed of De la Marck ; but, on the contrary, would have prevented it if they had had the means, and were struck with
horror when they beheld it.

"Speak not of the faithless, inconstant, plebeian rabble !"
said Crèvecœur. "When they took arms against a prince
who had no fault save that he was too kind and too good a
master for such a set of ungrateful slaves—when they armed
against him, and broke into his peaceful house, what could
there be in their intention but murder ? When they banded
themselves with the Wild Boar of Ardennes, the greatest
homicide in the marches of Flanders, what else could there
be in their purpose *but* murder, which is the very trade he
lives by ? And again, was it not one of their own vile rabble
who did the very deed, by thine own account ? I hope to
see their canals running blood by the light of their burning
houses. Oh, the kind, noble, generous lord whom they have
slaughtered ! Other vassals have rebelled under the pressure
of imposts and penury ; but the men of Liege in the fulness
of insolence and plenty." He again abandoned the reins of
his war-horse and wrung bitterly the hands which his mail-
gloves rendered untractable. Quentin easily saw that the
grief which he manifested was augmented by the bitter recollection of past intercourse and friendship with the sufferer,
and was silent accordingly, respecting feelings which he was
unwilling to aggravate, and at the same time felt it impossible to soothe.

But the Count of Crèvecœur returned again and again to
the subject—questioned him on every particular of the surprise of Schonwaldt, and the death of the bishop ; and then
suddenly, as if he had recollected something which had
escaped his memory, demanded what had become of the
Lady Hameline, and why she was not with her kinswoman.
"Not," he added contemptuously, " that I consider her absence as at all a loss to the Countess Isabelle ; for, although
she was her kinswoman, and upon the whole a well-meaning
woman, yet the court of Cocagne never produced such a
fantastic fool ; and I hold it for certain that her niece, whom
I have always observed to be a modest and orderly young
woman, was led into the absurd frolic of flying from Burgundy to France by that blundering, romantic, old match-
making and match-seeking idiot."

What a speech for a romantic lover to hear! and to hear, too, when it would have been ridiculous in him to attempt what it was impossible for him to achieve—namely, to convince the count, by force of arms, that he did foul wrong to the countess—the peerless in sense as in beauty—in terming her a modest and orderly young woman, qualities which might have been predicated with propriety of the daughter of a sunburnt peasant, who lived by goading the oxen, while her father held the plow. And, then, to suppose her under the domination and supreme guidance of a silly and romantic aunt—the slander should have been repelled down the slanderer's throat. But the open, though severe, physiognomy of the Count of Crèvecœur, the total contempt which he seemed to entertain for those feelings which were uppermost in Quentin's bosom, overawed him; not for fear of the count's fame in arms—that was a risk which would have increased his desire of making out a challenge—but in dread of ridicule, the weapon of all others most feared by enthusiasts of every description, and which, from its predominance over such minds, often checks what is absurd, and fully as often smothers that which is noble.

Under the influence of this fear of becoming an object of scorn rather than resentment, Durward, though with some pain, confined his reply to a confused account of the Lady Hameline having made her escape from Schonwaldt before the attack took place. He could not, indeed, have made his story very distinct without throwing ridicule on the near relation of Isabelle, and perhaps incurring some himself, as having been the object of her preposterous expectations. He added to his embarrassed detail, that he had heard a report, though a vague one, of the Lady Hameline having again fallen into the hands of William de la Marck.

"I trust in St. Lambert that he will marry her," said Crèvecœur; "as, indeed, he is likely enough to do, for the sake of her money-bags; and equally likely to knock her on the head so soon as these are either secured in his own grasp or, at farthest, emptied."

The count then proceeded to ask so many questions concerning the mode in which both ladies had conducted themselves on the journey, the degree of intimacy to which they admitted Quentin himself, and other trying particulars, that, vexed and ashamed and angry, the youth was scarce able to conceal his embarrassment from the keen-sighted soldier and courtier, who seemed suddenly disposed to take leave of him, saying, at the same time, "Umph—I see it is as I conjectured, on one side at least ; I trust the other party has kept her senses better. Come, sir squire, spur on and keep the van, while I fall back to discourse with the Lady Isabelle. I think I have learned now so much from you that I can talk to her of these sad passages without hurting her nicety, though I have fretted yours a little.   Yet stay, young gallant —one word ere you go.   You have had, I imagine, a happy journey through Fairyland—all full of heroic adventure, and high hope, and wild, minstrel-like delusion, like the gardens of *Morgaine la Fée*.   Forget it all, young soldier," he added, tapping him on the shoulder. '' Remember yonder lady only as the honored Countess of Croye ; forget her as a wandering and adventurous damsel.   And her friends—one of them I can answer for—will remember, on their part, only the services you have done her, and forget the unreasonable reward which you have had the boldness to propose to yourself."

Enraged that he had been unable to conceal from the sharpsighted Crèvecœur, feelings which the count seemed to consider as the object of ridicule, Quentin replied indignantly, '' My lord count, when I require advice of you, I will ask it ; when I demand assistance of you, it will be time enough to grant or refuse it ; when I set peculiar value on your opinion of me, it will not be too late to express it."

'' Heyday !'' said the count ; ''I have come between Amadis and Oriana, and must expect a challenge to the lists !''

'' You speak as if that were an impossibility," said Quentin. '' When I broke a lance with the Duke of Orleans, it was against a breast in which flowed better blood than that of Crèvecœur.   When I measured swords with Dunois, I engaged a better warrior."

'' Now Heaven nourish thy judgment, gentle youth !'' said Crèvecœur, still laughing at the chivalrous *inamorato.*   '' If thou speak'st truth, thou hast had singular luck in this world ; and, truly, if it be the pleasure of Providence exposes thee to such trials, without a beard on thy lip, thou wilt be mad with vanity ere thou writest thyself man.   Thou canst not move me to anger, though thou mayst to mirth. Believe me, though thou mayst have fought with princes, and played the champion for countesses, by some of those freaks which Fortune will sometimes exhibit, thou art by no means the equal of those of whom thou hast been either the casual opponent or more casual companion.   I can allow thee, like a youth who hath listened to romances till he fancied himself a paladin, to form pretty dreams for some time ; but thou must not be angry at a well-meaning friend, though he shake thee something roughly by the shoulders to awake thee."

"My Lord of Crèvecœur," said Quentin, "my family——"

"Nay, it was not utterly of family that I spoke," said the count ; "but of rank, fortune, high station, and so forth, which place a distance between various degrees and classes of persons. As for birth, all men are descended from Adam and Eve."

"My lord count," repeated Quentin, "my ancestors, the Durwards of Glen Houlakin——"

"Nay," said the count, "if you claim a farther descent for them than from Adam, I have done ! Good-even to you."

He reined back his horse, and paused to join the countess, to whom, if possible, his insinuations and advices, however well meant, were still more disagreeable than to Quentin, who, as he rode on, muttered to himself, "Cold-blooded, insolent, overweening coxcomb ! Would that the next Scottish archer who has his harquebuss pointed at thee may not let thee off so easily as I did ! "

In the evenng they reached the town of Charleroi, on the Sambre, where the Count of Crèvecœur had determined to leave the Countess Isabelle, whom the terror and fatigue of yesterday, joined to a flight of fifty miles since morning and the various distressing sensations by which it was accompanied, had made incapable of traveling farther, with safety to her health. The count consigned her, in a state of great exhaustion, to the care of the abbess of the Cistercian convent in Charleroi, a noble lady to whom both the families of Crèvecœur and Croye were related, and in whose prudence and kindness he could repose confidence.

Crèvecœur himself only stopped to recommend the utmost caution to the governor of a small Burgundian garrison who occupied the place, and required him also to mount a guard of honor upon the convent during the residence of the Countess Isabelle of Croye—ostensibly to secure her safety, but perhaps secretly to prevent her attempting to escape. The count only assigned as a cause for the garrison being vigilant some vague rumors which he had heard of disturbances in the bishopric of Liege. But he was determined himself to be the first who should carry the formidable news of the insurrection and the murder of the bishop, in all their horrible reality, to Duke Charles ; and for that purpose, having procured fresh horses for himself and suite, he mounted with the resolution of continuing his journey to Péronne without stopping for repose ; and informing Quentin Durward that he must attend him, he made, at the same time, a mock apology for parting fair company, but hoped that to so devoted a squire of dames a night's journey by moonshine would be more agreeable than supinely to yield himself to slumber like an ordinary mortal.

Quentin, already sufficiently afflicted by finding that he was to be parted from Isabelle, longed to answer this taunt with an indignant defiance ; but aware that the count would only laugh at his anger and despise his challenge, he resolved to wait some future time, when he might have an opportunity of obtaining some amends from this proud lord, who, though for very different reasons, had become nearly as odious to him as the Wild Boar of Ardennes himself. He therefore assented to Crèvecœur's proposal, as to what he had no choice of declining, and they pursued in company, and with all the despatch they could exert, the road between Charleroi and Péronne.

CHAPTER XXV

THE UNBIDDEN GUEST.

No human quality is so well wove
In warp and woof but there's some flaw in it.
I've known a brave man fly a shepherd's cur,
A wise man so demean him, driveling idiocy
Had wellnigh been ashamed on't. For your crafty,
Your worldly-wise man; he, above the rest,
Weaves his own snares so fine, he's often caught in them.
Old Play.

QUENTIN, during the earlier part of the night-journey, had to combat with that bitter heartache which is left when youth parts, and probably forever, with her he loves. As, pressed by the urgency of the moment and the impatience of Crèvecœur, they hasted on through the rich lowlands of Hainault, under the benign guidance of a rich and lustrous harvest-moon, she shed her yellow influence over rich and deep pastures, woodland, and corn-fields, from which the husbandmen were using her light to withdraw the grain, such was the industry of the Flemings even at that period ; she shone on broad, level, and fructifying rivers, where glided the white sail in the service of commerce, uninterrupted by rock or torrent, beside lively [lonely ?] quiet villages, whose external decency and cleanliness expressed the ease and comfort of the inhabitants ; she gleamed upon the feudal castle of many a gallant baron and knight, with its deep moat, battlemented court, and high belfry, for the chivalry of Hainault was renowned among the nobles of Europe ; and her light displayed at a distance, in its broad beam, the gigantic towers of more than one lofty minster.

Yet all this fair variety, however differing from the waste and wilderness of his own land, interrupted not the course of Quentin's regrets and sorrows. He had left his heart behind him, when he departed from Charleroi ; and the only reflection which the farther journey inspired was, that every step was carrying him farther from Isabelle. His imagination was taxed to recall every word she had spoken, every look she had directed towards him ; and, as happens frequently in such cases, the impression made upon his imagination by the recollection of these particulars was even stronger than the realities themselves had excited.

At length, after the cold hour of midnight was past, in spite alike of love and of sorrow, the extreme fatigue which Quentin had undergone the two preceding days began to have an effect on him, which his habits of exercise of every kind, and his singular alertness and activity of character, as well as the painful nature of the reflections which occupied his thoughts, had hitherto prevented his experiencing. The ideas of his mind began to be so little corrected by the exertions of his senses, worn out and deadened as the latter now were by extremity of fatigue, that the visions which the former drew superseded or perverted the information conveyed by the blunted organs of seeing and hearing ; and Durward was only sensible that he was awake by the exertions which, sensible of the peril of his situation, he occasionally made to resist falling into a deep and dead sleep. Every now and then a strong consciousness of the risk of falling from or with his horse roused him to exertion and animation ; but ere long his eyes again were dimmed by confused shades of all sorts of mingled colors, the moonlight landscape swam before them, and he was so much overcome with fatigue that the Count of Crèvecœur, observing his condition, was at length compelled to order two of his attendants, one to each rein of Durward's bridle, in order to prevent the risk of his falling from his horse.

When at length they reached the town of Landrecy, the count, in compassion to the youth, who had now been in a great measure without sleep for three nights, allowed himself and his retinue a halt of four hours for rest and refreshment.

Deep and sound were Quentin's slumbers, until they were broken by the sound of the count's trumpet, and the cry of his *fourriers* and harbingers, " *Debout! debout! Ha! Messires en route—en route!*" Yet, unwelcomely early as the tones came, they awaked him a different being in strength and spirits from what he had fallen asleep. Confidence in himself and his fortunes returned with his reviving spirits and with the rising sun. He thought of his love no longer as a desperate and fantastic dream, but as a high and invigorating principle, to be cherished in his bosom, although he might never propose to himself, under all the difficulties by which he was beset, to bring it to any prosperous issue. " The pilot," he reflected, " steers his bark by the polar star, although he never expects to become possessor of it ; and the thoughts of Isabelle of Croye shall make me a worthy man-at-arms, though I may never see her more. When she hears that a Scottish soldier named Quentin Durward distinguished himself in a well-fought field, or left his body on the breach of a disputed fortress, she will remember the companion of her journey, as one who did all in his power to avert the snares and misfortunes which beset it, and perhaps will honor his memory with a tear, his coffin with a garland."

In this manly mood of bearing his misfortune, Quentin felt himself more able to receive and reply to the jests of the Count of Crèvecœur, who passed several on his alleged effeminacy and incapacity of undergoing fatigue. The young Scot accommodated himself so good-humoredly to the count's raillery, and replied at once so happily and so respectfully, that the change of his tone and manner made obviously a more favorable impression on the count than he had entertained from his prisoner's conduct during the preceding evening, when, rendered irritable by the feelings of his situation, he was alternately moodily silent or fiercely argumentative.

The veteran soldier began at length to take notice of his young companion as a pretty fellow of whom something might be made ; and more than hinted to him that, would he but resign his situation in the Archer Guard of France, he would undertake to have him enrolled in the household of the Duke of Burgundy in an honorable condition, and would himself take care of his advancement. And although Quentin, with suitable expressions of gratitude, declined this favor at present until he should find out how far he had to complain of his original patron, King Louis, he, nevertheless, continued to remain on good terms with the Count of Crèvecœur ; and, while his enthusiastic mode of thinking, and his foreign and idiomatical manner of expressing himself, often excited a smile on the grave cheek of the count, that smile had lost all that it had of sarcastic and bitter, and did not exceed the limits of good humor and good manners.

Thus traveling on with much more harmony than on the preceding day, the little party came at last within two miles of the famous and strong town of Péronne, r ear which the Duke of Burgundy's army lay encamped, ready, as was supposed, to invade France ; and in opposition to which Louis XI. had himself assembled a strong force near St. Maxence, for the purpose of bringing to reason his over-powerful vassal.

Péronne,* situated upon a deep river, in a flat country,

* See Note 33.

and surrounded by strong bulwarks and profound moats, was accounted in ancient as in modern times one of the strongest fortresses in France. The Count of Crèvecœur, his retinue, and his prisoner were approaching the fortress about the third hour after noon ; when, riding through the pleasant glades of a large forest, which then covered the approach to the town on the east side, they were met by two men of rank, as appeared from the number of their attendants, dressed in the habits worn in time of peace ; and who, to judge from the falcons which they carried on their wrists, and the number of spaniels and greyhounds led by their followers, were engaged in the amusement of hawking. But on perceiving Crèvecœur, with whose appearance and liveries they were sufficiently intimate, they quitted the search which they were making for a heron along the banks of a long canal, and came galloping towards him.

"News—news, Count of Crèvecœur ! " they cried both together ; "will you give news or take news, or will you barter fairly ? "

" I would barter fairly, Messires," said Crèvecœur, after saluting them courteously, " did I conceive you had any news of importance sufficient to make an equivalent for mine."

The two sportsmen smiled on each other ; and the elder of the two, a fine baronial figure, with a dark countenance, marked with that sort of sadness which some physiognomists ascribe to a melancholy temperament, and some, as the Italian statuary augured of the visage of Charles I., consider as predicting an unhappy death,* turning to his companion, said, " Crèvecœur has been in Brabant, the country of commerce, and he has learned all its artifices : he will be too hard for us if we drive a bargain."

" Messires," said Crèvecœur, the Duke ought in justice to have the first of my wares, as the seigneur takes his toll before open market begins. But tell me, are your news of a sad or a pleasant complexion ? "

The person whom he particularly addressed was a lively-looking man, with an eye of great vivacity, which was corrected by an expression of reflection and gravity about the mouth and upper lip—the whole physiognomy marking a man who saw and judged rapidly, but was sage and slow in forming resolutions or in expressing opinions. This was the famous Knight of Hainault, son of Collart, or Nicolas de la Clite, known in history and amongst historians by the ven-

* See D'Hymbercourt. Note 34,

erable name of Philip des Comines,* at this time close to the person of Duke Charles the Bold, and one of his most esteemed counselors. He answered Crèvecœur's question concerning the complexion of the news of which he and his companion, the Baron d'Hymbercourt, were the depositaries. "They were," he said, "like the colors of the rainbow, various in hue, as they might be viewed from different points, and placed against the black cloud or the fair sky. Such a rainbow was never seen in France or Flanders since that of Noah's ark."

"My tidings," replied Crèvecœur, "are altogether like the comet—gloomy, wild, and terrible in themselves, yet to be accounted the forerunners of still greater and more dreadful evils which are to ensue."

"We must open our bales," said Comines to his companion, "or our market will be forestalled by some newcomers, for ours are public news. In one word, Crèvecœur, listen, and wonder—King Louis is at Péronne!"

"What!" said the count, in astonishment; "has the Duke retreated without a battle? and do you remain here in your dress of peace after the town is besieged by the French, for I cannot suppose it taken?"

"No, surely," said D'Hymbercourt, "the banners of Burgundy have not gone back a foot; and still King Louis is here."

"Then Edward of England must have come over the seas with his bowmen," said Crèvecœur, "and, like his ancestors, gained a second field of Poictiers."

"Not so," said Comines. "Not a French banner has been borne down, not a sail spread from England, where Edward is too much amused among the wives of the citizens of London to think of playing the Black Prince. Hear the extraordinary truth. You know, when you left us, that the conference between the commissioners on the parts of France and Burgundy was broken up, without apparent chance of reconciliation?"

"True; and we dreamed of nothing but war."

"What has followed has been indeed so like a dream," said Comines, "that I almost expect to awake and find it so. Only one day since, the Duke had in council protested so furiously against farther delay, that it was resolved to send a defiance to the King and march forward instantly into France. Toison d'Or, commissioned for the purpose, had put on his official dress, and had his foot in the stirrup to

*See Note 35.

mount his horse, when lo! the French herald Montjoie rode
into our camp. We thought of nothing else than that
Louis had been beforehand with our defiance; and began to
consider how much the Duke would resent the advice which
had prevented him from being the first to declare war. But
a council being speedily assembled, what was our wonder
when the herald informed us that Louis, King of France,
was scarce an hour's riding behind, intending to visit Charles
Duke of Burgundy with a small retinue, in order that their
differences might be settled at a personal interview!"

"You surprise me, Messires," said Crévecœur; "and yet
you surprise me less than you might have expected; for,
when I was last at Plessis-les-Tours, the all-trusted Cardinal
Balue, offended with his master, and Burgundian at heart,
did hint to me that he could so work upon Louis's peculiar
foibles as to lead him to place himself in such a position with
regard to Burgundy that the Duke might have the terms of
peace of his own making. But I never suspected that so old
a fox as Louis could have been induced to come into the trap
of his own accord. What said the Burgundian counselors?"

"As you may guess," answered D'Hymbercourt; "talked
much of faith to be observed and little of advantage to be
obtained by such a visit; while it was manifest they thought
almost entirely of the last, and were only anxious to find some
way to reconcile it with the necessary preservation of appearances."

"And what said the Duke?" continued the Count of
Crèvecœur.

"Spoke brief and bold, as usual," replied Comines.
"'Which of you was it,' he asked, 'who witnessed the meeting of my cousin Louis and me after the battle of Montl'héry,*
when I was so thoughtless as to accompany him back within
the intrenchments of Paris with half a score of attendants,
and so put my person at the King's mercy?' I replied, that
most of us had been present, and none could ever forget the
alarm which it had been his pleasure to give us. 'Well,'
said the Duke, 'you blamed me for my folly, and I confessed
to you that I had acted like a giddy-pated boy; and I am
aware, too, that, my father of happy memory being then
alive, my kinsman, Louis, would have had less advantage by
seizing on my person than I might now have by securing his.
But, nevertheless, if my royal kinsman comes hither on the
present occasion in the same singleness of heart under which
I then acted, he shall be royally welcome. If it is meant by

this appearance of confidence to circumvent and to blind me till he execute some of his politic schemes, by St. George of Burgundy, let him look to it!' And so, having turned up his mustachios and stamped on the ground, he ordered us all to get on our horses and receive so extraordinary a guest.'"

"And you met the King accordingly?" replied the Count of Crèvecœur. "Miracles have not ceased! How was he accompanied?"

"As slightly as might be," answered D'Hymbercourt: only a score or two of the Scottish Guard, and a few knights and gentlemen of his household, among whom his astrologer, Galeotti, made the gayest figure."

"That fellow," said Crèvecœur, "holds some dependence on the Cardinal Balue; I should not be surprised that he has had his share in determining the King to this step of doubtful policy. Any nobility of higher rank?"

"There are Monsieur of Orleans and Dunois," replied Comines,

"I will have a rouse with Dunois," said Crèvecœur, "wag the world as it will. But we heard that both he and the duke had fallen into disgrace, and were in prison?"

"They were both under arrest in the Castle of Loches, that delightful place of retirement for the French nobility," said d'Hymbercourt; "but Louis has released them, in order to bring them with him, perhaps because he cared not to leave Orleans behind. For his other attendants, faith, I think his gossip, the hangman marshall, with two or three of his retinue, and Oliver, his barber, may be the most considerable; and the whole bevy so poorly arrayed that, by my honor, the King resembles most an old usurer going to collect desperate debts, attended by a body of catch polls."

"And where is he lodged?" said Crèvecœur.

"Nay, that," replied Comines, "is the most marvelous of all. Our duke offered to let the King's Archer Guard have a gate of the town, and a bridge of boats over the Somme, and to have assigned to Louis himself the adjoining house, belonging to a wealthy burgess, Giles Orthen; but, in going thither, the King espied the banners of De Lau and Pencilde Rivière, whom he had banished from France, and scared, as it would seem, with the thought of lodging so near refugees and malcontents of his own making, he craved to be quartered in the Castle of Péronne, and *there* he hath his abode accordingly."

19

"Why, God ha' mercy!" exclaimed Crèvecœur, "this is not only venturing into the lion's den, but thrusting his head into his very jaws. Nothing less than the very bottom of the rat-trap would serve the crafty old politician!"

"Nay," said Comines, "D'Hymbercourt hath not told you the speech of Le Glorieux,* which, in my mind, was the shrewdest opinion that was given."

"And what said *his* most illustrious wisdom?" asked the count.

"As the Duke," replied Comines, "was hastily ordering some vessels and ornaments of plate and the like, to be prepared as presents for the King and his retinue, by way of welcome on his arival, 'Trouble not thy small brain about it, my friend Charles,' said Le Glorieux : 'I will give thy cousin Louis a nobler and a fitter gift than thou canst, and that is my cap and bells, and my bauble to boot ; for, by the mass, he is a greater fool than I am for putting himself in thy power.' 'But if I give him no reason to repent it, sirrah, how then?' said the Duke. 'Then, truly, Charles, thou shalt have cap and bauble thyself, as the greatest fool of the three of us.' I promise you this knavish quip touched the Duke closely. I saw him change color and bite his lip. And now our news are told, noble Crèvecœur, and what think you they resemble?"

"A mine full-charged with gunpowder," answered Crèvecœur, "which, I fear, it is my fate to bring the kindled linstock. Your news and mine are like flax and fire, which cannot meet without bursting into flame, or like certain chemical substances which cannot be mingled without an explosion. Friends—gentlemen, ride close by my rein ; and when I tell you what has chanced in the bishopric of Liege, I think you will be of opinion that King Louis might as safely have undertaken a pilgrimage to the infernal regions as this ill-timed visit to Péronne."

The two nobles drew up close on either hand of the count, and listened, with half-suppressed exclamations and gestures of the deepest wonder and interest, to his account of the transactions at Liege and Schonwaldt. Quentin was then called forward, and examined and re-examined on the particulars of the bishop's death, until at length he refused to answer any further interrogatories, not knowing wherefore they were asked, or what use might be made of his replies.

They now reached the rich and level banks of the Somme,

* The jester of Charles of Burgundy, of whom more hereafter.

and the ancient walls of the little town of Péronne la Pucelle, and the deep green meadows adjoining, now whitened with numerous tents of the Duke of Burgundy's army, amounting to about fifteen thousand men.

CHAPTER XXVI

When princes meet, astrologers may mark it
An ominous conjunction, full of boding,
Like that of Mars with Saturn.

Old Play.

ONE hardly knows whether to term it a privilege or a penalty annexed to the quality of princes, that, in their intercourse with each other, they are required, by the respect which is due to their own rank and dignity, to regulate their feelings and expressions by a severe etiquette, which precludes all violent and avowed display of passion, and which, but that the whole world are aware that this assumed complaisance is a matter of ceremony, might justly pass for profound dissimulation. It is no less certain, however, that the overstepping of these bounds of ceremonial, for the purpose of giving more direct vent to their angry passions, has the effect of compromising their dignity with the world in general, as was particularly noted when those distinguished rivals, Francis the First and the Emperor Charles, gave each other the lie direct, and were desirous of deciding their differences hand to hand, in single combat.

Charles of Burgundy, the most hasty and impatient, nay, the most imprudent, prince of his time, found himself, nevertheless, fettered within the magic circle which prescribed the most profound deference to Louis, as his suzerain and liege lord, who had deigned to confer upon him, a vassal of the crown, the distinguished honor of a personal visit. Dressed in his ducal mantle, and attended by his great officers and principal knights and nobles, he went in gallant cavalcade to receive Lous XI. His retinue absolutely blazed with gold and silver ; for the wealth of the court of England being exhausted by the wars of York and Lancaster, and the expenditure of France limited by the economy of the sovereign, that of Burgundy was for the time the most magnificent in Europe. The *cortège* of Louis, on the contrary, was few in number, and comparatively mean in appearance, and the exterior of the King himself, in a threadbare cloak, with his wonted old high-crowned hat struck full of images, rendered the contrast yet more striking ; and as the Duke, richly attired with the coronet and mantle of state, threw himself from his noble charger, and, kneeling on one knee, offered to hold the stirrup while Louis dismounted from his little ambling palfrey, the effect was almost grotesque.

The greeting between the two potentates was, of course, as full of affected kindness and compliment as it was totally devoid of sincerity. But the temper of the Duke rendered it much more difficult for him to preserve the necessary appearances in voice, speech, and demeanor ; while in the King every species of simulation and dissimulation seemed so much a part of his nature that those best acquainted with him could not have distinguished what was feigned from what was real.

Perhaps the most accurate illustration, were it not unworthy two such high potentates, would be to suppose the King in the situation of a stranger, perfectly acquainted with the habits and dispositions of the canine race, who, for some purpose of his own, is desirous to make friends with a large and surly mastiff, that holds him in suspicion, and is disposed to worry him on the first symptoms either of diffidence or of umbrage. The mastiff growls internally, erects his bristles, shows his teeth, yet is ashamed to fly upon the intruder, who seems at the same time so kind and so confiding, and therefore the animal endures advances which are far from pacifying him, watching at the same time the slightest opportunity which may justify him in his own eyes for seizing his friend by the throat.

The King was no doubt sensible, from the altered voice, constrained manner, and abrupt gestures of the Duke, that the game he had to play was delicate, and perhaps he more than once repented having even taken it in hand. But repentance was too late, and all that remained for him was that inimitable dexterity of management which the King understood equally at least with any man that ever lived.

The demeanor which Louis used towards the Duke was such as to resemble the kind overflowing of the heart in a moment of sincere reconciliation with an honored and tried friend, from whom he had been estranged by temporary circumstances now passed away, and forgotten as soon as removed. The King blamed himself for not having sooner taken the decisive step of convincing his kind and good kinsman, by such a mark of confidence as he was now be-

stowing, that the angry passages which had occurred betwixt
them were nothing in his remembrance when weighed
against the kindness which received him when an exile from
France, and under the displeasure of the King his father.
He spoke of the Good Duke of Burgundy, as Philip the
father of Duke Charles was currently called, and remembered a thousand instances of his paternal kindness.

"I think, cousin," he said, "your father made little
difference in his affection betwixt you and me ; for I remember, when by an accident I had bewildered myself in a
hunting-party, I found the Good Duke upbraided you with
leaving me in the forest, as if you had been careless of the
safety of an elder brother."

The Duke of Burgundy's features were naturally harsh and
severe, and when he attempted to smile, in polite acquiescence to the truth of what the King told him, the grimace
which he made was truly diabolical.

"Prince of dissemblers," he said in his secret soul, "would
that it stood with my honor to remind you *how* you have
requited all the benefits of our house !"

"And then," continued the King, "if the ties of consanguinity and gratitude are not sufficient to bind us together, my fair cousin, we have those of spiritual relationship ; for I am godfather to your fair daughter Mary, who is
as dear to me as one of my own maidens ; and when the
saints—their holy name be blessed !—sent me a little blossom
which withered in the course of three months, it was your
princely father who held it at the font, and celebrated the
ceremony of baptism with richer and prouder magnificence
than Paris itself could have afforded. Never shall I forget
the deep, the indelible impression which the generosity of
Duke Philip, and yours, my dearest cousin, made upon the
half-broken heart of the poor exile !"

"Your Majesty," said the Duke, compelling himself to
make some reply, "acknowledged that slight obligation in
terms which overpaid all the display which Burgundy could
make to show due sense of the honor you had done its
sovereign."

"I remember the words you mean, fair cousin," said the
King, smiling ; I think they were, that in guerdon of the
benefit of that day, I, poor wanderer, had nothing to offer
save the persons of myself, of my wife, and of my child. Well,
and I think I have indifferently well redeemed my pledge."

"I mean not to dispute what your Majesty is pleased to
aver," said the Duke ; "but——"

" But you ask," said the King, interrupting him, " how my actions have accorded with my words. Marry thus : the body of my infant child Joachim rests in Burgundian earth ; my own person I have this morning placed unreservedly in your power ; and for that of my wife—truly, cousin, I think, considering the period of time which has passed, you will scarce insist on my keeping my word in that particular. She was born on the day of the Blessed Annunciation (he crossed himself and muttered an *Ora pro nobis*), some fifty years since ; but she is no farther distant than Rheims, and if you insist on my promise being fulfilled to the letter, she shall presently wait your pleasure."

Angry as the Duke of Burgundy was at the barefaced attempt of the King to assume towards him a tone of friendship and intimacy, he could not help laughing at the whimsical reply of that singular monarch, and his laugh was as discordant as the abrupt tones of passion in which he often spoke. Having laughed longer and louder than was at that period, or would now be, thought fitting the time and occasion, he answered in the same tone, bluntly declining the honor of the Queen's company, but stating his willingness to accept that of the King's eldest daughter, whose beauty was celebrated.

" I am happy, fair cousin," said the King, with one of those dubious smiles of which he frequently made use, " that your gracious pleasure has not fixed on my younger daughter Joan. I should otherwise have had spear-breaking between you and my cousin of Orleans ; and, had harm come of it, I must on either side have lost a kind friend and affectionate cousin."

" Nay—nay, my royal sovereign," said Duke Charles, " the Duke of Orleans shall have no interruption from me in the path which he has chosen *par amours*. The cause in which I couch my lance against Orleans must be fair and straight."

Louis was far from taking amiss this brutal allusion to the personal deformity of the Princess Joan. On the contrary, he was rather pleased to find that the Duke was content to be amused with broad jests, in which he was himself a proficient, and which, according to the modern phrase, spared much sentimental hypocrisy. Accordingly, he speedily placed their intercourse on such a footing that Charles, though he felt it impossible to play the part of an affectionate and reconciled friend to a monarch whose ill offices he had so often encountered, and whose sincerity on the present occasion he so strongly doubted, yet had no difficulty in acting the hearty landlord towards a facetious guest; and so the want of reciprocity in kinder feelings between them was supplied by the tone of good fellowship which exists between two boon companions—a tone natural to the Duke from the frankness, and, it might be added, the grossness, of his character, and to Louis, because, though capable of assuming any mood of social intercourse, that which really suited him best was mingled with grossness of ideas and caustic humor of expression.

Both princes were happily able to preserve, during the period of a banquet at the town house of Péronne, the same kind of conversation, on which they met as on a neutral ground, and which, as Louis easily perceived, was more available than any other to keep the Duke of Burgundy in that state of composure which seemed necessary to his own safety.

Yet he was alarmed to observe that the Duke had around him several of those French nobles, and those of the highest rank and in situations of great trust and power, whom his own severity or injustice had driven into exile; and it was to secure himself from the possible effects of their resentment and revenge that (as already mentioned) he requested to be lodged in the castle or citadel of Péronne rather than in the town itself.* This was readily granted by Duke Charles, with one of those grim smiles of which it was impossible to say whether it meant good or harm to the party whom it concerned.

But when the King, expressing himself with as much delicacy as he could, and in the manner he thought best qualified to lull suspicion to sleep, asked whether the Scottish Archers of his Guard might not maintain the custody of the Castle of Péronne during his residence there, in lieu of the gate of the town which the Duke had offered to their care, Charles replied, with his wonted sternness of voice and abruptness of manner, rendered more alarming by his habit, when he spoke, of either turning up his mustachios or handling his sword or dagger, the last of which he used frequently to draw a little way and then return to the sheath†—"St. Martin! No, my liege. You are in your vassal's camp and city—so men call me in respect to your Majesty—my castle and town are yours and my men are yours; so it is indifferent whether my men-at-arms or the Scottish Archers guard either

* See Louis's Suspicious Character.   Note 37.
† This gesture, very indicative of a fierce character, is also by stage tradition a distinction of Shakespeare's Richard III.

the outer gate or defenses of the castle. No, by St. George! Péronne is a virgin fortress; she shall not lose her reputation by any neglect of mine. Maidens must be carefully watched, my royal cousin, if we would have them continue to live in good fame."

"Surely, fair cousin, and I altogether agree with you," said the King, " I being in fact more interested in the reputation of the good little town than you are—Péronne being, as you know, fair cousin, one of those upon the same river Somme which, pledged to your father of happy memory for redemption of money, are liable to be redeemed upon repayment. And, to speak truth, coming, like an honest debtor, disposed to clear off my obligations of every kind, I have brought here a few sumpter mules loaded with silver for the redemption—enough to maintain even your princely and royal establishment, fair cousin, for the space of three years."

"I will not receive a penny of it," said the Duke, twirling his mustachios ; " the day of redemption is past, my royal cousin ; nor was there ever serious purpose that the right should be exercised, the cession of these towns being the sole recompense my father ever received from France when, in a happy hour for your family, he consented to forget the murder of my grandfather, and to exchange the alliance of England for that of your father. St. George! if he had not so acted, your royal self, far from having towns on the Somme, could scarce have kept those beyond the Loire. No ; I will not render a stone of them, were I to receive for every stone so rendered its weight in gold. I thank God, and the wisdom and valor of my ancestors, that the revenues of Burgundy, though it be but a duchy, will maintain my state, even when a king is my guest, without obliging me to barter my heritage."

"Well, fair cousin," answered the King, with the same mild and placid manner as before, and unperturbed by the loud tone and violent gestures of the Duke, " I see that you are so good a friend to France that you are unwilling to part with aught that belongs to her. But we shall need some moderator in these affairs when we come to treat of them in council. What say you to St. Paul?"

"Neither St. Paul, nor St. Peter, nor e'er a saint in the calendar," said the Duke of Burgundy, "shall preach me out of the possession of Péronne."

"Nay, but you mistake me," said King Louis, smiling ; "I mean Louis de Luxembourg, our trusty constable, the Count of St. Paul. Ah ! St. Mary of Embrun ! we lack but

his head at our conference! the best head in France, and
the most useful to the restoration of perfect harmony betwixt us."

"By St. George of Burgundy!" said the Duke, "I marvel
to hear your Majesty talk thus of a man false and perjured
both to France and Burgundy—one who hath ever endeavored to fan into a flame our frequent differences, and that
with the purpose of giving himself the airs of a mediator.
I swear by the order I wear, that his marshes shall not be
long a resource for him!"

"Be not so warm, cousin," replied the King, smiling, and
speaking under his breath; "when I wished for the constable's *head*, as a means of ending the settlement of our
trifling differences, I had no desire for his *body*, which
might remain at St. Quentin's with much convenience."

"Ho! ho! I take your meaning, my royal cousin," said
Charles, with the same dissonant laugh which some other of
the King's coarse pleasantries had extorted, and added,
stamping with his heel on the ground, "I allow, in that
sense, the head of the constable *might* be useful at Péronne."

These, and other discourses, by which the King mixed
hints at serious affairs amid matters of mirth and amusement,
did not follow each other consecutively; but were adroitly
introduced during the time of the banquet at the *hôtel de
ville*, during a subsequent interview in the Duke's own apartments, and, in short, as occasion seemed to render the introduction of such delicate subjects easy and natural.

Indeed, however rashly Louis had placed himself in a risk
which the Duke's fiery temper, and the mutual subjects of
exasperated enmity which subsisted betwixt them, rendered
of doubtful and perilous issue, never pilot on an unknown
coast conducted himself with more firmness and prudence.
He seemed to sound, with the utmost address and precision,
the depths and shallows of his rival's mind and temper, and
manifested neither doubt nor fear when the result of his
experiments discovered much more of sunken rocks and of
dangerous shoals than of safe anchorage.

At length a day closed which must have been a weari-
some one to Louis, from the constant exertion, vigilance,
precaution, and attention which his situation required, as it
was a day of constraint to the Duke, from the necessity of
suppressing the violent feelings to which he was in the
general habit of giving uncontrolled vent.

No sooner had the latter retired into his own apartment,
after he had taken a formal leave of the King for the night,

than he gave way to the explosion of passion which he had
so long suppressed ; and many an oath and abusive epithet,
as his jester, Le Glorieux, said, " fell that night upon heads
which they were never coined for," his domestics reaping the
benefit of that hoard of injudicious language which he could
not in decency bestow on his royal guest, even in his absence,
and which was yet become too great to be altogether suppressed. The jests of the clown had some effect in tran-
quilizing the Duke's angry mood ; he laughed loudly, threw
the jester a piece of gold, caused himself to be disrobed in
tranquility, swallowed a deep cup of wine and spices, went
to bed, and slept soundly.

The *couchée* of King Louis is more worthy of notice than
that of Charles ; for the violent expression of exasperated
and headlong passion, as indeed it belongs more to the brutal
than the intelligent part of our nature, has little to interest
us in comparison to the deep workings of a vigorous and powerful mind.

Louis was escorted to the lodgings he had chosen in the
castle, or citadel, of Péronne by the chamberlains and harbingers of the Duke of Burgundy, and received at the entrance by a strong guard of archers and men-at-arms.

As he descended from his horse to cross the drawbridge,
over a moat of unusual width and depth, he looked on the
sentinel, and observed to Comines, who accompanied him,
with other Burgundian nobles, " They wear St. Andrew's
crosses, but not those of my Scottish Archers."

" You will find them as ready to die in your defense, sire,"
said the Burgundian, whose sagacious ear had detected in
the King's tone of speech a feeling which doubtless Louis
would have concealed if he could. " They wear the St.
Andrew's cross as the appendage of the collar of the Golden
Fleece, my master the Duke of Burgundy's order."

" Do I not know it ? " said Louis, showing the collar
which he himself wore in compliment to his host. " It is one
of the dear bonds of fraternity which exist between my kind
brother and myself. We are brothers in chivalry, as in
spiritual relationship—cousins by birth, and friends by every
tie of kind feeling and good neighborhood. No farther
than the base-court, my noble lords and gentlemen ! I can
permit your attendance no farther ; you have done me
enough of grace."

" We were charged by the Duke," said D'Hymbercourt,
" to bring your Majesty to your lodging. We trust your
Majesty will permit us to obey our master's command."

"In this small matter," said the King, "I trust you will allow my command to outweigh his, even with you his liege subjects. I am something indisposed, my lords—something fatigued. Great pleasure hath its toils as well as great pain. I trust to enjoy your society better to-morrow. And yours, too, Seignior Philip of Comines. I am told you are the annalist of the time ; we that desire to have a name in history must speak you fair, for men say your pen hath a sharp point, when you will. Good-night, my lords and gentles, to all and each of you."

The lords of Burgundy retired, much pleased with the grace of Louis's manner and the artful distribution of his attentions ; and the King was left with only one or two of his own personal followers, under the archway of the base-court of the Castle of Péronne, looking on the huge tower which occupied one of the angles, being in fact the donjon, or principal keep, of the place. This tall, dark, massive building was seen clearly by the same moon which was lighting Quentin Durward betwixt Charleroi and Péronne, which, as the reader is aware, shone with peculiar luster. The great keep was in form nearly resembling the White Tower in the citadel of London, but still more ancient in its architecture, deriving its date, as was affirmed, from the days of Charlemagne. The walls were of a tremendous thickness, the windows very small, and grated with bars of iron, and the huge clumsy bulk of the building cast a dark and portentous shadow over the whole of the courtyard.

"I am not to be lodged *there!*" the King said, with a shudder that had something in it ominous.

"No," replied the gray-headed seneschal, who attended upon him unbonneted. "God forbid ! Your Majesty's apartments are prepared in these lower buildings which are hard by, and in which King John slept two nights before the battle of Poictiers."

"Hum—that is no lucky omen either," muttered the King ; "but what of the tower, my old friend ? and why should you desire of Heaven that I may not be there lodged ?"

"Nay, my gracious liege," said the seneschal, "I know no evil of the tower at all—only that the sentinels say lights are seen, and strange noises heard in it at night ; and there are reasons why that may be the case, for anciently it was used as a state prison, and there are many tales of deeds which have been done in it."

Louis asked no farther questions ; for no man was more

bound than he to respect the secrets of a prison-house. At the door of the apartment destined for his use, which, though of later date than the tower, were still both ancient and gloomy, stood a small party of the Scottish Guard, which the Duke, although he declined to concede the point to Louis, had ordered to be introduced, so as to be near the person of their master. The faithful Lord Crawford was at their head.

"Crawford—my honest and faithful Crawford," said the King, "where hast thou been to-day? Are the lords of Burgundy so inhospitable as to neglect one of the bravest and most noble gentlemen that ever trod a court? I saw you not at the banquet."

"I declined it, my liege," said Crawford. "Times are changed with me. The day has been that I could have ventured a carouse with the best man in Burgundy, and that in the juice of his own grape; but a matter of four pints now flusters me, and I think it concerns your Majesty's service to set in this an example to my callants."

"Thou art ever prudent," said the King; "but surely your toil is the less when you have so few men to command? and a time of festivity requires not so severe self-denial on your part as a time of danger."

"If I have few men to command," said Crawford, "I have the more need to keep the knaves in fitting condition; and whether this business be like to end in feasting or fighting, God and your Majesty knows better than old John of Crawford."

"You surely do not apprehend any danger?" said the King hastily, yet in a whisper.

"Not I," answered Crawford. "I wish I did; for, as old Earl Tineman * used to say, apprehended dangers may be always defended dangers. The word for the night, if your Majesty pleases?"

"Let it be 'Burgundy,' in honor of our host and of a liquor that you love, Crawford."

"I will quarrel with neither duke nor drink so called," said Crawford, "provided always that both be sound. A good night to your Majesty!"

"A good night, my trusty Scot," said the King, and passed on to his apartments.

At the door of his bedroom Le Balafré was placed sentinel. "Follow me hither," said the King as he passed him; and the archer accordingly, like a piece of machinery put in

* An Earl of Douglas, so called.

motion by an artist, strode after him into the apartment, and remained there fixed, silent, and motionless, attending the royal command.

"Have you heard from that wandering paladin, your nephew?" said the king; "for he hath been lost to us since, like a young knight who had set out upon his first adventures, he sent us home two prisoners, as the first-fruits of his chivalry."

"My lord, I heard something of that," said Balafré; "and I hope your Majesty will believe that, if he hath acted wrongfully, it was in no shape by my precept or example, since I never was so bold as to unhorse any of your Majesty's most illustrious house, better knowing my own condition, and——"

"Be silent on that point," said the King; "your nephew did his duty in the matter."

"There, indeed," continued Balafré, "he had the cue from me. 'Quentin,' said I to him, 'whatever comes of it, remember you belong to the Scottish Archer Guard, and do your duty whatever comes on't.'"

"I guessed he had some such exquisite instructor," said Louis; "but it concerns me that you answer my first question. Have you heard of your nephew of late? Stand aback, my masters," he added, addressing the gentlemen of his chamber, "for this concerneth no ears but mine."

"Surely, please your Majesty," said Balafré, "I have seen this very evening the groom Charlet, whom my kinsman despatched from Liege, or some castle of the bishop's which is near it, and where he hath lodged the Ladies of Croye in safety."

"Now Our Lady of heaven be praised for it!" said the King. "Art thou sure of it?—sure of the good news?"

"As sure as I can be of aught," said Le Balafré. "The fellow, I think, hath letters for your Majesty from the Ladies of Croye."

"Haste to get them," said the King. "Give thy harquebuss to one of these knaves—to Oliver—to any one. Now Our Lady of Embrun be praised! and silver shall be the screen that surrounds her high altar!"

Louis, in this fit of gratitude and devotion, doffed, as usual, his hat, selected from the figures with which it was garnished that which represented his favorite image of the Virgin, placed it on a table, and, kneeling down, repeated reverently the vow he had made.

The groom, being the first messenger whom Durward had

despatched from Schonwaldt, was now introduced with his
letters. They were addressed to the King by the Ladies of
Croye, and barely thanked him in very cold terms for his
courtesy while at his court, and, something more warmly,
for having permitted them to retire, and sent them in safety
from his dominions, expressions at which Louis laughed
very heartily, instead of resenting them. He then demanded of Charlet, with obvious interest, whether they had
not sustained some alarm or attack upon the road? Charlet, a stupid fellow, and selected for that quality, gave a
very confused account of the affray in which his companion,
the Gascon, had been killed, but knew of no other. Again
Louis demanded of him, minutely and particularly, the
route which the party had taken to Liege ; and seemed much
interested when he was informed, in reply, that they had,
upon approaching Namur, kept the more direct road to
Liege, upon the right bank of the Maes, instead of the left
bank, as recommended in their route. The King then ordered the man a small present and dismissed him, disguising
the anxiety he had expressed, as if it only concerned the
safety of the Ladies of Croye.

Yet the news, though they inferred the failure of one of
his own favorite plans, seemed to imply more internal satisfaction on the King's part than he would have probably indicated in a case of brilliant success. He sighed like one
whose breast has been relieved from a heavy burden, muttered his devotional acknowledgments with an air of deep
sanctity, raised up his eyes, and hastened to adjust newer
and surer schemes of ambition.

With such purpose, Louis ordered the attendance of his
astrologer, Martius Galeotti, who appeared with his usual
air of assumed dignity, yet not without a shade of uncertainty on his brow, as if he had doubted the King's kind
reception. It was, however, favorable, even beyond the
warmest which he had ever met with at any former interview. Louis termed him his friend, his father in the
sciences, the glass by which a king should look into distant
futurity, and concluded by thrusting on his finger a ring of
very considerable value. Galeotti, not aware of the circumstances which had thus suddenly raised his character in
the estimation of Louis, yet understood his own profession
too well to let that ignorance be seen. He received with
grave modesty the praises of Louis, which he contended
were only due to the nobleness of the science which he
practised, a science the rather the more deserving of admi-

ration on account of its working miracles through means of so feeble an agent as himself ; and he and the King took leave for once much satisfied with each other.

On the astrologer's departure, Louis threw himself into a chair, and appearing much exhausted, dismissed the rest of his attendants, excepting Oliver alone, who, creeping around with gentle assiduity and noiseless step, assisted him in the task of preparing for repose.

While he received this assistance, the King, unlike to his wont, was so silent and passive, that his attendant was struck by the unusual change in his deportment. The worst minds have often something of good principle in them : banditti show fidelity to their captain, and sometimes a protected and promoted favorite has felt a gleam of sincere interest in the monarch to whom he owed his greatness. Oliver le Diable, le Mauvais, or by whatever other name he was called expressive of his evil propensities, was, nevertheless, scarcely so completely identified with Satan as not to feel some touch of grateful feeling for his master in this singular condition, when, as it seemed, his fate was deeply interested, and his strength seemed to be exhausted. After for a short time rendering to the King in silence the usual services paid by a servant to his master at the toilet, the attendant was at length tempted to say, with the freedom which his sovereign's indulgence had permitted him in such circumstances, " *Tête-dieu*, sire, you seem as if you had lost a battle ; and yet I, who was near your Majesty during this whole day, never knew you fight a field so gallantly."

" A field !" said King Louis, looking up, and assuming his wonted causticity of tone and manner ; " *Pasques-dieu*, my friend Oliver, say I have kept the arena in a bull-fight ; for a blinder, and more stubborn, untameable, uncontrollable brute, than our cousin of Burgundy, never existed, save in the shape of a Murcian bull, trained for the bull-feasts. Well, let it pass. I dodged him bravely. But, Oliver, rejoice with me that my plans in Flanders have not taken effect, whether as concerning those two rambling Princesses of Croye, or in Liege—you understand me ? "

" In faith, I do not, sire," replied Oliver ; " it is impossible for me to congratulate your Majesty on the failure of your favorite schemes, unless you tell me some reason for the change in your own wishes and views."

" Nay," answered the King, " there is no change in either, in a general view. But, *Pasques-dieu*, my friend, I have this day learned more of Duke Charles than I before knew.

When he was Count de Charalois, in the time of the old
Duke Philip and the banished Dauphin of France, we drank,
and hunted, and rambled together, and many a wild adventure we have had. And in those days I had a decided advantage over him, like that which a strong spirit naturally
assumes over a weak one. But he has since changed—has
become a dogged, daring, assuming, disputatious dogmatist,
who nourishes an obvious wish to drive matters to extremities,
while he thinks he has the game in his own hands. I was
compelled to glide as gently away from each offensive topic
as if I touched red-hot iron. I did but hint at the possibility
of those erratic Countesses of Croye, ere they attained Liege
—for thither I frankly confessed that, to the best of my
belief, they were gone—falling into the hands of some wild
snapper upon the frontiers, and, *Pasques-dieu!* you would
have thought I had spoken of sacrilege. It is needless to
tell you what he said, and quite enough to say, that I would
have held my head's safety very insecure, if, in that moment,
accounts had been brought of the success of thy friend, William with the Beard, in his and thy honest scheme of better-
ing himself by marriage."

"No friend of *mine*, if it please your Majesty," said Oliver ;
"neither friend nor plan of mine."

"True, Oliver," answered the king ; "thy plan had not
been to wed, but to shave, such a bridegroom. Well, thou
didst wish her as bad a one, when thou didst modestly hint
at thyself. However, Oliver, lucky the man who has her not ;
for hang, draw, and quarter were the most gentle words
which my gentle cousin spoke of him who should wed the
young countess, his vassal, without his most ducal permission."

"And he is, doubtless, as jealous of any disturbances in
the good town of Liege ?" asked the favorite.

"As much, or much more so," replied the king, "as
your understanding may easily anticipate ; but, ever since I
resolved on coming hither, my messengers have been in
Liege, to repress, for the present, every movement to insurrection ; and my very busy and bustling friends, Rouslaer
and Pavillon, have orders to be quiet as a mouse until this
happy meeting between my cousin and me is over."

"Judging, then, from your Majesty's account," said Oliver
dryly, "the utmost to be hoped from this meeting is, that
it should not make your condition worse ? Surely this is
like the crane that thrust her head into the fox's mouth,
and was glad to thank her good fortune that it was not bitten

off. Yet your Majesty seemed deeply obliged even now to the sage philosopher who encouraged you to play so hopeful a game."

"No game," said the King, sharply, "is to be despaired of until it is lost, and that I have no reason to expect it will be in my own case. On the contrary, if nothing occurs to stir the rage of this vindictive madman, I am sure of victory ; and surely, I am not a little obliged to the skill which selected for my agent, as the conductor of the Ladies of Croye, a youth whose horoscope so far corresponded with mine, that he hath saved me from danger, even by the disobedience of my own commands, and taking the route which avoided De la Marck's ambuscade."

"Your Majesty," said Oliver, "may find many agents who will serve you on the terms of acting rather after their own pleasure than your instructions."

"Nay, nay, Oliver," said Louis impatiently, "the heathen poet speaks of *vota diis exaudita malignis,*—wishes, that is, which the saints grant to us in their wrath ; and such, in the circumstances, would have been the success of William de la Marck's exploit, had it taken place about this time, and while I am in the power of this Duke of Burgundy. And this my own art foresaw—fortified by that of Galeotti ; that is, I foresaw not the miscarriage of De la Marck's undertaking, but I foresaw that the expedition of yonder Scottish archer should end happily for me. And such has been the issue, though in a manner different from what I expected ; for the stars, though they foretell general results, are yet silent on the means by which such are accomplished, being often the very reverse of what we expect, or even desire. But why talk I of these mysteries to thee, Oliver, who art in so far worse than the very devil, who is thy namesake, since he believes and trembles ; whereas thou art an infidel both to religion and to science, and wilt remain so till thine own destiny is accomplished, which, as thy horoscope and physiognomy alike assure me, will be by the intervention of the gallows ?"

"And if it indeed shall be so," said Oliver, in a resigned tone of voice, "it will be so ordered, because I was too grateful a servant to hesitate at executing the commands of my royal master."

Louis burst into his usual sardonic laugh. "Thou hast broken thy lance on me fairly, Oliver ; and, by Our Lady, thou art right, for I defied thee to it. But, prithee, tell me in sadness, does thou discover anything in these men's measures towards us, which may argue any suspicion of ill usage ? "

" My liege," replied Oliver, " your Majesty and yonder learned philosopher look for augury to the stars and heavenly host ; I am an earthly reptile, and consider but the things connected with my vocation. But, methinks, there is a lack of that earnest and precise attention on your Majesty, which men show to a welcome guest of a degree so far above them. The Duke, to-night, pleaded weariness, and saw your Majesty not farther than to the street, leaving to the officers of his household the task of conveying you to your lodgings. The rooms here are hastily and carelessly fitted up : the tapestry is hung up awry ; and, in one of the pieces, as you may observe, the figures are reversed and stand on their heads, while the trees grow with their roots uppermost."

" Pshaw ! accident, and the effect of hurry," said the King. " When did you ever know me concerned about such trifles as these ? "

" Not on their own account are they worth notice," said Oliver ; " but as intimating the degree of esteem in which the officers of the Duke's household observe your Grace to be held by him. Believe me, that had his desire seemed sincere that your reception should be in all points marked by scrupulous attention, the zeal of his people would have made minutes do the work of days. And when," he added, pointing to the basin and ewer, " was the furniture of your Majesty's toilet of other substance than silver ? "

" Nay," said the King, with a constrained smile, " that last remark upon the shaving utensils, Oliver, is too much in the style of thine own peculiar occupation to be combated by any one. True it is, that when I was only a refugee and an exile, I was served upon gold plate by order of the same Charles, who accounted silver too mean for the Dauphin, though he seems to hold that metal too rich for the King of France. Well, Oliver, we will to bed. Our resolution has been made and executed ; there is nothing to be done but to play manfully the game on which we have entered. I know that my cousin of Burgundy, like other wild bulls, shuts his eyes when he begins his career. I have but to watch that moment, like one of the tauridors whom we saw at Burgos, and his impetuosity places him at my mercy."

CHAPTER XXVII

THE EXPLOSION

'Tis listening fear, and dumb amazement all,
When to the startled eye the sudden glance
Appears far south, eruptive through the cloud.
THOMSON'S *Summer.*

THE preceding chapter, agreeable to its title, was designed as a retrospect, which might enable the reader fully to understand the terms upon which the King of France and the Duke of Burgundy stood together, when the former, moved, partly perhaps by his belief in astrology, which was represented as favorable to the issue of such a measure, and in a great measure doubtless by the conscious superiority of his own powers of mind over those of Charles, had adopted the extraordinary, and upon any other ground altogether inexplicable, resolution of committing his person to the faith of a fierce and exasperated enemy—a resolution also the more rash and unaccountable, as there were various examples in that stormy time to show, that safe-conducts, however solemnly plighted, had proved no assurance for those in whose favor they were conceived ; and indeed the murder of the Duke's grandfather, at the bridge of Montereau, in presence of the father of Louis, and at an interview solemnly agreed upon for the establishment of peace and amnesty, was a horrible precedent, should the Duke be disposed to resort to it.

But the temper of Charles, though rough, fierce, headlong and unyielding, was not, unless in the full tide of passion, faithless or ungenerous, faults which usually belong to colder dispositions. He was at no pains to show the King more courtesy than the laws of hospitality positively demanded ; but, on the other hand, he evinced no purpose of overleaping their sacred barriers.

On the following morning after the King's arrival, there was a general muster of the troops of the Duke of Burgundy, which were so numerous and so excellently appointed, that, perhaps, he was not sorry to have an opportunity of displaying them before his great rival. Indeed, while he paid the necessary compliment of a vassal to his suzerain, in declaring that these troops were the King's, and not his own, the curl of his upper lip and the proud glance of his eye intimated his consciousness that the words he used were but empty compliment, and that his fine army, at his own unlimited disposal, was as ready to march against Paris as in any other direction. It must have added to Louis's mortification, that he recognized, as forming part of this host, many banners of French nobility, not only of Normandy and Bretagne, but of provinces more immediately subjected to his own authority, who, from various causes of discontent, had joined and made common cause with the Duke of Burgundy.

True to his character, however, Louis seemed to take little notice of these malcontents, while, in fact, he was revolving in his mind the various means by which it might be possible to detach them from the banners of Burgundy and bring them back to his own, and resolved for that purpose, that he would cause those to whom he attached the greatest importance to be secretly sounded by Oliver and other agents.

He himself labored diligently, but at the same time cautiously, to make interest with the Duke's chief officers and advisers, employing for that purpose the usual means of familiar and frequent notice, adroit flattery, and liberal presents ; not, as he represented, to alienate their faithful services from their noble master, but that they might lend their aid in preserving peace betwixt France and Burgundy —an end so excellent in itself, and so obviously tending to the welfare of both countries, and of the reigning princes of either.

The notice of so great and so wise a king was in itself a mighty bribe ; promises did much, and direct gifts, which the customs of the time permitted the Burgundian courtiers to accept without scruple, did still more. During a boar hunt in the forest, while the Duke, eager always upon the immediate object, whether business or pleasure, gave himself entirely up to the ardor of the chase, Louis, unrestrained by his presence, sought and found the means of speaking secretly and separately to many of those who were reported to have most interest with Charles, among whom D'Hymbercourt and Comines were not forgotten ; nor did he fail to mix up the advances which he made towards those two distinguished persons with praises of the valor and military skill of the first, and of the profound sagacity and literary talents of the future historian of the period.

Such an opportunity of personally conciliating, or, if the reader pleases, corrupting, the ministers of Charles, was perhaps what the King had proposed to himself as a principal object of his visit, even if his art should fail to cajole the Duke himself. The connection betwixt France and Burgundy was so close, that most of the nobles belonging to the latter country had hopes or actual interests connected with the former, which the favor of Louis could advance or his personal displeasure destroy. Formed for this and every other species of intrigue, liberal to profusion when it was necessary to advance his plans, and skilful in putting the most plausible color upon his proposals and presents, the King contrived to reconcile the spirit of the proud to their profit, and to hold out to the real or pretended patriot the good of both France and Burgundy as the ostensible motive ; whilst the party's own private interest, like the concealed wheel of some machine, worked not the less powerfully that its operations were kept out of sight. For each man he had a suitable bait and a proper mode of presenting it : he poured the guerdon into the sleeve of those who were too proud to extend their hand, and trusted that his bounty, though it descended like the dew without noise and imperceptibly, would not fail to produce, in due season, a plentiful crop of goodwill at least, perhaps of good offices, to the donor. In fine, although he had been long paving the way by his ministers for an establishment of such an interest in the court of Burgundy as should be advantageous to the interests of France, Louis's own personal exertions, directed doubtless by the information of which he was previously possessed, did more to accomplish that object in a few hours than his agents had effected in years of negotiation.

One man alone the King missed whom he had been particularly desirous of conciliating, and that was the Count de Crèvecœur, whose firmness, during his conduct as envoy at Plessis, far from exciting Louis's resentment, had been viewed as a reason for making him his own if possible. He was not particularly gratified when he learnt that the count, at the head of an hundred lances, was gone towards the frontiers of Brabant to assist the bishop, in case of necessity, against William de la Marck and his discontented subjects ; but he consoled himself that the appearance of this force, joined with the directions which he had sent by faithful messengers, would serve to prevent any premature disturbances in that country, the breaking out of which might, he foresaw, render his present situation very precarious.

The court upon this occasion dined in the forest when the hour of noon arrived, as was common in those great hunting parties ; an arrangement at this time particularly agreeable to the Duke, desirous as he was to abridge that ceremonious and deferential solemnity with which he was otherwise under the necessity of receiving King Louis. In fact, the King's knowledge of human nature had in one particular misled him on this remarkable occasion. He thought that the Duke would have been inexpressibly flattered to have received such a mark of condescension and confidence from his liege lord ; but he forgot that the dependence of this dukedom upon the crown of France was privately the subject of galling mortification to a prince so powerful, so wealthy, and so proud as Charles, whose aim it certainly was to establish an independent kingdom. The presence of the King at the court of the Duke of Burgundy imposed on that prince the necessity of exhibiting himself in the subordinate character of a vassal, and of discharging many rites of feudal observance and deference, which, to one of his haughty disposition, resembled derogation from the character of a sovereign prince, which on all occasions he affected as far as possible to sustain.

But although it was possible to avoid much ceremony by having the dinner upon the green turf, with sound of bugles, broaching of barrels, and all the freedom of a sylvan meal, it was necessary that the evening repast should, even for that very reason, be held with more than usual solemnity.

Previous orders for this purpose had been given, and, upon returning to Péronne, King Louis found a banquet prepared with such a profusion of splendor and magnificence, as became the wealth of his formidable vassal, possessed as he was of almost all the Low Countries, then the richest portion of Europe. At the head of the long board, which groaned under plate of gold and silver, filled to profusion with the most exquisite dainties, sat the Duke, and on his right hand, upon a seat more elevated than his own, was placed his royal guest. Behind him stood on one side the son of the Duke of Gueldres, who officiated as his grand carver, on the other Le Glorieux, his jester, without whom he seldom stirred ; for, like most men of his hasty and coarse character, Charles carried to extremity the general taste of that age for court fools and jesters—experiencing that pleasure in their display of eccentricity and mental infirmity which his more acute, but not more benevolent, rival loved better to extract from marking the imperfections of humanity in its nobler specimens, and finding subject for mirth in the "fears of the brave and follies of the wise." And, indeed, if the anecdote related by Brantôme be true, that a court fool, having overheard Louis, in one of his agonies of repentant devotion, confess his accession to the poisoning of his brother, Henry Count of Guyenne, divulged it next day at dinner before the assembled court, that monarch might be supposed rather more than satisfied with the pleasantries of professed jesters for the rest of his life.

But, on the present occasion, Louis neglected not to take notice of the favorite buffoon of the Duke, and to applaud his repartees ; which he did the rather that he thought he saw that the folly of Le Glorieux, however grossly it was sometimes displayed, covered more than the usual quantity of shrewd and caustic observation proper to his class.

In fact, Tiel Wetzweiler, called Le Glorieux, was by no means a jester of the common stamp. He was a tall, fine-looking man, excellent at many exercises, which seemed scarce reconcilable with mental imbecility, because it must have required patience and attention to attain them. He usually followed the Duke to the chase and to the fight ; and at Montl'héry, when Charles was in considerable personal danger, wounded in the throat, and likely to be made prisoner by a French knight who had hold of his horse's rein, Tiel Wetzweiler charged the assailant so forcibly as to overthrow him and disengage his master. Perhaps he was afraid of this being thought too serious a service for a person of his condition, and that it might excite him enemies among those knights and nobles who had left the care of their master's person to the court fool. At any rate, he chose rather to be laughed at than praised for his achievement, and made such gasconading boasts of his exploits in the battle, that most men thought the rescue of Charles was as ideal as the rest of his tale ; and it was on this occasion he acquired the title of Le Glorieux (or the boastful), by which he was ever afterwards distinguished.

Le Glorieux was dressed very richly, but with little of the usual distinction of his profession, and that little rather of a symbolical than a very literal character. His head was not shorn ; on the contrary, he wore a profusion of long curled hair, which descended from under his cap, and joining with a well-arranged and handsomely trimmed beard, set off features which, but for a wild lightness of eye, might have been termed handsome. A ridge of scarlet velvet, carried across the top of his cap, indicated, rather than positively represented, the professional cock's-comb, which distinguished

the headgear of a fool in right of office. His bauble, made
of ebony, was crested, as usual, with a fool's head, with ass's
ears formed of silver ; but so small, and so minutely carved,
that, till very closely examined, it might have passed for an
official baton of a more solemn character. These were the
only badges of his office which his dress exhibited. In other
respects, it was such as to match with that of the most
courtly nobles. His bonnet displayed a medal of gold ; he
wore a chain of the same metal around his neck ; and the
fashion of his rich garments was not much more fantastic
than those of young gallants who have their clothes made in
the extremity of the existing fashion.

To this personage Charles, and Louis, in imitation of his
host, often addressed themselves during the entertainment ;
and both seemed to manifest, by hearty laughter, their
amusement at the answers of Le Glorieux.

"Whose seats be those that are vacant ? " said Charles to
the jester.

"One of those at least should be mine by right of succession, Charles," replied Le Glorieux.

"Why so, knave ? " said Charles.

"Because they belong to the Sieur D'Hymbercourt and
Des Comines, who are gone so far to fly their falcons that
they have forgot their supper. They who would rather look
at a kite on the wing than a peasant on the board are of kin
to the fool, and he should succeed to the stools, as a part of
their movable estate."

"That is but a stale jest, my friend Tiel," said the Duke ;
"but, fools or wise men, here come the defaulters."

As he spoke, Comines and D'Hymbercourt entered the
room, and, after having made their reverence to the two
princes, assumed in silence the seats which were left vacant
for them.

"What ho ! sirs," exclaimed the Duke, addressing them,
"your sport has been either very good or very bad, to lead
you so far and so late. Sir Philip des Comines, you are
dejected ; hath D'Hymbercourt won so heavy a wager on
you ? You are a philosopher, and should not grieve at bad
fortune. By St. George ! D'Hymbercourt looks as sad as
thou dost. How now, sirs ? Have you found no game ? or
have you lost your falcons ? or has a witch crossed your way ?
or has the Wild Huntsman* met you in the forest ? By my

---

* The famous apparition, sometimes called *Le Grand Veneur.*
Sully gives some account of this hunting specter.

honor, you seem as if you were come to a funeral, not a festival."

While the Duke spoke, the eyes of the company were all directed towards D'Hymbercourt and Des Comines ; and the embarrassment and dejection of their countenances, neither being of that class of persons to whom such expression of anxious melancholy was natural, became so remarkable, that the mirth and laughter of the company, which the rapid circulation of goblets of excellent wine had raised to a considerable height, was gradually hushed, and, without being able to assign any reason for such a change in their spirits, men spoke in whispers to each other, as on the eve of expecting some strange and important tidings.

"What means this silence, Messires ?" said the Duke, elevating his voice, which was naturally harsh. "If you bring these strange looks, and this stranger silence, into festivity, we shall wish you had abode in the marshes seeking for herons, or rather for woodcocks and howlets."

"My gracious lord," said Des Comines, "as we were about to return hither from the forest, we met the Count of Crèvecœur."

"How !" said the Duke ; "already returned from Brabant ? but he found all well there, doubtless ?"

"The count himself will presently give your Grace an account of his news," said D'Hymbercourt, "which we have heard but imperfectly."

"Body of me, where is the count ?" said the Duke.

"He changes his dress, to wait upon your Highness," answered D'Hymbercourt.

"His dress! *Saint-bleau!*" exclaimed the impatient prince, "what care I for his dress ? I think you have conspired with him to drive me mad."

"Or rather to be plain," said Des Comines, "he wishes to communicate these news at a private audience."

"*Teste-dieu!* my lord king," said Charles, "this is ever the way our counselors serve us. If they have got hold of aught which they consider as important for our ears, they look as grave upon the matter, and are as proud of their burden as an ass of a new pack-saddle. Some one bid Crévecœur come to us directly ! He comes from the frontiers of Liege, and we, at least (he laid some emphasis on the pronoun), have no secrets in that quarter which we would shun to have proclaimed before the assembled world."

All perceived that the Duke had drunk so much wine as to increase the native obstinacy of his disposition ; and though many would willingly have suggested that the present was neither a time for hearing news, nor for taking counsel, yet all knew the impetuosity of his temper too well to venture on farther interference, and sat in anxious expectation of the tidings which the count might have to communicate.

A brief interval intervened, during which the Duke remained looking eagerly to the door, as if in a transport of impatience, whilst the guests sat with their eyes bent on the table, as if to conceal their curiosity and anxiety. Louis alone maintaining perfect composure, continued his conversation alternately with the grand carver and with the jester.

At length Crèvecœur entered, and was presently saluted by the hurried question of his master, "What news from Liege and Brabant, sir count? The report of your arrival has chased mirth from our table ; we hope your actual presence will bring it back to us."

"My liege and master," answered the count, in a firm but melancholy tone, "the news which I bring you are fitter for the council-board than the feasting-table."

"Out with them, man, if they were tidings from Antichrist!" said the Duke ; "but I can guess them : the Liegeois are again in mutiny."

"They are my lord," said Crèvecœur, very gravely.

"Look there, man," said the Duke, "I have hit at once on what you have been so much afraid to mention to me : the harebrained burghers are again in arms. It could not be in better time, for we may at present have the advice of our own suzerain," bowing to King Louis, with eyes which spoke the most bitter, though suppressed, resentment, "to teach us how such mutineers should be dealt with. Hast thou more news in thy packet ? Out with them, and then answer for yourself why you went not forward to assist the bishop."

"My lord, the farther tidings are heavy for me to tell, and will be afflicting to you to hear. No aid of mine, or of living chivalry, could have availed the excellent prelate. William de la Marck, united with the insurgent Liegeois, has taken his castle of Schonwaldt, and murdered him in his own hall."

"*Murdered him!* " repeated the Duke, in a deep and low tone, but which nevertheless was heard from the one end of the hall in which they were assembled to the other ; "thou hast been imposed upon, Crèvecœur, by some wild report ; it is impossible ! "

"Alas, my lord ! " said the count, " I have it from an eyewitness, an archer of the King of France's Scottish Guard, who was in the hall when the murder was committed by William de la Marck's order."

"And who was doubtless aiding and abetting in the horrible sacrilege," exclaimed the Duke, starting up and stamping with his foot with such fury that he dashed in pieces the footstool which was placed before him. "Bar the doors of this hall, gentlemen—secure the windows—let no stranger stir from his seat, upon pain of instant death! Gentlemen of my chamber, draw your swords." And turning upon Louis, he advanced his own hand slowly and deliberately to the hilt of his weapon; while the King, without either showing fear or assuming a defensive posture, only said—

"These news, fair cousin, have staggered your reason."

"No!" replied the Duke, in a terrible tone, "but they have awakened a just resentment, which I have too long suffered to be stifled by trivial considerations of circumstance and place. Murderer of thy brother!—rebel against thy parent!—tyrant over thy subjects!—treacherous ally!—perjured king!—dishonored gentleman!—thou art in my power, and I thank God for it."

"Rather thank my folly," said the King; "for when we met on equal terms at Montl'héry, methinks you wished yourself farther from me than we are now."

The Duke still held his hand on the hilt of his sword, but refrained to draw his weapon, or to strike a foe who offered no sort of resistance which could in anywise provoke violence.

Meanwhile, wild and general confusion spread itself through the hall. The doors were now fastened and guarded by order of the Duke; but several of the French nobles, few as they were in number, started from their seats, and prepared for the defense of their sovereign. Louis had spoken not a word either to Orleans or Dunois since they were liberated from restraint at the Castle of Loches, if it could be termed liberation to be dragged in King Louis's train, objects of suspicion evidently rather than of respect and regard; but, nevertheless, the voice of Dunois was first heard above the tumult addressing himself to the Duke of Burgundy. "Sir duke, you have forgotten that you are a vassal of France, and that we, your guests, are Frenchmen. If you lift a hand against our monarch, prepare to sustain the utmost effects of our despair; for, credit me, we shall feast as high with the blood of Burgundy as we have done with its wine. Courage, my Lord of Orleans; and you, gentlemen of France, form yourselves round Dunois, and do as he does!"

It was in that moment when a king might see upon what tempers he could certainly rely. The few independent nobles and knights who attended Louis, most of whom had only received from him frowns or discountenance, unappalled by the display of infinitely superior force, and the certainty of destruction in case they came to blows, hastened to array themselves around Dunois, and, led by him, to press towards the head of the table where the contending princes were seated.

On the contrary, the tools and agents whom Louis had dragged forward out of their fitting and natural places into importance which was not due to them, showed cowardice and cold heart, and, remaining still in their seats, seemed resolved not to provoke their fate by intermeddling, whatever might become of their benefactor.

The first of the more generous party was the venerable Lord Crawford, who, with an agility which no one would have expected at his years, forced his way through all opposition, which was the less violent, as many of the Burgundians, either from a point of honor or a secret inclination to prevent Louis's impending fate, gave way to him, and threw himself boldly between the King and the Duke. He then placed his bonnet, from which his white hair escaped in disheveled tresses, upon one side of his head; his pale cheek and withered brow colored, and his aged eye lightened with all the fire of a gallant who is about to dare some desperate action. His cloak was flung over one shoulder, and his action intimated his readiness to wrap it about his left arm, while he unsheathed his sword with his right.

"I have fought for his father and his grandsire," that was all he said, "and, by St. Andrew, end the matter as it will, I will not fail him at this pinch."

What has taken some time to narrate happened, in fact, with the speed of light; for so soon as the Duke assumed his threatening posture, Crawford had thrown himself betwixt him and the object of his vengeance; and the French gentlemen, drawing together as fast as they could, were crowding to the same point.

The Duke of Burgundy still remained with his hand on his sword, and seemed in the act of giving the signal for a general onset, which must necessarily have ended in the massacre of the weaker party, when Crèvecœur rushed forward and exclaimed, in a voice like a trumpet, "My liege

Lord of Burgundy, beware what you do! This is *your* hall, you are the King's vassal; do not spill the blood of your guest on your hearth, the blood of your sovereign on the throne you have erected for him, and to which he came under your safeguard. For the sake of your house's honor, do not attempt to revenge one horrid murder by another yet worse!"

"Out of my road, Crèvecœur," answered the Duke, "and let my vengeance pass! Out of my path! The wrath of kings is to be dreaded like that of Heaven."

"Only when, like that of Heaven, it is *just*," answered Crèvecœur firmly. "Let me pray of you, my lord, to rein the violence of your temper, however justly offended. And for you, my lords of France, where resistance is unavailing, let me recommend you to forbear whatever may lead towards bloodshed."

"He is right," said Louis, whose coolness forsook him not in that dreadful moment, and who easily foresaw that if a brawl should commence, more violence would be dared and done in the heat of blood than was likely to be attempted if peace were preserved. "My cousin Orleans—kind Dunois—and you, my trusty Crawford—bring not on ruin and bloodshed by taking offense too hastily. Our cousin the Duke is chafed at the tidings of the death of a near and loving friend, the venerable Bishop of Liege, whose slaughter we lament as he does. Ancient, and, unhappily, recent subjects of jealousy lead him to suspect us of having abetted a crime which our bosom abhors. Should our host murder us on this spot—us, his king and his kinsman, under a false impression of our being accessory to this unhappy accident, our fate will be little lightened, but, on the contrary, greatly aggravated, by your stirring. Therefore, stand back, Crawford. Were it my last word, I speak as a king to his officers, and demand obedience. Stand back, and, if it is required, yield up your sword. I command you to do so, and your oath obliges you to obey."

"True—true, my lord," said Crawford, stepping back, and returning to the sheath the blade he had half drawn. "It may be all very true; but, by my honor, if I were at the head of threescore and ten of my brave fellows, instead of being loaded with more than the like number of years, I would try whether I could have some reason out of these fine gallants, with their golden chains and looped-up bonnets, with braw-warld dyes and devices on them."

The Duke stood with his eyes fixed on the ground for a considerable space, and then said, with bitter irony,

" Crèvecœur, you say well ; and it concerns our honor, that our obligations to this great king, our honored and loving guest, be not so hastily adjusted, as in our hasty anger we had at first proposed. We will so act that all Europe shall acknowledge the justice of our proceedings. Gentlemen of France, you must render up your arms to my officers ! Your master has broken the truce, and has no title to take farther benefit of it. In compassion, however, to your sentiments of honor, and in respect to the rank which he hath disgraced and the race which he hath degenerated, we ask not our cousin Louis's sword."

" Not one of us," said Dunois, " will resign our weapon, or quit this hall, unless we are assured of at least our king's safety, in life and limb."

" Nor will a man of the Scottish Guard," exclaimed Crawford, " lay down his arms, save at the command of the King of France, or his High Constable."

" Brave Dunois," said Louis, " and you, my trusty Crawford, your zeal will do me injury instead of benefit. I trust," he added, with dignity, " in my rightful cause more than in a vain resistance, which would but cost the lives of my best and bravest. Give up your swords ; the noble Burgundians who accept such honorable pledges will be more able than you are to protect both you and me. Give up your swords. It is I who command you."

It was thus that, in this dreadful emergency, Louis showed the promptitude of decision and clearness of judgment which alone could have saved his life. He was aware that until actual blows were exchanged he should have the assistance of most of the nobles present to moderate the fury of their prince ; but that, were a *mêlée* once commenced, he himself and his few adherents must be instantly murdered. At the same time, his worst enemies confessed that his demeanor had in it nothing either of meanness or cowardice. He shunned to aggravate into frenzy the wrath of the Duke ; but he neither deprecated nor seemed to fear it, and continued to look on him with the calm and fixed attention with which a brave man eyes the menacing gestures of a lunatic, whilst conscious that his own steadiness and composure operate as an insensible and powerful check on the rage even of insanity.

Crawford, at the King's command, threw his sword to Crèvecœur, saying, " Take it, and the devil give you joy of it ! It is no dishonor to the rightful owner who yields it, for we have had no fair play."

"Hold, gentlemen," said the Duke, in a broken voice, as one whom passion had almost deprived of utterance, "retain your swords ; it is sufficient you promise not to use them. And you, Louis of Valois, must regard yourself as my prisoner, until you are cleared of having abetted sacrilege and murder. Have him to the castle. Have him to Earl Herbert's Tower. Let him have six gentlemen of his train to attend him, such as he shall choose. My Lord of Crawford, your guard must leave the castle, and shall be honorably quartered elsewhere. Up with every drawbridge, and down with every portcullis. Let the gates of the town be trebly guarded. Draw the floating-bridge to the right-hand side of the river. Bring round the castle my band of Black Walloons, and treble the sentinels on every post ! You, D'Hymbercourt, look that patrols of horse and foot make the round of the town every half hour during the night, and every hour during the next day—if indeed such ward shall be necessary after daybreak, for it is like we may be sudden in this matter. Look to the person of Louis, as you love your life !"

He started from the table in fierce and moody haste, darted a glance of mortal enmity at the King, and rushed out of the apartment.

"Sirs," said the King, looking with dignity around him, "grief for the death of his ally hath made your prince frantic. I trust you know better your duty, as knights and noblemen, than to abet him in his treasonable violence against the person of his liege lord."

At this moment was heard in the streets the sound of drums beating and horns blowing, to call out the soldiery in every direction.

"We are," said Crèvecœur, who acted as the marshal of the Duke's household, "subjects of Burgundy, and must do our duty as such. Our hopes and prayers, and our efforts, will not be wanting to bring about peace and union between your Majesty and our liege lord. Meantime, we must obey his commands. These other lords and knights will be proud to contribute to the convenience of the illustrious Duke of Orleans, of the brave Dunois, and the stout Lord Crawford. I myself must be your Majesty's chamberlain, and bring you to your apartments in other guise than would be my desire, remembering the hospitality of Plessis. You have only to choose your attendants whom the Duke's commands limit to six."

"Then," said the King, looking around him, and think-

ing for a moment, "I desire the attendance of Oliver le
Dain, of a private of my Life Guard, called Balafré, who may
be unarmed, if you will, of Tristan l'Hermite, with two of
his people, and my right loyal and trusty philosopher,
Martius Galeotti."

"Your Majesty's will shall be complied with in all points,"
said the Count de Crèvecœur. "Galeotti," he added, after
a moment's inquiry, "is, I understand, at present supping
in some buxom company, but he shall instantly be sent for ;
the others will obey your Majesty's command upon the instant."

"Forward, then, to the new abode, which the hospitality
of our cousin provides for us," said the King. "We know
it is strong, and have only to hope it may be in a corresponding degree safe."

"Heard you the choice which King Louis has made of his
attendants?" said Le Glorieux to Count Crèvecœur apart,
as they followed Louis from the hall.

"Surely, my merry gossip," replied the count. "What
hast thou to object to them?"

"Nothing—nothing, only they are a rare election! A
panderly barber, a Scottish hired cut-throat, a chief hangman and his two assistants, and a thieving charlatan. I will
along with you, Crèvecœur, and take a lesson in the degrees
of roguery, from observing your skill in marshaling them.
The devil himself could scarce have summoned such a synod,
or have been a better president amongst them."

Accordingly, the all-licensed jester, seizing the count's
arm familiarly, began to march along with him, while, under
a strong guard, yet forgetting no semblance of respect, he
conducted the King towards his new apartment.*

* See Historical Epitome. Note 38.

21

CHAPTER XXVIII

UNCERTAINTY

Then happy low, lie down ;
Uneasy lies the head that wears a crown.
Henry IV., Part **II.**

FORTY men-at-arms, carrying alternately naked swords and
blazing torches, served as the escort, or rather the guard, of
King Lóuis, from the town-hall of Péronne to the castle ;
and as he entered within its darksome and gloomy strength,
it seemed as if a voice screamed in his ear that warning which
the Florentine has inscribed over the portal of the infernal
regions, " Leave all hope behind ! "

At that moment, perhaps, some feeling of remorse might
have crossed the King's mind, had he thought on the hundreds, nay thousands, whom, without cause, or in light suspicion, he had committed to the abysses of his dungeons,
deprived of all hope of liberty, and loathing even the life to
which they clung by animal instinct.

The broad glare of the torches outfacing the pale moon,
which was more obscured on this than on the former night,
and the red smoky light which they dispersed around the
ancient buildings, gave a darker shade to that huge donjon,
called the Earl Herbert's Tower. It was the same that Louis
had viewed with misgiving presentiment on the preceding
evening, and of which he was now doomed to become an inhabitant, under the terror of what violence soever the wrath-
ful temper of his overgrown vassal might tempt him to
exercise in those secret recesses of despotism.

To aggravate the King's painful feelings, he saw, as he
crossed the courtyard, several bodies, over each of which had
been hastily flung a military cloak. He was not long of discerning that they were corpses of slain archers of the Scottish Guard, who, having disputed, as the Count Crèvecœur
informed him, the command given them to quit the post
near the King's apartments, a brawl had ensued between
them and the Duke's Walloon bodyguards, and before it
could be composed by the officers on either side, several lives
had been lost.

" My trusty Scots ! " said the King, as he looked upon this melancholy spectacle ; " had they brought only man to man, all Flanders—ay, and Burgundy to boot—had not furnished champions to mate you."

" Yes, an it please your Majesty," said Balafré, who attended close behind the King, " Maistery mows the meadow : few men can fight more than two at once. I myself never care to meet three, unless it be in the way of special duty, when one must not stand to count heads."

"Art thou there, old acquaintance ? " said the King, looking behind him ; " then I have one true subject with me yet."

"And a faithful minister, whether in your councils, or in his offices about your royal person," whispered Oliver le Dain.

" We are all faithful," said Tristan l'Hermite, gruffly, " for should they put to death your Majesty, there is not one of us whom they would suffer to survive you, even if we would."

" Now, that is what I call good corporal bail for fidelity," said Le Glorieux, who, as already mentioned, with the restlessness proper to an infirm brain, had thrust himself into their company.

Meanwhile, the seneschal, hastily summoned, was turning with laborious effort the ponderous key which opened the reluctant gate of the huge Gothic keep, and was at last fain to call for the assistance of one of Crèvecœur's attendants. When they had succeeded, six men entered with torches, and showed the way through a narrow and winding passage, commanded at different points by shot-holes from vaults and casements constructed behind, and in the thickness of the massive walls. At the end of this passage arose a stair of corresponding rudeness, consisting of huge blocks of stone, roughly dressed with the hammer, and of unequal height. Having mounted this ascent, a strong iron-clenched door admitted them to what had been the great hall of the donjon, lighted but very faintly even during the daytime, for the apertures, diminished in appearance by the excessive thickness of the walls, resembled slits rather than windows, and now, but for the blaze of the torches, almost perfectly dark. Two or three bats, and other birds of evil presage, roused by the unusual glare, flew against the lights and threatened to extinguish them ; while the seneschal formally apologized to the King that the state-hall had not been put in order, such was the hurry of the notice sent to him ; and adding, that, in truth, the apartment had not been in use for twenty years, and rarely before that time, so far as ever he had heard, since the time of King Charles the Simple.

" King Charles the Simple ! " echoed Louis ; " I know the history of the tower now. He was here murdered by his treacherous vassal, Herbert, Earl of Vermandois,—so say our annals. I knew there was something concerning the Castle of Péronne which dwelt on my mind, though I could not recall the circumstance. *Here,* then, my predecessor was slain ? "

" Not here, not exactly here, and please your Majesty," said the old seneschal, stepping with the eager haste of a cicerone, who shows the curiosities of such a place—" not *here,* but in the side-chamber a little onward, which opens from your Majesty's bedchamber."

He hastily opened a wicket at the upper end of the hall, which led into a bedchamber, small, as is usual in such old buildings, but, even for that reason, rather more comfortable than the waste hall through which they had passed. Some hasty preparations had been here made for the King's accommodation. Arras had been tacked up, a fire lighted in the rusty grate, which had been long unused, and a pallet laid down for those gentlemen who were to pass the night in his chamber, as was then usual.

" We will get beds in the hall for the rest of your attendants," said the garrulous old man ; " but we have had such brief notice, if it please your Majesty. And if it please your Majesty to look upon this little wicket behind the arras, it opens into the little old cabinet in the thickness of the wall where Charles was slain, and there is a secret passage from below, which admitted the men who were to deal with him. And your Majesty, whose eyesight I hope is better than mine, may see the blood still on the oak floor, though the thing was done five hundred years ago."

While he thus spoke, he kept fumbling to open the postern of which he spoke, until the King said, " Forbear, old man —forbear but a little while, when thou mayst have a newer tale to tell, and fresher blood to show. My Lord of Crèvecœur, what say you ? "

" I can but answer, sire, that these two interior apartments are as much at your Majesty's disposal as those in your own castle at Plessis, and that Crèvecœur, a name never blackened by treachery or assassination, has the guard of the exterior defenses of it."

" But the private passage into that closet, of which the

old man speaks!" This King Louis said in a low and anxious tone, holding Crèvecœur's arm fast with one hand, and pointing to the wicket door with the other.

"It must be some dream of Mornay's," said Crèvecœur, "or some old and absurd tradition of the place ; but we will examine."

He was about to open the closet door, when Louis answered, "No, Crèvecœur, no ; your honor is sufficient warrant. But what will your duke do with me, Crèvecœur ? He cannot hope to keep me long a prisoner ; and in short, give me your opinion, Crèvecœur."

"My lord and sire," said the count, "how the Duke of Burgundy must resent this horrible cruelty on the person of his near relative and ally is for your Majesty to judge ; and what right he may have to consider it as instigated by your Majesty's emissaries you only can know. But my master is noble in his disposition, and made incapable, even by the very strength of his passions, of any underhand practises. Whatever he does will be done in the face of day and of the two nations. And I can but add, that it will be the wish of every counselor around him—excepting perhaps one—that he should behave in this matter with mildness and generosity, as well as justice."

"Ah! Crèvecœur," said Louis, taking his hand as if affected by some painful recollections, "how happy is the prince who has counsellors near him who can guard him against the effects of his own angry passions! Their names will be read in golden letters, when the history of his reign is perused. Noble Crèvecœur, had it been my lot to have such as thou art about *my* person !"

"It had in that case been your Majesty's study to have got rid of them as fast as you could," said Le Glorieux.

"Aha! Sir Wisdom, art thou there ?" said Louis, turning round, and instantly changing the pathetic tone in which he had addressed Crèvecœur, and adopting with facility one which had a turn of a gaiety in it ; "hast *thou* followed us hither ?"

"Ay, sir," answered Le Glorieux, "wisdom must follow in motley, where folly leads the way in purple."

"How shall I construe that, Sir Solomon," answered Louis ; "wouldst thou change conditions with me ?"

"Not I, by my halidome," quoth Le Glorieux, "if you would give me fifty crowns to boot."

"Why, wherefore so ? Methinks I could be well enough contented, as princes go, to have thee for my king."

"Ay, sire," replied Le Glorieux ; "but the question is, whether, judging of your Majesty's wit from its having lodged you here, I should not have cause to be ashamed of having so dull a fool."

"Peace, sirrah!" said the Count of Crèvecœur ; "your tongue runs too fast."

"Let it take its course," said the King ; "I know of no such fair subject of raillery as the follies of those who should know better. Here, my sagacious friend, take this purse of gold, and with it the advice, never to be so great a fool as to deem yourself wiser than other people. Prithee, do me so much favor as to inquire after my astrologer, Martius Galeotti, and send him hither to me presently."

"I will, without fail, my liege," answered the jester ; "and I wot well I shall find him at Jan Dopplethur's ; for philosophers, as well as fools, know where the best wine is sold."

"Let me pray for free entrance for this learned person through your guards, Seignior de Crèvecœur," said Louis.

"For his entrance, unquestionably," answered the count ; "but it grieves me to add, that my instructions do not authorize me to permit any one to quit your Majesty's apartments. I wish your Majesty a good-night," he subjoined, "and will presently make such arrangements in the outer hall as may put the gentlemen who are to inhabit it more at their ease."

"Give yourself no trouble for them, sir count," replied the King, "they are men accustomed to set hardships at defiance ; and, to speak truth, excepting that I wish to see Galeotti, I would desire as little further communication from without this night as may be consistent with your instructions."

"These are, to leave your Majesty," replied Crèvecœur, "undisputed possession of your own apartments. Such are my master's orders."

"Your master, Count Crèvecœur," answered Louis, "whom I may also term mine, is a right gracious master. My dominions," he added, "are somewhat shrunk in compass, now that they have dwindled to an old hall and a bed-chamber ; but they are still wide enough for all the subjects which I can at present boast of."

The Count of Crèvecœur took his leave ; and shortly after, they could hear the noise of the sentinels moving to their posts, accompanied with the word of command from the officers, and the hasty tread of the guards who were relieved.

At length all became still, and the only sound which filled
the air was the sluggish murmur of the river Somme, as it
glided, deep and muddy, under the walls of the castle.

"Go into the hall, my mates," said Louis to his train ;
"but do not lie down to sleep. Hold yourselves in readiness, for there is still something to be done to-night, and
that of moment."

Oliver and Tristan retired to the hall accordingly, in which
Le Balafré and the provost-marshal's two officers had remained when the others entered the bedchamber. They
found that those without had thrown fagots enough upon
the fire to serve the purpose of light and heat at the same
time, and, wrapping themselves in their cloaks, had sat down
on the floor, in postures which variously expressed the discomposure and dejection of their minds. Oliver and Tristan
saw nothing better to be done than to follow their example ;
and, never very good friends in the days of their court prosperity, they were both equally reluctant to repose confidence
in each other upon this strange and sudden reverse of fortune. So that the whole party sat in silent dejection.

Meanwhile, their master underwent, in the retirement of
his secret chamber, agonies that might have atoned for some
of those which had been imposed by his command. He
paced the room with short and unequal steps, often stood
still and clasped his hands together, and gave looce, in short,
to agitation, which, in public, he had found himself able to
suppress so successfully. At length, pausing, and wringing
his hands, he planted himself opposite to the wicket-door,
which had been pointed out by old Mornay as leading to the
scene of the murder of one of his predecessors, and gradually
gave voice to his feelings in a broken soliloquy.

"Charles the Simple—Charles the Simple ! What will
posterity call the Eleventh Louis, whose blood will probably
soon refresh the stains of thine ? Louis the Fool—Louis the
Driveller—Louis the Infatuated—all are terms too slight to
mark the extremity of my idiocy ! To think these hot-
headed Liegeois, to whom rebellion is as natural as their
food, would remain quiet—to dream that the Wild Beast of
Ardennes would, for a moment, be interrupted in his career
of force and bloodthirsty brutality—to suppose that I could
use reason and arguments to any good purpose with Charles
of Burgundy, until I had tried the force of such exhortations
with success upon a wild bull ! Fool, and double idiot that
I was ! But the villain Martius shall not escape. He has
been at the bottom of this, he and the vile priest, the de-

testable Balue.* If I ever get out of this danger, I will tear
from his head the cardinal's cap, though I pull the scalp
along with it! But the other traitor is in my hands: I am
yet king enough—have yet an empire roomy enough—for
the punishment of the quack-salving, word mongering, star-
gazing, lie-coining impostor, who has at once made a prisoner
and a dupe of me! The conjunction of the constellations—
ay, the conjunction! He must talk nonsense which would
scarce gull a thrice-sodden sheep's head, and I must be idiot
enough to think I understood him! But we shall see presently what the conjunction hath really boded. But first let
me to my devotions."

Above the little door, in memory perhaps of the deed
which had been done within, was a rude niche, containing
a crucifix cut in stone. Upon this emblem the King fixed his
eyes, as if about to kneel, but stopped short, as if he applied
to the blessed image the principles of worldly policy, and
deemed it rash to approach its presence without having
secured the private intercession of some supposed favorite.
He therefore turned from the crucifix as unworthy to look
upon it, and selecting from the images with which, as often
mentioned, his hat was completely garnished, a representation
of the Lady of Cléry, knelt down before it, and made the following extraordinary prayer, in which, it is to be observed, the
grossness of his superstition induced him, in some degree, to
consider the virgin of Cléry as a different person from the
Madonna of Embrun, a favorite idol, to whom he often paid
his vows:

"Sweet Lady of Cléry," he exclaimed, clasping his hands
and beating his breast while he spoke, "blessed mother of
Mercy! thou who art omnipotent with Omnipotence, have
compassion with me a sinner! It is true that I have something neglected thee for thy blessed sister of Embrun ; but I
am a king, my power is great, my wealth boundless ; and
were it otherwise, I would double the *gabelle* on my subjects,
rather than not pay my debts to you both. Undo these iron
doors—fill up these tremendous moats—lead me, as a mother
leads a child, out of this present and pressing danger! If *i*
have given thy sister the county of Boulogne to be held of
her forever, have I no means of showing devotion to thee
also? Thou shalt have the broad and rich province of
Champagne ; and its vineyards shall pour their abundance
into thy convent. I had promised the province to my brother
Charles; but he, thou knowest, is dead—poisoned by that

* See Punishment of Balue. Note 39.

wicked abbé of St. John d' Angély, whom, if I live, I will
punish! I promised this once before, but this time I will
keep my word. If I had any knowledge of the crime, believe,
dearest patroness, it was because I knew no better method of
quieting the discontents of my kingdom. O, do not reckon
that old debt to my account to-day; but be, as thou hast
ever been, kind, benignant, and easy to be entreated!
Sweetest Lady, work with thy Child, that He will pardon
all past sins, and one—one little deed which I must do this
night; nay, it is no *sin*, dearest Lady Cléry—no sin, but an
act of justice, privately administered, for the villain is the
greatest impostor that ever poured falsehood into a prince's
ear, and leans besides to the filthy heresy of the Greeks.
He is not deserving of thy protection, leave him to my care;
and hold it as good service that I rid the world of him, for
the man is a necromancer and wizard, that is not worth thy
thought and care—a dog, the extinction of whose life ought
to be of as little consequence in thine eyes as the treading
out a spark that drops from a lamp, or springs from a fire.
Think not of this little matter, gentlest, kindest Lady, but
only consider how thou canst best aid me in my troubles!
and I here bind my royal signet to thy effigy, in token that
I will keep my word concerning the county of Champagne,
and that this shall be the last time I will trouble thee in
affairs of blood, knowing thou art so kind, so gentle, and so
tender-hearted."

After this extraordinary contract with the object of his
adoration, Louis recited, apparently with deep devotion, the
seven penitential psalms in Latin, and several aves and
prayers especially belonging to the service of the Virgin.
He then arose, satisfied that he had secured the intercession
of the saint to whom he had prayed, the rather, as he
craftily reflected, that most of the sins for which he had requested her mediation on former occasions had been of a
different character, and that, therefore, the Lady of Cléry
was less likely to consider him as a hardened and habitual
shedder of blood, than the other saints whom he had more
frequently made confidents of his crimes in that respect.*

When he had thus cleared his conscience, or rather whited
it over like a sepulcher, the King thrust his head out at the
door of the hall, and summoned Le Balafré into his apartment. "My good soldier," he said, "thou hast served me
long, and hast had little promotion. We are here in a case
where I may either live or die; but I would not willingly

* See Prayer of Louis XI. Note 40.

die an ungrateful man, or leave, so far as the saints may place it in my power, either a friend or an enemy unrecompensed. Now, I have a friend to be rewarded, that is thyself—an enemy to be punished according to his deserts, and that is the base, treacherous villain, Martius Galeotti, who, by his impostures and specious falsehoods, has trained me hither into the power of my mortal enemy, with as firm a purpose of my destruction as ever butcher had of slaying the beast which he drove to the shambles."

"I will challenge him on that quarrel, since they say he is a fighting blade, although he looks somewhat unwieldy," said Le Balafré. "I doubt not but the Duke of Burgundy is so much a friend to men of the sword, that he will allow us a fair field within some reasonable space ; and if your Majesty live so long, and enjoy so much freedom, you shall behold me do battle in your right, and take as proper a vengeance on this philosopher as your heart could desire."

"I commend your bravery and your devotion to my service," said the King. "But this treacherous villain is a stout man-at-arms, and I would not willingly risk thy life, my brave soldier."

"I were no brave soldier, if it please your Majesty," said Balafré, "if I dare not face a better man than he. A fine thing it would be for me, who can neither read nor write, to be afraid of a fat lurdane, who has done little else all his life !"

"Nevertheless," said the King, "it is not our pleasure so to put thee in venture, Balafré. This traitor comes hither, summoned by our command. We would have thee, so soon as thou canst find occasion, close up with him, and smite him under the fifth rib. Dost thou understand me ?"

"Truly I do," answered Le Balafré ; "but, if it please your Majesty, this is a matter entirely out of my course of practise. I could not kill you a dog, unless it were in hot assault, or pursuit, or upon defiance given, or such like."

"Why sure *thou* dost not pretend to tenderness of heart ?" said the King ; "thou who hast been first in storm and siege, and most eager, as men tell me, on the pleasures and advantages which are gained on such occasions by the rough heart and the bloody hand ?"

"My lord," answered Le Balafré, "I have neither feared nor spared your enemies, sword in hand, And an assault is a desperate matter, under risks which raise a man's blood so, that, by St. Andrew, it will not settle for an hour or two, which I call a fair license for plundering after a storm. And

God pity us poor soldiers, who are first driven mad with danger, and then madder with victory. I have heard of a legion consisting entirely of saints ; and methinks it would take them all to pray and intercede for the rest of the army, and for all who wear plumes and corslets, buff-coats and broadswords. But what your Majesty purposes is out of my course of practise, though I will never deny that it has been wide enough. As for the astrologer, if he be a traitor, let him e'en die a traitor's death. I will neither meddle nor make with it. Your Majesty has your provost and two of his marshal's-men without, who are more fit for dealing with him than a Scottish gentleman of my family and standing in the service."

" You say well," said the King ; " but, at least, it belongs to thy duty to prevent interruption, and to guard the execution of my most just sentence."

"I will do so against all Péronne," said Le Balafré. " Your Majesty need not doubt my fealty in that which I can reconcile to my conscience, which, for mine own convenience and the service of your royal Majesty, I can vouch to be a pretty large one—at least, I know I have done some deeds for your Majesty, which I would rather have eaten a handful of my own dagger than I would have done for any else."

" Let that rest," said the King ; " and hear you ; when Galeotti is admitted, and the door shut on him, do you stand to your weapon, and guard the entrance on the inside of the apartment. Let no one intrude ; that is all I require of you. Go hence, and send the provost-marshal to me."

Balafré left the apartment accordingly, and in a minute afterwards Tristan l'Hermite entered from the hall.

" Welcome, gossip," said the King ; " what thinkest thou of our situation ? "

" As of men sentenced to death," said the provost-marshal, " unless there come a reprieve from the Duke."

" Reprieved or not, he that decoyed us into this snare shall go our *fourrier* to the next world, to take up lodgings . for us," said the King, with a grisly and ferocious smile. . " Tristan, thou hast done many an act of brave justice : *finis*—I should have said *funis—coronat opus*. Thou must stand by me to the end."

" I will, my liege," said Tristan ; " I am but a plain fellow, but I am grateful. I will do my duty within these walls, or elsewhere ; and while I live, your Majesty's breath shall pour as potential a note of condemnation, and your sentence be as literally executed, as when you sat on your own throne. They may deal with me the next hour for it if they will, I care not."

" It is even what I expected of thee, my loving gossip," said Louis ; " but hast thou good assistance ? The traitor is strong and able-bodied, and will doubtless be clamorous for aid. The Scot will do nought but keep the door ; and well that he can be brought to that by flattery and humoring. Then Oliver is good for nothing but lying, flattering, and suggesting dangerous counsels ; and, *Ventre Saint-Dieu!* I think is more like one day to deserve the halter himself than to use it to another. Have you men, think you, and means, to make sharp and sure work ? "

" I have Trois-Eschelles and Petit André with me," said he ; " men so expert in their office that out of three men they would hang up one ere his two companions were aware. And we have all resolved to live or die with your Majesty, knowing we shall have as short breath to draw when you are gone as ever fell to the lot of any of our patients. But what is to be our present subject, an it please your Majesty ? I love to be sure of my man : for, as your Majesty is pleased sometimes to remind me, I have now and then mistaken the criminal, and strung up in his place an honest laborer, who had given your Majesty no offense."

" Most true," said the other. " Know then, Tristan, that the condemned person is Martius Galeotti. You start, but it is even as I say. The villain has trained us all hither by false and treacherous representations, that he might put us into the hands of the Duke of Burgundy without defense."

" But not without vengeance ! " said Tristan ; " were it the last act of my life, I would sting him home like an expiring wasp, should I be crushed to pieces on the next instant ! "

" I know thy trusty spirit," said the King, " and the pleasure which, like other good men, thou dost find in the discharge of thy duty, since virtue, as the schoolmen say, is its own reward. But away, and prepare the priests, for the victim approaches."

" Would you have it done in your own presence, my gracious liege ? " said Tristan.

Louis declined this offer ; but charged the provost-marshal to have everything ready for the punctual execution of his commands the moment the astrologer left his apartment ; " For," said the King, " I will see the villain once more, just to observe how he bears himself towards the master whom he has led into the toils. I shall love to see the sense of approaching death strike the color from that ruddy cheek, and dim that eye which laughed as it lied. O, that there were but another with him, whose counsels aided his prognostications! But if I survive this—look to your scarlet, my Lord Cardinal! for Rome shall scarce protect you—be it spoken under favor of St. Peter and the blessed Lady of Cléry, who is all over mercy. Why do you tarry? Go get your grooms ready. I expect the villain instantly. I pray to heaven he take not fear and come not! that were indeed a baulk. Begone, Tristan; thou wert not wont to be so slow when business was to be done."

"On the contrary, an it like your Majesty, you were ever wont to say that I was too fast, and mistook your purpose, and did the job on the wrong subject. Now, please your Majesty to give me a sign, just when you part with Galeotti for the night, whether the business goes on or not. I have known your Majesty once or twice change your mind, and blame me for over-despatch." *

"Thou suspicious creature," answered King Louis, "I tell thee I will *not* change my mind. But to silence thy remonstrances, observe, if I say to the knave at parting, 'There is a Heaven above us!' then let the business go on; but if I say, 'Go in peace,' you will understand that my purpose is altered."

"My head is somewhat of the dullest out of my own department," said Tristan l'Hermite. "Stay, let me rehearse. If you bid him depart in peace, I am to have him dealt upon?"

"No, no—idiot, no!" said the King; "in that case you let him pass free. But if I say, '*There is a Heaven above us!*' up with him a yard or two nearer the planets he is so conversant with."

"I wish we may have the means here," said the provost.

"Then *up* with him or *down* with him, it matters not which," answered the King, grimly smiling.

"And the body," said the provost, "how shall we dispose of it?"

"Let me see an instant," said the King; "the windows of the hall are too narrow; but that projecting oriel is wide enough. We will over with him into the Somme, and put a paper on his breast, with the legend, 'Let the justice of the King pass toll-free. The Duke's officers may seize it for duties if they dare.'"

* See Louis's vengeance. Note 41.

The provost-marshal left the apartment of Louis, and summoned his two assistants to council in an embrasure in the great hall, where Trois-Eschelles stuck a torch against the wall to give them light. They discoursed in whispers little noticed by Oliver le Dain, who seemed sunk in dejection, and Le Balafré, who was fast asleep.

"Comrades," said the provost to his executioners, "perhaps you have thought that out vocation was over, or that at least, we were more likely to be the subjects of the duty of others than to have any more to discharge on our own parts. But courage, my mates! our gracious master reserved for us one noble cast of our office, and it must be gallantly executed as by men who would live in history."

"Ay, I guess how it is," said Trois-Eschelles; "our patron is like the old kaisers of Rome, who when things came to an extremity, or, as we would say, to the ladder-foot with them, were wont to select from their own ministers of justice some experienced person, who might spare their sacred persons from the awkward attempts of a novice or blunderer in our mystery. It was a pretty custom for ethnics; but, as a good Catholic, I should make some scruple at laying hands on the Most Christian King."

. "Nay, but brother, you are ever too scrupulous," said Petit-André. "If he issues word and warrant for his own execution, I see not how we can in duty dispute it. He that dwells at Rome must obey the Pope: the marshal's-men must do their master's bidding, and he the King's. "

"Hush, your knaves!" said the provost-marshal, "there is here no purpose concerning the King's person, but only that of the Greek heretic pagan and Mohammedan wizard, Martius Galeotti."

"Galeotti!" answered Petit-André; "that comes quite natural. I never knew one of these legerdemain fellows, who pass their life, as one may say, in dancing upon a tight-rope, but what they came at length to caper at the end of one—tohick!"

"My only concern is," said Trois-Eschelles, looking upwards, "that the poor creature must die without confession."

"Tush! tush!" said the provost-marshal, in reply, "he is a rank heretic and necromancer: a whole college of priests could not absolve him from the doom he has deserved. Besides, if he hath a fancy that way, thou hast a gift, Trois-Eschelles, to serve him for ghostly father thyself. But, what is more material, I fear you must use your poniards, my mates;

for you have not here the fitting conveniences for the exercise of your profession."

"Now, our Lady of the Isle of Paris forbid," said Trois-Eschelles, "that the king's command should find me destitute of my tools! I always wear around my body St. Francis's cord, doubled four times, with a handsome loop at the further end of it; for I am of the company of St. Francis, and may wear his cowl when I am *in extremis,* I thank God and the good fathers of Saumur."

"And for me," said Petit-André, "I have always in my budget a handy block and sheaf, or a pully as they call it, with a strong screw for securing it where I list in case we should travel where trees are scarce, or high branched from the ground. I have found it a great convenience."

"That will suit as well," said the provost-marshal; "you have but to screw your pulley into yonder beam above the door and pass the rope over it. I will keep the fellow in some conversation near the spot until you adjust the noose under his chin, and then——"

"And then we run up the rope," said Petit-André "and, tchick! our astrologer is so far in Heaven that he hath not a foot on earth."

"But, these gentlemen," said Trois-Eschelles, looking torwards the chimney, "do not these help, and so take a hansel of our vocation?"

"Hem! no," answered the provost; "the barber only contrives mischief, which he leaves other men to execute; and for the Scot, he keeps the door when the deed is a doing, which he hath not spirit or quickness sufficient to partake in more actively; every one to his trade."

With infinite dexterity, and even a sort of professional delight which sweetened the sense of their own precarious situation, the worthy executioners of the provost's mandates adapted their rope and pulley for putting in force the sentence which had been uttered against Galeotti by the captive monarch, seeming to rejoice that last action was to be one consistent with their past life. Tristan l'Hermite * sat eyeing their proceedings with a species of satisfaction; while Oliver paid no attention to them whatever; and Ludovic Lesly, if, awakened by the bustle, he looked upon them at all, considered them as engaged in matters entirely unconnected with his own duty, and for which he was not to be regarded as responsible in one way or other.

* See Note 42.

CHAPTER XXIX

RECRIMINATION

Thy time is not yet out : the devil thou servest
Has not as yet deserted thee. He aids
The friends who drudge for him, as the blind man
Was aided by the guide, who lent his shoulder
O'er rough and smooth, until he reached the brink
Of the fell precipice, then hurl'd him downward.
Old Play.

WHEN obeying the command, or rather the request, of Louis, for he was in circumstances in which, though a monarch, he could only *request* Le Glorieux to go in search of Martius Galeotti, the jester had no trouble in executing his commission, betaking himself at once to the best tavern in Péronne, of which he himself was rather more than an occasional frequenter, being a great admirer of that species of liquor which reduced all other men's brains to a level with his own.

He found, or rather observed, the astrologer in the corner of the public drinking-room—" stove," as it is called in German and Flemish, from its principal furniture—sitting in close colloquy with a female in a singular, and something like a Moorish or Asiatic, garb, who, as Le Glorieux approached Martius, rose as in the act to depart.

" These," said the stranger, " are news on which you may rely with absolute certainty " ; and with that disappeared among the crowd of guests who sat grouped at different tables in the apartment.

" Cousin philosopher," said the jester, presenting himself, " Heaven no sooner relieves one sentinel than it sends another to supply the place. One fool being gone, here I come another, to guide you to the apartments of Louis of France."

" And art thou the messenger ? " said Martius, gazing on him with prompt apprehension, and discovering at once the jester's quality, though less intimated, as we have before noticed, than was usual by his external appearance.

" Ay, sir, and like your learning," answered Le Glorieux ;

" when power sends folly to entreat the approach of wisdom,
'tis a sure sign what foot the patient halts upon."

" How if I refuse to come, when summoned at so late an
hour by such a messenger ? " said Galeotti.

" In that case we will consult your ease, and carry you,"
said Le Glorieux.   " Here are half a score of stout Burgundian yeomen at the door, with whom he of Crèvecœur has
furnished me to that effect.   For know that my friend
Charles of Burgundy and I have not taken away our kinsman
Louis's crown, which he was ass enough to put into our
power, but have only filed and clipt it a little ; and, though
reduced to the size of a spangle, it is still pure gold.   In
plain terms, he is still paramount over his own people, yourself included, and Most Christian King of the old dining-
hall in the Castle of Péronne, to which you, as his liege subject, are presently obliged to repair."

" I attend you, sir," said Martius Galeotti, and accompanied Le Glorieux accordingly, seeing, perhaps, that no
evasion was possible.

" Ay, sir," said the fool as they went towards the castle,
" you do well ; for we treat our kinsman as men use an old
famished lion in his cage, and thrust him now and then a
calf to mumble, to keep his old jaws in exercise."

" Do you mean," said Martius, " that the King intends
me bodily injury ? "

" Nay, that you can guess better than I," said the jester ;
" for though the night be cloudy, I warrant you can see the
stars through the mist.   I know nothing of the matter,
not I ; only my mother always told me to go warily near
an old rat in a trap, for he was never so much disposed to
bite,"

The astrologer asked no more questions ; and Le Glorieux
according to the custom of those of his class, continued to
run on in a wild and disordered strain of sarcasm and folly
mingled together, until he delivered the philosopher to the
guard at the castle gate of Péronne, where he was passed
from warder to warder, and at length admitted within
Herbert's Tower.

The hints of the jester had not been lost on Martius
Galeotti, and he saw something which seemed to confirm
them in the look and manner of Tristan, whose mode of addressing him, as he marshaled him to the King's bedchamber,
was lowering, sullen, and ominous.   A close observer of what
passed on earth, as well as among the heavenly bodies, the
pulley and the rope also caught the astrologer's eye ; and as
22

the latter was in a state of vibration, he concluded that some one who had been busy adjusting it had been interrupted in the work by his sudden arrival. All this he saw, and summoned together his subtilty to evade the impending danger, resolved, should he find that impossible, to defend himself to the last against whomsoever should assail him.

Thus resolved, and with a step and look corresponding to the determination he had taken, Martius presented himself before Louis, alike unabashed at the miscarriage of his predictions, and undismayed at the monarch's anger and its probable consequences.

"Every good planet be gracious to your Majesty!" said Galeotti, with an inclination almost Oriental in manner. "Every evil constellation withhold their influences from my royal master!"

"Methinks," replied the King, "that when you look around this apartment, when you think where it is situated, and how guarded, your wisdom might consider that my propitious stars had proved faithless, and that each evil conjunction had already done its worst. Art thou not ashamed, Martius Galeotti, to see me here and a prisoner, when you recollect by what assurances I was lured hither?"

"And art *thou* not ashamed, my royal sire?" replied the philosopher, "thou whose step in science was so forward, thy apprehension so quick, thy perseverance so unceasing,—art thou not ashamed to turn from the first frown of fortune, like a craven from the first clash of arms? Didst thou propose to become participant of those mysteries which raise men above the passions, the mischances, the pains, the sorrows of life, a state only to be attained by rivaling the firmness of the ancient Stoic; and dost thou shrink from the first pressure of adversity, and forfeit the glorious prize for which thou didst start as a competitor, frightened out of the course, like a scared racer, by shadowy and unreal evils?"

"Shadowy and unreal! frontless as thou art!" exclaimed the King, "is this dungeon unreal? the weapons of the guards of my detested enemy Burgundy, which you may hear clash at the gate, are those shadows? What, traitor, *are* real evils, if imprisonment, dethronement, and danger of life are not so?"

"Ignorance—ignorance, my brother, and prejudice," answered the sage with great firmness, "are the only real evils. Believe me, that kings in the plenitude of power, if immersed in ignorance and prejudice, are less free than sages in a dungeon and loaded with material chains. Towards this true happiness it is mine to guide you ; be it yours to attend to my instructions."

" And it is to such philosophical freedom that your lessons would have guided me ? " said the King, very bitterly. " I would you had told me at Plessis that the dominion promised me so liberally was an empire over my own passiors ; that the success of which I was assured related to my progress in philosophy ; and that I might become as wise and as learned as a strolling mountebank of Italy ? I might surely have attained this mental ascendency at a more moderate price than that of forfeiting the fairest crown in Christendom and becoming tenant of a dungeon in Péronne ! Go, sir, and think not to escape condign punishment. *There is a Heaven above us !* "

" I leave you not to your fate," replied Martius, " until I have vindicated, even in your eyes, darkened as they are, that reputation, a brighter gem than the brightest in thy crown, and at which the world shall wonder ages after all the race of Capet are mouldered into oblivion in the charnels of St. Denis."

" Speak on," said Louis ; " thine impudence cannot make me change my purposes or my opinion. Yet as I may never again pass judgment as a king, I will not censure thee unheard. Speak, then, though the best thou canst say will be to speak the truth. Confess that I am a dupe, thou an impostor, thy pretended science a dream, and the planets which shine above us as little influential of our destiny as their shadows, when reflected in the river, are capable of altering its course."

" And how know'st thou," answered the astrologer, boldly, " the secret influence of yonder blessed lights ? Speak'st thou of their inability to influence waters, when yet thou know'st that even the weakest, the moon herself,—weakest because nearest to this wretched earth of ours,—holds under her domination, not such poor streams as the Somme, but the tides of the mighty ocean itself, which ebb and increase as her disk waxes and wanes, and watch her influenc> as a slave waits the nod of a sultana ? And now, Louis of Valois, answer my parable in turn. Confess, art thou not like the foolish passenger, who becomes wroth with his pilot because he cannot bring the vessel into harbor without experiencing occasionally the adverse force of winds and currents ? I could indeed point to thee the probable issue of thine enterprise as prosperous, but it was in the power of Heaven alone to conduct thee thither ; and if the path be rough and dangerous, was it in my power to smooth or render it more safe ? Where is thy wisdom of yesterday, which taught thee so truly to discern that the ways of destiny are often ruled to our advantage, though in opposition to our wishes ? "

" You remind me—you remind me," said the King, hastily, " of one specific falsehood. You foretold yonder Scot should accomplish his enterprise fortunately for my interest and honor ; and thou knowest it has so terminated that no more mortal injury could I have received than from the impression which the issue of that affair is like to make on the excited brain of the Mad Bull of Burgundy. This is a direct falsehood. Thou canst plead no evasion here, canst refer to no remote favorable turn of the tide, for which, like an idiot sitting on the bank until the river shall pass away, thou wouldst have me wait contentedly. Here thy craft deceived thee. Thou wert weak enough to make a specific prediction, which has proved directly false."

" Which will prove most firm and true," answered the astrologer, boldly. " I would desire no greater triumph of art over ignorance than that prediction and its accomplishment will afford. I told thee he would be faithful in any honorable commission. Hath he not been so ? I told thee he would be scrupulous in aiding any evil enterprise. Hath he not proved so ? If you doubt it, go ask the Bohemian, Hayraddin Maugrabin."

The King here colored deeply with shame and anger.

" I told thee," continued the astrologer, " that the conjunction of planets under which he set forth augured danger to the person ; and hath not his path been beset by danger ? I told thee that it augured an advantage to the sender, and of that thou wilt soon have the benefit."

" Soon have the benefit ! " exclaimed the King ; " have I not the result already, in disgrace and imprisonment ? "

" No," answered the astrologer, " the end is not as yet ; thine own tongue shall ere long confess the benefit which thou hast received, from the manner in which the messenger bore himself in discharging thy commission."

" This is too—too insolent," said the King, " at once to deceive and to insult—— But hence ! think not my wrongs shall be unavenged. *There is a Heaven above us !* "

Galeotti turned to depart. " Yet stop," said Louis ; " thou bearest thine imposture bravely out. Let me hear your answer to one question, and think ere you speak. Can thy pretended skill ascertain the hour of thine own death ? "

" Only by referring to the fate of another," said Galeotti.

"I understand not thine answer," said Louis.

"Know then, O king," said Martius, "that this only I can tell with certainty concerning mine own death, that it shall take place exactly twenty-four hours before that of your Majesty."*

"Ha! say'st thou?" said Louis, his countenance again altering. "Hold—hold—go not—wait one moment. Saidst thou, *my* death should follow *thine* so closely?"

"Within the space of twenty-four hours," repeated Galeotti, firmly, "if there be one sparkle of true divination in those bright and mysterious intelligences, which speak, each on their courses, though without a tongue. I wish your Majesty good rest."

"Hold—hold—go not," said the King, taking him by the arm and leading him from the door. "Martius Galeotti, I have been a kind master to thee—enriched thee—made thee my friend—my companion—the instructor of my studies. Be open with me, I entreat you. Is there aught in this art of yours in very deed? Shall this Scot's mission be, in fact, propitious to me? And is the measure of our lives so very—*very* nearly matched? Confess, my good Martius, you speak after the trick of your trade. Confess, I pray you, and you shall have no displeasure at my hand. I am in years—a prisoner—likely to be deprived of a kingdom; to one in my condition truth is worth kingdoms, and it is from thee, dearest Martius, that I must look for this inestimable jewel."

"And I have laid it before your Majesty," said Galeotti, "at the risk that, in brutal passion, you might turn upon me and rend me."

"Who, I, Galeotti?" replied Louis, mildly. "Alas! thou mistakest me! Am I not captive, and should not I be patient, especially since my anger can only show my impotence? Tell me then in sincerity, have you fooled me, or is your science true, and do you truly report it?"

"Your Majesty will forgive me if I reply to you," said Martius Galeotti, "that time only—time and the event—will convince incredulity. It suits ill the place of confidence which I have held at the council-table of the renowned conqueror, Matthias Corvinus of Hungary—nay, in the cabinet of the Emperor himself—to reiterate assurances of that which I have advanced as true. If you will not believe me, I can but refer to the course of events. A day or two days' patience will prove or disprove what I have averred con-

* See Prediction of Louis XI's Death. Note 43.

cerning the young Scot ; and I will be contented to die on
the wheel, and have my limbs broken joint by joint, if your
Majesty have not advantage, and that in a most important
degree, from the dauntless conduct of that Quentin Durward. But if I were to die under such tortures, it would be
well your Majesty should seek a ghostly father ; for from the
moment my last groan is drawn only twenty-four hours will
remain to you for confession and penitence."

Louis continued to keep hold of Galeotti's robe as he led
him towards the door, and pronounced as he opened it, in a
loud voice, "To-morrow we'll talk more of this. Go in
peace, my learned father—*go in peace—go in peace!*"

He repeated these words three times ; and, still afraid that
the provost-marshal might mistake his purpose, he led the
astrologer into the hall, holding fast his robe, as if afraid that
he should be torn from him and put to death before his eyes.
He did not unloose his grasp until he had not only repeated
again and again the gracious phrase, "Go in peace," but
even made a private signal to the provost-marshal, to enjoin
a suspension of all proceedings against the person of the
astrologer.

Thus did the possession of some secret information, joined
to audacious courage and readiness of wit, save Galeotti from
the most imminent danger ; and thus was Louis, the most
sagacious as well as the most vindictive amongst the monarchs of the period, cheated of his revenge by the influence
of superstition upon a selfish temper, and a mind to which,
from the consciousness of many crimes, the fear of death
was peculiarly terrible.

He felt, however, considerable mortification at being
obliged to relinquish his purposed vengeance ; and the disappointment seemed to be shared by his satellites, to whom
the execution was to have been committed. Le Balafré
alone, perfectly indifferent on the subject, so soon as the
countermanding signal was given, left the door at which
he had posted himself, and in a few minutes was fast
asleep.

The provost-marshal, as the group reclined themselves to
repose in the hall after the King retired to his bedchamber,
continued to eye the goodly form of the astrologer, with the
look of the mastiff watching a joint of meat which the cook
had retrieved from his jaws, while his attendants comuni-
cated to each other in brief sentences their characteristic
sentiments.

"The poor blinded necromancer," whispered Trois-

Eschelles, with an air of spiritual unction and commiseration, to his comrade, Petit-André, "hath lost the fairest chance of expiating some of his vile sorceries, by dying through means of the cord of the blessed St. Francis! and I had purpose, indeed, to leave the comfortable noose around his neck, to scare the foul fiend from his unhappy carcass."

"And I," said Petit-André, "have missed the rarest opportunity of knowing how far a weight of seventeen stone will stretch a three-plied cord! It would have been a glorious experiment in our line, and the jolly old boy would have died so easily!"

While this whispered dialogue was going forward, Martius, who had taken the opposite side of the huge stone fireplace, round which the whole group was assembled, regarded them askance and with a look of suspicion. He first put his hand into his vest, and satisfied himself that the handle of a very sharp double-edged poniard, which he always carried about him, was disposed conveniently for his grasp ; for, as we have already noticed, he was, though now somewhat unwieldy, a powerful, athletic man, and prompt and active at the use of his weapon. Satisfied that this trusty instrument was in readiness, he next took from his bosom a scroll of parchment, inscribed with Greek characters and marked with cabalistic signs, drew together the wood in the fireplace, and made a blaze by which he could distinguish the features and attitude of all who sat or lay around : the heavy and deep slumbers of the Scottish soldier, who lay motionless, with his rough countenance as immovable as if it were cast in bronze ; the pale and anxious face of Oliver, who at one time assumed the appearance of slumber, and again opened his eyes and raised his head hastily, as if stung by some internal throe, or awakened by some distant sound ; the discontented, savage, bull-dog aspect of the provost, who looked

> Frustrate of his will,
> Not half sufficed, and greedy yet to kill ;

while the background was filled up by the ghastly hypocritical countenance of Trois-Echelles, whose eyes were cast up towards Heaven, as if he was internally saying his devotions ; and the grim drollery of Petit-André, who amused himself with mimicking the gestures and wry faces of his comrade before he betook himself to sleep.

Amidst these vulgar and ignoble countenances, nothing could show to greater advantage than the stately form, handsome mien, and commanding features of the astrologer, who might have passed for one of the ancient magi, imprisoned in a den of robbers, and about to invoke a spirit to accomplish his liberation. And, indeed, had he been distinguished by nothing else than the beauty of the graceful and flowing beard which descended over the mysterious roll which he held in his hand, one might have been pardoned for regretting that so noble an appendage had been bestowed on one who put both talents, learning, and the advantages of eloquence, and a majestic person, to the mean purposes of a cheat and an impostor.

Thus passed the night in Count Herbert's Tower, in the Castle of Péronne. When the first light of dawn penetrated the ancient Gothic chamber, the King summoned Oliver to his presence, who found the monarch sitting in his nightgown, and was astonished at the alteration which one night of mortal anxiety had made in his looks. He would have expressed some anxiety on the subject, but the King silenced him by entering into a statement of the various modes by which he had previously endeavored to form friends at the court of Burgundy, and which Oliver was charged to prosecute so soon as he should be permitted to stir abroad. And never was that wily minister more struck with the clearness of the King's intellect, and his intimate knowledge of all the springs which influence human actions, than he was during that memorable consultation.

About two hours afterwards, Oliver accordingly obtained permission from the Count of Crèvecœur to go out and execute the commissions which his master had entrusted him with ; and Louis, sending for the astrologer, in whom he seemed to have renewed his faith, held with him, in like manner, a long consultation, the issue of which appeared to give him more spirits and confidence than he had at first exhibited ; so that he dressed himself, and received the morning compliments of Crèvecœur with a calmness at which the Burgundian lord could not help wondering, the rather that he had already heard that the Duke had passed several hours in a state of mind which seemed to render the King's safety very precarious.

CHAPTER XXX

UNCERTAINTY

Our counsels waver like the unsteady bark,
That reels amid the strife of meeting currents.
Old Play.

IF the night passed by Louis was carefully anxious and agitated, that spent by the Duke of Burgundy, who had at no time the same mastery over his passions, and, indeed, who permitted them almost a free and uncontroled dominion over his actions, was still more disturbed.

According to the custom of the period, two of his principal and most favored counselors, D'Hymbercourt and Des Comines, shared his bedchamber, couches being prepared for them near the bed of the prince. Their attendance was never more necessary than upon this night, when, distracted by sorrow, by passion, by the desire of revenge, and by the sense of honor, which forbade him to exercise it upon Louis in his present condition, the Duke's mind resembled a volcano in eruption, which throws forth all the different contents of the mountain, mingled and molten into one burning mass.

He refused to throw off his clothes, or to make any preparation for sleep; but spent the night in a succession of the most violent bursts of passion. In some paroxysms he talked incessantly to his attendants so thick and so rapidly, that they were really afraid his senses would give way; choosing for his theme the merits and the kindness of heart of the murdered Bishop of Liege, and recalling all the instances of mutual kindness, affection, and confidence which had passed between them, until he had worked himself into such a transport of grief that he threw himself upon his face in the bed, and seemed ready to choke with the sobs and tears which he endeavored to stifle. Then starting from the couch, he gave vent at once to another and more curious mood, and traversed the room hastily, uttering incoherent threats, and still more incoherent oaths of vengeance, while, stamping with his foot, according to his customary action, he invoked St. George, St. Andrew, and whomsoever else he held most holy, to bear witness that he would take bloody vengeance on De la Marck, on the people of Liege, and on *him* who was the author of the whole. These last threats, uttered more obscurely than the others, obviously concerned the person of the King ; and at one time the Duke expressed his determination to send for the Duke of Normandy, the brother of the King, and with whom Louis was on the worst terms, in order to compel the captive monarch to surrender either the crown itself, or some of its most valuable rights and appanages.

Another day and night passed in the same stormy and fitful deliberations, or rather rapid transitions of passion ; for the Duke scarcely ate or drank, never changed his dress, and, altogether, demeaned himself like one in whom rage might terminate in utter insanity. By degrees he became more composed, and began to hold, from time to time, consultations with his ministers, in which much was proposed, but nothing resolved on. Comines assures us that at one time a courier was mounted in readiness to depart for the purpose of summoning the Duke of Normandy ; and in that event the prison of the French monarch would probably have been found, as in similar cases, a brief road to his grave.

At other times, when Charles had exhausted his fury, he sat with his features fixed in stern and rigid immobility, like one who broods over some desperate deed to which he is as yet unable to work up his resolution. And unquestionably it would have needed little more than an insidious hint from any of the counselors who attended his person, to have pushed the Duke to some very desperate action. But the nobles of Burgundy, from the sacred character attached to the person of a king, and a lord paramount, and from a regard to the public faith, as well as that of their Duke, which had been pledged when Louis threw himself into their power, were almost unanimously inclined to recommend moderate measures ; and the arguments which D'Hymbercourt and Des Comines had now and then ventured to insinuate during the night were, in the cooler hours of the next morning, advanced and urged by Crèvecœur and others. Possibly their zeal in behalf of the King might not be entirely disinterested. Many, as we have mentioned, had already experienced the bounty of the King, others had either estates or pretensions in France, which placed them a little under his influence ; and it is certain that the treasure, which had loaded four mules when the King entered Péronne, became much lighter in the course of these negotiations.

In the course of the third day the Count of Campo-basso brought his Italian wit to assist the counsels of Charles ; and well was it for Louis that he had not arrived when the Duke was in his first fury. Immediately on his arrival, a regular meeting of the Duke's counselors was convened, for conserving the measures to be adopted in this singular crisis.

On this occasion Campo-basso gave his opinion couched in the apologue of the traveler, the adder, and the fox ; and reminded the Duke of the advice which Reynard gave to the man, that he should crush his mortal enemy, now that chance had placed his fate at his disposal. Des Comines, who saw the Duke's eyes sparkle at a proposal which his own violence of temper had already repeatedly suggested, hastened to state the possibility that Louis might not be, in fact, so directly accessory to the sanguinary action which had been committed at Schonwaldt ; that he might be able to clear himself of the imputation laid to his charge, and perhaps to make other atonement for the distractions which his intrigues had occasioned in the Duke's dominions, and those of his allies ; and that an act of violence perpetrated on the King was sure to bring both on France and Burgundy a train of the most unhappy consequences, among which not the least to be feared was that the English might avail themselves of the commotions and civil discord which must needs . ensue to repossess themselves of Normandy and Guyenne, and renew those dreadful wars, which had only, and with difficulty, been terminated by the union of both France and Burgundy against the common enemy. Finally, he confessed, that he did not mean to urge the absolute and free dismissal of Louis ; but only that the Duke should avail himself no farther of his present condition than merely to establish a fair and equitable treaty between the countries, with such security on the King's part as should make it difficult for him to break his faith, or disturb the internal peace of Burgundy in future. D'Hymbercourt, Crèvecœur, and others signified their reprobation of the violent measures proposed by Campo-basso, and their opinion that in the way of treaty more permanent advantages could be obtained, and in a manner more honorable for Burgundy, than by an action which would stain her with a breach of faith and hospitality.

The Duke listened to these arguments with his looks fixed on the ground, and his brows so knitted together as to bring his bushy eyebrows into one mass. But when Crèvecœur proceeded to say that he did not believe Louis either knew of, or was accessory to, the atrocious act of violence committed at Schonwaldt, Charles raised his head, and darting a fierce look at his counselor, exclaimed, "Have you too, Crèvecœur, heard the gold of France clink? Methinks it rings in my councils as merrily as ever the bells of St. Denis. Dare any one say that Louis is not the fomenter of these feuds in Flanders?"

"My gracious lord," said Crèvecœur, "my hand has ever been more conversant with steel than with gold; and so far am I from holding that Louis is free from the charge of having caused the disturbances in Flanders, that it is not long since, in the face of his whole court, I charged him with that breach of faith, and offered him defiance in your name. But although his intrigues have been doubtless the original cause of these commotions, I am so far from believing that he authorized the death of the archbishop, that I believe one of his emissaries publicly protested against it; and I could produce the man, were it your Grace's pleasure to see him."

"It *is* our pleasure," said the Duke. "St. George! can you doubt that we desire to act justly? Even in the highest flight of our passion we are known for an upright and a just judge. We will see France ourself; we will ourself charge him with our wrongs, and ourself state to him the reparation which we expect and demand. If he shall be found guiltless of this murder, the atonement for other crimes may be more easy. If he hath been guilty who shall say that a life of penitence in some retired monastery, were not a most deserved and a most merciful doom? Who," he added, kindling as he spoke—"who shall dare to blame a revenge yet more direct and more speedy? Let your witness attend. We will to the castle at the hour before noon. Some articles we will minute down, with which he shall comply, or woe on his head! others shall depend upon the proof. Break up the council and dismiss yourselves. I will but change my dress, as this is scarce a fitting trim in which to wait on *my most gracious sovereign.*"

With a deep and bitter emphasis on the last expression, the Duke arose, and strode out of the room.

"Louis's safety, and, what is worse, the honor of Burgundy, depend on a cast of the dice," said D'Hymbercourt to Crèvecœur and to Des Comines. "Haste thee to the castle, Des Comines; thou hast a better filed tongue than either Crèvecœur or I. Explain to Louis what storm is approaching; he will best know how to pilot himself. I trust this Life Guardsman will say nothing which can aggravate; for who knows what may have been the secret commission with which he was charged?"

"The young man," said Crèvecœur, "seems bold, yet prudent and wary far beyond his years. In all which he said to me he was tender of the King's character, as of that of the prince whom he serves. I trust he will be equally so in the Duke's presence. I must go seek him, and also the young Countess of Croye."

"The countess! You told us you had left her at St. Bridget's nunnery?"

"Ay, but I was obliged," said the count, "to send for her express, by the Duke's orders; and she has been brought hither on a litter, as being unable to travel otherwise. She was in a state of the deepest distress, both on account of the uncertainty of the fate of her kinswoman, the Lady Hameline, and the gloom which overhangs her own, guilty as she has been of a feudal delinquency, in withdrawing herself from the protection of her liege lord, Duke Charles, who is not the person in the world most likely to view with indifference what trenches on his seigniorial rights."

The information that the young countess was in the hands of Charles added fresh and more pointed thorns to Louis's reflections. He was conscious that, by explaining the intrigues by which he had induced the Lady Hameline and her to resort to Péronne [Plessis], she might supply that evidence which he had removed by the execution of Zamet Maugrabin; and he knew well how much such proof of his having interfered with the rights of the Duke of Burgundy would furnish both motive and pretext for Charles's availing himself to the uttermost of his present predicament.

Louis discoursed on these matters with great anxiety to the Sieur Des Comines, whose acute and political talents better suited the King's temper than the blunt, martial character of Crèvecœur or the feudal haughtiness of D'Hymbercourt.

"These iron-handed soldiers, my good friend Comines," he said to his future historian, "should never enter a king's cabinet, but be left with the halberds and partizans in the ante-chamber. Their hands are indeed made for our use; but the monarch who puts their heads to any better occupation than that of anvils for his enemies' swords and maces ranks with the fool who presented his mistress with a dog-

leash for a carcanet.   It is with such as thou, Philip, whose
eyes are gifted with the quick and keen sense that sees beyond the exterior surface of affairs, that princes should
share their council-table, their cabinet—what do I say ?—
the most secret recesses of their soul."

Des Comines, himself so keen a spirit, was naturally gratified with the approbation of the most sagacious prince in
Europe ; and he could not so far disguise his internal satisfaction but that Louis was aware he had made some impression on him.

"I would" continued he, "that I had such a servant, or
rather that I were worthy to have such a one !   I had not
then been in this unfortunate situation ; which, nevertheless,
I should hardly regret, could I but discover any means of securing the services of so experienced a statist."

Des Comines said that all his faculties, such as they were,
were at the service of his Most Christian Majesty, saving
always his allegiance to his rightful lord, Duke Charles of
Burgundy.

"And am I one who would seduce you from that allegiance ?" said Louis, pathetically.   "Alas ! am I not now
endangered by having reposed too much confidence in my
vassal ? and can the cause of feudal good faith be more sacred
with any than with me, whose safety depends on an appeal
to it ?   No, Philip des Comines, continue to serve Charles
of Burgundy ; and you will best serve him by bringing
round a fair accommodation with Louis of France.   In doing
thus you will serve us both, and one, at least, will be grateful.   I am told your appointments in this court hardly match
those of the Grand Falconer ; and thus the services of the
wisest counselor in Europe are put on a level, or rather
ranked below, those of a fellow who feeds and physics kites !
France has wide lands ; her King has much gold.   Allow
me, my friend, to rectify this scandalous inequality.   The
means are not distant.   Permit me to use them."

The King produced a weighty bag of money ; but Des
Comines, more delicate in his sentiments than most courtiers
of that time, declined the proffer, declaring himself perfectly
satisfied with the liberality of his native prince, and assuring
Louis that his desire to serve him could not be increased by
the acceptance of any such gratuity as he had proposed.

"Singular man !" exclaimed the King ; let me embrace
the only courtier of his time at once capable and incorruptible.   Wisdom is to be desired more than fine gold ; and believe me, I trust in thy kindness, Philip, at this pinch, more

than I do in the purchased assistance of many who have received my gifts. I know you will not counsel your master to abuse such an opportunity as fortune, and, to speak plain, Des Comines, as my own folly, has afforded him."

" To *abuse* it, by no means," answered the historian ; " but most certainly to *use* it."

" How, and in what degree ? " said Louis. " I am not ass enough to expect that I shall escape without some ransom, but let it be a reasonable one ; reason I am ever willing to listen to, at Paris or at Plessis, equally as at Péronne."

" Ah, but if it like your Majesty," replied Des Comines, " reason at Paris or Plessis was used to speak in so low and soft a tone of voice, that she could not always gain an audience of your Majesty ; at Péronne she borrows the speaking-trumpet of necessity, and her voice becomes lordly and imperative."

" You are figurative," said Louis, unable to restrain an emotion of peevishness ; " I am a dull, blunt man, Sir of Comines. I pray you leave your tropes, and come to plain ground. What does your duke expect of me ? "

" I am the bearer of no proposition, my lord," said Des Comines ; " the Duke will soon explain his own pleasure. But some things occur to me as proposals, for which your Majesty ought to hold yourself prepared ; as, for example, the final cession of these towns here upon the Somme."

" I expected so much," said Louis.

" That you should disown the Liegeois and William de la Marck."

" As willingly as I disclaim Hell and Satan." said Louis.

"Ample security will be required, by hostages, or occupation of fortresses, or otherwise, that France shall in the future abstain from stirring up rebellion among the Flemings."

" It is something new," answered the King, " that a vassal should demand pledges from his sovereign ; but let that pass too."

" A suitable and independent appanage for your illustrious brother, the ally and friend of my master—Normandy or Champagne. The Duke loves your father's house, my liege."

" So well," answered Louis, " that, *mort Dieu !* he's about to make them all kings. Is your budget of hints yet emptied ? "

" Not entirely," answered the counselor : " it will certainly be required that your Majesty shall forbear molesting, as you have done of late, the Duke de Bretagne, and that you will

no longer contest the right which he and other grand feudatories have to strike money, to term themselves dukes and
princes by the grace of God——"

"In a word, to make so many kings of my vassals. Sir
Philip, would you make a fratricide of me? You remember
well my brother Charles: he was no sooner Duke of Guyenne
than he died. And what will be left to the descendant and
representative of Charlemagne, after giving away these rich
provinces, save to be smeared with oil at Rheims, and to eat
his dinner under a high canopy?"

"We will diminish your Majesty's concern on that score, by
giving you a companion in that solitary exaltation," said
Philip des Comines. "The Duke of Burgundy, though he
claims not at present the title of an independent king, desires
nevertheless to be freed in future from the abject marks of
subjection required of him to the crown of France; it is his
purpose to close his ducal coronet with an imperial arch, and
surmount it with a globe, in emblem that his dominions are
independent."

"And how dares the Duke of Burgundy, the sworn vassal
of France," exclaimed Louis, starting up and showing an
unwonted degree of emotion—"how dares he propose such
terms to his sovereign as, by every law of Europe, should
infer a forfeiture of his fief?"

"The doom of forfeiture it would in this case be difficult
to enforce," answered Des Comines, calmly. "Your Majesty
is aware that the strict interpretation of the feudal law is
becoming obsolete even in the Empire, and that superior and
vassal endeavor to mend their situation in regard to each
other as they have power and opportunity. Your Majesty's
interferences with the Duke's vassals in Flanders will prove
an exculpation of my master's conduct, supposing him to insist that, by enlarging his independence, France should in
future be debarred from any pretext of doing so."

"Comines—Comines!" said Louis, arising again and pacing the room in a pensive manner, "this is a dreadful lesson
on the text *væ victis!* You cannot mean that the Duke will
insist on all these hard conditions?"

"At least I would have your Majesty be in a condition to
discuss them all."

"Yet moderation, Des Comines—moderation in success is
—no one knows better than you—necessary to its ultimate
advantage."

"So please your Majesty, the merit of moderation is, I
have observed, most apt to be extolled by the losing party.

The winner holds in more esteem the prudence which calls on him not to leave an opportunity unimproved."

"Well, we will consider," replied the King; "but at least thou hast reached the extremity of your duke's unreasonable exaction? There can remain nothing—or if there does, for so thy brow intimates—what is it—what indeed can it be, unless it be my crown, which these previous demands, if granted, will deprive of all its luster?"

"My lord," said Des Comines, "what remains to be mentioned is a thing partly—indeed, in a great measure—within the Duke's own power, though he means to invite your Majesty's accession to it, for in truth it touches you nearly."

"*Pasques-dieu!*" exclaimed the King impatiently, "what is it? Speak out, Sir Philip; am I to send him my daughter for a concubine, or what other dishonor is he to put on me?"

"No dishonor, my liege; but your Majesty's cousin, the illustrious Duke of Orleans——"

"Ha!" exclaimed the King; but Des Comines proceeded without heeding the interruption.

"—Having conferred his affections on the young Countess Isabelle de Croye, the Duke expects your Majesty will, on your part, as he on his, yield your assent to the marriage, and unite with him in endowing the right noble couple with such an appanage as, joined to the countess's estates, may form a fit establishment for a child of France."

"Never—never!" said the King, bursting out into that emotion which he had of late suppressed with much difficulty, and striding about in a disordered haste, which formed the strongest contrast to the self-command which he usually exhibited—"never, never! Let them bring scissors and shear my hair like that of the parish fool, whom I have so richly resembled—let them bid the monastery or the grave yawn for me—let them bring red-hot basins to sear my eyes—axe or aconite—whatever they will; but Orleans shall not break his plighted faith to my daughter, or marry another while she lives!"

"Your Majesty," said Des Comines, "ere you set your mind so keenly against what is proposed, will consider your own want of power to prevent it. Every wise man, when he sees a rock giving way, withdraws from the bootless attempt of preventing the fall."

"But a brave man," said Louis, "will at least find his grave beneath it. Des Comines, consider the great loss—the utter destruction, such a marriage will bring upon my king-

23

dom. Recollect, I have but one feeble boy, and this Orleans
is the next heir ; consider that the church hath consented to
his union with Joan, which unites so happily the interests
of both branches of my family—think on all this, and think
too that this union has been the favorite scheme of my whole
life—that I have schemed for it, fought for it, watched for it
—prayed for it and sinned for it. Philip des Comines, I will
not forego it ! Think, man—think ! pity me in this extremity ; thy quick brain can speedily find some substitute for this
sacrifice—some ram to be offered up instead of that project
which is dear to me as the Patriarch's only son was to him.
Philip, pity me ! You, at least, should know that to men
of judgment and foresight the destruction of the scheme on
which they have long dwelt, and for which they have long
toiled, is more inexpressibly bitter than the transient grief
of ordinary men, whose pursuits are but the gratification of
some temporary passion—you, who know how to sympathize
with the deeper, the more genuine distress of baffled prudence
and disappointed sagacity, will you not feel for me ? "

" My lord and king ! " replied Des Comines, " I do sympathize with your distress, in so far as duty to my master——"

" Do not mention him ! " said Louis, acting, or at least
appearing to act, under an irresistible and headlong impulse,
which withdrew the usual guard which he maintained over
his language. " Charles of Burgundy is unworthy of your
attachment. He who can insult and strike his counselors
—he who can distinguish the wisest and most faithful among
them by the opprobrious name of Booted Head—— ! "

The wisdom of Philip des Comines did not prevent his
having a high sense of personal consequence ; and he was so
much struck with the words of the King uttered, as it were,
in the career of a passion which overleaped ceremony, that
he could only rely by repetition of the words " Booted Head!
It is impossible that my master the Duke could have so
termed the servant who has been at his side since he could
mount a palfrey, and that too before a foreign monarch—it
is impossible ! "

Louis instantly saw the impression he had made, and
avoiding alike a tone of condolence, which might have seemed
insulting, and one of sympathy, which might have savored
of affectation, he said, with simplicity, and at the same time
with dignity, " My misfortunes make me forget my courtesy,
else I had not spoken to you of what it must be unpleasant
for you to hear. But you have in reply taxed me with

having uttered impossibilities, this touches my honor ; yet I must submit to the charge, if I tell you not the circumstances which the Duke, laughing until his eyes ran over, assigned for the origin of that opprobrious name, which I will not offend your ears by repeating. Thus, then, it chanced. You, Sir Philip des Comines, were at a hunting-match with the Duke of Burgundy, your master ; and when he alighted after the chase, he required your services in drawing off his boots. Reading in your looks, perhaps, some natural resentment of this disparaging treatment, he ordered you to sit down in turn, and rendered you the same office he had just received from you. But, offended at your understanding him literally, he no sooner plucked one of your boots off than he brutally beat it about your head till the blood flowed, exclaiming against the insolence of a subject who had the presumption to accept of such a service at the hand of his sovereign ; and hence he, or his privileged fool Le Glorieux, is in the current habit of distinguishing you by the absurd and ridiculous name of *Tête-botté*, which makes one of the Duke's most ordinary subjects of pleasantry."*

While Louis thus spoke, he had the double pleasure of galling to the quick the person whom he addressed—an exercise which it was in his nature to enjoy, even where he had not, as in the present case, the apology that he did so in pure retaliation—and that of observing, that he had at length been able to find a point in Des Comines's character which might lead him gradually from the interests of Burgundy to those of France. But although the deep resentment which the offended courtier entertained against his master induced him at a future period to exchange the service of Charles for that of Louis, yet, at the present moment, he was contented to throw out only some general hints of his friendly inclination towards France, which he well knew the King would understand how to interpret. And indeed it would be unjust to stigmatize the memory of the excellent historian with the desertion of his master on this occasion, although he was certainly now possessed with sentiments much more favorable to Louis than when he entered the apartment.

He constrained himself to laugh at the anecdote which Louis had detailed, and then added, " I did not think so trifling a frolic would have dwelt on the mind of the Duke so long as to make it worth telling again. Some such passage there was of drawing off boots and the like, as your

* See Anecdote of the Boots. Note 44.

Majesty knows that the Duke is fond of rude play ; but it has been much exaggerated in his recollection. Let it pass on."

" Ay, *let* it pass on," said the King ; " it is indeed shame it should have detained us a minute. And now, Sir Philip, I hope you are French so far as to afford me your best counsel in these difficult affairs. You have, I am well aware, the clue to the labyrinth, if you would but impart it."

" Your Majesty may command my best advice and service, replied Des Comines, " under reservation always of my duty to my own master."

This was nearly what the courtier had before stated ; but he now repeated it in a tone so different, that whereas Louis understood from the former declaration that the reserved duty to Burgundy was the prime thing to be considered, so he now saw clearly that the emphasis was reversed, and that more weight was now given by the speaker to his promise of counsel than to a restriction which seemed interposed for the sake of form and consistency. The King resumed his own seat, and compelled Des Comines to sit by him, listening at the same time to that statesman, as if the words of an oracle sounded in his ears. Des Comines spoke in that low and impressive tone which implies at once great sincerity and some caution, and at the same time so slowly as if he was desirous that the King should weigh and consider each individual word as having its own peculiar and determined meaning. " The things," he said, " which I have suggested for your Majesty's consideration, harsh as they sound in your ear, are but substitutes for still more violent proposals brought forward in the Duke's councils by such as are more hostile to your Majesty. And I need scarce remind your Majesty that the more direct and more violent suggestions find readiest acceptance with our master, who loves brief and dangerous measures better than those that are safe, but at the same time circuitous."

" I remember," said the King, " I have seen him swim a river at the risk of drowning, though there was a bridge to be found for riding two hundred yards round."

" True, sire ; and he that weighs not his life against the gratification of a moment of impetuous passion will, on the same impulse, prefer the gratification of his will to the increase of his substantial power."

" Most true," replied the King ; " a fool will ever grasp rather at the appearance than the reality of authority. All this I know to be true of Charles of Burgundy. But, my dear friend Des Comines, what do you infer from these premises ?"

"Simply this, my lord," answered the Burgundian, "that as your Majesty has seen a skilful angler control a large and heavy fish, and finally draw him to land by a single hair, which fish had broken through a tackle tenfold stronger had the fisher presumed to strain the line on him, instead of giving him head enough for all his wild flourishes, even so your Majesty, by gratifying the Duke in these particulars on which he has pitched his ideas of honor and the gratification of his revenge, may evade many of the other unpalatable propositions at which I have hinted, and which—including, I must state openly to your Majesty, some of those through which France would be most especially weakened—will slide out of his remembrance and attention, and, being referred to subsequent conferences and future discussion, may be altogether eluded."

"I understand you, my good Sir Philip ; but to the matter," said the King. "To which of those happy propositions is your duke so much wedded that contradiction will make him unreasonable and untractable ? "

"To any or to all of them, if it please your Majesty, on which you may happen to contradict him. This is precisely what your Majesty must avoid ; and to take up my former parable, you must needs remain on the watch, ready to give the Duke line enough whenever he shoots away under the impulse of his rage. His fury, already considerably abated, will waste itself if he be unopposed, and you will presently find him become more friendly and more tractable."

"Still," said the King, musing, "there must be some particular demands which lie deeper at my cousin's heart than the other proposals. Were I but aware of these, Sir Philip——"

"Your Majesty may make the lightest of his demands the most important, simply by opposing it," said Des Comines ; "nevertheless, my lord, thus far I can say, that every shadow of treaty will be broken off, if your Majesty renounce not William de la Marck and the Liegeois."

"I have already said that I will disown them," said the King, "and well they deserve it at my hand : the villains have commenced their uproar at a moment that might have cost me my life."

"He that fires a train of powder," replied the historian, "must expect a speedy explosion of the mine. But more than mere disavowal of their cause will be expected of your Majesty by Duke Charles ; for know, that he will demand your Majesty's assistance to put the insurrection down, and your royal presence to witness the punishment which he destines for the rebels."

"That may scarce consist with our honor, Des Comines," said the King.

"To refuse it will scarcely consist with your Majesty's safety," replied Des Comines. "Charles is determined to show the people of Flanders that no hope, nay, no promise, of assistance from France will save them in their mutinies from the wrath and vengeance of Burgundy."

"But, Sir Philip, I will speak plainly," answered the King. "Could we but procrastinate the matter, might not these rogues of Liege make their own part good against Duke Charles? The knaves are numerous and steady, can they not hold out their town against him?"

"With the help of the thousand archers of France whom your Majesty promised them, they might have done something; but——"

"Whom I promised them!" said the King. "Alas! good Sir Philip! you much wrong me in saying so."

"—But without whom," continued Des Comines, not heeding the interruption, "as your Majesty will not *now* likely find it convenient to supply them, what chance will the burghers have of making good their town, in whose walls the large breaches made by Charles after the battle of St. Tron are still unrepaired; so that the lances of Hainault, Brabant, and Burgundy may advance to the attack twenty men in front?"

"The improvident idiots!" said the King. "If they have thus neglected their own safety, they deserve not my protection. Pass on; I will make no quarrel for their sake."

"The next point, I fear, will sit closer to your Majesty's heart," said Des Comines.

"Ah!" replied the King, "you mean that infernal marriage! I will not consent to the breach of the contract betwixt my daughter Joan and my cousin of Orleans; it would be wresting the scepter of France from me and my posterity, for that feeble boy the Dauphin is a blighted blossom, which will wither without fruit. This match between Joan and Orleans has been my thought by day, my dream by night. I tell thee, Sir Philip, I cannot give it up! Besides, it is inhuman to require me, with my own hand, to destroy at once my own scheme of policy and the happiness of a pair brought up for each other."

"Are they then so much attached?" said Des Comines.

"One of them at least is," said the King, "and the one

for whom I am bound to be most anxious. But you smile, Sir Philip, you are no believer in the force of love."

"Nay," said Des Comines, " if it please you, sire, I am so little an infidel in that particular that I was about to ask whether it would reconcile you in any degree to your acquiescing in the proposed marriage betwixt the Duke of Orleans and Isabelle de Croye, were I to satisfy you that the countess's inclinations are so much fixed on another that it is likely it will never be a match ?"

King Louis sighed. "Alas !" he said, "my good and dear friend, from what sepulcher have you drawn such dead man's comfort ? *Her* inclination, indeed ! Why, to speak truth, supposing that Orleans detested my daughter Joan, yet, but for this ill-raveled web of mischance, he must needs have married her ; so you may conjecture how little chance there is of this damsel being able to refuse him under a similar compulsion, and he a child of France besides. Ah, no, Philip ! little fear of her standing obstinate against the suit of such a lover. *Varium et mutabile*, Philip."

" Your Majesty may, in the present instance, undervalue the obstinate courage of this young lady. She comes of a race determinately wilful ; and I have picked out of Crèvecœur that she has formed a romantic attachment to a young squire, who, to say truth, rendered her many services on the road."

"Ha !" said the King, "an archer of my Guards, by name Quentin Durward ?"

"The same, as I think," said Des Comines ; "he was made prisoner along with the countess, traveling almost alone together."

"Now, Our Lord and Our Lady, and Monseigneur St. Martin, and Monseigneur St. Julian be praised every one of them !" said the King, "and all laud and honor to the learned Galeotti, who read in the stars that his youth's destiny was connected with mine ! If the maiden be so attached to him as to make her refractory to the will of Burgundy, this Quentin hath indeed been rarely useful to me."

" I believe, my lord," answered the Burgundian, "according to Crèvecœur's report, that there is some chance of her being sufficiently obstinate ; besides, doubtless, the noble Duke himself, notwithstanding what your Majesty was pleased to hint in way of supposition, will not willingly renounce his fair cousin, to whom he has been long engaged."

"Umph !" answered the King. "But you have never

seen my daughter Joan. A howlet, man!—an absolute owl, whom I am ashamed of! But let him be only a wise man, and marry her, I will give him leave to be mad *par amours* for the fairest lady in France. And now, Philip, have you given me the full map of your master's mind?"

"I have possessed you, sire, of those particulars on which he is at present most disposed to insist. But your Majesty well knows that the Duke's disposition is like a sweeping torrent, which only passes smoothly forward when its waves encounter no opposition; and what may be presented to chafe him into fury, it is impossible even to guess. Were more distinct evidence of your Majesty's practises—pardon the phrase, where there is so little time for selection—with the Liegeois and William de la Marck to occur unexpectedly, the issue might be terrible. There are strange news from that country: they say La Marck hath married Hameline the elder Countess of Croye."

"That old fool was so mad on marriage that she would have accepted the hand of Satan," said the King; "but that La Marck, beast as he is, should have married her rather more surprises me."

"There is a report also," continued Des Comines, "that an envoy, or herald, on La Marck's part, is approaching Péronne; this is like to drive the Duke frantic with rage. I trust that he has no letters, or the like, to show on your Majesty's part?"

"Letters to a Wild Boar!" answered the King. "No—no, Sir Philip, I was no such fool as to cast pearls before swine. What little intercourse I had with the brute animal was by message, in which I always employed such low-bred slaves and vagabonds that their evidence would not be received in a trial for robbing a hen-roost."

"I can then only further recommend," said Des Comines, taking his leave, "that your Majesty should remain on your guard, be guided by events, and, above all, avoid using any language or argument with the Duke which may better become your dignity than your present condition."

"If my dignity," said the King, "grow troublesome to me, which it seldom doth while there are deeper interests to think of, I have a special remedy for that swelling of the heart. It is but looking into a certain ruinous closet, Sir Philip, and thinking of the death of Charles the Simple; and it cures me as effectually as the cold bath would cool a fever. And now, my friend and monitor, must thou be gone? Well, Sir Philip, the time must come when thou wilt tire reading lessons of state policy to the Bull of Burgundy, who is incapable of comprehending your most simple argument. If Louis of Valois then lives, thou hast a friend in the court of France. I tell thee, my Philip, it would be a blessing to my kingdom should I ever acquire thee, who, with a profound view of subjects of state, hast also a conscience capable of feeling and discerning between right and wrong. So help me, Our Lord and Lady, and Monseigneur St. Martin, Oliver and Balue have hearts as hardened as the nether millstone; and my life is embittered by remorse and penances for the crimes they make me commit. Thou, Sir Philip, possessed of the wisdom of present and past times, canst teach how to become great without ceasing to be virtuous."

" A hard task, and which few have attained," said the historian, " but which is yet within the reach of princes who will strive for it. Meantime, sire, be prepared, for the Duke will presently confer with you."

Louis looked long after Philip when he left the apartment, and at length burst into a bitter laugh. "He spoke of fishing —I have sent him home, a trout properly tickled ! And he thinks himself virtuous because he took no bribe, but contented himself with flattery and promises, and the pleasure of avenging an affront to his vanity ! Why, he is but so much the poorer for the refusal of the money, not a jot the more honest. He must be mine, though, for he hath the shrewdest head among them. Well, now for nobler game ! I am to face this leviathan Charles, who will presently swim hitherward, cleaving the deep before him. I must, like a trembling sailor, throw a tub overboard to amuse him. But I may one day find the chance—of driving a harpoon into his entrails !" *

* See Philip des Comines. Note 45.

CHAPTER XXXI

THE INTERVIEW

Hold fast thy truth, young soldier. Gentle maiden,
Keep you your promise plight ; leave age its subtleties,
And gray-hair'd policy its maze of falsehood ;
But be you candid as the morning sky,
Ere the high sun sucks vapors up to stain it.
The Trial.

ON the perilous and important morning which preceded the
meeting of the two princes in the Castle of Péronne, Oliver
le Dain did his master the service of an active and skilful
agent, making interest for Louis in every quarter, both with
presents and promises ; so that, when the Duke's anger
should blaze forth, all around should be interested to
smother, and not to increase, the conflagration. He glided,
like night, from tent to tent, from house to house, making
himself friends, but not, in the Apostle's sense, with the
Mammon of unrighteousness. As was said of another active
political agent, "His finger was in every man's palm, his
mouth was in every man's ear"; and for various reasons,
some of which we have formerly hinted at, he secured the
favor of many Burgundian nobles, who either had something to hope or fear from France, or who thought that,
were the power of Louis too much reduced, their own duke
would be likely to pursue the road to despotic authority, to
which his heart naturally inclined him, with a daring and
unopposed pace.

Where Oliver suspected his own presence or arguments
might be less acceptable, he employed that of other servants
of the King ; and it was in this manner that he obtained,
by the favor of the Count de Crèvecœur, an interview betwixt Lord Crawford, accompanied by Le Balafré, and
Quentin Durward, who, since he had arrived at Péronne,
had been detained in a sort of honorable confinement.
Private affairs were assigned as the cause of requesting this
meeting ; but it is probable that Crèvecœur, who was afraid
that his master might be stirred up in passion to do something dishonorably violent towards Louis, was not sorry to

afford an opportunity to Crawford to give some hints to the young archer which might prove useful to his master.

The meeting between the countrymen was cordial, and even affecting.

"Thou art a singular youth," said Crawford, stroking the head of young Durward as a grandsire might do that of his descendant. "Certes, you have had as meikle good fortune as if you had been born with a lucky hood on your head."

"All comes of his gaining an archer's place at such early years," said Le Balafré ; "I never was so much talked of, fair nephew, because I was five-and-twenty years old before I was *hors de page*."

"And an ill-looking mountainous monster of a page thou wert, Ludovic," said the old commander, "with a beard like a baker's shool, and a back like old Wallace Wight."

"I fear," said Quentin, with downcast eyes, "I shall enjoy that title to distinction but a short time, since it is my purpose to resign the service of the Archer Guard."

Le Balafré was struck almost mute with astonishment, and Crawford's ancient features gleamed with displeasure. The former at length mustered words enough to say, "Resign !—leave your place in the Scottish Archers ! such a thing was never dreamt of. I would not give up my situation, to be made Constable of France."

"Hush ! Ludovic," said Crawford ; "this youngster knows better how to shape his course with the wind than we of the old world do. His journey hath given him some pretty tales to tell about King Louis ; and he is turning Burgundian, that he may make his own little profit by telling them to Duke Charles."

"If I thought so," said Le Balafré, "I would cut his throat with my own hand, were he fifty times my sister's son !"

"But you would first inquire whether I deserved to be so treated, fair kinsman ?" answered Quentin. "And you, my lord, know that I am no tale-bearer ; nor shall either question or torture draw out of me a word to King Louis's prejudice which may have come to my knowledge while I was in his service. So far my oath of duty keeps me silent. But I will not remain in that service, in which, besides the perils of fair battle with mine enemies, I am to be exposed to the dangers of ambuscade on the part of my friends."

"Nay, if he objects to lying in ambuscade," said the slow-witted Le Balafré, looking sorrowfully at the Lord Crawford, "I am afraid, my lord, that all is over with him ! I myself have had thirty bushments break upon me, and truly I think I have laid in ambuscade twice as often myself, it being a favorite practise in our King's mode of making war."

"It is so, indeed, Ludovic," answered Lord Crawford; "nevertheless, hold your peace, for I believe I understand this gear better than you do."

"I wish to Our Lady you may, my lord," answered Ludovic; "but it wounds me to the very midriff to think my sister's son should fear an ambushment."

"Young man," said Crawford, "I partly guess your meaning. You have met foul play on the road where you traveled by the King's command, and you think you have reason to charge him with being the author of it?"

"I have been threatened with foul play in the execution of the King's commission," answered Quentin; "but I have had the good fortune to elude it; whether his Majesty be innocent or guilty in the matter, I leave to God and his own conscience. He fed me when I was a-hungered, received me when I was a wandering stranger; I will never load him in his adversity with accusations which may indeed be unjust, since I heard them only from the vilest mouths."

"My dear boy—my own lad!" said Crawford, taking him in his arms, "ye think like a Scot, every joint of you! Like one that will forget a cause of quarrel with a friend whose back is already at the wall, and remember nothing of him but his kindness."

"Since my Lord Crawford has embraced my nephew," said Ludovic Lesly, "I will embrace him also, though I would have you to know, that to understand the service of an ambushment is as necessary to a soldier as it is to a priest to be able to read his breviary."

"Be hushed, Ludovic," said Crawford; "ye are an ass, my friend, and ken not the blessing Heaven has sent you in this braw callant. And now tell me, Quentin, my man, hath the King any advice of this brave, Christian, and manly resoultion of yours? for, poor man, he had need, in his strait, to ken what he has to reckon upon. Had he but brought the whole brigade of Guards with him—but God's will be done! Kens he of your purpose, think you?"

"I really can hardly tell," answered Quentin; "but I assured his learned astrologer, Martius Galeotti, of my resolution to be silent on all that could injure the King with the Duke of Burgundy. The particulars which I suspect I will not—under your favor—communicate even to your lordship ; and to the philosopher I was, of course, far less willing to unfold myself."

"Ha !—ay !" answered Lord Crawford. "Oliver did indeed tell me that Galeotti prophesied most stoutly concerning the line of conduct you were to hold ; and I am truly glad to find he did so on better authority than the stars."

"*He* prophesy !" said Le Balafré, laughing. "The stars never told him that honest Ludovic Lesly used to help yonder wench of his to spend the fair ducats he flings into her lap."

"Hush ! Ludovic," said his captain—"hush ! thou beast, man ! If thou dost not respect my gray hairs, because I have been e'en too much of a *routier* myself, respect the boy's youth and innocence, and let us have no more of such unbecoming daffing."

"Your honor may say your pleasure," answered Ludovic Lesly ; "but, by my faith, second-sighted Saunders Souplejaw, the town-souter of Glen Houlakin, was worth Gallotti, or Gallipotty, or whatever ye call him, twice told, for a prophet. He foretold that all my sister's children would die some day ; and he foretold it in the very hour that the youngest was born, and that is this lad Quentin, who, no doubt, will one day die, to make up the prophecy—the more's the pity ; the whole curney of them is gone but himself. And Saunders foretold to myself one day, that I should be made by marriage, which doubtless will also happen in due time, though it hath not yet come to pass, though how or when, I can hardly guess, as I care not myself for the wedded state, and Quentin is but a lad. Also, Saunders predicted——"

"Nay," said Lord Crawford, "unless the prediction be singularly to the purpose, I must cut you short, my good Ludovic ; for both you and I must now leave your nephew, with prayers to Our Lady to strengthen him in the good mind he is in ; for this is a case in which a light word might do more mischief than all the Parliament of Paris could mend. My blessing with you, my lad ; and be in no hurry to think of leaving our body, for there will be good blows going presently in the eye of day, and no ambuscade."

"And my blessing too, nephew," said Ludovic Lesly ; "for, since you have satisfied our most noble captain, I also am satisfied, as in duty bound."

"Stay, my lord," said Quentin, and led Lord Crawford a little apart from his uncle. "I must not forget to mention

that there is a person besides in the world, who, having
learned from me these circumstances which it is essential to
King Louis's safety should at present remain concealed, may
not think that the same obligation of secrecy which attaches
to me as the King's soldier, and as having been relieved by
his bounty, is at all binding on her."

"On *her!*" replied Crawford; "nay, if there be a woman
in the secret, the Lord ha' mercy, for we are all on the rocks
again!"

"Do not suppose so, my lord," replied Durward, "but
use your interest with the Count of Crèvecœur to permit me
an interview with the Countess Isabelle of Croye, who is the
party possessed of my secret, and I doubt not that I can
persuade her to be as silent as I shall unquestionably myself
remain concerning whatever may incense the Duke against
King Louis."

The old soldier mused for a long time, looked up to the
ceiling, then down again upon the floor, then shook his
head, and at length said, "There is something in all this
which, by my honor, I do not understand. The Countess
Isabelle of Croye! an interview with a lady of her birth,
blood, and possessions, and thou, a raw Scottish lad, so
certain of carrying thy point with her! Thou art either
strangely confident, my young friend, or else you have used
your time well upon the journey. But, by the cross of St.
Andrew! I will move Crèvecœur in thy behalf; and, as he
truly fears that Duke Charles may be provoked against the
King to the extremity of falling foul, I think it likely he
may grant thy request, though, by my honor, it is a comical
one."

So saying, and shrugging up his shoulders, the old lord
left the apartment, followed by Ludovic Lesly, who, forming
his looks on those of his principal, endeavored, though
knowing nothing of the cause of his wonder, to look as
mysterious and important as Crawford himself.

In a few minutes Crawford returned, but without his
attendant Le Balafré. The old man seemed in singular
humor, laughing and chuckling to himself in a manner which
strangely distorted his stern and rigid features, and at the
same time shaking his head, as at something which he could
not help condemning, while he found it irresistibly ludicrous.
"My certes, countryman," said he, "but you are not blate:
you will never lose fair lady for faint heart! Crèvecœur
swallowed your proposal as he would have done a cup of
vinegar, and swore to me roundly, by all the saints in Bur-

gundy, that were less than the honor of princes and the peace
of kingdoms at stake, you should never see even so much as
the print of the Countess Isabelle's foot on the clay.   Were
it not that he had a dame, and a fair one, I would have
thought that he meant to break a lance for the prize himself.
Perhaps he thinks of his nephew, the County Stephen.   A
countess! would no less serve you to be minting at ?   But
come along ; your interview with her must be brief.   But I
fancy you know how to make the most of little time—ho!
ho! ho!   By my faith, I can hardly chide thee for the
presumption, I have such a good will to laugh at it !"

With a brow like scarlet, at once offended and disconcerted
by the blunt inferences of the old soldier, and vexed at beholding in what an absurd light his passion was viewed by
every person of experience, Durward followed Lord Crawford
in silence to the Ursuline convent, in which the countess
was lodged, and in the parlor of which he found the Count
de Crèvecœur.

"So, young gallant," said the latter, sternly, "you must
see the fair companion of your romantic expedition once
more, it seems ?"

"Yes, my lord count," answered Quentin, firmly ; "and
what is more, I must see her alone."

"That shall never be," said the Count de Crèvecœur.
"Lord Crawford, I make you judge.   This young lady, the
daughter of my·old friend and companion in arms, the richest
heiress in Burgundy, has confessed a sort of a—what was I
going to say ?—in short, she is a fool, and your man-at-arms
here a presumptuous coxcomb.   In a word, they shall not
meet alone."

"Then will I not speak a single word to the countess in
your presence," said Quentin, much delighted.   "You have
told me much that I did not dare, presumptuous as I may
be, even to hope."

"Ay, truly said, my friend," said Crawford.   "You have
been imprudent in your communications ; and, since you
refer to me, and there is a good stout grating across the
parlor, I would advise you to trust to it, and let them do
the worst with their tongues.   What, man ! the life of a
king, and many thousands besides, is not to be weighed with
the chance of two young things whillywhawing in ilk other's
ears for a minute ?"

So saying, he dragged off Crèvecœur, who followed very
reluctantly, and cast many angry glances at the young archer
as he left the room.

In a moment after the Countess Isabelle entered on the other side of the grate, and no sooner saw Quentin alone in the parlor than she stopped short, and cast her eyes on the ground for the space of half a minute. " Yet why should I be ungrateful," she said, " because others are unjustly suspicious ? My friend—my preserver, I may almost say, so much have I been beset by treachery—my only faithful and constant friend ! "

As she spoke thus, she extended her hand to him through the grate, nay, suffered him to retain it until he had covered it with kisses, not unmingled with tears. She only said, " Durward, were we ever to meet again, I would not permit this folly."

If it be considered that Quentin had guarded her through so many perils, that he had been, in truth, her only faithful and zealous protector, perhaps my fair readers, even if countesses and heiresses should be of the number, will pardon the derogation.

But the countess extricated her hand at length, and stepping a pace back from the grate, asked Durward, in a very embarrassed tone, what boon he had to ask of her ? " For that you have a request to make I have learned from the old Scottish lord, who came here but now with my cousin of Crèvecœur. Let it be but reasonable," she said, " but such as poor Isabelle can grant with duty and honor uninfringed, and you cannot tax my slender powers too highly. But O ! do not speak hastily ; do not say," she added, looking around with timidity, " aught that might, if overheard, to prejudice to us both ! "

" Fear not, noble lady," said Quentin, sorrowfully ; " it is not *here* that I can forget the distance which fate has placed between us, or expose you to the censure of your proud kindred as the object of the most devoted love to one, poorer and less powerful, not perhaps less noble, than themselves. Let that pass like a dream of the night to all but one bosom, where, dream as it is, it will fill up the room of all existing realities."

" Hush—hush ! " said Isabelle ; " for your own sake, for mine, be silent on such a theme. Tell me rather what it is you have to ask of me."

"Forgiveness to one," replied Quentin, " who, for his own selfish views, hath conducted himself as your enemy."

" I trust I forgive all my enemies," answered Isabelle ; " but oh, Durward ! through what scenes have your courage and presence of mind protected me ! Yonder bloody hall !

the good bishop ! I knew not till yesterday half the horrors I had unconsciously witnessed."

" Do not think on them," said Quentin, who saw the transient color which had come to her cheek during conference fast fading into the most deadly paleness. " Do not look back, but look steadily forward, as they needs must who walk in a perilous road. Hearken to me. King Louis deserves nothing better at your hand, of all others, than to be proclaimed the wily and insidious politican which he really is. But to tax him as the encourager of your flight, still more as the author of a plan to throw you into the hands of De la Marck, will at this moment produce perhaps the King's death or dethronement ; and, at all events, the most bloody war between France and Burgundy which the two countries have ever been engaged in."

" These evils shall not arrive for my sake, if they can be prevented," said the Countess Isabelle ; " and indeed your slightest request were enough to make me forego my revenge, were that at any time a passion which I deeply cherish. Is it possible I would rather remember King Louis's injuries than your invaluable services ? Yet how is this to be ? When I am called before my sovereign, the Duke of Burgundy, I must either stand silent or speak the truth. The former would be contumacy ; and to a false tale you will not desire me to train my tongue."

" Surely not," said Durward ; " but let your evidence concerning Louis be confined to what you yourself positively know to be truth ; and when you mention what others have reported, no matter how credibly, let it be as reports only, and beware of pledging your own personal evidence to that which, though you may fully believe, you cannot personally know, to be true. The assembled council of Burgundy cannot refuse to a monarch the justice which in my country is rendered to the meanest person under accusation. They must esteem him innocent until direct and sufficient proof shall demonstrate his guilt. Now, what does not consist with your own certain knowledge should be proved by other evidence than your report from hearsay."

" I think I understand you," said the Countess Isabelle.

" I will make my meaning plainer," said Quentin ; and was illustrating it accordingly by more than one instance, when the convent-bell tolled.

" That," said the countess, " is a signal that we must part —part forever ! But do not forget me, Durward ; I will never forget you ; your faithful services——"

24

She could not speak more, but again extended her hand, which was again pressed to his lips; and I know not how it was that, in endeavoring to withdraw her hand, the countess came so close to the grating that Quentin was encouraged to press the adieu on her lips. The young lady did not chide him; perhaps there was no time, for Crèvecœur and Crawford, who had been from some loop-hole eye-witnesses, if not ear-witnesses also, of what was passing, rushed into the apartment, the first in a towering passion, the latter laughing and holding the count back.

"To your chamber, young mistress—to your chamber!" exclaimed the count to Isabelle, who, flinging down her veil, retired in all haste, "which should be exchanged for a cell and bread and water. And you, gentle sir, who are so malapert, the time will come when the interests of kings and kingdoms may not be connected with such as you are; and you shall then learn the penalty of your audacity in raising your beggarly eyes——"

"Hush—hush! enough said—rein up—rein up," said the old lord; "and you, Quentin, I command you, be silent, and begone to your quarters. There is no such room for so much scorn neither, Sir Count of Crèvecœur, that I must say now he is out of hearing. Quentin Durward is as much a gentleman as the King, only, as the Spaniards says, not so rich. He is as noble as myself, and I am chief of my name. Tush, tush! man, you must not speak to us of penalties."

"My lord—my lord," said Crèvecœur, impatiently, "the insolence of these foreign mercenaries is proverbial, and should receive rather rebuke than encouragement from you, who are their leader."

"My lord count," answered Crawford, "I have ordered my command for these fifty years without advice either from Frenchmen or Burgundian; and I intend to do so, under your favor, so long as I shall continue to hold it."

"Well—well, my lord," said Crèvecœur, "I meant you no disrespect; your nobleness, as well as your age, entitle you to be privileged in your impatience; and for these young people, I am satisfied to overlook the past, since I will take care that they never meet again."

"Do not take that upon your salvation, Crèvecœur," said the old lord, laughing; "mountains, it is said, may meet, and why not mortal creatures, that have legs, and life and love to put these legs in motion? Yon kiss, Crèvecœur, came tenderly off; methinks it was ominous."

"You are striving again to disturb my patience," said

Crèvecœur, "but I will not give you that advantage over me. Hark! they toll the summons to the castle : an awful meeting, of which God can only foretell the issue."

" This issue I can foretell," said the old Scottish lord, " that if violence is to be offered to the person of the King, few as his friends are, and surrounded by his enemies, he shall neither fall alone nor unrevenged ; and grieved I am that his own positive orders have prevented my taking measures to prepare for such an issue."

" My Lord of Crawford," said the Burgundian, " to anticipate such evil is the sure way to give occasion to it. Obey the orders of your royal master, and give no pretext for violence by taking hasty offense, and you will find that the day will pass over more smoothly than you now conjecture."

CHAPTER XXXII

THE INVESTIGATION

Me rather had, my heart might feel your love,
Than my displeased eye see your courtesy.
Up, cousin, up ; your heart is up, I know,
Thus high at least, although your knee—
King Richard II.

AT the first toll of the bell, which was to summon the
great nobles of Burgundy together in council, with the very
few French peers who could be present on the occasion,
Duke Charles, followed by a part of his train, armed with
partizans and battle-axes, entered the hall of Herbert's
Tower, in the Castle of Péronne. King Louis, who had expected the visit, arose and made two steps towards the Duke,
and then remained standing with an air of dignity, which,
in spite of the meanness of his dress and the familiarity of
his ordinary manners, he knew very well how to assume
when he judged it necessary. Upon the present important
crisis, the composure of his demeanor had an evident effect
upon his rival, who changed the abrupt and hasty step with
which he entered the apartment into one more becoming a
great vassal entering the presence of his lord paramount.
Apparently the Duke had formed the internal resolution to
treat Louis, in the outset at least, with the formalities due
to his high station ; but at the same time it was evident
that, in doing so, he put no small constraint upon the fiery
impatience of his own disposition, and was scarce able to
control the feelings of resentment and the thirst of revenge
which boiled in his bosom. Hence, though he compelled
himself to use the outward acts, and in some degree the
language, of courtesy and reverence, his color came and went
rapidly ; his voice was abrupt, hoarse, and broken ; his limbs
shook, as if impatient of the curb imposed on his motions ;
he frowned and bit his lip until the blood came ; and every
look and movement showed that the most passionate prince
who ever lived was under the dominion of one of his most
violent paroxysms of fury.
The King marked this war of passion with a calm and un-

troubled eye ; for, though he gathered from the Duke's looks a foretaste of the bitterness of death, which he dreaded alike as a mortal and a sinful man, yet he was resolved, like a wary and skilful pilot, neither to suffer himself to be disconcerted by his own fears, nor to abandon the helm, while there was a chance of saving the vessel by adroit pilotage. Therefore, when the Duke, in a hoarse and broken tone, said something of the scarcity of his accommodations, he answered with a smile, that he could not complain, since he had as yet found Herbert's Tower a better residence than it had proved to one of his ancestors.

" They told you the tradition then ? " said Charles. " Yes ; here he was slain, but it was because he refused to take the cowl, and finish his days in a monastery."

" The more fool he," said Louis, affecting unconcern, " since he gained the torment of being a martyr without the merit of being a saint."

" I come," said the Duke, " to pray your Majesty to attend a high council, at which things of weight are to be deliberated upon concerning the welfare of France and Burgundy. You will presently meet them—that is, if such be your pleasure——"

" Nay, my fair cousin," said the King, " never strain courtesy so far as to entreat what you may so boldly command. To council, since such is your Grace's pleasure. We are somewhat shorn of our train," he added, looking upon the small suite that arranged themselves to attend him ; " but you, cousin, must shine out for us both."

Marshaled by Toison d'Or, chief of the heralds of Burgundy, the princes left the Earl Herbert's Tower and entered the castleyard, which Louis observed was filled with the Duke's body-guard and men-at-arms, splendidly accoutered and drawn up in martial array. Crossing the court, they entered the council-hall, which was in a much more modern part of the building than that of which Louis had been the tenant, and, though in disrepair, had been hastily arranged for the solemnity of a public council. Two chairs of state were erected under the same canopy, that for the King being raised two steps higher than the one which the Duke was to occupy ; about twenty of the chief nobility sat, arranged in due order, on either hand of the chair of state ; and thus, when both the princes were seated, the person for whose trial, as it might be called, the council was summoned, held the highest place, and appeared to preside in it.

It was perhaps to get rid of this inconsistency, and the

scruples which might have been inspired by it, that Duke Charles, having bowed slightly to the royal chair, bluntly opened the sitting with the following words :—

" My good vassals and counselors, it is not unknown to you what disturbances have arisen in our territories, both in our father's time and in our own, from the rebellion of vassals against superiors, and subjects against their princes. And lately we have had the most dreadful proof of the height to which these evils have arrived in our case by the scandalous flight of the Countess Isabelle of Croye, and her aunt the Lady Hameline, to take refuge with a foreign power, thereby renouncing their fealty to us and inferring the forfeiture of their fiefs ; and in another more dreadful and deplorable instance, by the sacrilegious and bloody murder of our beloved brother and ally the Bishop of Liege, and the rebellion of that treacherous city, which was but too mildly punished for the last insurrection. We have been informed that these sad events may be traced not merely to the inconstancy and folly of women and the presumption of pampered citizens, but to the agency of foreign power, and the interference of a mighty neighbor, from whom, if good deeds could merit any return in kind, Burgundy could have expected nothing but the most sincere and devoted friendship. If this should prove truth," said the Duke, setting his teeth and pressing his heel against the ground, " what consideration shall withhold us, the means being in our power, from taking such measures as shall effectually, and at the very source, close up the main spring from which these evils have yearly flowed on us ? "

The Duke had begun his speech with some calmness, but he elevated his voice at the conclusion ; and the last sentence was spoken in a tone which made all the counselors tremble, and brought a transient fit of paleness across the King's cheek. He instantly recalled his courage, however, and addressed the council in his turn, in a tone evincing so much ease and composure that the Duke, though he seemed desirous to interrupt or stop him, found no decent opportunity to do so.

" Nobles of France and of Burgundy," he said, " knights of the Holy Spirit and of the Golden Fleece, since a king must plead his cause as an accused person he cannot desire more distinguished judges than the flower of nobleness and muster and pride of chivalry. Our fair cousin of Burgundy hath but darkened the dispute between us in so far that his courtesy has declined to state it in precise terms. I, who have no cause for observing such delicacy, nay, whose condition permits me not to do so, crave leave to speak more precisely. It is to us, my lords—to us, his liege lord, his kinsman, his ally—that unhappy circumstances, perverting our cousin's clear judgment and better nature, have induced him to apply the hateful charges of seducing his vassals from their allegiance, stirring up the people of Liege to revolt, and stimulating the outlawed William de la Marck to commit a most cruel and sacrilegious murder. Nobles of France and Burgundy, I might truly appeal to the circumstances in which I now stand as being in themselves a complete contradiction of such an accusation; for is it to be supposed that, having the sense of a rational being left me, I should have thrown myself unreservedly into the power of the Duke of Burgundy, while I was practising treachery against him such as could not fail to be discovered, and which, being discovered, must place me, as I now stand, in the power of a justly exasperated prince ? The folly of one who should seat himself quietly down to repose on a mine, after he had lighted the match which was to cause instant explosion, would have been wisdom compared to mine. I have no doubt that, amongst the perpetrators of those horrible treasons at Schonwaldt, villains have been busy with my name ; but am I to be answerable, who have given them no right to use it ? If two silly women, disgusted on account of some romantic cause of displeasure, sought refuge at my court, does it follow that they did so by my direction ? It will be found, when inquired into, that, since honor and chivalry forbade my sending them back prisoners to the court of Burgundy, —which, I think, gentlemen, no one who wears the collar of these orders would suggest,—that I came as nearly as possible to the same point by placing them in the hands of the venerable father in God, who is now a saint in Heaven." Here Louis seemed much affected, and pressed his kerchief to his eyes. " In the hands, I say, of a member of my own family, and still more closely united with that of Burgundy, whose situation, exalted condition in the church, and, alas ! whose numerous virtues qualified him to be the protector of these unhappy wanderers for a little while, and the mediator betwixt them and their liege lord. I say, therefore, the only circumstances which seem, in my brother of Burgundy's hasty view of this subject, to argue unworthy suspicions against me are such as can be explained on the fairest and most honorable motives ; and I say, moreover, that no one particle of credible evidence can be brought to support the injurious charges which have induced my brother to alter his friendly looks towards one who came to him in full confidence of friendship, have caused him to turn his festive hall into a court of justice, and his hospitable apartments into a prison.*

"My lord—my lord," said Charles, breaking in so soon as the King paused, "for your being here at a time so unluckily coinciding with the execution of your projects, I can only account by supposing that those who make it their trade to impose on others do sometimes egregiously delude themselves. The engineer is sometimes killed by the springing of his own petard. For what is to follow, let it depend on the event of this solemn inquiry. Bring hither the Countess Isabelle of Croye!"

As the young lady was introduced, supported on the one side by the Countess of Crèvecœur, who had her husband's commands to that effect, and on the other by the abbess of the Ursuline convent, Charles exclaimed with his usual harshness of voice and manner, "Soh! sweet princess, you, who could scarce find breath to answer us when we last laid our just and reasonable commands on you, yet have had wind enough to run as long a course as ever did hunted doe, what think you of the fair work you have made between two great princes and two mighty countries, that have been like to go to war for your baby face?"

The publicity of the scene and the violence of Charles's manner totally overcame the resolution which Isabelle had formed of throwing herself at the Duke's feet, and imploring him to take possession of her estates and permit her to retire into a cloister. She stood motionless like a terrified female in a storm, who hears the thunder roll on every side of her, and apprehends in every fresh peal the bolt which is to strike her dead. The Countess of Crèvecœur, a woman of spirit equal to her birth, and to the beauty which she preserved even in her matronly years, judged it necessary to interfere. "My lord duke," she said, "my fair cousin is under my protection. I know better than your Grace how women should be treated, and we will leave this presence instantly, unless you use a tone and language more suitable to our rank and sex."

The Duke burst out into a laugh. "Crèvecœur," he said, "thy tameness hath made a lordly dame of thy countess; but that is no affair of mine. Give a seat to yonder simple girl, to whom, so far from feeling enmity, I design the highest grace and honor. Sit down, mistress, and tell us at your leisure what fiend possessed you to fly from your native country, and embrace the trade of a damsel adventurous."

With much pain, and not without several interruptions, Isabelle confessed that, being absolutely determined against a match proposed to her by the Duke of Burgundy, she had indulged the hope of obtaining protection of the court of France.

"And under protection of the French monarch," said Charles. "Of that, doubtless, you were well assured?"

"I did indeed so think myself assured," said the Countess Isabelle, "otherwise I had not taken a step so decided." Here Charles looked upon Louis with a smile of inexpressible bitterness, which the King supported with the utmost firmness, except that his lip grew something whiter than it was wont to be. "But my information concerning King Louis's intentions towards us," continued the countess, after a short pause, "was almost entirely derived from my unhappy aunt, the Lady Hameline, and her opinions were formed upon the assertions and insinuations of persons whom I have since discovered to be the vilest traitors and most faithless wretches in the world." She then stated, in brief terms, what she had since come to learn of the treachery of Marthon, and of Hayraddin Maugrabin, and added that "she entertained no doubt that the elder Maugrabin, called Zamet, the original adviser of their flight, was capable of every species of treachery, as well as of assuming the character of an agent of Louis without authority."

There was a pause while the countess had continued her story, which she prosecuted, though very briefly, from the time she left the territories of Burgundy, in company with her aunt, until the storming of Schonwaldt, and her final surrender to the Count Crèvecœur. All remained mute after she had finished her brief and broken narrative, and the Duke of Burgundy bent his fierce dark eyes on the ground, like one who seeks for a pretext to indulge his passion, but finds none sufficiently plausible to justify himself in his own eyes. "The mole," he said at length, looking upwards, "winds not his dark subterranean path beneath our feet the less certainly, that we, though conscious of his motions, cannot absolutely trace them. Yet I would know of King Louis, wherefore he maintained these ladies at his court, had they not gone thither by his own invitation."

"I did not so entertain them, fair cousin," answered the King. "Out of compassion, indeed, I received them in privacy, but took an early opportunity of placing them under the protection of the late excellent bishop, your own ally, and who was—may God assoil him !—a better judge that I, or any secular prince, how to reconcile the protection due to fugitives with the duty which the king owes to his ally from whose dominions they have fled. I boldly ask this young lady whether my reception of them was cordial or whether it was not, on the contrary, such as made them express regret that they had made my court their place of refuge !"

"So much was it otherwise than cordial," answered the countess, "that it induced me, at least, to doubt how far it was possible that your Majesty should have actually given the invitation of which we had been assured by those who called themselves our agents ; since, supposing them to have proceeded only as they were duly authorized, it would have been hard to reconcile your Majesty's conduct with that to be expected from a king, a knight, and a gentleman."

The countess turned her eyes to the King as she spoke, with a look which was probably intended as a reproach, but the breast of Louis was armed against all such artillery. On the contrary, waving slowly his expanded hands, and looking around the circle, he seemed to make a triumphant appeal to all present upon the testimony borne to his innocence in the countess's reply.

Burgundy, meanwhile, cast on him a look which seemed to say that, if in some degree silenced, he was as far as ever from being satisfied, and then said abruptly to the countess, "Methinks, fair mistress, in this account of your wanderings, you have forgot all mention of certain love-passages. So, ho ! blushing already? Certain knights of the forest, by whom your quiet was for a time interrupted. Well, that incident hath come to our ear, and something we may presently form out of it. Tell me, King Louis, were it not well, before this vagrant Helen of Troy, or of Croye, set more kings by the ears—were it not well to carve out a fitting match for her ? "

King Louis, though conscious what ungrateful proposal was likely to be made next, gave a calm and silent assent to what Charles said ; but the countess herself was restored to courage by the very extremity of her situation. She quitted the arm of the Countess of Crèvecœur, on which she had hitherto leaned, came forward timidly, yet with an air of dignity, and, kneeling before the Duke's throne, thus addressed him : "Noble Duke of Burgundy, and my liege lord, I acknowledge my fault in having withdrawn myself from your dominions without your gracious permission, and will most humbly acquiesce in any penalty you are pleased to impose. I place my lands and castles at your rightful disposal, and pray you only of your own bounty, and for the sake of my father's memory, to allow the last of the line of Croye, out of her large estate, such a moderate maintenance as may find her admission into a convent for the remainder of her life."

" What think you, sire, of the young person's petition to us ? " said the Duke,addressing Louis.

"As of a holy and humble motion," said the King, " which doubtless comes from that grace which ought not to be resisted or withstood."

" The humble and lowly shall be exalted," said Charles. "Arise, Countess Isabelle ; we mean better for you than you have devised for yourself. We mean neither to sequestrate your estate nor to abase your honors but on the contrary, will add largely to both."

"Alas ! my lord," said the countess, continuing on her knees, " it is even that well-meant goodness which I fear still more than your Grace's displeasure, since it compels me——"

" St. George of Burgundy ! " said Duke Charles, " is our will to be thwarted, and our commands disputed, at every turn ? Up, I say, minion, and withdraw for the present ; when we have time to think of thee, we will so order matters that, *Teste-St.-Gris !* you shall either obey us or do worse."

Notwithstanding this stern answer, the Countess Isabelle remained at his feet, and would probably, by her pertinacity, have driven him to say upon the spot something yet more severe, had not the Countess of Crèvecœur, who better knew that prince's humor, interfered to raise her young friend, and to conduct her from the hall.

Quentin Durward was now summoned to appear, and presented himself before the King and Duke with that freedom, distant alike from bashful reserve and intrusive boldness, which becomes a youth at once well-born and well-nurtured, who gives honor where it is due, but without permitting himself to be dazzled or confused by the presence of those to whom it is to be rendered. His uncle had furnished him with the means of again equipping himself in the arms and dress of an archer of the Scottish Guard, and his complexion, mien, and air suited in an uncommon degree his splendid appearance. His extreme youth, too, prepossessed the coun-

selors in his favor, the rather that no one could easily believe
that the sagacious Louis would have chosen so very young a
person to be the confidant of political intrigues ; and thus the
King enjoyed, in this as in other cases, considerable advantage from his singular choice of agents, both as to age and
rank, where such election seemed least likely to be made.
At the command of the Duke, sanctioned by that of Louis,
Quentin commenced an account of his journey with the
Ladies of Croye to the neighborhood of Liege, premising a
statement of King Louis's instructions, which were that he
should escort them safely to the castle of the bishop.

" And you obeyed my orders accordingly ? " said the
King.

" I did, sire," replied the Scot.

" You omit a circumstance," said the Duke, " You were
set upon in the forest by two wandering knights."

" It does not become me to remember or to proclaim such
an incident," said the youth, blushing ingenuously.

" But it doth not become *me* to forget it," said the Duke
of Orleans. " This youth discharged his commission manfully, and maintained his trust in a manner that I shall long
remember. Come to my apartment, archer, when this
matter is over, and thou shalt find I have not forgot thy
brave bearing, while I am glad to see it is equalled by thy
modesty."

" And come to mine," said Dunois. " I have a helmet
for thee, since I think I owe thee one."

Quentin bowed low to both, and the examination was
resumed. At the command of Duke Charles, he produced
the written instructions which he had received for the direction of his journey.

" Did you follow these instructions literally, soldier ? "
said the Duke.

" No, if it please your Grace," replied Quentin. " They
directed me, as you may be pleased to observe, to cross the
Maes near Namur ; whereas I kept the left bank, as being
both the nigher and the safer road to Liege."

" And wherefore that alteration ? " said the Duke.

" Because I began to suspect the fidelity of my guide,"
answered Quentin.

" Now mark the questions I have next to ask thee," said
the Duke. " Reply truly to them, and fear nothing from
the resentment of any one. But if you palter or double in
your answers, I will have thee hung alive in an iron chain
from the steeple of the market-house, where thou shalt

wish for death for many an hour ere he come to relieve you !"

There was a deep silence ensued. At length, having given the youth time, as he thought, to consider the circumstances in which he was placed, the Duke demanded to know of Durward who his guide was, by whom supplied, and wherefore he had been led to entertain suspicion of him ? To the first of these questions Quentin Durward answered by naming Hayraddin Maugrabin, the Bohemian ; to the second, that the guide had been recommended by Tristan l'Hermite ; and in reply to the third point, he mentioned what had happened in the Franciscan convent, near Namur ; how the Bohemian had been expelled from the holy house, and how, jealous of his behavior, he had dogged him to a rendezvous with one of William de la Marck's lanzknechts, where he overheard them arrange a plan for surprising the ladies who were under his protection.

" Now, hark thee," said the Duke, " and once more remember thy life depends on thy veracity ; did these villains mention their having this king's—I mean this very King Louis of France's—authority for their scheme of surprising the escort and carrying away the ladies ?"

" If such infamous fellows had said so," replied Quentin, " I know not how I should have believed them, having the word of the King himself to place in opposition to theirs."

Louis, who had listened hitherto with most earnest attention, could not help drawing his breath deeply when he heard Durward's answer, in the manner of one from whose bosom a heavy weight has been at once removed. The Duke again looked disconcerted and moody ; and, returning to the charge, questioned Quentin still more closely, "Whether he did not understand, from these men's private conversation, that the plots which they meditated had King Louis's sanction ?"

" I repeat that I heard nothing which could authorize me to say so," answered the young man, who, though internally convinced of the King's accession to the treachery of Hayraddin, yet held it contrary to his allegiance to bring forward his own suspicions on the subject ; "and if I *had* heard such men make such an assertion, I again say that I would not have given their testimony weight against the instructions of the King himself."

" Thou art a faithful messenger," said the Duke, with a sneer ; and I venture to say that, in obeying the King's instructions, thou hast disappointed his expectations in a manner that thou mightst have smarted for, but that subsequent events have made thy bull-headed fidelity seem like good service."

" I understand you not, my lord," said Quentin Durward ; "all I know is, that my master King Louis sent me to protect these ladies, and that I did so accordingly, to the extent of my ability, both in the journey to Schonwaldt and through the subsequent scenes which took place. I understood the instructions of the King to be honorable, and I executed them honorably ; had they been of a different tenor, they would not have suited one of my name or nation."

" *Fier comme un Ecossois,*" said Charles, who, however disappointed at the tenor of Durward's reply, was not unjust enough to blame him for his boldness. " But hark thee, archer, what instructions were those which made thee, as some sad fugitives from Schonwaldt have informed us, parade the streets of Liege, at the head of those mutineers who afterwards cruelly murdered their temporal prince and spiritual father? And what harangue was it which thou didst make after that murder was committed, in which you took upon you, as agent for Louis, to assume authority among the villains who had just perpetrated so great a crime ? "

" My lord," said Quentin, " there are many who could testify that I assumed not the character of an envoy of France in the town of Liege, but had it fixed upon me by the obstinate clamors of the people themselves, who refused to give credit to any disclamation which I could make. This I told to those in the service of the bishop when I had made my escape from the city, and recommended their attention to the security of the castle, which might have prevented the calamity and horror of the succeeding night. It is, no doubt, true that I did, in the extremity of danger, avail myself of the influence which my imputed character gave me, to save the Countess Isabelle, to protect my own life, and, so far as I could, to rein in the humor for slaughter, which had already broke out in so dreadful an instance. I repeat, and will maintain it with my body, that I had no commission of any kind from the King of France respecting the people of Liege, far less instructions to instigate them to mutiny ; and that, finally, when I did avail myself of that imputed character, it was as if I had snatched up a shield to protect myself in a moment of emergency, and used it, as I should surely have done, for the defense of myself and others, without inquiring whether I had a right to the heraldic emblazonments which it displayed."

"And therein my young companion and prisoner," said Crèvecœur, unable any longer to remain silent, "acted with equal spirit and good sense ; and his doing so cannot justly be imputed as blame to King Louis."

There was a murmur of assent among the surrounding nobility which sounded joyfully in the ears of King Louis, whilst it gave no little offense to Charles. He rolled his eyes angrily around ; and the sentiments, so generally expressed by so many of his highest vassals and wisest counselors, would not perhaps have prevented his giving way to his violent and despotic temper, had not Des Comines, who foresaw the danger, prevented it by suddenly announcing a herald from the city of Liege.

"A herald from weavers and nailers ? " exclaimed the Duke, " but admit him instantly. By Our Lady, I will learn from this same herald something further of his employers' hopes and projects than this young French-Scottish man-at-arms seems desirous to tell me !"

CHAPTER XXXIII

THE HERALD

Ariel. —— Hark ! they roar,
Prospero. Let them be hunted soundly,

The Tempest.

THERE was room made in the assembly, and no small curiosity evinced by those present to see the herald whom the insurgent Liegeois had ventured to send to so haughty a prince as the Duke of Burgundy, while in such high indignation against them. For it must be remembered that at this period heralds were only despatched from sovereign princes to each other upon solemn occasions ; and that the inferior nobility employed pursuivants, a lower rank of officers-at-arms. It may be also noticed in passing, that Louis XI., an habitual derider of whatever did not promise real power or substantial advantage, was in especial a professed contemner of heralds and heraldry, " red, blue, and green, with all their trumpery," * to which the pride of his rival Charles, which was of a very different kind, attached no small degree of ceremonious importance.

The herald, who was now introduced into the presence of the monarchs, was dressed in a tabard, or coat, embroidered with the arms of his master, in which the boar's head made a distinguished appearance, in blazonry which, in the opinion of the skilful, was more showy than accurate. The rest of his dress—a dress always sufficiently tawdry—was overcharged with lace, embroidery, and ornament of every kind ; and the plume of feathers which he wore was so high, as if intended to sweep the roof of the hall. In short, the usual gaudy splendor of the heraldic attire was caricatured and overdone. The boar's head was not only repeated on every part of his dress, but even his bonnet was formed into that shape, and it was represented with gory tongue and bloody tusks, or, in proper language, " langued and dentated gules "; and there was something in the man's appearance which seemed to imply a mixture of boldness and apprehension,

---

*For a remarkable instance of this, see Disguised Herald. Note 46.

like one who has undertaken a dangerous commission, and is
sensible that audacity alone can carry him through it with
safety. Something of the same mixture of fear and effrontery
was visible in the manner in which he paid his respects, and
he showed also a grotesque awkwardness, not usual amongst
those who were accustomed to be received in the presence of
princes.

" Who art thou, in the devil's name ? " was the greeting
with which Charles the Bold received this singular envoy.

" I am Rouge Sanglier," answered the herald, " the officer-
at-arms of William de la Marck, by the grace of God and the
election of the chapter Prince Bishop of Liege——"

" Ha ! " exclaimed Charles ; but, as if subduing his own
passion, he made a sign to him to proceed.

" And, in right of his wife, the Honorable Countess Hameline of Croye, Count of Croye and Lord Bracquemont."

The utter astonishment of Duke Charles at the extremity
of boldness with which these titles were announced in his
presence seemed to strike him dumb ; and the herald, conceiving, doubtless, that he had made a suitable impression
by the annunciation of his character, proceeded to state his
errand.

"*Annuncio vobis gaudium magnum*," he said ; " I let you,
Charles of Burgundy and Earl of Flanders, to know, in my
master's name, that under favor of a dispensation of our Holy
Father of Rome, presently expected, and appointing a fitting
substitute *ad sacra*, he proposes to exercise at once the office
of Prince Bishop, and maintain the rights of Count of
Croye."

The Duke of Burgundy, at this and other pauses in the
herald's speech, only ejaculated, " Ha ! " or some similar
interjection, without making any answer ; and the tone of
exclamation was that of one who, though surprised and
moved, is willing to hear all that is to be said ere he commits
himself by making an answer. To the further astonishment
of all who were present he forbore from his usual abrupt and
violent gesticulations, remaining with the nail of his thumb
pressed against his teeth, which was his favorite attitude
when giving attention, and keeping his eyes bent on the
ground as if unwilling to betray the passion which might
gleam in them.

The envoy, therefore, proceeded boldly and unabashed in
the delivery of his message. " In the name, therefore, of
the Prince Bishop of Liege and Count of Croye, I am to require of you, Duke Charles, to desist from those pretensions

25

and encroachments which you have made on the free and imperial city of Liege, by connivance with the late Louis of Bourbon, unworthy bishop thereof."

" Ha ! " again exclaimed the Duke.

" Also to restore the banners of the community, which you took violently from the town, to the number of six-and-thirty, to rebuild the breaches in their walls, and restore the fortifications which you tyrannically dismantled, and to acknowledge my master, William de la Marck, as Prince Bishop, lawfully elected in a free chapter of canons, of which behold the *procès-verbal*."

" Have you finished ? " said the Duke.

" Not yet," replied the envoy : " I am further to require your Grace, on the part of the said right noble and venerable prince, bishop, and count, that you do presently withdraw the garrison from the Castle of Bracquemont, and other places of strength, belonging to the earldom of Croye, which have been placed there, whether in your own most gracious name, or in that of Isabelle, calling herself Countess of Croye, or any other, until it shall be decided by the Imperial Diet whether the fiefs in question shall not pertain to the sister of the late count, my most gracious Lady Hameline, rather than to his daughter, in respect of the *jus emphyteusis*."

" Your master is most learned," replied the Duke.

" Yet," continued the herald, " the noble and venerable prince and count will be disposed, all other disputes betwixt Burgundy and Liege being settled, to fix upon the Lady Isabelle such an appanage as may become her quality."

" He is generous and considerate," said the Duke, in the same tone.

" Now, by a poor fool's conscience," said Le Glorieux apart to the Count of Crèvecœur, " I would rather be in the worst cow's hide that ever died of the murrain than in that fellow's painted coat ! The poor man goes on like drunkards, who only look to the other pot, and not to the score which mine host chalks up behind the lattice."

" Have you yet done ? " said the Duke to the herald.

" One word more," answered Rouge Sanglier, " from my noble and venerable lord aforesaid, respecting his worthy and trusty ally, the Most Christian King——"

" Ha ! " exclaimed the Duke, starting, and in a fiercer tone than he had yet used ; but checking himself, he instantly composed himself again to attention.

" Which Most Christian King's royal person it is rumored

that you, Charles of Burgundy, have placed under restraint, contrary to your duty as a vassal of the crown of France, and to the faith observed among Christian sovereigns ; for which reason, my said noble and venerable master, by my mouth, charges you to put his Royal and Most Christian ally forthwith at freedom, or to receive the defiance which I am authorized to pronounce to you."

" Have you yet done ?" said the Duke.

" I have," answered the herald, " and await your Grace's answer, trusting it may be such as will save the effusion of Christian blood."

" Now, by St. George of Burgundy——" said the Duke ; but ere he could proceed further, Louis arose, and struck in with a tone of so much dignity and authority that Charles could not interrupt him.

" Under your favor, fair cousin of Burgundy," said the King ; " we ourselves crave priority of voice to replying to this insolent fellow. Sirrah herald, or whatever thou art, carry back notice to the perjured outlaw and murderer, William de la Marck, that the King of France will be presently before Liege, for the purpose of punishing the sacrilegious murderer of his late beloved kinsman, Louis of Bourbon ; and that he proposes to gibbet De la Marck alive, for the insolence of terming himself his ally, and putting his royal name into the mouth of one of his own base messengers."

" Add whatever else on my part," said Charles, " which it may not misbecome a prince to send to a common thief and murderer. And begone ! Yet stay. Never herald went from the court of Burgundy without having cause to cry, ' Largesse ! ' Let him be scourged till the bones are laid bare ! "

" Nay, but if it please your Grace," said Crèvecœur and D'Hymbercourt together, " he is a herald, and so far privileged."

" It is you, messires," replied the Duke, " who are such owls as to think that the tabard makes the herald. I see by that fellow's blazoning he is a mere impostor. Let Toison d'Or step forward, and question him in your presence."

In spite of his natural effrontery, the envoy of the Wild Boar of Ardennes now became pale, and that notwithstanding some touches of paint with which he had adorned his countenance. Toison d'Or, the chief herald, as we have elsewhere said, of the Duke, and king-at-arms within his dominions, stepped forward with the solemnity of one who knew what was due to his office, and asked his supposed brother in what college he had studied the science which he professed.

"I was bred a pursuivant at the Heraldic College of Ratisbon," answered Rouge Sanglier, "and received the diploma of *ehrenhold* from that same learned fraternity."

"You could not derive it from a source more worthy," answered Toison d'Or, bowing still lower than he had done before ; "and if I presume to confer with you on the mysteries of our sublime science, in obedience to the orders of the most gracious Duke, it is not in hopes of giving, but of receiving, knowledge."

"Go to," said the Duke, impatiently. "Leave off ceremony, and ask him some question that may try his skill."

"It were injustice to ask a disciple of the worthy College of Arms at Retisbon if he comprehendeth the common terms of blazonry," said Toison d'Or ; "but I may, without offense, crave of Rouge Sanglier to say if he is instructed in the more mysterious and secret terms of the science, by which the more learned do emblematically, and as it were parabolically express to each other what is conveyed to others in the ordinary language, taught in the very accidence as it were of heraldry ?"

"I understand one sort of blazonry as well as another," answered Rouge Sanglier, boldly ; "but it may be we have not the same terms in Germany which you have here in Flanders."

"Alas, that you will say so !" replied Toison d'Or ; "our noble science, which is indeed the very banner of nobleness and glory of generosity, being the same in all Christian countries, nay, known and acknowledged even by the Saracens and Moors. I would, therefore, pray of you to describe what coat you will after the celestial fashion, that is, by the planets."

"Blazon it yourself as you will," said Rouge Sanglier ; 'I will do no such apish tricks upon commandment, as an ape is made to come aloft."

"Show him a coat, and let him blazon it his own way," said the Duke ; "and if he fails, I promise him that his back shall be gules, azure, and sable."

"Here," said the herald of Burgundy, taking from his pouch a piece of parchment, "is a scroll, in which certain considerations led me to prick down, after my own poor fashion, an ancient coat. I will pray my brother, if indeed he belong to the honorable College of Arms at Ratisbon, to decipher it in fitting language."

Le Glorieux, who seemed to take great pleasure in this discussion, had by this time bustled himself close up to the two
heralds. "I will help thee, good fellow," said he to Rouge
Sanglier, as he looked hopelessly upon the scroll. "This,
my lords and masters, represents the cat looking out at the
dairy window."

This sally occasioned a laugh, which was something to the
advantage of Rouge Sanglier, as it led Toison d'Or, indignant
at the misconstruction of his drawing, to explain it as the
coat-of-arms assumed by Childebert, King of France, after
he had taken prisoner Gondemar, King of Burgundy; representing an ounce, or tiger-cat, the emblem of the captive
prince, behind a grating, or, as Toison d'Or technically defined it, "Sable, a musion passant or, oppressed with a trellis
gules, cloué of the second."

"By my bauble," said Le Glorieux, "if the cat resemble
Burgundy, she has the right side of the grating nowadays."

"True, good fellow," said Louis, laughing, while the rest
of the presence, and even Charles himself, seemed disconcerted at so broad a jest--"I owe thee a piece of gold for
turning something that looked like sad earnest into the merry
game which I trust it will end in."

"Silence, Le Glorieux," said the Duke; "and you, Toison d'Or, who are too learned to be intelligible, stand back;
and bring that rascal forward, some of you. Hark ye, villain," he said, in his harshest tone, "do you know the difference between argent and or, except in the shape of coined
money?"

"For pity's sake, your Grace, be good unto me! Noble
King Louis, speak for me!"

"Speak for thyself," said the Duke. "In a word, art thou
herald or not?"

"Only, for this occasion!" acknowledged the detected
official.

"Now, by St. George!" said the Duke, eyeing Louis askance, "we know no king—no gentleman—save *one*, who
would have so prostituted the noble science on which royalty
and gentry rest, save that king, who sent to Edward of England a serving man disguised as a herald." *

"Such a stratagem," said Louis, laughing or affecting to
laugh, "could only be justified at a court where no heralds
were at the time, and when the emergency was urgent. But,
though it might have passed on the blunt and thick-witted
islander, no one with brains a whit better than those of a wild

* See Note 46.

boar would have thought of passing such a trick upon the
accomplished court of Burgundy."

"Send him who will," said the Duke, fiercely, "he shall
return on their hands in poor case. Here !—drag him to
the market-place—slash him with bridle-reins and dog-whips
until the tabard hang about him in tatters ! Upon the
Rouge Sanglier !—ça—ça ! Haloo, haloo !"

Four or five large hounds, such as are painted in the hunt-
ing-pieces upon which Rubens and Schneiders labored in
conjunction, caught the well-known notes with which the
Duke concluded, and began to yell and bay as if the boar
were just roused from his lair.

"By the rood !" said King Louis, observant to catch the
vein of his dangerous cousin, " since the ass has put on the
boar's hide, I would set the dogs on him to bait him out of
it !"

"Right—right !" exclaimed Duke Charles, the fancy exactly chiming in with his humor at the moment—" it shall
be done ! Uncouple the hounds ! Hyke a Talbot ! hyke a
Beaumont ! We will course him from the door of the castle
to the east gate."

" I trust your Grace will treat me as a beast of chase," said
the fellow, putting the best face he could upon the matter,
" and allow me a fair law ?"

"Thou art but vermin," said the Duke, " and entitled to
no law, by the letter of the book of hunting ; nevertheless
thou shalt have sixty yards in advance, were it but for the
sake of thy unparalleled impudence. Away—away, sirs ! we
will see this sport." And the council breaking up tumult-
uously, all hurried, none faster than the two princes, to enjoy
the humane pastime which King Louis had suggested.

The Rouge Sanglier showed excellent sport ; for, winged
with terror, and having half a score of fierce boar-hounds
hard at his haunches, encouraged by the blowing of horns
and the woodland cheer of the hunters, he flew like the very
wind, and had he not been encumbered with his herald's
coat (the worst possible habit for a runner), he might fairly
have escaped dog-free ; he also doubled once or twice, in a
manner much approved of by the spectators. None of these,
nay, not even Charles himself, was so delighted with the
sport as King Louis, who, partly from political considerations, and partly as being naturally pleased with the sight of
human suffering when ludicrously exhibited, laughed till the
tears ran from his eyes, and in his ecstasies of rapture caught
hold of the Duke's ermine cloak, as if to support himself ;

whilst the Duke, no less delighted, flung his arm around the King's shoulder, making thus an exhibition of confidential sympathy and familiarity very much at variance with the terms on which they had so lately stood together.

At length the speed of the pseudo-herald could save him no longer from the fangs of his pursuers : they seized him, pulled him down, and would probably soon have throttled him, had not the Duke called out—"Stave and tail !—stave and tail !" Take them off him ! He hath shown so good a course that, though he has made no sport at bay, we will not have him despatched."

Several officers accordingly busied themselves in taking off the dogs ; and they were soon seen coupling some up, and pursuing others which ran through the streets, shaking in sport and triumph the tattered fragments of painted cloth and embroidery rent from the tabard, which the unfortunate wearer had put on in an unlucky hour.

At this moment, and while the Duke was too much engaged with what passed before him to mind what was said behind him, Oliver le Dain, gliding behind King Louis whispered into his ear—"It is the Bohemian, Hyraddin Maugrabin. It were not well he should come to speech of the Duke."

"He must die," answered Louis in the same tone ; "dead men tell no tales."

One instant afterwards, Tristan l'Hermite, to whom Oliver had given the hint, stepped forward before the King and the Duke, and said, in his blunt manner, "So please your Majesty and your Grace, this piece of game is mine, and I claim him ; he is marked with my stamp: the *fleur-de-lys* is branded on his shoulder, as all men may see. He is a known villain, and hath slain the King's subjects, robbed churches, deflowered virgins, slain deer in the royal park——"

"Enough—enough," said Duke Charles ; "he is my royal cousin's property by many a good title. What will your Majesty do with him ?"

"If he is left to my diposal," said the King. "I will at least give him one lesson in the science of heraldry, in which he is so ignorant—only explain to him practically the meaning of a cross *potence,* with a noose dangling proper."

"Not as to be by him borne, but as to bear him. Let him take the degrees under your gossip Tristan ; he is a deep professor in such mysteries."

Thus answered the Duke, with a burst of discordant laughter at his own wit, which was so cordially chorussed by

Louis that his rival could not help looking kindly at him, while he said—

"Ah, Louis—Louis! would to God thou wert as faithful a monarch as thou art a merry companion! I cannot but think often of the jovial time we used to spend together."

"You may bring it back when you will," said Louis: "I will grant you as fair terms as for very shame's sake you ought to ask in my present condition, without making yourself the fable of Christendom; and I will swear to observe them upon the holy relique which I have ever the grace to bear about my person, being a fragment of the true cross."

Here he took a small golden reliquary, which was suspended from his neck next to his shirt by a chain of the same metal, and having kissed it devoutly, continued—

"Never was false oath sworn on this most sacred relique but it was avenged within the year."

"Yet," said the Duke, "it was the same on which you swore amity to me when you left Burgundy, and shortly after sent the Bastard of Rubempré to murder or kidnap me."

"Nay, gracious cousin, now you are ripping up ancient grievances," said the King; "I promise you that you were deceived in that matter. Moreover, it was not upon *this* relique which I then swore, but upon another fragment of the true cross which I got from the Grand Seignior, weakened in virtue, doubtless, by sojourning with infidels. Besides, did not the war of the 'public good' break out within the year; and was not a Burgundian army encamped at St. Denis, backed by all the great feudatories of France; and was I not obliged to yield up Normandy to my brother? O God, shield us from perjury on such a warrant as this!"

"Well, cousin," answered the Duke, "I do believe thou hadst a lesson to keep faith another time. And now for once, without finesse and doubling, will you make good your promise, and go with me to punish this murdering La Marck and the Liegeois?"

"I will march against them," said Louis, "with the ban and arrière-ban of France, and the oriflamme displayed."

"Nay—nay," said the Duke, "that is more than is needful, or maybe advisable. The presence of your Scottish Guard and two hundred choice lances will serve to show that you are a free agent. A large army might——"

"Make me so in effect, you would say, my fair cousin?" said the King. "Well, you shall dictate the numbers of my attendants."

"And to put this fair cause of mischief out of the way,

you will agree to the Countess Isabelle of Croye wedding with the Duke of Orleans ? "

" Fair cousin," said the King, " you drive my courtesy to extremity. The duke is the betrothed bridegroom of my daughter Joan. Be generous—yield up this matter, and let us speak rather of the towns on the Somme."

" My council will talk to your Majesty of these," said Charles ; " I myself have less at heart the acquisition of territory than the redress of injuries. You have tampered with my vassals, and your royal pleasure must needs dispose of the hand of a ward of Burgundy. Your Majesty must bestow it within the pale of your own royal family, since you have meddled with it ; otherwise, our conference breaks off."

" Were I to say I did this willingly," said the King, " no one would believe me ; therefore do you, my fair cousin, judge of the extent of my wish to oblige you when I say, most reluctantly, that the parties consenting, and a dispensation from the Pope being obtained, my own objections shall be no bar to this match which you propose."

" All besides can be easily settled by our ministers," said the Duke, " and we are once more cousins and friends."

" May Heaven be praised ! " said Louis, " who, holding in his hand the hearts of princes, doth mercifully incline them to peace and clemency, and prevent the effusion of human blood. Oliver," he added apart to that favorite, who ever waited around him like the familiar beside a socerer, " hark thee—tell Tristan to be speedy in dealing with yonder runagate Bohemian."

CHAPTER XXXIV

THE EXECUTION

I'll take thee to the good green wood,
And make thine own hand choose the tree.
Old Ballad.

"Now God be praised that gave us the power of laughing and making others laugh, and shame to the dull cur who scorns the office of a jester! Here is a joke, and that none of the brightest, though it may pass, since it has amused two princes, which hath gone farther than a thousand reasons of state to prevent a war between France and Burgundy."

Such was the inference of Le Glorieux when, in consequence of the reconciliation of which we gave the particulars in the last chapter, the Burgundian guards were withdrawn from the Castle of Péronne, the abode of the King removed from the ominous Tower of Count Herbert, and, to the great joy both of French and Burgundians, an outward show at least of confidence and friendship seemed so established between Duke Charles and his liege lord. Yet still the latter, though treated with ceremonial observance, was sufficiently aware that he continued to be the object of suspicion, though he prudently affected to overlook it, and appeared to consider himself entirely at his ease.

Meanwhile, as frequently happens in such cases, whilst the principal parties concerned had so far made up their differences, one of the subaltern agents concerned in their intrigues was bitterly experiencing the truth of the political maxim, that if the great have frequent need of base tools, they make amends to society by abandoning them to their fate so soon as they find them no longer useful.

This was Hayraddin Maugrabin, who, surrendered by the Duke's officers to the King's provost-marshal, was by him placed in the hands of his two trusty aides-de-camp, Trois-Eschelles and Petit-André, to be despatched without loss of time. One on either side of him, and followed by a few guards and a multitude of rabble—this playing the *allegro,* that the *penseroso*—he was marched off (to use a modern comparison, like Garrick between Tragedy and Comedy) to the neighboring forest; where, to save all further trouble and ceremonial of a gibbet and so forth, the disposers of his fate proposed to knit him up to the first sufficient tree.

They were not long in finding an oak, as Petit-André facetiously expressed it, fit to bear such an acorn; and placing the wretched criminal on a bank, under a sufficient guard, they began their extemporaneous preparations for the final catastrophe. At that moment Hayraddin, gazing on the crowd, encountered the eyes of Quentin Durward, who, thinking he recognized the countenance of his faithless guide in that of the detected impostor, had followed with the crowd to witness the execution, and assure himself of the identity.

When the executioners informed him that all was ready, Hayraddin, with much calmness, asked a single boon at their hands.

" Anything, my son, consistent with our office," said Trois-Eschelles.

" That is," said Hayraddin, " anything but my life."

" Even so," said Trois-Eschelles, " and something more; for as you seem resolved to do credit to our mystery, and die like a man, without making wry mouths—why, though our orders are to be prompt, I care not if I indulge you ten minutes longer."

" You are even too generous," said Hayraddin.

" Truly we may be blamed for it," said Petit-André; " but what of that? I could consent almost to give my life for such a jerry-come-tumble, such a smart, tight, firm lad, who proposes to come from aloft with a grace, as an honest fellow should do."

" So that if you want a confessor," said Trois-Eschelles——

" Or a *lire* of wine," said his facetious companion——

" Or a psalm," said Tragedy——

" Or a song," said Comedy——

" Neither, my good, kind, and most expeditious friends," said the Bohemian; " I only pray to speak a few minutes with yonder archer of the Scottish Guard."

The executioners hesitated a moment; but Trois-Eschelles recollecting that Quentin Durward was believed, from various circumstances, to stand high in the favor of their master, King Louis, they resolved to permit the interview.

When Quentin, at their summons, approached the condemned criminal, he could not but be shocked at his appearance, however justly his doom might have been deserved. The remnants of his heraldic finery, rent to tatters by the fangs of the dogs, and the clutches of the bipeds who had rescued him from their fury to lead him to the gallows, gave him at once a ludicrous and a wretched appearance. His face was discolored with paint, and with some remnants of a fictitious beard, assumed for the purpose of disguise, and there was the paleness of death upon his cheek and upon his lip; yet, strong in passive courage, like most of his tribe, his eye, while it glistened and wandered, as well as the contorted smile of his mouth, seemed to bid defiance to the death he was about to die.

Quentin was struck partly with horror, partly with compassion, as he approached the miserable man, and these feelings probably betrayed themselves in his manner, for Petit-André called out, "Trip it more smartly, jolly archer this gentleman's leisure cannot wait for you, if you walk as if the pebbles were eggs, and you afraid of breaking them."

"I must speak with him in privacy," said the criminal, despair seeming to croak in his accent as he uttered the words.

"That may hardly consist with our office, my merry leap-the-ladder, said Petit-André; "we know you for a slippery eel of old."

"I am tied with your horse-girths, hand and foot," said the criminal. "You may keep guard around me, though out of earshot; the archer is your own King's servant. And if I give you ten guilders——"

"Laid out in masses, the sum may profit his poor soul," said Trois-Eschelles.

"Laid out in wine or *brantwein*, it will comfort my poor body," responded Petit-André. "So let them be forthcoming, my little crack-rope."

"Pay the bloodhounds their fee," said Hayraddin to Durward; "I was plundered of every stiver when they took me; it shall avail thee much."

Quentin paid the executioners their guerdon, and, like men of promise, they retreated out of hearing—keeping, however, a careful eye on the criminal's motions. After waiting an instant till the unhappy man should speak, as he still remained silent, Quentin at length addressed him, "And to this conclusion thou hast at length arrived?"

"Ay," answered Hayraddin, "it required neither astrologer, nor physiognomist, nor chiromantist, to foretell that I should follow the destiny of my family."

"Brought to this early end by thy long course of crime and treachery!" said the Scot.

"No, by the bright Alde aran and all his brother twinklers!" answered the Bohe i ian. "I am brought hither by my folly, in believing that the bloodthirsty cruelty of a Frank could be restrained even by what they themselves profess to hold most sacred. A priest's vestment would have been no safer garb for me than a herald's tabard, however sanctimonious are your professions of devotion and chivalry."

"A detected impostor has no right to claim the immunities of the disguise he had usurped," said Durward.

"Detected!" said the Bohemian. "My jargon was as much to the purpose as yonder old fool of a herald's; but let it pass. As well now as hereafter."

"You abuse time," said Quentin. "If you have aught to tell me, say it quickly, and then take some care of your soul."

"Of my soul!" said the Bohemian, with a hideous laugh. "Think ye a leprosy of twenty years can be cured in an instant? If I have a soul, it hath been in such a course since I was ten years old and more, that it would take me one month to recall all my crimes, and another to tell the priest; and were such space granted me, it is five to one I would employ it otherwise."

"Hardened wretch, blaspheme not! Tell me what thou hast to say, and I leave thee to thy fate," said Durward, with mingled pity and horror.

"I have a boon to ask," said Hayraddin, "but first I will buy it of you; for your tribe, with all their professions of charity, give nought for nought."

"I could wellnigh say 'Thy gift perish with thee,'" answered Quentin, "but that thou art on the very verge of eternity. Ask thy boon; reserve thy bounty, it can do me no good. I remember enough of your good offices of old."

"Why, I loved you," said Hayraddin, "for the matter that chanced on the banks of the Cher; and I would have helped you to a wealthy dame. You wore her scarf, which partly misled me; and indeed I thought that Hameline, with her portable wealth, was more for your market-penny than the other hen-sparrow, with her old roots at Bracquemont, which Charles has clutched, and is likely to keep his claws upon."

"Talk not so idly, unhappy man," said Quentin; "yonder officers become impatient."

"Give them ten guilders for ten minutes more," said the culprit, who, like most in his situation, mixed with his hardihood a desire of procrastinating his fate; "I tell thee it shall avail thee much."

"Use then well the minutes so purchased," said Durward, and easily made a new bargain with the marshal's-men.

This done, Hayraddin continued : "Yes, I assure you I meant you well ; and Hameline would have proved an easy and convenient spouse. Why, she has reconciled herself even with the Boar of Ardennes, though his mode of wooing was somewhat of the roughest, and lords it yonder in his sty, as if she had fed on mast-husks and acorns all her life."

"Cease this brutal and untimely jesting," said Quentin, "or, once more I tell you, I will leave you to your fate."

"You are right" said Hayraddin, after a moment's pause ; "what cannot be postponed must be faced ! Well, know then, I came hither in this accursed disguise, moved by a great reward from De la Marck, and hoping a yet mightier one from King Louis, not merely to bear the message of defiance which you may have heard of, but to tell the King an important secret."

"It was a fearful risk," said Durward.

"It was paid for as such, and such it hath proved," answered the Bohemian. "De la Marck attempted before to communicate with Louis by means of Marthon ; but she could not, it seems, approach nearer to him than the astrologer, to whom she told all the passages of the journey, and of Schonwaldt ; but it is a chance if her tidings ever reach Louis, except in the shape of a prophecy. But hear my secret, which is more important than aught she could tell. William de la Marck has assembled a numerous and strong force within the city of Liege, and augments it daily by means of the old priest's treasures. But he proposes not to hazard a battle with the chivalry of Burgundy, and still less to stand a siege in the dismantled town. This he will do : he will suffer the hot-brained Charles to sit down before the place without opposition, and in the night, make an outfall or sally upon the leaguer with his whole force. Many he will have in French armor, who will cry 'France,' 'St. Louis,' and 'Denis Montjoye,' as if there were a strong body of French auxiliaries in the city. This cannot choose but strike utter confusion among the Burgundians ; and if King Louis, with his guards, attendants, and such soldiers as he may have with him, shall second his efforts, the Boar of Ardennes nothing doubts the discomfiture of the whole Burgundian army. There is my secret, and I bequeath it to you. Forward, or prevent the enterprise—sell the intelli-

gence to King Louis or to Duke Charles, I care not. Save
or destroy whom thou wilt ; for my part, I only grieve that
I cannot spring it like a mine, to the destruction of them
all ! "

" It is indeed an important secret," said Quentin, instantly
comprehending how easily the national jealousy might be
awakened in a camp consisting partly of French, partly of
Burgundians.

" Ay, so it is," answered Hayraddin ; " and, now you have
it, you would fain begone, and leave me without granting
the boon for which I have paid beforehand."

" Tell me thy request," said Quentin ; " I will grant it if
it be in my power."

" Nay, it is no mighty demand : it is only in behalf of poor
Klepper, my palfrey, the only living thing that may miss
me. A due mile south you will find him feeding by a deserted collier's hut ; whistle to him thus (he whistled a
peculiar note), and call him by his name, Klepper, he will
come to you ; here is his bridle under my gaberdine—it is
lucky the hounds got it not, for he obeys no other. Take
him, and make much of him, I do not say for his master's
sake, but because I have placed at your disposal the event of
a mighty war. He will never fail you at need ; night and
day, rough and smooth, fair and foul, warm stables and the
winter sky, are the same to Klepper ; had I cleared the gates
of Péronne, and got so far as where I left him, I had not
been in this case. Will you be kind to Klepper ? "

" I swear to you that I will," answered Quentin, affected
by what seemed a trait of tenderness in a character so hardened.

" Then fare thee well ! " said the criminal. " Yet stay—
stay ; I would not willingly die in discourtesy, forgetting a
lady's commission. This billet is from the very gracious and
extremely silly Lady of the Wild Boar of Ardennes to her
black-eyed niece—I see by your look I have chosen a willing
messenger. And one word more—I forgot to say, that in
the stuffing of my saddle you will find a rich purse of gold
pieces, for the sake of which I put my life on the venture which
has cost me so dear. Take them, and replace a hundredfold
the guilders you have bestowed on these bloody slaves. I
make you mine heir."

" I will bestow them in good works, and masses for the
benefit of thy soul," said Quentin.

" Name not that word again," said Hayraddin, his countenance assuming a dreadful expression ; " there is—there

can be—there shall be—no such thing ! it is a dream of priestcraft !"

"Unhappy—most unhappy being ! Think better ! Let me speed for a priest; these men will delay yet a little longer, I will bribe them to it," said Quentin. "What canst thou expect, dying in such opinions, and impenitent ?"

"To be resolved into the elements," said the hardened atheist, pressing his fettered arms against his bosom ; "my hope, trust, and expectation is, that the mysterious frame of humanity shall melt into the general mass of nature, to be recompounded in the other forms with which she daily supplies those which daily disappear, and return under different forms—the watery particles to streams and showers, the earthly parts to enrich their mother earth, the airy portions to wanton in the breeze, and those of fire to supply the blaze of Aldebaran and his brethren. In this faith have I lived, and I will die in it ! Hence ! begone ! disturb me no farther ! I have spoken the last word that mortal ears shall listen to !"

Deeply impressed with the horrors of his condition, Quentin Durward yet saw that it was vain to hope to awaken him to a sense of his fearful state. He bid him, therefore, farewell ; to which the criminal only replied by a short and sullen nod, as one who, plunged in reverie, bids adieu to company which distracts his thoughts. He bent his course towards the forest, and easily found where Klepper was feeding. The creature came at his call, but was for some time unwilling to be caught, snuffing and starting when the stranger approached him. At length, however, Quentin's general acquaintance with the habits of the animal, and perhaps some particular knowledge of those of Klepper, which he had often admired while Hayraddin and he traveled together, enabled him to take possession of the Bohemian's dying bequest. Long ere he returned to Péronne, the Bohemian had gone where the vanity of his dreadful creed was to be put to the final issue—a fearful experience for one who had neither expressed remorse for the past nor apprehension for the future !

CHAPTER XXXV

A PRIZE FOR HONOR

'Tis brave for beauty when the best blade wins her.
The Count Palatine.

WHEN Quentin Durward reached Péronne, a council was sitting, in the issue of which he was interested more deeply than he could have apprehended, and which, though held by persons of a rank with whom one of his could scarce be supposed to have community of interest, had nevertheless the most extraordinary influence on his fortune.

King Louis, who, after the interlude of De la Marck's envoy, had omitted no opportunity to cultivate the returning interest which that circumstance had given him in the Duke's opinion, had been engaged in consulting him, or, it might be almost said, receiving his opinion, upon the number and quality of the troops, by whom, as auxiliary to the Duke of Burgundy, he was to be attended in their joint expedition against Liege. He plainly saw the wish of Charles was to call into his camp such Frenchmen as, from their small number and high quality, might be considered rather as hostages than as auxiliaries; but, observant of Crèvecœur's [Des Comines'] advice, he assented as readily to whatever the Duke proposed as if it had arisen from the free impulse of his own mind.

The King failed not, however, to indemnify himself for his complaisance by the indulgence of his vindictive temper against Balue, whose counsels had led him to repose such exuberant trust in the Duke of Burgundy. Tristan, who bore the summons for moving up his auxiliary forces, had the farther commission to carry the cardinal to the Castle of Loches, and there shut him up in one of those iron cages which he himself is said to have invented.

"Let him make proof of his own devices," said the King; "he is a man of holy church—we may not shed his blood; but, *Pasques-dieu!* his bishopric, for ten years to come, shall have an impregnable frontier to make up for its small extent! And see the troops are brought up instantly."

Perhaps, by this prompt acquiescence, Louis hoped to evade the more unpleasing condition with which the Duke had clogged their reconciliation. But if he so hoped, he greatly mistook the temper of his cousin ; for never man lived more tenacious of his purpose than Charles of Burgundy, and least of all was he willing to relax any stipulation which he had made in resentment, or revenge, of a supposed injury.

No sooner were the necessary expresses despatched to summon up the forces who were selected to act as auxiliaries than Louis was called upon by his host to give public consent to the espousals of the Duke of Orleans and Isabelle of Croye. The King complied with a heavy sigh, and presently after urged a slight expostulation, founded upon the necessity of observing the wishes of the duke himself.

"These have not been neglected," said the Duke of Burgundy : "Crèvecœur hath communicated with Monsieur d'Orleans, and finds him—strange to say—so dead to the honor of wedding a royal bride, that he acceded to the proposal of marrying the Countess of Croye as the kindest proposal which father could have made to him."

"He is the more ungracious and thankless," said Louis ; "but the whole shall be as you, my cousin, will, if you can bring it about with consent of the parties themselves."

"Fear not that," said the Duke ; and accordingly, not many minutes after the affair had been proposed, the Duke of Orleans and the Countess of Croye, the latter attended, as on the preceding occasion, by the Countess of Crèvecœur and the abbess of the Ursulines, were summoned to the presence of the princes, and heard from the mouth of Charles of Burgundy, unobjected to by that of Louis, who sat in silent and moody consciousness of diminished consequence, that the union of their hands was designed by the wisdom of both princes, to confirm the perpetual alliance which in future should take place betwixt France and Burgundy.

The Duke of Orleans had much difficulty in suppressing the joy which he felt upon the proposal, and which delicacy rendered improper in the presence of Louis ; and it required his habitual awe of that monarch to enable him to rein in his delight, so much as merely to reply, "that his duty compelled him to place his choice at the disposal of his sovereign."

"Fair cousin of Orleans," said Louis, with sullen gravity, "since I must speak on so unpleasant an occasion, it is needless for me to remind you that my sense of your merits had led me to propose for you a match into my own family. But, since my cousin of Burgundy thinks that the disposing of your hand otherwise is the surest pledge of amity between his dominions and mine, I love both too well not to sacrifice to them my own hopes and wishes."

The Duke of Orleans threw himself on his knees, and kissed,—and, for once, with sincerity of attachment,—the hand which the King, with averted countenance, extended to him. In fact he, as well as most present, saw, in the un-willing acquiescence of this accomplished dissembler, who, even with that very purpose, had suffered his reluctance to be visible, a king relinquishing his favorite project, and sub-jugating his paternal feelings to the necessities of state and interest of his country. Even Burgundy was moved, and Orleans' heart smote him for the joy which he involuntarily felt on being freed from his engagement with the Princess Joan. If he had known how deeply the King was cursing him in his soul, and what thoughts of future revenge he was agitating, it is probable his own delicacy on the occasion would not have been so much hurt.

Charles next turned to the young countess, and bluntly announced the proposed match to her, as a matter which neither admitted delay nor hesitation ; adding, at the same time, that it was but a too favorable consequence of her in-tractability on a former occasion.

" My Lord Duke and Sovereign," said Isabelle, summon-ing up all her courage, " I observe your Grace's commands, and submit to them."

" Enough, enough," said the Duke, interrupting her, " we will arrange the rest. Your Majesty," he continued, ad-dressing King Louis, " hath had a boar's hunt in the morn-ing ; what say you to rousing a wolf in the afternoon ? "

The young countess saw the necessity of decision. " Your Grace mistakes my meaning," she said, speaking, though timidly, yet loudly and decidedly enough to compel the Duke's attention, which, from some consciousness, he would otherwise have willingly denied to her. " My submission," she said, " only respected those lands and estates which your Grace's ancestors gave to mine, and which I resign to the house of Burgundy if my sovereign thinks my disobedience in this matter renders me unworthy to hold them."

" Ha ! St. George !" said the Duke, stamping furiously on the ground, " does the fool know in what presence she is, and to whom she speaks ? "

" My lord," she replied, still undismayed, " I am before my

suzerain, and, I trust, a just one. If you deprive me of my
lands, you take away all that your ancestors' generosity gave,
and you break the only bonds which attach us together.
You gave not this poor and persecuted form, still less the
spirit which animates me. And these it is my purpose to
dedicate to Heaven in the convent of the Ursulines, under
the guidance of this holy mother abbess."

The rage and astonishment of the Duke can hardly be conceived, unless we could estimate the surprise of a falcon
against whom a dove should ruffle its pinions in defiance.
" Will the holy mother receive you without an appanage ? "
he said, in a voice of scorn.

" If she doth her convent, in the first instance, so much
wrong," said the Lady Isabelle, "I trust there is charity
enough among the noble friends of my house to make up
some support for the orphan of Croye."

" It is false ! " said the Duke ; "it is a base pretext to cover
some secret and unworthy passion. My Lord of Orleans,
she shall be yours, if I drag her to the altar with my own
hands ! "

The Countess of Crèvecœur, a high-spirited woman, and
confident in her husband's merits and his favor with the
Duke, could keep silent no longer.   " My lord," she said,
" your passions transport you into language utterly unworthy.
The hand of no gentlewoman can be disposed of by force."

" And it is no part of the duty of a Christian prince,"
added the abbess, " to thwart the wishes of a pious soul, who,
broken with the cares and persecutions of the world, is desirous to become the bride of Heaven."

" Neither can my cousin of Orleans," said Dunois, " with
honor accept a proposal to which the lady has thus publicly stated her objections."

" If I were permitted," said Orleans, on whose facile mind
Isabelle's beauty had made a deep impression, " some time to
endeavor to place my pretensions before the countess in a
more favorable light——"

" My lord," said Isabelle, whose firmness was now fully
supported by the encouragement which she received from all
around, " it were to no purpose : my mind is made up to
decline this alliance, though far above my deserts."

" Nor have I time," said the Duke, " to wait till these
whimsies are changed with the next change of the moon.
Monseigneur d'Orleans, she shall learn within this hour that
obedience becomes matter of necessity."

" Not in my behalf, sire," answered the prince, who felt

that he could not, with any show of honor, avail himself of the Duke's obstinate disposition ; " to have been once openly and positively refused is enough for a son of France. He cannot prosecute his addresses farther."

The Duke darted one furious glance at Orleans, another at Louis ; and reading in the countenance of the latter, in spite of his utmost efforts to suppress his feelings, a look of secret triumph, he became outrageous.

" Write," he said to the secretary, " our doom of forfeiture and imprisonment against this disobedient and insolent minion. She shall to the *zuchthaus,* to the penitentiary, to herd with those lives have rendered them her rivals in effrontery ! "

There was a general murmur.

" My lord Duke," said the Count of Crèvecœur, taking the word for the rest, " this must be better thought on. We, your faithful vassals, cannot suffer such a dishonor to the nobility and chivalry of Burgundy. If the countess hath done amiss, let her be punished, but in the manner that becomes her rank and ours, who stand connected with her house by blood and alliance."

The Duke paused a moment, and looked full at his counselor with the stare of a bull which, when compelled by the neatherd from the road which he wishes to go, deliberates with himself whether to obey or to rush on his driver and toss him into the air.

Prudence, however, prevailed over fury ; he saw the sentiment was general in his council, was afraid of the advantages which Louis might derive from seeing dissension among his vassals ; and probably, for he was rather of a coarse and violent than of a malignant temper, felt ashamed of his own dishonorable proposal.

" You are right," he said, " Crèvecœur, and I spoke hastily. Her fate shall be determined according to the rules of chivalry. Her flight to Liege hath given the signal for the bishop's murder. He that best avenges that deed, and brings us the head of the Wild Boar of Ardennes, shall claim her hand of us ; and if she denies his right, we can at least grant him her fiefs, leaving it to his generosity to allow her what means he will to retire into a convent."

" Nay ! " said the countess, " think I am the daughter of Count Reinold—of your father's old, valiant, and faithful servant. Would you hold me out as a prize to the best sword-player ? "

" Your ancestress," said the Duke, " was won at a tourney ; you shall be fought for in real *mêlée.* Only thus far, for Count Reinold's sake, the successful prizer shall be a gentleman, of unimpeached birth and unstained bearings ; but, be he such, and the poorest who ever drew the strap of a sword-belt through the tongue of a buckle, he shall have at least the proffer of your hand. I swear it, by St. George, by my ducal crown, and by the order that I wear ! Ha ! messires," he added, turning to the nobles present, "this at least is, I think, in conformity with the rules of chivalry ? "

Isabelle's remonstrances were drowned in a general and jubilant assent, above which was heard the voice of old Lord Crawford, regretting the weight of years that prevented his striking for so fair a prize. The Duke was gratified by the general applause, and his temper began to flow more smoothly like that of a swollen river when it hath subsided within its natural boundries.

"Are we, to whom fate has given dames already," said Crèvecœur, "to be bystanders at this fair game ? It does not consist with my honor to be so, for I have myself a vow to be paid at the expense of that tusked and bristled brute, De la Marck."

"Strike boldly in, Crèvecœur," said the Duke ; "win her and since thou canst not wear her thyself, bestow her where thou wilt—on Count Stephen, your nephew, if you list."

"Gramercy, my lord ! " said Crèvecœur, "I will do my best in the battle ; and, should I be fortunate enough to be foremost, Stephen shall try his eloquence against that of the lady abbess."

"I trust," said Dunois, "that the chivalry of France are not excluded from this fair contest ? "

"Heaven forbid ! brave Dunois," answered the Duke, "were it but for the sake of seeing you do your uttermost. But," he added, "though there be no fault in the Lady Isabelle wedding a Frenchman, it will be necessary that the Count of Croye must become a subject of Burgundy."

"Enough, enough," said Dunois, "my bar sinister may never be surmounted by the coronet of Croye : I will live and die French. But yet, though I should lose the lands, I will strike a blow for the lady."

Le Balafré dared not speak aloud in such a presence, but he muttered to himself—"Now, Saunders Souplejaw, hold thine own ! Thou always saidst the fortune of our house was to be won by marriage, and never had you such a chance to keep your word with us."

"No one thinks of me," said Le Glorieux, "who am sure to carry off the prize from all of you."

"Right, my sapient friend," said Louis ; "when a woman is in the case, the greatest fool is ever the first in favor."

While the princes and their nobles thus jested over her fate, the abbess and the Countess of Crèvecœur endeavored in vain to console Isabelle, who had withdrawn with them from the council-presence. The former assured her, that the Holy Virgin would frown on every attempt to withdraw a true votress from the shrine of Saint Ursula ; while the Countess of Crèvecœur whispered more temporal consolation, that no true knight, who might succeed in the emprize proposed, would avail himself, against her inclinations, of the Duke's award ; and that perhaps the successful competitor might prove one who should find such favor in her eyes as to reconcile her to obedience. Love, like despair, catches at straws ; and, faint and vague as was the hope which this insinuation conveyed, the tears of the Countess Isabelle flowed more placidly while she dwelt upon it.*

* See Prize of Honor. Note 47.

CHAPTER XXXVI

The wretch condemn'd with life to part
  Still, still on hope relies,
And every pang that rends the heart
  Bids expectation rise.

Hope, like the glimmering taper's light,
  Adorns and cheers the way,
And still the darker grows the night,
  Emits a brighter ray.
                              GOLDSMITH.

FEW days had passed ere Louis had received, with a smile
of gratified vengeance, the intelligence that his favorite and
his counselor, the Cardinal Balue, was groaning within a
cage of iron, so disposed as scarce to permit him to enjoy
repose in any posture except when recumbent ; and of which
be it said in passing, he remained the unpitied tenant for
nearly twelve years. The auxiliary forces which the Duke
had required Louis to bring up had also appeared ; and he
comforted himself that their numbers were sufficient to protect his person against violence, although too limited to cope,
had such been his purpose, with the large army of Burgundy.
He saw himself also at liberty, when time should suit, to
resume his project of marriage between his daughter and
the Duke of Orleans ; and, although he was sensible to the
indignity of serving with his noblest peers under the banners
of his own vassal, and against the people whose cause he had
abetted, he did not allow these circumstances to embarrass
him in the meantime, trusting that a future day would bring
him amends. "For chance," said he to his trusty Oliver,
"may indeed gain one hit, but it is patience and wisdom
which win the game at last."

With such sentiments, upon a beautiful day in the latter
end of harvest, the King mounted his horse ; and indifferent
that he was looked upon rather as a part of the pageant of a
victor than in the light of an independent sovereign surrounded by his guards and his chivalry, King Louis sallied

from under the Gothic gateway of Péronne to join the Burgundian army, which commenced at the same time its march against Liege.

Most of the ladies of distinction who were in the place attended, dressed in their best array, upon the battlements and defenses of the gate, to see the gallant show of the warriors setting forth on the expedition. Thither had the Countess Crèvecœur brought the Countess Isabelle. The latter attended very reluctantly ; but the peremptory order of Charles had been, that she who was to bestow the palm in the tourney, should be visible to the knights who were about to enter the lists.

As they thronged out from under the arch, many a pennon and shield was to be seen, graced with fresh devices, expressive of the bearer's devoted resolution to become a competitor for a prize so fair. Here a charger was painted starting for the goal, there an arrow aimed at a mark ; one knight bore a bleeding heart, indicative of his passion, another a skull and a coronet of laurels, showing his determination to win or die. Many others there were ; and some so cunningly intricate, and obscure, that they might have defied the most ingenious interpreter. Each knight, too, it may be presumed, put his courser to his mettle, and assumed his most gallant seat in the saddle, as he passed for a moment under the view of the fair bevy of dames and damsels, who encouraged their valor by their smiles, and the waving of kerchiefs and of veils. The Archer Guard, selected almost at will from the flower of the Scottish nation, drew general applause, from the gallantry and splendor of their appearance.

And there was one among these strangers who ventured on a demonstration of acquaintance with the Lady Isabelle which had not been attempted even by the most noble of the French nobility. It was Quentin Durward, who, as he passed the ladies in his rank, presented to the Countess of Croye, on the point of his lance, the letter of her aunt.

"Now, by my honor," said the Count of Crèvecœur, "that is over insolent in an unworthy adventurer !"

"Do not call him so, Crèvecœur," said Dunois ; "I have good reason to bear testimony to his gallantry, and in behalf of that lady, too."

"You make words of nothing," said Isabelle, blushing with shame, and partly with resentment ; "it is a letter from my unfortunate aunt : she writes cheerfully, though her situation must be dreadful."

"Let us hear—let us hear what says the Boar's bride," said Crèvecœur.

The Countess Isabelle read the letter, in which her aunt seemed determined to make the best of a bad bargain, and to console herself for the haste and indecorum of her nuptials by the happiness of being wedded to one of the bravest men of the age, who had just acquired a princedom by his valor. She implored her niece not to judge of her William, as she called him, by the report of others, but to wait till she knew him personally. He had his faults, perhaps, but they were such as belonged to characters whom she had ever venerated. William was rather addicted to wine, but so was the gallant Sir Godfrey, her grandsire ; he was something hasty and sanguinary in his temper, such had been her brother, Reinold of blessed memory ; he was blunt in speech, few Germans were otherwise ; and a little wilful and peremptory, but she believed all men loved to rule. More there was to the same purpose ; and the whole concluded with the hope and request that Isabelle would, by means of the bearer, endeavor her escape from the tyrant of Burgundy, and come to her loving kinswoman's court of Liege, where any little differences concerning their mutual rights of succession to the earldom might be adjusted by Isabelle's marrying Carl Eberson—a bridegroom younger indeed than his bride, but that, as she (the Lady Hameline) might perhaps say from experience, was an inequality more easy to be endured than Isabelle could be aware of.*

Here the Countess Isabelle stopped ; the abbess observing, with a prim aspect, that she had read quite enough concerning such worldly vanities, and the Count of Crèvecœur breaking out, "Aroint thee, deceitful witch ! Why, this device smells rank as the toasted cheese in a rat-trap. Now fie, and double fie, upon the old decoy-duck !"

The Countess of Crèvecœur gravely rebuked her husband for his violence. "The Lady Hameline," she said, "must have been deceived by De la Marck with a show of courtesy."

"He show courtesy !" said the count; "I acquit him of all such dissimulation. You may as well expect courtesy from a literal wild boar ; you may as well try to lay leaf-gold on old rusty gibbet-irons. No—idiot as she is, she is not quite goose enough to fall in love with the fox who has snapped her, and that in his very den. But you women are all alike—fair words carry it ; and, I dare say, here is my

* See Bride of De la Marck. Note 48.

pretty cousin impatient to join her aunt in this fool's paradise, and marry the Boar-Pig."

"So far from being capable of such folly," said Isabelle, "I am doubly desirous of vengeance on the murderers of the excellent bishop, because it will, at the same time, free my aunt from the villain's power."

"Ah! there indeed spoke the voice of Croye!" exclaimed the count; and no more was said concerning the letter.

But while Isabelle read her aunt's epistle to her friends, it must be observed that she did not think it necessary to recite a certain *postscript*, in which the Countess Hameline, lady-like, gave an account of her occupations, and informed her niece that she had laid aside for the present a surcoat which she was working for her husband, bearing the arms of Croye and La Marck in conjugal fashion, parted per pale, because her William had determined, for purposes of policy, in the first action to have others dressed in his coat-armor, and himself to assume the arms of Orleans, with a bar sinister—in other words, those of Dunois. There was also a slip of paper in another hand, the contents of which the countess did not think it necessary to mention, being simply these words : " If you hear not of me soon, and that by the trumpet of Fame, conclude me dead, but not unworthy."

A thought, hitherto repelled as wildly incredible, now glanced with double keenness through Isabelle's soul. As female wit seldom fails in the contrivance of means, she so ordered it, that ere the troops were fully on march, Quentin Durward received from an unknown hand the billet of Lady Hameline, marked with three crosses opposite to the post-script, and having these words subjoined : " He who feared not the arms of Orleans when on the breast of their gallant owner cannot dread them when displayed on that of a tyrant and murderer." A thousand thousand times was this intimation kissed and pressed to the bosom of the young Scot! for it marshaled him on the path where both honor and love held out the reward, and possessed him with a secret unknown to others, by which to distinguish him whose death could alone give life to his hopes, and which he prudently resolved to lock up in his own bosom.

But Durward saw the necessity of acting otherwise respecting the information communicated by Hayraddin, since the proposed sally of De la Marck, unless heedfully guarded against, might prove the destruction of the besieging army ; so difficult was it, in the tumultuous warfare of those days, to recover from a nocturnal surprise. After pondering on the matter, he formed the additional resolution, that he would not communicate the intelligence save personally, and to both the princes while together; perhaps because he felt that, to mention so well-contrived and hopeful a scheme to Louis whilst in private might be too strong a temptation to the wavering probity of that monarch, and lead him to assist rather than repel the intended sally. He determined, therefore, to watch for an opportunity of revealing the secret whilst Louis and Charles were met, which, as they were not particularly fond of the constraint imposed by each other's society, was not likely soon to occur.

Meanwhile the march continued, and the confederates soon entered the territories of Liege. Here the Burgundian soldiers, at least a part of them, composed of those bands who had acquire the title of *écorcheurs,* or flayers, showed by the usage which they gave the inhabitants, under pretext of avenging the bishop's death, that they well deserved that honorable title; while their conduct greatly prejudiced the cause of Charles—the aggrieved inhabitants, who might otherwise have been passive in the quarrel, assuming arms in self-defense, harassing his march, by cutting off small parties, and falling back before the main body upon the city itself, thus augmenting the numbers and desperation of those who had resolved to defend it. The French, few in number, and those the choice soldiers of the country, kept, according to the King's orders, close by their respective standards, and observed the strictest discipline; a contrast which increased the suspicions of Charles, who could not help remarking that the troops of Louis demeaned themselves as if they were rather friends to the Liegeois than allies of Burgundy.

At length, without experiencing any serious opposition, the army arrived in the rich valley of the Maes, and before the large and populous city of Liege. The Castle of Schonwaldt they found had been totally destroyed, and learned that William de la Marck, whose only talents were of a military cast, had withdrawn his whole forces into the city, and was determined to avoid the encounter of the chivalry of France and Burgundy in the open field. But the invaders were not long of experiencing the danger which must always exist in attacking a large town, however open, if the inhabitants are disposed to defend it desperately.

A part of the Burgundian vanguard, conceiving that, from the dismantled and breached state of the walls, they had nothing to do but to march into Liege at their ease, entered one of the suburbs with the shouts of " Burgundy—Bur-

gundy! Kill—kill! All is ours! Remember Louis of
Bourbon!" But as they marched in disorder through the
narrow streets, and were partly dispersed for the purpose of
pillage, a large body of the inhabitants issued suddenly from
the town, fell furiously upon them, and made considerable
slaughter. De la Marck even availed himself of the breaches
in the walls, which permitted the defenders to issue out at
different points, and, by taking separate routes into the contested suburb, to attack, in the front, flank, and rear, at
once, the assailants, who, stunned by the furious, unexpected, and multiplied nature of the resistance offered, could
hardly stand to their arms. The evening, which began to
close, added to their confusion.

When this news was brought to Duke Charles, he was
furious with rage, which was not much appeased by the offer
of King Louis, to send the French men-at-arms into the
suburbs, to rescue and bring off the Burgundian vanguard.
Rejecting this offer briefly, he would have put himself at
the head of his own guards, to extricate those engaged in the
incautious advance; but D'Hymbercourt and Crèvecœur
entreated him to leave the service to them, and marching
into the scene of action at two points, with more order and
proper arrangement for mutual support, these two celebrated
captains succeeded in repulsing the Liegeois and in extricating the vanguard, who lost, besides prisoners, no fewer
than eight hundred men, of whom about a hundred were
men-at-arms. The prisoners, however, were not numerous,
most of them having been rescued by D'Hymbercourt, who
now proceeded to occupy the contested suburb, and to place
guards opposite to the town, from which it was divided by
an open space or esplanade of five or six hundred yards, left
free of buildings for the purposes of defence. There was no
moat betwixt the suburb and town, the ground being rocky
in that place. A gate fronted the suburb, from which sallies
might be easily made, and the wall was pierced by two or
three of those breaches which Duke Charles had caused to
be made after the battle of Saint Tron, and which had been
hastily repaired with mere barricades of timber. D'Hymbercourt turned two culverins on the gate, and placed two
others opposite to the principal breach, to repel any sally
from the city, and then returned to the Burgundian army,
which he found in great disorder.

In fact, the main body and rear of the numerous army of
the Duke had continued to advance while the broken and repulsed vanguard was in the act of retreating; and they had

come into collision with each other, to the great confusion of both. The necessary absence of D'Hymbercourt, who discharged all the duties of *maréchal du camp*, or, as we should now say, of quartermaster-general, augmented the disorder; and to complete the whole, the night sunk down dark as a wolf's mouth : there fell a thick and heavy rain, and the ground on which the beleaguering army must needs take up their position was muddy and intersected with many canals. It is scarce possible to form an idea of the confusion which prevailed in the Burgundian army, where leaders were separated from their soldiers and soldiers from their standards and officers. Every one, from the highest to the lowest, was seeking shelter and accommodation where he could individually find it; while the wearied and wounded, who had been engaged in the battle, were calling in vain for shelter and refreshment, and while those who knew nothing of the disaster were pressing on to have their share in the sack of the place, which they had no doubt was proceeding merrily.

When D'Hymbercourt returned he had a task to perform of incredible difficulty, and embittered by the reproaches of his master, who made no allowance for the still more necessary duty in which he had been engaged, until the temper of the gallant soldier began to give way under the Duke's unreasonable reproaches. " I went hence to restore some order in the van," he said, " and left the main body under your Grace's own guidance ; and now, on my return, I can neither find that we have front, flank, nor rear, so utter is the confusion."

" We are the more like a barrel of herrings," answered Le Glorieux, " which is the most natural resemblance for a Flemish army."

The jester's speech made the Duke laugh, and perhaps prevented a farther prosecution of the altercation betwixt him and his general.

By dint of great exertion, a small *lusthaus*, or country villa, of some wealthy citizen of Liege was secured and cleared of other occupants for the accommodation of the Duke and his immediate attendants ; and the authority of D'Hymbercourt and Crèvecœur at length established a guard in the vicinity, of about forty men-at-arms, who lighted a very large fire, made with the timber of the outhouses, which they pulled down for the purpose.

A little to the left of this villa, and betwixt it and the suburb, which, as we have said, was opposite to the city gate, and occupied by the Burgundian vanguard, lay another pleasure-house, surrounded by a garden and courtyard, and having two or three small inclosures or fields in the rear of it. In this the King of France established his own head-quarters. He did not himself pretend to be a soldier, further than a natural indifference to danger and much sagacity qualified him to be called such ; but he was always careful to employ the most skilful in that profession, and reposed in them the confidence they merited. Louis and his immediate attendants occupied this second villa ; a part of his Scottish Guard were placed in the court, where there were outhouses and sheds to shelter them from the weather; the rest were stationed in the garden. The remainder of the French men-at-arms were quartered closely together and in good order, with alarm-posts stationed, in case of their having to sustain an attack.

Dunois and Crawford, assisted by several old officers and soldiers, amongst whom Le Balafré was conspicuous for his diligence, contrived, by breaking down walls, making openings through hedges, filling up ditches, and the like, to facilitate the communication of the troops with each other, and the orderly combination of the whole in case of necessity.

Meanwhile, the King judged it proper to go without farther ceremony to the quarters of the Duke of Burgundy, to ascertain what was to be the order of proceeding and what cooperation was expected from him. His presence occasioned a sort of council of war to be held, of which Charles might not otherwise have dreamed.

It was then that Quentin Durward prayed earnestly to be admitted, as having something of importance to deliver to the two princes. This was obtained without much difficulty, and great was the astonishment of Louis when he heard him calmly and distinctly relate the purpose of William de la Marck to make a sally upon the camp of the besiegers under the dress and banners of the French. Louis would probably have been much better pleased to have had such important news communicated in private ; but as the whole story had been publicly told in presence of the Duke of Burgundy, he only observed, " that, whether true or false, such a report concerned them most materially."

" Not a whit—not a whit !" said the Duke, carelessly. " Had there been such a purpose as this young man announces, it had not been communicated to me by an archer of the Scottish Guard."

"However that may be," answered Louis, "I pray you, fair cousin, you and your captains, to attend, that to prevent the unpleasing consequences of such an attack, should it be made unexpectedly, I will cause my soldiers to wear white scarfs over their armor. Dunois, see it given out on the instant—that is," he added, "if our brother and general approves of it."

"I see no objection," replied the Duke, "if the chivalry of France are willing to run the risk of having the name of Knights of the Smock-sleeve bestowed on them in future."

"It would be a right well adapted title, friend Charles," said Le Glorieux, "considering that a woman is the reward of the most valiant."

"Well spoken, sagacity," said Louis. "Cousin, good-night, I will go arm me. By the way, what if I win the countess with mine own hand?"

"Your Majesty," said the Duke, in an altered tone of voice, "must then become a true Fleming."

"I cannot," answered Louis, in a tone of the most sincere confidence, "be more so than I am already, could I but bring you, my dear cousin, to believe it."

The Duke only replied by wishing the King good-night, in a tone resembling the snort of a shy horse, starting from the caress of the rider when he is about to mount, and is soothing him to stand still.

"I could pardon all his duplicity," said the Duke to Crèvecœur, "but cannot forgive his supposing me capable of the gross folly of being duped by his professions."

Louis, too, had his confidence with Oliver le Dain when he returned to his own quarters. "This Scot," he said, "is such a mixture of shrewdness and simplicity, that I know not what to make of him. *Pasques-Dieu!* think of his unpardonable folly in bringing out honest De la Marck's plan of a sally before the face of Burgundy, Crèvecœur, and all of them, instead of rounding it in my ear, and giving me at least the choice of abetting or defeating it!"

"It is better as it is, sir," said Oliver; "there are many in your present train who would scruple to assail Burgundy undefied, or to ally themselves with De la Marck."

"Thou art right, Oliver. Such fools there are in the world, and we have no time to reconcile their scruples by a little dose of self-interest. We must be true men, Oliver, and good allies of Burgundy, for this night at least; time may give us a chance of a better game. Go, tell no man to unarm himself; and let them shoot, in case of necessity, as sharply on those who cry 'France' and 'St. Denis' as if they cried 'Hell' and 'Satan.' I will myself sleep in my armor. Let Crawford place Quentin Durward on the extreme point of our line of sentinels, next to the city. Let him e'en have the first benefit of the sally which he has announced to us; if his luck bear him out, it is the better for him. But take an especial care of Martius Galeotti, and see he remain in the rear, in a place of the most absolute safety; he is even but too venturous, and, like a fool, would be both swordsman and philosopher. See to these things, Oliver, and good-night. Our Lady of Cléry, and Monseigneur St. Martin of Tours, be gracious to my slumbers!"*

* See Attack upon Liege. Note 49.

27

CHAPTER XXXVII

THE SALLY

He look'd, and saw what numbers numberless
The city-gates out-pour'd.
Paradise Regained.

A DEAD silence soon reigned over that great host which lay in leaguer before Liege. For a long time the cries of the soldiers repeating their signals, and seeking to join their several banners, sounded like the howling of bewildered dogs seeking their masters. But at length, overcome with weariness by the fatigues of the day, the dispersed soldiers crowded under such shelter as they could meet with, and those who could find none sunk down through very fatigue under walls, hedges, and such temporary protection, there to wait for morning—a morning which some of them were never to behold. A dead sleep fell on almost all, excepting those who kept a faint and weary watch by the lodgings of the King and the Duke. The dangers and hopes of the morrow—even the schemes of glory which many of the young nobility had founded upon the splendid prize held out to him who should avenge the murdered Bishop of Liege—glided from their recollection as they lay stupified with fatigue and sleep. But not so with Quentin Durward. The knowledge that he alone was possessed of the means of distinguishing La Marck in the contest—the recollection by whom that information had been communicated, and the fair augury which might be drawn from her conveying it to him—the thought that his fortune had brought him to a most perilous and doubtful crisis indeed, but one where there was still, at least, a chance of his coming off triumphant, banished every desire to sleep, and strung his nerves with vigor, which defied fatigue.

Posted, by the King's express order, on the extreme point between the French quarters and the town, a good way to the right of the suburb which we have mentioned, he sharpened his eye to penetrate the mass which lay before him, and excited his ears to catch the slightest sound which might announce any commotion in the beleaguered city. But its huge clocks had successively knelled three hours after midnight, and all continued still and silent as the grave.

At length, and just when Quentin began to think the attack would be deferred till daybreak, and joyfully recollected that there would be then light enough to descry the bar sinister across the fleur-de-lys of Orleans, he thought he heard in the city a humming murmur, like that of disturbed bees mustering for the defense of their hives. He listened ; the noise continued, but it was of a character so undistinguished by any peculiar or precise sound, that it might be the murmur of a wind rising among the boughs of a distant grove, or perhaps some stream swollen by the late rain, which was discharging itself into sluggish Maes with more than usual clamor. Quentin was prevented by these considerations from instantly giving the alarm, which, if done carelessly, would have been a heavy offense.

But when the noise rose louder, and seemed pouring at the same time towards his own post, and towards the suburb, he deemed it his duty to fall back as silently as possible, and call his uncle, who commanded the small body of archers destined to his support. All were on their feet in a moment, and with as little noise as possible. In less than a second, Lord Crawford was at their head, and, despatching an archer to alarm the King and his household, drew back his little party to some distance behind their watch-fire, that they might not be seen by its light. The rushing sound, which had approached them more nearly, seemed suddenly to have ceased ; but they still heard distinctly the more distant heavy tread of a large body of men approaching the suburb.

"The lazy Burgundians are asleep on their post," whispered Crawford ; "make for the suburb, Cunningham, and awaken the stupid oxen."

"Keep well to the rear as you go," said Durward ; "if ever I heard the tread of mortal men, there is a strong body interposed between us and the suburb."

"Well said, Quentin, my dainty callant," said Crawford ; "thou art a soldier beyond thy years. They only make halt till the others come forward. I would I had some knowledge where they are !"

"I will creep forward, my lord," said Quentin, "and endeavor to bring you information."

"Do so, my bonny child ; thou hast sharp ears and eyes, and goodwill ; but take heed, I would not lose thee for two and a plack."

Quentin, with his harquebuss ready prepared, stole for-

ward, through ground which he had reconnoitred carefully
in the twilight of the preceding evening, until he was not
only certain that he was in the neighborhood of a very large
body cf men, who were standing fast betwixt the King's
quarters and the suburbs, but also that there was a detached
party of smaller number in advance, and very close to him.
They seemed to whisper together, as if uncertain what to do
next.　At last, the steps of two or three *enfans perdus*, detached from that smaller party, approached him so near as
twice a pike's length.　Seeing it impossible to retreat undis-
covered, Quentin called out aloud, *Qui vive?*" and was answered by " *Vive Li—Li—ege—c'est à dire,*" added he who
spoke, correcting himself, " *Vive la France!*"　Quentin
instantly fired his harquebuss ; a man groaned and fell, and
he himself, under the instant but vague discharge of a number of pieces, the fire of which ran in a disorderly manner
alongst the column, and showed it to be very numerous,
hastened back to the main guard.

" Admirably done, my brave boy ! " said Crawford.　" Now,
callants, draw in within the courtyard ; they are too many
to mell with in the open field."

They drew within the courtyard and garden accordingly,
where they found all in great order, and the King prepared
to mount his horse.

" Whither away, sire ? " said Crawford ; " you are safest
here with your own people."

" Not so," said Louis ; " I must instantly to the Duke.
He must be convinced of our good faith at this critical
moment, or we shall have both Liegeois and Burgundians
upon us at once."　And springing on his horse, he bade
Dunois command the French troops without the house, and
Crawford the Archer Guard and other household troops to
defend the *lusthaue* and its inclosures.　He commanded
them to bring up two sakers and as many falconets (pieces
of cannon for the field), which had been left about half a
mile in the rear ; and, in the meantime, to make good their
posts, but by no means to advance, whatever success they
might obtain ; and having given these orders, he rode off,
with a small escort, to the Duke's quarters.

The delay which permitted these arrangements to be carried fully into effect was owing to Quentin's having fortunately shot the proprietor of the house, who acted as guide
to the column which was designed to attack it, and whose
attack, had it been made instantly, might have had a chance
of being successful.

Durward, who, by the King's order, attended him to the Duke's, found the latter in a state of choleric distemperature, which almost prevented his discharging the duties of a general, which were never more necessary ; for, besides the noise of a close and furious combat which had now taken place in the suburb upon the left of their whole army—besides the attack upon the King's quarters, which was fiercely maintained in the ćenter—a third column of Liegeois, of even superior numbers, had filed out from a more distant breach, and, marching by lanes, vineyards, and passes known to themselves, had fallen upon the right flank of the Burgundian army, who, alarmed at their war-cries of " *Vive la France!* " and " *Denis Montjoye!* " which mingled with those of " *Liege* " and " *Rouge Sanglier,*" and at the idea thus inspired, of treachery on the part of the French confederates, made a very desultory and imperfect resistance ; while the Duke, foaming, and swearing, and cursing his liege lord and all that belonged to him, called out to shoot with bow and gun on all that was French, whether black or white—alluding to the sleeves with which Louis's soldiers had designated themselves.

The arrival of the King, attended only by Le Balafré and Quentin, and half a score of archers, restored confidence between France and Burgundy.. D'Hymbercourt, Crèvecœur, and others of the Burgundian leaders, whose names were then the praise and dread of war, rushed devotedly into the conflict ; and, while some commanders hastened to bring up more distant troops, to whom the panic had not extended, others threw themselves into the tumult, reanimated the instinct of discipline, and while the Duke toiled in the front, shouting, hacking, and hewing, like an ordinary man-at-arms, brought their men by degrees into array, and dismayed the assailants, by the use of their artillery. The conduct of Louis, on the other hand, was that of a calm, collected, sagacious leader, who neither sought nor avoided danger, but showed so much self-possession and sagacity that the Burgundian leaders readily obeyed the orders which he issued.

The scene was now become in the utmost degree animated and horrible. On the left the suburb, after a fierce contest, had been set on fire, and a wide and dreadful conflagration did not prevent the burning ruins from being still disputed. On the center, the French troops, though pressed by immense odds, kept up so close and constant a fire that the little pleasure-house shone bright with the glancing flashes, as if surrounded with a martyr's crown of flames. On the left, the battle swayed backwards and forwards with varied success, as fresh reinforcements poured out of the town, or were brought forward from the rear of the Burgundian host; and the strife continued with unremitting fury for three mortal hours, which at length brought the dawn, so much desired by the besiegers. The enemy, at this period, seemed to be slackening their efforts upon the right and in the center, and several discharges of cannon were heard from the *lusthaus.*

"Go," said the King, to Le Balafré and Quentin, the instant his ear had caught the sound; "they have got up the sakers and falconets; the pleasure-house is safe, blessed be the Holy Virgin! Tell Dunois to move this way, but rather nearer the walls of Liege, with all our men-at-arms, excepting what he may leave for the defense of the house, and cut in between those thick-headed Liegeois on the right and the city, from which they are supplied with recruits."

The uncle and nephew galloped off to Dunois and Crawford, who, tired of their defensive war, joyfully obeyed the summons, and filing out at the head of a gallant body of about two hundred French gentlemen, besides squires, and the greater part of the archers and their followers, marched across the field, trampling down the wounded, till they gained the flank of the large body of Liegeois, by whom the right of the Burgundians had been so fiercely assailed. The increasing daylight discovered that the enemy were continuing to pour out from the city, either for the purpose of continuing the battle on that point, or of bringing safely off the forces who were already engaged.

"By Heaven!" said old Crawford to Dunois, "were I not certain it is *thou* that art riding in my side, I would say I saw thee among yonder banditti and burghers, marshalling and arraying them with thy mace—only, if you be thou, thou art bigger than thou art wont to be. Art thou sure yonder armed leader is not thy wraith, thy double-man, as these Flemings call it?"

"My wraith!" said Dunois; "I know not what you mean. But yonder is a caitiff with my bearings displayed on crest and shield, whom I will presently punish for his insolence."

"In the name of all that is noble, my lord, leave the vengeance to me!" said Quentin.

"To *thee* indeed, young man!" said Dunois; "that is a modest request. No—these things brook no substitution."

Then turning on his saddle, he called out to those around him, " Gentlemen of France, form your line, level your lances ! Let the rising sunbeams shine through the battalions of yonder swine of Liege and hogs of Ardennes, that masquerade in our ancient coats."

The men-at-arms answered with a loud shout of " A Dunois—a Dunois ! Long live the bold Bastard ! Orleans to the rescue ! " And, with their leader in the center, they charged at full gallop. They encountered no timid enemy. The large body which they charged consisted, excepting some mounted officers, entirely of infantry, who, setting the butt of their lances against their feet, the front rank kneeling, the second stooping, and those behind presenting their spears over their heads, offered such resistance to the rapid charge of the men-at arms as the hedgehog presents to his enemy. Few were able to make way through that iron wall ; but of those few was Dunois, who, giving spur to his horse, and making the noble animal leap more than twelve feet at a bound, fairly broke his way into the middle of the phalanx, and made towards the object of his animosity. What was his surprise to find Quentin still by his side, and fighting in the same front with himself—youth, desperate courage, and the determination to do or die having still kept the youth abreast with the best knight in Europe, for such was Dunois reported, and truly reported, at the period.

Their spears were soon broken ; but the lanzknechts were unable to withstand the blows of their long heavy swords ; while the horses and riders, armed in complete steel, sustained little injury from their lances. Still Dunois and Durward were contending with rival efforts to burst forward to the spot where he who had usurped the armorial bearings of Dunois was doing the duty of a good and valiant leader, when Dunois, observing the boar's head and tusks, the usual bearing of William de la Marck, in another part of the conflict, called out to Quentin, " Thou art worthy to avenge the arms of Orleans ! I leave thee the task. Balafré, support your nephew ; but let none dare to interfere with Dunois's boar-hunt."

That Quentin Durward joyfully acquiesced in this division of labor cannot be doubted, and each pressed forward upon his separate object, followed, and defended from behind, by such men-at arms as were able to keep up with them.

But at this moment the column which De la Marck had proposed to support, when his own course was arrested by the charge of Dunois, had lost all the advantages they had gained during the night; while the Burgundians, with returning day, had begun to show the qualities which belong to superior discipline. The great mass of Liegeois were compelled to retreat, and at length to fly; and, falling back on those who were engaged with the French men-at-arms, the whole became a confused tide of fighters, fliers, and pursuers, which rolled itself towards the city walls, and at last was poured into the ample and undefended breach through which the Liegeois had sailed.

Quentin made more than human exertions to overtake the special object of his pursuit, who was still in his sight, striving, by voice and example, to renew the battle, and bravely supported by a chosen party of lanzknechts. Le Balafré and several of his comrades attached themselves to Quentin, much marveling at the extraordinary gallantry displayed by so young a soldier. On the very brink of the breach De la Marck—for it was himself—succeeded in effecting a momentary stand, and repelling some of the most forward of the pursuers. He had a mace of iron in his hand, before which everything seemed to go down, and was so much covered with blood that it was almost impossible to discern those bearings on his shield which had so much incensed Dunois.

Quentin now found little difficulty in singling him out; for the commanding situation of which he had possessed himself, and the use he made of his terrible mace, caused many of the assailants to seek safer points of attack than that where so desperate a defender presented himself. But Quentin, to whom the importance attached to victory over this formidable antagonist was better known, sprung from his horse at the bottom of the breach, and letting the noble animal, the gift of the Duke of Orleans, run loose through the tumult, ascended the ruins to measure swords with the Boar of Ardennes. The latter, as if he had seen his intention, turned towards Durward with mace uplifted; and they were on the point of encounter when a dreadful shout of triumph, of tumult, and of despair announced that the besiegers were entering the city at another point, and in the rear of those who defended the breach. Assembling around him, by voice and bugle, the desperate partners of his desperate fortune, De la Marck, at those appalling sounds, abandoned the breach, and endeavored to effect his retreat towards a part of the city from which he might escape to the other side of the Maes. His immediate followers formed a deep body of well-disciplined men, who, never having given quarter, were resolved now not to ask it, and, who, in that hour of despair, threw themselves into such firm order that their front occupied the whole breadth of the street through which they slowly retired, making head from time to time, and checking the pursuers, many of whom began to seek a safer occupation by breaking into the houses for plunder. It is therefore probable that De la Marck might have effected his escape, his disguise concealing him from those who promised themselves to win honor and grandeur upon his head, but for the stanch pursuit of Quentin, his uncle Le Balafré, and some of his comrades. At every pause which was made by the lanzknechts a furious combat took place betwixt them and the archers, and in every *mêlée* Quentin sought De la Marck; but the latter, whose present object was to retreat, seemed to evade the young Scot's purpose of bringing him to single combat. The confusion was general in every direction. The shrieks and cries of women, the yelling of the terrified inhabitants, now subjected to the extremity of military license, sounded horribly shrill amid the shouts of battle, like the voice of misery and despair contending with that of fury and violence, which should be heard farthest and loudest.

It was just when De la Marck, retiring through this infernal scene, had passed the door of a small chapel of peculiar sanctity, that the shouts of "France—France! Burgundy—Burgundy!" apprised him that a part of the besiegers were entering the farther end of the street, which was a narrow one, and that his retreat was cut off. "Comrade," he said, "take all the men with you. Charge yonder fellows roundly, and break through if you can; with me it is over. I am man enough, now that I am brought to bay, to send some of these vagabond Scots to hell before me."

His lieutenant obeyed, and, with most of the few lanzknechts who remained alive, hurried to the farther end of the street, for the purpose of charging those Burgundians who were advancing, and so forcing their way so as to escape. About six of De la Marck's best men remained to perish with their master, and fronted the archers, who were not many more in number. "Sanglier! Sanglier! Hola! gentlemen of Scotland," said the ruffian but undaunted chief, waving his mace, "who longs to gain a coronet—who strikes at the Boar of Ardennes? You, young man, have, methinks, a hankering; but you must win ere you wear it."

Quentin heard but imperfectly the words, which were partly lost in the hollow helmet ; but the action could not be mistaken, and he had but time to bid his uncle and comrades, as they were gentlemen, to stand back, when De la Marck sprung upon him with a bound like a tiger, aiming at the same time a blow with his mace, so as to make his hand and foot keep time together, and giving his stroke full advantage of the descent of his leap ; but, light of foot and quick of eye, Quentin leaped aside, and disappointed an aim which would have been fatal had it taken effect.

They then closed, like the wolf and the wolf-dog, their comrades on either side remaining inactive spectators, for Le Balafré roared out for fair play, adding, " that he would venture his nephew on him, were he as wight as Wallace."

Neither was the experienced soldier's confidence unjustified ; for, although the blows of the despairing robber fell like those of the hammer on the anvil, yet the quick motions and dexterous swordsmanship of the young archer enabled him to escape, and to requite them with the point of his less noisy though more fatal weapon ; and that so often and so effectually, that the huge strength of his antagonist began to give way to fatigue, while the ground on which he stood became a puddle of blood.   Yet, still unabated in courage and ire, the Wild Boar of Ardennes fought on with as much mental energy as at first, and Quentin's victory seemed dubious and distant, when a female voice behind him called him by his name, ejaculating, " Help—help ! for the sake of the blessed Virgin !"

He turned his head, and with a single glance beheld Gertrude Pavillon, her mantle stripped from her shoulders, dragged forcibly along by a French soldier, one of several, who, breaking into the chapel close by, had seized, as their prey, on the terrified females who had taken refuge there.

" Wait for me but one moment," exclaimed Quentin to De la Marck, and sprung to extricate his benefactress from a situation of which he conjectured all the dangers.

" I wait no man's pleasure," said De la Marck, flourishing his mace, and beginning to retreat, glad, no doubt, of being free of so formidable an assailant.

" You shall wait mine, though by your leave," said Balafré ; " I will not have my nephew baulked."   So saying, he instantly assaulted De la Marck with his two-handed sword.

Quentin found, in the meanwhile, that the rescue of Gertrude was a task more difficult than could be finished in one moment.   Her captor, supported by his comrades, re-

fused to relinquish his prize ; and whilst Durward, aided by
one or two of his countrymen, endeavored to compel him to
do so, the former beheld the chance which Fortune had so
kindly afforded him for fortune and happiness glide out of
his reach ; so that, when he stood at length in the street
with the liberated Gertrude, there was no one near them.
Totally forgetting the defenseless situation of his companion, he was about to spring away in pursuit of the Boar of
Ardennes, as the greyhound tracks the deer, when, clinging
to him in her despair, she exclaimed, "For the sake of your
mother's honor, leave me not here ! As you are a gentleman, protect me to my father's house, which once sheltered you and the Lady Isabelle ! For her sake leave me
not !"

Her call was agonizing, but it was irresistible ; and bidding a mental adieu, with unutterable bitterness of feeling
to all the gay hopes which had stimulated his exertion, carried him through that bloody day, and which at one moment
seemed to approach consummation, Quentin, like an unwilling spirit who obeys a talisman which he cannot resist, protected Gertrude to Pavillon's house, and arrived in time to
defend that and the syndic himself against the fury of the
licentious soldiery.

Meantime, the King and the Duke of Burgundy entered
the city on horseback, and through one of the breaches.
They were both in complete armor, but the latter, covered
with blood from the plume to the spur, drove his steed furiously up the breach, which Louis surmounted with the
stately pace of one who leads a procession. They despatched
orders to stop the sack of the city, which had already commenced, and to assemble their scattered troops. The princes
themselves proceeded towards the great church, both for the
protection of many of the distinguished inhabitants, who
had taken refuge there, and in order to hold a sort of military council after they had heard high mass.

Busied like other officers of his rank in collecting those
under his command, Lord Crawford, at the turning of one
of streets which leads to the Maes, met Le Balafré sauntering
composedly towards the river, holding in his ·hand, by the
gory locks, a human head, with as much indifference as a
fowler carries a game-pouch.

"How now, Ludovic !" said his commander ; "what are
ye doing with that carrion ?"

"It is all is left of a bit of work which my nephew shaped
out, and nearly finished, and I put the last hand to," said

Le Balafré—"a good fellow that I despatched yonder, and who prayed me to throw his head into the Maes. Men have queer fancies when old Small Back * is gripping them ; but Small Back must lead down the dance with us all in our time."

" And you are going to throw that head into the Maes ? " said Crawford, looking more attentively on the ghastly memorial of mortality.

" Ay, truly am I," said Ludovic Lesly. " If you refuse a dying man his boon, you are likely to be haunted by his ghost, and I love to sleep sound at nights."

" You must take your chance of the ghaist, man," said Crawford ; "for, by my soul, there is more lies on that dead pow than you think for. Come along with me—not a word more—come along with me."

" Nay, for that matter," said Le Balafré, " I made him no promise ; for, in truth, I had off his head before the tongue had well done wagging ; and as I feared him not living, by St. Martin of Tours, I fear him as little when he is dead. Besides, my little gossip, the merry friar of St. Martin's will lend me a pot of holy water."

When high mass had been said in the cathedral church of Liege, and the terrified town was restored to some moderate degree of order, Louis and Charles, with their peers around, proceeded to hear the claims of those who had any to make for services performed during the battle. Those which respected the country of Croye and its fair mistress were first received, and,to the disappointment of sundry claimants who had thought themselves sure of the rich prize, there seemed doubt and mystery to involve their several pretensions. Crévecœur showed a boar's hide such as De la Marck usually wore ; Dunois produced a cloven shield, with his armorial bearings ; and there were others who claimed the merit of having despatched the murderer of the bishop, producing similar tokens—the rich reward fixed on De la Marck's head having brought death to all who were armed in his resemblance.

There was much noise and contest among the competitors, and Charles, internally regretting the rash promise which had placed the hand and wealth of his fair vassal on such a hazard, was in hopes he might find means of evading all these conflicting claims, when Crawford pressed forward into the circle, dragging Le Balafré after him, who, awkward

* A cant expression in Scotland for death, usually delineated as a skeleton.

and bashful, followed like an unwilling mastiff towed on in a leash, as his leader exclaimed,—" Away with your hoofs and hides, and painted iron ! No one, save he who slew the Boar, can show the tusks ! "

So saying, he flung on the floor the bloody head, easily known as that of De la Marck by the singular conformation of the jaws, which in reality had a certain resemblance to those of the animal whose name he bore, and which was instantly recognized by all who had seen him.*

" Crawford," said Louis, while Charles sat silent, in gloomy and displeased surprise, " I trust it is one of my faithful Scots who has won this prize ? "

" It is Ludovic Lesly, sire, whom we call Le Balafré," replied the old soldier.

" But is he noble," said the Duke—" is he of gentle blood ? Otherwise our promise is void."

" He is a cross ungainly piece of wood enough," said Crawford, looking at the tall, awkward, embarrassed figure of the archer ; " but I will warrant him a branch of the tree of Rothes for all that, and they have been as noble as any house in France or Burgundy, ever since it is told of their founder that,

> Between the less-lee † and the mair
> He slew the knight, and left him there.

" There is then no help for it," said the Duke, " and the fairest and richest heiress in Burgundy must be the wife of a rude mercenary soldier like this, or die secluded in a convent —and she the only child of our faithful Reginald (Reinold) de Croye ! I have been too rash."

And a cloud settled on his brow, to the surprise of his peers, who seldom saw him evince the slightest token of regret for the necessary consequences of an adopted resolution.

" Hold but an instant," said the Lord Crawford, " it may be better than your Grace conjectures. Hear but what this cavalier has to say. Speak out, man, and a murrain to thee," he added, apart to Le Balafré.

But that blunt soldier, though he could make a shift to express himself intelligibly enough to King Louis, to whose familiarity he was habituated, yet found himself incapable of enunciating his resolution before so splendid an assembly

---

* See Anachronisms. Note 50.
† See Descent of the Leslies. Note 51.

as that in presence of which he then stood ; and after having
turned his shoulders to the princes, and preluded with a
hoarse chuckling laugh, and two or three tremendous con-
tortions of countenance, he was only able to pronounce the
words, "Saunders Souplejaw"—and then stuck fast.

"May it please your Majesty and your Grace," said Crawford, "I must speak for my countryman and old comrade.
You shall understand that he has had it prophesied to him
by a seer in his own land, that the fortune of his house is to
be made by marriage ; but as he is, like myself, something
the worse for the wear,—loves the wine-house better than a
lady's summer-parlor, and, in short, having some barrack
tastes and likings which would make greatness in his own
person rather an encumbrance to him, he hath acted by my
advice, and resigns the pretensions acquired by the fate of
slaying William de la Marck to him by whom the Wild Boar
was actually brought to bay, who is his maternal nephew."

"I will vouch for that youth's services and prudence,"
said King Louis, overjoyed to see that fate had thrown so
gallant a prize to one over whom he had some influence.
"Without his prudence and vigilance we had been ruined.
It was he who made us aware of the night-sally."

"I then," said Charles, "owe him some reparation for
doubting his veracity."

"And I can attest his gallantry as a man-at-arms," said
Dunois.

"But," interrupted Crèvecœur, "though the uncle be a
Scottish *gentillâtre*, that makes not the nephew necessarily
so."

"He is of the house of Durward," said Crawford, "descended from that Allan Durward who was High Steward of
Scotland."

"Nay, if it be young Durward," said Crèvecœur, "I say
no more. Fortune has declared herself on his side too plainly
for me to struggle farther with her humorsome ladyship ;
but it is strange, from lord to horseboy, how wonderfully
these Scots stick by each other."

"Highlanders, shoulder to shoulder !" answered Lord
Crawford, laughing at the mortification of the proud Burgundian.

"We have yet to inquire," said Charles, thoughtfully,
"what the fair lady's sentiments may be towards this fortunate adventurer."

"By the mass !" said Crèvecœur, "I have but too much
reason to believe your Grace will find her more amenable to

authority than on former occasions. But why should I grudge this youth his preferment, since, after all, it is sense, firmness, and gallantry which have put him in possession of WEALTH, RANK, and BEAUTY ? "

I HAD already sent these sheets to the press, concluding, as I thought, with a moral of excellent tendency for the encouragement of all fair-haired, blue-eyed, long-legged, stout-hearted emigrants from my native country who might be willing in stirring times to take up the gallant profession of cavalieros of fortune. But a friendly monitor, one of those who like the lump of sugar which is found at the bottom of a tea-cup as well as the flavor of the souchong itself, has entered a bitter remonstrance, and insists that I should give a precise and particular account of the espousals of the young heir of Glenhoulakin and the lovely Flemish countess, and tell what tournaments were held, and how many lances were broken, upon so interesting an occasion ; nor withhold from the curious reader the number of sturdy boys who inherited the valor of Quentin Durward, and of bright damsels in whom were renewed the charms of Isabelle de Croye. I replied in course of post, that times were changed, and public weddings were entirely out of fashion. In days, traces of which I myself can remember, not only were the " fifteen friends " of the happy pair invited to witness their union, but the bridal minstrelsy still continued, as in the *Ancient Mariner*, to " nod their heads " till morning shone on them. The sack-posset was eaten in the nuptial chamber, the stocking was thrown, and the bride's garter was struggled for in presence of the happy couple whom Hymen had made one flesh. The authors of the period were laudably accurate in following its fashions. They spared you not a blush of the bride, not a rapturous glance of the bridegroom, not a diamond in her hair, not a button on his embroidered waistcoat ; until at length, with Astræa, " they fairly put their characters to bed." But how little does this agree with the modest privacy which induces our modern brides—sweet bashful darlings !—to steal from pomp and plate, and admiration and flattery, and, like honest Shenstone,

> Seek for freedom at an inn !

To these, unquestionably, an exposure of the circumstances of publicity with which a bridal in the 15th century was always celebrated must appear in the highest degree disgusting. Isabelle de Croye would be ranked in their estimation far below the maid who milks and does the meanest chores; for even she, were it in the church-porch, would reject the hand of her journeyman shoemaker should he propose "*faire des noces*," as it is called on Parisian signs, instead of going down on the top of the long coach to spend the honeymoon *incognito* at Deptford or Greenwich. I will not, therefore, tell more of this matter, but will steal away from the wedding as Ariosto from that of Angelica, leaving it to whom it may please to add farther particulars, after the fashion of their own imagination.

> Some better bard shall sing, in feudal state
> How Braquemont's Castle op'd its Gothic gate,
> When on the wand'ring Scot its lovely heir
> Bestow'd her beauty and an earldom fair.*

---

* E come a ritornare in sua contrada
Trovasse e buon naviglio e miglior tempo,
E dell' India a Medor desse lo scettro
Forse altri cantera con miglior plettro.
        Orlando Furioso, Canto xxx., Stanza 16.

NOTES TO QUENTIN DURWARD

Note 1.—Price on the Picturesque, p. xxvi

See Price's *Essay on the Picturesque*, in many passages ; but I would particularize the beautiful and highly poetical account which he gives of his own feelings on destroying, at the dictate of an improver, an ancient sequestrated garden, with its yew hedges, ornamented iron gates, and secluded wilderness.

Note 2.—Hughes's *ITINERARY*, xxxiii

This Journal, or *Itinerary*, with etchings by the author, was published at London, 1822, 8vo, and was followed by a volume in folio [4to], entitled *Views in the South of France, chiefly on the Rhone*, engraved by W. B. Cooke, etc., from drawings by P. De Wint, after original sketches by John Hughes, Lond. 1825.

Mr. Lockhart, in his *Life of Scott*, has, by some oversight, connected the late Mr. Skene's name with *Quentin Durward* instead of with *Anne of Geierstein*. There is good authority for correcting this (*Laing*).

Note 3.—Edition of *CENT NOUVELLES*, p. 4

This *editio princeps*, which, when in good preservation, is much sought after by connoisseurs, is entitled, *Les Cent Nouvelles Nouvelles, contenant Cent Histoires Nouveaux, qui sont moult plaisans à raconter en toutes bonnes compagnies par manière de joyeuxeté. Paris, Antoine Verard. Sans date d'année d'impression ; in folio gotique.* See De Bure.

Note 4.—St. Hubert, p. 16

Every vocation had, in the middle ages, its protecting saint. The chase, with its fortunes and its hazards, the business of so many and the amusement of all, was placed under the direction of St. Hubert. This silvan saint was the son of Bertrand Duke of Acquitaine, and, while in the secular state, was a courtier of King Pepin. He was passionately fond of the chase, and used to neglect attendance on divine worship for this amusement. While he was once engaged in this pastime, a stag appeared before him, having a crucifix bound between his horns, and he heard a voice which menaced him with eternal punishment if he did not repent of his sins. He retired from the world and took orders, his wife having also retreated into the cloister. Hubert afterwards became Bishop of Maestricht and Liege ; and from his zeal in destroying remnants of idolatry is called the Apostle of Ardennes and of Brabant. Those who were descended of his race were supposed to possess the power of curing persons bitten by mad dogs

Note 5.—Covin Tree, p. 23

The large tree in front of a Scottish castle was sometimes called so. It is difficult to trace the derivation ; but at that distance from the castle the laird received guests of rank, and thither he convoyed them on their departure.

Note 6.—Duke of Gueldres, p. 30

This was Adolphus, son of Arnold and of Catherine de Bourbon. The present story has little to do with him, though one of the most atrocious characters of his time. He made war against his father ; in which unnatural strife he made the old man prisoner, and used him with the most brutal violence, proceeding, it is said, even to the length of striking him with his hand. Arnold, in resentment of this usage, disinherited the unprincipled wretch, and sold to Charles of Burgundy whatever rights he had over the duchy of Gueldres and earldom of Zutphen. Mary of Burgundy, daughter of Charles, restored these possessions to the unnatural Adolphus, who was slain in 1477.

Note 7.—Constable St. Paul, p. 31

This part of Louis XI.'s reign was much embarrassed by the intrigues of the Constable St. Paul, who affected independence, and carried on intrigues with England, France, and Burgundy at the same time. According to the usual fate of such versatile politicians, the Constable ended by drawing upon himself the animosity of all the powerful neighbors whom he had in their turn amused and deceived. He was delivered up by the Duke of Burgundy to the King of France, tried, and hastily executed for treason, 1475.

Note 8.—Bishop and Stephens, p. 40

Sir Henry R. Bishop, the popular composer, and sometime professor of music in Edinburgh University, died in 1855. Miss Catherine Stephens was a delightful vocalist, who performed at the principal concerts and musical festivals about the time this was written. In 1838 she became Countess of Essex by her marriage with George, the fifth ear (*Laing*).

Note 9.—Use of Stilts, p. 44

The crutches or stilts which in Scotland are used to pass rivers. They are employed by the peasantry of the country near Bourdeaux to traverse those deserts of loose sand called Landes.

Note 10.—"Better Kind Fremit," etc., p. 55

"Better kind strangers than estranged kindred." The motto is engraved on a dirk belonging to a person who had but too much reason to choose such a device. It was left by him to my father, and is connected with a strange course of adventures, which may one day be told. The weapon is now in my possession.

Note 11.—Skene Dhu, p. 58

Black knife ; a species of knife without clasp or hinge, formerly much used by the Highlanders, who seldom traveled without such an ugly weapon, though it is now rarely used.

Note 12.—Gipsies or Bohemians, p. 59

In a former volume (*Guy Mannering*) of this edition of the Waverley Novels, the reader will find some remarks on the gipsies as they are found in Scotland. But it is well known that this extraordinary variety of the human race exists in nearly the same primitive state, speaking the same language, in almost all the kingdoms of Europe, and conforming in certain respects to the manners of the people around them, but yet remaining separated from them by certain material distinctions, in which they correspond with each other, and thus maintain their pretensions to be considered as a distinct race. Their first appearance in Europe took place in the beginning of the 15th century, when various bands of this singular people appeared in the different countries of Europe. They claimed an Egyptian descent, and their features attested that they were of Eastern origin. The account given by these singular people was, that it was appointed to them, as a penance, to travel for a certain number of years. This apology was probably selected as being most congenial to the superstitions of the countries which they visited. Their appearance, however, and manners strongly contradicted the allegation that they traveled from any religious motive.

Their dress and accoutrements were at once showy and squalid ; those who acted as captains and leaders of any horde, and such always appeared as their commanders, were arrayed in dresses of the most showy colors, such as scarlet or light green, were well mounted, assumed the title of dukes and counts, and affected considerable consequence. The rest of the tribe were most miserable in their diet and apparel, fed without hesitation on animals which had died of disease, and were clad in filthy and scanty rags, which hardly sufficed for the ordinary purposes of common decency. Their complexion was positively Eastern, approaching to that of the Hindoos.

Their manners were as depraved as their appearance was poor and beggarly. The men were in general thieves, and the women of the most abandoned character. The few arts which they studied with success were of a slight and idle, though ingenious, description. They practised working in iron, but never upon any great scale. Many were good sportsmen, good musicians, and masters, in a word, of all those trivial arts the practise of which is little better than mere idleness. But their ingenuity never ascended into industry. Two or three other peculiarities seem to have distinguished them in all countries. Their pretensions to read fortunes, by palmistry and by astrology, acquired them sometimes respect, but oftener drew them under suspicion as sorcerers; and lastly, the universal accusation that they augmented their horde by stealing children subjected them to doubt and execration. From this it happened that the pretension set up by these wanderers of being pilgrims in the act of penance, although it was at first admitted, and in many instances obtained them protection from the governments of the countries through which they traveled, was afterwards totally disbelieved, and they were considered as incorrigible rogues and vagrants; they incurred almost everywhere sentence of banishment, and, where suffered to remain, were rather objects of persecution than of protection from the law.

There is a curious and accurate account of their arrival in France in the journal of a doctor of theology, which is preserved and published by the learned Pasquier [*Les Recherches de la France*, iv. chap. xix. 1723]. The following is an extract:—
"On August 27th, 1427, came to Paris twelve penitents, *penanciers* (penance doers), as they called themselves, viz. a duke, an earl, and ten men, all on horseback, and calling themselves good Christians. They were of Lower Egypt, and gave out that, not long before, the Christians had subdued their country, and obliged them to embrace Christianity on pain of being put to death. Those who were baptized were great lords in their own country, and had a king and queen there. Soon after their conversion, the Saracens overran the country, and obliged them to renounce Christianity. When the Emperor of Germany, the King of Poland, and other Christian princess heard of this, they fell upon them, and obliged the whole of them, both great and small, to quit the country and go to the Pope at Rome, who enjoined them seven years' penance to wander over the world, without lying in a bed.

"They had been wandering five years when they came to Paris first; the principal people, and soon after the commonalty, about 100 or 120, reduced (according to their own account) from 1000 or 1200, when they went from home, the rest being dead, with their king and queen. They were lodged by the police at some distance from the city, at Chapel St. Denis.

"Nearly all of them had their ears bored, and wore two silver rings in each, which they said were esteemed ornaments in their country. The men were black, their hair curled; the women remarkably black, their only clothes a large old duffle garment, tied over the shoulders with a cloth or cord, and under it a miserable rocket. In short, they were the most poor miserable creatures that had ever been seen in France; and, notwithstanding their poverty, there were among them women who, by looking into people's hands, told their fortunes, and what was worse, they picked people's pockets of their money, and got it into their own, by telling these things through airy magic, *et cœtera.*"

Notwithstanding the ingenious account of themselves rendered by these gipsies, the Bishop of Paris ordered a friar, called Le Petit Jacobin, to preach a sermon, excommunicating all the men and women who had had recourse to these Bohemians on the subject of the future, and shown their hands for that purpose. They departed from Paris for Pontoise in the month of September.

Pasquier remarks upon this singular journal, that, however the story of a penance savors of a trick, these people wandered up and down France, under the eye, and with the knowledge, of the magistrates, for more than a hundred years; and it was not till 1561 that a sentence of banishment was passed against them in that kingdom.

The arrival of the Egyptians, as these singular people were called, in various parts of Europe corresponds with the period in which Timur or Tamerlane invaded Hindostan, affording its natives the choice between the Koran and death. There can be little doubt that these wanderers consisted originally of the Hindostanee tribes, who, displaced, and flying from the sabres of the Mahommedans, undertook this species of wandering life, without well knowing whither they were going. It is natural to suppose the band, as it now exists, is much mingled with Europeans; but most of these have been brought up from childhood among them, and learned all their practices.

It is strong evidence of this, that when they are in closest contact with the ordinary peasants around them, they still keep their language a mystery. There is little doubt, however, that it is a dialect of the Hindostanee, from the specimens produced by Grellmaen, Hoyland, and others, who have written on the subject. But the Author has, besides their authority, personal occasion to know that an individual, out of mere curiosity, and availing himself with patience and assiduity of such opportunities as offered, has made himself capable of conversing with any gipsy whom he meets, or can, like the royal Hal, drink with any tinker in his own language. The astonishment excited among these vagrants on finding a stranger participant of their mystery occasions very ludicrous scenes. It is hoped this gentleman will publish the knowledge he possesses on so singular a topic.

There are prudential reasons for postponing this disclosure at present ; for although much more reconciled to society since they have been less the objects of legal persecution, the gipsies are still a ferocious and vindictive people.

But notwithstanding this is certainly the case, I cannot but add, from my own observation of nearly fifty years, that the manners of these vagrant tribes are much ameliorated, that I have known individuals amongst them who have united themselves to civilized society, and maintain respectable characters, and that great alteration has been wrought in their cleanliness and general mode of life.

NOTE 13.—PETIT-ANDRÉ, p. 63

One of these two persons, I learned from the *Chronique de Jean de Troyes*, but too late to avail myself of the information, might with more accuracy have been called Petit-Jean than Petit-André. This was actually the name of the son of Henry de Cousin, master executioner of the High Court of Justice. The Constable St. Paul was executed by him with such dexterity that the head, when struck off, struck the ground at the same time with the body. This was in 1475.—

The History of Louis XI., King of France, attributed to Jean de Troyes, forms a supplement to the *Memoirs* of Philip de Comines. It was originally published under the title of *The Chronicles of the very Christian and very Victorious Louis of Valois*, etc., 1460 to 1483 ; but was afterwards vulgarly called *La Chronique Scandaleuse*.

A convenient edition of the translation of *Comines* and this supplement forms two volumes of Bohn's series of French Memoirs (*Laing*).

NOTE 14.—QUARRELS OF SCOTTISH ARCHERS, p. 72

Such disputes between the Scots Guards and the other constituted authorities of the ordinary military corps often occurred. In 1474, two [three] Scotsmen had been concerned in robbing John Pensart, a fishmonger, of a large sum of money. They were accordingly apprehended by Philip du Four, provost, with some of his followers. But ere they could lodge one of them, called Mortimer, in the prison of the Chastellet, they were attacked by two archers of the King's Scottish Guard, who rescued the prisoner. See *Chronique de Jean de Troyes*, at the said year, 1474.

NOTE 15.—SCOTTISH AUXILIARIES, p. 74

In both these battles, the Scottish auxiliaries of France, under Stewart Earl of Buchan, were distinguished. At Beaugé they were victorious, killing the Duke of Clarence, Henry V.'s brother, and cutting off his army. At Vernoil they were defeated and nearly extirpated.

NOTE 16.—OLIVER DAIN, p. 84

Oliver's name, or nickname, was Le Diable, which was bestowed on him by public hatred, in exchange for Le Daim, or Le Dain. He was originally the King's barber, but afterwards a favorite counselor.

NOTE 17.—CARD-PLAYING, p. 91

Dr. Dryasdust here remarks that cards, said to have been invented in a preceding reign, for the amusement of Charles V. [VI.] during the intervals of his mental disorder, seems speedily to have become common among the courtiers, since they already furnished Louis XI. with a metaphor. The same proverb was quoted by Durandarte, in the enchanted cave of Montesinos. The alleged origin of the invention of cards produced one of the shrewdest replies I have ever heard given in evidence. It was made by the late Dr. Gregory of Edinburgh to a counsel of great eminence at the Scottish bar. The Doctor's testimony went to prove the insanity of the party whose mental capacity was the point at issue. On a cross-interrogation, he admitted that the person in question played admirably at whist. "And do you seriously say, doctor," said the learned counsel, "that a person having a superior capacity for a game so difficult, and which requires in a pre-eminent degree memory, judgment, and combination, can be at the same time deranged in his understanding ?" "I am no card-player," said the doctor, with great address, "but I have read in history that cards were invented for the amusement of an insane king." The consequences of this reply were decisive.

NOTE 18.—ORDER OF GOLDEN FLEECE, p. 92

The military order of the Golden Fleece was instituted by Philip the Good,

Duke of Burgundy, in the year 1429, the King of Spain being grand-master of the order, as Duke of Burgundy. The number of knights was limited to thirty-one (*Laing*).

NOTE 19.—LOUIS AND HIS DAUGHTER, p. 101

Here the King touches on the very purpose for which he pressed on the match with such tyrannic severity, which was, that, as the Princess's personal deformity admitted little chance of its being fruitful, the branch of Orleans, which was next in succession to the crown, might be, by the want of heirs, weakened or extinguished. In a letter to the Compte de Dammartin, Louis, speaking of his daughter's match, says, " Qu'ils n'auroient pas beaucoup d'embarras à nourrir les enfans que naitroient de leur union ; mais cependant elle aura lieu, quelque chose qu'on en puisse dire."—Wraxall's *History of France*, vol. i. p. 143, note.

NOTE 20.—BALUE'S HORSEMANSHIP, p. 102

A friendly, though unknown, correspondent has pointed out to me that I have been mistaken in alleging that the cardinal was a bad rider. If so, I owe his memory an apology ; for there are few men who, until my latter days, have loved that exercise better than myself. But the cardinal may have been an indifferent horseman, though he wished to be looked upon as equal to the dangers of the chase. He was a man of assumption and ostentation, as he showed at the siege of Paris in 1465, where, contrary to the custom and usage of war, he mounted guard during the night with an unusual sound of clarions, trumpets, and other instruments. In imputing to the cardinal a want of skill in horsemanship, I recollected his adventure in Paris when attacked by assassins, on which occasion his mule, being scared by the crowd, ran away with the rider, and taking its course to a monastery, to the abbot of which he formerly belonged, was the means of saving his master's life.—See Jean de Troyes's *Chronicle*.

NOTE 21.—LOUIS XI. AND CHARLEMAGNE, p. 113

Charlemagne, I suppose on account of his unsparing rigor to the Saxons and other heathen, was accounted a saint during the dark ages ; and Louis XI., as one of his successors, honored his shrine with peculiar observance.

NOTE 22.—MURDER OF DOUGLAS, p. 117

The Princess Margaret, eldest daughter of King James the First, when only eleven years of age, was married to Louis, Dauphin of France, at the age of twelve, on the 6th of July 1436. It proved an unfortunate marriage. and the accomplished princess (her husband not succeeding till 1461 to the throne of France) died without issue, August 1445, in her twenty-third year, it is said of a broken heart. The allusion in the text is to the fate of James Earl of Douglas, who, upon the faith of a safe-conduct, after several acts of rebellion, visited James the Second in the Castle of Stirling. The king, irritated by some personal affront, but quite unpremeditated, drew his dagger and stabbed Douglas, who received his mortal wound from Sir Patrick Grey, one of the king's attendants (who had previously vowed revenge against the proud earl), on the 22d February 1452 (*Laing*).

NOTE 23.—LOUIS'S HUMOR, p. 121

The nature of Louis XI.'s coarse humor may be guessed at by those who have perused the *Cent Nouvelles Nouvelles*, which are grosser than most similar collections of the age.

The work is dedicated by its anonymous author to the Dauphin of France, afterwards Louis XI. It was first printed at Paris in 1486 by Antoine Verard, and, according to Burnet, afterwards passed through ten editions (*Laing*).

NOTE 24.—GALEOTTI, p. 148

Martius Galeotti was a native of Narni, in Umbria. He was secretary to Matthias Corvinus, King of Hungary, and tutor to his son, John Corvinus. While at his court, he composed a work, *De Jocose Dictis et Factis Regis Matthiæ Corvini*. He left Hungary in 1477, and was made prisoner at Venice on a charge of having propagated heterodox opinions in a treatise entitled, *De Homine Interiore et Corpore ejus*. He was obliged to recant some of these doctrines, and might have suffered seriously but for the protection of Sextus IV., then Pope, who had been one of his scholars. He went to France, attached himself to **Louis XI.**, and died in his service.

NOTE 25.—INVENTION OF PRINTING, p. 149

The invention of printing was really first practised at Mayence, on the Rhine. While the first book issued from that press bears the date 1457, the first from Frankfort is dated 1507 (*Laing*). [This ignores the claims made on behalf of Coster of Haarlem.]

NOTE 26.—RELIGION OF THE BOHEMIANS, p. 178

It was a remarkable feature of the character of these wanderers that they did not, like the Jews, whom they otherwise resembled in some particulars, possess or profess any particular religion, whether in form or principle. They readily conformed, as far as might be required, with the religion of any country in which they happened to sojourn, nor did they ever practise it more than was demanded of them. It is certain that in India they embraced neither the tenets of the religion of Bramah nor of Mahomet. They have hence been considered as belonging to the outcast East Indian tribes of Nuts or Parias. Their want of religion is supplied by a good deal of superstition. Such of their ritual as can be discovered, for example that belonging to marriage, is savage in the extreme, and resembles the customs of the Hottentots more than of any civilized people. They adopt various observances, picked up from the religion of the country in which they live. It is, or rather was, the custom of the tribes on the Borders of England and Scotland to attribute success to those journeys which are commenced by passing through the parish church; and they usually try to obtain permission from the beadle to do so when the church is empty, for the performance of divine service is not considered as essential to the omen. They are, therefore, totally devoid of any effectual sense of religion; and the higher or more instructed class may be considered as acknowledging no deity save those of Epicurus, and such is described as being the faith, or no faith, of Hayraddin Maugrabin.

I may here take notice that nothing is more disagreeable to this indolent and voluptuous people than being forced to follow any regular profession. When Paris was garrisoned by the Allied troops in the year 1815, the Author was walking with a British officer near a post held by the Prussian troops. He happened at the time to smoke a cigar, and was about, while passing the sentinel, to take it out of his mouth, in compliance with a general regulation to that effect, when, greatly to the astonishment of the passengers, the soldier addressed them in these words:—" *Rauchen sie immerfort; verdammt sey der Preussische Dienst!*" that is, "Smoke away; may the Prussian service be d—d!" Upon looking closely at the man, he seemed plainly to be a *zigeuner*, or gipsy, who took this method of expressing his detestation of the duty imposed on him. When the risk he ran by doing so is considered, it will be found to argue a deep degree of dislike which could make him commit himself so unwarily. If he had been overheard by a sergeant or corporal, the *prügel* would have been the slightest instrument of punishment employed.

NOTE 27.—WOLF SUPERSTITION, p. 201

Vox quoque Mœrim
Jam fugit ipsa; lupi Mœrim videre priores.
VIRGILII *Ecloga*, ix.

The commentators add, in explanation of this passage, the opinion of Pliny: "The being beheld by a wolf in Italy is accounted noxious, and is supposed to take away the speech of a man, if these animals behold him ere he sees them."

NOTE 28.—THE SQUIRE OF LOWE DEGREE, p. 211

There are two written black-letter editions of this old English poem or tale, but only one perfect copy is known, from which it was reprinted by Ritson, in his *Ancient National Romances*, 1802; and since, more accurately, in Mr. Hazlitt's collected *Remains of Early Popular Poetry of England*, 1866 (*Laing*)

NOTE 29.—QUENTIN'S ADVENTURE AT LIEGE, p. 220

The adventure of Quentin at Liege may be thought overstrained, yet it is extraordinary what slight circumstances will influence the public mind in a moment of doubt and uncertainty. Most readers must remember that, when the Dutch were on the point of rising against the French yoke, their zeal for liberation received a strong impulse from the landing of a person in a British volunteer uniform, whose presence, though that of a private individual, was received as a guaranty of succors from England.

NOTE 30.—BATTLE OF ST. TRON, p. 238

Fought by the insurgents of Liege against the Duke of Burgundy, Charles the Bold, when Count of Charolais, in which the people of Liege were defeated with great slaughter.

NOTE 31.—MURDER OF THE BISHOP OF LIEGE, p. 251

In assigning the present date to the murder of the Bishop of Liege, Louis de Bourbon, history has been violated. It is true that the bishop was made prisoner by the insurgents of that city. It is also true that the report of the insurrection came to Charles with a rumor that the bishop was slain, which excited his indignation against Louis, who was then in his power. But these things happened in 1467, and the bishop's murder did not take place till 1482. In the months of August and September of that year, William de la Marck, called the Wild Boar of Ardennes, entered into a conspiracy with the discontented citizens of Liege against their bishop, Louis of Bourbon, being aided with considerable sums of money by the King of France. By this means, and the assistance of many murderers and banditti, who thronged to him as to a leader befitting them, De la Marck assembled a body of troops, whom he dressed in scarlet as a uniform, with a boar's head on the left sleeve. With this little army he approached the city of Liege. Upon this the citizens, who were engaged in the conspiracy, came to their bishop, and, offering to stand by him to the death, exhorted him to march out against these robbers. The bishop, therefore, put himself at the head of a few troops of his own, trusting to the assistance of the people of Liege. But so soon as they came in sight of the enemy, the citizens, as before agreed, fled from the bishop's banner, and he was left with his own handful of adherents. At this moment De la Marck charged at the head of his banditti with the expected success. The bishop was brought before the profligate knight, who first cut him over the face, then murdered him with his own hand, and caused his body to be exposed naked in the great square of Liege before St. Lambert's cathedral.

Such is the actual narrative of a tragedy which struck with horror the people of the time. The murder of the bishop has been fifteen years antedated in the text, for reasons which the reader of romances will easily appreciate.

NOTE 32.—SCHWARZREITERS, p. 270

Fynes Morrison describes this species of soldiery as follows :—" He that at this day looks upon their *schwartz reytern* (that is, black horsemen) must confess that, to make their horses and boots shine, they make themselves as black as collyers. These horsemen wear black clothes, and poor though they be, yet spend no small time in brushing them. The most of them have black horses, which, while they painfully dress, and (as I said) delight to have their boots and shoes shine with blacking stuff, their hands and faces become black, and thereof they have their foresaid name. Yea I have heard Germans say that they do thus make themselves black to seem more terrible to their enemies."—*Itinerary*, edition 1617 [Part III.], p. 165.

NOTE 33.—PÉRONNE, p. 285

Indeed, though lying on an exposed and warlike frontier, it was never taken by an enemy, but preserved the proud name of Péronne la Pucelle, until the Duke of Wellington, a great destroyer of that sort of reputation, took the place in the memorable advance upon Paris in 1815.

NOTE 34.—D'HYMBERCOURT, p. 286

D'Hymbercourt, or Imbercourt, was put to death by the inhabitants of Ghent with the Chancellor of Burgundy in the year 1477. Mary of Burgundy, daughter of Charles the Bold, appeared in mourning in the market-place, and with tears besought the life of her servants from her insurgent subjects, but in vain.

NOTE 35.—PHILIP DES COMINES, p. 287

Philip des Comines was described in the former editions of this work as a little man, fitted rather for counsel than action. This was a description made at a venture, to vary the military portraits with which the age and work abound. Sleidan the historian, upon the authority of Matthieu d'Arves, who knew Philip des Comines, and had served in his household, says he was a man of tall stature and a noble presence. The learned Monsieur Petitot, editor of the edition of *Memoirs relative to the Hisotry of France*, a work of great value, intimates that Philip des Comines made a figure at the games of chivalry and pageants exhibited on the wedding of Charles of Burgundy with Margaret of England in 1468. See the *Chronicle* of Jean de Troyes, in Petitot's edition of the *Mémoires Relatifs à l'Histoire de France* [first series], vol. xiii. p. 375, note. I have looked into Olivier de la Marche, who, in lib. ii. chapter iv. of his *Memoirs*, gives an ample account of these "fierce vanities," containing as many miscellaneous articles as the reticule of the old merchant of *Peter Schlemihl*, who bought shadows, and carried with him in his bag whatever any one could wish or demand in return. There are in that splendid description knights, dames, pages, and archers, good store besides of castles, fiery dragons, and dromedaries ; there are leopards riding upon lions ; there are rocks, orchards, fountains, spears broken and whole, and the twelve labors of Hercules. In such a brilliant medley I had some trouble in finding Philip des Comines. He is the first named, however, of a gallant band of assailants, knights, and noblemen, to the number of twenty, who, with the Prince of Orange as their leader, encountered, in a general tourney, with a party of the same number under the profligate Adolf of Cleves, who acted as challenger, by the romantic title of *Arbre d'Or*. The encounter, though with arms of courtesy, was very fierce, and separated by main force, not without difficulty. Philip des Comines has, therefore, a title to be accounted *tam Marte quam Mercurio*, though, when we consider the obscurity which has settled on the rest of this *troupe dorée*, we are at no loss to estimate the most valuable of his qualifications. [Compare also Note 45, p. 443.]

NOTE 36.—MEETING OF LOUIS AND CHARLES AFTER THE BATTLE OF
MONTL'HÉRY, p. 288

After the battle of Montl'héry, in 1465, Charles, then Compte de Charolais, had an interview with Louis under the walls of Paris, each at the head of a small party. The two princes dismounted and walked together, so deeply engaged in discussing the business of their meeting, that Charles forgot the peculiarity of his situation ; and when Louis turned back towards the town of Paris, from which he came, the Count of Charolais kept him company so far as to pass the line of outworks with which Paris was surrounded, and enter a field-work which communicated with the town by a trench. At this period he had only five or six persons in company with him. His escort caught an alarm for his safety, and his principal followers rode forward from where he had left them, remembering that his grandfather had been assassinated at Montereau in a similar parley, on 10th September, 1419. To their great joy the count returned uninjured, accompanied with a guard belonging to Louis. The Burgundians taxed him with rashness in no measured terms. "Say no more of it," said Charles ; "I acknowledge the extent of my folly, but I was not aware what I was doing till I entered the redoubt."—*Mémoires de Philippe des Comines*, chap. xiii.

Louis was much praised for his good faith on this occasion ; and it was natural that the duke should call it to recollection when his enemy so unexpectedly put himself in his power by his visit to Péronne.

NOTE 37.—LOUIS'S SUSPICIOUS CHARACTER, p. 296

The arrival of three brothers, princes of the house of Savoy, of Monseigneur de Lau, whom the King had long detained in prison, of Sire Poncet de Rivière, and the Seigneur d'Urfé—who, by the way, as [ancestor of] a romance writer of a peculiar turn, might have been happily enough introduced into the present work, but the fate of the Euphuist was a warning to the Author—all of these nobles bearing the emblem of Burgundy, the cross, namely, of St. Andrew, inspired Louis with so much suspicion that he very impolitically demanded to be lodged in the old Castle of Péronne, and thus rendered himself an absolute captive.—See Comines's *Memoirs for the Year* 1468.

NOTE 38.—HISTORICAL EPITOME, p. 321

The historical facts attending this celebrated interview are expounded and enlarged upon in chapter xxvii. Agents sent by Louis had tempted the people of Liege to rebel against their superior, Duke Charles, and persecute and murder their bishop. But Louis was not prepared for their acting with such promptitude. They flew to arms with the temerity of a fickle rabble, took the bishop prisoner, menaced and insulted him, and tore to pieces one or two of his canons. The news was sent to the Duke of Burgundy at the moment when Louis had so unguardedly placed himself in his power ; and the consequence was, that Charles placed guards on the Castle of Péronne, and, deeply resenting the treachery of the King of France in exciting sedition in his dominions, while he pretended the most intimate friendship, he deliberated whether he should not put Louis to death.

Three days Louis was detained in this very precarious situation ; and it was only his profuse liberality amongst Charles's favorites and courtiers which finally ensured him from death or deposition. Comines, who was the Duke of Burgundy's chamberlain at the time and slept in his apartment, says Charles neither undressed nor slept, but flung himself from time to time on the bed, and at other times wildly traversed the apartment. It was long before his violent temper became in any degree tractable. At length he only agreed to give Louis his liberty on condition of his accompanying him in person against, and employing his troops in subduing, the mutineers whom his intrigues had instigated to arms.

This was a bitter and degrading alternative. But Louis, seeing no other mode of compounding for the effects of his rashness, not only submitted to this discreditable condition, but swore to it upon a crucifix said to have belonged to Charlemagne. These particulars are from Comines. There is a succinct epitome of them in Sir Nathaniel Wraxall's *History of France*, vol. i.

Note 39.—Punishment of Balue, p. 328

Louis kept his promise of vengeance against Cardinal La Balue, whom he always blamed as having betrayed him to Burgundy. After he had returned to his own kingdom, he caused his late favorite to be immured in one of the iron cages at Loches. These were constructed with horrible ingenuity, so that a person of ordinary size could neither stand up at his full height nor lie lengthwise in them. Some ascribe this horrible device to Balue himself. At any rate, he was confined in one of these dens for eleven years, nor did Louis permit him to be liberated till his last illness.

Note 40.—Prayer of Louis XI., p. 329

While I perused these passages in the old manuscript chronicle, I could not help feeling astonished that an intellect acute as that of Louis XI. certainly was could so delude itself by a sort of superstition of which one would think the stupidest savages incapable ; but the terms of the King's prayer, on a similar occasion, as preserved by Brantôme, are of a tenor fully as extraordinary. It is that which, being overheard by a fool or jester, was by him made public, and let in light on an act of fratricide which might never have been suspected. The way in which the story is narrated by the corrupted courtier, who could jest with all that is criminal as well as with all that is profligate, is worthy the reader's notice ; for such actions are seldom done where there are not men with hearts of the nether millstone, capable and willing to make them matters of laughter.

Among the numerous good tricks of dissimulation, feints, and finesses of gallantry which the good King (Louis XI.) did in his time, he put to death his brother, the Duke de Guyenne, at the moment when the Duke least thought of such a thing, and while the King was making the greatest show of love to him during his life, and of affection for him at his death, managing the whole concern with so much art that it would never have been known had not the King taken into his own service a fool who had belonged to his deceased brother. But it chanced that Louis, being engaged in his devout prayers and orisons at the high altar of Our Lady of Cléry, whom he called his good patroness, and no person nigh except this fool, who, without his knowledge, was within earshot, he thus gave vent to his pious homilies :

" Ah, my good Lady, my gentle mistress, my only friend, in whom alone I have resource, I pray you to supplicate God in my behalf, and to be my advocate with Him that He may pardon me the death of my brother, whom I caused to be poisoned by that wicked abbot of St. John. I confess my guilt to thee as to my good patroness and mistress. But then what could I do ? he was perpetually causing disorder in my kingdom. Cause me then to be pardoned, my good Lady, and I know what a reward I will give thee."

This singular confession did not escape the jester, who upbraided the King with the fratricide in the face of the whole company at dinner, which Louis was fain to let pass without observation, in case of increasing the slander.

Note 41.—Louis's Vengeance, p. 333

Varillas, in a history of Louis XI., observes, that his provost-marshal was often so precipitate in execution as to slay another person instead of him whom the King had indicated. This always occasioned a double execution, for the wrath or revenge of Louis was never satisfied with a vicarious punishment.

NOTE 42.—TRISTAN L'HERMITE, p. 335

The Author has endeavored to give to the odious Tristan l'Hermite a species of dogged and brutal fidelity to Louis similar to the attachment of a bull-dog to his master. With all the atrocity of his execrable character, he was certainly a man of courage, and was, in his youth, made knight on the breach of Fronsac, with a great number of other young nobles, by the honor-giving hand of the elder Dunois, the celebrated hero of Charles V. [VII.]'s reign.

NOTE 43.—PREDICTION OF LOUIS XI.'S DEATH, p. 341

The death of Martius Galeotti was in some degree connected with Louis XI. The astrologer was at Lyons, and hearing that the King was approaching the city, got on horseback in order to meet him. As he threw himself hastily from his horse to pay his respects to the King, he fell with a violence which, joined to his extreme corpulence, was the cause of his death in 1478.

But the acute and ready-witted expedient to escape instant death had no reference to the history of this philosopher. The same, or nearly the same, story is told of Tiberius, who demanded of a soothsayer, Thrasyllus, if he knew the day of his own death, and received for answer, "It would take place just three days before that of the Emperor." On this reply, instead of being thrown over the rocks into the sea, as had been the tyrant's first intention, he was taken great care of for the rest of his life.—*Taciti Annal.*, lib. vi. cap. 20–22.

The circumstances in which Louis XI. received a similar reply from an astrologer are as follow :—The soothsayer in question had presaged that a female favorite, to whom the King was very much attached, should die in a week. As he proved a true prophet, the King was as much incensed as if the astrologer could have prevented the evil he predicted. He sent for the philosopher, and had a party stationed to assassinate him as he retired from the royal presence. Being asked by the King concerning his own fortunes, he confessed that he perceived signs of some imminent danger. Being farther questioned concerning the day of his own death, he was shrewd enough to answer with composure, that it would be exactly three days before that of his Majesty. There was, of course, care taken that he should escape his destined fate ; and he was ever after much protected by the King, as a man of real science, and intimately connected with the royal destinies.

Although almost all the historians of Louis represent him as a dupe to the common but splendid imposture of judicial astrology, yet his credulity could not be deep-rooted, if the following anecdote, reported by Bayle, be correct :

Upon one occasion, Louis, intending to hunt, and doubtful of the weather, inquired of an astrologer near his person whether it would be fair. The sage, having recourse to his astrolabe, answered with confidence in the affirmative. At the entrance of the forest the royal cortège was met by a charcoalman, who expressed to some menials of the train his surprise that the King should have thought of hunting in a day which threatened tempest. The collier's prediction proved true. The King and his court were driven from their sport well drenched ; and Louis, having heard what the collier had said, ordered the man before him. "How were you more accurate in foretelling the weather, my friend," said he, "than this learned man ?" "I am an ignorant man, sire," answered the collier, "was never at school, and cannot read or write. But I have an astrologer of my own, who shall foretell weather with any of them. It is, with reverence, the ass who carries my charcoal, who always, when bad weather is approaching, points forward his ears, walks more slowly than usual, and tries to rub himself against walls ; and it was from these signs that I foretold yesterday's storm." The King burst into a fit of laughing, dismissed the astrological biped, and assigned the collier a small pension to maintain the quadruped, swearing he would never in future trust to any other astrologer than the charcoalman's ass.

But if there is any truth in this story, the credulity of Louis was not of a nature to be removed by the failure there mentioned. He is said to have believed in the prediction of Angelo Cattho, his physician, and the friend of Comines, who foretold the death of Charles of Burgundy in the very time and hour when it took place at the battle of Morat [Nancy]. Upon this assurance, Louis vowed a silver screen to the shrine of St. Martin, which he afterwards fulfilled at the expense of one hundred thousand francs. It is well known, besides, that he was the abject and devoted slave of his physicians. Coctier, or Cothier, one of their number, besides the retaining fee of ten thousand crowns, extorted from his royal patient great sums in lands and money, and, in addition to all, the bishopric of Amiens for his nephew. He maintained over Louis unbounded influence, by using to him the most disrespectful harshness and insolence. " I know," he said to the suffering King, " that one morning you will turn me adrift like so many others. But, by Heaven, you had better beware, for you will not live eight days after you have done so ! " It is unnecessary to dwell longer on the fears and superstitions of a prince whom the wretched love of life induced to submit to such indignities.

NOTE 44.—ANECDOTE OF THE BOOTS, p. 356

The story is told more bluntly, and less probably, in the French memoirs of the period, which affirm that Comines, out of a presumption inconsistent with his excellent good sense, had asked of Charles of Burgundy to draw off his boots, without having been treated with any previous familiarity to lead to such a freedom. I have endeavored to give the anecdote a turn more consistent with the sense and prudence of the great author concerned.

NOTE 45.—PHILIP DES COMINES, p. 362

There is little doubt that, during the interesting scene at Péronne, Philip des Comines first learned intimately to know the great powers of mind of Louis XI., by which he was so much dazzled that it is impossible, in reading his *Memoirs*, not to be sensible that he was blinded by them to the more odious shades of his character. He entertained from this time forward a partiality to France. The historian passed into France about 1472, and rose high in the good graces of Louis XI. He afterwards became the proprietor of the lordship of Argenton and others, a title which was given him by anticipation in the earliest editions of this work. He did not obtain it till he was in the French service. After the death of Louis, Philip des Comines fell under the suspicion of the daughter of Louis, called our Lady of Beaujeu, as too zealous a partisan of the rival house of Orleans. The historian himself was imprisoned for eight months in one of the iron cages which he has so forcibly described. It was there that he regretted the fate of a court life. " I have ventured on the great ocean," he said, in his affliction, " and the waves have devoured me." He was subjected to a trial, and exiled from court for some years by the Parliament of Paris, being found guilty of holding intercouse with disaffected persons. He survived this cloud, however, and was afterwards employed by Charles VIII. in one or two important missions, where talents were required. Louis XII. also transferred his favor to the historian, but did not employ him. He died at his Castle of Argenton in 1509, and was regretted as one of the most profound statesmen, and certainly the best historian, of his age. In a poem to his memory by the poet Ronsard, he received the distinguished praise, that he was the first to show the luster which valor and noble blood derived from being united with learning. [Compare also Note.35, p. 444.]

NOTE 46.—DISGUISED HERALD, p. 389

The heralds of the middle ages, like the *feciales* of the Romans, were invested with a character which was held almost sacred. To strike a herald was a crime which inferred a capital punishment ; and to counterfeit the character of such an august official was a degree of treason towards those men who were accounted the depositaries of the secrets of monarchs and the honor of nobles. Yet a prince so unscrupulous as Louis XI. did not hesitate to practise such an imposition, when he wished to enter into communication with Edward IV. of England.

Exercising that knowledge of mankind for which he was so eminent, he selected, as an agent fit for his purpose, a simple valet. This man, whose address had been known to him, he disguised as a herald, with all the insignia of his office, and sent him in that capacity to open a communication with the English army. Two things are remarkable in this transaction. First, that the stratagem, though of so fraudulent a nature, does not seem to have been necessarily called for, since all that King Louis could gain by it would be, that he did not commit himself by sending a more responsible messenger. The other circumstance worthy of notice is, that Comines, though he mentions the affair at great length, is so pleased with the King's shrewdness in selecting, and dexterity at indoctrinating, his pseudo-herald, that he forgets all remark on the impudence and fraud of the imposition, as well as the great risk of discovery ; from both which circumstances we are led to the conclusion, that the solemn character which the heralds endeavored to arrogate to themselves had already begun to lose regard among statesmen and men of the great world.

Even Ferne, zealous enough for the dignity of the herald, seems to impute this intrusion on their rights in some degree to necessity.

" I have heard some," he says, " but with shame enough, allow of the action of

Louis the Eleventh, King of France, who had so unknightly a regard both of his own honor and also of armes, that he had seldom about his court any officer-at-armes. And therefore, at such time as King Edward the Fourth, King of England, had entered France with hostile power, and lay before the town of St. Quentin, the same French king, for want of a herald to carry his mind to the English king, was constrained to subornate a vadelict, or common serving-man, with a trumpet, banner, having a hole made through the middest for this preposterous herauld to put his head through, and to cast it over his shoulders instead of a better coat-armor of France. And thus came this hastily-arrayed courier as a counterfeit officer-at-arms, with instructions from his sovereign's mouth to offer peace to our king. "Well," replies Torquatus, the other interlocutor in the dialogue, "that fault was never yet to be found in any of our English kings, nor ever shall be, I hope."—*Blazon of Gentrie*, 1586, pp. 161, 162.

In this curious book, the author, besides some assertions in favor of coat-armor, too nearly approaching blasphemy to be quoted, informs us that the Apostles were gentlemen of blood, and many of them descended from that worthy conqueror, Judas Maccabæus ; but through the course of time and persecution of wars, poverty oppressed the kindred, and they were constrained to servile works. So were the four doctors and fathers of the church (Ambrose, Augustine, Hierome, and Gregorie) gentlemen both of blood and arms (p. 98). The Author's copy of this rare tract (memorial of a hopeful young friend, now no more) exhibits a curious sally o the national and professional irritability of a Scottish herald.

This person appears to have been named Thomas Drysdale, Islay Herald, who purchased the volume in 1619, and seems to have perused it with patience and profit till he came to the following passage in Ferne, which enters into the distinction between sovereign and feudatory crowns. "There is also a king, and he a homager, or fœdatorie to the estate and majestie of another king, as to his superior lord, is that of Scotland to our English empire." This assertion set on fire the Scottish blood of Islay Herald, who, forgetting the book had been printed nearly forty years before, and that the author was probably dead, writes on the margin in great wrath, and in a half-text hand, "He is a traitor and lyar in his throat, and I offer him the combat, that says Scotland's kings were ever feudatorie to England."

NOTE 47.—PRIZE OF HONOR, p. 407.

The perilling the hand of an heiress upon the event of a battle was not so likely to take place in the 14th century as when the laws of chivalry were in more general observance. Yet it was not unlikely to occur to so absolute a prince as Duke Charles, in circumstances like those supposed.

NOTE 48.—BRIDE OF DE LA MARCK, p. 410.

It is almost unnecessary to add, that the marriage of William de la Marck with the Lady Hameline is as apocryphal as the lady herself. The real bride of the Wild Boar of Ardennes was Joan D'Arschel, Baroness of Schoonhoven.

NOTE 49.—ATTACK UPON LIEGE, p. 417.

The Duke of Burgundy, full of resentment for the usage which the bishop had received from the people of Liege (whose death, as already noticed, did not take place some years after), and knowing that the walls of the town had been repaired since they were breached by himself after the battle of St. Tron, advanced recklessly to their chastisement. His commanders shared his presumptuous confidence ; for the advanced guard of his army, under the Maréchal of Burgundy and Seigneur D'Hymbercourt, rushed upon one of the suburbs, without waiting for the rest of their army, which commanded by the Duke in person, remained about seven or eight leagues in the rear. The night was closing, and, as the Burgundian troops observed no discipline, they were exposed to a sudden attack from a party of the citizens commanded by Jean de Vilde, who, assaulting them in front and rear, threw them into great disorder, and killed more than eight hundred men, of whom one hundred were men-at-arms.

When Charles and the King of France came up, they took up their quarters in two villas situated near to the wall of the city. In the two or three days which followed, Louis was distinguished for the quiet and regulated composure with which he pressed the siege, and provided for defence in case of sallies ; while the Duke of Burgundy, no way deficient in courage, and who showed the rashness and want of order which was his principal characteristic, seemed also extremely suspicious that the King would desert him and join with the Liegeois.

They lay before the town for five or six days, and at length fixed the 30th of October 1468 for a general storm. The citizens, who had probably information of their intent, resolved to prevent their purpose, and determined on anticipating it by a desperate sally through the breaches in their walls. They placed at their head six hundred of the men of the little territory of Franchemont, belonging to the bishopric of Liege, and reckoned the most valiant of their troops. They burst out of the town on a sudden, surprised the Duke of Burgundy's quarters ere his guards could put on their armor, which they had laid off to enjoy some repose before the assault. The King of France's lodgings were also attacked and endangered. A great confusion ensued, augmented incalculably by the mutual jealousy and suspicions of the French and Burgundians. The people of Liege were, however, unable to maintain their hardy enterprise, when the men-at-arms of the King and Duke began to recover from their confusion, and were finally forced to retire within their walls, after narrowly missing the chance of surprising both King Louis and the Duke of Burgundy, the most powerful princes of their time. At daybreak the storm took place, as had been originally intended, and the citizens, disheartened and fatigued by the nocturnal sally, did not make so much resistance as was expected. Liege was taken and miserably pillaged, without regard to sex or age, things sacred or things profane. These particulars are fully related by Comines in his *Memoirs*, liv. ii. chaps. 11, 12, 13, and do not differ much from the account of the same events in chapters xxxv. and xxxvi.

Note 50.—Anachronisms, p. 429

We have already noticed the anachronism respecting the crimes of this atrocious baron; and it is scarce necessary to repeat, that if he in reality murdered the Bishop of Liege in 1482, the Count of La Marck could not be slain in the defence of Liege four[teen] years earlier. In fact, the Wild Boar of Ardennes, as he was usually termed, was of high birth, being the third son of John I., Count of La Marck and Aremberg, and ancestors of the branch called Barons of Lumain. He did not escape the punishment due to his atrocity, though it did not take place at the time, or in the manner, narrated in the text. Maximillian Emperor of Austria, caused him to be arrested at Utrecht, where he was beheaded in the year 1485, three years after the Bishop of Liege's death.

Note 51. Descent of the Leslies, p. 429

An old rhyme, by which the Leslies vindicate their descent from an ancient hero, who is said to have slain a gigantic Hungarian champion, and to have formed a proper name for himself by a play of words upon the place where he fought his adversary.

GLOSSARY

OF

WORDS, PHRASES, AND ALLUSIONS

Aberbrothock, now called *Arbroath*, a town in Forfarshire

Abonne, was, subscribed

Aboulcasem, of Basra, noted for his generosity and magnificence. *See* Weber, *Tales of the East*, vol. ii. p. 308

Abye, to pay the penalty for

Ad sacra, for holy things

Agnes Sorel, or *Soreau*, mistress of Charles VII. of France, who is said to have prompted the patriotic efforts of that king against the English in the 15th century

Aiguilettes, tagged points

Aldebaran, the name given to a star of the first magnitude in the constellation Taurus (Bull), one of the four "royal stars" of the ancient Egyptians

Allegro, joy, mirth. *Compare* Milton's *L'Allegro*

Amadis and Oriana, the hero and heroine of the romance of chivalry entitled *Amadis of Gaul*

Angelica, the heroine of Ariosto's *Orlando Furioso*, who falls in love with the obscure squire Medoro

Angelo, Henry, celebrated, riding and fencing master at the beginning of the 19th century. *See* his *Reminiscences* (2 vols. 1828–30)

Angus, the old name of Forfarshire

Annuncio vobis gaudium magnum, I announce to you tidings of great joy

Arbre d'Or, golden tree

Aroint, avaunt, begone

Assiettée, plateful

Astræa, the English dramatist, Aphra Behn (1640–89,) whose plays are

too frequently coarse and indelicate

Astucious, astute, crafty

Auberge, inn

Aught, possession

Autant de perdu, so much lost

Auvernat, red wine of Orleans

" *Auxerre est la boisson des rois*," Auxerre (wine, is the drink of kings

Azincour, Agincourt, fought in 1415

Back-friend, a backer, friend to fall back upon

Badaud, gazer, gossip

Bailey, a space between two circuits or walls of defence in a castle

Ban and arrière-ban, the entire feudal force

Bande Noire, a company of speculators who bought up the large estates of the old noble families of France, then demolished the château and sold the land in small parcels

Barbour, Scotch poet (14th century), author of a long poem on the exploits of Robert Bruce

Bastard of Rubempre, a nephew of the Count of Croye, who was accused of being an agent of Louis XI. employed to carry off (1464) the Count of Charolais (Charles of Burgundy)

Bavaroise, tea sweetened with vegetable syrup (capillaire)

Bayes. See The Rehearsal, Act iv. sc. 1

Beati pacifici, Blessed are the peaceful

Beati qui in Domino moriuntur, Blessed are the dead that die in the Lord

Benedicite, blessing, returning of thanks

Bifteck de mouton, beefsteak of mutton

Black Walloons. The Walloons, descendants of the Gallic Belgæ, live in the Ardennes and on both sides of the Franco-Belgian frontier. Black was no doubt the color of the uniform worn by Charles of Burgundy's Walloon soldiers

Blate, bashful

Bottrine, small leather flask

Bouilli, boiled meat

Brach, hound that hunts by scent

Braeman, one who lives on the southern slope of the Grampians

Brag, to challenge, proudly defy

Brantwein, brandy

Braw-warld, showy, gaudy

Brogue, a Highlander's shoe of undressed hide

Browst, brewage, beverage brewed

Bruder, brother

Buchan, John Stuart, Earl of, commanded the Scottish auxiliaries in France in the reign of Charles VII.; he was a son of Regent Albany, and grandson of Robert II. of Scotland

Bushment, or *ambushment*, an ambush

Cabaret, wine-shop, tavern

Callant, boy, stripling; *braw callant*, a fine fellow

Calthrop, or *caltrop*, a spiked iron ball; *gin*, trap

Canaille, rascal mob

Cap de Diou, God's head —a Gascon oath

447

Carcanet, necklace, chain of jewels

Carte, menu, bill of fare

Caserne, barracks

Catchpoll, a warrant-officer who arrests for debt

Cathay, China

Cense, reputed

Cerneau, the half kernel of an unripe walnut

Cham (of Tartary), khan, *i.e.* chief ruler of the Tartars in Muscovy

Chapeau à plumes, hat with feathers, plumed hat

Chapeau bras, three cornered hat with a low crown

Chares, household work

C h a s s e - c a f e, more correctly *pousse-cafe*, a small glass of brandy or liqueur taken after coffee

Château Margout, or *Margaux*, claret of the very first brand

Château of Sully, called Sully, on the left bank of the Loire (modern dept. Loiret), where the great minister of Henry IV. wrote his *Mémoires*

Chield, fellow

Chiromantist, one who tells fortunes by palmistry or the hand

Chouse, cheat, swindle

Cinq francs, five francs (the bottle)

Cléry, about 10 miles below Orleans on the Loire ; Louis XI. was buried there

C o c a g n e, an imaginary country, where good living and idleness are the chief objects or pursuits of the inhabitants

C o c k e r e d, pampered, brought up indulgently

C o l i n Maillard, blindman's buff

C o m b u s t, astrological term for a planet that is too near the sun

Comfiture, preparation of preserved fruit, confection

C o m i n g (*countess*), inclined to make advances, forward, eager

Condé, Louis Joseph de Bourbon, Prince of, French general in the Seven Years' War and the military chief of the *émigrés* on the Rhine, after the fall of the Bastille

Corbie, raven

Côtelette à la Maintenon, mutton cutlets served with parsley, mushrooms, and brown sauce

Couchée, a levee held just before retiring to sleep

Craig, neck

Croix de St. Louis, the decoration of a military order founded by Louis XIV. in 1693, for distinguished service by Roman Catholic officers, was a gold eight-armed cross bearing on one side the effigy of St. Louis of France, and on the other a flaming sword passed through a laurel crown

Cullion, poltroon

Curney, small number

Daffing, loose talk

Dariole, a pastry cake containing cream

Das ist, that is, *i.e.*

Deas, dais

Debout, etc. (p. 284), Arise —arise, gentlemen, it's time to be going !

De Bure, G. F., a celebrated French bibliographer of the 18th century

Demi-solde, half-pay

Denis Montjoye, the old war-cry of the French

Der bischoff, or *bischof*, the bishop

Doddered, covered with twining parasites, such as mistletoe

Dogberry. The allusion is to *Much Ado About Nothing*, Act iv. sc. 2

Dolly, a cook who gave her name to Dolly's Tavern in Paternoster Row, London ; her portrait was painted by Gainsborough

Donner and blitz, thunder and lightning ! a German oath ; *donner and hagel*, thunder and hail !

Dorff, or *dorf*, a village

D o u g l a s, A r c h i b a l d, fourth Earl of, entered the service of France and was made Duke of Touraine, in 1423

Du bist ein comischer man, you are a funny fellow

Duffle, a coarse woolen cloth with a thick nap

Du Guesclin, Bertrand, Constable of France, her greatest soldier during the 14th century

D u r i n d a r t e, should be *Durindana*, or *Durandana*, the sword of

Orlando (Roland) in the *Orlando Furioso*

Dyes, gewgaws, paltry ornaments

E b l i s, in Mohammedan mythology, the chief of the fallen angels

Ebro's temper. The allusion is doubtless to the celebrated weapons of Toledo, although that town is on the Tagus, not the Ebro

Échevin, sheriff, municipal magistrate

Éclaircissement, explanation

Ecosse, en avant, Scotland, (step) forward

E h r e n h o l d, German for " herald "

Ein wort, ein mann, a man of his word

Embrun, our Lady of, a figure of the Virgin much worshiped by Louis XI., preserved in a church at Embrun, in Dauphiné (modern dept. Hautes Alpes)

Enfans perdus, the forlorn hope

Ephemerides, an astronomical almanac

Escalier dérobé, private staircase

Étang, pond, lake

Ethnic, pagan

Etiam in cubiculo, even in the bedchamber

Euphuist, Sir Piercie Shafton in *The Monastery*

Fabliau, fable, moral tale

Fabtionnaire, sentry

Fähnlein, troop

F a i r e d e s n o c e s. The Paris innkeeper's notice runs *salle à faire des noces*, " a hall for wedding festivities "

Faitour, traitor, rascal

Faste, ostentation

F e c i a l e s, or *fesiales*, a college of priests who watched over the sanctity of treaties

Ferme ornée, a model farm

Fier comme un Écossais, proud as a Scotchman

Finis—I should have said, etc. (p. 331), Finis, I should have said the pope (*finis*), is the end of the work (book)

F l e u r - d e - l y s, lilies, the royal arms of France

Florentine (p. 322), Dante, in *Inferno*, iii. 9

Florio. The Italian-English dictionary of John

Florio, entitled *A World of Words* (1598), is doubtless what is alluded to (p. xxii)

Fossa cum furca, the right of life and death exercised by a feudal noble over his dependants—of hanging the males and drowning the females

Fourriers and Harbingers, both officers whose duty it was to procure and make all arrangements for the lodgings of people of high rank ; *fourrier*, avant-courier, messenger sent on in advance

Frampold, unruly, peevish

Free Companies, mercenary troops owning no master except their own captains, who sold their services to whomsoever paid them best

Fremit, strangers ; cold, indifferent

Gabelle, tax on salt

Garce, a young girl, now a dishonorable appellation

Garçon perruquier, hairdresser

Gauntois and Liegeois, people of Ghent (or Gand) and Liege

Gear, business, affair, thing owned ; *gear, let us to this*, set we about the matter in hand

Geb (up), give (up)

Geister-seers, or *geisterseher*, seer of ghosts

Gens de lettres, etc. (p. xxii), literary men, whom you call Sir Scott, I believe

Gentillâtre, country squire, poor gentleman

Ghaist, ghost

Gottfried, Godfrey

Grande chère, good living

Grand Seignior, the sultan of the Ottoman Turks

Grève, our Lady of. In the Place de Grève, Paris, criminals were executed

Gross sternendeuter, clever interpreters of the stars

Guilder, a Dutch florin = 1s. 8d.

Guildry, a guild, the members of a guild

Guinguette, a place of refreshment, tea-garden, outside Paris

Gut getroffen, well hit

Hagel and sturmwetter, hail and stormy weather ! a German oath

Hanap, a large drinking-cup

Handsel, earnest-money

Hanguisse, an *Angus*, an old name for the Scottish country of Forfar

Hauptmann, captain, leader

Haut-de-chausses à canon, knee - breeches ornamented with canons or indented ornamental rolls

Hermetical philosophy, a system ascribed to Hermes Trismegistus, *i.e.* the god Thoth, the traditional author of Egyptian culture

Herzog, duke

Hochheim, a celebrated Rhenish vintage

Hôpital des fous, lunatic asylum

Hors de page, finished serving one's apprenticeship as a page

Hôtel de ville, town-hall

Hyke a Talbot, a hunter's cry to his dog, occurs in Dame Berners, *Boke of Hawking and Hunting* (1486)

Impayable, excellent

Inamorato, lover

In commendam, in trust, along with

Jabot, frill

Jacques Bonhomme, equivalent to our Hodge, a generic name for the French peasant

Jaiza, or *Jaice*, formerly the capital of Bosnia, was captured after a long siege by Matthias Corvinus in 1463, and vainly stormed during three days by the sultan, Mahomet II., in 1464

Janus Pannonius, or *Jean de Cisnige*, Hungarian poet of the 15th century

Jardin Anglois, an English garden, the characteristic of which, as distinguished from a stiff, regularly - arranged French garden, is the appearance of untrammeled nature it exhibits

Jazeran, or *jaseran*, a flexible shirt of linked mail

Jean qui pleure, Weeping John ; *Jean qui rit*, Laughing John

Jerry-come-tumble, acrobat tumbler

Jeshurun, the chosen of Israel. *See* Deut. xxxii. 15

Johannisberg, the most valuable of the Rhenish wines

Jour maigre, fast day

Joyous science, *brethren of*, minstrels

Jus emphyteusis, the law whereby one person acquires a perpetual right to the use of land that belongs to another person

Kaisar, or *kaiser*, emperor

King of Castile, probably Philip III. of Spain, whose death was caused partly through his sitting too near to a brazier, and the punctilious etiquette of his attendants in refusing to move it until the proper functionary came

Klepper, hack, nag

Knight without fear and reproach, Chevalier Bayard (1476-1524)

Kurschenschaft, intended for *Kürschnerschaft*, the trade association of the furriers and skinners (*compare* p. 254) ; but this being an unusual compound, perhaps *Burschenschaft*, corporation association, was intended

La guerre est ma patrie, etc. (p. ix). The battle-field is my fatherland ; my armor my home ; my life a perpetual warfare

Landes, low flat deserts of loose sand bordering on the Bay of Biscay, in the south of France

Lanzknechts, or *lanz knechte*, also *landsknechte*, mercenary foot-soldiers, armed with pikes and swords, first organized by the Emperor Maximilian I. in 1487

Lapis offensionis, etc. (p. 185), a stone of offence and a stumbling-block

Largesse, a present, the heralds' cry when soliciting gratuities after the performance of some public function

Leaguer, a permanent fortified camp ; *Lie*

Leaguer, take up permanent quarters

"*Leave all hope behind*," from Dante's *Inferno*, iii. 9

Legion of saints, or *Theban legion*, were all massacred in the persecution of the Emperor Maximin, about the year 286

Liard, small French coin, current after the 14th century = 1-3d silver penny English

Linea vitæ, in palmistry, the line of life, the principal on the hand

Lire, should doubtless be *litre* = a little less than a quart

Loches, on the Indre, some 25 miles southeast of Tours

Loom, article, headpiece

Loon, fellow

Loretto, on the Adriatic coast of Italy, 15 miles from Ancona, where is preserved the reputed house in which the Virgin Mary lived at Nazareth—a celebrated shrine

Lower circles, or provinces in Lower (North) Germany, the principal of which were Westphalia and Saxony

Lucio, in Shakespeare's *Measure for Measure*, Act v. sc. 1

Lurdane, blockhead

Lusthaus, country villa

Macaronic Latin, a modern language used with Latin inflections and construction

Machiavel, or *Machiavelli*, *Niccolo di Bernardo dei*, a Florentine statesman of the 16th century, who taught that rulers may commit every treacherous and unlawful act in the interests of strong government

Mahomet's coffin, according to Mohammedan tradition, is suspended in mid-air between two magnets

Mahound, a contemptuous name given to a devil meant to represent Mahomet, in the mediæval mystery-plays

Maigre, thin, applied to soup made without meat

Maître de cuisine, head cook; *maître d'hôtel*, steward

Malvolio. See Shakespeare's *Twelfth Night*, Act ii. sc. 5

Maréchaussée, police horse-patrol

Marmoutier, *the abbey of*, in the environs of Tours, founded by St. Martin of Tours (4th century), and one of the most influential and powerful in France in the Middle Ages

Matelot, or *matelote*, a rich fish stew with wine sauce, flavored with onions and herbs

Meikle, much

Mein, my; *mein Gott*, my God ! *meinherr*, sir

Meister (*Æsop*), master, a title of honor given by Germans to an approved master in his art or craft

Mell, to interfere, meddle

Melpomene, in ancient Greek mythology, the Must of Tragedy

Melusina, in old French folklore was every Saturday transformed from a woman into a serpent from the waist downwards

Métairie, farmhouse

Mieux vault bon repas que bel habit, a good meal is better than a fine coat

Miladi Lac, *The Lady of the Lake*, Scott's poem

Minstrel, *the* (p. 49), or *Blind Harry*, author of a long doem descriptive of the exploits of Wallace (about 1460)

Minting, aiming

Molière's comedy, *L'Amour Medecin*. See Act i. sc. 1, the persons being, however, a dealer in tapestry and a goldsmith

More meo, in my own way

Morgaine la Fée, pupil of Merlin the Magician, and half-sister of King Arthur

Mumble, to chew gently with the gums

Murcian bull, one bred in Murcia, a province in the southeast of Spain

Musion, the wildcat, term of heraldry

Ne moliaris amico, etc. (p. 187), Devise not evil against thy neighbor, seeing he dwelleth securely by thee

Nom de guerre, nickname

Nostradamus, or *Michel de Notredame*, famous French astroioger (16th century)

Ora pro nobis, pray for us —a religious supplication

Ordonnance, *companies of*, independent companies, not enrolled among the ordinary regiments

Oriana. See Amadis and Oriana

Orlando, the Italian form of Roland

Par amours, by illicit love, in matters of love

Pasques-Dieu, the favorite oath of Louis XI.

Pasquier, *Etienne*, a French magistrate and historian (1529-1615), who wrote *Lettres* (1723) and other works

Pâté de Périgord, pasties of partridges with truffles

Paulus Jovius, or *Paolo Giovio*, an Italian historian of the 16th century, lived at the Pope's court, and wrote, amongst other works, *Elogia Doctorum Virorum* (Venice, 1546)

Pauvres revenants, poor ghosts

Paysage, landscape

Paysanne, country girl

Penseroso, sadness, melancholy. *Compare* Milton's *Il Penseroso*

Pereat improbus, etc., (p. 187), Let the wicked perish, Amen ! and let him be anathema

Pere pale, divided vertically

Peter Schlemihl, the hero of a tale by the German poet, Adelbert von Chamisso (1781-1838)

Petite pointe d'ail, slight flavor of garlic

Petit plat, little dish

Pigault le Brun, Charles A. G. Pigault de l'Epinoy, known as Pigault-Lebrun, a popular French novelist (1753-1835)

Pilleur, plunderer

Pirn, the bobbin of a spinning-wheel; *ill-winded pirns to ravel out*, knotty difficulties to solve or adjust

Pistol eating the leek. *See*

Shakespeare's *Henry V.*, Act v. sc. 1

Plack, an old Scotch copper coin=1-3d penny English

Pleached, with branches interwoven

Plexitium, a chase, woodlands inclosed for game

Polk, or *pulk*, a squadron, troop of Cossacks

Poortith, poverty

Post tot promissa, after so many promises

Potage, (formerly) vegetables; *potager*, kitchen garden

Potence, gallows

Potz tausend, the deuce

Pour passer le temps, to pass away the time

Pow, head

Prévenance, kind attention, obliging kindness

Prügel, cudgel, stick

Public Good, war of, grew out of a league formed by the great feudatory princes of France against Louis XI

Pucelle, virgin

Qui vive? Who goes there?

Regale, treat, entertainment

Rheims. *See* Smeared with oil, etc

Rheinwein, Rhenish wine

Rhinegrave, the title of the feudal lord of the *gau* or county of the Rhine

Rifacimento, restoration, repairing

Rochet, or *rocket*, a short cloak, worn formerly by both men and women; in Pasquier's passage the original French signifies "petticoat." Compare p. 438

Roman Comique, player in, a famous novel (1651-57), by Paul Scarron

Romaunt, a poetical romance of chivalry

Rouse, a bumper

Routier, an experienced man; *vieux routier*, an old stager

Rubempré, Bastard of. *See* Bastard of Rubempré

Runlet, a barrel (of spirits) holding 18½ gallons

St. Bartholomew, was flayed alive

St. Denis, 4 miles north of Paris; the abbey-church there was long the buri-

al-place of the sovereigns of France

St. Francis's cord, the founder of the monastic order of Franciscans, dressed in a coarse woolen tunic, girt about with a hempen cord

St. Gatien, the cathedral of Tours

St. John (Jean) d'Angely, about 16 miles southeast from La Rochelle. Jean Favre, abbot of St. Jean d'Angély was popularly believed to have poisoned (1472), at Louis XI.'s instigation, that king's brother, Charles Duke of Berri and of Guyenne

St. Jude, 28th October

St. Lambert, patron saint of Liege

St. Lambert's, the old cathedral of Liege, demolished by the French Revolutionists in 1794, and altogether removed in 1808

St. Martin, bishop of Tours, died just before the year 400

St. Patibularius, derived from Latin *patibulum*, a fork-shaped gibbet

St. Perpetuus, third successor of St. Martin of Tours, erected over that bishop's bones the church of St. Martin's consecrated in 472

St. Tron, more correctly *St. Trond*, about 20 miles northwest of Liege

Saints, legion of. *See* Legion of saints

Saker, a small gun formerly used in sieges

Sancte Huberte, etc., (p. 152), St. Hubert, St. Julian, St. Martin, St. Rosalia, all ye saints who hear me, pray for me a sinner

Suncte Juliane, etc. (p. 144), Holy Julian, listen to our prayers. Pray—pray for us

Sanglier, wild boar

Santon, a Mohammedan prophet or saint

Saumur, good fathers of, belonging to the ancient abbey of St. Laurent in Saumur, which dates back to the 11th century

Saus and braus, revelry in good things. *In Saus und Braus leben*=to live at heck and manger

Schakos, or *shako*, a military head-dress, a tall

cylindrical hat, with a shield in the front of it

Scheik Ebn Hali, or Ali ben Aben-Ragel, an Arab astrologer of the 11th century

Schelm, rogue, scoundrel

Schneiders, or *Snyders*, *Frans*, Flemish painter (1579-1657)

Schoppen, meant for *schöffen*, aldermen, municipal magistrates. *Schoppen* means pint-measures

Schwarzbier, black beer

Schwarzreiters, or *Schwarzreiter*, black horsemen, black troopers

Scotched (snake), slightly wounded

Sero venientibus ossa, the bones are for late comers

Sheerly, thoroughly, quite

Shenstone, William, English poet and landscape-gardener. The line "Seek for freedom at an inn," etc. (p. 432), is adapted from verses headed *Written at an Inn at Henley*

Shool, shovel

"*Showing the code*," etc. (p. xxxi), altered from *As You Like It*, Act iv. sc. 3

Sigillum confessionis, the seal of confession

Si non payatis, etc. (p. 187), If you do not pay, I will burn your monastery

Skaith, hurt, harm

Smeared with oil (p. 353). The coronation of the French kings usually took place at Rheims

Smock-faced, effeminate-looking, pale-faced

Snapped, snatched up, stolen

Souter, cobbler

Spreagh, cattle carried off in a raiding expedition

Stakt-house, or stadthaus, the town-house, town-hall

Statist, politician, statesman

Stave and tail, to strike the bear with a staff, and pull off the dogs by the tail, to separate them

Stoup, a flagon, deep narrow vessel for holding liquids

Straick, a measure of capacity=two bushels; the quantity of malt generally used for one brewing

Sully Maximilien de Be-thune, Duke of, author of *Mémoires des Sages et Royales Economies d'Estat de Henri le Grand* (1634–62)

Syndic, a magistrate, administrative officer

Tabatière, snuff-box

Tabouret, stool

Tam Marte quam Mercurio, as distinguished for arms as for diplomacy

Tasker, laborer

Tauridor, bull-fighter

Tender, to cherish, value, esteem

Termagund, or *Termagaunt*, an Oriental devil introduced into the mediæval mystery-plays. *Compare* Mahound

Teste St.-Gris, probably meant for "By the head of Christ"

Tête-Bleau, or *Tête-bleu*, *Tête-Dieu*, God's head—an oath

Teufel, the devil

Thebais, deserts of, in the neighborhood of Thebes on the Nile

" *The small rare volume*,

etc. (p. xxxix), from Dr. John Ferriar's *Bibliomania, an Epistle to Richard Heber, Esq.* (1809)

Tiffany, a kind of thin silk, gauze

Tocque, a small bonnet or low cap with narrow brim

To-name, nickname, honorary descriptive title

Triers, or *Trier*, Treves, in the Palatinate

Troupe dorée, choice company, *élite*

Trudchen, an affectionate diminutive of Gertrude

Two and a plack, two Scotch pennies and a plack=1-2d English

Un homme comme il faut a perfect gentleman

Vaconeldiablo, doubtless for *Baco el Diablo*, Bacchus (wine) the Devil

Væ victis, woe to the vanquished

Varium et mutabile, fickle and changeable (are women)

Ventre St. Gris, an oath, presumed to be translat-

able as "the body of St. Christ"

Vieux routier. *See* Routier

Vin ordinaire, the wine in common use

Vive Bourgogne, long live Burgundy !

Volée, flight

Vota diis exaudita malignis, vows listened to by unfriendly-disposed deities

Wallace Wight, Wallace the strong—a favorite designation of Scotland's great hero

Walloons. *See* Black Walloons

Was henker, what henker, what the deuce !

Weinkeller, wine-cellar

Wenceslaus, was emperor of Germany from 1378 to 1400. The reigning emperor at the time of this romance was Frederick IV. (1440–93)

Whillywhawing, talking in an intimate way like lovers

Yungfrau, or *jungfrau*, maiden, young woman

Zuchthaus, prison

INDEX

Lightning Source UK Ltd.
Milton Keynes UK
UKOW01f0635081016

284728UK00001B/64/P

9 781434 414854